Hippocrene
Practical Dictionaries

English–Deutsch
German–Englisch

Stephen Jones BA

HIPPOCRENE BOOKS, New York

Trademarks
The symbol ® designates entered words that we have reason to believe constitute trademarks. However, neither the presence or absence of such designation should be regarded as affecting the legal status of any trademark.

Schutzmarken
Das Symbol ® kennzeichnet Wörter, von denen wir glauben, daß sie eingetragene Schutzmarken darstellen. Allerdings beeinflusst weder das Vorhandensein noch das Fehlen eines solchen Zeichens den rechtlichen Status einer Schutzmarke.

Front cover photo © J.L. Stage/The Image Bank

First Hippocrene Edition, 1983

© Laurence Urdang Associates, 1982

Glossary of Menu Terms and special American usage entries © Hippocrene Books, 1983

ISBN 0-88254-813-1

Abbreviations/Abkürzungen

acc accusative, Akkusativ
adj adjective, Adjektiv
adv adverb, Adverb
anat anatomy, Anatomie
arch architecture, Architektur
art article, Artikel
astrol astrology, Astrologie
astron astronomy, Astronomie
biol biology, Biologie
bot botany, Botanik
chem chemistry, Chemie
coll colloquial,
    umgangssprachlich
comm commerce, Kommerz
dat dative, Dativ
derog derogatory, geringschätzig
elec electricity, Elektrizität
f feminine, Femininum
fig figurative, figürlich
gen genitive, Genetiv
geog geography, Erdkunde
gramm grammar, Grammatik
impol impolite, unhöflich
interj interjection, Ausruf
Jur Jura, Rechtswesen, law
Komm Kommerz, commerce
m masculine, Maskulinum
math mathematics, Mathematik
mech mechanics, machine,
    Mechanik
med medicine, Medizin

mil military, militärisch
mot motoring, Kraftfahrzeuge
n noun, Hauptwort, Substantiv
naut nautical, Schiffahrt
neut neuter, Neutrum
phone telephone, Telefon
phot photography, Photographie
pl plural, Plural
pol politics, Politik
poss possessive, possessiv
prep preposition, Präposition
pron pronoun, Pronomen,
    Fürwort
psychol psychology, Psychologie
rail railways, Eisenbahn
rel religion, Religion
Schiff Schiffahrt, nautical
sing singular, Singular, Einzahl
tech technical, Technik
Telef Telefon, telephone
TV television, Fernsehen
umg. umgangssprachlich,
    colloquial
univ university, Universität
unz. unzählbar, mass noun
US American, Amerikanisch
v verb, Verbum, Zeitwort
V vide (see, siehe)
Wissensch Naturwissenschaft,
    science
zool zoology, Zoologie

German pronunciation

a bald [balt]
a: sagen ['za:gən]
e Telefon [tele'fo:n]
e: nehmen ['ne:mən]
ɛ Geld [gɛlt]
ɛ: Bär [bɛ:r]
i Idee [i'de:]
i: bieten ['bi:tən]
ɔ Holz [hɔlts]
o Rosette [ro'zɛtə]
o: Mohn [mo:n]
u bunt [bunt]
u: Schnur [ʃnu:r]
y fünf [fynf]
y: kühl [ky:l]
ə Butter ['butər]
œ böse ['bœzə]
œ: Möbel ['mœbəl]
ai bei [bai]
au Haus [haus]
ɔy Freund [frɔynt]
ã Chance ['ʃã:sə]
ɛ̃ Terrain [tɛ'rɛ̃:]
ɔ̃ Champignon ['ʃampinjɔ̃]

b Bad [ba:t]
d Dank [daŋk]
f Frau [frau]
g gut [gu:t]
h halb [halp]
j ja [ja:]
k Kind [kint]
l Lied [li:t]
m Mensch [mɛnʃ]
n neu [nɔy]
p Person [pɛr'zo:n]
r Rad [ra:t]
s falls [fals]
t Gerät [gə'rɛ:t]
v Wein [vain]
z Reise ['raizə]
ç ich [iç]
x Buch [bu:x]
ʃ Schuh [ʃu:]
ʒ Garage [ga'ra:ʒə]
ŋ lang [laŋ]

The sign ' precedes a syllable having primary stress.

Aussprache auf Englisch

a hat [hat]
e bell [bel]
i big [big]
o dot [dot]
ʌ bun [bʌn]
u book [buk]
ə alone [ə'loun]
a: card [ka:d]
ə: word [wə:d]
i: team [ti:m]
o: torn [to:n]
u: spoon [spu:n]
ai die [dai]
ei ray [rei]
oi toy [toi]
au how [hau]
ou road [roud]
eə lair [leə]
iə fear [fiə]
uə poor [puə]

b back [bak]
d dull [dʌl]
f find [faind]
g gaze [geiz]
h hop [hop]
j yell [jel]
k cat [kat]
l life [laif]
m mouse [maus]
n night [nait]
p pick [pik]
r rose [rouz]
s sit [sit]
t toe [tou]
v vest [vest]
w week [wi:k]
z zoo [zu:]
θ think [θiŋk]
ð those [ðouz]
ʃ shoe [ʃu:]
ʒ treasure ['treʒə]
tʃ chalk [tʃo:k]
dʒ jump [dʒʌmp]
ŋ sing [siŋ]

Das Zeichen ' steht vor einer Silbe mit Hauptbetonung.
Das Zeichen ˌ steht vor einer Silbe mit Nebenbetonung.

Guide to the dictionary

English irregular plural forms are shown at the headword and in the text. The following categories of plurals forms are considered regular:

cat	cats
glass	glasses
fly	flies
half	halves
wife	wives

German plurals are shown for most words (for example, **Gemälde**) but not for many compounds (for example, **Wandgemälde**). The label *pl -* indicates that the plural does not vary.

Where no gender is shown for a German noun, it may be masculine or feminine, for example **Abgeordnete(r)**. Adjectival nouns are shown by -**(r)** or -**(s)**, the final letter being used according to the article, for example: **der Abgeordnete, ein Abgeordneter, die Abgeordnete, eine Abgeordnete, Abgeordnete** (*pl*).

Under a German headword, a sub-entry may be shown preceded by a dash. The full form may be obtained by adding the sub-entry to the nearest preceding full word, less that part after the vertical strokes, if any. Thus, **außerhalb** is shown as follows:

    außer‖dem *adv* besides. **-halb** *adv*, *prep* outside.

Irregular verbs listed in the verb tables are marked with an asterisk in the body of the dictionary.

Many English adverbs are not shown in the dictionary if they are regularly formed, that is, by the addition of -(*al*)*ly* to the adjective.

Leitfaden für das Wörterbuch

Englische unregelmäßige Plurale sind bei dem Stichwort und im Text gezeigt. Die folgenden Kategorien von Pluralformen sind als regelmäßig anzusehen:

cat	cats
glass	glasses
fly	flies
half	halves
wife	wives

Deutsche Plurale sind für die meisten Wörter angeführt (z.B. **Gemälde**), aber nicht für viele zusammengesetzte Wörter (z.B. **Wandgemälde**). Das Zeichen *pl* - deutet an, daß der Plural mit dem Singular identisch ist.

Wo kein Geschlecht für ein deutsches Hauptwort angegeben ist, kann es sowohl männlich als auch weiblich sein, z.B. **Abgeordnete(r)**. Hauptworte, die aus Adjektiven gebildet sind, sind folgendermaßen gekennzeichnet -(**r**) oder -(**s**), wobei der letzte Buchstabe von dem Artikel abhängt, z.B. **der Abgeordnete, ein Abgeordneter, die Abgeordnete, eine Abgeordnete, Abgeordnete** (*pl*).

Hinter einem deutschen Stichwort, findet man öfter eine weitere Eintragung hinter einem Strich. Das komplette Wort erhält man durch Hinzufügen dieses Wortes an das vorherige Wort ohne den Teil hinter die Vertikalen, wenn nötig. So ist z.B. **außerhalb** wie folgt gezeigt:

außer‖dem *adv* besides. **-halb** *adv*, *prep* outside.

Unregelmäßige Verben, die in der separaten Liste aufgeführt sind, sind mit einem Sternchen (*) bei den Stichwörtern angezeigt.

Viele englische Adverbien sind in dem Wörterbuch nicht aufgeführt, wenn sie aus den Adjektiven regelmäßig durch die Nachsilbe -(*al*)*ly* gebildet sind.

German irregular verbs

Infinitive	Preterite	Past Participle
backen	backte (buk)	gebacken
bedingen	bedang (bedingte)	bedungen
befehlen	befahl	befohlen
beginnen	begann	begonnen
beißen	biß	gebissen
bergen	barg	geborgen
bersten	barst	geborsten
bewegen	bewog	bewogen
biegen	bog	gebogen
bieten	bot	geboten
binden	band	gebunden
bitten	bat	gebeten
blasen	blies	geblasen
bleiben	blieb	geblieben
bleichen	blich	geblichen
braten	briet	gebraten
brauchen	brauchte	gebraucht (brauchen)
brechen	brach	gebrochen
brennen	brannte	gebrannt
bringen	brachte	gebracht
denken	dachte	gedacht
dreschen	drosch	gedroschen
dringen	drang	gedrungen
dürfen	durfte	gedurft
empfehlen	empfahl	empfohlen
erkiesen	erkor	erkoren
erlöschen	erlosch	erloschen
erschrecken	erschrak	erschrocken
essen	aß	gegessen
fahren	fuhr	gefahren
fallen	fiel	gefallen
fangen	fing	gefangen
fechten	focht	gefochten
finden	fand	gefunden
flechten	flocht	geflochten
fliegen	flog	geflogen

Infinitive	Preterite	Past Participle
fliehen	floh	geflohen
fließen	floß	geflossen
fressen	fraß	gefressen
frieren	fror	gefroren
gären	gor	gegoren
gebären	gebar	geboren
geben	gab	gegeben
gedeihen	gedieh	gediehen
gehen	ging	gegangen
gelingen	gelang	gelungen
gelten	galt	gegolten
genesen	genas	genesen
genießen	genoß	genossen
geschehen	geschah	geschehen
gewinnen	gewann	gewonnen
gießen	goß	gegossen
gleichen	glich	geglichen
gleiten	glitt	geglitten
glimmen	glomm	geglommen
graben	grub	gegraben
greifen	griff	gegriffen
haben	hatte	gehabt
halten	hielt	gehalten
hängen	hing	gehangen
hauen	haute (hieb)	gehauen
heben	hob	gehoben
heißen	hieß	geheißen
helfen	half	geholfen
kennen	kannte	gekannt
klimmen	klomm	geklommen
klingen	klang	geklungen
kneifen	kniff	gekniffen
kommen	kam	gekommen
können	konnte	gekonnt
kriechen	kroch	gekrochen
laden	lud	geladen
lassen	ließ	gelassen (lassen)
laufen	lief	gelaufen

Infinitive	Preterite	Past Participle
leiden	litt	gelitten
leihen	lieh	geliehen
lesen	las	gelesen
liegen	lag	gelegen
lügen	log	gelogen
mahlen	mahlte	gemahlen
meiden	mied	gemieden
melken	melkte (molk)	gemolken (gemelkt)
messen	maß	gemessen
mißlingen	mißlang	mißlungen
mögen	mochte	gemocht
müssen	mußte	gemußt
nehmen	nahm	genommen
nennen	nannte	genannt
pfeifen	pfiff	gepfiffen
preisen	pries	gepriesen
quellen	quoll	gequollen
raten	riet	geraten
reiben	rieb	gerieben
reißen	riß	gerissen
reiten	ritt	geritten
rennen	rannte	gerannt
riechen	roch	gerochen
ringen	rang	gerungen
rinnen	rann	geronnen
rufen	rief	gerufen
salzen	salzte	gesalzen (gesalzt)
saufen	soff	gesoffen
saugen	sog	gesogen
schaffen	schuf	geschaffen
schallen	schallte (scholl)	geschallt
scheiden	schied	geschieden
scheinen	schien	geschienen
sheißen	schiß	geschissen
schelten	schalt	gescholten
scheren	schor	geschoren
schieben	schob	geschoben
scheißen	schoß	geschossen
schinden	schund	geschunden

Infinitive	Preterite	Past Participle
schlafen	schlief	geschlafen
schlagen	schlug	geschlagen
schleichen	schlich	geschlichen
schleifen	schliff	geschliffen
schleißen	schliß	geschlissen
schließen	schloß	geschlossen
schlingen	schlang	geschlungen
schmeißen	schmiß	geschmissen
schmelzen	schmolz	geschmolzen
schnauben	schnob	geschnoben
schneiden	schnitt	geschnitten
schreiben	schrieb	geschrieben
schreien	schrie	geschrie(e)n
schreiten	schritt	geschritten
schweigen	schwieg	geschwiegen
schwellen	schwoll	geschwollen
schwimmen	schwamm	geschwommen
schwinden	schwand	geschwunden
schwingen	schwang	geschwungen
schwören	schwor	geschworen
sehen	sah	gesehen
sein	war	gewesen
senden	sandte	gesandt
sieden	sott	gesotten
singen	sang	gesungen
sinken	sank	gesunken
sinnen	sann	gesonnen
sitzen	saß	gesessen
sollen	sollte	gesollt (sollen)
spalten	spaltete	gespalten (gespaltet)
speien	spie	gespie(e)n
spinnen	spann	gesponnen
sprechen	sprach	gesprochen
sprießen	sproß	gesprossen
springen	sprang	gesprungen
stechen	stach	gestochen
stecken	steckte (stak)	gesteckt
stehen	stand	gestanden
stehlen	stahl	gestohlen

Infinitive	Preterite	Past Participle
steigen	stieg	gestiegen
sterben	starb	gestorben
stieben	stob	gestoben
stinken	stank	gestunken
stoßen	stieß	gestoßen
streichen	strich	gestrichen
streiten	stritt	gestritten
tragen	trug	getragen
treffen	traf	getroffen
treiben	trieb	getrieben
treten	trat	getreten
triefen	triefte (troff)	getrieft
trinken	trank	getrunken
trügen	trog	getrogen
tun	tat	getan
verderben	verdarb	verdorben
verdrießen	verdroß	verdrossen
vergessen	vergaß	vergessen
verlieren	verlor	verloren
verschleißen	verschliß	verschlissen
verzeihen	verzieh	verziehen
wachsen	wuchs	gewachsen
wägen	wog (wägte)	gewogen (gewägt)
waschen	wusch	gewaschen
weben	wob	gewoben
weichen	wich	gewichen
weisen	wies	gewiesen
wenden	wandte	gewandt
werben	warb	geworben
werden	wurde	geworden (worden)
werfen	warf	geworfen
wiegen	wog	gewogen
winden	wand	gewunden
wissen	wußte	gewußt
wollen	wollte	gewollt (wollen)
wringen	wrang	gewrungen
zeihen	zieh	geziehen
ziehen	zog	gezogen
zwingen	zwang	gezwungen

Unregelmäßige Verben

Infinitive	Präteritum	Partizip Perfekt
abide	abode	abode
arise	arose	arisen
awake	awoke	awoke
be	was	been
bear	bore	borne *or* born
beat	beat	beaten
become	became	become
begin	began	begun
bend	bent	bent
bet	bet	bet
beware		
bid	bid	bidden *or* bid
bind	bound	bound
bite	bit	bitten
bleed	bled	bled
blow	blew	blown
break	broke	broken
breed	bred	bred
bring	brought	brought
build	built	built
burn	burnt *or* burned	burnt *or* burned
burst	burst	burst
buy	bought	bought
can	could	
cast	cast	cast
catch	caught	caught
choose	chose	chosen
cling	clung	clung
come	came	come
cost	cost	cost
creep	crept	crept
cut	cut	cut
deal	dealt	dealt
dig	dug	dug
do	did	done
draw	drew	drawn
dream	dreamed *or* dreamt	dreamed *or* dreamt

Infinitive	Präteritum	Partizip Perfekt
drink	drank	drunk
drive	drove	driven
dwell	dwelt	dwelt
eat	ate	eaten
fall	fell	fallen
feed	fed	fed
feel	felt	felt
fight	fought	fought
find	found	found
flee	fled	fled
fling	flung	flung
fly	flew	flown
forbid	forbade	forbidden
forget	forgot	forgotten
forgive	forgave	forgiven
forsake	forsook	forsaken
freeze	froze	frozen
get	got	got
give	gave	given
go	went	gone
grind	ground	ground
grow	grew	grown
hang	hung *or* hanged	hung *or* hanged
have	had	had
hear	heard	heard
hide	hid	hidden
hit	hit	hit
hold	held	held
hurt	hurt	hurt
keep	kept	kept
kneel	knelt	knelt
knit	knitted *or* knit	knitted *or* knit
know	knew	known
lay	laid	laid
lead	led	led
lean	leant *or* leaned	leant *or* leaned
leap	leapt *or* leaped	leapt *or* leaped
learn	learnt *or* learned	learnt *or* learned
leave	left	left

Infinitive	Präteritum	Partizip Perfekt
lend	lent	lent
let	let	let
lie	lay	lain
light	lit *or* lighted	lit *or* lighted
lose	lost	lost
make	made	made
may	might	
mean	meant	meant
meet	met	met
mow	mowed	mown
must		
ought		
pay	paid	paid
put	put	put
quit	quitted *or* quit	quitted *or* quit
read	read	read
rid	rid	rid
ride	rode	ridden
ring	rang	rung
rise	rose	risen
run	ran	run
saw	sawed	sawn *or* sawed
say	said	said
see	saw	seen
seek	sought	sought
sell	sold	sold
send	sent	sent
set	set	set
sew	sewed	sewn *or* sewed
shake	shook	shaken
shear	sheared	sheared *or* shorn
shed	shed	shed
shine	shone	shone
shoe	shod	shod
shoot	shot	shot
show	showed	shown
shrink	shrank	shrunk
shut	shut	shut
sing	sang	sung

Infinitive	Präteritum	Partizip Perfekt
sink	sank	sunk
sit	sat	sat
sleep	slept	slept
slide	slid	slid
sling	slung	slung
slink	slunk	slunk
slit	slit	slit
smell	smelt *or* smelled	smelt *or* smelled
sow	sowed	sown *or* sowed
speak	spoke	spoken
speed	sped *or* speeded	sped *or* speeded
spell	spelt *or* spelled	spelt *or* spelled
spend	spent	spent
spill	spilt *or* spilled	spilt *or* spilled
spin	spun	spun
spit	spat	spat
split	split	split
spread	spread	spread
spring	sprang	sprung
stand	stood	stood
steal	stole	stolen
stick	stuck	stuck
sting	stung	stung
stink	stank *or* stunk	stunk
stride	strode	stridden
strike	struck	struck
string	strung	strung
strive	strove	striven
swear	swore	sworn
sweep	swept	swept
swell	swelled	swollen *or* swelled
swim	swam	swum
swing	swung	swung
take	took	taken
teach	taught	taught
tear	tore	torn
tell	told	told
think	thought	thought

Infinitive	Preterite	Past Participle
throw	threw	thrown
thrust	thrust	thrust
tread	trod	trodden
wake	woke	woken
wear	wore	worn
weave	wove	woven
weep	wept	wept
win	won	won
wind	wound	wound
wring	wrung	wrung
write	wrote	written

Glossary of menu terms

There is lots to eat in German-speaking countries: five meals a day are about standard, and there's plenty of scope for snacks — especially nice when traveling with children. **Frühstück** (breakfast) is usually light, perhaps coffee or chocolate and bread; **Zweites Frühstück** (second breakfast) is more serious and will probably feature food that seems like a U.S.-style light lunch. But in the middle of the day comes **Mittagessen** (lunch) which is usually the main meal of the day. In late afternoon, there is **Kaffee mit Kuchen** (coffee and cake and a lot more), and finally **Abendbrot** (supper).

German cuisine is based on the foods the countries produce. Expect to eat simple, hearty food quite fresh from the farm. In Austria, the influence of Hungarian cooking provides some diversion, and in German Switzerland, the French and Italian neighbors have left a pleasing mark. Game is often featured; it is certainly worth trying.

There are many designations in German for establishments which serve food. In large towns, most common is **Restaurant** (the German word is **Gaststätte**); in the country, you will find **Gasthaus** or **Gasthof**. A **Bierstube** or **Weinstube** will serve some food as well as beer or wine, rather like an English pub. Restaurants usually offer full meals, but the menu may not be broken into courses or types of food (appetizers, first courses, meat dishes, fish, etc.). Most restaurants offer one or more **Gedeck** (fixed-priced meal), usually including soup, entrée with one or more vegetable, and a light dessert, no substitutions or additions permitted. These meals are often excellent values. Be sure to tell the waiter that you are having the set meal before you order.

Hotel dining rooms generally offer good **Kaffee mit Kuchen**, but if you are away from your hotel, try a **Café** or **Konditorei**. These places are also good for a light breakfast or a snack at almost any time.

By law, German eating places must list all charges, including service, on the menu in the price of each item. It is still customary, however, to leave a small tip, perhaps 5%, on the table.

Vorspeisen (Hors d'Oeuvre)

Beefsteak Tartar raw ground beef served with raw egg and onion
Bismarckhering pickled herring with onion and spices
Eiersalat egg salad
Froschschenkel frogs' legs
Gänseleber goose liver
Käsebrot open-faced cheese sandwich
Kaviar caviar
Lachsbrot open-faced salmon sandwich
Lachsalm slices of smoked salmon
Ochsenzungesalat salad of sliced tongue
Rollmops bits of smoked herring with mustard, onion, and pickle
Westfälischer Schinken raw cured ham from Westphalia

Würste (Sausages)

Blutwurst blood sausage
Bratwurst grilled pork sausage (spiced)
Knackwurst (or **Knockwurst**) sausage of pork or beef, rather like our hot dog
Leberwurst liver sausage
Wienerwurst Vienna sausage, on the order of small hot dogs
Weisswurst white veal sausage flavored with herbs (a specialty of Munich)

Eierspeisen (Egg Dishes)

Omelette omelette, served plain (**natur**) or with various stuffings (**gefüllt**), e.g.:
mit Champignons with mushrooms;
mit Fines Herbes with herbs, as parsley, tarragon, chives; **mit Geflügelleber**

with chicken livers; **mit Schinken** with ham; **Spanisches** with tomato and onion sauce

Pfannkuchen a sort of egg pancake, also served plain (**natur**) or stuffed (**gefüllt**): **mit Käse** with cheese; **mit Schinken** with ham; **mit Speck** with bacon

Pochierte Eier poached eggs

Rührei scrambled eggs

Spiegeleier (or **Setzeier**) fried eggs

Weichgekochte Eier soft-cooked eggs

Wachsweiche Eier medium-cooked eggs

Fischgerichte (Seafood)

Aal eel

Austern oysters

Dorsch codfish

Forellen trout

Hecht pike

Heilbutt halibut

Hummer lobster

Jacobsmuscheln scallops, coquilles

Krabben shrimp; for the larger shrimp, Germans usually use the Italian word **scampi**

Schellfisch haddock

Seezunge sole; prepared in many different ways in Germany: fried, baked, in various sauces, etc.

Suppen (Soups)

Bauernsuppe "peasant soup": mixed vegetable soup

Biersuppe soup of beer with spices

Bohnensuppe bean soup

Brühe broth: **Fleischbrühe,** meat broth; **Geflügelbrühe,** chicken broth; **Fischbrühe,** fish broth

Champignonrahmsuppe cream of mushroom soup

Kartoffelsuppe potato soup

Leberknödelsuppe dumplings of chopped liver, onion, and spices, in broth

Linsensuppe lentil soup

Nudelsuppe mit Huhn chicken noodle soup

Tomatensuppe tomato soup

Zwiebelsuppe onion soup

Hauptgerichte (Main meat Dishes

Bauernschmaus "the peasant's delight": platter of bacon, sausages, sauerkraut, mashed potatoes, and dumplings

Burgunderschinken ham cooked in wine sauce with vegetables

Cordon Bleu slices of veal with ham and cheese dipped in batter and fried

Deutsches Beefsteak fried ground beef, with onion rings and potatoes (Note: the term "steak" on German menus often denotes what an American would call Salisbury steak, or hamburger; for something more like the American idea of steak, see **Lendensteak**)

Eisbein pickled ham hocks with sauerkraut and mashed potatoes

Filet Goulasch "Beef Stroganoff": strips of beef cooked in sour cream with onions and mushrooms

Frikadellen fried meat balls

Gulyas (Austria) goulash; spicy stew

Hackrahmsteak ground meat patty in browned cream gravy

Hammelkeule roast leg of lamb

Hammelkotelette lamb chop, grilled

Hasenpfeffer stew of pieces of hare, marinated in wine and spices, then cooked in the marinade with onions and mushrooms

Kalbsbrust Gefüllte mit Geflügelleber breast of veal, rolled and stuffed with chicken livers, ham, etc.

Kalbshirn mit Rührei calf brains with scrambled eggs

Kalbskotelette veal chop, grilled

Kalbsleber mit Zwiebeln calf liver with onions

Kalbsmilch sweetbreads

Kalbsschnitzel veal cutlet; see also **Wienerschnitzel**

Königsberger Klops large meat balls served in a sour cream sauce with capers

Lendensteak tenderloin steak (usually offered with a variety of sauces; if you prefer plain, ask for **"natur"**

Pfeffersteak steak coated with ground

peppercorns and grilled
Rehbraten roast venison; **Rehrücken** saddle of venison
Rostbraten roast beef (Germany); minute steak (Austria)
Roulades thin slices of veal rolled and stuffed with a variety of stuffings and garnishes
Sauerbraten roast beef marinated with wine and spices and vinegar, then pot-roasted with vegetables
Schmorbraten pot roast
Schnitzel usually a thin-sliced pan-fried veal cutlet; but sometimes pork (**Schweineschnitzel**) or other meat; prepared in a number of different ways, associated with different areas, as **Holstein-erschnitzel** (topped with a fried egg), **Schwäbischeschnitzel** (with sour cream sauce), and, the most famous, **Wiener-schnitzel** (breaded, with a lemon slice and various other garnishes)
Schweinefüsse pigs' feet
Schweinekotelette pork chop: **natur** (plain) or with a variety of sauces
Schweinslendchen pork tenderloin
Ungarischer Gulasch chunks of meat cooked with paprika, onions, and other vegetables
Wiener Rostbraten beef loin fried in butter with onions

Geflügel und Wild (Fowl and Game)

Backhuhn or **Brathuhn** fried chicken
Damwildkeule roast leg of venison
Fasan im Topf pheasant roasted in casserole
Förstertopf mit Pilzen casserole of venison with mushrooms
Frikassee vom Huhn fricasséed chicken
Gansbraten roast goose
Geflügelleber chicken livers
Geflügelragout chicken stew
Kapaun capon
Puterbraten roast turkey
Rebhuhn partridge
Rehbraten roast venison

Rehrücken saddle of venison
Supreme vom Masthuhn boned breast of chicken
Wiener Backhuhn chicken Vienna style: breaded and deep fried with parsley.
Wildschweinbraten roast of wild boar

Gemüse und Beilagen (Vegetables and Side dishes)

Apfelrotkohl or **-kraut** red cabbage cooked with apples
Artischockenhertzen artichoke hearts
Aubergine eggplant
Beete beets
Blumenkohl cauliflower
Dicke Bohnen broad beans (fava)
Erbsen peas
Grüne Bohnen green beans
Gurkensalat cucumber salad
Karotten carrots
Kartoffeln potatoes, the most common accompaniment to the meat dish in Germany; some of the more common ways they are listed on the menu: **Bratkartoffeln** potatoes boiled, sliced and panfried; **Gebackene Kartoffeln** baked potatoes; **Herzoginkartoffeln** "dutchess" potatoes: mashed, shaped and browned in oven; **Kartoffelknödel** potato dumplings; **Kartoffelpuffer** potato pancakes; **Pommes Frites** French-fried potatoes; **Würfelkartoffeln** fried diced potatoes
Kartoffelsalat German potato salad, served either hot (**heiss**), sautéed onions and bacon poured over sliced boiled potatoes with vinegar dressing; or cold (**kalt**), with vinegar dressing poured over sliced potatoes and chopped onions
Kohl cabbage
Krautsalat coleslaw
Lattich lettuce
Möhren carrots
Nudeln noodles
Obstsalat fruit salad
Pilzen mushrooms
Rosenkohl Brussel sprouts

Salatplatte salad; may indicate anything from a simple green salad to more elaborate affairs including vegetables, meats, and a variety of dressings

Spätzle short thick noodles often served with meat dishes; preparation varies from area to area

Spinat spinach

Steckrübe turnips

Succini zucchini

Zwiebeln onions

Süssspeisen (Desserts)

Apfelstrudel mixture of apples and spices rolled in very thin pastry and baked

Apfelsinen oranges

Arme Ritter a sort of French toast; bread dipped in batter and fried

Auflauf souffle; the German version may be heavier than the French

Eierschaum whipped custard of egg yolks and sugar, flavored with wine, similar to Italian zabaione

Eis or **Eiskrem** ice cream; may be served in a bowl (**Eisbecher**) with various syrups or fruit toppings; in German Switzerland, **Glace**

Eistorte ice cream cake

Englischer Kuchen pound cake

Erdbeeren strawberries

Haselnussrahm hazelnut cream

Himbeeren raspberries

Käsetorte cheesecake

Königskuchen "King's cake": rum-flavored layer cake with almonds, currants, and raisins

Mohrenkopf "Moor's head": dome-shaped cake filled with custard or whipped cream and topped with chocolate

Pfirsichen peaches

Schokoladencremetorte chocolate layer cake filled with a rich chocolate cream

Getränke (Beverages)

Apfelsinesaft orange juice

Bier beer; **Oktoberbier** is the dark beer enjoyed at the *Oktoberfest*

Himbeersaft raspberry juice; very popular with children

Kaffee coffee; in Austria often served **mit Schlag** or in Germany, **mit Schlagsahne** (whipped cream)

Kirsch brandy distilled from cherries

Kümmel caraway-seed-flavored liqueur

Milch milk

Mineralwasser mineral water

Schnapps brandy

Schokolade chocolate, usually served hot

Tee tea

Wasser water; **Eiswasser** ice water

English−Deutsch

A

a, an [ə, ən] *art* ein *m*, eine *f*, ein *neut*. *once a year* einmal im Jahr. *50 kilometres an hour* 50 Kilometer pro Stunde.

aback [ə'bak] *adv* **taken aback** verblüfft, überrascht.

abandon [ə'bandən] *v* (*leave*) verlassen; (*give up*) aufgeben. *n* **with abandon** ungezwungen. **abandoned** *adj* verfallen.

abashed [ə'baʃt] *adj* verlegen.

abate [ə'beit] *v* abnehmen.

abattoir ['abətwaɪ] *n* Schlachthaus *neut*.

abbey ['abi] *n Abtei f.* **abbess** *n* Äbtissin *f*. **abbot** *n* Abt *m*.

abbreviate [ə'briːvieit] *v* (ab)kürzen. **abbreviation** *n* Abkürzung *f*.

abdicate ['abdikeit] *v* abdanken. **abdication** *n* Abdankung *f*.

abdomen ['abdəmən] *n* Bauch *m*, Unterleib *m*. **abdominal** *adj* Leib-, abdominal.

abduct [əb'dʌkt] *v* entführen. **abduction** *n* Entführung *f*.

aberration [abə'reiʃən] *n* Abweichung *f*; (*optics, astron*) Aberration *f*. **mental aberration** Geistesverirrung *f*.

abet [ə'bet] *v* begünstigen, Vorschub leisten (+ *dat*).

abeyance [ə'beiəns] *n* **in abeyance** in der Schwebe.

abhor [əb'hoɪ] *v* hassen, verabscheuen. **abhorrence** *n* Abscheu (vor) *m*. **abhorrent** *adj* abscheulich.

*****abide** [ə'baid] *v* bleiben, verweilen; (*tolerate*) ausstehen. **abide by** festhalten an.

ability [ə'biləti] *n* Fähigkeit *f*; (*skill*) Geschicklichkeit *f*. **to the best of one's ability** nach besten Kräften.

abject [,abdʒekt] *adj* (*wretched*) elend; (*contemptible*) verächtlich, gemein.

ablaze [ə'bleiz] *adj, adv* brennend, in Flammen. **set ablaze** entflammen.

able ['eibl] *adj* fähig; (*talented*) geschickt, begabt. **be able** können, fähig sein; (*be in a position to*) in der Lage sein. **ably** *adv* geschickt.

abnormal [ab'noɪml] *adj* anormal, abnorm; (*unusual*) ungewöhnlich; (*malformed*) mißgestaltet. **abnormality** *n* Abnormität *f*; Mißbildung *f*.

aboard [ə'boɪd] *adj, adv* (*ship*) an Bord. **go aboard** an Bord gehen, einsteigen.

abode [ə'boud] *V* **abide**. *n* Wohnsitz *m*.

abolish [ə'boliʃ] *v* abschaffen, beseitigen.

abominable [ə'bominəbl] *adj* scheußlich. **abominate** *v* verabscheuen. **abomination** *n* Abscheu *m*.

aborigine [abə'ridʒini] *n* Ureinwohner *m*. **aboriginal** *adj* Ur-, ursprünglich.

abortion [ə'boɪʃən] *n* (*miscarriage*) Fehlgeburt *f*; (*termination of pregnancy*) Abtreibung *f*. **abortive** *adj* mißlungen.

abound [ə'baund] *v* im Überfluß vorhanden sein. **abound in** reich sein an.

about [ə'baut] *adv* (*approximately*) ungefähr, etwa; (*nearby*) in der Nähe. *prep* (*concerning*) über; (*around*) um ... herum. **be about to do something** etwas tun wollen. **walk about** hin- und herlaufen.

above [ə'bʌv] *prep* über. *adv* oben. **above-mentioned** oben erwähnt, obig. **above board** offen, ehrlich.

abrasion [ə'breiʒən] *n* Abschleifen *neut*, Abrieb *m*; (*wound*) Abschürfung *f*. **abrasive** *adj* abschleifend.

abreast [ə'brest] *adv* **keep abreast of** Schritt halten mit.

abridge [ə'bridʒ] *v* (ab)kürzen. **abridgement** *n* Abkürzung *f*.

abroad [ə'broɪd] *adv* (*go*) ins Ausland; (*be*) im Ausland.

abrupt [ə'brʌpt] *adj* (*sudden*) plötzlich; (*brusque*) kurz, unhöflich.
abscess ['abses] *n* Abszeß *m*.
abscond [əb'skɒnd] *v* flüchten.
absent ['absənt] *adj* abwesend. **absent-minded** geistesabwesend. **absentee** *n* Abwesende(r). **absence** *n* Abwesenheit *f*; (*lack*) Mangel *m*.
absolute ['absəluːt] *adj* völlig, vollkommen, absolut; (*unconditional*) bedingungslos; (*pure*) rein. **absolutely** *adv* völlig; (*interj*) gewiß! **absolutism** *n* Absolutismus *m*.
absolve [əb'zɒlv] *v* entbinden, freisprechen.
absorb [əb'zɔːb] *v* aufsaugen, absorbieren. **absorbed in thought** in Gedanken vertieft. **absorbent** *adj* absorbierend. **absorbent cotton** Watte *f*. **absorbing** *adj* fesselnd.
abstain [əb'stein] *v* (*voting*) seine Stimme enthalten. **abstain from** verzichten auf. **abstinence** *n* Enthaltsamkeit *f*.
abstemious [əb'stiːmiəs] *adj* mäßig, enthaltsam.
abstract ['abstrakt] *adj* abstrakt, theoretisch. **abstraction** *n* Abstraktion *f*.
absurd [əb'səːd] *adj* unsinnig, lächerlich. **absurdity** *n* Unsinn *m*.
abundance [ə'bʌndəns] *n* Überfluß *m*, Reichtum *m*. **abundant** *adj* reichlich. **abundant in** reich an.
abuse [ə'bjuːz, ə'bjuːs] *v* mißbrauchen; (*insult*) beleidigen. *n* Mißbrauch *m*; Beschimpfung *f*. **abusive** *adj* beleidigend.
abyss [ə'bis] *n* Abgrund *m*. **abysmal** *adj* abgrundtief; (*fig*) grenzenlos.
academy [ə'kadəmi] *n* Akademie *f*; (*private school*) Internat *m*. **academic** *adj* akademisch.
accede [ak'siːd] *v* (*agree*) zustimmen (+*dat*), (*join*) beitreten (+*dat*); (*throne*) besteigen.
accelerate [ək'seləreit] *v* (*mot*) gasgeben; (*make quicker*) beschleunigen; (*go faster*) schneller werden. **acceleration** *n* Beschleunigung *f*. **accelerator** *n* Gaspedal *neut*.
accent ['aksənt] *n* Akzent *m*. **accentuate** *v* betonen.
accept [ək'sept] *v* akzeptieren, annehmen; (*agree*) zusagen (+*dat*). **acceptable** *adj* annehmbar. **acceptance** *n* Annahme *f*.
access ['akses] *n* Zutritt *m*, Zugang *m*. **accessible** *adj* erreichbar.

accessory [ək'sesəri] *n* (*mot*) Zubehörteil *m*; (*law*) Mitschuldige(r).
accident ['aksidənt] *n* (*mishap*) Unfall *m*; (*chance*) Zufall *m*. **accidental** *adj* zufällig.
acclaim [ə'kleim] *v* zujubeln (+*dat*). *n* (*also acclamation*) Beifall *m*, Lob *neut*.
acclimatize [ə'klaimətaiz] *v* angewöhnen, akklimatisieren.
accolade ['akəleid] *n* Auszeichnung *f*.
accommodate [ə'kɒmədeit] *n* (*put up*) unterbringen; (*help*) aushelfen. **accommodating** *adj* hilfreich. **accommodation** *n* Unterkunft *f*.
accompany [ə'kʌmpəni] *v* begleiten. **accompaniment** *n* Begleitung *f*. **accompanist** *n* Begleiter(in).
accomplice [ə'kʌmplis] *n* Mittäter *m*.
accomplish [ə'kʌmpliʃ] *v* vollbringen, vollenden. **accomplished** *adj* gebildet, gewandt. **accomplishment** *n* Durchführung, Vollendung *f*.
accord [ə'kɔːd] *v* übereinstimmen. *n* Übereinstimmung *f*, Einklang *m*. **of one's own accord** freiwillig. **in accordance with** gemäß (+*dat*): *in accordance with the rules* den Regeln gemäß. **accordingly** *adv* dementsprechend, deswegen. **according to** laut (+*gen*).
accordion [ə'kɔːdiən] *n* Akkordeon *neut*.
accost [ə'kost] *v* ansprechen.
account [ə'kaunt] *n* (*bill*) Rechnung *f*; (*bank, etc*) Konto *neut*; (*report*) Bericht *m*. **accounts** *pl n* Bücher *pl*. **current account** Scheckkonto *neut*. **savings account** Sparkonto *neut*. **on account of** Konto. **on account of** wegen (+*gen*), *auf Grund* (+*gen*). **on no account** auf keinen Fall. **take into account** berücksichtigen. *v* **account for** erklären. **accountable** *adj* verantwortlich. **accountant** *n* Buchhalter *m*.
accrue [ə'kruː] *v* auflaufen.
accumulate [ə'kjuːmjuleit] *v* anhäufen, sich häufen. **accumulation** *n* Anhäufung *f*.
accurate ['akjurət] *adj* genau, exakt; (*correct*) richtig. **accuracy** *n* Genauigkeit *f*.
accuse [ə'kjuːz] *v* anklagen. **the accused** der/die Angeklagte(r). **accusation** *n* Anklage *f*. **accusative** *n* Akkusativ *m*.
accustom [ə'kʌstəm] *v* become accustomed to sich gewöhnen an. **accustomed** *adj* gewöhnlich, üblich.
ace [eis] *n* (*cards*) As *neut*. *adj* (*coll*) erstklassig.

ache [eik] n Schmerz m. v schmerzen, weh tun.
achieve [əˈtʃiːv] v durchführen, vollbringen; (reach) erlangen. achievement n Vollendung f. (success) Erfolg m.
acid [ˈasid] n Säure f. adj sauer.
acknowledge [əkˈnolidʒ] n anerkennen; (admit) zugeben. acknowledge receipt Empfang bestätigen. acknowledgment n Anerkennung f.
acne [ˈakni] n Pickel m, Akne f.
acorn [ˈeikɔːn] n Eichel f.
acoustic [əˈkuːstik] adj akustisch. acoustics pl n Akustik f sing.
acquaint [əˈkweint] v bekannt machen. be acquainted with kennen (+acc). get acquainted with kennenlernen (+acc). acquaintance n Bekannte(r).
acquiesce [akwiˈes] v sich fügen. acquiescence n Ergebung f. acquiescent adj fügsam.
acquire [əˈkwaiə] v erwerben, bekommen. acquisition n Erwerb m. acquisitive habsüchtig, gierig.
acquit [əˈkwit] v (law) freisprechen. acquittal n Freisprechung f.
acrid [ˈakrid] adj scharf, beißend.
acrimony [ˈakriməni] n Bitterkeit f. acrimonious adj bitter, beißend.
acrobat [ˈakrəbat] n Akrobat m. acrobatic adj akrobatisch. acrobatics pl n Akrobatik f sing.
across [əˈkros] adv hinüber, herüber. prep (quer) über (+acc), jenseits (+gen), auf der anderen Seite.
act [akt] v handeln, tun; (behave) sich verhalten; (theatre) (eine Rolle) spielen. act on wirken auf. n Handlung, Tat f; (law) Gesetz neut; (theatre) Aufzug m. acting adj amtierend; n (theatre) Spielen neut. actor n Schauspieler m. actress n Schauspielerin f.
action [ˈakʃən] n Handlung f; (deed) Tat f; (effect) Wirkung f; (law) Klage f; (battle) Gefecht neut.
active [ˈaktiv] adj tätig, aktiv. activate v aktivieren. activist n Aktivist m. activity n Tätigkeit f. activities n Unternehmungen pl.
actual [ˈaktʃuəl] adj wirklich, eigentlich, tatsächlich. actually adv wirklich, tatsächlich. interj eigentlich.
actuate [ˈaktjueit] v in Gang bringen.
acupuncture [ˈakjupʌŋktʃə] n Akupunktur f.

acute [əˈkjuːt] adj scharf, heftig; (angle) spitz; (person) scharfsinnig; (med) akut.
adamant [ˈadəmənt] adj unnachgiebig.
Adam's apple [adəmˈzapl] n Adamsapfel m.
adapt [əˈdapt] v anpassen; verändern. adapted to geeignet für. adaptable adj anpassungsfähig. adaptation n (theatre) Bearbeitung f. adaptor n (for plug) Zwischenstecker m.
add [ad] v (figures) addieren; (word, sentence) hinzufügen. add up addieren. addition n (math) Addition f; (something added) Zugabe f, Zutat m. in addition außerdem. in addition to zusätzlich zu. additional adj zusätzlich, weiter. additive n Zusatz m.
addendum [əˈdendəm] n Zusatz m.
adder [ˈadə] n (snake) Natter m.
addict [ˈadikt; v əˈdikt] n Süchtige(r); (coll) Fanatiker m. drug addict Rauschgiftsüchtige(r). addicted süchtig. addiction n Sucht f.
address [əˈdres] v (letter) addressieren; (person) anreden. n Adresse f, Anschrift f; (speech) Anrede f. address book Adreßbuch neut. addressee n Empfänger m.
adenoids [ˈadənoidz] pl n Polypen pl.
adept [əˈdept] adj geschickt, erfahren.
adequate [ˈadikwət] adj (quantity) ausreichend, genügend; (quality) annehmbar.
adhere [ədˈhiə] v adhere to haften or kleben an (+dat); (belief, etc.) festhalten an (+dat). adhesive adj klebrig, haftend. adhesive tape Klebeband neut. adherent n Anhänger m.
adjacent [əˈdʒeisənt] adj angrenzend.
adjective [ˈadʒiktiv] n Adjektiv neut, Eigenschaftswort neut.
adjoin [əˈdʒoin] v angrenzen (an). adjoining adj angrenzend, anliegend.
adjourn [əˈdʒəːn] v vertagen. adjournment n Vertagung f.
adjudicate [əˈdʒuːdikeit] v Recht sprechen, entscheiden. adjudicator n Schiedsrichter m.
adjust [əˈdʒʌst] v anpassen; berichtigen; (tech) einstellen. adjust to sich anpassen an. adjustable adj einstellbar. adjustment n Anpassung, Einstellung f.
ad-lib [ˈadlib] adv frei. v improvisieren.

administer [ǝd'ministǝ] v verwalten.
administer justice Recht sprechen.
administration n Verwaltung f. **administrative** adj Verwaltungs-. **administrator** n Verwalter m.

admiral ['admǝrǝl] n Admiral m.
admire [ǝd'maiǝ] v bewundern, hochschätzen. **admirable** adj bewundernswert. **admiration** n Bewunderung f.

admission [ǝd'miʃǝn] n Eintritt m; (acknowledgment) Zugeständnis neut.
admit [ǝd'mit] v (let in) hereinlassen, zulassen; (concede) zugeben. **admittance** n Zutritt, Eintritt m. **no admittance** Zutritt verboten.

adolescence [adǝ'lesns] Jugend f. **adolescent** adj jugendlich. n Jugendliche(r).
adopt [ǝ'dopt] v (child) adoptieren; (idea) annehmen, übernehmen. **adoption** n Adoption f; Übernahme f.
adore [ǝ'doi] v lieben; (rel) verehren. **adorable** adj entzückend. **adoration** n Verehrung f.
adorn [ǝ'doin] v schmücken. **adornment** n Schmuck m.

adrenaline [ǝ'drenǝlin] n Adrenalin neut.
adrift [ǝ'drift] adj, adv (naut) treibend; (fig) hilflos.
adroit [ǝ'droit] adj gewandt, geschickt.
adulation [adju'leiʃǝn] n Lobhudelei f.
adult ['adʌlt] n Erwachsene(r). adj erwachsen; (animal, plant) ausgewachsen.
adulterate [ǝ'dʌltǝreit] v verfälschen. **adulteration** n Verfälschung f.
adultery [ǝ'dʌltǝri] n Ehebruch m. **adulterer** n Ehebrecher(in).
advance [ǝd'vains] v vorwärts gehen, vorrücken; (make progress) Fortschritte machen; (cash) vorschießen; (cause) fördern; (tech) vorstellen. n Vorrücken neut, Fortschritt m; Vorschuß m. **in advance** im voraus. **advancement** n Beförderung f.
advantage [ǝd'vaintidʒ] n Vorteil m. **take advantage of** ausnutzen (+acc). **advantageous** adj vorteilhaft.
advent ['advǝnt] n Ankunft f; (rel) Advent m.
adventure [ǝd'ventʃǝ] n Abenteuer m. **adventurer** n Abenteurer m. **adventurous** adj gewagt.
adverb ['advǝib] n Adverb neut, Umstandswort neut.
adversary ['advǝsǝri] n Gegner m.

adverse ['advǝis] adj widrig, ungünstig.
adversity n Mißgeschick neut, Not f.
advertise ['advǝtaiz] v anzeigen. **advertisement** n Anzeige f. **advertising** n Reklame, Werbung f.
advise [ǝd'vaiz] v (be)raten, empfehlen; (comm) benachrichtigen. **advisable** adj ratsam. **adviser** n Berater m. **advice** n Rat m, Ratschlag m; (comm) Avis neut.
advocate ['advǝkeit] v befürworten.
aerial ['eǝriǝl] n Antenne f. adj Luft-.
aerodynamics [eǝrǝdai'namiks] n Aerodynamik f.
aeronautics [eǝrǝ'noitiks] n Aeronautik f, Flugwesen neut.
aeroplane ['eǝrǝplein] n Flugzeug neut.
aerosol ['eǝrǝsol] n Sprühdose f, Spray neut.
aesthetic [iis'θetik] adj ästhetisch.
affair [ǝ'feǝ] n Angelegenheit f, Sache f; (love affair) (Liebes) Affäre f.
affect[1] [ǝ'fekt] v (influence) (ein)wirken auf, beeinflüssen. **affected** adj (moved) bewegt.
affect[2] [ǝ'fekt] v (pretend) vorgeben. **affectation** n Affektation f. **affected** adj geziert.
affection [ǝ'fekʃǝn] n Zuneigung f, Liebe f. **affectionate** adj liebevoll.
affiliated [ǝ'filieitid] adj angeschlossen. **affiliated company** Tochtergesellschaft f. **affiliation** n Verbindung f, Mitgliedschaft f.
affinity [ǝ'finǝti] n Zuneigung f; (chem) Affinität f.
affirm [ǝ'fǝim] v behaupten. **affirmation** n Behauptung f. **affirmative** adj bestätigend.
affix [ǝ'fiks] v befestigen, ankleben (an).
afflict [ǝ'flikt] v betrüben. **affliction** n Leiden neut.
affluent ['afluǝnt] adj wohlhabend, reich. **affluence** n Wohlstand m.
afford [ǝ'foid] v sich leisten (können); (allow) gewähren.
affront [ǝ'frʌnt] v beleidigen. n Beleidigung f.
afloat [ǝ'flout] adj, adv schwimmend; (boat) auf dem Meere.
afoot [ǝ'fut] adv im Gang.
aforesaid [ǝ'foised] adj vorher erwähnt.
afraid [ǝ'freid] adj ängstlich, erschrocken, bange. **be afraid of** Angst haben vor. **be afraid to** sich scheuen. *I am afraid I must ...* ich muß leider ...

afresh [ə'freʃ] *adv* von neuem, noch einmal.

Africa ['afrikə] *n* Afrika *neut*. **African** *n* Afrikaner(in). *adj* afrikanisch.

aft [aɪft] *adj* Achter-. *adv* achtern.

after ['aɪftə] *conj* nachdem. *prep* nach, hinter. *adv* später, nachher. *adj* (*naut*) Achter-. **after all** schließlich. **shortly after** kurz danach.

after-effect *n* Nachwirkung *f*.

afterlife ['aɪftəlaif] *n* Leben nach dem Tode *neut*.

aftermath ['aɪftəmaθ] *n* Auswirkung *f*.

afternoon [ˌaɪftə'nuɪn] *n* Nachmittag *m*. **good afternoon!** guten Tag!

aftershave ['aɪftəʃeiv] *n* Rasierwasser *neut*.

after-taste *n* Nachgeschmack *m*.

afterthought ['aɪftəθɔɪt] *n* nachträglicher Einfall *m*.

afterwards ['aɪftəwədz] *adv* nachher, später, danach.

again [ə'gen] *adv* wieder, noch einmal, nochmals; (*moreover*) ferner. **again and again** immer wieder.

against [ə'genst] *prep* gegen. **as against** im Vergleich zu.

age [eidʒ] *n* (*person*) Alter *neut*; (*era*) Zeitalter *neut*. **age group** Altersgruppe *f*. **at the age of ...** im Alter von .... **of age** volljährig. **old age** (hohes) Alter *neut*. *v* alt werden. **aged** *adj* (*elderly*) betagt. *aged five years* fünf Jahre alt. **under age** minderjährig.

agency ['eidʒənsi] *n* Agentur *f*.

agenda [ə'dʒendə] *n* Tagesordnung *f*.

agent ['eidʒənt] *n* Agent *m*, Vermittler *m*; (*chem*) Wirkstoff *m*.

aggravate ['agrəveit] *v* verschlimmern; (*coll*) ärgern. **aggravation** *n* Verschlimmerung *f*; Ärger *m*.

aggregate ['agrigət] *adj* gesamt, ganz. *n* Summe *f*.

aggression [ə'greʃən] *n* Angriff *m*, Aggression *f*. **aggressive** *adj* aggressiv. **aggressor** *n* Angreifer *m*.

aghast [ə'gaɪst] *adj* entsetzt.

agile ['adʒail] *adj* agil, flink. **agility** *n* Flinkheit *f*.

agitate ['adʒiteit] *v* schütteln. **agitated** *adj* beunruhigt. **agitation** *n* Beunruhigung *f*.

agnostic [ag'nostik] *n* Agnostiker *m*. **agnosticism** *n* Agnostizismus *m*.

ago [ə'gou] *adv* vor: *a year ago* vor einem Jahr. **a moment ago** soeben. **a long time ago** schon lange her. **a short time ago** vor kurzem.

agog [ə'gog] *adj* gespannt.

agony ['agəni] *n* Qual *f*, Agonie *f*. **agonize over** sich quälen über.

agree [ə'griɪ] *v* (*concur*) übereinstimmen, einverstanden sein; (*date, etc*.) vereinbaren; (*consent*) zustimmen; (*be in agreement*) einig sein. *eggs do not agree with me* ich kann Eier nicht vertragen. **agreed!** einverstanden! **agreeable** *adj* angenehm. **agreement** *n* Übereinstimmung *f* (*written*) Abkommen *neut*.

agriculture ['agrikʌltʃə] *n* Landwirtschaft *f*. **agricultural** *adj* landwirtschaftlich.

aground [ə'graund] *adv* **run aground** stranden.

ahead [ə'hed] *adv* vorwärts. **straight ahead** gerade aus. **go ahead** fortfahren.

aid [eid] *n* Hilfe *f*. *v* helfen (+*dat*).

aim [eim] *v* (*gun*) richten; (*intend*) zielen. *n* Ziel *neut*. **aimless** *adj* ziellos.

air [eə] *n* Luft *f*; (*appearance*) Aussehen *neut*; (*music*) Lied *neut*. *v* (*laundry*) trocknen; (*views*) bekanntmachen. **go by air** fliegen. **airy** *adj* luftig.

airbed ['eəbed] *n* Luftmatratze *f*.

airborne ['eəbɔɪn] *adj* in der Luft; Luft-.

air-conditioned *adj* klimatisiert. **air-conditioning** *n* Klimaanlage *f*.

air-cooled *adj* (*mech*) luftgekühlt.

aircraft ['eəkraɪft] *n* Flugzeug *neut*.

airfield ['eəfiɪld] *n* Flugplatz *m*.

air force *n* Luftwaffe *f*.

air lift *n* Luftbrücke *f*.

airline ['eəlain] *n* Luftverkehrsgesellschaft *f*. **airline passenger** Fluggast *m*.

airmail ['eəmeil] *n* Luftpost *f*. **by airmail** mit Luftpost.

airport ['eəpɔɪt] *n* Flughafen *m*.

air-raid *n* Luftangriff *m*.

air steward *n* Steward *m*. **air stewardess** *n* Stewardeß *f*.

airtight ['eətait] *adj* luftdicht.

aisle [ail] *n* Gang *m*.

ajar [ə'dʒaɪ] *adj* halboffen.

akin [ə'kin] *adj* **akin to** ähnlich (+*dat*).

alabaster ['aləbaɪstə] *n* Alabaster *m*.

à la carte [alaɪ'kaɪt] *adv* nach der Speisekarte, à la carte.

alarm [ə'laɪm] *n* Alarm *m*; (*unrest*) Beunruhigung *f*. *v* beunruhigen. **alarm clock** Wecker *m*.

alas [ə'las] *interj* leider! o weh!
albatross ['albətros] *n* Albatros *m.*
albino [al'biɪnou] *n* Albino *m.*
album ['albəm] *n* Album *neut.*
alchemy ['alkəmi] *m* Alchimie *f.* **alchemist** *n* Alchimist *m.*
alcohol ['alkəhol] *n* Alkohol *m.* **alcoholic** *adj* alkoholisch. *n* Alkoholiker *m.* **alcoholism** *n* Alkoholismus *m.* **non-alcoholic** *adj* alkoholfrei.
alcove ['alkouv] *n* Nische *f.*
alderman ['oɪldəmən] *n* Ratsherr *m.*
ale [eil] *m* Bier *neut.*
alert [ə'ləɪt] *adj* wachsam, munter. *v* warnen. **on the alert** auf der Hut.
algebra ['aldʒibrə] *n* Algebra *f.*
alias ['eiliəs] *adv* sonst . . . genannt, alias. *n* Deckname *m.*
alibi ['alibai] *n* Alibi *neut.*
alien ['eiliən] *n* Fremde(r), Ausländer *m. adj* fremd. **alienate** *v* entfremden. **alienation** *n* Entfremdung *f.*
alight[1] [ə'lait] *v* (*from bus*) aussteigen.
alight[2] [ə'lait] *adj, adv* brennend, in Flammen. **set alight** entflammen.
align [ə'lain] *v* ausrichten. **alignment** *n* Ausrichtung *f.*
alike [ə'laik] *adj, adv* gleich.
alimentary canal [ali'mentəri] *m* Nährungskanal *m.*
alimony ['aliməni] *n* Unterhalt *m,* Alimente *pl.*
alive [ə'laiv] *adj* lebend, am Leben. **alive with** wimmelnd von.
alkali ['alkəlai] *n* Alkali *neut.* **alkaline** *adj* alkalisch.
all [oɪl] *adj* alle, sämtliche *pl. pron* alles, das Ganze. *adv* ganz. **all over** vorbei. **all gone** alle, weg. **above all** vor allem. **all at once** auf einmal. **at all** überhaupt. **all day** den ganzen Tag. **all right** in Ordnung, okay.
allay [ə'lei] *v* beruhigen.
allege [ə'ledʒ] *v* angeben, behaupten. **alleged** *adj* angeblich. **allegation** *n* Behauptung *f.*
allegiance [ə'liɪdʒəns] *n* Treue *f.*
allegory ['aligəri] *n* Allegorie *f.* **allegorical** *adj* allegorisch.
allergy ['alədʒi] *n* Allergie *f.* **allergic** *adj* allergisch (gegen).
alleviate [ə'liɪvieit] *v* erleichtern.
alley ['ali] *n* Gasse *f.* **bowling alley** Kegelbahn *f.*

alliance [ə'laiəns] *n* (*pol*) Bündnis *neut.* **form an alliance** ein Bündnis schließen.
allied ['alaid] *adj* verbündet, alliiert.
alligator ['aligeitə] *n* Alligator *m.*
alliteration [əlitə'reiʃən] *n* Alliteration *f.* **alliterative** *adj* alliterierend.
allocate ['aləkeit] *v* zuteilen.
allot [ə'lot] *v* (*distribute*) zuteilen; (*assign*) bestimmen. **allotment** *n* Zuteilung *f;* (*garden patch*) Schrebergarten *m.*
allow [ə'lau] *v* erlauben, gestatten. **allow for** berücksichtigen. **will you allow me** (*to*)? darf ich? **allowance** *n* Erlaubnis *f;* (*money*) Rente *f.*
alloy ['aloi; *v* ə'loi] *n* Legierung *f. v* legieren.
allude [ə'luɪd] *v* **allude to** anspielen auf (+*acc*). **allusion** *n* Anspielung *f.*
allure [ə'ljuə] *n* Reiz *m. v* verlocken. **alluring** *adj* verlockend.
ally ['alai; *v* ə'lai] *n* Verbündete(r); (*pol*) Alliierte(r). *v* **ally oneself with** sich verbünden mit. **the Allies** die Alliierten.
almanac ['oɪlmənak] *n* Jahrbuch *neut,* Almanach *m.*
almighty [oɪl'maiti] *adj* allmächtig; (*coll*) gewaltig. **the Almighty** der Allmächtige.
almond ['aɪmənd] *n* Mandel *f.*
almost ['oɪlmoust] *adv* fast, beinahe.
alms [aɪmz] *pl n* Almosen *neut sing.*
aloft [ə'loft] *adv* (*be*) oben; (*go*) nach oben.
alone [ə'loun] *adj, adv* allein. **leave alone** bleiben lassen. **leave me alone!** laß mich in Ruhe!
along [ə'loŋ] *prep* entlang (+*acc*): *along the coast* die Küste entlang. *adv* vorwärts, weiter; mit: **come along** mitkommen. **along with** zusammen mit. **get along with someone** mit jemandem gut auskommen. **alongside** *prep* neben (+*acc or dat*); (*ship*) längseits (+*gen*).
aloof [ə'luɪf] *adj* zurückhaltend.
aloud [ə'laud] *adv* laut. **read aloud** vorlesen.
alphabet ['alfəbit] *n* Alphabet *neut.* **alphabetical** *adj* alphabetisch.
Alps [alps] *pl n* Alpen *pl.* **alpine** *adj* Alpen-.
already [oɪl'redi] *adv* schon, bereits.
Alsatian [al'seiʃən] *n* (*dog*) Schäferhund *m. adj* elsässisch.
also ['oɪlsou] *adv* auch, ebenfalls; (*moreover*) ferner.

altar ['ɔːltə] *n* Altar *m*.
alter ['ɔːltə] *v* (*modify*) (ab-, ver)ändern; (*become changed*) sich (ver)ändern. **alteration** *n* (Ab-, Ver)Änderung *f*; (*building*) Umbau *m*.
alternate [ɔːl'tɔːnət; *v* 'ɔːltəneit] *adj* abwechselnd. *v* abwechseln.
alternative [ɔːl'tɔːnətiv] *adj* ander. *n* Alternative *f*. *there is no alternative* es gibt keine andere Möglichkeit.
although [ɔːl'ðou] *conj* obwohl, obgleich, wenn auch.
altitude ['altitjuːd] *m* Höhe *f*.
alto ['altou] *n* Alt *m*, Altstimme *f*.
altogether [ɔːltə'geðə] *adv* insgesamt, im ganzen; völlig.
altruistic [altru'istik] *adj* altruistisch.
aluminium [alju'miniəm] *n* Aluminium *neut*.
always ['ɔːlweiz] *adv* immer, stets; schon immer.
am [am] *V* be.
amalgamate [ə'malgəmeit] *v* (*tech*) amalgamieren; (*fig*) vereinigen.
amass [ə'mas] *v* aufhäufen.
amateur ['amətə] *n* Amateur *m*. *adj* Amateur-.
amaze [ə'meiz] *v* erstaunen, verblüffen. **amazed at** erstaunt über. **amazement** *n* Erstaunen *neut*. **amazing** *adj* erstaunlich; (*coll*) sagenhaft.
ambassador [am'basədə] *n* Botschafter *m*.
amber ['ambə] *n* Bernstein *m*. *adj* bernsteinfarb, gelb.
ambidextrous [ambi'dekstrəs] *adj* beidhändig.
ambiguous [am'bigjuəs] *adj* zweideutig, unklar.
ambition [am'biʃən] *n* Ehrgeiz *m*, Ambition *f*. **ambitious** *adj* ehrgeizig, ambitiös.
ambivalence [am'bivələns] *n* Ambivalenz *f*. **ambivalent** *adj* ambivalent.
amble ['ambl] *v* schlendern.
ambulance ['ambjuləns] *n* Krankenwagen *m*.
ambush ['ambuʃ] *n* Hinterhalt *m*. *v* aus dem Hinterhalt überfallen.
ameliorate [ə'miːliəreit] *v* (*make better*) verbessern; (*get better*) besser werden. **amelioration** *n* Verbesserung *f*.
amenable [ə'miːnəbl] *adj* zugänglich; (*accountable*) verantwortlich.
amend [ə'mend] *v* (ab)ändern; ergänzen, richtigstellen. **make amends for**

wiedergutmachen. **amendment** *n* (*to a motion*) Ergänzung *f*.
amenities [ə'miːnətiz] *pl n* Vorzüge *pl*, moderne Einrichtungen *pl*.
America [ə'merikə] *n* Amerika *neut*. **American** *n* Amerikaner(in); *adj* amerikanisch.
amethyst ['aməθist] *n* Amethyst *m*.
amiable ['eimiəbl] *adj* freundlich, liebenswürdig.
amicable ['amikəbl] *adj* freundschaftlich, friedlich.
amid [ə'mid] *prep* mitten unter (+*dat*).
amiss [ə'mis] *adj* verkehrt, nicht richtig. **take amiss** übelnehmen.
ammonia [ə'mouniə] *n* Ammoniak *neut*.
ammunition [amju'niʃən] *n* Munition *f*.
amnesia [am'niːziə] *n* Gedächtnisverlust *m*.
amnesty ['amnəsti] *n* Amnestie *f*.
amoeba [ə'miːbə] *n* Amöbe *f*.
among [ə'mʌŋ] *prep* unter, zwischen (+*dat*); bei (+*dat*). **among other things** unter anderem. **among ourselves/yourselves/themselves** miteinander, untereinander.
amoral [ei'morəl] *adj* amoralisch.
amorous ['amərəs] *adj* verliebt; liebevoll.
amorphous [ə'mɔːfəs] *adj* (*chem*) amorph; formlos.
amount [ə'maunt] *n* (*of money*) Betrag *m*, Summe *f*; (*quantity*) Menge *f*. **amount to** betragen. *it amounts to the same* es läuft auf das gleiche hinaus.
ampere ['ampeə] *n* Ampere *neut*.
amphibian [am'fibiən] *n* Amphibie *f*. **amphibious** *adj* amphibisch; (*vehicle*) Amphibien-.
amphitheatre ['amfiθiətə] *n* Amphitheater *neut*; (*lecture room*) Hörsaal *m*.
ample ['ampl] *adj* ausreichend, reichlich.
amplify ['amplifai] *v* verstärken. **amplification** *n* Verstärkung *f*. **amplifier** *n* Verstärker *m*.
amputate ['ampjuteit] *v* amputieren. **amputation** *n* Amputation *f*.
amuse [ə'mjuːz] *v* belustigen, amüsieren; (*entertain*) unterhalten. **be amused by** *or* **about** lustig finden. **amusing** *adj* lustig, unterhaltend. **amusement** *n* Unterhaltung *f*.
anachronism [ə'nakrənizəm] *n* Anachronismus *m*. **anachronistic** *adj* anachronistisch.

anaemia [ə'niːmiə] *n* Anämie, Blutarmut *f*. **anaemic** *adj* anämisch, blutarm.
anaesthetic [anəs'θetik] *n* Betäubungsmittel *neut*. **under anaesthetic** unter Narkose. **anaesthetize** *v* betäuben.
anagram ['anəgram] *n* Anagramm *neut*.
analogy [ə'nalədʒi] *n* Ähnlichkeit *f*, Analogie *f*. **analogous** *adj* analog, ähnlich.
analysis [ən'aləsis] *n* Analyse *f*. **analyse** *v* analysieren. **analytical** *adj* analytisch.
anarchy ['anəki] *n* Anarchie *f*. **anarchist** Anarchist *m*.
anathema [ə'naθəmə] *n* (*rel*) Kirchenbann *m*. **that is anathema to me** das ist mir ein Greuel.
anatomy [ə'natəmi] *n* Anatomie *f*. **anatomical** *adj* anatomisch.
ancestor ['ansestə] *n* Vorfahr *m*, Ahn *m*.
anchor ['aŋkə] *n* Anker *m*. *v* befestigen. **ride at anchor** vor Anker liegen. **weigh anchor** den Anker lichten.
anchovy ['antʃəvi] *n* Anschovis *f*.
ancient ['einʃənt] *adj* alt, uralt; aus alter Zeit, antik.
ancillary [an'siləri] *adj* zusätzlich, Hilfs-.
and [and] *conj* und.
anecdote ['anikdout] *n* Anekdote *f*.
anemone [ə'neməni] *n* Anemone *f*.
anew [ə'njuː] *adv* von neuem, wieder.
angel ['eindʒəl] *n* Engel *m*. **angelic** *adj* engelhaft.
angelica [an'dʒelikə] *n* Angelika *f*.
anger ['aŋgə] *n* Zorn *m*, Ärger *m*. *v* ärgern. **in anger** im Zorn. **angry** *adj* ärgerlich, zornig. **be angry** sich ärgern, böse sein.
angina [an'dʒainə] *n* Angina *f*.
angle¹ ['aŋgl] *n* Winkel *m*, Ecke *f*; (*coll*) Gesichtspunkt *m*. **be at an angle to** einen Winkel bilden mit.
angle² ['aŋgl] *v* angeln (nach). **angler** *n* Angler *m*. **angling** *n* Angeln *neut*.
anguish ['aŋgwiʃ] *n* Qual *f*.
angular ['aŋgjulə] *adj* winkelig, eckig.
animal ['animəl] *n* Tier *neut*. *adj* tierisch, animalisch. **animal fat** Tierfett *neut*. **animal kingdom** Tierreich *neut*.
animate ['animeit] *v* beleben; begeistern. **animated** *adj* lebhaft. **animated cartoon** Zeichentrickfilm *m*.
animosity [ani'mosəti] *n* Feindseligkeit *f*.
aniseed ['anisiːd] *n* Anis *m*.
anisette [ˌani'zet] *n* Anisett *m*.
ankle ['aŋkl] *n* (Fuß)Knöchel *m*.
annals ['anlz] *pl n* Annalen *pl*.

annex [ə'neks; *n* 'aneks] *n* (*to building*) Anbau *m*. *v* (*country*) annektieren. **annexation** *n* Annexion *f*.
annihilate [ə'naiəleit] *v* vernichten. **annihilation** *n* Vernichtung *f*.
anniversary [ˌani'vɔːsəri] *n* Jahrestag *m*. **wedding anniversary** Hochzeitstag *m*.
annotate ['anəteit] *v* kommentieren. **annotation** *n* Anmerkung *f*.
announce [ə'nauns] *v* ankündigen, ansagen, anzeigen. **announcement** *n* Ankündigung *f*, Ansage *f*; (*radio*) Durchsage *f*. **announcer** *n* (*radio*) Ansager *m*.
annoy [ə'noi] *v* belästigen, ärgern. **be annoyed at** *or* **with** sich ärgern über (+*acc*). **annoyance** *n* Belästigung *f*.
annual ['anjuəl] *adj* jährlich; Jahres-. *n* (*book*) Jahrbuch *neut*; (*plant*) einjährige Pflanze *f*.
annul [ə'nʌl] *v* annullieren. **annulment** *n* Annullierung *f*.
anode ['anoud] *n* Anode *f*.
anomaly [ə'noməli] *n* Anomalie *f*.
anonymous [ə'noniməs] *adj* anonym, ungenannt.
anorak ['anərak] *n* Anorak *m*.
another [ə'nʌðə] *pron, adj* (*a different*) ein anderer; (*an additional*) noch ein. **one another** einander, sich.
answer ['aːnsə] *n* Antwort *f*; (*solution*) Lösung *f*. *v* antworten, erwidern. **answer back** unverschämt antworten. **answer for** verantwortlich sein für. **answerable** *adj* verantwortlich.
ant [ant] *n* Ameise *f*.
antagonize [an'tagənaiz] *v* reizen, entfremden. **antagonist** *n* Gegner *m*, Feind *m*. **antagonistic** *adj* feindselig.
antecedent [anti'siːdənt] *adj* früher.
antelope ['antəloup] *n* Antilope *f*.
antenatal [anti'neitl] *adj* vor der Geburt. **antenatal care** Schwangerschaftsvorsorge *f*.
antenna [an'tenə] *m* (*insect*) Fühler *m*; (*radio*) Antenne *f*.
anthem ['anθəm] *n* Hymne *f*. **national anthem** Nationalhymne *f*.
anthology [an'θolədʒi] *n* Anthologie *f*.
anthropology [anθrə'polədʒi] *n* Anthropologie *f*. **anthropological** *adj* anthropologisch.
anti-aircraft [anti'eəkraːft] *adj* Fliegerabwehr-. **anti-aircraft gun** Fliegerabwehrkanone *f*.

antibiotic [antibai'otik] *n* Antibiotikum *neut. adj* antibiotisch.
antibody ['anti‚bodi] *n* Antikörper *m*.
anticipate [an'tisipeit] *v* (*expect*) erwarten; (*foresee*) voraussehen. **anticipation** *n* Erwartung *f*. **in anticipation of** in Erwartung (+ *gen*).
anticlimax [anti'klaimaks] *n* Enttäuschung *f*.
anticlockwise [anti'klokwaiz] *adj, adv* dem Uhrzeigersinn entgegen.
antics ['antiks] *pl n* Possen *pl*.
anticyclone [anti'saikloun] *n* Hochdruckgebiet *neut*.
antidote ['antidout] *n* Gegenmittel (gegen) *neut*.
antifreeze ['antifritz] *n* Frostschutzmittel *neut*.
antipathy [an'tipaθi] *n* Antipathie *f*, Abneigung *f*.
antique [an'tiik] *adj* antik, altertümlich. *n* Antiquität *f*. **antiquated** *adj* veraltet. **antiquity** *n* Altertum *neut*.
anti-Semitic [antisə'mitik] *adj* antisemitisch.
antiseptic [anti'septik] *n* Antiseptikum *neut. adj* antiseptisch.
antisocial [anti'souʃəl] *adj* gesellschaftsfeindlich; (*person*) unfreundlich.
antithesis [an'tiθəsis] *n* Gegensatz *m*.
antler ['antlə] *n* Geweihsprosse *f*.
antonym ['antənim] *n* Antonym *neut*.
anus ['einəs] *n* After *m*.
anvil ['anvil] *n* Amboß *m*.
anxious ['aŋkʃəs] *adj* (*worried*) beunruhigt, besorgt; (*desirous*) begierig (nach). **be anxious to do something** gespannt sein, etwas zu tun. **anxiety** *n* Angst *f*, Besorgnis *f*.
any ['eni] *pron* irgendein, welche. *adv* etwas. *any faster* schneller, etwas schneller. *any more?* noch mehr? *do you want any?* wollen sie welche? *I haven't any money* ich habe kein Geld. *I can't do it any longer* ich kann es nicht mehr machen. **anybody** *pron* (*irgend*) jemand; (*everybody*) jeder. **anyhow** *adv* jedenfalls. **anyone** *pron see* **anybody**. **anything** *pron* (*irgend*) etwas; (*everything*) alles. **anytime** *adv* jederzeit. **anyway** *adv* jedenfalls, sowieso. **anywhere** *adv* irgendwo(hin); (*everywhere*) überall.
apart [ə'part] *adv* auseinander, getrennt. **apart from** abgesehen von.

apartheid [ə'paɪteit] *n* Apartheid *f*.
apartment [ə'paɪtmənt] *n* Wohnung *f*.
apathy ['apəθi] *n* Apathie *f*. **apathetic** *adj* apathisch.
ape [eip] *n* Affe *m*. *v* nachäffen.
aperitive [ə'perətiv] *n* Aperitif *m*.
aperture ['apətjuə] *n* Öffnung *f*; (*phot*) Blende *f*.
apex ['eipeks] *n* Spitze *f*.
aphid ['eifid] *n* Blattlaus *f*.
aphrodisiac [afrə'diziak] *n* Aphrodisiakum *neut*.
apiece [ə'piːs] *adv* (*per person*) pro Person; (*for each article*) pro Stück.
apology [ə'polədʒi] *n* Entschuldigung *f*. **apologetic** ‚*adj* entschuldigend. **apologize** sich entschuldigen.
apoplexy ['apəpleksi] *n* Schlaganfall *m*.
apostle [ə'posl] *n* Apostel *m*.
apostrophe [ə'postrəfi] *n* Apostroph *m*, Auslassungszeichen *neut*.
appal [ə'poɪl] *v* entsetzen. **appalling** *adj* entsetzlich.
apparatus [apə'reitəs] *n* Apparat *m*, Gerät *neut*.
apparent [ə'parənt] *adj* (*obvious*) offenbar; (*seeming*) scheinbar. **apparently** allem Anschein nach.
apparition [apə'riʃən] *n* Erscheinung *f*, Geist *m*.
appeal [ə'piɪl] *n* Appell *m*, dringende Bitte *f*; (*charm*) Anziehungskraft *f*; (*law*) Berufung *f*. *v* **appeal against** (*law*) Berufung einlegen gegen. **appeal for** dringend bitten um. **appeal to** (*turn to*) appellieren, sich wenden an; (*please*) gefallen (+ *dat*). **appealing** *adj* reizvoll.
appear [ə'piə] *v* (*seem*) scheinen; (*become visible, present itself*) erscheinen; (*crop up*) auftauchen. **appearance** *n* Erscheinen *neut*; (*look*) Anschein *m*.
appease [ə'piɪz] *v* beruhigen; (*hunger*) stillen. **appeasement** *n* Beruhigung *f*.
appendix [ə'pendiks] *n* (*in book*) Anhang *m*; (*anat*) Blinddarm *m*. **appendicitis** *n* Blinddarmentzündung *f*.
appetite ['apitait] *n* Appetit *m*. **appetizer** *n* Appetitshappen *m*. **appetizing** *adj* appetitlich.
applaud [ə'ploɪd] *v* Beifall klatschen (+ *dat*); *applaudieren* (+ *dat*); (*fig*) loben.
apple ['apl] *n* Apfel *m*. **apple juice** Apfelsaft *m*. **apple tree** Apfelbaum *m*. **apple sauce** Apfelmus *neut*.

appliance [ə'plaiəns] n Gerät neut.
applicable ['aplikəbl] adj zutreffend.
applicant ['aplikənt] n Kandidat m.
apply [ə'plai] v anwenden; (be valid) gelten. **apply for** (job) sich bewerben um. **apply to** sich wenden an. **apply oneself to** sich bemühen um. **application** n Anwendung f; (job) Bewerbung f. **applied** adj angewandt.
appoint [ə'point] v anstellen, ernennen. **appointed** adj vereinbart. **well appointed** gut ausgestattet. **appointment** n Anstellung f; (meeting) Verabredung f.
apportion [ə'poːʃən] v zuteilen.
appraisal [ə'preizl] n Schätzung f.
appreciable [ə'priːʃəbl] adj merkbar.
appreciate [ə'priːʃieit] v schätzen; (understand) verstehen; (be grateful for) dankbar sein für; (increase in value) im Wert steigen. **appreciation** n (gratitude) Anerkennung f; (in value) Wertzuwachs m. **appreciative** adj anerkennend.
apprehend [apri'hend] v (understand) begreifen; (seize) verhaften. **apprehensive** adj angstvoll.
apprentice [ə'prentis] n Lehrling m. **apprenticeship** n Lehre f.
approach [ə'proutʃ] v (come near) sich nähern; (a place) nähern; (someone) sich wenden an. n Herankommen neut; (attitude) Einstellung f; (access) Zugang m. **approachable** adj zugänglich.
appropriate [ə'proupriət; v ə'prouprieit] adj geeignet (+ dat). v sich aneignen.
approve [ə'pruːv] v (agree) zustimmen; (pass, endorse) billigen, genehmigen. **approve of** billigen. **approved** adj bewährt. **approval** n Billigung f, Genehmigung f. **on approval** auf Probe.
approximate [ə'proksimət] adj ungefähr. **approximately** adv ungefähr, etwa.
apricot ['eiprikot] n Aprikose f.
April ['eiprəl] n April m.
apron ['eiprən] n Schürze f.
apt [apt] adj (remark) passend. **apt at** geschickt in. **be apt to do something** geneigt sein, etwas zu tun. **aptitude** n (gift) Begabung f.
aqualung ['akwəlʌŋ] n Unterwasseratmungsgerät neut.
aquarium [ə'kweəriəm] n Aquarium neut.
Aquarius [ə'kweəriəs] n Wassermann m.
aquatic [ə'kwatik] n Wasser-.
aqueduct ['akwidʌkt] n Aquädukt m.
Arab ['arəb] n Araber m. adj or **Arabian**,

Arabic arabisch. **Arabic** n arabische Sprache f.
arable ['arəbl] adj **arable land** Ackerland neut.
arbitrary ['aːbitrəri] adj willkürlich.
arbitrate ['aːbitreit] v entscheiden. **arbitration** n Schiedsspruch m. **arbitrator** n Schiedsrichter m.
arc [aːk] n Bogen m.
arcade [aːˈkeid] n Arkade f.
arch [aːtʃ] n (architecture) Bogen m. v (sich) wölben. adj Erz-. **archway** n Bogengang m.
archaeology [aːki'olədʒi] n Archäologie f. **archaeological** adj archäologisch. **archaeologist** n Archäologe m.
archaic [aːˈkeiik] adj altertümlich.
archbishop [aːtʃ'biʃəp] n Erzbischof m.
archduke [aːtʃ'djuːk] n Erzherzog m.
archer ['aːtʃə] n Bogenschütze m. **archery** n Bogenschießen neut.
archetype ['aːkitaip] n Vorbild neut; (psychol) Archetyp m.
archipelago [aːki'peləgou] n Archipel m.
architect ['aːkitekt] n Architekt m. **architecture** n Architektur f.
archives ['aːkaivz] pl n Archiv neut sing.
ardent ['aːdənt] adj eifrig, begeistert.
ardour ['aːdə] n Eifer m.
arduous ['aːdjuəs] adj mühsam, anstrengend.
are [aː] V be.
area ['eəriə] n (measurement) Fläche f; (region) Gebiet neut. Zone f.
arena [ə'riːnə] n Arena neut.
argue ['aːgjuː] v streiten; (case) diskutieren; (maintain) behaupten. **argument** n Streit m; (reasoning) Argument neut. **argumentative** adj streitlustig.
arid ['arid] adj trocken, dürr.
Aries ['eəriːz] n Widder m.
*arise [ə'raiz] v (come into being) entstehen; (get up) aufstehen.
arisen [ə'rizn] V arise.
aristocracy [ari'stokrəsi] n Adel m, Aristokratie f. **aristocrat** n Aristokrat m. **aristocratic** adj aristokratisch.
arithmetic [ə'riθmətik] n Arithmetik f. **arithmetical** adj arithmetisch.
arm¹ [aːm] n Arm m. (of chair) Seitenlehne f. **arm in arm** Arm in Arm. **with open arms** mit offenen Armen.
arm² [aːm] n (weapon) Waffe f. v bewaffnen. **arms race** Wettrüsten neut.

coat of arms Wappen *neut.* **armed forces** Streitkräfte *pl.*

armament ['ɑːməmənt] *n* Kriegsausrüstung *f.*

armchair ['ɑːmtʃeə] *n* Sessel, Lehnstuhl *m.*

armistice ['ɑːmistis] *n* Waffenstillstand *m.*

armour ['ɑːmə] *n* (*suit of*) Rüstung *f;* (*of ship, tank*) Panzerung *f.* **armoured** *adj* gepanzert.

armpit ['ɑːmpit] *n* Achselhöhle *f.*

army ['ɑːmi] *n* Armee *f,* Heer *neut.* **join the army** zum Militär gehen.

aroma [ə'roumə] *n* Aroma *neut,* Duft *m.*

arose [ə'rouz] *V* arise.

around [ə'raund] *adv* ringsherum, rundherum; auf allen Seiten; (*nearby*) in der Nähe. *prep* um ... herum, rings um; (*approximately*) ungefähr. **look around (for)** sich umsehen (nach). **turn around** sich umdrehen.

arouse [ə'rauz] *v* wecken; (*suspicion*) erregen.

arrange [ə'reindʒ] *v* (*put in order*) anordnen; (*meeting*) verabreden; (*holidays*) festsetzen. (*see to it*) arrangieren, einrichten; (*music*) bearbeiten. **arrangement** *n* Anordnung *f;* (*agreement*) Vereinbarung *f;* (*music*) Bearbeitung *f.* **make arrangements** Vorbereitungen treffen.

array [ə'rei] *n* Aufstellung *f.*

arrears [ə'riəz] *pl n* Rückstände *pl.* **in arrears** im Rückstand *m.*

arrest [ə'rest] *v* (*thief*) verhaften; (*halt*) anhalten; *n* Verhaftung *f.* **under arrest in** Haft, verhaftet. **arresting** *adj* fesselnd.

arrive [ə'raiv] *v* ankommen; (*fig*) gelangen. **arrival** *n* Ankunft *f.* **late arrival** Spätankömmling *m.*

arrogance ['ærəgəns] *n* Hochmut *m.* **arrogant** *adj* hochmütig, eingebildet.

arrow ['ærou] *n* Pfeil *m.*

arse [ɑːs] *n* (*vulgar*) Arsch *m.*

arsenal ['ɑːsənl] *n* Arsenal *neut.*

arsenic ['ɑːsnik] *n* Arsenik *neut.*

arson ['ɑːsn] *n* Brandstiftung *f.* **arsonist** *n* Brandstifter *m.*

art [ɑːt] *n* Kunst *f.* **arts** *pl* Geisteswissenschaften *pl.* **arts and crafts** Kunstgewerbe *neut sing.* **art gallery** Kunstgalerie *f.* **art school** Kunstschule *f.* **work of art** Kunstwerk *neut.*

artefact ['ɑːtifakt] *n* Artefakt *neut.*

artery ['ɑːtəri] *n* Arterie *f.*

arthritis [ɑː'θraitis] *n* Arthritis *f.*

artichoke ['ɑːtitʃouk] *n* Artischocke *f.*

article ['ɑːtikl] *n* Artikel *m;* (*newspaper*) Zeitungsartikel *m,* Bericht *m.* **article of clothing** Bekleidungstück *neut.*

articulate [ɑː'tikjulət] *adj.* **to be articulate** sich gut ausdrücken.

articulated lorry [ɑːtikjuleitid] *n* Sattelschlepper *m.*

artifice ['ɑːtifis] *n* Trick *m.*

artificial [ɑːti'fiʃəl] *adj* (*manmade*) künstlich, Kunst-; (*affected*) affektiert. **artificial respiration** künstliche Atmung *f.*

artillery [ɑː'tiləri] *n* Artillerie *f.*

artisan [ɑːti'zan] *n* Handwerker *m.*

artist ['ɑːtist] *n* Künstler *m;* (*painter*) Maler *m.* **artiste** *n* Artist(in). **artistic** *adj* künstlerisch.

as [az] *conj, prep* (*while*) als, während; (*in the way that*) wie, sowie; (*since*) da, weil; (*in role of*) als. **as ... as** (eben)so ... wie. **as far as** soweit. **as if** als ob. **as long as** solange. **as soon as** sobald. **as it were** sozusagen. **as well** auch.

asbestos [az'bestos] *n* Asbest *m.*

ascend [ə'send] *v* aufsteigen. **ascendant** *adj* vorherrschend. **ascent** *n* Aufstieg *m.* **Ascension** *n* Himmelfahrt *f.*

ascertain [asə'tein] *v* feststellen.

ascetic [ə'setik] *adj* asketisch. *n* Asket *m.*

ash[1] [aʃ] *n* (*cinder*) Asche *f.* **ashtray** *n* Aschenbecher *neut.*

ash[2] [aʃ] *n* (*tree*) Esche *f.*

ashamed [ə'ʃeimd] *adj* **be ashamed** sich schämen.

ashore [ə'ʃoɪ] *adv* am Ufer. **go ashore an** Land gehen.

Ash Wednesday *n* Aschermittwoch *m.*

Asia ['eiʃə] *n* Asien *neut.* **Asian** *n* Asiat *m;* *adj* asiatisch.

aside [ə'said] *adv* beiseite. **aside from** außer. **step aside** zur Seite treten. **turn aside from** sich wegwenden von.

ask [ɑːsk] *v* (*to question*) fragen; (*request*) bitten. **ask a question** eine Frage stellen.

askew [ə'skjuː] *adv* verschoben, schief.

asleep [ə'sliːp] *adj, adv* **be asleep** schlafen. **fall asleep** einschlafen.

asparagus [ə'spærəgəs] *n* Spargel *m.*

aspect ['aspekt] *n* (*appearance*) Aussehen *neut;* (*of a problem*) Aspekt *m.*

asphalt ['asfalt] *n* Asphalt *m.*

asphyxiate [əs'fiksieit] *v* ersticken. **asphyxiation** *n* Erstickung *f.*

aspic ['aspik] n Aspik m.
aspire [ə'spaiə] v **aspire to** streben nach.
aspiring adj hochstrebend.
aspirin ['aspərin] n Aspirin neut.
ass [as] n Esel m.
assail [ə'seil] v angreifen. **assailant** n Angreifer m.
assassin [ə'sasin] n Attentäter m, Mörder m. **assassinate** v ermordern. **assassination** n Ermordung f.
assault [ə'soilt] v angreifen, überfallen.. n Angriff m. **indecent assault** Sittlichkeitsverbrechen neut.
assemble [ə'sembl] v (congregate) sich versammeln; (put together) montieren, zusammenbauen; (bring together) versammeln. **assembly** n (people) Versammlung f; (tech) Montage f. **assembly hall** Aula f. **assembly line** Fließband.
assent [ə'sent] v zustimmen (+ dat). n Zustimmung f.
assert [ə'səit] v (insist on) bestehen auf; (declare) erklären. **assertion** n Behauptung f. (self-)assertive adj selbstsicher.
assess [ə'ses] v (for tax) bewerten; (estimate) schätzen. **assessment** n Bewertung f.
asset ['aset] n Vorteil m. **assets** pl Vermögen neut sing.
assiduous [ə'sidjuəs] adj fleißig.
assign [ə'sain] v zuteilen, bestimmen. **assignment** n Aufgabe f.
assimilate [ə'simileit] v aufnehmen. **assimilation** n Aufnahme f.
assist [ə'sist] v helfen (+ dat). **assistance** n Hilfe f. **assistant** n Helfer m. **sales assistant** n Verkäufer m.
associate [ə'sousieit] n ə'sousiət] v verbinden. n Kollege m, Mitarbeiter m; (comm) Partner m. **association** n (club) Verein m, Verband m; (link) Verbindung f.
assorted [ə'soitid] adj verschiedenartig,. gemischt. **assortment** n Sortiment neut.
assume [ə'sjuim] v (suppose) annehmen; (take over) übernehmen.
assure [ə'ʃuə] v (convince) versichern (+ dat), versprechen; (ensure) sicherstellen. **assurance** n (assertion) Versicherung f; (confidence) Selbstsicherheit f. **life assurance** Lebensversicherung f.
asterisk ['astərisk] n Sternchen neut.
asthma ['asmə] n Asthma neut.
astonish [ə'stoniʃ] v erstaunen, verblüffen.

be astonished (at) erstaunt sein (über), sich wundern (über). **astonishing** adj erstaunlich. **astonishment** n Erstaunen neut.
astound [ə'staund] v bestürzen, erstaunen.
astray [ə'strei] adv **go astray** in die Irre gehen. **lead astray** vom rechten Weg abführen.
astride [ə'straid] adv rittlings. prep rittlings auf (+ dat).
astringent [ə'strindʒənt] adj zusammenziehend.
astrology [ə'strolədʒi] n Astrologie f. **astrologer** n Astrologe m. **astrological** adj astrologisch.
astronaut ['astrənoıt] n Astronaut m.
astronomy [ə'stronəmi] n Astronomie f. **astronomer** n Astronom m. **astronomical** adj astronomisch.
astute [ə'stjuıt] adj scharfsinnig.
asunder [ə'sʌndə] adv auseinander.
asylum [ə'sailəm] n Asyl neut. **lunatic asylum** Irrenanstalt f. **political asylum** politisches Asyl neut.
at [at] prep (place) in, zu, bei, an, auf; (time) um, zu, in; (age, speed) mit; (price) zu. **at school** in der Schule. **at four o'clock** um vier Uhr. **at my house** bei mir. **at home** zuhause. **at (age) 65** mit 65. **at Christmas** zu Weihnachten. **at peace** in Frieden.
ate [et] V eat.
atheist ['eiθiist] n Atheist m.
Athens ['aθinz] n Athen neut.
athlete ['aθliıt] n Athlet m. **athletic** adj athletisch. **athletics** n (Leicht)Athletik f.
Atlantic [ət'lantik] n Atlantik m.
atlas ['atləs] n Atlas m.
atmosphere ['atməsfiə] n Atmosphäre f. **atmospheric** adj atmosphärisch, Luft-.
atom ['atəm] n Atom neut. **atomic** adj Atom-. **atomic bomb** Atombombe f. **atomic power** Atomkraft f. **atomic reactor** Atomreaktor m.
atone [ə'toun] v **atone for** büßen, wiedergutmachen. **atonement** n Buße f.
atrocious [ə'trouʃəs] adj grausam, brutal; (coll) scheußlich. **atrocity** n Greueltat f.
attach [ə'tatʃ] v (affix) befestigen, anhängen; (connect) anschließen; (to a letter) beifügen. **be attached to** mögen, lieb haben. **attach oneself to** sich anschließen an. **attachment** n (liking) Anhänglichkeit f; (fixture) Anschluß m.

attaché [ə'taʃei] *n* Attaché. **attaché case** Aktentasche *f.*

attack [ə'tak] *v* angreifen; (*criticize*) tadeln, kritisieren. *n* Angriff *m.* **heart attack** Herzanfall *m.*

attain [ə'tein] *v* erreichen, gelangen zu. **attainable** *adj* erreichbar.

attempt [ə'tempt] *v* versuchen, wagen. *n* Versuch *m.*

attend [ə'tend] *v* (*school*) besuchen; (*meeting*) beiwohnen (+*dat*); (*lecture*) hören. **attend to** sich kümmern um. **attendance** *n* Anwesenheit *f.* **good attendance** gute Teilnahme *f.* **attendant** *n* Wächter(in).

attention [ə'tenʃən] *n* Aufmerksamkeit *f*; (*care*) Pflege *f*; (*machine*) Wartung *f.* **pay attention to** aufpassen auf. **stand at attention** Haltung annehmen.

attic ['atik] *n* Dachkammer *f.*

attire [ə'taiə] *n* Kleidung *f.* *v* kleiden.

attitude ['atitjuːd] *n* Einstellung *f,* Verhalten *neut.*

attorney [ə'təːni] *n* (*lawyer*) Rechtsanwalt *m.* **power of attorney** Vollmacht *f.*

attract [ə'trakt] *v* anziehen; (*attention*) erregen. **attraction** *n* Anziehung f; (*charm*) Reiz *m,* Anziehungskraft *f.* **attractive** *adj* attraktiv.

attribute [ə'tribjuːt; *n* 'atribjuːt] *v* zuschreiben (+*dat*). *n* Eigenschaft *f.* **attributable** *adj* zuzuschreiben (+*dat*).

attrition [ə'triʃən] *n* Abnutzung *f.* **war of attrition** Zermürbungskrieg *m.*

aubergine ['oubəʒiːn] *n* Aubergine *f.*

auburn ['oːbən] *adj* kastanienbraun.

auction ['oːkʃən] *n* Auktion *f,* Versteigerung *f.* *v* versteigern. **auctioneer** *n* Versteigerer *m.*

audacious [oː'deiʃəs] *adj* kühn. **audacity** *n* (*boldness*) Wagemut *m;* (*cheek*) Frechheit *f.*

audible ['oːdəbl] *adj* hörbar.

audience ['oːdjəns] *n* (*people*) Publikum *neut,* Zuhörer *pl;* (*interview*) Audienz *f.*

audiovisual [oːdiou'viʒuəl] *adj* audiovisuell.

audit ['oːdit] *v* (Rechnungen) prüfen. *n* Rechnungsprüfung *f.* **auditor** *n* Rechnungsprüfer *m.*

audition [oː'diʃən] *n* (*theatre*) Sprech-, Hörprobe *f.* *v* eine Hörprobe abnehmen.

auditorium [oːdi'toːriəm] *n* Hörsaal *m.*

augment [oːg'ment] *v* vermehren; (*grow*) zunehmen.

August ['oːgəst] *n* August *m.*

aunt [aːnt] *n* Tante *f.*

au pair [ou 'peə] *n* Au-pair-Mädchen *neut.*

aura ['oːrə] *n* Aura *f*; (*med*) Vorgefühl *neut.*

auspicious [oː'spiʃəs] *adj* günstig.

austere [oː'stiə] *adj* (*person*) streng; (*surroundings*) nüchtern. **austerity** *n* Strenge *f.*

Australia [o'streiljə] *n* Australien *neut.* **Australian** *n* Australier(in); *adj* australisch.

Austria ['oːstriə] *n* Österreich *neut.* **Austrian** *n* Österreicher(in); *adj* österreichisch.

authentic [oː'θentik] *adj* echt, authentisch. **authenticity** *n* Echtheit *f.*

author ['oːθə] *n* (*writer*) Schriftsteller *m,* Autor *m;* (*of a particular item*) Verfasser *m.*

authority [oː'θorəti] *n* Autorität *f*; (*expert*) Fachmann *m.* **on good authority** aus guter Quelle. **the authorities** die Behörden *pl.* **authoritarian** *adj* autoritär.

authorize ['oːθəraiz] *v* genehmigen, bevollmächtigen. **authorization** *n* Genehmigung *f.*

autobiography [oːtoubai'ogrəfi] *n* Autobiographie *f.*

autocratic [oːtou'kratik] *adj* autokratisch.

autograph ['oːtəgraːf] *n* Autogramm *neut.* *v* unterschreiben.

automatic [oːtə'matik] *adj* automatisch, selbsttätig. **automatic transmission** Automatik *f.*

automobile ['oːtəməbiːl] *n* Wagen *m,* Auto *neut.*

autonomous [oː'tonəməs] *adj* autonom, unabhängig. **autonomy** *n* Autonomie *f.*

autopsy ['oːtopsi] *n* Autopsie *f.*

autumn ['oːtəm] *n* Herbst *m.* **autumnal** *adj* herbstlich, Herbst-.

auxiliary [oːg'ziljəri] *adj* Hilfs-, Zusatz-, zusätzlich. *n* Hilfskraft *f.*

avail [ə'veil] *n* **to no avail** nutzlos. *v* **avail oneself of** Gebrauch machen von, sich bedienen (+*gen*).

available [ə'veiləbl] *adj* (*obtainable*) erhältlich; (*usable*) verfügbar. **be available** zur Verfügung stehen. **availability** *n* Erhältlichkeit *f.*

avalanche ['avəlaːnʃ] *n* Lawine *f.*

avant-garde [avã'gaːd] *adj* avantgardistisch. *n* Avantgarde *f.*

avarice ['avəris] *n* Geiz *m*. **avaricious** *adj* geizig.

avenge [ə'vendʒ] *v* rächen. **avenge oneself on** sich rächen an.

avenue ['avinjuː] *n* Allee *f*.

average ['avəridʒ] *n* Durchschnitt *m. adj* durchschnittlich, Durchschnitts-. **on average** im Durchschnitt.

averse [ə'vəis] *adj* abgeneigt. **aversion** *n* Abneigung *f*.

avert [ə'vəit] *v* (*gaze*) abwenden; (*danger*) verhindern.

aviary ['eiviəri] *n* Vogelhaus *neut*.

aviation [eivi'eiʃən] *n* Luftfahrt *f*. **aviator** *n* Flieger *m*.

avid ['avid] *adj* gierig (auf). **avidity** *n* Begierde *f*.

avocado [avə'kaːdou] *n* Avocado(birne) *f*.

avoid [ə'void] *v* vermeiden; (*person*) aus dem Wege gehen (+*dat*). **avoidable** *adj* vermeidbar.

await [ə'weit] *v* erwarten.

***awake** [ə'weik] *v* (*wake up*) aufwachen; (*rouse*) wecken; (*arouse*) erwecken. **be awake** wach sein. **wide awake** munter. **awaken** *v* erwecken.

award [ə'woid] *v* verleihen. *n* Preis *m*.

aware [ə'weə] *adj* bewußt (+*gen*). **awareness** *n* Bewußtsein *neut*.

away [ə'wei] *adv* weg, fort. *adj* (*absent*) abwesend. *she is away* sie ist verreist.

awe [oi] *n* Ehrfurcht *f*. **awesome** *adj* (*impressive*) imponierend; (*frightening*) erschreckend.

awful ['oiful] *adj* furchtbar.

awhile [ə'wail] *adv* eine Weile, eine Zeitlang.

awkward ['oikwəd] *adj* (*clumsy*) ungeschickt, linkisch; (*embarrassing*) peinlich; (*contrary*) widerspenstig.

awning ['oiniŋ] *n* Markise *f*.

awoke [ə'wouk] *V* **awake**.

awoken [ə'woukn] *V* **awake**.

axe *or US* **ax** [aks] *n* Axt *f*.

axiom ['aksiəm] *n* Axiom *neut*.

axis ['aksis] *n* Achse *f*.

axle ['aksl] *n* Achse *f*.

B

babble ['babl] *v* plappern; (*water*) plätschern.

baboon [bə'buːn] *n* Pavian *m*.

baby ['beibi] *n* Baby *neut*, Säugling *m*. **baby carriage** Kinderwagen *m*. **babyish** *adj* kindisch. **babysit** *v* babysitten. **baby-sitter** *n* Babysitter *m*.

bachelor ['batʃələ] *n* Junggeselle *m*.

back [bak] *n* (*anat*) Rücken *m*; (*rear*) Rürckseite *f*; (*football*) Verteidiger *m. adj* hinter, Hinter-. *adv* zurück. *v* (*bet on*) wetten auf; (*support*) unterstützen; (*reverse*) rückwärts fahren. **back out** *v* sich zurückziehen.

backache ['bakeik] *n* Rückenschmerz *m*.

backbone ['bakboun] *n* Rückgrat *neut*, Wirbelsäule *f*.

backdate [bak'deit] *v* zurückdatieren.

backer ['bakə] *n* Förderer *m*.

backfire [bak'faiə] *v* (*car*) fehlzünden; (*plan*) fehlschlagen.

background ['bakgraund] *n* Hintergrund *m*.

backhand ['bakhand] *n* (*sport*) Rückhandschlag *m*.

backlash ['baklaʃ] *n* (politische) Reaktion *f*.

backlog ['baklog] *n* Rückstand *m*.

backside ['baksaid] *n* Hinterteil *neut*, Hintern *m*.

backstage ['baksteidʒ] *adj, adv* hinter den Kulissen.

backstroke ['bakstrouk] *n* Rückenschwimmen *neut*.

backward ['bakwəd] *adj* zurückgeblieben.

backwards ['bakwədz] *adv* zurück, rückwärts.

backwater ['bakwoitə] *n* Stauwasser *neut*.

backyard [bak'jaid] *n* Hinterhof *m*.

bacon ['beikən] *n* (Schinken)Speck *m*.

bacteria [bak'tiəriə] *pl n* Bakterien *pl*.

bad [bad] *adj* schlecht, schlimm; (*naughty*) böse; (*food*) faul, verfault. **bad-tempered** mißgelaunt.

bade [bad] *V* **bid**.

badge [badʒ] *n* Abzeichen *neut*.

badger ['badʒə] *n* Dachs *m*. *v* plagen.

badminton ['badmintən] *n* Federballspiel *neut*.

baffle ['bafl] *v* verblüffen.

bag [bag] *n* Beutel *m*, Sack *m*; (*paper*) Tüte *f*; (*handbag*) Tasche *f*. **baggage** *n* Gepäck *neut*. **baggy** *adj* bauschig. **bagpipes** *pl n* Dudelsack *m sing*.

bail¹ [beil] *n* (*security*) Kaution *f*. *v* gegen Kaution freilassen.

bail² *or* **bale** [beil] *v* **bail out** (*boat*) ausschöpfen; (*from aeroplane*) abspringen; (*help*) aushelfen.

bailiff ['beilif] *n* Gerichtsvollzieher *m*.

bait [beit] *n* Köder *m*. *v* ködern; (*tease*) quälen.

bake [beik] *v* backen. **baker** *n* Bäcker *m*. **bakery** Bäckerei *f*.

balance ['baləns] *n* Gleichgewicht *neut*; (*scales*) Waage *f*; (*of account*) Saldo *m*; (*amount left*) Rest *m*. *v* ausgleichen. **balance sheet** Bilanz *f*.

balcony ['balkəni] *n* Balkon *m*.

bald [boɪld] *adj* kahl.

bale¹ [beil] *n* Ballen *m*.

bale² [beil] *V* **bail²**.

ball¹ [boɪl] *n* (*sport*) Ball *m*; (*sphere*) Kugel *f*.

ball² [boɪl] *n* (*dance*) Ball *m*.

ballad ['baləd] *n* Ballade *f*.

ballast ['baləst] *n* Ballast *neut*.

ball bearing *n* Kugellager *neut*.

ballet ['balei] *n* Ballett *neut*. **ballet dancer** Ballettänzer(in).

ballistic [bə'listik] *adj* ballistisch.

balloon [bə'luɪn] *n* Ballon *m*; (*toy*) Luftballon *m*.

ballot ['balət] *n* Abstimmung *f*.

ball-point pen *n* Kugelschreiber *m*.

ballroom ['boɪlrum] *n* Tanzsaal *m*.

balmy ['baɪmi] *adj* sanft, lindernd.

bamboo [bam'buɪ] *n* Bambus *m*.

ban [ban] *v* verbieten. *n* Verbot *neut*.

banal [bə'naɪl] *adj* banal.

banana [bə'naɪnə] *n* Banane *f*.

band¹ [band] *n* Gruppe *f*; (*music*) Band *f*, Kapelle *f*; (*criminals*) Bande *f*. *v* **band together** sich vereinen.

band² [band] *n* (*strip*) Band *neut*, Binde *f*.

bandage ['bandidʒ] *n* Bandage *f*, Binde *f*. *v* bandagieren.

bandit ['bandit] *n* Bandit *m*.

bandy ['bandi] *adj* krummbeinig. *v* **bandy words** streiten.

bang [baŋ] *n* Knall *m*. *v* (*sound*) knallen; (*strike*) schlagen; (*door*) zuknallen.

bangle ['baŋgl] *n* (Arm)Spange *f*.

banish ['baniʃ] *v* verbannen.

banister ['banistə] *n* Treppengeländer *neut*.

banjo ['bandʒou] *n* Banjo *neut*.

bank¹ [baŋk] *n* (*river*) Ufer *neut*; (*sand*) Bank *f*.

bank² [baŋk] *n* (*comm*) Bank *f*. *v* (*money*) auf die Bank bringen. **bank on** sich verlassen auf. **bank account** *n* Bankkonto *neut*. **banker** *n* Bankier *m*. **banker's card** Scheckkarte *f*. **bank holiday** *n* Feiertag *m*. **banknote** *n* Banknote *f*.

bankrupt ['baŋkrʌpt] *adj* bankrott. *n* Bankrotteur *m*. **go bankrupt** Bankrott machen. **bankruptcy** Bankrott *m*.

banner ['banə] *n* Banner *neut*.

banquet ['baŋkwit] *n* Bankett *neut*.

banter ['bantə] *v* necken. *n* Neckerei *f*.

baptism ['baptizəm] *n* Taufe *f*. **baptize** *v* taufen.

bar [baɪ] *n* (*drink*) Bar *f*; (*rod*) Stange *f*, Barre *f*; (*chocolate*) Tafel *f*. *v* (*door*) verriegeln; (*ban*) verbieten.

barbarian [baɪ'beəriən] *n* Barbar *m*. **barbaric** *adj* barbarisch.

barbecue ['baɪbikjuɪ] *n* Barbecue *neut*. *v* am Spieß braten.

barbed wire [baɪbd] *n* Stacheldraht *m*.

barber ['baɪbə] *n* Barbier *m*, Friseur *m*.

barbiturate [baɪ'bitjurət] *n* Barbitursäure *f*.

bare [beə] *adj* nackt; (*trees*) kahl; (*empty*) leer; (*mere*) bloß. *v* entblößen. **barefoot** *adj* barfuß. **bare-headed** *adj* mit bloßem Kopf. **barely** *adv* kaum.

bargain ['baɪgin] *n* (*good buy*) Gelegenheitskauf *m*. (*deal*) Geschäft *neut*. *v* feilschen. **collective bargaining** tarifverhandlungen *pl*. **into the bargain** obendrein.

barge [baɪdʒ] *n* Lastkahn *m*. *v* **barge in** hereinstürzen.

baritone ['baritoun] *n* Bariton *m*.

bark¹ [baɪk] *v* (*dog*) bellen. *n* Bellen *neut*.

bark² [baɪk] *n* (*tree*) Rinde *f*.

barley ['baɪli] *n* (*crop*) Gerste *f*; (*in soup*) Graupen *pl*.

barmaid ['baɪmeid] *n* Barmädchen *neut*.

barman ['baɪman] *n* Barmann *m*.

barn [baɪn] *n* Scheune *f*.

barometer [bə'romitə] *n* Barometer *neut*.

baron ['barən] *n* Baron *m*.

baronet ['barənit] *n* Baronet *m*.

baroque [bə'rok] *adj* barock.

barracks ['baroks] *n* Kaserne *f*.

barrage ['baraɪʒ] *n* (*dam*) Damm *m*; (*mil*) Sperrfeuer *neut*; (*of questions*) Flut *f*.

barrel ['barəl] *n* Faß *neut*.

barren ['barən] *adj* unfruchtbar; (*desolate*) wüst.

barricade [bari'keid] *n* Barrikade *f*. *v* verbarrikadieren.
barrier ['bariə] *n* Schranke *f*.
barrister ['baristə] *n* Rechtsanwalt *m*.
barrow ['barou] *n* Schubkarren *m*.
bartender ['baitendə] *n* Barmann *m*.
barter ['baitə] *n* Tauschhandel *m*. *v* tauschen; (*haggle*) feilschen.
base[1] [beis] *n* (*bottom*) Fuß *m*, Boden *m*; (*basis*) Basis *f*; (*mil*) Stützpunkt *m*; (*chem*) Base *f*. *v* gründen. **be based on** basieren auf (+*dat*).
base[2] [beis] *adj* (*vile*) gemein.
baseball ['beisbɔil] *n* Baseball *m*.
basement ['beismənt] *n* Kellergeschoß *neut*.
bash [baʃ] *v* (heftig) schlagen. **have a bash!** versuch's mal!
bashful ['baʃful] *adj* schüchtern.
basic ['beisik] *adj* grundsätzlich, Grund-. **basically** *adv* im Grunde.
basil ['bazl] *n* Basilienkraut *neut*.
basin ['beisin] *n* (*washbasin, river basin*) Becken *neut*; (*dish*) Schale *f*.
basis ['beisis] *n* Basis *f*, Grundlage *f*.
bask [bask] *v* sich sonnen.
basket ['baiskit] *n* Korb *m*. **basketball** *n* Basketball *m*.
bass[1] [beis] *n* (*music*) Baß *m*. **bass guitar** Baßgitarre *f*. **double bass** Kontrabaß *m*.
bass[2] [bas] *n* Seebarsch *m*.
bassoon [bə'suin] *n* Fagott *neut*.
bastard ['baistəd] *n* Bastard *m*; (*derog*) Schweinehund *m*.
baste [beist] *v* (*meat*) mit Fett begießen.
bastion ['bastjən] *n* Bollwerk *neut*.
bat[1] [bat] *n* (*sport*) Schlagholz *neut*. *v* **without batting an eyelid** ohne mit der Wimper zu zucken.
bat[2] [bat] *n* (*zool*) Fledermaus *f*.
batch [batʃ] *n* Stoß *m*.
bath [baiθ] *n* Bad *neut*. *v* baden. **have or take a bath** ein Bad nehmen. **bathroom** *n* Badezimmer *neut*. **bathtub** *n* Badewanne *f*. **baths** *pl* *n* Schwimmbad *neut sing*.
baton ['batn] *n* (*music*) Taktstock *m*.
battalion [bə'taljən] *n* Bataillon *neut*.
batter[1] ['batə] *v* (*strike*) verprügeln.
batter[2] ['batə] *n* (*cookery*) Schlagteig *m*.
battery ['batəri] *n* Batterie *f*.
battle ['batl] *n* Schlacht *f*; (*fig*) Kampf *m*. *v* kämpfen. **battlefield** *n* Schlachtfeld *neut*. **battleship** *n* Schlachtschiff *neut*.
bawl [bɔil] *v* brüllen, heulen.
bay[1] [bei] *n* (*coast*) Bai *f*, Bucht *f*.

bay[2] [bei] *n* **keep at bay** abwehren.
bay[3] [bei] *n* (*tree*) Lorbeer *m*. **bay leaf** Lorbeerblatt *neut*.
bayonet ['beiənit] *n* Bajonett *neut*. *v* bajonettieren.
bay window *n* Erkerfenster *neut*.
bazaar [bə'zai] *n* Basar *m*.
***be** [bii] *v* sein; (*be situated*) liegen, stehen. *v* *aux* (*in passive*) werden. **There is/are** es gibt. *the book is on the table* das Buch liegt auf dem Tisch. *I want to be an engineer* ich will Ingenieur werden. *how much is that car?* wieviel kostet der Wagen
beach [biitʃ] *n* Strand *m*. *v* (*boat*) auf den Strand setzen.
beacon ['biikən] *n* Leuchtfeuer *neut*.
bead [biid] *n* Perle *f*.
beak [biik] *n* Schnabel *m*.
beaker ['biikə] *n* Becher *m*.
beam [biim] *n* (*wood*) Balken *m*; (*light*) Strahl *m*. *v* strahlen.
bean [biin] *n* Bohne *f*.
***bear**[1] [beə] *v* (*carry, yield*) tragen, (*tolerate*) ertragen, leiden; (*child*) gebären. **bring pressure to bear on** Druck ausüben auf. **bear right** sich nach rechts halten.
bear[2] [beə] *n* (*zool*) Bär *m*.
beard [biəd] *n* Bart *m*.
bearing ['beəriŋ] *n* (*posture*) Haltung *f*; (*relation*) Beziehung *f*; (*tech*) Lager *neut*. **bearings** *pl* *n* Orientierung *f* *sing*.
beast [biist] *n* Tier *neut*; (*cattle*) Vieh *neut*; (*person*) Bestie *f*. **beastly** *adj* (*coll*) scheußlich.
***beat** [biit] *v* schlagen. *n* (*stroke*) Schlag *m*; (*music*) Rhythmus *m*; (*policeman's*) Revier *neut*.
beaten ['biitn] *V* beat.
beautiful ['bjuitəful] *adj* schön. **beautifully** *adv* ausgezeichnet. **beauty** *n* Schönheit *f*.
beaver ['biivə] *n* Biber *m*.
became [bi'keim] *V* become.
because [bi'koz] *conj* weil. **because of** wegen (+*gen*).
***become** [bi'kʌm] *v* werden. **becoming** *adj* passend.
bed [bed] *v* Bett *neut*; (*garden*) Beet *neut*. **river bed** Flußbett *neut*. **seabed** *n* Meeresboden *m*. **bedclothes** *pl* *n* Bettwäsche *f* *sing*. **bedridden** *adj* bettlägerig. **bedroom** *n* Schlafzimmer *neut*. **bedsitter** *n* Einzimmerwohnung *f*. **bedspread** *n* Bettdecke *f*. **bedtime** *n* Schlafenzeit *f*.

betray

bee [biː] *n* Biene *f.*
beech [biːtʃ] *n* Buche *f.*
beef [biːf] *n* Rindfleisch *neut.*
beehive ['biːhaiv] *n* Bienenstock *m.*
been [biːn] *V* be.
beer [biə] *n* Bier *neut.*
beetle ['biːtl] *n* Käfer *m.*
beetroot ['biːtruːt] *n*.rote Bete *f.*
before [bi'foː] *conj* bevor, ehe; *prep* vor; *adv* (*time*) zuvor, früher; (*ahead*) voran. **beforehand** *adv* im voraus.
befriend [bi'frend] *v* befreunden.
beg [beg] *v* (*for money*) betteln; (*beseech*) bitten. **beggar** *n* Bettler *m.*
began [bi'gan] *V* begin.
***begin** [bi'gin] *v* beginnen, anfangen. **beginner** *n* Anfänger *m.* **beginning** *n* Anfang *m,* Beginn *m.*
begrudge [bi'grʌdʒ] *v* mißgönnen.
begun [bi'gʌn] *V* begin.
behalf [bi'haːf] *n* **on behalf of** im Namen von. **on my behalf** um meinetwillen.
behave [bi'heiv] *v* sich verhalten, sich betragen; (*behave well*) sich gut benehmen. **behave yourself!** benimm dich! **behaviour** *n* Benehmen *neut,* Verhalten *neut.*
behind [bi'haind] *prep* hinter. *adv* (*in the rear*) hinten; (*back*) zurück; (*behind schedule*) im Rückstand. *n* (*coll*) Hinterteil *neut.* **behindhand** *adv* im Rückstand.
***behold** [bi'hould] *v* sehen, betrachten. **beholder** *m* Betrachter *m.*
beige [beiʒ] *adj* beige.
being ['biːin] *n* (*existence*) (Da)Sein *neut;* (*creature*) Wesen *neut,* Geschöpf *neut.* **for the time being** einstweilen. **come into being** entstehen. **human being** Mensch *m.*
belated [bi'leitid] *adj* verspätet.
belch [beltʃ] *v* rülpsen; (*fumes*) ausspeien. *n* Rülpsen *neut.*
belfry ['belfri] *n* Glockenturm *m.*
Belgium ['beldʒəm] *n* Belgien *neut.* **Belgian** *n* Belgier(in). *adj* belgisch.
belief [bi'liːf] *n* Glaube *m;* (*conviction*) Überzeugung *f.* **believe** *v* glauben (+ *dat*). **believe in** glauben an (+ *acc*). **believable** *adj* glaublich. **believer** *n* Gläubige(r).
bell [bel] *n* Glocke *f;* (*on door*) Klingel *m.*
belligerent [bi'lidʒərənt] *adj* (*country*) kriegführend; (*person*) aggressiv.
bellow ['belou] *v* brüllen. *n* Gebrüll *neut.*

bellows ['belouz] *n* Blasebalg *m.*
belly ['beli] *n* Bauch *m.*
belong [bi'loŋ] *v* gehören (+ *dat*); (*be a member*) angehören (+ *dat*). **belongings** *pl n* Eigentum *neut sing;* Sachen *pl.*
beloved [bi'lʌvid] *adj* geliebt. *n* Geliebte(r).
below [bi'lou] *prep* unter. *adv* unten.
belt [belt] *n* Gürtel *m.* *v* (*coll*) verprügeln. **belt up!** halt die Klappe!
bemused [bi'mjuːzd] *adj* verwirrt.
bench [bentʃ] *n* Bank *f;* (*work table*) Arbeitstisch *m.*
***bend** [bend] *v* biegen; (*be bent*) sich beugen. *n* Kurve *f.*
beneath [bi'niːθ] *prep* unter.
benefactor ['benəfaktə] *n* Wohltäter *m.* **benefactress** *n* Wohltäterin *f.*
beneficent [bi'nefisənt] *adj* wohltätig.
beneficial [benə'fiʃəl] *adj* vorteilhaft, nützlich.
benefit ['benəfit] *n* Nutzen *m,* Gewinn *m.* *v* nützen. **benefit from** Nutzen ziehen aus.
benevolence [bi'nevələns] *n* Wohltätigkeit *f.* **benevolent** *adj* wohltätig.
benign [bi'nain] *adj* gütig; (*tumour*) gutartig.
bent [bent] *V* bend. *adj* krumm, verbogen; (*dishonest*) unehrlich. **be bent on** versessen sein auf (+ *acc*).
bequeath [bi'kwiːð] *v* vermachen.
beret ['berei] *n* Baskenmütze *f.*
berry ['beri] *n* Beere *f.*
berserk [bə'səːk] *adj* **go berserk** wild werden, toben.
berth [bəːθ] *n* (*mooring*) Liegeplatz *m;* (*bunk*) Koje *f.* **give a wide berth to** einen weiten Bogen machen um (+ *acc*).
beside [bi'said] *prep* neben. **be beside oneself with** außer sich sein vor (+ *dat*). **besides** *prep* außer. *adv* außerdem.
besiege [bi'siːdʒ] *v* belagern.
best [best] *adj* best. *adv* am besten, bestens. *n* das Beste. **do one's best** sein Bestes tun. **at best** höchstens. **best man** Trauzeuge *m.*
bestial ['bestjəl] *adj* bestialisch.
bestow [bi'stou] *v* **bestow upon** schenken (+ *dat*).
bestseller [best'selə] *n* Bestseller *m.*
bet [bet] *v* wetten. *n* Wette *f.*
betray [bi'trei] *v* verraten. **betrayal** *n* Verrat *m.*

better ['betə] *adj, adv* besser. *n* das Bessere. *v* verbessern. **get the better of** übertreffen. **better oneself** sich verbessern.

between [bi'twiːn] *prep* zwischen. *adv* dazwischen. **between you and me** unter uns.

beverage ['bevəridʒ] *n* Getränk *neut*.

***beware** [bi'weə] *v* sich hüten vor (+*dat*). **beware of the dog** Vorsicht Vorsicht–bissiger Hund!

bewilder [bi'wildə] *v* verwirren, verblüffen.

beyond [bi'jond] *prep* uber ... hinaus, jenseits (+*gen*); mehr als. *adv* jenseits, darüber hinaus. **beyond compare** unvergleichlich. *he is beyond help* ihm ist nicht mehr zu helfen.

bias ['baiəs] *n* Neigung *f*. **biased** *adj* voreingenommen.

bib [bib] *n* Latz *m*.

Bible ['baibl] *n* Bibel *f*.

bibliography [bibli'ogrəfi] *n* Bibliographie *f*.

biceps ['baiseps] *n* Bizeps *m*.

bicker ['bikə] *v* zanken.

bicycle ['baisikl] *n* Fahrrad *neut*.

***bid** [bid] *v* (*offer*) bieten; (*cards*) reizen. *n* (*offer*) Angebot *neut*; (*attempt*) Versuch *m*. **bid someone welcome** jemanden willkommen heißen. **bidder** *n* Bieter *m*.

bidden ['bidn] *V* **bid**.

bidet ['biːdei] *n* Bidet *neut*.

biennial [bai'eniəl] *adj* zweijährig.

big [big] *adj* groß. **big-headed** *adj* eingebildet. **big-hearted** *adj* großherzig.

bigamy ['bigəmi] *n* Bigamie *f*.

bigot ['bigət] *n* Frömmler *m*. **bigotted** *adj* bigott. **bigotry** *n* Bigotterie *f*.

bikini [bi'kiːni] *n* Bikini *m*.

bilateral [bai'latərəl] *adj* bilateral.

bilingual [bai'liŋwəl] *adj* zweisprachig.

bill¹ [bil] *n* (*in restaurant*) Rechnung *f*; Banknote *f*; (*comm*) Wechsel *m*; (*pol*) Gesetzentwurf *m*; (*poster*) Plakat *neut*. *v* fakturieren. **billboard** *n* Plakattafel *f*.

bill² [bil] *n* (*beak*) Schnabel *m*.

billiards ['biljədz] *n* Billard *neut*.

billion ['biljən] *n* Billion *f*; (*US*) Milliarde *f*.

bin [bin] *n* Kiste *f*; (*dustbin*) Mülleimer *m*.

binary ['bainəri] *adj* binär.

***bind** [baind] *v* (*tie*) binden; (*oblige*) verpflichten. **binding** *adj* bindend. *n* (*book*) Einband *m*.

binoculars [bi'nokjuləz] *pl n* Feldstecher *m*.

biography [bai'ogrəfi] *n* Biographie *f*. **biographer** *n* Biograph *m*. **biographical** *adj* biographisch.

biology [bai'olədʒi] *n* Biologie *f*. **biological** *adj* biologisch. **biologist** *n* Biologe *m*.

birch [bəːtʃ] *n* Birke *f*; (*rod*) Birkenrute *f*.

bird [bəːd] *n* Vogel *m*.

birth [bəːθ] *n* Geburt *f*. **date of birth** Geburtsdatum *neut*. **birth certificate** Geburtsurkunde *f*. **birth control** Geburtenregelung *f*. **birthday** Geburtstag *m*. **birthmark** Muttermal *neut*.

biscuit ['biskit] *n* Biskuit *m*, Keks *m*.

bisexual [bai'seksfuəl] *adj* bisexuell.

bishop ['biʃəp] *n* Bischof *m*.

bison ['baisən] *n* Bison *m*.

bit¹ [bit] *V* **bite**. *n* (*morsel*) Bißchen, Stückchen *neut*: *a bit of bread* ein Stückchen Brot. *a bit frightened* ein bißchen ängstlich.

bit² [bit] *n* (*harness*) Gebiß *neut*; (*drill*) Bohreisen *neut*.

bitch [bitʃ] *n* Hündin *f*; (*woman*) Weibsstück *neut*.

***bite** [bait] *v* beißen. *n* (*mouthful*) Bissen *m*; (*wound*) Biß *m*. **bite to eat** Imbiß *m*.

bitten ['bitn] *V* **bite**.

bitter ['bitə] *v* bitter; (*weather*) scharf. **to the bitter end** bis zum bitteren Ende. **bitterness** *n* Bitterkeit *f*.

bizarre [bi'zaː] *adj* bizarr, seltsam.

black ['blak] *adj* schwarz. *n* (*colour*) Schwarz *neut*; (*person*) Schwarze(r).

blackberry ['blakbəri] *n* Brombeere *f*.

blackbird ['blakbəːd] *n* Amsel *f*.

blackboard ['blakbɔːd] *n* Wandtafel *f*.

blackcurrant [ˌblakˈkʌrənt] *n* schwarze Johannisbeere *f*.

blacken ['blakn] *v* schwarz machen.

black eye *n* blaues Auge *neut*.

blackhead ['blakhed] *n* Mitesser *m*.

blackleg ['blakleg] *n* Streikbrecher *m*.

blackmail ['blakmeil] *n* Erpressung *f*. **blackmailer** *n* Erpresser *m*.

black market *n* schwarzer Markt *m*. **black marketeer** Schwarzhändler *m*.

black out *v* (*darken*) verdunkeln; (*faint*) ohnmächtig werden. **black-out** *n* Verdunkelung *f*; Ohnmachtsanfall *m*; (*elec*) Stromausfall *m*.

black pudding n Blutwurst f.
blacksmith ['blaksmiθ] n Schmied m.
bladder ['bladə] n Blase f.
blade [bleid] n (razor, knife) Klinge f;
(grass) Halm m; (tech) Blatt neut;
(propellor) Flügel m.
blame [bleim] v tadeln, die Schuld geben
(+ dat). n Schuld f, Tadel m. I am to
blame for this ich bin daran schuld.
blameless adj untadelig.
blancmange [blə'monʒ] n Pudding m.
bland [bland] adj sanft, mild.
blank [blaŋk] adj leer, unausgefüllt. n
(form) Formular neut; (cartridge)
Platzpatrone f. **blank cheque** Blankoscheck m.
blanket ['blaŋkit] n Decke f. adj Gesamt-,
allgemein.
blare [bleə] v schmettern. n Schmettern
neut.
blaspheme [blas'fiːm] v lästern. **blasphemy**
n Gotteslästerung f.
blast [blaːst] n Explosion f; (of wind)
(heftiger) Windstoß m. v sprengen.
blatant ['bleitənt] adj offenkundig.
blaze [bleiz] n Brand m, Feuer neut. v
lodern.
blazer ['bleizə] n Blazer m.
bleach [bliːtʃ] v bleichen. n Bleichmittel
neut.
bleak [bliːk] adj kahl; (fig) trostlos.
bleat [bliːt] v (sheep) blöken; (goat) meckern. n Blöken neut, Meckern neut.
bled [bled] V bleed.
*****bleed** [bliːd] v bluten; (brakes, radiators)
entlüften. **bleeding** adj blutend.
blemish ['blemiʃ] n Makel m.
blend [blend] v mischen. n Mischung f.
bless [bles] v segnen. **blessing** n Segen m.
blew [bluː] V blow[1].
blind [blaind] adj blind; (corner) unüber-
sichtlich. n (window) Rouleau neut. v
blenden; (fig) verblenden. **blind alley**
Sackgasse f. **blindfold** v die Augen
verbinden (+ dat). adv mit verbundenen
Augen.
blink [bliŋk] v blinzeln.
bliss [blis] n Wonne f. **blissful** glückselig.
blister ['blistə] n Blase f.
blizzard ['blizəd] n Schneesturm m.
blob [blob] n Tropfen m.
bloc [blok] n Block m.
block [blok] n (wood) Klotz m; (stone)
Block m; (US) Häuserblock m; (in pipe)
Verstopfung f; (barrier) Sperre f. v

blockieren; verstopfen. **writing block**
Schreibblock m. **blockade** n Blockade f.
blockage n Verstopfung f.
bloke [blouk] n Kerl m.
blond [blond] adj blond. **blonde** n
Blondine f.
blood [blʌd] n Blut neut. **in cold blood**
kaltblütig. **blood clot** Blutgerinnsel neut.
blood pressure Blutdruck m. **blood test**
Blutuntersuchung f. **bloodthirsty** adj
blutdurstig. **blood transfusion** Blutübertragung f. **blood vessel** Blutgefäß neut.
bloody adj blutig; (coll) verdammt.
bloom [bluːm] v blühen. n Blüte f.
blossom ['blosəm] n Blüte f. v blühen.
blot [blot] n Fleck m; (of ink) Tintenklecks m. v (make dirty) beschmieren.
blot out auslöschen.
blotch [blotʃ] n Fleck m; Klecks m.
blotting paper n Löschpapier neut.
blouse [blauz] n Bluse f.
*****blow[1]** [blou] v blasen; (of wind) wehen;
(fuse) durchbrennen. **blow over**
vorbeigehen. **blow up** (explode) sprengen.
blow the horn (mot) hupen. **blow one's
nose** sich die Nase putzen.
blow[2] [blou] n Schlag m; (misfortune)
Unglück neut.
blowlamp ['bloulamp] n Lötlampe f.
blown [bloun] V blow[1].
blowout ['blauaut] n (mot) geplatzter
Reifen m, Reifenpanne f.
blubber ['blʌbə] n Walfischspeck m.
blue [bluː] adj blau; (depressed)
niedergeschlagen. n Blau neut. **bluebell** n
Glockenblume f. **blueberry** n Heidelber-
ee f. **bluebottle** n Schmeißfliege f. **the
blues** Blues m sing.
bluff [blʌf] v bluffen. n Bluff m.
blunder ['blʌndə] n (dummer) Fehler m,
Schnitzer m. v (stumble) stolpern; (make
mistake) einen Schnitzer machen.
blunt [blʌnt] adj stumpf. v stumpf
machen; (enthusiasm) abstumpfen.
blur [blɔ:] v verwischen, verschmieren.
blurred adj verschwommen.
blush [blʌʃ] v erröten. n Erröten neut.
boar [bɔ:] n Eber m. **wild boar**
Wildschwein m.
board [bɔ:d] n (wooden) Brett neut;
(comm) Aufsichtsrat m. v (train) einsteigen in (+ acc). **board and lodging**
Unterkunft und Verpflegung f. **boarding
house** Pension f. **boarding school**
Internat neut.

boast [boust] v prahlen, angeben. n Prahlerei f. **boaster** n Prahler m.

boat [bout] n Boot neut. **in the same boat** in der gleichen Lage.

bob [bob] v sich auf- und abbewegen; (hair) kurz schneiden.

bobbin ['bobin] n Spule f.

bobsleigh ['bobslei] n Bobsleigh m.

bodice ['bodis] n Mieder neut.

body ['bodi] n Körper, Leib m; (corpse) Leiche f; (of people) Gruppe f; (car) Karosserie f. **bodily** adj körperlich.

bog [bog] n Sumpf m. v **get bogged down** steckenbleiben. **boggy** adj sumpfig.

bogus ['bougəs] adj falsch, unecht.

bohemian [bə'hiːmiən] adj zigeunerhaft, ungebunden. n (fig) Bohemien m.

boil¹ [boil] v kochen. **boiler** n Kessel m. **boiling** adj kochend.

boil² [boil] n (sore) Furunkel m.

boisterous ['boistərəs] adj ungestüm, laut.

bold [bould] adj kühn, tapfer; (cheeky) frech. **boldness** n Kühnheit f.

bolster ['boulstə] n Kissen neut. **bolster up** (fig) unterstützen.

bolt [boult] n (door) Riegel m; (screw) Bolzen m; (lightning) Blitzstrahl m; (cloth) Rolle f. v (door) verriegeln; (attach with bolts) anbolzen; (food) hinunterschlingen; (dash) (hastig) fliehen.

bomb [bom] n Bombe f. v bombardieren. **go down a bomb** einen Bombenerfolg haben. **bombard** v bombardieren. **bombardment** n Beschießung f. **bomber** n (aeroplane) Bombenflugzeug neut. **bombing** n Bombenangriff m.

bond [bond] n (tie) Bindung f; (comm) Schuldschein m.

bone [boun] n Knochen m, Bein neut; (fish) Gräte f. v (meat) die Knochen entfernen aus; (fish) entgräten.

bonfire ['bonfaiə] n Gartenfeuer neut.

bonnet ['bonit] n Haube f; (mot) Motorhaube f.

bonus ['bounəs] n Bonus m.

bony ['bouni] adj knochig.

book [buk] n Buch neut; (notebook) Heft neut. v (record) buchen; (reserve) reservieren. **bookcase** n Bücherschrank m. **booking office** Fahrtkartenschalter m. **bookkeeping** n Buchhaltung f. **bookmaker** n Buchmacher m. **bookshop** n Buchhandlung f.

boom [buːm] n (sound) Dröhnen neut; (econ) Konjunktur f; (naut) Baum m. v dröhnen.

boost [buːst] v Auftrieb geben (+ dat), (tech) verstärken. n Auftrieb m.

boot [buːt] n Stiefel m; (mot) Kofferraum m.

booth [buːð] n Bude f. **telephone booth** Telephonzelle f.

booze [buːz] (coll) v saufen. n alkoholisches Getränk neut. **boozer** n Säufer m.

border ['boːdə] n (of country) Grenze f; (edge) Rand m. v grenzen. **borderline** n Grenze f. **borderline case** Grenzfall m.

bore¹ [boː] V bear¹.

bore² [boː] v (drill) bohren; (a hole) ausbohren; (cylinder) ausschleifen. n Kaliber neut.

bore³ [boː] v (weary) langweilen. n langweiliger Mensch m. **be bored** sich langweilen. **boredom** n Langeweile f. **boring** adj langweilig.

born [boːn] adj geboren. she was born blind sie ist von der Geburt blind.

borne [boːn] V bear¹.

borough ['bʌrə] n Stadtbezirk m.

borrow ['borou] v borgen, entleihen. **borrower** n Entleiher m.

bosom ['buzəm] n Busen m. **bosom friend** Busenfreund m.

boss [bos] n Boß, Chef m. v **boss around** herumkommandieren. **bossy** adj herrisch.

botany ['botəni] n Botanik f. **botanical** adj botanisch. **botanical gardens** botanischer Garten m. **botanist** n Botaniker m.

both [bouθ] adj, pron beide(s). **both (of the) dogs** beide Hunde. **both ... and** sowohl ... als or wie auch.

bother ['boðə] v (disturb) belästigen, stören; (take trouble) sich Mühe geben. n Belästigung f. **bothersome** adj lästig.

bottle ['botl] n Flasche f. v in Flaschen füllen. **bottled** adj in Flaschen, Flaschen-. **bottleneck** n (fig) Engpaß m. **bottle opener** n Flaschenöffner m.

bottom ['botəm] n Boden m; (coll: anat) Hintern m. adj **bottom gear** erster Gang m.

bough [bau] n Ast m.

boulder ['bouldə] n Felsbrocken m.

bounce [bauns] v (of ball) hochspringen; (of cheque) platzen. **bounce around** herumhüpfen. **bouncer** n (coll) Rausschmeißer m.

bought [bɔɪt] V buy.
bound¹ [baund] V bind.
bound² [baund] n (leap) Sprung m, Satz m. v springen.
bound³ [baund] n (limit) Grenze f. out of bounds betreten verboten!
bound⁴ [baund] adj bound for unterwegs nach. outward/homeward bound auf der Ausreise/Heimreise.
bound⁵ [baund] adj (obliged) verpflichtet. He is bound to win er wird bestimmt gewinnen.
boundary ['baundəri] n Grenze f.
bouquet [buːkei] n (flowers) Blumenstrauß m; (of wine) Blume f.
bourgeois ['buəʒwai] adj bourgeois. n Bourgeois m. **bourgeoisie** n Bourgeoisie f.
bout [baut] n (of illness) Anfall m; (fight) Kampf m.
bow¹ [bau] v (lower head) sich verbeugen. n Verbeugung f.
bow² [bou] n (music, archery) Bogen m; (ribbon) Schleife f.
bow³ [bau] n (naut) Bug m.
bowels ['bauəlz] pl n Darm m sing; Eingeweide pl. open or move one's bowels sich entleeren.
bowl¹ [boul] n (basin) Schüssel f, Schale f.
bowl² [boul] v (ball) werfen. n Holzkugel f. bowls n Kegelspiel neut. play bowls kegeln.
box¹ [boks] n (container) Schachtel f, Kasten m; (theatre) Loge f; (court) Stand m.
box² [boks] v (sport) boxen. box someone's ears jemanden ohrfeigen. boxer n Boxer m. boxing n Boxen neut.
Boxing Day n zweiter Weihnachtsfeiertag m.
box office n (theatre) Kasse f.
boy [boi] n Junge m, Knabe m. **boyfriend** n Freund m. **boyhood** n Jugend f. **boyish** n knabenhaft.
boycott ['boikot] n Boykott m. v boykottieren.
bra [braː] n Büstenhalter m, BH m.
brace [breis] n Paar neut; (tech) Stütze f. v stützen. **braces** pl n Hosenträger pl.
bracelet ['breislit] n Armband neut.
bracing ['breisiŋ] adj erfrischend.
bracken ['brakən] n Farnkraut neut.
bracket ['brakit] n (parenthesis) Klammer f; (support) Träger m.

brag [brag] v prahlen, angeben. **braggart** n Prahler m.
braille [breil] n Brailleschrift f.
brain [brein] n Gehirn neut; Verstand m; Intelligenz f. **brainwashing** n Gehirnwäsche f. **brainwave** n Geistesblitz m. **brainy** adj klug.
braise [breiz] v schmoren.
brake [breik] n Bremse f. v bremsen. **brake pedal** Bremspedal neut.
bramble ['brambl] n (bush) Brombeerstrauch m; (berry) Brombeere f.
bran [bran] n (Weizen)Kleie f.
branch [braːntʃ] n Zweig m; (of bank) Zweigstelle f; (department) Abteilung f. v **branch off** abzweigen.
brand [brand] n (of goods) Marke f; (cattle) Brandzeichen neut. v (name) brandmarken. **brand-new** adj nagelneu.
brand name Markenname m.
brandish ['brandiʃ] v schwingen.
brandy ['brandi] n Weinbrand m.
brass [braːs] n Messing neut; (music) Blasinstrumente pl. adj Messing-.
brassiere ['brasiə] n Büstenhalter m.
brave [breiv] adj mutig, tapfer. v trotzen. **bravery** n Mut m, Tapferkeit f.
brawl [brɔːl] n Rauferei f. v raufen.
brawn [brɔːn] n Muskelkraft f. (cookery) Sülze f.
brazen ['breizn] adj (fig) unverschämt.
breach [briːtʃ] n Bruch m; (mil) Bresche f. v durchbrechen; (law) übertreten. **breach of contract** Vertragsbruch m. **breach of the peace** Friedensbruch m.
bread [bred] n Brot neut. v (cookery) panieren. **bread and butter** Butterbrot neut. **breadwinner** n Brotverdiener m.
breadth [bredθ] n Breite f, Weite f.
*break [breik] v brechen; (coll) kaputt machen; (law) übertreten; (promise) nicht halten; (day) anbrechen. n Bruch m; (gap) Lücke f; (rest) Pause f; (opportunity) Chance f. **break away** sich losreißen. **break down** (mot) eine Panne haben; (person) zusammenbrechen. **break in** (burgle) einbrechen; (animal) abrichten. **break out** ausbrechen. **break up** zerbrechen; (school) in die Ferien gehen.
breakable ['breikəbl] adj zerbrechlich.
breakage ['breikidʒ] n Bruchschaden m.
breakdown ['breikdaun] n (mot) Panne f. **nervous breakdown** Nervenzusammenbruch m.

breakfast ['brekfəst] n Frühstück neut. v frühstücken.
breakthrough ['breikθruː] n Durchbruch m.
breast [brest] n Brust f, Busen m. **breastbone** n Brustbein neut. **breast-stroke** n Brustschwimmen neut.
breath [breθ] n Atem m. **out of breath** außer Atem.
breathe [briːð] v atmen. **breathe in** einatmen. **breathe out** ausatmen.
bred [bred] V breed.
*breed [briːd] v (increase) sich vermehren; (animals) züchten; (fig) erzeugen. n (of dog) Rasse f. **breeding** n Zucht f; (education) Erziehung f.
breeze [briːz] n Brise f.
brew [bruː] v brauen. n Bräu neut. **brewery** n Brauerei f.
bribe [braib] v bestechen. n Bestechungsgeld neut. **bribery** n Bestechung f.
brick [brik] n Ziegelstein m. **bricklayer** n Maurer m.
bride [braid] n Braut f. **bridal** adj bräutlich, hochzeitlich. **bridegroom** n Bräutigam m. **bridesmaid** n Brautjungfer f.
bridge¹ [bridʒ] n Brücke f; (violin) Steg m. v überbrücken.
bridge² [bridʒ] n (card game) Bridge neut.
bridle ['braidl] n Zaum m.
brief [briːf] adj kurz. v instruieren. **briefcase** n Aktentasche f. **briefing** n Anweisung f. **briefly** adv kurz. **briefs** pl n Slip m sing.
brigade [bri'geid] n Brigade f. **brigadier** n Brigadegeneral m.
bright [brait] adj hell, leuchtend; (clever) klug. **brighten** v aufheitern. **brightness** n Glanz m (tech) Beleuchtungsstärke f.
brilliance ['briljəns] n Glanz m, Brillanz f. **brilliant** adj glänzend, brillant; (clever) scharfsinnig.
brim [brim] n Rand m; (hat) Krempe f.
brine [brain] n Salzwasser neut. **in brine** eingepökelt, Salz-.
*bring [briŋ] v bringen. **bring about** veranlassen. **bring along** mitbringen. **bring down** herunterbringen; (prices) herabsetzen. **bring up** (child) erziehen; (vomit) erbrechen.
brink [briŋk] n Rand m.
briquette [bri'ket] n Brikett m.
brisk [brisk] adj schnell, lebhaft.
bristle ['brisl] n Borste f.

Britain ['britn] n (Great Britain) Großbritannien neut. **British** adj britisch. **the British** die Briten. **Briton** Brite m, Britin f.
brittle ['britl] adj spröde.
broad [brɔːd] adj breit. **broadly** adv im allgemeinen.
broadcast ['brɔːdkaːst] v übertragen. n Sendung f. **broadcasting** n Rundfunk m.
broadcasting corporation n Rundfunkgesellschaft f.
brochure ['brəuʃuə] n Broschüre f.
broke [brəuk] V break. adj (coll) pleite.
broken ['brəukn] V break.
broker ['brəukə] n Makler m.
bronchitis [broŋ'kaitis] n Bronchitis f.
bronze [bronz] n Bronze f. adj aus Bronze, Bronze-; (colour) bronzefarben.
brooch [brəutʃ] n Brosche f.
brood [bruːd] n Brut f. v brüten. **broody** adj brütig.
brook [bruk] n Bach m.
broom [bruːm] n Besen m; (bot) Ginster m. **broomstick** n Besenstiehl m.
broth [broθ] n Brühe f.
brothel ['broθl] n Bordell neut.
brother ['brʌðə] n Bruder m. **Smith Bros.** Gebrüder Smith. **brothers and sisters** Geschwister pl. **brotherhood** n Bruderschaft f. **brother-in-law** n Schwager m. **brotherly** adj brüderlich.
brought [brɔːt] V bring.
brow [brau] n (forehead) Stirn f; (eyebrow) Augenbraue f; (of hill) Bergkuppe f.
brown [braun] adj braun. n Braun neut. v bräunen.
browse [brauz] v weiden; (in book) durchblättern.
bruise [bruːz] n blaue Flecke f, Quetschung f. v quetschen.
brunette [bruː'net] adj brünett. n Brünette f.
brush [brʌʃ] n Bürste f; (paintbrush) Pinsel m; (undergrowth) Unterholz neut. v bürsten. **brush past** vorbeistreichen.
brusque [brusk] adj brüsk.
Brussels ['brʌsəlz] n Brüssel neut. **Brussels sprouts** Rosenkohl m.
brute [bruːt] n Tier neut; (person) brutaler Mensch m. **brutal** adj brutal. **brutality** n Brutalität f.
bubble ['bʌbl] n Blase f. v sprudeln. **bubbly** adj sprudelnd.

buck¹ [bʌk] *n* Bock *m*; (*US coll*) Dollar *m*.

buck² [bʌk] *v* bocken. **buck up** (*hurry*) sich beeilen; (*cheer up*) munter werden.

bucket ['bʌkit] *n* Eimer *m*. **bucketful** *n* Eimervoll *m*.

buckle ['bʌkl] *n* Schnalle *f*. *v* anschnallen.

bud [bʌd] *n* Knospe *f*. *v* knospen. **nip in the bud** im Keim ersticken. **budding** *adj* angehend.

buddy ['bʌdi] *n* (*coll*) Kumpel *m*.

budge [bʌdʒ] *v* (sich) bewegen.

budgerigar ['bʌdʒərigaɪ] *n* Wellensittich *m*.

budget ['bʌdʒit] *n* Budget *neut*. *v* budgetieren.

buffalo ['bʌfəlou] *n* Büffel *m*; (*bison*) Bison *m*.

buffer ['bʌfə] *n* Puffer *m*.

buffet¹ ['bʌfit] *n* (*blow*) Schlag *m*. *v* stoßen.

buffet² ['bufei] *n* (*meal*) Büffett *neut*.

bug [bʌg] *n* Wanze *f*. *v* (*coll*) ärgern.

bugle ['bjuɪgl] *n* Signalhorn *neut*.

***build** [bild] *v* bauen. *n* Körperbau *m*. **build up** aufbauen. **builder** *n* Baumeister *m*. **building** *n* Gebäude *neut*, Haus *neut*. **built-in** *adj* eingebaut.

built [bilt] *V* build.

bulb [bʌlb] *n* (*flower*) Zwiebel *f*; (*lamp*) Glühbirne *f*. **bulbous** *adj* zwiebelförmig.

Bulgaria [bʌl'geəriə] *n* Bulgarien *neut*. **Bulgarian** *adj* bulgarisch. *n* Bulgare *m*. Bulgarin *f*.

bulge [bʌldʒ] *v* anschwellen. *n* Schwellung *f*, Ausbauchung *f*.

bulk [bʌlk] *n* Masse *f*; (*greater part*) Hauptteil *m*. **bulky** *adj* umfangreich.

bull [bul] *n* (*cattle*) Stier *m*; (*animal*) Bulle *f*; (*coll: nonsense*) Quatsch *m*. **bulldog** *n* Bulldogge *m*. **bulldozer** *n* Bulldozer *m*. **bullfight** *n* Stierkampf *m*.

bullet ['bulit] *n* (Gewehr)Kugel *f*.

bulletin ['bulətin] *n* Bulletin *neut*.

bullion ['buliən] *n* Gold-, Silberbarren *pl*.

bully ['buli] *v* einschüchtern. *n* Tyrann *m*.

bum [bʌm] *n* (*tramp*) Bummler *m*, Landstreicher *m*.

bump [bʌmp] *v* stoßen (gegen). *n* Stoß *m*; (*on the head*) Beule *f*. **bumper** *n* (*of car*) Stoßstange *f*. *adj* **bumper crop** Rekordernte *f*.

bun [bʌn] *n* (*hair*) Haarknoten *m*; (*cake*) Kuchen *m*; (*bread roll*) Brötchen *neut*.

bunch [bʌntʃ] *n* Bündel *neut*. **bunch of** flowers Blumenstrauß *m*. **bunch of grapes** Weintraube *f*. **bunch of keys** Schlüsselbund *m*.

bundle ['bʌndl] *n* Bündel *neut*. *v* zusammenbündeln.

bungalow ['bʌŋgəlou] *n* Bungalow *m*.

bungle ['bʌŋgl] *v* verpfuschen. **bungler** *n* Pfuscher.

bunion ['bʌnjən] *n* entzündeter Fußballen *m*.

bunk [bʌŋk] *n* Koje *f*.

bunker ['bʌŋkə] *n* Bunker *m*; (*golf*) Sandgrube *f*.

buoy [boi] *n* Boje *f*.

burden ['bəɪdn] *n* Last *f*. *v* belasten.

bureau ['bjuərou] *n* Büro *neut*; (*desk*) Schreibtisch *m*.

bureaucracy [bju'rokrəsi] *n* Bürokratie *f*. **bureaucrat** *n* Bürokrat *m*. **bureaucratic** *adj* bürokratisch.

burglar ['bəɪglə] *n* Einbrecher *m*. **burglary** *n* Einbruchsdiebstahl *m*.

burial ['beriəl] *n* Beerdigung *f*, Begräbnis *neut*.

***burn** [bəɪn] *v* brennen; (*set alight*) verbrennen. *n* Brandwunde *f*. **burn oneself** (*or one's fingers*) sich (die Finger) verbrennen.

burnt [bəɪnt] *V* burn. *adj* (*food*) angebrannt.

burrow ['bʌrou] *n* (*of rabbit*) Bau *m*. *v* graben.

***burst** [bəɪst] *v* platzen. *n* (*of shooting*) Feuerstoß *m*; (*of speed*) Spurt *m*. **burst out laughing/crying** in Lachen/Tränen ausbrechen. **burst tyre** geplatzter Reifen *m*.

bury ['beri] *v* begraben; (*one's hands, face*) vergraben.

bus [bʌs] *n* Bus *m*, Autobus *m*. **bus driver** Busfahrer *m*. **bus conductor** Busschaffner *m*. **bus stop** Bushaltestelle *f*.

bush [buʃ] *n* Busch *m*. **bushy** *adj* buschig.

business ['biznis] *n* Geschäft *neut*. **that's none of your business** das geht dich nichts an. **businessman** *n* Geschäftsmann *m*. **businesswoman** *n* Geschäftsfrau *f*.

bust¹ [bʌst] *n* (*breasts*) Busen *m*; (*sculpture*) Büste *f*.

bust² [bʌst] (*coll*) *adj* (*bankrupt*) pleite; (*broken*) kaputt. *v* zerbrechen, kaputt machen.

bustle ['bʌsl] *n* Aufregung *f*. *v* **bustle about** herumsausen.

busy ['bizi] n (occupied) beschäftigt; (hardworking) fleißig; (telephone) besetzt. v busy oneself with sich beschäftigen mit.
but [bʌt] conj aber. prep außer. adv (merely) nur. **not only ... but** also nicht nur ... sondern auch. **nothing but** nichts als. **but for** ohne.
butane ['bjuːtein] n Butan neut.
butcher [butʃə] n Fleischer m, Metzger m. **butcher's shop** Metzgerei f, Fleischerei f.
butler ['bʌtlə] n Butler m.
butt¹ [bʌt] n (thick end) dickes Ende neut; (of cigarette) Stummel m.
butt² [bʌt] n (of jokes) Zielscheibe f.
butt³ [bʌt] v (with the head) mit dem Kopf stoßen. n Kopfstoß.
butter ['bʌtə] n Butter f. v mit Butter bestreichen.
buttercup ['bʌtəkʌp] n Butterblume f.
butterfly ['bʌtəflai] n Schmetterling m.
buttocks ['bʌtəks] pl n Gesäß neut sing.
button ['bʌtn] n Knopf m. v (zu)knöpfen. **buttonhole** n Knopfloch neut.
buttress ['bʌtris] n Strebepfeiler m.
***buy** [bai] v kaufen. **buy in** einkaufen. **buyer** n Käufer(in).
buzz [bʌz] v summen. n Summen neut. **buzzer** n Summer m.
by [bai] prep (close to) bei, neben; (via) über; (past) an ... vorbei; (before) bis; (written by) von. adv vorbei. **by day** bei tage. **by bus** mit dem Bus. **by that** (mean, understand) damit. **by and by** nach und nach. **by-election** Nachwahl f. **bypass** n Umgehungstraße f. **by-product** n Nebenprodukt neut. **bystander** n Zuschauer m.

C

cab [kab] n (taxi) Taxi neut; (horse-drawn) Droschke f; (in truck) Fahrerhaus neut.
cabaret ['kabərei] n Kabarett neut.
cabbage ['kabidʒ] n Kohl m, Kraut neut.
cabin ['kabin] n Hütte f; (naut) Kabine f.
cabinet ['kabinit] n Schrank m; (pol) Kabinett neut. **cabinet-maker** n Möbeltischler m.
cable ['keibl] n (elec, telegram) Kabel neut; (rope) Tau neut, Seil neut. **cable address** Telegrammanschrift f. **cable railway** Drahtseilbahn f.
cackle ['kakl] v gackern. n Gegacker neut.
cactus ['kaktəs] n Kaktus m.
caddie ['kadi] n Golfjunge m.
cadence ['keidəns] n (music) Kadenz f. **cadenza** n Kadenz f.
cadet [kə'det] n Kadett m.
café ['kafei] n Café neut.
cafeteria [kafə'tiəriə] n Selbstbedienungsrestaurant neut.
caffeine ['kafiːn] n Koffein neut.
cage [keidʒ] n Käfig m. v in einen Käfig sperren.
cake [keik] n Kuchen m; (soap) Tafel f. v **be caked with mud** vor Schmutz starren.
calamine ['kaləmain] n Galmei m.
calamity [kə'laməti] n Unheil neut, Katastrophe f.
calcium ['kalsiəm] n Kalzium neut.
calculate ['kalkjuleit] v kalkulieren, berechnen. **calculating** adj berechnend. **calculation** n Berechnung f. **calculator** n (mech) Rechner m.
calendar ['kaləndə] n Kalender m.
calf¹ [kaːf] n (young cow) Kalb neut. **calfskin** n Kableder neut.
calf² [kaːf] n (anat) Wade f. **calf muscle** Wadenmuskel m.
calibre ['kalibə] n Kaliber neut.
call [koːl] v rufen; anrufen; (a doctor) holen; (regard as) halten für. n Ruf m; (phone) Anruf m; (demand) Aufforderung f. **call for** verlangen. **call off** (cancel) absagen. **callbox** n Telefonzelle f. **caller** n (visitor) Besucher m; (phone) Anrufer m. **calling** n Berufung f. **call-up** n Einberufung f.
callous ['kaləs] adj gefühllos, herzlos.
calm [kaːm] adj ruhig. n Ruhe, Stille f; (naut) Windstille f. v or **calm down** (sich) or beruhigen.
calorie ['kaləri] n Kalorie f.
came [keim] V come.
camel ['kaməl] n Kamel neut. **camelhair** n Kamelhaar neut.
camera ['kamərə] n Kamera f, Fotoapparat m. **cameraman** n Kameramann m.
camouflage ['kaməflaːʒ] n Tarnung f; (zool) Schutzfärbung f. v tarnen.
camp [kamp] n Lager neut. v lagern; (go camping) campen, zelten. **camp bed** n Feldbett neut. **camper** n Camper m. **camping** n Camping neut. **camp site** n Campingplatz m.

campaign [kam'pein] *n* (*mil, pol*) Feldzug *m*; Kampagne *f*. *v* **campaign for** (*fig*) werben um, kämpfen für.

campus ['kampəs] *n* Universitätsgelände *neut*.

camshaft ['kamʃɑːft] *n* Nockenwelle *f*.

***can*¹** [kan] *v* (*be able*) können; (*be allowed, may*) dürfen.

can² [kan] *n* (*tin*) Dose *f*, Büchse *f*. *v* konservieren.

Canada ['kanədə] *n* Kanada *neut*. **Canadian** *adj* kanadisch; *n* Kanadier(in).

canal [kə'nal] *n* Kanal *m*.

canary [kə'neəri] *n* Kanarienvogel *m*.

cancel ['kansəl] *v* (*meeting*) absagen; (*arrangement*) aufheben; (*stamp*) entwerten; (*cross out*) durchstreichen. **cancellation** *n* Absage *f*; Aufhebung *f*.

cancer ['kansə] *n* (*med*) Krebs *m*. **Cancer** (*astrol*) Krebs *m*. **breast cancer** Brustenkrebs *m*. **lung cancer** Lungenkrebs *m*.

candid ['kandid] *adj* offen, ehrlich.

candidate ['kandidət] *n* Kandidat *m*.

candle ['kandl] *n* Kerze *f*. **candle light** *n* Kerzenlicht *neut*. **candlestick** Leuchter *m*.

candour ['kandə] *n* Offenheit *f*; Ehrlichkeit *f*.

candy ['kandi] *n* Kandiszucker *m*; (*US: sweet*) Bonbon *neut*.

cane [kein] *n* (*walking stick*) Spazierstock *m*. **sugar cane** Zuckerrohr *m*. **cane sugar** Rohrzucker *m*.

canine ['keinain] *adj* Hunde-, Hunds-. **canine tooth** Eckzahn *m*.

canister ['kanistə] *n* Kanister *m*.

cannabis ['kanəbis] *n* Haschisch *neut*.

cannibal ['kanibəl] *n* Kannibale *m*.

cannon ['kanən] *n* Kanone *f*.

canoe [kə'nuː] *n* Kanu *neut*. *v* Kanu fahren.

canon ['kanən] *n* Domherr *m*; (*rule*) Kanon *m*.

can opener *n* Büchsenöffner *m*.

canopy ['kanəpi] *n* Baldachin *m*.

canteen [kan'tiːn] *n* (*restaurant*) Kantine *f*.

canter ['kantə] *n* Handgalopp *m*. *v* Handgalopp reiten.

canton ['kantən] *n* Kanton *m*.

canvas ['kanvəs] *n* Segeltuch *neut*; (*artist's*) Leinwand *f*.

canvass ['kanvəs] *v* werben.

canyon ['kanjən] *n* Cañon *m*, Schlucht *f*.

cap [kap] *n* (*hat*) Kappe *f*, Mütze *f*; (*lid*) Kappe *f*. *v* (*fig*) übertreffen.

capable ['keipəbl] *adj* (*able to do something*) fähig (zu); (*skilled*) begabt. **capability** *n* Fähigkeit *f*.

capacity [kə'pasəti] *n* (*volume*) Inhalt *m*; (*of ship*) Laderaum *m*; (*talent*) Talent *m*. **in the capacity of** als. **filled to capacity** voll (besetzt).

cape¹ [keip] *n* (*cloak*) Cape *neut*, Umhang *m*.

cape² [keip] *n* (*geog*) Kap *neut*.

caper¹ ['keipə] *n* Kapriole *f*. *v* kapriolen.

caper² ['keipə] *n* (*cookery*) Kaper *f*.

capital ['kapitl] *n* (*city*) Hauptstadt *f*; (*comm*) Kapital *neut*. *adj* (*main*) Haupt-; (*comm*) Kapital-; (*splendid*) großartig. **capitalism** *n* Kapitalismus *m*. **capitalist** *n* Kapitalist *m*. *adj* kapitalistisch. **capital punishment** Todesstrafe *n*.

capitulate [kə'pitjuleit] *v* kapitulieren (vor).

capricious [kə'priʃəs] *adj* launenhaft.

Capricorn ['kaprikoːn] *n* Steinbock *m*.

capsize [kap'saiz] *v* kentern.

capsule ['kapsjuːl] *n* Kapsel *f*.

captain ['kaptin] *n* (*mil*) Hauptmann *m*; (*naut*) Kapitän *m*; (*sport*) Mannschaftsführer *m*. *v* (*sport*) führen.

caption ['kapʃən] *n* (*picture*) Erklärung *f*; (*heading*) Überschrift *f*.

captive ['kaptiv] *n* Gefangene(r). *adj* gefangen. **captivity** *n* Gefangenschaft *f*. **captor** *n* Fänger *m*.

capture ['kaptʃə] *v* gefangennehmen; (*animal*) einfangen. *n* Genangennahme *f*.

car [kɑː] *n* (*mot*) Wagen *m*, Auto *neut*; (*rail*) Wagen *m*. **by car** mit dem Auto.

caramel ['karəmel] *n* Karamel *m*.

carat ['karət] *n* Karat *neut*.

caravan ['karəvan] *n* (*mot*) Wohnwagen *m*; (*oriental*) Karawane *f*.

caraway ['karəwei] *n* Kümmel *m*.

carbohydrate [kɑːbə'haidreit] *n* Kohlehydrat *neut*.

carbon ['kɑːbən] *n* Kohlenstoff *m*. **carbon copy** Durchschlag *m*. **carbon dioxide** Kohlendioxid *neut*; (*in drinks*) Kohlensäure *f*. **carbon paper** Kohlepapier *neut*.

carburettor ['kɑːbjuretə] **carburetor** *n* Vergaser *m*.

carcass ['kɑːkəs] *n* Kadaver *m*.

card [kɑːd] *n* Karte *f*. **cardboard** *n* Pappe *f*. **cardboard box** Pappschachtel *f*. **card**

game Kartenspiel *neut*. **card index** Kartei *f*.

cardiac ['kaɪdiak] *adj* Herz-.

cardigan ['kaɪdigən] *n* Wolljacke *f*.

cardinal ['kaɪdənl] *n* Kardinal *m*. *adj* grundsätzlich.

care [keə] *n* (*carefulness*) Sorgfalt *f*; (*looking after*) Pflege *f*; (*worry*) Sorge *f*. **take care** sich hüten; achtgeben. **take care of** (*look after*) pflegen; (*see to*) erledigen. *v* **care about** sich kümmern um. **care for** (*look after*) pflegen; (*see to*) sorgen für; (*like*) mögen. **carefree** *adj* sorgenfrei. **careful** *adj* sorgfältig; (*cautious*) vorsichtig. **carefulness** *n* Sorgfalt *f*; Vorsicht *f*. **careless** *adj* unachtsam, nachlässig. **carelessness** *n* Nachlässigkeit *f*.

career [kə'riə] *n* Laufbahn *f*, Karriere *f*.

caress [kə'res] *v* liebkosen. *n* Liebkosung *f*; Kuß *m*.

cargo ['kaɪgou] *n* Fracht *f*. **cargo plane** Transportflugzeug *neut*. **cargo ship** Frachtschiff *neut*.

caricature ['karikətjuə] *n* Karikatur *f*. *v* karikieren.

carnal ['kaɪnl] *adj* fleischlich.

carnation [kaɪ'neiʃən] *n* Nelke *f*.

carnival ['kaɪnivəl] *n* Karneval *m*, Fasching *m*.

carnivorous [kaɪ'nivərəs] *adj* fleischfressend.

carol ['karəl] *n* Weihnachtslied *neut*.

carpenter ['kaɪpəntə] *n* Zimmermann *m*, Tischler *m*. **carpentry** *n* Zimmerhandwerk *neut*.

carpet ['kaɪpit] *n* Teppich *m*. *v* mit einem Teppich belegen.

carriage ['karidʒ] *n* (*rail*) (Eisenbahn) Wagen *m*; (*transport*) Transport *f*; (*posture*) Haltung *f*. **carriageway** Fahrbahn *f*.

carrier ['kariə] *n* Träger *m*; (*med*) Keimträger *m*; (*comm*) Spediteur *m*. **carrier bag** Tragebeutel *m*.

carrot ['karət] *n* Mohrrübe *f*, Möhre *f*.

carry ['kari] *v* tragen; (*transport*) befördern. **carry out** ausführen. **carry cot** Tragbettchen *neut*.

cart [kaɪt] *n* Karren *m*.

cartilage ['kaɪtəlidʒ] *n* Knorpel *m*.

cartography [kaɪ'togrəfi] *n* Kartographie *f*.

carton ['kaɪtən] *n* Karton *m*.

cartoon [kaɪ'tuɪn] *n* Karikatur *f*; (*film*) Trickfilm *m*. **cartoonist** *n* Karikaturenzeichner *m*.

cartridge ['kaɪtridʒ] *n* Patrone *f*. **cartridge paper** Zeichenpapier *neut*.

carve [kaɪv] *v* (*in wood*) schnitzen; (*in stone*) meißeln; (*meat*) vorschneiden. **carving** *n* Schnitzerei *f*.

cascade [kas'keid] *n* Kaskade *f*.

case[1] [keis] *n* (*affair, instance*) Fall *m*; (*law*) Sache *f*. **in case** falls. **in case of** im Falle (+ *gen*). **in any case** auf jeden Fall.

case[2] [keis] *n* (*suitcase*) Koffer *m*; (*for cigarettes, camera*) Etui *neut*; (*tech*) Gehäuse *neut*.

cash [kaʃ] *n* Bargeld *neut*. *v* einlösen. **cash on delivery** per Nachnahme. **pay cash** bar zahlen. **cash desk** Kasse *f*.

cashier [ka'ʃiə] *n* Kassierer(in).

cashmere [kaʃ'miə] *n* Kaschmir *m*.

casing ['keisiŋ] *n* Gehäuse *neut*.

casino [kə'siɪnou] *n* Kasino *neut*.

casket ['kaɪskit] *n* Kästchen *neut*; (*coffin*) Sarg *m*.

casserole ['kasəroul] *n* (*vessel*) Kasserolle *f*; (*meal*) Schmorbraten *m*. *v* schmoren.

cassette [kə'set] *n* Kassette *f*. **cassette recorder** Kassettenrecorder *m*.

cassock ['kasək] *n* Soutane *f*.

***cast** [kaɪst] *v* werfen; (*metal*) gießen; (*theatre*) besetzen. *n* (*theatre*) Besetzung *f*.

caste [kaɪst] *n* Kaste *f*.

castle ['kaɪsl] *n* Burg *f*, Schloß *neut*; (*chess*) Turm *m*. *v* (*chess*) rochieren.

castor oil ['kaɪstə] *n* Möbelrolle *f*.

castrate [kə'streit] *v* kastrieren. **castration** *n* Kastration *f*.

casual ['kaʒuəl] *adj* beiläufig; (*careless*) nachlässig; (*informal*) leger. **casual labour** Gelegenheitsarbeit *f*.

casualty ['kaʒuəlti] *n* Verletzte(r). **casualties** *pl n* (*mil*) Ausfälle *pl*. **casualty department** Unfallstation *f*.

cat [kat] *n* Katze *f*. **tom cat** Kater *m*.

catalogue ['katələg] *n* Katalog *m*.

catalyst ['katəlist] *n* Katalysator *m*.

catamaran [katəmə'ran] *n* Katamaran *neut*.

catapult ['katəpʌlt] *n* Katapult *neut*.

cataract ['katərakt] *n* (*med*) grauer Star *m*; Wasserfall *m*.

catarrh [kə'taɪ] *n* Katarrh *m*.

catastrophe [kə'tastrəfi] *n* Katastrophe *f*. **catastrophic** *adj* katastrophal.

*catch [katʃ] v fangen; (bus, train) nehmen, erreichen; (surprise) ertappen; (illness) sich zuziehen. n Fang m.

category ['katəgəri] n Katagorie f. **categorical** adj kategorisch.

cater ['keitə] v cater for versorgen. **catering** n Bewirtung f.

caterpillar ['katəpilə] n Raupe f. **caterpillar track** Gleiskette f.

cathedral [kə'θiːdrəl] n Dom m, Kathedrale f.

cathode ['kaθoud] n Kathode f.

catholic ['kaθəlik] adj (rel) katholisch; universal. n Katholik(in). **Roman Catholic** römisch-katholisch.

catkin ['katkin] n Kätzchen neut.

cattle ['katl] pl n Vieh neut sing, Rindvieh neut sing. **cattle shed** Viehstall m.

catty ['kati] adj (coll) gehässig.

caught [kɔːt] V catch.

cauliflower ['kɔliflauə] n Blumenkohl m.

cause [kɔːz] n Ursache f; (reason) Grund m; (interests) Sache f. v verursachen, veranlassen.

causeway ['kɔːzwei] n Damm m.

caustic ['kɔːstik] adj ätzend; (fig) beißend.

caution ['kɔːʃən] n Vorsicht f. v warnen (vor). **cautious** adj vorsichtig.

cavalry ['kavəlri] n Kavallerie f.

cave [keiv] n Höhle f. v cave in einstürzen. **cavern** n Höhle f.

caviar ['kaviaː] n Kaviar m.

cavity ['kavəti] n Hohlraum m; (in tooth) Loch neut.

cease [siːs] v aufhören; (fire) einstellen. **ceasefire** n Feuereinstellung f. **ceaseless** adj unaufhörlich.

cedar ['siːdə] n Zeder f.

ceiling ['siːliŋ] n Decke f; (fig) Höchstgrenze f.

celebrate ['seləbreit] v feiern. **celebrated** adj berühmt. **celebration** n Feier f. **celebrity** n Berühmtheit f.

celery ['seləri] n Sellerie m or f.

celestial [sə'lestiəl] adj himmlisch.

celibacy ['selibəsi] n Zölibat neut or m, Ehelosigkeit f. **celibate** adj ehelos.

cell [sel] n Zelle f.

cellar ['selə] n Keller m.

cello ['tʃelou] n Cello neut.

cellophane ['seləfein] n Zellophan neut.

cellular ['seljulə] adj zellular.

cement [sə'ment] n Zement m. v zementieren; (fig) binden.

cemetery ['semətri] n Friedhof m.

cenotaph ['senətaːf] n Ehrenmal m.

censor ['sensə] n Zensor m. v zensieren. **censorship** n Zensur f.

censure ['senʃə] n Tadel m. v tadeln.

census ['sensəs] n Volkszählung f.

cent [sent] n Cent m. **per cent** Prozent neut.

centenary [sen'tiːnəri] n Hundertjahrfeier f.

centigrade ['sentigreid] adv Celsius.

centimetre ['sentimiːtə] n Zentimeter neut.

centipede ['sentipiːd] n Tausendfuß m.

centre ['sentə] n Zentrum neut, Mittelpunkt m. adj Zentral-. v centre around sich drehen um. centre on sich konzentrieren auf. centre forward (sport) Mittelstürmer m. centre half Mittelläufer m. centre of gravity Schwerpunkt m. centrepiece n Tafelaufsatz m. central adj zentral, Zentral-. Central America Mittelamerika neut. central heating Zentralheizung f. central station Hauptbahnhof m.

centrifugal [sen'trifjugəl] adj zentrifugal. **centrifugal force** Zentrifugalkraft f.

century ['sentʃuri] n Jahrhundert neut.

ceramic [sə'ramik] adj keramisch. **ceramics** n Keramik f.

cereal ['siəriəl] n Getreide neut. **breakfast cereal** Getreideflocken pl.

ceremony ['serəməni] n Zeremonie f. **ceremonial** adj zeremoniell. **ceremonious** adj zeremoniös.

certain ['sɔːtn] adj bestimmt, gewiß; (sure) sicher. **for certain** bestimmt. **certainly** adv sicherlich, gewiß. **certainty** n Sicherheit f.

certificate [sə'tifikət] n Bescheinigung f. **certification** n Bescheinigung f. **certify** v bestätigen.

cervix ['sɔːviks] n (anat) Gebärmutterhals m.

cesspool ['sespuːl] n Senkgrube f.

chafe [tʃeif] v reiben.

chaffinch ['tʃafintʃ] n Buchfink m.

chain [tʃein] n Kette f. v anketten. **chain reaction** Kettenreaktion f. **chain smoker** Kettenraucher m. **chainstore** n Kettenladen m.

chair [tʃeə] n Stuhl m; (armchair) Sessel m; (at meeting) Vorsitz m. v (meeting) den Vorsitz führen. **chairlift** n Sesselbahn f. **chairman** Vorsitzende(r).

chalet ['ʃalei] n Chalet neut.
chalk [tʃɔːk] n Kreide f. v mit Kreide schreiben.
challenge ['tʃalindʒ] n Aufforderung f; (objection) Einwand m. v auffordern; (question) bestreiten. challenger n Herausforderer m.
chamber ['tʃeimbə] n Kammer f. chamber music Kammermusik f. chamber pot Nachttopf m.
chameleon [kəmiːliən] n Chamäleon neut.
chamois ['ʃamwai] n Gemse f; (leather) Sämischleder neut.
champagne [ʃam'pein] n Champagner m.
champion ['tʃampiən] n (sport) Meister m, Sieger m; (defender) Verfechter m. v (cause) verfechten. championship n Meisterschaft f.
chance [tʃɑːns] n Zufall m; (opportunity) Gelegenheit f; (possibility) Chance f, Möglichkeit f. v riskieren. by chance zufällig. stand a chance Chancen haben. take a chance sein Glück versuchen. no chance! keine Spur!
chancellor [tʃɑːnsələ] n Kanzler m.
chandelier [ʃandə'liə] n Kronleuchter m.
change [tʃeindʒ] v (modify) (ab-, ver)ändern; (exchange) (aus)tauschen; (become changed) sich (ver)ändern; (trains) umsteigen; (clothes) sich umziehen; (money) wechseln. change gear schalten. change into (sich) verwandeln in. change over to übergehen zu. n (Ab-, Ver)Änderung f; (Ver)Wandlung f; (small change) Kleingeld neut. change of life Wechseljahre pl. for a change zur Abwechselung. changeable adj veränderlich. changeless adj unveränderlich.
channel ['tʃanl] n Kanal m; (fig) Weg m. v lenken. through official channels durch die Instanzen. English Channel der Ärmelkanal.
chant [tʃɑːnt] v intonieren. n Gesang m.
chaos ['keios] n Chaos neut; (mess) Durcheinander neut.
chap¹ [tʃap] v (skin) rissig machen; (become chapped) aufspringen.
chap² [tʃap] n (coll) Kerl m.
chapel ['tʃapəl] n Kapelle f.
chaperon ['ʃapəroun] n Anstandsdame f. v begleiten.
chaplain ['tʃaplin] n Kaplan m.
chapter ['tʃaptə] n Kapitel neut; (branch) Ortsgruppe f.

char¹ [tʃɑː] v (burn) verkohlen.
char² [tʃɑː] n (cleaning lady) Putzfrau f.
character ['karəktə] n Charakter m; (personality) Persönlichkeit f; (theatre) Person f; (reputation) Ruf m; (letter) Buchstabe m. characteristic n Kennzeichen neut; adj charakteristisch. characterize v charakterisieren.
charcoal ['tʃɑːkoul] n Holzkohle f; (for drawing) Reißkohle f.
charge [tʃɑːdʒ] n (cost) Preis m; (of firearm) Ladung f; (mil) Angriff m; (law) Anklage f; (elec) Ladung f. v (firearm, battery) laden; (price) verlangen; (attack) angreifen. be in charge of verantwortlich sein für. bring a charge against anklagen.
chariot ['tʃariət] n Streitwagen m.
charity ['tʃarəti] n Nächstenliebe f, Wohltätigkeit f; (organization) Wohlfahrtseinrichtung f. charitable adj wohltätig f.
charm [tʃɑːm] n (personal) Scharm m, Reiz m; (magic word) Zauberwort neut; (trinket) Amulett neut. v entzücken. charming entzückend, scharmant.
chart [tʃɑːt] n (naut) Seekarte f; Diagramm neut.
charter ['tʃɑːtə] n Verfassungsurkunde f; (naut, aero) Charter m. v chartern. adj Charter-.
chase [tʃeis] v verfolgen, jagen. n Verfolgung f, Jagd f.
chasm ['kazəm] n Abgrund m.
chassis ['ʃasi] n Fahrgestell neut.
chaste [tʃeist] adj keusch. chastity n Keuschheit f.
chastise [tʃas'taiz] v strafen.
chat [tʃat] v plaudern, sich unterhalten. n Plauderei f.
chatter ['tʃatə] v schnattern; (teeth) klappern. n Geschnatter neut; Klappern neut.
chauffeur ['ʃoufə] n Chauffeur m.
chauvinism ['ʃouvinizəm] n Chauvinismus m. chauvinist n Chauvinist m.
cheap [tʃiːp] adj billig, preiswert; (base) gemein.
cheat [tʃiːt] v betrügen. n Betrüger m, Schwindler m.
check [tʃek] v (inspect) prüfen, kontrollieren; (hinder) (ver)hindern; (look up) nachsehen; (tick) abhaken. check in sich anmelden. check out (hotel) abreisen. n Kontrolle f; (bill) Rechnung; (check) Scheck m; (chess) Schach m; (pattern) Karo neut. checklist n Kontrolliste f.

checkmate n Schachmatt neut. **checkpoint** Kontrollpunkt m. **check-up** n (med) ärztliche Untersuchung f.

cheek [tʃiːk] n (anat) Wange f, Backe f; (impudence) Frechheit f. **cheeky** adj frech.

cheer [tʃiə] v jubeln; (applaud) zujubeln (+dat); (encourage) aufmuntern. **cheer up** aufmuntern. n Beifallsruf m, Hurra neut. **cheers!** interj prost! **cheerful** adj fröhlich. **cheerio!** interj tschüs!

cheese [tʃiːz] n Käse f. **cheesecake** n Käsekuchen m; **cheesecloth** n Musselin m.

cheetah ['tʃiːtə] n Gepard m.

chef [ʃef] n Küchenchef m.

chemical ['kemikl] adj chemisch. **chemicals** pl n Chemikalien pl.

chemist ['kemist] n Chemiker m; (dispensing chemist) Apotheker m. **chemist's shop** Apotheke f.

chemistry ['kemistri] n Chemie f.

cheque [tʃek] n Scheck m. **chequebook** n Scheckbuch neut. **cheque card** Scheckkarte f.

cherish ['tʃeriʃ] v (feeling) hegen; (person) lieb haben.

cherry ['tʃeri] n Kirsche f; (tree) Kirschbaum m.

chess [tʃes] n Schach neut. **chessboard** n Schachbrett neut. **chessman** n Schachfigur f.

chest [tʃest] n (anat) Brust f; (container) Kiste f; (trunk) Truhe f. that's a weight off my chest da fällt mir ein Stein vom Herzen.

chestnut ['tʃesnʌt] n (sweet chestnut) (Eß)Kastanie f; (horse chestnut) (Roß)Kastanie f; (tree) Kastanienbaum m; (brown horse) Braune(r) m.

chew [tʃuː] v kauen. **chewing gum** Kaugummi m.

chick [tʃik] n Küken neut. **chicken** n Huhn neut; (for eating) Hähnchen neut. adj (coll) feige. **chicken soup** Hühnerbrühe f.

chicory ['tʃikəri] n Zichorie f; (salad plant) Chicorée f.

chief [tʃiːf] n (pl -s) Chef m, Leiter m; (of tribe) Häuptling m. adj Haupt-, erster. **chieftain** m Häuptling m.

chilblain ['tʃilblein] n Frostbeule f.

child [tʃaild] n (pl -ren) Kind neut. **with child** schwanger. **childbirth** n Entbindung

f. **childhood** n Kindheit f. **childish** adj kindisch. **childlike** adj kindlich.

Chile ['tʃili] n Chile neut. **Chilean** adj chilenisch. n Chilene m, Chilenin f.

chill [tʃil] n Kältegefühl neut; (fever) Schüttelfrost m. **chilled** adj (drink) gekühlt. **chilly** adj fröstelnd.

chilli ['tʃili] n Cayennepfeffer m.

chime [tʃaim] v (bell) läuten. n Geläut neut.

chimney ['tʃimni] n Schornstein m. **chimney sweep** Schornsteinfeger m.

chimpanzee [tʃimpən'ziː] n Schimpanse m.

chin [tʃin] n Kinn neut.

china ['tʃainə] n Porzellan neut. adj Porzellan-. **china clay** Kaolin neut.

China ['tʃainə] n China neut. **Chinese** adj chinesisch; n Chinese m, Chinesin f.

chink¹ [tʃiŋk] n (fissure) Ritze f, Spalt m.

chink² [tʃiŋk] v (sound) klirren. n Klirren neut.

chip [tʃip] n Splitter m. **chips** pl Pommes frites pl; (crisps) Chips pl. **chipped** adj (china) angestoßen.

chiropodist [ki'rɔpədist] n Fußpfleger(in). **chiropody** n Fußpflege f.

chirp [tʃəip] v zirpen. n Gezirp neut. **chirpy** adj munter.

chisel ['tʃizl] n Meißel m. v meißeln.

chivalrous [ʃivəlrəs] adj ritterlich. **chivalry** n Ritterlichkeit f.

chives [tʃaivz] pl n Schnittlauch m sing.

chlorine ['klɔːriːn] n Chlor neut. **chlorinate** v chlorieren.

chlorophyll ['klɔrəfil] n Chlorophyll neut.

chocolate ['tʃɔkələt] n Schokolade f. adj (colour) schokoladenbraun.

choice [tʃois] n Wahl f; (selection) Auswahl f. adj auserlesen.

choir ['kwaiə] n Chor m. **choirboy** Chorknabe m.

choke [tʃouk] v ersticken, würgen; (throttle) erwürgen. n (mot) Starterklappe f.

cholera ['kɔlərə] n Cholera f.

cholesterol [kə'lestərɔl] n Cholesterin neut.

***choose** [tʃuːz] v wählen; (select) auswählen; (prefer) vorziehen. **choosy** adj wählerisch.

chop¹ [tʃɔp] v (food) zerhacken; (wood) spalten. n Kotelett neut.

chop² [tʃɔp] v **chop and change** schwanken, wechseln.

chopsticks ['tʃɒpstiks] pl n Eßstäbchen pl.

chord [kɔːd] n (music) Akkord m.

chore [tʃɔː] n lästige Pflicht f.

choreographer [kɒriˈɒɡrəfə] n Choreograph m. **choreography** n Choreographie f.

chorus ['kɔːrəs] n Chor m; (of song) Refrain m.

chose [tʃəʊz] V choose.

chosen ['tʃəʊzn] V choose.

Christ [kraɪst] n Christus m.

christen ['krɪsn] v taufen. **christening** n Taufe f.

Christian ['krɪstʃən] adj christlich. n Christ m, Christin f. **Christian name** Vorname m. **Christianity** n Christentum neut.

Christmas ['krɪsməs] n Weihnachten pl. **Christmas card** Weihnachtskarte f. **Christmas present** Weihnachtsgeschenk neut. **Christmas tree** Weihnachtsbaum m.

chrome [krəʊm] n (plating) Verchromung f. adj (yellow) chromgelb. **chrome-plated** adj verchromt.

chromium ['krəʊmiəm] n Chrom neut.

chronic ['krɒnik] adj (med) chronisch.

chronicle ['krɒnikl] n Chronik f.

chronological [krɒnəˈlɒdʒikəl] adj chronologisch.

chrysalis ['krɪsəlis] n Puppe f.

chrysanthemum [kriˈsanθəməm] n Chrysantheme f.

chubby ['tʃʌbi] adj pausbäckig.

chuck [tʃʌk] v (coll) werfen.

chuckle ['tʃʌkl] v glucksen, kichern. n Kichern neut.

chunk [tʃʌŋk] n Klumpen m, Stück neut.

church [tʃɜːtʃ] n Kirche f. **church-goer** n Kirchgänger m. **churchyard** n Kirchhof m.

churn [tʃɜːn] n (butter) Butterfaß neut; (milk) Milchkanne f. v (fig) aufwühlen.

chute [ʃuːt] n Rutsche f.

cider ['saɪdə] n Apfelwein m.

cigar [siˈɡɑː] n Zigarre f.

cigarette [siɡəˈret] n Zigarette f. **cigarette end** Zigarettenstümmel m. **cigarette lighter** n Feuerzeug neut.

cinder ['sində] n Zinder m.

cine camera ['sini] n Filmkamera f.

cinema ['sinəmə] n Kino neut.

cinnamon ['sinəmən] n Zimt m.

circle ['sɜːkl] n Kreis m; (theatre) Rang m. v umkreisen. **circular** adj kreisförmig,

rund. **circulate** v zirkulieren, umlaufen; (send round) in Umlauf setzen. **circulation** n Umlauf m; (blood) Kreislauf m.

circuit ['sɜːkit] n Umlauf m; (elec) Stromkreis m.

circumcise ['sɜːkəmsaiz] n beschneiden. **circumcision** n Beschneidung f.

circumference [səˈkʌmfərəns] n Umfang m.

circumscribe ['sɜːkəmskraib] v umschreiben.

circumstance ['sɜːkəmstans] n Umstand m. **under the circumstances** unter diesen Umständen. **under no circumstances** auf keinen Fall.

circus ['sɜːkəs] n Zirkus m.

cistern ['sistən] n Zisterne f.

cite [sait] v zitieren.

citizen ['sitizn] n Bürger(in); (of country) Staatsangehörige(r). **citizenship** n Staatsangehörigkeit f.

citrus ['sitrəs] adj **citrus fruit** Zitrusfrucht f.

city ['siti] n Stadt f.

civic ['sivik] n städtisch.

civil ['sivl] adj (polite) höflich, freundlich; (not military) Zivil-. **civility** n Höflichkeit f. **civil engineer** Bauingenieur m. **civil rights** Bürgerrechte pl.

civilian [səˈviljən] adj Zivil-. n Zivilist m.

civilization [ˌsivilaiˈzeiʃən] n Zivilisation f. **civilize** v zivilisieren. **civilized** adj zivilisiert.

clad [klad] adj bekleidet; (tech) umkleidet.

claim [kleim] v verlangen, Anspruch erheben auf. n Anspruch m; (right) Anrecht neut. **claimant** n Antragsteller m.

clairvoyant [kleəˈvoiənt] n Hellseher(in).

clam [klam] n Muschel f.

clamber ['klambə] v klettern.

clammy ['klami] adj feucht, klebrig.

clamour ['klamə] n Geschrei neut. v **clamour for** rufen nach.

clamp [klamp] n Klammer f, Krampe f. v verklammern. **clamp down on** unterdrücken.

clan [klan] n Sippe f.

clandestine [klanˈdestin] adj heimlich.

clang [klaŋ] n Schall m, Klirren neut. v schallen, klirren.

clank [klaŋk] n Gerassel neut; Klappern neut. v rasseln, klappern.

clap [klap] v (*applaud*) klatschen, Beifall spenden (+dat); (*hit*) schlagen, klapsen. n (*tap*) Klaps m. clapper n (*bell*) Klöppel m. clapping n Klatschen *neut*.

claret ['klarət] n Rotwein m, Bordeaux m.

clarify ['klarəfai] v klären. clarification n Klärung f.

clarinet [klarə'net] n Klarinette f. clarinettist n Klarinettist m.

clash [klaʃ] v kollidieren, zusammenprallen; (*argue*) sich streiten; (*colours*) nicht zusammenpassen. n Knall m; (*conflict*) Konflikt m.

clasp [klaɪsp] v umklammern; n Haspe f, Klammer f.

class [klaɪs] n Klasse f; (*lesson*) Stunde f. v klassieren. class-conscious adj klassenbewußt. classroom n Klassenzimmer f. classy adj (*coll*) klasse, erstklassig.

classic ['klasik] adj klassisch. classics pl n die alten Sprachen pl. classical adj klassisch. classicism n Klassik f.

classify ['klasifai] v klassifizieren. classification n Klassifizierung f.

clatter ['klatə] v klappern. n Klappern *neut*.

clause [kloɪz] n (*in document*) Klausel f.

claustrophobia [kloɪstrə'foubiə] n Platzangst f.

claw [kloɪ] n Kralle f, Klaue f. v zerkratzen.

clay [klei] n Lehm m, Ton m.

clean [kliɪn] adj rein, sauber; (*paper*) weiß. adv ganz. v reinigen, putzen, saubermachen. clean up aufräumen. come clean gestehen. cleaner n (*woman*) Putzfrau f. cleaning n Reinigen *neut*. cleanness n Sauberkeit f. cleanly adj reinlich. clean-shaven adj glattrasiert.

cleanse [klenz] v reinigen.

clear [kliə] adj klar; (*sound, meaning*) deutlich, klar; (*road, way*) frei; (*glass*) durchsichtig. v räumen; (*table*) abräumen; (*road*) freimachen; (*forest*) roden; (*authorize*) freigeben. clearance n Räumung f; (*authorization*) Freigabe f; (*tech*) Spielraum m. clearcut adj (*fig*) eindeutig. clearing n Lichtung f. clearly adv offensichtlich.

clef [klef] n Notenschlüssel m.

clench [klentʃ] v (*fist*) zusammenballen.

clergy ['kləɪdʒi] n Klerus m. clergyman n Geistliche(r) m; Kleriker m.

clerical ['klerikəl] adj geistlich. clerical work Büroarbeit f.

clerk [klaɪk] n Büroangestellte(r); (*sales clerk*) Verkäufer(in).

clever ['klevə] adj klug, gescheit; (*crafty*) raffiniert. cleverness n Klugheit f.

cliché ['kliɪʃei] n Klischee *neut*.

click [klik] n Klicken *neut*. v klicken.

client ['klaiənt] n Kunde m, Kundin f. clientele n Kundschaft f.

cliff [klif] n Klippe f.

climate ['klaimət] n Klima *neut*.

climax ['klaimaks] n Höhepunkt m.

climb [klaim] v klettern; (*ascend*) steigen; (*mountain*) besteigen. n Aufstieg m. climb up hinaufklettern auf. climb down hinabsteigen. climber n (*mountaineer*) Bergsteiger m. climbing n (*mountaineering*) Bergsteigen *neut*.

*cling [kliŋ] v sich klammern (an); (*fig*) hängen (an).

clinic ['klinik] n Klinik f. clinical adj klinisch.

clink [kliŋk] n Klirren *neut*. v klirren.

clip[1] [klip] v (*hair*) schneiden; (*dog*) scheren; (*ticket*) knipsen. clipping n (*newspaper*) Zeitungsausschnitt m.

clip[2] [klip] n (*fastener*) Klammer f, Klemme f. v clip together zusammenklammern.

clitoris ['klitəris] n Kitzler m, Klitoris f.

cloak [klouk] n Umhang m. cloakroom n Garderobe f; (*WC*) Toilette f.

clock [klok] n Uhr f. clockwise adj, adv im Uhrzeigersinn. clockwork n Uhrwerk *neut*.

clog [klog] n Holzschuh m. v verstopfen.

cloister ['kloistə] n Kreuzgang m.

close[1] [klouz] v zumachen, schließen. n Ende *neut*; Schluß m. close down eingehen. closed adj (*shop*) geschlossen; (*road*) gesperrt.

close[2] [klous] adj nahe; (*intimate*) vertraut; (*careful*) genau; (*weather*) schwül. adv knapp. close to in der Nähe (+gen or von). close together dicht zusammen. that was close! das war knapp! closely adv genau, gründlich. close-up Nahaufnahme f.

closet ['klozit] n Schrank m.

clot [klot] n Klümpchen *neut*; (*of blood*) Blutgerinnsel *neut*. v gerinnen.

cloth [kloθ] n (*material*) Stoff m, Tuch *neut*; (*for wiping*) Lappen m.

clothe [klouð] v (be)kleiden. clothes pl n Kleider pl. clothes brush Kleiderbürste f.

32

clothes line Wäscheleine f. clothes peg
Wäscheklammer f. clothing n Kleidung f.
cloud [klaud] n Wolke f. cloud over sich
bewölken.
clove¹ [klouv] n (spice) Gewürznelke f.
clove² [klouv] n clove of garlic
Knoblauchzehe f.
clover ['klouvə] n Klee m.
clown [klaun] n Clown m.
club [klʌb] n (association) Klub m, Verein
m; (weapon) Keule f; (golf) Golfschläger
m. clubfoot n Klumpfuß m.
clue [kluː] n Spur f, Anhaltspunkt m. I
haven't a clue ich habe keine Ahnung f.
clump [klʌmp] n Klumpen neut; (of
bushes) Gebüsch neut.
clumsy ['klʌmzi] adj unbeholfen, linkisch.
clung [klʌŋ] V cling.
cluster ['klʌstə] n Traube f. v cluster
around schwärmen um.
clutch [klʌtʃ] n (fester) Griff m; (mot)
Kupplung f. v sich festklammern an.
clutch at greifen nach.
clutter ['klʌtə] n Unordnung f, Durcheinander neut. v vollstopfen.
coach [koutʃ] n Kutsche f; (rail) Wagen
m; (sport) Trainer m. v eintrainieren.
coagulate [kou'agjuleit] v gerinnen.
coal [koul] n Kohle f. coal-mine
Kohlenbergwerk neut.
coalition [kouə'liʃən] n (pol) Koalition f.
coarse [kɔːs] adj grob; (vulgar) ordinär.
coast [koust] n Küste f. coastal adj Küs-
ten-. coastline n Küstenlinie f.
coat [kout] n Mantel m; (of animal) Fell
neut, Pelz m; (of paint) Anstrich m. v
bestreichen. coated adj überzogen.
coathanger n Kleiderbügel m. coating n
Überzug m.
coax [kouks] v beschwatzen.
cobbler ['koblə] n Schuster m.
cobra ['koubrə] n Kobra neut.
cobweb ['kobweb] n Spinngewebe neut.
cocaine [kə'kein] n Kokain neut.
cock¹ [kok] n (male chicken) Hahn m;
(male bird) (Vogel)Männchen neut.
cock² [kok] v (gun) spannen; (ears)
spitzen.
cockle ['kokl] n (shellfish) Herzmuschel f.
cockpit ['kokpit] n Kanzel f, Kabine f.
cockroach ['kokroutʃ] n Küchenschabe f.
cocktail ['kokteil] n Cocktail neut.
cocoa ['koukou] n Kakao m.
coconut ['koukənʌt] n Kokosnuß m.
cocoon [kə'kuːn] n Kokon m, Puppe f.

cod [kod] n Kabeljau m.
code [koud] n Kode m.
codeine ['koudiːn] n Kodein neut.
coeducation [kouedju'keiʃən] n Gemein-
schaftserziehung f.
coerce [kou'əːs] v zwingen. coercion n
Zwang m.
coexist [kouig'zist] v koexistieren. coexistence n Koexistenz f.
coffee ['kofi] n Kaffee m. coffee bar Café
neut.
coffin ['kofin] n Sarg m.
cog [kog] n Radzahn neut. cogwheel Zahnrad neut.
cognac ['konjak] n Kognak m.
cohabit [kou'habit] v (ehelich) zusam-
menwohnen.
coherent [kou'hiərənt] adj zusam-
menhängend.
coil [koil] n Rolle f; v aufwickeln.
coin [koin] n Münze f. v prägen. coinbox
n (phone) Münzfernsprecher m.
coincide [kouin'said] v zusammenfallen;
(agree) übereinstimmen. coincidence n
Zufall m. coincidental zufällig.
colander ['koləndə] n Durchschlag m.
cold [kould] adj kalt. I am/feel cold mir
ist kalt. n Kälte f; (med) Erkältung f.
catch cold sich erkälten. in cold blood
kaltblütig. coldly adv (fig) gefühllos,
unfreundlich. cold store Kühlhaus neut.
coleslaw ['koulslɔ] n Krautsalat m.
colic ['kolik] n Kolik f.
collaborate [kə'labəreit] v zusammenarbeiten. collaboration n zusammenarbeit f. collaborator n Mitarbeiter
m; (in war) Kollaborateur m.
collapse [kə'laps] v einstürzen; (person)
zusammenbrechen. n Einsturz m; (fig,
med) Zusammenbruch m. collapsible adj
zusammenklappbar.
collar ['kolə] n Kragen m; (for dog) Hals-
band m. collarbone n Schlüsselbein
neut.
colleague ['koliːg] n Kollege m, Kollegin
f.
collect [kə'lekt] v sammeln; (fetch)
abholen; (taxes) einnehmen; (come
together) zusammenkommen. collect call
(phone) R-Gespräch neut. collected adj
(calm) gefaßt. collection n Sammlung f;
(rel) Kollekte f; (mail) Leerung f. collective adj kollektiv. collective bargaining
Tarifverhandlungen pl. collector n Sam-
mler m; (of taxes) Einnehmer m.

college ['kolidʒ] n Hochschule f; (at Oxford, etc.) College neut. **technical college** Realschule f.

collide [kə'laid] v kollidieren, zusammenprallen.

colloquial [kə'loukwiəl] adj umgangssprachlich.

Cologne [kə'loun] n Köln neut. **eau de Cologne** Kölnischwasser neut.

colon ['koulon] n (anat) Dickdarm m; (gram) Doppelpunkt m.

colonel ['kə:nl] n Oberst m.

colony ['koləni] n Kolonie f. **colonial** adj Kolonial-. **colonialism** Kolonialismus m. **colonize** v kolonisieren.

colossal [kə'losəl] adj kolossal, riesig.

colour ['kʌlə] n Farbe f; (fig) Ton m, Charakter m. **colours** pl Fahne f sing. v färben (also fig), kolorieren. **colour bar** Rassenschranke f. **colour-blind** adj farbenblind. **coloured** adj farbig. **coloured man/woman** Farbige(r). **colour film** Farbfilm m. **colourful** adj farbig, bunt. **colour television** Farbfernsehen neut.

colt [koult] n Fohlen neut.

column ['koləm] n Säule f; (in newspaper) Spalte f; (mil) Kolonne f. **columnist** n Kolumnist m.

coma ['koumə] n Koma f.

comb [koum] n Kamm m. v kämmen; (fig) durchkämmen.

combat ['kombat] v bekämpfen. n Kampf m, Gefecht neut.

combine [kəm'bain; n 'kombain] v vereinigen, verbinden; (come together) sich vereinigen. n Konzern m. **combine harvester** Mähdrescher m.

combustion [kəm'bʌstʃən] n Verbrennung f. **combustible** adj brennhar.

*come [kʌm] v kommen. **come about** geschehen. **come across** stoßen auf. **come back** zurückkommen. **come from** herkommen von stammen aus. **come near** sich nähern. **come on** weiterkommen; (make progress) fortschreiten. **come on!** los!; weiter! **come out** herauskommen. **come through** durchkommen. **come to** (arrive at) ankommen an, gelangen an; (amount to) sich belaufen auf; (regain consciousness) zu sich kommen. **comeback** n Comeback neut.

comedy ['komədi] n Komödie f. **comedian** n Komiker m.

comet ['komit] n Komet m.

comfort ['kʌmfət] n Bequemlichkeit f. Komfort m; (solace) Trost m. v trösten. **comfortable** adj bequem; (room, etc.) komfortabel.

comic ['komik] adj komisch, lustig; (theatre) Komödien-. n (person) Komiker m; (paper) Comic neut. **comical** adj komisch.

comma ['komə] n Komma neut.

command [kə'maind] n (order) Befehl m; (mil) Oberbefehl m; (mastery) Beherrschung f. v (instruct) befehlen; (be in charge of) kommandieren. **commander** n Befehlshaber m; (mil) Kommandant m. **commandment** n Gebot neut. **commando** n Kommando neut.

commemorate [kə'meməreit] v gedenken (+gen), feiern. **commemoration** n Gedächtnisfeier f.

commence [kə'mens] v beginnen, anfangen. **commencement** n Beginn m, Anfang m.

commend [kə'mend] v (praise) loben; (entrust) anvertrauen. **commendable** adj lobenswert.

comment ['koment] n (remark) Bemerkung f; (annotation) Anmerkung f. v kommentieren, Bemerkungen machen. **commentary** n Reportage f. **commentator** n Kommentator m.

commerce ['komə:s] n Handel m, Kommerz m. **commercial** adj kommerziell, geschäftlich, Handels-. **commercialize** v kommerzialisieren.

commiserate [kə'mizəreit] v **commiserate with** bemitleiden.

commission [kə'miʃən] n Auftrag m; (committee) Kommission f; (fee) Provision f; (mil) Offizierspatent neut. v (person) beauftragen; (thing) bestellen. **commissioner** n Bevollmächtigte(r).

commit [kə'mit] v (offence) begehen. **commit oneself** sich verpflichten. **commitment** n Verpflichtung f.

committee [kə'miti] n Ausschuß m, Kommission f.

commodity [kə'modəti] n Ware f. **commodities** pl Grundstoffe pl.

common ['komən] adj gemein, gemeinsam; (abundant) weit verbreitet; (vulgar) gemein, ordinär. **Common Market** Gemeinsamer Markt m. **commonplace** adj alltäglich. **commonsense** n gesunder Menschenverstand m.

commotion [kə'mouʃən] *n* Erregung *f*, Aufruhr *m*.

commune ['komjuːn] *n* Kommune *f*, Gemeinschaft *f*.

communicate [kə'mjuːnikeit] *v* mitteilen; (*illness*) übertragen. **communicative** *adj* gesprächig. **communication** *n* Kommunikation *f*; (*message*) Mitteilung *f*. **communications** *pl n* Verkehrswege *pl*.

communism ['komjunizəm] *n* Kommunismus *m*. **communist** *adj* kommunistisch. *n* Kommunist(in).

community [kə'mjuːnəti] *n* Gemeinschaft *f*.

commute [kə'mjuːt] *v* (*travel*) pendeln; (*a sentence*) herabsetzen. **commuter** *n* Pendler *m*.

compact¹ [kəm'pakt] *adj* kompakt, dicht.

compact² ['kompakt] *n* (*agreement*) Vertrag *m*, Pakt *m*.

companion [kəm'panjən] *n* Begleiter(in); Genosse *m*, Genossin *f*. **companionable** *adj* gesellig. **companionship** *n* Gesellschaft *f*.

company ['kʌmpəni] *n* Gesellschaft *f*; (*firm*) Gesellschaft *f*, Firma *f*; (*theatre*) Truppe *f*; (*mil*) Kompanie *f*.

compare [kəm'peə] *v* vergleichen; (*match up to*) sich vergleichen lassen. **comparable** *adj* vergleichbar. **comparative** *adj* relativ; (*gram*) steigernd. **comparatively** *adv* verhältnismäßig. **comparison** *n* Vergleich *m*. **in comparison with** im Vergleich zu.

compartment [kəm'paːtmənt] *n* Abteilung *f*.

compass ['kʌmpəs] *n* Kompaß *m*. **pair of compasses** Zirkel *m*.

compassion [kəm'paʃən] *n* Mitleid *neut*. **compassionate** *adj* mitleidig.

compatible [kəm'patəbl] *adj* vereinbar.

compel [kəm'pel] *v* zwingen.

compensate ['kompənseit] *v* (*money*) entschädigen; (*balance out*) ausgleichen. **compensation** *n* Entschädigung *f*; Ausgleich *m*.

compete [kəm'piːt] *v* konkurrieren, sich bewerben; (*take part*) teilnehmen. **competition** *n* Wettbewerb *m*; (*comm*) Konkurrenz *f*. **competitive** *adj* konkurrenzfähig. **competitor** *n* (*sport*) Teilnehmer(in); (*comm*) Konkurrent(in).

compile [kəm'pail] *v* kompilieren.

complacent [kəm'pleisnt] *adj* selbstzufrieden.

complain [kəm'plein] *v* klagen. **complain about/to** sich beschweren über/bei. **complaint** *n* Klage *f*, Beschwerde *f*.

complement ['kompləmənt] *n* Ergänzung *f*. *v* ergänzen; (*go together*) zusammenpassen. **complementary** *adj* komplementär.

complete [kəm'pliːt] *v* vollenden, vervollständigen; (*form*) ausfüllen. *adj* vollständig, vollendet. **completely** *adv* völlig, vollständig, ganz und gar. **completion** *n* Vollendung *f*.

complex ['kompleks] *adj* kompliziert. *n* (*psychol*) Komplex *m*.

complexion [kəm'plekʃən] *n* Teint *m*.

complicate ['komplikeit] *v* verwickeln, komplizieren. **complicated** *adj* kompliziert. **complication** *n* Komplikation *f*, Schwierigkeit *f*.

compliment ['kompləmənt] *n* Kompliment *neut*. *v* komplimentieren. **complimentary** *adj* höflich, artig. **complimentary ticket** Freikarte *f*.

comply [kəm'plai] *v* sich fügen. **comply with** (*rules*) sich halten an; (*request*) erfüllen.

component [kəm'pounənt] *n* Bestandteil *m*.

compose [kəm'pouz] *v* komponieren. **composed of** gefaßt. **be composed of** bestehen aus. **composer** *n* Komponist *m*. **composite** *adj* zusammengesetzt. **composition** *n* Komposition *f*; (*piece of music*) (Musik)Stück *neut*.

compost ['kompost] *n* Kompost *m*.

composure [kəm'pouʒə] *n* Gefaßtheit *f*.

compound ['kompaund] *n* Zusammensetzung *f*; (*chem*) Verbindung *f*; *adj* zusammengesetzt, gemischt.

comprehend [kompri'hend] *v* verstehen, begreifen. **comprehensible** *adj* verständlich. **comprehension** *n* Verständnis.

comprehensive [,kompri'hensiv] *adj* umfassend. **comprehensive school** *n* Gesamtschule *f*.

compress [kəm'pres; *n* 'kompres] *v* verdichten, zusammendrücken. *n* (*med*) Kompresse *f*. **compressed** *adj* zusammengedrückt. **compressed air** Preßluft *f*. **compression** *n* Verdichtung *f*. **compressor** *n* Verdichter *m*.

comprise [kəm'praiz] *v* bestehen aus.

compromise ['komprəmaiz] *n* Kompromiß *m or neut*. *v* einen Kompromiß schließen; (*expose*) kompromittieren.

compulsion [kəm'pʌlʃən] *n* Zwang *m*.
compulsive *adj* Zwangs-. **compulsory** *adj*
Zwangs-.
compunction [kəm'pʌŋkʃən] *n* Gewissensbisse *pl*, Reue *f*.
computer [kəm'pjuːtə] *n* Computer *m*.
comrade ['kɒmrid] *n* Genosse *m*, Genossin *f*; Kamerad(in). **comradeship** *n*
Kameradschaft *f*.
concave [kɒn'keiv] *adj* konkav, Hohl-.
conceal [kən'siːl] *v* verbergen, verstecken;
(*fact, etc.*) verschweigen.
concede [kən'siːd] *v* zugeben, einräumen;
(*right*) bewilligen.
conceit [kən'siːt] *n* Einbildung *f*, Eitelkeit
f. **conceited** *adj* eingebildet.
conceive [kən'siːv] *v* (*plan*) erdenken;
(*child*) empfangen; (*thoughts*) fassen.
conceive of sich vorstellen (+*acc*). **conceivable** *adj* denkbar, vorstellbar.
concentrate ['kɒnsəntreit] *v* konzentrieren. **concentrate on** sich konzentrieren
auf. **concentrated** *adj* konzentriert. **concentration** *n* Konzentration *f*.
concentric [kən'sentrik] *adj* konzentrisch.
concept ['kɒnsept] *n* Begriff *m*, Idee *f*.
conception *n* Vorstellung *f*; (*of child*)
Empfängnis *f*.
concern [kən'səːn] *v* betreffen, angehen;
(*worry*) beunruhigen. *n* (*worry*) Besorgnis
f, Sorge *f*; (*interest*) Interesse *neut*;
(*comm*) Betrieb *m*. **concern oneself with**
sich befassen mit. **as far as I am concerned** von mir aus. *that's not your concern!* das geht Sie nichts an! **concerning**
adj betreffend.
concert ['kɒnsət] *n* Konzert *neut*.
concerted [kən'səːtid] *adj* konzertiert.
concerto [kən'tʃəːtou] *n* Konzert *neut*.
concession [kən'seʃən] *n* Konzession *f*.
concessionnaire *n* Konzessionär *m*.
conciliate [kən'silieit] *v* versöhnen. **conciliation** *n* Versöhnung *f*. **conciliatory** *adj*
versöhnlich.
concise [kən'sais] *adj* kurz, knapp.
conclude [kən'kluːd] *v* schließen. **conclude
that** den Schluß ziehen, daß. **conclusive**
adj (*evidence*) schlüssig.
concoct [kən'kɒkt] *v* zusammenbrauen.
concrete ['kɒnkriːt] *adj* konkret; (*made of
concrete*) Beton-. *n* Beton *m*.
concussion [kən'kʌʃən] *n* (*med*) Gehirnerschütterung *f*.
condemn [kən'dem] *v* verurteilen. **condemnation** *n* Verurteilung *f*.

condense [kən'dens] *v* kondensieren. **condensation** *n* Kondensation *f*. **condensed
milk** Kondensmilch *f*.
condescend [kɒndi'send] *v* sich herablassen. **condescending** *adj* herablassend.
condescension *n* Herablassung *f*.
condition [kən'diʃən] *n* (*state*) Zustand
m; (*requirement*) Bedingung *f*, Voraussetzung *f*. **conditions** *pl* Umstände *pl*. **on
condition that** unter der Bedingung, daß.
out of condition (*sport*) in schlechter
Form. **conditional** *adj* bedingt.
condolence [kən'douləns] *n* Beileid *neut*.
condom ['kɒndɒm] *n* Kondom *neut*.
condone [kən'doun] *v* verzeihen.
conducive [kən'djuːsiv] *adj* förderlich.
conduct [kən'dʌkt; *n* 'kɒndʌkt]] *v* führen;
(*orchestra*) dirigieren; (*elec*) leiten. **conduct oneself** sich verhalten. *n* Führung *f*;
(*behaviour*) Verhalten *neut*.
conductor [kən'dʌktə] *n* (*music*) Dirigent
m; (*bus*) Schaffner(in).
cone [koun] *n* (*shape*) Kegel *m*; (*ice
cream*) Waffeltüte *f*; (*bot*) Zapfen *m*.
confectioner [kən'fekʃənə] *n*
Süßwarenhändler *m*. **confectionery** *n*
Süßwaren *pl*.
confederation [kənfedə'reiʃən] *n* Bund
m.
confer [kən'fəː] *v* (*bestow*) verleihen; (*discuss*) konferieren. **conference** *n* Konferenz *f*.
confess [kən'fes] *v* bekennen, gestehen;
(*rel*) beichten. **confession** *n* Geständnis
neut; (*rel*) Beichte *f*. **confessional** *n*
Beichtstuhl *m*.
confetti [kən'feti] *n* Konfetti *pl*.
confide [kən'faid] *v* anvertrauen. **confide
in** vertrauen (+*dat*). **confidence** *n* Vertrauen *neut*; (*in oneself*) Selbstvertrauen
neut. **confident** *adj* zuversichtlich; selbstsicher. **confidential** *adj* vertraulich.
confine [kən'fain] *v* (*limit*) beschränken;
(*lock up*) einsperren. **confinement** *n* (*in
prison*) Haft *f*; (*childbirth*) Niederkunft *f*.
confirm [kən'fəːm] *v* bestätigen; (*rel*)
konfirmieren. **confirmation** *n* Bestätigung
f; Konfirmation *f*.
confiscate ['kɒnfiskeit] *v* beschlagnahmen.
confiscation *n* Beschlagnahme *f*.
conflict ['kɒnflikt; *v* kən'flikt] *n* Konflikt
m, Streit *m*. *v* widerstreiten (+*dat*). **conflict of interests** Interessenkonflikt *m*.
conflicting *adj* widerstreitend.

conform [kən'fɔɪm] v (tally) übereinstimmen (mit); (to rules) sich fügen (+dat). **conformist** n Konformist.

confound [kən'faund] v (surprise) erstaunen; (mix up) verwechseln. **confound it!** verdammt!

confront [kən'frʌnt] v konfrontieren; (enemy) entgegentreten (+dat). **confrontation** n Konfrontation f.

confuse [kən'fjuɪz] v (mix up) verwechseln (mit); (perplex) verwirren. **confused** adj (person) verwirrt; (situation) verworren. **confusion** n Verwirrung f.

congeal [kən'dʒiːl] v gerinnen.

congenial [kən'dʒiːniəl] adj freundlich, gemütlich.

congenital [kən'dʒenitl] adj angeboren.

congested [kən'dʒestid] adj überfüllt. **congestion** n Stauung f; (traffic) Verkehrsstauung f.

conglomeration [kənˌglɔmə'reiʃən] n Anhäufung f, Konglomerat neut.

congratulate [kən'gratjuleit] v beglückwünschen. **congratulations** pl n Glückwünsche pl.

congregate ['kɔŋgrigeit] v sich versammeln. **congregation** n Versammlung f.

congress ['kɔŋgres] n Kongreß m. **congressman/woman** Abgeordnete(r).

conifer ['kɔnifə] n Nadelbaum m. **coniferous** adj Nadel-.

conjecture [kən'dʒektʃə] n Vermutung f.

conjugal ['kɔndʒugəl] adj ehelich.

conjugate ['kɔndʒugeit] v (gramm) konjugieren.

conjunction [kən'dʒʌŋkʃən] n Vereinigung f; (gramm, astrol) Konjunktion f.

conjunctivitis [kənˌdʒʌŋkti'vaitis] n Bindehautentzündung f.

conjure ['kʌndʒə] v **conjure up** heraufbeschwören. **conjurer** n Zauberkünstler m. **conjuring trick** Zauberkunststück neut.

connect [kə'nekt] v verbinden; (phone, etc.) anschließen. **connection** n Verbindung f; (phone, rail) Anschluß m. **in connection with** im Zusammenhang mit.

connoisseur [kɔnə'səɪ] n Kenner m.

connotation [kɔnə'teiʃən] n Nebenbedeutung f.

conquer ['kɔŋkə] v erobern, besiegen; (fig) überwinden, beherrschen. **conqueror** n Eroberer m. **conquest** n Eroberung f.

conscience ['kɔnʃəns] n Gewissen neut.

conscientious [kɔnʃi'enʃəs] adj pflichtbewußt.

conscious ['kɔnʃəs] adj bewußt. **consciousness** n Bewußtsein neut.

conscript ['kɔnskript] v einziehen. n Wehrpflichtige(r). **conscription** n Wehrpflicht f.

consecrate ['kɔnsikreit] v weihen.

consecutive [kən'sekjutiv] adj aufeinanderfolgend.

consensus [kən'sensəs] n Übereinstimmung f.

consent [kən'sent] v zustimmen (+dat). n Zustimmung f.

consequence ['kɔnsikwəns] n Folge f, Konsequenz f. **of no consequence** unbedeutend. **consequently** adv folglich.

conserve [kən'səɪv] v erhalten; (energy) sparen. **conservation** n Schutz m, Erhaltung f. **conservative** adj konservativ; n Konservative(r). **conservatory** n Treibhaus neut; (music) Musikhochschule f.

consider [kən'sidə] n (think about) überlegen; (regard as) halten für. **considerate** adj rücksichtsvoll. **consideration** n (thought) Überlegung f; (thoughtfulness) Rücksicht f. **considering** prep in Anbetracht (+gen).

consign [kən'sain] v versenden. **consignee** n Empfänger m. **consignment** n Sendung f. **consignor** n Absender m.

consist [kən'sist] v **consist of** bestehen aus. **consistency** n (of substance) Dichte f. **consistent** adj konsequent. **consistent with** vereinbar mit.

console [kən'soul] v trösten. **consolation** n Trost m. **consolation prize** Trostpreis m.

consolidate [kən'solideit] v stärken; (comm) konsolidieren. **consolidation** n Stärkung f.

consommé [kən'somei] n Fleischbrühe f.

consonant ['kɔnsənənt] n Konsonant m.

conspicuous [kən'spikjuəs] adj (visible) sichtbar; (striking) auffallend.

conspire [kən'spaiə] v sich verschwören. **conspiracy** n Verschwörung f. **conspirator** n Verschwörer m.

constable ['kʌnstəbl] n Polizist m.

constant ['kɔnstənt] adj beständig, konstant; (continual) dauernd. **constantly** adv ständig.

constellation [konstə'leiʃən] *n* Sternbild *neut.*

constipation [konsti'peiʃən] *n* (Darm)Verstopfung *f.*

constituency [kən'stitjuənsi] *n* Wahlkreis *m.* **constituent** *n* Wähler *m.*

constitute ['konstitjuːt] *v* bilden, darstellen. **constitution** *n* (*pol*) Grundgesetz *m,* Verfassung *f*; (*of person*) Konstitution *f.*

constrain [kən'strein] *v* zwingen **constraint** *n* Zwang *m,* Druck *m.*

constrict [kən'strikt] *v* zusammendrücken, einengen.

construct [kən'strʌkt] *v* bauen, konstruieren; (*argument*) aufstellen. **construction** *n* Bau *m,* Konstruktion *f.* **constructive** *adj* konstruktiv.

consul ['konsəl] *n* Konsul *m.* **consulate** *n* Konsulat *neut.*

consult [kən'sʌlt] *v* zu Rate ziehen, konsultieren; (*book*) nachsehen in. **consultant** *n* Berater *m.* **consultation** *n* Konsultation *f.* **consulting room** Sprechzimmer *neut.*

consume [kən'sjuːm] *v* verzehren; (*money, time*) verbrauchen. **consumer** *n* Verbraucher *m.*

contact ['kontakt] *n* Verbindung *f,* Kontakt *m.* *v* sich in Verbindung setzen mit. **be in contact with** in Verbindung stehen mit.

contagious [kən'teidʒəs] *adj* ansteckend.

contain [kən'tein] *v* enthalten; (*feelings*) beherrschen. **contain oneself** sich beherrschen. **container** *n* Behälter *m*; (*for goods transport*) Container *m.* **container ship** Containerschiff *m.*

contaminate [kən'taməneit] *v* verseuchen. **contamination** *n* Verseuchung *f.*

contemplate ['kontəmpleit] *v* (*observe*) nachdenklich betrachten; (*think about*) nachdenken über; (*doing something*) vorhaben. **contemplation** *n* Betrachtung *f*; Nachdenken *neut.*

contemporary [kən'tempərəri] *adj* zeitgenössisch; (*modern*) modern. *n* Zeitgenosse *m.*

contempt [kən'tempt] *n* Verachtung *f.* **contemptible** *adj* verächtlich. **contemptuous** *adj* voller Verachtung *f.*

contend [kən'tend] *v* kämpfen; (*assert*) behaupten.

content[1] ['kontent] *n* Inhalt *m.* **contents** *pl* Inhalt *m sing.* **table of contents** Inhaltsverzeichnis *neut.*

content[2] [kən'tent] *adj* zufrieden. **contentment** *n* Zufriedenheit *f.*

contention [kən'tenʃən] *n* Streit *m*; (*assertion*) Behauptung *f.*

contest ['kontest; *v* kən'test] *n* Wettkampf *m.* *v* bestreiten. **contestant** *n* Bewerber(in).

context ['kontekst] *n* Zusammenhang *m.*

continent ['kontinənt] *n* Festland *neut,* Kontinent *m.* **continental** *adj* Kontinental-.

contingency [kən'tindʒənsi] *n* Eventualität *f.*

continue [kən'tinjuː] *v* fortfahren, weitermachen; (*something*) fortsetzen; (*go further*) weitergehen. **continual** *adj* wiederholt. **continually** *adv* immer wieder. **continuation** *n* Fortsetzung *f.* **continuous** *adj* beständig.

contort [kən'toːt] *v* verdrehen. **contortion** *n* Verdrehung *f.* **contortionist** *n* Schlangenmensch *m.*

contour ['kontuə] *n* Umrißlinie *f.*

contraband ['kontrəband] *n* Schmuggelware *f.*

contraception [kontrə'sepʃən] *n* Empfängnisverhütung *f.* **contraceptive** *adj* empfängnisverhütend. *n* empfängnisverhütendes Mittel *neut.*

contract ['kontrakt; *v* kən'trakt] *n* Vertrag *m.* *v* (*become smaller*) sich zusammenziehen; (*illness*) sich zuziehen. **contraction** *n* Zusammenziehung *f.* **contractor** *n* (*building*) Bauunternehmer *m.*

contradict [kontrə'dikt] *v* widersprechen. **contradiction** *n* Widerspruch *m.* **contradictory** *adj* sich widersprechend.

contralto [kən'traltou] *n* (*voice*) Alt *m*; (*singer*) Altistin *f.*

contraption [kən'trapʃən] *n* komisches Ding *neut.*

contrary [kən'treəri; (*opposite*) 'kontrəri] *adj* (*person*) widerspenstig; (*opposite*) entgegengesetzt. *n* Gegenteil *m.* **on the contrary** im Gegenteil.

contrast [kən'traist; *n* 'kontraist] *v* (*compare*) vergleichen. **contrast with** kontrastieren mit. *n* Kontrast *m.* **in contrast to** im Gegensatz zu.

contravene [kontrə'viːn] *v* verstoßen gegen. **contravention** *n* Verstoß *m.*

contribute [kən'tribjut] *v* beitragen; (*money*) spenden. **contribution** *n* Beitrag *m.* **contributor** *n* Beitragende(r); (*to newspaper, etc.*) Mitarbeiter *m.*

contrive [kən'traɪv] v (*plan*) ausdenken. / *contrived to meet him* es gelang mir, ihn zu treffen.
control [kən'troul] v (*curb*) zügeln; (*machine*) steuern. n Leitung f. **controls** pl n Steuerung f. **under/out of control** unter/außer Kontrolle.
controversial [kɒntrə'vɜːʃəl] adj umstritten. **controversy** n Streitfrage f. Kontroverse f.
convalesce [kɒnvə'les] v genesen, gesund werden. **convalescence** n Genesungszeit f.
convection [kən'vekʃən] n Konvektion f.
convenience [kən'viːnjəns] n Bequemlichkeit f; (*advantage*) Vorteil m. **public convenience** Bedürfnisanstalt f. **convenient** adj (*suitable*) passend; (*time*) gelegen; (*advantageous*) vorteilhaft.
convent ['kɒnvənt] n Kloster neut; (*school*) Klosterschule f.
convention [kən'venʃən] n (*meeting*) Tagung f; (*agreement*) Konvention f; (*custom*) Brauch m, Konvention f. **conventional** adj konventionell.
converge [kən'vɜːdʒ] v konvergieren.
converse [kən'vɜːs] v sich unterhalten, sprechen. **conversation** n Unterhaltung f, Gespräch neut.
convert [kən'vɜːt; n 'kɒnvɜːt] v umwandeln; (*rel*) bekehren. n Bekehrte(r). **conversion** n Umwandlung f; (*rel*) Bekehrung f.
convertible [kən'vɜːtəbl] adj um-, verwandelbar. n (*mot*) Kabrio(lett) neut.
convex ['kɒnveks] adj konvex.
convey [kən'veɪ] v (*goods*) befördern; (*news*) übermitteln. **conveyance** n (*law*) Übertragung f; (*vehicle*) Fahrzeug neut.
convict [kən'vɪkt; n 'kɒnvɪkt] v verurteilen. n Verurteilte(r). **conviction** n (*belief*) Überzeugung f; (*law*) Verurteilung f.
convince [kən'vɪns] v überzeugen. **convincing** adj überzeugend.
convivial [kən'vɪvɪəl] adj fröhlich, heiter.
convoy ['kɒnvɔɪ] n (*mil*) Konvoi m.
convulsion [kən'vʌlʃən] n Zuckung f.
cook [kuk] v kochen; (*a meal*) zubereiten. n Koch m, Köchin f. **cooker** n Herd m. **cookery** n Küche f. **cookery book** Kochbuch neut. **cooking** n Küche f.
cool [kuːl] adj kühl. v abkühlen. **cooled** adj gekühlt. **coolness** n Kühle f.

coop [kuːp] n Hühnerkäfig m. v **coop up** einsperren.
cooperate [kou'ɒpəreɪt] v zusammenarbeiten. **cooperation** n Zusammenarbeit f, Kooperation f. **cooperative** adj (*helpful*) hilfsbereit; kooperativ. n Genossenschaft f, Kooperative f.
coordinate [kou'ɔːdɪneɪt] v koordinieren. n (*math*) Koordinate f. **coordination** n Koordination f.
cope [koup] v **cope with** fertigwerden mit.
copious ['koupiəs] adj reichlich.
copper[1] ['kɒpə] n (*metal*) Kupfer neut. adj kupfern; (*colour*) kupferfarben.
copper[2] ['kɒpə] n (*coll*) Polyp m.
copulate ['kɒpjuleɪt] v sich paaren. **copulation** n Paarung f.
copy ['kɒpi] n Kopie f; (*book*) Exemplar neut; (*newspaper*) Nummer f. v kopieren. **copyright** n Copyright neut.
coral ['kɒrəl] n Koralle f.
cord [kɔːd] n Schnur f.
cordial ['kɔːdiəl] adj herzlich.
cordon ['kɔːdn] n Absperrkette f. v **cordon off** absperren.
corduroy ['kɔːdərɔɪ] n Kord m.
core [kɔː] n (*apple*) Kernhaus neut. v entkernen. **to the core** durch und durch.
cork [kɔːk] n (*material*) Kork m; (*for bottle*) Korken m, Pfropfen m. adj korken. **corkscrew** n Korkenzieher m.
corn[1] [kɔːn] n Korn neut, Getreide neut; (*maize*) Mais m; (*wheat*) Weizen m.
corn[2] [kɔːn] n (*on foot*) Hühnerauge neut.
corner ['kɔːnə] n Ecke f, Winkel m; (*mot*) Kurve f; (*sport*) Eckball m. v in die Enge treiben.
cornet ['kɔːnit] n (*music*) Kornett neut; (*ice cream*) Eistüte f.
coronary ['kɒrənəri] adj koronar. **coronary thrombosis** Koronarthrombose f.
coronation [kɒrə'neɪʃən] n Krönung f.
coroner ['kɒrənə] n Leichenbeschauer m.
corporal[1] ['kɔːpərəl] adj körperlich. **corporal punishment** Prügelstrafe f.
corporal[2] ['kɔːpərəl] n (*mil*) Obergefreite(r) m.
corporation [kɔːpə'reɪʃən] n Körperschaft f; (*city authorities*) Gemeinderat m.
corps [kɔː] n Korps neut.
corpse [kɔːps] n Leiche f.
correct [kə'rekt] adj richtig; (*proper*) korrekt. v korrigieren. **correction** n Korrektur f.

correlation [korə'leiʃən] n Wechselbeziehung f.

correspond [korə'spond] v entsprechen (+dat); (write) korrespondieren. **correspondence** n Entsprechung f; Korrespondenz f. **corresponding** adj entsprechend.

corridor ['koridoɪ] n Gang m.

corrode [kə'roud] v zerfressen; (become corroded) rosten. **corrosion** n Korrosion f.

corrupt [kə'rʌpt] v bestechen. adj bestechlich, korrupt. **corruption** n Bestechung f, Korruption f.

corset ['koɪset] n Korsett neut.

cosmetic [koz'metik] adj kosmetisch. **cosmetic surgery** chirurgische Kosmetik f. **cosmetics** pl n Schönheitsmittel pl.

cosmic ['kozmik] adj kosmisch.

cosmopolitan [kozmə'politən] adj kosmopolitisch.

***cost** [kost] v kosten. n Preis m, Kosten pl. **costs** Unkosten pl. **cost of living** Lebenshaltungskosten pl.

costume ['kostjuɪm] n Kostüm neut.

cosy ['kouzi] adj gemütlich.

cot [kot] n Kinderbett neut.

cottage ['kotidʒ] n Hütte f, Häuschen neut. **cottage cheese** Hüttenkäse m.

cotton ['kotn] n Baumwolle f. adj Baumwoll-. **cotton wool** Watte f.

couch [kautʃ] n Couch f.

cough [kof] n Husten m. v husten.

could [kud] V can.

council ['kaunsəl] n Rat m. **councillor** m Rat m.

counsel ['kaunsəl] v beraten. n Rat m.

count[1] [kaunt] v zählen; (be valid) gelten. n (number) (Gesamt)Zahl f. **count on** rechnen mit.

count[2] [kaunt] n (noble) Graf m.

counter[1] ['kauntə] n (shop) Ladentisch m, Theke f; (bank) Schalter m; (game) Spielmarke f.

counter[2] ['kauntə] adv entgegen. adj entgegengesetzt. v entgegnen.

counteract [kauntə'rakt] v entgegenwirken (+dat).

counterattack ['kauntərə,tak] n Gegenangriff m.

counter-clockwise adj, adv dem Uhrzeigersinn entgegen.

counterfeit ['kauntəfit] adj gefälscht. v fälschen.

counterfoil ['kauntə,foil] n Kontrollabschnitt m.

counterpart ['kauntə,paɪt] n Gegenstück neut.

countess ['kauntis] n Gräfin f.

country ['kʌntri] n Land neut; (homeland) Heimat f; (pol) Land neut, Staat m. adj Land-. **in the country** auf dem Lande. **country house** Landhaus neut. **countryman** n Landmann m. **fellow countryman** Landsmann m. **countryside** Landschaft f.

county ['kaunti] n Grafschaft f.

coup [kuɪ] n Coup m; (pol) Staatsstreich m. **coup de grâce** Gnadenstoß m.

couple ['kʌpl] n Paar neut; (married couple) Ehepaar neut. **a couple of** ein paar.

coupon ['kuɪpon] n Coupon m, Gutschein m.

courage ['kʌridʒ] n Mut m, Tapferkeit f. **courageous** adj mutig, tapfer.

courier ['kuriə] n Kurier m; (tour guide) Reiseleiter(in).

course [koɪs] n Lauf m; (study) Kurs(us) m; (race) Bahn f; (of action) Richtung m. v laufen. **of course** natürlich, selbstverständlich. **in the course of** im Laufe (+gen).

court [koɪt] n (royal) Hof m; (law) Gericht neut. v (lover) werben um. **court martial** Kriegsgericht neut. **court-martial** v vor ein Kriegsgericht stellen. **courtroom** n Gerichtssaal m. **courtyard** n Hof m.

courtesy ['kəɪtəsi] n Höflichkeit f. **courteous** adj höflich.

cousin ['kʌzn] n Cousin m, Vetter m; Kusine f, Base f.

cove [kouv] n Bucht f.

cover ['kʌvə] v (be)decken; (extend over) sich erstrecken über; (include) einschließen. n (lid) Deckel m; (of book) (Schutz)Umschlag m. **covering** n (Be)Deckung f.

cow [kau] n Kuh f. v einschüchtern. **cowshed** n Kuhstall m.

coward ['kauəd] n Feigling m. **cowardice** n Feigheit f. **cowardly** adj feige.

cower ['kauə] v kauern.

coy [koi] adj spröde.

crab [krab] n Krebs m.

crack [krak] n (slit) Spalt m, Riß m; (sound) Krach m. v krachen; (break) brechen; (nut) knacken; (egg) aufschlagen; (joke) reißen. **crack up** (coll) zusammenbrechen. **cracker** n (firework)

Knallfrosch   m;   (*Christmas*)
Knallbonbon *m*; (*biscuit*) Keks *m*.
crackle ['krakl] *v* knistern. *n* Knistern
neut.
cradle ['kreidl] *n* Wiege *f*. *v* wiegen.
craft [kraift] *n* (*trade*) Handwerk *neut*,
Gewerbe *neut*; (*skill*) Kunstfertigkeit *f*;
(*ship*) Schiff *neut*. **craftsman** *n*
Handwerker *m*, Künstler *m*. **crafty** *adj*
schlau, listig.
cram [kram] *v* hineinstopfen; (*study*)
pauken.
cramp [kramp] *n* (*med*) Krampf *m*;
(*clamp*) Krampe *f*. *v* hemmen.
cranberry ['kranbəri] *n* Preiselbeere *f*.
crane [krein] *n* Kran *m*; (*bird*) Kranich
m.
crank [kraŋk] *n* Kurbel *f*; (*odd person*)
Kauz *m*. *v* ankurbeln. **crankshaft** *n*
Kurbelwelle *f*.
crap [krap] *n* (*vulgar*) Scheiße *f*.
crash [kraʃ] *n* (*sound*) Krach *m*; (*mot*)
Zusammenstoß *m*; (*aero*) Absturz *m*. *v*
stürzen (gegen); (*sound*) krachen. **crash
helmet** Sturzhelm *m*.
crate [kreit] *n* Kiste *f*.
crater ['kreitə] *n* Krater *m*.
cravat [krə'vat] *n* Halstuch *neut*,
Krawatte *f*.
crave [kreiv] *v* erbitten. **crave for** sehnen
nach. **craving** *n* Sehnsucht *f*.
crawl [kroːl] *v* kriechen. *n* Kriechen *neut*;
(*swimming*) Kraulstil *m*.
crayfish ['kreifiʃ] *n* Flußkrebs *m*.
crayon ['kreiən] *n* Farbstift *m*.
craze [kreiz] *n* (*coll*) Manie *f*. **crazy** *adj*
verrückt.
creak [kriːk] *v* knarren. *n* Knarren *neut*.
cream [kriːm] *n* Sahne *f*, Rahm *m*; (*skin*)
Creme *f*. **cream-coloured** *adj*
cremefarben. **creamy** *adj* sahnig.
crease [kriːs] *n* Falte *f*, Kniff *m*. *v* falten.
create [kri'eit] *v* erschaffen; (*cause*) verursachen. **creation** *n* Schöpfung *f*; (*product*)
Werk *neut*. **creative** *adj* schöpferisch. **creator** *n* Schöpfer *m*. **creature** *n* Lebewesen
neut, Geschöpf *neut*.
credentials [kri'denʃəlz] *pl n* (*identity
papers*) Ausweispapiere *pl*.
credible ['kredəbl] *adj* glaubhaft,
glaubwürdig.
credit ['kredit] *n* (*comm*) Guthaben *neut*,
Kredit *m*. *v* Glauben schenken (+*dat*).
on credit auf Kredit. **take the credit for**

sich als Verdienst anrechnen. **creditable**
adj rühmlich. **credit card** Kreditkarte *f*.
creditor *n* Gläubiger *m*.
credulous ['kredjuləs] *adj* leichtgläubig.
creed [kriːd] *n* Bekenntnis *neut*, Kredo
neut.
*****creep** [kriːp] *v* kriechen, schleichen. *n*
Kriechen *neut*.
cremate [kri'meit] *v* einäschern. **cremation**
n Einäscherung *f*. **crematorium** *n*
Krematorium *neut*.
crept [krept] *V* creep.
crescent ['kresnt] *n* Mondsichel *f*.
cress [kres] *n* Kresse *f*.
crest [krest] *n* (*of mountain*) Bergkamm
m; (*of wave*) Wellenkamm *m*; (*coat of
arms*) Wappen *neut*.
crevice ['krevis] *n* Spalte *f*, Sprung *m*.
crew [kruː] *n* Besatzung *f*, Mannschaft *f*.
crib [krib] *n* Kinderbett *neut*.
cricket[1] ['krikit] *n* (*insect*) Grille *f*.
cricket[2] ['krikit] *n* Kricket *neut*.
crime [kraim] *n* Verbrechen *neut*. **criminal**
adj verbrecherisch, kriminell. *n* Ver-
brecher(in).
crimson ['krimzn] *n* Karmesinrot *neut*.
cringe [krindʒ] *v* sich ducken.
crinkle ['kriŋkl] *v* kraus machen. *n*
Kräuselung *f*. **crinkly** *adj* kraus.
cripple ['kripl] *n* Krüppel *m*. *v* lähmen.
crisis ['kraisis] *n* (*pl* -ses) Krise *f*.
crisp [krisp] *adj* knusprig. **crisps** *pl n*
Chips *pl*. **crispy** *adj* knusprig.
criterion [krai'tiəriən] *n* (*pl* -a) Kriterium
neut.
critic ['kritik] *n* Kritiker *m*. **critical** *adj*
kritisch. **criticism** *n* Kritik *f*. **criticize** *v*
kritisieren.
croak [krouk] *v* (*person, crow*) krächzen;
(*frog*) quaken. *n* Krächzen *neut*; Quaken
neut.
crochet ['krouʃei] *v* häkeln. **crochet hook**
Häkelnadel *f*. **crochet work** Häkelarbeit
f.
crockery ['krokəri] *n* Geschirr *neut*.
crocodile ['krokədail] *n* Krokodil *neut*.
crocus ['kroukəs] *n* Krokus *m*.
crook [kruk] *n* (*shepherd's*) Hirtenstab *m*;
(*villain*) Gauner *m*. **crooked** *adj*
gekrümmt; (*dishonest*) krumm.
crop [krop] *n* (*harvest*) Ernte *f*; (*whip*)
Reitpeitsche *f*. *v* (*cut*) stutzen. **crop up**
auftauchen.
croquet ['kroukei] *n* Krocket *neut*.

cross [kros] *n* Kreuz *neut*; (*crossbreed*) Kreuzung *f*. *adj* Quer-; (*annoyed*) böse, ärgerlich. *v* kreuzen, überqueren. **cross over** hinübergehen. **cross one's mind** einfallen (+*dat*). **crossbow** *n* Armbrust *f*. **crossbreed** *n* Kreuzung *f*. **cross-country** *adj* Gelände-. **cross-examination** *n* Kreuzverhör *m*. **cross-eyed** *adj* schielend. **crossing** *n* Kreuzung *f*; (*rail*) Bahnübergang *m*; (*border*) Überfahrt *f*. **cross-legged** *adj* mit überschlagenen Beinen. **cross-reference** *n* Kreuzverweisung *f*. **crossroads** *n* Straßenkreuzung *f*; (*fig*) Scheideweg *m*. **cross-section** *n* Querschnitt *m*. **crosswind** *n* Seitenwind *m*. **crossword** *n* Kreuzworträtsel *neut*.

crotchet ['krotʃit] *n* (*music*) Viertelnote *f*.

crouch [krautʃ] *v* sich ducken.

crow [krou] *n* Krähe *f*. *v* krähen. **crow's feet** Krähenfüße *pl*. **crow's nest** (*naut*) Mastkorb *m*.

crowd [kraud] *n* Menge. *v* **crowd around** sich drängen um. **crowded** *adj* gedrängt.

crown [kraun] *n* Krone *f*. *v* krönen.

crucial ['kruːʃəl] *adj* kritisch, entscheidend.

crucifixion [,kruːsi'fikʃən] *n* Kreuzigung *f*. **crucify** *v* kreuzigen.

crude [kruːd] *adj* roh; (*person*) grob. **crude oil** Rohöl *neut*. **crudeness** *n* Roheit *f*.

cruel ['kruːəl] *adj* grausam. **cruelty** *n* Grausamkeit *f*.

cruise [kruːz] *v* (*boat*) kreuzen; (*aircraft*) fliegen. *n* Kreuzfahrt *f*. **cruiser** *n* (*naut*) Kreuzer *m*.

crumb [krʌm] *n* Krume *f*; (*coll*) Brocken *m*.

crumble ['krʌmbl] *v* zerkrümeln. **crumbly** *adj* krümelig.

crumple ['krʌmpl] *v* zerknittern.

crunch [krʌntʃ] *v* knirschen. *n* Knirschen *neut*. **crunchy** *adj* knusprig.

crusade [kruː'seid] *n* Kreuzzug *m*. **crusader** *n* Kreuzfahrer *m*.

crush [krʌʃ] *v* zerdrücken; unterdrücken. *n* Gedränge *neut*. **crushing** *adj* Überwältigend.

crust [krʌst] *n* Kruste *f*.

crustacean [krʌ'steiʃən] *n* Krustentier *neut*.

crutch [krʌtʃ] *n* Krücke *f*.

cry [krai] *v* (*shout*) schreien; (*weep*) weinen. *n* Schrei *m*, Ruf *m*. **cry out** auf-

schreien. **a far cry from** ein weiter Weg von.

crypt [kript] *n* Krypta *f*.

crystal ['kristl] *n* Kristall *m*.

cub [kʌb] *n* Junge(s) *neut*; (*fox, wolf*) Welpe *m*; (*scout*) Wölfling *m*.

cube [kjuːb] *n* Würfel *m*; (*math*) Kubikzahl *f*. **cubic** *adj* würfelförmig. **cubic centimetre** Kubikzentimeter *neut*. **cubic capacity** (*mot*) Hubraum *m*.

cubicle ['kjuːbikl] *n* Kabine *f*.

cuckoo ['kukuː] *n* Kuckuck *m*.

cucumber [kju'kʌmbə] *n* Gurke *f*.

cuddle ['kʌdl] *v* herzen, liebkosen.

cue¹ [kjuː] *n* (*theatre*) Stichwort *neut*.

cue² [kjuː] *n* (*billiards*) Billardstock *m*.

cuff¹ [kʌf] *n* (*shirt*) Manschette *f*; (*trousers*) AUfschlag *m*. **cufflink** *n* Manschettenknopf *m*.

cuff² [kʌf] *n* Ohrfeige *f*, Klaps *m*. *v* klapsen.

culinary ['kʌlinəri] *adj* kulinarisch, Küchen-.

culminate ['kʌlmi,neit] *v* kulminieren. **culmination** *n* Höhepunkt *m*.

culprit ['kʌlprit] *n* Täter *m*.

cult [kʌlt] *n* Kult *m*.

cultivate ['kʌlti,veit] *v* bebauen, kultivieren; (*fig*) pflegen. **cultivation** *n* Kultur *f*.

culture ['kʌltʃə] *n* Kultur *f*. **cultural** *adj* kulturell.

cumbersome ['kʌmbəsəm] *adj* sperrig, schwer zu handhaben.

cunning ['kʌniŋ] *adj* schlau, listig. *n* List *f*.

cup [kʌp] *n* Tasse *f*; (*trophy*) Pokal *m*. **cup final** Pokalendspiel *neut*. **cup tie** Pokalspiel *neut*.

cupboard ['kʌbəd] *n* Schrank *m*.

curate ['kjuərət] *n* Unterpfarrer *m*.

curator [kjuə'reitə] *n* Konservator *m*.

curb [kəːb] *v* zügeln. *n* Zaum *m*; (*kerb*) Bordstein *m*.

curdle ['kəːdl] *v* gerinnen.

cure [kjuə] *v* (*illness*) heilen; (*smoke*) räuchern; (*salt*) einsalzen. *n* Heilmittel *neut*.

curfew ['kəːfjuː] *n* Ausgehverbot *m*.

curious ['kjuəriəs] *adj* (*inquisitive*) neugierig; (*odd*) seltsam. **curiosity** *n* Neugier *f*.

curl [kəːl] *n* Locke *f*, Kräuselung *f*. *v* (sich) kräuseln. **curly** *adj* lockig, kraus.

currant ['kʌrənt] *n* Korinthe *f*.

currency ['kʌrənsi] n (*money*) Währung f.
current ['kʌrənt] adj (*present*) gegenwärtig; (*common*) gebräuchlich, üblich. n Strom m. current account Scheckkonto neut. current events Zeitgeschehen neut.
currently adv zur Zeit.
curry ['kʌri] n Curry neut. curry powder Curry(pulver) neut. curry sauce Currysoße f.
curse [kəːs] v verfluchen; (*swear*) fluchen. n Fluch m.
curt [kəːt] adj knapp, barsch.
curtail [kəːˈteil] v abkürzen. curtailment n Abkürzung f; Einschränkung f.
curtain ['kəːtn] n Gardine f; (*theatre*) Vorhang m.
curtsy ['kəːtsi] n Knicks m. v knicksen.
curve [kəːv] n Kurve f. v sich biegen. curved adj bogenförmig, gekrümmt.
cushion ['kuʃən] n Kissen neut. v polstern.
custard ['kʌstəd] n Vanillesoße f.
custody ['kʌstədi] n Aufsicht f; (*arrest*) Haft f.
custom ['kʌstəm] n (*habit*) Gewohnheit f; (*tradition*) Brauch m. (*customers*) Kundschaft f. customary adj gewöhnlich. customer n Kunde m, Kundin f. customs n Zoll m. customs duty Zoll m. customs official Zollbeamte(r) m.
*cut [kʌt] n Schnitt m; (*wound*) Schnittwunde f; (*in wages*) Kürzung f; (*coll: share*) Anteil m. v schneiden; (*prices*) herabsetzen; (*wages*) kürzen. cut off (*phone*) trennen.
cute [kjuːt] adj (*coll*) niedlich.
cuticle ['kjuːtikl] n Oberhaut f; (*on nail*) Nagelhaut f.
cutlery ['kʌtləri] n Besteck neut.
cutlet ['kʌtlit] n Kotelett neut.
cycle ['saikl] n Zyklus m; (*bicycle*) Fahrrad neut. v radfahren. cycling n Radsport m. cyclist n Radfahrer(in).
cyclone ['saikloun] n Zyklon m.
cylinder ['silində] n Zylinder m. cylinder block Motorblock m. cylinder capacity Hubraum m. cylinder head Zylinderkopf m.
cymbals ['simbəlz] pl n Becken neut sing.
cynic ['sinik] n Zyniker(in). cynical adj zynisch. cynicism n Zynismus m.
cypress ['saiprəs] n Zypresse f.
Cyprus ['saiprəs] n Zypern neut. Cypriot n Zypriot(in). adj zypriotisch.
cyst [sist] n Zyste f.

Czechoslovakia [ˌtʃekəsləˈvakiə] n die Tschechoslowakei f. Czechoslovakian n Tschechoslowake m, Tschechoslowakin f. adj tschechoslowakisch.

D

dab [dab] v betupfen. n Tupfen m.
dabble ['dabl] v plätschern. he dabbles in art er beschäftigt sich nebenbei mit Kunst. dabbler n Dilettant m.
dad [dad] n Vati m, Papa m.
daffodil ['dafədil] n Narzisse f.
daft [daːft] adj (*coll*) blöd(e), doof.
dagger ['dagə] n Dolch m.
daily ['deili] adj, adv täglich. daily paper Tageszeitung f.
dainty ['deinti] adj (*person*) niedlich; (*food*) lecker.
dairy ['deəri] n Molkerei f. dairy produce Milchprodukte pl.
daisy ['deizi] n Gänseblümchen neut.
dam [dam] n Damm m. v eindämmen.
damage ['damidʒ] v beschädigen; verletzen. n Schaden m. damages pl n (*compensation*) Schadenersatz m sing.
damn [dam] v verdammen. interj verdammt!
damp [damp] adj feucht. n Feuchtigkeit f. dampen v befeuchten.
damson ['damzən] n Pflaume f.
dance [daːns] n Tanz m. v tanzen. dancer n Tänzer(in). dance hall Tanzsaal m. dancing n Tanz m; Tanzen neut.
dandelion ['dandiˌlaiən] n Löwenzahn m.
dandruff ['dandrəf] n Schuppen pl.
Dane [dein] n Däne m, Dänin f. Danish adj dänisch.
danger ['deindʒə] n Gefahr f. in (or out of) danger in/außer Gefahr. dangerous adj gefährlich.
dangle ['daŋgl] v baumeln; baumeln lassen.
dare [deə] v wagen, riskieren; (*challenge*) herausfordern. daring adj wagemutig; (*risky*) gewagt; n Mut m.
dark [daːk] adj finster; (*esp colour*) dunkel. n Dunkelheit f. in the dark im Dunkeln; (*fig*) nicht im Bilde. darken v (sich) verdunkeln. darkness n Dunkelheit

decree

f. Finsternis *f.* **darkroom** *n* Dunkelkammer *f.*

darling ['dɑːlɪŋ] *n* Liebling *m. adj* lieb.

darn [dɑːn] *v* stopfen. **darning** *n* Stopfen *neut.*

dart [dɑːt] *v* schießen, sausen; *n* Pfeil *m.* **darts** *pl n* (*game*) (Pfeilwerfen) *neut sing.*

dash [daʃ] *v* (*smash*) zerschlagen; (*rush*) stürzen. *n* (*punctuation*) Gedankenstrich *m*; (*rush*) Stürzen *neut*; (*addition*) Schuß *m.* **dashboard** *n* Armaturenbrett *neut.*

dashing *adj* schneidig.

data ['deɪtə] *pl n* Daten *pl.* **data processing** Datenverarbeitung *f.*

date[1] [deɪt] *n* Datum *neut*; (*appointed day*) Termin *m*; (*with someone*) Verabredung *f. v* (*letter*) datieren. **dated** *adj* altmodisch.

date[2] [deɪt] *n* (*fruit*) Dattel *f.*

dative ['deɪtɪv] *n* Dativ *m.*

daughter ['dɔːtə] *n* Tochter *f.* **daughter-in-law** *n* Schwiegertochter *f.*

daunt [dɔːnt] *v* entmutigen.

dawdle ['dɔːdl] *v* trödeln.

dawn [dɔːn] *n* Tagesanbruch *m*; (Morgen)Dämmerung *f*; (*fig*) Anfang *m. v* dämmern (*also fig*).

day [deɪ] *n* Tag *m.* **daylight** Tageslicht *neut.*

daze [deɪz] *v* betäuben. **dazed** *adj* benommen.

dazzle ['dazl] *v* blenden.

dead [ded] *adj* tot. **dead man/woman** Tote(r). **the dead** die Toten *pl.* **deaden** *v* dämpfen. **dead certain** todsicher. **dead end** Sackgasse *f*; (*fig*) totes Geleise *neut.*

deadline *n* Termin *m.*

deaf [def] *adj* taub. **deaf aid** Hörgerät *neut.* **deaf mute** Taubstumme(r). **deafen** *v* taub machen.

*deal [diːl] *n* Geschäft *neut. v* handeln; (*cards*) austeilen. **deal with** (*attend to*) sich befassen mit; (*resolve*) erledigen. **a great/good deal of** viel. **dealer** *n* Händler *m*; (*cards*) Kartengeber *m.* **dealings** *pl n* Beziehungen *pl.*

dealt [delt] *V* **deal.**

dean [diːn] *n* Dekan *m.*

dear [dɪə] *adj* (*beloved*) lieb; (*expensive*) teuer. (*in letters*) **Dear Mr. Smith** Lieber Herr Smith, **Sehr geehrter Herr Smith.** *n* Liebling *m.* **dearly** *adv* herzlich.

death [deθ] *n* Tod *m*; (*case of death*) Todesfall *m.* **deathbed** *n* Sterbebett *neut.* **death penalty** Todesstrafe *f.*

debase [dɪ'beɪs] *v* entwerten.

debate [dɪ'beɪt] *n* Debatte *f. v* debattieren, diskutieren.

debit ['debɪt] *n* Soll *neut*; Lastschrift *f. v* belasten.

debris ['deɪbriː] *n* Schutt *m*, Trümmer *pl.*

debt [det] *n* Schuld *f.* **in debt** verschuldet. **debtor** *n* Schuldner *m.*

decade ['dekeɪd] *n* Jahrzehnt *neut*

decadence ['dekədəns] *n* Dekadenz *f.* **decadent** *adj* dekadent.

decanter [dɪ'kantə] *n* Karaffe *f.*

decapitate [dɪ'kapɪˌteɪt] *v* enthaupten. **decapitation** *n* Enthauptung *f.*

decay [dɪ'keɪ] *v* verfallen. *n* Verfall *m.* **tooth decay** Karies *f.*

deceased [dɪ'siːst] *adj* verstorben. **the deceased** der/die Verstorbene.

deceit [dɪ'siːt] *n* Täuschung, Betrug *m.* **deceitful** *adj* betrügerisch.

deceive [dɪ'siːv] *v* täuschen.

December [dɪ'sembə] *n* Dezember *m.*

decent ['diːsənt] *adj* (*respectable*) anständig; (*kind*) freundlich. **decency** *n* Anstand *m.*

deceptive [dɪ'septɪv] *adj* täuschend.

decibel ['desɪˌbel] *n* Dezibel *neut.*

decide [dɪ'saɪd] *v* entscheiden; (*make up one's mind*) sich entscheiden. **decided** *adj* entschieden. **decision** *n* Entscheidung *f*; (*of committee*) Beschluß *m.* **make a decision** eine Entscheidung treffen. **decisive** *adj* entscheidend.

deciduous [dɪ'sɪdjuəs] *adj* (*trees*) Laub-.

decimal ['desɪməl] *adj* Dezimal-.

decipher [dɪ'saɪfə] *v* entziffern.

deck [dek] *n* Deck *neut*; (*of cards*) Pack *neut.* **deckchair** *n* Liegestuhl *m.*

declare [dɪ'kleə] *v* erklären. **declaration** *n* Erklärung *f.*

decline [dɪ'klaɪn] *v* ablehnen; (*gram*) deklinieren.

decompose [ˌdiːkəm'pəʊz] *v* zerfallen.

decor ['deɪkɔɪ] *n* Ausstattung *f.*

decorate ['dekəˌreɪt] *v* schmücken; (*room*) tapezieren; (*mil*) auszeichnen. **decoration** *n* Verzierung *f*; (*of room*) Dekoration *f*; (*mil*) Orden *m.*

decoy ['diːkɔɪ] *n* Lockvogel *m.*

decrease [dɪ'kriːs] *v* (*make less*) vermindern; (*become less*) abnehmen. *n* Abnahme *f.*

decree [dɪ'kriː] *n* Erlaß *m.*

decrepit [di'krepit] *adj* hinfällig.
dedicate ['dedi̱keit] *v* widmen; *(rel)* weihen. **dedication** *n* (*book*) Widmung *f*; (*to duty, etc.*) Hingabe *f*; *(rel)* Einweihung *f*.
deduce [di'djuːs] *v* schließen (*aus*).
deduct [di'dʌkt] *v* abziehen. **deduction** *n* Abzug *m*.
deed [diːd] *n* Tat *f*; (*document*) Urkunde *f*.
deep [diːp] *adj* tief. **deep freeze** Tiefkühlschrank *m*. **deep-frozen** *adj* tiefgekühlt, Tiefkühl-.
deer [diə] *n* Hirsch *m*.
deface [di'feis] *v* entstellen.
default [di'fɔːlt] *n* Unterlassung *f*. *v* (*with payments*) in Verzug kommen.
defeat [di'fiːt] *v* schlagen, besiegen. *n* Niederlage *f*.
defect ['diːfekt; *v* di'fekt] *n* Fehler *m*, Defekt *m*. *v* (*pol*) überlaufen. **defective** *adj* fehlerhaft, defektiv.
defence [di'fens] *n* Verteidigung *f*. **defenceless** *adj* schutzlos.
defend [di'fend] *v* verteidigen. **defendant** *n* Angeklagte(r). **defender** *n* Verteidiger *m*. **defensive** *adj* defensiv, Verteidigungs-.
defer [di'fəː] *v* (*postpone*) verschieben. **defer to** (*yield to*) nachgeben (+ *dat*). **deferment** *n* Verschiebung *f*.
defiance [di'faiəns] *n* Trotz *m*. **defiant** *adj* trotzig, unnachgiebig.
deficiency [di'fiʃənsi] *n* Unzulänglichkeit *f*, Mangel *m*. **deficient** *adj* (*defective*) defektiv, mangelhaft; (*inadequate*) unzulänglich.
deficit ['defisit] *n* Defizit *neut*, Fehlbetrag *m*.
define [di'fain] *v* definieren, genau erklären. (**well**) **defined** *adj* deutlich. **definite** *adj* klar, deutlich. **definitely** *adv* bestimmt. **definition** *n* Erklärung *f*, Definition *f*; (*phot*) Schärfe *f*.
deflate [di'fleit] *v* die Luft ablassen aus. **deflation** (*pol*) Deflation *f*.
deform [di'fɔːm] *v* deformieren, entstellen. **deformed** *adj* deformiert, verformt. **deformity** *n* Mißbildung *f*.
defraud [di'frɔːd] *v* betrügen.
defrost [diːˈfrɒst] *v* abtauen.
deft [deft] *adj* flink.
defunct [di'fʌŋkt] *adj* verstorben; (*fig*) nicht mehr bestehend.
defy [di'fai] *v* (*resist*) trotzen; (*challenge*) herausfordern.

degenerate [di'dʒenə̱reit; *adj* di'dʒenərit] *v* degenerieren. *adj* degeneriert.
degrade [di'greid] *v* erniedrigen, entehren. **degradation** *n* Erniedrigung *f*. **degrading** *adj* erniedrigend.
degree [di'griː] *n* Grad *m*. **to a high degree** in hohem Maße.
dehydrate [diːˈhaidreit] *v* trocknen. **dehydrated** *adj* getrocknet, Trocken-.
deign [dein] *v* sich herablassen.
dejected [di'dʒektid] *adj* niedergeschlagen.
delay [di'lei] *v* (*postpone*) aufschieben. *n* Verzögerung *f*, Aufschub *m*. **be delayed** (*train, etc.*) Verspätung haben. **without delay** unverzüglich.
delegate ['deləgeit; 'deləgit] *v* delegieren. *n* Delegierte(r). **delegation** *m* Delegation *f*.
delete [di'liːt] *v* tilgen, streichen.
deliberate [di'libərət; *v* di'libəreit] *adj* (*intentional*) absichtlich. *v* nachdenken. **deliberately** *adv* absichtlich. **deliberation** *n* Überlegung *f*.
delicate ['delikət] *adj* (*fragile*) zart; (*fine*) fein; (*situation*) heikel. **delicacy** *n* Zartheit *f*; (*food*) Delikatesse *f*.
delicious [di'liʃəs] *adj* köstlich.
delight [di'lait] *n* Freude *f*, Vergnügen *neut*. *v* erfreuen. **delighted** *adj* erfreut, entzückt. **delightful** *adj* entzückend.
delinquency [di'liŋkwənsi] *n* Straffälligkeit *f*. **delinquent** *adj* delinquent. *n* Delinquent *m*.
delirious [di'liriəs] *adj* in Delirium. **delirium** *n* Delirium *neut*, Fieberwahn *m*.
deliver [di'livə] *v* (*goods*) (aus)liefern; (*rescue*) befreien; (*a woman in childbirth*) entbinden. **deliverance** *n* Befreiung *f*. **delivery** *n* (Aus)Lieferung *f*; Entbindung *f*.
delta ['deltə] *n* Delta *neut*.
delude [di'luːd] *v* täuschen. **delusion** *n* Täuschung *f*.
deluge ['deljuːdʒ] *n* Flut *f*.
delve [delv] *v* **delve into** erforschen.
demand [di'maːnd] *v* verlangen. *n* Verlangen *neut*; (*for a commodity, etc.*) Nachfrage *f*. **on demand** auf Verlangen. **demanding** *adj* anspruchsvoll.
demented [di'mentid] *adj* wahnsinnig.
democracy [di'mɒkrəsi] *n* Demokratie *f*. **democrat** *n* Demokrat *m*. **democratic** *adj* demokratisch.

demolish [di'moliʃ] v abbrechen. **demolition** n Abbruch m.

demon ['diːmən] n Teufel m.

demonstrate ['demən‚streit] v demonstrieren. **demonstration** n Demonstration f.

demoralize [di'morə‚laiz] v demoralisieren. **demoralization** n Demoralisation f.

demure [di'mjuə] adj bescheiden.

den [den] n Höhle f; (room) Bude f.

denial [di'naiəl] n Leugnung f.

denim ['denim] adj Denim-. **denims** pl n Jeans pl.

Denmark ['denmaɪk] n Dänemark neut.

denomination [di‚nomi'neiʃən] n (rel) Bekenntnis neut; (of banknote) Nennwert m. **denominator** n Nenner m. **common denominator** gemeinsamer Nenner m.

denote [di'nout] v bezeichnen.

denounce [di'nauns] v brandmarken.

dense [dens] adj dicht, dick. **density** n Dichte f.

dent [dent] n Beule f. v einbeulen.

dental ['dentl] adj Zahn-.

dentist ['dentist] n Zahnarzt m. **dentistry** n Zahnheilkunde f.

denture ['dentʃə] n (künstliches) Gebiß neut.

denude [di'njuːd] v entblößen.

denunciation [dinʌnsi'eiʃən] n Denunziation f.

deny [di'nai] v leugnen; (responsibility) ablehnen; (allegation) dementieren. **deny oneself** sich versagen.

deodorant [diː'oudərənt] n Desodorans neut.

depart [di'paɪt] v abfahren; (fig) abweichen. **departure** n (person) Weggehen neut; (train) Abfahrt f; (aeroplane) Abflug m.

department [di'paɪtmənt] n Abteilung f; (pol) Ministerium neut. **department store** Warenhaus neut.

depend [di'pend] v **depend on** abhängen von; (rely on) sich verlassen auf. **it (all) depends** es kommt darauf an. **dependable** adj zuverlässig. **dependant** n Familienangehörige(r). **dependent** adj abhängig (+ von).

depict [di'pikt] v schildern.

deplete [di'pliɪt] v erschöpfen. **depletion** n Erschöpfung f.

deplore [di'ploɪ] v bedauern. **deplorable** adj bedauernswert.

deport [di'poɪt] v deportieren. **deport oneself** sich verhalten. **deportation** n Deportation f. **deportment** n Haltung f.

depose [di'pouz] v absetzen.

deposit [di'pozit] v deponieren. n (surety) Kaution f; (down payment) Anzahlung f; (sediment) Niederschlag m. **deposit account** Sparkonto neut.

depot ['depou] n Depot neut.

depraved [di'preivd] adj lasterhaft, verworfen.

depreciate [di'priːʃi‚əit] v an Wert verlieren. **depreciation** n Wertminderung f.

depress [di'pres] v niederdrücken, deprimieren. **depressed** adj deprimiert. **depressing** adj deprimierend. **depression** n Depression f.

deprive [di'praiv] v berauben.

depth [depθ] n Tiefe f. **in depth** gründlich.

deputy ['depjuti] n Stellvertreter m. adj stellvertretend.

derail [di'reil] v entgleisen. **derailment** n Entgleisen neut.

derelict ['derilikt] adj (building) baufällig.

deride [di'raid] v verspotten. **derision** n Spott m. **derisory** adj spöttisch.

derive [di'raiv] v ableiten; (originate) stammen; (gain) gewinnen. **derivation** n Herkunft f.

derogatory [di'rogətəri] adj geringschätzig.

descend [di'send] v hinabsteigen; (from train) aussteigen. **be descended from** abstammen von. **descendant** n Nachkomme m. **descent** n Abstieg m; Abstammung f.

describe [di'skraib] v beschreiben. **description** n Beschreibung f.

desert[1] ['dezət] n Wüste f.

desert[2] [di'zəɪt] n (something deserved) Verdienst neut. **deserts** pl Lohn m sing.

desert[3] [di'zəɪt] v verlassen; (mil) desertieren. **deserter** n Deserteur m. **desertion** n Verlassen neut; (mil) Desertion f.

deserve [di'zəɪv] v verdienen.

design [di'zain] n Entwurf m; (drawing) Zeichnung f; (pattern) Muster neut. v entwerfen, planen.

designate ['dezig‚neit] v bezeichnen. **designation** n Bezeichnung f.

desire [di'zaiə] v wünschen, begehren; (ask for) wollen. n Wunsch m; (sexual) Begierde f. **desirous of** begierig nach.

desk [desk] n Schreibtisch m.
desolate ['desələt] v wüst, öde; (person) trostlos.
despair [di'speə] v verzweifeln. n Verzweiflung f.
desperate ['despərət] adj verzweifelt; (situation) hoffnungslos.
despicable [di'spikəbl] adj verächtlich.
despise [di'spaiz] v verachten.
despite [di'spait] prep trotz (+gen).
despondent [di'spondənt] adj mutlos.
despot ['despot] n Gewaltherrscher m, Despot m. **despotism** n Despotismus m.
dessert [di'zəːt] n Nachtisch m. **dessert spoon** Dessertlöffel m.
destiny ['destəni] n Schicksal neut. **destined** adj ausersehen, bestimmt. **destination** n (post) Bestimmungsort m; (travel) Reiseziel neut.
destitute ['destitjuːt] adj notleidend, bedürftig.
destroy [di'stroi] v zerstören, vernichten. **destroyer** n Zerstörer m. **destruction** n Zerstörung f. **destructive** adj zerstörerisch.
detach [di'tatʃ] v losmachen, abtrennen. **detached** adj (house) Einzel-; (fig) objektiv. **detachment** Objektivität f; (mil) Abteilung f.
detail ['diːteil] n Einzelheit f, Detail neut. **further details** Näheres neut; nähere Angaben pl. v detaillieren **detailed** adj eingehend.
detain [di'tein] v aufhalten; (arrest) verhaften.
detect [di'tekt] v entdecken. **detection** n Aufdeckung f. **detective** n Detektiv m. **detective story** Kriminalroman m.
détente [dei'tãːnt] n Entspannung f.
detention [di'tenʃən] n (law) Haft m; (school) Nachsitzen neut.
deter [di'təː] v abschrecken.
detergent [di'təːdʒənt] n Reinigungsmittel neut.
deteriorate [di'tiəriə reit] v sich verschlechtern. **deterioration** n Verschlechterung f.
determine [di'təːmin] v bestimmen; (decide) sich entschließen. **determined** adj entschlossen. **determination** n Entschlossenheit f.
detest [di'test] v hassen, verabscheuen. **detestable** adj abscheulich.
detonate ['detə neit] v detonieren.
detour ['diːtuə] n Umweg m.

detract [di'trakt] v **detract from** beeinträchtigen.
detriment ['detrimənt] n Schaden m, Nachteil m. **detrimental (to)** adj schädlich (für).
devalue [diː'valjuː] v abwerten. **devaluation** n Abwertung f.
devastate ['devə steit] v verwüsten. **devastating** adj vernichtend. **devastation** n Verwüstung f.
develop [di'veləp] v (sich) entwickeln. **developer** n Entwickler m. **developing** n Entwicklungs-. **development** n Entwicklung f.
deviate ['diːvi ait] v abweichen. **deviation** n Abweichung f.
device [di'vais] n Gerät neut, Vorrichtung f; (trick) Trick m.
devil ['devl] n Teufel m. **talk of the devil** den Teufel an die Wand malen. **devilish** adj teuflisch.
devious ['diːviəs] adj weitschweifig; (dishonest) krumm, unaufrichtig.
devise [di'vaiz] v ausdenken, erfinden.
devoid [di'void] adj **devoid of** ohne, frei von.
devolution [ˌdiːvə'luːʃən] n Dezentralisation f.
devote [di'vout] v widmen, hingeben. **devoted** adj ergeben. **be devoted to someone** sehr an jemandem hängen. **devotee** n Anhänger(in). **devotion** n Ergebenheit f.
devour [di'vauə] v verschlingen.
devout [di'vaut] adj fromm, andächtig.
dew [djuː] n Tau m.
dexterous ['dekstrəs] adj gewandt, flink. **dexterity** n Gewandtheit f.
diabetes [ˌdiə'biːtiːz] n Zuckerkrankheit f. **diabetic** adj zuckerkrank. n Diabetiker m.
diagnose [ˌdiəg'nouz] v diagnostizieren, erkennen. **diagnosis** n Diagnose f. **diagnostic** adj diagnostisch.
diagonal [dai'agənəl] adj diagonal. n Diagonale f.
diagram ['daiəgram] n Diagramm neut, Schaubild neut.
dial ['daiəl] n (phone) Wählscheibe f. v wählen. **dialling tone** Amtszeichen neut.
dialect ['daiəlekt] n Dialekt m.
dialogue ['daiəlog] n Dialog m.
diameter [dai'amitə] n Durchmesser m.
diamond ['daiəmənd]n Diamant m; (cards) Karo neut; (sport) Spielfeld neut. adj diamanten.

diaper ['daiəpə] *n* Windel *f*.
diaphragm ['daiə‚fram] *n* (*anat*) Zwerchfell *neut*; (*contraceptive*) (Okklusiv)Pessar *neut*.
diarrhoea [‚daiə'riə] *n* Durchfall *m*.
diary ['daiəri] *n* Tagebuch *neut*.
dice [dais] *pl n* Würfel *pl*. *v* (*cookery*) in Würfel schneiden.
dictate [dik'teit] *n* diktieren. **dictating machine** Diktiergerät *neut*. **dictation** *n* Diktat *neut*. **dictator** *n* Diktator *m*. **dictatorial** *adj* diktatorisch. **dictatorship** *n*.
dictionary ['dikʃənəri] *n* Wörterbuch *neut*.
did [did] *V* do.
die [dai] *v* sterben. **die away** schwächer werden. **die out** aussterben.
diesel ['diːzəl] *adj* Diesel-. **diesel engine** Dieselmotor *m*.
diet ['daiət] *n* Kost *f*, Nahrung *f*; (*for weight loss*) Abmagerungskur *f*; (*for convalescence, etc.*) Diät *f*, Schonkost *f*. *v* eine Abmagerungskur machen.
differ ['difə] *v* sich unterscheiden; (*think differently*) anderer Meinung sein. **difference** *n* Unterschied *m*. **different** *adj* verschieden, unterschiedlich; (*another*) ander. **differential** *adj* unterschiedlich. *n* (*mot*) Differentialgetriebe *neut*.
difficult ['difikəlt] *adj* schwer, schwierig. **difficulty** *n* Schwierigkeit *f*.
*dig [dig] *v* graben. **dig up** ausgraben.
digest [dai'dʒest; *n* 'daidʒest] *v* verdauen. *n* Auslese *f*. **digestible** *adj* verdaulich. **digestion** *n* Verdauung *f*.
digit ['didʒit] *n* (*figure*) Ziffer *f*; (*finger*) Finger *m*; (*toe*) Zehe *f*.
dignified ['digni‚faid] *adj* würdevoll.
dignity ['digniti] *n* Würde *f*.
digress [dai'gres] *v* abschweifen. **digression** *n* Abschweifung *f*.
digs [digz] *pl n* (*coll*) Bude *f sing*.
dilapidated [di'lapi‚deitid] *adj* baufällig.
dilate [dai'leit] *v* (sich) weiten.
dilemma [di'lemə] *n* Dilemma *neut*. **be in a dilemma** in der Klemme sitzen.
diligence ['dilidʒəns] *n* Fleiß *m*. **diligent** *adj* fleißig, gewissenhaft.
dilute [dai'luːt] *v* (*with water*) verwässern; verdünnen. *adj* (*also* **diluted**) verwässert.
dim [dim] *adj* trübe; (*light, vision*) schwach; (*coll: stupid*) dumm. *v* verdunkeln.
dimension [di'menʃən] *n* Dimension *f*. **dimensions** *pl* Ausmaße *pl*.

diminish [di'miniʃ] *v* (sich) vermindern. **diminishing** *adj* abnehmend.
diminutive [di'minjutiv] *adj* winzig.
dimple ['dimpl] *n* Grübchen *neut*.
din [din] *n* Lärm *m*, Getöse *neut*.
dine [dain] *v* speisen, essen. **diner** *n* (*person*) Tischgast *m*; (*rail*) Speisewagen *m*; (*restaurant*) Speiselokal *neut*. **dining car** Speisewagen *m*. **dining room** Eßzimmer *neut*. **dining table** Eßtisch *n*.
dinghy ['diŋgi] *n* Dingi *neut*, Beiboot *neut*. **rubber dinghy** Schlauchboot *neut*.
dingy ['dindʒi] *adj* trübe.
dinner ['dinə] *n* Abendessen *neut*; (*at midday*) Mittagessen *neut*; (*public*) Festessen *neut*. **dinner jacket** Smoking *m*. **dinner party** Diner *neut*.
dinosaur ['dainə‚soɪ] *n* Dinosaurier *m*.
dip [dip] *v* (ein)tauchen; (*slope down*) sich senken. **dip one's lights** (*mot*) abblenden. *n* Senkung *f*; (*bathe*) Bad *neut*. **dip switch** Abblendschalter *m*.
diploma [di'ploumə] *n* Diplom *neut*.
diplomacy [di'plouməsi] *n* Diplomatie *f*. **diplomat** *n* Diplomat *m*. **diplomatic** *adj* diplomatisch.
dipstick ['dipstik] *n* (*mot*) Ölmeßstab *m*.
dire [daiə] *adj* schrecklich; (*urgent*) dringend.
direct [di'rekt] *adj* direkt. *v* dirigieren, leiten; (*aim*) richten; (*give directions*) den Weg zeigen (+ *dat*); (*order*) anweisen. **direction** *n* Richtung *f*; Leitung *f*; **directions** *pl* (*for use*) Gebrauchsanweisung *f sing*; (*instructions*) Anweisungen *pl*. **directly** *adv* (*immediately*) unmittelbar; (*straight towards*) direkt, gerade. **director** *n* Direktor *m*, Leiter *m*; (*theatre, film*) Regisseur *m*. (*telephone*) **directory** *n* Telefonbuch *neut*.
dirt [dəɪt] *n* Schmutz *m*, Dreck *m*. **dirt cheap** spottbillig. **dirty** *adj* schmutzig, dreckig.
disability [disə'biləti] *n* Körperbehinderung *f*. **disability pension** Invalidenrente *f*.
disadvantage [‚disəd'vaɪntidʒ] *n* Nachteil *m*. **disadvantageous** *adj* ungünstig, unvorteilhaft.
disagree [‚disə'griɪ] *v* nicht übereinstimmen; (*argue*) sich streiten. **disagreeable** *adj* unangenehm. **disagreement** *n* Meinungsverschiedenheit *f*.

disappear [ˌdisə'piə] v verschwinden. **disappearance** n Verschwinden neut.

disappoint [ˌdisə'point] v enttäuschen. **disappointed** adj enttäuscht. **disappointing** adj enttäuschend. **disappointment** n Enttäuschung f.

disapprove [ˌdisə'pruːv] v disapprove of mißbilligen. **disapproval** n Mißbilligung f.

disarm [dis'aɪm] v entwaffnen; (pol) abrüsten. **disarmament** n Abrüstung f. **disarming** adj entwaffnend.

disaster [di'zaɪstə] n Katastrophe f, Unglück neut. **disastrous** adj katastrophal.

disband [dis'band] v (sich) auflösen.

disc or US **disk** [disk] n Scheibe f; (record) Schallplatte f.

discard [dis'kaɪd] v ablegen.

disc brake n Scheibenbremse f. **disc jockey** n Disk-Jockey m.

discern [di'səɪn] v (perceive) wahrnehmen; (differentiate) unterscheiden. **discernible** adj wahrnehmbar. **discerning** adj einsichtig.

discharge [dis'tʃaɪdʒ] v (dismiss) entlassen; (gun) abschießen; (duty) erfüllen; (ship) entladen; (of wound) eitern. n (med) Ausfluß m.

disciple [di'saipl] n Jünger m.

discipline ['disiplin] n Disziplin f. v disziplinieren; (train) schulen.

disclaim [dis'kleim] v ablehnen. **disclaimer** n Dementi neut.

disclose [dis'klouz] v enthüllen. **disclosure** n Bekanntmachung f.

discolour [dis'kʌlə] v (sich) verfärben. **discoloration** n Verfärbung f.

discomfort [dis'kʌmfət] n Unbehagen neut.

disconcert [diskən'səɪt] v aus der Fassung bringen.

disconnect [diskə'nekt] v trennen; (elec) abschalten.

disconsolate [dis'konsələt] adj trostlos.

discontinue [diskən'tinjuː] v aufhören; (something) einstellen.

discord ['diskoɪd] n (disagreement) Zwietracht f; (music) Diskordanz f. **discordant** adj diskordant.

discotheque ['diskətek] n Diskothek f.

discount ['diskaunt] v (ignore) außer Acht lassen. n Rabatt m.

discourage [dis'kʌridʒ] v entmutigen;

(dissuade) abraten. **discouraging** adj entmutigend.

discover [dis'kʌvə] v entdecken. **discoverer** n Entdecker m. **discovery** n Entdeckung f.

discredit [dis'kredit] v in Verruf bringen.

discreet [di'skriːt] adj diskret, verschwiegen.

discrepancy [di'skrepənsi] n Widerspruch m, Diskrepanz f.

discretion [di'skreʃən] n Diskretion f, Takt m. **at your discretion** nach Ihrem Gutdünken.

discriminate [di'skriminˌeit] v unterscheiden. **discriminate** (against) diskriminieren. **discriminating** adj anspruchsvoll. **discrimination** n (racial, etc.) Diskriminierung f.

discus ['diskəs] n Diskus m.

discuss [di'skʌs] v besprechen, diskutieren; (in writing) behandeln. **discussion** n Besprechung f, Diskussion f.

disease [di'ziːz] n Krankheit f. **diseased** adj krank.

disembark [disim'baɪk] v an Land gehen.

disengage [disin'geidʒ] v sich losmachen. **disengage the clutch** auskuppeln.

disfigure [dis'figə] v entstellen. **disfigurement** n Entstellung f.

disgrace [dis'greis] n Schande f. v Schande bringen über. **disgraceful** adj schändlich.

disgruntled [dis'grʌntld] adj mürrisch.

disguise [dis'gaiz] v verkleiden; (voice) verstellen. n Verkleidung f. **in disguise** verkleidet.

disgust [dis'gʌust] n Ekel m (vor). v anekeln. **disgusting** adj ekelhaft, widerlich.

dish [diʃ] n Schüssel f, Schale f; (meal) Gericht neut. **dishes** pl Geschirr neut sing. **wash the dishes** abspülen. **dishcloth** n (for drying) Geschirrtuch neut; (for mopping) Lappen m.

dishearten [dis'haɪtn] v entmutigen.

dishevelled [di'ʃevəld] adj in Unordnung; (hair) zerzaust.

dishonest [dis'onist] adj unehrlich, unaufrichtig. **dishonesty** n Unehrlichkeit f. **dishonour** n Unehre f, Schande f. v schänden. **dishonourable** adj unehrenhaft.

dishwasher ['diʃˌwoʃə] n Geschirrspülmaschine f.

disillusion [disi'luːʒən] v ernüchtern, desillusionieren. **be disillusioned about** die Illusion verloren haben über.

disinfect [disin'fekt] v desinfizieren. **disinfectant** n Desinfektionsmittel *neut.*

disinherit [disin'herit] v enterben.

disintegrate [dis'inti̩greit] v (sich) auflösen, (sich) zersetzen. **disintegration** n Auflösung *f.*

disinterested [dis'intristid] *adj* unparteiisch.

disjointed [dis'dʒointid] *adj* unzusammenhängend.

disk *V* disc.

dislike [dis'laik] v nicht mögen. n Abneigung *f* (gegen).

dislocate ['dislə̩keit] v verrenken. **dislocation** n Verrenkung *f.*

dislodge [dis'lodʒ] v verschieben.

disloyal [dis'loiəl] *adj* untreu. **disloyalty** n Untreue *f.*

dismal ['dizməl] *adj* trübe, niederdrückend.

dismantle [dis'mantl] v abmontieren.

dismay [dis'mei] v bestürzen. n Bestürzung *f,* Angst *f.*

dismiss [dis'mis] v wegschicken; (*employee*) entlassen; (*idea*) ablehnen. **dismissal** n Entlassung *f.*

dismount [dis'maunt] v absteigen.

disobey [disə'bei] v nicht gehorchen (+ *dat*). **disobedience** n Ungehorsam *m.* **disobedient** *adj* ungehorsam.

disorder [dis'oːdə] n Unordnung *f;* (*med*) Störung *f.*

disorganized [dis'oːgənaizd] *adj* unordentlich.

disown [dis'oun] v ableugnen; (*child*) verstoßen.

disparage [di'sparidʒ] v herabsetzen. **disparaging** v geringschätzig.

disparity [dis'pariti] n Unterschied *m.*

dispassionate [dis'paʃənit] *adj* unparteiisch.

dispatch [di'spatʃ] v absenden; (*person*) entsenden. n Versand *m,* Abfertigung *f;* (*report*) Meldung *f.*

dispel [di'spel] v vertreiben.

dispense [di'spens] v ausgeben. **dispense with** verzichten auf. **dispenser** n Verteiler *m.* **dispensing chemist** Apotheker(in).

disperse [di'spəːs] v zerstreuen.

displace [dis'pleis] v versetzen; (*replace*) ersetzen; (*water*) verdrängen. **displacement** n (*naut*) Wasserverdrängung *f.*

display [di'splei] v zeigen; (*goods, etc.*) auslegen. n (*goods*) Auslage *f;* (*feelings*) Zurschaustellung *f;* (*parade*) Entfaltung *f.*

displease [dis'pliːz] v mißfallen (+ *dat*). **displeased** *adj* ärgerlich. **displeasure** n Mißfallen *neut.*

dispose [di'spouz] v **dispose of** (get rid of) beseitigen, wegwerfen; (have at disposal) verfügen über. **disposed** *adj* geneigt. **disposable** *adj* zum Wegwerfen; Einweg-. **disposal** n Beseitigung *f.* **have at one's disposal** zur Verfügung haben. **be at someone's disposal** jemandem zur Verfügung stehen. **disposition** n Natur *f,* Art *f.*

disproportion [disprə'poːʃən] n Mißverhältnis *neut.* **disproportionate** *adj* unverhältnismäßig.

disprove [dis'pruːv] v widerlegen.

dispute [di'spjuːt] v (*contest*) bestreiten; (*argue*) disputieren. n Streit *m.* **trade dispute** Arbeitsstreitigkeit *f.*

disqualify [dis'kwoli̩fai] v disqualifizieren, ausschließen. **disqualification** n Disqualifikation *f.*

disregard [disrə'gaːd] v nicht beachten.

disrepute [disrə'pjuːt] n Verruf *m.* **bring into disrepute** in Verruf bringen. **disreputable** *adj* (*notorious*) verrufen.

disrespect [disrə'spekt] n Respektlosigkeit *f.* **disrespectful** *adj* respektlos.

disrupt [dis'rʌpt] v stören, unterbrechen. **disruption** n Störung *f.*

dissatisfied [dis'satis̩faid] *adj* unzufrieden.

dissect [di'sekt] v sezieren.

dissent [di'sent] n abweichende Meinung *f.* v anderer Meinung sein.

dissident ['disidənt] n Dissident *m.*

dissimilar [di'similə] v unähnlich.

dissociate [di'sousieit] v **dissociate oneself from** sich lossagen von.

dissolve [di'zolv] v (sich) auflösen; (*meeting*) aufheben.

dissuade [di'sweid] v abraten (+ *dat*).

distance ['distəns] n Ferne *f,* Entfernung *f.* (*gap*) Abstand *m.* **in the distance** in der Ferne. **keep one's distance** Abstand halten. **distant** *adj* fern, entfernt.

distaste [dis'teist] n Abneigung *f.* **distasteful** *adj* unangenehm.

distended [di'stendid] *adj* ausgedehnt.

distil [di'stil] v destillieren. **distillery** n Brennerei *f.*

distinct [di'stiŋkt] *adj* (*different*) verschieden; (*clear*) deutlich, ausgeprägt. **distinction** *n* (*difference*) Unterschied *m*; (*merit*) Würde *f*. **of distinction** von Rang. **gain a distinction** sich auszeichnen. **distinctive** *adj* kennzeichnend.

distinguish [di'stiŋgwiʃ] *v* unterscheiden; (*perceive*) erkennen. **distinguish oneself** sich auszeichnen. **distinguishable** *adj* erkennbar. **distinguished** *adj* hervorragend.

distort [di'stɔːt] *v* verdrehen; (*truth*) entstellen. **distortion** *n* Verdrehung *f*.

distract [di'strakt] *v* ablenken. **distracted** *adj* verwirrt, außer sich. **distraction** *n* Ablenkung *f*; (*amusement*) Unterhaltung *f*; (*madness*) Wahnsinn *m*.

distraught [di'strɔːt] *adj* verwirrt, bestürzt.

distress [di'stres] *n* Not *f*; (*suffering*) Leid *neut*, Qual *f*. *v* betrüben, quälen. **distress signal** Notsignal *m*.

distribute [di'stribjut] *v* verteilen. **distribution** *n* Verteilung *f*. **distributor** *n* Verteiler *m*.

district ['distrikt] *n* Gebiet *neut*, Gegend *f*; (*of town*) Viertel *neut*; (*administrative*) Bezirk *m*. *adj* Bezirks-. **district attorney** Staatsanwalt *m*.

distrust [dis'trʌst] *v* mißtrauen (+*dat*). *n* Mißtrauen *neut*.

disturb [di'stəːb] *v* stören; (*worry*) beunruhigen. **disturbance** *n* Störung *f*. **disturbances** *pl* (*pol*) Unruhen *pl*. **disturbing** *adj* beunruhigend.

disused [dis'juːzd] *adj* außer Gebrauch.

ditch [ditʃ] *n* Wassergraben *m*. *v* (*coll*) im Stich lassen.

ditto ['ditou] *adv* ebenfalls, dito. **ditto mark** Wiederholungszeichen *neut*.

divan [di'van] *n* Divan *m*, Sofa *neut*.

dive [daiv] *v* tauchen; (*from board*) einen Kopfsprung machen; (*aero*) stürzen. *n* Tauchen *neut*; Kopfsprung *m*; (*aero*) Sturzflug *m*. **diver** *n* Taucher *m*.

diverge [dai'vəːdʒ] *v* auseinandergehen.

diverse [dai'vəːs] *adj* verschieden.

divert [dai'vəːt] *v* ableiten; (*traffic*) umleiten. **diversion** *n* Ablenkung *f*; (*mot*) Umleitung *f*. **diversity** *n* Verschiedenheit *f*.

divide [di'vaid] *v* (sich) teilen.

dividend ['dividend] *n* Dividende *f*.

divine [di'vain] *adj* göttlich. *v* erraten.

division [di'viʒən] *n* Teilung *f*; (*math, mil*) Division *f*; (*comm*) Abteilung *f*.

divorce [di'vɔːs] *n* (Ehe)Scheidung *f*. *v* scheiden. **divorced** *adj* geschieden. **get divorced** sich scheiden lassen. **divorcee** *n* Geschiedene(r).

divulge [dai'vʌldʒ] *v* preisgeben.

dizzy ['dizi] *adj* schwindlig. **dizziness** *n* Schwindel *m*.

*do [duː] *v* tun, machen. **that will do!** (*that's enough*) das genügt! **that won't do** (*that's no good*) das geht nicht! **How do you do?** Guten Tag! *I could do with the money* ich könnte das Geld gut gebrauchen. **do away with** abschaffen. **do in** (*coll*) umbringen. **do up** (*coll*) überholen. **do without** verzichten auf.

docile ['dousail] *adj* fügsam.

dock[1] [dok] *n* Dock *neut*. **docks** *pl* Hafenanlagen *pl*. *v* (*ship*) docken.

dock[2] [dok] *n* (*law*) **in the dock** auf der Anklagebank *f*.

dock[3] [dok] *v* (*cut*) stutzen; (*pay*) kürzen.

doctor ['doktə] *n* (*of medicine*) Arzt *m*, Ärztin *f*; (*as title*) Doktor *m*.

doctrine ['doktrin] *n* Lehre *f*.

document ['dokjumənt] *n* Urkunde *f*, Dokument *neut*. **documents** *pl* Papiere *pl*. *v* urkundlich belegen. **documentary** *adj* urkundlich. *n* Lehrfilm *m*.

dodge [dodʒ] *v* beiseitespringen; (*avoid*) ausweichen. *n* Knitt *m*.

dog [dog] *n* Hund *m*. **dog-eared** *adj* mit Eselsohren. **dogged** *adj* hartnäckig. **dog kennel** Hundehütte *f*.

dogma ['dogmə] *n* Dogma *neut*. **dogmatic** *adj* dogmatisch.

do-it-yourself [‚duːitjɔː'self] *adj* zum Selbermachen; Bastler-.

dole [doul] *n* Stempelgeld *neut*. **go on the dole** stempeln gehen. *v* **dole out** verteilen.

doll [dol] *n* Puppe *f*.

dollar ['dolə] *n* Dollar *m*.

dolphin ['dolfin] *n* Delphin *m*.

domain [də'mein] *n* Bereich *neut*.

dome [doum] *n* Kuppel *f*.

domestic [də'mestik] *adj* häuslich, Haus-; (*national*) inländisch, Innen-. **domestic animal** Haustier *neut*. **domesticate** *v* (*tame*) zähmen.

dominate ['domi‚neit] *v* beherrschen. **dominant** *adj* (vor)herrschend; (*music, biol*) dominant. **domination** *n* Herrschaft *f*.

domineering [domi'niəriŋ] *adj* herrisch.

dominion [dəˈminjən] *n* Herrschaft *f*; (*country*) Dominion *neut.*
domino [ˈdominou] *n* Dominostein *m.* **dominoes** *pl* Dominospiel *neut sing.*
don [don] *v* (*clothes*) anziehen; (*hat*) aufsetzen.
donate [dəˈneit] *v* stiften, spenden. **donation** *n* Spende *f*, Stiftung *f*. **donor** *n* Spender *m.*
done [dʌn] *V* do.
donkey [ˈdoŋki] *n* Esel *m.*
doom [duːm] *n* Verhängnis *neut.* **doomed** *adj* verloren.
door [doː] *n* Tür *f.* **out of doors** draußen. **doorbell** Türklingel *f.* **doorhandle** *n* Türgriff *m.* **doorway** *n* Türöffnung *f*; Torweg *m.*
dope [doup] *n* (*coll*) Rauschgift *neut. v* (*sport*) dopen.
dormant [ˈdoːmənt] *adj* schlafend.
dormitory [ˈdoːmitəri] *n* Schlafsaal *m.* (*US: student house*) Wohnheim *m.*
dormouse [ˈdoːmaus] *n* Haselmaus *f.*
dose [dous] *n* Dosis *f. v* dosieren.
dot [dot] *n* Punkt *m.*
dote [dout] *v* **dote on** vernarrt sein in.
dotted [ˈdotid] *adj* übersät (mit). **dotted line** punktierte Linie *f.*
double [ˈdʌbl] *adj* doppelt, Doppel-. *adv* doppelt, zweimal. *n* das Doppelte; (*film*) Double *neut.* **doubles** *n* (*sport*) Doppelspiel *neut. v* verdoppeln; (*fold*) falten. **double-barrelled** *adj* doppelläufig. **double-bass** Kontrabaß *m.* **double-cross** *v* betrügen. **double-decker** Doppeldecker *m.* **double meaning** Zweideutigkeit *f.*
doubt [daut] *n* Zweifel *m. v* bezweifeln. **doubt whether** zweifeln, ob. **doubtful** *adj* zweifelhaft. **doubtless** *adv* ohne Zweifel, zweifellos.
dough [dou] *n* Teig *m.* **doughnut** *n* Krapfen *m.*
dove [dʌv] *n* Taube *f.*
dowdy [ˈdaudi] *adj* schäbig, schlampig.
down[1] [daun] *adv* hinab, herab; hinunter, herunter; unten. *I went down the road* ich ging die Straße hinunter. **up and down** auf und ab.
down[2] [daun] *n* (*feathers*) Daunen *pl.*
downcast [ˈdaunˌkaist] *adj* niedergeschlagen.
downfall [ˈdaunˌfoːl] *n* Sturz *m.*
downhearted [ˌdaunˈhaitid] *adj* mutlos.
downhill [ˌdaunˈhil] *adv* bergab.

downpour [ˈdaunˌpoː] *n* Wolkenbruch *m.*
downright [ˈdaunˌrait] *adv* völlig, höchst.
downstairs [ˌdaunˈsteəz] *adv* unten. *she came downstairs* sie kam nach unten.
downstream [ˌdaunˈstriːm] *adv* stromabwärts.
downtrodden [ˈdaunˌtrodn] *adj* unterworfen.
downward [ˈdaunwəd] *adj* Abwärts-, sinkend.
downwards [ˈdaunwədz] *adv* abwärts.
dowry [ˈdauəri] *n* Mitgift *f.*
doze [douz] *v* dösen. *n* Schläfchen *neut.*
dozen [ˈdʌzn] *n* Dutzend *neut.*
drab [drab] *adj* eintönig, farblos.
draft [draift] *n* (*plan*) Konzept *neut*, Entwurf *m*; (*comm*) Tratte *f*; (*mil*) Aushebung *f. v* entwerfen; (*mil*) ausheben.
drag [drag] *v* schleppen, schleifen. *n* **drag on** sich in die Länge ziehen.
dragon [ˈdragən] *n* Drache *m.* **dragonfly** *n* Libelle *f.*
drain [drein] *n* Abfluß *m*; (*fig*) Belastung *f. v* ablassen; (*water*) ableiten; (*fig*) erschöpfen. **drainage** *n* Entwässerung *f.* **drainpipe** *n* Abflußrohr *neut.*
drama [ˈdraimə] *n* Drama *neut.* **dramatic** *adj* dramatisch. **dramatize** *v* dramatisieren.
drank [draŋk] *V* drink.
drape [dreip] *v* drapieren. *n* (*curtain*) Vorhang *m.* **draper** *n* Tuchhändler *m.*
drastic [ˈdrastik] *adj* drastisch.
draught *or US* **draft** [draift] *n* Zug *m*; (*naut*) Tiefgang *m.* **draughts** *n* Damespiel *neut.* **draught beer** Bier vom Faß. **draughtsman** *n* Zeichner *m.* **draughty** *adj* zugig.
*draw [droː] *v* ziehen; (*curtain*) zuziehen; (*picture*) zeichnen; (*money*) abheben; (*public*) anziehen; (*water*) schöpfen; (*sport*) unentschieden spielen. *n* (*lottery*) Ziehung *f*; (*sport*) Unentschieden *neut.* **draw near** sich nähern. **draw up** (*document*) ausstellen. **drawback** *n* Nachteil *m.* **drawbridge** *n* Zugbrücke *f.* **drawer** *n* Schublade *f.* **drawing** *n* Zeichnung *f.* **drawing pin** *n* Heftzwecke *f.* **drawing room** Salon *m.*
drawl [droːl] *v* schleppend sprechen.
drawn [droːn] *V* draw.
dread [dred] *n* Furcht *f*, Angst *f. v* Angst haben vor. **dreadful** *adj* furchtbar.

*dream [driːm] *n* Traum *m. v* träumen.
dreamer *n* Träumer *n* **dreamy** *adj*
träumerisch.
dreamt [dremt] *V* **dream**.
dreary ['driəri] *adj* trübe, düster.
dredge [dredʒ] *v* (*river*) ausbaggern.
dredger *n* Bagger *m*.
dregs [dregz] *pl n* Bodensatz *m sing*; (*fig*)
Abschaum *m sing*.
drench [drentʃ] *v* durchnässen.
dress [dres] *v* (sich) anziehen; (*wound*)
verbinden. *n* (*clothes*) Kleidung *f*; (*woman's*) Kleid *neut*. **dress designer**
Modezeichner *m*. **dresser** *n* (*furniture*)
Küchenschrank *m*. **dressing** *n* (*salad*)
Soße *f*; (*med*) Verband *m*. **dressing gown**
Morgenrock *m*. **dressing room** (*theatre*)
Garderobe *f*. **dressing table** Toiletten-
tisch *m*. **dressmaking** *n* Damenschneide-
rei *f*. **dress suit** Gesellschaftsanzug *m*.
drew [druː] *V* **draw**.
dribble ['dribl] *v* tröpfeln; (*football*) drib-
beln. *n* Tröpfeln *neut*.
drier ['draiə] *n* Trockner *m*.
drift [drift] *v* treiben; (*coll*) sich treiben
lassen. *n* (*snow*) Verwehung *f*; (*tendency*)
Tendenz *f*. **drifter** *n* (*person*) Vagabund
m.
drill [dril] *n* Bohrmaschine *f*; (*training*)
Drill *m. v* (*holes*) bohren; (*train*) trainier-
en, drillen.
*drink [driŋk] *v* trinken; (*animal, coll*)
saufen. *n* Getränk *neut*; (*cocktail, etc.*)
Drink *m*. **drinker** *n* Trinker *m* (*coll*)
Säufer *m*.
drip [drip] *v* tropfen, triefen. *n* Tropfen *m*.
drip-dry *adj* bügelfrei. **dripping** *adj*
triefend. *n* Schmalz *neut*.
*drive [draiv] *v* treiben; (*vehicle*) fahren.
n Fahrt *f*; (*tech*) Antrieb *m*; (*mil*)
Kampagne *f*. **drive mad** verrückt
machen. **drive-in** (**cinema**) Autokino
neut.
drivel ['drivl] *v* sabbern, geifern. *n*
Quatsch *m*.
driver ['draivə] *n* Fahrer *m*, Chauffeur *m*.
driver's license Führerschein *m*.
driving ['draiviŋ] *adj* Treib-; (*mot*) Fahr-;
(*rain*) heftig. *n* Fahren *neut*. **driving lessons** Fahrunterricht *m*. **driving licence**
Führerschein *m*. **driving school** Fahr-
schule *f*. **driving test** Fahrprüfung *f*.
drizzle ['drizl] *n* Sprühregen *m. v* nieseln.
drone [droun] *v* summen. *n* Drohne *f*.

droop [druːp] *v* (*schlaff*) herunterhängen;
(*flower*) welken.
drop [drop] *n* (*of water*) Tropfen *m*; (*fall*)
Fall, Sturz *m. v* (*fall*) fallen; (*let fall*)
fallen lassen; (*passenger*) absetzen;
(*bomb*) abwerfen. **drop in** vorbeikommen.
drop off (**to sleep**) einschlafen. **drop-out** *n*
Dropout *m*.
drought [draut] *n* Dürre *f*.
drove [drouv] *V* **drive**.
drown [draun] *v* ertrinken. **drown out**
übertönen.
drowsy ['drauzi] *adj* schläfrig.
drudge [drʌdʒ] *n* Packesel *m*. **drudgery** *n*
Plackerei *f*.
drug [drʌg] *n* (*medicinal*) Droge *f*; (*narcotic*) Rauschgift *neut. v* betäuben. **drug
addict** Rauschgiftsüchtige(r).
drum [drʌm] *n* Trommel *f. v* trommeln.
drummer *n* Trommler *m*. **drumstick** *n*
Trommelstock *m*.
drunk [drʌŋk] *V* **drink**. *adj* betrunken;
(*coll*) besoffen. *n* Betrunkene(r). **get
drunk** sich betrinken; (*coll*) besoffen werden. **drunken** *adj* betrunken. **drunkard** *n*
Trinker *m*; (*coll*) Säufer *m*. **drunkenness** *n*
Betrunkenheit *f*.
dry [drai] *adj* trocken; (*wine*) herb. *v*
trocknen. **dry up** austrocknen; (*dishes*)
abtrocknen. **dry-clean** chemisch reinigen.
dry cleaner chemische Reinigung *f*. **dry
dock** Trockendock *neut*. **dry land** fester
Boden *m*.
dual ['djuəl] *adj* doppelt. **dual-purpose** *adj*
Mehrzweck-.
dubbed ['dʌbd] *adj* (*film*) synchronisiert.
dubious ['djuːbiəs] *adj* zweifelhaft, dubi-
ös.
duchess ['dʌtʃis] *n* Herzogin *f*.
duck[1] [dʌk] *n* Ente *f*.
duck[2] [dʌk] *v* sich ducken; (*under water*)
untertauchen.
duct [dʌkt] *n* Kanal *m*.
dud [dʌd] *adj* wertlos. *n* Niete *f*, Versager
m.
due [djuː] *adj* (*suitable*) gebührend; (*payment*) fällig. *the train is due at 7 o'clock*
der Zug soll (planmäßig) um 7 Uhr
ankommen. *adv due east* genau nach
Osten. **due to** infolge (+*gen*). **in due
course** zur rechten Zeit. *I am due to* ich
muß.
duel ['djuəl] *n* Duell *neut*.
duet [dju'et] *n* Duett *neut*.

dug [dʌg] V **dig.**
duke [djuːk] n Herzog m.
dull [dʌl] adj (colour) matt, düster; (pain)
dumpf; (boring) langweilig, uninteressant; (stupid) dumm. **dullness** n Düs-
terkeit f, Trübe f. v abstumpfen.
duly ['djuːli] adv gebührend, ordnungsgemäß.
dumb [dʌm] adj stumm; (coll: stupid)
doof. **deaf and dumb** taubstumm. **dumbfound** v verblüffen.
dummy ['dʌmi] n (baby's) Schnuller m;
(tailor's) Schneiderpuppe f; (imitation)
Attrappe f.
dump [dʌmp] n Müllhaufen m, Müllkippe
f. v abladen.
dumpling ['dʌmpliŋ] n Knödel m, Kloß
m.
dunce [dʌns] n Dummkopf m.
dune [djuːn] n Düne f.
dung [dʌŋ] n Mist m.
dungeon ['dʌndʒən] n Kerker m.
duplicate ['djuːplikət; v 'djuːplikeit] n
Duplikat neut. v verdoppeln; (make cop-
ies) vervielfältigen, kopieren. adj doppelt. **duplication** n Verdoppelung f. **dupli-
cator** n Vervielfältigungsmaschine f.
durable ['djuərəbl] adj dauerhaft.
duration [djuˈreifən] n Dauer f.
during ['djuəriŋ] prep während (+gen).
dusk [dʌsk] n (Abend)Dämmerung f.
dusky adj düster.
dust [dʌst] n Staub m. v abstauben.
dustbin n Mülleimer m. **dustcart** n
Müllwagen m. **duster** n Staubtuch neut.
dustman n Müllabfuhrmann m. **dusty** adj
staubig.
duty ['djuːti] n Pflicht f; (task) Aufgabe f;
(tax) Zoll m, Abgabe f. **off/on duty**
außer/im Dienst. **duty-free** adj zollfrei.
dutiful adj pflichtbewußt.
Dutch [dʌtʃ] adj holländisch. **Dutchman** n
Holländer m. **Dutchwoman** n Holländer-
in f.
duvet ['duːvei] n Federbett neut.
dwarf [dwɔːf] n Zwerg m. adj
zwergenhaft.
***dwell** [dwel] n wohnen. **dwell on** bleiben
bei. **dwelling** n Wohnung f.
dwelt [dwelt] V **dwell.**
dwindle ['dwindl] v abnehmen.
dye [dai] n Farbstoff m. v färben.
dyke [daik] n Deich m, Damm m.
dynamic [daiˈnamik] adj dynamisch.
dynamics n Dynamik f.

dynamite ['dainəˌmait] n Dynamit neut.
dynamo ['dainəˌmou] n Dynamo n.
dynasty ['dinəsti] n Dynastie f.
dysentery ['disəntri] n Ruhr f.
dyslexia [dis'leksiə] n Legasthenie f,
Wortblindheit f.
dyspepsia [dis'pepsiə] n Verdauungsstörung f.

E

each [iːtʃ] adj, pron jeder, jede, jedes. adv
je. **each other** einander, sich.
eager ['iːgə] adj eifrig. **eagerness** Eifer m.
eagle ['iːgl] n Adler m.
ear[1] [iə] n (anat) Ohr neut; (hearing)
Gehör neut. **earache** n Ohrenschmerzen
pl. **eardrum** n Trommelfell neut. **earlobe**
n Ohrläppchen neut. **earring** n Ohrring
m. **earshot** n **within/out of earshot**
in/außer Hörweite.
ear[2] [iə] n (of corn) Ähre f.
earl [əːl] n Graf m.
early ['əːli] adj, adv früh; (soon) bald.
earn [əːn] v verdienen. **earnings** pl n
Einkommen neut sing.
earnest ['əːnist] adj ernsthaft. n **in earnest**
im Ernst.
earth [əːθ] n Erde f. v (elec) erden. **earthly**
adj irdisch. **earthenware** n Steingut neut.
earthquake n Erdbeben neut. **earthworm**
n Regenwurm m.
earwig ['iəwig] n Ohrwurm m.
ease [iːz] n Leichtigkeit f; (comfort)
Behagen neut. v erleichtern. **at ease**
behaglich. **with ease** ohne Mühe.
easel ['iːzl] n Staffelei f.
east [iːst] n Osten m. adj also **easterly**
östlich, Ost-. adv also **eastwards** nach
Osten; ostwärts. **eastern** adj östlich;
orientalisch.
Easter ['iːstə] n Ostern neut.
easy ['iːzi] adj leicht. **easily** adv leicht,
mühelos; (by far) bei weitem. **easy-going**
adj ungezwungen.
***eat** [iːt] v essen; (of animals) fressen.
eaten ['iːtn] V **eat.**
eavesdrop ['iːvzdrop] v lauschen.
ebb [eb] n Ebbe f; (fig) Tiefstand m. v
verebben.

ebony ['ebəni] *n* Ebenholz *neut.*

eccentric [ik'sentrik] *adj* exzentrisch. *n* Sonderling *m.*

ecclesiastical [iklizzi'astikl] *adj* kirchlich.

echo ['ekou] *n* Echo *neut. v* widerhallen.

eclipse [i'klips] *n* Finsternis *f. v* verfinstern; (*fig*) in den Schatten stellen.

ecology [i'kolədʒi] *n* Ökologie *f.* **ecological** *adj* ökologisch.

economy [i'konəmi] *n* Wirtschaft *f*; (*thrift*) Sparsamkeit *f.* **economic** *adj* ökonomisch, wirtschaftlich, Wirtschafts-. **economical** *adj* sparsam, wirtschaftlich. **economics** *n* Volkswirtschaft *f.* **economist** *n* Volkswirtschaftler *m.* **economize** *v* sparen (an).

ecstasy ['ekstəsi] *n* Ekstase *f.* **ecstatic** *adj* ekstatisch.

eczema ['eksimə] *n* Ekzem *neut.*

edge [edʒ] *n* Rand *m.* **on edge** nervös.

edible ['edəbl] *adj* eßbar.

edit ['edit] *v* redigieren. **edition** *n* Ausgabe *f.* **editor** *n* Redakteur *m.*

editorial [,edi'toɪriəl] *adj* Redaktions-. *n* Leitartikel *m.*

educate ['edju,keit] *n* erziehen, ausbilden. **education** *n* Bildung *f*, Erziehung *f*; (*system*) Schulwesen *neut.* **educational** *adj* pädagogisch.

eel [iːl] *n* Aal *m.*

eerie ['iəri] *adj* unheimlich.

effect [i'fekt] *n* Wirkung *f*; (*impression*) Eindruck *m.* **have an effect on** wirken auf. **in effect** in Wirklichkeit. **effective** *adj* wirksam. **effectiveness** *n* Wirksamkeit *f.*

effeminate [i'feminət] *adj* weibisch.

effervesce [efə'ves] *v* sprudeln. **effervescent** *adj* sprudelnd.

efficiency [i'fiʃənsi] *n* Leistungsfähigkeit *f.* **efficient** *adj* (*person*) tüchtig; (*effective*) wirksam; (*machine*) leistungsfähig.

effigy ['efidʒi] *n* Abbild *neut.*

effort ['efət] *n* Anstrengung *f*, Mühe *f.* **make an effort** sich anstrengen. **make every effort** sich alle Mühe geben. **effortless** *adj* mühelos.

egg [eg] *n* Ei *neut. v* **egg on** reizen. **boiled egg** gekochtes Ei *neut.* **fried egg** Spiegelei *neut.* **scrambled egg** Rührei *neut.* **egg cup** Eierbecher *m.* **eggshell** *n* Eierschale *f.*

ego ['iːgou] *pron* Ich *neut.* **egoism** *n* Egoismus *m.* **egoist** *n* Egoist *m.*

Egypt ['iːdʒipt] *n* Ägypten *neut.* **Egyptian** *adj* ägyptisch; *n* Ägypter(in).

eiderdown ['aidədaun] *n* Federbett *neut.*

eight [eit] *adj* acht. *n* Acht *f.* **eighth** *adj* acht; *n* Achtel *neut.*

eighteen [ei'tiːn] *adj* achtzehn. **eighteenth** *adj* achtzehnt.

eighty ['eiti] *adj* achtzig. **eightieth** *adj* achtzigst.

either ['aiðə] *pron* einer (eine, eines) von beiden. **on either side** auf beiden Seiten. **either ... or ...** entweder ... oder ....

ejaculate [i'dʒakjuleit] *v* (*utter*) ausstoßen; ejakulieren.

eject [i'dʒekt] *v* ausstoßen.

eke [iːk] *v* **eke out** (*add to*) ergänzen.

elaborate [i'labərət; *v* i'labəreit] *adj* ausführlich, genau ausgearbeitet. *v* **elaborate on** eingehend erörtern. **elaboration** *n* Ausarbeitung *f.*

elapse [i'laps] *v* vergehen.

elastic [i'lastik] *adj* elastisch. **elastic band** Gummiband *neut.*

elated [i'leitid] *adj* begeistert, froh.

elbow ['elbou] *n* Ellbogen *m.*

elder[1] ['eldə] *adj* älter. *n* Ältere(r).

elder[2] ['eldə] *n* (*tree*) Holunder *m.*

elderly ['eldəli] *adj* älter.

eldest ['eldist] *adj* ältest. *n* Älteste(r).

elect [i'lekt] *v* wählen. **election** *n* Wahl *f.* **elector** *n* Wähler *m.* **electorate** *n* Wählerschaft *f.*

electric [ə'lektrik] *adj also* **electrical** elektrisch. **electrical engineering** Elektrotechnik *f.* **electric blanket** Heizdecke *f.* **electric chair** elektrischer Stuhl *m.* **electric cooker** Elektroherd *neut.* **electrician** *n* Elektriker *m.* **electricity** *n* Strom *m*, Elektrizität *f.*

electrify [ə'lektrifai] *v* elektrifizieren. **electrifying** *adj* (*fig*) elektrisierend.

electronic [elək'tronik] *n* elektronisch. **electronics** *n* Elektronik *f sing.*

elegant ['eligənt] *adj* elegant.

element ['eləmənt] *n* Element *neut.* **elementary** *adj* elementar.

elephant ['elifənt] *n* Elefant *m.*

elevate ['eliveit] *v* heben; (*promote*) erheben. **elevation** *n* Hochheben *neut*; (*promotion*) Erhebung *f.* **elevator** *n* Aufzug *m.*

eleven [i'levn] *adj* elf. **eleventh** *adj* elft.

eligible ['elidʒəbl] *adj* wählbar. **be eligible** in Frage kommen. **be eligible for** berechtigt sein zu. **eligibility** *n* Eignung *f.*

eliminate [i'limineit] *n* beseitigen; (*sport*) ausscheiden. **elimination** *n* Beseitigung *f*; Ausscheidung *f*.
élite [ei'liːt] *n* Elite *f*.
ellipse [i'lips] *n* Ellipse *f*. **elliptical** *adj* elliptisch.
elm [elm] *n* Ulme *f*.
elocution [elə'kjuːʃən] *n* Sprechkunde *f*.
elope [i'loup] *v* entlaufen. **elopement** *n* Entlaufen *neut*.
eloquent ['eləkwənt] *adj* (*person*) redegewandt. **eloquence** *n* Redegewandtheit *f*.
else [els] *adv* sonst. **anyone else?** sonst noch jemand? **someone else** jemand anders. **nothing else** nichts weiter. **elsewhere** *adv* anderswo, woanders.
elucidate [i'luːsideit] *v* aufklären. **elucidation** *n* Aufklärung *f*.
elude [i'luːd] *v* entgehen (*dat*).
emaciated [i'meisieitid] *adj* abgemagert.
emanate ['eməneit] *v* ausströmen (aus); (*fig*) herstammen (von).
emancipate [i'mansipeit] *v* befreien, emanzipieren. **emancipated** *adj* emanzipiert. **emancipation** *n* Befreiung *f*.
embalm [im'baːm] *v* einbalsamieren.
embankment [im'baŋkmənt] *n* Damm *m*; (*road*) Uferstraße *f*.
embargo [im'baːgou] *n* Handelssperre *f*.
embark [im'baːk] *v* sich einschiffen (nach); (*fig*) sich einlassen (in).
embarrass [im'barəs] *v* in Verlegenheit bringen. **be embarrassed** verlegen sein. **embarrassment** *n* Verlegenheit *f*.
embassy ['embəsi] *n* Botschaft *f*.
embellish [im'beliʃ] *v* verzieren.
embers 'embəz] *pl n* Glut *f sing*.
embezzle [im'bezl] *v* unterschlagen. **embezzlement** *n* Unterschlagung *f*.
embitter [im'bitə] *v* verbittern.
emblem ['embləm] *n* Sinnbild *neut*.
embody [im'bodi] *v* verkörpern. **embodiment** *n* Verkörperung *f*.
embossed [im'bost] *adj* erhaben.
embrace [im'breis] *v* umarmen; (*include*) umfassen. *n* Umarmung *f*.
embroider [im'broidə] *v* (be)sticken; (*story*) ausschmücken. **embroidery** *n* Stickerei *f*.
embryo ['embriou] *n* Embryo *m*.
emerald ['emərəld] *n* Smaragd *m*. **emerald green** smaragdgrün.
emerge [i'məːdʒ] *v* (*from water*) auftauchen; (*appear*) hervorkommen. **emergence** *n* Auftauchen *neut*.

emergency [i'məːdʒənsi] *n* Notfall *m*, *adj* Not-. **emergency exit** Notausgang *m*.
emigrate ['emigreit] *v* auswandern. **emigration** *n* Auswanderung *f*. **emigrant** *n* Auswanderer *m*.
eminent ['eminənt] *adj* hervorragend, erhaben. **eminence** *n* Erhöhung *f*.
emit [i'mit] *v* von sich geben. **emission** *n* Ausstrahlung *f*.
emotion [i'mouʃən] *n* Gefühl *neut*. **emotional** *adj* Gefühls-; (*excitable*) erregbar; (*full of feeling*) gefühlvoll.
empathy ['empəθi] *n* Einfühlung *f*.
emperor ['empərə] *n* Kaiser *m*.
emphasis ['emfəsis] *n* (*pl -ses*) Nachdruck *m*. **emphasize** *v* betonen, unterstreiken. **emphatic** *adj* nachdrücklich.
empire ['empaiə] *n* Reich *neut*.
empirical [im'pirikəl] *adj* empirisch.
employ [im'ploi] *v* (*use*) verwenden; (*appoint*) anstellen. **be employed** beschäftigt *or* tätig sein. **employee** *n* Angestellte(r); (*as opposed to employer*) Arbeitnehmer *m*. **employer** *n* Arbeitgeber *m*. **employment** *n* Arbeit *f*, Beschäftigung *f*.
empower [im'pauə] *v* ermächtigen.
empress ['empris] *n* Kaiserin *f*.
empty ['empti] *adj* leer. *v* leeren. **emptiness** *n* Leere *f*.
emulate ['emjuleit] *v* nacheifern (*dat*).
emulsion [i'mʌlʃən] *n* Emulsion *f*. **emulsify** *v* emulgieren.
enable [i'neibl] *v* ermöglichen.
enact [i'nakt] *v* verordnen; (*law*) erlassen.
enamel [i'naməl] *n* Emaille *f*; (*teeth*) Zahnschmelz *m*. *v* emaillieren.
enamour [i'namə] *v* **be enamoured of** verliebt sein in.
encase [in'keis] *v* umschließen.
enchant [in'tʃaint] *v* entzücken. **enchanting** *adj* entzückend. **enchantment** *n* Zauber *m*, Entzücken *neut*.
encircle [in'səːkl] *v* umringen.
enclose [in'klouz] *v* einschließen; (*in letter*) beifügen. **enclosed** *adj* (*in letter*) beigefügt. **enclosure** *n* Einzäunung *f*; (*in letter*) Anlage *f*.
encore ['oŋkoi] *interj* noch einmal! *n* Zugabe *f*.
encounter [in'kauntə] *v* treffen; (*difficulties*) stoßen auf. *n* Begegnung *f*; (*mil*) Gefecht *neut*.
encourage [in'kʌridʒ] *v* ermutigen; (*promote*) fördern. **encouragement** *n* Ermutigung *f*.

encroach [in'krout∫] v eindringen (in). **encroachment** n Eingriff m.

encyclopedia [insaiklə'piːdiə] n Enzyklopädie f.

end [end] n Ende neut; (finish) Schluß m; (purpose) Zweck m. v beend(ig)en; (come to an end) zu Ende gehen. **ending** n Ende neut. **endless** adj unendlich.

endanger [in'deindʒə] v gefährden.

endeavour [in'devə] v sich anstrengen, versuchen. n Versuch m, Bestrebung f.

endemic [en'demik] adj endemisch.

endive ['endiv] n Endivie f.

endorse [in'doːs] v indossieren; (approve of) billigen. **endorsement** n Vermerk m; Billigung f.

endow [in'dau] v stiften. **endowed with** begabt mit. **endowment** n Ausstattung f, Stiftung f.

endure [in'djuə] v ertragen. **enduring** adj beständig.

enemy ['enəmi] n Feind m. adj Feind-.

energy ['enədʒi] n Energie f. **energetic** adj energisch.

enforce [in'foːs] v durchsetzen. **enforcement** n Durchsetzung f.

engage [in'geidʒ] v (employ) anstellen; (tech) einschalten; (enemy) angreifen. **engaged** adj (to be married) verlobt; (occupied) besetzt. **get engaged** sich verloben. **engagement** n (to marry) Verlobung f; (appointment) Verabredung f.

engine ['endʒin] n Motor m; (rail) Lokomotive f. **engine driver** Lokomotivführer m.

engineer [endʒi'niə] n Ingenieur m. v (fig) organisieren. **engineering** n Technik f.

England ['iŋglənd] n England neut.

English ['iŋgliʃ] adj englisch. **(the) English (language)** (das) Englisch(e), die englische Sprache. I am English ich bin Engländer(in). **English Channel** Ärmelkanal m. **Englishman** n Engländer m. **Englishwoman** n Engländerin f.

engrave [in'greiv] v gravieren. **engraving** n Stich m.

engrossed [in'groust] adj vertieft.

engulf [in'gʌlf] v (overcome) überwältigen.

enhance [in'hɑːns] v verstärken.

enigma [i'nigmə] n Rätsel neut. **enigmatic** adj rätselhaft.

enjoy [in'dʒoi] v genießen, Freude haben an. **enjoy oneself** sich (gut) unterhalten.

enjoyment n Freude f. **enjoy yourself!** viel spaß/Vergnügen!

enlarge [in'lɑːdʒ] v (sich) vergrößern. **enlargement** n Vergrößerung f.

enlighten [in'laitn] v aufklären. **enlightened** adj aufgeklärt. **enlightenment** n Aufklärung f.

enlist [in'list] v (help) in Anspruch nehmen; (in army) sich melden.

enmity ['enməti] n Feindseligkeit f.

enormous [i'noːməs] adj riesig, ungeheuer.

enough [i'nʌf] adv genug. **be enough** genügen. **have enough of something** (be tired of) etwas satt haben.

enquire [in'kwaiə] adv sich erkundigen, fragen. **enquiry** n Nachfrage f.

enrage [in'reidʒ] v wütend machen. **enraged** adj wütend.

enrich [in'ritʃ] v bereichern.

enrol [in'roul] v einschreiben; (in club) als Mitglied aufnehmen; (oneself) beitreten (dat). **enrolment** n Aufnahme f.

ensign ['ensain] n (naut) (Schiffs)Flagge f.

enslave [in'sleiv] v versklaven.

ensue [in'sjuː] v (darauf) folgen. **ensuing** adj darauffolgend.

ensure [in'ʃuə] v gewährleisten, sichern.

entail [in'teil] v mit sich bringen.

entangle [in'taŋgl] v verstricken. **entangled** adj verstrickt.

enter ['entə] v (go in) eintreten; (a room) hineintreten in; (in book) einschreiben; (sport) sich anmelden.

enterprise ['entə,praiz] n (concern) Unternehmen neut; (initiative) Initiative f. **private enterprise** freie Wirtschaft f. **enterprising** adj unternehmungslustig.

entertain [entə'tein] v (amuse) unterhalten; (feelings) hegen; (as guests) gastlich bewirten. **entertaining** adj unterhaltsam. **entertainment** n Unterhaltung f.

enthral [in'θroːl] v entzücken. **enthralling** adj entzückend.

enthusiasm [in'θuːzi,azəm] n Begeisterung f, Enthusiasmus m. **enthusiastic** adj begeistert, enthusiastisch.

entice [in'tais] v verlocken. **enticement** n Anreiz m. **enticing** adj verlockend.

entire [in'taiə] adj ganz. **entirely** adv ganz, völlig, durchaus. **entirety** n Gesamtheit f.

entitle [in'taitl] v berechtigen (zu).

entity ['entəti] n Wesen neut.

entrails ['entreilz] *pl n* Eingeweide *pl.*

entrance¹ ['entrəns] *n* (*going in, fee*) Eintritt *m*; (*way in*) Eingang *m.*

entrance² [in'trains] *v* entzücken.

entrant ['entrənt] *n* (*sport*) Teilnehmer(in); (*for exam*) Kandidat *m.*

entreat [in'tri:t] *v* ernstlich bitten. **entreaty** *n* Bitte *f.*

entrenched [in'trentʃt] *v* **become entrenched** sich festsetzen.

entrepreneur [ˌɒntrəprə'nəː], *n* Unternehmer *m.*

entrust [in'trʌst] *v* (*thing*) anvertrauen (*dat*); (*person*) betrauen (mit).

entry ['entri] *n* Eintritt *m*; (*into country*) Einreise *f*; (*comm*) Posten *m*; (*theatre*) Auftritt *m.* **no entry** Eintritt verboten.

entwine [in'twain] *v* umwinden.

enunciate [i'nʌnsiˌeit] *v* aussagen; (*state*) ausdrücken.

envelop [in'veləp] *v* einwickeln; (*fig*) umhüllen.

envelope ['envəˌloup] *n* Umschlag *m.*

enviable ['enviəbl] *adj* beneidenswert.

envious ['enviəs] *adj* neidisch (*of* auf). **be envious of** beneiden.

environment [in'vaiərənmənt] *n* Umgebung *f*. **the environment** Umwelt *f*. **environmental** *adj* Umwelt-.

envisage [in'vizidʒ] *v* sich vorstellen.

envoy ['envɔi] *n* Bote *m.*

envy ['envi] *v* beneiden. *n* Neid *m.*

enzyme ['enzaim] *n* Enzym *neut.*

epaulet ['epəlet] *n* Epaulette *f.*

ephemeral [i'femərəl] *adj* vergänglich.

epic ['epik] *adj* (*poetry*) episch; heldenhaft. *n* Heldengedicht *neut.*

epicure ['epikjuə] *n* Feinschmecker *m.*

epidemic [epi'demik] *n* Epidemie *f. adj* epidemisch.

epilepsy ['epilepsi] *n* Epilepsie *f*. **epileptic** *adj* epileptisch; *n* Epileptiker(in).

epilogue ['epilog] *n* Epilog *m.*

Epiphany [i'pifəni] *n* Epiphanias *neut.*

episcopal [i'piskəpəl] *adj* bischöflich.

episode ['episoud] *n* Episode *f.*

epitaph ['epiˌtaːf] *n* Grabschrift *f.*

epitome [i'pitəmi] *n* Inbegriff *m.*

epoch ['iːpok] *n* Epoche *f.*

equable ['ekwəbl] *adj* (*person*) gelassen.

equal ['iːkwəl] *adj* gleich (+ *dat*). **be equal to** gleichen (+ *dat*); (*be able*) gewachsen sein (+ *dat*). **equal in size** von gleicher Größe. *n* Gleichgestellte(r). *v* gleichen (+ *dat*), gleich sein (+ *dat*). **equality** *n* Gleichheit *f*; (*pol*) Gleichberechtigung *f.*

equalize *v* gleichmachen. **equally** *adv* ebenso, in gleichem Maße.

equanimity [ekwə'nimiti] *n* Gleichmut *m.*

equate [i'kweit] *v* gleichstellen. **equation** *n* Gleichung *f.*

equator [i'kweitə] *n* Äquator *m.* **equatorial** *adj* äquatorial.

equestrian [i'kwestriən] *adj* Reit-, Reiter-.

equilateral [ˌiːkwi'latərəl] *adj* gleichseitig.

equilibrium [ˌiːkwi'libriəm] *n* Gleichgewicht *neut.*

equinox ['ekwinoks] *n* Tagundnachtgleiche *f.*

equip [i'kwip] *v* ausrüsten, ausstatten. **equipment** *n* Ausrüstung *f*, Einrichtung *f.*

equity ['ekwəti] *n* Billigkeit *f*; (*law*) Billigkeitsrecht *f.*

equivalent [i'kwivələnt] *adj* gleichwertig. **be equivalent to** gleichkommen (*dat*). *n* Gegenstück *neut.*

era ['iərə] *n* Epoche *f*, Ära *f.*

eradicate [i'radiˌkeit] *v* ausrotten. **eradication** *n* Ausrottung *f.*

erase [i'reiz] *v* ausradieren, tilgen. **eraser** *n* Radiergummi *m.*

erect [i'rekt] *v* errichten. *adj* aufrecht. **erection** *n* Errichtung *f*; (*anat*) Erektion *f.*

ermine ['əːmin] *n* Hermelin *m.*

erode [i'roud] *v* zerfressen. **erosion** *n* Zerfressung *f.*

erotic [i'rotik] *adj* erotisch. **eroticism** *n* Erotik *f.*

err [əː] *v* sich irren.

errand ['erənd] *n* (Boten)Gang *m.*

erratic [i'ratik] *adj* unberechenbar.

error ['erə] *n* Fehler *m*, Irrtum *m*; (*of compass*) Abweichung *f*; (*oversight*) Versehen *neut.* **erroneous** *adj* irrtümlich.

erudite ['erudait] *adj* gelehrt.

erupt [i'rupt] *v* (*volcano*) ausbrechen. **eruption** *n* Ausbruch *m*; (*skin*) Hautausschlag *m.*

escalate ['eskəleit] *v* (*a war*) steigern, eskalieren. **escalation** *n* Eskalation *f.*

escalator *n* Rolltreppe *f.*

escalope ['eskəlop] *n* Schnitzel *neut.*

escape [is'keip] *v* entkommen (+ *dat*); (*fig*) entgehen (+ *dat*). *n* Flucht *f*; (*of liquid*) Ausfluß *m.* **have a narrow escape** mit knapper Not entkommen.

escort [i'skɔːt; *n* 'eskɔːt] *v* begleiten. *n* (*mil*) Eskorte *f.*

esoteric [esə'terik] *adj* esoterisch.
especial [i'speʃəl] *adj* besonder, speziell.
especially *adv* besonders.
espionage ['espiə,naɾʒ] *n* Spionage *f*.
esplanade [,esplə'neid] *n* Esplanade *f*.
essay ['esei] *n* (*school*) Aufsatz *m*; (*literary*) Essay *m*.
essence ['esns] *n* Wesen *neut*; (*extract*) Essenz *f*.
essential [i'senʃəl] *adj* wesentlich; (*indispensable*) untentbehrlich, unbedingt notwendig. **essentially** *adv* im wesentlichen.
establish [i'stabliʃ] *v* einrichten, aufstellen; (*a fact*) feststellen; (*found*) gründen. **establishment** *n* Gründung *f*; (*comm*) Unternehmen *neut*.
estate [i'steit] *n* (*of deceased*) Nachlaß *m*; (*of noble*) Landsitz *m*. **housing estate** Siedlung *f*. **real estate** Immobilien *pl*. **estate agent** Grundstücksmakler *m*. **estate car** Kombiwagen *m*.
esteem [i'stiːm] *n* Achtung *f*. *v* hochschätzen.
estimate ['esti,meit; *n* 'estimət] *v* schätzen (auf). *n* (Ab)Schätzung. **estimation** *n* Ansicht (*opinion*) *f*.
estuary ['estjuəri] *n* (Fluß)Mündung *f*.
eternal [i'təinl] *adj* ewig. **eternity** *n* Ewigkeit *f*.
ether ['iiθə] *n* Äther *m*. **ethereal** *adj* ätherisch.
ethical ['eθikl] *adj* ethisch, sittlich. **ethics** *n* Ethik *f*.
ethnic ['eθnik] *adj* ethnisch, Volks-.
etiquette ['eti,ket] *n* Etikette *f*.
etymology [,eti'molədʒi] *n* Etymologie *f*.
Eucharist ['juːkərist] *n* heilige Messe *f*.
eunuch ['juːnək] *n* Eunuch *m*, Verschnittene(r) *m*.
euphemism ['juːfə,mizəm] *n* Euphemismus *m*. **euphemistic** *adj* beschönigend.
euphoria [ju'foɪriə] *n* Wohlbefinden *neut*, Euphorie *f*.
Europe ['juərəp] *n* Europa *neut*. **European** *adj* europäisch; *n* Europäer(in). **European Economic Community (EEC)** Europäische Wirtschaftsgemeinschaft (EWG) *f*. **European Community** Europäische Gemeinschaften (EG) *pl*.
euthanasia [juːθə'neiziə] *n* Euthanasie *f*, Gnadentod *m*.
evacuate [i'vakju,eit] *v* (*depart*) aussiedeln; (*empty*) entleeren; (*people*) evakuieren. **evacuation** *n* Evakuierung *f*.

evade [i'veid] *v* ausweichen, entgehen (+ *dat*); (*tax*) hinterziehen.
evaluate [i'valju,eit] *v* abschätzen. **evaluation** *n* Abschätzung *f*.
evangelical [,ivan'dʒelikəl] *adj* evangelisch. **evangelism** *n* Evangelismus *m*. **evangelist** *n* Evangelist *m*.
evaporate [i'vapə,reit] *v* verdampfen. **evaporated milk** Kondensmilch *f*. **evaporation** *n* Verdampfung *f*.
evasion [i'veiʒən] *n* Ausweichen *neut*. **tax evasion** Steuerhinterziehung *f*. **evasive** *adj* ausweichend. **evasive action** Ausweichmanöver *neut*.
eve [iːv] *n* Vorabend *m*. **Christmas Eve** Heiliger Abend *m*. **New Year's Eve** Sylvesterabend *m*.
even ['iːvən] *adj* eben, gerade. *adv* sogar. *even bigger* noch größer. **even more** noch mehr. **not even** nicht einmal. **even if** wenn auch. **even-handed** *adj* unparteiisch.
evening ['iːvniŋ] *n* Abend *m*. **in the evening** abends, am Abend. **this evening** heute abend. **evening dress** Gesellschaftsanzug *m*. **evening meal** Abendessen *neut*.
event [i'vent] *n* Ereignis *neut*; (*sport*) Disziplin *f*. **in the event of** im Falle (+ *gen*). **eventful** *adj* ereignisvoll.
ever ['evə] *adv* je(mals); (*always*) immer. *have you ever been to Berlin?* sind Sie schon einmal in Berlin gewesen? **ever so** sehr. **for ever** für immer. **evergreen** *adj* immergrün. **everlasting** *adj* ewig.
every ['evri] *adj* jede; alle *pl*. **every day** jeden Tag. **every one** jeder einzelne. **every other day** jeden zweiten Tag. **every so often** hin und wieder. **everybody/everyone** *pron* jeder. **everything** *pron* alles. **everywhere** *adv* überall.
evict [i'vikt] *n* exmittieren. **eviction** *n* Exmission *f*.
evidence ['evidəns] *v* Zeugnis *neut*; Beweis *m*. **give evidence** Zeugnis ablegen. *v* beweisen.
evil ['iːvl] *adj* übel, böse. *n* Übel *neut*, Böse *neut*.
evoke [i'vouk] *v* hervorrufen.
evolve [i'volv] *v* (sich) entwickeln. **evolution** *n* Entwicklung *f*; (*biol*) Evolution *f*.
ewe [juː] *n* Mutterschaf *neut*.
exacerbate [ig'zasə,beit] *v* verschlimmern.

exact [ig'zakt] *adj* genau, exakt. *v* verlangen; (*payment*) eintreiben. **exacting** *adj* anspruchsvoll. **exactly** *adv* genau.

exaggerate [ig'zadʒəˌreit] *v* übertreiben. **exaggerated** *adj* übertrieben. **exaggeration** *n* Übertreibung *f*.

exalt [ig'zolt] *v* erheben; (*praise*) preisen. **exaltation** *n* (*joy*) Wonne *f*. **exalted** *adj* erhaben; (*excited*) aufgeregt.

examine [ig'zamin] *v* untersuchen, prüfen; (*law*) verhören. **examination** *n* Prüfung *f*; (*inspection*) Untersuchung *f*. **medical examination** ärztliche Untersuchung *f*.

example [ig'zaːmpl] *n* Beispiel *neut*. **for example** zum Beispiel. **set an example** ein Beispiel geben.

exasperate [ig'zaːspəˌreit] *v* zum Verzweifeln bringen. **exasperation** *n* Verzweiflung *f*.

excavate ['ekskəˌveit] *v* ausgraben. **excavation** *n* Ausgrabung *f*. **excavator** *n* (*mech*) Bagger *m*.

exceed [ik'siːd] *v* überschreiten. **exceedingly** *adv* höchst.

excel [ik'sel] *v* sich auszeichnen. **excellence** *n* Vorzüglichkeit *f*. **Excellency** *n* Exzellenz *f*. **excellent** *adj* ausgezeichnet, vorzüglich.

except [ik'sept] *prep* außer. **except for** abgesehen von. *v* ausschließen. **exception** *n* Ausnahme *f*. **take exception to** übelnehmen.

excerpt ['eksəːpt] *n* Auszug *m*.

excess [ik'ses] *n* Übermaß *neut*, Überfluß *m* (an). *adj* Über-. **excess fare** Zuschlag *m*. **excessive** *adj* übermäßig.

exchange [iks'tʃeindʒ] *v* (aus-, um)tauschen; (*money*) wechseln. *n* Austausch *m*; (*phone*) Zentrale *f*. **foreign exchange** Devisen *pl*. **exchange rate** Wechselkurs *m*.

exchequer [iks'tʃekə] *n* Schatzamt *neut*.

excise ['eksaiz] *v* (*cut out*) herausschneiden. **excise duty** indirekter Steuer *m*.

excite [ik'sait] *v* erregen, aufregen. **get excited** sich aufregen. **excitement** *n* Aufregung *f*.

exclaim [ik'skleim] *v* ausrufen. **exclamation** *n* Ausruf *m*. **exclamation mark** Ausrufungszeichen *neut*.

exclude [ik'skluːd] *v* ausschließen. **exclusive** *adj* ausschließlich; (*fashionable*) exklusiv. **exclusive of** *also* **excluding** ausschließlich. **exclusion** *n* Ausschluß *m*.

excommunicate [ekskə'mjuːniˌkeit] *v* exkommunizieren. **excommunication** *n* Exkommunikation *f*.

excrement ['ekskrəmənt] *n* Exkrement *neut*, Kot *m*.

excrete [ik'skriːt] *v* ausscheiden. **excretion** *n* Ausscheidung *f*.

excruciating [ik'skruːʃieitiŋ] *adj* peinigend.

excursion [ik'skəːʃən] *n* Ausflug *m*.

excuse [ik'skjuːz] *n* Ausrede *f*. *v* entschuldigen, verzeihen. **excuse me!** Verzeihung!

execute ['eksiˌkjuːt] *v* (*carry out*) ausführen; (*person*) hinrichten. **execution** *n* Ausführung *f*; Hinrichtung *f*. **executioner** *n* Henker *m*. **executor** *n* Testamentvollstrecker *m*.

executive [ig'zekjutiv] *adj* vollziehend. *n* (*comm*) Geschäftsführer *m*.

exemplify [ig'zempliˌfai] *v* als Beispiel dienen für.

exempt [ig'zempt] *v* befreien (von). *adj* **exempt from** frei von.

exercise ['eksəˌsaiz] *n* Übung *f*; (*of duty*) Ausübung *f*. *v* üben; (*wield*) ausüben. **physical exercise** Leibesübung *f*. **exercise book** Schulheft *neut*.

exert [ig'zəːt] *v* ausüben. **exert oneself** sich anstrengen. **exertion** *n* Anstrengung *f*.

exhale [eks'heil] *v* ausatmen.

exhaust [ig'zoːst] *v* erschöpfen. **exhausted** *adj* erschöpft. **exhausting** *adj* anstrengend. **exhaustion** *n* Erschöpfung *f*. *n* **exhaust** (*gases*) Abgase *pl*. **exhaust pipe** Auspuffrohr *neut*.

exhibit [ig'zibit] *v* zeigen; (*goods*) ausstellen. **exhibition** *n* Ausstellung *f*. **exhibitor** *n* Aussteller *m*.

exhilarate [ig'ziləˌreit] *v* erheitern. **exhilarated** *adj* angeregt, heiter. **exhilarating** *adj* erheiternd. **exhilaration** *n* Erheiterung *f*.

exile ['eksail] *n* Verbannung *f*; (*person*) Verbannte(r). *v* verbannen.

exist [ig'zist] *v* existieren, sein. **existence** *n* Dasein *neut*, Existenz *f*. **existing** *adj* bestehend.

exit ['egzit] *n* Ausgang. *v* abtreten.

exodus ['eksədəs] *n* Auswanderung *f*; (*coll*) allgemeiner Ausbruch *m*.

exonerate [ig'zonəˌreit] *v* freisprechen (von).

exorbitant [ig'zɔːbitənt] *adj* übermäßig.
exorcize ['eksɔːsaiz] *v* austreiben.
exotic [ig'zotik] *adj* exotisch, fremdartig.
expand [ik'spand] *v* (sich) ausdehnen; (*develop*) entwickeln, erweitern. **expanse** *n* Weite *f*, weite Fläche *f*. **expansion** *n* Ausdehnung *f*; (*of firm*) Erweiterung *f*; (*pol*) Expansion *f*.
expatriate [eks'peitrieit; *n* eks'peitriət] *vv* ausbürgern. *n* im Ausland Lebende(r).
expect [ik'spekt] *v* erwarten; (*support*) annehmen. *She is expecting* sie ist in anderen Umständen. **expectation** *n* Erwartung *f*.
expedient [ik'spiːdiənt] *adj* zweckdienlich. *n* Notbehelf *m*.
expedition [ˌekspi'diʃən] *n* Expedition *f*.
expel [ik'spel] *v* ausstoßen; (*from school*) ausschließen.
expenditure [ik'spenditʃə] *n* Ausgabe *f*.
expense [ik'spens] *n* (Geld)Ausgabe *f*. **expenses** *pl* Unkosten *pl*. *at my expense* auf meine Kosten. *at the expense of* zum Schaden von. **expensive** *adj* teuer, kostspielig.
experience [ik'spiəriəns] *n* Erfahrung *f*; (*event*) Erlebnis *neut*. *v* erfahren, erleben. **experienced** *adj* erfahren.
experiment [ik'sperimənt] *m* Experiment *neut*, Probe *f*. *v* experimentieren. **experimental** *adj* Experimental-.
expert ['ekspəːt] *n* Fachmann *m*, Sachkundige(r). *adj* geschickt, gewandt. **expertise** *n* Sachkenntnis *f*.
expire [ik'spaiə] *v* (*breathe out*) ausatmen; (*lapse*) verfallen; (*die*) sterben. **expiry** *n also* **expiration** Ablauf *m*.
explain [ik'splein] *v* erklären. **explanation** *n* Erklärung *f*. **explanatory** *adj* erklärend. **be self-explanatory** sich von selbst verstehen.
explicit [ik'splisit] *adj* deutlich, ausdrücklich.
explode [ik'sploud] *v* explodieren. **explosion** *n* Explosion *f*.
exploit[1] ['eksploit] *n* Heldentat *f*, Abenteuer *m*.
exploit[2] [ik'sploit] *v* ausbeuten. **exploitation** *n* Ausbeutung *f*.
explore [ik'sploː] *v* erforschen. **explorer** *n* (Er)Forscher *m*. **exploration** *n* Erforschung *f*. **exploratory** *adj* forschend, Forschungs-.
exponent [ik'spounənt] *n* (*person*) Verfechter *m*.

export [ik'spoːt; *n* 'ekspoːt] *v* exportieren. *n* Export *m*. **exportation** *n* Ausfuhr *f*. **exporter** *n* Exporteur *m*. **export trade** *n* Exporthandel *m*.
expose [ik'spouz] *v* aussetzen; (*phot*) belichten; (*impostor*) aufdecken. **exposed** *adj* (*unprotected*) ungeschützt. **be exposed to** ausgesetzt sein (+ *dat*). **exposure** *n* (*phot*) Belichtung *f* (*med*) Unterkühlung *f*.
express [ik'spres] *v* ausdrücken. *adj* Eil-, Schnell-. **express letter** Eilbrief *m*. **express train** D-zug *m*. **expression** *n* Ausdruck *m*. **expressionism** *n* Expressionismus *m*. **expressionless** *adj* ausdruckslos. **expressive** *adj* ausdrucksvoll. **expressly** *adv* ausdrücklich.
expulsion [ik'spʌlʃən] *n* Ausweisung *f*.
exquisite ['ekswizit] *adj* ausgezeichnet; (*pain*) heftig.
extend [ik'stend] *v* ausdehnen; (*develop*) erweitern; (*hand*) ausstrecken; (*cover area*) sich erstrecken. **extension** *n* Erweiterung *f*; (*comm*) Verlängerung *f*; (*phone*) Nebenanschluß *f*; (*building*) Anbau *m*. **extensive** *adj* ausgedehnt. **extent** *n* Umfang *m*. **to a certain extent** bis zu einem gewissen Grade.
exterior [ik'stiəriə] *adj* äußer, Außen-. *n* das Äußere; (*appearance*) äußeres Ansehen *neut*.
exterminate [ik'stəːmiˌneit] *v* ausrotten. **extermination** *n* Ausrottung *f*.
external [ik'stəːnl] *adj* äußer, äußerlich, Außen-.
extinct [ik'stiŋkt] *adj* ausgestorben; (*volcano*) ausgebrannt. **become extinct** aussterben. **extinction** *n* Aussterben *neut*.
extinguish [ik'stiŋgwiʃ] *v* (aus)löschen. (*fire*) **extinguisher** Feuerlöscher *m*.
extort [ik'stɔːt] *v* erpressen. **extortion** *n* Erpressung *f*. **extortionate** *adj* erpresserisch. **extortionate price** Wucherpreis *m*.
extra ['ekstrə] *adj* zusätzlich, Extra-. *adv* besonders. **extras** *pl n* (*expenses*) Sonderausgaben *pl*; (*accessories*) Sonderzubehörteile *pl*.
extract [ik'strakt; *n* 'ekstrakt] *v* ausziehen; (*tooth*) ziehen; (*numerals*) gewinnen. *n* Auszug *m*. **extraction** *n* Ausziehen *neut*; (*tooth*, *minerals*) Extraktion *f*.
extradite ['ekstrəˌdait] *v* ausliefern. **extradition** *n* Auslieferung *f*.

extramural [,ekstrə'mjuərəl] *adj* außerplanmäßig.
extraordinary [ik'strɔːdənəri] *adj* außerordentlich, seltsam.
extravagant [ik'stravəgənt] *adj* verschwenderisch; (*exaggerated*) übertrieben.
extreme [ik'striːm] *adj* höchst, letzt; (*fig*) extrem; *n* Extrem *m*, äußerste Grenze *f*. **extremism** *n* Extremismus *m*. **extremist** *n* Extremist *m*.
extricate ['ekstri‚keit] *v* herauswickeln.
extrovert ['ekstrəvəit] *adj* (*psychol*) extravertiert. *n* Extravertierte(r).
exuberance [ig'zjuːbərəns] *n* Übermut *m*. **exuberant** *adj* übermütig.
exude [ig'zjuːd] *v* ausschlagen; ausstrahlen.
exultation [‚egzʌl'teiʃən] *n* Jubel *m*.
eye [ai] *n* Auge *neut*; (*of needle*) Öse *f*. *v* anschauen.
eyeball ['aibɔːl] *n* Augapfel *m*.
eyebrow ['aibrau] *n* Augenbraue *f*.
eye-catching ['aikatʃiŋ] *adj* auffallend.
eyelash ['ailaʃ] *n* Wimper *f*.
eyelid ['ailid] *n* Augenlid *neut*.
eye shadow *n* Lidschatten *m*.
eyesight ['aisait] *m* Sehkraft *f*.
eyewitness ['ai‚witnis] *n* Augenzeuge *m*.

F

fable ['feibl] *n* Fabel *f*.
fabric ['fabrik] *n* Stoff *m*, Gewebe *neut*. **fabricate** *v* herstellen; (*fig*) erfinden.
fabulous ['fabjuləs] *adj* fabelhaft, sagenhaft.
façade [fə'saːd] *n* Fassade *f*.
face [feis] *n* Gesicht *neut*; (*of clock*) Zifferblatt *neut*; (*surface*) Oberfläche *f*; (*cheek*) Stirn *f*. **pull faces** Fratzen schneiden. *v* gegenüberstehen; (*fig*) entgegentreten; (*of house, etc.*) liegen nach.
facet ['fasit] *n* Facette *f*; (*fig*) Aspekt *m*.
facetious [fə'siːʃəs] *adj* scherzhaft.
facial ['feiʃəl] *adj* Gesichts-.
facile ['fasail] *adj* (*easy*) leicht; (*superficial*) oberflächlich. **facilitate** *v* erleichtern.
facility *n* Leichtigkeit *f*. **facilities** *pl n* Einrichtungen *pl*.

facing ['feisiŋ] *prep* gegenüber. *n* Verkleidung *f*.
facsimile [fak'siməli] *n* Faksimile *neut*.
fact [fakt] *n* Tatsache *f*; (*reality*) Wirklichkeit *f*. **in fact** in der Tat, tatsächlich.
faction ['fakʃən] *n* Faktion *f*.
factor ['faktə] *n* Faktor *m*; (*comm*) Agent *m*.
factory ['faktəri] *n* Fabrik *f*. **factory worker** Fabrikarbeiter(in).
fad [fad] *n* Mode *f*.
fade [feid] *v* verschießen, verblassen; (*flower*) verwelken; (*sound*) schwinden. **faded** *adj* verschossen.
fag [fag] *n* (*coll: tiresome job*) Plackerei *f*. **fagged** *adj* erschöpft.
fail [feil] *v* fehlschlagen, scheitern; (*to do something*) unterlassen; (*in exam*) durchfallen; (*let down*) im Stich lassen. *n* **without fail** unbedingt.
faint [feint] *adj* (*colour*) blaß; (*sound*) leise; (*memory*) schwach. *v* ohnmächtig werden. *n* Ohnmacht *f*.
fair[1] [feə] *adj* (*hair*) hell, blond; (*beautiful*) schön; (*just*) gerecht, fair. **fair chance** aussichtsreiche Chance *f*. **play fair** fair spielen. **fair and square** offen und ehrlich. **fairly** *adv* (*quite*) ziemlich.
fair[2] [feə] *n* Messe *f*; (*funfair*) Jahrmarkt *m*. **fairground** Messegelände *neut*; Rummelplatz *m*.
fairy ['feəri] *n* Fee *f*. *adj* feenhaft, Feen-. **fairy tale** Märchen *neut*.
faith [feiθ] *n* Vertrauen *neut*; (*belief*) Glaube *m*. **faithful** *adj* treu; (*accurate*) getreu. **yours faithfully** hochachtungsvoll.
fake [feik] *v* fälschen. *n* Fälschung *f*; (*person*) Schwindler. *adj* vorgetäuscht.
falcon ['fɔːlkən] *n* Falke *m*.
*fall [fɔːl] *n* Sturz *m*, Fall *m*; (*fig*) Untergang *m*. *v* fallen; (*prices*) abnehmen; (*curtain*) niedergehen; (*fortress*) genommen werden. **fall asleep** einschlafen. **fall back** sich zurückziehen. **fall down** (*person*) hinfallen; (*building*) einstürzen. **fall in love with** sich verlieben in. **fall into** geraten in. **fall out with** zanken mit. **fall through** durchfallen.
fallacy ['faləsi] *n* Trugschluß *m*.
fallen ['fɔːlən] *V* fall.
fallible ['faləbl] *adj* fehlbar.
fall-out ['fɔːlaut] *n* Niederschlag *m*.
fallow ['falou] *adj* fahl.

false [fɔ:ls] *adj* falsch; *(person)* untreu; *(thing)* gefälscht. **false alarm** blinder Alarm *m*. **false start** Fehlstart *m*. **falsehood** *n* Lüge *f*. **falsify** fälschen.

falter ['fɔ:ltə] *v* stolpern; *(hesitate)* zögern; *(courage)* versagen.

fame [feim] *n* Ruhm *m*, Berühmtheit *f*.

familiar [fə'miljə] *adj* bekannt; *(informal)* ungezwungen. **familiarity** *n* Vertrautheit *f*.

family ['faməli] *n* Familie *f*; *(bot, zool)* Gattung *f*. *adj* Familien-.

famine ['famin] *n* Hungersnot *f*.

famished ['famiʃt] *n* **be famished** großen Hunger haben.

famous ['feiməs] *adj* berühmt. **famously** *adv* *(coll)* glänzend.

fan[1] [fan] *n* *(hand)* Fächer *m*; *(mot, elec)* Ventilator *m*. **fan belt** *n* Keilriemen *m*.

fan[2] [fan] *n* *(admirer)* Fan *m*.

fanatic [fə'natik] *n* Fanatiker(in). **fanatical** *adj* fanatisch.

fancy ['fansi] *n* Neigung *f* (zu); *(fantasy)* Phantasie *f*. **take a fancy to** eingenommen sein für. *v* gern haben *adj* schick. **fancy dress** Maskenkostüm *m*.

fanfare ['fanfeə] *n* Fanfare *f*.

fang [faŋ] *n* Fangzahn *m*; *(of snake)* Giftzahn *m*.

fantastic [fan'tastik] *adj* phantastisch; *(coll)* sagenhaft, toll.

fantasy ['fantəsi] *n* Phantasie *f*.

far [fa:] *adj* fern, entfernt. *adv* fern, weit. **as far as** bis (nach). **by far** bei weitem. **far and near** nahe und fern. **far better** viel besser. **far off** weit weg. **on the far side** auf der anderen Seite.

farce [fa:s] *n* Posse *f*; *(fig)* Farce *f*.

fare [feə] *n* Fahrpreis *m*; *(food)* Kost *f*. *v* ergehen.

farewell [feə'wel] *interj* lebe wohl! *n* Lebewohl *neut*. *adj* Abschieds-. **bid farewell to** Abschied nehmen von.

far-fetched [,fa:'fetʃt] *adj* weit hergeholt.

farm [fa:m] *n* Bauernhof *m*. **dairy farm** Meierei *f*. **poultry farm** Geflügelfarm *f*. *v* Landwirtschaft betreiben; *(land)* bebauen. **farm out** *(work)* weitergeben. **farmer** *n* Landwirt *m*, *Bauer m*. **farmhouse** *n* Bauernhaus *neut*. **farming** *n* Landwirtschaft *f*. **farmworker** Landarbeiter(in).

far-sighted [,fa:'saitid] *adj* weitsichtig.

fart [fa:t] *(vulgar)* Furz *m*. *v* furzen.

farther ['fa:ðə] *adj*, *adv* weiter, ferner.

farthest ['fa:ðist] *adj* fernst, weitest. *adv* am weitesten.

fascinate ['fasi,neit] *v* faszinieren. **fascinating** *adj* fesselnd, faszinierend. **fascination** *n* Bezauberung *f*, *Faszination f*.

fascism ['faʃizəm] *n* Faschismus *m*. **fascist** *adj* faschistisch. *n* Faschist *m*.

fashion ['faʃən] *n* Mode *f*; *(manner)* Art (und Weise) *f*. **in fashion** modisch. **out of fashion** unmodisch. *v* bilden, gestalten. **fashionable** *adj* modisch. **fashion show** Modeschau *f*.

fast[1] [fa:st] *adj*, *adv* *(quick)* schnell, rasch; *(firm)* fest; *(colour)* echt. *my watch is fast* meine Uhr geht vor.

fast[2] [fa:st] *v* fasten. *n* Fasten *neut*.

fasten ['fa:sn] *v* befestigen, festbinden; *(door)* verriegeln. **fastener** *n* Verschluß *m*.

fastidious [fa'stidiəs] *adj* wählerisch, anspruchsvoll.

fat [fat] *adj* *(person)* dick, fett; *(greasy)* fett, fettig. *n* Fett *neut*.

fatal ['feitl] *adj* tödlich. **fatalistic** *adj* fatalistisch. **fatality** *n* Todesfall *m*.

fate [feit] *n* Schicksal *neut*. **fateful** *adj* verhängnisvoll.

father ['fa:ðə] *n* Vater *m*. *v* zeugen. **Father Christmas** der Weihnachtsmann. **father-in-law** *n* Schwiegervater *m*. **fatherland** *n* Vaterland *neut*.

fathom ['faðəm] *n* Faden *m*. *v* sondieren; *(fig)* eindringen in.

fatigue [fə'ti:g] *n* Ermüdung *f*. *v* ermüden. **fatiguing** *adj* mühsam, ermüdend.

fatuous ['fatjuəs] *adj* albern.

fault [fɔ:lt] *n* Fehler *m*; *(tech)* Störung *f*; *(blame)* Schuld *f*. *It's my fault* es ist meine Schuld. *Whose fault is this?* wer ist daran schuld? **at fault** im Unrecht. **find fault (with)** tadeln.

fauna ['fɔ:nə] *n* Fauna *f*.

favour ['feivə] *n* Gunst *f*; *(kindness)* Gefallen *m*. **in favour of** zugunsten von *(or +gen)*. **be in favour of** einverstanden sein mit. **in his favour** zu seinen Gunsten. **find favour with** Gunst finden bei. *Do me a favour and ...* Tun sie nur den Gefallen und .... **favourable** *adj* günstig. **favourite** *adj* Lieblings-; *n* Liebling *m*; *(sport)* Favorit *m*.

fawn [fɔ:n] *n* Rehkalb *neut*. *adj* rehfarbig.

fear [fiə] *n* Furcht *f*, Angst *f*. **fears** *pl* *n* Befürchtungen *pl*. *v* sich fürchten (vor), Angst haben (vor). **fearful** *adj* *(person)*

ängstlich; (*thing*) furchtbar. **fearless** *adj*
furchtlos. **fearsome** *adj* schrecklich.
feasible ['fiːzəbl] *adj* möglich. **feasibility** *n*
Möglichkeit *f*.
feast [fiːst] *n* Fest *neut*; (*meal*) Festessen
neut. *v* sich ergötzen (von).
feat [fiːt] *n* Kunststück *neut*.
feather ['feðə] *n* Feder *f*. **featherweight** *n*
Federgewicht *neut*.
feature ['fiːtʃə] *n* (*of face*) Gesichtszug *m*;
(*characteristic*) Eigenschaft *f*,
Kennzeichen *neut*; (*newspaper*) Feature
neut. *v* darstellen. **feature film** Spielfilm
m.
February ['februəri] *n* Februar *m*.
fed [fed] *V* **feed**.
federal ['fedərəl] *adj* Bundes-; (*Swiss*)
eidgenössisch. **Federal Republic of Germany** Bundesrepublik Deutschland. **federalism** *n* Föderalismus *m*. **federalist** *n*
Föderalist *m*. **federation** *n* Bundesstaat
m; (*organization*) Verband *m*.
fee [fiː] *n* Gebühr *f*. **school fees** Schulgeld
neut sing.
feeble ['fiːbl] *adj* schwach, kraftlos. **feeble-minded** *adj* schwachsinnig. **feebleness**
n Schwachheit *f*.
*feed [fiːd] *v* essen; (*of animals*) fressen;
(*cattle*) füttern; (*person*) zu essen geben;
(*tech*) zuführen. *n* Futter *neut*; (*tech*)
Zufuhr *f*. **be fed up with** (*coll*) satt haben,
die Nase voll haben. **feedback** *n*
Rückkopplung; (*fig*) Rückwirkung. **feeding** *n* Nahrung *f*; (*animals*) Fütterung *f*.
*feel [fiːl] *v* (sich) fühlen; (*detect, sense*)
empfinden; (*pulse*) betasten. *I feel cold*
mir is kalt. *I feel better* es geht mir besser. *It feels hard* es fühlt sich hart an. *I
don't feel like working* ich habe keine
Lust zur Arbeit. *n* (*atmosphere*) Stimmung *f*. **feeler** *n* Fühler *m*. **feeling** *n*
Gefühl *neut*. **hurt someone's feelings**
jemanden verletzen.
feet [fiːt] *V* **foot**.
feign [fein] *v* simulieren.
feline ['fiːlain] *adj* Katzen-.
fell[1] [fel] *V* **fall**.
fell[2] [fel] *v* (*tree*) fällen.
fellow ['felou] *n* Genosse *m*, Genossin *f*;
(*coll*) Kerl *m*. **fellow-countryman** *n*
Landsmann *m*. **fellow men** Mitmenschen
pl. **fellowship** *n* Kameradschaft *f*; Gesellschaft *f*.
felony ['feləni] *n* Schwerverbrechen *neut*.
felon *n* Schwerverbrecher *m*.

felt[1] [felt] *V* **feel**.
felt[2] [felt] *n* Filz *m*.
female ['fiːmeil] *adj* weiblich. *n* Weib
neut; (*of animals*) Weibchen *neut*.
feminine ['feminin] *adj* weiblich. *n*
(*gramm*) Femininum *neut*. **femininity** *n*
Weiblichkeit *f*.
feminism ['feminizəm] *n* Frauenrechtlertum *neut*. **feminist** *n* Frauenrechtler(in),
Feminist(in).
fence [fens] *n* Zaun *m*. *v* (*sport*) fechten.
fence in *or* **off** einzäunen.
fend [fend] *v* **fend off** abwehren. **fend for
oneself** sich allein durchschlagen.
fender ['fendə] *n* (*US*) Kotflügel *m*.
(*fireguard*) Kaminvorsetzer *m*;\
fennel ['fenl] *n* Fenchel *m*.
ferment [fə'ment; *n* 'fɔːment] *v* gären (lassen). *n* (*fig*) Unruhe *f*. **fermentation** *n*
Gärung *f*.
fern [fəːn] *n* Farn *m*.
ferocious [fə'rouʃəs] *adj* wild, grausam;
(*dog*) bissig. **ferocity** *n* Wildheit *f*.
ferret ['ferit] *n* Frettchen *neut*. *v* **ferret out**
ausforschen. **ferret about** herumsuchen.
ferry ['feri] *n* Fähre *f*. *v* übersetzen.
fertile ['fəːtail] *adj* fruchtbar. **fertility** *n*
Fruchtbarkeit *f*. **fertilization** *n* Befruchtung *f*; (*of land*) Düngung *f*. **fertilize** *v*
befruchten; (*land*) düngen. **fertilizer** *n*
Düngemittel *neut*.
fervent ['fəːvənt] *adj* glühend, eifrig.
fester ['festə] *v* verfaulen; (*wound*) eitern.
festival ['festəvəl] *n* Fest *neut*.
festive ['festiv] *adj* festlich. **festivity** *n*
Fröhlichkeit *f*.
fetch [fetʃ] *v* holen; (*collect*) abholen;
(*price*) erzielen. **fetching** *adj* reizend.
fête [feit] *n* Gartenfest *neut*.
fetid ['fiːtid] *adj* übelriechend.
fetish ['fetiʃ] *n* Fetisch *m*.
fetter ['fetə] *v* fesseln. **fetters** *pl* Fessel *f*
sing.
feud [fjuːd] *n* Fehde *f*. *v* sich befehden.
feudal ['fjuːdl] *adj* feudal, Lehns-. **feudalism** *n* Feudalismus *m*.
fever ['fiːvə] *n* Fieber *neut*. **feverish** *adj*
fiebrig; (*activity*) fieberhaft.
few [fjuː] *adj, pron* wenige. **a few** einige,
ein paar.
fiancé [fi'onsei] *n* Verlobte(r) *m*. **fiancée** *n*
Verlobte *f*.
fiasco [fi'askou] *n* Fiasko *neut*, Mißerfolg
m.

fib [fib] *n* Flunkerei *f. v* flunkern. **fibber** *n* Flunkerer *m.*

fibre ['faibə] *n* Faser *f.* **fibreglass** *n* Glasfiber *f.*

fickle ['fikl] *adj* unbeständig. **fickleness** *n* Unbeständigkeit *f.*

fiction ['fikʃən] *n* Erdichtung *f;* (*as genre*) Erzählungsliteratur *f.* **work of fiction** Roman *m.* **fictitious** *adj* fiktiv. **fictitious character** erfundene Person *f.*

fiddle ['fidl] *v* tändeln, spielen. *n* Schwindel *m;* (*violin*) Fiedel *f.* **fiddler** *n* (*violinist*) Fiedler *m.*

fidelity [fi'deləti] *n* Treue *f.*

fidget ['fidʒit] *v* zappeln. **fidgety** *adj* zappelig.

field [fiːld] *n* Feld *neut;* (*mining*) Flöz *neut;* (*fig: sphere*) Bereich *m.* **field glasses** Feldstecker *m.* **fieldwork** *n* Feldforschung *f.*

fiend [fiːnd] *n* Teufel *m;* (*evil person*) Unhold *m.* **fiendish** *adj* teuflisch.

fierce [fiəs] *adj* wild, grausam. **fierceness** *n* Wildheit *f.*

fiery ['faiəri] *adj* feurig.

fifteen [fif'tiːn] *adj* fünfzehn. **fifteenth** *adj* fünfzehnt.

fifth [fifθ] *adj* fünft. *n* Fünftel *neut.*

fifty ['fifti] *adj* fünfzig. **fiftieth** *adj* fünfzigst. **fifty-fifty** *adv* halb und halb.

fig [fig] *n* Feige *f;* (*tree*) Feigenbaum *m.*

***fight** [fait] *v* kämpfen; (*fig*) bekämpfen. **have a fight** sich streiten. *n* Kampf *m;* (*quarrel*) Streit *m;* (*brawl*) Schlägerei *f.*

figment ['figmənt] *n* Erzeugnis der Phantasie *neut.*

figure ['figə] *n* (*number*) Ziffer *f;* (*of person*) Figur *f;* (*diagram*) Zeichnung *f,* Diagramm *neut.* **figure of speech** Redewendung *f. v* (*appear*) auftreten; (*coll: reckon*) meinen. **figure out** ausrechnen.

filament ['filəmənt] *n* (*elec*) Glühfaden *m.*

file¹ [fail] *n* (*documents*) Akte *f;* (*folder*) Mappe *f;* (*row*) Reihe *f. v* (*letters*) ablegen; (*suit*) vorlegen; (*mil*) difilieren. **filing cabinet** Aktenschrank *m.* **filing clerk** Registrator *m.*

file² [fail] *n* (*tool*) Feile *f. v* feilen.

filial ['filiəl] *adj* Kindes-.

fill [fil] *v* (an)füllen; (*with objects*) vollstopfen; (*tooth*) plombieren; (*hole*) zustopfen; (*become full*) sich füllen. **fill up** auffüllen; (*mot*) auftanken.

fillet ['filit] *n* Filet *neut.*

film [film] *n* Film *m. v* filmen. **make a film** einen Film drehen.

filter ['filtə] *n* Filter *m* or *neut. v* filtrieren. **filter-tip** *n* Filtermundstück *neut.*

filth [filθ] *n* Dreck *m,* Schmutz *m.* **filthy** *adj* dreckig, schmutzig; (*indecent*) unflätig; (*weather*) scheußlich.

fin [fin] *n* Flosse *f.*

final ['fainl] *adj* letzt, End-; (*definitive*) endgültig. *n* (*sport*) Endspiel *neut.* **finals** *pl n* (*exams*) Abschlußprüfung *f sing.* **finale** *n* Finale *neut.* **finalist** *n* Endspielteilnehmer(in). **finalize** *v* abschließen. **finally** *adv* schließlich, zum Schluß.

finance [fai'nans] *n* Finanzwesen *neut. v* finanzieren. **finances** *pl n* Finanzen *pl.* **financial** *adj* finanziell, Finanz-.

finch [fintʃ] *n* Fink *m.*

***find** [faind] *v* finden. **find guilty** für schuldig erklären. **find oneself** sich befinden. **find out** herausfinden; (*a person*) ertappen. *n* Fund *m.* **findings** *pl n* Beschluß *m sing.*

fine¹ [fain] *adj* fein; (*weather*) schön; (*splendid*) gut, herrlich; (*hair*) dünn; (*point*) spitz; (*clothes*) elegant.

fine² [fain] *n* Geldstrafe *f. v* mit einer Geldstrafe belegen.

finesse [fi'nes] *n* Feinheit *f;* (*cards*) Schneiden *neut.*

finger ['fiŋgə] *n* Finger *m. v* betasten. **fingernail** *n* Fingernagel *m.* **fingerprint** *n* Fingerabdruck *m.*

finish ['finiʃ] *v* aufhören, zu Ende gehen; beenden; (*complete*) vollenden; (*food*) aufessen; (*drink*) auftrinken. *n* Ende *neut;* Schluß *m.* **finished** *adj* fertig.

finite ['fainait] *adj* endlich.

Finland ['finlənd] *n* Finnland *neut.* **Finn** *n* Finne *m,* Finnin *f.* **Finnish** *adj* finnisch.

fir [fəː] *n* Tannenbaum *m.*

fire ['faiə] *n* Feuer *neut;* Brand *m.* **catch fire** Feuer fangen. **set fire to** in Brand stecken. *v* (*a gun*) abfeuern; (*with a gun*) schießen; (*mot*) zünden. **fire alarm** *n* Feueralarm *m;* (*device*) Feuermelder *m.* **firearms** ['faiərɑːmz] *pl n* Schußwaffen *pl.* **fire brigade** *n* Feuerwehr *f.* **fire drill** *n* Feueralarmübung *f.* **fire engine** *n* Feuerwehrauto *neut.* **fire escape** *n* Nottreppe *f.*

fire extinguisher n Feuerlöscher m.
fire-guard n Kaminvorsetzer m.
fireman ['faiəmən] n Feuerwehrmann m.
fireplace ['faiə‚pleis] n Kamin m.
fireproof ['faiə‚pruːf] adj feuerfest.
fireside ['faiə‚said] n Kamin m. adj häuslich.
fire station n Feuerwache f.
firewood ['faiə‚wud] n Brennholz m.
firework ['faiə‚wəːk] n Feuerwerkskörper m. **fireworks** pl n Feuerwerk neut sing.
firing squad n Exekutionskommando neut.
firm[1] [fəːm] adj erst. **fir st name** Vorname m. adv or **firstly** erstens, zuerst, zunächst. **at first** zuerst. **come first** (sport) gewinnen. **first aid** erste Hilfe. **first-class** adj erstklassig.
firm[2] [fəːm] n Firma f.
first [fəːst] adj erst. **first name** Vorname m. adv or **firstly** erstens, zuerst, zunächst. **at first** zuerst. **come first** (sport) gewinnen. **first aid** erste Hilfe. **first-class** adj erstklassig.
fiscal ['fiskəl] adj fiskalisch. **fiscal year** Finanzjahr neut.
fish [fiʃ] n Fisch m; v fischen; (in river) angeln. **fishbone** n Gräte f. **fisherman** n Fischer. **fishhook** n Angelhaken m. **fishing** n Fischen neut, Angeln neut. **fishing boat** Fischerboot neut. **fishing rod** Angelrute f. **fishmonger** n Fischhändler m. **fishy** n (coll: suspicious) verdächtig.
fission ['fiʃən] n Spaltung f.
fissure ['fiʃə] n Spalt m.
fist [fist] n Faust m.
fit[1] [fit] adj (suitable) geeignet, angemessen; (healthy) gesund; (sport) fit, in guter Form. n (clothes) Sitz m. v (clothes) sitzen; (insert) einsetzen. **fit in** sich einfügen. **fit into** sich hineinpassen in. **fitness** n Gesundheit f; (sport) Fitneß f. **fitter** n (mech) Monteur m. **fitting** adj passend. **fittings** pl n Zubehör neut sing.
fit[2] [fit] n (med) Anfall m.
five [faiv] adj fünf.
fix [fiks] v befestigen (an); (arrange) bestimmen; (eyes) richten (auf); (repair) reparieren; (coll) Klemme f; (drugs) Fix m.
fizz [fiz] v zischen, sprudeln. **fizzy** adj sprudelnd, sprudel-.
flabbergast ['flæbəgɑːst] v verblüffen.
flabby ['flæbi] adj schlaff.
flag[1] [flæg] n Fahne f; (naut) Flagge f. **flag down** stoppen.

flag[2] [flæg] v (wane) nachlassen.
flagrant ['fleigrənt] adj offenkundig.
flair [fleə] n natürliche Begabung f, feine Nase f.
flake [fleik] n (snow, cereals) Flocke f; (thin piece) Schuppe f. v **flake off** sich abschuppen.
flamboyant [flæm‚bɔiənt] adj auffallend.
flame [fleim] n Flamme f. **burst into flames** in Flammen aufgehen. **old flame** alte Flamme f.
flamingo [flə'miŋgou] n Flamingo m.
flan [flæn] n Torte f.
flank [flæŋk] n Flanke f. v flankieren.
flannel ['flænl] n (material) Flanell m; (facecloth) Waschlappen m.
flap [flæp] n Klappe f; (of skin, etc.) Lappen m. v flattern.
flare [fleə] v flackern; (dress) sich bauschen. **flare up** aufflackern. n (naut) Lichtsignal neut; (of dress) Ausbauchung f.
flash [flæʃ] n Blitz m; (phot) Blitzlicht neut. **news flash** Kurznachricht f. v aufblitzen; (fig) sich blitzartig bewegen. **flashback** n Rückblende f. **flashbulb** n Blitzlichtlampe f. **flasher** n (mot) Blinker m. **flashlight** n Taschenlampe f. **flashy** adj auffällig.
flask [flɑːsk] n Flasche f; (laboratory) Glaskolben m. **vacuum flask** Warmflasche f.
flat[1] [flæt] adj platt, flach; (level) eben; (refusal) glatt. **fall flat** ein glatter Versager sein.
flat[2] [flæt] n Wohnung f.
flatter ['flætə] v schmeicheln. **flattering** adj schmeichelnd. **flattery** n Schmeichelei f.
flatulence ['flætjuləns] n Blähsucht f.
flaunt [flɔːnt] v paradieren mit, prunken mit.
flautist ['flɔːtist] n Flötist(in).
flavour ['fleivə] n Geschmack m. v würzen. **flavouring** n Würze f.
flaw [flɔː] n (crack) Sprung m; (defect) Makel m. **flawless** adj tadellos.
flax [flæks] n Flachs m.
flea [fliː] n Floh m.
fleck [flek] n Flecken neut. v tüpfeln.
fled [fled] V **flee**.
*flee [fliː] v fliehen.
fleece [fliːs] n Vlies neut. v (coll) rupfen. **fleecy** adj flockig.
fleet [fliːt] n Flotte f.
fleeting ['fliːtiŋ] adj flüchtig.

Flemish ['flemiʃ] *adj* flämisch.
flesh [fleʃ] *n* Fleisch *neut*. **flesh-coloured**
adj fleischfarben. **fleshly** *adj* fleischlich.
fleshy *adj* fleischig.
flew [fluː] *V* **fly¹**.
flex [fleks] *n* Schnur *f*. *v* biegen; (*muscles*)
zusammenziehen. **flexibility** *n* Biegsamkeit *f*. **flexible** *adj* biegsam, flexibel.
flick [flik] *v* schnellen, schnippen. *n*
Schnippchen *neut*.
flicker ['flikə] *v* flackern. *n* Flackern *neut*.
flight¹ [flait] *n* (*flying*) Flug *m*. **flight of
stairs** Treppe *f*. **flighty** *adj* launisch.
flight² [flait] *n* (*fleeing*) Flucht *f*.
flimsy ['flimzi] *adj* dünn, schwach.
flinch [flintʃ] *v* zurückschrecken (vor).
***fling** [fliŋ] *v* schleudern, werfen. **fling
away** wegwerfen. **fling open** aufreißen.
flint [flint] *n* Feuerstein *m*.
flip [flip] *v* klapsen, schnellen. *n* Klaps *m*.
flippant ['flipənt] *adj* leichtfertig, keck.
flirt [fləːt] *v* flirten. **flirtatious** *adj* kokett.
flit [flit] *v* flitzen.
float [flout] *v* schwimmen, treiben; (*boat*)
flott sein. *n* (*angling*) Kokschwimmer *m*.
floating *adj* schwimmend.
flock [flok] *n* (*sheep*) Herde *f*; (*birds*) Flug
m. *v* sich scharen.
flog [flog] *v* peitschen, prügeln. **flogging**
adj Prügelstrafe *f*.
flood [flʌd] *n* Flut *f*. *v* fluten.
floor [floː] *n* (*Fuß*)Boden *m*; (*storey*)
Stock *m*. *v* (*coll*) verblüten.
flop [flop] *v* plumpsen; (*fail*) versagen. *n*
(*failure*) Niete *f*, Versager *m*.
flora ['floːrə] *m* Flora *f*. **floral** *adj* Blu-
men-.
florist ['florist] *n* Blümenhändler *m*.
flounder ['flaundə] *v* herumpflatschen,
stolpern.
flour ['flauə] *n* Mehl *neut*. **flour mill** *n*
Mühle *f*. **floury** *adj* mehlig.
flourish ['flʌriʃ] *v* (*thrive*) gedeihen. *n*
Schnörkel *m*.
flout [flaut] *v* verspotten.
flow [flou] *v* fließen, strömen. *n* Fluß *m*;
(*fig*) Strom *m*.
flower ['flauə] *n* (*plant*) Blume *f*; (*bloom*)
Blüte *f*. *v* blüten. **flowerbed** *n*
Blumenbeet *neut*. **flowerpot** *n* Blu-
mentopf *m*. **flower-seller** *n*
Blumenverkäufer(in). **flowery** *adj*
blumenreich.
flown [floun] *V* **fly¹**.

flu [fluː] *n* Grippe *f*.
fluctuate ['flʌktjuˌeit] *v* schwanken. **fluctuation** *n* Schwankung *f*.
flue [fluː] *n* Abzugsrohr *neut*.
fluent ['fluənt] *adj* fließend.
fluff [flʌf] *n* Flaum *m*, Federflocke *f*. *v*
(*coll*) verpfuschen. **fluffy** *adj* flaumig,
flockig.
fluid ['fluid] *n* Flüssigkeit *f*. *adj* flüssig.
fluke [fluːk] *n* (*coll*) Dusel *m*.
flung [flʌŋ] *V* **fling**.
fluorescent [fluə'resnt] *adj* fluoreszierend.
fluorescent light Leuchtstofflampe *f*.
fluoride ['fluəraid] *n* Fluorid *neut*.
flush¹ [flʌʃ] *v* (*blush*) erröten; (*WC*)
spülen. **flush out** ausspülen. *n* Erröten
neut. **flushed** *adj* erregt.
flush² [flʌʃ] *adj* (*level*) glatt. **be flush** (*coll*)
bei Kasse sein.
fluster ['flʌstə] *v* nervös machen, verwirren. **in a fluster** ganz verwirrt.
flute [fluːt] *n* Flöte *f*. **flute-player** *n*
Flötenspieler(in).
flutter ['flʌtə] *v* flattern. *n* Flattern *neut*.
flux [flʌks] *n* Fluß *m*; (*tech*) Schmelzmit-
tel *neut*. **in flux** im Fluß.
***fly¹** [flai] *v* fliegen; (*time*) entfliehen; (*flee*)
fliehen; (*goods*) im Flugzeug befördern. *n*
(*in trousers*) Hosenschlitz *m*. **flyer** *n*
(*aero*) Flieger *m*. **flying** *adj* fliegend.
flying visit Stippvisite *f*. **flyover** *n*
Überführung *f*. **flywheel** *n* Schwungrad
neut.
fly² [flai] *n* (*insect*) Fliege *f*.
foal [foul] *n* Fohlen *neut*.
foam [foum] *n* Schaum *m*. *v* schäumen.
foam rubber Schaumgummi *m*. **foaming**
adj schäumend.
focal ['foukəl] *adj* fokal. **focal point**
Brennpunkt *m*.
fodder ['fodə] *n* Futter *neut*.
foe [fou] *n* Feind *m*.
fog [fog] *n* Nebel *m*. **foggy** *adj* neblig.
foghorn *n* Nebelhorn *m*. **foglamp** *n*
Nebelscheinwerfer *m*.
foible ['foibl] *n* Schwäche *f*.
foil¹ [foil] *v* vereiteln, verhindern.
foil² [foil] *n* (*metal*) Folie *f*.
foist [foist] *v* **foist something on someone**
jemandem etwas andrehen.
fold¹ [fould] *v* (sich) falten; (*paper*) knif-
fen; (*arms*) kreuzen; (*business*) eingehen.
n Falte *f*; Kniff *m*. **folder** *n* (*for papers*)
Mappe *f*.

fold² [fould] n (*for sheep*) Pferch m.

foliage ['fouliidʒ] n Laub neut.

folk [fouk] n Leute pl. **folks** pl n (*relations*) Verwandte pl. **folk-dance** n Volkstanz m. **folklore** n Folklore f. **folk-song** n Volkslied neut.

follow ['folou] v folgen (+dat); (*instructions*) sich halten an; (*profession*) ausüben. **as follows** folgendermaßen. **follow from** sich ergeben aus. **follow up** verfolgen.

folly ['foli] n Narrheit f.

fond [fond] adj zärtlich; (*hopes*) kühn. **be fond of** gern or lieb haben. **fondness** n Vorliebe f.

fondle ['fondl] v streicheln.

font [font] n Taufbecken m.

food [fuːd] n Lebensmittel pl, Essen neut. **food and drink** Essen und Trinken neut. **foodstuff** n Nahrungsmittel pl.

fool [fuːl] n Narr m, Närrin f, Tor m. v zum Narren halten; betrügen. **fool around** herumalbern. **foolish** adj albern, dumm. **foolishness** n Torheit f.

foot [fut] n (pl feet) Fuß m; (*of bed, page*) Fußende neut. **on foot** zu Fuß. **football** n (*game*) Fußballspiel neut; (*ball*) Fußball m. **foothills** pl n Vorgebirge neut sing. **foothold** n Halt m. **gain a foothold** Fuß fassen. **footnote** n Anmerkung f. **footpath** n Fußweg m. **footprint** n (Fuß)Spur f. **footstep** n Schritt m. **footwear** n Schuhzeug neut.

for [foː] prep für. conj denn. **leave for London** nach London abreisen. **for fun** aus Spaß. **for joy** vor Freude. **stay for three weeks** drei Wochen bleiben. **what for?** wozu?

forage ['foridʒ] n Furage f. v furagieren.

forbade [foː'bad] V forbid.

***forbear** [foː'beə] v sich enthalten (+gen).

***forbid** [foː'bid] v verbieten. **forbidden** adj verboten. **forbidding** adj bedrohlich.

forbidden [foː'bidn] V forbid.

force [foːs] n Kraft f; (*violence*) Gewalt f. v (*compel*) zwingen; (*a door*) aufbrechen. **by force** gewaltsam. **in force** (*current*) in Kraft. **armed forces** Streitkräfte pl. **police force** Polizei f. **forced** adj gekünstelt. **forceful** adj eindringlich. **forcible** adj gewaltsam. **forcibly** adv zwangsweise.

forceps ['foːseps] pl n Zange f sing.

ford [foːd] n Furt f. v durchwaten.

fore [foː] adj Vorder-. **come to the fore** hervortreten.

forearm ['foːraːm] n Unterarm m.

forebear ['foːbə] n Vorfahr m.

foreboding [foː'boudiŋ] n Vorahnung f.

***forecast** ['foːkaːst] v voraussagen. n Voraussage f. **weather forecast** Wettervorhersage f.

forecourt ['foːkoːt] n Vorhof m.

forefather ['foːfaːdə] n Vorfahr m.

forefinger ['foːfiŋgə] n Zeigefinger m.

forefront ['foːfrʌnt] n **in the forefront** im Vordergrund.

foreground ['foːgraund] n Vordergrund m.

forehand ['foːhand] n (*sport*) Vorhandschlag m.

forehead ['forid] n Stirn f.

foreign ['forən] adj fremd, ausländisch, Auslands-. **foreign body** Fremdkörper m. **foreign language** Fremdsprache f. **foreign minister** Außenminister m. **foreign policy** Außenpolitik f. **foreigner** n Fremde(r), Ausländer(in).

foreleg ['foːleg] n Vorderbein neut.

foreman ['foːmən] n Vorarbeiter m, Aufseher m; (*jury*) Sprecher m.

foremost ['foːmoust] adj vorderst. **first and foremost** zu allererst.

forename ['foːneim] n Vorname m.

forensic [fə'rensik] adj forensisch.

forerunner ['foːrʌnə] n Vorgänger m.

***foresee** [foː'siː] v voraussagen.

foresight ['foːsait] n Vorsorge f.

foreskin ['foːskin] n Vorhaut f.

forest ['forist] n Forst m, Wald m. **forest fire** Waldbrand m.

forestall [foː'stoːl] v zuvorkommen (+dat).

foretaste ['foːteist] n Vorgeschmack m.

***foretell** [foː'tel] v vorhersagen.

forethought ['foːθoːt] n Vorbedacht m.

forever [fo'revə] adv immer, ständig.

foreword ['foːwəːd] n Vorwort neut.

forfeit ['foːfit] v verwirken. n Verwirkung f. adj verwirkt.

forgave [fə'geiv] V forgive.

forge [foːdʒ] v (*metal*) schmieden; (*plan*) ersinnen; (*document*) fälschen. n Schmiede f. **forgery** n Fälschung f.

***forget** [fə'get] v vergessen. **forgetful** adj vergeßlich.

***forgive** [fə'giv] v verzeihen, vergeben. **forgiveness** n Verzeihung f. **forgiving** adj versöhnlich.

forgiven [fə'gɪvn] V forgive.
*forgo [fɔɪ'gou] v verzichten auf.
forgot [fə'gɒt] V forget.
forgotten [fə'gɒtn] V forget.
fork [fɔɪk] n Gabel f; (in road) Gabelung
f. v fork out (coll: pay) blechen.
forlorn [fə'lɔɪn] adj verlassen, hilflos.
form [fɔɪm] n Gestalt f, Form f; (to fill
out) Formular neut. on form in Form. v
bilden.
formal ['fɔɪməl] adj formell.
format ['fɔɪmat] n Format neut.
formation [fɔɪ'meiʃən] n Bildung f; (geol,
mil) Formation f.
former ['fɔɪmə] adj vorig; (one-time)
ehemalig; (of two) jene(r). formerly adv
früher.
formidable ['fɔɪmidəbl] adj furchtbar.
formula ['fɔɪmjulə] n (pl -ae) Formel f;
(med) Rezept neut. formulate v formulieren. formulation n Formulierung f.
*forsake [fə'seik] v (person) verlassen.
forsaken [fə'seikn] V forsake.
forsook [fə'suk] V forsake.
fort [fɔɪt] n Festung f.
forte ['fɔɪtei] adv (music) laut. n Stärke f.
forth [fɔɪθ] adv (place) hervor; (time) fort.
and so forth und so weiter or fort. back
and forth hin und her.
fortify ['fɔɪti,fai] v (mil) befestigen; (heart-
en) ermutigen; (food) anreichern. fortification n Befestigung f; (fortress) Festung
f.
fortitude ['fɔɪti,tjuɪd] n Mut m.
fortnight ['fɔɪtnait] n vierzehn Tage. fortnightly adj vierzehntägig. adv alle
vierzehn Tage.
fortress ['fɔɪtris] n Festung f.
fortuitous [fɔɪ'tjuɪtəs] adj zufällig.
fortune ['fɔɪtʃən] n Glück neut; (fate)
Schicksal neut; (wealth) Vermögen neut.
fortunate adj glücklich. fortunately adv
glücklicherweise.
forty ['fɔɪti] adj vierzig.
forum ['fɔɪrəm] n Forum neut.
forward ['fɔɪwəd] adj vorder, Vorder-;
(impudent) vorlaut. adv vorwärts. v
(goods) spedieren; (letter) nachschicken.
n (sport) Stürmer m.
fossil ['fɒsl] n Fossil neut.
foster ['fɒstə] v pflegen; (feelings) Legen.
adj Pflege-.
fought [fɔɪt] V fight.
foul [faul] adj (dirty) schmutzig; (disgust-

ing) widerlich; (weather) schlecht. v
verschmutzen. n (sport) Regelverstoß m.
found¹ [faund] V find.
found² [faund] v gründen. be founded on
beruhen auf. foundation n (of building)
Grundmauer f; (of institute, firm, etc.)
Gründung f; (basis) Grundlage f; (institute) Stiftung f. founder n Gründer m.
foundry ['faundri] n Gießerei f.
fountain ['fauntin] n Springbrunnen m.
fountain pen Füllfeder f.
four [fɔɪ] adj vier. fourth adj viert; n
Viertel neut.
fourteen [fɔɪ'tiɪn] adj vierzehn.
fowl [faul] n Haushuhn neut.
fox [fɒks] n Fuchs m. v (coll) täuschen.
foyer ['fɔiei] n Foyer neut.
fraction ['frakʃən] n Bruchteil m; (math)
Bruch m.
fracture ['fraktʃə] n (med) Knochenbruch
m. v zerbrechen.
fragile ['fradʒail] adj zerbrechlich.
fragment ['fragmənt] n Bruchstück neut,
Brocken m.
fragrance ['freigrəns] n Duft m, Aroma
neut. fragrant adj duftig, wohlriechend.
frail [freil] adj schwach, gebrechlich. frail-
ty n Schwäche f.
frame [freim] n Rahmen m. v einrahmen.
spectacle frame Brillengestell neut.
France [fraɪns] n Frankreich neut.
franchise ['frantʃaiz] n (pol) Wahlrecht
neut; (comm) Konzession f.
frank [fraŋk] adj offen, freimütig. frankly
adv frei, offen. frankness n Freimut m.
frantic ['frantik] adj wild, rasend.
fraternal [frə'təɪnl] adj brüderlich.
fraud [frɔɪd] n Betrug m, Unterschlagung
f; (person) Schwindler(in). fraudulent adj
betrügerisch.
fraught [frɔɪt] adj voll. fraught with danger gefahrvoll.
fray¹ [frei] v (sich) ausfransen.
fray² [frei] n Rauferei f.
freak [friɪk] n (of nature) Mißbildung f;
(event, storm) Ausnahmeerscheinung f.
adj anormal.
freckle ['frekl] n Sommersprosse f.
free [friɪ] adj frei; kostenlos. v befreien,
freimachen. free and easy ungezwungen.
free speech Redefreiheit f. free will freier
Wille m. freedom n Freiheit. freely adv
reichlich.
freelance ['friɪlɑɪns] n freier Schriftsteller
m. adj freiberuflich tätig.

freemason ['friːmeisn] *n* Freimaurer *n.*
*freeze [friːz] *v* (*water*) frieren; (*food*)
tiefkühlen. **freeze to death** erfrieren. *I'm*
freezing ich friere. *n* (*comm*) Stopp *m.*
freezer *n* Tiefkühltruhe *f.* **freezing point**
Gefrierpunkt *m.*
freight [freit] *n* Fracht *f*; (*freight costs*)
Frachtgebühr *f.*
French [frentʃ] *adj* französisch. **French-**
man *n* Franzose *m.* **Frenchwoman** *n*
Französin *f.* **French horn** Waldhorn *neut.*
french fries *n pl* Pommes frites *pl.*
frenzy ['frenzi] *n* Raserei *f.*
frequency ['friːkwənsi] *n* Frequenz *f.* **fre-**
quent *adj* häufig, frequent; *v* häufig
besuchen. **frequently** *adv* öfters, häufig.
fresco ['freskou] *n* Fresko *neut.*
fresh [freʃ] *adj* frisch; (*water*) süß; (*air*)
erfrischend; (*cheeky*) frech. **fresh water**
Süßwasser *neut.* **freshen** *v* auffrischen.
freshness *n* Frische *f.*
fret [fret] *v* sich Sorgen machen.
friar ['fraiə] *n* Mönch *m.*
friction ['frikʃən] *n* Reibung *f.*
Friday ['fraidei] *n* Freitag *m.* **Good Friday**
Karfreitag *m.*
fridge [fridʒ] *n* Kühlschrank *m.*
fried [fraid] *adj* gebraten. **fried egg**
Spiegelei *neut.* **fried potatoes** Bratkartoffeln.
friend [frend] *n* Freund(in). **make friends**
with sich befreunden mit. **friendly** *adj*
freundlich, freundschaftlich. **friendship** *n*
Freundschaft *f.*
frieze [friːz] *n* Fries *m.*
frigate ['frigit] *n* Fregatte *f.*
fright [frait] *n* Schreck *m* **frighten** *v*
erschrecken. **frightening** *adj* erschreckend. **frightened** *adj* erschrocken. **be**
frightened of Angst haben vor. **frightful**
adj schrecklich.
frigid ['fridʒid] *adj* frigid. **frigidity** *n*
Frigidität *f.*
frill [fril] *n* Rüsche, Krause *f.* **frilly** *adj*
gekräuselt.
fringe [frindʒ] *n* Franse *f*; (*edge*)
Randzone *f*; (*hair*) Pony *neut.* **fringe**
benefits Nebenbezüge *pl.*
frisk [frisk] *v* herumhüpfen; (*search*)
absuchen. **frisky** *adj* munter, lebhaft.
fritter ['fritə] *v* **fritter away** verzetteln.
frivolity [fri'voliti] *n* Leichtfertigkeit *f.*
frivolous *adj* (*person*) leichtfertig; (*worth-*
less) nichtig.

frizz [friz] *v* (sich) kräuseln. **frizzy** *adj*
kraus.
fro [frou] *adv* **to and fro** auf und ab, hin
und her.
frock [frok] *n* Kleid *neut.*
frog [frog] *n* Frosch *m.*
frolic ['frolik] *n* Spaß *m*, Posse *f.* **frolic-**
some *adj* lustig, ausgelassen.
from [from] *prep* von; (*place*) aus, von;
(*to judge from*) nach. *Where are you*
from? wo kommen Sie her?
front [frʌnt] *n* Vorderseite *f*, vorderer Teil
m; (*mil, pol*) Front *f*; (*fa,cade*) Fassade *f.*
adj Vor-, Vorder-. **front door** Haustür *f.*
front room Vorderzimmer *neut.* **in front**
of vor.
frontier ['frʌntiə] *n* Grenze *f.*
frost [frost] *n* Frost *m.* *v* (*cookery*) glasier-
en. **frostbite** *n* Erfrieren *neut*; (*wound*)
Frostbeule *f.* **frostbitten** *adj* erfroren.
frosty *adj* frostig.
froth [froθ] *n* Schaum *m.* **frothy** *adj*
schäumig.
frown [fraun] *n* Stirnrunzeln *neut.* *v* die
Stirn runzeln. **frown on** mißbilligen.
froze [frouz] *V* **freeze.**
frozen ['frouzn] *V* **freeze.** *adj* gefroren;
(*comm*) eingefroren; (*food*) tiefgekühlt.
frozen over zugefroren.
frugal ['fruːgəl] *adj* sparsam.
fruit [fruːt] *n* Obst *neut*, Früchte *pl*;
(*result, yield*) Frucht *f.* **fruitful** *adj*
fruchtbar. **fruition** *n* Erfüllung *f.* **fruitless**
adj fruchtlos. **fruit machine** Spielautomat
neut. **fruit salad** Obstsalat *m.* **fruit tree**
Obstbaum *m.* **fruity** *adj* würzig.
frustrate [frʌ'streit] *v* vereiteln, frustrier-
en. **frustrated** *adj* vereitelt, frustriert.
frustration *n* Vereitelung *f*, Frustration *f.*
fry [frai] *v* (in der Pfanne) braten. **frying-**
pan *n* Bratpfanne *f.*
fuchsia ['fjuːʃə] *n* Fuchsia *f.*
fudge [fʌdʒ] *n* Karamelle *f.*
fuel ['fjuəl] *n* Brennstoff *m*; (*for engines*)
Treibstoff *m*; (*mot*) Benzin *neut.* *v*
tanken. **fuel gauge** Treibstoffmesser *m.*
fuel oil Brennöl *neut.*
fugitive ['fjuːdʒitiv] *adj* flüchtig. *n*
Flüchtling *m.*
fulcrum ['fulkrəm] *n* Drehpunkt *m.*
fulfil [ful'fil] *v* erfüllen. **fulfilment** *n* Erfüllung *f*; (*satisfaction*) Befriedigung *f.*
full [ful] *adj* voll; (*after meal*) satt. *adv*
direkt, gerade. **pay in full** voll bezahlen.
write out in full ausschreiben. **full-grown**

adj ausgewachsen. **full moon** Vollmond
m. **fullness** *n* Fülle *f*. **full stop** Punkt *m*.
full-time *adj* ganztägig. **fully** *adv* voll,
völlig.
fumble ['fʌmbl] *v* umhertasten. **fumble
with** herumfummeln an.
fume [fjuːm] *v* dampfen; (*coll*) wütend
sein. *n* Dunst *m*, Dampf *m*. **fumigate** *v*
ausräuchern.
fun [fʌn] *n* Spaß *m*. **it's fun** es macht
Spaß. **for fun** aus Spaß. **in fun** zum
Scherz. **have fun** sich amüsieren. **have
fun!** viel Spaß/vergnügen! **make fun of**
sich lustig machen über.
function ['fʌŋkʃən] *n* Funktion *f*; (*task*)
Aufgabe *f*; (*gathering*) Veranstaltung *f*. *v*
(*tech*) funktionieren; tätig sein. **function-
al** *adj* funktionell, zweckmäßig. **functionary** *n* Beamte(r).
fund [fʌnd] *n* Fonds *m*; (*fig*) Vorrat *m*. *v*
fundieren.
fundamental [fʌndə'mentl] *adj* grund-
legend, grundsätzlich.
funeral ['fjuːnərəl] *n* Begräbnis *neut*.
fungus ['fʌŋgəs] *n* (*pl* -**i**) Pilz *m*.
funnel ['fʌnl] *n* Trichter *m*; (*ship*) Schornstein *m*.
funny ['fʌni] *adj* (*amusing*) komisch, lustig, spaßhaft; (*strange*) komisch, seltsam.
funny-bone *n* Musikantenknochen *m*.
fur [fəː] *n* Pelz *m*; (*on tongue*) Belag *m*;
(*in boiler*) Kesselstein *m*. **fur coat**
Pelzmantel *m*. **furry** *adj* pelzartig, Pelz-;
belegt.
furious ['fjuəriəs] *adj* wütend.
furnace ['fəːnis] *n* (Brenn)Ofen *m*.
furnish ['fəːniʃ] *v* (*a room*) möblieren;
(*supply*) versehen, ausstatten. **furnishings**
pl n Möbel *pl*.
furniture ['fəːnitʃə] *n* Möbel *pl*.
furrow ['fʌrou] *n* Furche *f*.
further ['fəːðə] *adj, adv* weiter. **until further notice** bis auf weiteres. *v* fördern.
furthermore *adv* ferner, überdies. **furthest**
adj weitest; *adv* am weitestem.
furtive ['fəːtiv] *adj* (*person*) hinterlistig;
(*action*) verstohlen.
fury ['fjuəri] *n* Wut *f*.
fuse [fjuːz] *n* (*elec*) Sicherung *f*; (*explo-
sives*) Zünder *m*. *v* (*join, melt*)
(ver)schmelzen; (*elec*) sichern; (*elec:
blow a fuse*) durchbrennen. **fuse box**
Sicherungskasten *m*.
fuselage ['fjuːzə,laːʒ] *n* Rumpf *m*.
fusion ['fjuːʒən] *n* Verschmelzung *f*.

fuss [fʌs] *n* Getue, Theater *neut*. **make a
fuss** viel Wesens machen (um). **fussy** *adj*
kleinlich.
futile ['fjuːtail] *adj* zwecklos, wertlos. **futility** *n* Zwecklosigkeit *f*.
future ['fjuːtʃə] *n* Zukunft *f*. *adj* künftig.
in future in Zukunft. **futures** *pl n* (*comm*)
Termingeschäfte *pl*. **futuristic** *adj* futuris-
tisch.
fuzz [fʌz] *n* Fussel *f*. **fuzzy** *adj* (*hair*)
kraus; (*vision*) verschwommen.

G

gabble ['gabl] *v* schwätzen.
gable ['geibl] *n* Giebel *m*. **gabled** *adj*
gegiebelt.
gadget ['gadʒit] *n* Apparat *m*, Gerät *neut*.
gag¹ [gag] *v* knebeln. *n* Knebel *m*.
gag² [gag] (*coll: joke*) *n* Witz *m*. *v* einen
Witz reißen.
gaiety ['geiəti] *n* Heiterkeit *f*.
gain [gein] *n* Gewinn *m*. *v* gewinnen; (*of
clock*) vorgehen. **gain on** einholen. **gains**
pl (*comm*) Profit *m*.
gait [geit] *n* Gang *m*.
gala ['gaːlə] *n* Festlichkeit *f*.
galaxy ['galəksi] *n* Sternsystem *neut*;
(*ours*) Milchstraße *f*.
gale [geil] *n* heftiger Wind *m*, Sturmwind
m.
gallant ['galənt] *adj* tapfer; (*courteous*) ritterlich. **gallantry** *n* Tapferkeit *f*; Ritterlichkeit *f*.
gall bladder [goːl] *n* Gallenblase *f*.
galleon ['galiən] *n* Galeone *f*.
gallery ['galəri] *n* Galerie *f*.
galley ['gali] *n* Galeere *f*; (*kitchen*) Schiff-
sküche *f*.
gallon ['galən] *n* Gallone *f*.
gallop ['galəp] *n* Galopp *m*. *v* galoppier-
en.
gallows ['galouz] *n* Galgen *m*.
gallstone ['goːlstoun] *n* Gallenstein *m*.
galore [gə'loː] *adv* in Hülle and Fülle.
galvanize ['galvənaiz] *v* galvanisieren,
verzinken; (*fig: stimulate*) anspornen
(zu).
gamble ['gambl] *v* um Geld spielen. **gamble on** wetten auf. **gamble with** aufs Spiel

setzen. **gambler** *n* Spieler *m.* **gambling** *n* Spielen (um Geld) *neut. n* Wagnis *neut.*

game [geim] *n* Spiel *neut*; (*hunting*) Wild *neut.* **give the game away** den Plan verraten. *adj* (*leg*) lahm. **be game for** bereit sein zu. **gamekeeper** *n* Wildhüter *m.*

gammon ['gamən] *n* (geräucherter) Schinken *m.*

gang [gaŋ] *n* (*criminals*) Bande *f*; (*workers*) Kolonne *f. v* **gang up** sich zusammenrotten. **gangster** *n* Gangster *m.*

gangrene ['gaŋgriːn] *n* Brand *m.*

gangway ['gaŋwei] *n* (*theatre*) Gang *m*; (*naut*) Laufplanke *f.*

gaol [dʒeil] *V* jail.

gap [gap] *n* Lücke *f.*

gape [geip] *v* klaffen; (*person*) gähnen.

garage ['garɑːdʒ] *n* Garage *f*; (*mot: workshop*) Autowerkstatt *f. v* in eine Garage einstellen *or* unterbringen.

garbage ['gɑːbidʒ] *n* Müll *m.* **garbage can** Mülleimer *m.*

garble ['gɑːbl] *v* verstümmeln.

garden ['gɑːdn] *n* Garten *m. v* im Garten arbeiten. **gardening** *n* Gartenbau *m.* **garden party** Gartenfest *neut.*

gargle ['gɑːgl] *v* gurgeln. *n* Mundwasser *neut.*

gargoyle ['gɑːgoil] *n* (*arch*) Wasserspeier *m.*

garland ['gɑːlənd] *n* Girlande *f,* Blumengewinde *neut. v* bekränzen.

garlic ['gɑːlik] *n* Knoblauch *m.*

garment ['gɑːmənt] *n* Kleidungsstück *neut.*

garnish ['gɑːniʃ] *v* (*cookery*) garnieren. *n* Garnierung *f.*

garrison ['garisn] *n* Garnison *f. v* (*town*) besetzen; (*troops*) in Garnison legen.

garter ['gɑːtə] *n* Strumpfband *neut.*

gas [gas] *n* Gas *neut*; (*US: petrol*) Benzin *neut.* **step on the gas** Gas geben. *v* (*poison*) vergasen; (*slang: chatter*) schwätzen. **gasbag** *n* (*coll*) Windbeutel *m.* **gas cooker** Gasherd *m.* **gas fire** Gasheizung *f.*

gash [gaʃ] *v* aufschneiden. *n* klaffende Wunde *f.*

gasket ['gaskit] *n* Dichtung *f.*

gas main *n* Gasleitung *f.*

gas meter *n* Gasmesser *m.*

gasoline ['gasəˌliːn] *n* (*US*) Benzin *neut.*

gasp [gɑːsp] *v* keuchen. *n* Keuchen *neut.*

gas station *n* Tankstelle *f.*

gastric ['gastrik] *adj* gastrisch, Magen-.

gate [geit] *n* Tor *neut.*

gâteau ['gatou] *n* Torte *f.*

gateway ['geitwei] *n* Torweg *m.*

gather ['gaðə] *v* sammeln; (*people*) (sich) versammeln; (*flowers, etc.*) lesen; (*dress*) raffen; (*deduce*) schließen (aus). **gathering** *n* Versammlung *f.*

gaudy ['gɔːdi] *adj* (*colours*) grell, bunt.

gauge [geidʒ] *v* abmessen; (*judge*) schätzen. *n* Normalmaß *neut*; (*rail*) Spurweite *f.* **pressure gauge** Druckmesser *m.*

gaunt [gɔːnt] *adj* mager.

gauze [gɔːz] *n* Gaze *f.*

gave [geiv] *V* give.

gay [gei] *adj* (*colours*) bunt; (*person*) heiter, lustig; (*slang: homosexual*) warm.

gaze [geiz] *v* starren (auf). *n* (starrer) Blick *neut.*

gazelle [gəˈzel] *n* Gazelle *f.*

gazetteer [gazəˈtiə] *n* Namensverzeichnis *neut.*

gear [giə] *n* (*mot*) Gang *m*; (*gear wheel*) Zahnrad *neut*; (*equipment*) Gerät *neut,* Ausrüstung *f.* **in gear** eingeschaltet. **change gear** (*up or down*) Gang herauf *or* herab setzen. **gearbox** *n* Getriebe(gehäuse) *neut.*

geese [giːs] *V* goose.

gelatine ['dʒeləˌtiːn] *n* Gelatine *f*; (*explosive*) Sprenggelatine *f.*

gelignite ['dʒeligˌnait] *n* Gelatinedynamit *neut.*

gem [dʒem] *n* Edelstein *m,* Gemme *f.*

Gemini ['dʒemini] *n* Zwillinge *pl.*

gender ['dʒendə] *n* Geschlecht *neut*; (*gramm*) Genus *neut.*

gene [dʒiːn] *n* Gen *neut,* Erbeinheit *f.*

genealogy [dʒiːniˌalədʒi] *n* Genealogie *f.* **genealogist** *n* Genealoge *m.*

general ['dʒenərəl] *adj* allgemein. *n* General *m.* **in general** im Allgemeinen. **General Assembly** *n* Generalversammlung *f.* **general election** allgemeine Wahlen *pl.*

generate ['dʒenəreit] *v* erzeugen, verursachen. **generator** *n* Generator *m,* Stromerzeuger *m.* **generation** *n* Generation *f,* Zeitalter *m*; (*production*) Erzeugung *f.*

generic [dʒiˈnerik] *adj* allgemein, generell.

generous ['dʒenərəs] *adj* großzügig, freigebig. **generosity** *n* Großzügigkeit *f.*

genetic [dʒiˈnetik] *adj* genetisch, Entstehungs-. **genetics** *n* Genetik *f.*

Geneva [dʒi'niːvə] n Genf neut. **Lake Geneva** der Genfer See m.
genial ['dʒiːniəl] adj freundlich, herzlich. **geniality** n Freundlichkeit f.
genital ['dʒenitl] adj Geschlechts-. **genitals** pl n Geschlechtsteile pl.
genitive ['dʒenitiv] n Genitiv m.
genius ['dʒiːnjəs] n Genie neut; (talent) Begabung f.
genocide ['dʒenəsaid] n Völkermord m.
genteel [dʒen'tiːl] adj wohlerzogen, vornehm.
gentle ['dʒentl] adj sanft, mild. **gentleman** n Herr m. **gentleness** n Mildheit f.
gentry ['dʒentri] n Landadel m.
gents [dʒents] n (sign) Herren pl.
genuine ['dʒenjuin] adj echt, wahr. **genuineness** n Wahrheit f, Echtheit f.
genus ['dʒiːnəs] n Gattung f, Sorte f.
geography [dʒi'ogrəfi] n Erdkunde f, Geographie f. **geographical** adj geographisch. **geographer** n Geograph(in).
geology [dʒi'olədʒi] n Geologie f. **geologist** n Geologe m.
geometry [dʒi'omətri] n Geometrie f. **geometric** adj geometrisch.
geranium [dʒə'reiniəm] n Geranie f.
geriatric [dʒeri'atrik] adj geriatrisch. **geriatrics** n Geriatrie f.
germ [dʒəːm] n Keim m, Bakterie f. **German measles** n Röteln pl.
Germany ['dʒəːməni] n Deutschland neut. **German** adj deutsch; n Deutsche(r); (language) Deutsch neut. **Federal Republic of Germany** n Bundesrepublik Deutschland (BRD) f; **German Democratic Republic** n Deutsche Demokratische Republik (DDR) f.
germinate ['dʒəːmineit] v Keimen. **germination** n Keimen neut.
gesticulate [dʒe'stikju,leit] v wilde Gesten machen.
gesture ['dʒestʃə] n Geste f. v eine Geste machen.
*****get** [get] v (obtain) bekommen, erhalten; (become) werden. **get hold of** bekommen. **get in** einsteigen. **get married** sich verheiraten. **get off** aussteigen. **get ready** vorbereiten.
geyser ['giːzə] n Geiser m.
ghastly ['gaːstli] adj schrecklich, furchtbar.
gherkin ['gəːkin] n Essiggurke f.
ghetto ['getou] n Getto neut.

ghost [goust] n Gespenst neut, Geist m. **ghostly** adj gespenstisch.
giant ['dʒaiənt] n Riese m. adj riesenhaft.
gibberish ['dʒibəriʃ] n Quatsch m.
gibe [dʒaib] v spotten (über). n Spott m.
giblets ['dʒiblits] pl n Hühnerklein neut.
giddy ['gidi] adj schwind(e)lig. **giddiness** n Schwindel m.
gift [gift] n Geschenk neut; (talent) Begabung f. **gifted** adj begabt.
gigantic [dʒai'gantik] adj riesenhaft, gigantisch.
giggle ['gigl] v kichern. n Gekicher neut.
gill [gil] n (fish) Kieme f.
gilt [gilt] adj vergoldet. n Vergoldung f.
gimmick ['gimik] n Trick m.
gin [dʒin] n Gin m, Wacholderschnapps m.
ginger ['dʒindʒə] n Ingwer m. **gingerbread** n Pfefferkuchen m. **ginger-haired** adj rothaarig.
gingerly ['dʒindʒəli] adv vorsichtig.
gipsy ['dʒipsi] n Zigeuner(in). adj Zigeuner.
giraffe [dʒi'raːf] n Giraffe f.
*****gird** [gəːd] v umgürten, umlegen.
girder ['gəːdə] n Träger m, Tragbalken m.
girdle ['gəːdl] n Gurt m. v umgürten.
girl [gəːl] n Mädchen neut. **girl friend** Freundin f. **girlhood** n Mädchenjahre pl. **girlish** adj mädchenhaft.
girt [gəːt] V **gird**.
girth [gəːθ] n Umfang m; (horse) Gurt m.
gist [dʒist] n Wesentliche neut, Hauptpunkt m.
*****give** [giv] v geben; (gift) schenken (hand over) überreichen. n Elastizität f. **give away** (betray) verraten. **give back** zurückgeben. **give in** nachgeben. **give up** aufgeben.
given ['givn] V **give**. adj (an)gegeben.
glacier ['glasiə] n Gletscher m.
glad [glad] adj froh, fröhlich, glücklich. **gladness** n Fröhlichkeit, Glücklichkeit f.
glamour [glamə] n bezaubernde Schönheit f. **glamorous** adj bezaubernd.
glance [glaːns] v (flüchtig) blicken, einen Blick werfen. n flüchtiger Blick m.
gland [gland] n Drüse f. **glandular** adj drüsig, Drüsen-. **glandular fever** n Drüsenfieber m.
glare [gleə] v grell leuchten; (stare) starren. **glare at** anstarren. n blendendes Licht neut.

glass [glɑɪs] n Glas neut. **glasses** pl Brille f sing. **glassfibre** n Glaswolle f.
glaze [gleiz] n Glasur f. v verglasen; (windows) mit Glasscheiben versehen. **glazier** n Glaser m.
gleam [gliːm] n Schimmer m. v schimmern.
glean [gliːn] v (nach)lesen.
glee [gliː] n Fröhlichkeit f. **gleeful** adj fröhlich.
glib [glib] adj zungenfertig.
glide [glaid] v gleiten. **glider** n Segelflugzeug neut.
glimmer ['glimə] n Schimmer m. v schimmern.
glimpse [glimps] n flüchtiger Blick. v erspähen.
glint [glint] n Glitzern neut. v glitzern.
glisten ['glisn] n Glanz m. v glänzen.
glitter ['glitə] n Funkeln neut. v funkeln.
gloat [glout] v sich hämisch freuen über. **gloating** n Schadenfreude f.
globe [gloub] n (Erd)Kugel f. **global** adj global. **globular** adj kugelförmig.
gloom [gluːm] n Düsternis f, Dunkelheit f; (mood) Trübsinn m. **gloomy** adj düster.
glory ['gloːri] n Ruhm m, Ehre f. v sich freuen. **glorify** v verherrlichen. **glorious** adj glorreich, herrlich.
gloss [glos] n Glanz m. v polieren. **gloss paint** Ölfarbe f. **gloss over** vertuschen.
glossary ['glosəri] n Glossar neut, (spezielles) Wortverzeichnis neut.
glove [glʌv] n Handschuh m. **fit like a glove** passen wie angegossen.
glow [glou] n Glühen neut. v glühen.
glucose ['gluːkous] n Traubenzucker m.
glue [gluː] n Klebstoff neut. v kleben.
glum [glʌm] adj mürrisch.
glut [glʌt] n Überfluß m; (comm) Überangebot neut. v sättigen.
glutton ['glʌtən] n Vielfraß m. **gluttonous** adj gefräßig. **gluttony** n Gefräßigkeit f.
gnarled [nɑɪld] adj knorrig.
gnash [naʃ] v knirschen.
gnat [nat] n Mücke f.
gnaw [noɪ] v nagen an (+dat).
gnome [noum] n Zwerg m, Gnom m.
***go** [gou] v gehen; (travel) fahren, reisen; (machine) funktionieren, in Betrieb sein; (time) vergehen; (coll: become) werden. **go ahead** fortfahren. **go away** weggehen; (travel) verreisen. **go down** hinuntergehen; (price) fallen. **go out** hinausgehen; (fire) erlöschen. **go up** hinaufgehen; (prices) steigen. **have a go at** einen Versuch machen mit. **it's no go!** es geht nicht!
goad [goud] n Stachelstock m. v antreiben.
goal [goul] n Ziel neut; (sport) Tor m. **goalkeeper** n Torwart m.
goat [gout] n Ziege f.
gobble ['gobl] v **gobble (down)** (food) hinunterschlingen. **gobble up** verschlingen.
goblin ['goblin] n Kobold m.
god [god] n Gott m. **thank God!** Gott sei dank! **godchild** n Patenkind neut. **goddaughter** n Patentochter f. **goddess** n Göttin f. **godfather** n Pate m. **godmother** n Patin f. **godsend** n Glücksfall m. **godson** n Patensohn m.
goggles ['goglz] pl n Schutzbrille f sing.
gold [gould] n Gold neut. **golden** adj golden. **goldfish** n Goldfisch m. **gold leaf** n Blattgold neut. **gold mine** Goldgrube f. **gold-plated** adj vergoldet. **goldsmith** n goldschmied.
golf [golf] n Golf(spiel) neut. **golfclub** n Golfschläger m. **golf course** Golfplatz m. **golfer** n Golfspieler m.
gondola ['gondələ] n Gondel f.
gone [gon] V go.
gong [goŋ] n Gong m.
gonorrhoea [ˌgonəˈriə] n (med) Gonorrhöe f.
good [gud] adj gut; (pleasant) angenehm; (child) brav. n Gute neut, Wohl neut. **good afternoon** guten Tag. **goodbye** interj auf Wiedersehen. **good evening** guten Abend. **good for nothing** nichts Wert. **good-for-nothing** n Taugenichts m. **good-looking** adj gut aussehen. **good morning** guten Morgen. **good night** gute Nacht. **do (someone) good** (jemanden) wohltun. **it's no good** es nützt nichts. **goodness** n Güte f. **goods** pl n Güter pl.
Good Friday n Karfreitag m.
goose [guːs] n (pl geese) Gans f.
gooseberry ['guzbəri] n Stachelbeere f. **play gooseberry** Anstandswauwau spielen.
gore [goɪ] n Blut neut. v aufspießen.
gorge [goɪdʒ] n (geog) Schlucht f. v **gorge oneself** (coll) sich vollessen.
gorgeous ['goɪdʒəs] adj Wunderschön, prachtvoll.

gorilla [gə'rilə] n Gorilla m.
gorse [gɔːs] n Stechginster m.
gory [gɔːri] adj blutig.
gospel ['gɔspəl] n Evangelium neut.
gossip ['gɔsip] n Geschwätz neut; (person) Klatschbase f. v schwätzen.
got [gɔt] V get.
Gothic ['goθik] adj gotisch.
gotten ['gɔtn] V get.
gouge [gaudʒ] v aushöhlen. n Hohleisen neut.
goulash ['guːlaʃ] n Gulasch neut.
gourd [guəd] n Kürbis m.
gourmet ['guəmei] n Feinschmecker m.
gout [gaut] n Gicht f. gouty gichtkrank, gichtisch.
govern ['gʌvən] v (country) regieren; (determine) bestimmen; (tech) regeln. governess n Gouvernante f. government n Regierung f. governmental adj Regierungs-. governor n Gouverneur m.
gown [gaun] n Kleid neut.
grab [grab] v ergreifen, (an)packen. n (plötzlicher) Griff m.
grace [greis] n Gnade f, Güte f; (prayer) Tischgebet neut. 14 days' grace 14 Tage Aufschub. Your Grace Eure Hoheit. graceful adj anmutig. gracious adj angenehm, gnädig.
grade [greid] n Grad m, Stufe f; (comm) Qualität f; (US) (Schul)Klasse f; (slope) Gefälle neut. v sortieren, einordnen.
gradient ['greidiənt] n Gefälle neut.
gradual ['gradjuəl] adj stufenweise, allmählich.
graduate ['gradjuət; v 'gradjueit] n Graduierte(r); (high school) Absolvent(in). v abstufen; (university) promovieren. graduation n. Promovierung f; (high school) Absolvieren neut.
graffiti [grə'fiːtiː] pl n Graffiti neut sing.
graft¹ [graːft] n (bot) Pfropfreis neut; (med) Transplantat neut. v pfropfen; transplantieren.
graft² [graːft] n Korruption f.
grain [grein] n Getreide neut, Korn neut; (sand, etc.) Körnchen neut; (wood) n Maserung f. grainy adj körnig.
gram [gram] n Gramm neut.
grammar ['gramə] n Grammatik f. grammatical adj grammatisch. grammar school Gymnasium neut.
gramophone ['graməfoun] n Platten-

spieler m. gramophone record (Schall)Platte f.
granary ['granəri] n Kornkammer f.
grand [grand] adj groß, großartig. grand piano Flügel m. grandeur n Erhabenheit f.
grand-dad n also grandpa (coll) Opa m.
grand-daughter n Enkelin f.
grandfather ['gran,faːðə] n Großvater m.
grandma ['granmaɪ] n also granny (coll) Oma f.
grandmother ['gran,mʌðə] n Großmutter f.
grandparents ['gran,peərənts] pl n Großeltern pl.
grandson ['gransʌn] n Enkel m.
grandstand ['granstand] n Haupttribüne f.
grand total n Gesamtbetrag m.
granite ['granit] n Granit m.
grant [graːnt] v gewähren; (admit) zugestehen. n (student) Stipendium neut; (subsidy) Subvention f, Zuschuß m.
granule ['granjuːl] n Körnchen neut. granular adj körnig, granuliert.
grape [greip] n (Wein)Traube f. grapevine n Rebstock m.
grapefruit ['greipfruːt] n Grapefruit neut, Pampelmuse f.
graph [graːf] n graphische Darstellung f, Schaubild neut.
grapple ['grapl] v sich auseinandersetzen (mit), ringen (mit).
grasp [graːsp] v greifen, packen; (understand) begreifen. n Griff m. grasping adj habgierig.
grass [graːs] n Gras neut; (lawn) Rasen m. v (coll) pfeifen.
grate¹ [greit] n (Feuer)Rost m, Gitter neut.
grate² [greit] v (cookery) reiben; (teeth) knirschen. grate on one's nerves auf die Nerven gehen.
grateful ['greitful] adj dankbar.
gratify ['gratifai] v befriedigen. gratification n Befriedigung f. gratitude n Dankbarkeit f.
gratuity [grə'tjuəti] n Trinkgeld neut.
grave¹ [greiv] n Grab neut. gravedigger n Totengräber m. gravestone n Grabstein m. graveyard n Friedhof m.
grave² [greiv] adj ernsthaft, schwerwiegend.
gravel ['gravəl] n Kies m. gravelpit n Kiesgrube f.

gravity ['gravəti] n Schwerkraft f; (seriousness) Ernsthaftigkeit f, Ernst m.

gravy ['greivi] n (Braten)Soße f.

graze¹ [greiz] n (med) Abschürfung f. v abschürfen; (touch) leicht berühren.

graze² [greiz] v (animal) (ab)weiden. **grazing** n Weide f.

grease [griːs] n Fett neut, Schmalz neut; (tech, mot) Schmiere f. v schmieren.

great [greit] adj groß; (important) bedeutend; (coll) großartig, toll. **greatly** adv in hohem Maße. **great-grandparents** pl n Urgroßeltern pl. **greatness** n Größe f. **Great Britain** n Großbritannien neut.

Greece [griːs] n Griechenland neut. **Greek** adj griechisch; n Grieche m, Griechin f.

greed [griːd] n Gier f (nach). **greedy** adj gierig.

green [griːn] adj grün. n Grün neut. **greenfly** n grüne Blattlaus f. **greengage** n Reineclaude f. **greengrocer's** n Obst- und Gemüseladen m. **greenhouse** n Treibhaus neut. **greens** pl n (cookery) Grünzeug neut.

Greenland ['griːnlənd] n Grönland neut. **Greenlander** n Grönländer m.

greet [griːt] v grüßen, begrüßen. **greeting** n Gruß m, Begrüßung f.

gregarious [gri'geəriəs] adj gesellig.

grenade [grə'neid] n Granate f.

grew [gruː] V grow.

grey [grei] adj grau; (gloomy) trübe. n Grau neut. **greyhound** n Windhund m.

grid [grid] n Gitter neut; (network) Netz neut.

grief [griːf] n Trauer f. **grievance** n Beschwerde f. **grieve** v trauern.

grill [gril] v grillen; (question) einem strengen Verhör unterziehen. n Bratrost m, Grill m.

grille [gril] n Gitter neut.

grim [grim] adj (person) grimmig, verbissen; (prospect) schlimm, hoffnungslos.

grimace [gri'meis] n Grimasse f. v Grimassen schneiden.

grime [graim] n Schmutz m, Ruß m.

grin [grin] n Lächeln neut, Grinsen neut. v lächeln, grinsen.

*grind [graind] v mahlen; (knife) schleifen; (teeth) knirschen. n (coll) Plackerei f. **grinder** n (coffee, etc.) Mühle f.

grip [grip] v (an)packen, festhalten. n Griff m.

gripe [graip] v zwicken. n Kolik f; Bauchschmerzen pl.

grisly ['grizli] adj gräßlich.

gristle ['grisl] n Knorpel m. **gristly** adj knorpelig.

grit [grit] n Splitt m; (coll) Mut m, Entschlossenheit f. **grit one's teeth** die Zähne zusammenbeißen.

groan [groun] n Stöhnen neut. v stöhnen.

grocer ['grousə] n Lebensmittelhändler m. **grocer's shop** Lebensmittelgeschäft neut. **groceries** pl n Lebensmittel pl.

groin [groin] n (anat) Leistengegend f.

groom [gruːm] n (of bride) Bräutigam m; (for horse) (Pferde)Knecht m. v pflegen. **well groomed** gepflegt.

groove [gruːv] n Rinne f, Furche f.

grope [group] v tasten (nach). **gropingly** adv tastend, vorsichtig.

gross [grous] adj grob; (comm) Brutto-; (fat) dick. n Gros neut. **Gross National Product (GNP)** Bruttosozialprodukt neut. **gross weight** Bruttogewicht n.

grotesque [grə'tesk] adj grotesk.

grotto ['grotou] n Grotte f.

ground¹ [graund] V grind.

ground² [graund] n Boden m, Erde f. v (aero) still legen. **ground floor** Erdgeschoß neut. **grounds** pl (of house) Anlagen pl; (coffee) Bodensatz m; (reason) Grund m.

group [gruːp] n Gruppe f. v gruppieren.

grouse¹ [graus] n Birkhuhn neut.

grouse² [graus] v (coll: grumble) meckern. n Beschwerde f.

grove [grouv] n Hain m.

grovel ['grovl] v kriechen (vor). **grovelling** adj kriecherisch.

*grow [grou] v wachsen; (become) werden; (plants) züchten. **grow better** sich bessern. **grow old** alt werden. **grow out of** (clothes) herauswachsen aus; (habit) entwachsen (+ dat); (arise from) entstehen aus. **grow up** heranwachsen. **grower** n Züchter. **growing** adj wachsend.

growth n Wachstum neut; (increase) Zunahme f; (med) Gewächs neut.

grown [groun] V grow. adj erwachsen. **grown-up** Erwachsene(r) f.

grub [grʌb] n Made f; (slang: food) Futter neut. **grubby** adj schmutzig, dreckig.

grudge [grʌdʒ] v mißgönnen. n Mißgunst f.

gruelling ['gruəliŋ] adj mörderisch.
gruesome ['gru:səm] adj grausam.
gruff [grʌf] adj barsch.
grumble ['grʌmbl] v schimpfen, murren. n Murren neut.
grumpy ['grʌmpi] adj mürrisch.
grunt [grʌnt] n Grunzen neut. v grunzen.
guarantee [garən'ti:] n Garantie f, Gewährleistung f. v garantieren, gewährleisten. **guarantor** n Gewährsmann m.
guard [ga:d] n Wächter m, Wache f. v (be)schützen, bewachen. **guard against** sich hüten vor. **on one's guard** auf der Hut. **guard of honour** Ehrenwache f.
guerrilla [gə'rilə] n Guerillakämpfer m. **guerilla warfare** Guerillakrieg m.
guess [ges] n Schätzung f, Vermutung f. v schätzen, vermuten. **guesswork** n Mutmaßung f.
guest [gest] n Gast m. **guest house** Pension f. **guestroom** Fremdenzimmer neut.
guide [gaid] n Führer m; (book) Handbuch neut. v führen, leiten. **guide book** Reiseführer m.
guild [gild] n Gilde f, Vereinigung f.
guillotine ['giləti:n] n Guillotine f; (for paper) Papierschneidemaschine f. v guillotinieren.
guilt [gilt] n Schuld f; (feeling of) Schuldgefühl neut. **guilty** adj schuldig. **guilty conscience** schlechtes Gewissen neut. **find guilty** für schuldig erklären.
guinea pig ['gini] n Guinee f. **guinea pig** Meerschweinchen neut; (fig: in experiment) Versuchskaninchen neut.
guitar [gi'ta:] n Gitarre f. **guitar player** Gitarrenspieler(in).
gulf [gʌlf] n Golf m.
gull [gʌl] n Möwe f.
gullet [gʌlit] n Schlund m.
gullible ['gʌləbl] adj naiv, leichtgläubig. **gullibility** n Leichtgläubigkeit f.
gully ['gʌli] n Rinne f.
gulp [gʌlp] v hinunterschlucken. n Schluck m.
gum[1] [gʌm] n (glue) Klebstoff m; (from tree) Gummi neut; (sweet) Gummibonbon neut. **chewing gum** Kaugummi neut. v kleben.
gum[2] [gʌm] n (in mouth) Zahnfleisch neut.
gun [gʌn] n Gewehr neut; (hand gun) Pistole f; (large) Kanone f. **stick to one's guns** nicht nachgeben. v **gun down** erschießen.
gurgle ['gə:gl] n Gurgeln neut. v gurgeln.

gush [gʌʃ] v hervorquellen, entströmen. n Strom m, Guß m. **gushing** adj überschwenglich.
gust [gʌst] n Bö neut. v blasen.
gusto ['gʌstou] n Schwung m. **with gusto** eifrig.
gut [gʌt] n Darm m. **guts** pl Eingeweide pl; (coll) Mut m.
gutter ['gʌtə] n (roof) Dachrinne; (street) Gosse f. **gutter press** Schmutzpresse f.
guy[1] [gai] (coll) n Kerl m.
guy[2] [gai] n Halteseil neut. **guy-rope** n Spannschnur f.
gymnasium [dʒim'neiziəm] n Turnhalle f. **gymnast** n Turner(in). **gymnastic** adj gymnastisch. **gymnastics** n Gymnastik f.
gynaecology [gainə'kolədʒi] n Frauenheilkunde f, Gynäkologie f. **gynaecologist** n Frauenarzt m, Gynäkologe m. **gynaecological** adj gynäkologisch.
gypsum ['dʒipsəm] n Gips m.
gyrate [,dʒai'reit] v wirbeln.
gyroscope ['dʒairə,skoup] n Giroskop neut.

H

haberdasher ['habədaʃə] n Kurzwarenhändler m. **haberdashery** n Kurzwaren pl.
habit ['habit] n Gewohnheit f. **be in the habit of** gewöhnt sein. **habitual** adj gewohnt, üblich.
habitable ['habitəbl] adj bewohnbar. **habitat** n Heimat f. **habitation** n Wohnung f. **unfit for human habitation** für Wohnzwecke ungeeignet.
hack[1] [hak] v (zer)hacken. **hacksaw** n Metallsäge f.
hack[2] [hak] n (horse) Mietpferd neut, Gaul m; (writer) Lohnschreiber m.
hackneyed ['haknid] adj abgedroschen, banal.
had [had] V have.
haddock ['hadək] n Schellfisch m.
haemorrhage ['heməridʒ] n Blutung f, Blutsturz m. v bluten.
haemorrhoids ['heməroidz] pl n Hämorrhoiden pl.

haggard ['hagəd] *adj* hager, verstört.
haggle ['hagl] *v* feilschen.
Hague [heig] *n* Den Haag *m*.
hail¹ [heil] *n* Hagel *m*. *v* hageln. **hailstone**
n Hagelkorn *neut*. **hailstorm** *n* Hagel-
schauer *m*.
hail² [heil] *v* (*greet*) begrüßen; (*call up*)
zurufen. **hail from** herkommen von.
hair [heə] *n* (*single*) Haar *neut*; (*person's*)
Haar *neut*, Haare *pl*. **hairy** *adj* behaart,
haarig.
hairbrush ['heəbrʌʃ] *n* Haarbürste *f*.
haircut ['heəkʌt] *n* Haarschnitt *m*. **have a
haircut** sich die Haare schneiden lassen.
hair-do *n* Frisur *f*.
hairdresser ['heə,dresə] *n* Friseur *m*,
Friseuse *f*.
hair-dryer ['heə,draiə] *n* Haartrockner *m*.
hair-net *n* Haarnetz *neut*.
hairpin ['heəpin] *n* Haarnadel *f*.
hair-raising ['heə,reiziŋ] *adj* aufregend.
hake [heik] *n* Seehecht *m*.
half [haɪf] *n* Hälfte *f*. *adj* halb. *adv* halb,
zur Hälfte; (*almost*) beinahe. **at half price**
zum halben Preis.
half-and-half *adv* halb-und-halb.
half-back ['haɪfbak] *n* Läufer *m*.
half-baked [,haɪf'beikt] *adj* (*idea*) halbfer-
tig, nicht durchgedacht.
half-breed ['haɪfbriːd] *n* Mischling *m*.
half-brother ['haɪfbrʌðə] *n* Halbbruder *m*.
half-hearted [,haɪf'haɪtid] *adj* gleichgültig,
lustlos.
half-hour [,haɪf'auə] *n* halbe Stunde *f*.
half-hourly *adv* jede halbe Stunde.
half-mast [,haɪf'maɪst] *n* **at half-mast**
halbmast.
half-sister ['haɪfsistə] *n* Halbschwester *f*.
half-term [,haɪf'təɪm] *n* Semesterhalbzeit *f*.
half-time [,haɪf'taim] *n* Halbzeit *f*.
halfway [,haɪf'wei] *adv* in der Mitte,
halbwegs.
halfwit ['haɪfwit] *n* Schwachkopf *m*. **half-
witted** *adj* dumm, blöd.
halibut ['halibət] *n* Heilbutt *m*.
hall [hoɪl] *n* Halle *f*, Saal *m*; (*entrance*)
Diele *f*, Flur *m*. **hall of residence**
Studentenheim *neut*. **hall porter**
Hotelportier *m*.
hallmark ['hoɪlmaɪk] *n* Feingehaltsstempel
m; (*characteristic*) Kennzeichen *neut*.
hallowed ['haloud] *adj* verehrt.
Hallowe'en [halou'iɪn] *n* Abend vor
Allerheiligen *m*.

hallucinate [hə'luɪsineit] *v* halluzinieren.
hallucination *n* Halluzination *f*.
halo ['heilou] *n* Glorienschein *m*.
halt [hoɪlt] *n* Halt *m*, Pause *f*; (*railway*)
Haltestelle *f*. *v* Pause machen; (*put a stop
to*) halten lassen.
halter ['hoɪltə] *n* Halfter *f*.
halve [haɪv] *v* halbieren; (*reduce*) auf die
Hälfte reduzieren.
ham [ham] *n* Schinken *m*. (**radio**) **ham**
Radio-amateur *m*.
hamburger ['hambəɪgə] *n* Frikadelle *f*.
hamlet 'hamlit] *n* Dörfchen *neut*.
hammer ['hamə] *n* Hammer *m*. *v* hämmern. **hammer and tongs** (*coll*) mit aller
Kraft.
hammock ['hamək] *n* Hängematte *f*.
hamper¹ ['hampə] *v* behindern, hemmen.
hamper² ['hampə] *n* Packkorb *m*, Eßkorb
m.
hamster ['hamstə] *n* Hamster *m*.
hamstring ['hamstriŋ] *n* Knieflechse *f*. *v*
(*coll*) lähmen.
hand [hand] *n* Hand *f*; (*of clock*) Zeiger
m. *v* (*give*) geben. **at** *or* **to hand** zur
Hand. **hand in** einreichen. **hand out** austeilen. **hand over** übergeben. **in hand** im
Gange. **on the one hand ... on the other
hand ...** einerseits ... andererseits ....
handbag ['handbag] *n* Handtasche *f*.
handbook ['handbuk] *n* Handbuch *neut*;
(*travel*) Reiseführer *m*.
handbrake ['handbreik] *n* Handbremse *f*.
handcream ['handkriːm] *n* Handcreme *f*.
handcuff ['handkʌf] *v* Handschellen
anlegen (+*dat*). **handcuffs** *pl n* Handschellen *pl*.
handful ['handful] *n* Handvoll *f*.
handicap ['handikap] *n* Behinderung *f*;
(*sport*) Handikap *neut*. *v* (*horse*) extra
belasten; (*person*) hemmen. **handicapped**
adj (*med, etc*.) behindert.
handicraft ['handikraɪft] *n* Handwerk
neut.
handiwork ['handiwəɪk] *n* Handarbeit *f*.
handkerchief ['haŋkətʃif] *n* Taschentuch
neut.
handle ['handl] *n* Griff *m*; (*door*)
(Tür)Klinke *f*. *v* anfassen, handhaben;
(*deal with*) behandeln, sich befassen mit.
handlebar *n* Lenkstange *f*. **handling** *n*
Behandlung *f*.
handmade [,hand'meid] *adj* mit der Hand
gemacht.

hand-out ['handaut] n Almosen neut; (leaflet) Prospekt m, Werbezettel m.
hand-pick [hand'pik] v (sorgfältig) aus-wählen.
handrail ['handreil] n Geländer neut.
handshake ['handʃeik] n Händedruck m.
handsome ['hansəm] adj schön, stattlich.
handstand ['hand‚stand] n Handstand m.
hand-towel n Handtuch neut.
handwriting ['hand‚raitiŋ] n (Hand)Schrift f.
handy ['handi] adj greifbar, zur Hand; (adroit) geschickt, gewandt.
*****hang** [haŋ] v hängen; (person) erhängen. n (of a dress) Sitz m. **to get the hang of** beherrschen, begreifen. **hang on** (phone) am Apparat bleiben. **hang up** (phone) auflegen; (picture, coat) aufhängen.
hangar ['haŋə] n Flugzeughalle f.
hanger ['haŋə] n (for clothes) Kleiderbügel m.
hangover ['haŋouvə] n (coll) Kater m.
hanker ['haŋkə] v sich sehnen (nach). **hankering** n Verlangen neut.
haphazard [‚hap'hazəd] adj zufällig.
happen ['hapən] v geschehen, vorkom-men. **happen upon** finden. **happen along** erscheinen. **happening** n Ereignis neut.
happy ['hapi:] adj glücklich, zufrieden. **happy-go-lucky** adj sorglos. **happiness** n Glück neut, Glückseligkeit f.
harass ['harəs] v quälen, aufreiben.
harbour ['haɪbə] n Hafen m. v (protect) beherbergen.
hard [haɪd] adj hart; (difficult) schwer, schwierig; (callous) gefühllos. **hard-boiled** adj hartgekocht; (coll) hartnäckig. **hard-pressed** adj in schwerer Bedrängnis. **hard up** (coll) schlecht bei Kasse. **hard-of-hearing** adj schwerhörig.
harden ['haɪdn] v härten, hart machen; (become hard) hart werden.
hardly ['haɪdli] adj kaum. **hardly ever** fast nie.
hardware ['haɪdweə] n Eisenwaren pl; (computers) Hardware f.
hardy ['haɪdi] adj kräftig, abgehärtet; (plant) winterfest.
hare [heə] n Hase m.
haricot ['harikou] n weiße Bohne f.
hark [haɪk] v horchen. interj hör mal!
harm [haɪm] v schaden (+ dat), verletzen. n Schaden m, Leid neut. **harmful** adj schädlich. **harmfulness** n Schädlichkeit f.

harmless adj harmlos. **harmlessness** n Harmlosigkeit f.
harmonic [haɪ'monik] adj harmonisch.
harmonica [haɪ'monikə] n Mundharmonika f.
harmonious [haɪ'mouniəs] adj harmonisch, wohlklingend.
harmonize ['haɪmənaiz] v harmonisieren. **harmonization** n Harmonisierung f.
harmony ['haɪmɒni] n Harmonie f; (agreement) Einklang m, Übereinstim-mung f.
harness ['haɪnis] n (Pferde)Geschirr neut. v spannen; (fig) nutzbar machen.
harp [haɪp] n Harfe f. v **harp on** (coll) dauernd reden von.
harpoon [haɪ'puɪn] n Harpune f. v harpunieren.
harpsichord ['haɪpsi‚kɔɪd] n Cembalo neut.
harrowing ['harouiŋ] adj qualvoll, schrecklich.
harsh [haɪʃ] adj hart; (voice) rauh; (strict) streng. **harshness** n Strenge f, Härte f.
harvest ['haɪvist] n Ernte f. (time) Erntezeit f. v ernten, einbringen. **harvest-er** n (mech) Mähdrescher f. **Harvest Festival** Erntedankfest neut.
hash [haʃ] n Haschee neut. **make a hash of** (coll) verpfuschen.
hashish ['haʃi:ʃ] n Haschisch neut.
haste [heist] n Eile f. **make haste** sich beeilen. **hasten** v sich beeilen; beschleunigen. **hasty** adj eilig; (rushed) übereilt. **hastiness** Voreiligkeit f.
hat [hat] n Hut m. **eat one's hat** einen Besen fressen. **keep under one's hat** für sich halten.
hatch[1] [hatʃ] v ausbrüten. **hatch a plot** ein Komplott schmieden.
hatch[2] [hatʃ] n (naut) Luke f; (serving) Servierfenster neut.
hatchet ['hatʃit] n Beil neut. **bury the hatchet** das Kriegsbeil begraben.
hate [heit] v hassen, verabscheuen. n also **hatred** Haß m, Abscheu m. **hateful** adj hassenswert.
haughty ['hɔɪti] adj hochmutig. **haughti-ness** n Hochmut m.
haul [hɔɪl] v ziehen, schleppen. n (coll: booty) Fang m. **haulage** n Transport m, Spedition f. **haulier** n Transportun-ternehmer m, Spediteur m.
haunch [hɔɪntʃ] n Hüfte f; (of animal) Keule f, Lende f.

haunt [hoɪnt] v (*ghost*) spuken in. **haunted** *adj* gespenstig.

*have [hav] v haben. *I have to go* ich muß gehen. *I will have it repaired* ich werde es reparieren lassen. *I have got a car* ich habe ein Auto. *he's had it* es ist aus mit ihm. **be had** (*be cheated*) reingelegt sein. **have a tooth out** sich einen Zahn ziehen lassen. **have it out with** sich auseinandersetzen mit.

haven ['heivn] n Hafen m; (*fig*) Asyl neut.

havoc ['havək] n Verheerung f. **play havoc with** verheeren.

hawk [hoɪk] n Habicht m, Falke m.

hawthorn ['hoɪθoɪn] n Hagedorn m.

hay [hei] n Heu neut. **make hay** Heu machen, heuen. **hay fever** Heuschnupfen m. **haystack** n Heuschober m.

haywire ['heiwaiə] *adj* (*coll*) kaputt. **go haywire** kaputtgehen.

hazard ['hazəd] n (*danger*) Gefahr f; (*risk*) Risiko neut; (*chance*) Zufall m; (*golf*) Hindernis neut. v aufs Spiel setzen, wagen. **hazardous** *adj* gefährlich, riskant.

haze [heiz] n Dunst m, leichter Nebel m; (*fig*) Verschwommenheit f. **hazy** *adj* dunstig; verschwommen.

hazel ['heizl] n Haselstrauch m. *adj* (*colour*) nußbraun. **hazelnut** n Haselnuß f.

he [hiɪ] *pron* er.

head [hed] n Kopf m; (*leader*) Leiter m; (*top*) Spitze f. v leiten, führen. **head for** zugehen nach. **head off** umlenken. **per head** pro Kopf. **by a head** um eine Kopflänge f.

headache ['hedeik] n Kopfweh neut, Kopfschmerzen pl.

headfirst [,hed'fəɪst] *adj* kopfüber.

heading ['hediŋ] n Titel m, Überschrift f.

headlamp ['hedlamp] n Scheinwerfer m.

headland ['hedlənd] n Landzunge f, Landspitze f.

headline ['hedlain] n Schlagzeile f.

headlong ['hedloŋ] *adv* kopfüber; ungestüm, blindlings.

headmaster [,hed'maɪstə] n (Schul)Direktor m. **headmistress** n Direktorin f, Vorsteherin f.

head office n Hauptsitz m.

headphones ['hedfounz] pl n Kopfhörer m sing.

headquarters [,hed'kwoɪtəz] n (*mil*) Hauptquartier neut; (*comm*) Hauptsitz m.

headrest ['hedrest] n Kopfstütze f.

headscarf ['hedskaɪf] n Kopftuch neut.

headstrong ['hedstroŋ] *adj* eigensinning.

head waiter n Ober(kellner) m.

headway ['hedwei] n Fortschritte pl. **make headway** vorankommen, Fortschritte machen.

heal [hiɪl] v heilen. **healer** n Heiler m. **healing** n Heilung f. *adj* heilend, heilsam.

health [helθ] n Gesundheit f. **your health!** zum Wohl! **health insurance** Krankenversicherung f. **health resort** Kurort m. **healthy** *adj* gesund.

heap [hiɪp] n Haufe(n) m. v häufen. *heaps better* (*coll*) viel besser. **heap up** anhäufen.

*hear [hiə] v hören; (*listen*) zuhören. **hearing** n Gehör neut; (*law*) Verhör neut. **hearing aid** Horgerät neut. **hearsay** n Hörensagen neut. **preliminary hearing** Voruntersuchung f.

heard [həɪd] V **hear.**

hearse [həɪs] n Leichenwagen m.

heart [haɪt] n Herz neut. **change of heart** Gesinnungswechsel m.

heart attack n Herzanfall m.

heartbeat ['haɪtbiɪt] n Herzschlag m.

heart-breaking ['haɪtbreikiŋ] *adj* herzzerbrechend. **heart-broken** *adj* untröstlich.

heartburn ['haɪtbəɪn] n Sodbrennen neut.

heart failure n Herzschlag m.

heartfelt ['haɪtfelt] *adj* tiefempfunden.

hearth [haɪθ] n Kamin m.

hearty ['haɪti] *adj* herzlich. **heartily** adv herzlich, von Herzen.

heat [hiɪt] n Hitze f, Wärme f; (*sport*) Vorlauf m. **in the heat of passion** (*law*) im Affekt. v hitzen. **heated** *adj* (*fig*) erregt. **heating** n Heizung f. **heatproof** *adj* hitzebeständig. **heat-stroke** n Hitzschlag m. **heatwave** n Hitzewelle f.

heath [hiɪθ] n Heide f.

heathen ['hiɪðn] n Heide m. *adj* heidnisch, unzivilisiert.

heather ['heðə] n Heidekraut neut.

heave [hiɪv] v hieven; hochheben; (*sigh*) ausstoßen; (*anchor*) lichten. n Heben neut.

heaven ['hevn] n Himmel m. **go to heaven** in den Himmel kommen. **to move heaven and earth** (*fig*) Himmel und Erde in Bewegung setzen. **for heaven's sake** um Himmels Willen. **heavenly** *adj* himmlisch. **heavenly body** Himmelskörper m.

heavy ['hevi] *adj* schwer, schwerwiegend; (*mood*) träge; (*book*) langweilig. **heaviness** *n* Schwere *f*; (*mood*) Schwerfälligkeit *f*. **heavy-duty** *adj* Hochleistungs-. **heavyweight** *n* (*sport*) Schwergewichtler *m*.

Hebrew ['hiːbruː] *n* Hebräer *m*. *adj* hebräisch.

heckle ['hekl] *v* durch Fragen belästigen. **heckler** *n* Zwischenrufer *m*.

hectare ['hektaː] *n* Hektar *neut*.

hectic ['hektik] *adj* hektisch.

hedge [hedʒ] *n* Hecke *f*, Heckenzaun *m*. **hedgerow** *n* Hecke *f*.

hedgehog ['hedʒhog] *n* Igel *m*.

heed [hiːd] *v* achtgeben auf. *n* Beachtung. **heedful** *adj* achtsam. **heedless** *adj* achtlos.

heel [hiːl] *n* Ferse *f*; (*of shoe*) Absatz *m*. *v* (*shoes*) mit Absätzen versehen. **take to one's heels** die Beine in die Hand nehmen. **down-at-heel** (*fig*) schäbig. **well-heeled** *adj* wohlhabend.

hefty ['hefti] *adj* kräftig.

heifer ['hefə] *n* Färse *f*.

height [hait] *n* Höhe *f*; (*person*) Größe *f*; (*fig*) Höhepunkt *m*. **heighten** *v* verstärken.

heir [eə] *n* Erbe *m*. **heiress** *n* Erbin *f*. **heirloom** *n* Erbstück *neut*.

held [held] *V* **hold¹**

helicopter ['helikoptə] *n* Hubschrauber *m*.

hell [hel] *n* Hölle *f*. *interj* zum Teufel! **to hell with** zum Teufel mit. **hellish** *adj* höllisch.

hello [hə'lou] *interj* Guten Tag; (*on telephone*) hallo!

helm [helm] *n* Steuer *neut*, Ruder *neut*. **helmsman** *n* Steuermann *m*.

helmet ['helmit] *n* Helm *m*.

help [help] *v* helfen (+ *dat*). *n* Hilfe *f*. *I can't help it* ich kann nichts dafür, ich kann nicht anders. *help yourself* bedienen Sie Sich! **helper** *n* Helfer(in). **helpful** *adj* hilfreich. **helping** *n* Portion *f*. **helpless** *adj* hilflos.

hem [hem] *n* Saum *m*. *v* säumen. **hem in** einengen.

hemisphere ['hemi,sfiə] *n* Halbkugel *f*, Hemisphäre *f*.

hemp [hemp] *n* Hanf *m*.

hen [hen] *n* Huhn *neut*.

hence [hens] *adv* von hier; (*therefore*) deshalb, daher. *a week hence* in einer Woche. **henceforth** fortan, von jetzt an.

henna ['henə] *n* Henna *f*.

henpecked ['henpekt] *adj* **henpecked husband** Pantoffelheld *m*.

her [hə] *pron* (*acc*) sie; (*dat*) ihr. *poss adj* ihr.

herald ['herəld] *n* Herold *m*. *v* (*fig*) einleiten. **heraldic** *adj* heraldisch, Wappen-. **heraldry** *n* Heraldik *f*, Wappenkunde *f*.

herb [həːb] *n* Kraut *n*. **herbal** *adj* Kräuter-. **herbalist** *n* Kräuterkenner(in).

herd [həːd] *n* Herde *f*. *v* hüten, zusammentreiben.

here [hiə] *adv* hier; (*to here*) hierher. **hereafter** *adv* in Zukunft. **herewith** *adv* hiermit.

hereditary [hi'redətəri] *adj* erblich. **heredity** *n* Vererbung *f*, Erblichkeit *f*.

heresy ['herəsi] *n* Ketzerei *f*. **heretic** *n* Ketzer(in). **heretical** *adj* Ketzerisch.

heritage ['heritidʒ] *n* Erbe *neut*, Erbgut *neut*.

hermit ['həːmit] *n* Eremit *m*. **hermitage** *n* Klause *f*.

hernia ['həːniə] *n* Bruch *m*.

hero ['hiərou] *n* Held *m*. **heroine** *n* Heldin *f*. **heroic** *adj* heroisch, heldenmutig. **heroism** *n* Heldentum *neut*.

heron ['herən] *n* Reiher *m*.

herring ['heriŋ] *n* Hering *m*. **herringbone** *n* (*pattern*) Fischgrätenmuster *neut*. **pickled herring** Rollmops *m*.

hers [həːz] *poss pron* ihrer *m*, ihre *f*, ihres *neut*. **herself** *pron* (*reflexive*) sich; selbst. **by herself** allein.

hesitate ['heziteit] *v* zögern. **hesitant** *adj* zögernd. **hesitation** *n* Zögern *neut*, Bedenken *neut*.

heterosexual [hetərə'sekfuəl] *adj* heterosexuell.

***hew** [hjuː] *v* hauen.

hewn [hjuːn] *V* **hew**.

hexagon ['heksəgən] *n* Sechseck *neut*.

heyday ['heidei] *n* Höhepunkt *m*, Blütezeit *f*.

hiatus [hai'eitəs] *n* Lücke *f*.

hibernate ['haibəneit] *v* Winterschlafhalten. **hibernation** *n* Winterschlaf *m*.

hiccup ['hikʌp] *n* Schluckauf *m*, Schlucken *m*. *v* den Schluckauf haben.

hid [hid] *V* **hide¹**.

hidden ['hidn] *V* **hide¹**.
*hide¹ [haid] *v* (*conceal*) verstecken, verbergen; (*keep secret*) verheimlichen.
hide² [haid] *n* (*skin*) Fell *neut*, Haut *f*.
hideous ['hidiəs] *adj* abscheulich, schrecklich.
hiding¹ ['haidiŋ] *n* Versteck *neut*. **be in hiding** sich versteckt halten.
hiding² ['haidiŋ] *n* (*thrashing*) Prügel *neut*.
hierarchy ['haiəraɪki] *n* Hierarchie *f*, Rangordnung *f*. **hierarchical** *adj* hierarchisch.
high [hai] *adj* hoch; (*wind*) stark.
highbrow ['haibrau] *adj* intellektuell. *n* Intellektuelle(r).
hi-fi ['haifai] *adj* hi-fi. *n* Hi-Fi.
high frequency *n* Hochfrequenz *f*.
high jump *n* Hochsprung *m*.
highland ['hailənd] *n* Bergland *neut*.
highlight ['hailait] *n* Höhepunkt *m*.
highly ['haili] *adv* höchst, in hohem Grad, stark. **highly strung** überempfindlich.
highness ['hainis] *n* Höhe *f*. **Your Highness** Eure Hoheit.
highpitched [,hai'pitʃt] *adj* hoch.
high point *n* Höhepunkt *m*.
high-rise building *n* Hochhaus *neut*.
high-spirited *adj* lebhaft, temperamentvoll.
high street *n* Hauptstraße *f*.
high tide *n* Hochwasser *neut*.
highway ['haiwei] *n* Landstraße *f*.
hijack ['haidʒak] *v* (*aeroplane*) entführen. *n* Entführung *f*. **hijacker** *n* Entführer *m*, Hijacker *m*.
hike [haik] *v* wandern. *n* Wanderung *f*. **hiker** *n* Wanderer *m*.
hilarious [hi'leəriəs] *adj* lustig. **hilarity** *n* Lustigkeit *f*.
hill [hil] *n* Hügel *m*, Berg *m*. **hillside** *n* Hang *m*. **hilltop** *n* Bergspitze *f*.
him [him] *pron* (*acc*) ihn; (*dat*) ihm. **himself** *pron* (*reflexive*) sich; selbst. **by himself** allein.
hind [haind] *adj* hinter, Hinter-. **hindsight** *n* **with hindsight** im Rückblick.
hinder ['hində] *v* (ver)hindern. **hindrance** *n* Hindernis *neut*, Hinderung *f*.
Hindu [hin'duː] *n* Hindu *m*. *adj* Hindu-.
hinge [hindʒ] *n* Scharnier *neut*, Gelenk *neut*. **to hinge on** abhängen (von).
hint [hint] *n* Wink *m*. *v* andeuten.
hip [hip] *n* Hüfte *f*. **hip-bone** *n* Hüftbein *neut*. **hip-joint** *n* Hüftgelenk *neut*.

hippopotamus [hipə'potəməs] *n* Nilpferd *neut*.
hire [haiə] *v* (ver)mieten; (*staff*) anstellen. *n* Miete *f*. **hire-car** *n* Mietwagen *m*. **hire purchase** Ratenkauf *m*. **hire-purchase agreement** Teilzahlungsvertrag *m*.
his [hiz] *poss adj* sein. *poss pron* seiner *m*, seine *f*, seines *neut*.
hiss [his] *v* zischen. *n* Zischen *neut*.
history ['histəri] *n* Geschichte *f*. **history book** Geschichtsbuch *neut*. **historian** *n* Historiker(in). **historic** *adj* historisch. **historical** *adj* historisch, geschichtlich.
*hit [hit] *v* schlagen, stoßen. *n* Schlag *m*, Stoß *m*; (*record*) Schlager *m*. **make a hit** (*fig*) Erfolg haben. **hard hit** schwer getroffen. **hit upon** zufällig finden.
hitch [hitʃ] *v* befestigen; (*horse*) anspannen. *n* (*problem*) Haken *m*. **hitchhike** *v* per Anhalter fahren.
hitherto [,hiðə'tuː] *adv* bisher.
hive [haiv] *n* Bienenkorb *m*. *v* **hive off** abzweigen.
hoard [hɔːd] *n* Schatz *m*, Hort *m*. *v* sammeln, hamstern.
hoarding ['hɔːdiŋ] *n* Reklamewand *f*.
hoarse [hɔːs] *adj* rauh, heiser.
hoax [houks] *n* Falschmeldung *f*. *v* zum Besten haben.
hobble ['hobl] *v* hinken, hoppeln; (*horse*) fesseln.
hobby ['hobi] *n* Hobby *neut*. **hobby horse** *n* Steckenpferd *neut*.
hock¹ [hok] *n* (*joint*) Sprunggelenk *neut*.
hock² [hok] *n* (*wine*) Rheinwein *m*.
hockey ['hoki] *n* Hockey *neut*.
hoe [hou] *n* Hacke *f*. *v* hacken.
hog [hog] *n* (Schlacht)Schwein *neut*; (*coll*) Vielfraß *m*. **go the whole hog** aufs Ganze gehen.
hoist [hoist] *v* hochziehen. *n* Aufzug *m*, Kran *m*.
*hold¹ [hould] *v* halten; (*contain*) enthalten. *n* Halt *m*, Griff *m*; (*fig*) Einfluß *m*. **hold back** zurückhalten. **hold down** (*job*) behalten. **hold up** (*delay*) aufhalten; (*rob*) überfallen. **hold-up** *n* (*traffic*) Stockung *f*; (*robbery*) Überfall *m*.
hold² [hould] *n* (*naut*) Frachtraum *m*, Schiffsraum *m*.
holder ['houldə] *n* (*owner*) Inhaber *m*.
holding ['houldiŋ] *n* (*land*) Grundbesitz *m*, Guthaben *neut*. **holding company** Dachgesellschaft *f*.

hole [houl] *n* Loch *neut.*

holiday ['holədi] *n* Feiertag *m*, Ruhetag *m*. **holidays** *pl* Ferien *pl*, Urlaub *m sing*. **go on holiday** verreisen, in die Ferien gehen, auf Urlaub gehen. **holidaymaker** *n* Feriengast *m*, Urlauber(in).

Holland ['holənd] *n* Holland *neut*, die Niederlände *pl*.

hollow ['holou] *n* Höhle *f*, Loch *neut. adj* hohl, leer. *v* (aus)höhlen. **hollowness** *n* Hohlheit *f*, Leerheit *f*.

holly ['holi] *n* Steckpalme *f*.

holster ['houlstə] *n* Pistolenhalfter *f*.

holy ['houli] *adj* heilig.

homage ['homidʒ] *n* Huldigung *f*. **do or pay homage** huldigen.

home [houm] *n* Heim *neut*, Haus *neut*, Zuhause *neut*; (*institution*) Heim *neut*. **at home** zu Hause. **at home with** vertraut mit. **make yourself at home** mach dich bequem. **go home** nach Hause gehen. **hammer home** (*nail*) fest einschlagen. *adj* häuslich; (*national*) inner, Innen-. **home affairs** innere Angelegenheiten *pl*. **home market** Binnenmarkt *m*. **homecoming** *n* Heimkehr *f*. **homeland** *n* Heimat *f*, Vaterland *neut*. **homeless** *adj* obdachlos. **homely** *adj* heimisch, gemütlich. **be homesick** Heimweh haben. **homesickness** *n* Heimweh *neut*. **homeward** *adj* Heim-; *adv* heimwärts. **homework** *n* Hausaufgaben *pl*.

homicide ['homisaid] *n* Mord *m*; (*person*) Mörder *m*.

homogeneous [homə'dʒiːniəs] *adj* gleichartig, homogen.

homosexual [homə'sekʃuəl] *adj* homosexuell. *n* Homosexuelle(r). **homosexuality** *n* Homosexualität *f*.

honest ['onist] *adj* ehrlich, aufrecht. **honesty** *n* Ehrlichkeit *f*, Aufrichtigkeit *f*.

honey ['hʌni] *n* Honig *m*; (*darling*) Liebling *m*, Schatz *m*. **honey-bee** *n* Honigbiene *f*. **honeycomb** *n* Honigwabe *f*. **honeymoon** *n* Hochzeitsreise *f*.

honeysuckle ['hʌnisʌkl] *n* Geißblatt *neut.*

honour ['onə] *n* Ehre *f*; (*reputation*) guter Ruf *m*. **honours** *pl* Auszeichnungen *pl*. *v* (ver)ehren; (*cheque*) einlösen. **honourable** *adj* ehrenvoll; (*in titles*) ehrenwert.

hood [hud] *n* Kapuze *f*; (*US: on car*) Motorhaube *f*; (*coll*) Gangster *m*. **hoodwink** *v* täuschen.

hoof [huːf] *n* Huf *m*.

hook [huk] *n* Haken *m*. *v* haken. **hook up** (*coll*) anschließen.

hooligan ['huːligən] *n* Rowdy *m*. **hooliganism** *n* Rowdytum *neut.*

hoop [huːp] *n* Reif(en) *m.*

hoot [huːt] *v* hupen. *n* Hupen *neut.*

hop[1] [hop] *v* hüpfen. *n* Sprung *m.*

hop[2] [hop] *n* (*bot*) Hopfen *m.*

hope [houp] *v* hoffen (auf). *n* Hoffnung *f*. **hopeful** *adj* hoffnungsvoll; (*promising*) vielversprechend. **hopefully** *adv* hoffentlich. **hopeless** *adj* hoffnungslos. **hopelessness** *n* Hoffnungslosigkeit *f.*

horde [hoːd] *n* Horde *f.*

horizon [hə'raizn] *n* Horizont *m*. **horizontal** *adj* waagerecht, horizontal.

hormone ['hoːmoun] *n* Hormon *neut.*

horn [hoːn] *n* Horn *neut*; (*mot*) Hupe *f*. **horned** *adj* gehörnt. **hornrimmed spectacles** Hornbrille *f*. **horny** *adj* (*hands*) schwielig.

hornet ['hoːnit] *n* Hormisse *f.*

horoscope ['horəskoup] *n* Horoskop *neut.*

horrible ['horibl] *adj* schrecklich, fürchterlich.

horrid ['horid] *adj* scheußlich, abscheulich.

horrify ['horifai] *v* erschrecken, entsetzen. **horrifying** *adj* entsetzlich.

horror ['horə] *n* Entsetzen *neut*, Grausen *neut*. **horror-stricken** *adj* von Grausen gepackt.

hors d'oeuvre [oɪ'dəɪvr] *n* Vorspeise *f.*

horse [hoːs] *n* Pferd *neut*, Roß *neut*. **on horseback** zu Pferd. **horse chestnut** Roßkastanie *f*. **horseman** *n* Reiter *m*. **horsepower (hp)** *n* Pferdestärke (PS) *f*. **horse race** *n* Pferderennen *neut*. **horseradish** *n* Meerrettich *m.*

horticulture ['hoːtikʌltʃə] *n* Gartenbau *m.*

hose [houz] *n* (*stockings*) Strümpfe *pl*; (*tech*, *mot*) Schlauch *m*; (*in garden*) Gartenschlauch *m.*

hosiery ['houziəri] *pl n* Strumpfwaren *pl.*

hospitable [ho'spitəbl] *adj* gastfreundlich.

hospital ['hospitl] *n* Krankenhaus *neut*, Klinik *f.*

hospitality [hospi'taliti] *n* Gastfreundschaft *f.*

host[1] [houst] *n* Gastgeber *m*, Wirt *m.*

host[2] [houst] *n* (*large number*) Masse *f*, Menge *f.*

hostage ['hostidʒ] *n* Geisel *m*, *f.*

hostel ['hostəl] *n* Herberge *f*. **student hostel** Studentenheim *neut*. **youth hostel**

Jugendherberge *f.* **hostelry** *n* Wirtshaus *neut.*

hostess ['houstis] *n* Gastgeberin *f*, Wirtin *f*; (*air hostess*) Stewardeß *f.*

hostile ['hostail] *adj* feindlich, feindselig (gegen). **hostility** *n* Feindseligkeit *f*, Feindschaft *f.*

hot [hot] *adj* heiß; (*food, drink*) warm. **hotdog** *n* (heißes) Würstchen. **hot meal** warme Mahlzeit. **hot-water bottle** Wärmflasche *f.*

hotel [hou'tel] *n* Hotel *neut*, Gasthof *m.* **hotel register** *n* Fremdenbuch *neut.* **hotelier** *n* Hotelier *m.*

hound [haund] *n* Jagdhund *m.* *v* jagen, verfolgen.

hour ['auə] *n* Stunde *f.* **after hours** nach Geschäftsschluß. **for hours** stundenlang. **hourglass** *n* Sanduhr *f.* **hourly** *adj, adv* stündlich. **hourly wage** Stundenlohn *m.*

house [haus; *v* hauz] *n* Haus *neut*; (*theatre*) Publikum *neut.* **House of Commons** Unterhaus *neut.* **House of Lords** Oberhaus *neut.* **House of Representatives** Abgeordnetenhaus *neut.* *v* unterbringen.

houseboat ['hausbout] *n* Hausboot *neut.*

household ['haushould] *n* Haushalt *m.*

housekeeper ['haus‚kiːpə] *n* Haushälterin *f.* **housekeeping** *n* Haushaltung *f.* **housekeeping money** Haushaltsgeld *neut.*

housemaid ['hausmeid] *n* Dienstmächen *neut.* **housemaid's knee** (*med*) Kniescheibenentzündung *f.*

house-warming ['haus‚woːmiŋ] *n* Einzugsfest *neut.*

housewife ['hauswaif] *n* Hausfrau *f.*

housework ['hauswɔːk] *n* Hausarbeit *f.*

housing ['hauziŋ] *n* Unterbringung *f*, Wohnung *f*; (*tech*) Gehäuse *neut.* **housing estate** Siedlung *f.*

hovel ['hovəl] *n* Schuppen *m.*

hover ['hovə] *v* schweben. **hovercraft** *n* Luftkissenfahrzeug *neut.*

how [hau] *adv* wie. **how do you do?** guten Tag. **how are you?** wie geht es Ihnen? **how much** or **how many** wieviel. **however** *adv* aber, jedoch; (*in whatever way*) wie auch immer.

howl [haul] *v* heulen. *n* Heulen *neut.*

hub [hʌb] *n* Nabe *f*; (*fig*) Mittelpunkt *m.* **hub cap** Radkappe *f.*

huddle ['hʌdl] *v* sich zusammendrängen. **huddled** *adj* kauernd.

hue [hjuː] *n* Farbe *f*, Färbung *f.*

huff [hʌf] *n* **in a huff** gekränkt, beleidigt.

hug [hʌg] *v* umarmen. *n* Umarmung *f.*

huge [hjuːdʒ] *adj* riesig, riesengroß.

hulk [hʌlk] *n* (*naut*) Hulk *m.*

hull [hʌl] *n* (*naut*) Rumpf *m*; (*of seed, etc.*) Hülse *f*, Schale *f.* *v* enthülsen.

hum [hʌm] *v* summen, brummen. *n* Summen *neut*, Brummen *neut.*

human ['hjuːmən] *adj* menschlich. **human being** Mensch *m.* **human nature** Menschheit *f*, menschliche Natur *f.* **humane** *adj* human. **humanist** *n* Humanist(in). **humanitarian** *adj* menschenfreundlich. **humanity** *n* Menschheit *f.*

humble ['hʌmbl] *adj* demütig, bescheiden; (*lowly*) niedrig. **humiliate** *v* demütigen. **humiliating** *adj* demütigend. **humility** *n* Demut *f*, Bescheidenheit *f.*

humdrum ['hʌmdrʌm] *adj* langweilig, alltäglich.

humid ['hjuːmid] *adj* feucht. **humidity** *n* Feuchtigkeit *f.*

humour ['hjuːmə] *n* Humor *m*; (*mood*) Stimmung *f*, Laune *f.* *v* (*person*) nachgeben (+ *dat*). **sense of humour** Humor *m.* **humorous** *adj* lustig, humorvoll.

hump [hʌmp] *n* Buckel *m.* *v* (*coll: carry*) schleppen. **humpback** *n* Bucklige(r). **humpbacked** *adj* bucklig.

hunch [hʌntʃ] *n* (*coll*) Vorahnung *f.*

hundred ['hʌndrəd] *adj* hundert. *n* Hundert *neut.* **hundredth** *adj* hundertst; *n* Hundertstel *neut.* **hundredweight** Zentner *m.*

hung [hʌŋ] *V* hang.

Hungary ['hʌŋgəri] *n* Ungarn *neut.* **Hungarian** *adj* ungarisch; *n* Ungar(in).

hunger ['hʌŋgə] *n* Hunger *m.* *v* hungern. **hunger for** sehnen nach. **hungry** *adj* hungrig. **be hungry** Hunger haben.

hunt [hʌnt] *n* Jagd *f*, Jagen *neut*; (*for person*) Verfolgung *f.* *v* jagen; verfolgen. **hunter** *n* Jäger *m*; (*horse*) Jagdpferd *neut.* **hunting** *n* Jagd *f.*

hurdle ['həːdl] *n* Hürde *f*; (*fig*) Hindernis *neut.*

hurl [həːl] *v* werfen.

hurricane ['hʌrikən] *n* Orkan *m.* **hurricane lamp** Sturmlaterne *f.*

hurry ['hʌri] *v* eilen, sich beeilen; (*something*) beschleunigen. *n* Eile *f*, Hast *f.* **hurry up** mach schnell! **hurried** *adj* eilig, übereilt.

*hurt [hɔːt] v (*injure*) verletzen; *(ache)* schmerzen, weh tun; *(offend)* kränken, verletzen. n Verletzung f; Schmerzen *neut.* **hurtful** *adj* schädlich.

hurtle ['hɔːtl] v stürzen, sausen.

husband ['hʌzbənd] n (Ehe)Mann m. v (*resources*) sparsam umgehen mit. **husbandry** n Landwirtschaft f.

hush [hʌʃ] n Stille f, Ruhe f. v beruhigen.

husk [hʌsk] n Hülse f. v enthülsen.

husky ['hʌski] adj (*voice*) rauh, heiser.

hussar [hə'zaː] n Husar m.

hustle ['hʌsl] v drängen. **hustle and bustle** Gedränge *neut.*

hut [hʌt] n Hütte f.

hutch [hʌtʃ] n Stall m.

hyacinth ['haiəsinθ] n Hyazinthe f.

hybrid ['haibrid] n Kreuzung f, Mischling m. *adj* Misch-.

hydraulic [hai'drɔːlik] adj hydraulisch.

hydrocarbon [‚haidrou'kaːbən] n Kohlenwasserstoff m.

hydro-electric [‚haidroui'lektrik] adj hydroelektrisch.

hydrogen ['haidrədʒən] n Wasserstoff m. **hydrogen bomb** Wasserstoffbombe f. **hydrogen peroxide** Wasserstoffsuperoxyd *neut.*

hyena [hai'iːnə] n Hyäne f.

hygiene ['haidʒiːn] n Hygiene f, Gesundheitspflege f. **hygienic** adj hygienisch.

hymn [him] n Kirchenlied *neut*, Hymne f. **hymnbook** n Gesangbuch *neut.*

hypersensitive [haipə'sensətiv] adj überempfindlich.

hyphen ['haifən] n Bindestrich m.

hypnosis [hip'nousis] n Hypnose f. **hypnotic** adj hypnotisch. **hypnotist** n Hypnotiseur m. **hypnotize** v hypnotisieren.

hypochondria [haipə'kondriə] n Hypochondrie f. **hypochondriac** adj hypochondrisch. n Hypochonder m.

hypocrisy [hi'pokrəsi] n Heuchelei f. **hypocrite** n Heuchler(in). **hypocritical** adj heuchlerisch.

hypodermic [haipə'dəːmik] adj subkutan. **hypodermic syringe** Spritze f.

hypothesis [hai'poθəsis] n (pl -ses) Hypothese f. **hypothetical** adj hypothetisch.

hysterectomy [histə'rektəmi] n Hysterektomie f.

hysteria [his'tiəriə] n Hysterie f. **hysterical** adj hysterisch; *(coll: funny)* zum Schreien komisch.

I

I [ai] pron ich.

ice [ais] n Eis *neut.* v (*cookery*) mit Zuckerguß überziehen. **icing** n Zuckerguß m. **ice age** n Eiszeit f. **iceberg** n Eisberg m. **icebox** n Kühlschrank m. **ice cream** n Eis *neut.* **ice cube** n Eiswürfel m. **icy** adj eisig.

Iceland ['aislənd] n Island *neut.* **Icelandic** adj isländisch. **Icelander** n Isländer(in).

icicle ['aisikl] n Eiszapfen m.

icon ['aikon] n Ikone f.

idea [ai'diə] n Idee f; (*concept*) Begriff m. **I've no idea** ich habe keine Ahnung.

ideal [ai'diəl] n Ideal *neut. adj* ideal. **idealism** n Idealismus *neut.* **idealist** n Idealist m. **idealistic** adj idealistisch. **ideally** adv idealerweise.

identical [ai'dentikəl] adj identisch.

identify [ai'dentifai] v identifizieren; (*recognize*) erkennen. **identification** n Identifizierung f; (*pass*) Ausweis m.

identity [ai'dentiti] n Identität f. **identity card** Personalausweis m. **identity papers** Ausweispapiere pl.

ideology [aidi'olədʒi] n Ideologie f. **ideological** adj ideologisch. **ideologist** n Ideologe m, Ideologin f.

idiom ['idiəm] n Mundart f, Idiom *neut.* **idiomatic** adj idiomatisch.

idiosyncrasy [‚idiə'siŋkrəsi] n Eigenart f. **idiosyncratic** adj eigenartig.

idiot ['idiət] n (*coll*) Idiot m, Dummkopf m; (*med*) Blödsinnige(r). **idiocy** n Blödsinn m.

idle ['aidl] adj (*person*) faul, untätig; (*words, etc.*) eitel, unnütz. **idleness** n Faulheit f. **idler** n Faulenzer m.

idol ['aidl] n Idol *neut.* **idolize** v vergöttern.

idyllic [i'dilik] adj idyllisch.

if [if] conj wenn, falls; (*whether*) ob. **even if** selbst wenn. **if only** wenn … nur. **if not** falls nicht. **if so** in dem Fall.

ignite [ig'nait] v (ent)zünden.

ignition [ig'nifən] *n* Zündung *f*. **ignition key** Zündschlüssel *m*.

ignorant ['ignərənt] *adj* unwissend; (*uneducated*) ungebildet. **be ignorant of** nicht wissen *or* kennen. **ignorance** *n* Unkenntnis *f*.

ignore [ig'noɪ] *v* ignorieren, unbeachtet lassen.

ill [il] *adj* (*sick*) krank; (*bad*) schlimm, böse. **fall ill** krank werden. **ill-at-ease** *adj* unbehaglich. **ill-bred** schlecht erzogen. **ill-disposed** *adj* bösartig. **ill-fated** *adj* unselig. **ill-natured** *adj* boshaft. **illness** *n* Krankheit *f*. **ill-treat** *v* mißhandeln.

illegal [i'liɪgəl] *adj* illegal, gesetzwidrig. **illegality** *n* Ungesetzlichkeit *f*.

illegible [i'ledʒəbl] *adj* unleserlich. **illegibility** *n* Unleserlichkeit *f*.

illegitimate [ˌili'dʒitimit] *adj* (*child*) unehelich; (*unlawful*) ungesetzlich.

illicit [i'lisit] *adj* unzulässig, gesetzwidrig.

illiterate [i'litərit] *adj* analphabetisch, ungebildet. *n* Analphabet(in).

illogical [i'lodʒikəl] *adj* unlogisch.

illuminate [i'luɪmiˌneit] *v* erleuchten. **illuminated** *adj* beleuchtet. **illumination** *n* Beleuchtung *f*.

illusion [i'luɪʒən] *n* Illusion *f*. **illusory** *adj* illusorisch.

illustrate ['iləˌstreit] *v* (*book*) illustrieren; (*idea*) erklären. **illustration** *n* Illustration *f*, Bild *n*.

illustrious [i'lʌstriəs] *adj* berühmt.

image ['imidʒ] *n* Bild *neut*. (*idea*) Vorstellung *f*; (*public*) Image *neut*. **imagery** *n* Symbolik *f*.

imagine [i'madʒin] *v* sich vorstellen *or* denken. **imaginable** *adj* denkbar. **imaginary** *adj* eingebildet, Schein-. **imagination** *n* Phantasie *f*. **imaginative** *adj* phantasiereich.

imbalance [im'baləns] *n* Unausgeglichenheit *f*.

imbecile ['imbəˌsiɪl] *n* Schwachsinnige(r). *adj* schwachsinnig.

imitate ['imiˌteit] *v* nachahmen, imitieren. **imitation** *n* Nachahmung *f*; *adj* künstlich, Kunst-.

immaculate [i'makjulit] *adj* makellos.

immaterial [ˌimə'tiəriəl] *adj* belanglos.

immature [ˌimə'tjuə] *adj* unreif, unentwickelt. **immaturity** *n* Unreife *f*.

immediate [i'miɪdiət] *adj* unmittelbar, direkt. **immediately** *adv* sofort.

immense [i'mens] *adj* riesig, ungeheuer.

immerse [i'məɪs] *v* versenken, tauchen. **immersion** *n* Versunkenheit *f*, Immersion *f*. **immersion heater** Tauchsieder *m*.

immigrate ['imiˌgreit] *v* einwandern. **immigrant** *n* Einwanderer *m*, Einwanderin *f*. **immigration** *n* Einwanderung *f*.

imminent ['iminənt] *adj* drohend.

immobile [i'moubail] *adj* bewegungslos, unbeweglich. **immobility** *n* Unbeweglichkeit *f*. **immobilize** *v* unbeweglich machen.

immodest [i'modist] *adj* schamlos.

immoral [i'morəl] *adj* unsittlich, unmoralisch. **immorality** *n* Sittenlosigkeit *f*.

immortal [i'moɪtl] *adj* unsterblich, ewig. **immortality** *n* Unsterblichkeit *f*.

immovable [i'muɪvəbl] *adj* unbeweglich.

immune [i'mjuɪn] *adj* immun (gegen). **immunity** *n* Immunität *f*. **immunization** *n* Impfung *f*.

imp [imp] *v* Kobold *m*.

impact ['impakt] *n* Anprall *m*, Stoß *m*; (*effect*) Wirkung *f*, Einfluß *m*.

impair [im'peə] *v* beeinträchtigen. **impairment** *n* Beeinträchtigung *f*.

impart [im'paɪt] *v* geben, erteilen.

impartial [im'paɪʃəl] *adj* unparteiisch. **impartiality** *n* Unparteilichkeit *f*.

impassable [im'paɪsəbl] *adj* ungangbar, unpassierbar.

impasse [am'paɪs] *n* Sackgasse *f*.

impassive [im'pasiv] *adj* ungerührt.

impatient [im'peiʃənt] *adj* ungeduldig. **impatience** *n* Ungeduld *f*.

impeach [im'piɪtʃ] *v* anklagen. **impeachment** *n* Anklage *f*.

impeccable [im'pekəbl] *adj* tadellos. **impeccability** *n* Tadellosigkeit *f*.

impede [im'piɪd] *v* (be)hindern. **impediment** *n* Verhinderung *f*. **speech impediment** Sprachfehler *m*.

impel [im'pel] *v* (an)treiben. **impelled** *adj* gezwungen.

impending [im'pendiŋ] *adj* bevorstehend, drohend.

imperative [im'perətiv] *adj* dringend notwendig. *n* (*gramm*) Imperativ *m*.

imperfect [im'pəɪfikt] *adj* unvollkommen, fehlerhaft. **imperfection** *n* (*blemish*) Fehler *m*.

imperial [im'piəriəl] *adj* kaiserlich. **imperialism** *n* Imperialismus *m*. **imperialist** *adj* imperialistisch.

imperil [im'perəl] *v* gefährden.

impermanent [im'pəːmənənt] *adj* unbeständig.

impersonal [im'pəːsənl] *adj* unpersönlich. **impersonality** *n* Unpersönlichkeit *f*.

impersonate [im'pəːsə‚neit] *v* sich ausgeben als.

impertinent [im'pəːtinənt] *adj* frech, unverschämt. **impertinence** *n* Frechheit *f*, Unverschämtheit *f*.

impervious [im'pəːviəs] *adj* undurchdringlich.

impetuous [im'petjuəs] *adj* ungestüm, impulsiv. **impetuosity** *n* Ungestüm *neut*.

impetus ['impətəs] *n* Antrieb *m*, Schwung *m*.

impinge [im'pindʒ] *v* eingreifen (in), stoßen (an).

implement ['implimənt; *v* 'impliment] *n* Werkzeug *neut*, Gerät *neut*. *v* durchführen.

implicate ['implikeit] *v* hineinziehen. **implication** *n* Bedeutung *f*, Konsequenz *f*.

implicit [im'plisit] *adj* (*tacit*) unausgesprochen; (*unquestioning*) absolut. **implicitly** *adv* unbedingt.

implore [im'plɔː] *v* dringend bitten. **imploring** *adj* flehentlich.

imply [im'plai] *v* bedeuten.

impolite [impə'lait] *adj* unhöflich. **impoliteness** *n* Unhöflichkeit *f*.

import [im'pɔːt] *v* einführen, importieren. *n* Einfuhr *f*, Import *m*. **importer** *n* Importeur *m*, Einfuhrhändler *m*. **imports** *pl n* Importwaren *pl*.

importance [im'pɔːtəns] *n* Wichtigkeit *f*, Bedeutung *f*. **important** *adj* wichtig.

impose [im'pouz] *v* auferlegen. **impose upon** mißbrauchen. **imposing** *adj* imponierend. **imposition** *n* Auferlegung *f*; (*unreasonable demand*) Zumutung *f*.

impossible [im'posəbl] *adj* unmöglich. **impossibility** *n* Unmöglichkeit *f*.

impostor [im'postə] *n* Betrüger(in).

impotent ['impotənt] *adj* impotent. **impotence** *n* Impotenz *f*.

impound [im'paund] *v* beschlagnahmen.

impoverish [im'povəriʃ] *v* arm machen. **impoverished** *adj* verarmt.

impregnate ['impreg‚neit] *v* befruchten, schwanger machen; (*fabric, wood, etc.*) imprägnieren. **impregnable** *adj* uneinnehmbar.

impress [im'pres] *v* beeindrucken. **impres-**

sion *n* Eindruck *m*; (*book*) Auflage *f*. **impressionism** *n* (*painting*) Impressionismus *m*.

imprint [im'print; *n* 'imprint] *v* aufdrücken (auf); (*fig*) einprägen in. *n* Stempel *m*; (*fig*) Eindruck *m*.

imprison [im'prizn] *v* einsperren. **imprisonment** *n* Haft *f*, Gefangenschaft *f*.

improbable [im'probəbl] *adj* unwahrscheinlich. **improbability** *n* Unwahrscheinlichkeit *f*.

impromptu [im'promptjuː] *adj* improvisiert.

improper [im'propə] *adj* unpassend, unsittlich.

improve [im'pruːv] *v* verbessern; (*become better*) sich verbessern, besser werden. **improvement** *n* Verbesserung *f*.

improvise ['imprə‚vaiz] *v* improvisieren. **improvisation** *n* Improvisierung *f*.

impudent ['impjudənt] *adj* frech, unverschämt. **impudence** *n* Unverschämtheit *f*.

impulse ['impʌls] *n* Antrieb *m*, Drang *m*. **impulsive** *adj* impulsiv.

impure [im'pjuə] *adj* unrein. **impurity** *n* Unreinheit *f*; (*extraneous substance*) fremde Bestandteile *pl*.

in [in] *prep* (*place*) in, an auf; (*time*) in, während. (*into*) in ... hinein *or* herein. **in the street** auf der Straße. **in the evening** abends. **in bad weather** bei schlechtem Wetter. **in three days' time** nach drei Tagen. **in that** insofern als. **be in** (*at home*) zu Hause sein.

inability [‚inə'biləti] *n* Unfähigkeit *f*. **inability to pay** Zahlungsunfähigkeit *f*.

inaccessible [‚inak'sesəbl] *adj* unzugänglich, unerreichbar. **inaccessibility** *n* Unzugänglichkeit *f*.

inaccurate [in'akjurit] *adj* ungenau; (*incorrect*) falsch. **inaccuracy** *n* Ungenauigkeit *f*; Fehler *m*.

inactive [in'aktiv] *adj* untätig. **inactivity** *n* Untätigkeit *f*.

inadequate [in'adikwit] *adj* ungenügend, mangelhaft. **inadequacy** *n* Unzulänglichkeit *f*, Mangelhaftigkeit *f*.

inadvertent [‚inəd'vəːtənt] *adj* unabsichtlich, versehentlich.

inane [in'ein] *adj* leer, albern.

inanimate [in'animit] *adj* leblos.

inarticulate [‚inaːˈtikjulit] *adj* undeutlich. **be inarticulate** sich nicht gut ausdrücken können.

inasmuch [ˌinəz'mʌtʃ] conj **inasmuch as** da.

inaudible [in'ɔɪdəbl] adj unhörbar.

inaugurate [i'nɔɪgjuˌreit] v (feierlich) eröffnen. **inauguration** n (feierliche) Eröffnung f. **inaugural** adj Einführungs-.

inborn [ˌin'bɔɪn] adj angeboren.

incapable [in'keipəbl] adj unfähig. **incapacity** n Unfähigkeit f.

incendiary [in'sendiəri] adj Brand-. **incendiary bomb** Brandbombe f.

incense¹ [ˈinsens] n Weihrauch m.

incense² [in'sens] v wütend machen.

incentive [in'sentiv] n Ansporn m; (bonus) Leistungsanreiz m.

incessant [in'sesənt] adj ständig, unaufhörlich.

incest [ˈinsest] n Blutschande f. **incestuous** adj blutschänderisch.

inch [intʃ] n Zoll m.

incident [ˈinsidənt] n Vorfall m, Ereignis neut.

incinerator [in'sinəˌreitə] n Verbrennungsofen m. **incinerate** v verbrennen. **incineration** n Verbrennung f.

incite [in'sait] v anregen. **incitement** n Anregung f, Aufreizung f.

incline [in'klain] v neigen; (slope) abfallen. **inclination** n Neigung f. **inclined** adj geneigt.

include [in'kluɪd] v einschließen. **included** adj (in price) inbegriffen. **inclusive** adj einschließlich. **inclusive of** also including einschließlich. **inclusion** n Einbeziehung f.

incognito [ˌinkog'niɪtou] adv inkognito.

incoherent [ˌinkə'hiərənt] adj inkonsequent; (speech) unklar.

income [ˈinkʌm] n Einkommen neut, Einkünfte pl. **income tax** Einkommensteuer f. **income tax return** Einkommensteuererklärung f.

incompatible [inkəm'patəbl] adj unvereinbar. **incompatibility** n Unvereinbarkeit f.

incompetent [in'kompitənt] adj unfähig. **incompetence** n Unfähigkeit f.

incomplete [ˌinkəm'pliɪt] adj unvollständig.

incomprehensible [inˌkompri'hensəbl] adj unbegreiflich.

inconceivable [inkən'siɪvəbl] adj unfaßbar. **inconceivability** n Unfaßbarkeit f.

inconclusive [inkən'kluɪsiv] adj ohne Beweiskraft.

incongruous [in'koŋgruəs] adj unangemessen.

inconsiderate [ˌinkən'sidərit] adj rücksichtslos, besinnungslos.

inconsistent [ˌinkən'sistənt] adj inkonsequent; (person) unbeständig. **inconsistency** n Widerspruch m.

inconspicuous [inkən'spikjuəs] adj unauffällig.

incontinence [in'kontinəns] n (med) Inkontinenz f.

inconvenient [inkən'viɪnjənt] adj ungelegen. **inconvenience** n Ungelegenheit f. v stören, lästig sein (+ dat).

incorporate [in'kɔɪpəˌreit] v (combine) vereinigen; (comm) inkorporieren; (contain, include) enthalten. **incorporation** n (comm) Gründung f.

incorrect [inkə'rekt] adj unrichtig; (inexact) ungenau.

increase [in'kriɪs] v zunehmen; (in number) sich vermehren; (prices) steigen. n Vermehrung f, Zunahme f; Steigerung f; (wages) Lohnerhöhung f. **increasingly** adv immer mehr.

incredible [in'kredəbl] adj unglaublich. **incredibility** n Unglaublichkeit f. **incredibly** adv unglaublicherweise; (coll: extremely) unglaublich.

incredulous [in'kredjuləs] adj skeptisch, ungläubig. **incredulity** n Skepsis f.

increment [ˈiŋkrəmənt] n Zunahme f.

incriminate [in'krimineit] v beschuldigen. **incrimination** n Beschuldigung f.

incubate [ˈinkjuˌbeit] v ausbrüten. **incubation** n Ausbrütung f. **incubator** n (for babies) Brutkasten m.

incur [in'kəɪ] v sich zuziehen. **incur debts** Schulden machen. **incur losses** Verlüste erleiden.

incurable [in'kjuərəbl] adj unheilbar.

indebted [in'detid] adj verschuldet.

indecent [in'diɪsnt] adj unanständig. **indecency** n Unanständigkeit f.

indeed [in'diɪd] adv tatsächlich, wirklich.

indefinite [in'definit] adj unbestimmt. **indefinitely** adv auf unbestimmte Zeit.

indelible [in'deləbl] adj unauslöschlich; (ink) wasserfest.

indemnify [in'demnifai] v entschädigen. **indemnity** n Entschädigung f.

indent [in'dent] *v (type)* einrücken. **indentation** *n* Einrückung *f.*
independence [indi'pendəns] *n* Unabhängigkeit *f*, Selbstständigkeit *f.*
independent *adj* unabhängig, selbstständig; *(pol)* parteilos; *n (pol)* Unabhängige(r).
indescribable [indi'skraibəbl] *adj* unbeschreiblich.
indestructible [indi'strʌktəbl] *adj* unzerstörbar.
index ['indeks] *n (in book)* Register *neut*; *(file)* Kartei *f*; *(cost of living)* Index *m.* **index finger** Zeigefinger *m.*
India ['indjə] *n* Indien *neut.* **Indian** *adj* indisch; *(American)* indianisch; *n* Inder(in); *(American)* Indianer(in). **Indian ink** chinesische Tusche *f.* **Indian summer** Nachsommer *m.*
indicate ['indikeit] *v* anzeigen; *(hint)* andeuten. **indication** *n* Anzeichen *neut*; *(idea)* Andeutung *f*; *(information)* Angabe; *(med)* Indikation *f.* **indicative** *adj* anzeigend. **indicator** *n (sign)* Zeichen *neut*; *(mot)* Richtungsanzeiger *m*, Blinker *m.*
indict [in'dait] *v* anklagen (wegen). **indictment** *n* Anklageschrift *f.*
indifferent [in'difrənt] *adj* gleichgültig; *(poor quality)* mittelmäßig. **indifference** *n* Gleichgültigkeit *f*; Mittelmäßigkeit *f.*
indigenous [in'didʒinəs] *adj* einheimisch.
indigestion [indi'dʒestʃən] *n* Verdauungsstörung *f.* **indigestible** *adj* unverdaulich.
indignant [in'dignənt] *adj* empört. **indignation** *n* Empörung *f.*
indignity [in'dignəti] *n* Demütigung *f.*
indirect [indi'rekt] *adj* indirekt.
indiscreet [indi'skri:t] *adj* indiskret, taktlos. **indiscretion** *n* Vertrauensbruch *m*, Indiskretion *f.*
indiscriminate [indi'skriminit] *adj* rücksichtslos. **indiscriminately** *adv* ohne Unterschied.
indispensable [indi'spensəbl] *adj* unerläßlich, unentbehrlich. **indispensability** *n* Unerläßlichkeit *f*, Unentbehrlichkeit *f.*
indisposed [indi'spouzd] *adj* indisponiert, unpäßlich.
indisputable [indi'spju:təbl] *adj* unbestreitbar.
indistinct [indi'stiŋkt] *adj* unklar.

individual [indi'vidjuəl] *n* Individuum *neut*, Person *f. adj* einzeln, persönlich, individuell. **individualist** *n* Individualist(in). **individuality** *n* Individualität *f*, Eigenart *f.* **individually** *adv* einzeln.
indoctrinate [in'doktri,neit] *v* unterweisen. **indoctrination** *n* Unterweisung *f.*
indolent ['indələnt] *adj* lässig. **indolence** *n* Lässigkeit *f.*
indoor ['indoː] *adj* Haus-, Zimmer-. **indoor swimming pool** Hallenbad *neut.* **indoors** *adv* im Haus; *(go)* ins Haus.
induce [in'dju:s] *v (cause)* verursachen; *(persuade)* überreden. **inducement** *n* Anreiz *m.*
indulge [in'dʌldʒ] *v (a person)* nachgeben (+ *dat*); *(oneself)* verwöhnen. **indulgence** *n* Nachsicht *f*; Verwöhnung *f.* **indulgent** *adj* nachsichtig.
industry ['indəstri] *n* Industrie *f.* **industrial** *adj* industriell. **industrialist** *n* Industrielle(r). **industrious** *adj* fleißig.
inebriated [i'ni:brieitid] *adj* betrunken.
inedible [in'edibl] *adj* nicht eßbar.
inefficient [ini'fiʃnt] *adj* unfähig; *(thing)* unwirksam. **inefficiency** *n* Leistungsunfähigkeit *f.*
inept [i'nept] *adj* albern. **ineptitude** *n* Albernheit *f.*
inequality [ini'kwoləti] *n* Ungleichheit *f.*
inert [i'nəːt] *adj* inaktiv; *(person)* schlaff. **inertia** *n* Trägheit *f.*
inevitable [in'evitəbl] *adj* unvermeidlich. **inevitability** *n* Unvermeidlichkeit *f.*
inexpensive [inik'spensiv] *adj* billig, preiswert.
inexperienced [inik'spiəriənst] *adj* unerfahren.
infallible [in'faləbl] *adj* unfehlbar. **infallibility** *n* Unfehlbarkeit *f.*
infamous ['infəməs] *adj* schändlich. **infamy** *n* Schande *f.*
infancy ['infənsi] *n* frühe Kindheit *f.* **be still in its infancy** noch in den Kinderschuhen stehen. **infant** *(baby)* Säugling *m*; *(small child)* Kleinkind *neut.* **infantile** *adj* kindisch.
infantry ['infəntri] *n* Infanterie *f.* **infantryman** *n* Infanterist *m.*
infatuated [in'fatjueitid] *adj* vernarrt (in). **infatuation** *n* Vernarrtheit *f.*
infect [in'fekt] *v* infizieren, anstecken. **infection** *n* Infizierung *f*, Ansteckung *f.* **infectious** *adj* ansteckend.

infer [in'fəɪ] v folgern. **inference** n (conclusion) Schlußfolgerung f.

inferior [in'fiəriə] adj minderwertig. **inferiority** n Minderwertigkeit f. **inferiority complex** Minderwertigkeitskomplex m.

infernal [in'fəɪnl] adj höllisch; (coll) verdammt. **inferno** n Inferno neut.

infertile [in'fəɪtail] adj unfruchtbar. **infertility** n Unfruchtbarkeit f.

infest [in'fest] v heimsuchen, plagen. **infestation** n Plage f.

infidelity [ˌinfi'deliti] n Untreue f.

infiltrate [in'fil,treit] v einsickern in; (pol) unterwandern. **infiltration** n Einsickern neut; Unterwanderung f. **infiltrator** n Unterwanderer m.

infinite ['infinit] adj unendlich. **infinity** n Unendlichkeit f. **infinitesimal** adj winzig. **infinitive** [in'finitiv] n (gramm) Infinitiv m, Nennform f.

infirm [in'fəɪm] adj schwach. **infirmary** n Krankenhaus neut. **infirmity** n Krankheit f.

inflame [in'fleim] v entzünden; (fig) erregen. **inflamed** (med) entzündet. **inflammable** adj brennbar. **inflammation** n Entzündung f. **inflammatory** adj (fig) aufrührerisch.

inflate [in'fleit] v aufblasen; (price) übermäßig steigern. **inflatable** adj aufblasbar. **inflated** adj aufgebläht; (fig) aufgeblasen; (price) überhöht. **inflation** n Aufgeblasenheit; (comm) Inflation f. **inflationary** adj inflationistisch.

inflection [in'flekʃən] n Biegung f; (of voice) Modulation f.

inflict [in'flikt] v (blow) versetzen; (pain) zufügen; (burden) aufbürden. **infliction** n Zufügung f; (burden) Last f.

influence ['influəns] n Einfluß m; (power) Macht f. v beeinflussen, Einfluß ausüben auf. **influential** adj einflußreich.

influenza [ˌinflu'enzə] n Grippe f.

influx ['inflʌks] n Zustrom m.

inform [in'fɔɪm] v benachrichtigen, unterrichten. **inform against** anzeigen.

informal [in'fɔɪml] adj informell. **informality** n Ungezwungenheit f.

information [ˌinfə'meiʃən] n Auskunft f, Information f, Nachricht f; (data) Angaben pl. **information bureau** Auskunftsbüro neut. **informative** adj lehrreich. **informed** adj informiert. **informer** n Angeber(in).

infra-red [ˌinfrə'red] adj infrarot.

infringe [in'frindʒ] v verstoßen gegen; (rights) verletzen. **infringement** n Verletzung f.

infuriate [in'fjuəri,eit] v wütend machen. **infuriated** adj wütend.

ingenious [in'dʒiɪnjəs] adj (person) erfinderisch; (device) raffiniert. **ingenuity** n Erfindungsgabe f.

ingot ['iŋgət] n Barren m.

ingrained [in'greind] adj tief eingewurzelt.

ingredient [in'griɪdjənt] n Zutat f.

inhabit [in'habit] v bewohnen. **inhabitable** adj bewohnbar. **inhabitant** n Einwohner(in).

inhale [in'heil] v einatmen. **inhalation** n Einatmung f.

inherent [in'hiərənt] adj angeboren.

inherit [in'herit] v erben. **inheritance** n Erbe neut. **inherited** adj ererbt. **inheritor** n Erbe m, Erbin f.

inhibit [in'hibit] v hemmen; (prevent) hindern. **inhibition** n Hemmung f.

inhospitable [inhə'spitəbl] adj ungastlich.

inhuman [in'hjuɪmən] adj unmenschlich. **inhumanity** n Unmenschlichkeit f.

iniquitous [i'nikwətəs] adj (unjust) ungerecht; (sinful) frevelhaft. **iniquity** n Ungerechtigkeit f, (sin) Sünde f.

initial [i'niʃl] adj anfänglich, Anfangs-. n Anfangsbuchstabe m. **initials** pl n Monogramm neut. **initially** adv am Anfang.

initiate [i'niʃi,eit] v einführen (in); (start) beginnen. n Eingeweihte(r). **initiation** n Einweihung.

initiative [i'niʃiətiv] n Initiative f. **take the initiative** die Initiative ergreifen. **initiator** n Anstifter m.

inject [in'dʒekt] v einspritzen. **injection** n give/have an injection eine Spritze geben/bekommen.

injure ['indʒə] v verletzen. **injured party** Geschädigte(r). **injurious** adj schädlich. **injury** n Verletzung f, Wunde f.

injustice [in'dʒʌstis] n Unrecht neut, Ungerechtigkeit f.

ink [iŋk] n Tinte f, Tusche f. **inkblot** n Tintenklecks m. **inkwell** n Tintenfaß neut.

inkling ['iŋkliŋ] n Ahnung f.

inland ['inlənd] adj Binnen-. **Inland Revenue** Steuerbehörde f.

in-laws ['in,lɔts] pl n angeheiratete Verwandte pl. **daughter-in-law** Schwiegertochter f. **father-in-law**

Schwiegervater *m*. **mother-in-law** Schwiegermutter *f*. **son-in-law** Schwiegersohn *m*.

***inlay** ['inlei] *v* einlegen. *n* eingelegte Arbeit *f*; (*dentistry*) Plombe *f*.

inlet ['inlet] *n* Meeresarm *m*.

inmate ['inmeit] *n* Insasse *m*, Insassin *f*.

inn [in] *n* Gasthof *m*, Wirtshaus *neut*. **innkeeper** *n* Gastwirt(in).

innate [,i'neit] *adj* angeboren. **innately** *adv* von Natur.

inner ['inə] *adj* inner, Innen-. **innermost** *adj* innerst.

innocent ['inəsnt] *adj* unschuldig, schuldlos. **innocence** *n* Unschuld *f*, Schuldlosigkeit *f*.

innocuous [i'nokjuəs] *adj* harmlos, unschädlich.

innovation [inə'veiʃən] *n* Neuerung *f*. **innovator** *n* Neuerer *m*.

innuendo [,inju'endou] *n* Stichelei *f*.

innumerable [i'njuːmərəbl] *adj* zahllos, unzählig.

inoculate [i'nokjuˌleit] *v* (ein)impfen. **inoculation** *n* Impfung *f*.

inorganic [,inoːˈganik] *adj* unorganisch.

input ['input] *n* Eingabe *f*, Input *m*.

inquest ['inkwest] *n* gerichtliche Untersuchung *f*.

inquire [in'kwaiə] *v* sich erkundigen (nach). **inquiry** *n* Anfrage *f*; (*examination*) Untersuchung *f*, Prüfung *f*. **inquiry office** Auskunftsbüro *neut*.

inquisition [,inkwi'ziʃən] *n* Untersuchung *f*; (*rel*) Ketzergericht *neut*.

inquisitive [in'kwizətiv] *adj* neugierig.

insane [in'sein] *adj* geisteskrank; (*coll*) verrückt. **insanity** *n* Geisteskrankheit *f*.

insatiable [in'seiʃəbl] *adj* unersättlich. **insatiability** *n* Unersättlichkeit *f*.

inscribe [in'skraib] *v* (auf)schreiben. **inscription** *n* Beschriftung *f*; (*in book*) Widmung *f*.

insect ['insekt] *n* Insekt *neut*. **insecticide** *n* Insektizid *neut*.

insecure [,insi'kjuə] *adj* unsicher. **insecurity** *n* Unsicherheit *f*.

inseminate [in'semineit] *v* befruchten. **insemination** *n* Befruchtung *f*.

insensible [in'sensəbl] *adj* gefühllos; (*unconscious*) bewußtlos.

insensitive [in'sensətiv] *adj* unempfindlich. **insensitivity** *n* Unempfindlichkeit *f*.

inseparable [in'sepərəbl] *adj* untrennbar.

insert [in'səːt; *n* 'insəːt] *v* einfügen, einsetzen. *n* Beilage *f*. **insertion** *n* Einsatz *m*.

inshore [,in'ʃoː] *adj* Küsten-. *adv* zur Küste hin.

inside [,in'said] *adj* inner, Innen-. *adv* (*be*) drinnen; (*go*) nach innen. *prep* in, innerhalb; (*into*) in ... hinein. *n* Innenseite *f*, Innere *neut*. **insides** (*intestines*) Eingeweide *pl*.

insidious [in'sidiəs] *adj* heimtückisch.

insight ['insait] *n* Einblick *m*; (*understanding*) Verständnis *neut*.

insignificant [,insig'nifikənt] *adj* unbedeutend, unwichtig. **insignificance** *n* Bedeutungslosigkeit *f*.

insincere [,insin'siə] *adj* unaufrichtig. **insincerity** *n* Unaufrichtigkeit *f*.

insinuate [in'sinjueit] *v* zu verstehen geben, andeuten. **insinuation** *n* Andeutung *f*.

insipid [in'sipid] *adj* fade.

insist [in'sist] *v* bestehen (auf). **insistence** *n* Bestehen *neut*. **insistent** *adj* beharrlich.

insolent ['insələnt] *adj* unverschämt, frech. **insolence** *n* Unverschämtheit *f*, Frechheit *f*.

insoluble [in'soljubl] *adj* unauflöslich; (*problem*) unlösbar.

insolvent [in'solvənt] *adj* zahlungsunfähig.

insomnia [in'somniə] *n* Schlaflosigkeit *f*.

inspect [in'spekt] *v* untersuchen, besichtigen. **inspection** *n* Untersuchung *f*, Besichtigung *f*. **inspector** *n* Inspektor *m*.

inspire [in'spaiə] *v* inspirieren, begeistern; (*give rise to*) anregen. **inspiration** *n* Inspiration *f*, Anregung *f*. **inspiring** *adj* anregend.

instability [,instə'biləti] *n* Unbeständigkeit *f*.

install [in'stoːl] *v* einsetzen, einrichten. **installation** *n* Einrichtung *f*.

instalment [in'stoːlmənt] *n* Rate *f*. **instalment plan** Teilzahlungssystem *neut*.

instance ['instəns] *n* (*case*) Fall *f*; (*example*) Beispiel *neut*. **for instance** zum Beispiel (z.B.).

instant ['instənt] *n* Augenblick *m*. *adj* sofortig. **instant coffee** Pulverkaffee *m*. **instantaneous** *adj* augenblicklich. **instantly** *adv* sofort.

instead [in'sted] *adv* statt dessen. **instead of** (an)statt (+ *gen*).

instep ['instep] *n* Rist *m*, Spann *m*.
instigate ['instigeit] *v* anstiften. **instigation** *n* Anstiftung *f*. **instigator** *n* Anstifter(in).
instil [in'stil] *v* (*teach*) beibringen (+ *dat*).
instinct ['instiŋkt] *n* (Natur)Trieb *m*, Instinkt *m*. **instinctive** *adj* instinktiv; (*automatic*) unwillkürlich.
institute ['institjuɪt] *n* Institut *neut*. *v* einführen; (*found*) gründen. **institution** *n* Institut *neut*; (*home*) Anstalt *f*; (*foundation*) Stiftung *f*.
instruct [in'strʌkt] *v* unterweisen; (*teach*) unterrichten. **instruction** *n* Vorschrift *f*; (*teaching*) Unterrichtung *f*. **instructive** *adj* lehrreich. **instructor** *n* Lehrer(in). **instructions for use** Gebrauchsanweisung *f*.
instrument ['instrəmənt] *n* Instrument *neut*; (*tool*) Werkzeug *neut*; (*means*) Mittel *neut*. **instrumental** *adj* (*helpful*) förderlich. **be instrumental in** durchsetzen.
insubordinate [ˌinsəˈbɔidənət] *adj* widersetzlich. **insubordination** *n* Widersetzlichkeit *f*.
insufficient [ˌinsəˈfiʃənt] *adj* unzureichend. **insufficiency** *n* Unzulänglichkeit *f*.
insular ['insjulə] *adj* insular. **insularity** *n* Beschränktheit *f*.
insulate ['insjuleit] *v* isolieren. **insulation** *n* Isolierung *f*. **insulating tape** Isolierband *neut*.
insulin ['insjulin] *n* Insulin *neut*.
insult [in'sʌlt; *n* 'insʌlt] *v* beleidigen, beschimpfen. *n* Beleidigung *f*. **insulting** *adj* beleidigend.
insure [in'ʃuə] *v* versichern. **insurance** *n* Versicherung *f*. **insurance broker** Versicherungsmakler *m*. **insurance policy** Versicherungspolice *f*. **insurance premium** Versicherungsprämie *f*.
insurmountable [ˌinsəˈmauntəbl] *adj* unüberwindlich.
insurrection [insəˈrekʃən] *n* Aufstand *m*.
intact [in'takt] *adj* unberührt.
intake ['inteik] *n* Aufnahme *f*, Einlaß *m*.
intangible [in'tandʒəbl] *adj* unfaßbar.
integral ['intigrəl] *adj* wesentlich; (*math*) Integral-.
integrate ['intigreit] *v* integrieren; (*people*) eingliedern. **integration** *n* Integration *f*; Eingliederung *f*. **integrity** *n* Integrität *f*; (*completeness*) Vollständigkeit *f*.
intellect ['intilekt] *n* Intellekt *m*. **intellectual** *adj* intellektuell; *n* Intellektuelle(r).

intelligent [in'telidʒənt] *adj* intelligent.
intelligence *n* Intelligenz *f*; (*information*) Information *f*; (*secret service*) Geheimdienst *m*.
intelligible [in'telidʒəbl] *adj* verständlich, klar.
intend [in'tend] *v* beabsichtigen, die Absicht haben.
intense [in'tens] *adj* stark, intensiv; (*colour*) tief; (*person*) ernsthaft. **intensely** *adj* (*highly*) äußerst. **intensify** *v* verstärken. **intensity** *n* Stärke *f*. **intensive** *adj* intensiv.
intent[1] [in'tent] *n* Absicht *f*, Vorsatz *m*. **to all intents and purposes** im Grunde.
intent[2] [in'tent] *adj* **intent on** versessen auf.
intention [in'tenʃən] *n* Absicht *f*; (*plan*) Vorhaben *neut*; (*aim*) Ziel *neut*; (*meaning*) Sinn *m*. **intentional** *adj* absichtlich.
inter [in'tɔɪ] *v* beerdigen. **interment** *n* Beerdigung *f*.
interact [ˌintərˈakt] *v* aufeinander wirken. **interaction** *n* Wechselwirkung *f*.
intercede [ˌintəˈsiɪd] *v* sich verwenden (bei). **intercession** *n* Fürsprache *f*.
intercept [ˌintəˈsept] *v* abfangen. **interception** *n* Abfangen *neut*.
interchange [ˌintəˈtʃeindʒ] *n* Austausch *m*; (*roads*) (Autobahn) Kreuz/Dreieck *neut*. *v* austauschen.
intercom ['intəˌkom] *n* Sprechanlage *f*.
intercourse ['intəkɔis] *n* Verkehr *m*, Umgang *m*. **sexual intercourse** Geschlechtsverkehr *m*.
interest ['intrist] *n* Interesse *neut*; (*comm*) Zinsen *pl*; (*advantage*) Vorteil *m*. **interested** *adj* interessiert; (*biased*) beteiligt.
interfere [ˌintəˈfiə] *v* (*person*) sich einmischen; (*adversely affect*) stören. **interference** *n* Einmischung *f*; Störung *f*. **interfering** *adj* lästig, störend.
interim ['intərim] *n* Zwischenzeit *f*. *adj* vorläufig.
interior [in'tiəriə] *n* Innere *neut*. *adj* inner, Binnen-.
interjection [ˌintəˈdʒekʃən] *n* Ausruf *m*; (*gramm*) Interjektion *f*.
interlock [intəˈlok] *v* ineinandergreifen. **interlocking** *adj* verzahnt.
interlude ['intəluɪd] *n* (*interval*) Pause *f*.
intermediate [ˌintəˈmiɪdiət] *adj* Zwischen-. **intermediary** *n* Vermittler *m*.
interminable [in'tɔiminəbl] *adj* endlos.

intermission [ˌintə'miʃən] *n* Pause *f.* Unterbrechung *f.* **without intermission** pausenlos.

intermittent [ˌintə'mitənt] *adj* stoßweise, periodisch.

intern [in'təin] *v* internieren. *n* Assistentenarzt *m.* **internment** *n* Internierung *f.*

internal [in'təinl] *adj* inner; (*domestic*) Innen-, Inlands-; (*within organization*) intern.

international [ˌintə'naʃənl] *adj* international.

interpose [ˌintə'pouz] *v* dazwischenstellen. **interposition** *n* Zwischenstellung *f.*

interpret [in'təiprit] *v* dolmetschen; (*explain*) auslegen; (*theatre, music*) interpretieren. **interpreter** *n* Dolmetscher(in); Interpret(in). **interpretation** *n* Dolmetschen *neut*; Auslegung *f*; Interpretation *f.*

interrogate [in'terəgeit] *v* verhören. **interrogation** *n* Verhör *neut.* **interrogator** *n* Fragesteller *m.*

interrogative [ˌintə'rogətiv] *adj* fragend; (*gramm*) Frage-. *n* (*gramm*) Interrogativ *m.*

interrupt [ˌintə'rʌpt] *v* unterbrechen. **interruption** *n* Unterbrechung *f.*

intersect [ˌintə'sekt] *v* schneiden. **intersection** *n* Kreuzungspunkt *m*; (*mot*) Kreuzung *f.*

intersperse [ˌintə'spəis] *v* verstreuen.

interval ['intəvəl] *n* Zwischenraum *m*; (*break*) Pause *f*; (*timespan*) Abstand *m*; (*music*) Tonabstand *m.*

intervene [ˌintə'viin] *v* (*interfere*) eingreifen; (*come between*) dazwischentreten. **intervention** *n* Intervention *f*, Eingreifen *neut.*

interview ['intəvjui] *n* Interview *neut. v* interviewen. **interviewee** *n* Interviewte(r). **interviewer** *n* Interviewer *m.*

intestine [in'testin] *n* Darm *m.* **intestines** *pl* Eingeweide *pl.* **intestinal** *adj* Darm-.

intimate¹ ['intimət] *adj* vertraut. **intimacy** *n* Vertrautheit *f.*

intimate² ['intimeit] *v* andeuten. **intimation** *n* Andeutung *f*, Wink *m.*

intimidate [in'timideit] *v* einschüchtern. **intimidation** *n* Einschüchterung *f.*

into ['intu] *prep* in (+*acc*) hinein/herein. **be into** (*coll*) sich interessieren für. **get into** (*difficulties, etc.*) geraten in. **look into** (*investigate*) untersuchen.

intolerable [in'tolərəbl] *adj* unerträglich.

intolerant [in'tolərənt] *adj* intolerant. **intolerance** *n* Intoleranz *f.*

intonation [ˌintə'neiʃən] *n* Intonation *f.* **intone** *v* intonieren.

intoxicate [in'toksikeit] *v* berauschen. **intoxicated** *adj* berauscht; (*drunk*) betrunken. **intoxication** *n* Rausch *m.*

intransitive [in'transitiv] *adj* (*gramm*) intransitiv.

intravenous [ˌintrə'viinəs] *adj* intravenös.

intrepid [in'trepid] *adj* unerschrocken.

intricate ['intriket] *adj* kompliziert. **intricacy** *n* Kompliziertheit *f.*

intrigue ['intriig; *v* in'triig] *n* Intrige *f. v* faszinieren; (*plot*) intrigieren. **intriguing** *adj* faszinierend.

intrinsic [in'trinsik] *adj* wesentlich.

introduce [ˌintrə'djuis] *v* einführen; (*person*) vorstellen. **introduction** *n* Einführung *f*; (*in book*) Einleitung *f*, Vorwort *neut*; Vorstellung *f.* **introductory** *adj* einleitend. **letter of introduction** Empfehlungsbrief *m.*

introspective [ˌintrə'spektiv] *adj* selbstprüfend. **introspection** *n* Selbstprüfung *f.*

introvert ['intrə,vəit] *n* introvertierter Mensch *m.* **introverted** *adj* introvertiert.

intrude [in'truid] *v* hineindrängen; (*interfere*) sich einmischen. **intruder** *n* Eindringling *m.* **intrusion** *n* Eindrängen *neut*; Einmischung *f.* **intrusive** *adj* zudringlich; (*nuisance*) lästig.

intuition [ˌintjui'iʃən] *n* Intuition *f.* **intuitive** *adj* intuitiv.

inundate ['inʌndeit] *v* überschwemmen. **inundation** *n* Überschwemmung *f*; Flut *f.*

invade [in'veid] *v* überfallen. **invader** *n* Eindringling *m.* **invasion** *n* Einfall *m*, Invasion *f.*

invalid¹ ['invəlid] *n* Kranke(r), Invalide *m.*

invalid² [in'valid] *adj* ungültig. **invalidate** *v* fürungültig erklären. **invalidation** *n* Ungültigkeitserklärung *f.* **invalidity** *n* Ungültigkeit *f.*

invaluable [in'valjuəbl] *adj* unschätzbar.

invariable [in'veəriəbl] *adj* konstant, unveränderlich. **invariably** *adv* ausnahmslos.

invective [in'vektiv] *n* Beschimpfung *f.*

invent [in'vent] *v* erfinden. **invention** *n* Erfindung *f.* **inventor** *n* Erfinder(in).

inventory ['invəntri] *n* Inventar *neut*, Bestandsverzeichnis *neut*; (*stocktaking*) Bestandsaufnahme *f.*

invert [in'vəɪt] v umkehren. **inversion** n Umkehrung f.
invertebrate [in'vəɪtibrət] adj wirbellos. n wirbelloses Tier neut.
invest [in'vest] v investieren, anlegen. **investment** n Investition f, Anlage f. **investor** n Kapitalanleger m.
investigate [in'vestigeit] v untersuchen. **investigation** n Untersuchung f. **investigator** n Prüfer(in).
invigorating [in'vigəreitiŋ] adj stärkend.
invincible [in'vinsəbl] adj unüberwindlich. **invincibility** n Unüberwindlichkeit f.
invisible [in'vizəbl] adj unsichtbar. **invisibility** n Unsichtbarkeit f.
invite [in'vait] v einladen. **invitation** n Einladung f. **inviting** adj verlockend.
invoice ['invois] n Rechnung f. v in Rechnung stellen.
invoke [in'vouk] v anrufen. **invocation** n Anrufung f.
involuntary [in'voləntəri] adj unwillkürlich; (unintentional) unabsichtlich.
involve [in'volv] v (entail) mit sich bringen; (draw into) hineinziehen. **involved** adj verwickelt. **involvement** n Verwicklung f; Rolle f.
inward ['inwəd] adj inner. adv also **inwards** nach innen. **inwardly** adv im Innern.
iodine ['aiədiɪn] n Jod neut.
ion ['aiən] n Ion neut.
irate [ai'reit] adj wütend.
Ireland ['aiələnd] n Irland neut. **Irish** adj irisch. **Irishman/woman** n Irländer(in), Ire m, Irin f.
iris ['aiəris] n (eye) Iris f; (flower) Schwertlilie f.
irk [əɪk] v ärgern. **irksome** adj ärgerlich.
iron ['aiən] n Eisen neut; (ironing) Bügeleisen neut. adj eisern. v bügeln. **Iron Curtain** Eiserner Vorhang m. **ironing board** n Bügelbrett neut. **ironmonger** n Eisenwarenhändler m.
irony ['aiərəni] n Ironie f. **ironic** adj ironisch.
irrational [i'raʃənl] adj unlogisch; (unreasonable) unvernünftig. **irrationality** n Unvernunft f.
irredeemable [iri'diɪməbl] adj untilgbar; (beyond improvement) unverbesserlich.
irregular [i'regjulə] adj unregelmäßig. **irregularity** n Unregelmäßigkeit f.
irrelevant [i'reləvənt] adj belanglos. **irrelevance** n Belanglosigkeit f.

irreparable [i'repərəbl] adj nicht wiedergutzumachen.
irresistible [,iri'zistəbl] adj unwiderstehlich.
irrespective [,iri'spektiv] adj abgesehen (von), ohne Rücksicht (auf).
irresponsible [,iri'sponsəbl] adj unverantwortlich, verantwortungslos. **irresponsibility** n Unverantwortlichkeit f, Verantwortungslosigkeit f.
irrevocable [i'revəkəbl] adj unwiderruflich.
irrigate ['irigeit] v bewässern. **irrigation** n Bewässerung f.
irritate ['iriteit] v reizen. **irritable** adj reizbar. **irritant** n Reizmittel neut. **irritation** n Reizung f.
Islam ['izlaim] n Islam m. **Islamic** adj islamisch.
island ['ailənd] n Insel f. **islander** n Inselbewohner(in).
isolate ['aisəleit] v isolieren. **isolated** adj abgesondert; (lonely) einsam. **isolated case** Einzelfall m. **isolation** n Isolierung f; Einsamkeit f. **isolationism** n Isolationismus m.
issue ['iʃuɪ] n Frage f; (newspaper) Ausgabe f; (offspring) Nachkommenschaft f. v ausgeben; (orders) erteilen.
isthmus ['isməs] n Landenge f.
it [it] pron (nom, acc) es; (dat) ihm.
italic [i'talik] adj kursiv. **italics** pl n Kursivschrift f sing. **in italics** kursiv gedruckt.
Italy ['itəli] n Italien neut. **Italian** adj italienisch; n Italiener(in).
item ['aitəm] n Gegenstand m; (on agenda) Punkt m; (in newspaper) Artikel m. **itemize** v verzeichnen.
itinerary [ai'tinərəri] n Reiseplan m.
its [its] poss adj sein, ihr. **itself** pron sich; selbst. **by itself** von selbst.
ivory ['aivəri] n Elfenbein neut.
ivy ['aivi] n Efeu m.

J

jab [dʒab] *n* Stoß *m*, Stich *m*; *(coll: injection)* Spritze *f*. *v* Stechen.

jack [dʒak] *n* *(mot)* (Wagen)Heber *m*; *(cards)* Bube *m*. *v* **jack up** aufbocken.

jackal ['dʒakɔːl] *n* Schakal *m*.

jackdaw ['dʒakdɔː] *n* Dohle *f*.

jacket ['dʒakit] *n* Jacke *f*; *(book)* (Schutz)Umschlag *m*.

jack-knife ['dʒaknaif] *n* Klappmesser *neut*.

jackpot ['dʒakpot] *n* Jackpot *m*.

jade [dʒeid] *n* Nephrit *m*, Jade *m*.

jaded ['dʒeidid] *adj* erschöpft, abgemattet.

jagged ['dʒagid] *adj* zackig.

jaguar ['dʒagjuə] *n* Jaguar *m*.

jail [dʒeil] *n* Gefängnis *neut*. *v* ins Gefängnis werfen, einsperren. **jailer** *n* (Gefängnis)Wärter *m*.

jam¹ [dʒam] *v* einklemmen, verstopfen. **jam on the brakes** heftig auf die Bremse treten. **jam-packed** *adj* vollgestopft. *n* Engpaß *m*, Klemme *f*. **traffic jam** (Verkehrs)Stockung *f*.

jam² [dʒam] *n* Marmelade *f*.

janitor ['dʒanitə] *n* Hauswart *m*, Pförtner *m*.

January ['dʒanjuəri] *n* Januar *m*.

Japan [dʒə'pan] *n* Japan *neut*. **Japanese** *adj* japanisch; *n* Japaner(in).

jar¹ [dʒaː] *n* Glass *neut*.

jar² [dʒaː] *v* kreischen. **jar on one's nerves** einem auf die Nerven gehen. **jarring** *adj* mißtönend.

jargon ['dʒaːgən] *n* Jargon *m*, Kauderwelsch *neut*.

jasmine ['dʒazmin] *n* Jasmin *m*.

jaundice ['dʒɔːndis] *n* Gelbsucht *f*. **jaundiced** *adj* gelbsüchtig; *(fig)* neidisch, voreingenommen.

jaunt [dʒɔːnt] *n* Ausflug *m*. *v* einen Ausflug machen. **jaunty** *adj* lebhaft, flott.

javelin ['dʒavəlin] *n* Speer *m*.

jaw [dʒɔː] *n* Kiefer *m*. **jawbone** *n* Kinnbacken *m*.

jazz [dʒaz] *n* Jazz *m*. **jazz band** Jazzkapelle *f*.

jealous ['dʒeləs] *adj* eifersüchtig. **jealousy** *n* Eifersucht *f*.

jeans [dʒiːns] *pl n* Jeans *pl*.

jeep [dʒiːp] *n* Jeep *m*.

jeer [dʒiə] *v* spotten. **jeer at** verspotten. **jeering** *adj* höhnisch.

jelly ['dʒeli] *n* Gelee *neut*. **jellyfish** *n* Qualle *f*.

jeopardize ['dʒepədaiz] *v* gefährden. **jeopardy** *n* Gefahr *f*.

jerk [dʒəːk] *v* stoßen, rücken. *n* Ruck *m*, Stoß *m*. **jerkily** *adv* stoßweise.

jersey ['dʒəːzi] *n* Pullover *m*; *(fabric)* Jersey *m*.

Jerusalem [dʒə'ruːsələm] *n* Jerusalem *neut*.

jest [dʒest] *n* Scherz *m*. *v* scherzen. **jesting** *adj* scherzhaft. **jestingly** *adv* in Spaß.

jet [dʒet] *n* *(liquid)* Strahl *m*; *(tech)* Düse *f*; *(aero)* Düsenflugzeug *neut*. **jet-black** *adj* rabenschwarz. **jet engine** Düsenmotor *m*. **jet-propelled** *adj* mit Düsenantrieb.

jettison ['dʒetisn] *v* abwerfen; *(discard)* wegwerfen.

jetty ['dʒeti] *n* Landungssteg *m*, Mole *f*.

Jew [dʒuː] *n* Jude *m*, Judin *f*. **Jewish** *adj* jüdisch.

jewel ['dʒuːəl] *n* Edelstein *m*, Juwel *neut*; *(fig)* Perle *f*. **jeweller** *n* Juwelier *m*. **jewellery** *n* Schmuck *m*.

jig [dʒig] *n* Gigue *f*. *v* eine Gigue tanzen.

jigsaw ['dʒigsɔː] *n* Puzzlespiel *neut*, Geduldspiel *neut*.

jilt [dʒilt] *v* sitzenlassen.

jingle ['dʒiŋgl] *n* *(sound)* Geklingel *neut*; *(radio, etc.)* Werbelied *neut*. *v* klingeln.

jinx [dʒiŋks] *n* Unheil *neut*. *v* verhexen.

job [dʒob] *n* Arbeit *f*; *(post)* Stelle *f*; *(task)* Aufgabe *f*. **jobless** *adj* arbeitslos.

jockey ['dʒoki] *n* Jockei *m*.

jocular ['dʒokjulə] *adj* scherzhaft.

jodhpurs ['dʒodpəz] *pl n* Reithose *f*.

jog [dʒog] *v* stoßen; *(run)* trotten. *n* Stoß *m*. **jog trot** *n* Trott *m*.

join [dʒoin] *v* verbinden, vereinigen; *(club, etc.)* beitreten (+ *dat*). *(come together)* zusammenkommen. *n* Verbindungsstelle *f*; *(seam)* Naht *f*. **join in** mitmachen. **joiner** *n* Tischler *m*. **joinery** *n* Tischlerarbeit *f*.

joint [dʒoint] *n* *(anat)* Gelenk *neut*; Verbindung *f*; *(cookery)* Braten *m*; *(slang: place)* Lokal *neut*. *adj* Gesamt-. **jointed** *adj* gegliedert. **jointly** *adv* gemeinsam.

joist [dʒoist] *n* Querbalken *m*, Träger *m*.

joke [dʒouk] *n* Witz *m*, Scherz *m*. *v* scherzen. **joker** *n* Spaßvogel *m*; *(cards)* Joker *m*. **jokingly** *adv* im Spaß.

jolly ['dʒoli] *adj* lustig. **jolliness** *n* Lustigkeit *f*.

jolt [dʒoult] *n* Stoß *m. v* stoßen.
jostle ['dʒosl] *v* anstoßen. *n* Stoß *m.*
jot [dʒot] *n* Jota *neut. v* **jot down** notieren.
journal ['dʒɜːnl] *n* Zeitschrift *f; (diary)* Tagebuch *neut.* **journalism** *n* Zeitungswesen *neut.* **journalist** *n* Journalist(in).
journey ['dʒɜːni] *n* Reise *f. v* (ver)reisen.
jovial ['dʒouviəl] *adj* lustig, jovial. **joviality** *n* Lustigkeit *f.*
joy [dʒoi] *n* Freude *f*, Wonne *f.* **joyful** *adj* erfreut. **joyfulness** *n* Fröhlichkeit *f.*
jubilant ['dʒuːbilənt] *adj* jubelnd, frohlockend. **jubilation** *n* Jubel *m*, Frohlocken *neut.*
jubilee ['dʒuːbiliː] *n* Jubiläum *neut; (celebration)* Jubelfest *neut.*
Judaism ['dʒuːdeiˌizəm] *n* Judentum *neut.*
judge [dʒʌdʒ] *n (law)* Richter; *(expert)* Kenner *m. v* beurteilen; *(value)* (ein)schätzen. **judgment** *n* Beurteilung *f; (law)* Urteil *neut.*
judicial [dʒuːˈdiʃəl] *adj* gerichtlich. **judiciary** *n* Gerichtswesen *neut.*
judicious [dʒuːˈdiʃəs] *adj* wohlüberlegt; *(reasonable)* vernünftig.
judo ['dʒuːdou] *n* Judo *neut.*
jug [dʒʌg] *n* Krug *m*, Kanne *f.*
juggernaut ['dʒʌgənoːt] *n* Moloch *m; (mot)* Fernlastwagen *m.*
juggle ['dʒʌgl] *v* jonglieren. **juggler** *n* Jongleur *m.*
jugular ['dʒʌgjulə] *n* Drosselader *f.*
juice [dʒuːs] *n* Saft *m.* **juicy** *adj* saftig.
jukebox ['dʒuːkboks] *n* Jukebox *f.*
July [dʒuˈlai] *n* Juli *m.*
jumble ['dʒʌmbl] *n* Durcheinander *neut. v* durcheinander bringen. **jumble sale** Basar *m*, Ramschverkauf *m.*
jump [dʒʌmp] *n* Sprung *m. v* springen; *(be startled)* zusammenzucken. **jump at the chance** die Gelegenheit ergreifen. **jumpy** *adj* nervös.
jumper ['dʒʌmpə] *n* Pullover *m.*
junction ['dʒʌŋktʃən] *n (road)* Kreuzung *f; (rail)* Knotenpunkt *m.*
juncture ['dʒʌŋkʃə] *n* Augenblick *m.* **at this juncture** an dieser Stelle.
June [dʒuːn] *n* Juni *m.*
jungle ['dʒʌŋgl] *n* Dschungel *m.*
junior ['dʒuːnjə] *adj* junior, jünger. **junior school** Grundschule *f.*
juniper ['dʒuːnipə] *n* Wacholder *m.*
junk¹ [dʒʌŋk] *n* Trödel *m.* **junk shop** Trödelladen *m.*

junk² [dʒʌŋk] *n (naut)* Dschunke *f.*
junta ['dʒʌntə] *n* Junta *f.*
Jupiter ['dʒuːpitə] *n* Jupiter *m.*
jurisdiction [dʒuərisˈdikʃən] *n* Gerichtsbarkeit *f.*
jury ['dʒuəri] *n* die Geschworene *pl; (quiz, etc.)* Jury *f.* **trial by jury** Schwurgerichtsverhandlung *f.* **juror** *n* Geschworene(r).
just [dʒʌst] *adv (recently)* gerade, eben; *(only)* nur; *(exactly)* genau. **just about** so ungefähr. **just as good** ebenso gut. **just a little** ein ganz klein wenig. *adj* gerecht. **justly** *adv* mit Recht, gerecht.
justice ['dʒʌstis] *n* Gerechtigkeit *f; (judge)* Richter *m.* **Justice of the Peace** Friedensrichter *m.*
justify ['dʒʌstifai] *v* rechtfertigen. **justification** *n* Rechtfertigung *f.* **justifiable** *adj* berechtigt.
jut [dʒʌt] *v* jut out hervorragen.
jute [dʒuːt] *n* Jute *f.*
juvenile ['dʒuːvənail] *adj* jugendlich. **juvenile court** Jugendgericht *neut.* **juvenile delinquent** jugendlicher Straftäter *m.* **juvenile delinquency** Jugendkriminalität *f.*
juxtapose [ˌdʒʌkstəˈpouz] *v* nebeneinanderstellen.

K

kaleidoscope [kəˈlaidəskoup] *n* Kaleidoskop *neut.*
kangaroo [kaŋgəˈruː] *n* Känguruh *neut.*
karate [kəˈraːti] *n* Karate *neut.*
kebab [kiˈbab] *n* Kebab *m.*
keel [kiːl] *n* Kiel *m.*
keen [kiːn] *adj (sharp)* scharf; *(hearing)* fein; *(enthusiastic)* eifrig. **keenness** *n* Eifer *f.*
***keep** [kiːp] *v* halten, behalten; haben; *(remain)* bleiben; *(preserve, store)* aufbewahren; *(of food)* sich halten; *(support)* versorgen. **keep away** fernhalten. **keep fit** sich gesund erhalten. **keep in mind** im Gedächtnis behalten. **keep on** fortfahren. **keep out!** Eintritt verboten! **keep up with** Schritt halten mit. **keeper** *n* Wächter *m; (animals)* Züchter *m.* **be in keeping with** passen zu. **keepsake** *n* Andenken *neut.*

keg [keg] *n* Faß *neut.*
kennel ['kenl] *n* Hundehütte *f.*
kept [kept] *V* keep.
kerb [kɜːb] *n* Straßenkante *f.*
kernel ['kɜːnl] *n* Kern *m.*
kerosene ['kerəsiːn] *n* Petroleum *neut.*
ketchup ['ketʃəp] *n* Ketchup *m.*
kettle ['ketl] *n* Kessel *m.* **kettledrum** *n* Pauke *f.* **a pretty kettle of fish** eine schöne Bescherung. **a different kettle of fish** was ganz anderes.
key [kiː] *n* Schlüssel *m*; (*piano, typewriter*) Taste *f*; (*music*) Tonart *f.* **keyboard** *n* Tastatur *f.* **keyring** *n* Schlüsselring *m.*
khaki ['kɑːki] *adj* khaki.
kick [kik] *v* mit dem Fuß treten *or* stoßen. *n* Fußtritt *m*; (*football*) Schuß *m*; (*fig*) Schwung *m.* **kick-off** *n* Anstoß *m.* **kick off** anstoßen.
kid¹ [kid] *n* (*goat*) Zicklein *neut*; (*leather*) Ziegenleder *neut*; (*child*) Kind *neut.*
kid² [kid] *v* (*coll*) auf den Arm nehmen.
kidnap ['kidnap] *v* entführen. **kidnapper** *n* Entführer *m*, Kidnapper *m.*
kidney ['kidni] *n* Niere *f.* **kidney bean** weiße Bohne *f.* **kidney stone** Nierenstein *m.*
kill [kil] *v* töten, umbringen; (*animals*) schlachten. **kill oneself laughing** sich totlachen. **killer** *n* Mörder *m.* **killing** *n* Tötung *f. adj* tötend.
kiln [kiln] *n* Brennofen *m.*
kilo ['kiːlou] *n* Kilo *neut.*
kilogram ['kiləgram] *n* Kilogramm *neut.*
kilometre ['kiləmiːtə] *n* Kilometer *m.*
kin [kin] *n* Verwandte *pl.* **next of kin** nächste(r) Verwandte(r).
kind¹ [kaind] *adj* freundlich, gütig. **kindly** *adj* gütig. **kindness** *n* Güte *f.*
kind² [kaind] *n* Sorte *f,* Art *f*; (*species*) Gattung *f.* **all kinds of** allerlei. **in kind** in Waren.
kindergarten ['kindəgaːtn] *n* Kindergarten *m,* Krippe *f.*
kindle ['kindl] *v* entzünden.
kindred ['kindrid] *n* Verwandschaft *f.*
kinetic [kin'etik] *adj* kinetisch. **kinetics** *n* Kinetik *f.*
king [kiŋ] *n* König *m.* **kingdom** *n* Königreich *neut.* **animal kingdom** Tierreich *neut.*
kink [kiŋk] *n* Knick *m. v* knicken.
kiosk ['kiːɔsk] *n* Kiosk *m.* **telephone kiosk** Telephonzelle *f.*

kipper ['kipə] *n* Bückling *m,* Räucherhering *m.*
kiss [kis] *n* Kuß *m,* Küßchen *neut. v* küssen. **kiss goodbye** einen Abschiedskuß geben (+ *dat*).
kit [kit] *n* Ausrüstung *f*; (*mil*) Gepäck *neut.*
kitchen ['kitʃin] *n* Küche *f.* **kitchenette** *n* Kochnische *f.*
kite [kait] *n* Drachen *m*; (*bird*) Gabelweihe *f.*
kitten ['kitn] *n* Kätzchen *neut.*
kitty ['kiti] *n* Kasse *f.*
kleptomaniac [kleptə'meiniak] *n* Kleptomane *m.*
knack [nak] *n* Kniff *m,* Trick *m.* **get the knack of** den Dreh heraushaben (+ *gen*).
knapsack ['napsak] *n* Rucksack *m.*
knave [neiv] *n* Schurke *m*; (*cards*) Bube *m.*
knead [niːd] *v* kneten.
knee [niː] *n* Knie *neut.* **kneecap** *n* Kniescheibe *f.*
*kneel [niːl] *v* knien.
knelt [nelt] *V* kneel.
knew [njuː] *V* know.
knickers ['nikəz] *pl n* Schlüpfer *m sing*; Höschen *neut sing.*
knife [naif] *n* Messer *neut. v* (er)stechen.
knight [nait] *n* Ritter *m*; (*chess*) Springer *m.* **knighthood** *n* Rittertum *neut.* **knightly** *adj* ritterlich.
*knit [nit] *v* stricken; (*brow*) rünzeln. **knitted** *adj* Strick-. **knitting** *n* Strickzeug *neut.* **knitting needle** Stricknadel *f.* **knitwear** *n* Strickwaren *pl.*
knob [nob] *n* Knopf *m,* Griff *m.*
knobbly ['nobli] *adj* knorrig.
knock [nok] *v* (*strike*) schlagen; (*on door*) klopfen; (*criticize*) heruntermachen. *n* Schlag *m*; Klopfen *neut.* **knock off** (*coll: steal*) klauen; (*work*) Feierabend machen. **knock out** k.o. schlagen.
knot [not] *n* Knoten *m*; (*in wood*) Ast *m. v* knoten.
*know [nou] *v* wissen; (*be acquainted with*) kennen; (*know how to*) können; (*understand*) verstehen. **know-all** Besserwisser *m.* **know-how** *n* Knowhow *neut.* **knowing** *adj* geschickt; (*sly*) schlau. **knowingly** *adv* absichtlich. **be in the know** Bescheid wissen. **known** *adj* bekannt.
knowledge ['nolidʒ] *n* Kenntnis *f.* **knowledgeable** *adj* kenntnisreich.

known [noun] V **know**.
knuckle ['nʌkl] n Fingerknöchel m.
knuckle down eifrig herangehen. **knuckle under** nachgeben.

L

label ['leibl] n Zettel m; (sticky) Klebezettel neut; (luggage) Anhängezettel neut. v mit einem Zettel versehen; (fig) bezeichnen.
laboratory [lə'borətəri] n Labor neut. **laboratory assistant** Laborant(in).
labour ['leibə] n Arbeit; (work-force) Arbeitskräfte pl; (birth) Wehen pl. v (schwer) arbeiten, sich anstrengen. **laboured** adj schwerfällig; (style) mühsam. **labourer** n (ungelernter) Arbeiter m.
laburnum [lə'bəinəm] n Goldregen m.
labyrinth ['labərinθ] n Labyrinth neut.
lace [leis] n Spitze f; (shoe) Schnur f. v schnüren. **lacy** adj Spitzen-.
lacerate ['lasəreit] v zerreißen. **laceration** n Zerreißung f.
lack [lak] v mangeln (an). n Mangel m. **be lacking** fehlen.
lackadaisical [,lakə'deizikəl] adj schlapp.
lacquer ['lakə] n Lack m. v lackieren.
lad [lad] n Junge m, Bursche m.
ladder ['ladə] n Leiter f; (stocking) Laufmasche f. **ladder-resistant** adj maschenfest.
laden ['leidn] adj beladen.
ladle ['leidl] n Schöpflöffel m. v ausschöpfen.
lady ['leidi] n Dame f. **Ladies** n (sign) Damen pl. **ladies' man** Frauenheld m. **ladybird** Marienkäfer m. **lady-in-waiting** n Hofdame f. **ladylike** adj damenhaft.
lag¹ [lag] v **lag behind** zurückbleiben. n Zeitabstand m.
lag² [lag] v (cover) verkleiden.
lager ['laigə] n Lagerbier neut.
lagoon [lə'guin] n Lagune f.
laid [leid] V **lay¹**.
lain [lein] V **lie²**.
lair [leə] n Lager neut.
laity ['leiəti] n Laienstand m.
lake [leik] n (Binnen)See m.
lamb [lam] n Lamm neut; (meat) Lammfleisch neut.

lame [leim] adj lahm, hinkend; (excuse) schwach. v lahm machen. **lameness** n Lahmheit f; Schwäche f.
lament [lə'ment] v (weh)klagen; (regret) bedauern. n Klagelied neut. **lamentable** adj beklagenswert; bedauerlich. **lamentation** n Jammer m.
laminate ['lamineit] v schichten. **laminated** adj beschichtet.
lamp [lamp] n Lampe f; (street) Laterne f. **lamplight** n Lampenlicht neut. **lamppost** n Laternenpfahl m. **lampshade** n Lampenschirm m.
lance [lains] n Lanze f. v (med) mit einer Lanzette eröffnen, aufstechen. **lance corporal** n Hauptgefreite(r) m.
land [land] n Land neut. v an Land gehen; (aircraft) landen; (goods) abladen. **landing** n Landung f; (stairs) Treppenabsatz m. **landing craft** Landungsboot neut. **landing stage** Landesteg m.
landlady ['landleidi] n Wirtin f.
landlord ['landloid] n (Gast-)Wirt m.
landmark ['landmaik] n Wahrzeichen neut; (milestone) Markstein m.
landowner ['landounə] n Grundbesitzer m.
landscape ['landskeip] n Landschaft f. **landscape gardener** Kunstgärtner m. **landscape gardening** Kunstgärtnerei f. **landscape painter** Landschaftsmaler(in)
landslide ['landslaid] n Erdrutsch m. adj (pol) überwältigend.
lane [lein] n (country) (Feld)Weg m, Pfad m; (town) Gasse f; (mot) Spur f. (sport) Rennbahn f.
language ['langwidʒ] n Sprache f; (style) Stil m, Redeweise f. **bad language** Schimpfworte pl. **foreign language** Fremdsprache f.
languish ['langwiʃ] v schmachten.
lanky ['laŋki] adj schlaksig.
lantern ['lantən] n Laterne f.
lap¹ [lap] n (anat) Schoß m; (circuit) Runde f.
lap² [lap] v (drink) auflecken.
lapel [lə'pel] n Revers m or neut.
lapse [laps] n Versehen neut; (mistake) Irrtum m; (time) Zeitspanne f. v (time) vergehen; (from faith) abfallen.
larceny ['laisəni] n Diebstahl m.
larch [laitʃ] n Lärche f.

lard [laɪd] n Schmalz neut. v spicken. **lard-ing needle** Sticknadel f.
larder ['laɪdə] n Speisekammer f.
large [laɪdʒ] adj groß; (considerable) beträchtlich. **at large** auf freiem Fuß m. **large as life** in Lebensgröße. **large-scale** adj Groß-. **largesse** n Freigiebigkeit f. **largely** adv weitgehend. **largeness** n Größe f.
lark¹ [laɪk] n (bird) Lerche f.
lark² [laɪk] n Spaß m. v **lark about** Possen treiben.
larva ['laɪvə] n Larve f. **larval** adj Larven-.
larynx ['larɪŋks] n Kehlkopf m. **laryngitis** n Kehlkopfentzündung f.
laser ['leɪzə] n Laser m. **laser beam** Laserstrahl m.
lash [laʃ] v (whip) peitschen; (tie) festbinden. n Peitschenschnur f; (eyelash) Wimper f. **lash out** ausschlagen.
lass [las] n Mädchen neut, Mädel neut.
lassitude ['lasɪtjuːd] n Mattigkeit f.
lasso [la'suː] n Lasso m. v mit einem Lasso fangen.
last [laɪst] adj letzt. **at last** endlich, schließlich. **last but not least** nicht zuletzt. **last year** im vorigen Jahr. adv also **lastly** zuletzt. v (time) dauern; (supply) ausreichen; (be preserved) (gut) halten. **lasting** adj anhaltend, dauernd.
latch [latʃ] n Klinke f. v einklinken. **latch onto** (understand) spitzkriegen.
late [leɪt] adj spät; (tardy) verspätet; (deceased) selig; (former) ehemalig. **be late** Verspätung haben. **lately** adv neuerdings. **lateness** n Verspätung f. **later** adj später. **latest** adj spätest; (newest) neuest. **at the latest** spätestens.
latent ['leɪtənt] adj latent.
lateral ['latərəl] adj seitlich. **laterally** adv seitwärts.
lathe [leɪð] n Drehbank f.
lather ['laɪðə] n Seifenschaum m. v schäumen; (beat) verprügeln.
Latin ['latɪn] adj lateinisch. n Latein neut. **Latin America** n Lateinamerika neut. **Latin-American** adj lateinamerikanisch.
latitude ['latɪtjuːd] n Breite f; (fig) Spielraum m. **latitudinal** adj Breiten-.
latrine [lə'triːn] n Klosett neut, Latrine f.
latter ['latə] adj letzt. **latterly** adv neuerdings.
lattice ['latɪs] n Gitter neut; (pattern) Gitterwerk neut.
laugh [laɪf] v lachen. **laugh at** sich lustig

machen über. **laugh off** mit einem Scherz abtun. **laughable** adj lächerlich. n Lachen neut. **laughter** Gelächter neut.
launch [lɔːntʃ] n (boat) Barkasse f; (of boat) Stapellauf m; (of rocket) Abschuß m; (start) Start m. v (boat) vom Stapel lassen; (fig) in Gang setzen.
launder ['lɔːndə] v waschen. **launderette** n Waschsalon m. **laundry** n Wäscherei f; (washing) Wäsche f.
laurel ['lɔrəl] n Lorbeer m.
lava ['laɪvə] n Lava f.
lavatory ['lavətəri] n Klosett neut, Toilette f.
lavender ['lavɪndə] n Lavendel m. adj (colour) lavendelfarben.
lavish ['lavɪʃ] adj verschwenderisch. **lavishness** n Verschwendung f.
law [lɔ] n (single law) Gesetz neut; (system) Recht neut; (study) Jura pl. **law-abiding** adj friedlich. **lawcourt** Gerichtshof m. **lawful** adj rechtmäßig, gesetzlich. **lawless** adj gesetzwidrig. **lawsuit** n Prozeß m. **lawyer** n Rechtsanwalt m.
lawn [lɔːn] n Rasen m; (fabric) Batist m. **lawnmower** n Rasenmäher m. **lawn tennis** Tennis neut.
lax [laks] adj locker.
laxative ['laksətɪv] n Abführmittel neut.
***lay¹** [leɪ] v legen; (put down) setzen, stellen; (table) decken. **lay down** hinlegen; (law) vorschreiben. **lay off** (dismiss) entlassen.
lay² [leɪ] adj Laien-. **layman** n Laie m.
lay-by ['leɪbaɪ] n Parkstreifen m.
layer ['leɪə] n Schicht f.
lazy ['leɪzi] adj faul. **laze** v faulenzen. **laziness** n Faulheit f. **lazybones** n Faulpelz m.
***lead¹** [liːd] v leiten, führen. **leader** n Führer m, Leiter m; (in newspaper) Leitartikel m. **leadership** n Führerschaft f. **leading** adj führend, Haupt-. n (dog's) Leine f; (theatre) Hauptrolle f; (cable) Schnur f; (hint) Hinweis m.
lead² [led] n Blei neut; (in pencil) Bleistiftmine f.
leaf [liːf] n Blatt neut. **leaflet** n (pamphlet) Prospekt m. v **leaf through** durchblättern. **leafy** adj belaubt.
league [liːg] n (association) Bund neut; (sport) Liga f.
leak [liːk] n Leck neut; (pol) Durchsickern neut. v lecken; durchsickern. **leakage** n Lecken neut. **leaky** adj leck.

*lean¹ [liːn] *v* (sich) lehnen. **lean on** sich stützen auf; (*rely on*) sich verlassen auf. **leaning** *n* Neigung *f.*

lean² [liːn] *adj* mager.

leant [lent] *V* **lean¹**

*leap [liːp] *v* hüpfen, springen. *n* Sprung *m.* **look before you leap** erst wägen, dann wagen. **by leaps and bounds** sprunghaft. **leap frog** Bockspringen *neut.* **leapyear** *n* Schaltjahr *neut.*

leapt [lept] *V* **leap.**

*learn [ləɪn] *v* lernen; (*find out*) erfahren. **learned** *adj* gelehrt. **learner** *n* Anfänger *m*; (*driver*) Fahrschüler(in). **learning** *n* Wissen *neut.*

learnt [ləɪnt] *V* **learn.**

lease [liːs] *n* Mietvertrag *m*, Pachtvertrag *m. v* (ver)mieten, pachten. **leaseholder** *n* Pächter(in).

leash [liːʃ] *n* Leine *f.*

least [liːst] *adj* (*smallest*) kleinst; (*slightest*) geringst. **at least** mindestens. **not in the least** nicht im geringsten.

leather ['leðə] *n* Leder *neut. adj* ledern. **leathery** *adj* lederartig.

*leave¹ [liːv] *v* verlassen, lassen; (*go away*) (ab-, ver)reisen, weggehen. **leave off** aufhören. **leave out** ·auslassen. **left-luggage office** Gepäckaufbewahrung *f.*

leave² [liːv] *n* (*permission*) Erlaubnis *f*; (*holiday*) Urlaub *m.* **take one's leave of** Abschied nehmen von.

lecherous ['letʃərəs] *adj* wollustig. **lechery** *n* Wollust *f.*

lectern ['lektən] *n* Lesepult *neut.*

lecture ['lektʃə] *n* Vortrag *m*, Vorlesung *f. v* einen Vortrag halten. **lecturer** *n* Dozent *m.* **lecture hall** Hörsaal *m.*

led [led] *V* **lead¹.**

ledge [ledʒ] *n* Sims *m* or *neut.*

ledger ['ledʒə] *n* Hauptbuch *neut.*

lee [liː] *n* (*naut*) Leeseite *f.*

leech [liːtʃ] *n* Blutegel *m.*

leek [liːk] *n* Porree *m.*

leer [liə] *n* anzügliches Grinsen. *v* anzüglich grinsen.

leeway ['liːwei] *n* Abtrift *f*; (*fig*) Spielraum *m.*

left¹ [left] *V* **leave¹.**

left² [left] *adj* link. *adv* (nach) links. **on the left** links. **left-handed** *adj* linkshändig. **left-wing** *adj* Links-.

leg [leg] *n* Bein *neut*; (*cookery*) Keule *f*; (*sport*) Lauf *m.* **be on one's last legs** auf

dem letzten Loch pfeifen. **leggy** *adj* langbeinig.

legacy ['legəsi] *n* Legat *neut.*

legal ['liːgəl] *adj* gesetzlich, rechtlich. **legality** *n* Gesetzlichkeit *f.* **legalize** *v* legalisieren.

legend ['ledʒənd] *n* Sage *f*, Legende *f.* **legendary** *adj* sagenhaft, legendär.

legible ['ledʒəbl] *adj* leserlich. **legibility** *n* Leserlichkeit *f.*

legion ['liːdʒən] *n* Legion *f.* **legionary** *n* Legionär *m.*

legislate ['ledʒisleit] *v* Gesetze geben. **legislation** *n* Gesetzgebung *f.* **legislative** *adj* gesetzgebend. **legislator** *n* Gesetzgeber *m.*

legitimate [lə'dʒitimət] *adj* rechtmäßig; (*child*) ehelich; (*justified*) berechtigt. **legitimacy** *n* Rechtmäßigkeit; Ehelichkeit *f.*

leisure ['leʒə] *n* Freizeit *f.* **leisurely** *adv* ohne Hast.

lemon ['lemən] *n* Zitrone *f. adj* zitronengelb. **lemonade** *n* Zitronenlimonade *f.* **lemon squeezer** Zitronenpresse *f.*

*lend [lend] *v* (ver)leihen. **lend a hand** helfen. **lending library** Leihbibliothek *f.*

length [leŋθ] *n* Länge *f*; (*of cloth*) Stück *neut*; (*time*) Dauer *f.* **at length** (*in detail*) ausführlich; (*at last*) schließlich. **lengthen** *v* (sich) verlängern. **lengthways** *adv* längs. **lengthy** *adj* übermäßig lang.

lenient ['liːniənt] *adj* nachsichtig (gegenüber). **leniency** Nachsicht *f.*

lens [lenz] *n* Linse *f*; (*photographic*) Objektiv *neut.*

lent [lent] *V* **lend.**

Lent [lent] *n* Fastenzeit *f.*

lentil ['lentil] *n* Linse *f.*

Leo ['liːou] *n* Löwe *m.* **leonine** *adj* Löwen-.

leopard ['lepəd] *n* Leopard *m.*

leper ['lepə] *n* Leprakranke(r). **leprosy** *n* Lepra *f.*

lesbian ['lezbiən] *adj* lesbisch. *n* Lesbierin *f.*

less [les] *adv* weniger. *adj* geringer. *prep* minus. **lessen** *v* (sich) vermindern. **lesser** *adj* kleiner, geringer.

lesson ['lesn] *n* (*in school*) Stunde *f*; (*warning*) Warnung *f.* **lessons** *pl* Unterricht *m sing.*

lest [lest] *conj* damit ... nicht.

*let [let] v lassen; (*rooms, etc.*) vermieten.
let's go gehen wir. **let alone** (*not annoy*)
in Ruhe lassen; (*much less*) geschweige
denn **let down** enttäuschen, im Stich
lassen. **let go** gehen lassen. **let go of** loslassen. **let up** (*coll*) nachlassen.

lethal ['liːθəl] *adj* tödlich.

lethargy ['leθədʒi] n Lethargie f. **lethargic**
adj lethargisch.

letter ['letə] n Brief m; (*of alphabet*)
Buchstabe m. **letter box** Briefkasten m.

lettuce ['letis] n Kopfsalat m.

leukaemia [luːˈkiːmiə] n Leukämie f.

level ['levl] *adj* gerade, eben; (*equal*)
gleich. **level crossing** Bahnübergang m.
level-headed *adj* nüchtern. **draw level
with** einholen. v ebnen; (*make equal*)
gleichmachen. n Ebene f, Niveau *neut*.

lever ['liːvə] n Hebel m.

levy ['levi] n Abgabe f. v erheben.

lewd [luːd] *adj* lüstern. **lewdness** n Lüs-
ternheit f.

liable ['laiəbl] *adj* (*responsible*) verantwortlich. **be liable to** neigen zu. **liability** n
Verantwortlichkeit. **limited liability**
(*comm*) mit beschränkter Haftung. **be
liable for** haften für. **liable to prosecution**
strafbar.

liaison [liˈeizon] n Verbindung f; (*love
affair*) (Liebes)Verhältnis *neut*.

liar ['laiə] n Lügner(in).

libel ['laibəl] n Verleumdung f. v (*schrift-
tlich*) verleumden. **libellous** *adj*
verleumderisch.

liberal ['libərəl] *adj* liberal; (*generous*)
großzügig. n Liberale(r). **liberalize** v
liberalisieren.

liberate ['libəreit] v befreien. **liberation** n
Befreiung f. **liberator** n Befreier m.

liberty ['libəti] n Freiheit f. **at liberty** frei.

Libra ['liːbrə] n Waage f.

library ['laibrəri] n Bibliothek f, Bücherei
f. **librarian** n Bibliothekar(in).

libretto [liˈbretou] n Libretto *neut*,
Textbuch *neut*.

lice [lais] V **louse**.

licence ['laisəns] n Genehmigung f,
Lizenz f. **driving licence** Führerschein m.
marriage licence Eheerlaubnis f. **license** v
genehmigen. **licensed** *adj* konzessioniert.

lichen ['laikən] n Flechte f.

lick [lik] v lecken; (*coll: defeat*) besiegen;
(*flames*) züngeln. n Lecken *neut*.

lid [lid] n Deckel m; (*eyelid*) Lid *neut*.

lie¹ [lai] n Lüge. v lügen.

*lie² [lai] v liegen. **lie down** sich hinlegen.
lie in (*coll*) sich ausschlafen.

lieutenant [ləfˈtenənt] n Leutnant m.

life [laif] n Leben *neut*. **lifebelt** n Rettungs-
gürtel m. **lifeboat** n Rettungsboot *neut*.
lifeguard n Bademeister m. **life insurance**
Lebensversicherung f. **life jacket**
Schwimmweste f. **lifeless** *adj* leblos. **life-
like** *adj* naturgetreu. **lifesize** *adj* lebens-
groß. **lifetime** n Lebenszeit f.

lift [lift] n Aufzug m, Fahrstuhl m. v
(auf)heben. **give a lift to** (im Auto)
mitnehmen.

*light¹ [lait] n Licht *neut*; (*lamp*) Lampe
f. **a light** (*for cigarette*) Feuer *neut*. v
anzünden.

light² [lait] *adj* leicht; (*colour*) hell.

lighten¹ ['laitn] v (*reduce weight*) erleichtern, leichter machen.

lighten² ['laitn] v (*brighten*) sich erhellen,
heller werden.

lighter ['laitə] n (*cigarette*) Feuerzeug
neut.

lighthouse ['laithaus] n Leuchtturm m.

lighting ['laitiŋ] n Beleuchtung f.

lightning ['laitniŋ] n Blitz m. **lightning
conductor** Blitzableiter m. **flash of lightning** Blitzschlag m.

light ['laitweit]**weight** *adj* leicht. n
Leichtgewichtler m.

light-year ['laitjiə] n Lichtjahr *neut*.

like¹ [laik] *adj* gleich (+ *dat*), ähnlich
(+ *dat*). *prep* wie. **what's it like?** wie ist
es? **like-minded** *adj* gleichgesinnt. **likewise** *adv* gleichfalls.

like² [laik] v gern haben; mögen. *do you
like it?* gefällt es Ihnen? (*food*) schmeckt
es (Ihnen)? **likeable** *adj* liebenswürdig.
liking n Zuneigung f; (*taste*) Geschmack
m.

likely ['laikli] *adj* wahrscheinlich. **likeli-
hood** n Wahrscheinlichkeit f.

lilac ['lailək] n (*colour*) Lila *neut*. *adj*
lilafarben.

lily ['lili] n Lilie f.

limb [lim] n Glied *neut*. **limbs** *pl*
Gliedmaßen *pl*.

limbo ['limbou] n (*rel*) Vorhölle f. **in limbo** (*fig*) in der Schwebe, in Vergessenheit.

lime¹ [laim] n (*mineral*) Kalk *neut*.

lime² [laim] n (*tree*) Linde f, Lindenbaum
m; (*fruit*) Limonelle f.

limit ['limit] *n* Grenze *f*, Schranke *f*. *v* begrenzen, beschränken. **limited** *adj* beschränkt; (*comm*) mit beschränkter Haftung.

limousine ['liməˌziːn] *n* Limousine *f*.

limp[1] [limp] *v* hinken. *n* Hinken *neut*.

limp[2] [limp] *adj* schlaff.

line [lain] *n* Linie *f*, Strich *m*; (*row*) Reihe *f*; (*of print*) Zeile *f*; (*washing*) Leine *f*; (*wrinkle*) Falte *f*. *v* linieren; (*coat, etc.*) füttern. **lineage** *n* Abstammung *f*. **linear** *adj* Linear-.

linen ['linin] *n* Leinen *neut*. **bed linen** Wäsche *f*.

liner ['lainə] *n* (*ship*) Linienschiff *neut*, Überseedampfer *m*.

linesman ['lainzman] *n* Linienrichter *m*.

linger ['liŋgə] *v* verweilen. **lingering** *adj* (*illness*) schleichend.

lingerie ['lãʒəriː] *n* (Damen)Unterwäsche *f*.

linguist ['liŋgwist] *n* Linguist(in). **linguistic** *adj* linguistisch. **linguistics** *n* Linguistik *f*.

lining ['lainiŋ] *n* Futter *neut*, Fütterung *f*.

link [liŋk] *n* (*of chain*) Glied *neut*; (*connection*) Verbindung *f*. *v* verbinden. **link arms** sich einhaken (bei).

linoleum [li'nouliəm] *n* Linoleum *neut*.

linseed ['linˌsiːd] *n* Leinsamen *m*. **linseed oil** Leinöl *neut*.

lint [lint] *n* Zupfleinen *neut*.

lion ['laiən] *n* Löwe *m*. **lioness** *n* Löwin *f*. **lion's share** Löwenanteil *m*.

lip [lip] *n* Lippe *f*; (*edge*) Rand *m*; (*coll: impudence*) Frechheit *f*. **lip service** Lippendienst *m*. **lipstick** *n* Lippenstift *m*.

liqueur [li'kjuə] *n* Likör *m*.

liquid ['likwid] *n* Flüssigkeit *f*. *adj* flüssig. **liquidate** *v* (*comm*) liquidieren. **liquidation** *n* Liquidierung *f*. **liquidator** *n* Liquidator *m*. **liquidity** *n* Flüssigkeit *f*.

liquor ['likə] *n* alkoholisches Getränk *neut*.

liquorice ['likəris] *n* Lakritze *f*.

lisp [lisp] *n* Lispeln *neut*. *v* lispeln.

list[1] [list] *n* Liste *f*, Verzeichnis *neut*. *v* verzeichnen.

list[2] [list] *n* (*naut*) Schlagseite *f*. *v* Schlagseite haben.

listen ['lisn] *v* hören auf, zuhören (+ *dat*). **listener** *n* Zuhörer *m*. **listening device** Abhörgerät *neut*.

listless ['listlis] *adj* lustlos.

lit [lit] *V* **light**[1].

litany ['litəni] *n* Litanei *f*.

literacy ['litərəsi] *n* die Fähigkeit, lesen und schreiben zu können *f*. **literate** *adj* gelehrt. **be literate** lesen und schreiben können.

literal ['litərəl] *adj* buchstäblich.

literary ['litərəri] *adj* literarisch.

literature ['litrətʃə] *n* Literatur *f*.

lithe [laið] *adj* geschmeidig.

litigation [liti'geiʃən] *n* Prozeß *m*.

litre ['liːtə] *n* Liter *neut*.

litter ['litə] *n* (*rubbish*) Abfall *m*; (*stretcher*) Tragbahre *f*; (*animals*) Wurf *m*. **litter bin** Abfallkorb *m*.

little ['litl] *adj* klein. *adv* wenig. **a little** ein bißchen, ein wenig.

liturgy ['litədʒi] *n* Liturgie *f*.

live[1] [liv] *v* leben; (*reside*) wohnen.

live[2] [laiv] *adj* (*alive*) lebendig; (*radio, etc.*) live; (*electricity*) stromführend. **live broadcast** Livesendung *f*.

livelihood ['laivlihud] *n* Lebensunterhalt *m*.

lively ['laivli] *adj* lebhaft. **liveliness** *n* Lebhaftigkeit *f*.

liver ['livə] *n* Leber *f*.

livestock ['laivstok] *n* Vieh *neut*.

livid ['livid] *adj* (*coll: angry*) wütend.

living ['liviŋ] *adj* lebendig, am Leben. *n* Lebensunterhalt *m*. **make a living** sein Brot verdienen. **living room** Wohnzimmer *neut*.

lizard ['lizəd] *n* Eidechse *f*.

load [loud] *n* Last *f*, Belastung *f*. *v* (be)laden.

loaf[1] [louf] *n* Laib *m*, Brot *neut*.

loaf[2] [louf] *v* **loaf around** faulenzen. **loafer** *n* Bummler *m*, Faulenzer *m*.

loan [loun] *n* Anleihe *f*; (*credit*) Darlehen *neut*. *v* leihen.

loathe [louð] *v* hassen, nicht ausstehen können. **loathing** *n* Abscheu *m*. **loathsome** *adj* abscheulich.

lob [lob] *v* (*sport*) lobben. *n* Lob *m*.

lobby ['lobi] *n* Vorhalle *f*; (*pol*) Interessengruppe *f*.

lobe [loub] *n* Lappen *m*.

lobster ['lobstə] *n* Hummer *m*.

local ['loukəl] *adj* örtlich, Orts-. *n* Ortsbewohner *m*. **local government** Gemeindeverwaltung *f*. **locality** *n* Ort *m*. **localize** *v* lokalisieren.

locate [lə'keit] *v* ausfindig machen. **location** *n* Standort *m*.

lock¹ [lok] *n* Schloß *neut*; (*canal*) Schleuse *f*. *v* verschließen. **lock in** einsperren. **lock out** aussperren. **lock up** verschließen.

lock² [lok] *n* (*of hair*) Locke *f*.

locker ['lokə] *n* Schließfach *neut*.

locket ['lokit] *n* Medaillon *neut*.

locomotive [ˌloukə'moutiv] *n* Lokomotive *f*.

locust ['loukəst] *n* Heuschrecke *f*.

lodge [lodʒ] *v* (*a person*) unterbringen; (*complaint*) einreichen. *n* (*hunting*) Jagdhütte *f*. **lodger** *n* Untermieter *m*.

lodgings *pl* Wohnung *f sing*, Zimmer *neut sing*.

loft [loft] *n* (Dach)Boden *m*. **lofty** *adj* hoch.

log [log] *n* Klotz *m*; (*naut*) Log *neut*. *v* (*naut*) loggen, ins Logbuch eintragen.

logarithm ['logəriðəm] *n* Logarithmus *m*.

loggerheads ['logəhedz] *pl n* **be at loggerheads with** in den Haaren liegen mit.

logic ['lodʒik] *n* Logik *f*. **logical** *adj* logisch.

loins [loinz] *pl n* Lenden *pl*. **loincloth** *n* Lendentuch *neut*.

loiter ['loitə] *v* schlendern. **loiterer** *n* Schlenderer *m*.

lollipop ['loli,pop] *n* Lutscher *m*.

London ['lʌndən] *n* London *neut*.

lonely ['lounli] *adj* einsam. **loneliness** *n* Einsamkeit *f*.

long¹ [loŋ] *adj* lang.

long² [loŋ] *v* sich sehnen (nach).

long-distance *adj* Fern-.

longevity [lon'dʒevəti] *n* Langlebigkeit *f*.

longing ['loŋiŋ] *n* Sehnsucht *f*.

longitude ['londʒitjuːd] *n* Länge *f*. **longitudinal** *adj* Längen-.

long-playing record *n* Langspielplatte *f*.

long-term *adj* langfristig.

long-winded *adj* langatmig.

loo [luː] (*coll*) Klo *neut*.

look [luk] *n* (*glance*) Blick *m*; (*appearance*) Aussehen *neut*; (*expression*) Miene *f*. *v* schauen, blicken, gucken (auf); (*appear*) aussehen. **look after** aufpassen auf; (*care for*) sorgen für. **look for** suchen. **look forward to** sich freuen auf. **look into** untersuchen. **look out!** paß auf! **loom¹** [luːm] *v* **loom up** aufragen.

loom² [luːm] *n* Webstuhl *m*, Webmaschine *f*.

loop [luːp] *n* Schleife *f*, Schlinge *f*. *v* eine Schleife machen.

loophole ['luːphoul] *n* Lücke *f*.

loose [luːs] *adj* schlaff, locker; (*free*) los.

loosen *v* lösen, lockern. **loose change** Kleingeld *neut*. **loose translation** freie Übersetzung *f*.

loot [luːt] *n* Beute *f*. *v* plündern. **looter** *n* Plünderer *m*. **looting** *n* Plünderung *f*.

lop [lop] *v* **lop off** abhacken.

lopsided [ˌlop'saidid] *adj* schief.

lord [loːd] *n* Herr *m*; (*noble*) Edelmann *m*. **House of Lords** Oberhaus *neut*.

lorry ['lori] *n* Lastkraftwagen (Lkw) *m*.

***lose** [luːz] *v* verlieren; (*clock*) nachgehen. **lose one's way** sich verlieren. **loser** *n* Verlierer(in). **loss** *n* Verlust *m*; (*decrease*) Abnahme *f*. **dead loss** (*coll*) Niete *f*, Versager *m*.

lost [lost] *V* **lose**.

lot [lot] *n* Los *neut*; (*fate*) Schicksal *neut*; (*land*) Bauplatz *m*. **draw lots** Lose ziehen. **a lot of** viel, eine Menge.

lotion ['louʃən] *n* Lotion *f*.

lottery ['lotəri] *n* Lotterie *f*.

lotus ['loutəs] *n* Lotos *m*.

loud [laud] *adj* laut; (*colour*) schreiend. **loudmouth** *n* Maulheld *m*. **loudness** *n* Lautstärke *f*. **loudspeaker** *n* Lautsprecher *m*.

lounge [laundʒ] *n* Wohnzimmer *neut*; (*hotel*) Foyer *neut*. *v* faulenzen.

louse [laus] *n* (*pl* **lice**) Laus *f*. **lousy** *adj* (*slang*) saumäßig.

love [lʌv] *n* Liebe *f*; (*person*) Liebling *m*; (*sport*) null. *v* lieben. **love doing something** etwas gern tun. **love affair** Liebesaffäre *f*. **loveless** *adj* lieblos. **love letter** Liebesbrief *m*. **loveliness** *n* Schönheit *f*. **lovely** *adj* lieblich, schön. **lover** *n* Liebhaber(in), Geliebte(r). **lovesick** *adj* liebeskrank. **loving** *adj* liebend.

low [lou] *adj* niedrig; (*deep*) tief; (*sad*) niedergeschlagen; (*base*) ordinär. **lowly** *adj* bescheiden. **low tide** Niedrigwasser *neut*.

lower ['louə] *v* senken, niederlassen; (*fig*) erniedrigen.

loyal ['loiəl] *adj* treu. **loyalty** *n* Treue *f*.

lozenge ['lozindʒ] *n* Pastille *f*.

lubricate ['luːbrikeit] *v* schmieren, ölen. **lubricant** *n* Schmiermittel *neut*. **lubrication** *n* Schmierung *f*.

lucid ['luːsid] *adj* deutlich, klar.

luck [lʌk] *n* (*happiness, fortune*) Glück *neut*; (*fate*) Schicksal *neut*; (*chance*) Zufall *m*. **luckily** *adv* glücklicherweise. **lucky** *adj* glücklich.

lucrative ['luːkrətiv] adj gewinnbringend.
ludicrous ['luːdikrəs] adj lächerlich.
lug [lʌg] v (carry, drag) schleppen.
luggage ['lʌgidʒ] n Gepäck neut. **luggage rack** Gepäcknetz neut.
lukewarm ['luːkwoːm] adj lauwarm.
lull [lʌl] n (pause) Pause f; (calm) Stille f.
lullaby ['lʌləbai] n Wiegenlied neut.
lumbago [lʌm'beigou] n Hexenschuß m, Lumbago f.
lumber¹ ['lʌmbə] n (timber) Bauholz neut; (junk) Plunder m. **lumber room** Rumpelkammer f.
lumber² ['lʌmbə] v schwerfällig gehen.
luminous ['luːminəs] adj leuchtend.
lump [lʌmp] n Klumpen m, Beule f. **lump sugar** Würfelzucker m. **lump sum** Pauschalsumme f. v **lump together** zusammenfassen. **lumpy** adj klumpig.
lunar ['luːnə] adj Mond-.
lunatic ['luːnətik] n Wahnsinnige(r). **lunacy** n Wahnsinn m.
lunch [lʌntʃ] n Mittagessen neut. v zu Mittag essen. **lunchtime** Mittagspause f.
lung [lʌŋ] n Lunge f. **lung cancer** Lungenkrebs m.
lunge [lʌndʒ] v losstürzen (auf).
lurch¹ [ləːtʃ] v taumeln.
lurch² [ləːtʃ] n **leave in the lurch** im Stich lassen.
lure [luə] v (an)locken. n Köder m.
lurid ['luərid] adj grell.
lurk [ləːk] v lauern.
luscious ['lʌʃəs] adj köstlich, lecker.
lush [lʌʃ] adj saftig.
lust [lʌst] n Wollust f, Begierde f. v **lust after** begehren. **lustful** adj lüstern.
lustre ['lʌstə] n Glanz m. **lustrous** adj strahlend.
lute [luːt] n Laute f.
Luxembourg ['lʌksəmbəɪg] n Luxemburg neut.
luxury ['lʌkʃəri] n Luxus m; (article) Luxusartikel m. **luxuriant** adj üppig. **luxurious** adj luxuriös.
lynch [lintʃ] v lynchen.
lynx [links] n Luchs m.
lyrical ['lirikəl] adj lyrisch.
lyrics ['liriks] pl n Lyrik f sing, Text m sing.

M

mac [mak] n Regenmantel m.
macabre [mə'kaːbr] adj grausig.
macaroni [makə'rouni] n Makkaroni pl.
mace¹ [meis] n Amtsstab m.
mace² [meis] n (cookery) Muskatblüte f.
machine [mə'ʃiːn] n Maschine f. v maschinell herstellen. **machine gun** Maschinengewehr neut. **machinery** n Maschinerie f. **machine tool** Werkzeugmaschine f. **machinist** n Maschinenarbeiter(in).
mackerel ['makrəl] n Makrele f.
mackintosh ['makinˌtoʃ] n Regenmantel m.
mad [mad] adj wahnsinnig, verrückt; (angry) wütend. **madhouse** n Irrenhaus neut. **madly** adv wie verrückt. **madman** n Verrückte(r) m. **madness** n Wahnsinn m.
madam ['madəm] n gnädige Frau f.
made [meid] V **make.**
magazine [ˌmagə'ziːn] n (publication) Zeitschrift f, Illustrierte f; (also warehouse, rifle) Magazin neut.
maggot ['magət] n Made f. **maggoty** adj madig.
magic ['madʒik] n Zauberei f. adj also **magical** Zauber-, zauberhaft. **magician** n Zauberer m; (entertainer) Zauberkünstler m.
magistrate ['madʒistreit] n Friedensrichter m.
magnanimous [mag'nanimǝs] adj großmütig. **magnanimity** n Großmut f.
magnate ['magneit] n Magnat m.
magnet ['magnǝt] n Magnet m. **magnetic** adj magnetisch. **magnetism** n Magnetismus m; (fig) Anziehungskraft f. **magnetize** v magnetisieren.
magnificent [mag'nifisnt] adj prächtig. **magnificence** n Pracht f.
magnify ['magnifai] v vergrößern. **magnifying glass** Lupe f. **magnification** n Vergrößerung f.
magnitude ['magnitjuːd] n Größe f, Ausmaß neut.
magnolia [mag'nouliǝ] n Magnolie f.
magpie ['magpai] n Elster f.
mahogany [mǝ'hogǝni] n (wood) Mahagoni neut. adj Mahagoni-.
maid [meid] n Mädchen neut; (servant)

Dienstmädchen *neut.* **old maid** alte Jungfer *f.*

maiden ['meidǝn] *n* Mädchen *neut.* **maiden name** Mädchenname *m.* **maiden speech** Jungfernrede *f.*

mail [meil] *n* Post *f. v* schicken, absenden. **mailbox** Briefkasten *m.* **mail-order company** Versandhaus *neut.* **mailboat** *n* Paketboot *neut.*

maim [meim] *v* lähmen.

main [mein] *adj* Haupt-, hauptsächlich. **mains** *pl n* (*gas, water*) Hauptleitung *f;* (*elec*) Netz *neut sing.* **mainstay** *n* (*fig*) Hauptstütze *f.* **main street** Hauptstraße *f.*

maintain [mein'tein] *v* erhalten; behaupten. **maintenance** *n* Erhaltung *f;* (*tech, mot*) Wartung *f.*

maisonette [meizǝ'net] *n* Wohnung *f.*

maize [meiz] *n* Mais *m.*

majesty ['madʒǝsti] *n* Majestät *f.* **His/Her/Your Majesty** Seine/Ihre/Eure Majestät. **majestic** *adj* majestätisch.

major ['meidʒǝ] *n* (*mil*) Major *m;* (*music*) Dur *neut. adj* (*significant*) bedeutend; (*greater*) größer. **majority** *n* Mehrheit *f;* (*law*) Mündigkeit *f.*

*make [meik] *v* machen; (*produce*) herstellen; (*force*) zwingen; (*build*) bauen; (*reach*) erreichen. *n* (*brand*) Marke *f;* (*type*) Art *f.* **make good** (*succeed*) Erfolg haben. **make out** vergeben. **makeshift** *adj* Behelfs-. **make-up** *n* Schminke *f.*

maladjusted [malǝ'dʒʌstid] *adj* verhaltensgestört.

malaria [mǝ'leǝriǝ] *n* Malaria *f.*

male [meil] *n* Mann *m;* (*animals*) Männchen *neut. adj* männlich. **male nurse** Krankenpfleger *m.*

malevolent [mǝ'levǝlǝnt] *adj* mißgünstig. **malevolence** *n* Mißgunst *f.*

malfunction [mal'fʌŋkʃǝn] *n* Funktionsstörung *f.*

malice ['malis] *n* Böswilligkeit. **malicious** *adj* böswillig.

malignant [mǝ'lignǝnt] *adj* böswillig; (*med*) bösartig.

malinger [mǝ'liŋgǝ] *v* sich krank stellen, simulieren.

mallet ['malit] *n* Schlegel *m.*

malnutrition [malnju'triʃǝn] *n* Unterernährung *f.*

malt [moɪlt] *n* Malz *neut.*

Malta ['moɪltǝ] *n* Malta *neut.* **Maltese** *n* Malteser(in) *adj* maltesisch.

maltreat [mal'triɪt] *v* mißhandeln, schlecht behandeln. **maltreatment** *n* schlechte Behandlung *f.*

mammal ['mamǝl] *n* Säugetier *neut.*

mammoth ['mamǝθ] *n* Mammut *neut. adj* riesig.

man [man] *n* (*pl* **men**) Mann *m;* (*human*) Mensch *m. v* bemannen. **manliness** *n* Mannhaftigkeit *f.* **manly** *adj* mannhaft.

manslaughter *n* Totschlag *m.*

manage ['manidʒ] *v* (*control*) leiten, führen; (*cope*) zurechtkommen, auskommen. **management** *n* Geschäftsleitung *f,* Direktion *f.* **manager** *n* Leiter *m,* Manager *m.*

mandarin ['mandǝrin] *n* Mandarin *m;* (*fruit*) Mandarine *f.*

mandate ['mandeit] *n* Mandat *neut.* **mandatory** *adj* verbindlich.

mandolin ['mandǝlin] *n* Mandoline *f.*

mane [mein] *n* Mähne *f.*

maneuver [mǝ'nuɪvǝ] *n* (*US*) Manöver *neut. v* manövrieren.

mange [meindʒ] *n* Räude *f.*

mangle[1] ['maŋgl] *n* (Wäsche)Mangel *f. v* mangeln.

mangle[2] ['maŋgl] *v* (*disfigure*) verstümmeln.

manhandle [man'handl] *v* grob behandeln, mißhandeln.

mania ['meiniǝ] *n* Manie *f.* **maniac** *n* Wahnsinnige(r). **manic** *adj* manisch.

manicure ['manikjuǝ] *n* Maniküre *f. v* maniküren. **manicurist** *n* Maniküre *f.*

manifest ['manifest] *adj* offenbar. *v* erscheinen. **manifestation** *n* Offenbarung *f;* (*symptom*) Anzeichen *neut.*

manifesto [mani'festou] *n* Manifest *neut.*

manifold ['manifould] *adj* mannigfaltig.

manipulate [mǝ'nipjuleit] *v* manipulieren. **manipulation** *n* Manipulation *f.*

mankind [,man'kaind] *n* Menschheit *f.*

man-made [,man'meid] *adj* künstlich.

manner ['manǝ] *n* (*way*) Art *f,* Weise *f;* (*behaviour*) Manier *f,* Benehmen *neut.* **mannered** *adj* manieriert. **mannerism** *n* Manierismus *m.*

manoeuvre [mǝ'nuɪvǝ] *n* Manöver *neut. v* manövrieren.

manor ['manǝ] *n* Herrensitz *m,* Herrenhaus *neut.*

manpower ['man,pauǝ] *n* Arbeitskräfte *pl.*

mansion ['manʃǝn] *n* (herrschaftliches) Wohnhaus *neut.*

mantelpiece ['mantlpiːs] *n* Kaminsims *m* or neut.

manual ['manjuəl] *adj* manuell, Hand-. *n* Handbuch *neut.*

manufacture [manjuˈfaktʃə] *v* herstellen, erzeugen. *n* Herstellung *f*, Erzeugung *f*. **manufacturer** *n* Hersteller *m*, Fabrikant *m.*

manure [məˈnjuə] *n* Dünger *m*, Mist *m*. *v* düngen.

manuscript ['manjuskript] *n* Manuskript *neut. adj* handschriftlich.

many ['meni] *adj* viele. **how many?** wieviele? **many times** oft. **a good many** ziemlich viele.

map [map] *n* (Land)Karte *f*; (*of town*) Stadtplan *m*. *v* eine karte machen von.

maple ['meipl] *n* Ahorn *m.*

mar [maɪ] *v* verderben, beeinträchtigen.

marathon ['marəθən] *n* Marathonlauf *m. adj* Marathon-.

marble ['maːbl] *n* Marmor *m*; (*toy*) Marmel *f.*

march [maːtʃ] *n* Marsch *m*. *v* marschieren. **march past** vorbeimarschieren an. **March** [maːtʃ] *n* März *m.*

marchioness [ˌmaːʃəˈnes] *n* Marquise *f.*

mare [meə] *n* Stute *f.*

margarine [ˌmaːdʒəˈriːn] *n* Margarine *f.*

margin ['maːdʒin] *n* Rand *m*; (*limit*) Grenze *f*; (*profit*) Gewinnspanne *f*. **marginal** *adj* Rand-; (*slight*) geringfügig.

marguerite [ˌmaːgəˈriːt] *n* Gänseblümchen *neut.*

marigold ['marigould] *n* Ringelblume *f.*

marijuana [mariˈwaːnə] *n* Marihuana *neut.*

marina [məˈriːnə] *n* Yachthafen *m.*

marinade [ˌmariˈneid] *v* marinieren. *n* Marinade *f.*

marine [məˈriːn] *adj* See-, Meeres-. *n* (*shipping*) Marine *f*; (*mil*) Marineinfanterist *m*. **mariner** *n* Matrose *m.*

marital ['maritl] *adj* ehelich.

maritime ['maritaim] *adj* See-, Schiffahrts-.

marjoram ['maːdʒərəm] *n* Majoran *m.*

mark[1] [maːk] *n* Marke *f*. Zeichen *neut*; (*school*) Note *f*; (*stain*) Fleck *m*; (*distinguishing feature*) Kennzeichen *neut*. *v* bezeichnen; (*note*) notieren, vermerken. **marked** *adj* markant, ausgeprägt. **markedly** *adv* ausgesprochen.

mark[2] [maːk] *n* (*currency*) Mark *f.*

market ['maːkit] *n* Markt *m*. *v* auf den Markt bringen. **marketing** *n* Marketing *neut*. **market place** Marktplatz *m*. **market research** Marktforschung *f.*

marmalade ['maːməleid] *n* Orangenmarmelade *f.*

maroon[1] [məˈruːn] *adj* (*colour*) rotbraun.

maroon[2] [məˈruːn] *v* (*naut*) aussetzen.

marquee [maːˈkiː] *n* großes Zelt *neut.*

marquess ['maːkwis] *n* Marquis *m.*

marriage ['maridʒ] *n* Heirat *f*, Ehe *f*; (*wedding*) Hochzeit *f*; (*ceremony*) Trauung *f*. **marriage certificate** Trauschein *m.*

marrow ['marou] *n* (*of bone*) Mark *neut*; (*vegetable*) Eierkürbis *m*. **marrowbone** *n* Markknochen *m.*

marry ['mari] *v* heiraten; (*get married*) sich verheiraten mit. **married couple** Ehepaar *neut.*

Mars [maːz] *n* Mars *m*. **Martian** *adj* Mars-; *n* Marsbewohner *m.*

marsh [maːʃ] *n* Sumpf *m*. **marshy** *adj* sumpfig.

marshal ['maːʃəl] *n* Marschall *m*. *v* einordnen; (*troops*) aufstellen.

martial ['maːʃəl] *adj* militärisch, Kriegs-.

martin ['maːtin] *n* Mauerschwalbe *f.*

martyr ['maːtə] *n* Märtyrer(in). **martyrdom** *n* Martyrium *neut.*

marvel ['maːvəl] *n* Wunder *neut*. *v* staunen (über). **marvellous** *adj* wunderbar.

marzipan [maːziˈpan] *n* Marzipan *neut.*

mascara [maˈskaːrə] *n* Wimperntusche *f.*

mascot ['maskət] *n* Maskottchen *neut.*

masculine ['maskjulin] *adj* männlich; (*manly*) mannhaft; (*of woman*) männisch. *n* (*gramm*) Maskulinum *m*. **masculinity** *n* Männlichkeit *f*, Mannhaftigkeit *f.*

mash [maʃ] *v* zerquetschen. **mashed potatoes** Kartoffelpüree *neut.*

mask [maːsk] *n* Maske *f*. *v* maskieren.

masochist ['masəkist] *n* Masochist *m*. **masochism** *n* Masochismus *m.*

mason ['meisn] *n* Maurer *m*. **masonic** *adj* Freimaurer-. **masonry** *n* Mauerwerk *neut.*

masquerade [maskəˈreid] *n* Maskerade *f*. *v* sich ausgeben (als).

mass[1] [mas] *n* Masse *f*. *v* sich ansammeln. *adj* Massen-. **the masses** die breite Masse. **mass meeting** Massenversammlung *f*. **mass-produce** *v* serienmäßig herstellen. **mass production** Massenherstellung *f.*

mass² [mas] *n* (*rel*) Messe *f.*
massacre ['masəkə] *n* Massaker *neut*, Blutbad *neut*. *v* massakrieren.
massage ['masaɪʒ] *n* Massage *f*. *v* massieren. **masseur** *n* Masseur *m*. **masseuse** *n* Masseuse *f.*
massive ['masiv] *adj* massiv.
mast [maɪst] *n* Mast *m.*
mastectomy [ma'stektəmi] *n* Brustamputation *f.*
master ['maɪstə] *n* Herr *m*; (*school*) Lehrer *m*; (*artist*) Meister m. *v* meistern. **masterful** *adj* meisterhaft. **masterpiece** *n* Meisterwerk *neut*. **mastery** *n* Beherrschung *f.*
masturbate ['mastəbeit] *v* onanieren. **masturbation** *n* Onanie *f.*
mat [mat] *n* Matte *f*; (*beer*) Untersetzer *m*. **matted** *adj* mattiert.
match¹ [matʃ] *n* Streichholz *neut.*
match² [matʃ] *n* (*equal*) Gleiche(r); (*sport*) Spiel *neut*. *v* anpassen. **meet one's match** seinen Meister finden. **matchless** *adj* unvergleichlich.
mate [meit] *n* (*friend*) Kamarad(in); (*chess*) (Schach)Matt *neut*; (*animal*) Männchen *neut*, Weibchen *neut*; (*naut*) Schiffsoffizier *m*. *v* sich paaren; (*chess*) matt setzen.
material [mə'tiəriəl] *n* Stoff *m*. *adj* materiell; (*important*) wesentlich. **materials** *pl* Werkstoffe *pl*. **materialist** *n* Materialist *m*. **materialistic** *adj* materialistisch.
maternal [mə'təɪnl] *adj* mütterlich; mütterlicherseits. **maternal grandfather** Großvater. **maternity** *n* Mutterschaft *f*. **maternity dress** Umstandskleid *neut*. **maternity home** Entbindungsheim *neut.*
mathematics [maθə'matiks] *n* Mathmatik *f*. **mathematical** *adj* mathematisch. **mathematician** *n* Mathematiker *m.*
matinee ['matinei] *n* Matinee *f.*
matins ['matinz] *n* Frühgottesdienst *m.*
matrimony ['matriməni] *n* Ehestand *m*, Ehe *f*. **matrimonial** *adj* ehelich, Ehe-.
matrix ['meitriks] *n* Matrix *f.*
matron ['meitrən] *n* (*school*) Hausmutter *f*; (*nurse*) Oberin *f.*
matter ['matə] *n* Stoff *m*, Materie *f*; (*affair*) Sache *f*; (*pus*) Eiter *m*. *v* von Bedeutung sein. *what's the matter?* was ist los? *it doesn't matter* es macht nichts. **matter-of-fact** *adj* sachlich.
mattress ['matris] *n* Matratze *f.*

mature [mə'tjuə] *adj* reif. *v* reifen. **maturity** *n* Reife *f.*
maudlin ['moɪdlin] *adj* weinerlich.
maul [moɪl] *v* zerreißen.
mausoleum [moɪsə'liəm] *n* Mausoleum *neut*, Grabmal *neut.*
mauve [mouv] *adj* malvenfarben.
maxim ['maksim] *n* Grundsatz *m.*
maximum ['maksiməm] *n* Maximum *neut*. *adj* Höchst-, Maximal-.
*may [mei] *v* mögen, können. *may I?* darf ich? **maybe** *adv* vielleicht.
May [mei] *n* Mai *m*. **mayday** (*SOS*) Maydaysignal *neut.*
mayonnaise [ˌmeiə'neiz] *n* Mayonnaise *f.*
mayor [meə] *n* Bürgermeister *m*. **mayoress** *n* Bürgermeisterin *f.*
maze [meiz] *v* Labyrinth *neut*, Irrgarten *m.*
me [miɪ] *pron* (*acc*) mich; (*dat*) mir.
meadow ['medou] *n* Wiese *f.*
meagre ['miɪgə] *adj* mager, dürr.
meal¹ [miɪl] *n* Mahlzeit *f*, Essen *neut.*
meal² [miɪl] *n* (*flour*) Mehl *neut.*
*mean¹ [miɪn] *v* (*word, etc.*) bedeuten; (*person*) meinen; (*intend*) vorhaben, beabsichtigen.
mean² [miɪn] *adj* (*slight*) gering; (*base*) gemein; (*tight-fisted*) geizig. **meanness** *n* Gemeinheit *f.*
mean³ [miɪn] *n* Durchschnitt *m*. *adj* mittler, Durschnitts-.
meander [mi'andə] *v* sich winden. *n* Windung *f.*
meaning ['miɪniŋ] *n* (*significance*) Bedeutung *f*; (*sense*) Sinn *m*. **meaningful** *adj* bedeutsam. **meaningless** *adj* sinnlos.
means [miɪnz] *n* Mittel *neut*. **by means of** durch, mittels. **by no means** auf keinen Fall. **by all means** selbstverständlich.
meant [ment] *V* **mean¹**.
meanwhile ['miɪnwail] *adv* mittlerweile.
measles ['miɪzlz] *n* Masern *pl*. **German measles** Röteln *pl.*
measure ['meʒə] *v* messen. *n* Maß *neut*. **measurement** *n* Messung *f*, Maß *neut.*
meat [miɪt] *n* Fleisch *neut*. **meatball** *n* Fleischklößchen *neut*. **meaty** *adj* fleischig.
mechanic [mi'kanik] *n* Mechaniker *m*. **mechanical** *adj* mechanisch. **mechanics** *n* Mechanik *f*. **mechanism** *n* Mechanismus *m*. **mechanize** *v* mechanisieren.
medal ['medl] *n* Medaille *f*, Orden *m*. **medallion** *n* Schaumünze *f.*

meridian

meddle ['medl] v sich (ein)mischen (in).
meddlesome adj zudringlich.
media ['miːdiə] pl n Medien pl. **mass
media** Massenmedien pl.
mediate ['miːdieit] v vermitteln. **mediation**
n Vermittlung f. **mediator** n Vermittler
m.
medical ['medikəl] adj medizinisch, ärztlich. **medical certificate** Krankenschein
m. **medical student** Medizinstudent m.
medicament n Arzneimittel neut. **medicinal** adj heilkräftig. **medicine** n Arznei f,
Arzneimittel neut; (science) Medizin f.
medieval [medi'iːvəl] adj mittelalterlich.
mediocre [miːdi'oukə] adj mittelmäßig.
mediocrity n Mittelmäßigkeit f.
meditate ['mediteit] v meditieren; (reflect)
nachdenken (über). **meditation** n (rel)
Meditation f; Nachdenken neut.
Mediterranean [meditə'reiniən] n Mit-
telmeer neut. adj Mittelmeer-.
medium ['miːdiəm] adj mittler, Mittel-. n
Mitte f; (spiritualist) Medium neut. **medi-
um-sized** adj mittelgroß.
medley ['medli] n Gemisch neut; (music)
Potpourri neut.
meek [miːk] adj mild, sanft. **meekness** n
Milde f, Sanftmut f.
***meet** [miːt] v treffen, begegnen (+dat);
(by appointment) sich treffen (mit);
(requirements) erfüllen; (call for)
abholen. **meeting** n Treffen neut; (session) Versammlung f, Sitzung f.
megaphone ['megəfoun] n Megaphon
neut.
melancholy ['melənkəli] n Melancholie f,
Trübsinn m. **melancholic** adj
melancholisch.
mellow ['melou] adj reif; (person) freundlich, heiter.
melodrama ['melədraːmə] n Melodrama
neut. **melodramatic** adj melodramatisch.
melody ['melədi] n Melodie f. **melodious**
adj wohlklingend.
melon ['melən] n Melone f.
melt [melt] v schmelzen. **melt away**
zergehen. **melting point** Schmelzpunkt m.
member ['membə] n Mitglied m. **membership** n Mitgliedschaft f.
membrane ['membrein] n Membrane f.
memento [mə'mentou] n Andenken neut.
memo ['memou] n (note) Notiz f;
(message) Mitteilung f.
memoirs ['memwaːz] pl n Memoiren pl.

memorable ['memərəbl] adj denkwürdig.
memorandum [memə'randəm] n (note)
Notiz f; (message) Mitteilung f.
memorial [mi'moːriəl] n Denkmal neut.
adj **memorial service** Gedenkgottesdienst
m.
memory ['meməri] n (power of)
Gedächtnis neut; (of something) Erinnerung f. **memorize** v auswendig lernen.
men [men] V **man**.
menace ['menis] n Drohung f. v
bedrohen. **menacing** adj drohend.
menagerie [mi'nadʒəri] n Menagerie f.
mend [mend] v reparieren; (clothes)
flicken; (socks, etc.) stopfen. n ausgebes-
serte Stelle f. **on the mend** (coll) auf dem
Wege der Besserung.
menial ['miːniəl] adj niedrig.
menopause ['menəpoːz] n Wechseljahre
pl, Menopause f.
menstrual ['menstruəl] adj Menstrua-
tions-. **menstruate** v die Regel haben,
menstruieren. **menstruation** n Menstruation f, Monatsblutung f.
mental ['mentl] adj geistig, Geistes-;
(slang) verrückt. **mental deficiency**
Schwachsinn m. **mental hospital**
Nervenheilanstalt f. **mental illness** Geisteskrankheit f. **mentality** n Mentalität f,
Gesinnung f. **mentally ill** geisteskrank.
menthol ['menθəl] n Menthol neut.
mention ['menʃən] v erwähnen. n
Erwähnung f. **don't mention it!** bitte
sehr!
menu ['menjuː] n Speisekarte f, Menü
neut.
mercantile ['məːkəntail] adj kaufmännisch, Handels-.
mercenary ['məːsinəri] adj gewinnsüchtig,
geldgierig. n Söldner m.
merchandise ['məːtʃəndaiz] n Waren pl,
Handelsgüter pl. v verkaufen.
merchant ['məːtʃənt] n Kaufmann m;
(wholesaler) Großhändler m. **merchant
navy** Handelsflotte f.
mercury ['məːkjuri] n Quecksilber neut.
Mercury n Merkur m.
mercy ['məːsi] n Erbarmen neut, Gnade f.
merciful adj barmherzig. **merciless** adj
erbarmungslos.
mere [miə] adj bloß, rein.
merge [məːdʒ] v verschmelzen; (comm)
fusionieren. **merger** n Fusion f.
meridian [mə'ridiən] n Meridian m.

meringue [məˈraŋ] n Meringe f, Baiser neut.

merit [ˈmerit] n Verdienst neut; (value) Wert m. v verdienen.

mermaid [ˈmɔːmeid] n Seejungfrau f.

merry [ˈmeri] adj lustig, fröhlich. make merry feiern. merry-go-round n Karussell neut. merriment n Lustigkeit f.

mesh [meʃ] n Masche f. v ineinandergreifen. meshed adj maschig.

mesmerize [ˈmezməraiz] n hypnotisieren; (fig) faszinieren.

mess [mes] n Durcheinander neut, Unordnung f; (mil) Messe f. v beschmutzen. mess about herumpfuschen. mess up verderben, verpfuschen. messy adj unordentlich.

message [ˈmesidʒ] n Mitteilung f; (news) Nachricht f. messenger n Bote m.

met [met] V meet.

metabolism [miˈtabəlizm] n Stoffwechsel m. metabolic adj metabolisch.

metal [ˈmetl] n Metall neut. metallic adj metallisch. metallurgy n Metallurgie f.

metamorphosis [metəˈmɔːfəsis] n Metamorphose f, Verwandlung f. metamorphose v verwandeln.

metaphor [ˈmetəfə] n Metapher f. metaphorical adj metaphorisch.

metaphysics [ˌmetəˈfiziks] n Metaphysik f. metaphysical adj metaphysisch.

meteor [ˈmiːtiə] n Meteor m. meteoric adj meteorartig, plötzlich.

meteorology [ˌmiːtiəˈrolədʒi] n Meteorologie f, Wetterkunde f. meteorological adj meteorologisch, Wetter-.

meter [ˈmiːtə] n Messer m. gas meter Gasuhr f. parking meter Parkuhr f.

methane [ˈmiːθein] n Methan neut.

method [ˈmeθəd] n Methode f; (procedure) Verfahren neut. methodical adj methodisch.

methylated spirits [ˈmeθileitid] n Brennspiritus m.

meticulous [miˈtikjuləs] adj übergenau, peinlich genau.

metre [ˈmiːtə] n Meter m or neut. metric adj metrisch.

metronome [ˈmetrənoum] n Metronom neut, Taktmesser m.

metropolis [məˈtropəlis] n Metropole f, Hauptstadt f.

mice [mais] V mouse.

microbe [ˈmaikroub] n Mikrobe f.

microfilm [ˈmaikrəˌfilm] n Mikrofilm m.

microphone [ˈmaikrəfoun] n Mikrophon neut.

microscope [ˈmaikrəskoup] n Mikroscop neut. microscopic adj mikroskopisch; (tiny) verschwindend klein.

mid [mid] adj mittler, Mittel-. in mid air mitten in der Luft. midday n Mittag m.

middle [ˈmidl] n Mitte f. adj mittler, Mittel-. middle-aged adj im mittleren Alter. middle-class adj bürgerlich, bourgeois. middle classes Mittelstand m.

Middle Ages pl n Mittelalter neut.

Middle East n Naher Osten m.

midge [midʒ] n Mücke f.

midget [ˈmidʒit] n Zwerg m.

midnight [ˈmidnait] n Mitternacht f.

midsummer [ˈmidˌsʌmə] n Hochsommer m.

midst [midst] n Mitte f. in the midst of mitten unter (+ dat).

midwife [ˈmidwaif] n Hebamme f. midwifery n Geburtshilfe f.

might[1] [mait] V may.

might[2] [mait] n Macht f; (force) Gewalt f.

mighty [ˈmaiti] adj mächtig. adv sehr.

migraine [ˈmiːgrein] n Migräne f.

migrate [maiˈgreit] v abwandern. migrant adj Wander-; n Umsiedler m. migration n Wanderung f.

mike [maik] n (coll) Mikrophon neut.

mild [maild] adj mild, sanft. to put it mildly gelinde gesagt. mildness n Sanftheit f.

mildew [ˈmildjuː] n Mehltau m, Moder m.

mile [mail] n Meile f. mileage n Meilenzahl f. milestone n (fig) Markstein m.

militant [ˈmilitənt] adj militant, kämpferisch. n (pol) Radikale(r).

military [ˈmilitəri] adj militärisch, Militär-, Kriegs-.

milk [milk] n Milch f. v melken. milk tooth n Milchzahn m. milky adj milchig. Milky Way Milchstraße f.

mill [mil] n Mühle f; (works) Fabrik f. v mahlen. run-of-the-mill adj mittelmäßig. miller n Müller m.

millennium [miˈleniəm] n Jahrtausend neut.

milligram [ˈmiliˌgram] n Milligramm neut.

millilitre [ˈmiliˌliːtə] n Milliliter neut.

millimetre [ˈmiliˌmiːtə] n Millimeter neut.

millinery [ˈmilinəri] n Müte pl.

million ['miljən] *n* Million *f*. **millionaire** *n* Millionär *n*. **millionairess** *n* Millionärin *f*.

milometer [mai'lomitə] *n* Meilenzähler *m*, Kilometerzähler *m*.

mime [maim] *n* (*actor*) Mime *m*. *v* mimen.

mimic ['mimik] *v* nachäffen. **mimicry** *n* Nachäffung *f*.

mince [mins] *v* zerhacken. *n* (*mincemeat*) Hackfleisch *neut*. **mincer** *n* Fleischwolf *m*. **mince about** geziert gehen. **mincing** *adj* geziert, affektiert. **not mince one's words** kein Blatt vor den Mund nehmen.

mind [maind] *n* Geist *m*, Verstand *m*; (*opinion*) Meinung *f*. *v* etwas dagegen haben; (*look after*) aufpassen auf. **frame of mind** Gesinnung *f*, Stimmung *f*. **make up one's mind** sich entschließen. **mind out!** paß auf! Achtung! **Never mind!** macht nichts! *I don't mind* ist mir egal.

mine[1] [main] *poss pron* meiner *m*, meine *f*, meines *neut*; der, die, das meine *or* meinige. **a friend of mine** ein Freund von mir. **it's mine** es gehört mir.

mine[2] [main] *n* (*coal, etc.*) Bergwerk *neut*; (*mil*) Mine *f*. *v* minieren. **miner** *n* Bergarbeiter *m*. **minefield** *n* Minenfeld. **mining** *n* Bergbau *m*. **minesweeper** *n* Minensuchboot *neut*.

mineral ['minərəl] *n* Mineral *neut*. *adj* mineralisch. **mineral water** Mineralwasser *neut*.

mingle ['miŋgl] *v* (sich) vermischen.

miniature ['minitʃə] *n* Miniatur *f*. *adj* Klein-.

minimum ['miniməm] *n* Minimum *neut*. **minimal** *adj* Mindest-, Minimal-.

minister ['ministə] *n* (*pol*) Minister *m*; (*rel*) Pfarrer *m*. **ministry** *n* (*pol*) Ministerium *neut*.

mink [miŋk] *n* Nerz *m*.

minor ['mainə] *adj* kleiner, geringer; (*trivial*) geringfügig. *n* (*under age*) Minderjährige(r); (*music*) Moll *neut*. **minority** *n* Minderheit *f*; (*under age*) Minderjährigkeit *f*.

minstrel ['minstrəl] *n* Minnesänger *m*.

mint[1] [mint] *n* (*cookery*) Minze *f*.

mint[2] [mint] *n* (*money*) Münzanstalt *f*. *v* münzen.

minuet [minju'et] *n* Menuett *neut*.

minus ['mainəs] *prep* weniger, minus. *it's minus 20 degrees* wir haben 20 Grad Kälte.

minute[1] ['minit] *n* Minute *f*. **just a minute!** Moment mal!

minute[2] [mai'njuːt] *adj* winzig.

miracle ['mirəkl] *n* Wunder *neut*, Wundertat *f*. **miraculous** *adj* wunderbar. **miraculously** *adv* durch ein Wunder.

mirage ['miraːʒ] *n* Luftspiegelung *f*.

mirror ['mirə] *n* Spiegel *m*. *v* widerspiegeln.

mirth [məːθ] *n* Fröhlichkeit *f*, Lustigkeit *f*.

misadventure [misəd'ventʃə] *n* Unfall *m*, Unglück *neut*.

misanthropist [miz'anθrəpist] *n* Menschenfeind *m*. **misanthropic** *adj* menschenfeindlich.

misapprehension [misapri'henʃən] *n* Mißverständnis *neut*.

misbehave [misbi'heiv] *v* sich schlecht benehmen. **misbehaviour** *n* schlechtes Benehmen *neut*.

miscalculate [mis'kalkjuleit] *v* sich verrechnen.

miscarriage [mis'karidʒ] *n* Fehlgeburt *f*. **miscarriage of justice** Fehlspruch *m*, Rechtsbeugung *f*. **miscarry** *v* eine Fehlgeburt haben; (*go wrong*) mißlingen.

miscellaneous [misə'leiniəs] *adj* vermischt. *n* Verschiedenes *neut*. **miscellany** *n* Gemisch *neut*.

mischance [mis'tʃaɪns] *n* Unfall *m*.

mischief ['mistʃif] *n* Unfug *m*. **mischievous** *adj* schelmisch, durchtrieben. **mischief-maker** *n* Störenfried *m*.

misconception [miskən'sepʃən] *n* Mißverständnis *neut*.

misconduct [mis'kɔndʌkt] *n* schlechtes Benehmen *neut*.

misconstrue [miskən'struː] *v* mißdeuten.

misdeed [mis'diːd] *n* Untat *f*, Verbrechen *neut*.

misdemeanour [misdi'miːnə] *n* Vergehen *neut*.

miser ['maizə] *n* Geizhals *m*. **miserly** *adj* geizig. **miserliness** *n* Geiz *m*.

miserable ['mizərəbl] *adj* (*unhappy*) unglücklich; (*wretched*) elend.

misery ['mizəri] *n* Elend *neut*, Not *f*.

misfire [mis'faiə] *v* versagen; (*mot*) fehlzünden. *n* Versager *m*; Fehlzündung *f*.

misfit ['misfit] *n* Einzelgänger *m*.

misfortune [mis'fɔːtʃən] *n* Unglück *neut*.

misgiving [mis'giviŋ] *n* Zweifel *m*.

misguided [mis'gaidid] *adj* (*erroneous*) irrig.
mishap ['mishap] *n* Unglück *neut.*
***mishear** [mis'hiə] *v* sich verhören.
misinterpret [misin'tə:prit] *v* mißdeuten.
***mislay** [mis'lei] *v* verlegen.
***mislead** [mis'li:d] *v* irreführen. **misleading** *adj* irreführend.
misnomer [mis'noumə] *n* falsche. Bezeichnung *f.*
misplace [mis'pleis] *v* verlegen. **misplaced** *adj* (*inappropriate*) unangebracht.
misprint ['misprint] *n* Druckfehler *m.*
miss¹ [mis] *v* (*shot*) verfehlen; (*train, opportunity*) verpassen, versäumen; (*absent friend*) vermissen. *n* Fehlschuß *m.* **missing** *adj* fehlend; (*person*) vermißt.
miss² [mis] *n* (*title*) Fräulein *neut.*
missile ['misail] *n* Rakete *f,* Geschoß *neut.* **guided missile** Fernlenkrakete *f.*
mission ['miʃən] *n* Mission *f;* (*task*) Auftrag *m;* (*pol*) Gesandschaft *f.* **missionary** *n* Missionar(in).
mist [mist] *n* (feuchter) Dunst *m,* Nebel *m.*
***mistake** [mi'steik] *n* Fehler *m,* Irrtum *m.* *v* verwechseln. **be mistaken** im Irrtum sein.
mister ['mistə] *n* Herr *m.*
mistletoe ['misltou] *n* Mistel *f.*
mistress ['mistris] *n* (*lover*) Mätresse *f;* (*school*) Lehrerin *f;* (*of house or animal*) Herrin *f.*
mistrust [mis'trʌst] *v* mißtrauen. *n* Mißtrauen *neut,* Argwohn *m.* **mistrustful** *adj* mißtrauisch.
***misunderstand** [misʌndə'stand] *v* mißverstehen. **misunderstanding** *n* Mißverständnis *neut.*
misuse [mis'ju:s; *v* mis'ju:z] *v* mißbrauchen. *n* Mißbrauch *m.*
mitigate ['mitigeit] *v* mildern. **mitigating circumstances** strafmildernde Umstände *pl.*
mitre ['maitə] *n* Bischofsmütze *f.*
mitten ['mitn] *n* Fausthandschuh *m.*
mix [miks] *v* (ver)mischen. *n* Mischung *f.* **mix up** verwechseln. **mixer** *n* Mixer *m.* **mixture** *n* Mischung *f;* (*med*) Mixtur *f.*
moan [moun] *n* Stöhnen *neut. v* stöhnen.
mob [mob] *n* Pöbel *m,* Gesindel *neut.*
mobile ['moubail] *adj* beweglich; (*motorized*) motorisiert. *n* Mobile *neut.* **mobility** *n* Beweglichkeit *f.* **mobilization** *n* Mobilisierung *f.* **mobilize** *v* mobilisieren.

moccasin ['mokəsin] *n* Mokassin *m.*
mock [mok] *v* verhöhnen, verspotten. *adj* Schein-. **mock trial** Scheinprozeß *m.*
mockery *n* Verhöhnung *f.* (*travesty*) Zerrbild *neut.* **mocking** *adj* spöttisch.
mode [moud] *n* Weise *f.* Methode *f.*
model ['modl] *n* Modell *neut;* (*pattern*) Muster *neut,* Vorbild *neut;* (*fashion*) Mannequin *neut. adj* vorbildlich, musterhaft. *v* modellieren; (*clothes*) vorführen.
moderate ['modərət; *v* 'modəreit] *adj* gemäßigt, mäßig. *v* mäßigen. **moderation** *n* Mäßigung *f.* **in moderation** mit Maß.
modern ['modən] *adj* modern. **modernity** *n* Modernität *f.* **modernize** *v* modernisieren. **modernization** *n* Modernisierung *f.*
modest ['modist] *adj* bescheiden; (*reasonable*) vernünftig. **modesty** *n* Bescheidenheit *f.*
modify ['modifai] *v* abändern, modifizieren. **modification** *n* Abänderung *f,* Modifikation *f.*
modulate ['modjuleit] *v* modulieren.
mohair ['mouheə] *n* Mohair *m.*
moist [moist] *adj* feucht. **moisture** *n* Feuchtigkeit *f.*
molar ['moulə] *n* Backenzahn *m.*
molasses [mə'lasiz] *n* Melasse *f.*
mold (*US*) *V* **mould.**
mole¹ [moul] *n* (*birthmark*) Muttermal *neut,* Leberfleck *m.*
mole² [moul] *n* (*zool*) Maulwurf *m.*
molecule ['molikju:l] *n* Molekül *neut.* **molecular** *adj* molekular.
molest [mə'lest] *v* belästigen.
mollusc ['moləsk] *n* Weichtier *neut.*
molt (*US*) *V* **moult.**
molten ['moultən] *adj* geschmolzen, flüssig.
moment ['moumənt] *n* Moment *m,* Augenblick *m.* **momentary** *adj* momentan, augenblicklich.
monarch ['monək] *n* Monarch(in). **monarchy** *n* Monarchie *f.*
monastery ['monəstəri] *n* Kloster *neut.* **monastic** *adj* kloster-.
Monday ['mʌndi] *n* Montag *m.*
money ['mʌni] *n* Geld *neut.* **money box** Sparbüchse *f.* **money order** Zahlungsanweisung *f.* **monetary** *adj* Währungs-.
mongolism ['moŋgəlizm] *n* Mongolismus *m.*

mongrel ['mʌŋgrəl] *n* Mischling *m*, Kreuzung *f*.

monitor ['monitə] *n* (*TV*) Monitor *m*. *v* überwachen, kontrollieren.

monk [mʌŋk] *n* Mönch *m*. **monkish** *adj* mönchisch.

monkey ['mʌŋki] *n* Affe *m*. *v* **monkey around** herumalbern.

monogamy [mə'nogəmi] *n* Monogamie *f*. **monogamous** *adj* monogam.

monogram ['monəgram] *n* Monogramm *neut*.

monologue ['monəlog] *n* Monolog *m*.

monopolize [mə'nopəlaiz] *v* monopolisieren. **monopoly** *n* Monopol *neut*.

monosyllable ['monəsiləbl] *n* einsilbiges Wort *neut*.

monotonous [mə'notənəs] *adj* monoton. **monotony** *n* Monotonie *f*.

monsoon [mon'suːn] *n* Monsun *m*.

monster ['monstə] *n* Ungeheuer *neut*; (*malformation*) Mißbildung *f*. **monstrous** *adj* ungeheuer.

month [mʌnθ] *n* Monat *m*. **monthly** *adj* monatlich; *n* (*magazine*) Monatsschrift *f*.

monument ['monjument] *n* Denkmal *neut*. **monumental** *adj* kolossal.

mood [muːd] *n* Laune *f*, Stimmung *f*. **be in a good/bad mood** guter/schlechter Laune sein. **moody** *adj* launisch.

moon [muːn] *n* Mond *m*. **full moon** Vollmond *m*. **moonlight** *n* Mondschein *m*.

moor[1] [muə] *n* Heide *f*, Moor *neut*.

moor[2] [muə] *v* (*boat*) vertäuen. **mooring** *n* Liegeplatz *m*.

mop [mop] *n* Mop *m*. *v* aufwischen.

mope [moup] *v* traurig sein, (*coll*) Trübsal blasen.

moped ['mouped] *n* Moped *neut*.

moral ['morəl] *adj* moralisch. *n* (*of story*) Lehre *f*. **morals** *pl* Moral *f sing*, Sitten *pl*. **morale** *n* Morale *f*. **morality** *n* Sittlichkeit *f*. **mores** *pl n* Sitten *pl*.

morbid ['moːbid] *adj* (*fig*) schauerlich.

more [moː] *adj* mehr; (*in number*) weitere, mehr. *adv* mehr, weiter. *more rapid* schneller. **more and more** immer mehr. **more or less** mehr oder weniger. **once more** noch einmal. **moreover** *adv* überdies, fernerhin.

morgue [moːg] *n* Leichenhaus *neut*.

morning ['moːniŋ] *n* Morgen *m*, Vormittag *m*. **in the mornings** morgens. **this morning** heute früh.

moron ['moːron] *n* Schwachsinnige(r). **moronic** *adj* schwachsinnig.

morose [mə'rous] *adj* mürrisch.

morphine ['moːfiːn] *n* Morphium *neut*.

morse code [moːs] *n* Morsealphabet *neut*.

morsel ['moːsəl] *n* Bissen *m*, Stückchen *neut*.

mortal ['moːtl] *adj* sterblich; (*wound*) tödlich. **mortality** *n* Sterblichkeit *f*.

mortar ['moːtə] *n* (*for bricks*) Mörtel *m*; (*mil*) Granatwerfer *m*.

mortgage ['moːgidʒ] *n* Hypothek *f*.

mortify ['moːtifai] *v* demütigen. **mortification** *n* Demütigung *f*.

mortuary ['moːtʃuəri] *n* Leichenhaus *neut*.

mosaic [mə'zeiik] *n* Mosaik *neut*.

mosque [mosk] *n* Moschee *f*.

mosquito [mə'skiːtou] *n* Moskito *m*.

moss [mos] *n* Moos *neut*. **mossy** *adj* bemoost.

most [moust] *adj* die meisten. *adv* äußerst, höchst; am meisten. *n* das Meiste. *most people* die meisten Leute. **at most** höchstens. **mostly** *adv* meistens, größtenteils.

motel [mou'tel] *n* Motel *neut*.

moth [moθ] *n* Motte *f*. **mothball** *n* Mottenkugel *f*.

mother ['mʌθə] *n* Mutter *f*. *v* bemuttern. **on one's mother's side** mütterlicherseits. **mother country** Mutterland *neut*. **motherhood** *n* Mutterschaft *f*. **mother-in-law** Schwiegermutter *f*. **motherless** *adj* mutterlos. **motherly** *adj* mütterlich. **mother-of-pearl** *n* Perlmutt *neut*.

motion ['mouʃən] *n* Bewegung *f*; (*pol*) Antrag *m*. *v* zuwinken. **set in motion** in Gang setzen.

motivate ['moutiveit] *v* motivieren. **motivation** *n* Motivierung *f*.

motif [mou'tiːf] *n* Motiv *m*.

motive ['moutiv] *n* Beweggrund *m*.

motor ['moutə] *n* Motor *m*. **motor accident** Autounfall *m*. **motorcar** *n* Wagen *m*, Auto *neut*. **motor cycle** *n* Mottorrad *neut*. **motorist** *n* Autofahrer *m*.

mottled ['motld] *adj* gefleckt.

motto ['motou] *n* Motto *neut*.

mould[1] [mould] *or US* **mold** *n* (*tech*) Form *f*; (*type*) Art *f*. *v* bilden, formen; (*tech*) gießen.

mould[2] [mould] *or US* **mold** *n* (*mildew*) Schimmel *m*. **mouldy** *adj* schimmelig.

moult [moult] *or US* **molt** *v* sich mausern.
mound [maund] *n* (Erd)Hügel *m*.
mount[1] [maunt] *v* (*horse*) besteigen. *n* (*frame*) Gestell *neut*; (*horse*) Reittier *neut*.
mount[2] [maunt] *n* Berg *m*, Hügel *m*.
mountain ['mauntən] *n* Berg *m*. **mountaineer** *n* Bergsteiger *m*.
mourn [moɪn] *v* trauern (um). **mourning** *n* Trauer *f*. **go into mourning** Trauer anlegen.
mouse [maus] *n* (*pl* **mice**) Maus *f*. **mousetrap** *n* Mausefalle *f*.
mousse [muɪs] *n* Kremeis *neut*.
moustache [mə'staɪʃ] *or US* **mustache** *n* Schnurrbart *m*.
mouth [mauθ] *n* Mund *m*; (*opening*) Öffnung *f*; (*river*) Mündung *f*; (*animal*) Maul *neut*. **mouthful** *n* Mundvoll *m*. **mouthpiece** *n* Mundstück *neut*. **mouthwash** *n* Mundwasser *neut*.
move [muɪv] *v* (sich) bewegen; (*emotionally*) rühren; (*house*) umziehen. **movable** *adj* beweglich. **movement** *n* Bewegung *f*. **moving** *adj* rührend. **moving staircase** Rolltreppe *f*.
movie ['muɪvi] *n* Film *m*. **go to the movies** ins Kino gehen.
***mow** [mou] *v* mähen. **mower** *n* (Rasen)Mäher *m*.
mown [moun] *V* **mow**.
Mr ['mistə] *n* Herr *m*.
Mrs ['misiz] *n* Frau *f*.
much [mʌtʃ] *adj, adv* viel. **how much?** wieviel?
muck [mʌk] *n* (*dung*) Mist *m*; (*dirt*) Dreck *m*. **mucky** *adj* schmutzig, dreckig.
mucus ['mjuːkəs] *n* Schleim *m*.
mud [mʌd] *n* Schlamm *m*. **muddy** *adj* schlammig. **mudguard** *n* Kotflügel *m*. **mudslinger** *n* Verleumder(in).
muddle ['mʌdl] *n* Durcheinander *neut*, Wirrwarr *m*. *v* **muddle through** sich durchwursteln. **muddled** *adj* konfus.
muff [mʌf] *n* Muff *m*.
muffle ['mʌfl] *v* (*noise*) dämpfen. **muffler** *n* Schal *m*; (*mot*) Schalldämpfer *m*.
mug [mʌg] *n* Krug *m*, Becher *m*. *v* (*rob*) überfallen. **muggy** *adj* (*weather*) schwül.
mulberry ['mʌlbəri] *n* Maulbeere *f*.
mule [mjuːl] *n* Maulesel *m*. **mulish** *adj* störrisch.
multicoloured [,mʌlti'kʌləd] *adj* bunt, vielfarbig.

multiple ['mʌltipl] *adj* mehrfach, vielfach.
multiply ['mʌltiplai] *v* (sich) vermehren; (*math*) multiplizieren. **multiplication** *v* Vermehrung; (*math*) Multiplikation *f*. **multiplicity** *n* Vielfalt *f*.
multiracial [,mʌlti'reiʃəl] *adj* gemischtrassig.
multitude ['mʌltitjuːd] *n* Menge *f*. **multitudinous** *adj* zahlreich.
mumble ['mʌmbl] *v* murmeln. *n* Gemurmel *neut*.
mummy[1] ['mʌmi] *n* (*embalmed*) Mumie *f*.
mummy[2] ['mʌmi] *n* (*coll*) Mutti *f*.
mumps [mʌmps] *n* Ziegenpeter *m*.
munch [mʌntʃ] *v* schmetzend kauen.
mundane [mʌn'dein] *adj* alltäglich, banal.
municipal [mju'nisipəl] *adj* städtisch, Stadt-. **municipality** *n* Stadt *f*, Stadtbezirk *m*.
mural ['mjuərəl] *n* Wandgemälde *neut*.
murder ['məɪdə] *n* Mord *m*, Ermordung *f*. *v* (er)morden. **murderer** *n* Mörder *m*. **murderous** *adj* mörderisch, tödlich.
murmur ['məɪmə] *v* murmeln. *n* Murmeln *neut*.
muscle ['mʌsl] *n* Muskel *m*. **muscular** *adj* (*person*) muskulös.
muse [mjuːz] *n* Muse *f*. *v* (nach)denken.
museum [mju'ziəm] *n* Museum *neut*.
mushroom ['mʌʃrum] *n* Pilz *m*, Champignon *m*. *v* (*coll*) sich ausbreiten.
music ['mjuːzik] *n* Musik *f*. **musical** *adj* musikalisch. **musician** *n* Musiker *m*. **music stand** Notenständer *m*.
musk [mʌsk] *n* Moschus *m*.
musket ['mʌskit] *n* Flinte *f*, Muskete *f*. **musketeer** *n* Musketier *m*.
Muslim ['mʌzlim] *n* Mohammedaner(in). *adj* mohammedanisch.
muslin ['mʌzlin] *n* Musselin *m*.
mussel ['mʌsl] *n* Muschel *f*.
***must**[1] [mʌst] *v* müssen.
must[2] [mʌst] *n* Most *m*. **musty** *adj* muffig, schimmelig.
mustard ['mʌstəd] *n* Senf *m*.
muster ['mʌstə] *v* antreten lassen. **muster one's courage** sich zusammennehmen. *n* **pass muster** Zustimmung finden.
mutation [mju'teiʃən] *n* Veränderung *f*; (*biol*) Mutation *f*.
mute [mjuːt] *adj* stumm. *n* Stumme(r); (*music*) Sordine *f*.
mutilate ['mjuːtileit] *v* verstümmeln. **mutilation** *n* Verstümmelung *f*.

mutiny ['mjuːtini] *n* Meuterei *f.* *v* meutern. **mutineer** *n* Meuterer *m.* **mutinous** *adj* meuterisch.
mutter ['mʌtə] *v* murmeln.
mutton ['mʌtn] *n* Hammelfleisch *neut.*
mutual ['mjuːtʃuəl] *adj* gegenseitig.
muzzle ['mʌzl] *n* Maul *neut;* (*protection*) Maulkorb *m.*
my [mai] *poss adj* mein, meine, mein. **myself** *pron* mich (selbst). **by myself** allein.
mystery ['mistəri] *n* Rätsel *neut,* Geheimnis *neut.* **mysterious** *adj* geheimnisvoll, mysteriös. **mystic** *n* Mystiker(in). *adj* mystisch. **mysticism** *n* Mystizismus *m.* **mystify** *v* täuschen, verblüffen.
myth [miθ] *n* Mythos *m.* **mythical** *adj* mythisch. **mythological** *adj* mythologisch. **mythology** *n* Mythologie *f.*

N

nag [nag] *v* herumnörgeln an. *n* Gaul *m.*
nail [neil] *n* Nagel *m.* *v* (an)nageln. **nail down** zunageln. **nailbrush** *n* Nagelbürste *f.* **nail-file** *n* Nagelfeile *f.* **nail polish** Nagellack *m.* **nail scissors** Nagelschere *f sing.*
naive [nai'iːv] *adj* naiv. **naïveté** *n* Naivität *f.*
naked ['neikid] *adj* nackt. **nakedness** *n* Nacktheit *f.*
name [neim] *n* Name *m;* (*reputation*) Ruf *m.* **by name** namentlich. **by the name of** namens. **what's your name?** wie heißen Sie? *v* nennen; (*mention*) erwähnen. **namely** *adv* nämlich.
nanny ['nani] *n* Kindermädchen *neut.*
nap [nap] *n* Nickerchen *neut.*
napkin ['napkin] *n* (*table*) Serviette *f.*
nappy ['napi] *n* Windel *f.*
narcotic [naɪ'kotik] *n* Narkotikum *neut.* *adj* narkotisch.
narrate [nə'reit] *v* erzählen. **narration** *also* **narrative** Erzählung *f.* **narrative** *adj* Erzählungs-. **narrator** *n* Erzähler(in).
narrow ['narou] *adj* eng, schmal; (*fig*) beschränkt. *v* sich verengen. **narrowly** *adv* (*just*) mit Mühe. **narrow-minded** *adj* engstirnig.

nasal ['neizəl] *adj* Nasen-; (*voice*) nasal.
nasturtium [nə'stəɪʃəm] *n* Kapuzinerkresse *f.*
nasty ['naɪsti] *adj* ekelhaft, widerlich; (*serious*) ernst, schlimm; (*person*) gemein, böse.
nation ['neiʃən] *n* Nation *f,* Volk *neut.* **national** *adj* national, Volks-. **nationalism** *n* Nationalismus *m.* **nationality** *n* Staatsangehörigkeit *f.* **nationalization** *n* Verstaatlichung *f.* **nationalize** *v* verstaatlichen. **national anthem** Nationalhymne *f.* **National Insurance** Sozialversicherung *f.*
native ['neitiv] *adj* eingeboren. *n* Eingeborene(r).
nativity [nə'tivəti] *n* Geburt *f.* **nativity play** Krippenspiel *neut.*
natural ['natʃərəl] *adj* natürlich, Natur-. **natural resources** Naturschätze *pl.* **naturalist** *n* Naturforscher *m.* **naturalize** *v* einbürgern.
nature ['neitʃə] *n* Natur *f.*
naughty ['noːti] *adj* unartig, ungezogen. **naughtiness** *n* Ungezogenheit *f.*
nausea ['noːziə] *n* Übelkeit *f,* Brechreiz *m;* (*seasickness*) Seekrankheit *f.* **nauseating** *adj* widerlich.
nautical ['noːtikəl] *adj* nautisch, Schiffs-. **nautical mile** Seemeile *f.*
naval ['neivəl] *adj* Flotten-, See-. **naval battle** Seeschlacht *f.*
navel ['neivəl] *n* Nabel *m.*
navigate ['navigeit] *v* navigieren. **navigable** *adj* schiffbar. **navigation** *n* Navigation *f.* **navigator** *n* Navigator *m.*
navy ['neivi] *n* Flotte *f,* Kriegsmarine *f.* **navy-blue** *adj* marineblau.
near [niə] *adj* nahe. *adv* nahe, in der Nähe. *prep* in der Nähe (von *or* + *gen*), nahe an. **nearby** *adv* in der Nähe; *adj* nahe gelegen. **nearly** *adv* fast, beinahe.
neat [niːt] *adj* ordentlich; (*alcohol*) rein, unverdünnt. **neatness** *n* Ordentlichkeit *f.*
necessary ['nesisəri] *adj* nötig, erforderlich. **necessarily** *adv* notwendigerweise. **necessitate** *v* erfordern. **necessity** *n* Notwendigkeit *f.* **necessities** *pl* Bedarfsartikel *pl.*
neck [nek] *n* Hals *m.* **neckerchief** *n* Halstuch *neut.* **necklace** *n* Halskette *f.* **necktie** *n* Krawatte *f.*
nectar ['nektə] *n* Nektar *m.*

née [nei] *adj* geborene.
need [niːd] *v* Bedürfnis *neut*, Bedarf *m*; (*necessity*) Notwendigkeit *f*. **if need arise** im Notfall. **needful** *adj* nötig. **neediness** Armut *f*. **needless** *adj* unnötig. **needy** *adj* arm.
needle ['niːdl] *n* Nadel *f*; (*indicator*) Zeiger *m*. *v* (*coll*) reizen. **needlework** *n* Handarbeit *f*.
negate [ni'geit] *v* annullieren, verneinen. **negation** *n* Annullierung *f*, Verneinung *f*. **negative** *adj* negativ; (*answer*) ablehnend. *n* (*phot*) Negativ *neut*.
neglect [ni'glekt] *v* vernachlässigen. *n* Vernachlässigung *f*.
negligée ['negliʒei] *n* Negligé *neut*.
negligence ['neglidʒəns] *n* Nachlässigkeit *f*. **negligent** *adj* nachlässig. **negligible** *adj* geringfügig.
negotiate [ni'gouʃieit] *v* verhandeln. **negotiation** *n* Verhandlung *f*. **negotiator** Vermittler *m*.
Negro ['niːgrou] *n* Neger *m*. *adj* Neger-. **Negress** *n* Negerin *f*.
neigh [nei] *v* wiehern. *n* Wiehern *neut*.
neighbour ['neibə] *n* Nachbar(in). **neighbourhood** *n* Nachbarschaft *f*. **neighbourly** *adj* freundlich.
neither ['naiðə] *adj*, *pron* kein (von beiden). **neither ... nor ...** weder ... noch ... .
neon ['niːon] *n* Neon *neut*.
nephew ['nefjuː] *n* Neffe *m*.
nepotism ['nepətizəm] *n* Vetternwirtschaft *f*.
nerve [nəːv] *n* Nerv *m*; (*cheek*) Frechheit *f*. **nerves** *pl* Nervosität *f sing*. **nervous** *adj* Nerven-; (*on edge*) nervös. **nervousness** *n* Nervosität *f*. **nervy** *adj* nervös. **nerve-racking** nervenaufreibend.
nest [nest] *n* Nest *neut*. *v* nisten.
nestle ['nesl] *v* sich anschmiegen.
net[1] [net] *n* Netz *neut*; (*fabric*) Tüll *m*. *v* fangen.
net[2] [net] *adj* (*comm*) netto, Netto-. **net amount** Nettobetrag *m*. **net price** Nettopreis *m*. **net profit** Reingewinn *m*.
Netherlands ['neðələndz] *pl n* Niederlände *pl*.
nettle ['netl] *n* Nessel *f*. *v* ärgern. **nettle rash** Nesselausschlag *m*. **grasp the nettle** die Schwierigkeit anpacken.
neurosis [nju'rousis] *n* Neurose *f*. **neurotic** *adj* neurotisch; *n* Neurotiker(in).

neuter ['njuːtə] *adj* (*gramm*) sächlich. *n* Neutrum *neut*. *v* (*male*) kastrieren; (*female*) sterilisieren.
neutral ['njuːtrəl] *adj* neutral. *n* (*mot*) Leerlauf *m*. **neutrality** *n* Neutralität *f*. **neutralize** *v* neutralisieren.
never ['nevə] *adv* nie, niemals. **never-ending** *adj* endlos. **never-failing** *adj* unfehlbar. **nevermore** *adv* nimmermehr. **nevertheless** *adv* nichtsdestoweniger.
new [njuː] *adj* neu; (*strange*) unbekannt. **newborn** *adj* neugeboren. **newcomer** *n* Neuankömmling *m*. **new-fangled** *adj* neumodisch. **newish** *adj* ziemlich neu. **newly** *adv* neulich. **newly-wed** *adj* jungvermählt. **newness** *n* Neuheit *f*. **news** *pl n* Nachrichten *pl*. **newspaper** *n* Zeitung *f*. **newsagent** Zeitungshändler *m*. **news flash** Kurznachricht *f*. **newsstand** *n* Zeitungskiosk *m* **newsworthy** *adj* aktuell.
newt [njuːt] *n* Wassermolch *m*.
New Testament *n* Neujahr *neut*. **New Year's Day** Neujahr *neut*. **New Year's Eve** Sylvester *neut*.
next [nekst] *adj* nächst, nächstfolgend; *adv* gleich daran, nächstens. *prep* neben, bei. **next door** nebenan.
nib [nib] *n* (Füllfeder)Spitze *f*.
nibble ['nibl] *v* nagen, knabbern (an). *n* Nagen *neut*, Knabbern *neut*; (*morsel*) Happen *m*.
nice [nais] *adj* nett; (*kind*) freundlich. **nicely** *adv* nett. **nicety** *n* Feinheit *f*.
niche [nitʃ] *n* Nische *f*.
nick [nik] *v* einkerben; (*coll*: *catch*) erwischen. *n* Kerbe *f*; (*coll*) Gefängnis *neut*; Polizeiwache *f*.
nickel ['nikl] *n* Nickel *neut*; (*US*) Fünfcentstück *neut*. *adj* Nickel-. **nickel-plated** *adj* vernickelt.
nickname ['nikneim] *n* Spitzname *m*.
nicotine ['nikətiːn] *n* Nikotin *neut*.
niece [niːs] *n* Nichte *f*.
niggle ['nigl] *v* trödeln.
night [nait] *n* Nacht *f*; (*evening*) Abend *m*. **all night** die ganze Nacht. **goodnight** gute Nacht. **nightclub** *n* Nachtlokal *neut*. **nightdress** *n* Nachthemd *neut*. **nightly** *adj* nächtlich. **nightmare** *n* Alptraum *m*. **nighttime** *n* Nacht *f*.
nightingale ['naitiŋˌgeil] *n* Nachtigall *f*.
nil [nil] *n* Null *f*.
nimble ['nimbl] *adj* flink. **nimbleness** *n* Gewandtheit *f*.

nine [nain] adj neun. n Neun f. **ninth** adj neunt; n Neuntel neut.

nineteen [nain'tiːn] adj neunzehn. n Neunzehn f. **nineteenth** adj neunzehnt.

ninety ['nainti] adj neunzig. n Neunzig f. **ninetieth** adj neunzigst.

nip [nip] v kneifen, zwicken. **nip in the bud** im Keim ersticken.

nipple ['nipl] n Brustwarze f; (baby's bottle) Lutscher m; (tech) Nippel m.

nit [nit] n Niß f, Nisse f.

nitrogen ['naitrədʒən] n Stickstoff m.

no [nou] adv nein. adj kein. **on no account** auf keinen Fall. **in no way** keineswegs. **no more** nicht mehr. **no smoking** Rauchen verboten. **no-smoking compartment** Nichtraucher m.

noble ['noubl] adj edel, adlig. **nobility** n Adel m, Adelsstand m. **nobleman** n Edelmann m.

nobody ['noubodi] pron niemand, keiner.

nocturnal [nok'təːnəl] adj nächtlich, Nacht-.

nod [nod] v nicken. n Nicken neut. **nod off** einschlafen.

noise [noiz] n Lärm m, Geräusch neut. **noiseless** adj geräuschlos. **noisy** adj laut.

nomad ['noumad] n Nomade m, Nomadin f. **nomadic** adj nomadisch.

nominal ['nominl] adj nominell, Nenn-.

nominate ['nomineit] v ernennen. **nomination** n Ernennung f.

nominative ['nominətiv] n (gramm) Nominativ m.

nonchalant ['nonʃələnt] adj unbekümmert. **nonchalance** n Gleichgültigkeit f.

nondescript ['nondiskript] adj nichtssagend.

none [nʌn] pron kein; (person) niemand. adv keineswegs.

nonentity [non'entəti] n Unding neut; (coll: person) Null f.

nonetheless [ˌnʌnðəˈles] adv nichtsdestoweniger.

nonsense ['nonsəns] n Unsinn m. interj Unsinn! Quatsch! **nonsensical** adj sinnlos. **stand no nonsense** sich nichts gefallen lassen.

non-smoker [non'smoukə] n Nichtraucher(in). **non-smoking compartment** Nichtraucher(abteil) m.

non-stop [non'stop] adj pausenlos; (train) durchgehend.

noodles ['nuːdlz] pl n Nudeln pl.

noon [nuːn] n Mittag m. **at noon** zu Mittag.

no-one ['nouwʌn] pron keiner, niemand.

noose [nuːs] n Schlinge f.

nor [noː] adj noch. **nor do I** ich auch nicht.

norm [noːm] n Norm f. **normal** adj normal. **normality** n Normalität f. **normalize** v normalisieren. **normally** adv normalerweise.

north [noːθ] n Norden m. adj also **northerly, northern** nördlich, Nord-. adv also **northwards** nach Norden, nordwärts. **North America** Nordamerika neut. **north-east** n Nordosten m. **North Pole** Nordpol m. **north-west** n Nordwesten m.

Norway ['noːwei] n Norwegen neut. **Norwegian** adj norwegisch; n Norweger(in).

nose [nouz] n Nase f. **nosy** adj (coll) neugierig.

nostalgia [no'staldʒə] n Nostalgie f. **nostalgic** adj wehmütig.

nostril ['nostril] n Nasenloch neut.

not [not] adv nicht. **not a** kein. **is it not? or isn't it?** nicht wahr?

notch [notʃ] n Kerbe f. v einkerben.

note [nout] n Vermerk m, Notiz f; (letter) Zettel m; (music) Note f; (money) Schein m; (importance) Bedeutung f. v merken. **take notes** Notizen machen.

nothing ['nʌθiŋ] pron nichts. n Nichts neut. **nothing but** nichts als.

notice ['noutis] n Notiz f; (law) Kündigung f. v bemerken. **period of notice** Kündigungsfrist f. **take notice (of)** achtgeben (auf). **give notice** kündigen. **until further notice** bis auf weiteres. **noticeable** adj bemerkenswert. **noticeboard** n Anschlagtafel f.

notify ['noutifai] v melden, benachrichtigen. **notification** n Meldung f; Benachrichtigung f.

notion ['nouʃən] n Begriff m. **have no notion** keine Ahnung haben.

notorious [nou'toːriəs] adj notorisch.

notwithstanding [notwið'standiŋ] prep trotz (+gen).

nougat ['nuːgaɪ] n Nugat m.

nought [noːt] n Null f. **come/bring to nought** zunichte kommen/bringen.

noun [naun] n Hauptwort neut.

nourish ['nʌriʃ] v (er)nähren. **nourishing** adj nahrhaft. **nourishment** n Ernährung f.

116

novel ['novəl] *adj* neu, neuartig. *n* Roman *m*. **novelist** *n* Romanschriftsteller(in). **novelty** *n* Neuheit *f*.
November [nə'vembə] *n* November *m*.
novice ['novis] *n* Anfänger(in); *(rel)* Novize *m, f*.
now [nau] *adv* jetzt, nun; *(straightaway)* sofort. **now and again** ab und zu, hin und wieder. **nowadays** *adv* heutzutage.
nowhere ['nouweə] *adv* nirgends, nirgendwo. **from nowhere** aus dem Nichts.
noxious ['nokʃəs] *adj* schädlich.
nozzle ['nozl] *n* Schnauze *f*, Ausguß *m*.
nuance ['njuːãs] *n* Nuance *f*, Schattierung *f*.
nuclear ['njuːkliə] *adj* Kern-. **nuclear energy** Atomkraft *f*. **nuclear reactor** Kernreaktor *m*.
nucleus ['njuːkliəs] *n* Kern *m*.
nude ['njuːd] *adj* nackt. **nudist** *n* Nudist(in). **nudity** *n* Nacktheit *f*.
nudge [nʌdʒ] *n* Rippenstoß *m*. *v* leicht anstoßen.
nugget ['nʌgit] *n* Goldklumpen *m*.
nuisance ['njuːsns] *n* Ärgernis *neut*.
null [nʌl] *adj* nichtig, ungültig. **null and void** null und nichtig.
numb [nʌm] *adj* starr, erstarrt. *v* taub machen.
number ['nʌmbə] *n* Nummer *f*; *(amount)* Anzahl *f*; *(figure)* Ziffer *f*. *v* numerieren. **number-plate** *n* Nummernschild *neut*. **numeral** *n* Ziffer *f*. **numerous** *adj* zahlreich.
nun [nʌn] *n* Nonne *f*.
nurse [nəːs] *n* Krankenschwester *f*, Krankenpfleger(in). *v* pflegen; *(feed baby)* stillen. **nursemaid** *n* Kindermädchen *neut*. **nursing** *n* Krankenpflege *f*. **nursing home** Privatklinik *f*.
nursery ['nəːsəri] *n* *(in house)* Kinderzimmer *neut*; *(institution)* Krippe *f*, Kindertagesstätte *f*; *(bot)* Gärtnerei *f*. **nurseryman** *n* Pflanzenzüchter *m*. **nursery rhyme** *n* Kinderlied *neut*, Kinderreim *m*. **nursery school** *n* Kindergarten *m*.
nurture ['nəːtʃə] *v* erziehen.
nut [nʌt] *n* Nuß *f*; *(for bolt)* Mutter *f*. **nutcracker** Nußknacker *m*. **nuts** *adj (coll)* verrückt. **nutmeg** *n* Muskatnuß *f*.
nutrient ['njuːtriənt] *n* Nährstoff *m*. *adj* nährend. **nutrition** *n* Ernährung *f*. **nutritious** *adj* nahrhaft.

nuzzle ['nʌzl] *v* sich schmiegen (an).
nylon ['nailon] *n* Nylon *neut*. **nylons** *pl* Strümpfe *pl*.
nymph [nimf] *n* Nymphe *f*.

O

oak [ouk] *n* Eiche *f*, *(wood)* Eichenholz *neut*. **oaken** *adj* eichen.
oar [oɪ] *n* Ruder *neut*, Riemen *m*. **oarsman** *n* Ruderer *m*.
oasis [ou'eisis] *n* *(pl -ses)* Oase *f*.
oath [ouθ] *n* Eid *m*; *(swear word)* Fluch *m*.
oats [outs] *pl n* Hafer *m sing*. **oatmeal** *n* Hafermehl *neut*.
obedient [ə'biːdiənt] *adj* gehorsam. **obedience** *n* Gehorsam *m*.
obese [ə'biːs] *adj* fettleibig. **obesity** *n* Fettleibigkeit *f*.
obey [ə'bei] *v* gehorchen (+*dat*); *(an order)* befolgen.
obituary [ə'bitjuəri] *n* Todesanzeige *f*.
object ['obʒikt; *v* əb'ʒekt] *n* Gegenstand *m*; *(aim)* Ziel *neut*; *(gramm)* Objekt *neut*. **money is no object** Geld spielt keine Rolle. **objective** *adj* objektiv. *v* einwenden (gegen). **objection** *n* Einwand *m*, Einspruch *m*. **objectionable** *adj* unangenehm.
oblige [ə'blaidʒ] *v* *(coerce)* zwingen. **be obliged to do something** etwas tun müssen. **much obliged!** besten Dank! **obligation** *n* Verpflichtung *f*. **obligatory** *adj* verbindlich.
oblique [ə'bliːk] *adj* schräg.
obliterate [ə'blitəreit] *v* auslöschen, tilgen. **obliteration** *n* Auslöschung *f*, Vertilgung *f*.
oblivion [ə'bliviən] *n* Vergessenheit *f*. **oblivious (to)** *adj* blind (gegen).
oblong ['oblon] *n* Rechteck *neut*. *adj* rechteckig.
obnoxious [əb'nokʃəs] *adj* gehässig.
oboe ['oubou] *n* Oboe *f*. **oboist** *n* Oboist(in).
obscene [əb'siːn] *adj* obszön. **obscenity** *n* Obszönität *f*, Unzüchtigkeit *f*.
obscure [əb'skjuə] *adj* *(dark)* dunkel, düster; *(meaning, etc.)* obskur, udeutlich.

obscurity n Dunkelheit f; Undeutlichkeit f.

observe [əb'zəɪv] v beobachten; (remark) bemerken. **observer** n Beobachter m. **observation** n Beobachtung f; Bemerkung f.

obsess [əb'ses] v quälen, heimsuchen. **obsessed** adj besessen. **obsession** n Besessenheit f.

obsolescent [obsə'lesnt] adj veraltend. **obsolescence** n Veralten neut.

obsolete ['obsəliːt] adj überholt, veraltet.

obstacle ['obstəkl] n Hindernis neut.

obstetrics [ob'stetriks] n Geburtshilfe f. **obstetrician** n Geburtshelfer(in).

obstinate ['obstinət] adj hartnäckig. **obstinacy** n Hartnäckigkeit f.

obstruct [əb'strʌkt] v versperren, blockieren; (hinder) hemmen. **obstruction** n Versperrung f; Hemmung f; (obstacle) Hindernis neut.

obtain [əb'tein] v erhalten, bekommen. **obtainable** adj erhältlich.

obtrusive [əb'truːsiv] adj aufdringlich.

obtuse [əb'tjuːs] adj stumpf.

obvious ['obviəs] adj offensichtlich.

occasion [ə'keiʒən] n Gelegenheit f; (possibility) Möglichkeit f; (cause) Anlaß m. **occasional** adj gelegentlich.

occult ['okʌlt] adj okkult. **the occult** okkulte Wissenschaften pl.

occupy ['okjupai] v (person) beschäftigen; (house) bewohnen; (mil) besetzen. **occupied** adj (phone booth, etc.) besetzt. **occupant** n Bewohner(in). **occupation** n Beschäftigung f; (profession) Beruf m; (mil) Besatzung f. **occupational** adj beruflich.

occur [ə'kəɪ] v vorkommen. **it occurs to me** es fällt mir ein. **occurrence** n Ereignis neut.

ocean ['ouʃən] n Ozean m, Meer neut. **oceanic** adj ozeanisch. **ocean-going** adj Hochsee-.

ochre ['oukə] adj ockerfarbig.

octagon ['oktəgən] n Achteck neut. **octagonal** adj achteckig.

octave ['oktiv] n Oktave f.

October [ok'toubə] n Oktober m.

octopus ['oktəpəs] n Tintenfisch m.

oculist ['okjulist] n Augenarzt m.

odd [od] adj (strange) seltsam; (numbers) ungerade. **oddity** n Seltsamkeit f. **oddly (enough)** seltsamerweise. **oddments** pl n Reste pl. **oddness** n Seltsamkeit f. **odds** pl

n (Gewinn)Chancen pl. **at odds with** uneins mit. **odds and ends** Krimskrams m.

ode [oud] n Ode f.

odious ['oudiəs] adj verhaßt.

odour ['oudə] n Geruch m. **odourless** adj geruchlos.

oesophagus [iː'sofəgəs] n Speiseröhre f.

of [ov] prep von or gen.

off [of] prep fort, weg. adv weg, entfernt; ab. adj (food) verdorben, nicht mehr frisch. **go off** weggehen; (food) verderben. **take off** (clothes) ausziehen; (holiday) frei nehmen. **switch off** ausschalten. **off and on** ab und zu. **off duty** dienstfrei.

offal ['ofəl] n Innereien pl.

offend [ə'fend] v kränken, beleidigen. **offender** n Missetäter(in). **offence** n Vergehen neut, Verstoß m. **take offence (at)** Anstoß nehmen (an). **offensive** adj widerwärtig; n (mil) Angriff m.

offer ['ofə] v (an)bieten. n Angebot neut. **offering** n (gift) Spende f.

offhand ['of'hand] adj lässig.

office ['ofis] n Büro neut; (official position or department) Amt neut. **officer** n (mil) Offizier. **take office** das Amt antreten. **office staff** Büropersonal neut.

official [ə'fiʃəl] n Beamte(r). adj amtlich; (report, function) offiziell. **officially** adj offiziell.

officious [ə'fiʃəs] adj aufdringlich.

offing ['ofiŋ] n **in the offing** in Sicht, drohend.

off-licence ['oflaisns] n Wein- und Spirituosenhandlung f.

off-peak [of'piːk] adj außerhalb der Hauptverkehrszeit.

off-putting ['of,putiŋ] adj abstoßend.

off-season [of'siːzn] n stille Saison f.

offset [of'set; n 'ofset] v ausgleichen. n (printing) offsetdruck m.

offshore ['ofʃoɪ] adj Küsten-. adv von der Küste entfernt, auf dem Meere.

offside [of'said] adj abseits.

offspring ['ofspriŋ] n Nachkommenschaft f.

offstage ['ofsteidʒ] adv hinter den Kulissen.

often ['ofn] adv oft, häufig.

ogre ['ougə] n Ungeheuer neut, Riese m.

oil [oil] n Öl n; (petroleum) Erdöl neut. v ölen. **oilfield** Ölfeld neut. **oil-paint** n

Ölfarbe *f*. **oil-painting** *n* Ölgemalde *neut*.
oily *adj* fettig.
ointment ['ointmənt] *n* Salbe *f*.
old [ould] *adj* alt. **grow old** alt werden.
five years old fünf Jahre alt. **old age** Alter
neut. **old-fashioned** *adj* altmodisch.
olive ['oliv] *n* Olive *f*. **olive-green** *adj* oliv-
grün. **olive branch** *n* Ölzweig *m*. **olive oil**
Olivenöl *neut*. **olive tree** Ölbaum *m*.
Olympics [ə'limpiks] *pl n* Olympische
Spiele *pl*, Olympiade *f*.
omelette ['omlit] *n* Omelett *neut*.
omen ['oumən] *n* Vorzeichen *neut*. **omi-
nous** *adj* verhängnisvoll, drohend.
omit [ou'mit] *v* auslassen; (*to do something*) unterlassen. **omission** *n* Unterlassung *f*.
omnipotent [om'nipətənt] *adj* allmächtig.
omnipotence *n* Allmacht *f*.
on [on] *prep* (*position*) an, auf; (*concerning*) über. *adv* (*forward*) fort, weiter. **have
on** one bei sich haben. **on fire** in Brand.
on foot zu Fuß. **on time** pünktlich. **put
on** (*clothes*) anziehen; (*manner*) affektier-
en. **switch on** einschalten.
once [wʌns] *adv*, *conj* einmal. **at once**
sofort. **once and for all** ein für allemal.
all at once auf einmal, plötzlich.
one [wʌn] *adj* ein, eine, ein. *n* Eins *f*. *pron*
man. **oneself** *pron* sich (selbst). **by oneself** allein. **one-piece** *adj* einteilig. **one-
way street** Einbahnstraße *f*.
onion ['ʌnjən] *n* Zwiebel *f*.
onlooker ['onlukə] *n* Zuschauer(in).
only ['ounli] *adj* einzig. *adv* nur; (*with
times*) erst. *conj* jedoch. **only just** gerade.
not only ... but also ... nicht nur ...
sondern auch ....
onset ['onset] *n* Anfang *m*.
onslaught ['onsloit] *n* Angriff *m*.
onus ['ounəs] *n* Last *f*, Verpflichtung *f*.
onward ['onwəd] *adv* vorwärts, weiter.
ooze [uiz] *v* (aus)sickern.
opal ['oupəl] *n* Opal *m*.
opaque [ou'peik] *adj* undurchsichtig.
open ['oupən] *v* öffnen, aufmachen;
(*book*) aufschlagen; (*event, shop*)
eröffnen; (*begin*) anfangen. *adj* offen,
auf. **open-air** *adj* Freiluft-. **in the open air**
im Freien. **with open arms** herzlich.
open-handed *adj* freigiebig. **opening** *n*
Öffnung *f*. (*shop*) Eröffnung *f*. **open-
minded** *adj* aufgeschlossen.
opera ['opərə] *n* Oper *f*. **opera house** Oper

f, Opernhaus *neut*. **opera singer** Opern-
sänger(in). **operatic** *adj* Opern-.
operate ['opəreit] *v* funktionieren, laufen;
(*med, tech, comm*) operieren. **operation** *n*
Arbeitslauf *m*, Betrieb *m*; Operation *f*.
operative *adj* tätig, wirksam; *n* Arbeiter
m.
ophthalmic [of'θalmik] *adj* Augen-. **ophthalmologist** *n* Augenarzt *m*. **ophthalmol-
ogy** *n* Ophthalmologie *f*.
opinion [ə'pinjən] *n* Meinung *f*, Ansicht *f*.
in my opinion meines Erachtens. **opinion
poll** Meinungsumfrage *f*.
opium ['oupiəm] *n* Opium *neut*.
opponent [ə'pounənt] *n* Gegner(in).
opportune [opə'tjuin] *adj* rechtzeitig.
opportunist *n* Opportunist(in).
opportunity [opə'tjuinəti] *n* Gelegenheit
f; (*possibility*) Möglichkeit *f*. **take the
opportunity** die Gelegenheit ergreifen.
oppose [ə'pouz] *v* bekämpfen, sich widersetzen (+*dat*). **opposed** *adj* feindlich
(gegen). **as opposed to** im Vergleich zu.
opposing *adj* (*ideas*) widerstreitend.
opposition *n* Widerstand *m*; (*pol*) Opposition *f*.
opposite ['opəzit] *adj* gegenüberliegend. *n*
Gegenteil *neut*.
oppress [ə'pres] *v* unterdrücken. **oppres-
sion** *n* Unterdrückung *f*. **oppressive** *adj*
bedrückend; (*weather*) schwül.
opt [opt] *v* sich entscheiden (für).
optical ['optikl] *adj* optisch. **optician** *n*
Optiker *m*. **optics** *n* Optik *f*.
optimism ['optimizəm] *n* Optimismus *m*.
optimist *n* Optimist(in). **optimistic** *adj*
optimistisch.
optimum ['optiməm] *n* Optimum *neut*. *adj*
optimal.
option ['opʃən] *n* Wahl *f*; (*comm*) Option
f. **have no option (but to)** keine andere
Möglichkeit haben (, als zu). **optional** *adj*
wahlfrei.
opulent ['opjulənt] *adj* opulent, üppig.
opulence *n* Opulenz *f*, Üppigkeit *f*.
or [oi] *conj* oder. **or else** sonst.
oracle ['orəkl] *n* Orakel *neut*.
oral ['oirəl] *adj* mündlich; (*med*) oral. *n*
mündliche Prüfung *f*.
orange ['orindʒ] *n* Apfelsine *f*, Orange *f*.
adj orange.
orator ['orətə] *n* Redner *m*. **oration** *n*
Rede *f*. **oratory** *n* Redekunst *f*.
orbit ['oibit] *n* Umlaufbahn *f*. *v*
umkreisen.

orchard ['ɔɪtʃəd] *n* Obstgarten *m*.
orchestra ['ɔɪkəstrə] *n* Orchester *neut*.
orchestral *adj* Orchester-, orchestral.
orchid ['ɔɪkid] *n* Orchidee *f*.
ordain [ɔɪ'dein] *v* ordinieren, weihen;
(*decree*) anordnen.
ordeal [ɔɪ'diɪl] *n* schwere Prüfung *f*.
order ['ɔɪdə] *n* Ordnung *f*; (*series*)
Reihenfolge *f*; (*comm*) Bestellung *f*, Auftrag *m*; (*command*) Befehl *m*; (*rel*) Orden
m. *v* (*comm*) bestellen; (*command*)
befehlen. **put in order** ordnen. **in order to**
... um ... zu ...
orderly ['ɔɪdəli] *adj* ordentlich. *n* (*med*)
Sanitäter *m*.
ordinal ['ɔɪdinl] *adj* Ordinal-.
ordinary ['ɔɪdənəri] *adj* gewöhnlich, normal. **out-of-the-ordinary** außerordentlich.
ordinarily *adv* normalerweise.
ore [ɔɪ] *n* Erz *neut*.
oregano [ori'gaɪnou] *n* Origanum *neut*.
organ ['ɔɪgən] *n* Organ *neut*; (*music*)
Orgel *f*. **organist** *n* Organist(in).
organic [ɔɪ'ganik] *adj* organisch.
organism ['ɔɪgənizəm] *n* Organismus *m*.
organize ['ɔɪgənaiz] *v* organisieren. **organization** *n* Organisation *f*; (*association*)
Verband *m*. **organizer** *n* Organisator *m*.
orgasm ['ɔɪgazəm] *n* Orgasmus *m*.
orgy ['ɔɪdʒi] *n* Orgie *f*.
orient ['ɔɪriənt] *v* orientieren. **the Orient**
Morgenland *neut*, Orient *m*. **oriental** *adj*
orientalisch; *n* Orientale *m*, Orientalin *f*.
orientate ['ɔɪriənteit] *v* orientieren. **orientation** *n* Orientierung *f*.
origin ['ɔridʒin] *n* Ursprung *f*; Herkunft
f, Entstehung *f*. **original** *adj* ursprünglich; (*unusual*) originell; *n* Original
neut. **originality** *n* Originalität *f*. **originate**
v entstehen.
ornament ['ɔɪnəmənt] *n* Ornament *neut*. *v*
verzieren, schmücken. **ornamental** *adj*
ornamental.
ornate [ɔɪ'neit] *adj* reich verziert.
ornithology [ɔɪni'θolodʒi] *n* Ornithologie
f, Vogelkunde *f*. **ornithologist** *n* Ornitho-
loge *m*, Ornithologin *f*.
orphan ['ɔɪfən] *n* Waise *f*, Waisenkind
neut. *v* verwaisen. **orphanage** *n*
Waisenhaus *neut*.
orthodox ['ɔɪθədoks] *adj* orthodox.
orthopaedic [ɔɪθə'piɪdik] *adj*
orthopädisch. **orthopaedics** *n* Orthopädie
f.

oscillate ['osileit] *v* oszillieren, schwingen.
oscillation *n* Schwingung *f*.
ostensible [o'stensəbl] *adj* scheinbar.
ostentatious [osten'teiʃəs] *adj*
großtuerisch. **ostentation** *n* Prahlerei *f*.
osteopath ['ostiəpaθ] *n* Osteopath(in).
ostracize ['ostrəsaiz] *v* verbannen.
ostrich ['ostritʃ] *n* Strauß *m*.
other ['ʌðə] *adj*, *pron* ander. **other than**
anders als. **each other** einander. **somebody or other** irgend jemand. **one after
the other** einer/eine/eins nach dem/der
andern.
otherwise ['ʌðəwaiz] *adv* sonst.
otter ['otə] *n* Otter *m*.
*****ought** [ɔɪt] *v* sollen. **you ought to do it**
Sie sollten es tun.
ounce [auns] *n* Unze *f*.
our [auə] *adj* unser. **Our Father**
Vaterunser *neut*. **ours** *poss pron* unsere.
ourselves uns (selbst).
oust [aust] *v* vertreiben.
out [aut] *adv* aus, hinaus, heraus;
(*outside*) draußen. **come out** herauskommen; (*book, etc.*) erscheinen. **go out**
hinausgehen. **out of** the bounds ausgeschlossen. **out-of-date** *adj* veraltet.
outboard ['autbɔɪd] *adj* Außenbord-. *n*
Außenbordmotor *m*.
outbreak ['autbreik] *n* Ausbruch *m*.
outbuilding ['autbildiŋ] *n* Nebengebäude
neut.
outburst ['autbɔɪst] *n* Ausbruch *m*.
outcast ['autkaɪst] *n* Ausgestoßene(r).
outcome ['autkʌm] *n* Ergebnis *neut*.
outcry ['autkrai] *n* Aufschrei *m*.
*****outdo** [aut'duɪ] *v* übertreffen.
outdoor ['autdɔɪ] *adj* Außen-. **outdoor
swimming pool** Freibad *neut*. **outdoors**
adv draußen.
outer ['autə] *adj* äußer, Außen-. **outer
garments** Oberkleidung *f*. **outer space**
Weltraum *m*.
outfit ['autfit] *n* Ausstattung *f*; (*coll*:
team) Mannschaft *f*. **outfitter** *n* (Herren)Ausstatter *m*.
outgoing ['autgouiŋ] *adj* (*pol*) abtretend;
(*friendly*) gesellig.
*****outgrow** [aut'grou] *v* hinauswachsen
über; (*clothes*) herauswachsen aus.
outhouse ['authaus] *n* Anbau *m*,
Nebengebäude *neut*.
outing ['autiŋ] *n* Ausflug *m*.
outlandish [aut'landiʃ] *adj* seltsam,
grotesk.

outlaw ['autlɔɪ] *n* Vogelfreie(r). *v* ächten.
outlay ['autlei] *n* Auslage *f*, Ausgabe *f*.
outlet ['autlit] *n* Auslaß *m*.
outline ['autlain] *n* Umriß *m*. *v* umreißen.
outlive [aut'liv] *v* überleben.
outlook ['autluk] *n* Aussicht *f*; *(attitude)* Auffassung *f*.
outlying ['autlaiiŋ] *adj* entlegen.
outnumber [aut'nʌmbə] *v* (zahlenmäßig) überlegen sein (+ *dat*).
outpatient ['autpeiʃənt] *n* ambulanter Patient *m*.
outpost ['autpoust] *n* Vorposten *m*.
output ['autput] *n* Leistung *f*, Output *m*.
outrage ['autreidʒ] *n* Schande *f*. **outraged** *adj* beleidigt, schockiert. **outrageous** *adj* frevelhaft.
outright ['autrait; *adv* aut'rait] *adj*, *adv* ganz, völlig; *(immediately)* sogleich, auf der Stelle.
outside [aut'said; *adj* 'autsaid] *n* Äußere *neut*; Außenseite *f*. *adj* äußer, Außen-. *prep* außerhalb (+ *gen*). *adv* (*go*) hinaus; (*be*) draußen. **outsider** *n* Außenseiter(in).
outsize ['autsaiz] *adj* übergroß. *n* Übergröße *f*.
outskirts ['autskɔːtz] *pl n* Umgebung *f sing*, Staatrand *m sing*.
outspoken [aut'spoukən] *adj* freimütig.
outstanding [aut'standiŋ] *adj* hervorragend; *(not settled)* unerledigt.
outstrip [aut'strip] *v* überholen.
outward ['autwəd] *adj* äußer. *adv* also **outwards** nach Außen. **outward-bound** *adj* auf der Ausreise. **outwardly** *adv* äußerlich.
outweigh [aut'wei] *v* überwiegen.
outwit [aut'wit] *v* überlisten.
oval ['ouvəl] *n* Oval *neut*. *adj* oval.
ovary ['ouvəri] *n* Eierstock *m*.
ovation [ou'veiʃən] *n* Ovation *f*, Beifallssturm *m*.
oven ['ʌvn] *n* *(cookery)* Backofen *m*; *(industrial, etc.)* Ofen *m*.
over ['ouvə] *adv* über, hinüber, herüber; *(finished)* zu Ende; *(during)* während; *(too much)* allzu. *prep* über; *(more than)* mehr als. **over and over again** immer wieder. **over there** drüben. **all over England** in ganz England. **it's all over** es ist aus.
overall ['ouvərɔːl] *adj* gesamt. *adv* insgesamt. *n also* **overalls** *pl* Overall *m*, Schutzanzug *m*.
overbalance [ouvə'baləns] *v* umkippen.

overbearing [ouvə'beəriŋ] *adj* anmaßend, arrogant.
overboard ['ouvəbɔːd] *adv* über Bord.
overcast [ouvə'kaɪst] *adj* bedeckt, bewölkt.
overcharge [ouvə'tʃaɪdʒ] *v* zuviel verlangen von.
overcoat ['ouvəkout] *n* Mantel *m*.
*overcome [ouvə'kʌm] *v* überwinden. *adj* *(with emotion)* tief bewegt.
overcrowded [ouvə'kraudid] *adj* überfüllt.
*overdo [ouvə'duɪ] *v* übertreiben. **overdo it** zu weit gehen. **overdone** *adj* *(cookery)* übergar.
overdose ['ouvədous] *n* Überdosis *f*.
*overdraw [ouvə'drɔː] *v* überziehen. **overdraft** *n* (Konto)Überziehung *f*.
overdrive ['ouvədraiv] *n* Schongang *m*.
overdue [ouvə'djuɪ] *adj* überfällig; *(train)* verspätet.
overestimate [ouvə'estimeit] *v* überschätzen.
overexpose [ouvəik'spouz] *v* *(phot)* überbelichten.
overfill [ouvə'fil] *v* überfüllen.
overflow [ouvə'flou; *n* 'ouvəflou] *v* überlaufen. *n* Überlauf *m*.
overgrown [ouvə'groun] *adj* überwachsen.
*overhang [ouvə'haŋ; *n* 'ouvəhaŋ] *v* überhängen. *n* Überhang *m*.
overhaul [ouvə'hɔːl] *v* überholen. *n* Überholung *f*.
overhead [ouvə'hed] *adj* obenliegend. **overheads** *pl n* allgemeine Unkosten *pl*.
*overhear [ouvə'hiə] *v* (zufällig) hören.
overheat [ouvə'hiːt] *v* überheizen; *(mot)* heißlaufen.
overjoyed [ouvə'dʒɔid] *adj* entzückt, außer sich vor Freude.
overland [ouvə'land] *adj* Überland-.
overlap [ouvə'lap; *n* 'ouvəlap] *v* sich überschneiden (mit). *n* Überschneiden *neut*, Übergreifen *neut*.
*overlay [ouvə'lei; *n* 'ouvəlei] *v* bedecken, belegen. *n* Auflage *f*, Bedeckung *f*.
overleaf [ouvə'liːf] *adv* umseitig, umstehend.
overload [ouvə'loud; *n* 'ouvəloud] *v* überbelasten. *n* Überbelastung *f*.
overlook [ouvə'luk] *v* *(room, etc.)* überblicken; *(let pass)* nicht beachten.
overnight [ouvə'nait] *adv* über Nacht. **stay overnight** übernachten. *adj* Nacht-. **overnight case** Handkoffer *m*.

overpower [ouvə'pauə] v überwältigen.
overrate [ouvə'reit] v überschätzen.
overrule [ouvə'ruːl] v zurückweisen; (person) überstimmen.
***overrun** [ouvə'rʌn] v überschwemmen, überlaufen.
overseas [ouvə'siːz] adv in Übersee. adj überseeisch, Übersee-.
overseer [ouvə'siə] n Vorarbeiter m.
overshadow [ouvə'ʃadou] v überschatten.
***overshoot** [ouvə'ʃuːt] v hinausschießen über.
oversight ['ouvəsait] n Versehen neut.
***oversleep** [ouvə'sliːp] v sich verschlafen.
overspill ['ouvəspil] n Überschuß m.
overt [ou'vəːt] adj offenkundig.
***overtake** [ouvə'teik] v überholen.
***overthrow** [ouvə'θrou; n 'ouvəθrou] v (um)stürzen. n Umsturz m.
overtime ['ouvətaim] n Überstunden pl. **work overtime** Überstunden machen.
overtone ['ouvətoun] n Nuance f.
overture ['ouvətjuə] n (music) Ouvertüre f.
overturn [ouvə'təːn] v umkippen.
overweight [ouvə'weit] adj (zu) dick, fettleibig.
overwhelm [ouvə'welm] v überwältigen. **overwhelming** adj überwältigend.
overwork [ouvə'wəːk] v (sich) überanstrengen.
overwrought [ouvə'rɔːt] adj nervös, überreizt.
ovulate ['ovjuleit] v ovulieren. **ovulation** n Ovulation f. **ovum** n Ei neut, Eizelle f.
owe [ou] v schulden; (have debts) Schulden haben. **owing** adj zu zahlen. **owing to** infolge or wegen (+gen).
owl [aul] n Eule f.
own [oun] adj eigen. v besitzen; (admit) zugeben. **own up** gestehen. **owner** n Inhaber(in). **ownership** n Besitz m.
ox [oks] n (pl oxen) Ochse m, Rind neut. **oxtail** Ochsenschwanz m.
oxygen ['oksidʒən] n Sauerstoff m.
oyster ['oistə] n Auster f.

P

pace [peis] n (step) Schritt m; (speed) Geschwindigkeit f, Tempo neut. v schreiten. **keep pace with** Schritt halten mit. **pacemaker** n Schrittmacher m.
Pacific [pə'sifik] n Pazifik m.
pacify ['pasifai] v befrieden. **pacifier** n (for baby) Schnuller m. **pacifism** n Pazifismus m. **pacifist** n Pazifist(in).
pack [pak] n Pack m, Packung f; (cards) Spiel neut; (dogs) Meute f. v einpacken; (stuff) vollstopfen. **package** n Paket neut.
packaging n Verpackung f. **packet** n Packung f, Päckchen neut. **packhorse** n Lastpferd neut.
pact [pakt] n Pakt m, Vertrag m.
pad¹ [pad] n Polster neut; (paper) Block m; (sport) Schützer m; (ink) Stempelkissen neut. **padding** n Polsterung f.
pad² [pad] v trotten.
paddle¹ ['padl] n Paddel neut. v paddeln.
paddle-steamer n Raddampfer m.
paddle² ['padl] v (wade) planschen, herumpaddeln.
paddock ['padək] n Pferdekoppel f; (on racecourse) Sattelplatz m.
paddyfield ['padifiːld] n Reisfeld neut.
padlock ['padlok] n Vorhängeschloß neut. v (mit einem Vorhängeschloß) verschließen.
paediatric [piːdi'atrik] adj pädiatrisch. **paediatrician** n Kinderarzt m, Kinderärztin f. **paediatrics** n Kinderheilkunde f.
pagan ['peigən] adj heidnisch. n Heide m, Heidin f.
page¹ [peidʒ] n (book) Seite f.
page² [peidʒ] n (boy) Page m.
pageant ['padʒənt] n Festzug m. **pageantry** n Prunk m.
paid [peid] V **pay**.
pail [peil] n Eimer m.
pain [pein] n Schmerz m, Schmerzen pl; (suffering) Leid neut. v peinigen. **take pains** sich Mühe geben. **on pain of** bei Strafe von. **painful** adj schmerzhaft. **painkiller** n schmerzstillendes Mittel neut. **painless** adj schmerzlos. **painstaking** adj sorgfältig.
paint [peint] n Farbe f, Lack m. v anstreichen; (pictures) malen. **paintbrush** n Pinsel m. **painted** adj bemalt. **painter** n Maler(in). **painting** n Gemälde neut.
pair [peə] n Paar neut; (animals) Pärchen neut; (married couple) Ehepaar neut. v **pair off** paarweise anordnen. **a pair of trousers** eine Hose.

pal [pal] *n* (*coll*) Kamerad *m*, Kumpel *m*.
palace ['paləs] *n* Palast *m*.
palate ['palit] *n* (Vorder)Gaumen *m*; (*taste*) Geschmack *m*. **palatable** *adj* schmackhaft.
pale [peil] *adj* blaß, bleich. *v* blaßwerden. **pale ale** helles Bier *neut*. **paleness** *n* Blässe *f*.
palette ['palit] *n* Palette *f*.
pall¹ [poil] *v* (*become boring*) jeden Reiz verlieren.
pall² [poil] *n* (*for coffin*) Leichentuch *neut*; (*fig*) Hülle *f*. **pall-bearer** *n* Sargträger *m*.
palm¹ [paim] *n* (*of hand*) Handfläche *f*. **palmist** *n* Handwahrsager(in). **palmistry** *n* Handlesekunst *f*.
palm² [paim] *n* (*tree*) Palme *f*.
palpitate ['palpiteit] *v* (*heart*) unregelmäßigschlagen; (*tremble*) beben, zittern.
pamper ['pampə] *v* verwöhnen.
pamphlet ['pamflit] *n* Broschüre *f*.
pan [pan] *n* Pfanne *f*.
pancreas ['paŋkriəs] *n* Bauchspeicheldrüse *f*.
panda ['pandə] *n* Panda *m*.
pander ['pandə] *v* nachgeben (+*dat*).
pane [pein] *n* (Fenster)Scheibe *f*.
panel ['panl] *n* Tafel *f*; (*door*) Füllung *f*; (*dress*) Einsatzstück *m*; (*instrument*) Armaturenbrett *neut*. *v* täfeln. **panelling** *n* Täfelung *f*.
pang [paŋ] *n* (*of remorse*) Gewissensbisse *pl*.
panic ['panik] *n* Panik *f*. *v* hinreißen (zu). **panic-stricken** *adj* von panischer Angst erfüllt. **panicky** *adj* überängstlich.
pannier ['paniə] *n* (Trag)Korb *m*; (*motorcycle*) Satteltasche *f*.
panorama [,panə'raimə] *n* Panorama *neut*, Rundblick *m*. **panoramic** *adj* panoramisch.
pansy ['panzi] *n* Stiefmütterchen *neut*.
pant [pant] *v* keuchen, schnaufen.
panther ['panθə] *n* Panther *m*.
panties ['pantiz] *pl n* (*coll*) Schlüpfer *m sing*, Höschen *neut sing*.
pantomime ['pantəmaim] *n* Pantomime *f*.
pantry ['pantri] *n* Speiseschrank *m*.
pants [pants] *pl n* (*trousers*) Hose *f sing*; (*underpants*) Unterhose *f sing*. **pantyhose** Strumpfhose *f*.
papal ['peipl] *adj* päpstlich.
paper ['peipə] *n* Papier *neut*; (*newspaper*) Zeitung *f*; (*scientific*) Abhandlung *f*. *v* (a

room) tapezieren. **paperback** *n* Taschenbuch *neut*. **paper bag** Tüte *f*. **paperclip** *n* Büroklammer *f*. **paper-thin** *adj* hauchdünn. **paperweight** *n* Briefbeschwerer *m*. **paperwork** *n* Büroarbeit *f*.
paprika ['paprikə] *n* Paprika *m*.
par [paı] *n* Nennwert *m*, (*golf*) Par *neut*. **on a par with** gleich (+*dat*).
parable ['parəbl] *n* Parabel *f*.
parachute ['parəʃuit] *n* Fallschirm *m*. *v* mit dem Fallschirm abspringen.
parade [pə'reid] *n* Parade *f*. *v* (*march past*) vorbeimarschieren. **parade ground** Paradeplatz *m*.
paradise ['parədais] *n* Paradies *neut*.
paradox ['parədoks] *n* Paradox *neut*. **paradoxical** *adj* paradox.
paraffin ['parəfin] *n* Paraffin *neut*.
paragraph ['parəgraıf] *n* Absatz *m*.
parallel ['parəlel] *n* Parallele *f*. *adj* parallel. *v* entsprechen (+*dat*).
paralyse ['parəlaiz] *v* paralysieren. **paralysed** *adj* gelähmt. **paralysis** *n* (*pl* -ses) Lähmung *f*, Paralyse *f*. **paralytic** *adj* paralytisch; (*coll*) besoffen.
paramilitary [,parə'militəri] *adj* paramilitärisch.
paramount ['parəmaunt] *adj* äußerst wichtig, überragend.
paranoia [,parə'noiə] *n* Paranoia *f*. **paranoid** *adj* paranoid.
parapet ['parəpit] *n* Brüstung *f*.
paraphernalia [,parəfə'neiliə] *n* Zubehör *neut*.
paraphrase ['parəfreiz] *n* Umschreibung *f*, Paraphrase *f*. *v* umschreiben.
paraplegia [parə'pliidʒə] *n* Paraplegie *f*. **paraplegic** *adj* paraplegisch.
parasite ['parəsait] *n* Parasit *m*, Schmarotzer *m*. **parasitic** *adj* parasitisch.
parasol ['parəsol] *n* Sonnenschirm *m*.
paratrooper ['parə,truipə] *n* Fallschirmjäger *m*.
parcel ['paisəl] *n* Paket *neut*, Päckchen *neut*; (*of land*) Parzelle *f*. **parcel post** Paketpost *f*. **parcels office** Gepäckabfertigung *f*. *v* **parcel out** austeilen.
parch [paitʃ] *v* dörren. **parched** *adj* ausgetrocknet; (*coll*) sehr durstig.
parchment ['paitʃmənt] *n* Pergament *neut*.
pardon ['paidn] *n* Verzeihung *f*. *v* verzeihen (+*dat*); (*law*) begnadigen. **I beg your pardon** *or* **pardon me** Verzeihung! **pardonable** *adj* verzeihlich.

pare [peə] v schälen; (*prices, costs, etc.*) herabsetzen, beschneiden.

parent ['peərənt] n Vater m, Mutter f. **parents** pl Eltern pl. **parentage** n Abkunft f. **parental** adj elterlich.

parenthesis [pə'renθəsis] n (pl -ses) Parenthese f.

parish ['pariʃ] n (Kirchen)gemeinde f. adj Gemeinde-.

parity ['pariti] n Parität f.

park [paɪk] n Park m. v (*mot*) parken. **car park** Parkplatz m. **no parking** Parken verboten. **parking place** or **lot** Parkplatz m. **parking light** Standlicht neut. **parking meter** Parkuhr f.

parliament ['paɪləmənt] n Parlament neut. **member of parliament** Abgeordnete(r), Parlamentarier m. **parliamentary** adj parlamentarisch, Parlaments-.

parlour ['paɪlə] n Wohnzimmer neut. **ice-cream parlour** Eisdiele f.

parochial [pə'roukiəl] adj Gemeinde-; (*fig*) engstirnig.

parody ['parədi] n Parodie f. v parodieren.

parole [pə'roul] n Bewährung f. **release on parole** auf Bewährung entlassen.

paroxysm ['parəksizəm] n Anfall m.

parrot ['parət] n Papagei m.

parsley ['paɪsli] n Petersilie f.

parsnip ['paɪsnip] n Pastinake f.

parson ['paɪsn] n Pfarrer m. **parsonage** n Pfarrhaus neut.

part [paɪt] n Teil m; (*theatre*) Rolle f. adj Teil-. v trennen; (*people*) sich trennen; (*hair*) scheiteln. **for my part** meinerseits. **in part** teilweise. **take part (in)** teilnehmen (an).

*partake [paɪteik] v **partake of** (*eat*) zu sich nehmen.

partial ['paɪʃəl] adj Teil-; (*biased*) eingenommen. **be partial to** (*coll*) eine Vorliebe haben für. **partially** adv teilweise.

participate [pa'tisipeit] v teilnehmen (an). **participant** n Teilnehmer(in). **participation** n Teilnahme f.

participle ['paɪtisipl] n Partizip neut.

particle ['paɪtikl] n Teilchen neut.

particular [pə'tikjulə] adj besonder, speziell; (*fussy*) wählerisch. **particulars** pl n Einzelheiten pl. **particularly** adv besonders.

parting ['paɪtiŋ] n Abschied neut; (*hair*) Scheitel m.

partisan [paɪti'zan] n Anhänger m.

partition [pa'tiʃən] n Aufteilung f, Trennung f; (*wall, etc.*) Scheidewand f.

partly ['paɪtli] adv zum Teil, teils.

partner ['paɪtnə] n Partner(in). **partnership** n Partnerschaft f.

partridge ['paɪtridʒ] n Rebhuhn neut.

party ['paɪti] n (*pol, law*) Partei f; (*social gathering*) Party f. **be a party to** beteiligt sein an.

pass [paɪs] v (*go past*) vorbeigehen(an); (*go beyond*) überschreiten, übertreffen; (*exam*) bestehen; (*of time*) vergehen; (*time*) vertreiben; (*hand*) überreichen; (*approve*) billigen; (*sport*) zuspielen. n (*travel document*) Zeitkarte f. **pass away** sterben. **pass off (as)** ausgeben (als). **pass out** (*coll*) ohmächtig werden. **pass up** verzichten auf.

passage ['pasidʒ] n Durchfahrt f, Reise f; (*in book*) Stelle f; (*corridor*) Gang m; (*of time*) Verlauf m.

passenger ['pasindʒə] n Fahrgast m, Reisende(r); (*aeroplane*) Fluggast m.

passion ['paʃən] n Leidenschaft f; (*anger*) Zorn m; (*rel*) Passion f. **passionate** adj leidenschaftlich.

passive ['pasiv] adj passiv. **passivity** n Passivität f.

Passover ['paɪsouvə] n Passahfest neut.

passport ['paɪspoɪt] n (Reise)Paß m.

password ['paɪswoɪd] n Kennwort neut.

past [paɪst] n Vergangenheit f. adj vergangen. prep nach, über; (*in front of*) an ... vorbei. **ten past six** zehn (Minuten) nach sechs. **half past six** halb sieben. **in the past** früher.

pasta ['pastə] n Teigwaren pl.

paste [peist] n Paste f; (*glue*) Klebstoff m. v kleben.

pastel ['pastəl] adj **pastel colour** Pastellfarbe f.

pasteurize ['pastʃəraiz] v pasteurisieren.

pastime ['paɪstaim] n Zeitvertreib m.

pastor ['paɪstə] n Pfarrer m, Pastor m. **pastoral** adj (*poetry*) Hirten-; (*rel*) pastoral.

pastry ['peistri] n Teig m; (*cake*) Tortengebäck neut.

pasture ['paɪstʃə] n Weide f, Grasland neut.

pasty[1] ['peisti] adj teigig; (*complexion*) bleich.

pasty[2] ['pasti] n Pastete f.

pat

pat [pæt] *n* (leichter) Schlag *m*. *v* klopfen, patschen. **pat on the back** (*v*) beglückwünschen.
patch [pætʃ] *n* Flicken *m*, Lappen *m*; (*on eye*) Augenbinde *f*. *v* flicken. **patchwork** *n* Flickwerk *neut*. **patchy** *adj* ungleichmäßig.
pâté ['pætei] *n* Pastete *f*.
patent ['peitənt] *n* Patent *neut. adj* patentiert, Patent-; (*obvious*) offenkundig. *v* patentieren.
paternal [pə'tə:nl] *adj* väterlich. **paternal grandfather** Großvater väterlicherseits. **paternity** *n* Vaterschaft *f*.
path [pɑːθ] *n* Weg *m*, Pfad *m*. **pathway** *n* Weg *m*, Bahn *f*.
pathetic [pə'θetik] *adj* (*moving*) rührend; (*pitiable*) kläglich.
pathology [pə'θolədʒi] *n* Pathologie *f*. **pathological** *adj* pathologisch. **pathologist** *n* Pathologe *m*, Pathologin *f*.
patience ['peiʃəns] *n* Geduld *f*. **patient** *adj* geduldig, duldsam. *n* Patient(in).
patio ['pætiou] *n* Patio *m*.
patriarchal ['peitriɑːkəl] *adj* patriarchalisch.
patriot ['pætriət] *n* Patriot(in). **patriotic** *adj* patriotisch. **patriotism** *n* Patriotismus *m*.
patrol [pə'troul] *n* Patrouille *f*. *v* durchstreifen. **patrol car** Streifenwagen *m*. **patrolman** *n* Streifenpolizist *m*.
patron ['peitrən] *n* Patron *m*, Gönner *m*. **patronage** *n* Gönnerschaft *f*. **patronize** *v* (*theatre, restaurant*) besuchen; (*person*) gönnerhaft behandeln. **patronizing** *adj* gönnerhaft.
patter¹ ['pætə] *n* (*rain*) Prasseln *neut. v* prasseln.
patter² ['pætə] *n* (*speech*) Geplapper *neut*, Rotwelsch *neut. v* plappern.
pattern ['pætən] *n* Muster *neut*.
paunch [pɔːntʃ] *n* Wanst *m*. **paunchy** *adj* dickbäuchig.
pauper ['pɔːpə] *n* Arme(r).
pause [pɔːz] *n* Pause *f*. *v* anhalten, zögern.
pave [peiv] *v* pflastern. **pave the way** den Weg bahnen. **pavement** *n* Bürgersteig *m*.
pavilion [pə'viljən] *n* Pavillon *m*.
paw [pɔː] *n* Pfote *f*, Tatze *f*. *v* (*ground*) stampfen auf.
pawn¹ [pɔːn] *n* (*chess*) Bauer *m*.
pawn² [pɔːn] *v* verpfänden. **pawnbroker** *n* Pfandleiher *m*.

*pay [pei] *n* Lohn *m*, Gehalt *neut. v* zahlen; (*bill*) bezahlen; (*be worthwhile*) sich lohnen; (*visit, compliment*) machen. **pay attention** achtgeben (auf). **pay homage** huldigen (+ *dat*). **pay for** bezahlen. **payable** *adj* fällig. **payday** *n* Zahltag *m*. **paying guest** zahlender Gast *m*. **payload** *n* Nutzlast *f*. **payment** *n* (Be)Zahlung *f*; (*cheque*) Einlösung *f*.
pea [piː] *n* Erbse *f*.
peace [piːs] *n* Frieden *m*; (*quiet*) Ruhe *f*. **make one's peace with** sich aussöhnen mit. **leave in peace** in Ruhe lassen. **peace of mind** Seelenruhe *f*. **peace treaty** Friedensvertrag *m*. **peaceable** *adj* friedlich. **peaceful** *adj* ruhig.
peach [piːtʃ] *n* Pfirsich *m*.
peacock ['piːkok] *n* Pfau *m*.
peak [piːk] *n* Spitze *f*, Gipfel *m*. *adj* Höchst-, Spitzen-. **peaked** *adj* spitz.
peal [piːl] *v* (*bells*) läuten. *n* Geläute *neut*. **peal of thunder** Donnerschlag *m*.
peanut ['piːnʌt] *n* Erdnuß *f*.
pear [peə] *n* Birne *f*. **pear-shaped** *adj* birnenförmig.
pearl [pəːl] *n* Perle *f*. *adj* Perlen-.
peasant ['peznt] *n* Bauer *m*. *adj* bäuerlich.
peat [piːt] *n* Torf *m*.
pebble ['pebl] *n* Kieselstein *m*.
peck [pek] *v* picken, hacken. *n* Picken *neut*; (*kiss*) (flüchtiger) Kuß *m*. **peckish** *adj* (*coll*) hungrig.
peculiar [pi'kjuːljə] *adj* (*strange*) seltsam. **peculiar to** eigentümlich (+ *dat*). **peculiarity** *n* Eigentümlichkeit *f*.
pedal ['pedl] *n* Pedal *neut*, Fußhebel *m*. *v* (*a bicycle*) fahren.
pedantic [pi'dæntik] *adj* pedantisch.
peddle ['pedl] *v* hausieren. **peddler** *n* Hausierer *m*.
pedestal ['pedistl] *n* Sockel *m*. **put on a pedestal** vergöttern.
pedestrian [pi'destriən] *n* Fußgänger(in). *adj* Fußgänger-; (*humdrum*) langweilig, banal. **pedestrian crossing** Fußgängerüberweg *m*. **pedestrian precinct** Fußgängerzone *f*.
pedigree ['pedigriː] *n* Stammbaum *m*.
pedlar ['pedlə] *n* Hausierer *m*.
peel [piːl] *n* Schale *f*. *v* schälen. **peeler** *n* Schäler *m*.
peep [piːp] *v* gucken, verstohlen blicken. *n* verstohlener Blick *m*. **peephole** *n* Guckloch *neut*.

peer[1] [piə] v (look) spähen, gucken.
peer[2] [piə] n (equal) Ebenbürtige(r); (noble) Peer m. **peerage** n Peerwürde f. **peerless** adj unvergleichlich.
peevish ['piːviʃ] adj verdrießlich.
peg [peg] n Pflock m; (coathook) Haken m; (clothes) Klammer f. v anpflöcken; (prices) festlegen. **off the peg** von der Stange.
pejorative [pə'dʒorətiv] adj herabsetzend.
pelican ['pelikən] n Pelikan m.
pellet ['pelit] n Kügelchen neut; (shot) Schrotkorn neut.
pelmet ['pelmit] n Falbel f.
pelt[1] [pelt] v (throw) bewerfen.
pelt[2] [pelt] n (skin) Fell neut, Pelz m.
pelvis ['pelvis] n (anat) Becken neut.
pen[1] [pen] n (writing) (Schreib)Feder f, Federhalter m.
pen[2] [pen] n (animals) Pferch m, Hürde f. v einpferchen.
penal ['piːnl] adj Straf-. **penalize** v bestrafen. **penalty** n (gesetzliche) Strafe f. **penalty kick** Elfmeterstoß m.
penance ['penəns] n Buße f.
pencil ['pensl] n Bleistift m. v **pencil in** (a date) vorläufig festsetzen. **pencil-sharpener** n Bleistiftspitzer m.
pendant ['pendənt] n Anhänger m.
pending ['pendiŋ] adj (noch) unentschieden. prep bis.
pendulum ['pendjuləm] n Pendel neut.
penetrate ['penitreit] v durchdringen, eindringen (in). **penetrating** adj durchdringend. **penetration** n Durchdringen neut.
penguin ['peŋgwin] n Pinguin m.
penicillin [peni'silin] n Penizillin neut.
peninsula [pə'ninsjulə] n Halbinsel f. **peninsular** adj Halbinsel-.
penis ['piːnis] n Penis m.
penitent ['penitənt] adj bußfertig. n Büßer(in). **penitence** n Buße f.
penknife ['nennaif] n Taschenmesser neut.
pen-name n Pseudonym neut.
pennant ['penənt] n Wimpel m.
penny ['peni] n Penny m, Pfennig m. **penniless** adj mittellos.
pension ['penʃən] n Rente f. **pensioner** n Rentner(in).
pensive ['pensiv] adj gedankenvoll.
pent [pent] adj **pent up** (feelings) angestaut, zurückgehalten.
pentagon ['pentəgən] n Fünfeck neut.

Pentagon (US) Pentagon neut. **pentagonal** adj fünfeckig.
penthouse ['penthaus] n Dachwohnung f.
penultimate [pi'nʌltimit] adj vorletzt.
people ['piːpl] pl n Leute pl, Menschen pl; sing (nation) Volk neut.
pepper ['pepə] n Pfeffer m. **peppercorn** n Pfefferkorn neut. **peppermint** n Pfefferminze f. **peppery** adj pfefferig, scharf.
per [pə] prep pro. **per capita** pro Kopf.
perceive [pə'siːv] v wahrnehmen; (understand) begreifen. **perceptible** adj spürbar. **perception** n Wahrnehmung f. **perceptive** adj (person) scharfsinnig.
per cent adv, n Prozent neut. **sixty per cent** sechzig Prozent. **percentage** n Prozentsatz m.
perch [pəːtʃ] n Sitzstange f; (fish) Barsch m. v sitzen.
percolate ['pəːkəleit] v durchsickern. **percolator** n Kaffeemaschine f.
percussion [pə'kʌʃən] n (music) Schlaginstrumente pl.
perennial [pə'reniəl] adj beständig; (plant) perennierend. n perennierende Pflanze f.
perfect ['pəːfikt; v pə'fekt] adj vollkommen, vollendet, perfekt. v vervollkommnen. **perfection** n Vollkommenheit f. **perfectionist** n Perfektionist(in). **perfectly** adv (coll) ganz, völlig.
perforate ['pəːfəreit] v perforieren. **perforation** n Perforation f.
perform [pə'fɔːm] v machen, ausführen; (music, play) aufführen, spielen. n (work, output) Leistung f; (music, theatre) Aufführung f. **performer** n Artist(in).
perfume ['pəːfjuːm] n (fragrance) Duft m; (woman's) Parfüm neut. v parfümieren.
perhaps [pə'haps] adv vielleicht.
peril ['peril] n Gefahr f. **perilous** adj gefährlich.
perimeter [pə'rimitə] n Umkreis ; (outer area) Peripherie f.
period ['piəriəd] n Periode f, Frist f; (lesson) Stunde f; (menstrual) Regel f, Periode f; (full stop) Punkt m. **periodic** adj periodisch. **periodical** n Zeitschrift f. **periodically** adv periodisch, von Zeit zu Zeit.
peripheral [pə'rifərəl] adj peripherisch, Rand-. **periphery** n Peripherie f.
periscope ['periskoup] n Periskop neut.
perish ['periʃ] v umkommen, sterben;

(*materials*) verwelken. **perishable** *adj* leicht verderblich.

perjure ['pɔːdʒə] *v* **perjure oneself** meineidig werden. **perjurer** *n* Meineidige(r). **perjury** *n* Meineid *m*.

perk¹ [pɔːk] *v* **perk up** munter werden. **perky** *adj* munter.

perk² [pɔːk] *n* (*coll: of job*) Vorteil *m*, Vergünstigung *f*.

perm [pɔːm] *n* Dauerwelle *f*.

permanent ['pɔːmənənt] *adj* dauernd, ständig, permanent. **permanence** *n* Permanenz *f*, Ständigkeit *f*.

permeate ['pɔːmieit] *v* durchdringen. **permeable** *adj* durchlässig.

permit [pə'mit; *n* 'pɔːmit] *v* erlauben, gestatten; (*officially*) zulassen, genehmigen. *n* Genehmigung *f*; (*certificate*) Zulassungsschein *m*. **permissible** *adj* zulässig. **permission** *n* Erlaubnis *f*, Genehmigung *f*. **permissive** *adj* freizügig.

permutation [pɔːmju'teiʃən] *n* Permutation *f*.

pernicious [pə'niʃəs] *adj* bösartig.

perpendicular [pɔːpen'dikjulə] *adj* senkrecht. *n* Senkrechte *f*.

perpetrate ['pɔːpitreit] *v* begehen. **perpetration** *n* Begehung *f*. **perpetrator** *n* Täter *m*.

perpetual [pə'petʃuəl] *adj* beständig, ewig. **perpetuate** [pə'petʃueit] *v* verewigen, fortsetzen.

perplex [pə'pleks] *v* verwirren, verblüffen. **perplexed** *adj* perplex, verwirrt.

persecute ['pɔːsikjuːt] *v* verfolgen. **persecution** *n* Verfolgung *f*. **persecutor** *n* Verfolger(in).

persevere [pɔːsi'viə] *v* beharren, nicht aufgeben. **perseverance** *n* Beharrlichkeit *f*. **persevering** *adj* beharrlich.

persist [pə'sist] *v* (*person*) beharren (bei); (*thing*) fortdauern. **persistence** *n* Beharren *neut*, Hartnäckigkeit *f*. **persistent** *adj* (*person*) hartnäckig; (*questions, etc.*) anhaltend.

person ['pɔːsn] *n* Person *f*. **personal** *adj* persönlich. **personal matter** Privatsache *f*. **personality** *n* Personalität *f*; (*personage*) Persönlichkeit *f*.

personnel [pɔːsə'nel] *n* Personal *neut*, Belegschaft *f*. **personnel department** Personalabteilung *f*. **personnel manager** Personalchef *m*.

perspective [pə'spektiv] *n* Perspektive *f*.

perspire [pə'spaiə] *v* schwitzen, transpirieren. **perspiration** *n* Schweiß *m*.

persuade [pə'sweid] *v* überreden; (*convince*) überzeugen. **persuasion** *n* Überredung *f*; Überzeugung *f*. **persuasive** *adj* überredend; überzeugend.

pert [pɔːt] *adj* keck.

pertain [pə'tein] *v* betreffen. **pertaining to** betreffend. **pertinacious** *adj* hartnäckig. **pertinent** *adj* angemessen.

perturb [pə'tɔːb] *v* beunruhigen.

peruse [pə'ruːz] *v* durchlesen.

pervade [pə'veid] *v* erfüllen, durchdringen. **pervasive** *adj* durchdringend.

perverse [pə'vɔːs] *adj* pervers, widernatürlich. **perversion** *n* Perversion *f*, Verdrehung *f*. **perversion of justice** Rechtsbeugung *f*. **pervert** *v* verdrehen. *n* perverser Mensch *m*.

pest [pest] *n* Schädling *m*; (*coll: person*) lästiger Mensch *m*. **pesticide** *n* Pestizid *neut*.

pester ['pestə] *v* quälen, plagen.

pet [pet] *n* Haustier *neut*; (*darling*) Schätzchen *neut*. *adj* Lieblings-. *v* liebkosen. **pet name** Kosename *m*.

petal ['petl] *n* Blumenblatt *neut*.

petition [pə'tiʃən] *n* Bittschrift *f*.

petrify ['petrifai] *v* versteinen. **petrified** *adj* (*coll*) starr, bestürzt.

petrol ['petrəl] *n* Benzin *neut*. **petrol station** Tankstelle *f*. **petroleum** *n* Erdöl *neut*.

petticoat ['petikout] *n* Unterrock *m*.

petty ['peti] *adj* (*unimportant*) unbedeutend; (*mean*) kleinlich. **petty cash** Kleinkasse *f*.

petulant ['petjulənt] *adj* verdrießlich.

pew [pjuː] *n* Kirchensitz *m*.

pewter ['pjuːtə] *n* Hartzinn *neut*.

phantom ['fantəm] *n* Phantom *neut*, Gespenst *neut*. *adj* Schein-.

pharmacy ['fɑːməsi] *n* Apotheke *f*. **pharmacist** *n* Apotheker(in).

pharynx ['fariŋks] *n* Schlundkopf *m*.

phase [feiz] *n* (*tech*) Phase *f*; (*stage*) Stadium *neut*, Etappe *f*.

pheasant ['feznt] *n* Fasan *m*.

phenomenon [fə'nɔmənən] *n* (*pl* -a) Phänomen *neut*. **phenomenal** *adj* phänomenal.

phial ['faiəl] *n* Ampulle *f*.

philanthropy [fi'lanθrəpi] *n* Philanthropie *f*. **philanthropic** *adj* philanthropisch, menschenfreundlich. **philanthropist** *n* Philanthrop, Menschenfreund *m*.

philately [fi'lætəli] *n* Briefmarkensammeln *neut.* **philatelist** *n* Briefmarkensammler(in).

philosophy [fi'losəfi] *n* Philosophie *f.* **philosopher** *n* Philosoph *m.* **philosophical** *adj* philosophisch.

phlegm [flem] *n* Schleim *m,* Phlegma *neut.* **phlegmatic** *adj* phlegmatisch.

phobia ['foubiə] *n* Phobie *f.*

phone [foun] *n* (*coll*) Fernsprecher *m.* *v* anrufen. **phone booth** *or* **box** Telefonzelle *f.*

phonetic [fə'netik] *adj* phonetisch. **phonetics** *n* Phonetik *f.*

phoney ['founi] *adj* (*coll*) falsch, fingiert. *n* Schwindler *m.*

phosphate ['fosfeit] *n* Phosphat *neut.*

phosphorescence [fosfə'resəns] *n* Phosphoreszenz *f.* **phosphorescent** *adj* phosphoreszierend.

phosphorus ['fosfərəs] *n* Phosphor *m.*

photo ['foutou] *n* Foto *neut.*

photocopy ['foutou,kopi] *n* Fotokopie *f.* *v* fotokopieren.

photogenic [,foutou'dʒenik] *adj* fotogen.

photograph ['foutəgrɑːf] *n* Lichtbild *neut,* Foto *neut.* *v* aufnehmen, fotografieren. **photographer** *n* Fotograf *m.* **photographic** *adj* fotografisch. **photography** *n* Fotografie *f.*

phrase [freiz] *n* (*expression*) Ausdruck *m,* Redewendung *f*; (*music*) Phrase *f.* *v* fassen.

physical ['fizikəl] *adj* physisch, körperlich. **physical education** Leibeserziehung *f.*

physician [fi'ziʃən] *n* Arzt *m,* Ärztin *f.*

physics ['fiziks] *n* Physik *f.* **physicist** *n* Physiker *m.*

physiology [,fizi'olədʒi] *n* Physiologie *f.* **physiological** *adj* physiologisch.

physiotherapy [,fiziou'θerəpi] *n* Physiotherapie *f.*

physique [fi'ziːk] *n* Körperbau *m.*

piano [pi'ænou] *n* Klavier *neut.* **pianist** *n* Klavierspieler(in).

pick¹ [pik] *v* (*choose*) auswählen, (*fruit*) pflücken; (*lock*) knacken. **pick of the bunch** (*coll*) das Beste (von allen).

pick² [pik] *or* **pickaxe** *n* Spitzhacke *f.*

picket ['pikit] *n* Pfahl *m*; (*strike*) Streikposten *m.* *v* (*factory, etc.*) Streikposten aufstellen vor.

pickle ['pikl] *n* Pökel *m.* *v* einpökeln. **pickled** *adj* gepökelt; (*coll: drunk*) blau. **pickles** *pl* Eingepökeltes *neut sing.*

picnic ['piknik] *n* Picknick *neut.*

pictorial [pik'tɔːriəl] *adj* Bilder-.

picture ['piktʃə] *n* Bild *neut*; (*painting*) Gemälde *neut*; (*film*) Film *m.* *v* (*imagine*) sich vorstellen. **pictures** *pl* Kino *neut sing.* **picture book** Bilderbuch *neut.* **picture postcard** Ansichtskarte *f.*

picturesque [piktʃə'resk] *adj* pittoresk.

pidgin ['pidʒən] *n* Mischsprache *f.*

pie [pai] *n* (*meat*) Pastete *f*; (*fruit*) Torte *f.*

piece [piːs] *n* Stück *neut*; (*part*) Teil *m*; (*paper*) Blatt *neut.* **piece of advice** Ratschlag *m.* **fall to pieces** in Stücke gehen, zerfallen. **go to pieces** zusammenbrechen. *v* **piece together** zusammenstellen. **piecemeal** *adv* stückweise. **piecework** *n* Akkordarbeit *f.*

pier [piə] *n* Pier *m,* Kai *m.*

pierce [piəs] *v* durchbohren, durchstechen. **piercing** *adj* durchdringend.

piety ['paiəti] *n* Frömmigkeit *f.*

pig [pig] *n* Schwein *m.* **pigheaded** *adj* störrisch. **piglet** *n* Schweinchen *neut.* **pigskin** *n* Schweinsleder *neut.* **pigsty** *n* Schweinestall *m.* **pigtail** *n* Zopf *m.*

pigment ['pigmənt] *n* Pigment *neut,* Farbstoff *m.* **pigmentation** *n* Pigmentation *f.*

pike [paik] *n* (*fish*) Hecht *m*; (*weapon*) Pike *f,* Spieß *m.*

pilchard ['piltʃəd] *n* Sardine *f.*

pile¹ [pail] *n* (*heap*) Haufen *m,* Stapel *m.* *v* (an)häufen, stapeln. **pile-up** *n* (*mot*) (Massen)Karambolage *f.*

pile² [pail] *n* (*post*) Pfahl *m,* Joch *neut.*

pile³ [pail] *n* (*of carpet*) Flor *m.*

piles [pailz] *pl n* Hämorrhoiden *pl.*

pilfer ['pilfə] *v* klauen. **pilferage** *n* Dieberei *f.*

pilgrim ['pilgrim] *n* Pilger(in). **pilgrimage** *n* Pilgerfahrt *f,* Wallfahrt *f.*

pill [pil] *n* Pille *f,* Tablette *f.* **the pill** (*contraceptive*) die Pille.

pillage ['pilidʒ] *v* (aus)plündern. *n* Plünderung *f.*

pillar ['pilə] *n* Pfeiler *m,* Säule *f.* **pillarbox** *n* Briefkasten *m.*

pillion ['piljən] *n* Soziussitz *m.* **ride pillion** auf dem Sozius fahren.

pillow ['pilou] *n* Kopfkissen *neut.* **pillow case** *n* Kissenbezug *m.*

pilot ['pailət] *n* Pilot *m.* *v* steuern, lenken. **pilot light** Zündflamme *f.*

pimento [pi'mentou] n Piment m or neut.

pimp [pimp] n Zuhälter m.

pimple ['pimpl] n Pustel f, Pickel m. **pimply** adj pickelig.

pin [pin] n Stecknadel f. v befestigen. **pin down** festnageln. **pincushion** n Nadelkissen neut.

pinafore ['pinəfɔ:] n Schürze f. **pinafore dress** Kleiderrock m.

pincers ['pinsəz] pl n Zange f sing; (crab's) Krebsschere f sing.

pinch [pintʃ] v zwicken, kneifen; (coll) klauen. n Kneifen neut, Zwicken neut; (salt, etc.) Prise f.

pine[1] [pain] n Kiefer f, Pinie f. **pine cone** n Kiefernzapfen m.

pine[2] [pain] v sich sehnen (nach). **pine away** verschmachten.

pineapple ['painapl] n Ananas f.

ping-pong ['piŋpoŋ] n (coll) Tischtennis neut.

pinion ['pinjən] n (tech) Ritzel m. v fesseln.

pink [piŋk] adj rosa, blaßrot. n (flower) Nelke f. v (mot) klopfen. **in the pink** kerngesund.

pinnacle ['pinəkl] n Spitzturm m; (fig) Gipfel m.

pinpoint ['pinpoint] v ins Auge fassen, hervorheben.

pint [paint] n Pinte f.

pioneer [,paiə'niə] n Pionier m, Bahnbrecher m. v den Weg bahnen für. **pioneering** adj bahnbrechend.

pious ['paiəs] adj fromm.

pip[1] [pip] n (fruit) (Obst)Kern m.

pip[2] [pip] n (sound) Ton m; (mil) Stern m; (on card) Auge neut; (on dice) Punkt m.

pipe [paip] n Rohr neut, Röhre f; (tobacco, music) Pfeife f; (sound) Pfeifen neut. v (liquid) durch Röhren leiten; (play pipes, etc.) pfeifen; (cookery) spritzen. **pipedream** n Luftschloß neut. **pipeline** n Rohrleitung f.

piquant ['pi:kənt] adj pikant.

pique [pi:k] n Groll m.

pirate ['paiərət] n Seeräuber m. **piracy** n Seeräuberei f.

pirouette [piru'et] n Pirouette f. v pirouettieren.

Pisces ['paisi:z] n Fische pl.

piss [pis] v (vulgar) pissen. n Pisse f.

pistachio [pi'sta:ʃiou] n Pistazie f.

pistol ['pistl] n Pistole f.

piston ['pistən] n Kolben m.

pit [pit] n Grube f; (mining) Zeche f, Bergwerk neut. **pitted** adj vernarbt; (corroded) zerfressen.

pitch[1] [pitʃ] v werfen; (tent) aufschlagen. n Wurf m; (sport) Feld neut; (music) Tonhöhe f; (level) Grad m. **pitcher** n Werfer m; (jug) Krug m. **pitchfork** n Mistgabel f.

pitch[2] [pitʃ] n (tar) Pech neut.

pitfall ['pitfɔ:l] n Fallgrube f, Falle f.

pith [piθ] n Mark neut. **pithy** adj markig.

pittance ['pitəns] n Hungerlohn m.

pituitary [pi'tju:titəri] n Hirnanhangdrüse f, Hypophyse f.

pity ['piti] n Mitleid neut. v bemitleiden. **it's a pity** es ist schade, es ist ein Jammer m.

pivot ['pivət] n Drehpunkt m. v sich drehen.

placard ['plaka:d] n Plakat neut.

placate [plə'keit] v beschwichtigen.

place [pleis] n Platz m; (town, locality) Ort m; (spot) Stelle f. **go places** (coll) es weit bringen. **out-of-place** adj (remark) unangebracht. **placename** n Ortsname m. **place of interest** Sehenswürdigkeit f. **take place** stattfinden. v stellen, legen, setzen; (identify) identifizieren, erkennen.

placenta [plə'sentə] n Plazenta f.

placid ['plasid] adj ruhig, gelassen.

plagiarize ['pleidʒəraiz] v plagiieren. **plagiarism** n Plagiat m.

plague [pleig] n Seuche f, Pest f. v plagen, quälen.

plaice [pleis] n Scholle f.

plain [plein] adj einfach, schlicht; (obvious) klar; (not pretty) unansehnlich. adv einfach. n Ebene f. **plainly** adv offensichtlich. **speak plainly** offen reden.

plaintiff ['pleintif] n Kläger(in).

plaintive ['pleintiv] adj traurig, wehmütig.

plait [plat] n Zopf m, Flechte f. v flechten.

plan [plan] n Plan m; (drawing) Entwurf m, Zeichnung f. v planen; (intend) vorhaben. **according to plan** planmäßig.

plane[1] [plein] adj flach, eben. n Ebene f; (aeroplane) Flugzeug neut.

plane[2] [plein] n (tool) Hobel m. v (ab)hobeln.

planet ['planit] n Planet m.

plank [plaŋk] n Planke f, Diele f.

plankton ['plaŋktən] n Plankton neut.

planning ['planiŋ] *n* Planung *f.*
plant [plɑːnt] *n* Pflanze *f*; (*factory*) Betrieb *m*, Fabrik *f.* *v* pflanzen. **plantation** *n* Pflanzung *f.*
plaque [plɑːk] *n* Gedenktafel *f.*
plasma ['plazmə] *n* Plasma *neut.*
plaster ['plɑːstə] *n* (*med*) Pflaster *neut*; (*of Paris*) Gips *m.* *v* bepflastern. **adhesive plaster** Heftpflaster *neut.* **plaster cast** Gipsabdruck *m*; (*med*) Gipsverband *m.*
plastic ['plastik] *n* Kunststoff *m.* *adj* Kunststoff-.
plate [pleit] *n* (*for food*) Teller *m*; (*tech*) Platte *f*, Scheibe *f.* *v* (*metal*) plattieren. **gold-plated** *adj* vergoldet.
plateau ['platou] *n* Hochebene *f*, Plateau *neut.*
platform ['platfɔːm] *n* (*rail*) Bahnsteig *m*; (*speaker's*) Tribüne *f*; (*fig: pol*) Parteiprogramm *neut.*
platinum ['platinəm] *n* Platin *neut.*
platonic [plə'tonik] *adj* platonisch.
platoon [plə'tuːn] *n* (*mil*) Zug *m.*
plausible ['plɔːzəbl] *adj* glaubhaft.
play [plei] *n* Spiel *neut*; (*theatre*) Schauspiel *neut*, Stück *neut*; (*tech*) Spielraum *m.* *v* spielen. **play safe** kein Risiko eingehen. **playboy** *n* Playboy *m.* **player** *n* Spieler(in); (*actor*) Schauspieler(in). **playful** *adj* scherzhaft. **playground** *n* Spielplatz *m*; (*school*) Schulhof *m.* **playing card** Spielkarte *f.* **playing field** Sportplatz *m.* **playmate** *n* Spielkamerad(in). **plaything** *n* Spielzeug *neut.* **playwright** *n* Dramatiker *m.*
plea [pliː] *n* dringende Bitte *f*; (*law*) Plädoyer *neut.*
plead [pliːd] *v* (*law*) plädieren. **plead for** flehen um.
please [pliːz] *v* gefallen (+ *dat*), Freude machen (+ *dat*). *adv* bitte! **pleasant** *adj* angenehm; (*person*) freundlich, nett. **pleased** *adj* zufrieden. **pleasing** *adj* angenehm. **pleasurable** *adj* vergnüglich. **pleasure** *n* Vernügen *neut.*
pleat [pliːt] *n* Falte *f.* *v* in Falten legen.
plebiscite ['plebisait] *n* Volksabstimmung *f*, Plebiszit *neut.*
pledge [pledʒ] *n* Pfand *neut*; (*promise*) Versprechen *neut.* *v* versprechen.
plenty ['plenti] *n* Fülle *f*, Reichtum *m.* **plenty of** eine Menge, viel.
pleurisy ['pluərisi] *n* Rippenfellentzündung *f.*

pliable ['plaiəbl] *adj* biegsam. **pliability** *n* Biegsamkeit *f.*
pliers ['plaiəz] *pl n* Zange *f sing.*
plight [plait] *n* Notlage *f.*
plimsoll ['plimsəl] *n* Turnschuh *m.*
plod [plod] *v* sich hinschleppen, schwerfällig gehen.
plonk[1] [ploŋk] *v* **plonk down** hinschmeißen.
plonk[2] [ploŋk] *n* (*coll*) billiger Wein.
plot[1] [plot] *n* Komplott *neut*; (*in novel*) Handlung *f.* *v* sich verschwören; (*on map*) einzeichnen. **plotter** *n* Verschwörer(in).
plot[2] [plot] *n* (*land*) Parzelle *f*, Grundstück *neut.*
plough [plau] *n* Pflug *m*; (*astron*) Großer Bär *m.* *v* (um)pflügen. **ploughman** *n* Pflüger *m.*
pluck [plʌk] *v* pflücken; (*poultry*) rupfen; (*music*) zupfen. *n* (*courage*) Mut *m.* **plucky** *adj* mutig. **pluck up courage** Mut fassen.
plug [plʌg] *n* (*elec*) Stecker *m*; (*stopper*) Stöpsel *m.* *v* verstopfen; (*coll*) befürworten. **plug in** anschließen, einstecken.
plum [plʌm] *n* Pflaume *f*, Zwetschge *f.*
plumage ['pluːmidʒ] *n* Gefieder *neut.*
plumb [plʌm] *n* Senkblei *neut.* *adj* senkrecht. *v* (*sound*) sondieren. **plumber** *n* Klempner *m.* **plumbing** *n* Klempnerarbeit *f*; (*pipes*) Rohrleitungen *pl f.*
plume [pluːm] *n* Feder *f*; (*of smoke*) Streifen *m.*
plummet ['plʌmit] *v* abstürzen.
plump[1] [plʌmp] *adj* (*fat*) rundlich, mollig. **plumpness** *n* Rundlichkeit *f.*
plump[2] [plʌmp] *v* (*fall*) plumpsen. **plump for** sich entscheiden für.
plunder ['plʌndə] *v* plündern. *n* (*spoils*) Beute *f.*
plunge [plʌndʒ] *v* tauchen; (*fall*) stürzen. *n* Sturz *m.*
pluperfect [pluː'pəfikt] *n* (*gramm*) Vorvergangenheit *f.*
plural ['pluərəl] *adj* Plural-. *n* Plural *m*, Mehrzahl *f.*
plus [plʌs] *prep* plus. *adj* Plus-. *n* Plus *neut.*
plush [plʌʃ] *adj* (*fig*) luzuriös.
Pluto ['pluːtou] *n* Pluto *m.*
ply[1] [plai] *v* (*trade*) ausüben; (*travel*) verkehren.

ply² [plai] *n (of yarn)* Strähne *f.* **plywood** *n* Sperrholz *neut.*

pneumatic [nju'matik] *adj* pneumatisch. **pneumatic tyre** *n* Luftreifen *m.* **pneumatic drill** Preßluftbohrer *m.*

pneumonia [nju'mouniə] *n* Lungenentzündung *f.*

poach¹ [poutʃ] *v (cookery)* pochieren. **poached egg** verlorenes Ei *neut.*

poach² [poutʃ] *v* wildern. **poacher** *n* Wilddieb *m.*

pocket ['pokit] *n* Tasche *f. adj* Taschen-. *v* in die Tasche stecken, einstecken. **to be in pocket** gut bei Kasse sein. **pocketknife** *n* Taschenmesser *neut.* **pocket-money** Taschengeld *neut.*

pod [pod] *n* Schote *f.*

podgy ['podʒi] *adj (coll)* mollig, dick.

poem ['pouim] *n* Gedicht *neut.* **poet** *n* Dichter *m.* **poetess** *n* Dichterin *f.* **poetic** *adj* poetisch, dichterisch. **poetry** *n* Dichtkunst *f; (poems)* Gedichte *f.*

poignant ['poinjənt] *adj* schmerzlich; *(wit)* scharf; *(grief)* bitter.

point [point] *n (tip)* Spitze *f; (place, spot)* Punkt *m; (in time)* Zeitpunkt *m; (main thing)* Hauptsache *f.* **be on the point of doing** eben tun wollen. **point of view** Standpunkt *m.* **points** *pl n (rail)* Weichen *pl.* **that's the point!** das is es ja! **there's no point in** es hat keinen Zweck, zu. *v* spitzen; *(indicate)* (mit dem Finger) zeigen. **point out** hinweisen auf. **pointed** *adj* zugespitzt; *(remark)* treffend, beißend. **pointless** *adj* sinnlos.

poise [poiz] *n* Haltung *f; (calmness)* Gelassenheit *f.*

poison ['poizən] *n* Gift *neut. v* vergiften. **poisoner** *n* Giftmörder(in). **poisonous** *adj* giftig.

poke [pouk] *n* Stoß *m,* Puff *m. v* stoßen; *(fire)* schüren.

poker¹ ['poukə] *n (for fire)* Feuerhaken *m.*

poker² ['poukə] *n (gambling)* Poker(spiel) *neut.*

Poland ['poulənd] *n* Polen *neut.* **Pole** *n* Pole *m,* Polin *f.* **Polish** *adj* polnisch.

polar ['poulə] *adj* polar. **polar bear** Eisbär *m.*

pole¹ [poul] *n (geog)* Pol *m.* **pole star** *n* Polarstern *m.*

pole² [poul] *n* Pfosten *m,* Pfahl *m; (telegraph, etc.)* Stange *f.* **pole-vault** *n* Stabhochsprung *m.*

police [pə'liːs] *n* Polizei *f. n* (polizeilich) überwachen. *adj* polizeilich, Polizei-. **police force** Polizei *f.* **policeman** *n* Polizist *m,* Schutzmann *m.* **police station** Polizeiwache *f,* Polizeirevier *neut.*

policy¹ ['poləsi] *n* Politik *f; (personal)* Methode *f.*

policy² ['poləsi] *n (insurance)* Police *f.*

polio ['pouliou] *n* Kinderlähmung *f.*

polish ['poliʃ] *n* Politur *f; (floors, furniture)* Bohnerwachs *neut; (shoes)* Schuhcreme *f. v* polieren; *(furniture)* bohnern; *(shoes)* wichsen. **polished** *adj* poliert; *(fig)* fein, elegant. **polisher** *n* Polierer *m.*

polite [pə'lait] *adj* höflich. **politeness** *n* Höflichkeit *f.*

politics ['politiks] *n* Politik *f.* **political** *adj* politisch. **politician** *n* Politiker *m.*

polka ['polkə] *n* Polka *f.*

poll [poul] *n (voting)* Abstimmung *f; (opinion poll)* Meinungsumfrage *f.*

pollen ['polən] *n* Pollen *m,* Blütenstaub *m.* **pollinate** *v* befruchten.

pollute [pə'luːt] *v* verschmutzen, verunreinigen. **pollution** *n (environmental)* Umweltverschmutzung *f.*

polo ['poulou] *n* Polo *neut.* **polo-neck** *n* Rollkragen *m.*

polygamy [pə'ligəmi] *n* Polygamie *f.* **polygamous** *adj* polygam.

polygon ['poligən] *n* Polygon *neut.*

polytechnic [,poli'teknik] *n* Polytechnikum *neut.*

polythene ['poliθiːn] *n* Polyäthylen *neut. adj* **polythene bag** Plastiktüte *f.*

pomegranate ['pomigranit] *n* Granatapfel *m.*

pomp [pomp] *n* Prunk *m,* Pracht *f.* **pomposity** *n* Bombast *m.* **pompous** *adj* bombastisch.

pond [pond] *n* Teich *m.*

ponder ['pondə] *v* nachdenken (über). **ponderous** *adj* schwer; *(movement)* schwerfällig.

pony ['pouni] *n* Pony *neut,* Pferdchen *neut.* **pony-tail** Pferdeschwanz *m.*

poodle ['puːdl] *n* Pudel *m.*

poof [puːf] *n (derog)* Schwule(r) *m.*

pool¹ [puːl] *n (pond)* Teich *m; (blood, etc.)* Lache *f; (swimming)* (Schwimm)Bad *neut.*

pool² [puːl] *n (game)* Pool *m; (fund)* Kasse *f. v (resources)* vereinigen. **football pools** Fußballtoto *m.*

poor [puə] *adj* arm, bedürftig; (*earth*) dürr; (*bad*) schlecht. **the poor** die Armen *pl.* **poorly** *adj* (*coll*) krank, unwohl.
pop[1] [pop] *n* Knall *m*, Puff *m*; (*drink*) Limonade *f.* *v* knallen; (*burst*) platzen. **pop in** schnell vorbeikommen. **pop up** (*appear*) auftauchen.
pop[2] [pop] *adj* **pop music** Popmusik *f.* **pop song** Schlager *m.*
pope [poup] *n* Papst *m.*
poplar ['poplə] *n* Pappel *f.*
poppy ['popi] *n* Mohn *m.*
popular ['popjulə] *adj* populär; (*well-liked*) beliebt; (*of the people*) Volks-. **popularity** *n* Popularität *f.*
population [‚popju'leiʃən] *n* Bevölkerung *f.* **populate** *v* bevölkern. **populous** *adj* volkreich.
porcelain ['poslin] *n* Porzellan *neut. adj* Porzellan-.
porch [poɪtʃ] *n* Vorhalle *neut.*
porcupine ['poɪkjupain] *n* Stachelschwein *neut.*
pore[1] [poɪ] *n* Pore *f.*
pore[2] [poɪ] *v* **pore over** eifrig studieren, brüten über.
pork [poɪk] *n* Schweinefleisch *neut.* **pork butcher** Schweineschlächter *m.* **pork chop** Schweinskotelett *neut.* **roast pork** Schweinebraten *m.*
pornography [poɪ'nogrəfi] *n* Pornographie *f.* **pornographic** *adj* pornographisch; (*film, book*) Porno-.
porous ['poɪrəs] *adj* porös.
porpoise ['poɪpəs] *n* Tümmler *m.*
porridge ['poridʒ] *n* Haferflockenbrei *m.* **porridge oats** Haferflocken *pl.*
port[1] [poɪt] *n* (*harbour*) Hafen *m*; (*town*) Hafenstadt *f.*
port[2] [poɪt] *n* (*naut*) Backbord *neut. adj* Backbord-.
port[3] [poɪt] *n* (*wine*) Portwein *m.*
portly ['poɪtli] *adj* wohlbeleibt.
portable ['poɪtəbl] *adj* tragbar. **portable radio** Kofferradio *neut.*
portent ['poɪtent] *n* Omen *neut*, Vorzeichnung *f.* **portentous** *adj* ominös.
porter ['poɪtə] *n* (*rail, etc.*) Gepäckträger *m.*
portfolio [poɪt'fouliou] *n* Mappe *f*; (*pol*) Portefeuille *neut.* **minister without portfolio** Minister ohne Geschäftsbereich *m.*
porthole ['poɪthoul] *n* Luke *f.*
portion ['poɪʃən] *n* (*food*) Portion *f*; (*share*) (An)Teil *m.*

portrait ['poɪtrət] *n* Porträt *neut.* **portray** *v* malen; (*fig*) schildern. **portrayal** *n* Porträt *neut*, Schilderung *f.*
Portugal ['poɪtʃugəl] *n* Portugal *neut.* **Portuguese** *adj* portugiesisch; *n* Portugiese *m*, Portugiesin *f.*
pose [pouz] *n* Pose *f.* *v* sitzen, posieren; (*problem*) stellen. **pose as** sich ausgeben als. **poseur** *n* Poseur *m.*
posh [poʃ] *adj* vornehm.
position [pə'ziʃən] *n* Position *f*, Stellung *f*; (*situation*) Lage *f*; (*attitude*) Standpunkt *m*; (*standing*) Rang *m.* *v* stellen.
positive ['pozətiv] *adj* positiv.
possess [pə'zes] *v* besitzen. **possessed** *adj* besessen. **possession** *n* Besitz *m.* **take possession of** in Besitz nehmen. **possessive** *adj* (*person*) besitzgierig. **possessor** *n* Inhaber(in).
possible ['posəbl] *adj* möglich; (*imaginable*) eventuell. **possibility** *n* Möglichkeit *f.* **possibly** *adv* möglicherweise.
post[1] [poust] *n* (*pole*) Pfahl *m*, Pfosten *m.* **deaf as a post** stocktaub.
post[2] [poust] *n* (*mil*) Posten *m*; (*job*) Stelle *f.* *v* aufstellen.
post[3] [poust] *n* (*mail*) Post *f.* **by post** per Post. **postage stamp** Briefmarke *f.* **postcard** *n* Postkarte *f.* **postman** *n* Briefträger *m.* **post office** Postamt *neut.* *v* zur Post bringen; (*send*) (mit der Post) schicken. **keep someone posted** jemanden auf dem laufenden halten. **postage** *n* Porto *neut*, Postgebühr *f.* **postal** *adj* Post-.
poste restante [poust'testãt] *adv* postlagernd.
poster ['poustə] *n* Plakat *neut.*
posterior [po'stiəriə] *adj* später, hinter. *n* Hintern *m.*
posterity [po'sterəti] *n* Nachwelt *f.*
postgraduate [poust'gradjuit] *n* Doktorand(in).
post-haste *adv* schnellstens.
posthumous ['postjuməs] *adj* postum.
post-mortem [poust'moɪtəm] *n* Autopsie *f.*
post-natal [pous'neitl] *adj* postnatal.
postpone [pous'poun] *v* verschieben. **postponement** *n* Verschiebung *f.*
postscript ['pousskript] *n* Postskriptum *neut.*
postulate ['postjuleit] *v* voraussetzen, annehmen,

posture ['postʃə] n (Körper)Haltung f.
post-war adj Nachkriegs-.
pot [pot] n Topf m; (tea, coffee) Kanne f.
v (coll) schießen. **go to pot** vor die
Hunde gehen. **pot-bellied** adj
dickbäuchig.
potassium [pə'tasjəm] n Kalium neut.
potato [pə'teitou] n Kartoffel f. **boiled
potatoes** Salzkartoffeln pl. **chipped** or
french-fried potatoes Pommes frites pl.
roast or **fried potatoes** Bratkartoffeln pl.
potent ['poutənt] adj stark; (sexually)
potent. **potency** n Stärke f; Potenz f.
potential [pə'tenʃəl] adj möglich, potential. n Potential neut.
pothole ['pothoul] n Höhle f.
potion ['pouʃən] n Arzneitrank m. **love
potion** Liebestrank m.
potluck [pot'lʌk] n **take potluck with** (coll)
probieren, es riskieren mit/bei.
potted ['potid] adj (meat) eingemacht;
(plant) Topf-; (version) gekürzt.
potter ['potə] v **potter around**
herumhantieren, herumbasteln.
pottery ['potəri] n Töpferwaren pl, Steingut neut.
potty ['poti] n Töpfchen neut.
pouch [pautʃ] n Beutel m.
poultice ['poultis] n Breiumschlag m.
poultry ['poultri] n Geflügel neut.
pounce [pauns] v springen, sich stürzen.
n Sprung m, Satz m.
pound¹ [paund] v zerstampfen; (hit) hämmern, klopfen.
pound² [paund] n (currency, weight)
Pfund neut.
pour [poɪ] v gießen. **pour out** (a liquid)
ausgießen; (drink) einschenken; (come
out) herausströmen.
pout [paut] v schmollen, maulen.
poverty ['povəti] n Armut f. **poverty-
stricken** adj verarmt.
powder ['paudə] n Pulver neut; (face)
Puder m. v (face) pudern. **powder room**
Damentoilette f. **powdery** adj pulverig.
power ['pauə] n Macht f; (tech) Kraft f;
(elec) Strom m. v betreiben, antreiben.
great power (pol) Großmacht f. **powerful**
adj mächtig. **powerless** adj machtlos.
power station Kraftwerk neut.
practicable ['praktikəbl] adj
durchführbar.
practical ['praktikəl] adj praktisch.
practice ['praktis] n Praxis f; (exercise)

Übung f; (custom) Brauch m; (procedure)
Verfahren neut. v see **practise**.
practise ['praktis] v üben; (profession)
ausüben; (med, law) praktizieren. **practised** adj geübt.
practitioner [prak'tiʃənə] n Praktiker m.
medical practitioner praktischer Arzt m.
pragmatic [prag'matik] adj pragmatisch.
pragmatism n Pragmatismus m. **pragmatist** n Pragmatiker m.
Prague [praɪg] n Prag neut.
prairie ['preəri] n Prärie f.
praise [preiz] v loben. v Lob neut. **praise-
worthy** adj lobenswert.
pram [pram] n Kinderwagen m.
prance [prains] v tänzeln.
prank [praŋk] n Streich m, Possen m.
prattle ['pratl] v plappern, schwatzen. n
Geplapper neut, Geschwätz neut.
prawn [proɪn] n Garnele f.
pray [prei] v beten; (ask) bitten. **prayer** n
Gebet neut. **prayerbook** Gebetbuch neut.
preach [priitʃ] v predigen. **preacher** n
Prediger(in). **preaching** n Lehre f.
precarious [pri'keəriəs] adj unsicher,
gefährlich.
precaution [pri'koɪʃən] n Vorkehrung f.
precautionary adj vorbeugend.
precede [pri'siid] v vorhergehen. **precedence** n Vorrang m. **precedent** n
Präzedenzfall m. **order of precedence**
Rangordnung f. **preceding** adj
vorhergehend.
precinct ['priisiŋkt] n Bezirk m. **precincts**
pl Umgebung f.
precious ['preʃəs] adj kostbar, wertvoll;
(jewels) edel. adv (coll) äußerst.
precipice ['presipis] n Abgrund m.
precipitate [pri'sipiteit] v (bring about)
herbeiführen; (chem) fällen. **precipitation**
n (haste) Hast f; (chem) Fällung f; (rain,
etc.) Niederschlag m.
précis ['preisi] n Zusammenfassung f. v
zusammenfassen.
precise [pri'sais] adj präzis, genau. **precisely** adv genau. **precision** n Genauigkeit
f; (tech) Präzision f.
preclude [pri'kluɪd] v ausschließen; (prevent) vorbeugen.
precocious [pri'kouʃəs] adj frühreif. **pre-
cociousness** n Frühreife f.
preconceive [,priːkən'siːv] v vorher ausdenken. **preconception** n Vorurteil neut.
precondition [,priːkən'diʃən] n Voraussetzung f.

precursor [ˌpriː'kɔːsə] *n* Vorläufer(in). **precursory** *adj* vorausgehend.

predatory ['predətəri] *adj* räuberisch. **predator** *n* Raubtier *neut*.

predecessor ['priːdisesə] *n* Vorgänger(in). **predestine** [pri'destin] *v* prädestinieren. **predestination** *n* Vorbestimmung *f*, Prädestination *f*.

predicament [pri'dikəmənt] *n* schwierige Lage *f*.

predicate ['predikət] *n* (*gramm*) Prädikat *neut*. *v* aussagen.

predict [pri'dikt] *v* voraussagen. **predictable** *adj* voraussagbar. **prediction** *n* Voraussage *f*.

predominate [pri'domineit] *v* vorwiegen. **predominance** *n* Vorherrschaft *f*. **predominant** *adj* vorwiegend.

pre-eminent [priː'eminənt] *adj* hervorragend. **pre-eminence** *n* Überlegenheit *f*.

preen [priːn] *v* (sich) putzen.

prefabricate [priː'fabrikeit] *v* vorfabrizieren. **prefabricated** *adj* Fertig-.

preface ['prefis] *n* Vorwort *neut*. *v* einleiten.

prefect ['priːfekt] *n* (*pol*) Präfekt *m*; (*school*) Aufsichtsschüler(in).

prefer [pri'fɔː] *v* vorziehen, lieber haben. **preferable** *adj* vorzuziehen. **preferably** *adv* am besten. **preference** *n* Vorzug *m*. **preferential** *adj* bevorzugt.

prefix ['priːfiks] *n* Präfix *neut*, Vorsilbe *f*.

pregnant ['pregnənt] *adj* schwanger; (*animals*) trächtig; (*fig*) bedeutend, vielsagend. **pregnancy** *n* Schwangerschaft *f*.

prehistoric [ˌpriːhis'torik] *adj* vorgeschichtlich. **prehistory** *n* Vorgeschichte *f*.

prejudice ['predʒədis] *n* Vorurteil *neut*. *v* beeinträchtigen; (*person*) beeinflussen. **prejudiced** *adj* voreingenommen. **prejudicial** *adj* nachteilig, schädlich.

preliminary [pri'liminəri] *adj* vorläufig, Vor-.

prelude ['preljuːd] *n* Vorspiel *neut*, Präludium *neut*.

premarital [priː'maritl] *adj* vorehelich.

premature [premə'tʃuə] *adj* frühzeitig. **premature birth** Frühgeburt *f*. **prematurity** *n* Frühzeitigkeit *f*.

premeditate [priː'mediteit] *v* vorher überlegen. **premeditated** *adj* (*crime*) vorsätzlich. **premeditation** *n* Vorbedacht *m*.

premier ['premiə] *adj* erst. *n* Premierminister *m*.

premiere ['premieə] *n* Erstaufführung *f*, Premiere *f*.

premise ['premis] *n* Voraussetzung *f*, Prämisse *f*.

premises ['premisis] *pl n* Gelände *neut sing*. **business premises** Büro *neut*, Geschäftsräume *pl*. **on the premises** im Hause.

premium ['priːmiəm] *n* Prämie *f*.

premonition [ˌpremə'niʃən] *n* Vorahnung *f*.

prenatal [priː'neitl] *adj* prenatal, vor der Geburt.

preoccupied [priː'okjupaid] *adj* vertieft (in).

prepare [pri'peə] *v* vorbereiten; (*food*) zubereiten; (*produce*) herstellen. **prepare for** sich vorbereiten auf. **preparation** *n* Vorbereitung *f*; (*med*) Präparat *neut*; (*homework*) Hausaufgaben *pl*. **preparatory** *adj* vorbereitend. **prepared** *adj* bereit.

preposition [ˌprepə'ziʃən] *n* Präposition *f*.

preposterous [pri'postərəs] *adj* absurd, lächerlich.

prerogative [pri'rogətiv] *n* Vorrecht *neut*.

prescribe [pri'skraib] *v* vorschreiben, anordnen; (*med*) verordnen. **prescription** *n* Verordnung *f*.

present[1] ['preznt] *adj* (*time*) gegenwärtig; (*people*) anwesend; (*things*) vorhanden. *n* Gegenwart *f*. **at the present time** im Moment, zur Zeit. **be present at** Beiwohnen (+ *dat*). **presently** *adv* gleich. **presence** *n* (*people*) Anwesenheit *f*, Beisein *neut*; (*things*) Vorhandensein *neut*. **presence of mind** Geistesgegenwart *f*.

present[2] ['preznt] *v* pri'zent] *n* Geschenk *neut*. *v* vorlegen; (*gift*) schenken; (*person*) vorstellen; (*play*) vorführen. **presentation** *n* Vorlegung *f*; Schenkung *f*; Übergabe *f*; Vorführung *f*.

preserve [pri'zɔːv] *v* bewahren; (*food*) einmachen. *n* Konserve *f*.

preside [pri'zaid] *v* den Vorsitz führen. **preside over** (*meeting*) leiten.

president ['prezidənt] *n* Präsident *m*; (*comm*) Generaldirektor *m*. **presidency** *n* (*pol*) Präsidentschaft *f*; (*meeting*) Vorsitz *m*. **presidential** *adj* Präsidenten-.

press [pres] *v* drücken; (*iron*) bügeln. *n* Presse *f*. **press conference** Pressekonferenz *f*. **press stud** Druckknopf *m*. **press-up** *n* Liegestütz *m*. **pressing** *adj* dringend.

pressure ['preʃə] n Druck m. pressure
cooker Schnellkochtopf m. pressure
gauge Druckmesser m. pressure group
Interessengruppe f. pressurize (aircraft)
auf Normaldruck halten; (person) unter
Druck setzen.
prestige [pre'stiːʒ] n Prestige neut. prestig-
ious adj Prestige-.
presume [pri'zjuːm] v annehmen; (dare
to) sich erlauben. presumably adv
vermutlich. presumption n Vermutung f;
(cheek) Unverschämtheit f. presumptuous adj unverschämt.
pretend [pri'tend] v vorgeben. pretend to
so tun, als ob; (claim) Anspruch erheben
(auf). pretence n Vorwand m, Anschein
m. under false pretences unter Vorspiegelung falscher Tatsachen. preten-
tious adj ammaßend. pretentiousness n
Anmaßung f.
pretext ['priːtekst] n Vorwand m, Ausrede
f.
pretty ['priti] adj hübsch, niedlich. adv
(coll) ziemlich. prettify v hübsch machen.
prettiness n Schönheit f.
prevail [pri'veil] v (win) siegen (über); (be
prevalent) vorwiegen, vorherrschen. pre-
vailing adj vorherrschend; (opinion)
allgemein. prevalence n Herrschen neut.
prevalent adj (vor)herrschend.
prevent [pri'vent] v verhindern, verhüten.
prevention n Verhütung f. preventive adj
vorbeugend. preventive measure Vorsichtsmaßnahme f.
preview ['priːvjuː] n Vorschau f,
Probeaufführung f.
previous ['priːviəs] adj vorhergehend,
früher. previously adv vorher.
prey [prei] n Opfer neut. v prey on
erbeuten.
price [prais] n Preis m, Kosten pl. v den
Preis festsetzen für; (evaluate) bewerten.
priceless adj unschätzbar. price-tag n
Preiszettel m.
prick [prik] n Stich m. v stechen.
prickle ['prikl] n Stachel m, Dorn m. v
prickeln, kribbeln. prickly adj stachelig;
(person) reizbar, übellaunig.
pride [praid] n Stolz m; (arrogance)
Hochmut m; (lions) Rudel neut. v pride
oneself on stolz sein auf.
priest [priːst] n Priester m. priestess n
Priesterin f. priesthood n Priesterschaft f.
priestly adj priesterlich.

prim [prim] adj steif, affektiert. primness
n Steifheit f.
primary ['praiməri] adj erst, ursprünglich;
(main) primär, Haupt-; (basic) grun-
dlegend. primary school Grundschule f.
primarily adv hauptsächlich.
primate ['praimət] n (biol) Primat m.
prime [praim] adj erst; (main) Haupt-;
(number) unteilbar; (best) erstklassig.
prime minister Premierminister(in). n
Blüte f. v (gun) laden; (paint) grundier-
en; (fig) vorbereiten. primer n (paint)
Grundierfarbe f; (book) Elementarbuch
neut. priming n Vorbereitung f.
primeval [prai'miːvəl] adj urzeitlich.
primitive ['primitiv] adj (early) urzeitlich,
Ur-; (crude, unrefined) primitiv. primi-
tiveness n Primitivität f.
primrose ['primrouz] n Primel f.
prince [prins] n (ruler) Fürst m; (king's
son) Prinz m. princely adj fürstlich. princess n Fürstin f, Prinzessin f. principality
n Fürstentum neut.
principal ['prinsəpəl] adj erst, Haupt-. n
Vorsteher(in); (comm) Kapital neut. principally adv hauptsächlich.
principle ['prinsəpəl] n Prinzip neut,
Grundsatz m; (basis) Grundlage f. prin-
cipled adj mit hohen Grundsätzen.
print [print] v drucken. printed matter
Drucksache f. printer n Drucker m.
printing n Druck m. printing press
Druckerei f. n Druck m; (of photograph)
Abzug m, Kopie f.
prior ['praiə] adj früher. adv prior to vor.
priority n Priorität f; (precedence) Vorrang m.
prise [praiz] v prise open aufbrechen.
prism ['prizm] n Prisma neut.
prison ['prizn] n Gefängnis neut. prisoner
n Gefangene(r), Häftling m.
private ['praivət] adj privat; (personal)
persönlich. n gemeiner Soldat m. privacy
n Privatleben neut, Ruhe f.
privet ['privət] n Liguster m.
privilege ['privilidʒ] n Privilegium neut,
Sonderrecht neut; (honour) Ehre f. privileged adj bevorrechtet. be privileged to
die Ehre haben, zu.
privy ['privi] n Abort m. adj be privy to
eingeweiht sein in. privy council
Geheimer Rat m.
prize [praiz] n Preis m; (lottery) Los neut.
adj Preis-. v hochschätzen.

probable ['probəbl] *adj* wahrscheinlich. **probability** *n* Wahrscheinlichkeit *f*.
probation [prə'beiʃən] *n* Probezeit *f*; (*law*) bedingte Freilassung *f*. **probationary** *adj* Probe-.
probe [proub] *n* (*tech*) Sonde *f*; (*enquiry*) Untersuchung *f*. *v* **probe into** eindringen in, erforschen.
problem ['probləm] *n* Problem *neut*. **problematical** *adj* problematisch.
proceed [prə'siid] *v* weitergehen; (*continue*) fortfahren; (*begin*) beginnen. **procedure** *n* Vorgehen *neut*. **proceedings** *pl n* (*law*) Verfahren *neut sing*. **proceeds** *pl n* Erlös *m sing*, Ertrag *m sing*.
process ['prouses] *v* bearbeiten, verarbeiten. *n* Verfahren *neut*, Prozeß *m*. **processing** *n* Verarbeitung *f*.
procession [prə'seʃən] *n* Prozession *f*, Zug *m*.
proclaim [prə'kleim] *v* proklamieren, verkünden. **proclamation** *n* Proklamation *f*.
procreate ['proukrieit] *v* erzeugen. **procreation** *n* Zeugung *f*.
procure [prə'kjuə] *v* beschaffen, besorgen.
prod [prod] *v* stechen, stoßen; (*coll: induce*) anspornen (zu). *n* Stich *m*, Stoß *m*.
prodigy ['prodidʒi] *n* Wunder *neut*; (*child*) Wunderkind *neut*. **prodigious** *adj* riesig, erstaunlich.
produce [prə'djuis; *n* 'prodjuis] *v* (*goods*) erzeugen, herstellen; (*submit*) vorlegen; (*cause, call forth*) hervorrufen; (*theatre*) aufführen; (*films*) herausbringen. *n* Erzeugnis *neut*, Produkte *pl*. **producer** *n* Hersteller; (*theatre, film*) Regisseur *m*.
product *n* Produkt *neut*, Erzeugnis *neut*; (*result*) Ergebnis *neut*. **production** *n* Herstellung *f*, Produktion *f*; (*theatre*) Aufführung *f*; (*film*) Regie *f*. **production line** Fließband *neut*. **productive** *adj* fruchtbar, leistungsfähig. **productivity** *n* Leistungsfähigkeit *f*, Produktivität *f*.
profane [prə'fein] *adj* profan. **profanity** *n* Fluchen *neut*.
profess [prə'fes] *v* erklären. **profession** *n* (*occupation*) Beruf *m*; (*assertion*) Beteuerung *f*. **professional** *adj* Berufs-, beruflich; (*education*) fachlich, Fach-.
professor [prə'fesə] *n* Professor(in). **professorship** *n* Lehrstuhl *m*.
proficient [prə'fiʃənt] *adj* erfahren. **proficiency** *n* Erfahrenheit *f*.

profile ['proufail] *n* Profil *neut*. *v* profilieren.
profit ['profit] *n* (*comm*) Gewinn *m*, Profit *m*; (*advantage*) Vorteil *m*. *v* **profit from** Nutzen ziehen aus. **profitable** *adj* rentabel; (*advantageous*) vorteilhaft. **profiteer** *n* Profitmacher *m*; *v* sich bereichern.
program ['prougram] *n* (*computer*) Programm *neut*. *v* programmieren. **programmer** *n* Programmierer(in).
programme ['prougram] *n* Programm *neut*; (*TV, radio: broadcast*) Sendung *f*. *v* planen.
progress ['prougres] *n* Fortschritt *m*; (*development*) Entwicklung *f*. *v* fortschreiten, sich entwickeln. **in progress** im Gange. **progression** *n* Fortbewegung *f*. **progressive** *adj* fortschrittlich.
prohibit [prə'hibit] *v* verbieten. **prohibition** *n* Verbot *neut*; (*of drinking*) Alkoholverbot *neut*. **prohibitive** *adj* verbietend; (*excessively high*) untragbar.
project ['prodʒekt; *v* prə'dʒekt] *n* Projekt *neut*, Plan *m*; (*school*) Planaufgabe *f*. *v* (*film, etc.*) projizieren; (*plan*) planen. **projection** *n* Projektion *f*. **projector** *n* Projektionsapparat *m*.
proletariat [proulə'teəriət] *n* Proletariat *neut*. **proletarian** *adj* proletarisch. *n* Proletarier(in).
proliferate [prə'lifəreit] *v* sich vermehren, wuchern. **proliferation** *n* Wucherung *f*.
prolific [prə'lifik] *adj* fruchtbar.
prologue ['proulog] *n* Prolog *m*.
prolong [prə'loŋ] *v* verlängern. **prolonged** *adj* anhaltend. **prolongation** *n* Verlängerung *f*.
promenade [promə'naid] *n* Promenade *f*; (*walk*) Spaziergang *m*. *v* promenieren, spazieren.
prominent ['prominənt] *adj* (*person*) prominent, maßgebend. **prominence** *n* Prominenz *f*, hervorragende Bedeutung *f*.
promiscuous [prə'miskjuəs] *adj* promiskuitiv. **promiscuity** *n* Promiskuität *f*.
promise ['promis] *n* Versprechen *neut*. *v* versprechen. **promising** *adj* vielversprechend.
promontory ['promontəri] *n* Landspitze *f*.
promote [prə'mout] *v* (*person*) befördern; (*encourage, support*) fördern, Vorschub leisten (+ *dat*); (*comm*) Reklame machen für. **promoter** *n* (*sport*) Promoter *m*. **pro-**

prompt   **136**

motion *n* Beförderung; (*publicity*) Werbung *f*, Reklame *f*.
prompt [prompt] *adj* sofortig, prompt. *v* (*theatre*) soufflieren; (*cause*) hervorrufen. **promptness** *n* Pünktlichkeit *f*.
prone [proun] *adj* hingestreckt. **prone to** geneigt zu.
prong [proŋ] *n* Zinke *f*. **pronged** *adj* gezinkt.
pronoun ['prounaun] *n* Pronomen *neut*.
pronounce [prə'nauns] *v* aussprechen. **pronouncement** *n* Ausspruch *m*. **pronunciation** *n* Aussprache *f*.
proof [pruːf] *n* Beweis *m*, Nachweis *m*; (*printing*) Korrekturabzug *m*. *adj* undurchlässig, fest. **proof against** sicher vor. **proof-reader** *n* Korrektor(in).
prop[1] [prop] *n* Stütze *f*. *v* **prop up** stützen.
prop[2] [prop] *n* (*theatre*) Requisit *neut*.
propaganda [propə'gandə] *n* Propaganda *f*. **propagandist** *n* Propagandist(in).
propagate ['propəgeit] *v* fortpflanzen. **propagation** *n* Fortpflanzung *f*.
propel [prə'pel] *v* (an)treiben. **propellant** *n* Treibstoff *m*. **propeller** *n* Propeller *m*.
proper ['propə] *adj* (*fitting*) richtig, passend, geeignet; (*thorough*) ordentlich. **properly** *adv* richtig, wie es sich gehört.
property ['propəti] *n* Eigentum *neut*; (*characteristic*) Eigenschaft *f*; (*real estate*) Immobilien *pl*.
prophecy ['profəsi] *n* Weissagung *f*. **prophesy** *v* prophezeien. **prophet** *n* Prophet *m*. **prophetic** *adj* prophetisch.
proportion [prə'pɔːʃən] *n* Verhältnis *neut*; (*part*) Anteil *m*; (*measurement*) Ausmaß *neut*. **in proportion to** im Verhältnis zu. **be out of proportion to** in keinem Verhältnis stehen zu. **well-proportioned** *adj* wohlgestaltet. **proportional** *adj* verhältnismäßig, proportional.
propose [prə'pouz] *v* vorschlagen; (*a motion*) beantragen; (*marriage*) einen Heiratsantrag machen (+ *dat*). **proposal** *n* Vorschlag *m*; (*offer*) Angebot *neut*; (*marriage*) Heiratsantrag *m*. **proposer** *n* Antragsteller *n*. **proposition** *n* Vorschlag *m*; (*project*) Projekt *neut*, Plan *m*.
proprietor [prə'praiətə] *n* Besitzer(in), Inhaber(in).
propriety [prə'praiəti] *n* Schicklichkeit *f*, Anstand *m*.
propulsion [prə'pʌlʃən] *n* Antrieb *m*.
prose [prouz] *n* Prosa *f*. *adj* Prosa-.

prosecute ['prosikjuːt] *v* (*law*) gerichtlich verfolgen. **prosecution** *n* Verfolgung *f*; (*law*) Anklage *f*.
prospect ['prospekt; *v* prə'spekt] *n* Aussicht *f*. *v* **prospect for** (*gold, etc.*) graben nach. **prospective** *adj* künftig, voraussichtlich.
prospectus [prə'spektəs] *n* (Werbe)-Prospekt *m*.
prosper ['prospə] *v* gedeihen. **prosperity** *n* Wohlstand *m*. **prosperous** *adj* erfolgreich, wohlhabend.
prostitute ['prostitjuːt] *n* Prostituierte *f*. *v* prostituieren. **prostitution** *n* Prostitution *f*.
prostrate ['prostreit; *v* pro'streit] *adj* hingestreckt. *v* zu Boden werfen. **prostrate oneself** sich demütigen (vor).
protagonist [prou'tagənist] *n* Hauptfigur *f*.
protect [prə'tekt] *v* (be)schützen. **protection** *n* Schutz *m*. **protectionism** *n* Schutzzollpolitik *f*. **protective** *adj* (be)schützend. **protector** *n* Beschützer *m*. **protectorate** *n* Schutzgebiet *neut*.
protégé ['protəʒei] *n* Schützling *m*.
protein ['proutiːn] *n* Protein *neut*, Eiweiß *neut*.
protest ['proutest; *v* prə'test] *n* Protest *m*, Einspruch *m*. *v* protestieren, Einspruch erheben (auf).
Protestant ['protistənt] *n* Protestant(in). *adj* protestantisch. **Protestantism** *n* Protestantismus *m*.
protocol ['proutəkol] *n* Protokoll *neut*.
prototype ['proutətaip] *n* Prototyp *m*.
protractor [prə'traktə] *n* Winkelmesser *m*.
protrude [prə'truːd] *v* herausstehen, hervorstehen.
proud [praud] *adj* stolz (auf); (*arrogant*) hochmütig.
prove [pruːv] *v* beweisen. **prove to be** sich erweisen als.
proverb ['provəːb] *n* Sprichwort *neut*. **proverbial** *adj* sprichwörtlich.
provide [prə'vaid] *v* versehen, versorgen. **provide for** sorgen für. **provided** *conj* vorausgesetzt.
provident ['providənt] *adj* fürsorglich. **providence** *n* Vorsehung *f*. **providential** *adj* glücklich.
province ['provins] *n* Provinz *f*. **provincial** *adj* Provinz-, provinzial; (*limited, narrow*) provinziell.

puny

provision [prə'viʒən] *n* Vorrichtung *f*; (*regulation*) Vorschrift *f*. **provisions** *pl* Vorrat *m*. **provisional** *adj* vorläufig, provisorisch.
proviso [prə'vaizou] *n* Vorbehalt *m*, Klausel *f*.
provoke [prə'vouk] *v* (*cause*) veranlassen; (*person*) provozieren; (*annoy*) ärgern. **provocation** *n* Provokation *f*; (*challenge*) Herausforderung *f*.
prow [prau] *n* Bug *m*.
prowess ['prauis] *n* Tüchtigkeit *f*.
prowl [praul] *v* herumstreichen. **prowler** *n* Herumtreiber *m*.
proximity [prok'siməti] *n* Nähe *f*.
proxy ['proksi] *n* Vollmacht *f*; (*person*) Bevollmächtigte(r).
prude [pruːd] *n* prüder Mensch *m*. **prudery** *n* Prüderie *f*. **prudish** *adj* prüde.
prudent ['pruːdənt] *adj* vernünftig, umsichtig. **prudence** *n* Klugheit *f*.
prune[1] [pruːn] *n* Backpflaume *f*.
prune[2] [pruːn] *v* (*tree*) beschneiden.
pry [prai] *v* herumschnuffeln. **pry into** die Nase stecken in. **prying** *adj* neugierig.
psalm [saːm] *n* Psalm *m*.
pseudonym ['sjuːdənim] *n* Pseudonym *neut*, Deckname *m*.
psychedelic [ˌsaikə'delik] *adj* psychedelisch.
psychiatry [sai'kaiətri] *n* Psychiatrie *f*. **psychiatric** *adj* psychiatrisch. **psychiatrist** *m* Psychiater(in).
psychic ['saikik] *adj* psychisch.
psychoanalysis [ˌsaikouə'naləsis] *n* Psychoanalyse *f*. **psychoanalyst** *n* Psychoanalytiker(in).
psychology [sai'kolədʒi] *n* Psychologie *f*. **psychological** *adj* psychologisch. **psychologist** *n* Psycholog(in).
psychopath ['saikəpaθ] *n* Psychopath(in).
psychosomatic [ˌsaikəsə'matik] *adj* psychosomatisch.
pub [pʌb] *n* (*coll*) Kneipe *f*.
puberty ['pjuːbəti] *n* Pübertät *f*, Geschlechtsreife *f*.
pubic ['pjuːbik] *adj* Scham-.
public ['pʌblik] *adj* öffentlich; (*national*) Volks-, national. *n* Öffentlichkeit *f*, Publikum *neut*. **public house** *n* Wirtshaus *neut*. **public school** Privatschule *f*. **public-spirited** *adj* gemeinsinnig. **publication** *n* Veröffentlichung *f*, Publikation *f*. **publicity** *n* Reklame *f*, Werbung *f*. **publicize** *v* veröffentlichen.

publish ['pʌbliʃ] *v* (*publicize*) veröffentlichen; (*book*) herausbringen. **publisher** *n* Verleger(in), Herausgeber(in); (*firm*) Verlag *m*. **publishing** *n* Verlagswesen *neut*.
pucker ['pʌkə] *v* runzeln; (*mouth*) spitzen.
pudding ['pudiŋ] *n* Pudding *m*. **black pudding** *n* Blutwurst *f*.
puddle ['pʌdl] *n* Pfütze *f*, Lache *f*.
puerile ['pjuərail] *adj* pueril.
puff [pʌf] *n* Hauch *m*; (*on cigar, etc.*) Zug *m*. *v* blasen, pusten. **powder puff** Puderquaste *f*. **puffed-up** *adj* (*coll*) aufgeblasen. **puff pastry** Blätterteig *m*. **puffy** *adj* angeschwollen.
pull [pul] *v* ziehen; (*tug*) zerren; (*rip*) reißen. *n* Zug *m*. **pull through** (*survive*) durchkommen.
pulley ['puli] *n* Rolle *f*.
pullover ['pulˌouvə] *n* Pullover *m*.
pulp [pʌlp] *n* Brei *m*; (*fruit*) Fruchtfleisch *neut*; (*paper*) Pulpe *f*. **pulpy** *adj* breiig, weich.
pulpit ['pulpit] *n* Kanzel *f*.
pulsate [pʌl'seit] *v* pulsieren. **pulsation** *n* Pulsieren *neut*.
pulse [pʌls] *n* Puls *m*, Pulsschlag *m*. *v* pulsieren.
pulverize ['pʌlvəraiz] *v* pulverisieren, zermahlen. **pulverization** *n* Pulverisierung *f*.
pump [pʌmp] *n* Pumpe *f*. *v* pumpen.
pumpkin ['pʌmpkin] *n* Kürbis *m*.
pun [pʌn] *n* Wortspiel *neut*.
punch[1] [pʌntʃ] *n* (*blow*) (Faust)Schlag *m*. *v* (mit der Faust) schlagen.
punch[2] [pʌntʃ] *n* (*drink*) Punsch *m*. **punchbowl** *n* Punschbowle *f*.
punch[3] [pʌntʃ] *n* (*tool*) Locher *m*, Lochzange *f*. *v* lochen; (*tickets*) knipsen. **punchcard** *n* Lochkarte *f*.
punctual ['pʌŋktʃuəl] *adj* pünktlich. **punctuality** *n* Pünktlichkeit *f*.
punctuate ['pʌŋktʃueit] *v* interpunktieren; (*fig*) unterbrechen. **punctuation** *n* Interpunktion *f*.
puncture ['pʌŋktʃə] *v* durchstechen, perforieren; (*tyre*) platzen. *n* Loch *neut*; (*tyre*) Reifenpanne *f*.
pungent ['pʌndʒənt] *adj* scharf.
punish ['pʌniʃ] *v* (be)strafen. **punishment** *n* Strafe *f*.
puny ['pjuːni] *adj* schwächlich.

pupil¹ ['pjuːpl] *n* Schüler(in).
pupil² ['pjuːpl] *n* (*eye*) Pupille *f*.
puppet ['pʌpit] *n* Marionette *f*. **puppet show** Puppenspiel *neut*, Marionettentheater *neut*.
puppy ['pʌpi] *n* junger Hund *m*, Welpe *m*.
purchase ['pɔːtʃəs] *n* Einkauf *m*. *v* (ein)kaufen. **purchaser** *n* Käufer(in).
pure ['pjuə] *adj* rein. **purebred** *adj* reinrassig. **purify** *v* reinigen; (*tech*) klären. **purification** *n* Reinigung *f*; Klärung *f*. **purity** *n* Reinheit *f*.
purée ['pjuərei] *n* Purée *neut*.
purgatory ['pɔːgətəri] *n* Fegefeuer *neut*.
purge [pɔːdʒ] *v* reinigen, säubern. *n* Reinigung *f*; (*pol*) Säuberung *f*.
puritan ['pjuəritən] *n* Puritaner(in). **puritanical** *adj* puritanisch. **puritanism** *n* Puritanismus *m*.
purl [pɔːl] *n* Linksstricken *neut*. *v* linksstricken.
purple ['pɔːpl] *adj* purpurn, purpurrot. *n* Purpur *m*.
purpose ['pɔːpəs] *n* Zweck *m*, Ziel *neut*. **for the purpose of** zwecks (+ *gen*). **on purpose** absichtlich. **purposeful** *adj* zielbewußt. **purposeless** *adj* zwecklos. **purposely** *adv* absichtlich.
purr [pɔː] *v* schnurren, summen. *n* Schnurren *neut*.
purse [pɔːs] *n* Portemonnaie *neut*, Geldbeutel *m*; Handtasche *f*; (*prize*) Börse *f*. *v* (*lips*) spitzen.
purser ['pɔːsə] *n* Zahlmeister *m*.
pursue [pə'sjuː] *v* verfolgen; (*studies*) betreiben; (*continue*) fortfahren in. **pursuit** *n* Verfolgung *f*; (*activity*) Beschäftigung *f*; (*of happiness, etc.*) Jagd *f*, Suche *f*.
pus [pʌs] *n* Eiter *m*.
push [puʃ] *n* Stoß *m*, Schub *m*. **get the push** (*coll*) entlassen werden. *v* stoßen, schieben; (*button*) drücken; (*in crowd*) drängen. **be pushed for time** keine zeit haben. **push aside** beiseite schieben. **push open/to** (*door*) auf/zuschieben. **push off** (*coll*) abhauen. **push through** durchsetzen. **pushbike** *m* (*coll*) Rad *neut*. **pushbutton** *n* Druckknopf *m*. **pushchair** *n* Kinderwagen. **pusher** *n* (*drugs*) Pusher *m*. **pushing** *adj* aufdringlich.
pussy ['pusi] *n* (*coll*) Mieze *f*.
*put [put] *v* stellen, setzen, legen; (*express*) ausdrücken; (*shot*) werfen. **put away** weglegen. **put back** (*clock*) nach-

stellen; (*postpone*) aufschieben. **put by** aufsparen. **put down** hinlegen; (*revolt*) unterdrücken; (*animal*) töten. **put off** verschieben; (*discourage*) davon abraten (+ *dat*). **put through** durchführen; (*phone*) verbinden. **put up** (*coll*) unterbringen. **put up with** dulden, ausstehen.
putrid ['pjuːtrid] *adj* verfault.
putt [pʌt] *v* putten.
putty ['pʌti] *n* Kitt *m*.
puzzle ['pʌzl] *n* Rätsel *neut*; (*jigsaw*) Puzzlespiel *neut*. *v* verwirren. **puzzlement** *n* Verwirrung *f*. **puzzling** *adj* rätselhaft.
pyjamas [pə'dʒaːməz] *n* Schlafanzug *m*.
pylon ['pailən] *n* (*elec*) Leitungsmast *m*.
pyramid ['pirəmid] *n* Pyramide *f*.
python ['paiθən] *n* Pythonschlange *f*.

Q

quack¹ [kwak] *n* (*duck*) Quaken *neut*. *v* quaken.
quack² [kwak] *n* (*doctor*) Quacksalber *m*. *adj* quacksalberisch.
quadrangle ['kwodraŋgl] *n* Viereck *neut*; Hof *m*. **quadrangular** *adj* viereckig.
quadrant ['kwodrənt] *n* Quadrant *m*.
quadrilateral [kwodrə'latərəl] *adj* vierseitig.
quadruped ['kwodruped] *n* Vierfüßer *m*.
quadruple [kwod'ruːpl] *adj* vierfach, vierfältig. *v* vervierfachen.
quagmire ['kwagmaiə] *n* Morast *m*.
quail¹ [kweil] *n* (*bird*) Wachtel *f*.
quail² [kweil] *v* verzagen, den Mut verlieren.
quaint [kweint] *adj* kurios, merkwürdig.
quake [kweik] *v* beben. *n* Erdbeben *neut*.
qualify ['kwolifai] *v* (sich) qualifizieren; (*limit*) einschränken. **qualification** *n* Qualifikation *f*; Einschränkung *f*. **qualified** *adj* qualifiziert, geeignet; eingeschränkt.
quality ['kwoləti] *n* Qualität *f*; (*property*) Eigenschaft *f*; (*type*) Sorte *f*. *adj* erstklassig, guter Qualität *f*.
qualm [kwaːm] *n* Skrupel *m*.
quandary ['kwondəri] *n* Verlegenheit *f*.
quantify ['kwontifai] *v* messen, (quantitativ) bestimmen.

quantity ['kwontəti] *n* Quantität *f*, Menge *f*.

quarantine ['kworəntiːn] *n* Quarantäne *f*. *v* unter Quarantäne stellen.

quarrel ['kworəl] *n* Streit *m*, Zank *m*. *v* (sich) streiten, (sich) zanken. **quarrelsome** *adj* streitsüchtig, zankig.

quarry[1] ['kwori] *n* (*hunting*) Jagdbeute *f*; (*fig*) Opfer *neut*.

quarry[2] ['kwori] *n* Steinbruch *m*. *v* brechen, hauen.

quart [kwoːt] *n* Quart *neut*.

quarter ['kwoːtə] *n* (*fourth, of town, etc.*) Viertel *neut*; (*of year*) Quartal *neut*, Vierteljahr *neut*. *v* vierteln; (*to house*) unterbringen. **quarter of an hour** Viertelstunde *f*. **quarter to/past** Viertel vor/nach. **quarterdeck** *n* Achterdeck *neut*. **quarter-final** *n* Viertelfinale *neut*. **quarterly** *adj* vierteljährlich.

quartet [kwoːˈtet] *n* Quartett *neut*.

quartz [kwoːts] *n* Quartz *m*.

quash [kwoʃ] *v* annullieren; (*resistance, etc.*) unterdrücken.

quaver ['kweivə] *v* zittern. *n* (*music*) Achtelnote *f*.

quay [kiː] *n* Kai *m*.

queasy ['kwiːzi] *adj* übel. *I feel queasy* mir ist übel.

queen [kwiːn] *n* Königin *f*; (*cards, chess*) Dame *f*. **queen bee** Bienenkönigin *f*. **queen mother** Königinmutter *f*.

queer [kwiə] *adj* seltsam, sonderbar; (*odd*) komisch; (*coll: homosexual*) schwul. *n* (*coll*) Homo *m*, Schwule(r).

quell [kwel] *v* unterdrücken.

quench [kwentʃ] *v* löschen.

query ['kwiəri] *n* Frage *f*, Erkundigung *f*. *v* in Frage stellen.

quest [kwest] *n* Suche *f* (nach).

question ['kwestʃən] *n* Frage *f*. *v* (be)fragen. **put** *or* **ask a question** eine Frage stellen. **out of the question** ausgeschlossen. **the question is** es handelt sich darum. **questionable** *adj* fragwürdig. **questioning** *adj* fragend. *n* Befragung *f*. **questionnaire** *n* Fragebogen *m*.

queue [kjuː] *n* Schlange *f*. *v* Schlange stehen, sich anstellen.

quibble ['kwibl] *v* Haare spalten, spitzfindig sein.

quick [kwik] *adj* schnell; (*nimble*) flink; (*temper*) hitzig; (*ear, eye*) scharf. **quicken** *v* beschleunigen. **quickness** *n* Schnel-

ligkeit *f*. **quicksand** *n* Treibsand *m*. **quicksilver** *n* Quecksilber *neut*. **quick-tempered** *adj* hitzig, reizbar. **quick-witted** *adj* scharfsinnig.

quid [kwid] *n* (*coll*) Pfund *neut*.

quiet ['kwaiət] *adj* ruhig, still. **quieten** *v* beruhigen. **quietness** *n* Ruhe *f*, Stille *f*.

quill [kwil] *n* Feder *f*.

quilt [kwilt] *n* Steppdecke *f*.

quinine [kwiˈniːn] *n* Chinin *neut*.

quinsy ['kwinzi] *n* Mandelentzündung *f*.

quintet [kwinˈtet] *n* Quintett *neut*.

quirk [kwəːk] *n* Eigenart *f*.

*****quit** [kwit] *v* (*stop*) aufhören; (*leave*) verlassen; (*job*) aufgeben. **notice to quit** Kündigung *f*. **quits** *adj* (*coll*) quitt.

quite [kwait] *adv* (*fairly*) ziemlich; (*wholly*) ganz, durchaus.

quiver[1] ['kwivə] *v* zittern.

quiver[2] ['kwivə] *n* (*arrows*) Köcher *m*.

quiz [kwiz] *n* Quiz *neut*. *v* (aus)fragen.

quizzical ['kwizikl] *adj* spöttisch.

quota ['kwoutə] *n* Quote *f*, Anteil *m*.

quote [kwout] *v* zitieren. **quotation** *n* Zitat *f*; (*comm*) Preisangabe *f*. **quotation marks** Anführungszeichen *pl*.

R

rabbi ['rabai] *n* Rabbiner *m*.

rabbit ['rabit] *n* Kaninchen *neut*. **rabbit hutch** Kaninchenstall *m*.

rabble ['rabl] *n* Pöbel *m*.

rabies ['reibiːz] *n* Tollwut *f*. **rabid** *adj* tollwütig; (*coll: angry*) wütend.

race[1] [reis] *n* Rennen *neut*, Wettlauf *m*. *v* um die Wette laufen (mit), rennen. **the races** Pferderennen *pl*. **racecourse** *n* Rennbahn *f*. **racehorse** *n* Rennpferd *neut*. **racing** *n* Pferderennen *neut*; *adj* Renn-. **racing driver** Rennfahrer *m*.

race[2] [reis] *n* (*group*) Rasse *f*. **racial** *adj* rassisch, Rassen-. **racialism** *or* **racism** *n* Rassismus *m*. **racialist** *or* **racist** *n* Rassist(in); *adj* rassistisch.

rack [rak] *n* Gestell *neut*; (*luggage*) Gepäcknetz *neut*. *v* **rack one's brains** sich den Kopf zerbrechen.

racket[1] ['rakit] *n* (*sport*) Rakett *neut*, Schläger *m*.

racket² ['rakit] *n* (*noise*) Krach *m*, Trübel *m*; (*coll: swindle*) Schwindel *m*. **racketeer** *n* Schwindler *m*, Gangster *m*.

radar ['reidaɪ] *n* Radar *m or neut.*

radial ['reidiəl] *adj* radial. *n* (*tyre*) Gürtelreifen *m*.

radiant ['reidiənt] *adj* strahlend. **radiance** *n* Strahlung *f*.

radiate ['reidieit] *v* ausstrahlen. **radiation** *n* Strahlung *f*. **radiator** *n* (*house*) Heizkörper *m*; (*mot*) Kühler *m*.

radical ['radikəl] *adj* radikal. *n* Radikale(r). **radicalism** *n* Radikalismus *m*.

radio ['reidiou] *n* (*set*) Radio *neut*; (*network*) Rundfunk *m*. *v* senden, durchgeben. **radio ham** (*coll*) Funkamateur *m*. **radio station** Sender *m*, Funkstation *f*. **radio wave** Radiowelle *f*.

radioactive [reidiou'aktiv] *adj* radioaktiv. **radioactivity** *n* Radioaktivität *f*.

radiology [reidi'olədʒi] *n* Radiologie *f*, Röntgenlehre *f*. **radiologist** *n* Radiologe *m*.

radiotherapy [reidiou'θerəpi] *n* Radiotherapie *f*, Strahlenbehandlung *f*.

radish ['radiʃ] *n* Radieschen *neut*.

radium ['reidiəm] *n* Radium *neut*.

radius ['reidiəs] *n* Radius *m*.

raffia ['rafiə] *n* Raffiabast *m*.

raffle ['rafl] *n* Tombola *f*. *v* verlosen.

raft [raɪft] *n* Floß *neut*.

rafter ['raɪftə] *n* Dachsparren *m*.

rag¹ [rag] *n* Fetzen *m*, Lumpen *m*; (*coll: newspaper*) Blatt *neut*. **rag doll** Stoffpuppe *f*. **ragged** *adj* zerfetzt.

rag² [rag] *v* (*coll: tease*) necken, piesacken.

rage [reidʒ] *n* Wut *f*. *v* wüten. **in a rage** wütend. **be all the rage** die große Mode sein.

raid [reid] *n* Angriff *m*, Überfall *m*; (*police*) Razzia *f*. *v* überfallen; eine Razzia machen auf.

rail [reil] *n* Riegel *m*, Schiene *f*. **by rail** mit der Bahn. **railing** *n* Geländer *neut*. **railway** *or* **railroad** *n* Eisenbahn *f*. **railway station** Bahnhof *m*.

rain [rein] *n* Regen *m*. *v* regnen. **rainbow** *n* Regenbogen *m*. **raincoat** *n* Regenmantel *m*. **rainfall** *n* Niederschlag *m*. **rainproof** *adj* wasserdicht. **rainstorm** *n* Regenguß. **rainy** *adj* regnerisch.

raise [reiz] *v* erheben, aufrichten; (*pro-*

voke) hervorrufen; (*money*) beschaffen. *n* (*in pay*) Erhöhung *f*. **raised** *adj* erhöht.

raisin ['reizən] *n* Rosine *f*.

rake [reik] *n* Rechen *m*. *v* rechen.

rally ['rali] *n* (*meeting*) (Massen)Versammlung *f*; (*mot*) Sternfahrt *f*, Rallye *f*. *v* (wieder) sammeln; (*spirits*) sich erholen. **rally round** sich scharen um.

ram [ram] *n* (*zool*) Widder *m*; (*tech*) Ramme *f*. *v* rammen.

ramble ['rambl] *v* wandern; (*speech*) drauflos reden. *n* Wanderung *f*, Bummel *m*. **rambler** *n* Wanderer *m*; (*rose*) Kletterrose *f*. **rambling** *adj* wandernd; (*speech*) unzusammenhängend, weitschweifig.

ramp [ramp] *n* Rampe *f*.

rampage [ram'peidʒ] *v* (herum)toben.

rampant ['rampənt] *adj* üppig, wuchernd.

rampart ['rampaɪt] *n* Festungswall *m*.

ramshackle ['ramʃakl] *adj* wackelig.

ran [ran] *V* **run**.

ranch [raɪntʃ] *n* Ranch *f*.

rancid ['ransid] *adj* ranzig.

rancour ['raŋkə] *n* Erbitterung *f*, Böswilligkeit *f*.

random ['randəm] *adj* zufällig. *n* **at random** wahllos, aufs Geratewohl.

randy ['randi] *adj* (*coll*) geil, wollüstig.

rang [raŋ] *V* **ring²**.

range [reindʒ] *n* Reihe *f*; (*mountains*) Kette *f*; (*reach*) Tragweite *f*. *v* anordnen; (*vary*) variieren, schwanken; (*rove*) wandern.

rank¹ [raŋk] *n* (*status*) Rang *m*; (*row*) Reihe *f*. *v* **rank with** zählen zu. **the ranks** (*mil*) die Mannschaften *pl*.

rank² [raŋk] *adj* (*plants*) üppig; (*offensive*) widerlich; (*coarse*) grob.

rankle ['raŋkl] *v* nagen.

ransack ['ransak] *v* plündern, durchwühlen.

ransom ['ransəm] *n* Lösegeld *neut*. *v* loskaufen.

rap [rap] *n* Klopfen *neut*. *v* klopfen.

rape [reip] *n* Vergewaltigung *f*. *v* vergewaltigen. **rapist** *n* Vergewaltiger *m*.

rapid ['rapid] *adj* schnell, rasch. **rapidity** *n* Schnelligkeit *f*. **rapids** *pl n* Stromschnelle *f*.

rapier ['reipiə] *n* Rapier *neut*.

rapture ['raptʃə] *n* Verzückung *f*, Begeisterung *f*. **rapturous** *adj* hingerissen.

rare¹ ['reə] *adj* selten, rar; (*air*) dünn. **rarely** *adv* selten. **rarity** *n* Seltenheit *f.*

rare² ['reə] *adj* (*cookery*) nicht durchgebraten, englisch.

rascal ['raɪskəl] *n* Schurke *m.* **rascally** *adj* schurkisch.

rash¹ [raʃ] *n* (*on skin*) Hautausschlag *m.*

rash² [raʃ] *adj* hastig, übereilt. **rashness** *n* Hast *f.*

rasher ['raʃə] *n* (Schinken)Schnitte *f.*

raspberry ['raɪzbəri] *n* Himbeere *f.*

rat [rat] *n* Ratte *f. v* **rat on** (*coll*) verraten.

rate [reit] *n* (*comm*) Satz *m,* Kurs *m;* (*charge*) Gebühr *f;* (*speed*) Geschwindigkeit *f: v* schätzen. **rates** *pl* Gemeindesteuer *f.* **birth rate** Geburtenziffer *f.* **at any rate** auf jeden Fall. **first-rate** *adj* erstklassig. **second-rate, third-rate,** *etc. adj* minderwertig.

rather ['raɪðə] *adv* (*quite*) ziemlich, etwas; (*preferably*) lieber, eher. *I would rather* ich möchte lieber.

ratify ['ratifai] *v* ratifizieren. **ratification** *n* Ratifizierung *f.*

ratio ['reiʃiou] *n* Verhältnis *neut.*

ration ['raʃən] *n* Ration *f. v* rationieren. **rations** *pl* Verpflegung *f sing.*

rational ['raʃənl] *adj* rational, vernünftig. **rationale** *n* Grundprinzip *neut.* **rationalization** *n* Rationalisierung *f.* **rationalize** *v* rationalisieren.

rattle ['ratl] *v* klappern, rasseln. *n* Gerassel *neut,* Klappern *neut.* **rattlesnake** *n* Klapperschlange *f.*

raucous ['rɔɪkəs] *adj* rauh, heiser.

ravage ['ravidʒ] *v* verwüstern. *n* Verwüstung. **ravages of time** Zahn der Zeit *m.*

rave [reiv] *v* irre reden, toben. **rave about** (*coll*) schwärmen von. **raving** *adj* delirierend. **ravings** *pl* *n* Fieberwahn *m,* Delirien *pl.*

raven ['reivən] *n* Rabe *m.*

ravenous ['ravənəs] *adj* heißhungrig.

ravine [rə'viɪn] *n* Schlucht *f.*

ravish ['raviʃ] *v* (*delight*) hinreißen; (*rape*) vergewaltigen. **ravishing** *adj* entzückend.

raw [rɔɪ] *adj* roh; (*voice*) rauh; (*sore*) wund. **rawhide** *n* Rohleder *neut.* **rawness** *n* Rohzustand *m.*

ray [rei] *n* Strahl *m.* **ray of light** Lichtstrahl *m.*

rayon ['reiɔn] *n* Kunstseide *f.*

razor ['reizə] *n* Rasiermesser *neut.* **electric razor** Elektrorasierer *m.* **razor blade**

Rasierklinge *f.* **razor-sharp** *adj* messerscharf.

reach [riɪtʃ] *v* (*arrive at*) erreichen; (*stretch to*) sich erstrecken (bis). *n* Reichweite *f.* **reach (out) for** reichen *or* greifen nach.

react [ri'akt] *v* reagieren. **reaction** *n* Reaktion *f.* **reactionary** *adj* reaktionär; *n* Reaktionär(in).

*read [riɪd] *v* lesen; (*interpret*) auslegen, deuten. **read aloud** vorlesen. **read through** durchlesen. **readable** *adj* leserlich; (*worth reading*) lesenswert. **reader** *n* Leser(in); (*university*) Dozent *m.* **readership** *n* Leserkreis *m.* **reading** *n* Lesen *neut;* (*public*) Vorlesung *f.* **reading matter** Lektüre *f.*

readjust [riɪə'dʒʌst] *v* wieder in Ordnung bringen; (*tech*) wieder einstellen; (*person*) (sich) wieder anpassen (an). **readjustment** *n* Wiederanpassung *f.*

ready ['redi] *adj* bereit, fertig; (*quick*) prompt. **get** *or* **make ready** sich vorbereiten; (*thing*) fertig machen. **readiness** *n* Bereitschaft *f.* **ready-made** *adj* Fertig-. **ready-reckoner** *n* Rechentabelle *f.* **readily** *adv* ohne weiteres.

real [riəl] *adj* wirklich, wahr; (*genuine*) echt. **real estate** Immobilien *pl.* **realism** n Realismus *m.* **realist** *n* Realist(in). **realistic** *adj* realistisch. **reality** *n* Wirklichkeit *f,* Realität *f.* **really** *adv* tatsächlich, in der Tat; (*very, actually*) wirklich.

realize ['riəlaiz] *v* begreifen, erkennen; (*bring about*) verwirklichen. **realizable** *adj* durchführbar. **realization** *n* Erkenntnis *f;* Verwirklichung *f.*

realm [relm] *n* Königreich *neut;* (*sphere*) Gebiet *neut.*

reap [riɪp] *v* ernten, mähen. **reaper** *n* Mäher(in).

reappear [riɪə'piə] *v* wieder erscheinen. **reappearance** *n* Wiedererscheinen *neut.*

rear¹ [riə] *adj* hinter, Hinter-. *n* Hinterseite *f,* Rückseite *f.* **rear lamp** Schlußlicht *neut.* **rear wheel** Hinterrad *neut.*

rear² [riə] *v* (*child*) erziehen; (*animals*) züchten.

rearrange [riɪə'reindʒ] *v* neu ordnen, umordnen; (*date, etc.*) ändern. **rearrangement** *n* Neuordnung *f;* Änderung *f.*

reason ['riɪzn] *n* Grund *m;* (*good sense*) Vernunft *f. v* folgern. **for this reason** aus diesem Grund. **by reason of** wegen (+ *gen*). **reason with** zu überzeugen ver-

suchen. **reasonable** adj vernünftig. **reasonableness** n Vernünftigkeit. **reasonably** adv vernünftigerweise; (fairly) ziemlich. **reasoning** n Schlußfolgerung f, Argument neut.
reassure [riə'ʃuə] v beruhigen. **reassurance** n Beruhigung f.
rebate ['riːbeit] n Rabatt m.
rebel ['rebl] n Rebell(in), Aufrührer(in). adj aufrührerisch. v rebellieren. **rebellion** n Aufstand m. **rebellious** adj aufrührerisch.
rebound [ri'baund; n 'riːbaund] v zurückprallen. n Rückprall m.
rebuff [ri'bʌf] v abweisen. n Abweisung f.
*rebuild [riː'bild] v wiederaufbauen.
rebuke [ri'bjuːk] v zurechtweisen, rüffeln. n Rüffel m.
recall [ri'koːl] v (call back) zurückrufen; (remember) sich erinnern an. n Rückruf m; Erinnerung f.
recap ['riːkap] v kurz zusammenfassen. n Zusammenfassung f.
recede [ri'siːd] v zurückgehen, zurückweichen.
receipt [rə'siːt] n (of letter) Empfang m; (of goods) Annahme f; (bill) Quittung f. **receipts** pl Einnahmen pl. **acknowledge receipt** Empfang bestätigen.
receive [rə'siːv] v empfangen, bekommen. **receiver** n (phone) Hörer m; (comm) Konkursverwalter m; (radio) Empfänger m. **receivership** n Konkursverwaltung f.
recent ['riːsnt] adj neu, modern, neulich entstanden. **recently** adv neulich, vor kurzem.
receptacle [rə'septəkl] n Behälter m, Gefäß neut.
reception [rə'sepʃən] n Empfang m. **receptionist** n Empfangsdame f. **reception room** Empfangszimmer neut.
recess [ri'ses] n Pause f, Unterbrechung f; (holiday) Ferien pl; (niche) Nische f.
recession [rə'seʃən] n (comm) Rezession f.
recharge [riː'tʃaːdʒ] v (battery) wieder aufladen.
recipe ['resəpi] n Rezept neut.
recipient [rə'sipiənt] n Empfänger(in).
reciprocate [rə'siprəkeit] v erwidern. **reciprocal** adj gegenseitig. **reciprocation** n Erwiderung f.
recite [rə'sait] v vortragen, rezitieren. **piano/song recital** Klavier-/Liederabend m.

reckless ['rekləs] adj rücksichtslos. **recklessness** n Rücksichtslosigkeit f.
reckon ['rekən] v rechnen, zählen; (believe) meinen. **reckon on** sich verlassen auf. **reckon with** rechnen mit. **reckoning** n Abrechnung f.
reclaim [ri'kleim] v (ask for back) zurückfordern; (land from sea) gewinnen.
recline [rə'klain] v sich zurücklehnen (an).
recluse [rə'kluːs] n Einsiedler(in).
recognize ['rekəgnaiz] v (wieder) erkennen; (acknowledge) anerkennen; (concede) zugeben. **recognition-** n (Wieder)Erkennen neut; Anerkennung f. **recognizable** adj erkennbar.
recoil [rə'koil; n 'riːkoil] v zurückprallen; (in fear) zurückschrecken. n Rückprall m.
recollect [rekə'lekt] n sich erinnern an. **recollection** n Erinnerung f.
recommence [riːkə'mens] v wieder beginnen.
recommend [rekə'mend] v empfehlen. **to be recommended** empfehlenswert. **recommendation** n Empfehlung f; (suggestion) Vorschlag m.
recompense ['rekəmpens] n Belohnung f. v belohnen.
reconcile ['rekənsail] v versöhnen. **reconcile oneself to** sich abfinden mit. **reconcilable** adj vereinbar (mit). **reconciliation** n Versöhnung f.
reconstruct [riːkən'strʌkt] v wiederaufbauen; (events) rekonstruieren. **reconstruction** n Wiederaufbau m; Rekonstruktion f.
record [rə'koːd; n 'rekoːd] v (film, tape) aufnehmen; (write down) aufschreiben, eintragen. n (disc) Schallplatte f; (of proceedings, etc.) Protokoll neut, Bericht m; (sport) Rekord m. **break the record** den Rekord brechen. **off the record** inoffiziell. **recorder** n (music) Blockflöte f. **recording** n Aufnahme f. **record-player** n Plattenspieler m.
recount [ri'kaunt] v (narrate) erzählen.
recoup [ri'kuːp] v (loss) wieder einholen.
recover [rə'kʌvə] v zurückgewinnen; (get better) sich erholen. **recovery** n Zurückgewinnung f; Erholung f.
recreation [rekri'eifən] n Erholung f, Entspannung f. **recreation ground** n Spielplatz neut.

recrimination [ri,krimi'neiʃən] *n* Gegenbeschuldigung *f*.

recruit [rə'kruːt] *n* Rekrut *m*. *v* rekrutieren. **recruitment** *n* Rekrutierung *f*.

rectangle ['rektaŋgl] *n* Rechteck *neut*. **rectangular** *adj* rechteckig.

rectify ['rektifai] *v* richtigstellen, korrigieren; (*elec*) gleichrichten. **rectification** *n* Richtigstellung *f*, Korrektur *f*.

rectum ['rektəm] *n* Mastdarm *m*. **rectal** *adj* rektal.

recuperate [rə'kjuːpəreit] *v* sich erholen. **recuperation** *n* Erholung *f*.

recur [ri'kəːr] *v* wieder auftreten, sich wiederholen. **recurrence** *n* Wiederauftreten *neut*. **recurrent** *adj* wiederkehrend.

red [red] *adj* rot. *n* Rot *neut*. **red tape** Amtsschimmel *m*. **redden** *v* erröten, rot werden. **redness** *n* Röte *f*. **red-handed** *adj* auf frischer Tat.

redeem [rə'diːm] *v* (*pledge*) einlösen; (*prisoner*) loskaufen; (*promise*) einhalten. **redemption** *n* Ablösung *f*; Rückkauf *m*.

redevelop [,riːdi'veləp] *v* neu entwickeln; (*town*) umbauen.

redress [rə'dres] *n* (*legal*) Rechtshilfe *f*; (*compensation*) Wiedergutmachung *f*. *v* wiedergutmachen. **redress the balance** das Gleichgewicht wiederherstellen.

reduce [rə'djuːs] *v* vermindern, verringern; (*prices*) herabsetzen; (*tech*) reduzieren; (*slim*) eine Abmagerungskur machen. **in reduced circumstances** verarmt. **reduction** *n* Verminderung *f*; Herabsetzung *f*; (*tech*) Reduktion *f*.

redundant [rə'dʌndənt] *adj* überflüssig; (*jobless*) arbeitslos. **be made redundant** entlassen werden. **redundancy** *n* Überflüssigkeit *f*; (*worker*) Entlassung *f*.

reed [riːd] *n* Rohr *neut*; (*music*) (Rohr)Blatt *neut*. **reedy** *adj* (*voice*) piepsig.

reef [riːf] *n* (Felsen)Riff *neut*.

reek [riːk] *v* stinken (nach). *n* Gestank *m*.

reel¹ [riːl] *n* Spule *f*; (*cotton*) Rolle *f*.

reel² [riːl] *v* taumeln, schwanken.

refectory [rə'fektəri] *n* Speisesaal *m*; (*university*) Mensa *f*.

refer [rə'fəːr] *v* **refer to** hinweisen auf, sich beziehen auf; (*mention*) erwähnen; (*a book*) nachschlagen in. **reference** *n* Bezug *m*, Hinweis *m*; Erwähnung *f*; (*in book*) Verweis *m*. **with reference to** in Bezug auf, hinsichtlich (+ *gen*). **reference book** Nachschlagewerk *neut*.

referee [refə'riː] *n* Schiedsrichter *m*.

referendum [refə'rendəm] *n* Volksentscheid *m*.

refill [riː'fil; *n* 'riːfil] *v* nachfüllen. *n* (*for pen*) Ersatzmine *f*.

refine [rə'fain] *v* (*tech*) raffinieren; (*improve*) verfeinern. **refined** *adj* raffiniert; (*person, etc.*) kultiviert **refinement** *n* Verfeinerung *f*; (*good breeding*) Kultiviertheit *f*. **refinery** *n* Raffinerie *f*.

reflation [rə'fleiʃn] *n* Wirtschaftsbelebung *f*.

reflect [rə'flekt] *v* widerspiegeln; (*consider*) nachdenken. **reflection** *n* Widerspiegelung *f*. (*thought*) Überlegung *f*; (*remark*) Bemerkung *f*. **reflective** *adj* zurückstrahlend; (*thoughtful*) nachdenklich. **reflector** *n* (*mot*) Rückstrahler *m*.

reflex ['riːfleks] *n* Reflex *m*.

reform [rə'fɔːm] *n* Reform *f*, Verbesserung *f*. *v* reformieren, (ver)bessern. **reformation** *n* Verbesserung *f*; (*history*) Reformation *f*. **reformatory** *n* Besserungsanstalt *f*. **reformed** *adj* verbessert. **reformer** *n* Reformer(in).

refract [rə'frakt] *v* brechen.

refrain¹ [rə'frein] *v* **refrain from** sich enthalten (+ *gen*).

refrain² [rə'frein] *n* Refrain *m*.

refresh [rə'freʃ] *v* erfrischen; (*memory*) auffrischen. **refresher course** Wiederholungskurs *m*. **refreshing** *adj* erfrischend. **refreshment** *n* Erfrischung *f*. **refreshments** *pl* Imbiß *m sing*.

refrigerator [rə'fridʒəreitə] *n* Kühlschrank *m*. **refrigerate** *v* kühlen. **refrigeration** *n* Kühlung *f*.

refuel [riː'fjuːəl] *v* tanken.

refuge ['refjuːdʒ] *n* Zuflucht *f*, Schutz *m*. **refugee** *n* Flüchtling *m*.

refund ['riːfʌnd; *v* ri'fʌnd] *n* Rückvergütung *f*. *v* zurückzahlen.

refuse¹ [rə'fjuːz] *v* ablehnen, verweigern. **refusal** *n* Verweigerung *f*, Ablehnung *f*.

refuse² ['refjuːs] *n* Abfall *m*, Müll *m*. **refuse collection** Müllabfuhr *f*.

refute [ri'fjuːt] *v* widerlegen.

regain [ri'gein] *v* wiedergewinnen.

regal ['riːgəl] *adj* königlich.

regard [rə'gaːd] *v* ansehen, betrachten. *n* (*esteem*) (Hoch)Achtung *f*; (*consideration*) Rücksicht *f*, Hinblick *m*. **in this regard** in dieser Hinsicht. **with regard to** in bezug auf. **as regards** was ... betrifft. **regarding** *prep* hinsichtlich (+ *gen*), bezüglich (+*gen*). **regardless** *adj* ohne Rücksicht (auf).

regatta [rə'gatə] *n* Regatta *f*.

regent ['riːdʒənt] *n* Regent(in).

regime [rei'ʒiːm] *n* Regime *f*.

regiment ['redʒimənt] *n* Regiment *neut*.

region ['riːdʒən] *n* Gebiet *neut*, Gegend *f*. **in the region of** etwa, ungefähr. **regional** *adj* regional, örtlich.

register ['redʒistə] *v* registrieren; (*report*) sich eintragen lassen. *n* Register *neut*. **registered** *adj* eingetragen. **registered letter** Einschreibebrief *m*. **send by registered post** per Einschreiben schicken. **registrar** *n* (*births*, *etc*.) Standesbeamte(r); (*hospital*, *etc*.) Direktor *m*. **registration** *n* Registrierung *f*. **registration number** (*mot*) polizeiliches Kennzeichen *neut*. **registry office** Standesamt *neut*.

regress [ri'gres] *v* zurückgehen. **regression** *n* Regression *f*. **regressive** *adj* rückläufig.

regret [rə'gret] *v* bedauern. *n* Reue *f*, Bedauern *neut*. **regrettable** *adj* bedauerlich.

regular ['regjulə] *adj* regelmäßig; (*normal*) gewöhnlich; (*correct*) ordnungsgemäß. **regular (customer)** Stammgast *m*. **regularity** *n* Regelmäßigkeit *f*.

regulate ['regjuleit] *v* regeln, ordnen. **regulation** *n* (*rule*) Vorschrift *f*; (*tech*) Regelung *f*. **regulator** *n* Regler *m*.

rehabilitate [riːhə'biliteit] *n* rehabilitieren. **rehabilitation** *n* Rehabilitation *f*.

rehearse [rə'həːs] *v* proben. **rehearsal** *n* Probe *f*.

reign [rein] *n* Regierung(szeit) *f*. *v* regieren, herrschen.

reimburse [riːim'bəːs] *v* (*person*) entschädigen. **reimbursement** *n* Entschädigung *f*.

rein [rein] *n* Zügel *m*.

reincarnation [riːinkɑː'neiʃən] *n* Reinkarnation *f*, Wiederverkörperung *f*.

reindeer ['reindiə] *n* Ren(tier) *neut*.

reinforce [riːin'fɔːs] *v* verstärken; (*concrete*) armieren. **reinforcement** *n* Verstärkung *f*.

reinstate [riːin'steit] *v* wiedereinsetzen. **reinstatement** *n* Wiedereinsetzung *f*.

reinvest [riːin'vest] *v* wiederinvestieren.

reissue [riː'iʃuː] *v* neu herausgeben. *n* Neuausgabe *f*.

reject [rə'dʒekt]; *n* 'riːdʒekt] *v* ablehnen, verwerfen. **rejection** *n* Ablehnung *f*, Verwerfung *f*. *n* Ausschußartikel *m*.

rejoice [rə'dʒois] *v* sich freuen. **rejoicing** *adj* froh; *n* Freude *f*.

rejoin [rə'dʃoin] *v* sich wieder anschließen; (*reply*) erwidern. **rejoinder** *n* Erwiderung *f*.

rejuvenate [rə'dʒuːvəneit] *v* verjüngen. **rejuvenation** *n* Verjüngung *f*.

relapse [rə'laps] *v* zurückfallen; (*med*) einen Rückfall bekommen. *n* Rückfall *m*.

relate [rə'leit] *v* (*tell*) erzählen; (*link*) verbinden. **related** *adj* verwandt. **relating to** in bezug auf.

relation [rə'leiʃn] *n* Verhältnis *neut*; (*business*) Beziehung *f*; (*person*) Verwandte(r). **relationship** *n* Verhältnis *neut*; (*family*) Verwandtschaft *f*.

relative ['relətiv] *n* Verwandte(r). *adj* relativ, verhältnismäßig. **relatively** *adv* verhältnismäßig. **relativity** *n* Relativität *f*.

relax [rə'laks] *v* entspannen. **relaxation** *n* Entspannung *f*.

relay ['riːlei] *v* ri'lei] *n* (*race*) Staffellauf *m*; (*tech*) Relais *neut*. *v* weitergeben.

release [rə'liːs] *v* freilassen, entlassen; (*film*, *etc*.) freigeben; (*news*) bekanntgeben; (*let go*) loslassen. *n* Entlassung *f*; Freigabe *f*.

relent [rə'lent] *v* nachgiebig werden. **relentless** *adj* unbarmherzig.

relevant ['reləvənt] *adj* erheblich, relevant; (*appropriate*) entsprechend. **relevance** *n* Relevanz *f*.

reliable [ri'laiəbl] *adj* zuverlässig. **reliability** *n* Zuverlässigkeit *f*. **reliance** *n* Vertrauen *neut*.

relic ['relik] *n* Überbleibsel *neut*; (*rel*) Reliquie *f*.

relief [rə'liːf] *n* Erleichterung *f*; (*mil*) Ablösung *f*; (*help*) Hilfe *f*; (*geog*) Relief *neut*. **tax relief** Steuerbegünstigung *f*.

relieve [rə'liːv] *v* erleichtern; (*from burden*) entlasten; (*person*) ablösen; (*reassure*) beruhigen.

religion [rə'lidʒən] *n* Religion *f*. **religious** *adj* religiös.

relinquish [rə'liŋkwiʃ] *v* aufgeben, verzichten auf.

relish ['reliʃ] *v* sich erfreuen an. *n* (*fig*) Vergnügen *neut*; (*sauce*) Soße *f*.

reluctant [rə'lʌktənt] *adj* widerwillig. **be reluctant to do** ungern tun. **reluctance** *n* Widerstreben *neut*. **reluctantly** *adv* ungern.

rely [rə'lai] v sich verlassen (auf).

remain [rə'mein] v bleiben; (*be left over*) übrigbleiben. **remains** pl n Überreste pl; (*person*) die sterblichen Überreste pl. **remainder** n Rest m, Restbestand m. **remaining** adj übriggeblieben.

remand [rə'maind] v in Untersuchungshaft zurückschicken.

remark [rə'maːk] n Bemerkung f. v bemerken. **remarkable** adj bemerkenswert.

remarry [riː'mari] v wieder heiraten.

remedy ['remədi] n Gegenmittel neut; (*med*) Heilmittel neut. v berichtigen.

remember [ri'membə] v sich erinnern an. *remember me to your mother* grüße deine Mutter von mir. **remembrance** n Erinnerung f.

remind [rə'maind] v erinnern (an); (*someone to do something*) mahnen. **reminder** n Mahnung f.

reminiscence [remə'nisens] n Erinnerung f. **be reminiscent of** erinnern an.

remiss [rə'mis] adj nachlässig.

remit [rə'mit] v überweisen. **remittance** n Überweisung f.

remnant ['remnənt] n (Über)Rest m, Überbleibsel neut.

remorse [rə'mois] n Gewissensbisse pl, Reue f. **remorseful** n reumütig. **remorseless** adj unbarmherzig.

remote [rə'mout] adj fern, entfernt. **remote control** Fernsteuerung f. **remoteness** n Ferne f.

remove [rə'muːv] v beseitigen, entfernen; (*move house*) umziehen. **removal** n Beseitigung f; Umzug m. **remover** n (Möbel)Spediteur m.

remunerate [rə'mjuːnəreit] v belohnen. **remuneration** n Lohn m, Vergütung f.

renaissance [rə'neisəns] n Renaissance f.

rename [riː'neim] v umbenennen.

render ['rendə] v (*make*) machen; (*give back*) wiedergeben; (*service*) leisten.

rendezvous ['rondivuː] n Verabredung f, Stelldichein neut.

renegade ['renigeid] n Abtrünnige(r). adj abtrünnig.

renew [rə'njuː] v erneuern; (*contract*) verlängern. **renewal** n Erneuerung f.

renounce [ri'nauns] v verzichten auf; (*person*) verleugnen; (*beliefs*) abschwören.

renovate ['renəveit] v erneuern, renovieren. **renovation** n Renovierung f, Erneuerung f.

renown [rə'naun] n Ruhm m, Berühmtheit f. **renowned** adj berühmt.

rent [rent] n Miete f. v mieten; (*let*) vermieten. **rental** n Mietbetrag m.

renunciation [ri,nʌnsi'eiʃən] n (*rejection*) Ablehnung f.

reopen [riː'oupən] v wieder öffnen; (*shop, etc.*) wiedereröffnen.

reorganize [riː'oɪgənaiz] v reorganisieren, neugestalten. **reorganization** n Reorganisation f.

rep [rep] n (*coll: representative*) Vertreter(in).

repair [ri'peə] v reparieren, ausbessern; (*clothes*) flicken. n Reparatur f. **in good repair** in gutem Zustand. **in need of repair** reparaturbedürftig. **repair kit** Flickzeug neut. **reparation** n Wiedergutmachung f.

repartee [repaɪ'tiː] n Schlagabtausch m.

repatriate [riː'patrieit] v repatriieren. **repatriation** n Repatriierung f.

*repay [ri'pei] v zurückzahlen; (*kindness*) erwidern. **repayable** adj rückzahlbar. **repayment** n Rückzahlung f.

repeal [rə'piːl] v aufheben, widerrufen. n Aufhebung f.

repeat [rə'piːt] v wiederholen. n Wiederholung f. **repeated** adj wiederholt.

repel [rə'pel] v abweisen. **repellent** adj abstoßend, widerlich.

repent [rə'pent] v bereuen. **repentance** n Reue f. **repentant** adj bußfertig.

repercussions [riːpə'kʌʃənz] pl n Rückwirkungen pl.

repertoire ['repətwaɪ] n Repertoire neut.

repetition [repə'tiʃn] n Wiederholung f. **repetitive** adj sich wiederholend.

replace [rə'pleis] v ersetzen. **replacement** n Ersatz m. **replacement part** Ersatzteil neut.

replay ['riːplei] n (*sport*) Wiederholungsspiel neut; (*tape*) Wiedergabe f.

replenish [rə'pleniʃ] v ergänzen.

replica ['replikə] n Kopie f.

reply [rə'plai] v antworten, erwidern. n Antwort f, Erwiderung f. **reply to** (*person*) antworten (+ dat); (*question, letter*) antworten auf. **in reply to** in Erwiderung auf.

report [rə'poɪt] n Bericht m; (*factual statement*) Meldung f. v berichten;

(denounce) melden; *(present oneself)* sich melden. **reporter** *n* Reporter *m*.

repose [rə'pouz] *n* Ruhe *f*. *v* ruhen.

represent [reprə'zent] *v* darstellen; *(act as representative)* vertreten. **representation** *n* Darstellung *f*; Vertretung *f*. **representative** *n* Vertreter(in). *adj (typical)* typisch.

repress [rə'pres] *v* unterdrücken; *(psychol)* verdrängen. **repression** *n* Unterdrückung *f*; Verdrängung *f*.

reprieve [rə'priːv] *v* begnadigen. *n* Strafaufschub *m*; *(fig)* Gnadenfrist *f*.

reprimand ['reprimaːnd] *v* rügen. *n* Rüge *f*, Verweis *m*.

reprint [riː'print; *n* 'riːprint] *v* neu drucken. *n* Neudruck *m*.

reprisal [rə'praizəl] *n* Repressalie *f*.

reproach [rə'proutʃ] *n* Vorwurf *m*, Tadel *m*. *v* Vorwürfe machen (+ *dat*). **reproachful** *adj* vorwurfsvoll.

reproduce [riːprə'djuːs] *v* (sich) fortpflanzen; *(copy)* kopieren. **reproduction** *n* Fortpflanzung *f*; *(copy)* Reproduktion *f*.

reproof [rə'pruːf] *n* Verweis *m*, Rüge *f*. **reprove** *v* rügen.

reptile ['reptail] *n* Reptil *neut*, Kriechtier *neut*.

republic [rə'pʌblik] *n* Republik *f*. **republican** *adj* republikanisch; *n* Republikaner(in).

repudiate [rə'pjuːdieit] *v* zurückweisen, nicht anerkennen. *n* Nichtanerkennung *f*.

repugnant [rə'pʌgnənt] *adj* widerlich, widerwärtig.

repulsion [rə'pʌlʃn] *n* Abscheu *m*. **repulsive** *adj* widerwärtig, abscheulich.

repute [rə'pjuːt] *n* Ruf *m*. **reputation** *n* Ruf *m*. **reputed** *adj* angeblich. **be reputed** betrachtet sein (als).

request [ri'kwest] *n* Bitte *f*. *v* bitten (um). **on request** auf Wunsch.

requiem ['rekwiəm] *n* Requiem *neut*.

require [rə'kwaiə] *v* *(need)* brauchen; *(person)* verlangen (von); *(call for)* erfordern. **be required** erforderlich sein. **requirement** *n* Anforderung *f*; *(need)* Bedürfnis *neut*.

requisite ['rekwizit] *adj* erforderlich, notwendig.

re-route [riː'ruːt] *v* umleiten.

resale [riː'seil] *n* Weiterverkauf *m*.

rescue ['reskjuː] *v* retten, befreien. *n* Rettung *f*. **come to the rescue of** zur Hilfe kommen (+ *dat*). **rescuer** *n* Retter *m*.

research [ri'səːtʃ] *n* Forschung *f*. *v* forschen. **researcher** *n* Forscher *m*.

resemble [rə'zembl] *v* ähnlich sein (+ *dat*). **resemblance** *n* Ähnlichkeit *f*.

resent [ri'zent] *v* übelnehmen. **resentful** *adj* ärgerlich (auf). **resentment** *n* Groll *m*, Unwille *m*.

reserve [rə'zəːv] *v* reservieren (lassen). *n* Reserve *f*; *(for animals)* Schutzgebiet *neut*; *(sport)* Ersatzmann *m*. **reserved** *adj* reserviert. **reservation** *n* Vorbehalt *m*; Reservierung *f*.

reservoir ['rezvwaː] *n* Reservoir *neut*.

reside [rə'zaid] *v* wohnen. **residence** *n* Wohnung *f*; *(domicile)* Wohnsitz *m*. **resident** *adj* wohnhaft. **residential** *adj* Wohn-.

residue ['rezidjuː] *n* Rest *m*, Rückstand *m*. **residual** *adj* übrig, Rest-.

resign [rə'zain] *v* zurücktreten. **resign oneself to** sich abfinden mit. **resignation** *n* Rücktritt *m*; *(mood)* Resignation *f*. **hand in one's resignation** seinen Rücktritt einreichen. **resigned** *adj* resigniert, ergeben.

resilient [rə'ziliənt] *adj* elastisch; *(person)* unverwüstlich.

resin ['rezin] *n* Harz *neut*.

resist [rə'zist] *v* widerstehen. **resistance** *n* Widerstand *m*. **resistant** *adj* widerstehend, beständig.

*resit [riː'sit] *v* *(exam)* wiederholen.

resolute ['rezəluːt] *adj* entschlossen. **resolution** *n* *(determination)* Entschlossenheit *f*; *(decision)* Beschluß *m*.

resolve [rə'zolv] *v* *(problem)* lösen; *(tech)* auflösen; *(decide)* beschließen. *n* *(determination)* Entschlossenheit *f*. **resolved** *adj* entschlossen.

resonant ['rezənənt] *adj* widerhallend; *(voice)* volltönend. **resonance** *n* Resonanz *f*.

resort [rə'zoːt] *n* *(hope)* Ausweg *m*; *(place)* Ferienort *m*; *(use)* Anwendung *f*. **seaside resort** Seebad *neut*. *v* **resort to** zurückgreifen auf.

resound [rə'zaund] *v* widerhallen.

resource [rə'zoːs] *n* Mittel *neut*. **natural resources** Bodenschätze *pl*. **resourceful** *adj* findig.

respect [rə'spekt] *v* (hoch)achten; *(take account of)* berücksichtigen. *n* *(for person)* Hochachtung *f*, Respekt *m*; Rücksicht *f*. **in this respect** in dieser Hinsicht. **respectable** *adj* ansehnlich, respektabel.

respectful *adj* achtvoll. **respective** *adj* entsprechend. **respectively** *adv* beziehungsweise.

respiration [respə'reiʃn] *n* Atmung *f.*

respite ['respait] *n* **without respite** ohne Unterlaß.

respond [rə'spond] *v* **respond to** (*question*) antworten (auf); (*react*) reagieren (auf). **response** *n* Antwort *f;* Reaktion *f.* **responsible** [rə'sponsəbl] *adj* verantwortlich. **responsibility** *n* Verantwortung *f;* (*commitment*) Verpflichtung *f.*

rest¹ [rest] *n* Ruhe *f.* **day of rest** Ruhetag *m.* **have a rest** sich ausruhen. **without rest** unaufhörlich. *v* ruhen. **rested** *adj* ausgeruht. **restful** *adj* ruhig. **restive** *adj* unruhig. **restless** *adj* ruhelos. **restlessness** *n* Unruhe *f.*

rest² [rest] *n* (*remainder*) Rest *m.*

restaurant ['restront] *n* Restaurant *neut,* Gaststätte *f.* **restaurant car** Speisewagen *m.*

restore [rə'stoɪ] *v* wiederherstellen. **restoration** *n* Wiederherstellung *f;* (*of painting, etc.*) Restauration *f.*

restrain [rə'strein] *v* zurückhalten. **restrained** *adj* zurückhaltend. **restraint** *n* Zurückhaltung *f;* (*limitation*) Einschränkung *f.*

restrict [rə'strikt] *v* einschränken, beschränken. **restricted** *adj* eingeschränkt, beschränkt. **restriction** *n* Einschränkung *f,* Beschränkung *f.* **restrictive** *adj* einschränkend.

result [rə'zʌlt] *n* Ergebnis *neut,* Resultat *neut;* (*consequence*) Folge *f.* *v* sich ergeben. **result in** enden mit. **resultant** *adj* daraus enstehend.

resume [rə'zjuːm] *v* wieder beginnen; (*work*) wieder aufnehmen. **resumption** *n* Wiederaufnahme *f.*

résumé ['reizumei] *n* Resümee *neut.*

resurgence [ri'səɪdʒəns] *n* Wiederaufstieg *m.*

resurrect [rezə'rekt] *v* (*thing*) ausgraben, wieder einführen. **resurrection** *n* Auferstehung *f.*

resuscitate [rə'sʌsəteit] *v* wiederbeleben. **resuscitation** *n* Wiederbelebung *f.*

retail ['riːteil] *n* Einzelhandel *m. adj* Einzelhandels-. **retail price** Ladenpreis *m.* **retail shop** Einzelhandelsgeschäft *neut.* *v* im Einzelhandel verkaufen. **retailer** *n* Einzelhändler(in).

retain [rə'tein] *v* behalten. **retention** *n* Beibehaltung *f.*

retaliate [rə'talieit] *v* sich rächen. **retaliation** *n* Vergeltung *f.* **relaliatory** *adj* Vergeltungs-.

retard [rə'taɪd] *v* hindern. **retarded** *adj* zurückgeblieben.

reticent ['retisənt] *adj* schweigsam. **reticence** *n* Schweigsamkeit *f,* Zurückhaltung *f.*

retina ['retinə] *n* Netzhaut *f.*

retinue ['retinjuɪ] *n* Gefolge *neut.*

retire [rə'taiə] *v* sich zurückziehen; (*from work*) in den Ruhestand treten. **retired** *adj* pensioniert. **retirement** *n* Ruhestand *m;* (*resignation*) Rucktritt *m.* **retiring** *adj* zurückhaltend.

retort¹ [rə'toɪt] *v* (*scharf*) erwidern. *n* (schlagfertige) Antwort *f.*

retort² [rə'toɪt] *n* (*vessel*) Retorte *f.*

retrace [ri'treis] *v* zurückverfolgen.

retract [rə'trakt] *v* (*draw in*) einziehen; (*take back*) zurücknehmen, widerrufen. **retractable** *adj* einziehbar.

retreat [rə'tritt] *v* sich zurückziehen. *n* Rückzug *m;* (*place*) Zufluchtsort *m.*

retrieve [rə'triɪv] *v* wiederfinden, herausholen. **retriever** *n* Apporthund *m.*

retrograde ['retrəgreid] *adj* rückläufig.

retrospect ['retrəspekt] *n* Rückblick *m.* **in retrospect** rückschauend. **retrospective** *adj* rückwirkend.

return [rə'təɪn] *v* zurückkommen, wiederkehren; (*give back*) zurückgeben; (*answer*) erwidern. *n* Rückkehr *f;* (*ticket*) Rückfahrkarte *f;* (*comm*) Ertrag *m.* **tax return** Steuererklärung *f.* **many happy returns** herzlichen Glückwunsch.

reunite [riɪju'nait] *v* wiedervereinigen. **reunion** *n* Wiedervereinigung *f;* (*meeting*) Treffen *neut.*

rev [rev] *v* (*coll: mot*) auf Touren bringen. **revs** *pl n* Drehzahl *f sing.*

reveal [rə'viɪl] *v* enthüllen, offenbaren; (*display*) zeigen. **revealing** *adj* aufschlußreich. **revelation** *n* Enthüllung *f,* Offenbarung *f.*

revel ['revl] *v* feiern. **revel in** schwelgen in. **reveller** *n* Feiernde(r). **revelry** *n* Festlichkeit *f.*

revenge [rə'vendʒ] *n* Rache *f.* *v* rächen. **take revenge on** sich rächen an.

revenue ['revinjuɪ] *n* Einnahmen *pl.*

reverberate [rə'vəɪbəreit] *v* (*sound*)

widerhallen. **reverberation** *n* Widerhall *m*.

reverence ['revərəns] *n* Verehrung *f*, Ehrfurcht *f*. **revere** *v* (ver)ehren. **reverend** *adj* ehrwürdig. **reverent** *adj* ehrerbietig.

reverse [rə'vəːs] *v* umkehren; (*mot*) rückwarts fahren. *n* (*opposite*) Gegenteil *neut*; (*of coin, etc.*) Rückseite *f*; (*mot*) Rückwärtsgang *m*. **reverse-charge call** R-Gespräch *neut*. **reversible** *adj* (*coat*) wendbar; (*law*) umstoßbar.

revert [rə'vəːt] *v* zurückkehren.

review [rə'vjuː] *n* Nachprüfung *f*; (*magazine*) Rundschau *f*; (*troops*) Parade *f*. *v* nachprüfen. **reviewer** *n* Kritiker *m*.

revise [rə'vaiz] *v* revidieren; (*book*) überarbeiten. **revision** *n* Revision *f*; Überarbeitung *f*.

revive [rə'vaiv] *v* wiederbeleben. **revival** *n* Wiederbelebung *f*; (*play*) Wiederaufführung *f*.

revoke [rə'vouk] *n* widerrufen. **revocable** *adj* widerruflich. **revocation** *n* Widerruf *m*.

revolt [rə'voult] *n* Aufruhr *m*, Aufstand *m*. *v* revoltieren, sich empören; (*disgust*) abstoßen. **revolting** *adj* abstoßend.

revolution [revə'luːʃən] *n* (*pol*) Revolution *f*; (*turning*) Umdrehung *f*, Rotation *f*. **revolutions per minute** Drehzahl *f*. **revolutionary** *adj* revolutionär; *n* Revolutionär(in).

revolve [rə'volv] *v* (sich) drehen. **revolver** *n* Revolver *m*. **revolving** *adj* drehbar.

revue [rə'vjuː] *n* Revue *f*.

revulsion [rə'vʌlʃən] *n* Ekel *m*.

reward [rə'woːd] *n* Belohnung *f*; *v* belohnen. **rewarding** *adj* lohnend.

rhetoric ['retərik] *n* Rhetorik *f*; (*empty*) Redeschwall *m*. **rhetorical** *adj* rhetorisch.

rheumatism ['ruːmətizəm] *n* Rheumatismus *m*. **rheumatic** *adj* rheumatisch.

rhinoceros [rai'nosərəs] *n* Nashorn *neut*.

rhododendron [roudə'dendrən] *n* Rhododendron *m or neut*.

rhubarb ['ruːbaːb] *n* Rhabarber *m*.

rhyme [raim] *n* Reim *m*. *v* reimen. **nursery rhyme** Kinderreim *n*.

rhythm ['riðəm] *n* Rhythmus *m*. **rhythmic** *adj* rhythmisch.

rib [rib] *n* Rippe *f*. **ribbed** *adj* (*material*) gerippt.

ribbon ['ribən] *n* Band *neut*; (*typewriter*) Farbband *neut*. **ribbons** *pl n* (*rags*) Fetzen *pl*. **ribboned** *adj* gestreift.

rice [rais] *n* Reis *m*.

rich [ritʃ] *adj* reich, wohlhabend; (*earth*) fruchtbar; (*food*) schwer. **rich man/woman** Reiche(r). **the rich** die Reichen. **riches** *pl n* Reichtum *m*. **richness** *n* Reichtum *m*; (*food*) Schwere *f*; (*finery*) Pracht *f*.

rickety ['rikəti] *adj* (*wobbly*) wackelig.

***rid** [rid] *v* befreien, frei machen. **be rid of** los sein (+*acc*). **get rid of** loswerden (+*acc*). **good riddance to him!** Gott sei Dank ist man ihn los!

ridden ['ridn] *V* ride.

riddle ['ridl] *n* Rätsel *neut*.

riddled ['ridld] *adj* durchlöchert.

***ride** [raid] *v* reiten; (*bicycle, motor cycle*) fahren. **riding whip** Reitpeitsche *f*. *n* Ritt *m*; Fahrt *f*. **take for a ride** (*coll*) übers Ohr hauen. **rider** *n* Reiter(in); (*cycle*) Fahrer(in). **riding** *n* Reitsport *m*.

ridge [ridʒ] *n* Kamm *m*, Grat *m*; (*roof*) First *m*.

ridicule ['ridikjuːl] *n* Spott *m*. *v* verspotten, lächerlich machen. **ridiculous** *adj* lächerlich.

rife [raif] *adj* **be rife** vorherrschen, grassieren. **rife with** voll von.

rifle[1] ['raifl] *n* (*gun*) Gewehr *neut*. **riflerange** *n* Schießstand *m*.

rifle[2] ['raifl] *v* ausplündern.

rift [rift] *n* Spalte *f*, Riß *m*.

rig [rig] *n* Takelung *f*; (*coll*) Vorrichtung *f*, Anlage *f*. *v* auftakeln. **rig out** (*coll*) ausstatten. **rigging** *n* Takelwerk *neut*.

right [rait] *adj* (*correct*) recht, richtig; (*proper*) angemessen; (*right-hand*) recht. **all right** in Ordnung. **be right** (*thing*) recht sein; (*person*) recht haben. **feel all right** sich wohl befinden. **right-handed** *adj* rechtshändig. **right-wing** *adj* Rechts-. *adv* (*correctly*) recht, richtig; (*completely*) ganz; (*to the right*) (nach) rechts. **right away** sofort. *n* Recht *neut*. **right of way** (*mot*) Vorfahrt *f*. *v* berichtigen. **rightly** *adv* mit Recht.

righteous ['raitʃəs] *adj* rechtschaffen, gerecht.

rigid ['ridʒid] *adj* starr, steif; (*person*) streng, unbeugsam. **rigidity** *n* Starrheit *f*.

rigmarole ['rigməroul] *n* (*coll*) Theater *neut*.

rigour ['rigə] *n* Strenge *f*, Härte *f*. **rigorous** *adj* streng.

rim [rim] n Rand m.
rind [raind] n (cheese) Rinde f; (bacon) Schwarte f.
ring¹ [riŋ] n Ring m; (comm) Kartell neut. **wedding ring** n Trauring m. **ringleader** n Rädelsführer m.
*ring² [riŋ] v (sound) läuten, klingeln; (echo) widerhallen. n (Glocken)Klang m, Klingeln neut. **there's a ring at the door** es klingelt. **ring (up)** (coll: phone) anrufen. **ringing** n Läuten neut.
rink [riŋk] n (ice) Eisbahn f.
rinse [rins] v ausspülen. n Spülung f.
riot ['raiət] n Aufruhr m, Tumult m. v randalieren. **rioter** n Aufrührer(in). **riotous** adj aufrührerisch; (laughter) zügellos.
rip [rip] v reißen, zerreißen. n Riß m. **ripcord** n Reißleine f.
ripe [raip] adj reif. **ripen** v reifen, reif werden.
ripple ['ripl] n Kräuselung f; (noise) Platschern neut. v (sich) kräuseln.
*rise [raiz] v sich erheben; (get up) aufstehen; (meeting) vertagen; (prices) steigen. n Aufstieg m; (prices) Steigen neut; (increase) Zuwachs m; (pay) Erhöhung f. **give rise to** hervorrufen, veranlassen. **rising** adj steigend.
risen ['rizn] V rise.
risk [risk] n Risiko neut; (danger) Gefahr f. v riskieren. **take a risk** ein Risiko eingehen. **risky** adj riskant.
rissole ['risoul] n Boulette f, Frikadelle f.
rite [rait] n Ritus m, Zeremonie f.
ritual ['ritʃuəl] n Ritual neut. adj rituell.
rival ['raivəl] n Rivale m, Rivalin f. adj rivalisierend. v rivalisieren or wetteifern mit. **rivalry** n Rivalität f.
river ['rivə] n Fluß m. **down river** stromabwärts. **up river** stromaufwärts. **riverside** n Flußufer neut; adj Ufer-.
rivet ['rivit] n Niet m. v vernieten; (captivate) fesseln.
road [roud] n Straße f; (esp. fig) Weg m. **main road** Landstraße f. **on the road to** auf dem Wege zu. **road accident** Verkehrsunfall m. **road block** Straßensperre f. **road sign** Straßenschild neut. **roadworks** pl n Straßenbauarbeiten pl.
roam [roum] v (umher)wandern.
roar [rɔː] v brüllen; (person) laut schreien; (wind) toben. n Gebrüll neut. **roaring** adj (coll) enorm, famos.

roast [roust] v braten, rösten. n Braten m.
rob [rob] v rauben. **robber** n Räuber m. **robbery** n Raub m.
robe [roub] n Talar m. **bathrobe** Bademantel m. v kleiden.
robin ['robin] n Rotkehlchen neut.
robot ['roubot] n Roboter m.
robust [rə'bʌst] adj robust, kräftig. **robustness** n Robustheit f.
rock¹ [rok] n (stone) Fels m, Felsen m; (naut) Klippe f. **steady as a rock** felsenfest. **on the rocks** (fig) gescheitert; (drink) mit Eis. **rockery** n Steingarten m. **rocky** adj felsig.
rock² [rok] v schaukeln; (baby) wiegen. **rocking-horse** n Schaukelpferd neut. **rock 'n' roll** n Rock and Roll m.
rocket ['rokit] n Rakete f. v hochschießen.
rod [rod] n Rute f.
rode [roud] V ride.
rodent ['roudənt] n Nagetier neut.
roe [rou] n Rogen m.
rogue [roug] n Schurke m. **roguish** adj schurkisch.
role [roul] n Rolle f.
roll [roul] v rollen. **roll out** ausrollen. **roll over** sich herumdrehen. **roll up** aufwickeln, aufrollen. **roller** n Walze f. **roller blind** Rouleau neut. **roller-skate** n Rollschuh. **rolling-pin** n Nudelholz neut. **roll-neck** n Rollkragen m. n Rolle f; (bread) Brötchen neut; (meat) Roulade f. **roll-call** n Namensaufruf m.
romance [rou'mans] n Romanze f. **romantic** romantisch; n Romantiker(in).
Rome [roum] n Rom neut. **Roman** adj römisch. n Römer(in). **Roman Catholic** römisch-katholisch.
romp [romp] v sich herumbalgen. **romp through** leicht hindurchkommen.
roof [ruːf] n (pl -s) Dach neut. v bedachen. **roofing** n Dachwerk neut.
rook¹ [ruk] n Saatkrähe f. v (coll) schwindeln, betrügen.
rook² [ruk] n (chess) Turm m.
room [ruːm] n (house) Zimmer neut; (space) Raum m, Platz m. v logieren (bei). **rooms** pl n Wohnung f. **room-mate** n Zimmergenosse m, -genossin f. **roomy** adj geräumig.
roost [ruːst] n Hühnerstall m. v (bird) auf der Stange sitzen, schlafen. **rooster** n Hahn m.

root¹ [ruːt] n Würzel f; (source) Quelle f.
take root Wurzel schlagen. **rooted** adj
eingewürzelt. **rootless** adj wurzellos.
root² [ruːt] v **root for** (pigs) wühlen nach.
root out ausgraben.
rope [roup] n Seil neut; (naut) Tau neut. v
festbinden. **know the ropes** sich auskennen. **ropeladder** n Strickleiter f. **ropy** adj
(coll) kläglich, schäbig.
rosary ['rouzəri] n Rosenkranz m.
rose¹ [rouz] V **rise**.
rose² [rouz] n Rose f. **rosebush** n Rosenstrauch m. **rose-coloured** adj rosenrot.
through rose-coloured spectacles durch
eine rosarote Brille. **rosette** n Rosette f.
rosy adj rosig.
rosemary ['rouzməri] n Rosmarin m.
rot [rot] v verfaulen. n Fäulnis f; (nonsense) Quatsch m. **rotten** adj faul,
verfault; (corrupt) morsch, faul. **rottenness** n Fäule f. **rotter** n (coll)
Schweinehund m.
rota ['routə] n Turnus m.
rotate [rou'teit] v sich drehen, rotieren;
(crops) wechseln lassen. **rotary** adj rotierend, kreisend. **rotation** n Umdrehung f,
Rotation f; (crops, etc.) Abwechselung f.
rotor n Rotor m.
rouge [ruːʒ] n (make-up) Rouge neut.
rough [rʌf] adj rauh; (sea) stürmisch;
(hair) struppig; (person) grob, roh;
(approximate) ungefähr. **roughage** n Ballaststoffe pl. **roughen** v aufrauhen. **roughly** adv ungefähr. **roughness** n Rauhheit f.
roulette [ruː'let] n Roulette f.
round [raund] adj rund. adv rundherum.
n Runde f. v runden; (corner)
(herum)fahren um. **round off** abrunden.
round up (cattle) zusammentreiben;
(criminals) ausheben. **round trip** (Hinund) Rückfahrt f. **roundabout** n Karussell neut; (mot) Kreisverkehr m; adj
weitschweifig. **roundly** adv gründlich.
roundness n Rundheit f.
route [ruːt] n Weg m, Route f.
routine [ruː'tiːn] n Routine f. adj üblich.
rove [rouv] v herumwandern. **rover** n
Wanderer m.
row¹ [rou] n Reihe f. **in rows** reihenweise.
row² [rou] v (boat) rudern. **rowing** n
Rudern neut; (sport) Rudersport m. **rowing boat** Ruderboot neut.
row³ [rau] n (quarrel) Streit m; (noise)
Krach m. v sich streiten, zanken.

rowdy ['raudi] adj lärmend, flegelhaft. n
Rowdy m.
royal ['roiəl] adj königlich. **royalist** n
Royalist m. **royalty** n Königtum neut.
royalties pl Tantieme f.
rub [rʌb] v reiben. **rub off** abreiben. **rub
out** (erase) ausradieren. n Reiben neut.
rubber ['rʌbə] n Gummi m; (eraser)
Radiergummi m. **rubber band** Gummiband neut. **rubber stamp** Gummistempel
m.
rubbish ['rʌbiʃ] n Abfall m, Müll m; (nonsense) Quatsch m. **rubbishy** adj wertlos.
rubble ['rʌbl] n Trümmer pl, Schutt m.
ruby ['ruːbi] n Rubin m. adj (colour)
rubinrot.
rucksack ['rʌksak] n Rucksack m.
rudder ['rʌdə] n Ruder neut.
rude [ruːd] adj grob, unverschämt;
(rough) roh, wild. **rudeness** n Grobheit f;
Roheit f.
rudiment ['ruːdimənt] n Rudiment neut.
rudiments pl Grundlagen pl.
rueful ['ruːfəl] adj kläglich, traurig. **ruefulness** n Traurigkeit f.
ruff [rʌf] n Krause f; (bird's) Halskrause
f.
ruffian ['rʌfiən] n Schurke m, Raufbold
m.
ruffle ['rʌfl] v kräuseln. n Krause f.
rug [rʌg] n (floor) Vorleger m; (blanket)
Wolldecke f.
rugby ['rʌgbi] n Rugby neut.
rugged ['rʌgid] adj wild, rauh; (face)
runzelig. **ruggedness** n Rauheit f.
ruin ['ruːin] n Verfall m, Vernichtung f;
(building) Ruine f. v vernichten, ruinieren. **ruins** pl Trümmer pl. **ruinous** adj
ruinierend.
rule [ruːl] n Regel f; (pol) Regierung f;
(drawing) Lineal neut. **rule of thumb**
Faustregel f. v (govern) regieren; (decide)
entscheiden. **ruler** n (pol) Herrscher(in);
(drawing) Lineal neut. **ruling** adj herrschend; n Entscheidung f.
rum [rʌm] n Rum m.
Rumania [ruː'mainjə] n Rumänien neut.
Rumanian n Rumäne m, Rumänin f; adj
rumänisch.
rumble ['rʌmbl] v poltern, knurren. n
Dröhnen neut, Gepolter neut.
rummage ['rʌmidʒ] v **rummage through**
durchsuchen, herumwühlen in.
rumour ['ruːmə] n Gerücht neut.

rump [rʌmp] *n* Hinterteil *neut*. **rump
steak** Rumpsteak *neut*.

***run** [rʌn] *v* rennen, laufen; (*river*)
fließen; (*machine*) laufen, in Gang sein;
(*nose*) laufen. **run away** weglaufen. **run
down** (*person*) heruntermachen. **run-down**
adj erschöpft. **run out** zu Ende laufen.
run out of knapp werden mit. **run over**
(flüchtig) durchsehen. **runway** *n*
Rollbahn *f*. *n* Lauf *m*, Rennen *neut*. **in
the long run** auf die Dauer. **on the run**
auf der Flucht. **runner** *n* Läufer(in). **running** *adj* laufend; (*water*) fließend.

rung[^1] [rʌn] *V* ring[^2].

rung[^2] [rʌn] *n* Sprosse *f*.

rupture ['rʌptʃə] *n* Bruch *m*. *v* brechen,
zerreißen.

rural ['ruərəl] *adj* ländlich, Land-.

rush[^1] [rʌʃ] *v* stürzen, rasen. *n* Stürzen
neut. **be in a rush** es eilig haben. **rush
hour** Hauptverkehrszeit *f*.

rush[^2] [rʌʃ] *n* (*bot*) Binse *f*.

rusk [rʌsk] *n* Zwieback *m*.

Russia ['rʌʃə] *n* Rußland *neut*. **Russian**
adj russisch; *n* Russe *m*, Russin *f*.

rust [rʌst] *n* Rost *m*. *v* rosten, rostig werden. **rust-coloured** *adj* rostfarben. **rustproof** *adj* rostfrei. **rusty** *adj* rostig.

rustic ['rʌstik] *adj* ländlich, bäuerlich. *n*
Bauer *m*.

rustle ['rʌsl] *v* rascheln, rauschen. *n* Rascheln *neut*.

rut [rʌt] *n* Furche *f*. **be stuck in a rut**
beim alten Schlendrian verbleiben.

ruthless ['ruːθlis] *adj* unbarmherzig, rücksichtslos. **ruthlessness** *n* Unbarm-
herzigkeit *f*.

rye [rai] *n* Roggen *m*.

S

Sabbath ['sabəθ] *n* Sabbat *m*.

sabbatical [sə'batikəl] *adj* **sabbatical year**
Urlaubsjahr *neut*.

sable ['seibl] *n* Zobel *m*; (fur) Zobelpelz
m. *adj* Zobel-.

sabotage ['sabətaːʒ] *n* Sabotage *f*. *v* sabotieren. **saboteur** *n* Saboteur *m*.

sabre ['seibə] *n* Säbel *m*.

saccharin ['sakərin] *n* Saccharin *neut*.

sachet ['saʃei] *n* Kissen *neut*, Täschchen
neut.

sack [sak] *n* Sack *m*. *v* entlassen. **get the
sack** (*coll*) entlassen werden.

sacrament ['sakrəmənt] *n* Sakrament
neut. **sacramental** *adj* sakramental.

sacred ['seikrid] *adj* heilig.

sacrifice ['sakrifais] *v* opfern. *n* Opfer
neut. **sacrificial** *adj* Opfer-.

sacrilege ['sakrəlidʒ] *n* Sakrileg *neut*. **sacrilegious** *adj* gotteslästerlich.

sad [sad] *adj* traurig. **sadden** *v* traurig
machen. **sadness** *n* Traurigkeit *f*.

saddle ['sadl] *n* Sattel *m*. (*meat*) Rücken
m. *v* satteln; (*with task*) belasten. **saddlebag** *n* Satteltasche *f*. **saddler** *n* Sattler *m*.

sadism ['seidizəm] *n* Sadismus *m*. **sadist** *n*
Sadist(in). **sadistic** *adj* sadistisch.

safe [seif] *adj* (*secure*) sicher; (*not dangerous*) ungefährlich; (*careful*) vorsichtig;
(*dependable*) verläßlich. *n* Safe *m*, Geld-
schrank *m*. **safe and sound** gesund und
munter. **safe conduct** Geleitbrief *m*. **safe-
guard** *n* Sicherung *f*, Vorsichtsmaßnahme
f. **safety** *n* Sicherheit *f*. **safety belt**
Sicherheitsgurt *m*. **safety pin** Sicherheit-
snadel *f*.

saffron ['safrən] *n* Safran *m*. *adj*
safrangelb.

sag [sag] *v* absacken, herabhängen.

saga ['saɡə] *n* Saga *f*.

sage[^1] [seidʒ] *adj* weise. *n* Weise(r). **saga-
cious** *adj* scharfsinnig, klug. **sagacity** *n*
Klugheit *f*.

sage[^2] [seidʒ] *n* (*bot*) Salbei *f*.

Sagittarius [sadʒi'teəriəs] *n* Schütze *m*.

sago ['seigou] *n* Sago *m*.

said [sed] *V* say.

sail [seil] *n* Segel *neut*. *v* segeln; (*depart*)
fahren. **sailing** *n* Segelsport *m*. **sailing
boat** *n* Segelboot *neut*. **sailor** *n* Matrose
m.

saint [seint] *n* Heilige(r). **saintliness** *n*
Heiligkeit *f*. **saintly** *adj* fromm.

sake [seik] *n* **for the sake of** wegen
(+ *gen*), um … (+ *gen*) willen. **for heav-
en's sake** um Himmels willen. **for my
sake** um meinetwillen.

salad ['saləd] *n* Salat *m*. **salad dressing**
Salatsoße *f*.

salami [sə'laːmi] *n* Salami *f*.

salary ['saləri] *n* Gehalt *neut*. **salaried
employee** Gehaltsempfänger(in). **salary
increase** Gehaltserhöhung *f*.

sale [seil] *n* Verkauf *m*; (*end of season*) Schlußverkauf *m*. **on** or **for sale** zu verkaufen. **sales** *pl* Absatz *m*, Umsatz *m*. **sales department** Verkaufsabteilung *f*. **salesgirl** or **saleswoman** *n* Verkäuferin. **salesman** *n* Verkäufer *m*; (*travelling*) Geschäftsreisende(r).

saline ['seilain] *adj* salzig. **salinity** *n* Salzigkeit *f*.

saliva [sə'laivə] *n* Speichel *m*. **salivary** *adj* Speichel-.

sallow ['salou] *adj* bläßlich.

salmon ['samən] *n* Lachs *m*. *adj* (*colour*) lachsrot.

salon ['salon] *n* Salon *m*.

saloon [sə'luɪn] *n* Saal *m*, Salon *m*; (*bar*) Kneipe *f*, Ausschank *m*.

salt [soɪlt] *n* Salz *neut*. *v* salzen; (*pickle*) einsalzen. **salt beef** gepökeltes Rindfleisch *neut*. **salt cellar** Salzfäßchen *neut*. **salted** *adj* gesalzen. **saltiness** *n* Salzigkeit *f*. **salt water** Salzwasser *neut*. **salty** *adj* salzig.

salute [sə'luɪt] *v* grüßen. *n* Gruß *m*; (*of guns*) Salut *m*.

salvage ['salvidʒ] *n* Bergung *f*, Rettung *f*. *v* bergen, retten.

salvation [sal'veifən] *n* Rettung *f*, Heil *neut*. **Salvation Army** Heilsarmee *f*.

same [seim] *pron, adj* derselbe, dieselbe, dasselbe; der/die/das gleiche. **all the same** trotzdem. **it's all the same to me** es ist mir gleich or egal. **the same old story** die alte Leier *f*. **sameness** *n* Gleichheit *f*; (*monotony*) Eintönigkeit *f*.

sample ['saɪmpl] *n* Muster *neut*, Probe *f*. *v* probieren.

sanatorium [sanə'toɪriəm] *n* Sanatorium *neut*.

sanction ['saŋkʃən] *n* Sanktion *f*. *v* billigen.

sanctity ['saŋktəti] *n* Heiligkeit *f*.

sanctuary ['saŋktʃuəri] *n* Heiligtum *neut*; (*place of safety*) Asyl *neut*.

sand [sand] *n* Sand *m*. *v* **sand down** abschmirgeln. **sandbag** *n* Sandsack *m*. **sandbank** *n* Sandbank *f*. **sandpaper** *n* Sandpapier *neut*. **sand-pit** *n* Sandgrube *f*. **sandy** *adj* sandig.

sandal ['sandl] *n* Sandale *f*.

sandwich ['sanwidʒ] *n* Sandwich *neut*.

sane [sein] *adj* geistig gesund. **sanity** *n* geistige Gesundheit *f*.

sang [saŋ] *V* sing.

sanitary ['sanitəri] *adj* hygienisch. **sanita-** ry towel Damenbinde *f*. **sanitation** *n* Sanierung *f*, sanitäre Einrichtungen *pl*.

sank [saŋk] *V* sink.

sap [sap] *n* Saft *m*. **sapling** *n* junger Baum *m*.

sapphire ['safaiə] *n* Saphir *m*.

sarcasm ['saɪkazəm] *n* Sarkasmus *m*. **sarcastic** *adj* sarkastisch, höhnisch.

sardine [saɪ'diɪn] *n* Sardine *f*.

sardonic [saɪ'donik] *adj* sardonisch, zynisch.

sash[1] [saʃ] *n* (*garment*) Schärpe *f*.

sash[2] [saʃ] *n* (*window*) Fensterrahmen *m*. **sash window** Fallfenster *neut*.

sat [sat] *V* sit.

satchel ['satʃəl] *n* Schulmappe *f*.

satellite ['satəlait] *n* Satellit *m*; (*pol*) Satellitenstaat *m*.

satin ['satin] *n* Satin *m*. *adj* Satin-.

satire ['sataiə] *n* Satire *f*. **satirical** *adj* satirisch. **satirist** *n* Satiriker(in).

satisfy ['satisfai] *v* befriedigen. **satisfaction** *n* Befriedigung *f*; (*contentment*) Zufriedenheit *f*. **satisfactory** *adj* befriedigend. **satisfied** *adj* zufrieden.

saturate ['satʃəreit] *v* sättigen. **saturation** *n* Sättigung *f*.

Saturday ['satədi] *n* Sonnabend *m*, Samstag *m*.

Saturn ['satən] *n* Saturn *m*. **saturnine** *adj* (*person*) stillschweigend, verdrießlich.

sauce [soɪs] *n* Soße *f*; (*cheek*) Frechheit *f*. **sauce-boat** *n* Soßenschüssel *f*.

saucepan ['soɪspən] *n* Kochtopf *m*, Kasserolle *f*.

saucer ['soɪsə] *n* Untertasse *f*. **flying saucer** fliegende Untertasse *f*.

saucy ['soɪsi] *adj* frech, keck.

sauna ['soɪnə] *n* Sauna *f*.

saunter ['soɪntə] *v* schlendern.

sausage ['sosidʒ] *n* Wurst *f*.

savage ['savidʒ] *adj* (*animal*) wild; (*tribe, etc.*) primitiv, barbarisch; (*behaviour*) brutal, roh. *n* Wilde(r). **savageness** *n* Wildheit *f*. **savagery** *n* Unzivilisiertheit *f*.

save[1] [seiv] *v* (*rescue*) (er)retten; (*money*) sparen; (*avoid*) ersparen; (*time*) gewinnen; (*protect*) schützen. *n* (*football*) Abwehr *f*. **saving** *n* Ersparnis *f*. **savings** *pl* Ersparnisse *pl*. **savings account** Sparkonto *neut*. **savings bank** Sparkasse *f*. **savings book** Sparbuch *neut*.

save[2] [seiv] *prep, conj* außer (+*dat*), mit Ausnahme von (+*dat*).

saviour ['seivjə] *n* Retter *m*.
savoir-faire [savwɑː'feə] *n* Gewandtheit *f*,
Feingefühl *neut*.
savoury ['seivəri] *adj* wohlschmeckend,
würzig. *n* (*piquant*) Vorspeise *f*.
saw¹ [sɔː] *V* **see¹**.
*****saw²** [sɔː] *n* Säge *f*. *v* sägen. **sawdust** *n*
Sägemehl *neut*. **sawmill** *n* Sägewerk *neut*.
sawn [sɔːn] *V* **saw²**.
saxophone ['saksəfoun] *n* Saxophon *neut*.
saxophonist *n* Saxophonist(in).
*****say** [sei] *v* sagen; (*maintain*) behaupten.
saying *n* Sprichwort *neut*. **have one's say**
seine Meinung äußern. **it goes without
saying** selbstverständlich.
scab [skab] *n* Schorf *m*; (*strike-breaker*)
Streikbrecher *m*.
scaffold ['skafəld] *n* (*execution*) Schafott
m. **scaffolding** *n* Baugerüst *neut*, Gestell
neut.
scald [skɔːld] *v* verbrühen. *n* Verbrühung
f. **scalding** *adj* brühheiß.
scale¹ [skeil] *n* (*fish, etc.*) Schuppe *f*; (*kettle*) Kesselstein *m*. *v* schuppen. **scaly** *adj*
schuppig.
scale² [skeil] *n also* **scales** *pl* Waage *f*.
scale³ [skeil] *n* (*gradation*) Skala *f*;
(*music*) Tonleiter *f*; (*proportion*) Maßstab
m. *v* (*climb*) erklettern. **to scale**
maßstabgetreu.   **scale   model**
maßstabgetreues Modell *neut*.
scallop ['skaləp] *n* Kammuschel *f*.
scalp [skalp] *n* Kopfhaut *f*; (*as trophy*)
Skalp *m*. *v* skalpieren.
scalpel ['skalpəl] *n* Skalpell *neut*.
scampi ['skampi] *pl n* Scampi *pl*.
scan [skan] *v* (*carefully*) prüfen, genau
untersuchen; (*briefly*) (flüchtig) überblicken.
scandal ['skandl] *n* Skandal *m*. **scandalize**
v schockieren. **scandalous** *adj* skandalös.
scandalmonger *n* Lästermaul *neut*.
scant [skant] *adj* knapp, spärlich. **scanty**
adj knapp; (*insufficient*) unzulänglich.
scapegoat ['skeipgout] *n* Sündenbock *m*.
scar [skɑː] *n* Narbe *f*. *v* vernarben.
scarce [skeəs] *adj* knapp, selten. **scarcely**
adv kaum. **scarcity** *n* Mangel *m*.
scare [skeə] *v* erschrecken, in Schrecken
versetzen. *n* Schreck *m*. **scarecrow** *n*
Vogelscheue *f*. **scary** *adj* erschreckend.
scarf [skɑːf] *n* Halstuch *neut*, Schal *m*.
scarlet ['skɑːlit] *adj* scharlachrot. **scarlet
fever** Scharlachfieber *neut*.

scathing ['skeiðiŋ] *adj* (*fig*) verletzend,
beißend.
scatter ['skatə] *v* (ver)streuen; bestreuen
(mit). **scatterbrain** *n* Wirrkopf *n*.
scavenge ['skavindʒ] *v* durchsuchen,
herumwühlen (in). **scavenger** *n* (*zool*)
Aasfresser *m*.
scene [siːn] *n* Szene *f*; (*situation*) Ort *m*.
scenery *n* Landschaft *f*; (*theatre*)
Bühnenbild *neut*. **scenic** *adj* malerisch.
scent [sent] *n* Duft *m*; (*perfume*) Parfüm
neut. *v* (*smell*) riechen; (*perfume*)
parfümieren. **scented** *adj* parfümiert.
sceptic ['skeptik] *n* Skeptiker(in). **sceptical**
adj skeptisch. **scepticism** *n* Skeptizismus
m.
sceptre ['septə] *n* Zepter *neut*.
schedule ['ʃedjuːl] *n* Plan *m*; (*list*)
Verzeichnis *neut*; (*trains*) Fahrplan *m*. *v*
planen.
scheme [skiːm] *n* Schema *neut*; (*plan*)
Plan *m*, Programm *neut*. *v* (*coll*) intrigier-
en. **schemer** *n* Ränkeschmied *m*.
schizophrenia   [ˌskitsə'friːniə]   *n*
Schizophrenie *f*. **schizophrenic** *adj*
schizophren; *n* Schizophrene(r).
scholar ['skolə] *n* Gelehrte(r); (*pupil*)
Schüler(in). **scholarly** *adj* gelehrt. **scholarship** *n* Gelehrsamkeit *f*; (*grant*)
Stipendium *neut*.
scholastic [skə'lastik] *adj* akademisch.
school¹ [skuːl] *n* Schule *f*. *v* schulen.
schoolboy *n* Schüler *m*. **schoolgirl** *n*
Schülerin *f*. **schooling** *n* Unterricht *m*.
schoolteacher *n* Lehrer(in).
school² [skuːl] *n* (*fish*) Zug *m*; (*whales*)
Schar *f*.
schooner ['skuːnə] *n* Schoner *m*; (*glass*)
Humpen *m*.
sciatica [sai'atikə] *n* Ischias *m or neut*.
science ['saiəns] *n* Wissenschaft *f*; (*natural science*) Naturwissenschaft *f*. **scientific** *adj* wissenschaftlich. **scientist** *n* Wis-
senschaftler(in).
scissors ['sizəz] *pl n* Schere *f sing*.
scoff¹ [skof] *v* spotten (über). *n* Spott *m*,
Hohn *m*.
scoff² [skof] *v* (*coll: eat*) fressen,
hinunterschlingen.
scold [skould] *v* schimpfen. **give a scold-
ing** ausschelten (+*acc*).
scone [skon] *n* Teegebäck *neut*.
scoop [skuːp] *n* Schaufel *f*, Schöpfer *m*;
(*newspaper*) (sensationelle) Erstmeldung
f. *v* schöpfen.

scooter ['skuːtə] n Roller m.

scope [skoup] n Umfang m, Gebiet neut.

scorch [skɔːtʃ] v verbrennen. **scorching** adj (weather) brennend.

score [skɔː] n (score) Punktzahl f, Spielergebnis neut; (20) zwanzig (Stück); (music) Partitur f. v (points) zählen, machen. **know the score** (coll) Bescheid wissen. **scoreboard** n Anzeigetafel f.

scorn [skɔːn] n Verachtung f, Spott m. v verachten. **scornful** adj verächtlich.

scorpion ['skɔːpiən] n Skorpion m.

Scotland ['skɔtlənd] n Schottland neut. **Scotch** n (schottischer) Whisky m. **Scotsman** n Schotte m. **Scotswoman** n Schottin f. **Scottish** adj schottisch.

scoundrel ['skaundrəl] n Schurke m, Schuft m.

scour[1] [skauə] v (clean) scheuern, schrubben. **scourer** n Scheuerlappen m.

scour[2] [skauə] v (search) durchsuchen.

scout [skaut] n (mil) Späher m; (boy scout) Pfadfinder m.

scowl [skaul] v finster (an)blicken. n finsterer Blick m.

scramble ['skrambl] v krabbeln, klettern; (eggs) rühren. **scramble for** balgen um. **scrambled egg(s)** Rührei neut.

scrap [skrap] n (piece) Stück neut, Fetzen m; (metal) Schrott m; (fight) Prügelei f. v (metal) verschrotten; (plan) verwerfen. **scrapbook** n Sammelalbum neut, Einklebebuch neut.

scrape [skreip] v schaben, kratzen. n Kratzen neut; (coll) Klemme f.

scratch [skratʃ] v (zer)kratzen. n Kratzstelle f, Riß m; (wound) Schramme f. **scratchy** adj kratzend.

scrawl [skrɔːl] v kritzeln. n Gekritzel neut.

scream [skriːm] n Schrei m. v schreien. **it's a scream** es ist zum Schreien.

screech [skriːtʃ] n Gekreisch neut; (cry) (durchdringender) Schrei m. v kreischen.

screen [skriːn] n (Schutz)Schirm m, (Schutz)Wand f; (film) Leinwand f; (TV) Bildschirm m. v abschirmen. **screenplay** n Drehbuch neut.

screw [skruː] n Schraube f. v schrauben. **screwdriver** n Schraubenzieher m.

scribble ['skribl] n Gekritzel neut. v kritzeln. **scribbler** n Kritzler m.

script [skript] n Schrift f; (handwriting) Handschrift f; (film) Drehbuch neut.

scripture ['skriptʃə] n Heilige Schrift f.

scroll [skroul] n Schriftrolle f; (decoration) Schnörkel m.

scrounge [skraundʒ] v (coll) schmarotzen, schnorren. **scrounger** n Schmarotzer m.

scrub[1] [skrʌb] v schrubben, scheuern. n Schrubben neut. **scrubbing brush** n Scheuerbürste f.

scrub[2] [skrʌb] n (bush) Gestrüpp neut, Busch m.

scruffy ['skrʌfi] adj schäbig.

scruple ['skruːpl] n Skrupel m. **scrupulous** adj peinlich, voller.

scrutiny ['skruːtəni] n (genaue) Untersuchung f. **scrutinize** v genau untersuchen.

scuffle ['skʌfl] n Rauferei f. v sich raufen.

sculpt [skʌlpt] v formen, schnitzen. **sculptor** n Bildhauer m. **sculpture** n Skulptur f.

scum [skʌm] n Abschaum m.

scurf [skəːf] n Schorf m; (dandruff) Schuppen pl.

scurvy ['skəːvi] n Skorbut m.

scuttle ['skʌtl] n Kohleneimer m.

scythe [saið] n Sense f. v (ab)mähen.

sea [siː] n See f, Meer neut. **at sea** auf See. **all at sea** (coll) perplex, im Dunkeln. **on the high seas** auf hoher see. **go to sea** zur See gehen.

seabed ['siːbed] n Meeresgrund m.

sea front n Strandpromenade f.

seagoing ['siːgouiŋ] adj Hochsee-.

seagull ['siːgʌl] n Möwe f.

seahorse ['siːhɔːs] n Seepferdchen neut.

seal[1] [siːl] n Siegel neut. v besiegeln. **seal up** versiegeln. **sealing wax** Siegellack m.

seal[2] [siːl] n (zool) Robbe f, Seehund m. **sealskin** n Seehundsfell neut.

sea-level n Meeresspiegel m.

sea-lion n Seelöwe m.

seam [siːm] n Saum m, Naht f; (minerals) Flöz neut. v säumen.

seaman ['siːmən] n Seemann m, Matrose m. **seamanlike** adj seemännisch. **seamanship** n Seemannskunst f.

search [səːtʃ] v suchen, forschen (nach); (for criminal) fahnden (nach); (person, place) durchsuchen (nach). **searchlight** n Scheinwerfer m. **search party** Suchtrupp m. **search warrant** Haussuchungsbefehl m. n Suche f; Untersuchung f. **searcher** n Sucher m, Forscher m. **searching** adj (enquiry) gründlich.

sea-shore n Seeküste f.

seasick ['siːsik] *adj* seekrank. **seasickness** *n* Seekrankheit *f.*

seaside ['siːsaid] *n* See *f.* **at the seaside** an der See. **to the seaside** an die See. **seaside town** Küstenstadt *f.*

season ['siːzn] *n* Jahreszeit *f*; (*comm*) Saison *f. v* (*cookery*) würzen; (*wood*) ablagern. **seasonal** *adj* saisonbedingt. **seasoning** *n* Würze *f.* **season-ticket** *n* Zeitkarte *f*; (*theatre*) Abonnement *neut.*

seat [siːt] *n* Sitz *m*; (*train, theatre*) Platz *m*; (*residence*) Wohnsitz *m. v* setzen. *please be seated!* bitte setzen Sie sich! **seating** *n* Sitzgelegenheit *f.*

seaweed ['siːwiːd] *n* Tang *m*, Alge *f.*

seaworthy ['siːwəːði] *adj* seetüchtig.

secluded [si'kluːdid] *adj* abgelegen. **seclusion** *n* Zurückgezogenheit *f.*

second¹ ['sekənd] *n* (*time*) Sekunde *f. wait a second!* moment mal!

second² ['sekənd] *adj* zweit; (*next*) nächst, folgend. *adv* an zweiter Stelle. *n* Zweite(r). **for the second time** zum zweiten Mal. **on second thoughts** bei näherer Überlegung. **play second fiddle** die Nebenrolle spielen. **secondary** *adj* nebensächlich, sekundär. **secondary school** Sekundarschule *f.* **second-best** *adj* zweitbest. **second-class** *adj* zweitrangig. **second-hand** *adj* gebraucht, Gebraucht-. **secondly** *adv* zweitens. **second-rate** *adj* minderwertig.

secret ['siːkrit] *adj* geheim, heimlich. **keep secret** geheimhalten. *n* Geheimnis *neut.* **in secret** *or* **secretly** *adv* heimlich. **secrecy** *n* Verborgenheit *f*, Heimlichkeit *f.* **secretive** *adj* verschlossen. **secretiveness** *n* Verschlossenheit *f.*

secretary ['sekrətəri] *n* Sekretär(in). **secretarial** *adj* Sekretär-. **secretary general** Generalsekretär *m.*

secrete [si'kriːt] *v* absondern. **secretion** *n* Absonderung *f.*

sect [sekt] *n* Sekte *f.* **sectarian** *adj* sektiererisch.

section ['sekʃən] *n* (*part*) Teil *m*; (*of firm*) Abteilung *f*; (*of book, document*) Abschnitt *m. v* **section off** abteilen.

sector ['sektə] *n* Sektor *m.*

secular ['sekjulə] *adj* weltlich. **secularism** *n* Säkularismus *f.*

secure [si'kjuə] *adj* sicher. *v* sichern; (*affix*) festmachen (an); (*procure*) sich beschaffen. **security** *n* Sicherheit *f*; (*bond*)

Bürgschaft *f.* **securities** *pl* (*comm*) Wertpapiere *pl.*

sedate [si'deit] *adj* ruhig, gelassen. **sedateness** *n* Gelassenheit *f.* **sedative** *n* Beruhigungsmittel *neut.* **sedation** *n* (Nerven)Beruhigung *f.*

sediment ['sedimənt] *n* Sediment *neut.* **sedimentation** *n* Sedimentation *n.*

seduce [si'djuːs] *v* verführen. **seducer** *n* Verführer *m.* **seduction** *n* Verführung *f.* **seductive** *adj* verlockend.

*see¹ [siː] *v* sehen; (*understand*) einsehen, verstehen; (*consult*) konsultieren, besuchen. **see home** (*person*) nach Hause begleiten. **seeing that** da. **see through** (*understand*) durchschauen; (*finish*) zu Ende führen. **see to** sich kümmern um. **see to it that** darauf achten, daß. **wait and see** abwarten.

see² [siː] *n* Bistum *neut.*

seed [siːd] *n* Same *m*; (*pip*) Kern *m.* **seedy** *adj* schäbig.

*seek [siːk] *v* suchen. **seeker** *n* Sucher(in).

seem [siːm] *v* scheinen. **seeming** *adj* scheinbar. **seemly** *adj* schicklich.

seen [siːn] *V* see¹.

seep [siːp] *v* (durch)sickern.

seesaw ['siːsoː] *n* Wippe *f. v* schaukeln.

seethe [siːð] *v* sieden. **seething** *adj* (*coll*) wütend.

segment ['segmənt] *n* Abschnitt *m*, Segment *neut.*

segregate ['segrigeit] *v* trennen, absondern. **segregation** *n* Absonderung *f*; (*racial*) Rassentrennung *f.*

seize [siːz] *v* ergreifen. **seize up** festfahren. **seizure** *n* Ergreifung *f*; (*med*) Anfall *m.*

seldom ['seldəm] *adv* selten.

select [sə'lekt] *v* auswählen, auslesen. *adj* exklusiv. **selected** *adj* ausgewählt. **selection** *n* Auswahl *f.* **selective** *adj* auswählend.

self [self] *n* Selbst *neut*, Ich *neut.*

self-assured *adj* selbstsicher. **self-assurance** *n* Selbstsicherheit *f.*

self-centred *adj* ichbezogen.

self-confident *adj* selbstbewußt, selbstsicher. **self-confidence** *n* Selbstbewußtsein *neut.*

self-conscious *adj* gehemmt, befangen. **self-consciousness** *n* Befangenheit *f.*

self-contained *adj* (*flat*) separat; (*person*) zurückhaltend.

self-control n Selbstbeherrschung f.
self-defence n Selbstverteidigung f.
self-denial n Selbstverleugnung f.
self-discipline n Selbstdisziplin f.
self-employed adj selbständig.
self-esteem n Selbstachtung f.
self-evident adj selbstverständlich.
self-important adj wichtigtuerisch.
self-indulgent adj selbstgefällig.
self-interest n Eigennutz m. self-interested adj eigennützig.
selfish ['selfiʃ] adj selbstisch, selbstsüchtig. selfishness n Egoismus m.
selfless ['selflis] adj selbstlos.
self-made adj self-made man Emporkömmling m.
self-pity n Selbstmitleid neut.
self-portrait n Selbstporträt neut.
self-respect n Selbstachtung f.
self-righteous adj selbstgerecht.
self-sacrifice n Selbstaufopferung f. self-sacrificing adj aufopferungsvoll.
selfsame ['selfseim] adj ebenderselbe, ebendieselbe, ebendasselbe.
self-satisfied adj selbstzufrieden.
self-service adj Selbstbedienung f. adj Selbstbedienungs-.
self-sufficient adj unabhängig; (person) selbstgenügsam.
self-will n Eigensinn m. self-willed adj eigensinnig.
*sell [sel] v verkaufen. seller n Verkäufer(in). sell out (betray) verraten. sold out ausverkauft.
Sellotape ® ['seləteip] n Tesa-Film m.
semantic [sə'mantik] adj semantisch. semantics n Semantik f.
semaphore ['seməfoɪ] n Semaphor m.
semen ['siɪmən] n Samen m, Sperma neut.
semicircle ['semisəɪkl] n Halbkreis m. semicircular adj halbkreisförmig.
semicolon [,semi'koulən] n Strichpunkt m.
semi-detached (house) adj halbfreistehend.
semifinal [semi'fainl] n Vorschlußrunde f; Halbfinale neut.
seminal ['seminl] adj Samen-; (influential) einflußreich, wichtig.
seminar ['seminaɪ] n Seminar neut.
semiprecious [semi'preʃəs] adj halbedel.
semolina [,semə'liɪnə] n Grieß m; (pudding) Grießbrei m.
senate ['senit] n Senat m. senator n Senator m. senatorial adj senatorisch.

*send [send] v schicken, senden. send away fortschicken. send for (person) schicken nach. send off (letter) absenden. send-off n Abschiedsfeier f. sender n Absender(in).
senile ['siɪnail] adj senil. senility n Senilität f.
senior ['siɪnjə] adj älter; (school) Ober-. n Ältere(r).
sensation [sen'seiʃən] n Gefühl neut, Empfindung f; (excitement) Sensation f. sensational adj sensationell. sensationalism n Effekthascherei f.
sense [sens] n Sinn m; (feeling) Gefühl neut. common sense Vernunft f. make sense sinnvoll sein. sense of humour Sinn für Humor m. v empfinden, spüren. senseless adj sinnlos.
sensible ['sensəbl] adj vernünftig. sensibility n Sensibilität f. sensibleness n Vernünftigkeit f.
sensitive ['sensitiv] adj empfindlich (gegen). sensitivity n Empfindlichkeit f; (appreciativeness) Sensibilität f. Feingefühl neut.
sensual ['sensjuəl] adj sinnlich. sensuality n Sinnlichkeit f.
sensuous ['sensjuəs] adj sinnlich. sensuousness n Sinnlichkeit f.
sent [sent] V send.
sentence ['sentəns] n Satz m; (punishment) Strafe f, Urteil neut. v verurteilen.
sentiment ['sentimənt] n Empfindsamkeit f; (feeling) Gefühl neut. sentiments pl Meinungen pl, Gesinnung f sing. sentimental adj sentimental. sentimentality n Sentimentalität f.
sentry ['sentri] n Wachposten m.
separate ['sepərət; v 'sepəreit] adj getrennt. v trennen; (couple) sich trennen. separable adj trennbar. separateness n Getrenntheit f. separation n Trennung f.
September [sep'tembə] n September m.
septic ['septik] adj septisch.
sequel ['siɪkwəl] n (novel, etc.) Fortsetzung f; (consequence) Folge f.
sequence ['siɪkwəns] n (Reihen)Folge f, Reihe f; (film) Szene f. sequential adj (aufeinander)folgend.
sequin ['siɪkwin] n Paillette f.
serenade [serə'neid] n Serenade f.
serene [sə'riɪn] adj heiter, gelassen. serenity n Heiterkeit f.

serf [səɪf] *n* Leibeigene(r). **serfdom** *n* Leibeigenschaft *f*.

sergeant ['saɪdʒənt] *n* (*mil*) Feldwebel *m*; (*police*) Wachtmeister *m*.

serial ['siəriəl] *n* (*book*) Fortsetzungsroman *m*; (*TV, radio*) Sendereihe *f*. *adj* Fortsetzungs-. **serial number** Seriennummer *f*.

series ['siəriz] *n* Serie *f*.

serious ['siəriəs] *adj* ernst(haft); (*illness*) gefährlich. **seriously** *adv* ernstlich, im Ernst; (*injured*) schwer. **seriousness** *n* Ernst *m*.

sermon ['saɪmən] *n* Predigt *f*.

serpent ['saɪpənt] *n* Schlange *f*.

servant ['saɪvənt] *n* Diener(in). **domestic servant** Hausangestellte(r). **public servant** *n* Beamte(r), Beamtin *f*.

serve [saɪv] *v* dienen (+ *dat*); (*customer*) bedienen; (*food*) servieren; (*tennis*) aufschlagen. **serve no purpose** nichts nützen. *it serves him right* es geschieht ihm recht.

service ['saɪvis] *n* Dienst *m*; (*shop, restaurant*) Bedienung *f*; (*after-sales*) Kundendienst *m*; (*mot*) Inspektion; (*favour*) Gefallen *m*; (*church*) Gottesdienst *m*. **military service** Wehrdienst *m*. **service station** Tankstelle *f*. *v* (*mot*) warten, überholen. **serviceable** *adj* brauchbar.

serviette [ˌsaɪvi'et] *n* Serviette *f*.

servile ['saɪvail] *adj* servil. **servility** *n* Unterwürfigkeit *f*.

session ['seʃən] *n* Sitzung *f*; (*university*) Semester *neut*.

*****set** [set] *v* setzen, stellen; (*date, etc.*) festsetzen; (*table*) decken; (*sun*) untergehen; (*become solid*) gerinnen. **set aside** aufheben. **setback** *n* Rückschlag *m*. **set fire to** in Brand stecken. **set off** (*on journey*) sich auf den Weg machen, aufbrechen. **set one's heart on** sein Herz hängen an. **set to** darangehen. **setting** *n* Hintergrund *m*. *n* Satz *m*; (*crockery*) Service *f*; (*radio*) Apparat *m*; (*clique*) Kreis *m*, Clique *f*.

settee [se'tiɪ] *n* Sofa *neut*.

settle ['setl] *v* (*arrange*) festsetzen; (*dispute*) schlichten; (*debt*) bezahlen; (*come to rest*) sich niederlassen; (*subside*) sich senken; (*in place*) sich ansiedeln. **settle down** (*calm down*) sich beruhigen; (*in place*) sich niederlassen. **settle for** (*coll*) annehmen. **settle in** sich einleben. **settle up** bezahlen. **settled** *adj* abgemacht, erledigt. **settlement** *n* (*place*) Siedlung *f*; (*agreement*) Übereinkommen *neut*. **settler** *n* Siedler(in).

seven ['sevn] *adj* sieben. *n* Sieben *f*. **seventh** *adj* siebt, siebent; *n* Siebtel *neut*.

seventeen [sevn'tiɪn] *adj* siebzehn. *n* Siebzehn *f*. **seventeenth** *adj* siebzehnt.

seventy ['sevnti] *adj* siebzig. *n* Siebzig *f*.

sever ['sevə] *v* trennen. **severance** *n* Trennung *f*. **severance pay** Abfindungsentschädigung *f*.

several ['sevrəl] *adj* mehrere; (*separate*) getrennt. **severally** *adv* getrennt.

severe [sə'viə] *adj* streng, hart; (*weather*) rauh; (*difficult*) schwierig. **severity** *n* Strenge *f*; Härte *f*; (*seriousness*) Ernst *m*.

*****sew** [sou] *v* nähen. **sewing** *n* Näharbeit *f*. **sewing machine** Nähmaschine *f*.

sewage ['sjuidʒ] *n* Abwasser *neut*. **sewer** *n* Abwasserkanal *m*. **sewerage** *n* Kanalisation *f*.

sewn [soun] *V* sew.

sex [seks] *n* Geschlecht *neut*, Sex *m*. *adj* Geschlechts-, sexual. **sexual** *adj* sexual. **sexual intercourse** Geschlechtsverkehr *m*. **sexuality** *n* Sexualität *f*. **sexy** *adj* sexy.

sextet [seks'tet] *n* Sextett *neut*.

shabby ['ʃabi] *adj* schäbig.

shack [ʃak] *n* Hütte *f*.

shackle ['ʃakl] *v* fesseln. **shackles** *pl n* Fesseln *pl*.

shade [ʃeid] *n* Schatten *m*. *v* beschatten; (*protect*) schützen; (*drawing*) schattieren. **shading** *n* Schattierung *f*. **shady** *adj* schattig; (*dubious*) fragwürdig.

shadow ['ʃadou] *n* Schatten *m*. **without a shadow of doubt** ohne den geringsten Zweifel. **shadow cabinet** Schattenkabinett *neut*. **shadowy** *adj* schattig.

shaft [ʃaɪft] *n* (*handle*) Schaft *m*; (*lift*) Schacht *m*; (*tech*) Welle *f*.

shaggy ['ʃagi] *adj* zottig.

*****shake** [ʃeik] *v* schütteln; (*shock*) erschüttern; (*tremble*) zittern; (*hand*) drücken. **shake hands with** die Hand geben (+ *dat*). **shake off** (*coll*) loswerden. *n* Schütteln *neut*. **shaky** *adj* wackelig.

shall [ʃal] *v* (*to form future*) werden; (*implying permission*) sollen, dürfen. *I shall go* ich werde gehen. *shall I go?* soll ich gehen?

shallot [ʃə'lot] *n* Schalotte *f*.

shallow ['ʃalou] *adj* flach, seicht; *(superficial)* oberflächlich, seicht. **shallows** *pl n* Untiefe *f*. **shallowness** *n* Seichtheit *f*.

sham [ʃam] *n* Betrug *m*; *(person)* Schwindler *m*. *adj* falsch.

shambles ['ʃamblz] *n* Durcheinander *neut*.

shame [ʃeim] *n* Scham *f*, Schamgefühl *neut*; *(scandal)* Schande *f*. **it's a shame that ...** schade, daß ... **shame-faced** *adj* verschämt. **shamefacedness** *n* Verschämtheit *f*. **what a shame!** (wie) shade! *v* schämen. **shameful** *adj* schändlich. **shamefulness** *n* Schändlichkeit *f*. **shameless** *adj* schamlos. **shamelessness** *n* Schamlosigkeit *f*.

shampoo [ʃam'puː] *n* Shampoo *neut*, Haarwaschmittel *neut*. *v* shampooieren.

shamrock ['ʃamrok] *n* Kleeblatt *neut*.

shanty[1] ['ʃanti] *n* *(hut)* Hütte *f*. **shanty town** Elendsviertel *neut*.

shanty[2] ['ʃanti] *n* *(song)* Matrosenlied *neut*.

shape [ʃeip] *n* Gestalt *f*, Form *f*. *v* gestalten, formen. **shaped** *adj* geformt. **shapeless** *adj* formlos. **shapelessness** *n* Formlosigkeit *f*. **shapely** *adj* wohlgeformt.

share [ʃeə] *n* (An)Teil *m*; *(comm)* Aktie *f*. *v* teilen. **shareholder** *n* Aktionär *m*.

shark [ʃaɪk] *n* Hai(fisch) *m*.

sharp [ʃaɪp] *adj* scharf; *(pointed)* spitz; *(outline)* deutlich. *adv* *(coll)* pünktlich. **look sharp!** mach schnell! **sharpen** *v* *(knife)* schleifen; *(pencil)* spitzen. **sharp-eyed** *adj* scharfsichtig. **sharpness** *n* Schärfe *f*. **sharpshooter** *n* Scharfschütze *m*. **sharp-witted** *adj* scharfsinnig.

shatter ['ʃatə] *v* zerschmettern; *(glass)* zersplittern; **shattered** *adj* *(coll)* erschüttert.

shave [ʃeiv] *v* (sich) rasieren. **clean-shaven** *adj* glattrasiert. **shaving brush** Rasierpinsel *m*. **shaving soap** Rasierseife *f*. **shaving foam** Rasierschaum *m*. *n* Rasur *f*. **shaver** *n* Rasierapparat *m*.

shawl [ʃoːl] *n* Schal *m*.

she [ʃiː] *pron* sie.

sheaf [ʃiːf] *n* *(pl* **sheaves)** Garbe *f*.

*shear [ʃiə] *v* scheren. **shears** *pl n* Schere *f sing*. **shearer** *n* Scherer *m*. **shearing** *n* Schur *f*.

sheath [ʃiːθ] *n* Scheide *f*. **sheathe** *v* *(sword)* in die Scheide stecken. **sheathed** *adj* *(tech)* verkleidet.

*shed[1] [ʃed] *v* *(tears, blood)* vergießen; *(leaves)* abwerfen.

shed[2] [ʃed] *n* *(hut)* Schuppen *m*; *(cows)* Stall *m*.

sheen [ʃiːn] *n* Glanz *m*, Schimmer *m*.

sheep [ʃiːp] *n* *(pl* **sheep)** Schaf *neut*. **sheepdog** *n* Schäferhund. **sheepskin** *n* Schaffell *neut*. **sheepish** *adj* einfältig, verlegen.

sheer [ʃiə] *adj* *(pure)* bloß; *(steep)* steil.

sheet [ʃiːt] *n* *(bed)* Bettuch *neut*, (Bett)Laken *neut*; *(paper, metal)* Blatt *neut*.

shelf [ʃelf] *n* *(pl* **shelves)** Regal *neut*, Fach *neut*. **on the shelf** sitzengeblieben.

shell [ʃel] *n* Schale *f*; *(snail)* Schneckenhaus *neut*; *(mil)* Granate *f*. **shellfish** *n* Schalentier *neut*. **shell-shock** *n* Kriegsneurose *f*. *v* *(egg)* schälen; *(nuts)* enthülsen. **shelling** *n* *(mil)* Artilleriefeuer *neut*.

shelter ['ʃeltə] *n* Obdach *neut*; *(little hut)* Schutzhütte *f*. *v* beschützen; *(take shelter)* Schutz suchen.

shelve [ʃelv] *v* *(plan)* auf die lange Bank schieben, aufschieben.

shepherd ['ʃepəd] *n* Schäfer *m*, Hirt *m*. **shepherdess** *n* Schäferin *f*, Hirtin *f*.

sheriff ['ʃerif] *n* Sheriff *m*.

sherry ['ʃeri] *n* Sherry *m*.

shield [ʃiːld] *n* Schild *m*; *(fig)* Schutz *m*. *v* beschirmen.

shift [ʃift] *v* (sich) verschieben; *(get rid of)* beseitigen; *(coll: move fast)* schnell fahren; *(gear)* schalten. *n* Verschiebung *f*; *(work)* Schicht *f*. **shifty** *adj* schlau.

shimmer ['ʃimə] *n* Schimmer *m*. *v* schimmern.

shin [ʃin] *n* Schienbein *neut*. *v* **shin up** hinaufklettern.

*shine [ʃain] *v* scheinen, leuchten; *(shoes)* putzen. *n* Glanz *m*. **shiny** *adj* glänzend, strahlend.

shingle ['ʃingl] *n* *(on beach)* Strandkies *m*.

shingles ['ʃinglz] *n* *(med)* Gürtelrose *f*.

ship [ʃip] *n* Schiff *neut*. **shipowner** *n* Reeder *m*. **shipwreck** *n* Schiffbruch *m* **be shipwrecked** Schiffbruch erleiden. **shipyard** *n* Werft *f*. *v* verschiffen, spedieren. **shipment** *n* Verladung *f*. **shipper** *n* Spediteur *m*.

shirk [ʃəːk] *v* sich drücken (vor). **shirker** *n* Drückeberger(in).

shirt [ʃəːt] *n* Hemd *neut*. **shirty** *adj* *(coll)* verdrießlich.

shit [ʃit] *n* *(vulgar)* Scheiße *f*. *v* scheißen. **shitty** *adj* beschissen.

shiver ['ʃivə] v zittern. n Zittern neut.
shoal [ʃoul] n Schwarm m, Zug m.
shock [ʃok] v (impact) Stoß m, Anprall m; (fright) Schreck m, Schock m; (med) Nervenschock m; (elec) Schlag m. v schockieren, entsetzen. **shocked** adj schockiert. **shocking** adj schockierend.
shod [ʃod] V shoe.
shoddy ['ʃodi] adj schäbig.
*shoe [ʃuː] n Schuh m; (horse) Hufeisen neut. shoe-horn n Schuhlöffel m. **shoelace** n Schnürsenkel m. v beschuhen. **shoemaker** n Schuhmacher m.
shone [ʃon] V shine.
shook [ʃuk] V shake.
*shoot [ʃuːt] v schießen; (hit) anschießen; (kill) erschießen; (film) drehen. **shoot down** (aeroplane) abschießen. **shooting** n (game, etc.) Jagd f. **shooting star** Sternschnuppe f.
shop [ʃop] n Laden m, Geschäft neut; (factory) Werkstatt f. **shop assistant** Verkäufer(in). **shopkeeper** n Ladenbesitzer m. **shop-lifting** n Ladendiebstahl m. **shop-steward** n Betriebsrat m. **shop-window** n Schaufenster neut. v (also go shopping) einkaufen gehen. **shopper** n Einkäufer(in). **shopping** n Einkäufe pl.
shore [ʃoː] n Küste f, Strand m.
shorn [ʃoːn] V shear.
short [ʃoːt] adj kurz; (person) klein. adv plötzlich. **short of** knapp an.
shortage ['ʃoːtidʒ] n Mangel m, Knappheit f.
shortbread ['ʃoːtbred] n Mürbekuchen m.
short-circuit n Kurzschluß m. v kurzschließen.
shortcoming ['ʃoːtkʌmiŋ] n Fehler m, Unzulänglichkeit f.
short cut n Abkürzung f.
shorthand ['ʃoːthand] n Kurzschrift f. **shorthand typist** Stenotypist(in).
short list v in die engere Wahl ziehen.
short-lived adj kurzlebig.
shortly ['ʃoːtli] adv bald, in kurzer Zeit.
short-sighted adj kurzsichtig. **short-sightedness** n Kurzsichtigkeit f.
shorts [ʃoːts] pl n kurze Hose f sing.
short-tempered adj reizbar.
short-term adj kurzfristig.
short-time adj **short-time work** Kurzarbeit f.
short-wave adj Kurzwellen-.
shot [ʃot] V shoot. n Schuß m; (pellets)

Schrot m; (sport) Kugel f; (films) Aufnahme f; (injection) Spritze f. adj (coll) erschüttert. **have a shot** (coll) versuchen. **shotgun** n Schrotflinte f. **shot put** Kugelstoß m.
should [ʃud] v sollen. I should go ich sollte gehen. I should like (to) Ich möchte.
shoulder ['ʃouldə] n Schulter f, Achsel f. **shoulder-blade** n Schulterblatt neut.
shout [ʃaut] v rufen, schreien. n Schrei m, Ruf m. **shouting** n Geschrei neut.
shove [ʃʌv] v schieben, stoßen. n Stoß m, Schub m.
*show v zeigen; (goods, etc.) ausstellen. **showcase** n Schaukasten m. **showman** n Schausteller m. **show off** angeben, sich großtun. **show-off** n Angeber m, Großtuer m. **showpiece** n Paradestück neut. **showroom** n Ausstellungsraum m. n Ausstellung f; (theatre) Vorstellung f. **mere show** leerer Schein m.
shower ['ʃauə] n (rain) Schauer m; (bath) Dusche f. v sich duschen.
shown [ʃoun] V show.
shred [ʃred] n Fetzen m. v zerfetzen. **not a shred of** keine Spur von.
shrew [ʃruː] n Spitzmaus f; (woman) zankisches Weib neut.
shrewd [ʃruːd] adj scharfsinning, schlau. **shrewdness** n Scharfsinn m.
shriek [ʃriːk] n Schrei m, Gekreisch neut. v schreien, kreischen.
shrill [ʃril] adj schrill, gellend.
shrimp [ʃrimp] n Garnele f.
shrine [ʃrain] n Schrein m.
*shrink [ʃriŋk] v einschrumpfen. **shrink from** zurückweichen von. **shrinkage** n Schrumpfung f.
shrivel ['ʃrivl] v runzelig werden, schrumpfen.
shroud [ʃraud] n Leichentuch neut. v (fig) umhüllen.
Shrove Tuesday [ʃrouv] n Fastnachtsdienstag m.
shrub [ʃrʌb] n Strauch m, Busch m. **shrubbery** n Gebüsch neut.
shrug [ʃrʌg] v zucken. n (Achsel)Zucken neut.
shrunk [ʃrʌŋk] V shrink.
shudder ['ʃʌdə] v schaudern. n Schauder m.
shuffle ['ʃʌfl] v (mit den Füßen) scharren, schlurfen; (cards) mischen. n Schlurfen neut; (cards) (Karten)Mischen neut.

shun [ʃʌn] v vermeiden.
shunt [ʃʌnt] v (rail) rangieren.
*shut [ʃʌt] v schließen, zumachen; (book) zuklappen. **shut down** stillegen. **shut off** abstellen. **shut out** aussperren. **shut up** (be silent) den Mund halten. adj geschlossen, zu.
shutter ['ʃʌtə] n Fensterladen m; (phot) Verschluß m.
shuttle ['ʃʌtl] n Pendelverkehr m.
shuttlecock ['ʃʌtlkok] n Federball m.
shy [ʃai] adj schüchtern. v (horse) scheuen. **shy away from** zurückschrecken vor. **shyness** n Schüchternheit f.
sick [sik] adj krank. I feel sick mir ist übel. **sick humour** schwarzer Humor m. **sicken** v erkranken; (disgust) anekeln. **sickening** adj ekelhaft. **sick leave** Krankheitsurlaub m. **sickly** adj kränklich. **sickness** n Krankheit f; (vomiting) Erbrechen neut.
sickle ['sikl] n Sichel f.
side [said] n Seite f; (edge) Rand m; (team) Mannschaft f. adj seitlich, Seiten-. **sideboard** n Buffet neut. **sideboards** or **sideburns** pl n Koteletten pl. **sidelight** n (mot) Standlicht neut. **sideline** n Nebenbeschäftigung f. **sidelong** adj seitlich. **sideshow** n Jahrmarktsbude f. **siding** n Nebengleis neut.
sidle ['saidl] v sich schlängeln. **sidle up to** heranschleichen an.
siege [siːdʒ] n Belagerung f. **lay siege to** belagern.
sieve [siv] n Sieb neut. v (durch)sieben.
sift [sift] v (durch)sieben; (evidence, etc.) sorgfältig überprüfen.
sigh [sai] v seufzen. n Seufzer m.
sight [sait] n (power of) Sehvermögen neut; (instance of seeing) Anblick m; (range of vision) Sicht f; (of gun) Visier neut; (place of interest) Sehenswürdigkeit f. **at sight** (comm) bei Sicht. **at first sight** beim ersten Anblick. **sighted** adj sichtig. **sightless** adj blind. **go sightseeing** die Sehenswürdigkeiten besichtigen.
sign [sain] n Zeichen neut; (noticeboard, etc.) Schild neut. v unterschreiben. **signwriter** n Schriftmaler m. **signpost** n Wegweiser m.
signal ['signəl] n Signal neut. v signalisieren.
signature ['signətʃə] n Unterschrift f. **signature tune** Kennmelodie f. **signatory** n Unterzeichner m; (pol) Signatar m.

signify ['signifai] v bedeuten. **significance** n Bedeutung f. **significant** adj wichtig.
silence ['sailəns] n Ruhe f, Stille f; (absence of talking, etc.) Schweigen neut. v zum Schweigen bringen.
silent ['sailənt] adj still, ruhig; stillschweigend. **be** or **fall silent** schweigen. **silent film** Stummfilm m.
silhouette [silu'et] n Silhouette f.
silk [silk] n Seide f. adj Seiden-.
sill [sil] n Fensterbrett neut; (door) Schwelle f.
silly ['sili] adj dumm, albern. **silly season** Sauregurkenzeit f.
silt [silt] n Schlamm m. v **silt up** verschlammen.
silver ['silvə] n Silber neut. adj silbern, Silber-. **silver plate** Tafelsilber neut. **silver-plated** adj versilbert.
similar ['similə] adj ähnlich (+dat). **similarity** n Ähnlichkeit f. **similarly** adv gleichermaßen.
simile ['siməli] n Gleichnis neut.
simmer ['simə] v leicht kochen (lassen).
simple ['simpl] adj einfach. **simple-minded** adj einfältig. **simpleton** n Einfaltspinsel m. **simplicity** n Einfachheit f. **simplify** v vereinfachen. **simply** adv einfach.
simulate ['simjuleit] v simulieren. **simulation** n Simulation f. **simulator** n Simulator m.
simultaneous [siməl'teinjəs] adj gleichzeitig.
sin [sin] n Sünde f. v sündigen. **sinful** adj sündig. **sinner** n Sünder(in).
since [sins] prep seit. I've been living here since 1960 ich wohne hier seit 1960. conj (time) seit(dem); (because) da. adv seitdem, seither; (in the meantime) inzwischen.
sincere [sin'siə] adj aufrichtig, ehrlich. **yours sincerely** mit freundlichen Grüßen. **sincerity** n Aufrichtigkeit f.
sinew ['sinjuː] n Sehne f. **sinewy** adj sehnig.
*sing [siŋ] v singen. **singer** n Sänger(in). **singing** n Singen neut, Gesang m.
singe [sindʒ] v (ver)sengen.
single ['siŋgl] adj einzig; (individual) einzeln; (room, bed, etc.) Einzel-; (unmarried) ledig. v **single out** auslesen. **single ticket** einfache Fahrkarte f. **single-handed** adj eigenhändig. **single-minded** adj zielstrebig. **singly** adv einzeln, allein.

singular ['siŋgjulə] *adj* einzigartig; (*gramm*) im Singular. *n* (*gramm*) Singular *m*.

sinister ['sinistə] *adj* drohend, unheilvoll.

*sink [siŋk] *v* sinken; (*cause to sink*) senken. *n* Spülbecken *neut*.

sinuous ['sinjuəs] *adj* gewunden, sich windend.

sinus ['sainəs] *n* (Nasen) Nebenhöhle *f*. **sinusitis** *n* Nebenhöhlenentzündung *f*.

sip [sip] *v* nippen an, schlürfen. *n* Schlückchen *neut*.

siphon ['saifən] *n* Heber *m*; (*soda*) Siphon *m*. *v* aushebern.

sir [səɪ] *n* (mein) Herr. **Dear Sir** (*in letters*) sehr geehrter Herr!

siren ['saiərən] *n* Sirene *f*.

sirloin ['səːloin] *n* Lendenstück *neut*.

sister ['sistə] *n* Schwester *f*; (*nurse*) Oberschwester *f*. **sister-in-law** *n* Schwägerin *f*. *adj* Schwester-. **sisterly** *adj* schwesterlich.

*sit [sit] *v* sitzen; (*exam*) machen; (*hen*) brüten. **sit down** sich (hin)setzen. **sitting** *n* Sitzung *f*. **sitting duck** leichtes Opfer *neut*. **sitting-room** *n* Wohnzimmer *neut*.

site [sait] *n* Stelle *f*. **building site** Baustelle *f*. *v* placieren.

situation [sitju'eiʃən] *n* Lage *f*; (*state of affairs*) Situation *f*; (*Sach*)Lage *f*; (*job*) Stelle *f*, Posten *m*. **situated** *adj* gelegen.

six [siks] *adj* sechs. *n* Sechs *f*. **sixth** *adj* sechst; *n* Sechstel *neut*. **sixth form** Prima *f*.

sixteen [siks'tiːn] *adj* sechzehn. *n* Sechzehn *f*.

sixty ['siksti] *adj* sechzig. *n* Sechzig *f*.

size [saiz] *n* Größe *f*. *v* **size up** (*coll*) abschätzen.

sizzle ['sizl] *v* zischen.

skate[1] [skeit] *n* (*ice*) Schlittschuh *m*; (*roller*) Rollschuh *m*. *v* Schlittschuh/Rollschuh laufen. **skater** *n* Eisläufer(in); Rollschuhläufer(in).

skate[2] [skeit] *n* (*fish*) Rochen *m*.

skeleton ['skelitn] *n* Skelett *neut*, Knochengerüst *neut*. **skeleton key** Dietrich *m*.

sketch [sketʃ] *n* Skizze *f*; (*theatre*) Sketch *m*. *v* skizzieren. **sketchy** *adj* oberflächlich.

skewer ['skjuə] *n* Fleischspieß *m*. *v* spießen.

ski [skiː] *n* Ski *m*. *v* Ski laufen. **skier** *n* Skiläufer(in), Skifahrer(in). **skiing** *n* Skilaufen *neut*, Skifahren *neut*.

skid [skid] *v* schleudern. *n* Schleudern *neut*.

skill [skil] *n* (*skilfulness*) Geschicklichkeit *f*, Gewandtheit *f*; (*expertise*) Fachkenntnis *f*. **skilled** *adj* geschickt. **skilled worker** Facharbeiter *m*. **skilful** *adj* geschickt.

skim [skim] *v* abschöpfen; (*milk*) entrahmen. **skim through** (*read*) überfliegen. **skim milk** Magermilch *f*.

skimp [skimp] *v* geizen (mit); (*work*) nachlässig machen.

skin [skin] *n* Haut *f*; (*animal*) Fell *neut*, Pelz *m*; (*fruit*) Schale *f*, Rinde *f*. **skin-deep** *adj* oberflächlich. **skin-diving** *n* Schwimmtauchen *neut*. **skinflint** *n* Geizhals *m*. **skin-tight** *adj* hauteng. *v* enthäuten. **skinny** *adj* mager.

skip [skip] *v* hüpfen; (*with rope*) seilspringen; (*miss*) auslassen. **skip through** (*read*) überfliegen. *n* Sprung *m*. **skipping-rope** *n* Hüpfseil *neut*.

skipper ['skipə] *n* (*coll: naut*) Kapitän *m*.

skirmish ['skəːmiʃ] *n* Gefecht *neut*.

skirt [skəːt] *n* Rock *m*. *v* (*go around*) herumgehen um. **skirting board** Wandleiste *f*.

skittle ['skitl] *n* Kegel *m*. **play skittles** kegeln. **skittle alley** Kegelbahn *f*.

skull [skʌl] *n* Schädel *m*. **skull-cap** *n* Käppchen *neut*.

skunk [skʌŋk] *n* Skunk *m*, Stinktier *neut*.

sky [skai] *n* Himmel *m*. **sky-blue** *adj* himmelblau. **sky-high** *adj*, *adv* himmelhoch. **skylark** *n* Lerche *f*. **skylight** *n* Dachfenster *neut*. **skyscraper** *n* Hochhaus *neut*, Wolkenkratzer *m*.

slab [slab] *n* (*stone*) (Stein)Platte *f*; (*chocolate*) Tafel *f*.

slack [slak] *adj* schlaff, locker; (*person*) nachlässig; (*trade*) flau. **slacken** *v* lockern, entspannen; (*pace, etc.*) vermindern. **slackness** *n* Schlaffheit *f*.

slacks [slaks] *pl n* Hose *f sing*.

slag [slag] *n* Schlacke *f*. **slagheap** *n* Halde *f*.

slalom ['slaːləm] *n* Slalom *m*.

slam [slam] *v* (*door*) zuknallen. *n* Knall *m*.

slander ['slaːndə] *n* Verleumdung *f*. *v* verleumden. **slanderer** *n* Verleumder *m*. **slanderous** *adj* verleumderisch.

slang [slaŋ] *n* Jargon *m*. *v* beschimpfen.

slant [slaːnt] *n* Schräge *f*; (*attitude*) Einstellung *f*. *v* schräg liegen. **slant-eyed** *adj* mit schräggestellten Augen. **slanting** *adj* schräg.

slap [slap] *v* klapsen, schlagen. *n* Klaps *m*, Schlag *m*. **slapdash** *adj* schlampig.

slash [slaʃ] *v* schlitzen, zerfetzen. *n* Schnitt *m*, Schlitz *m*.

slat [slat] *n* Latte *f*. Leiste *f*.

slate [sleit] *n* Schiefer *m*; (*writing*) Schiefertafel *f*; (*on roof*) Dachschiefer *m*. *v* (*coll*) heftig tadeln, kritisieren.

slaughter [slɔːtə] *v* schlachten. *n* Schlachten *neut*. **slaughterhouse** *n* Schlachthaus *neut*. **slaughterer** *n* Schlächter *m*.

slave [sleiv] *n* Sklave *m*, Sklavin *f*. **slave-driver** *n* Leuteschinder *m*. *v* **slave away** schuften. **slavery** *n* Sklaverei *f*. **slavish** *adj* sklavisch.

sledge [sledʒ] *n* Schlitten *m*.

sledgehammer ['sledʒˌhamə] *n* Schmiedehammer *m*, Schlägel *m*.

sleek [sliːk] *adj* glatt. **sleekness** *n* Glätte *f*.

***sleep** [sliːp] *v* schlafen; (*spend the night*) übernachten. *n* Schlaf *m*. **go to sleep** einschlafen. **sleeper** *n* Schläfer(in) *m*, (*railway*) Schwelle *f*. **sleeping bag** Schlafsack *m*. **sleeping car** Schlafwagen *m*. **sleepless** *adj* schlaflos. **sleeplessness** *n* Schlaflosigkeit *f*. **sleepwalker** *n* Nachtwandler *m*. **sleepy** *adj* schläfrig, müde.

sleet [sliːt] *n* Schneeregen *m*.

sleeve [sliːv] *n* Ärmel *m*. **sleeved** *adj* mit Ärmeln. **sleeveless** *adj* ärmellos.

sleigh [slei] *n* Schlitten *m*.

slender ['slendə] *adj* schlank, schmal. **slenderness** *n* Schlankheit *f*.

slept [slept] *V* **sleep**.

slice [slais] *n* Scheibe *f*, Schnitte *f*. *v* aufschneiden. **sliced** *adj* geschnitten, in Scheiben. **slicer** *n* Schneidemaschine *f*.

slick [slik] *adj* glatt; (*person*) raffiniert. **slicker** *n* Gauner *m*.

slid [slid] *V* **slide**.

***slide** [slaid] *v* gleiten, rutschen. **slide rule** Rechenschieber *m*. **sliding door** Schiebetür *f*. **sliding scale** gleitende Skala *f*. *n* (*phot*) Dia(positiv) *neut*; (*playground*) Schlitterbahn *f*.

slight [slait] *adj* gering, unbedeutend, klein; (*person*) schmächtig, dünn. **not in the slightest** nicht im geringsten. *v* (*person*) kränken. *n* Beleidigung *f*. **slightly** *adv* leicht, ein bißchen.

slim [slim] *adj* schlank, dünn; (*chance, etc.*) gering. *v* eine Schlankheitskur machen, abnehmen. **slimness** *n* Schlankheit *f*.

slime [slaim] *n* Schleim *m*. **slimy** *adj* schleimig.

***sling** [sliŋ] *n* (*weapon*) Schleuder *m*; (*arm*) Schlinge *f*. *v* schleudern.

***slink** [sliŋk] *v* schleichen.

slip [slip] *n* Fehltritt *m*; (*underskirt*) Unterrock *m*. *v* gleiten, rutschen. **slip away** sich davonmachen. **slip off** (*clothes*) ausziehen. **slip on** (*clothes*) anziehen. **slip up** sich irren, sich vertun. **slipknot** *n* Laufknoten *m*. **slipshod** *adj* schlampig.

slipper ['slipə] *n* Pantoffel *m*.

slippery ['slipəri] *adj* schlüpfrig, glitschig; (*person*) aalglatt.

***slit** [slit] *n* Schlitz *m*. *v* aufschlitzen. **slit-eyed** *adj* schlitzäugig.

slither ['sliðə] *v* rutschen, schlittern. **slithery** *adj* schlüpfrig.

slobber ['slobə] *v* sabbern, geifern. *n* Geifer *m*. **slobbery** *adj* sabbernd.

sloe [slou] *n* Schlehe *f*.

slog [slog] *v* hart schlagen; (*work hard*) schuften. *n* (harter) Schlag *m*.

slogan ['slougən] *n* Slogan *m*, Schlagwort *neut*.

slop [slop] *v* verschütten. *n* Pfütze *f*. **slops** *pl n* Abwasser *neut*.

slope [sloup] *n* Abhang *m*. *v* abfallen. **sloping** *adj* schräg.

sloppy ['slopi] *adj* matschig; (*slapdash*) schlampig. **sloppiness** *n* Matschigkeit *f*; Schlampigkeit *f*.

slot [slot] *n* Schlitz *m*; (*for coin*) Münzeinwurf *m*.

slouch [slautʃ] *v* latschen. **slouching** *adj* latschig.

slovenly ['slʌvnli] *adj* schlampig.

slow [slou] *adj* langsam; (*boring*) langweilig. *v* *also* **slow down** *or* **up** (sich) verlangsamen. **slow-down** *n* Verlangsamung *f*. **slow motion** Zeitlupentempo *neut*. **slowness** *n* Langsamkeit *f*; (*wits*) Schwerfälligkeit *f*.

sludge [slʌdʒ] *n* Schlamm *m*.

slug [slʌg] *n* Schnecke *f*.

sluggish ['slʌgiʃ] *adj* träge, schwerfällig; (*river*) langsam fließend. **sluggishness** *n* Schwerfälligkeit *f*.

sluice [sluːs] *n* Schleuse *f*. *v* ausspülen.

slums [slʌmz] *pl n* Elendsviertel *neut.*
slumber ['slʌmbə] *v* schlummern. *n*
Schlummer *m.*
slump [slʌmp] *v* hinplumpsen; (*prices*)
stürzen. *n* (*comm*) Geschäftsrückgang *m,*
Wirtschaftskrise *f.*
slung [slʌŋ] *V* sling.
slunk [slʌŋk] *V* slink.
slur [sləɪ] *v* (*words*) verschlucken, undeutlich aussprechen. *n* Vorwurf *m.*
slush [slʌʃ] *n* Matsch *m;* (*snow*)
Schneematsch *m;* (*sentimentality*)
Schmalz *m.* **slushy** *adj* matschig;
schmalzig.
slut [slʌt] *n* Schlampe *f.* **sluttish** *adj*
schlampig.
sly [slai] *adj* schlau, hinterhältig. **slyness**
n Schlauheit *f.*
smack¹ [smak] *n* Klaps *m,* Klatsch *m. v*
schlagen, einen Klaps geben (+ *dat*).
smack² [smak] *n* (*flavour*) Geschmack *m.*
v schmecken (nach).
small [smɔɪl] *adj* klein; (*number, extent*)
gering. **small change** Kleingeld *neut.*
small talk Geplauder *neut.* **smallness** *n*
Kleinheit *f.*
smallpox ['smɔɪlpoks] *n* Pocken *pl.*
smart [smaɪt] *adj* schick, gepflegt; (*coll:
clever*) gescheit, raffiniert. **smart aleck**
(*coll*) Naseweis *m. v* (*suffer*) leiden.
smarten up zurechtmachen.
smash [smaʃ] *v* zerschmettern,
zerschlagen; (*enemy, etc.*) vernichten. *n*
(*mot*) Zusammenstoß *m.* **smash hit**
Bombenerfolg *m.* **smashing** *adj* (*coll*) toll,
sagenhaft.
smear [smiə] *v* (be)schmieren. *n*
(Schmutz) Fleck *m;* (*med*) Abstrich *m.*
smear campaign Verleumdung-
skampagne *f.*
*****smell** [smel] *n* Geruch *m;* (*pleasant*)
Duft *m. v* riechen. **smell of** riechen nach.
smelly *adj* übelriechend.
smelt [smelt] *V* smell.
smile [smail] *v* lächeln. *n* Lächeln *neut.*
smiling *adj* lächelnd.
smirk [smɔɪk] *v* schmunzeln.
smock [smok] *n* Kittel *m.*
smog [smog] *n* Smog *m,* Rauchnebel *m.*
smoke [smouk] *v* rauchen; (*meat, fish*)
räuchern. *n* Rauch *m.* **smokescreen** *n*
Nebelvorhang *m.* **smokestack** *n* Schornstein *m.* **smoker** *n* Raucher(in); (*train*)
Raucherabteil *m.* **smoking** *n* Rauchen
neut. **no smoking** Rauchen verboten.

smooth [smuɪð] *adj* glatt. **smoothness** *n*
Glätte *f.* **smooth-tongued** *adj*
schmeichlerisch. *v* glätten.
smother ['smʌðə] *v* ersticken; (*with gifts,
etc.*) überhäufen.
smoulder ['smouldə] *v* schwelen.
smudge [smʌdʒ] *n* Schmutzfleck *m,*
Klecks *m. v* beschmutzen.
smug [smʌg] *adj* selbstgefällig.
smuggle ['smʌgl] *v* schmuggeln. **smuggler**
n Schmuggler *m.* **smuggling** *n* Schmuggel
m.
snack [snak] *n* Imbiß *m.* **snack bar**
Imbißstube *f.*
snag [snag] *n* (*difficulty*) Haken *m.*
snail [sneil] *n* Schnecke *f.* **at a snail's pace**
im Schneckentempo.
snake [sneik] *n* Schlange *f.*
snap [snap] *v* (*break*) (zer)brechen; (*dog*)
schnappen; (*noise*) knacken; (*phot*) knipsen. **snap at** (*person*) anschnauzen. **snap-
dragon** *n* Löwenmaul *neut.* **snap-fastener**
n Druckknopf *m.* **snapshot** *n* Schnapp-
schuß *m.* **snappy** *adj* (*coll*) schnell,
lebhaft.
snare [sneə] *n* Schlinge *f. v* fangen.
snare drum *n* Schnarrtrommel *f.*
snarl [snaɪl] *n* Knurren *neut. v* knurren.
snatch [snatʃ] *v* schnell ergreifen. **snatch
at** greifen nach.
sneak [sniɪk] *v* schleichen; (*tell tales*)
petzen. *n* Petzer *m.* **sneakers** *pl n* Turn-
schuhe *pl.* **sneaking** *adj* heimlich. **sneaky**
adj heimtückisch.
sneer [sniə] *v* spötteln (über). *v* höhnisch
lächeln. *n* Hohnlächeln *neut.*
sneeze [sniɪz] *v* niesen. *n* Niesen *neut.*
sniff [snif] *v* schnüffeln. *n* Schnüffeln
neut.
snigger ['snigə] *v* kichern. *n* Kichern *neut.*
snip [snip] *v* schneiden. *n,* Schnitt *m.*
snipe [snaip] *n* Schnepfe *f. v* aus dem
Hinterhalt schießen. **sniper** *n* Hecken-
schütze *m.*
snivel ['snivl] *v* wimmern. **snivelling** *adj*
weinerlich.
snob [snob] *n* Snob *m.* **snobbery** *n* Snob-
ismus *m.* **snobbish** *adj* snobistisch.
snooker ['snuɪkə] *n* Snooker *neut.*
snoop [snuɪp] *v* herumschnüffeln. *n*
Schnüffler *m.*
snooty ['snuɪti] *adj* hochnäsig.
snooze [snuɪz] *n* Nickerchen *neut. v* ein
Nickerchen machen.

snore [snɔː] v schnarchen. n Schnarchen neut.

snorkel ['snɔːkəl] n Schnorchel m.

snort [snɔːt] n Schnauben neut. v schnauben.

snout [snaut] n Schnauze f.

snow [snou] n Schnee m. **snowball** n Schneeball m; v (develop) lawinenartig anwachsen. **snowdrift** n. Schneewehe f. **snowdrop** n Schneeglöckchen neut. v schneien.

snub [snʌb] n Rüffel m, Verweis m. v rüffeln. adj stumpf.

snuff [snʌf] n Schnupftabak m. **take snuff** schnupfen.

snug [snʌg] adj gemütlich, bequem.

snuggle ['snʌgl] v sich schmiegen (an).

so [sou] adv so; (very) sehr. conj also, daher. **so that** damit. **so am/do I** ich auch. **so what?** na und? **I think so** ich glaube schon.

soak [souk] v durchtränken; (washing) einweichen. **soaking wet** triefend naß.

soap [soup] n Seife f. v (ein)seifen. **soapy** adj seifig. **soapy water** Seifenwasser neut.

soar [sɔː] v (fly up) hochfliegen; (rise) hoch aufsteigen.

sob [sob] v schluchzen. n Schluchzen neut.

sober ['soubə] adj nüchtern. v **sober up** nüchtern werden. **sobriety** n Nüchternheit f.

sociable ['souʃəbl] adj gesellig. **sociability** n Geselligkeit f.

social ['souʃəl] adj (animals) gesellig; (gathering) gesellschaftlich, gesellig; (of society) Gesellschafts-, Sozial-, gesellschaftlich. **social security** Sozialversicherung f. **social services** soziale Einrichtungen pl. **social worker** Sozialarbeiter(in). **socialism** n Sozialismus m. **socialist** n Sozialist(in).

society [sə'saiəti] n Gesellschaft f.

sociology [sousi'olədʒi] n Soziologie f. **sociological** adj soziologisch. **sociologist** n Soziologe m.

sock [sok] n Socke f.

socket ['sokit] n (elec) Steckdose f; (eye) Höhle f; (bone) Gelenkpfanne f.

soda ['soudə] n Soda; also **soda water** Soda(wasser) neut.

sodden ['sodn] adj durchnäßt.

sofa ['soufə] n Sofa neut.

soft [soft] adj weich; (voice, etc.) leise; (gentle) sanft, mild. **soften** v weich

machen or werden; (water) enthärten. **soft-hearted** adj weichherzig.

soggy ['sogi] adj feucht.

soil¹ [soil] n Boden m, Erde f.

soil² [soil] n (dirt) Schmutz m. v beschmutzen.

solar ['soulə] adj Sonnen-.

sold [sould] V sell.

solder ['soldə] v löten. n Lot neut. **soldering iron** Lötkolben m.

soldier ['souldʒə] n Soldat m.

sole¹ [soul] adj (only) einzig, alleinig.

sole² [soul] n (of shoe) Sohle f. v besohlen.

sole³ [soul] n (fish) Seezunge f.

solemn ['soləm] adj feierlich; (person) ernst. **solemnity** n Feierlichkeit f.

solicitor [sə'lisitə] n (law) Anwalt m.

solicitous [sə'lisitəs] adj fürsorglich; (eager) eifrig.

solid ['solid] adj (not liquid) fest; (pure) massiv. **solidarity** n Solidarität f. **solidify** v fest werden.

solitary ['solitəri] adj (person) einsam; (single) einzeln.

solitude ['solitjuːd] n Einsamkeit f.

solo ['soulou] n Solo neut. adj Solo-, Allein-. adv allein. **soloist** n Solist(in).

solstice ['solstis] n Sonnenwende f.

solve [solv] v lösen. **soluble** adj löslich; (problem) lösbar. **solution** n Lösung f. **solvent** n Lösungsmittel neut; adj (comm) zahlungsfähig.

sombre ['sombə] adj düster.

some [sʌm] adj (several) einige; (a little) etwas; (some ... or other) (irgend)ein; (approx.) ungefähr. **somebody** or **someone** pron jemand. **some day** eines Tages. **something** pron etwas. **sometime** adv irgendwann. **sometimes** adv manchmal. **somewhat** adv ziemlich. **somewhere** adv irgendwo(hin).

somersault ['sʌməsɔːlt] n Purzelbaum m. v (person) einen Purzelbaum schlagen; (thing) sich überschlagen.

son [sʌn] n Sohn m. **son-in-law** n Schwiegersohn m.

sonata [sə'naːtə] n Sonata f.

song [soŋ] n Lied neut, Gesang m. **songbird** n Singvogel m.

sonic ['sonik] adj Schall-. **sonic barrier** Schallgrenze f.

sonnet ['sonit] n Sonett neut.

soon [suːn] adv bald. **as soon as** sobald. **as soon as possible** so bald wie möglich. **sooner** adv früher.

soot [sut] *n* Ruß *m.* **sooty** *adj* rußig.
soothe [suːð] *v* beruhigen; (*pain*) lindern.
  soothing *adj* lindernd, besänftigend.
sophisticated [sə'fistikeitid] *adj* (*person*)
  kultiviert; (*machinery, etc.*) kompliziert,
  hochentwickelt. **sophistication** *n* Kultiviertheit *f.*
sopping ['sopiŋ] *adj* patschnaß.
soprano [sə'praːnou] *n* Sopranistin *f;*
  (*voice*) Sopran *m. adj* Sopran-.
sordid ['soːdid] *adj* schmutzig, gemein.
sore [soː] *adj* wund; (*inflamed*) entzündet;
  (*coll: annoyed*) verärgert. *n* Wunde *f.*
  sorely *adv* äußerst. **soreness** *n* Empfindlichkeit *f.*
sorrow ['sorou] *n* Kummer *m,* Leid *neut;*
  (*regret*) Reue *f.* **sorrowful** *adj* betrübt,
  traurig.
sorry ['sori] *adj* traurig, betrübt; (*sight,*
  etc.) jämmerlich, traurig. *interj*
  Verzeihung! *I am sorry* es tut mir leid. *I*
  am/feel sorry for you Sie tun mir leid.
sort [soːt] *n* Sorte *f,* Art *f;* (*brand*) Marke
  f. **all sorts of** allerlei. **a sort of** eine Art.
  sort of (*coll*) gewissermaßen. **that sort of**
  thing so etwas. *v* sortieren.
soufflé ['suːflei] *n* Auflauf *m.*
sought [soːt] *V* seek. **sought-after** *adj*
  gesucht.
soul [soul] *n* Seele *f.* **not a soul** kein
  Mensch.   **soul-destroying**   *adj*
  seelentötend. **soulful** *adj* seelenvoll. **soul-**
  less *adj* seelenlos.
sound[1] [saund] *n* Schall *m;* (*noise*) Geräusch *neut,* Klang *m.* **soundproof** *adj*
  schalldicht. **sound wave** Schallwelle *f. v*
  klingen. **sound the alarm** den Alarm
  schlagen. **sound the horn** hupen. **sound-**
  less *adj* geräuschlos.
sound[2] [saund] *adj* (*healthy*) gesund;
  (*safe*) sicher; (*reasoning*) stichhaltig.
sound[3] [saund] *v* loten, sondieren.
soup [suːp] *n* Suppe *f,* Brühe *f.*
sour [sauə] *adj* sauer.
source [soːs] *n* Quelle *f.*
south [sauθ] *n* Süden *m. adj* also *souther-*
  ly, **southern** südlich, Süd-. *adv* also
  southwards nach Süden, südwärts. **South**
  America Südamerika *neut.* **south-east** *n*
  Südosten. **South Pole** Südpol *m.* **south-**
  west *n* Südwesten *m.*
souvenir [suːvə'niə] *n* Andenken *neut.*
sovereign ['sovrin] *n* Souverän *m. adj*
  souverän. **sovereignty** *n* Souveränität *f.*
Soviet Union ['souviət] *n* Sowjetunion *f.*

***sow**[1] [sou] *v* säen; (*field*) besäen. **sower** *n*
  Säer *m.*
sow[2] [sau] *n* Sau *f.*
sown [soun] *V* **sow**[1].
soya ['soiə] *n* Sojabohne *f.*
spa [spaː] *n* Badekurort *m.*
space [speis] *n* Raum *m;* (*gap*) Zwischenraum *m,* Abstand *m;* (*astron*) Weltraum *m.* **space flight** Raumflug *m.*
  spaceship *n* Raumschiff *neut. v* (räumlich) einteilen. **spacious** *adj* geräumig.
spade[1] [speid] *n* Spaten *m.* **spadework** *n*
  (*fig*) Vorarbeit *f.*
spade[2] [speid] *n* (*cards*) Pik *neut.*
Spain [spein] *n* Spanien *neut.* **Spaniard** *n*
  Spanier(in). **Spanish** *adj* spanisch.
span [span] *n* (*arch*) Spannweite *f;* (*time*)
  Zeitspanne *f.*
spaniel ['spanjəl] *n* Spaniel *m.*
spank [spaŋk] *v* verhauen, prügeln.
spanner ['spanə] *n* Schraubenschlüssel *m.*
spare [speə] *adj* Ersatz-; (*over*) übrig;
  (*thin*) hager, dürr. **spare time** Freizeit *f.*
  spare tyre Ersatzreifen *m.* **spare rib** Rip-
  penspeer *m. v* (*pains, expense*) scheuen;
  (*give*) übrig haben (für); (*feelings, etc.*)
  verschonen. **sparing** *adj* sparsam. *n* also
  spare part Ersatzteil *m.*
spark [spaːk] *n* Funke *m. v* funkeln. **spark**
  or **sparking plug** Zündkerze *f.*
sparkle ['spaːkl] *v* funkeln, glänzen. *n*
  Funkeln *neut,* Glanz *m.* **sparkler** *n*
  Wunderkerze *f.* **sparkling** *adj* funkelnd;
  (*wine*) schäumend.
sparrow ['sparou] *n* Spatz *m,* Sperling *m.*
sparse [spaːs] *adj* spärlich, dünn. **sparse-**
  ness *n* Spärlichkeit *f.*
spasm ['spazəm] *n* (*med*) Krampf *m;* (*fig*)
  Anfall *m.* **spasmodic** *adj* (*fig*) sprunghaft.
spastic ['spastik] *adj* spastisch. *n* Spas-
  tiker(in).
spat [spat] *V* **spit**[1].
spatial ['speiʃl] *adj* räumlich.
spatula ['spatjulə] *n* Spachtel *m.*
spawn [spoːn] *n* Laich *m. v* (*eggs*)
  ablegen; (*fig*) hervorbringen.
***speak** [spiːk] *v* sprechen, reden. **speak**
  out frei herausreden. **speak to** reden mit.
  speak up laut sprechen. **speak up for sich**
  einsetzen für. **speaker** *n* Redner *m.*
spear [spiə] *n* Speer *m. v* aufspießen.
special ['speʃəl] *adj* besonder, speziell;
  (*train, case*) Sonder-. **specialist** *n*
  Fachmann *m.* **speciality** *n* Spezialität *f.*
  specialization *n* Spezialisierung *f.* **special-**

ize *v* spezialisieren. **specially** *adv* besonders.

species ['spiːʃɪz] *n* Art *f*; (*biol*) Spezies *f*.

specify ['spesifai] *v* spezifizieren, im einzeln angeben. **specific** *adj* spezifisch. **specifications** *n* *pl* (*tech*) technische Daten *pl*.

specimen ['spesimin] *n* Muster *neut*, Probe *f*.

speck [spek] *n* Fleck *m*. **speckle** *v* flecken.

spectacle ['spektəkl] *n* Schauspiel *neut*. **spectacles** *pl* Brille *f sing*. **spectacular** *adj* sensationell.

spectator [spek'teitə] *n* Zuschauer(in).

spectrum ['spektrəm] *n* Spektrum *neut*.

speculate ['spekjuleit] *v* nachdenken; (*comm*) spekulieren. **speculation** *n* Mutmaßung *f*, Annahme *f*; (*comm*) Spekulation *f*. **speculative** *adj* spekulativ. **speculator** *n* Spekulant *m*.

sped [sped] *V* **speed**.

speech [spiːtʃ] *n* Sprache *f*; (*a talk*) Rede *f*. **make a speech** eine Rede halten.

*****speed** [spiːd] *n* Geschwindigkeit *f*, Tempo *neut*. *v* rasen, eilen; (*exceed limit*) (zu) schnell fahren. **speed up** beschleunigen. **speed limit** Geschwindigkeitsbegrenzung *f*. **speedboat** *n* Schnellboot *neut*. **speedometer** *n* Tachometer *m*. **speedy** *adj* schnell.

*****spell**[1] [spel] *v* (*name the letters in*) buchstabieren; (*signify*) bedeuten. **how do you spell . . . ?** wie schreibt man . . . ? **spell out** deutlich erklären. **spelling** *n* Rechtschreibung *f*.

spell[2] [spel] *n* (*magic*) Zauber *m*, Zauberspruch *m*. **cast a spell on** bezaubern. **spellbound** *adj* fasziniert.

spell[3] [spel] *n* (*period*) Periode *f*, Weile *f*. **spelt** [spelt] *V* **spell**[1].

*****spend** [spend] *v* (*money*) ausgeben; (*time*) verbringen. **spending money** Taschengeld *neut*. **spendthrift** *n* Verschwender(in); *adj* verschwenderisch. **spent** [spent] *V* **spend**.

sperm [spəːm] *n* Sperma *neut*.

sperm whale *n* Pottwal *m*.

spew [spjuː] *v* (*vulgar*) sich erbrechen, kotzen. **spew out** ausspeien.

sphere [sfiə] *n* Kugel *f*; (*fig*) Bereich *m*. **spherical** *adj* kugelförmig.

spice [spais] *n* Gewürz *neut*. *v* würzen. **spiced** *adj* gewürzt. **spicy** *adj* pikant, scharf.

spider ['spaidə] *n* Spinne *f*. **spider's web** Spinngewebe *neut*. **spidery** *adj* spinnenartig.

spike [spaik] *n* Spitze *f*, Dorn *m*.

*****spill** [spil] *v* verschütten; (*blood*) vergießen. *n* (*coll*) Sturz, Fall *m*. **spilt** [spilt] *V* **spill**.

*****spin** [spin] *v* (*thread, web*) spinnen; (*turn*) (herum)wirbeln, spinnen; (*washing*) schleudern. *n* (*coll: in car, etc.*) Spazierfahrt *f*. **spin-dryer** *n* Wäscheschleuder *f*. **spinning wheel** Spinnrad *neut*.

spinach ['spinidʒ] *n* Spinat *m*.

spindle ['spindl] *n* Spindel *f*. **spindly** *adj* spindeldürr.

spine [spain] *n* (*thorn, etc.*) Stachel *m*; (*anat*) Rückgrat *neut*, Wirbelsäule *f*. **spiny** *adj* stachelig.

spinster ['spinstə] *n* unverheiratete Frau *f*; (*elderly*) alte Jungfer *f*.

spiral ['spaiərəl] *adj* schraubenförmig, spiral. **spiral staircase** Wendeltreppe *f*. *n* Spirale *f*.

spire ['spaiə] *n* Turmspitze *f*.

spirit ['spirit] *n* Geist *m*. **spirits** *pl* (*drinks*) Spirituosen *pl*, Alkohol *m*. **high spirits** Frohsinn *m*, gehobene Stimmung *f*. *v* **spirit away** hinwegzaubern. **spirited** *adj* lebhaft. **spiritual** *adj* geistig, geistlich.

*****spit**[1] [spit] *n* (*saliva*) Spucke *f*, Speichel *m*. *v* spucken.

spit[2] [spit] *n* (*roasting*) (Brat)Spieß *m*; (*geog*) Landzunge *f*.

spite [spait] *n* Boshaftigkeit *f*. **in spite of** trotz (+*gen*). **spiteful** *adj* boshaft.

splash [splaʃ] *v* (be)spritzen. *n* Spritzen *neut*; (*mark*) Fleck *m*.

spleen [spliːn] *n* Milz *f*.

splendid ['splendid] *adj* prächtig, herrlich. **splendour** *n* Pracht *f*.

splice [splais] *v* (*ropes*) spleißen; (*tapes, films*) zusammenfügen.

splint [splint] *n* Schiene *f*. **splinter** *n* Splitter *m*. *v* zersplittern. **splinter group** Splittergruppe *f*.

*****split** [split] *v* (zer)spalten, sich spalten. **split up** sich trennen. **split hairs** Haarspalterei treiben. **splitting headache** rasende Kopfschmerzen *pl*. *n* Spalt *m*, Riß *m*. *adj* gespalten.

splutter ['splʌtə] *v* stottern.

*****spoil** [spoil] *v* verderben; (*child*) verwöhnen. **spoils** *pl n* Beute *f*. **spoilsport** *n* Spielverderber(in).

spoke[1] [spouk] *V* **speak.**
spoke[2] [spouk] *n* (*wheel*) Speiche *f.*
spoken ['spoukn] *V* **speak.**
spokesman ['spouksmən] *n* Sprecher *m.*
sponge [spʌndʒ] *n* Schwamm *m. v* **sponge down** (mit einem Schwamm) abwaschen. **sponge-cake** *n* Sandtorte *f.* **sponger** *n* (*coll*) Schmarotzer *m.* **spongy** *adj* schwammig.
sponsor ['sponsə] *n* Förderer *m*, Schirmherr *m*; (*radio, TV*) Sponsor *m. v* unterstützen, fördern. **sponsorship** *n* Schirmherrschaft *f.*
spontaneous [spon'teinjəs] *adj* spontan. **spontaneity** *n* Freiwilligkeit *f*, Spontaneität *f.*
spool [spuːl] *n* Spule *f.*
spoon [spuːn] *n* Löffel *m. v* **spoon out** auslöffeln. **spoon-feed** *v* verhätscheln. **spoonful** *n* Löffelvoll *m.*
sporadic [spə'radik] *adj* verstreut, sporadisch.
sport [spoːt] *n* Sport *m*; (*fun*) Spaß *m.* **play sports** Sport treiben. **sportscar** *n* Sportwagen *m.* **sportsman** *n* Sportler *m.* **sportswoman** *n* Sportlerin *f. v* scherzen; (*wear*) tragen. **sporting** *adj* sportlich.
spot [spot] *n* (*mark*) Fleck *m*; (*place*) Stelle *f*; (*pimple*) Pickel *m.* **spot check** Stichprobe *f.* **spotlight** *n* Scheinwerfer *m.* **spotless** *adj* fleckenlos. *v* beflecken; (*notice*) entdecken, erspähen. **spotted** *adj* fleckig. **spotty** *adj* pickelig.
spouse [spaus] *n* Gatte *m*, Gattin *f*, Gemahl(in).
spout [spaut] *n* Tülle *f*, Schnauze *f. v* (*coll*) deklamieren.
sprain [sprein] *n* Verrenkung *f. v* verrenken.
sprang [spraŋ] *V* **spring.**
sprawl [sproːl] *v* (*person*) sich rekeln; (*town*) sich ausbreiten.
spray[1] [sprei] *v* (be)sprühen. *n* (*aerosol, etc.*) Sprühdose *f*, Spray *m*; (*sea*) Schaum *m.*
spray[2] [sprei] *n* (*of flowers*) Blütenzweig *m.*
*spread [spred] *v* ausbreiten; (*butter, etc.*) streichen; (*rumour*) (sich) verbreiten. *n* Ausbreitung *f*; (*extent*) Umfang *m*, Spanne *f*; (*for bread*) Aufstrich *m.*
spree [spriː] *n* (*shopping*) Einkaufsbummel *m.*
sprig [sprig] *n* Schößling *m.*

sprightly ['spraitli] *adj* lebhaft, munter.
*spring [spriŋ] *n* (*season*) Frühling *m*; (*tech*) Feder *f*; (*water*) Brunnen *m*, Quelle *f.* **springboard** *n* Sprungbrett *neut. v* springen. **spring a leak** ein Leck bekommen. **springing** *n* Federung *f.* **springy** *adj* elastisch.
sprinkle ['spriŋkl] *v* sprenkeln. **sprinkler** *n* Brause *f.* **a sprinkling of** ein bißchen.
sprint [sprint] *n* Sprint *m. v* sprinten. **sprinter** *n* Sprinter *m.*
sprout [spraut] *v* sprießen. n Sprößling *m.* (**Brussels**) **sprouts** Rosenkohl *m sing.*
spruce [spruːs] *n* (*tree*) Fichte *f.*
sprung [sprʌŋ] *V* **spring.**
spur [spəː] *n* Sporn *m*; (*fig*) Ansporn *m. v* (*horse*) die Sporen geben (+ *dat*); (*fig*) anspornen.
spurious ['spjuəriəs] *adj* falsch, unecht.
spurn [spəːn] *v* zurückweisen.
spurt [spəːt] *v* (*water*) hervorspritzen. *n* (*sport*) Spurt *m.*
spy [spai] *v* (*espy*) erspähen; (*pol*) spionieren. *n* Spion(in). **spy-glass** *n* Fernglas *neut.* **spying** *n* Spionage *f.*
squabble ['skwobl] *v* sich zanken. *n* Kabbelei *f*, Zank *m.*
squad [skwod] *n* Gruppe *f*; (*mil*) Zug *m*; (*police*) Kommando *neut.* **flying squad** Überfallkommando *neut.* **squad car** Streifenwagen *m.*
squadron ['skwodrən] *n* (*naut*) Geschwader *neut*; (*aero*) Staffel *f.* **squadron leader** Major *m.*
squalid ['skwolid] *adj* schmutzig. **squalor** *n* Schmutz *m.*
squall [skwoːl] *n* heftiger Windstoß *m*; (*storm*) Gewitter *neut.*
squander ['skwondə] *v* verschwenden, vergeuden.
square [skweə] *n* Quadrat *neut*, Viereck *neut*; (*in town*) Platz *m. adj* viereckig, quadratisch.
squash [skwoʃ] *n* (*people*) Gedränge *neut*; (*game*) Squash *neut. v* zerquetschen. **fruit squash** Fruchtsaft *m.*
squat [skwot] *v* hocken; (*ein Haus*) unberechtigt besetzen. *adj* gedrungen. **squatter** *n* Squatter *m.*
squawk [skwoːk] *n* Kreischen *neut. v* kreischen.
squeak [skwiːk] *v* (*wheel, etc.*) quietschen; (*mouse, etc.*) piepsen. *n* Quietschen *neut*; Piepsen *neut.* **squeaky** *adj* quietschend.

squeal [skwiːl] v schreien, quieken; (criminal) pfeifen. n Schrei m, Quieken neut.
squeamish ['skwiːmiʃ] adj überempfindlich. **squeamishness** n Überempfindlichkeit f.
squeeze [skwiːz] v drücken; (fruit) auspressen, ausquetschen. n Druck m. **credit squeeze** Kreditbeschränkung f. **squeezer** n Presse f.
squid [skwid] n Tintenfisch m.
squiggle ['skwigl] n Kritzelei f.
squint [skwint] n Schielen neut. v schielen. **squint-eyed** adj schielend.
squire ['skwaiə] n Junker m, Gutsherr m.
squirm [skwəːm] v sich winden.
squirrel ['skwirəl] n Eichhörnchen neut.
squirt [skwəːt] v spritzen. n Spritze f.
stab [stab] v (kill) erstechen. n Stich m. **stab wound** Stichwunde f. **make a stab at** versuchen.
stabilize ['steibilaiz] v stabilisieren. **stability** n Stabilität f. **stabilization** n Stabilisierung f.
stable[1] ['steibl] n Stall m. v einstallen. **stable-lad/man** n Stallknecht m.
stable[2] ['steibl] adj stabil.
staccato [stə'kaːtou] adj, adv staccato.
stack [stak] n Schober m; (wood, etc.) Stapel m. v aufschobern.
stadium ['steidiəm] n Stadion neut.
staff [staːf] n (stick) Stock m; (work force) Personal neut; (mil) Stab m. adj Personal-; stabs-.
stag [stag] n Rothirsch m. **stag party** Herrengesellschaft f.
stage [steidʒ] n (of development, etc.) Stufe f, Stadium neut; (theatre) Bühne. **stage fright** Lampenfieber neut. **stage-manager** n Inspizient m. v (play) aufführen; (fig) veranstalten.
stagger ['stagə] v schwanken, taumeln; (amaze) verblüffen. **staggering** adj taumelnd; phantastisch.
stagnant ['stagnənt] adj stillstehend, stagnierend. **stagnate** v stagnieren. **stagnation** n Stagnation f.
staid [steid] adj gesetzt, seriös.
stain [stein] adj Fleck m; (for wood, etc.) Färbung f. v beflecken; färben. **stainless** adj (steel) rostfrei.
stair [steə] n Treppenstufe f. (flight of) **stairs** Treppe f. **stair-carpet** n Treppenläufer m.
stake[1] [steik] n (post) Pfahl m, Pfosten m.

stake a claim (to) Anspruch erheben (auf).
stake[2] [steik] n (betting) Einsatz m; (share) Anteil m. v (money) setzen. **put at stake** aufs Spiel setzen.
stale [steil] adj (bread) alt, altbacken; (beer, etc.) abgestanden; (thing) abgedroschen.
stalemate ['steilmeit] n (chess) Patt neut; (fig) Stillstand m. v pattsetzen.
stalk[1] [stoːk] n (bot) Stiel m.
stalk[2] [stoːk] v sich anpirschen an.
stall[1] [stoːl] n (stable) Stand m; (market) Bude f. **stalls** pl (theatre) Parkett neut sing. v (engine) aussetzen; (car) stehenbleiben.
stall[2] [stoːl] v (delay) ausweichen, Ausflüchte machen.
stallion ['staljən] n Hengst m.
stamina ['staminə] n Durchhaltevermögen neut, Ausdauer f.
stammer ['stamə] v stottern, stammeln. n Stottern neut, Gestammel neut. **stammerer** n Stotterer m. **stammering** adj stotternd.
stamp [stamp] v (with foot) stampfen; (rubber stamp) stempeln; (letters) frankieren. n Stempel m; (letter) Briefmarke f. **stamp album** Briefmarkenalbum neut. **stamp collector** Briefmarkensammler m.
stampede [stam'piːd] n wilde Flucht f.
*****stand** [stand] n (sales, etc.) Bude f, Stand m; (attitude) Standpunkt m; (for spectators) (Zuschauer)Tribüne f; (resistance) Widerstand m. v stehen. I can't stand him ich kann ihn nicht ausstehen. I can't stand it ich kann es nicht aushalten. **as things stand** unter den Umständen. **my offer stands** mein Angebot gilt noch. **stand aside** beiseite treten. **stand back** zurücktreten. **stand by** (be loyal to) treu bleiben (+dat). **stand for** (mean) bedeuten, stehen für; (tolerate) sich gefallen lassen; (parliament) kandidieren. **stand in for** einspringen für. **stand up** aufstehen. **stand up to** sich verteidigen gegen. **standby** n Stütze f; (alert) Alarmbereitschaft f. **standing** n Stand m, Rang m. **standing order** (bank) Dauerauftrag m. **stand-offish** adj hochmütig.
standard ['standəd] n Standard m, Norm f. (flag) Standarte f. adj Normal-; (usual) gewöhnlich, normal. **standardize** v

normen, standardisieren. **standardization** *n* Normung *f*.

stank [staŋk] *V* stink.

stanza ['stanzə] *n* Strophe *f*, Stanza *f*.

staple¹ [steipl] *n* Heftklammer *f*. *v* heften. **stapler** *n* Heftmaschine *f*.

staple² [steipl] *adj* Haupt-.

star [staɪ] *n* Stern *m*; (*films, etc.*) Star *m*. **starlight** *n* Sternenlicht *neut*. *v* die Hauptrolle spielen. **starring** in der Hauptrolle. **starry** *adj* (*sky*) Sternen-; (*night*) sternhell.

starboard ['staɪbəd] *n* Steuerbord *neut*. *adj* Steuerbord-.

starch [staɪtʃ] *n* (Wäsche)Stärke *f*. *v* stärken. **starched** *adj* gestärkt. **starchy** *adj* (*person*) steif, förmlich.

stare [steə] *n* starrer Blick *m*, Starrblick *m*. *v* starren. **stare at** anstarren.

stark [staɪk] *adj* kahl, öde. *adv* **stark naked** splitternackt. **stark-staring mad** total verrückt.

starling ['staɪliŋ] *n* Star *m*.

start [staɪt] *v* anfangen, beginnen; (*leave*) abfahren; (*arise*) entstehen; (*sport*) starten (lassen); (*engine*) anlassen; (*jump*) hochschrecken. *n* Anfang *m*, Beginn *m*; (*sport*) Start *m*; (*journey*) Abreise *f*. **from the start** vom Anfang an. **starter** *n* (*sport*) Starter *m*. **starter motor** Anlaßmotor *m*.

startle ['staɪtl] *v* erschrecken, überraschen. **startling** *adj* erschreckend.

starve [staɪv] *v* verhungern. **starvation** *n* Hungern *neut*, Verhungern *neut*.

state [steit] *n* (*pol*) Staat *m*; (*condition*) Zustand *m*; (*situation*) Lage *f*. *v* erklären, behaupten. *adj* Staats-, staatlich. **stated** *adj* angegeben. **stateless** *adj* staatenlos. **stately** *adj* stattlich. **statement** *n* Erklärung *f*. **statement of account** Kontoauszug *m*. **statesman** *n* Staatsmann *m*. **statesmanship** *n* Staatskunst *f*.

static ['statik] *adj* statisch. *n* statische Elekrizität *f*.

station ['steiʃən] *n* Platz *m*, Posten *m*; (*rail*) Bahnhof *m*; (*standing*) Stand *m*. **station master** Bahnhofsvorsteher *m*. **station wagon** Kombi(wagen) *m*. *v* stationieren.

stationary ['steiʃənəri] *adj* stillstehend, stationär.

stationer ['steiʃənə] *n* Schreibwarenhändler *m*. **stationery** *n* Schreibwaren *pl*; (*office*) Büromaterial *neut*.

statistics [stə'tistiks] *n* Statistik *f*. **statistical** *adj* statistisch.

statue ['statjuɪ] *n* Standbild *neut*, Statue *f*.

stature ['statʃə] *n* Körpergröße *f*, Statur *f*; (*moral, etc.*) Kaliber *neut*.

status ['steitəs] *n* Status *m*; (*rank*) Stand *m*, Rang *m*. **status quo** Status quo *m*. **status symbol** Statussymbol *neut*.

statute ['statjuɪt] *n* Gesetz *neut*. **statutory** *adj* gesetzlich (vorgeschrieben).

staunch [stoɪntʃ] *adj* getreu, zuverlässig.

stay [stei] *v* bleiben; (*in hotel*) logieren, unterkommen; (*with friends, etc.*) zu Besuch sein (bei). **stay the night** übernachten. **stay behind** zurückbleiben. **stay in** zu Hause bleiben. *n* Aufenthalt *m*; Besuch *m*.

steadfast ['stedfaɪst] *adj* fest, treu.

steady ['stedi] *adj* sicher, fest, stabil; (*regular*) regelmäßig, gleichmäßig; (*cautious*) vorsichtig. *v* festigen. **steady on!** langsam!, vorsichtig! **steadiness** *n* Festigkeit *f*, Sicherheit *f*.

steak [steik] *n* Steak *neut*.

*steal [stiɪl] *v* stehlen. **steal away** sich davonstehlen.

stealthy ['stelθi] *adj* heimlich. **stealth** *n* Heimlichkeit *f*.

steam [stiɪm] *n* Dampf *m*. *v* dampfen; (*food*) dünsten. **steam-boiler** *n* Dampfkessel *m*. **steamer** *n* (*naut*) Dampfer *m*, Dampfschiff *neut*; (*cookery*) Dampfkochtopf *m*. **steam-roller** *n* Dampfwalze *f*; *v* (*opposition*) niederwalzen. **steamy** *adj* dampfig.

steel [stiɪl] *n* Stahl *m*. *adj* stählern, Stahl-. **steelworks** *pl n* Stahlwerk *neut* *sing*. **steely** hart.

steep¹ [stiɪp] *adj* steil, jäh; (*coll: improbable*) unwahrscheinlich; (*prices*) gepfeffert.

steep² [stiɪp] *v* (*soak*) einweichen.

steeple ['stiɪpl] *n* Kirchturm *m*, Spitzturm *m*.

steeplechase ['stiɪpltʃeis] *n* Steeplechase *f*. **steeplejack** *n* Turmarbeiter *m*.

steer [stiə] *v* steuern, lenken. **steering column** *n* Lenksäule *f*. **steering lock** Lenkradschloß *m*. **steering wheel** Lenkrad *neut*, Steuer *neut*.

stem¹ [stem] *n* (*stalk*) Stiel *m*; (*line of descent*) Stamm *m*. *v* **stem from** stammen von, zurückgehen auf.

stem² [stem] *v* eindämmen; (*blood*) stillen.

stench [stentʃ] *n* Gestank *m.*
stencil ['stensl] *n* Schablone *f. v* schablonieren.
step [step] *v* treten, schreiten. *n* Schritt *m;* (*measure*) Maßnahme *f;* (*stage, gradation*) Stufe *f.* **step by step** Schritt für Schritt. **step on it** (*coll*) Gas geben. **step aside** zur seite treten. **step-ladder** *n* Trittleiter *f.* **stepping-stone** *n* Trittstein *m;* (*fig*) Sprungbrett *neut.*
stepbrother ['stepbrʌðə] *n* Stiefbruder *m.*
stepdaughter ['stepdɔːtə] *n* Stieftochter *f.*
stepfather ['stepfɑːðə] *n* Stiefvater *m.*
stepmother ['stepmʌðə] *n* Stiefmutter *f.*
stepsister ['stepsistə] *n* Stiefschwester *f.*
stepson ['stepsʌn] *n* Stiefsohn *m.*
stereo ['steriou] *n* Stereoanlage *f. adj* Stereo-. **stereophonic** *adj* stereophonisch.
stereotyped ['steriətaipt] *adj* stereotyp.
sterile ['sterail] *adj* steril. **sterility** *n* Sterilität *f.*
sterling ['stɔːliŋ] *n* Sterling *m.*
stern[1] [stɔːn] *adj* streng, hart. **sternness** *n* Strenge *f.* Härte *f.*
stern[2] [stɔːn] *n* (*naut*) Heck *neut.*
stethoscope ['steθəskoup] *n* Stethoskop *neut.*
stew [stjuː] *n* Eintopfgericht *neut. v* schmoren. **stewed** *adj* geschmort.
steward ['stjuəd] *n* (*ship, aeroplane*) Steward *m;* (*race, etc.*) Ordner *m.* **stewardess** *n* Stewardeß *f.*
stick[1] [stik] *n* (*wood*) Stock *m;* (*hockey*) Schläger *m.*
***stick**[2] [stik] *v* (*with glue, etc.*) kleben *or* heften (an); (*pointed instrument*) stecken; **stick out** (*tongue*) herausstrecken; (*protrude*) hervorstehen. **stick to** (*remain with*) bleiben bei. **stick up for** sich einsetzen für. **be stuck** steckenbleiben. **stuck-up** *adj* hochnäsig. **sticking plaster** Heftpflaster *neut.* **sticky** *adj* klebrig.
stiff [stif] *adj* steif, starr; (*drink*) stark; (*difficult*) schwierig. *n* (*coll*) Leiche *f.* **stiffen** *v* (ver)steifen, (ver)stärken. **stiffnecked** *adj* halsstarrig. **stiffness** *n* Steife *f,* Starrheit *f.*
stifle ['staifl] *v* ersticken. **stifling** *adj* zum Ersticken.
stigma ['stigmə] *n* Brandmal *neut,* Stigma *neut.*
stile [stail] *n* Zauntritt *m.*
still[1] [stil] *adj* still. *adv* (immer)noch. *conj* und doch, dennoch. *v* beruhigen. **still**

birth Totgeburt *f.* **stillborn** *adj* totgeboren. **stillness** *n* Stille *f.*
still[2] [stil] *n* (*for spirits*) Brennerei *f.*
stilt [stilt] *n* Stelze *f.* **stilted** *adj* gespreizt.
stimulus ['stimjuləs] *n* (*pl* -i) Stimulus *m.* **stimulant** *n* Reizmittel *neut.* **stimulate** *v* anregen. **stimulating** *adj* anregend. **stimulation** *n* Anreiz *m.*
***sting** [stiŋ] *v* (*insect*) stechen; (*be painful*) brennen; (*remark*) kränken. *n* Stich *m.* **stinging** *adj* brennend; schmerzend. **stinging nettle** Brennessel *f.*
stingy ['stindʒi] *adj* geizig.
***stink** [stiŋk] *v* stinken, übel riechen. *n* Gestank *m;* (*coll: scandal*) Skandal *m.*
stint [stint] *v* knausern mit. *n* (*of work*) Schicht *f.*
stipulate ['stipjuleit] *v* festsetzen; (*insist on*) bestehen auf. **stipulation** Bedingung *f.*
stir [stɔː] *v* (*liquids*) (an)rühren; (*move*) sich rühren *or* bewegen; (*excite*) aufrühren, bewegen. *n* Rühren *neut;* (*sensation*) Sensation *f.* **stirring** *adj* aufregend.
stirrup ['stirəp] *n* Steigbügel *m.*
stitch [stitʃ] *n* Stich *m;* (*knitting*) Masche *f;* (*pain*) Stechen *m. v* nähen. **stitch up** vernähen. **stitching** *n* Näherei *f.*
stoat [stout] *n* Hermelin *neut.*
stock [stok] *n* (*of goods*) Vorrat *m,* Lager *neut;* (*cookery*) Brühe; (*descent*) Stamm *m.* **stocks** *pl* (*comm*) Aktien *pl.* **stockbroker** *n* Börsenmakler *m.* **stock exchange** Börse *f.* **stockpile** *v* aufstapeln. **stock-still** *adj* bewegungslos. **stocktaking** *n* Bestandaufnahme *f. v* (*goods*) führen, vorrätig haben.
stocking ['stokiŋ] *n* Strumpf *m.*
stocky ['stoki] *adj* stämmig, untersetzt.
stodge [stodʒ] *n* schwerverdauliches Zeug *neut.* **stodgy** *adj* schwer(verdaulich).
stoical ['stouikl] *adj* stoisch.
stoke [stouk] *v* schüren. **stoker** *n* Heizer *m.*
stole[1] [stoul] *V* steal.
stole[2] [stoul] *n* Stola *f.*
stolen ['stoulən] *V* steal.
stomach ['stʌmək] *n* Magen *m;* (*coll: abdomen*) Bauch *m;* (*taste for*) Appetit (zu) *f. v* ertragen. **stomach-ache** *n* Magenschmerzen *pl.*
stone [stoun] *n* Stein *m;* (*fruit*) Kern *m. adj* steinern, Stein-. *v* (*fruit*) entkernen; (*to death*) steinigen. **stone age** Steinzeit *f.*

stoned adj (coll) besoffen. **stone-deaf** adj stocktaub. **stonemason** n Steinmetz m.
stony adj steinig.
stood [stud] V stand.
stool [stuːl] n Hocker m, Stuhl m; (med) Stuhlgang m.
stoop [stuːp] v sich bücken; (posture) gebeugt gehen. n Beugen neut, krumme Haltung f.
stop [stop] v (activity) aufhören; (motion) anhalten, stoppen; (clock) stehenbleiben; (put a stop to) einstellen; (bus, train) anhalten; (pipe, etc.) verstopfen. n Halt m, Stillstand m; (break) Pause f; (bus) Haltestelle f. **stoppage** n Stillstand m. **stopper** n Stöpsel m. **stop-watch** n Stoppuhr f.
store [stoː] v aufbewahren. n Vorrat m, Lager neut; (shop) Laden m. **storage** n Lagerung f. **storekeeper** n (shop) Ladenbesitzer m.
storey ['stoːri] n Stockwerk neut. **four-storied** adj vierstöckig.
stork [stoːk] n Storch m.
storm [stoːm] n Sturm m, Unwetter neut; (thunderstorm) Gewitter neut. **storm-tossed** adj sturmgepeitscht. v stürmen. **storm-troops** Sturmtruppen pl. **stormy** adj stürmisch.
story ['stoːri] n Geschichte f, Erzählung f. **to cut a long story short** um es ganz kurz zu sagen. **story-book** n Märchenbuch neut. **story-teller** n Erzähler(in).
stout [staut] adj dick, beleibt; (strong) kräftig. n dunkles Bier neut, Malzbier neut.
stove [stouv] n Ofen m; (cooking) Kochherd m. **stove-pipe** Ofenrohr neut.
stow [stou] v verstauen. **stowaway** blinder Passagier m.
straddle ['stradl] v (sitting) rittlings sitzen auf.
straggle ['stragl] v umherstreifen. **straggle behind** nachhinken. **straggler** n Nachzügler m.
straight [streit] adj gerade; (hair) glatt; (candid) offen, freimütig. adv gerade, direkt. **get straight** (clarify) klarstellen. **think straight** logisch denken. **straight on** or **ahead** gerade aus. **straightaway** adv sofort. **straighten** v gerademachen. **straighten out** (put in order) in Ordnung bringen. **straightforward** adj (thing) einfach, schlicht; (person) offen, aufrichtig. n (sport) Gerade f.

strain¹ [strein] v spannen; (muscle) zerren; (tech) verzerren; (filter) sieben, filtern. **strain oneself** sich (über)anstrengen. n Überanstrengung f; (emotional) Streß m, Anspannung f; (med) Zerrung. **strained** adj (relations, etc.) gespannt.
strain² [strein] n (race) Abstammung f, Rasse f.
straits [streits] pl n Straße f, Meerenge f. **dire straits** Notlage f. **strait-jacket** n Zwangsjacke f.
strand¹ [strand] n (rope) Strang m; (hair) Strähne f; (thought) Faden m.
strand² [strand] n (shore) Strand m, Ufer neut. v stranden. **stranded** adj gestrandet.
strange [streindʒ] adj (odd) seltsam, sonderbar; (alien) fremd. **strangeness** n Seltsamkeit f; Fremdartigkeit f. **stranger** n Fremde(r). **be a stranger to** nicht vertraut sein mit. **strangely** adv seltsamerweise.
strangle ['strangl] v erwürgen, erdrosseln. **stranglehold** n Würgegriff m.
strap [strap] n Riemen m; (dress) Träger m. v festschnallen. **strapless** adj trägerlos. **strapping** adj stramm.
strategy ['stratədʒi] n Strategie f. **strategic** adj strategisch.
stratum ['straitəm] n (pl -a) Schicht f.
straw [stroː] n Stroh neut; (single) Strohhalm m; (drinking) Trinkhalm m. adj Stroh-. **straw hat** Strohhut m.
strawberry ['stroːbəri] n Erdbeere f.
stray [strei] v sich verirren; (from path, etc.) abgehen (von); (attention) wandern. adj verirrt. n verirrtes Tier neut.
streak [striːk] n Streifen neut; (in character) Einschlag m. **streak of lightning** Blitzstrahl m. v streifen; (race, fly) rasen, sausen. **streaked** adj gestreift.
stream [striːm] n Bach m; (current) Strom m, Strömung f. v strömen. **streamer** n (party) Papierschlange f. **streamline** v (fig) rationalisieren. **streamlined** adj windschnittig.
street [striːt] n Straße f. **streetcar** n Straßenbahn f. **street lamp** Straßenlaterne f. **street-walker** n Straßendirne f.
strength [streŋθ] n Stärke f, Kraft f, Kräfte pl; (liquids) Stärke f; (mil) Macht f, Schlagkraft f. **strengthen** v (ver)stärken. **strengthening** n Verstärkung f.

strenuous ['strenjuǝs] *adj* anstrengend.
stress [stres] *n (emphasis)* Nachdruck *m*;
(psychological) Streß *m*; *(pronunciation)*
Akzent *m*. *v* betonen. **stressful** *adj* belas-
tend.
stretch [stretʃ] *v* (aus)strecken, ausdehnen; *(person)* sich strecken; *(e.g.
land, town)* sich erstrecken. *n (time)* Zeitspanne *f*; *(place)* Strecke *f*. **stretcher** *n*
Tragbahre *f*. **stretchy** *adj* dehnbar.
stricken ['strikǝn] *adj (sickness)* befallen
(von); *(emotion)* ergriffen (von).
strict [strikt] *adj* streng. **strictness** *n*
Strenge *f*.
stridden ['stridn] *V* **stride**.
***stride** [straid] *v* schreiten. *n* Schritt *m*.
make great strides Fortschritte machen.
get into one's stride in Schwung kommen.
strident ['straidǝnt] *adj* grell.
strife [straif] *n* Kampf *m*.
***strike** [straik] *v* schlagen; *(target)* tref-
fen; *(workers)* streiken; *(match)*
entzünden. **it strikes me** es fällt mir ein.
strike off streichen von. *n* Schlag *m*, Stoß
m; *(labour)* Streik *m*. **striking** *adj* auffallend.
***string** [striŋ] *n* Schnur *f*, Bindfaden *m*;
(instrument) Saite *f*. **strings** *pl (mus)*
Streicher *pl*. *v (instrument)* besaiten.
string together verknüpfen. **stringed
instrument** Streichinstrument *neut*.
stringent ['strindʒǝnt] *adj* streng. **strin-
gency** *n* Strenge *f*.
strip¹ [strip] *v* abziehen; *(clothes)* ausziehen.
strip² [strip] *n (narrow piece)* (schmaler)
Streifen *m*.
stripe [straip] *n* Streifen *m*, Strich *m*. *v*
streifen. **striped** *adj* gestreift.
***strive** [straiv] *v (for)* streben (nach); *(to
do)* sich anstrengen (zu).
striven ['strivn] *V* **strive**.
strode [stroud] *V* **stride**.
stroke¹ [strouk] *n (blow)* Schlag *m*; *(pen)*
Strich *m*; *(med)* Schlaganfall *m*.
stroke² [strouk] *v* streicheln.
stroll [stroul] *v* schlendern. *n* Bummel *m*,
Spaziergang *m*.
strong [stroŋ] *adj (person, thing)* stark;
(person) kräftig; *(flavour, etc.)* scharf. **be
going strong** wohlauf sein. **strong-room** *n*
Tresor *m*. **strong-willed** *adj* willensstark.
strongly *adv* kräftig.

strove [strouv] *V* **strive**.
struck [strʌk] *V* **strike**.
structure ['strʌktʃǝ] *n* Struktur *f*. **structural** *adj* strukturell.
struggle ['strʌgl] *v* kämpfen, ringen. *n*
Kampf *m*.
strum [strʌm] *v* klimpern (auf).
strung [strʌŋ] *V* **string**.
strut¹ [strʌt] *v* (herum)stolzieren. **strutting**
adj prahlerisch.
strut² [strʌt] *n* Stütze *f*, Spreize *f*.
stub [stʌb] *n* Stumpf *m*; *(cheque)* Kontrollabschnitt *m*, Talon *m*; *(cigarette)*
(Zigaretten)Stummel *m*. *v* **stub out** ausdrücken.
stubble ['stʌbl] *n* Stoppel *f*; *(beard)* Stop-
peln *pl*. **stubbly** *adj* stoppelig.
stubborn ['stʌbǝn] *adj* hartnäckig, eigensinnig. **stubbornness** *n* Hartnäckigkeit *f*.
stuck [stʌk] *V* **stick²**.
stud¹ [stʌd] *n* Beschlagnagel *m*; *(button)*
Knopf *m*.
stud² [stʌd] *n (farm)* Gestüt *neut*; *(horse)*
Zuchthengst *m*.
student ['stjuːdǝnt] *n* Student(in); *(at
school, also fig)* Schüler(in).
studio ['stjuːdiou] *n* Studio *neut*.
study ['stʌdi] *n* Studium *neut*; *(piece of
research, etc.)* Studie *f*, Untersuchung *f*;
(room) Studierzimmer *neut*. *v* studieren.
stuff [stʌf] *n* Stoff *m*; *(coll)* Zeug *neut*,
Kram *m*. *v* vollstopfen; *(taxidermy)* auss-
topfen; *(cookery)* füllen. **stuffing** *n* Füllung *f*.
stuffy ['stʌfi] *adj (air)* dumpf, schwül;
(thing) langweilig; *(person)* pedantisch;
(nose) verstopft.
stumble [stʌmbl] *v* stolpern. **stumbling-
block** *n* Hindernis *neut*.
stump [stʌmp] *n* Stumpf *m*. *v (coll)* verblüffen. **stumpy** *adj* stumpfartig.
stun [stʌn] *v* betäuben; *(fig)* bestürzen.
stunning *adj (coll)* phantastisch.
stung [stʌŋ] *V* **sting**.
stunk [stʌŋk] *V* **stink**.
stunt¹ [stʌnt] *v (growth)* hindern, hemmen. **stunted** *adj* verkümmert.
stunt² [stʌnt] *n (feat)* Kunststück *neut*.
stupid ['stjuːpid] *adj* dumm, blöd. **stupidity** *n* Dummheit *f*.
stupor ['stjuːpǝ] *n* Erstarrung *f*; *(dullness)*
Stumpfsinn *m*.
sturdy ['stǝːdi] *adj* robust, kräftig.
sturgeon ['stǝːdʒǝn] *n* Stör *m*.

stutter ['stʌtə] *n* Stottern *neut. v* stottern.
stutterer *n* Stotterer *m*.
sty [stai] *n* Schweinestall *m*.
style [stail] *n* Stil *m. v (name)* benennen; *(shape)* formen. **latest style** neueste Mode *f*. **hairstyle** *n* Frisur *f*. **stylish** *adj* elegant.
stylus ['stailəs] *n* Griffel *m; (record-player)* Nadel *f*.
suave [swaɪv] *adj* weltmännisch, zuvorkommend.
subconscious [sʌb'konʃəs] *adj* unterbewußt. *n* das Unterbewußte *neut*.
subcontract [sʌbkən'trakt] *n* Nebenvertrag *m*. **subcontractor** *n* Unterkontrahent *m*.
subdue [səb'djuɪ] *v* unterwerfen. **subdued** *adj (person)* zurückhaltend; *(lights)* gedämpft.
subject ['sʌbdʒikt; *v* səb'dʒekt] *n (school, etc.)* Fach *neut; (theme)* Thema *neut*, Gegenstand *m; (gramm)* Subjekt *neut; (citizen)* Staatsangehörige(r). *adj (to ruler)* untertan *(+dat); (liable)* geneigt (zu); *(exposed)* ausgesetzt *(+dat). v* unterwerfen; *(expose)* aussetzen *(+dat)*. **subjection** *n* Unterwerfung *f*. **subjective** *adj* subjektiv.
subjunctive [səb'dʒʌŋktiv] *n* Konjunktiv *m*.
***sublet** [ˌsʌb'let] *n* untervermieten.
sublime [sə'blaim] *adj* sublim, erhaben.
submarine [sʌbmərɪn] *n* Unterseeboot (U-Boot) *neut. adj* Untersee-.
submerge [səb'mɔɪdʒ] *v* (ein)tauchen. **submerged** *adj* untergetaucht.
submit [səb'mit] *v* sich unterwerfen; *(maintain)* behaupten; *(hand in)* einreichen, vorlegen. **submission** *n* Unterwerfung *f; (documents)* Vorlage *f*. **submissive** *adj* gehorsam.
subnormal [sʌb'noɪməl] *adj (child, etc.)* minderbegabt.
subordinate [sə'bɔɪdinət] *v* unterordnen. *adj* untergeordnet. *n* Untergebene(r).
subscribe [səb'skraib] *v (money)* zeichnen. **subscribe to** *(newspaper)* abonnieren auf; *(view, etc.)* billigen. **subscriber** *n* Abonnent(in); *(phone)* Teilnehmer(in). **subscription** *n* Abonnement *neut*.
subsequent ['sʌbsikwənt] *adj* (nach)folgend. **subsequently** *adv* nachher, hinterher.
subservient [səb'sɜɪviənt] *adj* unterwürfig. **subservience** *n* Unterwürfigkeit *f*.

subside [səb'said] *v (noise, etc.)* nachlassen, abnehmen; *(sink)* sich senken. **subsidence** *n* (Boden)Senkung *f*.
subsidiary [səb'sidiəri] *adj* Hilfs-, Neben-. *n (company)* Tochtergesellschaft.
subsidize ['sʌbsidaiz] *v* subventionieren. **subsidy** *n* Subvention *f*.
subsist [səb'sist] *v* existieren. **subsist on** sich ernähren von. **subsistence** *n* Existenz *f*.
substance ['sʌbstəns] *n* Substanz *f*, Stoff *m; (of argument, etc.)* Gehalt *neut*, Kern *m*. **substantial** *adj* beträchtlich. **substantiate** *v* begründen.
substitute ['sʌbstitjuɪt] *n* Ersatz *m; (sport)* Ersatzspieler(in). *adj* Ersatz-. *v* ersetzen. **substitution** *n* Einsetzung *f*.
subtitle ['sʌbtaitl] *n* Untertitel *m*.
subtle ['sʌtl] *adj* fein, subtil. **subtlety** *n* Feinheit *f*.
subtract [səb'trakt] *v* abziehen. **subtraction** *n* Abziehen *neut; (thing subtracted)* Abzug *m*.
suburb ['sʌbəɪb] *n* Vorort *m*. **suburban** *adj* Vororts-; *(coll: provincial)* kleinstädtisch.
subvert [səb'vɔɪt] *v (government)* stürzen; *(morals)* untergraben. **subversion** *n* Sturz *m*; Untergrabung *f*. **subversive** *adj* umstürzlerisch.
subway ['sʌbwei] *n (in UK)* Fußgängerunterführung *f; (in US)* U-Bahn *f*.
succeed [sək'siɪd] *v (follow)* folgen auf, nachfolgen *(+dat); (be successful)* Erfolg haben, erfolgreich sein; gelingen *(impers). I succeeded in doing it* es gelang mir, es zu tun. **success** *n* Erfolg *m*. **successful** *adj* erfolgreich. **succession** *n* Reihenfolge *f*, Folge *f*. **successive** *adj* (aufeinander)folgend. **successor** *n* Nachfolger(in).
succinct [sək'siŋkt] *adj* kurz(gefaßt).
succulent ['sʌkjulənt] *adj* saftig. *n (bot)* Sukkulente *f*. **succulence** *n* Saftigkeit *f*.
succumb [sə'kʌm] *v* nachgeben *(+dat)*.
such [sʌtʃ] *adj* solch, derartig. *such a big house* ein so großes Haus. **no such thing** nichts dergleichen. **such as** wie zum Beispiel. **as such** an sich. **such is life** so ist das Leben.
suck [sʌk] *v* saugen; *(sweet, thumb)* lutschen. **sucker** *n (coll)* Gimpel *m; (bot)* Wurzelschößling *m*. **sucking pig** *n* Spanferkel *neut*. **suckle** *v* stillen. **suckling** *n* Säugling *m*.

suction ['sʌkʃən] v Saugwirkung f, Sog m.
sudden ['sʌdən] adj plötzlich. suddenness
n Plötzlichkeit f.
suds [sʌdz] n Seifenlauge f.
sue [suː] v verklagen (auf).
suede [sweid] n Wildleder neut.
suet ['suːit] n Nierenfett neut, Talg m.
suffer ['sʌfə] v leiden (an). sufferer n
Leidende(r). suffering n Leiden neut; adj
leidend (an).
sufficient [sə'fiʃənt] adj genügend, ausreichend.
suffocate ['sʌfəkeit] v ersticken. suffocating adj erstickend. suffocation n Erstick-
en neut.
sugar ['ʃugə] n Zucker m. v zuckern;
süßen. sugar cane n Zuckerrohr neut.
sugared adj gezuckert. sugary adj
süßlich; (fig) zuckersüß.
suggest [sə'dʒest] v vorschlagen; (maintain) behaupten; (indicate) hindeuten
auf. suggestion n Vorschlag m; (trace)
Spur f. suggestive adj anzüglich,
zweideutig. be suggestive of deuten auf.
suicide ['suːisaid] n Selbstmord m. suicid-
al adj selbstmörderisch.
suit [suːt] n (man's) Anzug m; (woman's)
Kostüm neut; (cards) Farbe f; (law)
Klage f. follow suit dasselbe tun. suitcase
n Handkoffer m. v (an)passen; (clothes)
(gut) stehen (+dat); (food) bekommen
(+dat). suitable adj geeignet, passend.
suite [swiːt] n (furniture) Garnitur f;
(rooms) Zimmerflucht f.
sulk [sʌlk] v schmollen, trotzen. sulky adj
mürrisch, schmollend.
sullen ['sʌlən] adj mürrisch.
sulphur ['sʌlfə] n Schwefel m. sulphurous
adj schwefelig; (fig) hitzig.
sultan ['sʌltən] n Sultan m.
sultana [sʌl'taːnə] n (dried fruit) Sultanine
f.
sultry ['sʌltri] adj schwül. sultriness n
Schwüle f.
sum [sʌm] n Summe f; (money) Betrag m;
(calculation) Rechenaufgabe f. v sum up
zusammenfassen.
summarize ['sʌməraiz] v zusammenfassen. summary n Zusammenfassung f.
summer ['sʌmə] n Sommer m. adj som-
merlich, Sommer-. summerhouse n
Gartenhaus neut. summery adj sommer-
lich.
summit ['sʌmit] n Gipfel m. summit conference Gipfelkonferenz f.

summon ['sʌmən] v aufrufen, kommen
lassen; (meeting) einberufen; (courage)
fassen. summons n Berufung f; (law)
(Vor)Ladung f. take out a summons
against vorladen lassen.
sump [sʌmp] n Ölwanne f.
sumptuous ['sʌmptʃuəs] adj prächtig,
kostspielig.
sun [sʌn] n Sonne f. v sun oneself sich
sonnen.
sunbathe ['sʌnbeið] v ein Sonnenbad
nehmen, sich sonnen.
sunbeam ['sʌnbiːm] n Sonnenstrahl m.
sunburn ['sʌnbəːn] n Sonnenbrand m.
sunburnt adj sonnenverbrannt.
sundae ['sʌndei] n Eisbecher m.
Sunday ['sʌndi] n Sonntag m. Sunday
best Sonntagskleider pl.
sundial ['sʌndaiəl] n Sonnenuhr f.
sundry ['sʌndri] pl adj verschiedene,
diverse. sundries pl n Verschiedenes neut
sing.
sunflower ['sʌn,flauə] n Sonnenblume f.
sung [sʌŋ] V sing.
sun-glasses pl n Sonnenbrille f sing.
sunk [sʌŋk] V sink.
sunlight ['sʌnlait] n Sonnenlicht neut.
sunny ['sʌni] adj sonnig.
sunrise ['sʌnraiz] n Sonnenaufgang m.
sunset ['sʌnset] n Sonnenuntergang m.
sunshine ['sʌnʃain] n Sonnenschein m.
sunstroke ['sʌnstrouk] n Sonnenstich m.
sun-tan n (Sonnen)Bräune f.
super ['suːpə] adj (coll) prima.
superannuation [,suːpərənju'eiʃən] n (contribution) Altersversicherungsbeitrag m;
(pension) Pension f. superannuated adj
pensioniert.
superb [suː'pəːb] adj herrlich, prächtig.
supercilious [,suːpə'siliəs] adj herablassend, hochmütig.
superficial [,suːpə'fiʃəl] adj oberflächlich.
superfluous [suː'pəːfluəs] adj überflüssig.
superhuman [,suːpə'hjuːmən] adj
übermenschlich.
superimpose [,suːpərim'pouz] v legen
(auf); (add) hinzufügen (zu). superim-
posed adj darübergelegt.
superintendent [,suːpərin'tendənt] n
Inspektor m, Vorsteher m.
superior [suː'piəriə] adj überlegen;
(higher) höherliegend; (quality) hervorragend, erlesen. n Überlegene(r). mother
superior Oberin f. superiority n
Überlegenheit f.

superlative [suɪ'pəɪlətiv] *adj* unübertreff-lich, hervorragend. *n* Superlativ *m*.

supermarket ['suɪpə‚maɪkit] *n* Supermarkt *m*.

supernatural [‚suɪpə'natʃərəl] *adj* übernatürlich. *n* das Übernatürliche *neut*.

supersede [‚suɪpə'siːd] *v* ersetzen.

supersonic [‚suɪpə'sonik] *adj* Überschall-.

superstition [suɪpə'stiʃən] *n* Aberglaube *m*. **superstitious** *adj* abergläubig.

supervise ['suɪpəvaiz] *v* beaufsichtigen, kontrollieren. **supervision** *n* Beaufsichtigung *f*, Kontrolle *f*. **supervisor** *n* Aufseher *m*, Kontrolleur *m*. **supervisory** *adj* Aufsichts-.

supper ['sʌpə] *n* Abendessen *neut*.

supple ['sʌpl] *adj* geschmeidig, biegsam. **suppleness** *n* Geschmeidigkeit *f*.

supplement ['sʌpləmənt] *n* Ergänzung *f*; (*newspaper*) Beilage *f*. **supplementary** *adj* ergänzend, Zusatz-.

supply [sə'plai] *v* liefern, versorgen; (*a need*) decken. *n* Lieferung *f*. (*stock*) Vorrat *m*; (*water, electricity, etc.*) Versorgung *f*. **supply and demand** Angebot und Nachfrage. **supplies** *pl n* Zufuhren *pl*. **supplier** *n* Lieferant *m*.

support [sə'poɪt] *v* tragen, stützen; (*withstand*) ertragen; (*family*) unterhalten; (*cause*) befürworten. *n* (*tech*) Stütze *f*; Unterstützung *f*. **supporter** *n* Anhänger *m*.

suppose [sə'pouz] *v* annehmen, sich vorstellen; (*believe, think*) meinen. **supposed** *adj* angenommen. **be supposed to** sollen. **supposition** *n* Vermutung *f*, Annahme *f*.

suppository [sə'pozitri] *n* (Darm-) Zäpfchen *neut*.

suppress [sə'pres] *v* unterdrücken; (*truth*) verheimlichen. **suppression** *n* Unterdrückung *f*; Verheimlichung *f*.

supreme [su'priːm] *adj* oberst, höchst. **supremacy** *n* Obergewalt *neut*.

surcharge ['səɪtʃaidʒ] *n* Zuschlag *m*.

sure [ʃuə] *adj* sicher, gewiß. *adv* (*coll*) sicherlich. **for sure** gewiß. **make sure** sich vergewissern. **you can be sure** du kannst dich darauf verlassen. **sure-fire** *adj* todsicher. **surely** *adv* sicherlich. **sureness** *n* Sicherheit *f*. **surety** *n* Bürge *f*.

surf [səɪf] *n* Brandung *f*. *v* wellenreiten. **surfboard** *n* Wellenreiterbrett *neut*. **surfer** *n* Wellenreiter(in).

surface ['səɪfis] *n* Oberfläche *f*. *adj* ober-flächlich. *v* auftauchen. **surface mail** gewöhnliche Post *f*.

surfeit ['səɪfit] *n* Übermaß *neut*. *v* übersättigen.

surge [səɪdʒ] *n* (*water*) Woge *f*; (*emotion*) Aufwallung *f*. *v* (*waves*) branden; (*crowd*) (vorwärts)drängen.

surgeon ['səɪdʒən] *n* Chirurg *m*. **surgery** *n* Chirurgie *f*; (*consulting room*) Sprechzimmer *neut*. **surgical** *adj* chirurgisch.

surly ['səɪli] *adj* verdrießlich, mürrisch. **surliness** *n* Verdrießlichkeit *f*.

surmount [sə'maunt] *v* überwinden. **surmountable** *adj* überwindlich.

surname ['səɪneim] *n* Familienname *m*, Zuname *m*.

surpass [sə'pais] *v* übertreffen. **surpass oneself** sich selbst übertreffen.

surplus ['səɪpləs] *n* Überschuß *m*. *adj* überschüssig.

surprise [sə'praiz] *v* überraschen. *n* Überraschung *f*. *adj* unerwartet. **surprised** *adj* überrascht. **surprising** *adj* erstaunlich.

surrealism [sə'riəlizəm] *n* Surrealismus *m*. **surrealist** *n* Surrealist(in). **surrealistic** *adj* surrealistisch.

surrender [sə'rendə] *v* sich ergeben, kapitulieren; (*office*) aufgeben; (*prisoner*) ausliefern. *n* Kapitulation *f*; Auslieferung *f*.

surreptitious [‚sʌrəp'tiʃəs] *adj* erschlichen; (*stealthy*) heimlich.

surround [sə'raund] *v* umgeben, umringen. *n* Einfassung *f*. **surrounding** *adj* umgebend. **surroundings** *pl n* Umgebung *f*.

survey ['səɪvei; *v* sə'vei] *n* Überblick *m*; (*land, house, etc.*) Vermessung *f*; (*questionnaire*) Umfrage *f*. *v* überblicken; vermessen. **surveyor** *n* Landmesser *m*.

survive [sə'vaiv] *v* (*outlive*) überleben; (*continue to exist*) weiterleben, weiterbestehen. **survival** *n* Überleben *neut*. **survivor** *n* Überlebende(r).

susceptible [sə'septəbl] *adj* anfällig, empfänglich (für). **susceptibility** *n* Anfälligkeit *f*, Empfänglichkeit *f*.

suspect [sə'spekt; *n* 'sʌspekt] *v* verdächtigen; (*believe*) vermuten. *n* Verdachtsperson *f*. *adj* verdächtig.

suspend [sə'spend] *v* aufhängen; (*person*) suspendieren; (*regulation*) (zeitweilig) aufheben. **suspended** *adj* ausgesetzt, verschoben. **suspender** *n* Strumpfhalter *m*. **suspenders** *pl* (*for trousers*) Hosenträger *pl.* **suspense** *n* Spannung *f.* **suspension** *n* (*mot*) Federung *f*; (*person*) Suspension *f.* **suspension bridge** Hängebrücke *f.* **suspension railway** Schwebebahn *f.*

suspicion [sə'spiʃən] *n* Verdacht *m*; (*mistrust*) Mißtrauen *neut*; (*trace*) Spur *f.* **suspicious** *adj* mißtrauisch; (*behaviour*) verdächtig. **suspiciousness** *n* Mißtrauen *neut.*

sustain [sə'stein] *v* (*suffer*) erleiden; (*family*) ernähren. **sustained** *adj* anhaltend. **sustenance** *n* Ernährung *f.*

suture ['suːtʃə] *n* Naht *f.* *v* vernähen.

swab [swob] *n* (*med*) Abstrich *m.*

swagger ['swagə] *v* (herum)stolzieren. **swaggering** *adj* stolzierend.

swallow[1] ['swolou] *v* schlucken. *n* Schluck *m.*

swallow[2] ['swolou] *n* (*bird*) Schwalbe *f.*

swam [swam] *V* **swim.**

swamp [swomp] *n* Sumpf *m*, Moor *neut.* *v* überschwemmen. **swampy** *adj* sumpfig.

swan [swon] *n* Schwan *m.*

swank [swaŋk] *v* protzen, prahlen. **swanky** *adj* protzig.

swap [swop] *v* (aus)tauschen. *n* Tausch *m.*

swarm [swoːm] *n* Schwarm *m.* *v* schwärmen.

swarthy ['swoːði] *adj* dunkelhäutig, schwärzlich.

swat [swot] *v* zerquetschen.

sway [swei] *v* schwanken, schaukeln. *n* Schwanken *neut*; (*power*) Macht *f*, Einfluß *m.*

*swear [sweə] *v* schwören; (*bad language*) fluchen. **swearword** *n* Fluch *m*, Fluchwort *neut.*

sweat [swet] *n* Schweiß *m.* *v* schwitzen. **sweater** *n* Pullover *m.* **sweaty** *adj* verschwitzt.

swede [swiːd] *n* Kohlrübe *f.*

Sweden ['swiːdn] *n* Schweden *neut.* **Swede** *n* Schwede *m*, Schwedin *f.* **Swedish** *adj* schwedisch.

*sweep [swiːp] *v* kehren, fegen; (*mines*) suchen. **sweep aside** beiseite schieben, abtun. **sweepstake** *n* Toto *neut.* *n* Schornsteinfeger *m.* **make a clean sweep** reinen Tisch machen. **sweeper** *n* Kehrer *m.* **sweeping** *adj* radikal, weitreichend. **sweepings** *pl* Kehricht *m sing.*

sweet [swiːt] *adj* süß; (*kind*) nett. **sweet corn** Mais *m.* **sweeten** *v* süßen. **sweetheart** *n* Schatz *m.* **sweet-tempered** *adj* gutmütig. *n* Bonbon *m*; (*dessert*) Nachspeise *f.* **sweetshop** *n* Süßwarengeschäft *neut.* **sweetness** *n* Süßigkeit *f*; (*person*) Lieblichkeit *f.*

*swell [swel] *v* (auf)schwellen. *n* (*sea*) Wellengang *m. adj* (*coll*) prima. **swelling** *n* (*med*) Schwellung *f.*

swelter ['sweltə] *v* vor Hitze kochen. **sweltering** *adj* schwül.

swept [swept] *V* **sweep.**

swerve [swəːv] *v* ausscheren.

swift [swift] *n* (*zool*) Segler *m. adj* schnell, rasch. **swift-footed** *adj* schnellfüßig. **swiftness** *n* Schnelligkeit *f.*

swill [swil] *n* Schweinefutter *neut.* *v* spülen.

*swim [swim] *v* schwimmen. *my head is swimming* mir ist schwindlig. *n* Schwimmen *neut*, Bad *neut.* **in the swim** auf dem laufenden. **swimmer** *n* Schwimmer(in). **swimming** *n* Schwimmen *neut.* **swimming pool** Schwimmbad *neut.*

swindle ['swindl] *v* betrügen. *n* Schwindel *m*, Betrug *m.* **swindler** *n* Schwindler(in).

swine [swain] *n* (*pl* **swine**) Schwein *neut.*

*swing [swiŋ] *v* schwingen. *n* (*child's*) Schaukel *f.* **swing a door open/shut** eine Tür auf/zustoßen.

swipe [swaip] *v* hauen; (*coll: steal*) klauen. *n* Hieb *m.*

swirl [swəːl] *v* wirbeln. *n* Wirbel *m.*

swish [swiʃ] *v* rascheln. *n* Rascheln *neut.*

Swiss [swis] *n* Schweizer(in). *adj* schweizerisch. **Swiss German** Schweizerdeutsch *neut.*

switch [switʃ] *n* Schalter *m*; (*change*) Wechsel *m*; (*whip*) Rute *f.* **on/off-switch** *n* Ein/Ausschalter *m.* *v* (*change*) wechseln. **switchboard** *n* (*phone*) Vermittlung *f.* **switch on** einschalten. **switch off** ausschalten. **switch over to** übergehen zu.

Switzerland ['switsələnd] *n* die Schweiz *f.*

swivel ['swivl] *v* (sich) drehen.

swollen ['swoulən] *V* **swell.** *adj* geschwollen. **swollen-headed** *adj* eingebildet, aufgeblasen.

swoop [swuːp] *v* niederschießen, sich stürzen (auf).

swop [swop] *V* **swap.**

sword [soːd] *n* Schwert *neut.* **swordfish** *n* Schwertfisch *m.* **swordsman** *n* Fechter *m.*

swore [swoː] *V* **swear.**

sworn [swoːn] *V* **swear.** *adj* vereidigt; (*enemy*) geschworen.

swot [swɔt] *v (coll)* büffeln, pauken. *n* Büffler *m*.

swum [swʌm] *V* swim.

swung [swʌŋ] *V* swing.

sycamore ['sikəmɔɪ] *n* Sykamore *f*.

syllable ['siləbl] *n* Silbe *f*.

syllabus ['siləbəs] *n* Lehrplan *m*.

symbol ['simbl] *n* Sinnbild *neut*, Symbol *neut*. **symbolic** *adj* sinnbildlich, symbolisch (für). **symbolism** *n* Symbolik *f*. **symbolize** *v* symbolisieren.

symmetry ['simitri] *n* Symmetrie *f*. **symmetrical** *adj* symmetrisch.

sympathy ['simpəθi] *n* Mitleid *neut*, Mitgefühl *neut*. **sympathetic** *adj* mitleidend.

symphony ['simfəni] *n* Sinfonie *f*. **symphonic** *adj* sinfonisch.

symposium [sim'pouziəm] *n* Symposion *neut*.

symptom ['simptəm] *n* Symptom *neut*. **symptomatic** *adj* symptomatisch.

synagogue ['sinəgog] *n* Synagoge *f*.

synchromesh ['siŋkroumeʃ] *n* Synchrongetriebe *neut*.

synchronize ['siŋkrənaiz] *v* synchronisieren.

syndicate ['sindikit] *n* Syndikat *neut*. **syndication** *n* Syndikatsbildung *f*.

syndrome ['sindroum] *n (med)* Syndrom *neut*.

synonym ['sinənim] *n* Synonym *neut*. **synonymous** *adj* synonym.

synopsis [si'nopsis] *n (pl -ses)* Synopse *f*, Zusammenfassung *f*. **synoptic** *adj* synoptisch.

syntax ['sintaks] *n* Syntax *f*. **syntactic** *adj* syntaktisch.

synthesis ['sinθisis] *n (pl -ses)* Synthese *f*. **synthetic** *adj* synthetisch, Kunst-.

syphilis ['sifilis] *n* Syphilis *f*.

syringe [si'rindʒ] *n* Spritze *f*.

syrup ['sirəp] *n* Sirup *m*, Zuckersaft *m*. **syrupy** *adj* sirupartig.

system ['sistəm] *n* System *neut*; *(geol)* Formation *f*. **systematic** *adj* systematisch.

T

tab [tab] *n (in garment)* Aufhänger *m*; *(label)* Etikett *neut*; *(coll: bill)* Rechnung *f*.

table ['teibl] *n* Tisch *m*; *(math, etc.)* Tabelle *f*. **table of contents** Inhaltsverzeichnis *neut*. **table-cloth** *n* Tischtuch *neut*. **table-spoon** *n* Eßlöffel *m*.

table d'hôte [taɪblə'dout] *n* Table d'hôte *f*.

tablet ['tablit] *n* Tablette *f*; *(stone)* Tafel *f*.

taboo [ta'buː] *adj* tabu. *n* Tabu *neut*.

tacit ['tasit] *adj* stillschweigend. **taciturn** *adj* schweigsam.

tack [tak] *n* Reißnagel *m*; *(naut)* Lavieren *neut*; *(sewing)* Heftstich *m*. *v* lavieren; heften. **tacky** *adj* klebrig.

tackle ['takl] *n (naut)* Takel *neut*; *(equipment, etc.)* Zeug *neut*, Ausrüstung *f*. *v (sport)* angreifen; *(person)* angehen; *(problem)* anpacken.

tact [takt] *n* Takt *m*. **tactful** *adj* taktvoll. **tactless** *adj* taktlos.

tactics ['taktiks] *pl n* Taktik *f*. **tactical** *adj* taktisch.

tadpole ['tadpoul] *n* Kaulquappe *f*.

taffeta ['tafitə] *n* Taft *m*.

tag [tag] *n (loop)* Anhänger *m*, *(label)* Etikett *neut*. **price-tag** Preiszettel *m*.

tail [teil] *n* Schwanz *m*. *v (coll: follow)* beschatten. **tail end** Schluß *m*. **tailcoat** *n* Frack *m*. **tail-lamp** *n* Schlußlicht *neut*.

tailor ['teilə] *n* Schneider *m*. *v* schneidern. **tailor-made** *adj* nach Maß angefertigt.

taint [teint] *n* Fleck *m*, Makel *m*. *v* verderben.

*take [teik] *v* nehmen; *(something somewhere)* bringen; *(prisoner)* fassen; *(photo, exam)* machen. *how long does it take?* wie lange dauert es? wie lange braucht man? **take aback** verblüffen. **take along** mitnehmen. **take away** wegnehmen; *(subtract)* abziehen. **take back** *(retract)* zurücknehmen. **take down** *(on paper)* aufschreiben. **take off** *(clothes)* ausziehen; *(mimic)* nachäffen. **take over** übernehmen. **take up** aufnehmen.

taken ['teikn] *V* take.

talcum powder ['talkəm] *n* Talkumpuder *m*.

tale [teil] *n* Erzählung *f*. **old wives' tale** Ammenmärchen *neut*.

talent ['talənt] *n* Talent *neut*, Begabung *f*. **talented** *adj* begabt.

talk [tɔːk] *n* Rede *neut*; *(conversation)* Gespräch *neut*; *(chat)* Unterhaltung *f*; *(lecture)* Vortrag *m*. *v* reden, sprechen. **talk over** besprechen. **talkative** *adj* geschwätzig.

tall [tɔːl] *adj* groß, hoch. **tallness** *n* Größe, Höhe *f*. **tall story** unglaubliche Geschichte *f*.

tally ['tali] *v (coll)* übereinstimmen (mit), entsprechen (+ *dat*).

talon ['talən] *n* Klaue *f*.

tambourine [tambə'riːn] *n* Tamburin *neut*.

tame [teim] *adj* zahm, gezähmt. *v* zähmen.

tamper ['tampə] *v* herumfuschen (an), sich einmischen (in).

tampon ['tampon] *n* Tampon *m*.

tan [tan] *v* gerben; *(skin)* sich bräunen. *n (colour)* Gelbbraun *neut*; *(skin)* Sonnenbräunung *f*.

tandem ['tandəm] *n* Tandem *neut*.

tangent ['tandʒənt] *n* Tangente *f*.

tangerine [tandʒə'riːn] *n* Mandarine *f*.

tangible ['tandʒəbl] *adj* greifbar.

tangle ['tangl] *n* Gewirr *neut*. *v* verwickeln.

tank [taŋk] *n* Tank *m*, Behälter *m*; *(mil)* Panzer *m*. **tanker** *n (ship)* Tanker *m*.

tankard ['taŋkəd] *n* Krug *m*.

tantalize ['tantəlaiz] *v* quälen.

tantamount ['tantəmaunt] *adj* **be tantamount to** gleichkommen (+ *dat*).

tantrum ['tantrəm] *n* Wutanfall *m*.

tap¹ [tap] *v* leicht schlagen, klopfen. *n* leichter Schlag *m*. **tap-dance** *n* Steptanz *m*.

tap² [tap] *n* Hahn *m*. *v* anzapfen. **taproom** *n* Schankstube *f*.

tape [teip] *n* Band *neut*, Streifen *m*; *(recording)* Tonband *neut*; *(sport)* Zielband *m*. *v* heften. **adhesive tape** Klebestreifen. **tape measure** *n* Metermaß *m*. **tape-recorder** *n* Tonbandgerät *neut*. **tape-recording** *n* Bandaufnahme *f*.

taper ['teipə] *n* (dünne) Wachskerze *f*. *v* spitz zulaufen. **tapered** *adj* spitz (zulaufend).

tapestry ['tapəstri] *n* Wandteppich *m*.

tapioca [tapi'oukə] *n* Tapioka *f*.

tar [taː] *n* Teer *m*.

tarantula [tə'rantjulə] *n* Tarantel *f*.

target ['taːgit] *n (sport)* Zielscheibe *f*; *(ambition)* Ziel *neut*.

tariff ['tarif] *n (imports)* Zolltarif *m*; *(price list)* Preisverzeichnis *neut*.

tarmac ® ['taːmak] *n* Asphalt *m*; *(runway)* Rollbahn *f*.

tarnish ['taːniʃ] *v (metal)* anlaufen; *(reputation)* beflecken.

tarpaulin [taː'pɔːlin] *n* Persenning *f*.

tarragon ['tarəgən] *n* Estragon *m*.

tart¹ [taːt] *n* Torte *f*; *(prostitute)* Dirne *f*.

tart² [taːt] *adj* sauer, herb.

tartan ['taːtən] *n* Tartan *m*, Schottenmuster *neut*.

tartar ['taːtə] *n* Weinstein *m*; *(teeth)* Zahnstein *m*.

task [taːsk] *n* Aufgabe *f*. **take to task** zur Rede stellen.

tassel ['tasəl] *n* Quaste *f*.

taste [teist] *n* Geschmack *neut*; *(sample)* Kostprobe *f*; *(liking)* Neigung *f*. *v* schmecken. **tasteful** *adj* geschmackvoll. **tasteless** *adj* geschmacklos. **tasty** *adj* schmackhaft.

tattered ['tatəd] *adj* zerrissen.

tattoo [tə'tuː] *n* Tätowierung *f*. *v* tätowieren.

taught [tɔːt] *V* teach.

taunt [tɔːnt] *v* sticheln, verspotten. *n* Stichelei *f*.

Taurus ['tɔːrəs] *n* Stier *m*.

taut [tɔːt] *adj* stramm, straff.

tavern ['tavən] *n* Taverne *f*, Kneipe *f*.

tax [taks] *n* Steuer *f*. **tax-free** *adj* steuerfrei. **taxpayer** *n* Steuerzahler(in). **tax return** *n* Steuererklärung *f*. *v* besteuern; *(test)* anstrengen. **taxable** *adj* steuerpflichtig.

taxi ['taksi] *n* Taxi *neut*. **taxi-driver** *n* Taxifahrer *m*.

tea [tiː] *n* Tee *m*; *(meal)* Abendbrot *neut*. **tea-cloth** *n* Geschirrtuch *neut*. **teacup** *n* Teetasse *f*. **teapot** *n* Teekanne *f*. **teaspoon** *n* Teelöffel *m*.

***teach** [tiːtʃ] *v* lehren; *(animals)* dressieren. **teacher** *n* Lehrer(in). **teaching** *n* Unterricht *m*. **teachings** *pl* Lehre *f sing*.

teak [tiːk] *n* Teakholz *neut*.

team [tiːm] *n (sport)* Mannschaft *f*; *(horses)* Gespann *neut*. *v* **team up** sich zusammentun (mit). **teamwork** *n* Zusammenarbeit *f*.

***tear¹** [teə] *v* reißen, zerreißen. *n* Riß *m*. **tear away** wegreißen. **tear oneself away** sich losreißen.

tear² [tiə] *n* Träne *f*. **tear gas** *n* Tränengas *neut*. **tearful** *adj* weinerlich.

tease [tiːz] v necken.

teat [tiːt] n (bottle) Sauger m; (anat) Brustwarze f; (zool) Zitze f.

technical ['teknikəl] adj technisch. **technician** n Techniker m. **technique** n Technik f. **technological** adj technologisch. **technology** n Technologie f.

tedious ['tiːdiəs] adj langweilig. **tedium** n Langeweile f.

tee [tiː] n (golf) Abschlagstelle f.

teem [tiːm] v wimmeln (von).

teenage ['tiːneidʒ] adj Jugend-. **teenager** n Teenager m.

teeth [tiːθ] V tooth.

teethe [tiːð] v zahnen. **teething troubles** (fig) Kinderkrankheiten pl.

teetotal [tiː'toutl] adj abstinent. **teetotaller** n Abstinenzler(in).

telecommunications [ˌtelikəmjuːni-'keiʃənz] pl n Fernmeldewesen neut sing.

telegram ['teligram] n Telegramm neut. **by telegram** telegraphisch.

telegraph ['teligraːf] n Telegraph m. v telegraphieren. **telegraphic** adj telegraphisch.

telepathy [tə'lepəθi] n Telepathie f, Gedankenübertragung f. **telepathic** adj telepathisch.

telephone ['telifoun] n Fernsprecher m, Telefon neut. v anrufen, telefonieren. **by telephone** telefonisch. **telephone booth** Telefonzelle f. **telephone call** Telefongespräch neut, Anruf m. **telephone directory** Telefonbuch neut. **telephone exchange** (Telefon)Zentrale f. **telephonist** n Telefonist(in).

telescope ['teliskoup] n Fernrohr neut, Teleskop neut. **telescopic** adj teleskopisch.

television ['teliviʒən] n Fernsehen neut. **televize** v (im Fernsehen) übertragen. **on television** im Fernsehen.

telex ['teleks] n Fernschreiber m, Telex neut. v (durch Telex) übertragen.

*tell [tel] v sagen; (story) erzählen; (recognize) erkennen. **telltale** n Klatschbase f. **tell the truth** die Wahrheit sagen. **teller** n Kassierer m. **telling** adj wirkungsvoll.

temper ['tempə] n Wut f, Zorn m; (mood) Laune f. **lose one's temper** in Wut geraten. v mildern; (steel) härten. **temperament** n Temperament neut. **temperamental** adj temperamentvoll. **temperance** n

Mäßigkeit f. **temperate** adj maßvoll; (climate) gemäßigt. **tempered** adj gehärtet.

temperature ['temprətʃə] n Temperatur f. **have a temperature** Fieber haben. **take (a person's) temperature** die Temperatur messen (+ dat).

tempestuous [tem'pestjuəs] adj stürmisch.

temple¹ ['templ] n (arch) Tempel m.

temple² ['templ] n (anat) Schläfe f.

tempo ['tempou] n Tempo neut.

temporary ['tempərəri] adj provisorisch, vorläufig.

tempt [tempt] v verlocken. **temptation** n Verlockung f. **tempting** adj verlockend; (food) appetitanregend.

ten [ten] adj zehn. n Zehn f. **tenth** adj zehnt; n Zehntel neut.

tenable ['tenəbl] adj haltbar.

tenacious [tə'neiʃəs] adj zäh. **tenacity** n Zähigkeit f.

tenant ['tenənt] n Mieter m. **tenancy** n Mietverhältnis neut.

tend¹ [tend] v (be inclined) neigen (zu), eine Tendenz haben (zu).

tend² [tend] v (care for) bedienen, sich kümmern um.

tendency ['tendənsi] n Tendenz f.

tender¹ ['tendə] adj zart; (affectionate) zärtlich. **tender-hearted** adj weichherzig. **tenderloin** n Filet neut. **tenderness** n Zartheit f; Zärtlichkeit f.

tender² ['tendə] v anbieten; (comm) ein Angebot machen. n Angebot neut.

tendon ['tendən] n Sehne f.

tendril ['tendril] n Ranke f.

tenement ['tenəmənt] n Mietshaus neut.

tennis ['tenis] n Tennis neut. **tennis ball** Tennisball m. **tennis court** Tennisplatz m. **tennis racket** (Tennis)Schläger m.

tenor ['tenə] n Tenor m. adj Tenor-.

tense¹ [tens] adj gespannt. v (sich) straffen. **tensile** adj dehnbar. **tension** n Spannung f.

tense² [tens] n (gramm) Zeitform f, Tempus neut.

tent [tent] n Zelt neut.

tentacle ['tentəkl] n Tentakel m, Fühler m; (octopus) Fangarm m.

tentative ['tentətiv] adj versuchend, Versuchs-; (temporary) vorläufig. **tentatively** adv versuchsweise.

tenterhooks ['tentəhuks] n **be on tenterhooks** wie auf heißen Kohlen sitzen.

tenuous ['tenjuəs] adj dünn; (argument) schwach.

tepid ['tepid] *adj* lauwarm. **tepidness** *n* Lauheit *f*.

term [tɜːm] *n (expression)* Ausdruck *m*; *(period of time)* Frist *f*; *(academic, two per year)* Semester *neut*; *(academic, three per year)* Trimester *neut*. **end of term** *(school)* Schulschluß *m*. **terms** *pl* Bedingungen *pl*. **be on good terms with** gut auskommen mit. **come to terms with** sich abfinden mit.

terminal ['tɜːminəl] *adj* End-, Schluß-; *(med)* unheilbar. *n* Terminal *neut*.

terminate ['tɜːmineit] *v* beendigen; *(contract)* kündigen. **termination** *n* Ende *neut*, Schluß *m*.

terminology [tɜːmi'nolədʒi] *n* Terminologie *f*.

terminus ['tɜːminəs] *n* Endstation *f*.

terrace ['terəs] *n* Terrasse *f*; *(houses)* Häuserreihe *f*.

terrain [tə'rein] *n* Terrain *neut*, Gelände *neut*.

terrestrial [tə'restriəl] *adj* irdisch.

terrible ['terəbl] *adj* schrecklich, furchtbar. **terribleness** *n* Schrecklichkeit *f*, Fürchterlichkeit *f*.

terrier ['teriə] *n* Terrier *m*.

terrify ['terifai] *v* erschrecken. **terrific** *adj (coll)* klasse, unwahrscheinlich. **terrified** *adj* erschrocken. **be terrified of** sich fürchten vor.

territory ['teritəri] *n* Gebiet *neut*, Territorium *neut*; *(pol)* Staatsgebiet *neut*. **territorial waters** Hoheitsgewässer *pl*.

terror ['terə] *n* Schrecken *m*, Entsetzen *neut*; *(pol)* Terror *m*. **terrorism** *n* Terrorismus *m*. **terrorist** *n* Terrorist(in); *adj* terroristisch.

test [test] *n* Versuch *m*, Probe *f*; *(examination)* Prüfung *f*. *v* prüfen, erproben. **test-case** *n* Präzedenzfall *m*.

testament ['testəmənt] *n* Testament *neut*.

testicle ['testikl] *n* Hoden *m*.

testify ['testifai] *v* bezeugen.

testimony ['testiməni] *n* Zeugnis *neut*. **testimonial** *n* Zeugnis *neut*, Empfehlungsschreiben *f*.

tetanus ['tetənəs] *n* Wundstarrkrampf *m*, Tetanus *m*.

tether ['teðə] *n* Haltestrick *m*. **be at the end of one's tether** mit seiner Geduld am Ende sein. *v* anbinden.

text [tekst] *n* Text *m*. **textbook** *n* Lehrbuch *neut*. **textual** *adj* textlich.

textile ['tekstail] *n* Gewebe *neut*, Faserstoff *m*. **textiles** *pl* Textilien *pl*.

texture ['tekstjuə] *n* Textur *f*.

than [ðən] *conj* als.

thank [θaŋk] *v* danken (+*dat*), sich bedanken bei. **thanks** *pl n* Dank *m sing*. *interj* danke! **thankful** *adj* dankbar. **thankless** *adj* undankbar. **thank you!** danke! **many thanks!** dankeschön! **thank goodness!** Gott sei Dank!

that [ðat] *adj* der, die, das; jener, jene, jenes. *pron* das; *(who, which)* der, die, das, welch. **that is** (i.e.) das heißt (d.h.). **that's it!** so ist es! **like that** so. **that which** das, was. **the man that I saw** der Mann, den ich sah. **in order that** damit. *conj* daß. *adv (coll)* so, dermaßen.

thatch [θatʃ] *n* Dachstroh *neut*. **thatched roof** Strohdach *neut*.

thaw [θɔ:] *v* tauen. *n* Tauwetter *neut*.

the [ðə] *art* der, die, das *sing*; die *pl*.

theatre ['θiətə] *n* Theater *neut*; *(operating)* Operationssaal *m*. **theatre-goer** *n* Theaterbesucher(in). **theatrical** *adj* theatralisch.

theft [θeft] *n* Diebstahl *m*.

their [ðeə] *poss adj* ihr, ihre, ihr. **theirs** *pron* der/die/das ihrige. **a friend of theirs** ein Freund von ihnen.

them [ðem] *pron (acc)* sie; *(dat)* ihnen.

theme [θiːm] *n* Thema *neut*.

then [ðen] *adv (at that time)* damals; *(next)* dann, darauf. *conj* also. *adj* damalig.

theology [θi'olədʒi] *n* Theologie *f*. **theologian** *n* Theologe *m*. **theological** *adj* theologisch.

theorem ['θiərəm] *n* Theorem *m*.

theory ['θiəri] *n* Theorie *f*. **theoretical** *adj* theoretisch. **theorist** *n* Theoretiker(in). **theorize** *v* theoretisieren.

therapy ['θerəpi] *n* Therapie *f*, Behandlung *f*. **therapeutic** *adj* therapeutisch. **therapist** *n* Therapeut(in).

there [ðeə] *adv* dort, da; *(to that place)* dahin, dorthin. **here and there** hier und da. **over there** da drüben. **thereabouts** *adv* so ungefähr. **thereafter** *adv* danach. **there and back** hin und zurück. **there are** es sind, es gibt. **there is** es ist, es gibt. **up there** da oben. *interj* na!

thermal ['θɜːməl] *adj* thermal, Wärme-. *n (aero)* Thermik *f*.

thermodynamics [θɜːmoudai'namiks] *n* Thermodynamik *f*.

thermometer [θə'mɒmitə] *n* Thermometer *neut.*

thermonuclear [θəɪmou'njukliə] *adj* thermonuklear.

thermos ® ['θəɪmɒs] *n* Thermosflasche *f.*

thermostat ['θəɪməstat] *n* Thermostat *m.*

these [ðiɪz] *pl adj, pron* diese. **one of these days** eines Tages. **these are** dies sind.

thesis ['θiɪsis] *n* (*pl* -ses) These *f,* Satz *m;* (*university*) Dissertation *f.*

they [ðei] *pl pron* sie. **they say** man sagt.

thick [θik] *adj* dick; (*hair, woods*) dicht; (*coll: stupid*) dumm. **thicken** *v* dick machen *or* werden, (sich) verdicken; (*cookery*) legieren. **thickness** *n* Dicke *f,* Stärke *f.* **thick-skinned** *adj* (*fig*) dickfellig.

thief [θiɪf] *n* (*pl* thieves) Dieb(in). **thieve** *v* stehlen. **thievish** *adj* diebisch.

thigh [θai] *n* (Ober)Schenkel *m.* **thighbone** *n* Schenkelknochen *m.*

thimble ['θimbl] *n* Fingerhut *m.*

thin [θin] *adj* dünn; (*person*) mager; (*weak*) schwach. *v* dünn machen *or* werden; (*cookery*) verdünnen. **thinner** *n* Verdünner *m.* **thinness** *n* Dünne *f;* Magerkeit *f.* **thin-skinned** *adj* empfindlich.

thing [θiŋ] *n* Ding *neut.* **things** *pl* Sachen *pl,* Zeug *neut sing.* **how are things?** wie geht es?

***think** [θiŋk] *v* denken; (*hold opinion*) denken, meinen. **think about** denken an; (*consider*) überlegen, nachdenken über. **think of** (*doing*) daran denken, vorhaben. *what do you think of it?* was halten sie davon? *I think so* ich glaube schon. **thinker** *n* Denker(in). **thinking** *n* (*opinion*) Meinung *f.*

third [θəɪd] *adj* dritt. *n* Drittel *neut.* **third party** Dritte(r). **third-party insurance** Haftpflichtversicherung *f.* **third-rate** *adj* (*coll*) minderwertig.

thirst [θəɪst] *n* Durst (nach) *m.* **die of thirst** verdursten. *v* dursten. **thirsty** *adj* durstig. **be thirsty** Durst haben.

thirteen [θəɪ'tiɪn] *adj* dreizehn. *n* Dreizehn *f.* **thirteenth** *adj* dreizehnt.

thirty ['θəɪti] *adj* dreißig. *n* Dreißig *f.* **thirtieth** *adj* dreißigst.

this [ðis] *adj* (*pl* these) dieser, diese, dieses. *pron* dies, das. **like this** so, folgendermaßen. **this morning** heute früh. **this year** dieses Jahr.

thistle ['θisl] *n* Distel *f.*

thorn [θɔin] *n* Dorn *m.* **thorny** *adj* dornig.

thorough ['θʌrə] *adj* gründlich; (*person*) genau, sorgfältig. **thoroughbred** *n* Vollblut *neut. adj* Vollblut-. **thoroughfare** *n* Durchgangsstraße *f.* **thoroughness** *n* Gründlichkeit *f.*

those [ðouz] *pl adj, pron* jene.

though [ðou] *conj* obwohl, obgleich. *adv* aber, dennoch, jedoch. **as though** als ob. **even though** wenn ... auch.

thought [θɔit] *V* think. *n* Gedanke *m;* (*thinking*) Denken *neut;* (*reflection*) Überlegung *f.* **thoughtful** *adj* gedankenvoll; (*considerate*) rücksichtsvoll. **thoughtless** *adj* gedankenlos; rücksichtslos.

thousand ['θauzənd] *adj* tausend. *n* Tausend *neut.* **thousandth** *adj* tausendst; *n* Tausendstel *neut.*

thrash [θraʃ] *v* verdreschen; (*defeat*) heftig schlagen. **thrash about** hin und her schlagen. **thrashing** *n* Prügel *pl,* Dresche *f.*

thread [θred] *n* Faden *m;* (*screw*) Gewinde *neut.* **threadbare** *adj* fadenscheinig. *v* (*needle*) einfädeln; (*beads*) einreihen. **thread one's way through** sich winden durch.

threat [θret] *n* Drohung *f;* (*danger*) Gefahr *f,* Bedrohung *f.* **threaten** *v* bedrohen; (*endanger*) gefährden. **threatening** *adj* drohend.

three [θriɪ] *adj* drei. *n* Drei *f.* **three-cornered** dreieckig. **three-dimensional** *adj* dreidimensional. **threefold** *adv, adj* dreifach. **three-ply** *adj* dreifach. **three-quarters of an hour** eine Dreiviertelstunde *f.*

thresh [θreʃ] *v* dreschen.

threshold ['θreʃould] *n* (Tür)Schwelle *f.*

threw [θruɪ] *V* throw.

thrift [θrift] *n* Sparsamkeit *f.* **thrifty** *adj* sparsam.

thrill [θril] *v* erregen, begeistern. *n* Zittern *neut,* Erregung *f.* **thriller** *n* Reißer *m.* **thrilling** *adj* sensationell.

thrive [θraiv] *v* gedeihen. **thriving** *adj* blühend.

throat [θrout] *n* Kehle *f,* Rachen *m;* (*neck*) Hals *m.* **throaty** *adj* rauh.

throb [θrob] *v* pulsieren, klopfen. *n* Pulsieren *neut.*

thrombosis [θrom'bousis] *n* Thrombose *f.*

throne [θroun] *n* Thron *m*.
throng [θroŋ] *n* Gedränge *neut*. *v* sich scharen.
throttle ['θrotl] *v* erwürgen. *n* (*tech*) Drosselklappe *f*. **open the throttle** (*mot*) Gas geben.
through [θru:] *prep*, *adv* durch. **fall through** (*coll*) ins Wasser fallen. **get through** fertig sein mit; (*exam*) bestehen. **go through with** zu Ende führen. **wet through** durchnäßt. **throughout** *adv* (*place*) überall in. **throughout the night** die ganze Nacht hindurch. *adj* (*ticket*, *train*) durchgehend.
***throw** [θrou] *v* werfen. **throw away** wegwerfen; (*chance*) verpassen. **throwback** *n* Rückkehr *f*. **throw up** (*coll*) kotzen. **throw-in** (*sport*) Einwurf *m*. *n* Wurf *m*.
thrush [θrʌʃ] *n* Drossel *f*.
***thrust** [θrʌst] *v* stecken, schieben. *n* Stoß *m*, Hieb *m*; (*tech*) Schubkraft *f*.
thud [θʌd] *n* (dumpfer) Schlag *m*. *v* dumpfer schlagen.
thumb [θʌm] *n* Daumen *m*. *v* **thumb through** durchblättern. **thumb a lift** per Anhalter fahren. **thumbtack** Reißnagel *m*.
thump [θʌmp] *n* Puff *m*, Schlag *m*. *v* puffen.
thunder ['θʌndə] *n* Donner *m*. *v* donnern. **thunderbolt** *n* Blitz *m*. **thunderclap** *n* Donnerschlag *m*. **thunderstorm** *n* Gewitter *neut*. **thunderstruck** *adj* wie vom Blitz getroffen.
Thursday ['θə:zdi] *n* Donnerstag *m*. **on Thursdays** donnerstags.
thus [ðʌs] *adv* so, folgendermaßen. **thus far** bis jetzt, soweit.
thwart [θwɔːt] *v* (*person*) entgegenarbeiten (+*dat*); (*plan*) vereiteln.
thyme [taim] *n* Thymian *m*.
thyroid ['θairoid] *n* Schilddrüse *f*. *adj* Schilddrüsen-.
tiara [ti'aːrə] *n* Tiara *f*.
tick[1] [tik] *v* (*clock*) ticken; (*with pen*) abhaken. **tick over** (*mot*) im Leerlauf sein. *n* Ticken *neut*; Häkchen *neut*.
tick[2] [tik] *n* (*parasite*) Zecke *f*.
ticket ['tikit] *n* (*label*) Etikett *neut*, Zettel *m*; (*travel*) Fahrkarte *f*, Fahrschein *m*; (*theatre*) Karte *f*. **ticket-collector** *n* Schaffner *m*. **ticket-office** *n* Fahrkartenschalter *m*.

tickle ['tikl] *v* kitzeln; (*fig*) amüsieren. *n* Kitzel *m*, Juckreiz *m*. **ticklish** *adj* kitzlig.
tide [taid] *n* Gezeiten *pl*, Ebbe und Flut *f*. **high tide** Flut *f*, Hochwasser *neut*. **low tide** Ebbe *f*, Niedrigwasser *neut*. **tidal** *adj* Gezeiten-, Flut-.
tidy ['taidi] *adj* ordentlich, sauber. *v* **in Ordnung bringen. tidy up** aufräumen.
tie [tai] *v* (an)binden, festbinden; (*knot*) machen; (*necktie*) binden. **tie in with** übereinstimmen mit. **tie up** verbinden. **be tied up** nicht abkömmlich sein. *n* (*necktie*) Schlips *m*, Krawatte *m*; (*sport*) Unentschieden *neut*; (*obligation*) Verpflichtung *f*, Last *f*.
tier [tiə] *n* Reihe *f*, Rang *m*.
tiger ['taigə] *n* Tiger *m*. **tigress** *n* Tigerin *f*.
tight [tait] *v* fest, stramm; (*clothes*) eng, knapp; (*watertight, etc.*) dicht; (*in short supply*) knapp; (*coll: mean*) geizig. **tighten** *v* festziehen, straffen. **tight-fisted** *adj* geizig. **tights** *pl n* Strumpfhose *f sing*. *adv* **hold tight** festhalten. **sit tight** sitzenbleiben.
tile [tail] *n* (*roof*) (Dach)Ziegel *m*; (*wall*) Fliese *f*.
till[1] [til] *V* until.
till[2] [til] *n* (*in shop*) Kasse *f*.
till[3] [til] *v* (*land*) bebauen, pflügen.
tiller ['tilə] *n* (*naut*) (Ruder)Pinne *f*.
tilt [tilt] *v* kippen, (sich) neigen. *n* Neigung *f*, Schräglage *f*. **tilt over** umkippen.
timber ['timbə] *n* (Bau)Holz *neut*. **timber forest** Hochwald *m*.
time [taim] *n* Zeit *f*; (*occasion*) Mal *neut*; (*era*) Zeitalter *neut*, (*music*) Takt *m*. **at all times** stets. **at this time** zu dieser Zeit. **behind the times** rückständig. **have a good time** sich gut unterhalten. **in good time** rechtzeitig. **time limit** *n* Frist *f*. **timepiece** *n* Uhr *f*. **timetable** *n* (*bus, train*) Fahrplan *m*; (*school*) Stundenplan *m*. **what time is it?** wieviel Uhr ist es? *or* wie spät ist es? *v* (mit der Uhr) messen, zeitlich abstimmen. **timeless** *adj* ewig. **timely** *adj* rechtzeitig.
timid ['timid] *adj* ängstlich, schüchtern. **timidity** *n* Ängstlichkeit *f*, Schüchternheit *f*.
tin [tin] *n* Zinn *neut*; (*can*) Dose *f*, Büchse *f*. *adj* zinnern, Zinn-. **tin can** Blechdose *f*. **tin foil** *n* Stanniol *neut*. **tinopener** *n* Dosenöffner *m*.

tinge [tindʒ] v (leicht) färben. n Färbung f; (fig) Anstrich m.

tingle ['tiŋgl] v prickeln, kribbeln. n Prickeln neut.

tinker ['tiŋkə] n Kesselflicker m. v tinker with herumbasteln an.

tinkle ['tiŋkl] v klingeln. n Klingeln neut, Geklingel neut.

tinsel ['tinsəl] n Lametta neut.

tint [tint] n Farbton m. v tönen, leicht färben.

tiny ['taini] adj winzig.

tip¹ [tip] n (sharp end) Spitze f; (summit) Gipfel m. **tipped** adj (cigarette) Filter-. **on tiptoe** auf den Zehenspitzen.

tip² [tip] n (for rubbish) (Müll)Abladeplatz m. v kippen. **tip over** umkippen.

tip³ [tip] n (gratuity) Trinkgeld neut; (hint) Wink m, Tip m. v ein Trinkgeld geben (+ dat); einen Tip geben (+ dat). **tip off** n rechtzeitiger Wink m.

tipsy ['tipsi] adj (coll) beschwipst.

tire¹ ['taiə] v ermüden; (become tired) müde werden. **tire out** erschöpfen. **tired** adj müde. **tiredness** n Müdigkeit f. **tireless** adj unermüdlich. **tiresome** adj lästig.

tire² ['taiə] (US) V tyre.

tissue ['tiʃuː] n Gewebe neut; (paper handkerchief) Papiertaschentuch neut. **tissue paper** n Seidenpapier neut.

tit [tit] n (bird) Meise f.

title ['taitl] n Titel m; (right) Rechtstitel m. **titled** adj betitelt. **title-deed** Eigentumsurkunde f. **title-holder** n (sport) Titelverteidiger(in). **title-role** Titelrolle f.

to [tu] prep zu; (motion, travel) nach; (time of day) vor; (in order to) um zu. adv (shut) zu, geschlossen. **to and fro** auf und ab. fix to the wall an die Wand befestigen. go to bed/the movies/school ins Bett/ins Kino/in die Schule gehen. go to Berlin nach Berlin fahren. I gave it to him ich gab es ihm. ten to one (o'clock) zehn vor eins; (odds) zehn gegen eins. **to-do** n Getue neut.

toad [toud] n Kröte f. **toadstool** n Pilz m.

toast [toust] n Toast m; (drink) Trinkspruch m, Toast m. v toasten. **toaster** n Toaster m. **toastmaster** n Toastmeister m.

tobacco [tə'bakou] n Tabak m. **tobacconist** n Tabakhändler m.

toboggan [tə'bogən] n Schlitten m, Rodel(schlitten) m. v rodeln.

today [tə'dei] n, adv heute. **today's** or of

today heutig, von heute; (of nowadays) der heutigen Zeit.

toddler ['todlə] n Kleinkind neut.

toe [tou] n Zehe f. **on one's toes** auf Draht. **toe-cap** n Kappe f. **toe-nail** n Zehennagel m.

toffee ['tofi] n Karamelle f.

together [tə'geðə] adv zusammen; (at the same time) gleichzeitig. **get together** (coll) sich treffen.

toil [toil] n Mühe f, schwere Arbeit f. v mühselig arbeiten, schuften (an).

toilet ['toilit] n (all senses) Toilette f; (WC) Klosett neut. **toilet-paper** Klosettpapier neut. **toilet soap** Toilettenseife f.

token ['toukən] n Zeichen neut, Beweis m; (voucher) Gutschein m, Bon m. adj nominell.

told [tould] V tell.

tolerate ['toləreit] v dulden, tolerieren. **tolerable** adj erträglich. **tolerance** n Toleranz f. **tolerant** adj duldsam, tolerant.

toll¹ [toul] n Zoll m.

toll² [toul] v (bell) läuten.

tomato [tə'martou] n (pl tomatoes) Tomate f.

tomb [tuːm] n Grabmal neut, Grab neut. **tombstone** n Grabstein m.

tomorrow [tə'morou] n, adv morgen. **tomorrow morning** morgen früh. **tomorrow's** or of tomorrow morgig, von morgen. **the day after tomorrow** übermorgen.

ton [tʌn] n Tonne f.

tone [toun] n Ton m; (muscle) Tonus m. **tone down** v mildern. **tonal** adj tonal.

tongs [toŋz] pl n Zange f sing.

tongue [tʌŋ] n Zunge f; (language) Sprache f. **tongue-tied** adj zungenlahm. **tongue-twister** n Zungenbrecher m.

tonic ['tonik] adj tonisch, Ton-. **tonic water** Tonic neut. n Tonikum neut.

tonight [tə'nait] adv heute abend, heute nacht.

tonsil ['tonsil] n Mandel f. **tonsillectomy** n Mandelentfernung f. **tonsillitis** n Mandelentzündung f.

too [tuː] adv (excessively) zu, allzu; (as well) auch, ebenfalls.

took [tuk] V take.

tool [tuːl] n Werkzeug neut. **toolbox** n Werkzeugkasten m. **tooling** n Bearbeitung f.

tooth [tuːθ] *n* (*pl* **teeth**) Zahn *m*. **toothache** *n* Zahnweh *neut*. **toothbrush** *n* Zahnbürste *f*. **toothless** *adj* zahnlos. **toothpaste** *n* Zahnpasta *f*. **toothpick** *n* Zahnstocher *m*.

top[1] [top] *n* oberes Ende *neut*, obere Seite *f*; (*hill*) Gipfel *m*; (*lid*) Deckel *m*; (*page*) Kopf *m*. **on top of** oben auf; (*besides*) über. **top hat** Zylinder *m*. **top-heavy** *adj* kopflastig. **topsoil** *n* Ackerkrume *f*. *adj* oberst, höchst; (*chief*) Haupt-. *v* krönen.

top[2] [top] *n* (*toy*) Kreisel *m*.

topaz ['toupaz] *n* Topas *m*.

topic ['topik] *n* Thema *neut*, Gegenstand *m*. **topical** *adj* aktuell.

topography [tə'pogrəfi] *n* Topographie *f*.

topple ['topl] *v* (um)kippen.

topsy-turvy [topsi'təːvi] *adv* durcheinander, in Unordnung.

torch [toːtʃ] *n* Fackel *f*; (*elec*) Taschenlampe *f*.

tore [toː] *V* **tear**[1].

torment [toː'ment; *n* 'toːment] *v* quälen. *n* Qual *f*. **tormentor** *n* Quälgeist *m*.

torn [toːn] *V* **tear**[1]. *adj* zerrissen.

tornado [toː'neidou] *n* Tornado *m*, Wirbelsturm *m*.

torpedo [toː'piːdou] *n* Torpedo *m*.

torrent ['torənt] *n* Wildbach *m*; (*of abuse, etc.*) Strom *m*, Ausbruch *m*. **torrential** *adj* strömend. **torrential rain** Wolkenbruch *m*.

torso ['toːsou] *n* Torso *m*.

tortoise ['toːtəs] *n* Schildkröte *f*. **tortoiseshell** *n* Schildpatt *m*.

tortuous ['toːtʃuəs] *adj* gekrümmt.

torture ['toːtʃə] *n* Folter *f*, Folterung *f*; Tortur *f*. *v* foltern. **torturer** *n* Folterer *m*.

toss [tos] *v* (hoch)werfen; (*coin*) hochwerfen; *tossed about by the waves* von den Wellen hin und her geworfen.

tot[1] [tot] *n* (*whisky, etc.*) Schlückchen *neut*; (*child*) Knirps *m*.

tot[2] [tot] *v* **tot up** zusammenzählen.

total ['toutəl] *adj* total, ganz, Gesamt-. *n* Summe *f*, Gesamtbetrag *m*. **in total** als Ganzes. **totalitarian** *adj* totalitär. **totalisator** *n* Totalisator *m*. *v* sich belaufen auf; (*person*) zusammenzählen. **totality** *n* Gesamtheit *f*. **totally** *adv* völlig, total.

totter ['totə] *v* taumeln, wanken. **tottering** *adj* wackelig.

touch [tʌtʃ] *v* anrühren, anfassen; (*feel*) betasten; (*border on*) grenzen an; (*emotionally*) berühren. **touch down** landen.

touching *adj* rührend. **touchline** *n* Marklinie *f*. **touchstone** *n* Prüfstein *m*. *n* Berührung *f*, Anrühren *neut*; (*sense*) Tastsinn *m*, (*trace*) Spur *f*. **be/keep in touch** with in Verbindung stehen/bleiben mit. **touchy** *adj* empfindlich, reizbar.

tough [tʌf] *adj* zäh; (*person*) zäh, robust; (*difficult*) schwierig, sauer. **toughen** *v* zäher machen *or* werden. **toughness** *n* Zähigkeit *f*, Härte *f*.

toupee ['tuːpei] *n* Toupet *neut*.

tour [tuə] *n* Tour *f*, Rundreise *f*, (*of inspection*) Rundgang *m*; (*theatre*) Tournee *f*. *v* bereisen. **touring** *adj* Touren-. **tourism** *n* Tourismus *m*. **tourist** *n* Tourist(in).

tournament ['tuənəmənt] *n* Turnier *neut*.

tow [tou] *v* bugsieren, schleppen. *n* Schlepptau *neut*. **have in tow** im Schlepptau haben. **towline** *or* **towrope** *n* Schlepptau *neut*.

towards [tə'woːdz] *prep* (*place*) auf ... zu, nach ... hin; (*behaviour, attitude*) gegen(über). *towards midday* gegen Mittag.

towel ['tauəl] *n* Handtuch *neut*. **towelling** *n* Handtuchstoff *m*.

tower ['tauə] *n* Turm *m*. *v* (hoch)ragen.

town [taun] *n* Stadt *f*. *adj* Stadt-. **town council** Stadtrat *m*. **town hall** Rathaus *neut*. **town planning** Stadtplanung *f*.

toxic ['toksik] *adj* giftig, toxisch. **toxin** *n* Toxin *neut*.

toy [toi] *n* Spielzeug *neut*. **toys** *pl* Spielwaren *pl*. *v* **toy with** spielen mit.

trace [treis] *n* Spur *f*. *v* nachspüren, verfolgen; (*draw*) pausen, durchzeichnen. **tracing** *n* Pause *f*. **tracing paper** Pauspapier *neut*.

track [trak] *n* Spur *f*, Fährte *f*; (*rail*) Gleis *neut*; (*road*) Weg *m*, Pfad *m*; (*sport*) Bahn *f*. **track suit** Trainingsanzug *m*.

tract[1] [trakt] *n* (*land*) Strecke *f*. **digestive tract** Verdauungssystem *neut*.

tract[2] [trakt] *n* (*treatise*) Traktat *neut*.

tractor ['traktə] *n* Traktor *m*.

trade [treid] *n* Handel *m*; (*job, skill*) Gewerbe *neut*. **trade balance** *n* Handelsbilanz *f*. **trade fair** Messe *f*. **trademark** *n* Warenzeichen *neut*. **tradesman** *n* Lieferant *m*. **trade union** *n* Gewerkschaft *f*. **trade-unionist** *n* Gewerkschaftler(in). *v* handeln; (*exchange*) eintauschen. **trader** *n* Händler *m*.

tradition [trə'diʃən] *n* Tradition *f*. **traditional** *adj* traditionell.
traffic ['trafik] *n* Verkehr *m*. **traffic jam** Verkehrsstockung *f*. **trafficker** *n* Händler *m*. **traffic lights** Verkehrsampel *f sing*.
tragedy ['tradʒədi] *n* (*theatre*) Tragödie *f*; (*fig*) Unglück *neut*. **tragic** *adj* tragisch.
trail [treil] *n* Spur *f*, Fährte *f*. *v* schleifen, (nach)schleppen; (*follow*) verfolgen; (*lag behind*) nachhinken.
train [trein] *n* Zug *m*; (*of dress*) Schleppe *f*. *v* (*person for job, etc.*) ausbilden; (*sport*) trainieren; (*child*) schulen; (*animal*) dressieren. **trainee** *n* Lehrling *m*. **trainer** *n* (*sport*) Trainer *m*. **training** *n* Ausbildung *f*; (*sport*) Training *neut*.
trait [treit] *n* Zug *m*, Merkmal *neut*.
traitor ['treitə] *n* Verräter(in). **traitorous** *adj* verräterisch.
tram [tram] *n* Straßenbahn *f*.
tramp [tramp] *n* Landstreicher *m*. *v* stampfen.
trample ['trampl] *v* trampeln.
trampoline ['trampəliːn] *n* Trampoline *f*.
trance [trains] *n* Trance *f*.
tranquil ['traŋkwil] *adj* ruhig, friedlich. **tranquillity** *n* Ruhe *f*. **tranquillizer** *n* Beruhigungsmittel *neut*.
transact [tran'zakt] *v* durchführen. **transaction** *n* Geschäft *neut*, Transaktion *f*.
transcend [tran'send] *v* überschreiten. **transcendental** *adj* transzendental.
transcribe [tran'skraib] *v* abschreiben. **transcription** *n* Abschrift *f*.
transept ['transept] *n* Querschiff *neut*.
transfer [trans'fəː; *n* 'transfəː] *v* übertragen; (*money*) überweisen; (*trains*) umsteigen. *n* Übertragung *f*; Überweisung *f*; Umsteigen *neut*; (*design*) Abziehbild *neut*. **transferable** *adj* übertragbar. **transferred-charge call** R-Gespräch *neut*.
transform [trans'fɔːm] *v* umwandeln. **transformation** *n* Umwandlung *f*. **transformer** *n* (*elec*) Transformator *m*.
transfuse [trans'fjuːz] *v* (*blood*) übertragen. **transfusion** *n* (*blood*) Blutübertragung *f*.
transient ['tranziənt] *adj* vorübergehend.
transistor [tran'zistə] *n* Transistor *m*.
transit ['transit] *n* Durchfahrt *f*; (*of goods*) Transport *f*. *adj* Durchgangs-. **in transit** unterwegs.
transition [tran'ziʃən] *n* Übergang *m*. **transitional** *adj* Übergangs-.

transitive ['transitiv] *adj* transitiv.
translate [trans'leit] *v* übersetzen. **translation** *n* Übersetzung *f*. **translator** *n* Übersetzer(in).
translucent [trans'luːsnt] *adj* lichtdurchlässig.
transmit [tranz'mit] *v* übersenden; (*radio, TV*) senden. **transmitter** *n* (*radio, TV*) Sender *m*. **transmission** *n* (*mot*) Getriebe *neut*; (*radio, TV*) Sendung *f*.
transparent [trans'peərənt] *adj* durchsichtig, transparent; (*fig*) offensichtlich. **transparency** *n* Durchsichtigkeit *f*; (*phot*) (Dia)Positiv *neut*.
transplant [trans'plaint; *n* 'transplaint] *v* verpflanzen; (*med*) transplantieren. *n* (*operation*) Transplantation *f*; (*actual organ*) Transplantat *neut*. **transplantation** *n* Verpflanzung *f*.
transport [trans'pɔːt; *n* 'transpɔːt] *v* befördern, transportieren. *n* Beförderung *f*, Transport *m*. **transportable** *adj* transportierbar. **transportation** *n* Transport *m*.
transpose [trans'pouz] *v* umstellen, versetzen.
transverse ['tranzvəːs] *adj* quer, Quer-.
trap [trap] *n* Falle *f*. **lay a trap** eine Falle stellen. **shut your trap!** (*impol*) halt die Klappe! **trapdoor** *n* Falltür *f*. *v* fangen.
trapper *n* Trapper *m*.
trapeze [trə'piːz] *n* Trapez *neut*.
trash [traʃ] *n* Abfall *m*; (*film, book, etc.*) Kitsch *m*. **trash-can** *n* Abfalleimer *m*. **trashy** *adj* wertlos.
trauma ['troimə] *n* Trauma *neut*. **traumatic** *adj* traumatisch.
travel ['travl] *v* reisen. *n* Reisen *neut*. **travel agency** Reisebüro *neut*. **traveller** Reisende(r). **travelling** *adj* Reise-. **travelling expenses** Reisespesen *pl*.
travesty ['travəsti] *n* Travestie *f*.
trawl [troil] *n* Grundschleppnetz *neut*, Trawl *neut*. **trawler** *n* Trawler *m*.
treachery ['tretʃəri] *n* Verrat *m*. **treacherous** *adj* verräterich; (*dangerous*) gefährlich.
treacle ['triːkl] *n* Sirup *m*, Melasse *f*.
*tread [tred] *n* Tritt *m*, Schritt *m*; (*tyre*) Profil *neut*; (*ladder*) Sprosse *f*. *v* treten. **treadmill** *n* Tretmühle *f*.
treason ['triːzn] *n* Verrat *m*.
treasure ['treʒə] *n* Schatz *m*. *v* hochschätzen. **treasurer** *n* Schatzmeister(in); (*club*) Kassenwart *m*. **treasury** *n*

Schatzkammer *f.* **Treasury** *n* (*pol*) Finanzministerium *neut.*
treat [tritt] *v* behandeln. **treat someone to something** jemandem zu etwas einladen. *n* (*coll*) Genuß *m*, Vergnügen *neut.* **treatment** *n* Behandlung *f.*
treatise ['triːtiz] *n* Abhandlung *f.*
treaty ['triːti] *n* Vertrag *m*, Pakt *m.*
treble ['trebl] *adj* dreifach; (*music*) Diskant-. *v* (sich) verdreifachen.
tree [triː] *n* Baum *m.* **family tree** Stammbaum *m.*
trek [trek] *n* Treck *m.* *v* trecken.
trellis ['trelis] *n* Gitter *neut*, Gitterwerk *neut.*
tremble ['trembl] *v* zittern. *n* Zittern *neut.*
tremendous [trə'mendəs] *adj* enorm, kolossal; (*coll: excellent*) ausgezeichnet.
tremor ['tremə] *n* Beben *neut.*
trench [trentʃ] *n* Graben *m*; (*mil*) Schützengraben *m.* **trench coat** *n* Trenchcoat *m.*
trend [trend] *n* Tendenz *f*, Trend *m.* **trendy** *adj* (neu)modisch.
trespass ['trespəs] *v* unbefugt betreten. **trespasser** *n* Unbefugte(r). **trespassers will be prosecuted** Eintritt bei Strafe verboten.
trestle ['tresl] *n* Gestell *m.*
trial ['traiəl] *n* Probe *f*, Versuch *m*; (*legal*) Prozeß *m.* *adj* Probe-. **on trial** vor Gericht.
triangle ['traiaŋgl] *n* Dreieck *neut*; (*music*) Triangel *m.* **triangular** *adj* dreieckig.
tribe [traib] *n* Stamm *m.* **tribal** *adj* Stammes-. **tribesman** *n* Stammesangehörige(r).
tribunal [trai'bjuːnl] *n* Gerichtshof *m*, Tribunal *neut.*
tributary ['tribjutəri] *n* Nebenfluß *m.*
tribute ['tribjutt] *n* Tribut *m.* **pay tribute** (*fig*) Anerkennung zollen.
trick [trik] *n* Trick *m*, Kniff *m*; (*practical joke*) Streich *m*; (*cards*) Stich *m.* *adj* Trick-. *v* betrügen. **trickery** *n* Betrügerei *f.* **trickster** *n* Schwindler(in). **tricky** *adj* knifflig.
trickle ['trikl] *v* tröpfeln, sickern. *n* Tröpfeln *neut.*
tricycle ['traisikl] *n* Dreirad *neut.*
tried [traid] *adj* erprobt, bewährt.
trifle ['traifl] *n* Kleinigkeit *f*; (*cookery*) Trifle *m*, (süßer) Auflauf *m.* **a trifle** ein bißchen. *v* spielen. **trifling** *adj* belanglos.
trigger ['trigə] *n* Abzug *m.* **pull the trigger** abdrücken. *v* **trigger off** auslösen.

trigonometry [trigə'nɔmətri] *n* Trigonometrie *f.*
trilby ['trilbi] *n* weicher Filzhut *m.*
trim [trim] *adj* gepflegt, nett; (*slim*) schlank. *v* zurechtmachen; (*hair, etc.*) ausputzen, beschneiden. **trimming** *n* Verzierung *f.*
trinket ['triŋkit] *n* Schmuckstück *neut.*
trio ['triːou] *n* Trio *neut.*
trip [trip] *n* Reise *f*, Ausflug *m*; (*stumble*) Fehltritt *m*, Stolpern *neut.* *v* stolpern; (*dance*) tänzeln, trippeln. **trip up** (*someone else*) ein Bein stellen (+ *dat*). **tripper** *n* Ausflügler(in).
tripe [traip] *n* Kaldaunen *pl*; (*coll: nonsense*) Quatsch *m.*
triple ['tripl] *adj* dreifach, Drei-. *v* verdreifachen. **triplet** *n* Drilling *m.* **triplex glass** Sicherheitsglas *neut.*
tripod ['traipɔd] *n* Dreifuß *m*; (*phot*) Stativ *neut.*
trite [trait] *adj* platt, banal.
triumph ['traiʌmf] *n* Triumph *m*; Sieg *m.* *v* triumphieren. **triumphal** *adj* Triumph-, Sieger-. **triumphant** *adj* triumphierend, siegreich.
trivial ['triviəl] *adj* geringfügig, trivial. **triviality** *n* Trivialität *f.*
trod [trɔd] *V* tread.
trodden ['trɔdn] *V* tread.
trolley ['trɔli] *n* (*supermarket*) Einkaufswagen *m*; (*tea*) Servierwagen *m*; (*airport, etc.*) Kofferkuli *m*; (*tram*) Straßenbahn *f.* **trolleybus** *n* O-Bus *m.*
trombone [trɔm'boun] *n* Posaune *f.* **trombonist** *n* Posaunist(in).
troop [truːp] *n* Trupp *m.* **troops** *pl* Truppen *pl.* **trooping the colour** Fahnenparade *f.*
trophy ['troufi] *n* (*sport*) Preis *m*; (*mil, hunting*) Trophäe *f.*
tropic ['trɔpik] *n* Wendekreis *m.* **tropics** *pl* Tropen *pl.* **tropical** *adj* tropisch.
trot [trɔt] *n* Trott *m*, Trab *m.* *v* trotten, traben.
trouble ['trʌbl] *n* Schwierigkeiten *pl*; (*effort*) Mühe *f*; (*burden*) Belästigung *f*; (*tech*) Störung *f.* *v* beunruhigen, stören. **troubles** *pl* (*pol*) Unruhe *f*, Aufruhr *f.* **be in trouble** Schwierigkeiten haben. **be troubled** bekümmert sein. **get into trouble** Ärger bringen (+ *dat*) *or* bekommen. **take (the) trouble** sich die Mühe ge' ˀn. **trouble-maker** *n* Unruhestifter(in). **trou-**

ble-shooter n Störungssucher(in). **troublesome** adj lästig.
trough [trof] n Trog m.
trousers ['trauzəz] pl n Hose f sing.
trout [traut] n Forelle f.
trowel ['trauəl] n Kelle f; (gardening) Pflanzenheber m.
truant ['truːənt] n Schwänzer(in). **play truant** (die Schule) schwänzen. **truancy** n Schwänzerei f.
truce [truːs] n Waffenstillstand m.
truck [trʌk] n (road) Lastkraftwagen (Lkw) m; (rail) Güterwagen m. **truck-driver** n Lastwagenfahrer m.
trudge [trʌdʒ] v sich mühsam schleppen.
true [truː] adj wahr; (genuine) echt; (loyal) treu; (rightful) rechtmäßig. **truism** n Binsenwahrheit f. **truly** adv wirklich, in der Tat. **yours truly** hochachtungsvoll.
truffle ['trʌfl] n Trüffel f.
trump [trʌmp] n Trumpf m. **trump card** Trumpfkarte f. v (über)trumpfen. **trumped up** falsch, erdichtet.
trumpet ['trʌmpit] n Trompete f. v trompeten. **trumpeter** n Trompeter m.
truncheon ['trʌntʃən] n Knüppel m.
trunk [trʌŋk] n (tree) Baumstamm m; (anat) Leib m; (case) Schankkoffer m. (rnot) n Kofferaum m. **trunks** pl Badehose f sing. **trunk-call** Ferngespräch neut. **trunk-road** Fern'straße f.
truss [trʌs] n (med) Bruchband neut. v zusammenbinden; (cookery) dressieren.
trust [trʌst] v trauen (+dat); (hope) hoffen. n Vertrauen neut; (expectation) Erwartung f; (comm) Trust m. **hold in trust** als Treuhänder verwalten. **trustee** n Treuhänder m. **trusting** adj vertrauensvoll. **trustworthy** adj vertrauenswürdig. **trusty** adj treu.
truth [truːθ] n Wahrheit f. **truthful** adj wahr, wahrhaftig. **truthfulness** n Wahrhaftigkeit f.
try [trai] v (attempt) versuchen; (test, sample) probieren; (law) vor Gericht stellen, verhandeln gegen (wegen). **try on** (clothes) anprobieren. **try out** probieren. n Versuch m. **trying** adj peinlich, schwierig; (person) belästigend.
tsar [zaː] n Zar m.
T-shirt ['tiːʃəːt] n T-Shirt neut.
tub [tʌb] n (Bade)Wanne f; (barrel) Faß neut, Tonne f. **tubby** adj (coll) rundlich.
tuba ['tjuːbə] n Tuba f.
tube [tjuːb] n Rohr neut, Röhre f; (of

tyre) (Luft)Schlauch m; (coll: underground railway) U-Bahn f.
tuber ['tjuːbə] n Knolle f.
tuberculosis [tjubəːkjuˈlousis] n Tuberkulose f.
tuck [tʌk] n Einschlag m. v **tuck in** (shirt) einstecken; (food) einhauen, zugreifen; (sheet) feststecken; (person) warm zudecken.
Tuesday ['tjuːzdi] n Dienstag m. **on Tuesdays** dienstags.
tuft [tʌft] n Büschel neut, Schopf m.
tug [tʌg] v ziehen, zerren; (boat) schleppen. n Zerren neut, Zug m; (boat) Schlepper m, Bugsierdampfer m.
tuition [tjuˈiʃən] n Unterricht m.
tulip ['tjuːlip] n Tulpe f.
tumble ['tʌmbl] v hinfallen, umstürzen. **tumbledown** adj baufällig. **tumble-dryer** (Wäsche)Trockner m. n Fall m, Sturz m. **tumbler** n Glas neut.
tummy ['tʌmi] n (coll) Bauch m, Bäuchlein neut. **tummy-ache** n Bauchweh neut.
tumour ['tjuːmə] n Geschwulst f, Tumor m.
tumult ['tjuːmʌlt] n Tumult m, Lärm m. **tumultuous** adj stürmisch.
tuna ['tjuːnə] n Thunfisch m.
tune [tjuːn] n Melodie f. **in/out of tune** gestimmt/verstimmt. **to the tune of** (coll) im Ausmaß von. v (ab)stimmen. **tune in to** einstellen auf. **tuneful** adj melodisch, wohlklingend. **tuner** n (pianos, etc.) Stimmer m.
tunic ['tjuːnik] n (school) Kittel m. (mil) Uniformrock m.
tunnel ['tʌnl] n Tunnel m, Unterführung f. v **tunnel through** einen Tunnel bauen durch.
tunny ['tʌni] V tuna.
turban ['təːbən] n Turban m.
turbine ['təːbain] n Turbine f.
turbot ['təːbət] n Steinbutt m.
turbulent ['təːbjulənt] adj unruhig, stürmisch. **turbulence** n Turbulenz f.
tureen [təˈriːn] n Terrine f.
turf [təːf] n Rasen m; (sport) Turf m, Rennbahn f. v **turf out** (coll) hinausschmeißen.
turkey ['təːki] n (cock) Truthahn m; (hen) Truthenne f.
Turkey ['təːki] n die Türkei f. **Turk** n Türke m, Türkin f. **Turkish** adj türkisch.

turmeric ['tə:mərik] *n* Gelbwurz *f*.
turmoil ['tə:moil] *n* Aufruhr *m*.
turn [tə:n] *v* (sich) drehen; *(become)* werden. **turn around** *or* **round** *(person)* sich umdrehen; *(thing)* herumdrehen. **turn back** umkehren. **turn down** *(offer)* ablehnen; *(radio)* leiser stellen. **turning** *n* *(mot)* Abzweigung *f*. **turning point** Wendepunkt *m*. **turn left/right** links/rechts abbiegen. **turn loose** freilassen. **turn off** *(light)* ausschalten; *(radio)* abstellen; *(mot)* abbiegen. **turn on** einschalten. **turn out** *(expel)* ausweisen; *(produce)* herstellen. **turn-out** *n* *(spectators)* Teilnahme *f*. **turn over** (sich) umdrehen. **turnover** *n* *(comm)* Umsatz *m*. **turnstile** *n* Drehkreuz *neut*. **turntable** *n* *(records)* Plattenteller *m*. **turn up** *(appear)* auftauchen; *(radio)* lauter stellen. **turn-up** *n* *(trousers)* Umschlag *m*. *n* Umdrehung *f*; *(change of direction)* Wendung *f*. **it's my turn** ich bin an der Reihe. **do someone a good turn** jemandem einen Gefallen tun.
turnip ['tə:nip] *n* (weiße) Rübe *f*.
turpentine ['tə:pəntain] *n* Turpentin *neut*.
turquoise ['tə:kwoiz] *n* Türkis *m*. *adj* *(colour)* türkisblau.
turret ['tʌrit] *n* Türmchen *neut*; *(gun)* Geschützturm *m*, Panzerturm *m*.
turtle ['tə:tl] *n* Schildkröte *f*. **turtle dove** Turteltaube *f*.
tusk [tʌsk] *n* Stoßzahn *m*.
tussle ['tʌsl] *n* Balgerei *f*, Ringen *neut*. *v* sich balgen, kämpfen.
tutor ['tju:tə] *n* Privatlehrer *m*; *(university)* Tutor *m*.
tuxedo [tʌk'si:dou] *n* Smoking *m*.
tweed [twi:d] *n* Tweed *m*.
tweezers ['twi:zəz] *pl n* Pinzette *f* *sing*.
twelve [twelv] *adj* zwölf. *n* Zwölf *f*. **twelfth** *adj* zwölft.
twenty ['twenti] *adj* zwanzig. *n* Zwanzig *f*. **twentieth** *adj* zwanzigst.
twice [twais] *adv* zweimal. **twice as much** zweimal so viel. **think twice about** sich gründlich überlegen.
twiddle ['twidl] *v* herumdrehen, spielen mit.
twig [twig] *n* Zweig *m*.
twilight ['twailait] *n* (Abend)Dämmerung *f*, Zwielicht *neut*. *adj* Zwielicht-.
twin [twin] *n* Zwilling *m*. *adj* Zwillings-. **twin-cylinder engine** Zweizylindermotor *m*.

twine [twain] *n* Bindfaden *m*, Schnur *f*. *v* *(threads)* zusammendrehen. **twine around** winden um.
twinge [twindʒ] *n* Stich *m*, Stechen *neut*. **twinge of conscience** Gewissensbiß *m*. *v* zwicken, kneifen.
twinkle ['twiŋkl] *v* glitzern, funkeln; *(eyes)* blinzeln. *n* Glitzern *neut*; Blinzeln *neut*. **in a twinkle** im Nu.
twirl [twə:l] *v* wirbeln. *n* Wirbel *m*.
twist [twist] *v* (sich) drehen, (sich) winden; *(meaning)* verdrehen; *(features)* verzerren. **twist one's ankle** sich den Fuß verrenken. **twisted** *adj* *(person)* verschroben. **twisting** *adj* sich windend. *n* Drehung *f*, Windung *f*; *(in story)* Wendung *f*.
twit [twit] *n* *(coll)* Dummkopf *m*.
twitch [twitʃ] *v* zucken. *n* Zucken *neut*.
twitter ['twitə] *v* zwitschern. *n* Gezwitscher *neut*, Zwitschern *neut*.
two [tu:] *adj* zwei. **two-faced** *adj* heuchlerisch. **twofold** *adj* zweifach. **two-stroke engine** Zweitaktmotor *m*. *n* Zwei *f*; *(pair)* Paar *neut*.
tycoon [tai'ku:n] *n* Industriemagnat *m*.
type [taip] *n* Typ *m*, Sorte *f*, Klasse *f*; *(person)* Typ *m*; *(print)* Druck *m*, Druckschrift *f*. *v* (mit der Maschine) schreiben, tippen. **typed** *adj* maschinengeschrieben. **typewriter** *n* Schreibmaschine *f*. **typing error** Tippfehler *m*. **typist** *n* Typist(in).
typhoid ['taifoid] *n* Typhus *m*.
typhoon [tai'fu:n] *n* Taifun *m*.
typical ['tipikəl] *adj* typisch. **typify** *v* verkörpern.
tyrant ['tairənt] *n* Tyrann(in). **tyrannical** *adj* tyrannisch. **tyrannize** *v* tyrannisieren. **tyranny** *n* Tyrannei *f*.
tyre ['taiə] *or US* **tire** *n* Reifen *m*.

U

ubiquitous [ju'bikwitəs] *adj* überall zu finden(d).
udder ['ʌdə] *n* Euter *neut*.
ugly ['ʌgli] *adj* häßlich. **ugliness** *n* Häßlichkeit *f*.
ulcer ['ʌlsə] *n* Geschwür *neut*.

ulterior [ʌl'tiəriə] *adj* **ulterior motives** Hintergedanken *pl.*

ultimate ['ʌltimət] *adj* allerletzt; (*conclusive*) endgültig, entscheidend. **ultimately** *adv* schließlich. **ultimatum** *n* Ultimatum *neut.*

ultraviolet [ʌltrə'vaiələt] *adj* ultraviolett.

umbilical [ʌm'bilikəl] *n* Nabelschnur *f.*

umbrella [ʌm'brelə] *n* Regenschirm *m.*

umlaut ['umlaut] *n* Umlaut *m.*

umpire ['ʌmpaiə] *n* Schiedsrichter *m.*

umpteen [ʌmp'tiːn] *adj* zahllos. **umpteen times** x-mal.

unable [ʌn'eibl] *adj* unfähig. **be unable** nicht können.

unacceptable [ʌnək'septəbl] *adj* unannehmbar.

unaccompanied [ʌnə'kumpənid] *adj* unbegleitet; (*music*) ohne Begleitung.

unanimous [juː'naniməs] *adj* einstimmig. **unanimity** *n* Einstimmigkeit *f.*

unannounced [ʌnə'naunst] *adj* unangekündigt.

unarmed [ʌn'aːmd] *adj* unbewaffnet.

unassuming [ʌnə'sjuːmiŋ] *adj* bescheiden.

unattractive [ʌnə'traktiv] *adj* reizlos, nicht anziehend.

unauthorized [ʌn'ɔːθəraizd] *adj* unbefugt.

unavoidable [ʌnə'voidəbl] *adj* unvermeidlich.

unaware [ʌnə'weə] *adj* **be unaware of** sich nicht bewußt sein (+ *gen*). **unawares** *adv* **take unawares** überraschen.

unbalanced [ʌn'balənst] *adj* unausgeglichen; (*mentally disturbed*) geistesgestört.

unbearable [ʌn'beərəbl] *adj* unerträglich.

unbelievable [ʌnbi'liːvəbl] *adj* unglaublich. **unbeliever** *n* Ungläubige(r). **unbelieving** *adj* ungläubig.

*****unbend** [ʌn'bend] *v* (*person*) freundlicher werden. **unbending** *adj* unbeugsam.

unbounded [ʌn'baundid] *adj* unbegrenzt, grenzenlos.

unbreakable [ʌn'breikəbl] *adj* unzerbrechlich.

unbridled [ʌn'braidld] *adj* zügellos.

unbroken [ʌn'broukn] *adj* (*continuous*) ununterbrochen.

uncalled-for [ʌn'kɔːldfɔː] *adj* unangebracht.

uncanny [ʌn'kani] *adj* unheimlich.

uncertain [ʌn'səːtn] *adj* unsicher, ungewiß. **uncertainty** *n* Unsicherheit *f*, Ungewißheit *f.*

uncle ['ʌŋkl] *n* Onkel *m.*

unclean [ʌn'kliːn] *adj* unrein.

uncomfortable [ʌn'kʌmfətəbl] *adj* unbequem; (*fact, etc.*) beunruhigend.

uncommon [ʌn'komən] *adj* ungewöhnlich, selten. **uncommonly** *adv* (*extremely*) außerordentlich.

unconditional [ʌnkən'diʃənl] *adj* bedingungslos, uneingeschränkt.

unconfirme [ʌnkən'fəːmd]d *adj* unbestätigt.

unconscious [ʌn'konʃəs] *adj* (*unknowing*) unbewußt; (*med*) bewußtlos. **unconsciousness** *n* Bewußtlosigkeit *f.*

uncontrollable [ʌnkən'trouləbl] *adj* unbeherrscht, unkontrollierbar.

unconventional [ʌnkən'venʃənl] *adj* unkonventionell.

unconvinced [ʌnkən'vinst] *adj* nicht überzeugt. **unconvincing** *adj* nicht überzeugend.

uncooked [ʌn'kukt] *adj* roh, ungekocht.

uncork [ʌn'kɔːk] *v* entkorken.

uncouth [ʌn'kuːθ] *adj* ungehobelt, unfein.

uncover [ʌn'kʌvə] *v* aufdecken.

uncut [ʌn'kʌt] *adj* (*gem*) ungeschliffen; (*grass*) ungemäht; (*book*) unabgekürzt.

undecided [ʌndi'saidid] *adj* (*thing*) unentschieden; (*person*) unentschlossen.

undeniable [ʌndi'naiəbl] *adj* unbestreitbar.

under ['ʌndə] *prep* unter; (*less than*) weniger als. **under age** minderjährig. **under construction** im Bau. **under cover of** im Schutz (+ *gen*). *adv* unten. **go under** zugrunde gehen. *adj* Unter-.

undercharge [ʌndə'tʃaɪdʒ] *v* zu wenig berechnen.

underclothes ['ʌndəklouðz] *pl n* Unterwäsche *f sing.*

undercoat ['ʌndəkout] *n* Grundierung *f*, Grundanstrich *m.*

undercover [ʌndə'kʌvə] *adj* Geheim-.

*****undercut** [ʌndə'kʌt] *v* (*comm*) unterbieten.

underdeveloped [ʌndədi'veləpt] *adj* unterentwickelt. **underdeveloped country** Entwicklungsland *neut.*

underdone [ʌndə'dʌn] *adj* (*meat*) nicht durchgebraten.

underestimate [ʌndə'estimeit] *adj* unterschätzen.

underexpose [ʌndərik'spouz] *v* unterbelichten. **underexposure** *n* Unterbelichtung *f.*

underfoot [ʌndə'fut] adv am Boden.
*undergo [ʌndə'gou] v erleben; (operation) sich unterziehen (+dat).
undergraduate [ʌndə'grædjuət] n Student(in).
underground ['ʌndəgraund; adv ʌndə'graund] adj unterirdisch, Untergrund-; (pol) geheim, Untergrund-. n (rail) Untergrundbahn f, (coll) U-Bahn f. adv unter der Erde. **go underground** (hide) untertauchen.
undergrowth ['ʌndəgrouθ] n Unterholz neut.
underhand [ʌndə'hænd] adj heimlich, hinterlistig.
*underlie [ʌndə'lai] v zugrunde liegen (+dat).
underline [ʌndə'lain] v unterstreichen; (stress) betonen.
undermine [ʌndə'main] v unterminieren, untergraben.
underneath [ʌndə'niːθ] prep unter, unterhalb. adv unten, darunter.
underpants ['ʌndəpænts] pl n Unterhose f sing.
underpass ['ʌndəpɑis] n Unterführung f.
underprivileged [ʌndə'privilidʒd] adj benachteiligt.
underrate [ʌndə'reit] v unterschätzen.
*understand [ʌndə'stænd] v verstehen. **understandable** adj verständlich. **understanding** n Verständnis neut; (agreement) Verständigung f; adj verständnisvoll.
understate [ʌndə'steit] v untertreiben. **understatement** n Untertreibung f.
understudy ['ʌndəstʌdi] n Ersatzschauspieler(in).
*undertake [ʌndə'teik] v übernehmen. **undertaker** n Leichenbestatter m. **undertaking** n Unternehmen neut; (promise) Versprechen neut.
undertone ['ʌndətoun] n Unterton m.
underwear ['ʌndəweə] n Unterwäsche f.
underweight [ʌndə'weit] adj untergewichtig.
underworld ['ʌndəwəːld] n Unterwelt f.
*underwrite [ʌndə'rait] v unterzeichnen, versichern. **underwriter** n Versicherer m.
undesirable [ʌndi'zaiərəbl] adj nicht wünschenswert, unerwünscht.
*undo [ʌn'duː] v (package) öffnen, aufmachen; (coat, knot) aufknöpfen; (work) zunichte machen. **undoing** n Ruin m, Vernichtung f.

undoubted [ʌn'dautid] adj unbestritten. **undoubtedly** adv ohne Zweifel.
undress [ʌn'dres] v (sich) ausziehen. **undressed** adj unbekleidet.
undue [ʌn'djuː] adj übermäßig, übertrieben; (improper) unschicklich. **unduly** adv übertrieben.
undulate ['ʌndjuleit] v wogen, wallen. **undulation** n Wallen neut.
unearth [ʌn'əːθ] v ausgraben; (fig) ans Tageslicht bringen.
uneasy [ʌn'iːzi] adj (person) beunruhigt, ängstlich; (feeling) unbehaglich.
uneducated [ʌn'edjukeitid] adj ungebildet.
unemployed [ʌnem'ploid] adj arbeitslos. **unemployment** n Arbeitslosigkeit f.
unending [ʌn'endiŋ] adj endlos.
unequal [ʌn'iːkwəl] adj ungleich. **unequalled** adj unübertroffen.
uneven [ʌn'iːvn] adj uneben. **unevenness** n Unebenheit f.
uneventful [ʌni'ventfəl] adj ereignislos.
unexpected [ʌneks'pektid] adj unerwartet.
unfailing [ʌn'feiliŋ] adj unfehlbar.
unfair [ʌn'feə] adj ungerecht, unfair. **unfairness** n Unbilligkeit f.
unfaithful [ʌn'feiθfəl] adj untreu. **unfaithfulness** n Untreue f.
unfamiliar [ʌnfə'miljə] adj unbekannt.
unfasten [ʌn'faisn] v aufmachen, losbinden.
unfit [ʌn'fit] adj ungeeignet; (sport) nicht fit.
unfold [ʌn'fould] v (sich) entfalten.
unforeseen [ʌnfoː'siːn] adj unvorhergesehen.
unforgettable [ʌnfə'getəbl] adj unvergeßlich.
unfortunate [ʌn'foːtʃənət] adj unglücklich; (regrettable) bedauerlich. n Unglückliche(r). **unfortunately** adv unglücklicherweise, leider.
unfurnished [ʌn'fəːnifd] adj unmöbliert.
ungrateful [ʌn'greitfəl] adj undankbar.
unhappy [ʌn'hæpi] adj unglücklich; (with something) unzufrieden. **unhappily** adv leider. **unhappiness** n Unglück neut.
unhealthy [ʌn'helθi] adj (person) ungesund; (damaging to health) gesundheitsschädlich.
unhurt [ʌn'həːt] adj unverletzt.
unicorn ['juːnikoːn] n Einhorn m.

uniform ['juːnifoːm] *n* Uniform *f*, Dienstkleidung *f*. *adj* einförmig, gleichförmig.
uniformity *n* Gleichheit *f*.
unify ['juːnifai] *v* vereinigen. **unification** *n* Vereinigung *f*.
unilateral [juːni'latərəl] *adj* einseitig.
uninhabited [ʌnin'habitid] *adj* unbewohnt. **uninhabitable** *adj* unbewohnbar.
unintelligible [ʌnin'telidʒəbl] *adj* unverständlich.
uninterested [ʌn'intristid] *adj* uninteressiert. **uninteresting** *adj* uninteressant.
union ['juːnjən] *n* Vereinigung *f*; (*pol*) Staatenbund *m*; (*agreement*) Eintracht *f*; (*trade union*) Gewerkschaft *f*. **unionize** *v* gewerkschaftlich organisieren.
unique [juːˈniːk] *adj* einzigartig; (*only*) einzig.
unison ['juːnisn] *n* Einklang *m*.
unit ['juːnit] *n* Einheit *f*.
unite [juˈnait] *v* (sich) vereinigen. **united** *adj* vereint, vereinigt. **unity** *n* Einheit *f*; (*accord*) Einigkeit *f*.
United Kingdom *n* Vereinigtes Königreich.
United Nations *pl n* Vereinte Nationen.
United States of America *n* Vereinigte Staaten von Amerika.
universe ('juːnivəːs] *n* Weltall *neut*, Universum *neut*. **universal** *adj* universal.
university [juːni'vəːsəti] *n* Universität *f*, Hochschule *f*. *adj* Universitäts-, Hochschul-.
unjust [ʌn'dʒʌst] *adj* ungerecht.
unkempt [ʌn'kempt] *adj* ungepflegt.
unkind [ʌn'kaind] *adj* unfreundlich. **unkindness** *n* Unfreundlichkeit *f*.
unknown [ʌn'noun] *adj* unbekannt. *n* das Unbekannte.
unlawful [ʌn'loːfəl] *adj* rechtswidrig, unzulässig.
unless [ʌn'les] *conj* wenn ... nicht, es sei denn.
unlike [ʌn'laik] *adj*, *prep* unähnlich, (*in contrast to*) im Gegensatz zu. **unlikely** *adv* unwahrscheinlich.
unload [ʌn'loud] *v* (*goods*) abladen; (*truck, etc.*) entladen.
unlock [ʌn'lok] *v* aufschließen, öffnen. **unlocked** *adj* unverschlossen.
unlucky [ʌn'lʌki] *adj* unglücklich.
unmarried [ʌn'marid] *adj* ledig, unverheiratet.
unnatural [ʌn'natʃərəl] *adj* unnatürlich.

unnecessary [ʌn'nesəsəri] *adj* unnötig, nicht notwendig.
unobtainable [ʌnəb'teinəbl] *adj* unerhältlich.
unoccupied [ʌn'okjupaid] *adj* unbesetzt; (*house*) unbewohnt; (*person*) unbeschäftigt.
unofficial [ʌnə'fiʃəl] *adj* inoffiziell.
unorthodox [ʌn'oːθədoks] *adj* unorthodox.
unpack [ʌn'pak] *v* auspacken.
unpleasant [ʌn'pleznt] *adj* unangenehm. **unpleasantness** *n* Unannehmlichkeit *f*.
unpopular [ʌn'popjulə] *adj* unbeliebt.
unprecedented [ʌn'presidentid] *adj* unerhört.
unpretentious [ʌnpri'tenʃəs] *adj* anspruchslos.
unravel [ʌn'ravəl] *v* auftrennen; (*fig*) enträtseln.
unreal [ʌn'riəl] *adj* unwirklich. **unrealistic** *adj* unrealistisch.
unreasonable [ʌn'riːzənəbl] *adj* übertrieben, übermäßig; (*person*) unvernünftig.
unrelenting [ʌnri'lentiŋ] *adj* unerbittlich.
unreliable [ʌnri'laiəbl] *adj* unzuverlässig. **unreliability** *n* Unzuverlässigkeit *f*.
unrest [ʌn'rest] *n* Unruhe *f*.
unruly [ʌn'ruːli] *adj* unlenksam.
unsafe [ʌn'seif] *adj* unsicher, gefährlich.
unsatisfactory [ʌnsatis'faktəri] *adj* unbefriedigend. **unsatisifed** *adj* unzufrieden.
unscrew [ʌn'skruː] *v* aufschrauben.
unsettle [ʌn'setl] *v* beunruhigen. **unsettled** *adj* unruhig.
unsightly [ʌn'saitli] *adj* unansehnlich.
unskilled [ʌn'skild] *adj* ungelernt.
unsound [ʌn'saund] *adj* (*advice, etc.*) unzuverlässig. **of unsound mind** geistesgestört.
unspeakable [ʌn'spiːkəbl] *adj* unbeschreiblich; (*horrible*) scheußlich, entsetzlich.
unstable [ʌn'steibl] *adj* nicht fest, schwankend; (*person*) labil.
unsteady [ʌn'stedi] *adj* wackelig, unsicher.
unsuccessful [ʌnsək'sesfəl] *adj* erfolglos.
unsuitable [ʌn'suːtəbl] *adj* ungeeignet.
untangle [ʌn'taŋgl] *v* entwirren.
untidy [ʌn'taidi] *adj* unordentlich. **untidiness** *n* Unordentlichkeit *f*.

untie [ʌn'tai] v losbinden.
until [ən'til] prep, conj bis. **not until** erst.
untoward [ʌntə'wɔːd] adj ungünstig.
untrue [ʌn'truː] adj unwahr, falsch; (friend) untreu. **untruth** n Unwahrheit f, Falschheit f. **untruthful** adj unwahr, unaufrichtig.
unusual [ʌn'juːʒuəl] adj ungewöhnlich, außergewöhnlich.
unwell [ʌn'wel] adj unwohl.
unwieldy [ʌn'wiːldi] adj unhandlich.
***unwind** [ʌn'waind] v loswickeln, abspulen; (rest) sich entspannen, (sich) ausruhen.
unworthy [ʌn'wəːði] adj unwürdig.
unwrap [ʌn'rap] v auswickeln.
up [ʌp] prep auf, hinauf. adv auf, hoch; hinauf, herauf; (out of bed) auf; (sun) aufgegangen. **it's up to me** es liegt an mir. **up to now** bis jetzt. **up for trial** vor Gericht. **what's up?** was ist los?
upbringing ['ʌpbriŋiŋ] n Erziehung f.
update [ʌp'deit] v modernisieren; (book) neu bearbeiten.
upheaval [ʌp'hiːvl] n Umwälzung f.
uphill [ʌp'hil] adv bergauf. adj (fig) mühsam.
***uphold** [ʌp'hould] v unterstützen, billigen.
upholster [ʌp'houlstə] v ' (auf)polstern. **upholsterer** n Polsterer m. **upholstery** n Polsterung f.
upkeep ['ʌpkiːp] n Instandhaltung f; (cost) Unterhaltskosten pl.
uplift [ʌp'lift] v erbauen.
upon [ə'pon] prep auf. **once upon a time** es war einmal.
upper ['ʌpə] adj ober, höher. **uppermost** adj oberst, höchst. n (shoe) Oberleder neut.
upright ['ʌprait] adj, adv gerade, aufrecht; (honest) aufrecht, aufrichtig.
uprising [ʌ'praiziŋ] n Aufstand m.
uproar ['ʌprɔː] n Aufruhr m, Tumult m.
uproot [ʌp'ruːt] v ausreißen, entwurzeln.
***upset** [ʌp'set; n 'ʌpset] v (person) bestürzen, beunruhigen; (plan) vereiteln; (tip over) umkippen. adj bestürzt, außer Fassung; (stomach) verstimmt. n (stomach) Verstimmung f.
upshot ['ʌpʃot] n Ergebnis neut.
upside down [ʌpsai'daun] adv verkehrt herum, mit dem Kopf nach unten. **turn upside down** sich auf den Kopf stellen.
upstairs [ʌp'steəz] adv (go) nach oben, die

Treppe hinauf; (be) oben. adj (room) obere(r).
upstream [ʌp'striːm] adv stromaufwärts.
uptight ['ʌptait] adj (coll) nervös, aufgeregt.
up-to-date [ʌptə'deit] adj modern, aktuell.
upward ['ʌpwəd] adj nach oben (gerichtet). **upward glance** Blick nach oben m. adv also **upwards** aufwärts, nach oben.
uranium [ju'reiniəm] n Uran neut.
Uranus [juə'reinəs] n Uranus m.
urban ['əːbən] adj städtisch, Stadt-. **urbanization** n Verstädterung f. **urbanize** v verstädtern.
urchin ['əːtʃin] n (boy) Bengel m.
urge [əːdʒ] v (implore) (dringend) bitten, raten (+dat); (insist on) betonen, bestehen auf. **urge on** antreiben. n Drang m, (An)Trieb m.
urgent ['əːdʒənt] adj dringend. **urgency** n Dringlichkeit f.
urine ['juːrin] n Urin m, Harn m. **urinal** n Urinbecken neut, Pissoir neut. **urinary** adj Urin-. **urinate** v urinieren.
urn [əːn] n Urne f.
us [ʌs] pron uns. **both of us** wir beide. **all of us** wir alle.
usage ['juːzidʒ] n Brauch m, Gebrauch m.
use [juːz; n juːs] v benutzen, gebrauchen; (apply) anwenden; (coll: exploit) ausbeuten. n Gebrauch m, Verwendung f. **be of use** von Nutzen sein, helfen. **for the use of** zum Nutzen von. **it's no use** es hilft nichts. **make use of** Gebrauch machen von. **use up** verbrauchen. I used to live here ich wohnte (früher) hier. she used to say sie hat immer gesagt, sie pflegte zu sagen. **useful** adj nützlich, brauchbar. **usefulness** n Nützlichkeit f. **useless** adj nutzlos, unnütz. **user** Benutzer(in). **uselessness** n Nutzlosigkeit f.
usher ['ʌʃə] n Platzanweiser(in). v **usher in** (fig) einleiten.
usual ['juːʒuəl] adj üblich, gewöhnlich. **usually** adv gewöhnlich, normalerweise.
usurp [ju'zəːp] v gewaltsam nehmen, usurpieren. **usurpation** n Usurpation f. **usurper** n Usurpator m.
utensil [ju'tensl] n Gerät neut, Werkzeug neut; (pl) Utensilien pl.
uterus ['juːtərəs] n Gebärmutter f, Uterus m. **uterine** adj Gebärmutter-.

utility [ju'tilǝti] *n* Nutzen *m*. **public utility** *n* öffentlicher Versorgungsbetrieb *m*.
utilize ['juttilaiz] *v* verwenden. **utilization** *n* Verwendung *f*.
utmost ['ʌtmoust] *adj* äußerst. **do one's utmost** sein möglichstes tun.
utter[1] ['ʌtǝ] *v* äußern, aussprechen. **utterance** *n* Äußerung *f*.
utter[2] ['ʌtǝ] *adj* rein, bloß, höchst.
U-turn ['juttǝin] *n* Wende *f*; (*pol*) Kehrtwendung *f*.

V

vacant ['veikǝnt] *adj* leer. **vacancy** *n* Leere *f*; (*job*) freie Stelle. **vacate** *v* verlassen; (*seat*) freimachen. **vacation** *n* Urlaub *m*.
vaccine ['vaksiin] *n* Impfstoff *m*. **vaccinate** *v* impfen. **vaccination** *n* Impfung *f*.
vacillate ['vasileit] *v* schwanken. **vacillation** *n* Schwanken *neut*.
vacuum ['vakjum] *n* Vakuum *neut*. **vacuum-cleaner** *n* Staubsauger *m*. *v* (*coll*) mit dem Staubsauger reinigen. **vacuous** *adj* leer.
vagina [vǝ'dʒainǝ] *n* Scheide *f*, Vagina *f*.
vagrant ['veigrǝnt] *n* Vagabund *m*, Landstreicher *m*.
vague [veig] *adj* vage, undeutlich; (*person*) zerstreut. **vagueness** *n* Verschwommenheit *f*.
vain [vein] *adj* (*person*) eitel, eingebildet; (*thing*) eitel, leer; (*effort*) vergeblich. **in vain** umsonst, vergeblich.
valiant ['valiǝnt] *adj* tapfer, heroisch.
valid ['valid] *adj* gültig. **validate** *v* für gültig erklären. **validity** *n* Gültigkeit *f*.
valley ['vali] *n* Tal *neut*.
value ['valjuɪ] *n* Wert *neut*. **value-added tax (VAT)** Mehrwertsteuer (Mwst) *f*. *v* (*establish value of*) einschätzen; (*treasure*) bewerten. **valuable** *adj* wertvoll, kostbar. **valuables** *pl n* Wertsachen *pl*. **valuation** *n* Schätzung *f*. **valued** *adj* hochgeschätzt. **valueless** *adj* wertlos.
valve [valv] *n* Ventil *neut*; (*anat*) Klappe *f*; (*elec*) Röhre *f*.
vampire ['vampaiǝ] *n* Vampir *m*.
van [van] *n* Lastwagen *m*, Lieferwagen *m*. **luggage van** Gepäckwagen *m*.

vandal ['vandl] *n* Vandale *m*, Vandalin *f*. **vandalism** *n* Vandalismus *m*.
vanilla [vǝ'nilǝ] *n* Vanille *f*.
vanish ['vaniʃ] *v* verschwinden. **vanishing cream** Tagescreme *f*.
vanity ['vanǝti] *n* Eitelkeit *f*. **vanity bag** Kosmetiktasche *f*.
vapour ['veipǝ] *n* Dampf *m*. **vaporize** *v* verdampfen.
varicose veins ['varikous] *pl n* Krampfadern *pl*.
varnish ['vaɪniʃ] *n* Lack *m*, Firnis *m*. *v* lackieren.
vary ['veǝri] *v* (*modify*) (ab)ändern, variieren; (*become changed*) sich ändern, variieren. **variable** *adj* veränderlich. **variation** *n* Veränderung; (*music, biology*) Variation *f*. **varied** *adj* verschiedenartig, abwechslungsvoll. **variety** *n* Verschiedenheit, Mannigfaltigkeit *f*; (*species*) Art *f*, Varietät *f*. **variety show** Variété *neut*. **various** *adj* verschieden; (*several*) mehrere. **varying** *adj* wechselnd, unterschiedlich.
vase [vaɪz] *n* Vase *f*.
vasectomy [vǝ'sektǝmi] *n* Vasektomie *f*.
vast [vaɪst] *adj* ungeheuer, riesig; (*wide*) weit, ausgedehnt. **vast majority** überwiegende Mehrheit *f*. **vast numbers of** zahllos(e). **vastly** *adv* gewaltig. **vastness** *n* Weite *f*.
vat [vat] *n* großes Faß *neut*.
vault[1] [voɪlt] *n* (*ceiling*) Gewölbe *neut*; (*cellar*) Keller *m*; (*safe*) Stahlkammer *f*.
vault[2] [voɪlt] *v* (*jump*) springen (über). *n* Sprung *m*. **vaulting-horse** *n* Sprungpferd *neut*.
veal [viɪl] *n* Kalbfleisch *neut*.
veer [viǝ] *v* sich drehen; (*mot*) ausscheren.
vegetable ['vedʒtǝbl] *n* Gemüse *neut*. *adj* pflanzlich. **vegetarian** *n* Vegetarier(in); *adj* vegetarisch. **vegetation** *n* Pflanzenwuchs *m*, Vegetation *f*.
vehement ['viɪǝmǝnt] *adj* heftig, gewaltig.
vehicle ['viǝkl] *n* Fahrzeug *neut*; (*medium*) Mittel *neut*, Vehikel *neut*.
veil [veil] *n* Schleier *m*. *v* verschleiern. **veiled** *adj* verschleiert.
vein [vein] *n* Vene *f*; (*mood*) Stimmung *f*; (*in rock*) Ader *f*. **veined** *adj* geädert.
velocity [vǝ'losǝti] *n* Geschwindigkeit *f*.
velvet ['velvit] *n* Samt *m*. *adj* Samt-. **velvety** *adj* samtweich, samtartig.

vending machine ['vendiŋ] *n* (Verkaufs)Automat *m*.

veneer [və'niə] *n* Furnier *neut*; (*fig*) Anstrich *m*. *v* furnieren.

venerate ['venəreit] *v* verehren, bewundern. **venerable** *adj* ehrwürdig. **veneration** *n* Verehrung *f*.

venereal disease [və'niəriəl] *n* Geschlechtskrankheit *f*.

Venetian blind [və'niːʃən] *n* Jalousie *f*.

vengeance ['vendʒəns] *n* Rache *f*. **take vengeance on** sich rächen an. **vengeful** *adj* rachsüchtig.

venison ['venisn] *n* Reh *neut*, Wildbret *neut*.

venom ['venəm] *n* (Tier)Gift *neut*. **venomous** *adj* giftig.

vent [vent] *n* Öffnung *f*, Luftloch *neut*; (*in jacket*) Schlitz *m*. *v* lüften; (*feelings*) freien Lauf lassen (+*dat*), äußern.

ventilate ['ventileit] *v* ventilieren, lüften. **ventilation** *n* Ventilation *f*, Lüftung *f*. **ventilator** *n* Ventilator *m*, Lüftungsanlage *f*.

venture ['ventʃə] *n* (*risk*) Risiko *neut*, Wagnis *neut*; (*undertaking*) Unternehmen *neut*. *v* wagen.

venue ['venjuː] *n* Schauplatz *m*; (*meeting place*) Treffpunkt *m*.

Venus ['viːnəs] *n* Venus *f*.

verb [vəːb] *n* Verbum *neut*, Zeitwort *neut*. **verbal** *adj* mündlich. **verbalize** *v* formulieren. **verbatim** *adv* wortwörtlich. **verbose** *adj* wortreich.

verdict ['vəːdikt] *n* Urteil *neut*.

verge [vəːdʒ] *n* Rand *m*, Grenze *f*; (*grass*) Grasstreifen *m*. **verge on** grenzen an.

verify ['verifai] *v* beweisen, bestätigen, beglaubigen. **verification** *n* Beglaubigung *f*.

vermin ['vəːmin] *pl n* Schädlinge *pl*.

vermouth ['vəːməθ] *n* Wermut *m*.

vernacular [və'nakjulə] *n* Volkssprache *f*.

versatile ['vəːsətail] *adj* (*person*) vielseitig. **versatility** *n* Vielseitigkeit *f*.

verse [vəːs] *n* (*stanza*) Strophe *f*; (*line*) Vers *m*; (*poetry*) Poesie *f*, Dichtung *f*. **versed** *adj* versiert.

version ['vəːʃən] *n* Fassung *f*, Version *f*; (*Bible, etc*.) Übersetzung *f*.

versus ['vəːsəs] *prep* gegen.

vertebra ['vəːtibrə] *n* (*pl* -ae) Wirbel *m*. **vertebral column** Wirbelsäule *f*. **vertebrate** *n* Wirbeltier *neut*.

vertical ['vəːtikl] *adj* senkrecht, lotrecht. *n* Senkrechte *f*.

vertigo ['vəːtigou] *n* Schwindelgefühl *neut*.

very ['veri] *adj* sehr. *very best* allerbest. *adj that very day* an ebendemselben Tag. *at the very beginning* gerade am Anfang.

vessel ['vesl] *n* Gefäß *neut*; (*ship*) Schiff *neut*.

vest [vest] *n* (*undershirt*) Unterhemd *neut*; (*waistcoat*) Weste *f*.

vestige ['vestidʒ] *n* Spur *f*.

vestments ['vestmənts] *pl n* (*rel*) Amtstracht *f*.

vestry ['vestri] *n* Sakristei *f*.

vet [vet] *n* (*animals*) Tierarzt *m*. *v* prüfen, überholen.

veteran ['vetərən] *n* Veteran *m*.

veterinary ['vetərinəri] *n* Tierarzt *m*.

veto ['viːtou] *n* Veto *neut*, Einspruch *m*. *v* Veto einlegen gegen.

vex [veks] *v* ärgern, belästigen. **vexation** *n* Ärger *m*. **vexed** *adj* ärgerlich; (*question*) strittig.

via [vaiə] *prep* über.

viable ['vaiəbl] *adj* lebensfähig; (*practicable*) durchführbar.

viaduct ['vaiədʌkt] *n* Viadukt *m*.

vibrate [vai'breit] *v* vibrieren. **vibration** *n* Vibrieren *neut*, Vibration *f*.

vicar ['vikə] *n* Pfarrer *m*. **vicarage** *n* Pfarrhaus *neut*.

vicarious [vi'keəriəs] *adj* aus zweiter Hand.

vice¹ [vais] *n* (*evil*) Laster *neut*, Untugend *f*.

vice² [vais] *n* (*tool*) Schraubstock *m*, Zwinge *f*.

vice-chancellor [vais'tʃɑːnsələ] *n* (*university*) Rektor *m*.

vice-president [vais'prezidənt] *n* Vizepräsident *m*.

vice versa [vaisi'vəːsə] *adv* umgekehrt.

vicinity [vi'sinəti] *n* Nähe *f*, Nachbarschaft *f*.

vicious ['viʃəs] *adj* bösartig, gemein; (*blow, etc*) heftig, gewaltig. **vicious circle** Teufelskreis *m*. **viciousness** *n* Gemeinheit *f*.

victim ['viktim] *n* Opfer *neut*. **victimize** *v* ungerecht behandeln.

victor ['viktə] *n* Sieger(in). **victorious** *adj* siegreich. **victory** *n* Sieg *m*.

video-tape ['vidiouteip] *n* Magnetbildband *neut*.

view [vjuː] n Ausblick m, Aussicht f; (picture, opinion) Ansicht f. **in view** in Sicht. **viewfinder** n Sucher m. **viewpoint** n Gesichtspunkt m, Standpunkt m. **with a view to** mit der Absicht, zu. **v** ansehen, betrachten. **viewer** n (TV) Zuschauer(in).

vigil ['vidʒil] n Wachen neut. **keep vigil** wachen. **vigilance** n Wachsamkeit f. **vigilant** adj wachsam.

vigour ['vigə] n Kraft f, Vitalität f. **vigorous** adj kräftig, energisch.

vile [vail] adj gemein, ekelerregend, widerlich.

villa ['vilə] n Villa f.

village ['vilidʒ] n Dorf neut. adj dörflich, Dorf-. **villager** n Dorfbewohner(in).

villain ['vilən] n Schurke m; (coll) Schelm m. **villainous** adj schurkisch. **villainy** n Schurkerei f.

vindictive [vin'diktiv] adj rachsüchtig. **vindictiveness** n Rachsucht f.

vine [vain] n Rebe f, Weinstock m. **vineleaf** n Weinblatt m. **vineyard** n Weinberg m. **viniculture** n Weinbau m.

vinegar ['vinigə] n Essig m. **vinegary** adj sauer.

vintage ['vintidʒ] n Weinernte f; (particular year) Jahrgang m.

vinyl ['vainil] n Vinyl neut. adj Vinyl-.

viola [vi'oulə] n Viola f.

violate ['vaiəleit] v (law) übertreten; (woman) vergewaltigen. **violation** n Übertretung f.

violence ['vaiələns] n Gewalt f, Gewalttätigkeit f. **violent** adj (blow) heftig, gewaltig; (person, action) gewaltsam.

violet ['vaiəlit] n Veilchen neut. adj violett.

violin [vaiə'lin] n Geige f, Violine f. **violinist** n Geiger(in).

viper ['vaipə] n Viper f, Natter f.

virgin ['vəːdʒin] n Jungfrau f. adj jungfräulich; (soil) unbebaut. **virginity** n Jungfernschaft f.

Virgo ['vəːgou] n Jungfrau f.

virile ['virail] adj männlich, kräftig. **virility** n Männlichkeit f.

virtual ['vəːtʃuəl] adj eigentlich; (coll) praktisch. **virtually** adv praktisch.

virtue ['vəːtʃuː] n Tugend f. **by virtue of** wegen (+ gen). **virtuous** adj tugendhaft, rechtschaffen.

virtuoso [ˌvəːtju'ouzou] n Virtuose m, Virtuosin f. **virtuosity** n Virtuosität f.

virus ['vaiərəs] n Virus neut.

visa ['viːzə] n Visum neut.

viscount ['vaikaunt] n Vicomte m.

viscous ['viskəs] adj zähflüssig. **viscosity** n Viskosität f.

visible ['vizəbl] adj sichtbar. **visibility** n Sichtbarkeit f. **visibly** adj offenbar.

vision ['viʒən] n (power of sight) Sehvermögen neut; (insight) Einsicht f; (mystical, etc.) Vision f. **field of vision** Blickfeld neut. **visionary** adj phantastisch; n Hellseher(in).

visit ['vizit] v besuchen. n Besuch m. **visitation** n Besuchen neut. **visiting** adj Besuchs-. **visitor** n Besucher(in). **visitor's book** Gästebuch neut.

visor ['vaizə] n Visier neut; (peak) Schirm m.

visual ['viʒuəl] adj visuell. **visual aids** Anschauungsmaterial neut. **visualize** v vergegenwärtigen.

vital ['vaitl] adj lebenswichtig. **vitality** n Lebenskraft f.

vitamin ['vitəmin] n Vitamin neut.

vivacious [vi'veiʃəs] adj lebhaft, munter. **vivacity** n Lebhaftigkeit f.

vivid ['vivid] adj (description) lebendig; (colour) leuchtend; (imagination) lebhaft.

vixen ['viksn] n Füchsin f.

vocabulary [və'kabjuləri] n Wortschatz m; (glossary) Wörterverzeichnis neut.

vocal ['voukəl] adj stimmlich; (music) Vokal-. **vocal cords** pl Stimmbänder pl. **vocalist** n Sänger(in).

vocation [vou'keiʃən] n (rel) Berufung f; (occupation) Beruf m. **vocational** adj Berufs-.

vociferous [və'sifərəs] adj brüllend, lärmend.

vodka ['vodkə] n Wodka m.

voice [vois] n Stimme f. v ausdrücken, äußern.

void [void] adj leer; (invalid) nichtig, ungültig.

volatile ['volətail] adj flüchtig; (person) wankelmütig, sprunghaft.

volcano [vol'keinou] n Vulkan m. **volcanic** adj vulkanisch. **volcanic eruption** Vulkanausbruch m.

volley ['voli] n (mil) Salve f; (tennis) Flugschlag m.

volt [voult] n Volt neut. **voltage** n Spannung f.

volume ['voljum] n Volumen neut, Inhalt m; (book) Band m; (noise level) Lautstärke f.

voluntary ['vɒləntri] *adj* freiwillig.
volunteer [vɒlən'tiə] *n* Freiwillige(r). *adj* Freiwilligen-. *v* sich freiwillig melden.
voluptuous [və'lʌptʃuəs] *adj* wollüstig. **voluptuousness** *n* Wollust *f*.
vomit ['vɒmit] *v* (sich) erbrechen.
voodoo ['vuːduː] *n* Wodu *m*.
voracious [və'reiʃəs] *adj* gierig.
vote [vout] *n* (*individual*) Stimme *f*; (*right to vote*) Stimmrecht *neut*; (*election*) Abstimmung *f*, Wahl *f*. **vote of no confidence** Mißtrauensvotum *neut*. *v* abstimmen. **vote for** stimmen für. **voter** *n* Wähler(in).
vouch [vautʃ] *v* (sich) bürgen für. **voucher** *n* Gutschein *m*. **vouchsafe** *v* gewähren.
vow [vau] *n* Gelübde *neut*. *v* schwören, geloben.
vowel ['vauəl] *n* Vokal *m*. *adj* vokalisch.
voyage ['vɒiidʒ] *n* Reise *f*. *v* reisen. **voyager** *n* Reisende(r).
vulgar ['vʌlgə] *adj* vulgär, ordinär. **vulgarity** *n* Ungezogenheit *f*.
vulnerable ['vʌlnərəbl] *adj* verwundbar.
vulture ['vʌltʃə] *n* Geier *m*.

W

wad [wɒd] *n* Bausch *m*; (*money*) Rolle *f*.
waddle ['wɒdl] *v* watscheln.
wade [weid] *v* waten.
wafer ['weifə] *n* Waffel *f*; (*rel*) Hostie *f*. **wafer-thin** *adj* hauchdünn.
waffle ['wɒfl] *n* Waffel *f*.
waft [wɒft] *v* wehen.
wag [wag] *v* **wag one's head** mit dem Kopf wackeln. **wag one's tail** wedeln.
wage [weidʒ] *n also* **wages** Lohn *m*. **wage agreement** Tarifvertrag *m*. **wage-earner** *n* Lohnempfänger(in). **wage freeze** *n* Lohnstopp *m*. **wage-packet** *n* Lohntüte *f*. *v* (*war*) führen.
waggle ['wagl] *v* wackeln (mit).
wagon ['wagən] *n* Wagen *m*; (*rail*) Waggon *m*.
waif [weif] *n* verwahrlostes Kind *neut*.
wail [weil] *v* jammern, wehklagen. **wailing** *n* Jammern *neut*.
waist [weist] *n* Taille *f*. **waistband** n Bund *m*. **waistcoat** *n* Weste *f*.
wait [weit] *v* warten. **no waiting** Parken

verboten. **wait and see** abwarten. **wait for** warten auf. **waiting-room** *n* Wartesaal *m*. **wait on** bedienen. *n* Wartezeit *f*. **waiter** *n* Kellner *m*. **waitress** *n* Kellnerin *f*.
waive [weiv] *v* verzichten auf.
*wake [weik] *v also* **waken** *or* **wake up** aufwachen, erwachen; (*awaken*) (auf)wecken, erwecken. **wakeful** *adj* wachsam. **waking** *adj* wach.
walk [wɔːk] *v* laufen, (zu Fuß) gehen. **walk out** streiken. **walk out on** im Stich lassen. **walk-over** *n* leichter Sieg *m*, Spaziergang *m*. *n* Spaziergang *m*; (*path*) Weg *m*. **go for a walk** einen Spaziergang machen, spazierengehen. **walk of life** Lebensstellung *f*.
wall [wɔːl] *n* Mauer *f*; (*internal*) Wand *f*. **wallpaper** *n* Tapete *f*; *v* tapezieren.
wallet ['wɒlit] *n* Brieftasche *f*, Geldtasche *f*.
wallop ['wɒləp] *v* prügeln. *n* (heftiger) Schlag *m*.
wallow ['wɒlou] *v* sich wälzen.
walnut ['wɔːlnʌt] *n* Walnuß *f*.
walrus ['wɔːlrəs] *n* Walroß *neut*.
waltz [wɔːlts] *n* Walzer *m*. *v* Walzer tanzen, walzen.
wand [wɒnd] *n* Rute *f*; (*magic*) Zauberstab *m*.
wander ['wɒndə] *v* wandern. **wander about** umherwandern. **wanderlust** *n* Wanderlust *f*. **wanderer** *n* Wanderer *m*. **wandering** *n* Wandern *neut*. *adj* wandernd.
wane [wein] *v* abnehmen.
wangle ['waŋɡl] *v* organisieren, (hinterherum) beschaffen. **wangler** *n* Schieber *m*.
want [wɒnt] *v* wollen; (*need*) benötigen; (*wish*) wünschen. **wants** *pl n* Bedürfnisse *pl*. **wanted** *adj* gesucht. **be found wanting** den Erwartungen nicht entsprechen.
wanton ['wɒntən] *adj* lüstern; (*cruelty, etc.*) rücksichtslos.
war [wɔː] *n* Krieg *m*. **be at war with** Kriegführen mit. **prisoner-of-war** Kriegsgefangene(r) *m*. **war crime** *n* Kriegsverbrechen *neut*. **warfare** *n* Kriegführung *f*. **warlike** *adj* kriegerisch. **war memorial** Kriegerdenkmal *neut*.
warble ['wɔːbl] *v* trillern.
ward [wɔːd] *n* (*town*) Bezirk *n*; (*hospital*) Station *f*; (*of court*) Mündel *neut*. *v* **ward off** abwehren. **warden** *n* Vorsteher *m*.
warder *n* Gefängniswärter *m*.

wardrobe ['wɔːdroub] *n* Kleiderschrank *m*; (*clothes*) Garderobe *f*.

wares [weɔz] *pl n* Waren *pl*.

warehouse ['weɔhaus] *n* Lager(haus) *neut*.

warm [wɔːm] *adj* warm. **warm-blooded** *adj* warmblütig. **warm-hearted** *adj* warmherzig. *v* (auf)wärmen. **warm up** *v* (*become warm*) warm werden; (*engine*) warmlaufen (lassen). **warmish** *adj* lauwarm. **warmth** *n* Wärme *f*.

warn [wɔːn] *v* warnen. **warn off** verwarnen. **warning** *n* Warnung *f*. *adj* warnend. **warning light** Warnlicht *neut*.

warp [wɔːp] *v* sich verziehen, krumm werden. **warped** *adj* verzogen.

warrant ['worɔnt] *n* Vollmacht *f*, Berechtigung *f*. **warrant of arrest** Haftbefehl *m*.

warren ['worɔn] *n* Kaninchengehege *neut*.

warrior ['woriɔ] *n* Krieger *m*.

wart [wɔːt] *n* Warze *f*.

wary ['weɔri] *adj* vorsichtig, behutsam. **wary of** auf der Hut vor.

was [woz] *V* be.

wash [woʃ] *v* waschen; (*oneself*) sich waschen; (*dishes*) spülen. **washbasin** *n* Waschbecken *neut*. **wash down** abwaschen. **washed-out** *adj* verblaßt; (*coll*) ermüdet. **washed-up** *adj* (*coll*) ruiniert, fertig. **washing** *n* (*laundry*) Wäsche *f*. **washing machine** Waschmaschine *f*. **washing powder** Waschmittel *neut*. **wash up** (ab)spülen, abwaschen. *n* Waschen *neut*, Wäsche *f*. **washable** *adj* waschecht. **washer** *n* (*tech*) Scheibe *f*, Dichtungsring *m*.

wasp [wosp] *n* Wespe *f*. **waspish** *adj* reizbar.

waste [weist] *v* verschwenden, vergeuden. **waste away** abnehmen, verfallen. *n* Verschwendung *f*; (*rubbish*) Abfall *m*. **waste of time** Zeitverschwendung *f*. *adj* (*land*) wüst; Abfall-. **lay waste** verwüsten. **waste-bin** *n* Abfalleimer *m*. **waste-paper basket** *n* Papierkorb *neut*. **wasteful** *adj* verschwenderisch.

watch [wotʃ] *v* (*guard*) bewachen; (*observe*) zusehen, beobachten; (*pay attention to*) achtgeben auf. **watch out!** paß auf! **watch out for** auf der Hut sein vor. **watch television** fernsehen. *n* Wache *f*; (*wristwatch*) Armbanduhr *f*. **keep watch** Wache halten. **watchdog** *n* Wachhund *m*. **watchman** *n* Wächter *m*. **watchful** *adj* wachsam.

water ['wɔːtɔ] *n* Wasser *neut*. *v* wässern. **water down** verwässern.

water-closet *n* (Wasser)Klosett *neut*, WC *neut*.

water-colour *n* Aquarell *neut*. *adj* Aquarell-.

watercress ['wɔːtɔkres] *n* Brunnenkresse *f*.

waterfall ['wɔːtɔfɔːl] *n* Wasserfall *m*.

watering-can *n* Gießkanne *f*.

water-lily *n* Seerose *f*, Wasserlilie *f*.

waterlogged ['wɔːtɔlogd] *adj* vollgesogen.

watermark ['wɔːtɔmaːk] *n* (*in paper*) Wasserzeichen *neut*.

water-melon *n* Wassermelone *f*.

water-mill *n* Wassermühle *f*.

waterproof ['wɔːtɔpruːf] *adj* wasserdicht. *n* Regenmantel *m*. *v* imprägnieren.

watershed ['wɔːtɔʃed] *n* Wasserscheide *f*.

water-ski *n* Wasserski *m*. *v* Wasserski fahren.

watertight ['wɔːtɔtait] *adj* wasserdicht; (*argument*) unanfechtbar.

water-way *n* Wasserstraße *f*.

waterworks ['wɔːtɔwɔːks] *pl n* Wasserwerk *neut sing*.

watery ['wɔːtɔri] *adj* wässerig; (*eyes*) tränend.

watt [wot] *n* Watt *neut*. **wattage** *n* Wattleistung *f*.

wave [weiv] *n* Welle *f*; (*gesture*) Wink *m*. **waveband** *n* Wellenband *neut*. **wavelength** *n* Wellenlänge *f*. *v* winken; (*hair*) in Wellen legen. **wavy** *adj* wellig; (*hair*) gewellt.

waver ['weivɔ] *v* schwanken.

wax¹ [waks] *n* Wachs *neut*. *v* (*floor*) bohnern. **waxen** *adj* wächsern. **waxwork** *n* Wachsfigur *f*.

wax² [waks] *v* (*increase*) wachsen; (*become*) werden.

way [wei] *n* Weg *m*; (*direction*) Richtung *f*; (*method*) Art *f*, Weise *f*; (*respect*) Hinsicht *f*, Beziehung *f*. **by the way** übrigens. **on the way** unterwegs. **out-of-the-way** *adj* abgelegen; (*odd*) ungewöhnlich.

*****waylay** [wei'lei] *v* auflauern (+ *dat*).

wayward ['weiwɔd] *adj* eigensinnig. **waywardness** *n* Eigensinn *m*.

we [wiː] *pl pron* wir.

weak [wiːk] *adj* schwach; (*liquids*) dünn. **weak-minded** *adj* charakterschwach. **weaken** *v* schwächen. *n* Schwächling *m*. **weakly** *adj*, *adv* schwächlich. **weakness** *n* Schwäche *f*; (*disadvantage*) Nachteil *m*; (*liking*) Vorliebe *f*.

wealth [welθ] *n* Reichtum *m*; (*fortune*) Vermögen *neut*. **wealthy** *adj* reich, wohlhabend.

wean [wiin] *v* entwöhnen.

weapon ['wepən] *n* Waffe *f*.

***wear** [weə] *v* tragen; (*wear out*) abnutzen; (*become worn*) abgenutzt werden; *n* Tragen *neut*; (*wear and tear*) Abnutzung *f*, Verschleiß *m*. **wear off** (*fig*) sich verlieren. **wear out** (*person*) ermüden.

weary ['wiəri] *adj* müde; (*task*) lästig. *v* ermüden; (*become tired of*) müde werden (+*gen*). **weariness** *n* Müdigkeit *f*. **wearisome** *adj* ermüdend, langweilig.

weasel ['wizl] *n* Wiesel *neut*.

weather ['weðə] *n* Wetter *neut*. **weather-beaten** *adj* verwittert. **weathercock** *n* Wetterhahn *m*. **weather forecast** Wettervorhersage *f*. **weatherman** *n* (*coll*) Meteorologe *m*. **weather-proof** *adj* wetterfest.

***weave** [wiiv] *v* weben. **weave into** einflechten in. **weaving** *n* Weberei *f*; *adj* Web-.

web [web] *n* (*spider's*) Spinngewebe *neut*. **webbed foot** Schwimmfuß *m*. **webbing** *n* Gewebe *neut*. **web-footed** *adj* schwimmfüßig.

wedding ['wedin] *n* Hochzeit *f*. **wedding cake** Hochzeitskuchen *m*. **wedding day** Hochzeitstag *m*. **wedding ring** Trauring *m*.

wedge [wedʒ] *n* Keil *m*; (*of cheese*) Ecke *f*. **wedge-shaped** *adj* keilförmig. *v* einkeilen.

Wednesday ['wenzdi] *n* Mittwoch *m*. **on Wednesdays** mittwochs.

weed [wiid] *n* Unkraut *neut*. *v* (*Unkraut*) jäten. **weedy** *adj* (*coll*) schmächtig.

week [wiik] *n* Woche *f*. **weekday** *n* Wochentag *m*. **weekend** *n* Wochenende *neut*. **weekly** *adj* wöchentlich; *n* (*magazine*) Wochenzeitschrift *f*.

***weep** [wiip] *v* weinen. **weeping** *adj* weinend; *n* Weinen *neut*. **weeping willow** Trauerweide *f*.

weigh [wei] *v* wiegen. **weigh one's words** seine Worte abwägen. **weigh up** abschätzen. **weight** *n* Gewicht *neut*. **carry weight with** viel gelten bei. **lose weight** abnehmen. **put on weight** zunehmen. **weight-lifting** *n* Gewichtheben *neut*. **weighty** *adj* schwerwiegend.

weir [wiə] *n* Wehr *neut*.

weird [wiəd] *adj* unheimlich.

welcome ['welkəm] *n* Willkommen *neut*. *adj*, *interj* willkommen. **you're welcome** (*coll*) bitte, nichts zu danken. *v* willkommen heißen; (*fig*) begrüßen.

weld [weld] *v* (ver)schweißen. *n* Schweißstelle *f*, Schweißnaht *f*. **welder** *n* Schweißer *m*. **welding** *n* Schweißen *neut*.

welfare ['welfeə] *n* Wohlfahrt *f*. **welfare state** Wohlfahrtsstaat *m*.

well¹ [wel] *n* (*for water*) Brunnen *m*, Quelle *f*.

well² [wel] *adv* gut. **as well** auch. **as well as** sowohl ... als auch. **you may well ask** du kannst wohl fragen. *adj* (*healthy*) wohl, gesund. **feel well** sich wohl fühlen. **I'm not well** mir ist nicht wohl. *interj* na, schön.

well-being *n* Wohlergehen *neut*.

well-behaved *adj* artig.

well-bred *adj* wohlerzogen.

well-built *adj* gut gebaut; (*person*) kräftig gebaut.

well-done *adj* (*meat*) gut durchgebraten.

wellingtons ['welintənz] *pl n* Gummistiefel *pl*.

well-known *adj* (wohl)bekannt.

well-meaning *adj* wohlmeinend.

well-off *adj* wohlhabend.

well-paid *adj* gut bezahlt.

well-spoken *adj* höflich.

well-to-do *adj* wohlhabend.

well-worn *adj* abgenutzt; (*phrase*) abgedroschen.

went [went] *V* go.

wept [wept] *V* weep.

west [west] *n* Westen *m*. *adj* also **westerly** westlich, West-. *adv* also **westwards** nach Westen; westwärts. **western** *adj* westlich; *n* Wildwestfilm *m*.

wet [wet] *adj* naß. **wet through** durchnäßt. **wet weather** Regenwetter *neut*. *n* Nässe *f*. *v* anfeuchten, naßmachen. **wetness** *n* Nässe *f*.

whack [wak] *v* schlagen, verhauen. *n* Schlag *m*.

whale [weil] *n* Wal *m*, Walfisch *m*. **whaler** *n* Walfänger *m*. **whaling** *n* Walfang *m*.

wharf [woif] *n* Kai *m*.

what [wot] *pron* was. **so what?** na und? **what about ... ?** wie wäre es mit ... ? **whatever** *pron* was auch immer. **nothing whatever** überhaupt nichts. **what for?** wozu? **what's up?** was ist los? **what's your**

name? wie heißt du? *or* (*polite*) wie ist Ihr Name? *adj* was für ein, welch.
wheat [wiːt] *n* Weizen *m.*
wheel [wiːl] *n* Rad *neut*; (*steering*) Lenkrad *neut*. **at the wheel** am Steuer. *v* rollen. **wheelbarrow** *n* Schubkarren *m.*
wheelchair *n* Rollstuhl *m.*
wheeze [wiːz] *n* Keuchen *neut*; (*coll*) Plan *m. v* keuchen, schnaufen.
whelk [welk] *n* Wellhornschnecke *f.*
when [wen] *adv* (*question*) wann. *conj* (*with past tense*) als; (*with present tense*) wenn. **whenever** *conj* wann auch immer.
where [weə] *adv*, *conj* wo; (*motion*) wohin. **where from?** woher? **where to?** wohin? *where do you come from?* wo kommen Sie her? *where are you going?* wo gehen Sie hin? **whereabouts** *adv* wo; *n* Verbleib *m*. **whereas** *conj* wohingegen, während. **whereby** *adv* wodurch, womit. **whereupon** *adv* woraufhin. **wherever** *adv* wo auch immer.
whether ['weðə] *conj* ob.
which [witʃ] *pron* (*question*) welch; (*the one that*) welch, der/die/das.
whiff [wif] *n* Hauch *m.*
while [wail] *conj* während; (*whereas*) wogegen. *n* Weile *f.* **a long while ago** schon lange her. **for a while** eine Zeitlang. **in a while** bald. *v* **while away the time** sich die Zeit vertreiben.
whim [wim] *n* Laune *f*, Einfall *m.*
whimper ['wimpə] *n* Wimmer *neut. v* wimmern.
whimsical ['wimzikl] *adj* launenhaft.
whine [wain] *n* Gewinsel *neut. v* winseln. **whining** *adj* weinerlich.
whip [wip] *n* Peitsche *f. v* peitschen; (*cream*) schlagen. **whipped cream** Schlagsahne *f.* **whipping** *n* Peitschen *neut.* **whipround** *n* (*coll*) Geldsammlung *f.*
whippet ['wipit] *n* Whippet *m.*
whirl [wəːl] *n* Wirbel *m. v* wirbeln. **whirlwind** *n* Wirbelwind *m.*
whisk [wisk] *n* Schneebesen *m. v* schlagen. **whisk away/off** *v* wegzaubern.
whiskers ['wiskəz] *pl n* (*animals*) Schnurrhaare *pl*; (*man's*) Barthaare *pl.*
whisky ['wiski] *n* Whisky *m.*
whisper ['wispə] *v* flüstern. *n* Flüstern *m.*
whist [wist] *n* Whist *neut.*
whistle ['wisl] *v* pfeifen. *n* Pfiff *m*; (*instrument*) Pfeife *f.*
white [wait] *adj* weiß; (*pale*) blaß. **white**

bread Weißbrot *neut.* **white lie** Notlüge *f.* **white man** Weiße(r) *m.* **whitewash** *v* tünchen. **white wine** Weißwein *m. n* Weiß *neut*; (*person*) Weiße(r). **whiten** *v* weiß machen; (*bleach*) bleichen. **whiteness** *n* Weiße *f.*
whiting ['waitiŋ] *n* Weißfisch *m.*
Whitsun ['witsn] *n* Pfingsten *neut sing.*
whiz [wiz] *v* zischen.
who [huː] *pron* (*question*) wer; (*the one which, that*) wer, welch, der/die/das. **whoever** *pron* wer auch immer.
whole [houl] *adj* ganz; (*undamaged*) heil, unverletzt. *n* das Ganze *neut*; (*collective*) Gesamtheit *f.* **on the whole** im großen und ganzen.
whole-hearted *adj* rückhaltlos.
wholemeal ['houlmiːl] *adj* Vollkorn-.
wholesale ['houlseil] *adv* en gros; (*fig*) unterschiedslos. *adj* Großhandels-. *n* Großhandel *m.* **wholesaler** *n* Großhändler *m.*
wholesome ['houlsəm] *adj* bekömmlich, gesund.
whom [huːm] *pron* (*question*) (*acc*) wen, (*dat*) wem; (*that, the one whom*) den, dem.
whooping cough ['huːpiŋ] *n* Keuchhusten *m.*
whore [hoː] *n* Hure *f. v* huren.
whose [huːz] *pron* (*question*) wessen; (*of whom*) dessen, deren. *whose is this?* wem gehört dies?
why [wai] *adv* warum. *interj* nun, ja. **that is why** deshalb. **the reason why** der Grund, weshalb.
wick [wik] *n* Docht *m.*
wicked ['wikid] *adj* böse. **wickedness** *n* Bosheit *f.*
wicker ['wikə] *adj* Weiden-, Korb-. **wickerwork** *n* Korbwaren *pl.*
wicket ['wikit] *n* (*gate*) Pförtchen *neut.*
wide [waid] *adj* breit. *adv* weit. **far and wide** weit und breit. **wide awake** hellwach. **widespread** *adj* weitverbreitet. **widely** *adv* weit. **widely known** allgemein bekannt. **widen** *v* breiter machen *or* werden. **wideness** *n* Breite *f.*
widow ['widou] *n* Witwe *f.* **widowed** *adj* verwitwet. **widower** *n* Witwer *m.* **widowhood** *n* Witwenstand *m.*
width [widθ] *n* Breite *f*, Weite *f.*
wield [wiːld] *v* (*weapon*) handhaben; (*influence*) ausüben.

wife [waif] *n* (*pl* **wives**) Frau *f*.
wig [wig] *n* Perücke *f*.
wiggle ['wigl] *v* wackeln. *n* Wackeln *neut*.
wild [waild] *adj* wild; (*coll*: *angry*) wütend. **be wild about** (*coll*) schwärmen für. **wildcat strike** wilder Streik *m*. **wild flower** Feldblume *f*. **Wildness** *n* Wildheit *f*.
wilderness ['wildənəs] *n* Wüste *f*.
wilful ['wilfəl] *adj* eigensinnig. **wilfulness** *n* Eigensinn *m*.
will[1] [wil] *v* (*to form future*) werden; (*expressing wish or determination*) wollen.
will[2] [wil] *n* Wille *m*; (*testament*) Testament *neut*. **will-power** *n* Willenskraft *f*.
willing [wiliŋ] *adj* bereit. **willingly** *adv* bereitwillig. **willingness** *n* Bereitschaft *f*.
willow ['wilou] *n* Weide *f*.
wilt [wilt] *v* verwelken.
wily ['waili] *adj* schlau, listig.
***win** [win] *v* gewinnen; (*mil*) siegen. *n* Seig *m*.
wince [wins] *v* zusammenzucken. *n* (Zusammen)Zucken *neut*.
winch [wintʃ] *n* Winde *f*.
wind[1] [wind] *n* Wind *m*. **wind instrument** Blasinstrument *neut*.
***wind**[2] [waind] *v* (sich) winden; (*yarn*) aufwickeln; (*clock*) aufziehen. **wind up** (*come to a close*) Schluß machen. (*business*) auflösen. **winder** *n* Winde *f*. **winding** *adj* sich windend, schlängelnd.
windlass ['windləs] *n* Winde *f*.
windmill ['wind,mil] *n* Windmühle *f*.
windpipe ['windpaip] *n* Luftröhre *f*.
window ['windou] *n* Fenster *neut*; (*ticket office, etc.*) Schalter *m*; (*shop*) Schaufenster *neut*. **window-box** *n* Blumenkasten *m*. **window-frame** *n* Fensterrahmen *m*. **window-pane** *n* Fensterscheibe *f*. **window-shopping** *n* Schaufensterbummel *m*. **window-sill** Fensterbrett *neut*.
windshield ['windʃild] *n* Windschutzscheibe *f*. **windshield-wiper** Scheibenwischer *m*.
windy ['windi] *adj* windig.
wine [wain] *n* Wein *m*. **wine bar** Weinstube *f*. **wineglass** *n* Weinglas *neut*.
wing [wiŋ] *n* Flügel *m*; (*theatre*) Kulisse *f*; (*mot*) Kotflügel *m*. **on the wing** im Fluge. **winged** *adj* geflügelt. **winger** *n* (*sport*) Außenstürmer *m*. **wing-nut** *n* Flügelmutter *f*.
wink [wiŋk] *n* Zwinkern *neut*. *v* **wink at** zuzwinkern (+ *dat*).

winkle ['wiŋkl] *n* Strandschnecke *f*.
winner ['winə] *n* Sieger(in), Gewinner(in).
winnings *pl n* Gewinn *m sing*.
winter ['wintə] *n* Winter *m*. *v* überwintern. **wintry** *adj* winterlich.
wipe [waip] *v* wischen. **wipe out** (*destroy*) ausrotten. **wipe up** (*dishes*) abtrocknen. **wiper** *n* Wischer *m*.
wire [waiə] *n* Draht *m*; (*telegram*) Telegramm *neut*. **wire netting** Maschendraht *m*. *v* (*house, etc.*) Leitungen legen in. **wireless** *n* Radio *neut*. **wiring** *n* Leitungsnetz *neut*.
wiry ['waiəri] *adj* (*person*) sehnig, zäh, (*hair*) borstig.
wisdom ['wizdəm] *n* Weisheit *f*. **wisdom tooth** *n* Weisheitszahn *m*.
wise [waiz] *adj* weise, klug. **wise guy** (*coll*) Besserwisser *m*. **wise man/woman** Weise(r).
wish [wiʃ] *v* wünschen. **wish for** sich wünschen. *I wish to know* ich möchte wissen. **wished-for** *adj* erwünscht. *n* Wunsch *m*.
wisp [wisp] *n* (*hair*) Strähne *f*. **wispy** *adj* (*hair*) wuschelig.
wistful ['wistfəl] *adj* sehnsüchtig. **wistfulness** *n* Sehnsucht *f*.
wit [wit] *n* Witz *m*, Esprit *m*. **wits** *pl* Verstand *m*.
witch [witʃ] *n* Hexe *f*. **witchcraft** *n* Hexerei *f*. **witch-doctor** *n* Medizinmann *m*.
with [wið] *prep* mit; (*among people*) bei. **weep with joy** vor Freude weinen. **stay with** bleiben bei.
***withdraw** [wið'drɔ] *v* (sich) zurückziehen; (*remark*) zurücknehmen; (*money*) abheben. **withdrawal** *n* Zurückziehung *f*; Zurücknahme *f*; Abhebung *f*. **withdrawn** *adj* zurückgezogen.
wither ['wiðə] *v* verdorren, verwelken. **withered** *adj* welk.
***withhold** [wið'hould] *v* zurückhalten.
within [wi'ðin] *prep* innerhalb (+ *gen*). *adv* darin, innen. **within a short time** binnen kurzem.
without [wi'ðaut] *prep* ohne (+ *acc*).
***withstand** [wið'stand] *v* widerstehen (+ *dat*).
witness ['witnis] *n* Zeuge *m*, Zeugin *f*. **bear witness to** Zeuge ablegen von. **witness-box** *n* Zeugenstand *m*. *v* bezeugen; (*be present at*) erleben, sehen.

wrap

witty ['witi] *adj* witzig. **witticism** *n* Witz *m*.

wizard ['wizəd] *n* Zauberer *m*. **wizardry** *n* Zauberei *f*.

wobble ['wobl] *v* wackeln, schwanken. *n* Wackeln *neut*. **wobbly** *adj* wackelig.

woke [wouk] *V* **wake**.

woken ['woukn] *V* **wake**.

wolf [wulf] *n* (*pl* **wolves**) Wolf *m*. *v* (*gobble*) verschlingen. **she-wolf** *n* Wölfin *f*.

woman ['wumən] *n* (*pl* **women**) Frau *f*. **woman doctor** Ärztin *f*. **womanly** *adj* weiblich, fraulich.

womb [wuːm] *n* Gebärmutter *f*.

won [wʌn] *V* **win**.

wonder ['wʌndə] *n* (*marvel*) Wunder *neut*; (*astonishment*) Erstaunen *neut*, Verwunderung *f*. **no wonder** kein Wunder. *v* (*be surprised*) sich wundern; (*ask oneself*, *muse*) sich fragen, gespannt sein. **wonderful** *adj* wunderbar. **wondrous** *adj* erstaunlich.

wonky ['woŋki] *adj* wackelig.

wood [wud] *n* Holz *neut*; (*forest*) Wald *m*. **wooden** *adj* hölzern, Holz-.

woodcock ['wudkok] *n* Waldschnepfe *f*.

woodpecker ['wudpekə] *n* Specht *m*.

wood-pigeon *n* Ringeltaube *f*.

woodwind ['wudwind] *n* Holzblasinstrument *neut*; Holzbläser *m*.

woodwork ['wudwəːk] *n* Holzarbeit *f*, Tischlerei *f*.

woodworm ['wudwəːm] *n* Holzwurm *m*.

woody ['wudi] *adj* Holz-, holzig; (*countryside*) Wald-, waldig.

wool [wul] *n* Wolle *f*. **woollen** *adj* wollen, Woll-. **woolly** *adj* wollig.

word [wəːd] *n* Wort *neut*. **break/keep one's word** sein Wort brechen/halten. **wording** *n* Fassung *f*. **wordy** *adj* wortreich, langatmig.

wore [woː] *V* **wear**.

work [wəːk] *n* Arbeit *f*; (*piece of work, art, music, etc.*) Werk *neut*. **works** *pl* Werk *neut*. *v* arbeiten; (*of machine*) laufen, funktionieren; (*succeed*) klappen; (*land*) bebauen; (*metal*) schmieden; (*operate* (*machine*)) bedienen. **work off** (*debt*) abarbeiten; (*feelings*) abreagieren. **work out** ausrechnen. **out of work** arbeitslos. **worked-up** *adj* aufgeregt, aufgebracht. **worker** *n* Arbeiter(in). **working** *adj* Arbeits-; (*person*) berufstätig. **working class** Arbeiterklasse *f*; *adj* Arbeiter-. **in working order** betriebsfähig.

working party Arbeitsgruppe *f*. **workman** *n* Handwerker *m*. **work-to-rule** *n* Bummelstreik *m*.

world [wəːld] *n* Welt *f*. **not for all the world** nicht um alles in der Welt. **the world to come** das Jenseits *neut*. **world champion** Weltmeister(in). **world-famous** *adj* weltberühmt. **worldly-wise** *adj* weltklug. **world-wide** *adj* weitverbreitet. **worldly** *adj* irdisch.

worm [wəːm] *n* Wurm *m*.

worn [woːn] *v* **wear**. *adj* (*worn out*) abgenutzt. **worn out** *adj* (*thing*) abgenutzt; (*person*) todmüde.

worry ['wʌri] *v* (*bother*) beunruhigen; (*be worried*) sich Sorgen machen, sich beunruhigen. *n* Sorge *f*, Besorgnis *f*. **worrying** *adj* beunruhigend. **worried** *adj* beunruhigt, besorgt.

worse [wəːs] *adj, adv* schlimmer, schlechter. **worse and worse** immer schlechter. **worsen** *v* (sich) verschlechtern *or* verschlimmern.

worship ['wəːʃip] *n* Anbetung *f*, Verehrung *f*; (*in church*) Gottesdienst *m*. *v* anbeten, verehren. **worshipful** *adj* ehrwürdig. **worshipper** *n* Anbeter(in).

worst [wəːst] *adj* schlechtest, schlimmst. *adv* am schlechtesten *or* schlimmsten. **at the worst** im schlimmsten Falle.

worsted ['wustid] *n* Kammgarn *neut*.

worth [wəːθ] *n* Wert *m*. *adj* wert. **it's worth ten marks** es ist zehn Mark wert. **it's not worth it** es lohnt sich nicht. **worthless** *adj* wertlos. **worthwhile** *adj* der Mühe wert. **worthy** *adj* würdig, wert.

would [wud] *v* (*to form conditional*) würde, würdest, etc. (*used to*) pflegte, pflegtest, etc; (*expressing desire, volition*) wollte, wolltest, etc. *he would go* (*if*) er würde gehen(wenn). *I would like* ich möchte. *he would come in the summer* er pflegte im Sommer zu kommen. *he would not come* er wollte durchaus nicht kommen.

wound¹ [waund] *V* **wind²**.

wound² [wuːnd] *n* Wunde *f*. *v* verwunden. **wounded** *adj* verletzt.

wove [wouv] *V* **weave**.

woven ['wouvn] *V* **weave**.

wrangle ['raŋgl] *v* zanken, streiten. *n* Zank *m*, Streit *m*.

wrap [rap] *v* wickeln. **wrap up** einwickeln. *n* Schal *m*. **wrapper** *n* Umschlag *m*. **wrap-**

ping n Verpackung f. **wrapping paper** Einwickelpapier neut.
wreath [riːθ] n Kranz m.
wreck [rek] n wrack neut; (naut) Schiffbruch m. v zerstören. **wreckage** n Trümmer pl.
wren [ren] n Zaunkönig m.
wrench [rentʃ] v zerren, ziehen. n (tool) Schraubenschlüssel m.
wrestle ['resl] v ringen. **wrestler** n Ringer m. **wrestling** n Ringkampf m, Ringen neut.
wretch [retʃ] n Elende(r), armes Wesen neut. **wretched** adj unglücklich, elend.
wriggle ['rigl] v sich schlängeln. n Schlängeln neut.
***wring** [riŋ] v (hands) ringen; (clothes) auswringen. **wringer** n Wringermaschine f. **wringing wet** triefend naß.
wrinkle ['riŋkl] n (face, brow) Runzel f, Falte f; (paper) Knitter m. **wrinkled** adj runzlig.
wrist [rist] n Handgelenk neut. **wristwatch** n Armbanduhr f.
writ [rit] n (law) (Vor)Ladung f. **Holy Writ** Heilige Schrift f.
***write** [rait] v schreiben. **write down** aufschreiben. **write off** abschreiben. **write out** (cheque) ausstellen. **writer** n Schriftsteller(in). **writing** n Schreiben neut. **in writing** schriftlich. **writing-paper** n Schreibpapier neut.
written ['ritn] V write. adj schriftlich.
writhe [raið] v sich winden.
wrong [roŋ] adj (incorrect) falsch; (bad, immoral) unrecht. **be wrong** sich irren, unrecht haben. **what's wrong with ... ?** was ist los mit ... ? that was wrong of you das war unrecht von dir. **go wrong** (mech) kaputtgehen; (plan) schiefgehen. **get it wrong** es ganz falsch verstehen. **wrongdoer** n Missetäter(in). **wrongdoing** n Missetat f. **wrongly** adv mit Unrecht.
wrote [rout] V write.
wrought iron [,roit'aiən] n Schweißeisen neut.
wrung [rʌŋ] V wring.
wry [rai] adj verschroben.

X

xenophobia [,zenə'foubiə] n Fremdenfeindlichkeit f.
Xerox ® ['ziəroks] n Fotokopiergerät neut. v fotokopieren.
X-ray [eks'rei] n Röntgenstrahl m; (picture) Röntgenbild neut. v röntgen. adj Röntgen-.
xylophone ['zailəfoun] n Xylophon neut.

Y

yacht [jot] n Jacht f. **yachting** n Segeln neut.
yank [jaŋk] v (coll) heftig ziehen (an). n Ruck m.
yap [jap] v kläffen; (coll) schwätzen. n Kläffen neut.
yard¹ [jaɪd] n (measure) Yard neut. **yardstick** n Maßstab m.
yard² [jaɪd] n Hof m.
yarn [jaɪn] n Garn neut; (story) Geschichte f.
yawn [joɪn] n Gähnen neut. v gähnen.
year [jiə] n Jahr neut. **5 years old** fünf Jahre alt. **for years** jahrelang. **yearbook** n Jahrbuch neut. **yearly** adj jährlich.
yearn [jəɪn] v sich sehnen (nach). **yearning** n Sehnsucht f.
yeast [jiɪst] n Hefe f.
yell [jel] v (gellend) aufschreien. n Schrei m.
yellow ['jelou] adj gelb. n Gelb neut.
yelp [jelp] v jaulen. n Jaulen neut.
yes [jes] adv ja, jawohl. **yes-man** n Jasager m.
yesterday ['jestədi] n, adv gestern. **yesterday morning** gestern früh. **yesterday's** or **of yesterday** gestrig, von gestern. **the day before yesterday** vorgestern.
yet [jət] adv noch, immer noch. conj aber.
yew [juɪ] n Eibe f.
yield [jiɪld] n Ertrag m. **yielding** adj ergiebig.
yoga ['jougə] n Joga m.
yoghurt ['jogət] n Joghurt m.
yoke [jouk] n Joch m. v verbinden.
yolk [jouk] n Eidotter m, Eigelb neut.
yonder ['jondə] adv da, dort drüben. adj jene(r).

you [juː] *pron* (*fam sing*) du; (*fam pl*) ihr; (*polite sing or pl*) Sie; (*impers, one*) man. *acc*: dich; euch; Sie; einen. *dat*: dir; euch; Ihnen; einem.

young [jʌŋ] *adj* jung. *n* (Tier)Junge *pl*. young children kleine Kinder *pl*.

your [jɔː] *adj* (*fam sing*) dein; (*fam pl*) euer; (*polite sing or pl*) Ihr; (*impers, one's*) sein. yours (der/die/das) deine *or* eure *or* Ihre *or* seine. *a friend of yours* ein Freund von dir.

youth [juːθ] *n* Jugend *f*; (*lad*) Jüngling *m*. *adj* Jugend-. youth hostel Jugendherberge *f*. youthful *adj* jugendlich, jung.

Yugoslavia [juːgouˈslɑːvjə] *n* Jugoslawien *neut*. Yugoslav *n* Jugoslawe *m*, Jugoslawin *f*. *adj* jugoslawisch.

Z

zeal [ziːl] *n* Eifer *m*. zealous *adj* eifrig.

zebra [ˈzebrə] *n* Zebra *neut*. zebra crossing *n* Zebrastreifen *m*.

zero [ˈziərou] *n* Null *f*.

zest [zest] *n* Lust *f*, Begeisterung *f*.

zigzag [ˈzigzag] *adj* Zickzack-. *n* Zickzack *m*.

zinc [ziŋk] *n* Zink *neut*.

zip [zip] *n also* zipper Reißverschluß *m*. zip code Postleitzahl *f*.

zodiac [ˈzoudiak] *n* Tierkreis *m*. signs of the zodiac Tierkreiszeichen *pl*.

zone [zoun] *n* Zone *f*.

zoo [zuː] *n* Zoo *m*. zoological *adj* zoologisch. zoologist *n* Zoologe *m*. zoology *n* Zoologie *f*, Tierkunde *f*.

zoom [zuːm] *v* summen, brummen; (*coll: rush*) sausen; (*prices*) Hochschnellen. zoom lens *n* Zoom(objektiv) *neut*.

German—Englisch

German–English

A

Aal [aːl] *m* (*pl* **-e**) eel.
ab [ap] *adv* off; *prep* (*abwärts, nach unten*) from; (*weg, fort*) from. **ab und zu** now and again, from time to time. **auf und ab** up and down, to and fro.
abänderlich ['apɛndərliç] *adj* variable. **abändern** *v* change, modify. **Abänderung** *f* modification; (*Pol*) amendment.
abarbeiten ['aparbaitən] (*Schuld*) work off; (*Werkzeug*) wear out. **sich die Finger abarbeiten** work one's fingers to the bone.
Abbau ['apbau] *m* (*unz.*) demolition; (*Personal*) reduction of staff, staff-cut. **abbauen** *v* demolish; (*Personal*) cut.
abbestellen ['apbəʃtɛlən] *v* cancel.
*abbiegen ['apbiːgən] *v* deflect, turn aside; (*Straße*) bend; (*Mot*) turn off.
Abbild ['apbilt] *neut* image, likeness. **abbilden** *v* illustrate, depict. **Abbildung** *f* illustration, drawing.
abblenden ['apblɛndən] *v* (*Mot*) dip one's headlights.
*abbrechen ['apbrɛçən] *v* break off; (*Blumen, Obst*) pick; (*abbauen*) demolish; (*Lager*) break.
*abbringen ['apbriŋən] *v* dissuade, put off; (*entfernen*) remove.
Abbruch ['apbrux] *m* (*unz.*) (*Haus*) demolition; (*Einstellung*) stop, cessation.
abdanken ['apdaŋkən] *v* (*König*) abdicate; (*Beamter*) resign. **Abdankung** *f* (*pl* **-en**) abdication; resignation.
abdecken ['apdɛkən] *v* uncover; (*Tisch*) clear; (*schützen*) shield, cover; (*Verlust*) make good.
abdichten ['apdiçtən] *v* seal up; (*wasserdicht machen*) make watertight.
Abdomen [ap'doːmən] *neut* abdomen. **abdominal** *adj* abdominal.
abdrehen ['apdreiən] *v* unscrew, twist off; (*Hals*) wring.
Abdruck ['apdruk] *m* reprint, new impression; (*Finger-*) print. **abdrucken** *v* print.
abdrücken ['apdrykən] *v* (*Pistole*) fire.
Abend ['aːbənt] *m* (*pl* **-e**) evening. **gestern abend** yesterday evening, last night. **–brot** *or* **–essen** *neut* supper, dinner. **–land** *neut* West, Occident. **–mahl** *neut* Holy Communion. **abends** *adv* in the evening(s).
Abenteuer ['aːbəntɔyər] *neut* (pl **-**) adventure. **abenteuerlich** *adj* adventurous. **Abenteurer** *m* adventurer.
aber ['aːbər] *conj* but; (*jedoch*) however. **das ist aber schrecklich!** that's just awful!
Aberglaube ['aːbərglaubə] *m* superstition. **abergläubisch** *adj* superstitious.
aberkennen ['apɛrkɛnən] *v* deprive, dispossess.
abermals ['aːbərmals] *adv* again, once more.
*abfahren ['apfaːrən] *v* set off, depart; (*Mot*) drive off. **Abfahrt** *f* departure; (*Ski*) descent, downhill run.
Abfall ['apfal] **1** (*unz.*) falling off, decline; (*Neigung*) slope. **2** *m* waste, rubbish. **–eimer** *m* dustbin. **abfallen** *v* fall off, decline. **abfällig** *adj* disparaging.
abfassen ['apfasən] *v* compose, draw up, formulate. **Abfassung** *f* wording.
abfertigen ['apfɛrtigən] *v* (*Güter*) (prepare for) dispatch; (*Fahrzeug*) check over, prepare (for departure); (*Kundschaft*) see to.

abfinden ['apfindən] v pay off. **sich abfinden mit** come to terms with (auch fig) **Abfindung** f (pl -en) settlement, agreement.

***abfliegen** ['apfli:gən] fly away; (Flugzeug) take off.

***abfließen** ['apfli:sən] v flow away, drain off.

Abflug ['apflu:k] m (Flugzeug) take-off.

Abfluß ['apflus] m outflow, draining off. **-rohr** neut waste-pipe.

Abfuhr ['apfu:r] m removal. **abführen** v lead away. **Abführmittel** n laxative.

Abgabe ['apga:bə] f delivery, handing over; (Steuer) tax, duty. **Abgaben** pl (Verkauf) sales. **abgabenfrei** adj tax-free, duty-free.

Abgang ['apgaŋ] m (Zug, usw.) departure; (Abtreten) retirement; (Verlust) loss, depreciation.

Abgas ['apga:s] neut exhaust gas.

***abgeben** ['apge:bən] v give up, hand over; (Stimme) cast.

abgedroschen ['apgədrɔʃən] adj commonplace, hackneyed.

abgegriffen ['apgəgrifən] adj (Münze) worn; (Buch) dog-eared, well-thumbed.

***abgehen** ['apge:ən] v go away, depart; (Straße) branch off; (Knopf, usw.) come off.

abgemacht ['apgəmaxt] adj agreed.

Abgeordnete(r) ['apgəɔrdnətə(r)] delegate; (Parlament) Member of Parliament; (US) congressman. **Abgeordnetenhaus** neut parliament; (GB) House of Commons.

abgesehen ['apgəze:ən] prep **abgesehen von** apart from, except for.

abgestanden ['apgəʃtandən] adj stale; (Bier, usw.) flat.

abgestorben ['apgəʃtɔrbən] adj numb.

Abgott ['apgɔt] m idol.

abgrenzen ['apgrɛntsən] v (Gebiete) limit, mark off. **Abgrenzung** f demarcation, definition.

Abgrund ['apgrunt] m abyss.

abhalten ['aphaltən] v keep away; (hindern) hinder, stop; (Versammlung, usw.) hold.

Abhandlung ['aphandluŋ] f essay, written report.

Abhang ['aphaŋ] m slope.

abhauen ['aphauən] v cut off; (umg.) go away, (umg.) buzz off.

abhelfen ['aphɛlfən] v remedy, correct.

abholen ['apho:lən] v call for, pick up.

abhören ['aphœ:rən] v (Platte) listen to; (Gespräch) eavesdrop on; (Telef) monitor, listen in, tap; (Zeugen) question. **Abhörgerät** neut (electronic) listening device, bug.

Abitur [abi'tu:r] neut school-leaving exam, 'A'-levels.

abkanzeln ['apkantsəln] v scold, reprimand.

abkehren ['apke:rən] v sweep up. **sich abkehren** turn away.

abknöpfen ['apknœpfən] v unbutton.

Abkommen ['apkɔmən] neut (pl -) agreement, settlement.

abkühlen ['apky:lən] v cool, cool off.

Abkunft ['apkunft] f descent, lineage.

abkürzen ['apkyrtsən] v shorten; (Wort) abbreviate. **Abkürzung** f abbreviation; (Weg) short cut.

***abladen** ['apla:dən] v unload.

Ablauf ['aplauf] m (Abfluß) outlet, drain; (Verlauf) sequence of events; (Ende) expiry, end. **ablaufen** v drain, flow off; (Zeit) elapse; (Schuhe) wear out.

ablegen ['aple:gən] v put down; (Kleider) take off; (Gewohnheiten) give up.

ablehnen ['aple:nən] v reject, refuse; (Einladung) decline. **Ablehnung** f (pl -en) refusal.

ableiten ['aplaitən] v divert, lead away; (Flüssigkeit) draw off. **Ableitung** f diversion.

ablenken ['aplɛŋkən] v turn away, divert.

abliefern ['apli:fərn] v deliver. **Ablieferung** f delivery.

ablösen ['aplœ:zən] v (Person) relieve, replace; (Schuld) settle; (loslösen) loosen, free. **Ablösung** f relief; loosening.

abmachen ['apmaxən] v detach; (Geschäft) arrange, agree about. **Abmachung** f (pl -en) arrangement, agreement.

abmelden ['apmɛldən] v **sich abmelden** v give notice (of one's departure).

***abmessen** ['apmɛsən] v measure off; (Grundstück) survey; (Worte) weigh. **Abmessung** f measurement, dimension.

Abnahme ['apna:mə] f (pl -n) reduction, decrease; (Entfernung) removal.

***abnehmen** ['apne:mən] v take off, take away; (sich vermindern) decrease; (schlanker werden) lose weight, grow slim. **Abnehmer** m (pl -) customer, consumer.

Abneigung ['apnaiguŋ] f dislike, aversion.
abnorm [ap'nɔrm] adj abnormal.
Abnormität f (pl -en) abnormality.
abnutzen ['apnutsən] v wear out.
Abnutzung f wear (and tear).
Abonnement [abɔn'mã] neut (pl -s) subscription. **Abonnent** m (pl -en) subscriber. **abonnieren** v subscribe.
Abort [a'bɔrt] m (pl -e) lavatory.
abquälen ['apkvɛɪlən] v sich abquälen take great pains.
abraten ['apraɪtən] v advise against, dissuade from.
abräumen ['aprɔymən] v clear away.
abrechnen ['apreçnən] v settle; (abziehen) deduct. **abrechnen mit** settle up with.
Abrede ['apreɪdə] f agreement. **in Abrede stellen** deny. **abreden** v agree.
abreiben ['apraibən] v rub off; (trocknen) rub down.
Abreise ['apraizə] f departure. **abreisen** v depart, leave.
***abreißen** ['apraisən] v tear off; (Haus) demolish, tear down; (sich ablösen) break off.
Abrieb ['apriɪp] m abrasion, wear.
***abrufen** ['apruɪfən] v cancel, call off; (Person) recall.
abrüsten ['aprystən] v disarm. **Abrüstung** f disarmament.
Absage ['apzaːgə] f (pl -n) refusal. **absagen** v cancel, call off; (Einladung) decline, refuse.
Absatz ['apzats] **1** m (Pause) stop, break; (Schuh) heel; paragraph. **2** m (unz.) (Waren) sales (pl), turnover.
abschaffen ['apʃafən] v abolish, do away with. **Abschaffung** f abolition.
abschalten ['apʃaltən] v switch off.
abschätzen ['apʃɛtsən] v estimate, appraise. **Abschätzung** f estimate, assessment.
Abscheu ['apʃɔy] m or f horror, revulsion. **abscheulich** adj horrible, revolting.
abschicken ['apʃikən] v send off or away.
Abschied ['apʃiɪt] m (pl -e) departure, leaving. **Abschied nehmen von** say goodbye to, take one's leave of.
***abschießen** ['apʃiɪsən] v (Gewehr) fire; (Flugzeug) shoot down.
Abschlag ['apʃlaɪk] m reduction, rebate. **abschlagen** v strike off; (ablehnen) refuse.
***abschließen** ['apʃliɪsən] v lock up; (Geschäft, Vertrag) conclude, settle; end, close.

Abschluß ['apʃlus] m conclusion; (Geschäft, Vertrag) settlement. **-prüfung** f final exam(s), finals.
abschnallen ['apʃnalən] v unbuckle.
***abschneiden** ['apʃnaidən] v cut off.
Abschnitt ['apʃnit] m section, part; (Kontroll-) counterfoil.
abschrauben ['apʃraubən] v unscrew.
abschrecken ['apʃrɛkən] v scare off, deter. **-d** adj deterrent. **Abschreckung** f deterrence. **-smittel** neut deterrent.
***abschreiben** ['apʃraibən] v copy out, write out; (Verlust, usw.) abschreiben; (plagiieren) plagiarize.
Abschrift ['apʃrift] f copy.
Abschuß ['apʃus] m (Gewehr) firing; (Flugzeug) shooting down.
***absehen** ['apzɛɪən] v see, perceive; (voraussehen) foresee. **absehbar** adj within sight; (Zeit) foreseeable.
abseits ['apzaits] adv aside.
***absenden** ['apzɛndən] v send (off). **Absender** m sender.
absetzen ['apzɛtsən] v set down; (verkaufen) sell; (entlassen) dismiss; (aussteigen lassen) drop off.
Absicht ['apziçt] f (pl -en) intention, purpose. **absicht‖lich** adj deliberate; adv on purpose, deliberately. **-slos** adj unintentional.
absolut [apzo'luɪt] adj absolute.
absondern ['apzɔndərn] v isolate, cut off, separate; (Med, Bot) secrete. **Absonderung** f (pl -en) isolation.
absorbieren [apzɔr'biɪrən] v absorb. **Absorption** f absorption.
absperren ['apʃpɛrən] v block off; (Gas, Strom) cut off; (Straße) block, cordon off.
abspielen ['apʃpiɪlən] v (Schallplatte, usw.) play; (Musik) sight-read; (Ball) pass.
***abspringen** ['apʃpriŋən] v jump down (from), jump off; (Flugzeug) bale out; (Splitter) chip or break off; (Farbe) flake off.
abspülen ['apʃpyɪlən] v wash, wash up. **Abspülwasser** neut dishwater.
abstammen ['apʃtamən] v be descended from. **Abstammung** f descent, lineage.
Abstand ['apʃtant] m distance. **Abstand halten** keep one's distance.
abstatten ['apʃtatən] v (Besuch) pay; (Dank) give.

*absteigen ['apʃtaigən] v climb down, descend; (vom Pferd) dismount.

abstellen ['apʃtɛlən] v (Gerät, Licht) turn off; (niederlegen) put down; (Mot) park.

Abstieg ['apʃtiːk] m (pl -e) descent.

abstimmen ['apʃtimən] v vote, (Instrument, Radio) tune. **sich abstimmen** agree. **aufeinander abstimmen** collate, coordinate. **Abstimmung** f vote, poll.

Abstinenz [apsti'nɛnts] f abstinence; (Alkohol) teetotalism. **–ler** m (pl -) abstainer; teetotaller.

abstoßend ['apʃtoːsənt] adj repulsive, repellent.

abstrakt [ap'strakt] adj abstract.

Absturz ['apʃturts] m fall; (Flugzeug) crash; (Abgrund) precipice. **abstürzen** v fall, plummet; (Flugzeug) crash.

absurd [ap'zurt] adj absurd.

Abszeß [aps'tsɛs] m (pl Abszesse) abcess.

Abt [apt] m (pl Äbte) abbott. **Abtei** f (pl -en) abbey.

Abteil [ap'tail] neut (pl -e) compartment. **abteilen** v separate, divide off. **Abteilung** f (auch Mil) division; (einer Firma) department. **–sleiter** m head of department.

Äbtissin [ɛp'tisin] f (pl -nen) abbess.

*abtreiben ['aptraibən] v drive away; (Med) abort. **Abtreibung** f (pl -en) (induced) abortion.

Abtritt ['aptrit] m departure; (Theater) exit.

abtrocknen ['aptrɔknən] v wipe dry; (Geschirr) wipe up, dry.

abtrünnig ['aptryniç] adj disloyal, rebellious.

*abtun ['aptun] put aside; (Kleider) take off; (erledigen) close, settle; (Tier) put down.

abwandeln ['apvandəln] v vary. **Abwandlung** f variation.

abwarten ['apvartən] v wait for, expect; wait and see.

abwärts ['apvɛrts] adv downwards, down.

abwaschen ['apvaʃən] v wash off; (Geschirr) wash up.

Abwasser ['apvasər] neut waste water, effluent.

abwechseln ['apvɛksəln] v take turns; (wechseln) change, vary. **–d** adj alternating. adv alternately, in turns. **Abwechslung** f change.

Abwehr ['apvɛir] f defence; (Widerstand) resistance. **abwehren** v ward off; (Feind) repel.

*abweichen ['apvaiçən] v deviate. **–d** adj discrepant, anomalous; (Meinung) dissenting.

*abweisen ['apvaisən] v turn away, refuse; (Bewerber) turn down. **–d** adj unfriendly, dismissive.

*abwenden ['apvɛndən] v turn away or aside; (Gefahr) avert, prevent.

*abwerfen ['apvɛrfən] v throw off; (Bomben) drop; (Zinsen) yield.

abwerten ['apvɛrtən] v devalue. **Abwertung** f devaluation.

abwesend ['apveːzənt] adj absent; (zerstreut) absent-minded. **Abwesenheit** f absence.

abzahlen ['aptsaːlən] v pay off.

abzählen ['aptsɛilən] v count; (Geld) count out.

abzäunen ['aptsɔynən] v fence off.

Abzeichen ['aptsaiçən] neut badge; (Kennzeichen) mark.

*abziehen ['aptsiːən] v draw off, remove; (Math) subtract; (fortgehen) go away, withdraw.

Abzug ['aptsuːk] m departure; (Geld) deduction; (Foto) print; (Abdruck) copy.

abzweigen ['aptsvaigən] v branch off. **Abzweigung** f (pl -en) branch; (Mot) turning.

ach! [ax] interj oh! ah!

Achse ['aksə] f (pl -n) (Rad) axle; (Math, Pol) axis.

Achsel ['aksəl] f (pl -n) shoulder. **–bein** neut shoulder-blade. **–höhle** f armpit. **–zucken** neut (pl -) shrug (of the shoulders).

acht [axt] adj eight. **(heute) vor acht Tagen** a week ago (today).

Acht [axt] f (unz.) attention. **außer acht lassen** ignore, disregard. **sich in acht nehmen** be careful, take care. **acht||en** v esteem. **–en auf** pay attention to, heed. **–geben** v pay attention. **–los** adj careless. **–sam** adj attentive. **Achtung** f attention; (Wertschätzung) esteem; interj watch out! look out!

achtzig ['axtsiç] adj eighty.

ächzen ['ɛçtsən] v groan.

Acker ['akər] m (pl Äcker) field. **–bau** m agriculture, farming.

addieren [a'diːrən] v add (up). **Addiermaschine** f adding machine.

Adel ['aɪdəl] *m* nobility, aristocracy. **ad(e)lig** *adj* noble, aristocratic. **Ad(e)lige(r)** noble(man), aristocrat.
Ader ['aɪdər] *f* (*pl* -n) blood vessel; vein, artery.
Adjektiv ['atjɛktiːf] *neut* (*pl* -e) adjective.
Adler ['aɪdlər] *m* (*pl* -) eagle.
Admiral [atmi'raːl] *m* (*pl* -e) admiral. **–ität** *f* admiralty.
adoptieren [adɔp'tiɪrən] *v* adopt. **Adoptiv-** adopted, adoptive.
Adrenalin [adrena'liːn] *neut* adrenaline.
Adresse [a'drɛsə] *f* (*pl* -n) address. **Adreßbuch** *neut* address book, directory. **adressieren** *v* address.
Advokat [atvo'kaɪt] *m* (*pl* -en) lawyer.
Affäre [a'fɛɪrə] *f* (*pl* -n) affair; (*Liebes-*) (love) affair.
Affe ['afə] *m* (*pl* -n) ape, monkey.
affektiert [afɛk'tiɪrt] *adj* affected, conceited.
äffen ['ɛfən] *v* ape, imitate.
Afrika ['aɪfrika] *neut* Africa. **Afrikaner** *m* African. **afrikanisch** *adj* African.
After ['aftər] *m* (*pl* -) anus.
Agent [a'gɛnt] *m* (*pl* -en) agent. **–ur** *f* (*pl* -en) agency.
Agnostiker [a'gnɔstikər] *m* (*pl* -) agnostic. **agnostisch** *adj* agnostic.
Ägypten [ɛ'gyptən] *neut* Egypt. **Ägypter** *m* (*pl* -) Egyptian. **ägyptisch** *adj* Egyptian.
Ahn [aɪn] *m* (*pl* -en) ancestor.
ähneln ['ɛɪnəln] *v* look like, resemble.
ahnen ['aɪnən] *v* suspect, guess.
ähnlich ['ɛɪnliç] *adj* like, similar (to). **Ähnlichkeit** *f* (*pl* -en) likeness, similarity.
Ahorn ['aɪhɔrn] *m* (*pl* -e) maple.
Ähre ['ɛɪrə] *f* (*pl* -n) ear (of corn).
Akadem||ie [akade'miː] *f* (*pl* -n) academy; (*Hochschule, Fachschule*) college. **–iker** *m* (*pl* -) university graduate. **akademisch** *adj* academic.
Akkord [a'kɔrt] *m* (*pl* -e) agreement; (*Musik*) chord. **–arbeit** *f* piece-work.
Akrobat [akro'baɪt] *m* (*pl* -en) acrobat. **akrobatisch** *adj* acrobatic.
Akt [akt] *m* (*pl* -e) act, action, deed; document; (*Kunst*) nude.
Akte ['aktə] *f* (*pl* -n) file, dossier. **zu den Akten legen** file (away). **Akten||schrank** *m* filing cabinet. **–tasche** *f* briefcase.
Aktie ['aktsiə] *f* (*pl* -n) share. **Aktien||gesellschaft** *f* joint-stock company. **–makler** *m* stockbroker.

Aktionär [aktsio'nɛɪr] *m* (*pl* -e) shareholder.
aktiv [ak'tiːf] *adj* active. **–ieren** *v* activate.
aktuell [aktu'ɛl] *adj* current, contemporary, up-to-date.
Akzent [ak'tsɛnt] *m* (*pl* -e) accent. **akzeptieren** [aktsɛp'tiɪrən] *v* accept.
Alarm [a'larm] *m* (*pl* -e) alarm. **alarm||bereit** *adj* standing by, on the alert. **–ieren** *v* alarm.
albern ['albərn] *adj* silly, foolish.
Album ['album] *neut* (*pl* **Alben**) album.
Alge ['algə] *f* (*pl* -n) seaweed.
Algebra ['algebra] *f* algebra.
Alimente [ali'mɛntə] *pl* alimony *sing*.
Alkohol [alko'hoːl] *m* (*pl* -e) alcohol. **alkoholfrei** *adj* non-alcoholic. **Alkoholiker** *m* alcoholic. **alkoholisch** *adj* alcoholic.
all [al] *pron, adj* all. **All** *neut* universe. **alle** *pl* all; everybody *sing*. **alle beide** both. **wir alle** we all, all of us. **die Milch ist alle** the milk is all gone. **alle zwei Tage** every other day. **alles** everything. **alledem** *pron* trotz alledem nevertheless.
Allee [a'leɪ] *f* (*pl* -n) avenue.
Allegorie [alego'riː] (*pl* -n) allegory. **allegorisch** *adj* allegorical.
allein [a'lain] *adj, adv* alone; (*ohne Hilfer*) (by) oneself. *conj* but. **alleinstehend** *adj* (*Haus*) detached; (*Person*) single.
allemal ['aləmal] *adv* always. **ein für allemal** once and for all.
allenfalls ['alənfals] *adv* if need be; (*höchstens*) at most.
aller||best [a'lɔrbɛst] *adj* very best, best of all. **–dings** *adv* certainly, surely, indeed. **–erst** *adj* first of all, very first. **–höchst** *adj* supreme, highest of all. **–lei** *adj* (*undeklinierbar*) various, all kinds of. **–liebst** *adj* (most) delightful, dearest. **–wenigst** *adj* very least.
allezeit ['alətsait] *adv* always, at any time.
allgemein ['algəmain] *adj* common, general. **im allgemeinen** in general.
Alliierte(r) [ali'iɪrtə(r)] *m* allied.
alljährlich ['alˈjɛɪrliç] *adj* annual.
allmächtig [al'mɛçtiç] *adj* all-powerful, almighty.
allmählich [al'mɛːliç] *adj* gradual.
allseitig ['alzaitiç] *adj* universal, comprehensive.
alltäglich ['al'tɛɪkliç] *adj* everyday. *adv* every day.

allzu ['altsuː] *adv* much too, all too.

Almanach ['almanax] *m* (*pl* -e) almanac.

Alpen ['alpən] *pl* Alps *pl*.

Alphabet [alfa'beɪt] *neut* (*pl* -e) alphabet. **alphabetisch** *adj* alphabetical.

Alptraum ['alptraum] *m* nightmare.

als [als] *conj* as; (*da, zu der Zeit*) when; (*nach Komparativen*) than. **als ob** as if. **nichts als** nothing but. *als dein Freund möchte ich sagen ...* as your friend, I would like to say ... *als ich noch ein Kind war* when I was a child.

also ['alzo] *conj* so, therefore.

alt [alt] *adj* old.

Alt [alt] *m* (*unz.*) alto (voice).

Altar [al'taɪr] *m* (*pl* Altäre) altar.

Alter ['altər] *neut* (*unz.*) age; (*hohes Alter*) old age. **Alters∥fürsorge** *f* care of the aged. **–heim** *neut* old people's home. **altersschwach** *adj* (*Person*) senile, feeble. **Altertum** *neut* (*unz.*) antiquity. **altertümlich** *adj* ancient, archaic.

Aluminium [alu'miːnium] *neut* aluminium.

am [am] *prep* + *art* an dem.

Amboß ['ambɔs] *m* (*pl* Ambosse) anvil.

Ameise ['aɪmaizə] *f* (*pl* -n) ant.

Amerika [a'meːrika] *neut* America. **Amerikaner** *m* American. **amerikanisch** *adj* American.

Ampel ['ampəl] *f* (*pl* -n) (*Verkehrs-*) traffic light; (*Hängelampe*) hanging lamp.

Amsel ['amzəl] *f* (*pl* -n) blackbird.

Amt [amt] *neut* (*pl* Ämter) office; (*Stellung*) official position, post; (*Telef*) exchange. *das Auswärtige Amt* the Foreign Office. *das Amt antreteten* take office. **amtieren** *v* officiate. **amtlich** *adj* official. **Amts∥geheimnis** *neut* offical secret. **–gericht** *neut* district court. **–zeichen** *neut* dial tone.

amüsant [amy'zant] *adj* amusing. **amüsieren** *v* amuse. **sich amüsieren** amuse *or* enjoy oneself.

an [an] *prep* at; (*nahe*) near; (*auf*) on. *adv* on. *an diesem Tag* on this day. *an diesem Ort* at this place. *der Ort, an dem* the place where. *an der Wand* on the wall. *an die Tür klopfen* knock at *or* on the door. *von heute an* from today. *von jetzt an* from now on. *sie hat nichts an* she has nothing on.

analog [ana'loːk] *adj* analagous. **Analogie** *f* analogy. **analogisch** *adj* analogous.

Analphabet [analfa'beɪt] *m* (*pl* -en) illiterate.

Analyse [ana'lyːzə] *f* (*pl* -n) analysis. **analysieren** *v* analyse. **Analytiker** *m* analyst. **analytisch** *adj* analytical.

Ananas ['ananas] *f* (*pl* -se) pineapple.

Anarchie [anar'çiː] *f* (*pl* -n) anarchy. **Anarchist** *m* (*pl* -en) anarchist.

Anatomie [anato'miː] *f* (*pl* -n) anatomy. **anatomisch** *adj* anatomical.

Anbau ['anbau] **1** *m* (*unz.*) cultivation, tillage. **2** *m* extension, annexe.

***anbeißen** ['anbaisən] *v* bite into; (*Fisch*) bite, take the bait.

anbelangen ['anbəlaŋən] *v* concern, relate to. *was mich anbelangt* as to me, as far as I am concerned.

anbeten ['anbeɪtən] *v* worship, adore.

***anbieten** ['anbiːtən] *v* offer.

Anblick ['anblik] *m* sight, view; (*Aussehen*) appearance. **anblicken** *v* look at, gaze at.

***anbrechen** ['anbrɛçən] *v* (*Essen, Vorrat*) break into, begin; (*Tag*) dawn, break; (*Nacht*) fall.

***anbrennen** ['anbrɛnən] *v* (*Speisen*) burn; (*Zigarette, Lampe*) light.

***anbringen** ['anbriŋən] *v* bring, place; (*befestigen*) attach; (*Klage*) lodge, bring.

Anbruch ['anbrux] *m* (*unz.*) beginning. *bei Anbruch der Nacht* at nightfall.

Andacht ['andaxt] *f* (*pl* -en) devotion.

Andenken ['andɛŋkən] *neut* (*pl* -) memory, remembrance; (*Erinnerungstück*) souvenir.

ander ['andər] *adj, pron* other, different. *ein andermal* another time.

ändern ['ɛndərn] *v* alter, change. **Änderung** *f* (*pl* -en) alteration, change.

ander∥thalb ['andərthalp] *adj* one-and-a-half. **–nfalls** *adv* otherwise, else. **–s** *adv* differently. **–seits** *adv* on the other hand. **–swo** *adv* elsewhere.

andeuten ['andɔytən] *v* indicate, point to; (*anspielen*) imply, suggest, allude to. **Andeutung** *f* indication; suggestion, allusion.

andrehen ['andreɪən] *v* turn on, switch on; (*Mot*) start up; (*umg.*) wangle, fix up.

andrer ['andrər] *pron* anderer. *V* ander.

aneignen ['anaignən] *v* sich aneignen appropriate; (*Kenntnisse*) acquire. **Aneignung** *f* (*pl* -en) appropriation; acquisition.

aneinander [anain'andər] *adv* to *or* against one another, together. **–liegend** *adj* neighbouring, adjacent. **–schließen** *v* join together.
*anerkennen ['anɛrkɛnən] *v* recognize, acknowledge. **Anerkennung** *f* recognition, approval.
*anfahren ['anfaɪrən] *v* begin (to move); (*bringen*) convey, carry; (*ankommen*) arrive; (*zusammenstoßen*) drive into. **Anfahrt** *f* arrival; (*Zufahrtsstraße*) drive.
Anfall ['anfal] *m* attack.
Anfang ['anfaŋ] *m* beginning, start. **anfangen** *v* begin, start. **Anfänger** *m* (*pl* -) beginner. **anfangs** *adv* at first, initially. **Anfangsbuchstabe** *m* (*pl* -n) initial letter.
anfassen ['anfasən] *v* touch; (*ergreifen*) hold, grasp; (*Aufgabe*) set *or* go about.
*anfecht‖en ['anfɛçtən] *v* contest, dispute; (*beunruhigen*) trouble; (*Versuchung*) tempt. **–bar** *adj* questionable, contestable.
Anforderung ['anfɔrdərʊŋ] *f* demand, claim; (*Bedürfnis*) requirement.
Anfrage ['anfraɪgə] *f* inquiry.
anfühlen ['anfyɪlən] *v* touch, feel. **sich anfühlen** feel (to the touch).
anführen ['anfyɪrən] *v* lead, command; (*Worte*) quote, state; (*täuschen*) trick, deceive. **Anführungszeichen** *pl* quotation marks.
anfüllen ['anfylən] *v* fill (up).
Angabe ['angaɪbə] *f* declaration, statement. **–n** *pl* specifications, data. **nähere Angaben** details, particulars.
*angeben ['angeɪbən] *v* state, declare; (*anzeigen*) inform against; (*vorgeben*) pretend; (*prahlen*) brag, boast, show off. **Angeber** *m* (*pl* -) informer; (*Prahler*) show off, boaster. **angeblich** *adj* supposed, alleged.
angeboren ['angəbɔɪrən] *adj* innate, inherent.
Angebot ['angəbɔɪt] *neut* (*pl* -e) offer. **Angebot und Nachfrage** supply and demand.
*angehen ['angeɪən] *v* begin; (*angreifen*) attack; (*betreffen*) concern. *das geht mich nichts an* that is none of my business.
angehören ['angəhœɪrən] *v* belong (to). **Angehörige(r)** *m* member.
Angeklagte(r) ['angəklaɪktə(r)] (*Jur*) (the) accused, defendant.
Angelegenheit ['angəleɪgənhait] *f* matter, concern, business.

angeln ['aŋəln] *v* fish, angle. **Angeln** *neut* angling, fishing. **Angelrute** *f* fishing rod.
Angelsachse ['aŋɔlzaksə] *m* Anglo-Saxon. **angelsächsisch** *adj* Anglo-Saxon.
angemessen ['angəmɛsən] *adj* proper, suitable.
angenehm ['angəneɪm] *adj* pleasant, agreeable.
angenommen ['angənɔmən] *adj* supposing, assuming.
angesehen ['angəzeɪən] *adj* respected.
Angesicht ['angəziçt] *neut* face, countenance. **angesichts** *prep* considering, in view of.
Angestellte(r) ['angəʃtɛltə(r)] employee, office worker.
angewandt ['angəvant] *adj* applied, practical.
angewöhnen ['angəvœɪnən] *v* accustom. **sich angewöhnen** get used to, make a habit of. **Angewohnheit** *f* habit, custom.
Angler ['aŋlər] *m* (*pl* -) angler, fisherman.
*angreifen ['angraifən] *v* (*anfassen*) take hold of; (*feindlich*) attack; (*unternehmen*) set about. **Angreifer** *m* (*pl* -) aggressor, attacker.
angrenzen ['angrɛntsən] *v* border on, adjoin.
Angriff ['angrif] *m* attack. **angriffslustig** *adj* aggressive.
Angst [aŋst] *f* (*pl* Ängste) fear, anxiety. **Angst haben vor** be afraid of.
ängst‖igen ['ɛŋstigən] *v* frighten. **–lich** *adj* fearful, timid; (*peinlich*) scrupulous, (over-)careful.
*anhaben ['anhaɪbən] *v* wear, have on.
Anhalt ['anhalt] *m* support, prop; (*fig*) clue. **anhalten** *v* stop; (*andauern*) continue, last. **Anhalter** *m* hitchhiker. **per Anhalter fahren** hitchhike.
Anhang ['anhaŋ] *m* appendix, supplement. **anhängen** *v* hang on, attach; (*hinzufügen*) add. **Anhänger** *m* follower; (*Fußball*) supporter; (*Mot*) trailer. **Anhängeschloß** *neut* padlock. **anhänglich** *adj* affectionate.
Anhöhe ['anhœɪə] *f* (low) hill.
anhören ['anhœɪrən] *v* listen (to).
Ankauf ['ankauf] *m* purchase. **ankaufen** *v* purchase, buy.
Anker ['aŋkər] *m* (*pl* -) anchor. **den Anker lichten/werfen** weigh/cast anchor. **ankern** *v* anchor.

Anklage ['anklaːgə] *f* accusation, charge. **–bank** *f* dock. **anklagen** *v* accuse. **Ankläger** *m* plaintiff.
Anklang ['anklaŋ] *m* approval, recognition; (*Spur*) touch, echo.
anknüpfen ['anknypfən] *v* fasten (on), tie (on); (*fig*) take up, establish.
***ankommen** ['ankɔmən] *v* arrive; (*abhängen*) depend (on). *es kommt darauf an* it depends.
ankündigen ['ankyndigən] *v* announce, publicize. **Ankündigung** *f* announcement.
Ankunft ['ankunft] *f* (*pl* Ankünfte) arrival.
Anlage ['anlaːgə] *f* installation; (*Entwurf*) plan, layout; park, gardens *pl*; (*Brief*) enclosure; (*Begabung*) talent; (*Neigung*) tendency, susceptibility; (*Komm*) investment; (*Fabrik*) plant, works.
anlangen ['anlaŋən] *v* (*ankommen*) arrive; (*betreffen*) concern.
Anlaß ['anlas] *m* (*pl* Anlässe) occasion, cause. **Anlaß geben** cause, give rise to.
anlassen *v* leave on; (*Mot*) start.
anläßlich *prep* on the occasion of.
Anlasser *m* (*pl* -) (*Mot*) starter-motor.
Anlauf ['anlauf] *m* start; (*kurzer Lauf*) run, dash. **anlaufen** *v* run at, rush at; (*Hafen*) put into; (*wachsen*) rise, increase.
anlegen ['anleːgən] *v* put on *or* against; (*Gewehr*) aim at; (*gründen*) found; (*Geld*) invest; (*Schiff*) lie alongside.
Anleihe ['anlaiə] *f* (*pl* -n) loan.
Anleitung ['anlaituŋ] *f* instruction.
***anliegen** ['anliːgən] *v* (*Schiff*) lie beside; (*Kleidung*) fit well. **Anliegen** *neut* (*pl* -) request. **anliegend** *adj* adjoining.
anlocken ['anlɔkən] *v* entice, attract.
anmachen ['anmaxən] *v* attach; (*Speisen*) prepare; (*Feuer*) kindle; (*Licht*) turn on.
Anmarsch ['anmarʃ] *m* advance, approach. **anmarschieren** *v* advance on, march on.
anmaßen ['anmaːsən] *v* sich anmaßen, zu presume to, take it upon oneself to. **Anmaßung** *f* presumptuousness.
anmelden ['anmɛldən] *v* announce, report. **sich anmelden** *v* report; (*polizeilich*) register (with the police). **Anmeldung** *f* announcement; (*polizeilich*) registration.
anmerken ['anmɛrkən] *v* note, observe. **Anmerkung** *f* note, observation.
Anmut ['anmuːt] *f* grace, charm, elegance. **anmutig** *adj* graceful.

annähern ['annɛːərn] *v* bring closer; (*ähnlich machen*) make similar. **sich annähern** approach. **annähernd** *adj* approaching. *adv* almost, close to.
Annahme ['annaːmə] *f* (*pl* -n) acceptance; (*Vermutung*) assumption.
***annehm||en** ['anneːmən] *v* accept, take; (*vermuten*) assume, suppose. **–bar** *adj* acceptable.
anonym [ano'nyːm] *adj* anonymous. **Anonymität** *f* anonymity.
anordnen ['anɔrdnən] *v* put in order, arrange; (*befehlen*) direct, command. **Anordnung** *f* arrangement; (*Befehl*) order, instruction.
anpacken ['anpakən] *v* grasp, seize.
anpassen ['anpasən] *v* fit, adapt. **sich anpassen** *v* adapt, adjust. **Anpassung** *f* adaptation, adjustment. **anpassungsfähig** *adj* adaptable. **Anpassungsfähigkeit** *f* adaptability.
anrechnen ['anrɛçnən] *v* charge; (*hochschätzen*) value, esteem highly.
Anrede ['anreːdə] *f* speech, address. **anreden** *v* address, speak to.
anregen ['anreːgən] *v* stimulate, incite; (*geistig*) excite, inspire. **–d** *adj* exciting. **Anregung** *f* excitement.
anrichten ['anriçtən] *v* (*Schaden*) cause, do; (*Essen*) prepare.
Anruf ['anruːf] *m* call, shout; (*Telef*) call. **anrufen** *v* call, hail; (*Telef*) ring up, call.
anrühren ['anryːrən] *v* touch, handle; (*Küche*) stir.
ans [ans] *prep+art* an das.
Ansage ['anzaːgə] *f* announcement; (*Kartenspiel*) bidding. **ansagen** *v* announce, declare; bid. **Ansager** *m* (*pl* -) announcer.
ansammeln ['anzaməln] *v* collect. **sich ansammeln** gather. **Ansammlung** *f* collection, accumulation; (*Menge*) crowd, gathering.
Ansatz ['anzats] *m* (*Anfang*) start, beginning; (*Zusatzstück*) (added) piece, fitting. **–punkt** *m* starting point.
anschaffen ['anʃafən] *v* procure, obtain.
anschalten ['anʃaltən] *v* switch, turn on.
anschau||en ['anʃauən] *v* look at, view. **–lich** *adj* obvious, evident.
Anschein ['anʃain] *m* (*unz.*) (outer) appearance. **allem Anschein nach** to all appearances.

Anschlag ['anʃlaɪk] *m* (*Med*) stroke, attack; (*Plakat*) poster; (*Kosten-*) estimate; (*Angriff*) (criminal) attack, outrage.
***anschließen** ['anʃliːsən] *v* connect; (*anketten*) chain up. **-d** *adj* subsequent.
Anschluß ['anʃlus] *m* connection; (*pol*) annexation.
anschnallen ['anʃnalən] *v* fasten, buckle.
Anschove [an'ʃoːvə] *f* (*pl* -n), **Anschovis** *f* (*pl* -) anchovy.
Anschrift ['anʃrift] *f* address.
anschuldigen ['ənʃuldigən] *v* accuse (of), charge (with).
***ansehen** ['anzeɪən] *v* look at, consider. **Ansehen** *neut* appearance; (*Hochachtung*) respect, esteem. **ansehnlich** *adj* notable.
ansetzen ['anzɛtsən] *v* put on, attach; (*Gewicht*) put on; (*anfangen*) begin; (*versuchen*) try.
Ansicht ['anzɪçt] *f* view, sight; (*Meinung*) opinion.
Anspiel ['anʃpiːl] *neut* (*Tennis*) service; (*Fußball*) kick-off. **anspielen** *v* play first; (*Tennis*) serve; (*Fußball*) kick off. **anspielen auf** hint at, allude to. **Anspielung** *f* (*pl* -en) allusion.
ansprechen ['anʃprɛçən] speak to, address; (*auf der Straße, usw.*) accost.
Anspruch ['anʃprux] *m* claim. **Anspruch haben auf** have a right to. **in Anspruch nehmen** lay claim to, claim; (*Zeit*) take up. **Ansprüche stellen** make demands. **anspruchsvoll** *adj* demanding.
Anstalt ['anʃtalt] *f* (*pl* -en) (*Heim*) institution; (*Schule*) institute; (*Vorbereitung*) arrangement.
Anstand ['anʃtant] *m* (*unz.*) decency. **anständig** *adj* decent, proper. **Anstandsdame** *f* chaperone.
anstatt ['anʃtat] *prep* instead of. **anstatt daß** rather than.
anstecken ['anʃtɛkən] *v* pin on (to); (*Ring*) put on; (*Med*) infect; (*Feuer*) light. **-d** *adj* infectious. **Ansteckung** *f* infection.
anstellen ['anʃtɛlən] *v* carry out, do; (*Person*) appoint, employ; (*Mot*) start; (*Radio*) switch on. **Anstellung** *f* appointment.
anstiften ['anʃtiftən] *v* cause, instigate.
Anstoß ['anʃtoːs] *m* impulse; (*Sport*) kick-off. **Anstoß geben/nehmen** give/take offence (*US* offense). **anstoßen** *v* knock against; (*Haus, usw.*) adjoin.

anstrengen ['anʃtrɛŋən] *v* strain, exert; (*Prozeß*) bring in. **sich anstrengen** strain or exert oneself; make an effort.
Antarktika [an'tarktika] *f* Antarctica. **Antarktis** *f* Antarctic. **antarktisch** *adj* antarctic.
antasten ['antastən] *v* touch, handle; (*Thema*) touch on; (*Recht, usw.*) injure.
Anteil ['antail] *m* share, portion; (*Mitgefühl*) sympathy. **-nahme** *f* sympathy.
Antenne [an'tɛnə] *f* (*pl* -n) aerial.
Antibiotikum [antibi'ɔːtikum] *neut* (*pl* -biotika) antibiotic.
antik [an'tiːk] *adj* ancient, classical.
Antikörper ['antikœrpər] *m* antibody.
Antiquität [antikvi'tɛːt] *f* (*pl* -en) antique. **-enhändler** *m* antique dealer.
antisemitisch [antize'miːtiʃ] *adj* antisemitic.
Antiseptikum [anti'sɛptikum] *m* (*pl* -septika) antiseptic. **antiseptisch** *adj* antiseptic.
Antrag ['antraɪk] *m* (*pl* **Anträge**) offer, proposal; (*Pol*) motion. **einen Antrag stellen** propose a motion. **Antragsteller** *m* applicant; (*Pol*) mover (of a motion).
***antreffen** ['antrɛfən] *v* encounter.
***antreiben** ['antraibən] *v* drive, propel; (*Person*) urge; (*ans Ufer*) drift ashore.
***antreten** ['antreɪtən] *v* (*Amt*) enter, take over; (*Reise*) set out on.
Antrieb ['antriːp] *m* drive, impulse; (*Tech*) drive. **aus eigenem Antrieb** of one's own free will.
Antritt ['antrit] *m* beginning; (*Amt*) entrance.
***antun** ['antuɪn] *v* (*Kleidung*) put on; (*Verletzung*) do, inflict.
Antwort ['antvɔrt] *f* (*pl* -en) answer, reply. **antworten** *v* answer, reply (to).
anvertrauen ['anfɛrtrauən] *v* entrust.
Anwalt ['anvalt] *m* (*pl* **Anwälte**) (defending) lawyer, solicitor.
anwärmen ['anvɛrmən] *v* warm (up).
***anweisen** ['anvaisən] *v* (*zuweisen*) assign; (*anleiten*) direct, show; (*Geld*) transfer. **Anweisung** *f* instruction, order; (*Geld*) remittance, transfer.
***anwend‖en** ['anvɛndən] *v* employ, use; (*Gewalt, Methode, Wissenschaft, usw.*) apply. **-bar** *adj* applicable. **Anwendung** *f.* application.

anwesend ['anvɛɪzənt] *adj* present. **Anwesenheit** *f* presence.

Anzahl ['antsaɪl] *f* number. **Anzahlung** *f* deposit, down payment.

Anzeichen ['antsaɪçən] *neut* mark, sign.

Anzeige ['antsaɪgə] *f* (*pl* -n) announcement; (*Inserat*) advertisement; (*bei der Polizei*) report. **–blatt** *neut* advertiser, advertising journal. **anzeig‖en** *v* announce; (*person*) inform against, report (to the police). **–epflichtig** *adj* notifiable.

***anziehen** ['antsiːən] *v* (*Kleider*) put on; (*Schraube*) tighten; (*Person*) dress; (*heranlocken*) attract. **sich anziehen** get dressed. **anziehend** *adj* attractive. **Anziehung** *f* attraction. **–skraft** *f* power of attraction; (*Person*) attractiveness.

Anzug ['antsuːk] **1** *m* (*unz.*) approach. **2** *m* suit.

anzünden ['antsyndən] *v* light, ignite.

Apfel ['apfəl] *m* (*pl* **Äpfel**) apple. **–baum** *m* apple tree. **–garten** *m* apple orchard. **–kuchen** *m* apple cake. **–mus** *neut* apple sauce. **–saft** *m* apple juice. **–sine** *f* orange. **–wein** *m* cider.

Apostel [a'pɔstəl] *m* (*pl* -) apostle. **–geschichte** *f* Acts of the Apostles.

Apostroph [apo'stroːf] *m* (*pl* -e) apostrophe.

Apotheke [apo'teːkə] *f* (*pl* -n) chemist's (shop), pharmacy. **–r** *m* (*pl* -) chemist, pharmacist. **–rkunst** *f* pharmacy, pharmaceutics.

Apparat [apa'raːt] *m* (*pl* -e) apparatus; (*Vorrichtung*) appliance, device; (*Foto*) camera; (*Telef*) telephone, handset. **am Apparat!** speaking! **am Apparat bleiben** hold the line.

appellieren [apɛ'liːrən] *v* appeal.

Appetit [apə'tiːt] *m* (*pl* -e) appetite.

Aprikose [apri'koːzə] *f* (*pl* -n) apricot.

April [a'pril] *m* (*pl* -e) April. **der erste April** April Fools' Day.

Aquarell [akva'rɛl] *neut* (*pl* -e) water-colour.

Aquarium [a'kvaːrium] *neut* (*pl* **Aquarien**) aquarium.

Äquator [ɛ'kvaːtɔr] *m* equator. **äquatorial** *adj* equatorial.

Arab‖er ['arabər] *m* (*pl* -) Arab. **–ien** *neut* Arabia. **arabisch** *adj* Arab, Arabian.

Arbeit ['arbaɪt] *f* (*pl* -en) work; (*Beschäftigung*) job. **arbeiten** *v* work. **Arbeiter** *m* worker, workman. **–klasse** *f* working class. **Arbeitgeber** *m* employer. **Arbeits‖amt** *neut* employment office. **–erlaubnis** *f* work permit. **arbeits‖fähig** *adj* able to work. **–los** *adj* unemployed. **–losenunterstützung** *f.* unemployment benefit. **–losigkeit** *f* unemployment.

Archäolog‖ie [arçəolo'giː] *f* archaeology. **–e** *m* archaeologist. **archäologisch** *adj* archaeological.

Architekt [arçi'tɛkt] *m* (*pl* -en) architect. **–ur** *f* (*pl* -en) architecture.

Archiv [ar'çiːf] *neut* (*pl* -e) archives *pl*, records *pl*.

arg [ark] *adj* bad, evil; (*ernst*) serious.

Ärger ['ɛrgər] *m* (*unz.*) (*Verdruß*) annoyance, irritation; (*Zorn*) anger. **ärgerlich** *adj* (*Person*) angry, annoyed; (*Sache*) annoying. **ärgern** *v* annoy, irritate. **sich ärgern über** be angry about.

Argument [argu'mɛnt] *neut* (*pl* -e) argument, reasoning.

Argwohn ['arkvoːn] *m* (*unz.*) distrust, suspicion. **argwöhnisch** *adj* suspicious, mistrustful.

Aristokrat [aristo'kraːt] *m* (*pl* -en) aristocrat. **–ie** *f* aristocracy. **aristokratisch** *adj* aristocratic.

Arithmetik [arit'mɛtik] *f* arithmetic. **arithmetisch** *adj* arithmetical.

Arktis ['arktis] *f* Arctic. **arktisch** *adj* arctic.

arm [arm] *adj* poor. **–arm** *adj* poor in . . . . **nikotinarm** *adj* low-nicotine.

Arm [arm] *m* (*pl* -e) arm; (*Fluß*) branch, tributary.

Armaturenbrett [arma'tuːrənbrɛt] *neut* dashboard, instrument panel.

Armband ['armbant] *neut* bracelet. **–uhr** *f* (wrist)watch.

Armee [ar'meː] *f* (*pl* -n) army.

Ärmel ['ɛrməl] *m* (*pl* -) sleeve. **–kanal** *m* English Channel.

ärmlich ['ɛrmliç] *adj* poor, miserable.

armselig ['armzɛɪliç] *adj* wretched, miserable.

Arm‖sessel *m* armchair. **–stuhl** *m* armchair.

Armut ['armuːt] *f* poverty.

Arrest [a'rɛst] *m* (*pl* -e) arrest, detention.

Arsch [arʃ] *m* (*pl* **Ärsche**) (*vulgär*) arse.

Art [art] *f* (*pl* -en) type, kind, sort; (*Weise*) way, method; (*Biol*) species; (*Brauch*) habit.

artig ['artiç] *adj* (*Kind*) good, well-behaved.
-artig [-artiç] *adj* –like.
Artikel [ar'tiːkəl] *m* (*pl* -) article.
Artillerie [artilə'riː] *f* (*pl* -n) artillery.
Artischocke [arti'ʃɔkə] *f* (*pl* -n) artichoke.
Artist [ar'tist] *m* (*pl* -en) artiste.
Arznei [arts'nai] *f* (*pl* -en) medicine, medicament, drug. **–mittel** *neut* medicine.
Arzt [artst] *m* (*pl* **Ärzte**) doctor, physician.
Ärztin ['ɛrtstin] *f* (*pl* -nen) (woman) doctor. **ärztlich** *adj* medical.
As [as] *neut* (*pl* -se) ace.
Asbest [as'bɛst] *m* asbestos.
Asche ['aʃə] *f* (*pl* -n) ash. **–nbecher** *m* ashtray.
Aspekt [as'pɛkt] *m* (*pl* -e) aspect.
Asphalt [as'falt] *m* asphalt, tarmac.
Assistent [asis'tɛnt] *m* (*pl* -en) assistant.
Ast [ast] *m* (*pl* **Äste**) bough, branch.
ästhetisch [ɛs'teːtiʃ] *adj* aesthetic.
Astronaut [astro'naut] *m* (*pl* -en) astronaut. **–ik** *f* astronautics. **astronautisch** *adj* astronautical.
Astronom [astro'noːm] *m* (*pl* -en) astronomer. **–ie** *f* astronomy. **astronomisch** *adj* astronomical.
Asyl [a'zyːl] *neut* (*pl* -e) asylum.
Atelier [atə'ljeː] *neut* (*pl* -s) studio.
Atem ['aːtəm] *m* (*pl* -) breath. **Atem holen** take breath.
Atheis‖mus [ate'ismus] *m* atheism. **–t** *m* (*pl* -en) atheist.
Äther ['ɛːtər] *m* ether. **ätherisch** *adj* ethereal.
Athlet [at'leːt] *m* (*pl* -en) athlete. **–ik** *f* athletics. **athletisch** *adj* athletic.
Atlantik [at'lantik] *m* Atlantic (Ocean).
Atlas¹ ['atlas] *m* (*pl* **Atlanten**) (*Buch*) atlas.
Atlas² *m* (*pl* -se) (*Stoff*) satin.
atmen ['aːtmən] *v* breathe.
Atmosphäre [atmos'fɛːrə] *f* (*pl* -n) atmosphere.
Atmung ['aːtmuŋ] *f* respiration, breathing. **–sapparat** *m* respirator.
Atom [a'toːm] *neut* (*pl* -e) atom. **–abfall** *m* atomic waste. **–antrieb** *m* nuclear propulsion. **–bombe** *f* atom bomb. **–kraft** *f* nuclear power. **–kraftwerk** *f* nuclear power station.
Attentat [atɛn'taːt] *neut* (*pl* -e) assassination (attempt). **Attentäter** *m* assassin, assailant.

ätzen ['ɛtsən] *v* corrode; (*Med*) cauterize; (*Kupferstich*) etch. **–d** *adj* corrosive, caustic.
Aubergine [obɛr'ʒiːnə] *f* (*pl* -n) aubergine.
auch [aux] *conj* also, too; (*sogar*) even; (*tatsächlich*) indeed, but. **nicht nur ... sondern auch ...** not only ... but also **.... sowohl ... als auch ...** both ... and ... . **auch wenn** even if, (even) though. *ich auch!* me too! *ich auch nicht* nor me, me neither. *was er auch sagen mag* whatever he may say. **wer auch immer** whoever.
Audienz [audi'ɛnts] *f* (*pl* -en) audience, interview.
auf [auf] *prep* on. *adv* up; (*offenstehend*) open. **auf und ab** up and down. *auf den Tisch stellen* put on the table. *auf dem Tisch finden* find on the table. *auf die Schule gehen* go to school. *auf der Schule sein* be at school. *auf deutsch* in German. **auf einmal** at once.
Aufbau ['aufbau] *m* (*unz.*) building, construction; structure.
aufbessern ['aufbɛsərn] *v* improve; (*Gehalt*) increase. **Aufbesserung** *f* improvement; (*Gehalt*) increase, rise.
aufbewahren ['aufbəvaːrən] *v* store (up), keep. **Aufbewahrung** *f* storage, safe-keeping.
***aufblasen** ['aufblaːzən] *v* blow up, inflate.
aufblicken ['aufblikən] *v* look up.
aufbrauchen ['aufbrauxən] *v* use up.
***aufbrechen** ['aufbrɛçən] *v* break open; (*Knospen, Wunden*) open; (*abreisen*) set off.
***aufbringen** ['aufbriŋən] *v* bring up, raise; (*ärgern*) imitate, provoke.
Aufbruch ['aufbrux] *m* departure, start.
aufdecken ['aufdɛkən] *v* uncover, reveal; (*Tisch*) spread. **Aufdeckung** *f* revealing, unveiling.
aufdrehen ['aufdreːən] *v* switch *or* turn on; (*Schraube*) unscrew.
aufdringlich ['aufdriŋliç] *adj* intrusive, importunate.
aufeinander [aufain'andər] *adv* (one) after another; (*gegeneinander*) one against the other. **–folgen** *v* follow (one after another). **–folgend** *adj* successive. **–stoßen** *v* (*Mot*) collide; (*Meinungen*) clash. **–treffen** *v* meet.

Aufenthalt ['aufənthalt] *m* (*pl* -e) (*kurze Wartezeit*) delay, stop; (*längerer Besuch usw.*) stay. **-serlaubnis** *f* residence permit.

auferlegen ['aufɛrleːgən] *v* impose.

***auferstehen** ['aufɛrʃteːən] *v* rise from the dead. **Auferstehung** *f* resurrection.

***auffahren** ['auffaːrən] *v* rise, go up; (*herauffahren*) draw up; (*aufspringen*) start, jump; (*zornig werden*) flare up; (*wagen*) collide. **Auffahrt** *f* ascent; (*in den Himmel*) Ascension; (*Zufahrtsweg*) drive.

***auffallen** ['auffalən] *v* strike, come to one's attention. *es fiel mir ein* it struck me, I realized. **auffallend** *or* **auffällig** *adj* striking, remarkable.

auffassen ['auffasən] *v* pick up; (*begreifen*) understand; (*deuten*) interpret. **Auffassung** *f* comprehension; (*Auslegung*) interpretation; (*Meinung*) opinion.

***auffliegen** ['auffliːgən] *v* fly up; (*Flugzeug*) take off; (*Tür*) fly open; (*explodieren*) explode.

auffordern ['auffɔrdərn] *v* challenge; (*einladen*) ask, invite. **Aufforderung** *f* challenge; (*Recht*) summons; (*Einladung*) invitation, request.

***auffressen** ['auffrɛsən] *v* devour.

auffrischen ['auffriʃən] *v* freshen up; (*Kenntnisse*) refresh.

aufführen ['auffyːrən] *v* (*Theater*) put on, perform; (*Film*) show; (*Konzert*) give; (*zitieren*) cite; (*aufbauen*) erect. **Aufführung** *f* performance; (*Film*) showing; (*Benehmen*) behaviour.

Aufgabe ['aufgaːbə] *f* task, duty; (*Übergabe*) handing in.

Aufgang ['aufgaŋ] *m* rise, ascent.

***aufgeben** [aufgeːbən] *v* give up; (*Gepäck*) check in.

aufgeblasen ['aufgəblaːzən] *adj* arrogant, conceited.

aufgeklärt ['aufgəklɛːrt] *adj* enlightened.

aufgelegt ['aufgəleːkt] *adj* inclined, in the mood. **gut/schlecht aufgelegt** in a good/bad mood.

aufgeregt ['aufgərɛːkt] *adj* excited.

aufgeschlossen ['aufgəʃlɔsən] *adj* enlightened, open-minded.

***aufhalten** ['aufhaltən] *adj* keep open; (*anhalten*) stop; (*hinhalten*) delay. **sich aufhalten** stay.

***aufhängen** ['aufhɛŋən] *v* hang up.

***aufheben** ['aufheːbən] *v* lift, raise; (*aufbewahren*) store, keep; (*abschaffen*) abolish, cancel. **Aufhebung** *f* raising, abolition.

aufheitern ['aufhaitərn] *v* cheer up. **sich aufheitern** (*Wetter*) brighten up.

aufhören ['aufhœːrən] *v* stop, cease.

aufklären ['aufklɛːrən] *v* (*Person*) enlighten; (*Sache*) clarify, explain. **Aufklärung** *f* clarification; (*the*) Enlightenment.

aufkleben ['aufkleːbən] *v* stick on, paste on.

aufknöpfen ['aufknœpfən] *v* unbutton.

***aufkommen** ['aufkɔmən] *v* arise. **aufkommen für** take responsibility for.

***aufladen** ['auflaːdən] *v* load.

Auflage ['auflaːgə] *f* (*Buch*) edition; (*Zeitung*) circulation.

***auflassen** ['auflasən] *v* leave open.

Auflauf ['auflauf] *m* riot; (*Speise*) trifle, soufflé. **auflaufen** *v* run up; (*Schiff*) run aground; (*Geld*) increase.

auflegen ['aufleːgən] *v* put on; (*Buch*) print, publish; (*Telef*) hang up.

auflösbar ['auflœːtzbaːr] *adj* soluble. **auflösen** *v* (*Knoten*) loosen; (*in Wasser, usw.*) dissolve; (*Rätsel*) solve; (*Vertrag*) cancel; (*Geschäft*) close down; (*Ehe*) break up. **Auflösung** *f* loosening, solution; cancellation; closure; break-up.

***aufmachen** ['aufmaxən] *v* open; (*Knoten, Knöpfe*) undo. **sich aufmachen** set off. **Aufmachung** *f* outward appearance.

aufmerksam ['aufmɛrkzam] *adj* attentive. **jemanden auf etwas aufmerksam machen** draw something to someone's attention. **Aufmerksamkeit** *f* attentiveness, attention.

aufmuntern ['aufmuntərn] *v* encourage, cheer up.

Aufnahme ['aufnaːmə] *f* (*pl* -n) taking up; (*Foto*) shot, picture; (*Tonband, usw.*) recording; (*Zulassung*) admission; (*Empfang*) reception. **aufnahmefähig** *adj* receptive. **Aufnahmeprüfung** *f* entrance exam.

***aufnehmen** ['aufneːmən] *v* take up; (*zulassen*) admit; (*empfangen*) receive; (*Radio*) pick up; (*Foto*) photograph; (*Protokoll, Tonband*) record.

aufopfern ['aufopfərn] *v* sacrifice.

aufpassen ['aufpasən] *v* pay attention; (*vorsichtig sein*) take care. **aufpassen auf** take care of, look after.

Aufprall ['aufpral] *m* (*pl* -e) impact, collision. **aufprallen** *v* strike, collide.

aufputzen ['aufputsən] *v* dress up, adorn; (*reinigen*) clean up.

aufräumen ['aufrɔymən] *v* tidy up, clean up; (*wegschaffen*) clear away. **Aufräumung** *f* cleaning up.

aufrecht ['aufrɛçt] *adj* upright, erect; (*fig*) upright, honest. **–erhalten** *v* maintain, keep up.

aufregen ['aufreɪgən] *v* excite, upset. **sich aufregen** get excited *or* upset. **Aufregung** *f* excitement, agitation.

aufrichten ['aufrɪçtən] *v* erect, set up; (*trösten*) console.

aufrichtig ['aufrɪçtɪç] sincere, honest. **Aufrichtigkeit** *f* sincerity, honesty.

aufrücken ['aufrykən] *v* move up; (*Dienstgrad*) be promoted.

Aufruf ['aufruːf] *m* call, appeal. **aufrufen** *v* call out.

Aufruhr ['aufruːr] *m* (*pl* -e) tumult; (*Erhebung*) revolt. **aufrühren** *v* stir up; (*Erhebung*) incite to revolt. **Aufrührer** *m* (*pl* -) agitator, rebel. **aufrührerisch** *adj* rebellious, riotous.

aufrüsten ['aufrystən] *v* (re)arm. **Aufrüstung** *f* (re)armament.

aufs [aufs] *prep + art* auf das.

aufsagen ['aufzagən] *v* recite, repeat.

Aufsatz ['aufzats] *m* essay; (*Tech*) top (piece); (*Tafel-*) centre-piece.

*****aufsaugen** ['aufzaugən] *v* suck up. **–d** *adj* absorbent.

*****aufschieben** ['aufʃiːbən] *v* push open; (*fig*) put off, delay. **Aufschiebung** *f* postponement, delay.

Aufschlag ['aufʃlaːk] *m* surcharge, extra charge; (*Hose*) turn-up; (*Jacke*) lapel; (*Auftreffen*) impact; (*Tennis*) service. **aufschlagen** *v* (*Preis*) raise; (*Stoff*) turn up; (*auftreffen*) hit; (*Buch*) open, consult; (*Tennis*) serve.

*****aufschließen** ['aufʃliːsən] *v* open up, unlock; (*erklären*) explain.

Aufschluß ['aufʃlus] *m* unlocking; (*Erklärung*) explanation. **aufschlußreich** *adj* informative.

*****aufschneiden** ['aufʃnaɪdən] *v* cut open; (*Fleisch*) carve.

Aufschnitt ['aufʃnɪt] *m* (cold) sliced meat.

Aufschrei ['aufʃraɪ] *m* scream, shriek; (*fig*) outcry.

*****aufschreiben** ['aufʃraɪbən] *v* write down, note.

Aufschrift ['aufʃrɪt] *f* (*Briefumschlag*) address; (*Etikett*) labelling, information; (*Inschrift*) inscription.

Aufschub ['aufʃuːp] *m* delay, deferment.

Aufschwung ['aufʃvuŋ] *m* swinging up, rising up; (*Komm*) boom, upturn (in economy).

*****aufsehen** ['aufzeːən] *v* look up. **Aufsehen** *neut* (*unz.*) stir, sensation. **Aufseher** *m* (*pl* -) overseer, inspector.

aufsetzen ['aufzɛtsən] *v* put on; (*Schriftliches*) draft, draw up.

Aufsicht ['aufzɪçt] *f* supervision, control; (*Verantwortung*) charge, care. **–srat** *m* board of directors.

*****aufspringen** ['aufʃprɪŋən] *v* spring up; (*Tür*) fly open; (*Riß*) crack, open.

Aufstand ['aufʃtant] *m* revolt, rebellion.

aufstapeln ['aufʃtaːpəln] *v* stack up, pile up.

aufstauen ['aufʃtauən] *v* dam (up).

*****aufstehen** ['aufʃteːən] *v* stand up; (*morgens, usw.*) get up, rise; (*revoltieren*) revolt; (*offenstehen*) stand open.

*****aufsteigen** ['aufʃtaɪgən] *v* climb up, ascend, rise; (*Pferd*) mount.

aufstellen ['aufʃtɛlən] *v* set up; (*Kandidat*) nominate; (*Mil*) draw up; (*Theorie, usw.*) propose, advance.

Aufstieg ['aufʃtiːk] *m* ascent, rise.

aufsuchen ['aufzuːxən] *v* (*Arzt, Gasthaus*) visit; (*Person*) visit, look up.

auftanken ['auftaŋkən] *v* refuel.

*****auftauchen** ['auftauxən] *v* (*aus Wasser*) emerge; (*fig*) turn up, crop up.

auftauen ['auftauən] *v* thaw (out), melt.

aufteilen ['auftaɪlən] *v* divide up; (*verteilen*) share out.

Auftrag ['auftraɪk] *m* (*pl* **Aufträge**) (*Komm*) order; (*Aufgabe*) task. **auftragen** *v* (*Farbe*) apply; (*Essen*) serve. **Auftrag‖geber** *m* customer, purchaser. **–nehmer** *m* contractor, supplier.

*****auftreiben** ['auftraɪbən] *v* (*auffinden*) hunt out, find; (*Staub*) stir up; (*Geld*) raise.

*****auftreten** ['auftreːtən] *v* come forward, appear.

Auftritt ['auftrɪt] *m* (*Szene*) scene; (*Schauspieler*) appearance, entrance.

*****auftun** ['auftuːn] *v* open.

aufwachen ['aufvaxən] *v* wake up.

*****aufwachsen** ['aufvaksən] grow up.

Aufwand ['aufvant] *m* (*unz.*) expenditure.
aufwärmen ['aufvɛrmən] *v* (*Sport*) warm up; (*speisen*) heat up.
aufwärts ['aufvɛrts] *adv* up(wards).
aufwecken ['aufvɛkən] *v* wake up.
*****aufwend‖en** ['augvɛndən] *v* (*Geld*) spend; (*Zeit*) devote; (*Energie*) expend. **–ig** *adj* expensive. **Aufwendung** *f* expenditure.
*****aufwerfen** ['aufvɛrfən] *v* throw up.
aufwerten ['aufvɛrtən] *v* raise the value of, revalue. **Aufwertung** *f* revaluation.
*****aufwinden** ['aufvindən] *v* wind up; (*mit der Winde*) winch up.
aufwirbeln ['aufvirbəln] *v* whirl up.
aufwischen ['aufviʃən] *v* wipe up.
aufwühlen ['aufvyːlən] *v* root up; (*fig*) stir up, agitate.
aufzählen ['auftsɛːlən] *v* count out.
aufzeichnen ['auftsaiçnən] *v* sketch; (*niederschreiben*) write down.
*****aufziehen** ['auftsiːən] *v* (*Kind, Tier, Flagge*) raise; (*Vorhang*) open; (*Pflanze*) grow; (*necken*) tease.
Aufzug ['auftsuːk] *m* lift, (*US*) elevator; (*Festzug*) procession, parade; (*Theater*) act.
Augapfel ['aukapfəl] *m* eyeball.
Auge ['augə] *neut* (*pl* **-n**) eye. **unter vier Augen** in private. **ins Auge fallen** be conspicuous, catch the eye. **Augen‖arzt** *m* oculist, ophthalmologist. **–blick** *m* moment, instant. **–braue** *f* eyebrow. **–lid** *neut* eyelid. **–loch** *neut* eye socket.
August [au'gust] *m* (*pl* **-e**) August.
Aula ['aula] *f* (*pl* **Aulen**) (great) hall.
Au-pair-Mädchen [o'pɛirmɛitçən] *neut* au-pair girl.
aus [aus] *prep* from. *adv* out; (*vorbei*) over, finished. *aus London* from London. *aus dem Fenster* out of the window. *aus Liebe zu* for love of. *aus Holz* (made) of wood, wooden. *von mir aus* as far as I'm concerned. *es ist aus* it's over.
ausarbeiten ['ausarbaitən] *v* work out; (*vervollkommnen*) perfect, finish off. **Ausarbeitung** *f* working out; finishing off, completion.
ausarten ['ausarrtən] *v* degenerate.
ausatmen ['ausaːtmən] *v* exhale, breathe out.
ausbaggern ['ausbagərn] *v* dredge.
Ausbau ['ausbau] *m* (*pl* **-ten**) extension; (*Fertigstellung*) completion.

ausbauchen ['ausbauxən] *v* bulge. **Ausbauchung** *f* bulge.
ausbessern ['ausbɛsərn] *v* repair, mend.
Ausbeute ['ausbɔytə] *f* profit, gain; (*Ernte*) crop, yield. **ausbeuten** *v* exploit. **Ausbeut‖er** *m* exploiter. **–ung** *f* exploitation.
ausbilden ['ausbildən] *v* educate; (*Lehrling*) train; (*gestalten*) develop, shape. **Ausbildung** *f* education; training; (*Gestaltung*) development, shaping.
*****ausbleiben** ['ausblaibən] *v* stay away; (*aufhören*) stop.
Ausblick ['ausblik] *m* view; (*fig*) prospect, outlook.
*****ausbrechen** ['ausbrɛçən] *v* break out.
ausbreiten ['ausbraitən] *v* spread (out), stretch (out), extend.
Ausbruch ['ausbrux] *m* outbreak; (*vom Gefängnis*) escape, break-out; (*Zorn, Vulkan*) eruption.
ausbrüten ['ausbryːtən] *v* hatch.
Ausdauer ['ausdauər] *f* endurance, perseverance. **ausdauern** *v* persevere, endure.
ausdehnen ['ausdeinən] *v* extend; (*Metall*) expand. **Ausdehnung** *f* extension; expansion.
*****ausdenken** ['ausdɛŋkən] *v* invent, think out; (*sich vorstellen*) imagine.
ausdrehen ['ausdreiən] *v* turn off, switch off; (*Gelenk*) dislocate.
Ausdruck ['ausdruk] *m* expression, phrase. **ausdrück‖en** *f* express; (*auspressen*) squeeze out. **–lich** *adj* express, explicit. **ausdrucks‖los** *adj* expressionless, vacant. **–voll** *adj* expressive.
auseinander [ausain'andər] *adv* apart. **–bauen** *v* take apart, dismantle. **–fallen** *v* fall to pieces. **–gehen** *v* break up; (*sich trennen*) part. **–nehmen** *v* take apart. **–setzen** *v* explain. **Auseinandersetzung** *f* (vigorous) discussion; (*Streit*) argument.
auserlesen ['ausɛrleːzən] *adj* selected.
ausersehen ['ausɛrzeiən] *v* choose, select.
auserwählen ['ausɛrvɛilən] *v* choose, select.
*****ausfahren** ['ausfarrən] *v* drive out; (*Person*) take for a drive *or* walk. **Ausfahrt** *f* exit; (*Ausflug*) excursion; (*Ausfahren*) departure.
Ausfall ['ausfal] *m* loss; (*Fehlbetrag*) deficiency, deficit; (*Ergebnis*) result; (*Mil*) attack, sally. **ausfallen** *v* fall out; (*unterbleiben*) fail, be wanting; attack.

ausfertigen ['ausfɛrtigən] v (Schriftliches) draw up; (ausstellen) issue.

ausfindig ['ausfindiç] adj **ausfindig machen** find out.

Ausflug ['ausfluːk] m excursion, outing.

ausfragen [ausfraːgən] v question, interrogate.

Ausfuhr ['ausfuːr] f (pl -en) export.

ausführ‖en ['ausfyːrən] v carry out, perform; (Waren) export; (erklären) explain, set out (in detail). **–bar** adj feasible. **–lich** adj detailed, extensive; adv in full. **Ausführung** f execution, performance; (Darstellung) explanation.

ausfüllen ['ausfylən] v fill; (Formular) fill out.

Ausgabe ['ausgaːbə] f expenditure, expense; (Buch) edition.

Ausgang ['ausgaŋ] m going out; (Tür) way out, exit; (Ergebnis) result, issue; (freier Tag) day off.

*ausgeben ['ausgeːbən] v (Geld) spend; (herausgeben) distribute; (Karten) deal. **sich ausgeben für** pose as.

ausgeglichen ['ausgəgliçən] adj (well-)balanced.

*ausgehen ['ausgeːən] v go out; (enden) come to an end; (Vorrat) run out. **Ausgehverbot** neut curfew.

ausgelassen ['ausgəlasən] adj wild, unrestrained, boisterous.

ausgemacht ['ausgəmaxt] adj agreed, settled.

ausgenommen ['ausgənɔmən] prep except for.

ausgeprägt ['ausgəprɛkt] adj marked, distinct.

ausgerechnet ['ausgəreçnət] adv precisely, just.

ausgeschlossen ['ausgəʃlɔsən] adj impossible, out of the question.

ausgesprochen ['ausgəʃprɔxən] adj pronounced, distinct. adv distinctly, very.

ausgewachsen ['ausgəvaksən] adj fullgrown.

ausgezeichnet ['ausgətsaiçnət] adj excellent.

*ausgießen ['ausgiːsən] v pour out.

Ausgleich ['ausglaiç] m (pl -e) settlement; (Entschädigung) compensation; (Sport) equalizer. **ausgleichen** v equalize, make even; (Verlust) compensate; (Konto) balance.

Ausguß ['ausgus] m outlet; (Kanne) spout.

*aushalten ['aushaltən] v bear, endure; (durchhalten) persevere.

*ausheben ['aushɛːbən] v pull out, lift out; (Truppen) enlist. **Aushebung** f enlistment; (Wehrdienst) conscription.

*aushelfen ['aushɛlfən] v help (out), assist.

Aushilfe ['aushilfə] f (temporary) help, assistance.

aushöhlen ['aushøːlən] v hollow out, excavate.

*auskennen ['auskɛnən] v **sich auskennen** (umg.) know what's what; (in ɛiner Sache) know well.

auskleiden ['ausklaidən] v line. **sich auskleiden** undress.

*auskommen ['auskɔmən] v (mit etwas) manage or cope with; (mit einer Person) get on well with.

Auskunft ['auskunft] f (pl **Auskünfte**) information.

auslachen ['auslaxən] v laugh at.

*ausladen ['auslaːdən] v unload.

Auslage ['auslaːgə] f display; (Schaufenster) shop window. **–n** pl expenses pl.

Ausland ['auslant] neut foreign country or countries. **ins** or **im Ausland** abroad. **Ausländer** m (pl -), **Ausländerin** f (pl -nen) foreigner. **ausländisch** adj foreign.

*auslassen ['auslasən] v omit, leave out; (Butter) melt; (Kleider) let down. **Auslassung** f omission; (Äußerung) utterance. **–szeichen** neut apostrophe.

Auslauf ['auslauf] m outflow; (Schiff) sailing, departure; (Bewegungsfreiheit) room to move. **auslaufen** v run out; (Schiff) put to sea.

ausleeren ['auslɛːrən] v empty. **Ausleerung** f emptying, draining.

auslegen ['auslɛːgən] v lay out; (Geld) spend; (erklären) explain, interpret. **Auslegung** f display; (Erklärung) interpretation.

Auslese ['auslɛːzə] f (pl -n) selection; (Wein) choice wine. **auslesen** v select; (Buch) read to the end.

ausliefern ['ausliːfərn] v deliver; (Verbrecher) extradite. **Auslieferung** f delivery; extradition.

auslösen ['ausløːzən] v loosen; (Gefangene) ransom; (veranlassen) cause, spark off.

ausmachen ['ausmaxən] v (Feuer, Licht) put out; (betragen) amount to; (ver-

abreden) agree, fix. **das macht nichts aus** that doesn't matter.

Ausmaß ['ausmaɪs] *neut* scale, extent.

Ausnahme ['ausnaɪmə] *f* (*pl* -n) exception. **mit Ausnahme von** excepting, with the exception of. **-fall** *m* exception, special case. **-zustand** *m* (*Pol*) state of emergency. **ausnahms‖los** *adj* without exception. **-weise** *adv* by way of exception, just for once.

*****ausnehmen** ['ausneɪmən] *v* take out; (*ausschließen*) exclude, make an exception of.

ausnutzen ['ausnutsən] *v* take advantage of.

auspacken ['auspakən] *v* unpack.

ausprobieren ['ausprobiɪrən] *v* try (out), test.

Auspuff ['auspuf] *m* (*pl* -e) exhaust. **-rohr** *neut* exhaust pipe. **-topf** *m* silencer.

ausradieren ['ausradiɪrən] *v* erase, rub out.

ausräumen ['ausrɔymən] *v* clear out, clean out.

ausrechnen ['ausrɛçnən] *v* calculate, work out. **Ausrechnung** *f* calculation.

Ausrede ['ausreɪdə] *f* excuse.

ausreichen ['ausraiçən] *v* be enough *or* sufficient. **-d** *adj* sufficient, enough.

Ausreise ['ausraizə] *f* outward journey; (*Grenzübertritt*) departure, exit. **ausreisen** *v* depart.

ausrichten ['ausriçtən] *v* adjust, align; (*durchsetzen*) accomplish, do; (*Botschaft*) convey.

ausrotten ['ausrɔtən] *v* stamp out, root out.

Ausruf ['ausruɪf] *m* cry, exclamation; (*Bekanntmachung*) proclamation. **ausrufen** *v* cry out, exclaim; (*Namen*) call out. **Ausrufung** *f* exclamation. **-zeichen** *neut* exclamation mark.

ausruhen ['ausruɪən] *v* rest.

ausrüsten ['ausrystən] *v* equip; (*Mil*) arm. **Ausrüstung** *f* equipment; (*Mil*) armament.

Aussage ['auszaɪgə] *f* (*pl* -n) statement, declaration; (*Jur*) evidence, testimony. **aussagen** *v* declare, state; (*Jur*) give evidence, make a statement, testify.

ausschalten ['ausʃaltən] *v* switch off; (*fig*) exclude.

Ausschank ['ausʃaŋk] *m* (*Ausgabe*) service (of alcoholic drinks); (*Kneipe*) bar, pub. **Ausschank über die Straße** off-sales, off-licence.

*****ausscheiden** ['ausʃaidən] *v* withdraw, retire; (*absondern*) separate. **Ausscheidung** *f* withdrawal; separation.

ausschicken ['ausʃikən] *v* send out.

ausschiffen ['ausʃifən] *v* disembark, land. **Ausschiffung** *f* disembarkation.

ausschimpfen ['ausʃimpfən] *v* scold, abuse.

*****ausschlafen** ['ausʃlaɪfən] *v* lie in, sleep until completely rested.

Ausschlag ['ausʃlaɪk] *m* (*Med*) rash; (*Bot*) shoot; (*Zeiger*) deflection. **ausschlagen** *v* knock out; (*ablehnen*) refuse; (*Pferd*) kick out.

*****ausschließen** ['ausʃliɪsən] *v* shut out, lock out; (*fig*) exclude. **ausschließlich** *adj* exclusive; *prep* excluding, exclusive of. **Ausschließung** *f* exclusion; (*Arbeiter*) lock-out.

*****ausschneiden** ['ausʃnaidən] *v* cut out.

Ausschnitt ['ausʃnit] *m* (*Teil*) section; (*Zeitung*) press cutting; (*Kleid*) low neckline.

ausschöpfen ['ausʃœpfən] *v* (*Wasser*) scoop out; (*Boot*) bail out; (*Möglichkeiten*) exhaust.

*****ausschreiben** ['ausʃraibən] *v* write out, copy out; (*Formular*) fill out; (*ankündigen*) announce.

Ausschreitung ['ausʃraituŋ] *f* excess, transgression.

Ausschuß ['ausʃus] **1** *m* committee, board. **2** *m* (*unz.*) (*Abfall*) refuse, rejects *pl*.

ausschweifen ['ausʃwaifən] *v* (*moralisch*) lead a dissolute life; (*von Thema*) digress. **Ausschweifung** *f* debauchery, immorality; digression.

*****aussehen** ['auszeɪən] *v* appear, look. *sie sieht hübsch aus* she looks pretty. *es sieht nach Regen aus* it looks like rain.

außen ['ausən] *adv* (to the) outside, outwards. **Außenbordmotor** *m* outboard motor.

*****aussenden** ['auszɛndən] *v* send out; (*Strahlen*) emit; (*Radio*) transmit.

Außen‖handel *m* foreign trade. **-läufer** *m* wing-half. **-minister** *m* foreign minister. **-politik** *f* foreign policy; (*allgemein*) foreign affairs. **-seite** *f* outside. **-seiter** *m* outsider. **-stürmer** *m* wing (forward).

außer ['ausər] *prep (räumlich)* out of, outside; *(ausgenommen)* except. **außer Betrieb** out of order.

äußer ['ɔysər] *adj* external, exterior, outer.

außer‖dem *adv* besides. **–halb** *adv, prep* outside.

äußerlich ['ɔysərliç] *adj* external.

äußern ['ɔysərn] *v* express, utter; *(zeigen)* manifest, reveal.

außerordentlich [ausər'ɔrdəntliç] *adj* extraordinary.

äußerst ['ɔysərst] *adj* the utmost.

aussetzen ['auszɛtzən] *v (Pflanze)* plant out; *(Kind)* abandon; *(Tier)* set free; *(Geld)* offer; *(einer Gefahr, dem Spott, usw.)* expose (to); *(aufhören)* stop; *(Mot)* stall.

Aussicht ['auziçt] *f* outlook, prospect; *(Blick)* view. **aussichts‖los** *adj* unpromising, hopeless. **–voll** *adj* promising.

aussondern ['auszɔndərn] *(auswählen)* select; excrete. **Aussonderung** *f* separation; selection; excretion.

ausspeien ['ausʃpaiən] *v* spit out; *(Rauch)* belch out.

Aussprache ['ausʃpraixə] *f* pronunciation. ***aussprechen** ['ausʃprɛçən] *v* pronounce.

Ausspruch ['ausʃprux] *m* remark, saying; *(Jur)* verdict.

ausspülen ['ausʃpyːlən] *v* wash out, rinse.

Ausstand ['ausʃtant] *m* strike.

ausstatten ['ausʃtatən] *v* equip, furnish; *(Tochter)* provide with a dowry. **Ausstattung** *f (pl* **-en)** equipment, outfit; dowry.

*ausstehen ['ausʃteːən] *v* be missing; *(Geld)* be owed; *(ertragen)* endure, bear. *ich kann ihn nicht ausstehen* I can't stand him.

*aussteigen ['ausʃtaigən] *v* get off, alight.

ausstellen ['ausʃtɛlən] *v* display, exhibit; *(Paß, Urkunde)* issue; *(Quittung)* write out. **Aussteller** *m (pl* **-)** exhibiter. **Ausstellung** *f* exhibition; issue; writing out.

*aussterben ['ausʃtɛrbən] *v* die out.

Ausstieg ['ausʃtiːg] *m (pl* **-e)** exit door.

*ausstoßen ['ausʃtoːsən] *v* push out, thrust out; *(Schrei)* give.

ausstrahlen ['ausʃtraːlən] *v* radiate.

ausstrecken ['ausʃtrɛkən] *v* stretch out, extend.

*ausstreichen ['ausʃtraiçən] *v (Wort)* strike out, cross out; *(Teig)* roll out.

ausströmen ['ausʃtrœːmən] *v (Flüssigkeit)* pour out; *(Gas)* escape.

aussuchen ['auszuːxən] *v* search (out), select.

Austausch ['austauʃ] *m* exchange. **austauschen** *v* exchange.

austeilen ['austailən] *v* distribute, share out.

Auster ['austər] *f (pl* **-n)** oyster.

Austrag ['austraik] *m (pl* **Austräge)** decision, end, result. **austragen** *v* carry out; *(Kampf)* decide; *(Post)* deliver.

Australi‖en [au'straːliən] *neut* Australia. **–er** *m (pl* **-)**, **–erin** *f (pl* **-nen)** Australian. **australisch** *adj* Australian.

*austreiben ['austraibən] *v* expel.

*austreten ['austreitən] *v* leave, withdraw (from); *(Schuhe, usw.)* wear out.

*austrinken ['austriŋkən] *v* drain, drink off.

Austritt ['austrit] *m* leaving, departure.

ausüben ['ausyːbən] *v* practise; *(Druck, Einfluß)* exert; *(Macht)* wield. **–d** *adj* practising. **Ausübung** *f* practice, exercise.

Ausverkauf ['ausfɛrkauf] *m* (clearance) sale. **ausverkauft** *adj* sold out.

Auswahl ['ausvail] *f* choice, selection.

Auswanderer ['ausvandərər] *m* emigrant. **auswandern** *v* emigrate. **Auswanderung** *f* emigration.

auswärtig ['ausvɛrtiç] *adj* foreign. **das Auswärtige Amt** the Foreign Office.

auswärts ['ausvɛrts] *adv* outwards; *(nach draußen)* outside.

auswechseln ['ausvɛksəln] *v* change (for), exchange.

Ausweg ['ausveik] *m* way out.

*ausweichen ['ausvaiçən] *v* make way; *(Frage)* evade, dodge. **–d** *adj* evasive, elusive. **Ausweichung** *f* evasion.

Ausweis ['ausvais] *m (pl* **-e)** identity card *or* papers; *(Paß)* passport. **ausweisen** *v* expel, turn out. **Ausweisung** *f* expulsion.

auswendig ['ausvɛndiç] *adj* external. **auswendig lernen** learn by heart.

*auswerfen ['ausvɛrfən] *v* throw out; *(Anker)* cast.

auswirken ['ausvirkən] *v* obtain. **sich auswirken auf** have an effect on. **Auswirkung** *f* effect.

auswischen ['ausviʃən] *v* wipe out.

Auswuchs ['ausvuks] *m* growth; *(Nebenerscheinung)* (unwelcome) product, side-effect.

auszahlen ['austsailən] *v* pay out. **Auszahlung** *f* payment.

auszeichnen ['austsaiçnən] *v* (*Ware*) label; (*ehren*) honour; (*hervorheben*) distinguish, mark out. **sich auszeichnen** distinguish oneself. **Auszeichnung** *f* distinction, honour, award.

*****ausziehen** ['austsiːən] *v* pull out, extract; (*Person*) undress; (*aus einer Wohnung*) move out. **sich ausziehen** undress.

Auszug ['austsuːk] *m* removal; (*Abmarsch*) departure; (*Exzerpt*) excerpt.

authentisch [au'tɛntiʃ] *adj* authentic.

Auto ['auto] *neut* (*pl* -s) car, automobile. **–ausstellung** *f* motor show. **–bahn** *f* motorway. **–fahrer** *m* driver, motorist.

Autogramm [auto'gram] *neut* (*pl* -e) autograph.

Automat [auto'maɪt] *m* (*pl* -en) vending machine. **automatisch** *adj* automatic. **automatisieren** *v* automate.

autonom [auto'noːm] *adj* autonomous.

Autor ['autor] *m* (*pl* -en) author.

autoritär [autori'tɛːr] *adj* authoritarian. **Autorität** *f* authority.

Auto‖unfall *m* road accident. **–vermietung** *f* car hire.

avantgardistisch [avãgar'distiʃ] *adj* avantgarde.

Axt [akst] *f* (*pl* Äxte) axe.

B

Baby ['beɪbi] *neut* (*pl* -s) baby.

Bach [bax] *m* (*pl* Bäche) stream, brook.

Backbord ['bakbɔrt] *neut* (*naut*) port (side).

Backe ['bakə] *f* (*pl* -n) cheek.

backen ['bakən] *v* bake.

Bäcker ['bɛkər] *m* (*pl* -) baker. **–ei** *f* (*pl* -en) bakery.

Back‖ofen *m* oven. **–pulver** *neut* baking powder. **–stein** *m* brick.

Bad [baːt] *neut* (*pl* Bäder) bath; (*Badeort*) spa. **Bade‖anstalt** *f* baths, swimming pool. **–anzug** *m* bathing costume. **–hose** *f* bathing trunks *pl*. **baden** *v* bathe. **Bade‖wanne** *f* bath tub. **–zimmer** *neut* bathroom.

Bagger ['bagər] *m* (*pl* -) dredger, excavator. **baggern** *v* dredge, excavate.

Bahn [baɪn] *f* (*pl* -en) railway; (*Weg*) path. **–brecher** *m* pioneer. **bahnen** *v* **den Weg bahnen** pave the way (for).

Bahn‖hof *m* (railway) station. **–steig** *m* (railway) platform.

Bahre ['baɪrə] *f* (*pl* -n) stretcher; (*Toten-*) bier.

Bai [bai] *f* (*pl* -en) (*Bucht*) bay.

Bajonett [bajo'nɛt] *neut* (*pl* -e) bayonet.

Bakterium [bak'teɪrium] *neut* (*pl* **Bakterien**) bacterium (*pl* -a).

balancieren [balã'siːrən] *v* balance.

bald [balt] *adv* soon. **–ig** *adj* early, quick. **–möglichst** *adv* as soon as possible.

Balken ['balkən] *m* (*pl* -) beam.

Balkon [nal'kõː] *m* (*pl* -e) balcony.

Ball¹ [bal] *m* (*pl* Bälle) ball.

Ball² *m* (*pl* Bälle) (*Tanz*) dance, ball.

Ballade [ba'laɪdə] *f* (*pl* -n) ballad.

ballen ['balən] *v* (*Faust*) clench. **sich ballen** cluster, clump together.

Ballen ['balən] *m* (*pl* -) bale, bundle; (*Anat*) palm. **–entzündung** *f* bunion.

Ballett [ba'lɛt] *neut* (*pl* -e) ballet. **Ballett‖tänzer** *m* (*pl* -), **–tänzerin** *f* (*pl* -nen) ballet dancer. **Balletteuse** *f* (*pl* -n) ballerina.

Ballistik [ba'listik] *f* (*unz.*) ballistics. **ballistisch** *adj* ballistic.

Ballon [ba'lõː] *m* (*pl* -e) balloon.

Balsam ['balzam] *m* (*pl* -e) balsam; (*fig*) balm. **balsamieren** *v* embalm.

baltisch ['baltiʃ] *adj* Baltic.

Bambus ['bambus] *m* (*pl* -se) bamboo.

Banane [ba'naɪnə] *f* (*pl* -n) banana.

Band¹ [bant] **1** *neut* (*pl* Bänder) tape; (*Haar*) ribbon; (*Anat*) ligament; (*Radio*) waveband. **2** *neut* (*pl* -e) bond, tie.

Band² *m* (*pl* Bände) (*Buch*) volume.

Band³ [bɛnt] *f* (*pl* -s) (*Jazz*) band.

Bandage [ban'daɪʒə] *f* (*pl* -n) bandage. **bandagieren** *v* bandage.

Bandaufnahme ['bantaufnaɪmə] *f* tape recording.

Bande ['bandə] *f* (*pl* -n) gang, band.

bändigen ['bɛndigən] *v* tame, subdue; (*Wut*) control.

Bandit [ban'diːt] *m* (*pl* -en) bandit.

Bandscheibe ['bantʃaibə] *f* (*Anat*) disc. **–nverfall** *m* slipped disc.

bang(e) ['baŋ(ə)] *adj* afraid, anxious. **bangen** *v* be afraid *or* anxious.

Bank¹ [baŋk] *f* (*pl* Bänke) (*zum Sitzen*) bench, seat.

Bank² *f* (*pl* -en) (*Komm*) bank.

Bankett [baŋ'kɛt] *neut* (*pl* -e) banquet.

bankrott [baŋ'rɔt] *adj* bankrupt. **Bankrott** *m* (*pl* -e) bankruptcy. **Bankrott machen**

go bankrupt. **Bankrotteur** m (pl -e) bankrupt.
Bank‖konto neut bank account. **–note** f banknote.
Bann [ban] m (pl -e) ban; (Kirche) excommunication; (Zauber) spell.
bar [baɪr] adj bare; (Geld) ready, in cash. **für bare Münze nehmen** accept, take at face value.
Bar [baɪr] f (pl -s) bar, tavern.
Bär [bɛɪr] m (pl -en) bear.
Barbar [bar'baɪr] m (pl -en) barbarian. **Barbarei** f (pl -en) barbarism. **barbarisch** adj barbarian.
barfuß ['baɪrfuɪs] adv barefoot. **barfüßig** adj barefoot.
Bargeld ['baɪrgɛlt] neut cash.
Bariton ['bariton] m (pl -e) baritone.
Barmädchen ['baɪrmɛtçən] neut barmaid.
barmherzig [barm'hɛrtsiç] adj merciful, compassionate. **Barmherzigkeit** f mercifulness, mercy.
Barock [ba'rɔk] neut or m baroque. **barock** adj baroque.
Barometer [ba'romɛtər] neut barometer.
Baron [ba'roɪn] m (pl -e) baron. **–in** f (pl -nen) baroness.
Barre ['barə] f (pl -n) bar; (Gold) ingot.
Barriere [bari'ɛɪrə] f (pl -n) barrier, gate.
barsch [barʃ] adj rude, brusque.
Bart [baɪrt] m (pl Bärte) beard. **bärtig** ['bɛɪrtiç] adj bearded.
Base¹ [baɪzə] f (pl -n) (female) cousin.
Base² f (pl -n) alkali, base.
Basel ['baɪzəl] neut Basle, Bâle.
basieren [ba'ziɪrən] v be based (on). **Basis** f (pl Basen) basis (pl -ses), base.
Baß [bas] m (pl Bässe) bass. **–geige** f double-bass.
Bassist [ba'sist] m (pl -en) (Sänger) bass (singer); (Baßgeigenspieler) double-bass (player).
Bastard ['bastart] m (pl -e) bastard.
basteln ['bastəln] v put together, rig up; (umg.) do-it-yourself. **er bastelt gern** he loves to tinker around. **Bastler** m (pl -) handyman, tinkerer.
Bataillon [batai'ljoɪn] neut (pl -e) battalion.
Batterie [batə'riɪ] f (pl -n) battery.
Bau [bau] **1** m (unz.) building, construction; (Getreide, usw.) cultivation, growing. **2** m (pl -e) (Bergwerk) mine; (Tiere) burrow. **3** m (pl -ten) building. **–arbeiter** m construction worker.

Bauch [baux] m (pl Bäuche) belly, abdomen. **bauchig** adj bellied, bulging, convex. **Bauchweh** neut or **Bauschmerzen** pl stomach-ache.
bauen ['bauən] build; (Bot) grow, cultivate.
Bauer ['bauər] m (pl -n) (small) farmer, peasant; (Schach) pawn.
Bäuerin ['bɔyərin] f (pl -nen) farmer's wife, peasant woman. **bäuerlich** adj rustic, rural.
Bauern‖haus neut farmhouse. **–hof** m farm(yard).
baufällig ['baufɛliç] adj dilapidated.
Bau‖genossenschaft f building society. **–ingenieur** m structural or civil engineer. **–stelle** f building site.
Baum [baum] m (pl Bäume) tree; (Schiff) boom. **–garten** m orchard. **–wolle** f cotton.
Bayer ['baiər] m (pl -) Bavarian. **–n** neut Bavaria. **bay(e)risch** adj Bavarian.
beabsichtigen [bə'apziçtigən] v intend, propose.
beachten [bə'axtən] v pay attention to. **beachtungswert** adj noteworthy. **Beachtung** f attention, notice.
Beamte(r) [bə'amtə(r)] m, **Beamtin** f (Staats-) civil servant, official; (Privat-) officer, representative.
beängstigen [bə'ɛŋstigən] v worry, frighten.
beanspruchen [bə'anʃpruxən] v claim, demand; (Person) make demands on. **Beanspruchung** f claim; (Belastung) strain, load.
***beantragen** [bə'antraɪgən] v propose.
beantworten [bə'antvɔrtən] v answer, reply to.
bearbeiten [bə'arbaitən] v work on; (Metall, Holz, Land) work; (Buch) edit, revise; (Musik) arrange; (Theaterstück) adapt. **Bearbeiter** m editor, reviser; arranger. **Bearbeitung** f working; (Verbesserung) revision, adaptation; (Musik) arrangement.
beaufsichtigen [bə'aufziçtigən] v supervise, control. **Beaufsichtigung** f supervision, control.
***beauftragen** [bə'auftraɪgən] v commission, authorize. **Beauftragte(r)** m deputy, agent.
bebauen [bə'bauən] v (Gelände) build on; (Land) cultivate. **bebaute Fläche** f built-up area.

beben ['beɪbən] v tremble, shake.
Becher ['bɛçər] m (pl -) tumbler, glass.
–glas neut (laboratory) beaker.
Becken ['bɛkən] neut (pl -) basin; (Anat) pelvis; (Musik) cymbal.
bedacht [bə'daxt] adj thoughtful, mindful. **Bedacht** m consideration; (Überlegung) deliberation. **bedächtig** adj thoughtful, careful.
Bedarf [bə'darf] m (unz.) need; (Nachfrage) demand.
bedauerlich [bə'dauərliç] adj regrettable, unfortunate. **bedauern** v (Sache) regret, deplore; (Person) be or feel sorry for.
bedecken [bə'dɛkən] v cover. **bedeckt** adj (Himmel) overcast. **Bedeckung** f (pl -en) cover(ing).
***bedenken** [bə'dɛnkən] v consider, think over. **sich bedenken** deliberate, weigh the consequences (of).
bedeuten [bə'dɔytən] v mean, signify. **–d** adj important. **Bedeutung** f meaning; (Wichtigkeit) significance, importance. **bedeutungs‖los** adj meaningless. **–voll** adj significant.
bedienen [bə'diːnən] v serve, wait on; (Maschine) operate, work. **Bedienung** f service; (Maschine) operation; (Diener) staff, servants pl.
bedingt [bə'dɪŋkt] adj conditional, limited. **Bedingung** f (pl -en) condition.
Bedrängnis [bə'drɛŋnis] f (pl -se) distress, trouble.
bedrohen [bə'droːən] v threaten. **Bedrohung** f (pl -en) threat.
***bedürfen** [bə'drfən] v need, require. **Bedürfnis** neut (pl -se) need, requirement. **Bedürfnisanstalt** f public toilet.
beeilen [bə'ailən] v **sich beeilen** hurry.
beeindrucken [bə'aindrukən] v impress.
beeinflussen [bə'ainflusən] v influence, have an influence or effect on.
beeinträchtigen [bə'aintrɛçtigən] v reduce, inhibit, be detrimental to.
beenden [bə'ɛndigən] v end, finish. **Beendigung** f end, termination.
Beerdigung [bə'eːrdiguŋ] f burial, funeral.
Beere ['beːrə] f (pl -n) berry.
Beet [beɪt] neut (pl -e) bed; (Blumen-) flowerbed; (Gemüse) vegetable patch.
befähigen [bə'fɛːigən] v enable, make fit. **befähigt** adj able, qualified. **Befähigung** f (pl -en) capacity, fitness.

befahrbar [bə'faːrbaːr] adj passable, usable. **befahren** v travel or drive on.
***befallen** [bə'falən] v befall; (Krankheit) attack, strike.
befangen [bə'faŋən] adj shy, self-conscious; (parteiisch) biased.
befassen [bə'fasən] v **sich befassen mit** engage in, occupy oneself with.
***befehlen** [bə'feːlən] v command, order. **Befehl** m (pl -e) command, order. **Befehlshaber** m (pl -) commander, commanding officer.
befestigen [bə'fɛstigən] v fasten; (stärken) strengthen; (Mil) fortify. **Befestigung** f (pl -en) fastening; strengthening; (Mil) fortification.
***befinden** [bə'findən] v find. **sich befinden** be, be situated; (Person) be, find oneself. **sich wohl befinden** feel well. **befindlich** adj present, to be found.
beflecken [bə'flɛkən] v stain, soil.
befolgen [bə'folgən] v obey, follow.
befördern [bə'fœdərn] v convey, dispatch; (Rang) promote. **Beförderung** f (pl -en) transport, conveyance; promotion.
befragen [bə'fraɪgən] v question. **sich befragen** enquire, inquire.
befreien [bə'fraiən] v liberate, free. **Befreier** m (pl -) liberator. **Befreiung** f (pl -en) liberation; (Entlastung) exemption.
befreunden [bə'frɔyndən] v **sich befreunden mit** make friends with. **befreundet** adj friendly (with); intimate. **eng befreundet sein mit** be a close friend of.
befriedigen [bə'friːdigən] v satisfy. **–d** adj satisfactory. **Befriedigung** f (pl -en) satisfaction.
befruchten [bə'fruxtən] v fertilize; (anregen) stimulate. **Befruchtung** f (pl -en) fertilization.
befugen [bə'fuːgən] v authorize, empower. **Befugnis** f (pl -se) authority, right.
befürchten [bə'fyrçtən] v fear; (vermuten) suspect. **Befürchtung** f (pl -en) fear, apprehension.
befürworten [bə'fyrvortən] v recommend, advocate.
begabt [bə'gaːpt] adj talented, gifted. **Begabung** f talent, gift.
begatten [bə'gatən] v **sich begatten** mate, copulate. **Begattung** f (pl -en) mating, copulation.
***begeben** [bə'geːbən] v **sich begeben** go, proceed; (verzichten) renounce, give up.

begegnen [bə'geɪgnən] v meet, encounter.
Begegnung f (pl -en) meeting, encounter.
*begehen [bə'geɪən] (Unrecht) commit,
do; (gehen auf) walk on.
begehren [bə'geɪrən] v desire, covet.
begeistern [bə'gaɪstərn] v inspire, fill with
enthusiasm. **begeistert** adj inspired,
enthusiastic. **Begeisterung** f enthusiasm.
Begier [bə'giːr], f (unz.), also **Begierde** f
(pl -n) desire, craving. **begierig** adj desirous, covetous.
begießen [bə'giːsən] v water, sprinkle;
(Braten) baste.
Beginn [bə'gin] m (unz.) beginning.
beginnen v begin.
beglaubigen [bə'glaubigən] v certify,
attest. **Beglaubigung** f (pl -en) certification.
begleiten [bə'glaitən] v accompany.
Begleit‖er m (pl -) attendant; (Musik)
accompanist. **—schreiben** neut covering
letter. **—ung** f (pl -en) attendants pl,
escort; (Musik) accompaniment.
beglücken [bə'glykən] v make happy.
beglückwünschen v congratulate.
Beglückwünschung f (pl -en) congratulations pl.
begnadigen [bə'gnaɪdigən] v pardon.
begnügen [bə'gnyːgən] v **sich begnügen
mit** content oneself with, be satisfied
with.
*begraben [bə'graɪbən] v bury. **Begräbnis**
neut (pl -se) burial, funeral.
*begreifen [bə'graifən] v understand,
grasp, apprehend. **begreiflich** adj comprehensible.
begrenzt [bə'grɛntst] adj restricted, limited.
Begriff [bə'grif] m (pl -e) concept, idea.
Begriffsvermögen neut comprehension.
begründen [bə'gryndən] v found, establish; (Behauptung) substantiate.
Begründer m founder.
begrüßen [bə'gryːsən] v greet, welcome.
begünstigen [bə'gynstigən] v (vorziehen)
favour; (fördern) promote, further.
begütert [bə'gyːtərt] adj wealthy, well-to-
do.
begütigen [bə'gyːtigən] v placate, appease.
behäbig [bə'hɛːbiç] adj (beleibt) portly,
corpulent; (bequem, langsam) comfortable.
behagen [bə'haɪgən] v please, suit.
Behagen neut (pl -) ease, comfort. **behaglich** adj comfortable, at ease.

*behalten [bə'haltən] v keep, retain; (im
Gedächtnis) remember. **Behälter** m (pl -)
container; (Flüssigkeiten) tank.
behandeln [bə'handəln] v treat, handle.
Behandlung f treatment, handling; (Med)
treatment, therapy.
beharren [bə'harən] v persist. **beharrlich**
adj persistent, pertinacious.
behaupten [bə'hauptən] v maintain, asset,
state. **Behauptung** f (pl -eu) statement,
assertion.
behend(e) [bə'hɛnt, bə'hɛndə] adj, also
behendig nimble, agile. **Behendigkeit** f
agility.
beherbergen [bə'hɛrbɛrgən] v rule, govern.
beherrschen [bə'hɛrʃən] v (Zorn, usw.)
control; (meistern, können) master. **sich
beherrschen** control oneself. **Beherrschung** f rule, control; mastery.
beherzigen [bə'hɛrtsigən] v take to heart.
behilflich [bə'hilfliç] adj helpful.
behindern [bə'hindərn] v hinder,
obstruct. **Behinderung** f (pl -en) hindrance.
Behörde [bə'hoerdə] f (pl -n) authority,
authorities pl.
behüten [bə'hyːtən] v guard, protect.
Behüter m (pl -) protector, guard.
bei [bai] prep at; (neben) near. **bei mir** at
(my) home; (in der Tasche) on me. **bei
Herrn Schmidt** at Herr Schmidt's
(house). **bei der Post arbeiten** work for
the Post Office. **bei der Hand nehmen**
take by the hand. **beim Aussteigen** while
or when getting out. **bei Nacht** at night.
bei Tag during the day. **bei der Arbeit** at
work. **bei weitem** by far. **bei Shakespeare**
in Shakespeare.
*beibehalten ['baibəhaltən] v retain;
keep.
*beibringen ['baibriŋən] v bring forward;
(Verlust, Wunde) inflict; (lehren) teach.
Beichte ['baiçtə] f (pl -n) (Rel) confession.
beichten v confess. **Beichtvater** m confes-
sor.
beide ['baidə] adj, pron both. **alle beide**
both. **einer von beiden** either of two. **in
beiden Fällen** in either case. **wir beide**
both of us. **zu beiden Seiten** on both
sides. **beider‖lei** adj of both sorts. **—seitig** adj mutual, reciprocal. **—seits** adv
mutually. **beidhändig** adj ambidextrous.

Beifahrer ['baifaɪrər] *m* (*pl* -) passenger.
Beifall ['baifal] *m* (*unz.*) applause; (*Billigung*) approval. **Beifall klatschen** applaud.
beifügen ['baifyːgən] *v* enclose, attach.
***beigeben** ['baigeːbən] *v* add. **klein beigeben** draw in one's horns, yield.
Beigeschmack ['baigəʃmak] *m* (after)taste; (*fig*) tinge.
Beihilfe ['baihilfə] *f* financial aid, subsidy; (*Jur*) aiding and abetting.
***beikommen** ['baikɔmən] *v* get at, get near, reach.
Beil [bail] *neut* (*pl* -e) (*Holz*) hatchet; (*Fleisch*) cleaver.
Beilage ['bailaːgə] *f* enclosure, insert; (*Zeitung*) supplement.
beiläufig ['bailɔyfiç] *adj* incidental. *adv* incidentally, by the way.
beilegen ['baileːgən] *v* add; (*zuschreiben*) attribute, ascribe; (*schlichten*) settle.
Beileid ['bailait] *neut* (*unz.*) condolence.
beiliegend ['bailiːgənt] *adj* enclosed.
beim [baim] *prep + art* **bei dem**.
***beimessen** ['baimɛsən] *v* attribute, credit with.
Bein [bain] *neut* (*pl* -e) leg; (*Knochen*) bone.
beinah(e) ['bainaː(ə)] *adv* almost, nearly.
Beiname ['bainaːmə] *m* nickname. **mit dem Beinamen ...** known as ..., called ....
beirren [bəˈirən] *v* **sicht nicht beirren lassen** stick to one's opinions, not be misled.
beisammen [bai'zamən] *adv* together.
Beischlaf ['baiʃlaːf] *m* (sexual) intercourse.
beiseite [bai'zaitə] *adv* to one side, aside. **-legen** *v* put aside or by.
Beispiel ['baiʃpiːl] *neut* (*pl* -e) example. **zum Beispiel** for example *or* instance. **beispielsweise** *adv* for instance, as an example.
***beißen** ['baisən] *v* bite. **beißend** *adj* biting; (*Säure*) caustic. **Beiß‖zahn** *m* incisor. **-zange** *f* pincers.
Beistand ['baiʃtant] *m* help, assistance.
***beistehen** ['baiʃteːən] *v* help, assist.
beistimmen ['baiʃtimən] *v* agree, consent. **Bestimmung** *f* agreement, consent.
Beitrag ['baitraːk] *m* (*pl* Beiträge) contribution; (*Klub*) subscription. **beitragen** *v* contribute. **Beiträger** *m* (*pl* -) contributor.

***beitreten** ['baitreːtən] *v* join; (*Meinung*) agree to, accept.
Beiwagen ['baivaːgən] *m* sidecar.
beiwohnen ['baivoːnən] *v* be present at, attend; (*beischlafen*) have sex with.
beizeiten [bai'tsaitən] *adv* early.
beizen ['baitsən] *v* (*Holz*) stain; (*Metall*) etch; (*Fleisch*) salt, pickle.
bejahen [bə'jaːən] *v* affirm, agree to.
bejahrt [bə'jaɪrt] *adj* aged.
bekämpfen [bə'kɛmpfən] *v* fight (against), combat.
bekannt [bə'kant] *adj* known. **bekannt werden** mit become acquainted with. **sich bekanntmachen mit** acquaint oneself with. **Bekannt‖e(r)** acquaintance. **-gabe** *f* announcement, notification. **bekannt‖geben** *v* make known, disclose. **-lich** *adv* as is well known. **Bekanntschaft** *f* acquaintance.
bekehren [bə'keɪrən] *v* convert. **Bekehr‖te(r)** convert. **-ung** *f* conversion.
***bekennen** [bə'kɛnən] *v* acknowledge, confess. **Bekenntnis** *neut* (*pl* -se) confession; (*Glaube*) faith, creed.
beklagen [bə'klaːgən] *v* lament, deplore. **-swert** *adj* lamentable. **Baklagte(r)** *m* accused, defendant.
bekleiden [bə'klaidən] *v* clothe; (*beziehen*) coat; (*Amt*) occupy. **Bekleidung** *f* clothing; (*Material*) coating.
***beklemmen** [bə'klɛmən] *v* oppress, frighten; (*ersticken*) stifle. **Angst beklemmt mich** I am seized by fear.
***bekommen** [bə'kɔmən] *v* obtain, get, receive; (*Zug*) catch; (*Krankheit*) catch, get. **bekömmlich** *adj* wholesome, beneficial.
bekräftigen [bə'krɛftigən] *v* confirm, strengthen.
bekreuzigen [bə'krɔytsigən] *v* **sich bekreuzigen** cross oneself.
bekümmern [bə'kymərn] *v* trouble, distress. **bekümmert sein** be anxious *or* troubled.
bekunden [bə'kundən] *v* state; (*zeigen*) show, manifest.
***beladen** [bə'laidən] *v* load.
Belag [bə'laːk] *m* (*pl* Beläge) covering, coating; (*Aufstrich*) spread. **Butterbrot mit Belag** sandwich.
belagern [bə'laɪgərn] *v* besiege. **Belagerung** *f* siege.

belangen [bə'laŋgən] v concern; (Jur) prosecute. **belanglos** adj unimportant.

belasten [bə'lastən] v burden; (Konto) debit, charge; (Jur) accuse.

belästigen [bə'lɛstigən] v pester, bother; (umg.) bug. **Belästigung** f bother, annoyance.

Belastung [bə'lastuŋ] f (pl -en) load; (Konto) debit, charge.

***belaufen** [bə'laufən] v sich belaufen auf amount to, total.

belauschen [bə'lauʃən] v eavesdrop on, listen to (secretly).

beleben [bə'leːbən] v animate; (Med) revive. **belebt** adj animated, lively; (Ort) crowded, bustling. **Beleb||theit** f liveliness. **-ung** f animation; revival.

Beleg [bə'leːk] m (pl -e) proof, evidence; (Urkunde) voucher. **belegen** v cover; (Platz) reserve; (Kursus) enrol for; (Brot) spread. **belegtes Brötchen** filled roll, sandwich. **Belegschaft** f personnel, staff.

belehren [bə'leːrən] v instruct, teach.

beleibt [bə'laipt] adj portly, stout.

beleidigen [bə'laidigən] v insult. **beleidigend** adj insulting, offensive. **Beleidigung** f (pl -en) insult.

beleuchten [bə'lɔyçtən] v illuminate, light (up). **Beleuchtung** f lighting, illumination.

Belgien ['bɛlgiən] neut Belgium. **Belgier** m (pl -), **Belgierin** f (pl -nen) Belgian. **belgisch** adj Belgian.

belichten [bə'liçtən] v (Foto) expose. **Belichtung** f (pl -en) exposure. **Belichtungsmesser** m light meter.

belieben [bə'liːbən] v (gefallen) please; (wünschen) like, wish. **Belieben** neut pleasure, will. **nach Belieben** at will, as you like. **beliebig** adj any (you like), whatever. **beliebt** adj loved, popular.

bellen ['bɛlən] v bark.

belohnen [bə'loːnən] v reward, recompense. **Belohnung** f reward, recompense.

belüften [bə'lyftən] v ventilate. **Belüftung** f ventilation.

belustigen [bə'lustigən] v amuse. **Belustigung** f amusement.

bemächtigen [bə'mɛçtigən] v sich bemächtigen seize, take possession of.

bemerkbar [bə'mɛrkbaːr] adj noticeable, observable. **bemerken** v notice; (sagen) remark. **-swert** adj remarkable, noteworthy. **Bemerkung** f (pl -en) remark.

***bemessen** [bə'mɛsən] v measure. adj restricted.

bemitleiden [bə'mitlaidən] v pity, feel sorry for.

bemühen [bə'myːən] v trouble (oneself), take pains. **Bemühen** neut or **Bemühung** f (pl -en) effort, exertion.

benachbart [bə'naxbaːrt] adj neighbouring.

benachrichtigen [bə'naxriçtigən] v inform. **Benachrichtigung** f report.

benannt [bə'nant] adj named.

***benehmen** [bə'neːmən] v sich benehmen behave. **Benehmen** neut behaviour.

beneiden [bə'naidən] v envy.

***benennen** [bə'nɛnən] v name, call. **Benennung** f (pl -en) name, title.

Bengel ['bɛŋəl] m (pl -) brat, little rascal.

benommen [bə'nɔmən] adj confused.

benötigen [bə'nœtigən] v need, require.

benutzen [bə'nutsən] v use, make use of. **Benutzung** f use, employment.

Benzin [bɛn'tsiːn] neut petrol, (US) gasoline. **-uhr** f petrol or fuel gauge. **-verbrauch** m fuel consumption.

beobachten [bə'oːbaxtən] v observe, watch; (bemerken) notice. **Beobach||ter** m (pl -) observer, onlooker. **-tung** f (pl -en) observation.

bepflanzen [bə'pflantsən] v plant.

bequem [bə'kveːm] adj comfortable; (mühelos) convenient. **bequemlich** adj lazy, comfort-loving.

***beraten** [bə'raːtən] v advise. sich beraten confer. **beratend** adj advisory. **Berater** m adviser, counsellor. **Beratung** f consultation.

berauben [bə'raubən] v rob or deprive of.

berauschen [bə'rauʃən] v intoxicate.

berechenbar [bə'rɛçənbaːr] adj calculable. **berechnen** v calculate, evaluate. **berechnend** adj (Person) selfish, calculating. **Berechnung** f calculation, evaluation.

berechtigen [bə'rɛçtigən] v entitle, authorize. **berechtigt** adj entitled. **Berechtigung** f authorization, entitlement.

bereden [bə'reːdən] v persuade. **beredsam** adj eloquent.

Bereich [bə'raiç] m (pl -e) region, domain; (fig) field, sphere, realm.

bereichern [bə'raiçərn] v enrich. sich bereichern acquire wealth, get rich.

bereit [bə'rait] adj ready, prepared. **bereiten** v prepare, make ready. **bereit||halten** v keep in readiness. **-machen**

v make ready. **Bereitschaft** *f* readiness.
bereit‖stehen *v* be ready. **–stellen** *v*
make ready, prepare. **Bereitung** *f* (*pl* -en)
preparation. **bereitwillig** *adj* ready.
bereuen [bə'rɔyən] *v* regret, repent.
Berg [bɛrk] *m* (*pl* -e) mountain. **bergab**
adv downhill. **Bergarbeiter** *m* miner. **bergauf**
adv uphill. **Bergbau** *m* mining.
***bergen** ['bɛrgən] *v* conceal; (*schützen*)
protect; (*Güter*) recover.
Bergführer ['bɛrkfyrər] *m* mountain
guide.
bergig ['bɛrgiç] *adj* mountainous, hilly.
Berg‖leute *pl* miners. **–mann** *m* miner.
bergmännisch *adj* mining. **Berg‖rutsch** *m*
landslide. **–steigen** *neut* mountain
climbing. **–steiger** *m* (mountain) climber,
mountaineer.
Bergung ['bɛrguŋ] *f* (*pl* -en) rescue;
(*Schiff*) salvage. **–sarbeiten** *f pl* salvage
or rescue operations.
Bergwerk ['bɛrkvɛrk] *neut* mine, pit.
Bericht [bə'riçt] *m* (*pl* -e) report, account.
berichten *v* report, give an account. **Berichterstatter**
m (*pl* -) reporter; (*Radio*)
commentator, correspondent.
berichtigen [bə'riçtigən] *v* correct,
amend; (*Schulden*) pay. **Berichtigung** *f*
correction; (*Schulden*) settlement.
beritten [bə'ritən] *adj* mounted.
Bernstein ['bɛrnʃtain] *m* amber.
berüchtigt [bə'ryçtiçt] *adj* notorious, infamous.
berücksichtigen [bə'rykziçtigən] *v* keep in
mind, consider, take account of. **Berücksichtigung**
f consideration.
Beruf [bə'ruːf] *m* (*pl* -e) occupation, job,
profession; (*Gewerbe*) trade. **beruf‖en** *v*
appoint; (*kommen lassen*) summon, send
for. **–lich** *adj* professional, vocational.
Berufs‖ausbildung *f* vocational training.
–krankheit *f* occupational disease.
–schule *f* vocational school, technical
college. **berufstätig** *adj* employed. **Berufstätigkeit**
f employment, professional
activity. **Berufung** *f* (*pl* -en) appointment;
(*Jur*) appeal.
beruhen [bə'ruːən] *v* rest (on), be founded
(on).
beruhigen [bə'ruːigən] *v* pacify, calm.
beruhigend *adj* calming. **Beruhigung** *f*
calming, pacification. **Beruhigungsmittel**
neut sedative.
berühmt [bə'ryːmt] *adj* famous, celebrated.

Berühmtheit *f* fame; (*Person*) celebrity.
berühren [bə'ryːrən] *v* touch, handle;
(*angrenzen*) border; (*angehen*) concern;
(*erwähnen*) touch on.
besäen [bə'zɛːən] *v* sow.
besänftigen [bə'zɛnftigən] *v* soothe, calm
(down).
Besatzung [bə'zatsuŋ] *f* (*Mil*) garrison;
(*Schiff, Flugzeug*) crew; (*Pol*) occupation.
–szone *f* occupied area (of a country).
beschädigen [bə'ʃɛːdigən] *v* damage.
Beschädigung *f* damage.
beschaffen [bə'ʃafən] *v* get, procure. *adj*
constituted.
beschäftigen [bə'ʃɛftigən] *v* employ; (*zu
tun geben*) occupy, keep busy. **beschäftigt**
adj employed; occupied, busy. **Beschäftigung**
f (*pl* -en) employment, occupation.
beschämen [bə'ʃɛːmən] *v* shame.
beschatten [bə'ʃatən] *v* shade; (*verfolgen*)
shadow.
beschauen [bə'ʃauən] *v* look at; (*prüfen*)
examine, look over. **Beschauer** *m* (*pl* -)
spectator, inspector. **beschaulich** *adj* contemplative.
Bescheid [bə'ʃait] *m* (*pl* -e) information;
(*Entscheidung*) decision, ruling. **Bescheid
geben/sagen** give information, inform.
Bescheid wissen know the situation, be
well informed.
bescheinigen [bə'ʃainigən] *v* certify,
attest. **Bescheinigung** *f* (*pl* -en) certificate;
(*Quittung*) receipt.
beschenken [bə'ʃɛnkən] *v* give a present
to, present (with).
bescheren [bə'ʃeːrən] *v* give presents.
Bescherung *f* giving (of presents). **eine
schöne Bescherung** a fine mess.
***beschießen** [bə'ʃiːsən] *v* fire on, shell.
Beschießung *f* shelling, bombardment.
beschimpfen [bə'ʃimpfən] *v* insult.
Beschlag [bə'ʃlaːk] *m* (*pl* Beschläge)
clasp, catch; (*Jur*) seizure. **in Beschlag
nehmen** seize, confiscate. **beschlagen** *v*
cover, fit; (*Pferd*) shoe. **Beschlagnahme** *f*
(*pl* -n) confiscation, seizure.
beschlagrahmen *v* seize, confiscate.
beschleunigen [bə'ʃlɔynigən] *v* accelerate.
Beschleunigung *f* acceleration.
***beschließen** [bə'ʃliːsən] *v* decide,
resolve; (*beendigen*) terminate, end.

Beschluß [bə'ʃlus] *m* (*pl* **Beschlüsse**) decision, resolution; (*Ende*) end, close.
beschmutzen [bə'ʃmutsən] *v* dirty, soil.
*****beschneiden** [bə'ʃnaidən] *v* cut, prune, clip; (*Kind*) circumcize. **Beschneidung** *f* circumcision.
beschränken [bə'ʃrɛnkən] *v* restrict, limit. **beschränkt** *adj* limited, confined. **Beschränkung** *f* limitation.
*****beschreiben** [bə'ʃraibən] *v* describe. **Beschreibung** *f* description.
beschuldigen [bə'ʃuldigən] *v* accuse. **Beschuldigte(r)** *m* accused, defendant. **Beschuldigung** *f* accusation.
beschützen [bə'ʃytsən] *v* protect.
Beschwerde [bə'ʃveɪrdə] *f* (*pl* -n) complaint. **beschweren** *v* burden. **sich beschweren über** complain about. **beschwerlich** *adj* troublesome; (*mühselig*) tedious.
beschwichtigen [bə'ʃviçtigən] *v* appease, pacify. **Beschwichtigung** *f* allaying, appeasement.
beschwipst [bə'ʃvipst] *adj* (*umg.*) tipsy.
*****beschwören** [bə'ʃvœɪrən] *v* swear (on oath); (*Person*) implore, beg; (*Erinnerungen, Geister*) conjure up.
*****besehen** [bə'zeɪən] *v* look at, inspect.
beseitigen [bə'zaitigən] *v* remove, get rid of, eliminate; (*Schwierigkeiten*) overcome. **Beseitigung** *f* removal, elimination.
Besen ['beɪzən] *m* (*pl* -) broom.
besessen [bə'zɛsən] *adj* possessed.
besetzen [bə'zɛtsən] *v* (*Platz*) occupy, take; (*Mil*) occupy; (*Kleid*) trim, decorate; (*Posten*) fill. **besetzt** *adj* (*Theater*) full; (*Platz*) taken; (*WC*) occupied, engaged; (*Telef*) engaged. **Besetzung** *f* occupation; (*Theater*) casting.
besichtigen [bə'ziçtigən] *v* inspect, view. **Besichtigung** *f* inspection; (*Sehenswürdigkeiten*) sightseeing.
besiedeln [bə'ziːdəln] *v* colonize.
besiegen [bə'ziːgən] *v* conquer.
*****besinnen** [bə'zinən] *v* **sich besinnen** remember, recollect. **Besinnen** *neut* reflection, consideration. **Besinnung** *f* contemplation; (*Bewußtsein*) consciousness. **besinnungslos** *adj* unconscious, senseless.
Besitz [bə'zits] *m* (*pl* -e) possession. **besitzen** *v* possess, own. **Besitzer** *m* (*pl* -) owner.
besoffen [bə'zɔfən] *adj* (*vulgär*) drunk.

Besoldung [bə'zɔlduŋ] *f* (*pl* -en) salary, wages *pl*.
besonder [bə'zɔndər] *adj* special, particular. **besonders** *adv* especially, particularly. **nichts Besonderes** nothing special, not up to much.
besonnen [bə'zɔnən] *adj* sensible, prudent. **Besonnenheit** *f* prudence.
besorgen [bə'zɔrgən] *v* take care of, see to; (*beschaffen*) obtain. **Besorgnis** *f* (*pl* -se) apprehension, anxiety. **besorgniserregend** *adj* giving cause for worry. **besorgt** *adj* anxious, worried. **Besorgung** *f* (*pl* -en) management; (*Einkauf*) purchase.
bespannen [bə'ʃpanən] *v* (*verkleiden*) cover; (*Fahrzeug*) harness; (*Musik*) string. **Bespannung** *f* (*pl* -en) covering; (*Pferde*) team (of horses).
*****besprechen** [bə'ʃprɛçən] *v* discuss; (*Buch, Film*) review. **Besprechung** *f* discussion; (*Buch, Film*) review.
besser ['bɛsər] *adj* better. **desto besser** so much the better. **um so besser** all the better. **er ist besser dran** he is better off. **bessern** *v* improve, make better. **Besserung** *f* (*pl* -en) improvement.
best [bɛst] *adj* best. **am besten** *adv* best. **aufs Beste** in the best possible way. **besten Dank!** many thanks!
Bestand [bə'ʃtant] *m* (*pl* **Bestände**) continuance, duration; (*Vorrat*) stock, supply.
beständig [bə'ʃtɛndiç] *adj* constant, lasting.
Bestandteil [bə'ʃtanttail] *m* component, part.
bestärken [bə'ʃtɛrkən] *v* strengthen; (*bestätigen*) confirm. **Bestärkung** *f* strengthening; confirmation.
bestätigen [bə'ʃtɛɪtigən] *v* confirm, verify. **bestätigend** *adj* confirmatory. **Bestätigung** *f* (*pl* -en) confirmation.
bestatten [bə'ʃtatən] *v* bury. **Bestattung** *f* (*pl* -en) funeral, burial.
*****bestechen** [bə'ʃtɛçən] *v* bribe, corrupt. **bestechlich** *adj* corrupt, bribable. **Bestechung** *f* bribery, corruption.
Besteck [bə'ʃtɛk] *neut* (*pl* -e) cutlery; knife, fork, and spoon; (*Med*) (medical) instruments *pl*.
*****bestehen** [bə'ʃteɪən] *v* exist, be; (*überstehen*) undergo; (*Examen*) pass; (*fortdauern*) endure, survive. **bestehen auf** insist on. **bestehen aus** consist of.

*besteigen [bə'ʃtaigən] v climb, ascend; (*Pferd*) mount. **Besteigung** f ascent; mounting.

bestellen [bə'ʃtɛlən] v (*Waren*) order; (*Zimmer*) reserve; (*Boden*) cultivate. **Bestellung** f order; reservation; cultivation.

bestenfalls ['bɛstənfals] adv at best. **bestens** adv in the best manner.

besteuern [bə'ʃtɔyərn] v tax. **Besteuerung** f taxation.

Bestie ['bɛstiə] f (pl -n) beast.

bestimmen [bə'ʃtimən] v determine, fix; (*ernennen*) appoint. **bestimmt** adj definite, certain. **Bestimmung** f determination; (*Vorschrift*) regulation; (*Ernennung*) appointment.

bestrafen [bə'ʃtraɪfən] v punish. **Bestrafung** f punishment.

Bestrahlung [bə'ʃtraɪluŋ] f radiation; (*Med*) radiotherapy.

bestreben [bə'ʃtreɪbən] v **sich bestreben** strive, endeavour. **Bestreben** neut or **Bestrebung** f endeavour, exertion.

*bestreiten [bə'ʃtraitən] v dispute, contest.

bestürmen [bə'ʃtyrmən] v assault, storm.

bestürzen [bə'ʃtyrtsən] v startle, disconcert. **bestürzt** adj taken aback, dismayed.

Besuch [bə'zuːx] m (pl -e) visit, call. **Besuch haben** have visitors. *ich bin zu Besuch hier* I am visiting, I am a visitor. **besuchen** v visit, see; (*Schule*) go to, attend. **Besucher** m (pl -) visitor, caller; (*Gast*) guest.

betagt [bə'taɪkt] adj aged, elderly.

betasten [bə'tastən] v finger, touch.

betätigen [bə'tɛɪtigən] v put into action; (*Maschine*) operate; (*Bremse*) apply. **sich betätigen** occupy oneself, work; (*activ sein*) be active, participate. **Betätigung** f operation; (*Teilnahme*) participation.

betäuben [bə'tɔybən] v stun; (*narkotisieren*) anaesthetize. **Betäubung** f anaesthesia. **Betäubungsmittel** neut anaesthetic.

Bete ['beːtə] f beet, beetroot.

beteiligen [bə'tailigən] v give a share to. **sich beteiligen** participate in. **beteiligt sein an** be involved in. **Beteiligung** f (pl -en) participation; (*Anteil*) share.

beten ['beːtən] v pray.

beteuern [bə'tɔyərn] v affirm, declare; (*Unschuld*) protest. **Beteuerung** f (pl -en) affirmation, declaration.

Beton [be'tɔ̃] m concrete.

betonen [bə'toːnən] v stress, emphasize. **Betonung** f stress, emphasis.

Betracht [bə'traxt] m (unz.) consideration. **außer Betracht lassen** leave aside, not consider. **in Betracht ziehen** take into consideration. **betrachten** v look at; (*ansehen als*) consider. **beträchtlich** adj considerable. **Betrachtung** f consideration.

Betrag [bə'traɪk] m (pl Beträge) amount. **betragen** v amount to. **sich betragen** behave. **Betragen** neut behaviour.

betrauen [bə'trauən] v entrust.

Betreff [bə'trɛf] m (unz.) **in Betreff** with regard to, concerning. **betreff‖en** v concern; (*befallen*) befall; (*erwischen*) surprise. **-end** adj in question. prep concerning. **-s** prep concerning.

*betreiben [bə'traibən] v carry on, follow; (*Studien*) pursue; (*Maschine*) operate.

*betreten [bə'treitən] v tread on; (*eintreten*) enter. adj surprised, disconcerted.

Betrieb [bə'triːp] m (pl -e) firm, concern, business; (*Wirken*) running; (*Verkehr*) bustle, activity. **außer Betrieb** out of order. **in Betrieb** in operation, working, in use. **in Betrieb setzen** put into operation. **Betriebs‖anlage** f industrial plant, works. **-anweisung** f operating instructions pl. **-führer** m works manager. **-kosten** pl operating costs. **-rat** m works council. **-unfall** m industrial accident.

*betrinken [bə'triŋkən] v **sich betrinken** get drunk.

betroffen [bə'trɔfən] adj perplexed, disconcerted.

betrüben [bə'tryːbən] v grieve, depress. **betrübt** adj sad.

Betrug [bə'truːk] m (unz.) fraud, swindle, deception. **betrügen** v cheat, deceive. **Betrüger** m (pl -) cheat, swindler. **betrügerisch** adj deceitful.

betrunken [bə'truŋkən] adj drunk. **Betrunkenheit** f drunkenness.

Bett [bɛt] neut (pl -en) bed. **ins Bett gehen** go to bed. **-decke** f bedspread.

betteln ['bɛtəln] v beg.

bettlägerig ['bɛtlɛɪɡəriç] adj bedridden.

Bettler ['bɛtlər] m (pl -) beggar.

Bett‖wäsche f bed linen. **-zeug** neut bedding.

beugen ['bɔygən] v bend; (*Gramm*) inflect. **sich beugen** bow; (*sich fügen*) submit. **Beugung** f bow, bend(ing).

Beule ['bɔylə] f (pl -n) swelling, lump; (*Metall*) dent.

beunruhigen [bə'unruːigən] v disturb, make anxious. **beunruhigt sein** be anxious or alarmed. **Beunruhigung** f agitation, uneasiness.

beurkunden [bə'uːrkundən] v certify, attest. **Beurkundung** f certification.

beurlauben [bə'uːrlaubən] v grant leave to, send on holiday.

beurteilen [bə'uːrtailən] v judge. **Beurteilung** f judgment.

Beute ['bɔytə] f (*unz.*) booty, loot.

Beutel ['bɔytəl] m (pl -) bag; (*Geld*) purse; (*Zool*) pouch. **beuteln** v be baggy, bulge. **Beuteltier** neut marsupial.

bevölkern [bə'fœlkərn] v populate. **dicht/spärlich bevölkert** densely/sparsely populated. **Bevölkerung** f population.

bevollmächtigen [bə'fɔlmɛçtigən] v authorize. **bevollmächtigt** adj authorized. **Bevollmächtigte(r)** m authorized agent or representative; (*Jur*) attorney.

bevor [bə'fɔr] conj before.

*****bevorstehen** [bə'fɔːrʃteɪən] v be imminent, be at hand.

bevorzugen [bə'fɔːrtsuːgən] v favour, prefer.

bewachen [bə'vaxən] v guard.

bewaffnen [bə'vafnən] v arm. **bewaffnet** adj armed. **Bewaffnung** f armament.

bewahren [bə'vaːrən] v keep, preserve.

bewähren [bə'vɛːrən] v **sich bewähren** prove true. **bewährt** adj tried, proved.

Bewahrung [bə'vaːruŋ] f (pl -en) preservation.

Bewährung [bə'vɛːruŋ] f trial, test; (*Jur*) probation. **-sfrist** f probation (period).

bewältigen [bə'vɛltigən] v overpower; (*Schwierigkeit*) master, overcome.

bewässern [bə'vɛsərn] v irrigate. **Bewässerung** f irrigation.

*****bewegen** [bə'veɪgən] v move; (*rühren*) move, touch; (*überreden*) persuade. **sich bewegen** move. **Beweggrund** m motive. **beweglich** adj movable, mobile. **bewegt** adj excited; (*gerührt*) touched, moved. **Bewegung** f (pl -en) motion, movement; (*Rührung*) emotion. **in Bewegung setzen** set in motion.

Beweis [bə'vais] m (pl -e) proof, evidence. **beweisen** v prove, demonstrate.

Beweis‖führung f reasoning, demonstration. **-stück** neut (piece of) evidence, exhibit.

bewerben [bə'vɛrbən] v **sich bewerben um** apply for. **Bewerber** m applicant, candidate. **Bewerbung** f application, candidacy.

bewerkstelligen [bə'vɛrkʃtɛligən] v accomplish, achieve.

bewerten [bə'veɪrtən] v value, rate.

bewilligen [bə'viligən] v allow, grant. **Bewilligung** f (pl -en) grant, permission.

bewirken [bə'virkən] v bring about, cause.

bewirten [bə'virtən] v entertain. **bewirtschaften** v manage, administer. **Bewirtung** f hospitality.

bewohnbar [bə'voɪnbaɪr] adj inhabitable. **bewohnen** v live in, inhabit. **Bewohner** m (pl -) inhabitant, resident.

bewölken [bə'vœlkən] v **sich bewölken** (*Himmel*) become cloudy. **bewölkt** adj overcast, cloudy.

Bewunderer [bə'vundərər] m (pl -) admirer. **bewundern** v admire. **bewundernswert** adj admirable. **Bewunderung** f admiration.

bewußt [bə'vust] adj conscious, deliberate; (*klar*) aware, conscious. **ich bin mir meines Fehlers bewußt** I am aware of my mistake. **Bewußtheit** f awareness. **bewußtlos** adj unconscious. **Bewußt‖losigkeit** f unconsciousness. **-sein** neut consciousness. **zu Bewußtsein kommen** regain consciousness.

bezahlen [bə'tsaɪlən] v pay for; (*Rechnung*) pay. **Bezahlung** f payment, settlement.

bezaubern [bə'tsaubərn] v enchant, charm, bewitch. **Bezauberung** f spell.

bezeichnen [bə'tsaiçnən] v designate; (*Zeichen*) mark. **Bezeichnung** f (*Beschreibung*) description; (*Name*) designation; (*Zeichen*) mark.

bezeugen [bə'tsɔygən] v testify (to), provide evidence of.

*****beziehen** [bə'tsiːən] v cover; (*Geige*) string; (*Wohnung*) move into; (*Posten*) take up; (*Gehalt*) draw; (*erhalten, kaufen*) procure. **das Bett frisch beziehen** change the sheets. **sich beziehen auf** refer to, relate to. **Beziehung** f relation(ship). **in Beziehung auf** with regard or respect to. **beziehungsweise** adv respectively, or.

Bezirk [bə'tsɪrk] *m* (*pl* -e) district, area.
Bezug [bə'tsuːk] *m* (*pl* Bezüge) covering; (*Kopfkissen*) pillow-case; (*Waren*) supply, purchase. **bezüglich** *prep* concerning, relating to.
bezweifeln [bə'tsvaifəln] *v* doubt.
***bezwingen** [bə'tsvɪŋən] *v* conquer, overcome. **sich bezwingen** control *or* restrain oneself.
Bibel ['biːbəl] *f* (*pl* -n) Bible. **-stelle** *f* (biblical) text *or* passage.
Biber ['biːbər] *m* (*pl* -) beaver.
Bibliographie [bibliogra'fiː] *f* (*pl* -n) bibliography. **bibliographisch** *adj* bibliographic.
Bibliothek [biblio'teːk] *f* (*pl* -en) library. **-ar** *m* (*pl* -e) librarian.
biblisch ['biːblɪʃ] *adj* biblical.
bieder ['biːdər] *adj* honest, upright, respectable. **Biedermann** *m* honest man *or* fellow.
***biegen** ['biːgən] *v* bend; (*beim Fahren, usw.*) turn. **biegsam** *adj* supple; (*ügsam*) yielding. **Biegung** *f* (*pl* -en) bend; curve.
Biene ['biːnə] *f* (*pl* -n) bee. **Bienen‖stich** *m* bee sting; (*Kuchen*) almond pastry. **-stock** *m* beehive. **-wabe** *f* honeycomb. **-zucht** *f* beekeeping. **-züchter** *m* beekeeper.
Bier [biːr] *neut* (*pl* -e) beer. **-faß** *neut* beer barrel, cask. **-garten** *m* beer garden.
Biest [biːst] *neut* (*pl* -er) beast; (*fig*) brute.
***bieten** ['biːtən] *v* offer; (*Versteigerung*) bid.
Bigamie [biga'miː] *f* bigamy. **bigamisch** *adj* bigamous.
bigott [bi'gɔt] *adj* bigoted.
Bikini [bi'kiːniː] *m* (*pl* -s) bikini.
Bilanz [bi'lants] *f* (*pl* -en) balance (sheet), annual accounts.
Bild [bɪlt] *neut* (*pl* -er) picture; (*Buch*) illustration; (*Vorstellung*) idea.
bilden ['bɪldən] *v* form, shape; (*erziehen*) educate; (*darstellen*) constitute.
Bilder‖buch *neut* picture book. **-galerie** *f* (picture) gallery. **Bild‖feld** *neut* field of vision. **-hauer** *m* sculptor. **bildhübsch** *adj* very pretty, lovely. **Bildnis** *neut* (*pl* -se) image, likeness. **bildsam** *adj* plastic, flexible; (*fig*) docile. **Bildsäule** *f* statue. **Bildung** ['bɪlduŋ] *f* (*pl* -en) formation; (*Erziehung*) education.

Billard ['bɪljart] *neut* (*pl* -e) billiards; (*Tisch*) billiard table. **-stock** *m* cue.
Billett [bɪl'jɛt] *neut* (*pl* -s *or* -e) ticket; (*Zettel*) note.
billig ['bɪlɪç] *adj* cheap, inexpensive; (*gerecht*) fair. **-en** *v* approve. **Billig‖keit** *f* cheapness, fairness. **-ung** *f* approval.
Billion [bɪl'joːn] *f* (*pl* -en) billion, (*US*) trillion.
Bimsstein ['bɪmsʃtain] *m* pumice stone.
binär [bɪ'nɛːr] *adj* binary.
Binde ['bɪndə] *f* (*pl* -n) bandage; (*Arm*) sling. **-haut** *f* conjunctiva.
***binden** ['bɪndən] *v* bind, tie. **Bind‖estrich** *m* hyphen. **-faden** *m* string. **-ung** *f* binding; (*Verpflichtung*) obligation.
binnen ['bɪnən] *prep* within. **Binnenhandel** *m* internal trade.
Biograph [bio'graːf] *m* (*pl* -en) biographer. **-ie** *f* biography. **biographisch** *adj* biographical.
Biologe [bio'loːgə] *m* (*pl* -n) biologist. **Biologie** *f* biology. **biologisch** *adj* biological.
Birke ['bɪrkə] *f* (*pl* -n) birch.
Birne ['bɪrnə] *f* (*pl* -n) pear; (*Glühbirne*) light-bulb.
bis [bɪs] *prep* (*räumlich*) as far as, (up) to; (*zeitlich*) until, till, to. *conj* until, till. **bis an, bis nach,** *or* **bis zu** up to, as far as. **bis jetzt** until now. **bis morgen** by tomorrow; (*Gruß*) see you tomorrow.
Bischof ['bɪʃɔf] *m* (*pl* Bischöfe) bishop. **bischöflich** *adj* episcopal.
bisher [bɪs'heːr] *adv* until now, hitherto. **-ig** *adj* until now, previous.
Biß [bɪs] *m* (*pl* Bisse) bite. **ein bißchen** a bit, a little.
bisweilen [bɪs'vailən] *adv* occasionally, sometimes.
bitte ['bɪtə] *interj* please. **Bitte** *f* request. **bitten** *v* request, ask; (*anflehen*) beg, implore.
bitter ['bɪtər] *adj* bitter. **Bitter‖keit** *f* bitterness. **-salz** *neut* Epsom salts. **bittersüß** *adj* bittersweet.
Bizeps ['biːtsɛps] *m* (*pl* -e) biceps.
Blamage [bla'maːʒə] *f* (*pl* -n) disgrace. **blamieren** *v* disgrace, compromise.
blank [blaŋk] *adj* bright, polished; (*rein*) clean; (*bloß*) bare.
blanko ['blaŋko] *adj* blank. **Blankoscheck** *m* blank cheque.

Blase ['blaːzə] *f* (*pl* **-n**) bubble; (*Haut*) blister; (*Harn*) bladder. **blasen** *v* blow.
blasiert [bla'ziːrt] *adj* blasé, conceited.
Blasinstrument ['blaːzinstrumɛnt] *neut* wind instrument.
blaß [blas] *adj* pale. **Blässe** *f* paleness, pallor. **bläßlich** *adj* pale, palish.
Blatt [blat] *neut* (*pl* **Blätter**) leaf; (*Papier*) sheet; (*Zeitung*) newspaper; (*Klinge*) blade. **blätterabwerfend** *adj* deciduous.
blättern *v* (*Buch*) leaf through. **Blätterteig** *m* puff pastry. **Blatt‖grün** *neut* chlorophyll. **–laus** *f* greenfly, aphid.
blau [blau] *adj* blue; (*umg.*) drunk. **blaues Auge** black eye. **Blau** *neut* blue.
Blech [blɛç] *neut* (*pl* **-e**) sheet metal, tin. **–bläser** *pl* (*Musik*) brass (section). **–dose** *f* tin-can.
blecken ['blɛkən] show, bare (teeth).
Blei [blai] *neut* (*pl* **-e**) lead.
***bleiben** ['blaibən] *v* remain, stay. **bleiben bei** keep *or* stick to.
bleich [blaiç] *adj* pale, faded. **Bleiche** *f* paleness. **bleichen** *v* black; (*farblos werden*) grow pale, fade. **Bleich‖mittel** *neut* bleach(ing agent). **–sucht** *f* anaemia. **bleichsüchtig** *adj* anaemic.
Bleistift ['blaiʃtift] *m* (*pl* **-e**) pencil.
Blende ['blɛndə] *f* (*pl* **-n**) blind, shutter; (*Foto*) shutter. **blenden** *v* blind, dazzle. **–d** *adj* dazzling, brilliant.
Blick [blik] *m* (*pl* **-e**) glance, look; (*Aussicht*) view. **blicken** *v* look.
blind [blint] *adj* blind. **Blind‖darm** *m* (*Anat*) appendix. **–darmentzündung** *f* appendicitis. **–e(r)** *m* blind man. **–enhund** *m* guide dog. **–enschrift** *f* braille. **–gänger** *m* dud (bomb *or* shell). **–heit** *f* blindness. **blindlings** *adv* blindly.
blinken ['bliŋkən] *v* sparkle, twinkle, glitter. **Blinker** *m* (*Mot*) indicator. **Blinklicht** *neut* flashing light.
blinzeln ['blintsəln] *v* blink, wink.
Blitz [blits] *m* (*pl* **-e**) lightning. **blitzen** *v* flash, emit flashes. **Blitzlicht** *neut* (*Foto*) flash, flashlight. **blitz‖sauber** *adj* spruce, very clean. **–schnell** *adj* quick as lightning. **Blitzschlag** *m* flash of lightning.
Block [blɔk] *m* (*pl* **Blöcke**) block; (*Papier*) pad. **–ade** *f* blockade. **–flöte** *f* (*Musik*) recorder. **blockieren** *v* blockade, block. **Blockschrift** *f* block letters.
blöd(e) [blœt, 'blœːdə] *adj* silly, daft. **Blöd‖heit** *f* stupidity, silliness. **–sinn** *m* idiocy. **blödsinnig** *adj* idiotic, silly.

blöken ['blœːkən] *v* bleat.
blond [blɔnt] *adj* blond, fair-haired. **Blondine** *f* blonde.
bloß [blɔs] *adj* bare, simple. *adv* only, merely.
Blöße ['blœːsə] *f* nakedness; (*fig*) weakness.
bloßlegen ['blosleːgən] *v* reveal, expose.
blühen ['blyːən] *v* bloom, flower. **blühend** *adj* blooming; (*fig*) flourishing.
Blume ['bluːmə] *f* (*pl* **-n**) flower; (*Wein*) bouquet. **Blumen‖beet** *neut* flowerbed. **–blatt** *neut* petal. **–kohl** *m* cauliflower. **–muster** *neut* floral pattern. **–strauß** *m* bunch of flowers, bouquet. **–topf** *m* flowerpot. **–zwiebel** *f* bulb.
Bluse ['bluːzə] *f* (*pl* **-n**) blouse.
Blut [bluːt] *neut* blood. **–druck** *m* blood pressure. **blutdurstig** *adj* bloodthirsty.
Blüte ['blyːtə] *f* (*pl* **-n**) blossom, bloom.
bluten ['bluːtən] *v* bleed. **Blut‖gefäß** *neut* blood vessel. **–gerinnsel** *neut* blood clot. **–gruppe** *f* blood group. **blutig** *adj* bloody. **Blut‖übertragung** *f* blood transfusion. **–untersuchung** *f* blood test.
Bö [bœː] *f* (*pl* **-en**) squall, gust of wind.
Bock [bɔk] *m* (*pl* **Böcke**) (*Schaf-*) ram; (*Ziegen-, Reh-*) buck; (*Sport*) horse. **bockig** *adj* obstinate. **Bockwurst** *f* saveloy, large Frankfurter.
Boden ['boːdən] *m* (*pl* **Böden**) (*Erde*) ground; (*Fuß-*) floor; (*Dach-*) loft; (*Fluß-, Meeres-*) bottom, bed. **bodenlos** *adj* bottomless.
Bogen ['boːgən] *m* (*pl* **-**) curve, arch; (*Waffe, auch für Geige*) bow. **–schießen** *neut* archery. **–schütze** *m* archer.
Bohne ['boːnə] *f* (*pl* **-n**) bean.
bohren ['boːrən] *v* bore, drill. **Bohrer** *m* (*pl* **-**) borer, drill. **Bohrmaschine** *f* drill.
Boje ['boːjə] *f* (*pl* **-n**) buoy.
Bollwerk ['bɔlvɛrk] *neut* (*pl* **-e**) bulwark.
Bolzen ['bɔltsən] *m* (*pl* **-**) peg; (*Tech*) bolt; (*Pfeil*) arrow, bolt.
bombardieren [bɔmbair'diːrən] *v* bombard.
Bombe ['bɔmbə] *f* (*pl* **-n**) bomb. **Bomben‖angriff** *m* bombing raid. **–anschlag** *m* (terrorist) bombing. **–flugzeug** *neut* bomber.
Bonbon [bõ'bõ] *neut* (*pl* **-s**) sweet, (*US*) candy.
Boot [boːt] *neut* (*pl* **-e**) boat.

Bord¹ [bɔrt] *neut* (*pl* -e) board.
Bord² *m* (*pl* -e) edge, rim. **an Bord gehen** go aboard, board.
Bordell [bɔr'dɛl] *neut* (*pl* -e) brothel.
borgen ['bɔrgən] *v* (*entleihen*) borrow; (*verleihen*) lend. **Borger** *m* (*pl* -) (*Entleiher*) borrower; (*Verleiher*) lender.
Borke ['bɔrkə] *f* (*pl* -n) bark.
Börse ['bœrzə] *f* (*pl* -n) stock exchange; (*Beutel*) purse. **-nmakler** *m* stockbroker.
Borste ['bɔrstə] *f* (*pl* -n) bristle.
bös(e) ['bœːz(ə)] *adj* bad; (*Mensch*) wicked; (*Geist*) evil; (*Kind*) naughty; (*wütend*) cross. **bösartig** *adj* malicious; (*Med*) malignant. **Böse** *neut* mischief; *m* evil person, devil.
boshaft ['bɔshaft] *adj* malicious, spiteful.
Boß [bɔs] *m* (*pl* **Bosse**) boss.
böswillig ['bœːzviliç] *adj* malicious, malevolent. **Böswilligkeit** *f* malice.
Botanik [bo'taːnik] *f* botany. **-er** *m* (*pl* -) botanist. **botanisch** *adj* botanical.
Bote ['boːtə] *m* (*pl* -n) messenger.
Bot‖engang *m* errand. **-schaft** *f* message; (*Gesandschaft*) embassy. **-schafter** *m* ambassador.
Bottich ['bɔtiç] *m* (*pl* -e) tub, vat.
Bowle ['boːlə] *f* (*pl* -n) (*Getränk*) punch, fruit cup; (*Gefäß*) punchbowl.
boxen ['bɔksən] *v* box. **Boxer** *m* (*pl* -) boxer. **Boxkampf** *m* boxing match.
brach [braːx] *adj* fallow, untilled.
Branche ['brãːʃə] *f* (*pl* -n) (*Geschäftszweig*) line of business, trade; (*Abteilung*) department.
Brand [brant] *m* (*pl* **Brände**) fire, blaze; (*Med*) gangrene; (*Bot*) mildew. **-bombe** *f* incendiary bomb. **brandmarken** *v* brand, stigmatize. **Brand‖stifter** *m* arsonist, fire-raiser. **-stiftung** *f* arson.
Brandung ['branduŋ] *f* (*pl* -en) surf, breakers *pl*.
Branntwein ['brantvain] *m* brandy.
*braten ['braːtən] *v* roast; (*in der Pfanne*) fry; (*auf dem Rost*) grill. **Braten** *m* roast (meat), joint. **Brat‖fisch** *m* fried fish. **-hähnchen** *neut* roast chicken. **-kartoffeln** *pl* fried potatoes. **-pfanne** *f* frying pan. **-wurst** *f* fried sausage.
Bräu [brɔy] *neut* brew; (*Brauerei*) brewery.
Brauch [braux] *m* (*pl* **Bräuche**) custom, usage. **brauchbar** *adj* serviceable; usable; (*nützlich*) useful. **brauchen** *v* need, require; (*gebrauchen*) use.

brauen ['brauən] *v* brew. **Brauerei** *f* brewery.
braun [braun] *adj* brown. **Braun** *neut* brown.
Braunschweig ['braunʃvaik] *neut* Brunswick.
Brause ['brauzə] *f* (*pl* -n) (*Dusche*) shower; (*Gießkanne*) rose; (*Limonade*) lemonade, pop. **-bad** *neut* shower.
Braut [braut] *f* (*pl* **Bräute**) (*am Hochzeitstag*) bride; (*Verlobte*) fiancée.
Bräutigam ['brɔytigam] *m* bridegroom.
Braut‖jungfer *f* bridesmaid. **-kleid** *neut* wedding dress.
bräutlich ['brɔytliç] *adj* bridal.
brav [braːf] *adj* honest, worthy; (*tapfer*) brave; (*artig*) good, well-behaved.
*brechen ['brɛçən] *v* break; (*Marmor*) quarry. **Bahn brechen** (*fig*) blaze a trail. **Brech‖bohne** *f* French bean. **-mittel** *neut* emetic.
Brei [brai] *m* (*pl* -e) paste, pulp.
breit [brait] *adj* broad, wide. **Breite** *f* breadth, width; (*Geog*) latitude.
Bremse¹ ['brɛmzə] *f* (*pl* -n) brake. **bremsen** *v* brake. **Brems‖licht** *f* brake light, stop light. **-pedal** *neut* brake pedal.
Bremse² *f* (*pl* -n) horse-fly.
brennbar ['brɛnbaːr] *adj* combustible, inflammable. **brennen** *v* burn; (*Branntwein*) distill. **Brenn‖erei** *f* distillery. **-nessel** *f* stinging nettle. **-punkt** *m* focus. **-stoff** *m* fuel.
Brett [brɛt] *neut* (*pl* -er) board; (*Regal*) shelf.
Brezel ['brɛtsəl] *f* (*pl* -n) pretzel.
Brief [briːf] *m* (*pl* -e) letter. **-kasten** *m* letterbox. **-kopf** *m* letterhead. **brieflich** *adj* written. **Brief‖marke** *f* (*postage*) stamp. **-tasche** *f* wallet, pocket book. **-träger** *m* postman.
Brigade [bri'gaːdə] *f* (*pl* -n) brigade.
brillant [bril'jant] *adj* brilliant.
Brille ['brilə] *f* (*pl* -n) spectacles, glasses; (*Schutz*) goggles.
*bringen ['briŋən] *v* bring; (*mitnehmen, begleiten*) take; (*Zeitung*) print, publish; (*Theater*) present, put on. **es weit bringen** do well, go far. **ans Licht bringen** bring to light.
Brite ['britə] *m* (*pl* -n), **Britin** *f* (*pl* -nen) Briton.
bröckelig ['brœkəliç] *adj* crumbly. **bröckeln** *v* crumble.

Brocken ['brɔkən] m (pl -) crumb; (pl) scraps, bits and pieces.
Brombeere ['brɔmbeɪrə] f blackberry. **Brombeerstrauch** m blackberry bush, bramble.
Bronze ['brõsə] f (pl -n) bronze. **bronzefarben** adj bronze(-coloured).
Brosche ['brɔʃə] f (pl -n) brooch.
Broschüre [brɔ'ʃyɪrə] f (pl -n) brochure.
Brot [broɪt] neut (pl -e) bread; (Laib) loaf.
Brötchen ['brœɪtçən] neut bread roll.
Brot||**schnitte** f slice (of bread). **-verdiener** m bread-winner.
Bruch [brux] m (pl **Brüche**) break; (Knochen) fracture; (Math) fraction; (Versprechen, Vertrag) breech; (Gesetz) violation, breech. **bruchfest** adj unbreakable.
brüchig ['bryçiç] adj brittle.
Bruch||**landung** f crash landing. **-stück** neut fragment. **-teil** m fraction.
Brücke ['brykə] f (pl -n) bridge.
Bruder ['bruɪdər] m (pl **Brüder**) brother. **brüderlich** ['brydəarliç] adj brotherly. **Brüderschaft** f brotherhood.
Brühe ['bryɪə] f (pl -n) broth; (Suppengrundlage) stock. **brühen** v scald. **brühheiß** adj boiling hot.
brüllen ['brylən] v bellow; (Sturm, Raubtier) roar. **Brüllfrosch** m bullfrog.
brummen ['brumən] v growl; (Insekten) buzz, hum; (mürrisch sein) grumble; (umg.) go to prison, do time.
brünett [bry'nɛt] adj brunette, dark brown. **Brünette** f brunette.
Brunnen ['brunən] m (pl -) well; (Quelle) spring.
Brunst [brunst] f (pl **Brünste**) lust, ardour; (Tier) heat. **brünstig** adj lusty; (Tier) in heat.
Brüssel ['brysəl] neut Brussels.
Brust [brust] f (pl **Brüste**) breast, chest; (Frauen) breast. **-kasten** m chest. **-krebs** m breast cancer. **-schwimmen** neut breaststroke. **-warze** f nipple.
brutal [bru'taɪl] adj brutal.
brüten ['brytən] v brood.
brutto ['bruto] adj gross. **Bruttogewicht** neut gross weight. **Bruttosozialprodukt** neut gross national product.
Bube ['buɪbə] m (pl -n) boy, lad; (Karten) jack, knave.
Buch [buɪx] neut (pl **Bücher**) book.
Buche ['buɪxə] f (pl -n) beech (tree).

buchen ['buçən] v record, enter (in a book).
Bücherei ['byçərai] f (pl -en) library. **Bücherschrank** m bookcase.
Buchfink [buçfiŋk] m chaffinch.
Buch||**halter** m book-keeper. **-haltung** f book-keeping; accounts department. **-händler** m bookseller. **-handlung** f bookshop. **-macher** m bookmaker.
Büchse ['byksə] f (pl -n) box; (Blechdose) tin, can; (Gewehr) rifle.
Buchstabe ['buːxʃtaɪbə] f (pl -n) letter (of the alphabet). **buchstabieren** v spell. **Buchstabierung** f spelling. **buchstäblich** adj literal.
Bucht [buxt] f (pl -en) bay.
Buckel ['bukəl] m (pl -) hump, mound; (am Rücken) humpback. **buckelig** adj hunchbacked.
bücken ['bykən] v sich bücken stoop, bow.
Bude ['buːdə] f (pl -n) booth; (Markt) stall; (umg.) lodgings, digs, room(s).
Budget [by'dʒɛɪ] neut (pl -s) budget.
Büfett [by'fɛt] neut (pl -s) sideboard, dresser. **kaltes Büfett** cold buffet.
Büffel ['byfəl] m (pl -) buffalo.
Bug [buk] m (pl -e) (Schiff) bow; (Flugzeug) nose; (Pferd) shoulder.
Bügel ['byɪgəl] m (pl -) hoop, handle; (Kleider-) hanger; (Steig-) stirrup. **-brett** neut ironing board. **-eisen** neut iron. **bügelt** adj permanent press, non-iron. **bügeln** v iron.
bugsieren ['bugziɪrən] v tow. **Bugsierer** m tugboat.
Bühne ['byɪnə] f (pl -n) stage. **Bühnen**||**bild** neut set, scenery. **-dichter** m playwright. **-deutsch** neut high German, standard German.
Bulgare [bul'gaɪrə] m (pl -n), **Bulgarin** f (pl -nen) Bulgarian. **Bulgarien** neut Bulgaria. **bulgarisch** adj Bulgarian.
Bulle ['bulə] m (pl -n) bull; (umg.) cop.
Bummel ['buməl] m (pl -) stroll. **bummeln** v stroll; (nichts tun) loaf, loiter. **Bummel**||**streik** m work-to-rule, go-slow. **-zug** m slow train, local (train).
Bund[1] [bunt] neut (pl -e) bundle; (Schlüssel, Radieschen, usw.) bunch.
Bund[2] m (pl **Bünde**) band; (Verein) association, league; (Staat) federation.
Bündel ['byndəl] neut (pl -) bundle, bunch. **bündeln** bundle (up).

Bundes‖bahn f federal railway, West German railway. **–haus** parliament buildings. **–präsident** m federal (West German) president. **–rat** m (*BRD, Österreich*) upper house (of parliament); (*Schweiz*) (Swiss) government. **–republik Deutschland (BRD)** f Federal Republic of Germany, West Germany. **–tag** m West German parliament, federal parliament. **–staat** m federal state.

Bündnis ['byntnɪs] *neut* (*pl* **-se**) alliance.

Bunker ['bʊnkər] m (*pl* **-**) bunker.

bunt [bʊnt] *adj* brightly coloured, gay.

Bürde ['byrdə] f (*pl* **-n**) burden.

Burg [bʊrk] f (*pl* **-en**) castle; (*Festung*) fort.

Bürge ['byrgə] m (*pl* **-n**) surety, guarantor. **bürgen** v guarantee, vouch for; (*Jur*) stand bail for.

Bürger ['byrgər] m (*pl* **-**) citizen; (*Stadt*) townsman; bourgeois. **–krieg** m civil war. **bürgerlich** *adj* bourgeois, middle-class; (*Küche*) simple, plain; (*zivil*) civilian. **Bürger‖meister** m mayor. **–recht** *neut* civil rights. **–schaft** f citizenry, citizens. **–stand** m middle class(es). **–steig** m pavement, (*US*) sidewalk.

Bürgschaft ['byrgʃaft] f (*pl* **-en**) surety, bond.

Büro [by'roː] *neut* (*pl* **-s**) office. **–klammer** f paperclip. **–krat** m (*pl* **-en**) bureaucrat. **–kratie** f bureaucracy. **bürokratisch** *adj* bureaucratic.

Bursche ['bʊrʃə] m (*pl* **-n**) lad, fellow.

Bürste ['byrstə] f (*pl* **-n**) brush. **bürsten** v brush.

Busch [bʊʃ] m (*pl* **Büsche**) bush, shrub.

Büschel ['byʃəl] *neut* (*pl* **-**) bunch; (*Haare*) tuft.

buschig ['bʊʃɪç] *adj* bushy.

Busen ['buːzən] m (*pl* **-**) breast. **–freund** m bosom friend.

Buße ['buːsə] f (*pl* **-n**) penance; (*Geld*) fine.

büßen ['byːsən] v do penance (for).

Büste ['byːstə] f (*pl* **-n**) bust. **–nhälter** m brassière.

Butter ['bʊtər] f (*unz.*) butter. **–blume** f buttercup. **–brot** *neut* (slice of) bread and butter. **–brotpapier** *neut* greaseproof paper.

C

Café [ka'feː] *neut* (*pl* **-s**) café, coffee house.

campen ['kɛmpən] v camp. **Camper** m camper. **Camping** *neut* camping. **–platz** m camp(ing) site.

Caravan ['karavaɪn] m (*pl* **-s**) caravan; (*Kombiwagen*) estate car.

Cellist [tʃe'lɪst] m (*pl* **-en**), **Cellistin** f (*pl* **-nen**) cellist. **Cello** *neut* cello.

Cembalo ['tʃɛmbalo] *neut* (*pl* **-s**) harpsichord.

Champagner [ʃam'panjər] m (*pl* **-**) champagne.

Champignon ['ʃampinjɔ̃] m (*pl* **-s**) mushroom.

Chance ['ʃãsə] f (*pl* **-n**) chance. **Chancengleichheit** f equality of opportunity.

Chaos ['kaɪɔs] *neut* (*unz.*) chaos. **chaotisch** *adj* chaotic.

Charakter ['karaktər] m (*pl* **-e**) character. **charakterisieren** v characterize. **charakteristisch** *adj* characteristic.

Chauffeur [ʃɔ'fœɪr] m (*pl* **-e**) driver, chauffeur.

Chaussee [ʃo'seɪ] f (*pl* **-n**) highway, main road.

Chef [ʃɛf] m (*pl* **-s**) boss, head; (*Arbeitgeber*) employer.

Chemie [çe'miː] f (*unz.*) chemistry. **Chemikalien** f pl chemicals. **Chemiker** m (*pl* **-**) (industrial *or* research) chemist. **chemisch** *adj* chemical. **–e Reinigung** f dry cleaning.

China ['çiːna] *neut* China. **Chinese** m (*pl* **-n**), **Chinesin** f (*pl* **-nen**) Chinese (person). **chinesisch** *adj* Chinese.

Chirurg [çi'rʊrk] m (*pl* **-en**) surgeon. **–ie** f surgery. **chirurgisch** *adj* surgical.

Chlor [kloːr] *neut* (*unz.*) chlorine. **Chloroform** *neut* chloroform. **Chlorophyll** *neut* chlorophyll. **Chlorwasser** *neut* chlorinated water.

Cholera ['kolera] f (*unz.*) cholera.

Chor [koːr] m (*pl* **Chöre**) choir; (*Gesang*) chorus. **–direktor** m choirmaster.

Christ [krɪst] m (*pl* **-en**) Christian. **christlich** *adj* Christian. **Christ‖nacht** f Christmas Eve. **–us** m Christ.

Chrom [kroːm] *neut* (*unz.*) chromium; (*Verchromung*) chrome, chrome-plating. **chromiert** *adj* chrome-plated.

Chronik ['kroːnik] f (*pl* **-en**) chronicle. **chronisch** *adj* chronic.

Computer [kɔm'pjuːtər] *m* (*pl* -) computer.

Coupé [ku'peɪ] *neut* (*pl* -s) railway carriage.

Cousin [ku'zɛ̃] *m* (*pl* -s) (male) cousin. **–e** *f* (female) cousin.

Creme [kreɪm] *f* (*pl* -s) cream; (*Süßspeise*) cream pudding; (*Hautsalbe*) handcream, skincream.

D

da [da] *adv* (*örtlich*) there; (*zeitlich*) then. *conj* because, since. **da draußen/drinnen** out/in there. **da sein** be present. **da bin ich** here I am. **da siehst Du!** see! **da hingegen** whereas.

dabei [da'bai] *adv* close (by), near; (*bei diesem*) thereby; (*außerdem*) moreover. **dabei sein** be present. **es bleibt dabei** that is *or* remains settled. **was ist dabei?** what does it matter? **dabei sein, es zu tun** be on the point of doing it. **dabei bleiben** stick to one's opinion.

Dach [dax] *neut* (*pl* **Dächer**) roof. **–boden** *m* attic. **–fenster** *neut* skylight. **–gesellschaft** *f* holding company. **–kammer** *f* attic, garret. **–rinne** *f* gutter.

Dachs [daks] *m* (*pl* -e) badger. **–hund** *m* dachshund.

Dachziegel ['daxtsiːɡəl] *m* roof tile.

dadurch [da'durç] *adv* for this reason, in this way. **dadurch daß** because, since.

dafür [da'fyːr] *adv* for that; (*Gegenleistung*) in return. **dafür sein** be in favour (of it). **er kann nichts dafür** he can't help it.

dagegen [da'ɡeɪɡən] *adv* against it; (*Vergleich*) in comparison. *conj* on the contrary, however. **ich habe nichts dagegen** I have no objections. **er stimmt dagegen** he is voting against it.

daher [da'heɪr] *adv* from there. *conj* hence, accordingly. **daher kommt es** hence it follows. **daher, daß** since, because.

dahin [da'hin] *adv* there, to that place.

dahinten [da'hintən] *adv* back there.

dahinter [da'hintər] *adv* behind it *or* that. **–kommen** *v* find out (about it), get to the bottom of it. **–stecken** *v* lie behind, be the cause.

damals ['daːmaːls] *adv* then, at that time.

Dame ['daːmə] *f* (*pl* -n) lady; (*Karten*) queen. **–brett** *neut* draughtboard, (*US*) checker-board. **Damen‖binde** *f* sanitary towel. **–toilette** *f* ladies' lavatory. **–wäsche** *f* lingerie. **Dame‖spiel** *neut* draughts. **–stein** *m* draughtsman, (*US*) checker.

Damm [dam] *m* (*pl* **Dämme**) dam; dike; (*Bahn-, Straßen-*) embankment.

dämmen ['dɛmən] *v* dam (up).

dämmern ['dɛmərn] *v* (*morgens*) dawn, grow light; (*abends*) grow dark. **es dämmert** dawn is breaking. **Dämmerung** *f* (*pl* -en) (*morgens*) dawn; (*abends*) twilight, dusk.

Dampf [dampf] *m* (*pl* **Dämpfe**) steam, vapour. **dampfen** *v* steam; (*Rauch*) smoke, fume.

dämpfen ['dɛmpfən] *v* (*Ofen*) damp down; (*Schall*) muffle; (*Licht*) soften; (*Küche*) steam.

Dampf‖er ['dampfər] *m* (*pl* -) steamer, steamship. **–kessel** *m* boiler. **–kochtopf** *m* pressure cooker. **–maschine** *f* steam engine. **–schiff** *neut* steamship, steamer.

danach [da'naːx] *adv* after it; (*darauf*) afterwards; (*entsprechend*) accordingly.

Däne ['dɛnə] *m* (*pl* -n), **Dänin** (-nen) Dane. **Dänemark** *neut* Denmark. **dänisch** *adj* Danish.

daneben [da'neːbən] *adv* beside (it); (*außerdem*) besides.

Dank [daŋk] *m* (*unz.*) thanks. **dankbar** *adj* grateful, thankful. **Dankbarkeit** *f* gratitude. **danken** *v* thank.

dann [dan] *adv* then.

daran [da'ran] *adv* on *or* at *or* by it. **nahe daran sein zu** be on the point of. **nahe daran close** by. **gut daran sein** be well off.

darauf [da'rauf] *adv* on it; (*nachher*) afterwards. **es kommt darauf an (ob)** it depends (whether). **wie kommt er darauf?** why does he think so?

daraus [da'raus] *adv* out of it, from it. **es ist nichts daraus geworden** nothing has come of that.

*darbieten ['daːrbiːtən] *v* offer, present.

darein [da'rain] *adv* in(to) it; (*hierin*) therein.

darin [da'rin] *adv* in it, within; (*hierin*) therein.

darlegen ['daːrleɪɡən] *v* explain, expound. **Darlegung** *f* explanation.

Darlehen ['darrleɪən] *neut* (*pl* -) loan.
Darm [darm] *m* (*pl* **Därme**) intestines *pl.*
−verstopfung *f* constipation.
darstellen ['darrʃtɛlən] *v* represent. **Darsteller** *m* (*Theater*) actor, performer. **Darstellung** *f* exhibition.
darüber [da'ryːbər] *adv* over it; (*davon*) about it; (*hinüber*) across. **darüber hinaus** over and above that, furthermore.
darum [da'rum] *adv* around *or* about it, for it. *conj* therefore.
darunter [da'runtər] *adv* under *or* beneath it; (*dazwischen*) among them; (*weniger*) less.
das [das] *art* the. *pron* which, that.
Dasein ['daɪzaɪn] *neut* (*unz.*) existence, being; (*Vorhandensein*) presence. **Daseinskampf** *m* struggle for existence.
daß [das] *conj* that.
Daten ['daɪtən] *neut pl* data *pl.* **-verarbeitung** *f* data processing.
datieren [da'tiːrən] *v* date.
Datum ['daɪtum] *neut* (*pl* **Daten**) date; (*Tatsache*) datum, fact.
Dauer ['dauər] *f* (*unz.*) period (of time), duration. **−auftrag** *m* (*Bank*) standing order. **dauerhaft** *adj* lasting, durable. **Dauerkarte** *f* season ticket. **dauern** *v* last, continue. **−d** *adj* lasting, permanent. **Dauerwelle** *f* perm, permanent wave.
Daumen ['daumən] *m* (*pl* -) thumb.
Daunendecke ['daunəndɛkə] *f* eiderdown, continental quilt.
davon [da'fɔn] *adv* of *or* from it; (*weg*) away; (*darüber*) about it. **−kommen** *v* escape. **sich davonmachen** *v* (*umg.*) make one's escape, slide off.
davor [da'foːr] *adv* (*örtlich*) before it, in front of it; (*zeitlich*) before that *or* then. **Angst haben davor** be afraid of it. **eine Stunde davor** an hour earlier.
dawider [da'viːdər] *adv* against it.
dazu [da'tsuː] *adv* to it; (*Zweck*) for this (purpose), to that end; (*überdies*) in addition.
dazwischen [da'tsviʃən] *adv* between *or* among them. **−treten** *v* intervene.
Debatte [de'batə] *f* (*pl* -n) debate. **debattieren** *v* debate.
Debet ['deɪbɛt] *neut* (*pl* -s) debit.
Debüt [de'byː] *neut* (*pl* -s) début.
Deck [dɛk] *neut* (*pl* -e) deck.
Decke ['dɛkə] *f* (*pl* -n) cover(ing); (*Bett*) blanket; (*Zimmer*) ceiling. **−l** *m* lid.
decken *v* cover; set (the table).

Deck∥mantel *m* pretext. **−name** *m* pseudonym. **−ung** *f* cover(ing); (*Verteidigung*) protection.
definieren [defi'niːrən] *v* define. **definitiv** *adj* definite.
Defizit ['deɪfitsit] *neut* (*pl* -e) deficit.
degenerieren [degene'riːrən] *v* degenerate.
dehnbar ['deɪnbaɪr] *adj* elastic, malleable; (*Begriff*) loose, vague. **Dehnbarkeit** *f* elasticity, malleability. **dehnen** *v* stretch. **Dehnung** *f* stretching, expansion.
Deich [daɪç] *m* (*pl* -e) dike.
Deichsel ['daɪksəl] *f* (*pl* -n) shaft, pole. **deichseln** *v* (*umg.*) wangle.
dein [daɪn] *adj* your. *pron* yours. **deinerseits** *adv* on *or* for your part. **deinesgleichen** *pron* your likes, people like you. **deinethalben, deinetwegen,** *or* **deinetwillen** *adv* for your sake. **deinige** *pron* **der, die, das deinige** yours.
dekadent [deka'dɛnt] *adj* decadent. **Dekadenz** *f* decadence.
Dekan [de'kaɪn] *m* (*pl* -e) dean.
deklamieren [dekla'miːrən] *v* declaim.
deklarieren [dekla'riːrən] *v* declare.
Deklination [deklinatsi'oɪn] *f* (*pl* -en) declension. **deklinieren** *v* decline.
Dekor [de'koːr] *m* (*pl* -s) decoration(s). **dekorieren** *v* decorate.
Dekret [de'kreɪt] *neut* (*pl* -e) decree.
delegieren [dele'giːrən] *v* delegate. **Delegierte(r)** *m* delegate.
delikat [deli'kaɪt] *adj* (*Person, Angelegenheit*) delicate; (*Speise*) delicious. **Delikatesse** *f* (*pl* -n) delicacy.
Delikt [de'likt] *neut* (*pl* -e) crime.
Delphin [dɛl'fiːn] *m* (*pl* -e) dolphin.
dem [deɪm] *art* to the. *pron* to this *or* that (one); (*wem*) to whom, to which.
Dementi [de'mɛnti] *neut* (*pl* -s) (official) denial. **dementieren** *v* deny.
demgemäß ['deɪmgəmɛːs] *adv* accordingly.
Demission [demisi'oɪn] *f* (*pl* -en) resignation. **demissionieren** *v* resign.
demnach [deɪmnaɪx] *adv* accordingly.
demnächst ['deɪmnɛːçst] *adv* shortly, soon.
Demokrat [demo'kraɪt] *m* (*pl* -en) democrat. **−ie** *f* democracy. **demokratisch** *adj* democratic.
demolieren [demo'liːrən] *v* demolish.
Demonstrant [demɔn'strant] *m* (*pl* -en) demonstrator. **Demonstration** *f* (*pl* -en)

demonstration. **demonstrieren** v demonstrate. **demonstrativ** adj demonstrative.
Demut ['deːmuːt] f (unz.) humility. **demütig** adj humble. **–en** v humiliate, humble. **Demütigung** f (pl -en) humiliation.
demzufolge ['deːmtsufɔlgə] adv accordingly. pron according to which.
den [deɪn] art the. pl to the. pron whom, which. pl to these. **denen** pron to whom or which.
Denkart ['deŋkaːrt] f way of thinking. **denk∥bar** adj conceivable, thinkable. **–en** v think. **Denk∥en** neut thinking, thought. **–er** m (pl -) thinker. **–freiheit** f freedom of thought. **–mal** neut monument. **denkwürdig** adj memorable. **Denkzettel** m lesson, punishment.
dennoch ['dɛnɔx] conj nevertheless.
Denunziant [denuntsi'ant] m (pl -en) informer. **denunzieren** v denounce, inform against.
Depesche [de'pɛʃə] f (pl -n) telegram, dispatch.
deponieren [depo'niːrən] v deposit.
Depot [de'poɪ] neut (pl -s) warehouse, storehouse, depot.
Depression [depresi'oɪn] f (pl -en) depression. **depressiv** adj depressed.
deprimieren [depri'miːrən] v depress. **–d** adj depressing.
der [deɪr] art the; (to) the; pl of the. pron who, which; (to) whom or which.
derart ['deːraɪrt] adv in such a way, so. **–ig** adj of such a type, such, of that kind.
derb [dɛrp] adj crude, coarse; (Person) rough, tough. **Derbheit** f crudeness; (Person) roughness.
deren ['deːrən] pron whose, of which. **derenthalben, derentwegen,** or **derentwillen** adv on whose account, for whose sake.
dergleichen [deːr'glaiçən] adv suchlike, of the kind.
derjenige ['deːrjeːnigə] **diejenige, dasjenige** pron he who, she who, that which.
dermaßen ['deːrmaɪsən] adv to such a degree, in such a way.
derselbe [deːr'zɛlbə] pron **dieselbe, dasselbe** the same.
derzeitig ['deːrtsaitiç] adj present; (damalig) of that time.
des [dɛs] art of the.
desgleichen [dɛs'glaiçən] adv likewise.
deshalb ['dɛshalp] adv therefore.

Desillusion [dɛziluzi'oɪn] f disillusionment.
Desinfektion [dɛzinfɛktsi'oɪn] f disinfection. **–smittel** neut disinfectant. **desinfizieren** v disinfect.
dessen ['dɛsən] pron whose, of which.
destillieren [dɛsti'liːrən] v distil.
desto ['dɛsto] adv the, all the, so much. **je ... desto ...** the ... the ... .
deswegen ['dɛsveːgən], **deswillen** adv therefore.
Detail [de'tai] neut (pl -s) detail, item. **–geschäft** neut retail firm or business. **–handel** m retail trade. **detaillieren** v detail, particularize.
deuten ['dɔytən] v explain, interpret. **deuten auf** point to, indicate, suggest. **deutlich** adj clear, plain. **Deutlichkeit** f clearness, distinctness.
deutsch [dɔytʃ] adj German. **Deutsch** neut German (language). **Deutsche(r)** German. **Deutschland** neut Germany.
Devise [de'viːzə] f (pl -n) motto; pl foreign currency or exchange. **Devisenkurs** m rate of exchange.
Dezember [de'tsɛmbər] m (pl -) December.
dezimal [detsi'maɪl] adj, decimal.
Dia ['diːa] neut (pl -s), also **Diapositiv** slide, transparency.
Dialekt [dia'lɛkt] m (pl -e) dialect.
Dialog [dia'loɪk] m (pl -e) dialogue.
Diamant [dia'mant] m (pl -en) diamond. **diamanten** adj diamond.
Diät [di'ɛɪt] f (pl -en) diet.
dich [diç] pron sing you.
dicht [diçt] adj dense; (Wald, Nebel, Stoff) thick; (nahe) close (by); (wasserdicht) watertight.
dichten¹ ['diçtən] v seal, make watertight or airtight.
dichten² v write (poetry); (erträumen) invent. **Dichter** m (pl -), **Dichterin** f (pl -nen) poet. **dichterisch** adj poetic.
Dichtheit f ['diçthait] or **Dichtigkeit** f density.
Dichtung ['diçtuŋ] f poetry, literature.
dick [dik] adj think; (Person) fat. **Dick∥darm** m large intestine. **–e** f fatness, thickness. **–icht** neut thicket.
die [diː] art the; pron who, which.
Dieb [diːp] m (pl -e) thief. **diebisch** adj thieving. **Diebstahl** m theft.
Diele ['diːlə] f (pl -n) board, plank; (Vor-

raum) hall, vestibule; (*Eis-*) ice-cream parlour. **Dielenbrett** *neut* floorboard.

dienen ['diːnən] *v* serve. **Diener** *m* (*pl -*), **Dienerin** *f* (*pl -nen*) servant. **Dienerschaft** *f* servants *pl*, domestics *pl*. **Dienst** *f* (*pl -e*) service; (*Amt*) duty.

Dienstag ['diːnstaːk] *m* Tuesday. **Dienst‖entlassung** *f* dismissal. –**grad** *m* rank. –**leistung** *f* service. **dienstlich** *adj*, *adv* official(ly). **Dienst‖mädchen** *neut* (serving) maid. –**pflicht** *f* conscription. –**stunden** *f pl* working hours. –**wohnung** *f* official residence.

dieser ['diːzər] **diese, dieses** *pron, adj* this. **dies‖jährig** *adj* this year's. –**mal** *adv* this time. –**seits** *adv* on this side.

Dietrich ['diːtriç] *m* (*pl -e*) skeleton key.

diffizil [difi'tsiːl] *adj* difficult, awkward.

Diktat [dik'taːt] *neut* (*pl -e*) dictation. **Diktator** *m* (*pl -en*) dictator. **diktatorisch** *adj* dictatorial. **Diktatur** *f* (*pl -en*) dictatorship. **diktieren** *v* dictate. **Diktiergerät** *neut* dictaphone, dictating machine.

Diner [di'neː] *neut* (*pl -s*) dinner, dinner-party.

Ding [diŋ] *neut* (*pl -e*) thing. **vor allen Dingen** above all. **Dingelchen** *neut* (pretty) little thing. **Dingsbums** *neut* (*umg.*) what's-it's-name, what's-his-name.

Diplom [di'ploːm] *neut* (*pl -e*) diploma. –**at** *m* (*pl -en*) diplomat. –**atie** *f* diplomacy. **diplomatisch** *adj* diplomatic. **Diplomingenieur** *m* graduate engineer.

dir [diːr] *pron sing* to you.

Dirigent [diri'gɛnt] *m* (*pl -en*) (*Musik*) conductor. **dirigieren** *v* conduct.

Dirne ['dirnə] *f* (*pl -n*) prostitute, whore; wench.

diskontieren [diskɔn'tiːrən] *v* discount. **Diskontsatz** *m* bank-rate.

Diskothek [diskɔ'teːk] *f* (*pl -en*) disco(theque).

diskriminieren [diskrimi'niːrən] *v* discriminate (against). **Diskriminierung** *f* discrimination.

Diskussion [diskusi'oːn] *f* (*pl -en*) discussion. **diskutieren** *v* discuss.

disponieren [dispo'niːrən] *v* arrange, dispose (of). **disponieren über** have at one's disposal.

Dissident [disi'dɛnt] *m* (*pl -en*) dissident, dissenter.

Distel ['distəl] *f* (*pl -n*) thistle.

Disziplin [distsi'pliːn] *f* (*pl -en*) discipline.

disziplinarisch *adj* disciplinary. **Disziplinarverfahren** *neut* disciplinary action.

D-Mark ['deːmark] *f* (*pl -*) (*West*) German mark.

doch [dɔx] *conj* nevertheless, yet, but; *adv* indeed, oh yes.

Docht [dɔxt] *m* (*pl -e*) wick.

Dock [dɔk] *neut* (*pl -e*) dock. –**arbeiter** *m* docker, (*US*) longshoreman.

Dogge ['dɔgə] *f* (*pl -n*) Great Dane; bulldog.

Dogma ['dɔgma] *f* (*pl* **Dogmen**) Dogma. **dogmatisch** *adj* dogmatic.

Doktor ['dɔktɔr] *m* (*pl -en*) doctor. –**arbeit** *f* doctoral *or* PhD thesis. –**at** *neut* doctorate, PhD.

Dolch [dɔlç] *m* (*pl -e*) dagger.

dolmetschen ['dɔlmɛtʃən] *v* interpret. **Dolmetscher** *m* interpreter.

Dom [doːm] *m* (*pl -e*) cathedral. –**herr** *m* canon. –**pfaff** (*Zool*) *m* bullfinch.

Domino ['doːmino] *neut* (*pl -s*) dominoes. –**stein** *m* domino.

Donau ['doːnau] *f* Danube.

Donner ['dɔnər] *m* (*pl -*) thunder. **donnern** *v* thunder.

Donnerstag ['dɔnərstaːk] *m* Thursday. **Donnerwetter** ['dɔnərvɛtər] *neut* thunderstorm. *interj* damn!

doof [doːf] *adj* (*umg.*) daft, dumb, stupid.

Doppel ['dɔpəl] *neut* (*pl -*) duplicate. **Doppel-** *adj* double-. **Doppel‖bett** *neut* double bed. –**ehe** *f* bigamy. –**gänger** *m* ghostly double; doppelgänger **doppeln** *v* double. **Doppel‖punkt** *m* colon. –**sinn** *m* ambiguity. **doppelt** *adj* double(d).

Dorf [dɔrf] *neut* (*pl* **Dörfer**) village. –**bewohner** *m* villager.

Dorn [dɔrn] *m* (*pl -en*) thorn. –**röschen** *neut* Sleeping Beauty.

Dorsch [dɔrʃ] *m* (*pl -e*) cod.

dort [dɔrt] *adv* there. –**her** *adv* (from) there. –**herum** *adv* around there. –**hin** (to) there. –**ig** *adj* of that place.

Dose ['doːzə] *f* (*pl -n*) tin, box; (*Konserven-*) tin, can. **Dosenöffner** *m* tin-opener, can-opener.

dosieren [do'ziːrən] *v* measure out (a dose of). **Dosis** *f* (*pl* **Dosen**) dose.

Dotter ['dɔtə] *m* (*pl -*) (egg) yolk.

Dozent [do'tsɛnt] *m* (*pl -en*) university *or* college lecturer.

Drache ['draxə] *m* (*pl -n*) dragon.

Drachen ['draxən] *m* (*pl* -) kite.

Draht [drait] *m* (*pl* Drähte) wire, (*Kabel*) cable. **–anschrift** *f* telegraphic address. **–seil** *neut* cable. **–seilbahn** *f* cable car, funicular.

Drama ['drɑːma] *neut* (*pl* Dramen) drama. **–tiker** *m* (*pl* -) dramatist. **dramatisch** *adj* dramatic.

dran [dran] *V* daran.

Drang [draŋ] *m* (*pl* Dränge) drive, urge; (*Druck*) pressure.

drängeln ['drɛŋəln] *v* jostle, shove.

drängen ['drɛŋən] *v* press, urge.

drapieren [dra'piːrən] *v* drape.

drastisch ['drastiʃ] *adj* drastic.

drauf [drauf] *V* darauf.

draußen ['drausən] *adv* outside, out of doors.

Dreck [drɛk] *m* (*unz.*) filth, dirt; (*Kot*) excrement; (*Kleinigkeit*) trifle. **dreckig** *adj* filthy, dirty.

Dreh [dreɪ] *m* (*pl* -e) turn. **den Dreh heraushaben** get the hang *or* knack of it. **–bank** *f* lathe. **–buch** *neut* film-script, scenario. **drehen** *v* turn, rotate. **Dreh‖punkt** *m* pivot. **–ung** *f* (*pl* -en) turn, rotation, revolution. **–zahl** *f* revolutions per minute, rpm.

drei [drai] *adj* three. **Dreieck** *neut* triangle. **dreieckig** *adj* triangular. **dreifach** *adj* triple, treble. **Dreifuß** *m* tripod. **dreimal** *adv* three times. **Dreirad** *neut* tricycle.

dreißig ['draisiç] *adj* thirty.

dreist [draist] *adj* cheeky, impudent.

dreiviertel ['draifiːrtəl] *adj* three-quarter. *adv* three-quarters. **Dreiviertelstunde** *f* three-quarters of an hour.

dreizehn ['draitsein] *adj* thirteen.

***dreschen** ['drɛʃən] *v* thresh.

dressieren [drɛ'siːrən] *v* train.

Drillich ['driliç] *m* (*pl* -e) (*Stoff*) drill, canvas.

Drilling ['driliŋ] *m* (*pl* -e) triplet.

drin [drin] *V* darin.

***dringen** ['driŋən] *v* penetrate. **dringen auf** insist on. **dringen in** implore, urge.

dritte ['dritə] *adj* third. **Drittel** *neut* (*pl* -) third.

Droge ['droːgə] *f* (*pl* -n) drug. **Drogerie** *f* (*pl* -n) chemist's (shop), pharmacy. **Drogist** *m* (*pl* -en) pharmacist, chemist.

drohen ['droːən] *v* threaten. **–d** *adj* threatening; (*Gefahr, usw.*) impending, imminent.

Drohne ['droːnə] *f* (*pl* -n) drone.

dröhnen ['drœːnən] *v* roar; (*Kanone*) boom; (*Donner*) rumble.

Drohung ['droːuŋ] *f* (*pl* -en) threat.

Droschke ['drɔʃkə] *f* (*pl* -n) taxi; (*Pferde-*) cab.

Drossel ['drɔsəl] *f* (*pl* -n) (*Vogel*) thrush; (*Mot*) throttle. **–ader** *f* jugular vein. **drosseln** *v* throttle.

drüben ['dryːbən] *adv* over there.

Druck[1] [druk] *m* (*pl* Drücke) pressure.

Druck[2] *m* (*pl* -e) print; (*Auflage*) impression. **drucken** *v* print.

drücken ['drykən] *v* press, push; (*Hand*) shake; (*bedrücken*) oppress. **sich drücken** get out of, avoid.

Druck‖er ['drukər] *m* (*pl* -) printer. **–erei** *f* (*pl* -en) printing plant, press. **–fehler** *m* misprint. **–knopf** *m* push button; (*Kleidung*) snap fastener. **–luft** *f* compressed air. **–messer** *m* pressure gauge. **–sache** *f* printed matter. **–schrift** *f* publication; (*Buchstaben*) block letter.

drum [drum] *V* darum.

drunter ['druntər] *V* darunter.

Drüse ['dryːzə] *f* (*pl* -n) gland.

Dschungel ['dʒuŋəl] *m* (*pl* -) jungle.

du [duː] *pron* you.

Dübel ['dyːbəl] *m* (*pl* -) dowel, wall-plug.

ducken ['dukən] *v* humble, humiliate. **sich ducken** duck; (*fig*) cower.

Dudelsack ['duːdəlzak] *m* bagpipes *pl.*

Duell [du'ɛl] *neut* (*pl* -e) duel. **–ant** *m* duellist.

Duett [du'ɛt] *neut* (*pl* -e) duet.

Duft [duft] *m* (*pl* Düfte) fragrance, aroma; (*Blumen*) scent. **dufte** *adj* (*umg.*) splendid, fine. **duften** *v* smell (sweet), be fragrant. **–d** *adj* fragrant, aromatic.

dulden ['duldən] *v* endure; (*erlauben*) tolerate, allow. **duldsam** *adj* tolerant, patient.

dumm [dum] *adj* stupid. **–heit** *f* stupidity; (*Tat*) foolish action, blunder. **–kopf** *m* idiot, fool.

dumpf [dumpf] *adj* (*Klang*) dull, hollow, muffled; (*schwül*) close, sultry; (*muffig*) musty.

Düne ['dyːnə] *f* (*pl* -n) dune.

Düngemittel ['dyŋəmitəl] *neut* fertilizer. **düngen** *v* fertilize, manure. **Dünger** *m* manure.

dunkel ['duŋkəl] *adj* dark; (*düster*) gloomy, dim; (*ungewiß*) obscure. **Dunkel‖heit** *f* darkness, obscurity.

–kammer f (Foto) darkroom. **dunkeln** v
es dunkelt it is growing dark.
Dünkel ['dyŋkɔl] m arrogance.
dünn [dyn] adj thin. **Dünn‖darm** m small
intestine.
Dunst [dunst] m (pl Dünste) haze, mist.
dunsten v steam.
dünsten ['dynstən] v steam; (Küche) stew.
Dur [duɪr] neut (Musik) major (key).
durch [durç] prep through; (mittels) by,
through; (Zeit) during. adv through(out).
durch Zufall by chance. **durch und durch**
thoroughly.
durchaus [durç'aus] adv completely, thoroughly.
durchblättern [durç'blɛtərn] v leaf
through, skim through.
durchbohren ['durçboɪrən] v pierce, bore
through.
*****durchbrechen** ['durçbrɛçən] v break
through. **Durchbruch** m break-through;
(Öffnung) breach.
*****durchdringen** ['durçdriŋən] v penetrate;
['driŋən] (durchsickern) permeate.
durcheinander [durçain'andər] adv in
confusion, in disorder, in a mess.
Durcheinander neut muddle. **durchei-
nanderbringen** v muddle up; (aufregen)
upset, excite.
Durchfahrt ['durçfaɪrt] f passage; (Tor)
gate. **keine Durchfahrt** no thoroughfare.
Durchfall ['durçfal] m failure; (Med) diarrhoea. **durchfallen** v fall through;
(Prüfung) fail.
durchführen ['durçfyɪrən] v carry out,
perform; (begleiten) lead through.
Durchführung f implementation, execution.
Durchgabe ['durçgaɪbə] f transmission.
Durchgang ['durçgaŋ] m passage.
durchgeben ['durçgeɪbən] v transmit, pass
on.
durchgehen ['durçgeɪən] v walk or go
through, (fliehen) run away; (durchdringen) penetrate. **–d** adj continuous;
(Zug) through.
*****durchkommen** ['durçkɔmən] v come or
pass through.
*****durchlaufen** ['durçlaufən] v run through.
durchleuchten [durç'lɔyçtən] v (Med) x-
ray.
durchmachen ['durçmaxən] v endure, live
through.
Durchmesser ['durçmɛsər] m diameter.

Durchreise ['durçraizə] f journey
through, passage, transit.
durchs [durçs] prep + art **durch das.**
Durchsage ['durçzaɪgə] f announcement.
durchsagen v announce.
Durchschlag ['durçʃlaɪk] m carbon
(copy); (Sieb) strainer, sieve. **–papier**
neut carbon paper.
Durchschnitt ['durçʃnit] m cutting
through; (Querschnitt) cross-section;
(Mittelwert) mean, average. **durchschnittlich** adj average. **Durchschnittsmensch** m
average person, man in the street.
Durchschrift ['durçʃrift] f (carbon) copy.
*****durchsehen** ['durçzeɪən] v look or see
through; (prüfen) look through or over.
Durchsicht ['durçziçt] f (pl -en) perusal,
inspection. **durchsichtig** adj transparent.
durchsuchen ['durçzuɪxən] v search.
durchtrieben [durç'triɪbən] adj cunning,
sly.
*****durchwinden** ['durçvindən] v **sich
durchwinden** struggle through.
*****durchziehen** ['durçtsiɪən] v pass
through; (etwas durch etwas) pull or
draw through; [-'tsiɪən] traverse; (durchdringen) fill, permeate.
*****dürfen** ['dyrfən] v be allowed or permit-
ted to, may. **darf ich?** may I? **wenn ich
bitten darf** if you please. **du darfst nicht**
you may or must not.
dürftig ['dyrftiç] adj needy, poor. **Dürf-
tigkeit** f poverty.
dürr [dyr] adj arid, dry; (hager) lean.
Dürre f drought; (Magerkeit) leanness.
Durst [durst] m thirst. **durst‖en** v be
thirsty. **–ig** adj thirsty. **–stillend** adj
thirst-quenching.
Dusche ['duʃə] f (pl -n) shower. **duschen** v
shower, have or take a shower.
Düse ['dyzə] f (pl -n) jet, nozzle.
Düsen‖antrieb m jet propulsion.
–flugzeug neut jet (plane).
düster ['dystər] adj dark; (fig) gloomy.
Dutzend ['dutsənt] neut (pl -e) dozen.
duzen ['duɪtsən] v address familiarly
(using du), be on first-name terms with.
Dynamik [dy'naɪmik] f dynamics.
dynamisch adj dynamic.
Dynamit [dyna'miɪt] neut (unz.) dynamite.
Dynamo [dy'naɪmo] m (pl -s) dynamo.
Dynastie [dynas'tiɪ] f (pl -n) dynasty.
D-Zug ['deɪtsuk] m (pl D-Züge) express
train.

E

Ebbe ['ɛbə] f (pl -n) ebb; (Niedrigwasser) low tide. **ebben** v ebb.

eben ['eːbən] adj level, even. adv just. ich war eben abgereist I had just left. **eben deswegen** for that very reason. **Ebenbild** neut image. **ebenbürtig** adj equal (in rank). **Ebene** f (pl -n) plain; (Math) plane. **ebenfalls** adv likewise. **Eben‖heit** f evenness, smoothness. **-holz** neut ebony. **ebenso** adv just so. **-gut** adv just as well. **-viel** adv just as much.

Eber ['eːbər] m (pl -) boar.

ebnen ['eːbnən] v level, smooth.

Echo ['ɛçoː] neut (pl -s) echo.

echt [ɛçt] adj genuine, real. **Echtheit** f genuineness, authenticity.

Eck [ɛk] neut (pl -e) corner. **-ball** m corner (kick). **-e** f corner, angle. **eckig** adj angular. **Eckzahn** m eyetooth.

edel ['eːdəl] adj noble. **Edel‖mann** m nobleman. **-metall** neut precious metal. **-stein** m precious stone, gemstone.

Edikt [e'dikt] neut (pl -e) edict.

Efeu ['eːfɔy] m ivy.

Effekten [ɛ'fɛktən] pl effects, personal belongings; (Komm) bonds, shares. **Effekthascherei** f sensationalism. **effekt‖iv** adj effective, actual. **-voll** adj effective.

egal [e'gaːl] adj equal, (all) the same. das ist mir ganz egal it's all the same to me.

Egoismus [ego'ismus] m (pl Egoismen) selfishness, egotism. **Egoist** m egotist. **egoistisch** adj egotistic, selfish.

ehe ['eːə] conj, adv before. **-malig** adj former.

Ehe ['eːə] f (pl -n) marriage. **-brecher** m adulterer. **-brecherin** f adulteress. **ehebrecherisch** adj adulterous. **Ehe‖bruch** m adultery. **-frau** f wife, married woman. **ehe‖lich** adj matrimonial, conjugal. **-los** adj unmarried, single. **Ehe‖mann** m husband. **-paar** neut married couple.

eher ['eːər] adv sooner; (lieber) rather.

Ehre ['eːrə] f (pl -n) honour. **ehren** v honour. **-haft** adj honourable. **Ehrenmal** neut war memorial. **ehrenvoll** adj honourable.

Ehrfurcht ['eːrfurçt] f awe. **ehrfürchtig** adj full of awe or reverence.

Ehr‖gefühl neut sense of honour, self-

respect. **-geiz** m ambition. **ehrgeizig** adj ambitious.

ehrlich ['eːrliç] adj honest, sincere. **Ehrlichkeit** f honesty. **ehrlos** adj dishonourable. **Ehrung** f (pl -en) honour, award. **ehrwürdig** adj venerable.

Ei [ai] neut (pl -er) egg. **-abstoßung** f ovulation. **-dotter** m yolk.

Eiche ['aiçə] f (pl -n) oak. **Eich‖el** f acorn. **-hörnchen** neut squirrel.

Eid [ait] m (pl -e) oath. **einen Eid ablegen** swear an oath.

Eidechse ['aidɛksə] f (pl -n) lizard.

Eidgenosse m confederate. **-nschaft** f confederacy; (Schweiz) Switzerland. **eidgenössisch** adj confederate; (schweizerisch) Swiss.

Eier‖becher ['aiərbɛçər] m eggcup. **-kuchen** m omelette. **-schale** f eggshell. **-stock** m ovary.

Eifer ['aifər] m (unz.) fervour, zeal. **-sucht** f jealousy. **eifersüchtig** adj jealous. **eifrig** adj eager, zealous. **Eifrigkeit** f zeal.

Eigelb ['aigɛlp] neut (pl -e) (egg) yolk.

eigen ['aigən] adj own; (eigentümlich) particular; (eigenartig) peculiar. **sich etwas zu eigen machen** get or acquire something. **etwas auf eigene Faust unternehmen** do something of one's own accord.

Eigenart f (pl -en) peculiarity. **eigenartig** adj peculiar.

eigen‖händig adj by oneself. **-mächtig** adj arbitrary.

Eigen‖name m proper name. **-nutz** m self-interest.

Eigenschaft f (pl -en) quality, attribute, trait. **-swort** neut adjective.

Eigensinn m obstinacy. **eigensinnig** adj obstinate, headstrong.

eigen‖ständig adj independent. **-süchtig** adj egoistic.

eigentlich ['aigəntliç] adv actually, really. adj real, actual.

Eigentum ['aigəntuːm] neut (pl Eigentümer) property. **Eigentümer** m owner. **eigentümlich** adj peculiar.

eignen ['aignən] v sich eignen für or zu be suited for.

Eil‖bote ['ailboːtə] m (pl -n) courier, express messenger. **-brief** m express letter.

Eile ['ailə] f haste, hurry. **eilen** v hurry, hasten. **eilig** adj hasty, fast. **Eil‖sendung** f

(*Post*) special delivery. **–zug** *m* fast train, limited-stop train.

Eimer ['aimər] *m* (*pl* -) bucket, pail.

ein [ain], **eine, ein** *art* a, an. *pron, adj* one.

einander [ain'andər] *pron* each other, one another.

einatmen ['ainaɪtmən] *v* inhale, breathe in. **Einatmung** *f* inhalation.

Einbahnstraße ['ainbaɪnʃtraɪsə] *f* one-way street.

einbalsamieren [ainbaɪlza'miɪrən] *v* embalm.

Einband ['ainbant] *m* binding, cover (of book).

Einbau ['ainbau] *m* installation. **einbauen** *v* install, build in; (*fig*) incorporate (into).

*einbegreifen ['ainbəgraifən] *v* include, comprise. **mit einbegriffen** included.

*einbiegen ['ainbiɪgən] *v* bend in; (*Straße*) turn into.

einbilden ['ainbildən] *v* **sich einbilden** imagine. **Einbildung** *f* imagination; (*Dünkel*) conceit. **–svermögen** *neut* (power of) imagination.

Einblick ['ainblik] *m* insight.

*einbrechen ['ainbrɛçən] *v* break open; (*Haus*) break into, burgle. **Einbrecher** *m* burglar. **Einbruch** *m* break-in, burglary; (*Mil*) invasion. **–sdiebstahl** *m* burglary.

einbürgern ['ainbyrgən] *v* naturalize. **sich einbürgern** become naturalized; (*Wort, usw.*) come into use, gain acceptance. **Einbürgerung** *f* naturalization.

eindeutig ['aindɔytiç] *adj* unequivocal, clear.

*eindringen ['aindriŋən] *v* enter by force; (*Mil*) invade. **eindringlich** *adj* urgent.

Eindruck ['aindruk] *m* impression. **eindrücken** *v* press in. **sich eindrücken** leave an impression. **eindrucksvoll** *adj* impressive.

einerlei ['ainərlai] *adj* of one kind. **es ist einerlei** it makes no difference.

einerseits ['ainərzaits] *adv* on (the) one hand.

einfach ['ainfax] *adj* simple; (*nicht doppelt*) single. **Einfachheit** *f* simplicity.

*einfahren ['ainfaɪrən] *v* drive in; (*Mot*) run in; (*einbringen*) bring in. **Einfahrt** *f* entrance, way in; (*Hineinfahren*) arrival, entrance.

Einfall ['ainfal] *m* idea, inspiration; (*Mil*) invasion, assault. **einfallen** *v* fall in;

(*idee*) occur (to). **es fällt mir ein** it strikes me.

einfältig ['ainfɛltiç] *adj* naive, artless. **Einfältigkeit** *f* naivety, artlessness.

einfetten ['ainfɛtən] *v* grease, lubricate.

*einfinden ['ainfindən] *v* **sich einfinden** appear, turn up.

*einflechten ['ainflɛçtən] *v* interweave; (*Wort*) put in.

Einflug ['ainfluːk] *m* incursion; (*Aero*) approach.

Einfluß ['ainflus] *m* influence. **einflußreich** *adj* influential.

einförmig ['ainfœrmiç] *adj* monotonous, uniform.

einfügen ['ainfyːgən] *v* fit in.

einfühlen ['ainfyːlən] *v* **sich einfühlen in** sympathize with, get into the spirit of. **Einfühlung** *f* sympathizing, sympathy.

Einfuhr ['ainfuːr] *f* (*pl* -en) import. **einführen** *v* bring in; (*Waren*) import; (*Gebrauch*) introduce. **Einfuhrhandel** *m* import trade. **Einführung** *f* introduction. **Einfuhrverbot** *neut* import ban.

Eingang ['aingaŋ] *m* way in; (*Ankunft*) arrival; (*Einleitung*) introduction.

eingebildet ['aingəbildət] *adj* conceited; (*erfunden*) imaginary.

eingeboren ['aingəboːrən] *adj* native; (*angeboren*) innate. **Eingeborene(r)** *m* native.

Eingebung ['aingəbuŋ] *f* (*pl* -en) inspiration.

*eingehen ['aingeːən] *v* go *or* enter into; (*aufhören*) stop; (*welken*) decay; (*Risiko*) run; (*zustimmen*) agree. **–d** *adj* thorough, detailed.

eingemacht ['aingəmaxt] *adj* bottled; canned; (*Fleisch*) potted.

eingenommen ['aingənɔmən] *adj* biased (in favour of).

Eingeweide ['aingəvaidə] *neut* (*pl* -) intestines *pl*, entrails *pl*.

Eingeweihte(r) ['aingəvaitə(r)] *m* (*pl* -) initiate.

eingewöhnen ['aingəvœnən] *v* accustom. **sich eingewöhnen** become accustomed (to).

*eingießen ['aingiɪsən] *v* pour in *or* out.

eingliedern ['aingliɪdərn] *v* incorporate; (*einordnen*) classify. **Eingliederung** *f* incorporation; classification.

*eingreifen ['aingraifən] *v* catch (hold of); (*einmischen*) interfere. **Eingriff** *m* catch; interference; (*Übergriff*) encroachment.

*einhalten ['ainhaltən] *v* restrain, check; observe; stop.

einhändig ['ainhɛndig] *adj* with one hand. **–en** *v* hand in.

einheimisch ['ainhaimiʃ] *adj* native, indigenous.

Einheit ['ainhait] *f* (*pl* **-en**) unit; (*Pol*) unity. **einheitlich** *adj* uniform.

einholen ['ainhoːlən] *v* collect; (*einkaufen*) shop, buy; (*erreichen*) catch up with.

einig ['ainiç] *adj* united, at one. **einig sein** be in agreement. **–en** *v* unite. **sich einigen** agree.

einiger ['ainigər], **einige, einiges** *pron* some, any. **einigermaßen** *adv* to some extent.

Einigkeit *f* (*unz.*) unity; (*Eintracht*) agreement. **Einigung** *f* unification; agreement.

einjährig ['ainjɛːriç] *adj* one-year-old; (*Bot*) annual.

einkassieren ['ainkasiːrən] *v* cash (in).

Einkauf ['ainkauf] *m* (*pl* **Einkäufe**) purchase. **einkaufen** *v* buy, purchase. **einkaufen gehen** go shopping.

einkehren ['ainkeːrən] *v* call in (at).

Einklang ['ainklaŋ] *m* (*pl* **Einklänge**) harmony.

*einkommen ['ainkɔmən] *v* come in, arrive. **Einkommen** *neut* income.

einkreisen ['ainkraisən] *v* encircle.

Einkünfte ['ainkynftə] *pl* revenue, income *sing*.

*einladen ['ainlaːdən] *v* invite. **Einladung** *f* (*pl* **-en**) invitation.

Einlage ['ainlaːgə] *f* (*pl* **-n**) lining, filler; (*Brief*) enclosure; (*Geld*) deposit.

Einlaß ['ainlas] *m* (*pl* **Einlässe**) admission; (*Öffnung*) inlet. **einlassen** *v* let in, admit.

*einlaufen ['ainlaufən] *v* arrive; (*Wasser*) run in.

einleben ['ainleːbən] *v* **sich einleben in** accustom oneself to.

einlegen ['ainleːgən] *v* enclose, insert; (*Beschwerde*) file; (*Fleisch*) salt, pickle.

einleiten ['ainlaitən] *v* introduce, initiate; (*beginnen*) start. **Einleitung** *f* introduction.

einlösen ['ainlœːzən] *v* redeem. **Einlösung** *f* payment, redemption.

einmachen ['ainmaxən] *v* (*Obst*) preserve, bottle.

einmal ['ainmal] *adv* once. **auf einmal** all at once. **noch einmal** (once) again. **nicht einmal** not even. **–ig** *adj* unique.

Einmarsch ['ainmarʃ] *m* (*pl* **Einmärsche**) marching in, entry. **einmarschieren** *v* enter, march in (to).

einmischen ['ainmiʃən] *v* **sich einmischen in** interfere *or* meddle in.

einmünden ['ainmyndən] *v* run *or* flow (into), join.

Einnahme ['ainnaːmə] *f* (*pl* **-n**) receipts *pl*, takings *pl*, revenue.

*einnehmen ['ainneːmən] *v* take (in); (*Geld*) receive.

Einöde ['ainœːdə] *f* (*pl* **-n**) desert, wasteland.

einölen ['ainœːlən] *v* oil.

einordnen ['ainɔrdnən] *v* order, arrange; (*Mot*) get in lane.

einpacken ['ainpakən] *v* pack, wrap up.

einpökeln ['ainpœːkəln] *v* pickle.

einprägen ['ainpreːgən] *v* imprint. **jemandem etwas einprägen** impress something on somebody.

einrahmen ['ainraːmən] *v* frame.

einräumen ['ainrɔymən] *v* tidy up, put away; (*zugeben*) concede; (*einrichten*) furnish; (*Platz*) vacate, give up.

Einrede ['ainreːdə] *f* (*pl* **-n**) objection. **einreden** *v* persuade; (*widersprechen*) contradict.

einreichen ['ainraiçən] *v* hand over *or* in.

Einreise ['ainraizə] *f* (*pl* **-n**) entry.

einrichten ['ainriçtən] *v* arrange, set up; (*gründen*) establish; (*Zimmer*) furnish. **Einrichtung** *f* establishment; arrangement; (*Anstalt*) institution; (*Zimmer*) fittings *pl*, furnishings *pl*.

einrücken ['ainrykən] *v* enter.

eins [ains] *pron* one.

einsam ['ainzaːm] *adj* lonely, solitary. **Einsamkeit** *f* loneliness.

Einsatz ['ainzats] *m* (*pl* **Einsätze**) insertion; insert, filling; (*Spiel*) stake; (*Mil*) mission, operation.

einschalten ['ainʃaltən] *v* switch on; (*einfügen*) insert, put in. **Einschaltung** *f* switching on; insertion.

einschiffen ['ainʃifən] *v* bring on board, load (into a ship). **sich einschiffen** go on board, embark.

*einschlafen ['ainʃlaːfən] *v* go to sleep, fall asleep.

Einschlag ['ainʃlaık] m (pl **Einschläge**) impact; (*Umschlag*) wrapper. **einschlagen** v drive in, break; (*einwickeln*) wrap; (*Weg*) take, follow; (*Hände*) shake hands; (*zustimmen*) agree.

***einschließen** ['ainʃliːsən] v lock up or in; (*umfassen*) comprise, include; (*umzingeln*) encircle. **einschließlich** adj inclusive; *prep* including, inclusive of. **Einschluß** m (pl **Einschlüsse**) inclusion.

einschmeicheln ['ainʃmaiçəln] v sich einschmeicheln bei ingratiate oneself with.

einschränken ['ainʃrɛnkən] v restrict, limit. **Einschränkung** f restriction, limitation.

Einschreibebrief ['ainʃraibəbriːf] m registered letter. **einschreiben** v register; (*eintragen*) inscribe, write in. **per Einschreiben** adv (by) registered mail. **Einschreibung** f registration.

einschüchtern ['ainʃyçtərn] v intimidate.

***einsehen** ['ainzeːən] v inspect, look over; (*prüfen*) examine; (*begreifen*) realize.

einseitig ['ainzaitiç] adj one-sided; (*Pol*) unilateral.

einsenden ['ainzɛndən] v send in.

einsetzen ['ainzɛtsən] v set in, put in; (*Amt*) install; begin; (*Geld*) deposit.

Einsicht ['ainziçt] f (pl -en) insight; (*Verständnis*) understanding. **einsichtsvoll** adj judicious, sensible.

Einsiedler ['ainziːdlər] m (pl -) hermit.

einspannen ['ainʃpanən] v (*Pferd*) harness; (*mit Rahmen*) stretch.

einsperren ['ainʃpɛrən] v lock in or up; (*Gefängnis*) imprison, jail.

einspritzen ['ainʃpritsən] v inject.

Einspruch ['ainʃprux] m (pl **Einsprüche**) objection, protest. **Einspruch erheben gegen** raise an objection against.

einst [ainst] adv (*Vergangenheit*) once, at one time; (*Zukunft*) some day, one day.

einstecken ['ainʃtɛkən] v put in; (*in die Tasche*) pocket.

***einsteigen** ['ainʃtaigən] v (*Auto, Schiff, usw.*) get in, get on, board.

einstellen ['ainʃtɛlən] v cease, stop; (*tech*) adjust; (*phot*) focus; (*radio, usw.*) tune. **–bar** adj adjustable. **Einstellung** f stop, suspension; adjustment; (*Ansicht*) attitude.

einstig ['ainstiç] adj former.

einstimmen ['ainʃtimən] v agree; join (in). **einstimmig** adj unanimous.

einstmalig ['ainstmaːliç] adj former.

einstöckig ['ainʃtœkiç] adj one-storeyed.

***einstoßen** ['ainʃtoːsən] v push or drive in(to); (*Tür*) knock or break down.

einströmen ['ainʃtrœːmən] v flow or stream in(to).

einstufen ['ainʃtuːfən] v classify, grade.

einstürmen ['ainʃtyrmən] v rush in; (*angreifen*) attack.

Einsturz ['ainʃturts] m (pl **Einstürze**) downfall, collapse. **einstürzen** v collapse; (*niederreißen*) knock down, demolish.

einstweilen ['ainstvailən] adv meanwhile, for the time being. **einstweilig** adj temporary, provisional.

eintägig ['aintɛːgiç] adj one-day.

Eintausch ['aintauʃ] m exchange. **eintauschen** v exchange, trade.

einteilen ['aintailən] v divide up, classify; (*Skala*) graduate; (*Arbeit*) plan out.

eintönig ['aintœːniç] adj monotonous.

Eintopf ['aintɔpf] m stew, casserole.

Eintracht ['aintraxt] f (*unz.*) harmony, unity.

Eintrag ['aintraık] m (pl **Einträge**) (*Komm*) entry; (*Schaden*) damage. **eintragen** v carry in; (*einschreiben*) enter; (*einbringen*) yield. **einträglich** adj profitable. **Eintragung** f entry.

***eintreten** ['aintreːtən] v come in; (*eindrücken*) kick in; (*beitreten*) join; (*geschehen*) occur.

Eintritt ['aintrit] m entrance; (*Anfang*) beginning. **–skarte** f admission ticket.

einverleiben ['ainfɛrlaibən] v incorporate.

einverstanden ['ainfɛrʃtandən] adj in agreement. **einverstanden sein mit** agree with, approve of.

Einwand ['ainvant] m (pl **Einwände**) objection. **einwandfrei** adj perfect, faultless.

Einwanderer ['ainvandərər] m (pl -) immigrant. **einwandern** v immigrate. **Einwanderung** f immigration.

einwärts ['ainvɛrts] adv inwards.

einwechseln ['ainvɛksəln] v change; exchange.

Einwegflasche ['ainvɛkflaʃə] f non-returnable bottle.

einweichen ['ainvaiçən] v soak, steep.

einweihen ['ainvaiən] v inaugurate; (*Person*) initiate; (*Kirche*) consecrate. **Einweihung** f inauguration; initiation; consecration.

Einwendung ['ainvɛnduŋ] ƒ (pl -en) objection.

einwickeln ['ainvikəln] v wrap (up).

einwilligen ['ainviligən] v consent, agree. **Einwilligung** ƒ consent.

einwirken ['ainvirkən] v **einwirken auf** influence, affect. **Einwirkung** ƒ influence.

Einwohner ['ainvoinər] m (pl -) inhabitant.

Einzahl ['aintsail] ƒ (unz.) (Gramm) singular.

einzahlen ['aintsailən] v pay in, deposit.

Einzel‖erscheinung ['aintsələrʃainuŋ] ƒ (isolated) phenomenon. **-fall** m individual case. **-handel** m retail trade. **-handelsgeschäft** neut retail shop. **-händler** m retailer. **-haus** neut detached house. **-heit** ƒ detail. **-kind** neut only child. **einzeln** adj single; (getrennt) isolated; (alleinstehend) detached. **einzelnstehend** adj detached. **Einzelzimmer** neut single room.

einziehen ['aintsiiən] v pull or draw in; (einkassieren) collect; (beschlagnahmen) confiscate; (Rekruten) draft; (Wohnung) move in.

einzig ['aintsiç] adj only, single.

Einzug ['aintsuik] m entry, entrance; (Wohnung) moving in.

Eis [ais] neut (unz.) ice; (Speise) ice-cream. **-bahn** ƒ ice/skating rink. **-bär** m polar bear. **-bein** neut knuckle of pork. **-berg** m iceberg.

Eischale ['aiʃailə] ƒ eggshell.

Eisen ['aizən] neut (pl -) iron. **-bahn** ƒ railway. **-händler** m ironmonger. **-waren** ƒ pl ironmongery.

eisern ['aizərn] adj iron.

eisig ['aiziç] adj icy. **eiskalt** adj ice-cold. **Eis‖lauf** m skating. **-läufer** m (pl -) skater. **-laufbahn** ƒ skating rink. **-meer** neut polar sea. **-regen** m freezing rain. **-tüte** ƒ ice-cream cone/cornet. **-vogel** m kingfisher. **-würfel** m ice cube. **-zapfen** m icicle.

eitel ['aitəl] adj vain. **Eitelkeit** ƒ vanity.

Eiter ['aitər] m (unz.) pus. **eitern** v fester, suppurate.

Eiweiß ['aivais] neut (pl -e) egg-white; protein; albumen. **-stoff** m protein.

Ekel ['eikəl] m (unz.) disgust, repugnance. **ekelhaft** adj loathsome, disgusting. **sich ekeln** be disgusted by.

Ekzem [ɛk'tseim] neut (pl -e) eczema.

elastisch [e'lastiʃ] adj elastic.

Elefant [ele'fant] m (pl -en) elephant.

elegant [ele'gant] adj elegant. **Eleganz** ƒ elegance.

elektrifizieren [elɛktrifi'tsiirən] v also **elektrisieren** electrify. **Elektriker** m electrician. **elektrisch** adj electric(al). **Elektrizität** ƒ electricity.

Elektro‖gerät [e'lɛktrogərɛit] neut electric appliance. **-installateur** m electrician. **-motor** m electric motor.

Elektronik [elɛk'troinik] ƒ electronics. **elektronisch** adj electronic.

Elektrotechnik [elɛktro'teçnik] ƒ electrical engineering.

Element [ele'mɛnt] neut (pl -e) element; (Zelle) battery. **elementar** adj elementary.

elend ['eilɛnt] adj miserable. **Elend** neut misery. **-sviertel** neut slums pl.

elf [ɛlf] pron, adj eleven.

Elf [ɛlf] m (pl -en) elf, fairy.

Elfenbein ['ɛlfənbain] neut (unz.) ivory.

elfte ['ɛlftə] adj eleventh.

Elite [e'liitə] ƒ (pl -n) elite.

Ellbogen ['ɛlboigən] m (pl -) elbow.

Ellipse [ɛ'lipsə] ƒ (pl -n) ellipse. **elliptisch** adj elliptical.

Elsaß ['ɛlsas] neut Alsace. **Elsässer** m (pl -), **Elsässerin** ƒ (pl -nen) Alsatian. **elsässisch** adj Alsatian.

Elster ['ɛlstər] ƒ (pl -n) magpie.

Eltern ['ɛltərn] pl parents. **elterlich** adj parental.

Email [e'maij] neut (pl -s) enamel.

emanzipieren [emantsi'piirən] v emancipate. **Emanzipation** ƒ emancipation.

Empfang [ɛm'pfaŋ] m (pl Empfänge) welcome, reception. **empfangen** v welcome, receive; (Kind) conceive. **Empfänger** m receiver. **empfänglich** adj susceptible. **Empfängnis** ƒ conception. **-verhütung** ƒ contraception.

***empfehlen** [ɛm'pfeilən] v recommend. **-swert** adj to be recommended. **Empfehlung** ƒ recommendation. **-sschreiben** letter of recommendation.

empfinden [ɛm'pfindən] v feel. **empfindlich** adj sensitive; (reizbar) touchy. **Empfindung** ƒ feeling; (Wahrnehmung) perception.

empor [ɛm'poir] adv up(wards). **-ragen** v tower (up/over). **-streben** v struggle up(wards).

empören [ɛm'pœɪrən] v shock, revolt; (*erregen*) stir up. **sich empören** rebel.

emsig ['ɛmziç] adj diligent, industrious.

Ende ['ɛndə] neut (pl -n) end.

endemisch [ɛn'deɪmɪʃ] adj endemic.

enden ['ɛndən] v finish, end. **end‖gültig** adj final. **–lich** adv finally, at last; adj final; (*beschränkt*) finite. **–los** adj endless, infinite.

End‖punkt m end (point). **–spiel** neut (*Sport*) final. **–station** f terminus. **–zweck** m (ultimate) goal or purpose.

Energie [enɛr'giː] f (pl -n) energy. **–krise** energy crisis. **energisch** adj energetic.

eng [ɛŋ] adj narrow; (*dicht*) tight, close; (*Freund*) close. **Enge** f narrowness; tightness; (*Klemme*) difficulty.

Engel ['ɛŋəl] m (pl -) angel. **engelhaft** adj angelic.

England ['ɛŋlant] neut England. **Engländer** m (pl -) Englishman. **Engländerin** f (pl -nen) Englishwoman. *ich bin Engländer(in)* I am English. **englisch** adj English.

Engpaß ['ɛŋpas] m narrow pass; (*verkehr*) bottleneck; (*Klemme*) difficulty, tight spot.

engros [ã'groɪ] adv wholesale.

engstirnig ['ɛŋʃtɪrnɪç] adj narrow-minded.

Enkel ['ɛŋkəl] m (pl -) grandson. **–in** f granddaughter. **–kind** neut grandchild.

enorm [e'nɔrm] adj enormous.

entarten [ɛnt'aɪrtən] v degenerate. **Entartung** f degeneracy, degeneration.

entbehrlich [ɛnt'beɪrlɪç] adj dispensable, (to) spare.

*entbinden [ɛnt'bɪndən] v release, set free; (*eine Frau*) deliver. **Entbindung** f release, setting free; (*Geburt*) delivery.

entblößen [ɛnt'blœɪsən] v uncover; (*berauben*) deprive, rob.

entdecken [ɛnt'dɛkən] v discover. **Entdecker** m discoverer. **Entdeckung** f discovery.

Ente ['ɛntə] f (pl -n) duck; (*Falschmeldung, Lüge*) hoax, canard.

entehren [ɛnt'eɪrən] v dishonour, disgrace.

enteignen [ɛnt'aɪgnən] v expropriate, dispossess. **Enteignung** f expropriation; seizure.

enterben [ɛnt'ɛrbən] v disinherit.

*entfallen [ɛnt'falən] v fall or slip from; (*Gedächtnis*) slip, escape.

entfalten [ɛnt'faltən] v unfold; (*zeigen*) display. (*Mil*) deploy; **Entfaltung** f unfolding; display; deployment; development.

entfernen [ɛnt'fɛrnən] v remove. **sich entfernen** go away, withdraw. **Entfernung** f distance; (*Wegbringen*) removal.

entflammen [ɛnt'flamən] v inflame, kindle.

*entfliehen [ɛnt'fliɪən] v flee from.

entfremden [ɛnt'frɛmdən] v alienate, estrange. **Entfremdung** f alienation, estrangement.

entführen [ɛnt'fyɪrən] v abduct; (*Flugzeug*) hijack. **Entführer** m abductor, kidnapper; hijacker. **Entführung** f abduction, kidnapping; hijacking.

entgegen [ɛnt'geɪgən] prep against, contrary to; (*hinzu*) towards. adv towards. **–kommen** v meet; (*Kompromiß*) make concessions. **–sehen** v look forward to. **–treten** v move towards; (*widerstehen*) oppose. **–wirken** v work against.

entgegnen [ɛnt'geɪgnən] v retort, answer back.

*entgehen [ɛnt'geɪən] v escape from.

Entgelt [ɛnt'gɛlt] neut (unz.) compensation.

entgiften [ɛnt'gɪftən] v decontaminate.

entgleisen [ɛnt'glaɪzən] v be or become derailed. **Entgleisung** f derailment.

entgräten [ɛnt'greɪtən] v bone; fillet (fish).

enthaaren [ɛnt'haɪrən] v remove hair from, depilate.

*enthalten [ɛnt'haltən] v hold, contain. **sich enthalten** refrain (from). **enthaltsam** adj abstemious. **Enthaltung** f abstention.

enthaupten [ɛnt'hauptən] v behead, decapitate.

enthüllen [ɛnt'hylən] v uncover, reveal.

Enthusiasmus [ɛntuzi'asmus] m (unz.) enthusiasm. **enthusiastisch** adj enthusiastic.

entkernen [ɛnt'kɛrnən] v (*Obst*) stone.

entkleiden [ɛnt'klaɪdən] v (*Person*) undress, strip; (*wegnehmen*) divest. **sich entkleiden** undress.

*entkommen [ɛnt'kɔmən] v escape.

entkuppeln [ɛnt'kupəln] v disconnect; (*Mot*) declutch.

entladen [ɛnt'laɪdən] v unload; (*Gewehr, Batterie*) discharge.

entlang [ɛnt'laŋ] prep, adv along. **–fahren** v travel along. **–gehen** walk along.

*entlassen [ɛnt'lasən] v dismiss, discharge, (*umg.*) fire, sack; (*Gefangene*) release. **entlassen werden** be dismissed,

(*coll*) get the sack. **Entlassung** *f* dismissal, discharge; release.
entlasten [ɛnt'lastən] *v* unburden; (*erleichtern*) relieve; (*Bank*) credit; (*Verdachtsperson*) clear, exonerate.
entleeren [ɛnt'leɪrən] *v* empty. **sich entleeren** relieve oneself.
entlegen [ɛnt'leɪgən] *adj* remote.
entmilitarisieren [ɛntmilitari'ziɪrən] *v* demilitarize.
entmutigen [ɛnt'mutigən] *v* discourage. **Entmutigung** *f* discouragement.
Entnahme [ɛnt'naɪmə] *f* (*unz.*) taking *or* drawing out; (*Geld*) withdrawal; (*Strom*) use.
entnazifizieren [ɛntnatsifi'tsiɪrən] *v* denazify.
*****entnehmen** [ɛnt'neɪmən] *v* take away *or* out; (*folgern*) conclude, infer; (*Geld*) withdraw; (*Strom*) use. **Entnehmer** *m* (*Komm*) drawer (of bills); (*Strom*) user.
entrahmen [ɛnt'raɪmən] *v* skim (milk).
entrüsten [ɛnt'rystən] *v* irritate, anger. **Entrüstung** *f* indignation, anger.
entsagen [ɛnt'zaɪgən] *v* renounce, give up.
entschädigen [ɛnt'ʃɛɪdigən] *v* compensate. **Entschädigung** *f* compensation.
Entscheid [ɛnt'ʃaɪt] *m* (*pl* -e) decision.
entscheiden *v* decide. **sich entscheiden** decide, resolve, make up one's mind. **entscheidend** *adj* decisive. **Entscheidung** *f* decision; (*Urteil*) sentence.
entschieden [ɛnt'ʃiɪdən] *adj* determined, resolute. *adv* decidedly. **Entschiedenheit** *f* determination.
*****entschließen** [ɛnt'ʃliɪsən] *v* **sich entschließen** decide, determine.
entschlossen [ɛnt'ʃlɔsən] *adj* determined, resolute.
Entschluß [ɛnt'ʃlus] *m* (*pl* **Entschlüsse**) decision. **-kraft** *f* power of decision, decisiveness.
entschuldigen [ɛnt'ʃuldigən] *v* excuse, pardon. **sich entschuldigen** apologize, excuse oneself. **entschuldigen Sie!** excuse me! **Entschuldigung** *f* apology; *interj* I'm sorry! pardon me!
entsetzen [ɛnt'zɛtsən] *v* horrify, appal; (*von einem Posten*) dismiss; (*Mil*) relieve. **Entsetzen** *neut* horror. **entsetzlich** *adj* dreadful, horrible. **entsetzt** *adj* horrified, shocked.
entspannen [ɛnt'ʃpanən] *v* relax, release. **sich entspannen** relax, calm down. **Entspannung** *f* relaxation; (*Pol*) détente.

*****entsprechen** [ɛnt'ʃprɛçən] *v* correspond (to); (*Anforderung*) comply with. **entsprechend** *adj* corresponding, appropriate.
*****entspringen** [ɛnt'ʃpriŋən] *v* escape from, run away from.
entstammen [ɛnt'ʃtamən] *v* descend (from).
*****entstehen** [ɛnt'ʃteɪən] *v* arise, originate. **Entstehung** *f* origin.
enttäuschen [ɛnt'tɔyʃən] *v* disappoint. **enttäuscht** *adj* disappointed. **Enttäuschung** *f* disappointment.
entvölkern [ɛnt'fœlkərn] *v* depopulate.
*****entwachsen** [ɛnt'vaksən] *v* grow out of.
entwaffnen [ɛnt'vafnən] *v* disarm.
entwässern [ɛnt'vɛsərn] *v* drain; (*austrocknen*) dehydrate. **Entwässerung** *f* drainage; dehydration.
entweder [ɛnt'veɪdər] *conj* either.
*****entweichen** [ɛnt'vaɪçən] *v* escape.
entweihen [ɛnt'vaɪən] *v* desecrate, profane.
*****entwerfen** [ɛnt'vɛrfən] *v* design, plan; (*skizzieren*) sketch; (*Fassung*) draft, draw up.
entwerten [ɛnt'vertən] *v* devalue; (*Briefmarke*) cancel. **Entwertung** *f* devaluation; cancellation.
entwickeln [ɛnt'vikəln] *v* develop. **sich entwickeln** develop. **Entwicklung** *f* development. **Entwicklungs‖land** *neut* developing country. **−lehre** *f* theory of evolution.
entwirren [ɛnt'virən] *v* disentangle.
entwischen [ɛnt'viʃən] *v* slip *or* steal away from.
entwürdigen [ɛnt'vyrdigən] *v* degrade, debase.
Entwurf [ɛnt'vurf] *m* (*pl* **Entwürfe**) design, plan; (*Skizze*) sketch; (*Fassung*) draft.
entwurzeln [ɛnt'vurtsəln] *v* uproot; (*vernichten*) eradicate.
*****entziehen** [ɛnt'tsiɪən] *v* take away, withdraw; (*rauben*) deprive.
entziffern [ɛnt'tsifərn] *v* decipher, make out.
entzücken [ɛnt'tsykən] *v* delight, enchant. **Entzücken** *neut* delight, enchantment. **entzückt** *adj* delighted, enchanted. **entzückend** *adj* delightful, enchanting.
entzündbar [ɛnt'tsyntbair] *adj* inflammable. **entzünden** *adj* kindle, light. **sich entzünden** catch fire. **Entzündung** *f* ignition; (*med*) inflammation.

entzwei [ɛnt'tsvai] *adv* in two, asunder.
-brechen *v* break in two.

Enzyklopädie [ɛntsyklope'diː] *f* (*pl* -n)
encyclopedia.

Epidemie [epide'miː] *f* (*pl* -n) epidemic.
epidemisch *adj* epidemic.

Epilepsie [epilɛp'siː] *f* (*unz.*) epilepsy.
Epileptiker *m* epileptic. **epileptisch** *adj*
epileptic.

Episode [epi'zoɪdə] *f* (*pl* -n) episode.

er [ɛr] *pron* he.

erachten [ɛr'axtən] *v* think, consider.
Erachten *neut* opinion, judgment. **meines
Erachtens** in my opinion.

Erbarmen [ɛr'barmən] *neut* (*unz.*) pity,
compassion. **erbärmlich** *adj* pitiful, pitiable. **erbarmungs∥los** *adj* merciless, piti-
less. **-voll** *adj* compassionate, merciful.

erbauen [ɛr'bauən] *v* build, erect.

Erbe ['ɛrbə] *m* (*pl* -n) heir; *neut* (*unz.*)
inheritance. **Erbeinheit** *f* gene. **erben** *v*
inherit. **Erb∥fehler** *m* hereditary defect.
-feind *m* traditional enemy. **-gut** *neut*
inheritance; (*Erbhof*) ancestral estate.
erblich *adj* hereditary.

erbittern [ɛr'bitərn] *v* embitter. **erbittert**
adj embittered, bitter.

erblassen [ɛr'blasən] *v* grow pale.

erblicken [ɛr'blikən] *v* glimpse, catch
sight of.

erblinden [ɛr'blindən] *v* blind.

***erbrechen** [ɛr'brɛçən] *v* **sich erbrechen**
vomit.

Erbschaft ['ɛrpʃaft] *v* (*pl* -en) legacy,
inheritance.

Erbse ['ɛrpsə] *f* (*pl* -n) pea.

Erd∥beben ['ɛrtbeɪbən] *neut* (*pl* -) earthquake. **-beere** *f* strawberry. **-boden** *m*
earth, soil.

Erde ['ɛrdə] *v* (*pl* -n) earth. **erden** *v*
(*Strom*) earth.

***erdenken** [ɛr'dɛŋkən] *v* think of, think
out; (*erfinden*) invent.

Erdgas *neut* natural gas.

erdichten [ɛr'diçtən] *v* fabricate, invent.
Erdichtung *f* fabrication, invention.

Erd∥kreis *m* globe, earth. **-kunde** *f*
geography. **erdkundlich** *adj* geograph-
ic(al). **Erd∥nuß** *f* peanut. **-öl** *neut* oil,
petroleum.

erdrosseln [ɛr'drɔsəln] *v* strangle.

erdulden [ɛr'duldən] *v* endure.

ereignen [ɛr'aignən] *v* **sich ereignen** happen. **Ereignis** *neut* event, occurrence.

***erfahren** [ɛr'faɪrən] *v* experience; (*hören,
lernen*) learn, hear of. *adj* experienced,
proficient. **Erfahrung** *f* experience.

erfassen [ɛr'fasən] *v* seize; (*einschließen*)
include; (*begreifen*) understand, grasp.

***erfinden** [ɛr'findən] *v* invent. **Erfinder** *m*
inventor. **erfinderisch** *adj* inventive.
Erfindung *f* invention.

Erfolg [ɛr'fɔlk] *m* (*pl* -e) success;
(*Ergebnis*) result, outcome. **Erfolg haben**
achieve success, succeed. **erfolgen** *v*
result, follow. **erfolg∥los** *adj* unsuccessful. **-reich** *adj* successful.

erforderlich [ɛr'fɔrdərliç] *adj* necessary.
erfordern *v* require, need; (*verlangen*)
demand. **Erfordernis** *neut* necessity;
(*Voraussetzung*) requirement.

erforschen [ɛr'fɔrʃən] *v* investigate.
Erforsch∥er *m* investigator. **-ung** *f*
investigation.

erfreuen [ɛr'frɔyən] *v* delight. **sich
erfreuen an** enjoy, take delight in. **erfreu-
lich** *adj* gratifying. **erfreut** *adj* gratified.

***erfrieren** [ɛr'friːrən] *v* freeze to death.
Erfrierung *f* frostbite.

erfrischen [ɛr'friʃən] *v* refresh. **-d** *adj*
refreshing. **Erfrischung** *f* refreshment.

erfüllen [ɛr'fylən] *v* fill; (*Aufgabe*) carry
out; (*Bitte, Forderung*) comply with, fulfil. **Erfüllung** *f* accomplishment, fulfilment.

ergänzen [ɛr'gɛntsən] *v* supplement, add
to; (*vervollständigen*) complete.
Ergänzung *f* supplement; completion.

***ergeben** [ɛr'geɪbən] *v* yield. **sich ergeben**
surrender; (*folgen*) result. **Ergebenheit** *f*
devotion; (*Fügsamkeit*) submissiveness.
Ergebnis *neut* result.

***ergehen** [ɛr'geɪən] *v* (*Gesetz*) be promul-
gated, come out.

ergiebig [ɛr'giːbiç] *adj* productive, profitable.

***ergreifen** [ɛr'graifən] *v* grasp, seize;
(*rühren*) touch, move (deeply). **-d** *adj*
touching, affecting. **Ergreifung** *f* seizure.

erhaben [ɛr'haɪbən] *adj* exalted, sublime.

***erhalten** [ɛr'haltən] *v* receive, obtain;
(*bewahren*) preserve, maintain. **erhältlich**
adj available, obtainable. **Erhaltung** *f*
preservation, maintenance.

***erheben** [ɛr'heɪbən] *v* lift up; (*Einspruch*)
raise. **sich erheben** rise (up). **Anspruch
erheben auf** lay claim to. **erheblich** *adj*
considerable. **Erhebung** *f* uprising.

erheitern [ɛr'haitərn] *v* cheer up; (*unterhalten*) amuse. **sich erheitern** (*Himmel*) brighten, clear up.

erhitzen [ɛr'hitsən] *v* heat (up); (*Person*) inflame.

erhöhen [ɛr'høːən] *v* raise, heighten. **Erhöhung** *f* raising, heightening.

erholen [ɛr'hoilən] *v* **sich erholen** recover, get better; (*sich ausruhen*) rest. **Erholung** *f* recovery; rest; (*Unterhaltung*) recreation.

erinnern [ɛr'inərn] *v* remind. **sich erinnern an** remember. **Erinnerung** *f* (*pl* -en) memory, remembrance.

erkälten [ɛr'kɛltən] *v* cool. **sich erkälten** catch (a) cold. **Erkältung** *f* (*pl* -en) (*Med*) cold.

erkennbar [ɛr'kɛnbair] *adj* recognizable.

erkennen *v* recognize; (*Fehler*) acknowledge; (*merken*) perceive.

Erkenntnis¹ [ɛr'kɛntnis] *neut* (*pl* -se) judgment, sentence.

Erkenntnis² *f* (*pl* -se) recognition; (*Einsicht*) understanding.

Erkenn‖ung [ɛr'kɛnuŋ] *f* (*pl* -en) recognition. **–ungswort** *neut* password. **–ungszeichen** *neut* distinguishing mark.

Erkerfenster ['ɛrkərfɛnstər] *neut* bay window.

erklären [ɛr'klɛirən] *v* explain; (*aussprechen*) declare. **sich erklären** declare oneself. **Erklärung** *f* explanation; declaration.

erkranken [ɛr'krankən] *v* fall ill, become sick.

erkundigen [ɛr'kundigən] *v* **sich erkundigen** (**nach**) inquire (about). **Erkundigung** *f* inquiry.

erlangen [ɛr'laŋən] *v* obtain, acquire; (*erreichen*) get to, reach.

Erlaß [ɛr'las] *m* (*pl* **Erlässe**) decree, edict.

*erlassen [ɛr'lasən] *v* issue; (*befreien*) release, absolve.

erlauben [ɛr'laubən] *v* permit. **Erlaubnis** *f* permission.

erläutern [ɛr'lɔytərn] *v* explain, elucidate. **Erläuterung** *f* explanation; *pl* commentary, notes.

erleben [ɛr'leibən] *v* live through, experience. **Erlebnis** *neut* (*pl* -se) experience.

erledigen [ɛr'leidigən] *v* take care of, deal with; (*beenden*) finish (off). **erledigt** *adj* settled; (*erschöpft*) exhausted. **Erledigung** *f* (*pl* -en) carrying out, execution.

erlegen [ɛr'leigən] *v* kill.

erleichtern [ɛr'laiçtərn] *v* ease, aid, lighten. **Erleichterung** *f* (*pl* -en) relief.

*erleiden [ɛr'laidən] *v* suffer, undergo.

erlernen [ɛr'lɛrnən] *v* learn, acquire.

Erlös [ɛr'løis] *m* (*pl* -e) proceeds *pl*.

*erlöschen [ɛr'lœʃən] *v* go *or* die out.

ermächtigen [ɛr'mɛçtigən] *v* authorize, empower.

ermahnen [ɛr'mainən] *v* admonish.

Ermangelung [ɛr'maŋəluŋ] *f* (*pl* -) **in Ermangelung** in the absence *or* default (of).

ermäßigen [ɛr'mɛisigən] *v* reduce, lower. **Ermäßigung** *f* reduction.

ermitteln [ɛr'mitəln] *v* ascertain, find out.

ermöglichen [ɛr'møːkliçən] *v* enable, render possible.

ermorden [ɛr'mɔrdən] *v* murder, assassinate.

ermüden [ɛr'myidən] *v* tire out; grow tired.

ermuntern [ɛr'muntərn] *v* encourage, cheer up.

ermutigen [ɛr'muitigən] *v* encourage. **Ermutigung** *f* encouragement.

ernähren [ɛr'nɛirən] *v* feed, nourish. **sich ernähren** support oneself. **Ernährer** *m* breadwinner. **Ernährung** *f* nourishment.

*ernennen [ɛr'nɛnən] *v* appoint, designate. **Ernennung** *f* appointment.

erneuern [ɛr'nɔyərn] *v* renew; renovate, restore. **Erneuerung** *f* renewal; renovation. **erneut** *adj* repeated; *adv* again.

erniedrigen [ɛr'niidrigən] *v* lower; (*degradieren*) degrade, humble.

ernst [ɛrnst] *adj* serious, grave. **Ernst** *m* seriousness, gravity. **im Ernst** in earnest. **ernsthaft** *adj* earnest, serious. **–lich** *adj* serious.

Ernte ['ɛrntə] *f* (*pl* -n) harvest; (*Wein*) vintage. **ernten** *v* harvest, reap.

ernüchtern [ɛr'nyçtərn] *v* disillusion, disenchant; (*vom Rausch*) sober (up). **sich ernüchtern** sober up. **Ernüchterung** *f* disillusionment; sobering up.

Eroberer [ɛr'ɔibərər] *m* (*pl* -) conqueror. **erobern** *v* conquer. **Eroberung** *f* conquest.

eröffnen [ɛr'œfnən] *v* open; (*anfangen*) open, begin. **Eröffnung** *f* opening, beginning.

erörtern [ɛr'œrtərn] *v* discuss. **Erörterung** *f* discussion.

Erotik [e'roɪtik] ƒ (*unz.*) eroticism. **erotisch** *adj* erotic.
erpressen [ɛr'prɛsən] *v* (*Sache*) extort; (*Person*) blackmail. **Erpresser** *m* blackmailer. **erpresserisch** *adj* extortionate. **Erpressung** ƒ blackmail, extortion.
erproben [ɛr'proɪbən] *v* try (out), test. **Erprobung** ƒ trial, test.
*****erraten** [ɛr'raɪtən] *v* guess.
errechnen [ɛr'rɛçnən] *v* calculate.
erregen [ɛr'reɪgən] *v* excite; (*hervorrufen*) create, produce. **erregbar** *adj* excitable. **erregend** *adj* exciting. **erregt** *adj* excited. **Erregung** ƒ excitement.
erreichen [ɛr'raiçən] *v* attain, reach. **erreichbar** *adj* attainable. **Erreichung** ƒ attainment.
errichten [ɛr'riçtən] *v* erect, build; (*gründen*) set up, establish.
erröten [ɛr'rœɪtən] *v* blush.
Errungenschaft [ɛr'ruŋənʃaft] ƒ (*pl* -en) achievement.
Ersatz [ɛr'zats] *m* (*unz.*) substitute; (*Wiedergutmachung*) compensation; (*Nachschub*) reinforcements *pl*. **-kaffee** *m* coffee substitute. **-rad** *neut* spare wheel. **-spieler** *m* (*Sport*) substitute. **-teil** *neut* spare part.
*****erschaffen** [ɛr'ʃafən] *v* create. **Erschaffer** *m* creator. **Erschaffung** ƒ creation.
*****erscheinen** [ɛr'ʃainən] *v* appear. **Erscheinung** ƒ phenomenon; (*Aussehen*) appearance.
*****erschießen** [ɛr'ʃiɪsən] *v* shoot (dead). **Erschießungskommando** *neut* firing squad.
*****erschließen** [ɛr'ʃliɪsən] *v* open up; (*folgern*) infer, deduce.
erschöpfen [ɛr'ʃœpfən] *v* exhaust, use up; (*Person*) exhaust, tire out. **erschöpft** *adj* exhausted. **Erschöpfung** ƒ exhaustion.
*****erschrecken** [ɛr'ʃrɛkən] *v* scare, frighten; be frightened *or* scared. **Erschrecken** *neut* fright. **erschreckend** *adj* frightening.
erschrocken [ɛr'ʃrɔkən] *adj* frightened, terrified. **Erschrockenheit** ƒ fright, terror.
erschüttern [ɛr'ʃytərn] *v* shake; (*Person*) shake, disturb, shock. **Erschütterung** ƒ shock.
erschweren [ɛr'ʃveɪrən] *v* make (more) difficult, aggravate.
*****ersehen** [ɛr'zeɪən] *v* perceive, see.
ersetzen [ɛr'zɛtsən] *v* replace; (*Schaden*) make good. **ersetzlich** *adj* replaceable, renewable.

ersichtlich [ɛr'ziçtliç] *adj* evident.
*****ersinnen** [ɛr'zinən] *v* contrive, devise.
ersparen [ɛr'ʃpaɪrən] *v* save.
erst [eɪrst] *adj* first. *adv* at first; (*nur*) only, just.
erstarren [ɛr'ʃtarən] *v* stiffen, become rigid; (*Flüssigkeit*) congeal, solidify. **Erstarrung** ƒ stiffness.
erstatten [ɛr'ʃtatən] *v* restore; (*ersetzen*) replace. **Bericht erstatten** report, make a report. **Erstattung** ƒ restitution.
Erstaufführung ['eɪrstauffyɪruŋ] ƒ (*pl* -en) première, first performance.
erstaunen [ɛr'ʃtaunən] *v* astonish; be astonished. **Erstaunen** *neut* astonishment, amazement. **erstaunlich** *adj* astonishing.
erste(r) ['eɪrstə(r)], **erste**, **erste(s)** *adj* first.
erstens ['eɪrstəns] *adv* first(ly).
ersticken [ɛr'ʃtikən] *v* suffocate; (*fig*) stifle. **erstickend** *adj* suffocating. **Erstickung** ƒ suffocation; stifling.
erst‖klassig *adj* first-class. **–malig** *adj* for the first time, first-time.
erstrecken [ɛr'ʃtrɛkən] *v* **sich erstrecken** stretch, extend.
ertappen [ɛr'tapən] *v* catch, surprise. **auf frischer Tat ertappen** catch red-handed.
Ertrag [ɛr'traɪk] *m* (*pl* Erträge) profit; (*Boden*) yield. **ertragen** *v* bear, stand. **erträglich** *adj* bearable, tolerable.
ertränken [ɛr'trɛŋkən] *v* (cause to) drown.
*****ertrinken** [ɛr'triŋkən] *v* drown, be drowned.
erwachen [ɛr'vaxən] *v* awake, wake up.
*****erwachsen** [ɛr'vaksən] *v* grow up. **Erwachsene(r)** *m* adult.
*****erwägen** [ɛr'vɛɪgən] *v* consider, weigh. **Erwägung** ƒ consideration.
erwähnen [ɛr'vɛɪnən] *v* mention. **Erwähnung** ƒ mention.
erwärmen [ɛr'vɛrmən] *v* warm, heat.
erwarten [ɛr'vartən] *v* expect. **über Erwarten** better than expectation. **wider Erwarten** contrary to expectation. **Erwartung** ƒ (*pl* -en) expectation.
erwecken [ɛr'vɛkən] *v* awaken; (*erregen*) arouse, rouse.
*****erweisen** [ɛr'vaizən] *v* prove; (*Dienst*) render, do; (*Ehrung*) pay. **sich erweisen als** prove to be.
erweitern [ɛr'vaitərn] *v* enlarge, widen, extend. **Erweiterung** ƒ (*pl* -en) extension, enlargement.

Erwerb [ɛr'vɛrp] *m* (*pl* -e) acquisition; (*Lohn*) earnings. **erwerben** *v* acquire; (*Verdienen*) earn. **erwerbstätig** *adj* (gainfully) employed. **Erwerbung** *f* acquisition.
erwidern [ɛr'viːdərn] *v* reply; (*vergelten*) retaliate. **Erwiderung** *f* reply.
erwischen [ɛr'vifən] *v* (*Person*) catch.
erwünscht [ɛr'vynʃt] *adj* desired, wished-for.
erwürgen [ɛr'vyrgən] *v* strangle.
Erz [eɪrts] *neut* (*pl* -e) ore.
erzählen [ɛr'tsɛɪlən] *v* tell, relate. **Erzähler** *m* narrator; story-teller. **erzählerisch** *adj* narrative. **Erzählung** *f* story.
Erz‖bischof *n* archbishop. **–engel** *m* archangel.
erzeugen [ɛr'tsɔygən] *v* (*herstellen*) produce; (*Strom*) generate; (*Kinder*) procreate. **Erzeuger** *m* producer; father, procreator. **Erzeugnis** *neut* product(ion); (*Boden*) produce.
Erz‖feind *m* arch-enemy. **–herzog** *m* archduke. **–herzogin** *f* archduchess.
*erziehen [ɛr'tsiːən] *v* (*Tiere, Menschen*) bring up; (*Bildung*) educate. **Erzieher** *m* educator. **erzieherisch** *adj* educational. **Erziehung** *f* upbringing; (*Bildung*) education.
erzogen [ɛr'tsoɡən] *adj* **gut/schlecht erzogen** well/badly brought up.
es [ɛs] *pron* it.
Esche ['ɛʃə] *f* (*pl* -n) ash (tree).
Esel ['eɪzəl] *m* (*pl* -) donkey, ass. **eselhaft** *adj* asinine. **Eselsohr** *neut* dog's-ear (on page).
esoterisch [ezo'teɪriʃ] *adj* esoteric.
Essay ['ɛsɛ] *m*, *neut* (*pl* -s) essay.
eßbar ['ɛsbar] *adj* edible.
essen ['ɛsən] *v* eat. **zu Mittag essen** lunch, have lunch. **zu Abend essen** dine, have supper. **Essen** *neut* food; (*Mahlzeit*) meal.
Essig ['ɛsiç] *m* (*pl* -e) vinegar. **–gurke** *f* pickled cucumber, gherkin.
Eß‖kastanie *f* sweet chestnut. **–löffel** *m* tablespoon. **–tisch** *m* dinner table. **–zimmer** *neut* dining room.
etablieren [eta'bliːrən] *v* establish.
Etage [e'taːʒə] *f* (*pl* -n) storey, floor. **–nwohnung** *f* flat, (*US*) apartment.
Etat [e'taɪ] *m* (*pl* -s) budget; (*Komm*) balance-sheet.
Ethik ['eɪtik] *f* (*unz.*) ethics. **ethisch** *adj* ethical.

ethnisch ['ɛtniʃ] *adj* ethnic.
Etikett [eti'kɛt] *neut* (*pl* -e) tag, label.
Etikette [eti'kɛtə] *f* (*pl* -n) etiquette.
etliche ['ɛtliçə] *pron pl* some, several.
Etui [ɛt'viː] *neut* (*pl* -s) (small) case; (*Zigaretten*) cigarette-case; (*Brillen*) spectacles-case.
etwa ['ɛtva] *adv* about, around; (*vielleicht*) perhaps.
etwas ['ɛtvas] *pron* something, anything. *adj* some, any, a little.
Etymologie [etymolo'giː] *f* (*pl* -n) etymology.
euch [ɔyç] *pron* you; (*to*) you.
euer ['ɔyər] *pl adj* your. *pron* yours.
Eule ['ɔylə] *f* (*pl* -n) owl.
Eunuch [ɔy'nuːx] *m* (*pl* -en) eunuch.
Europa [ɔy'roːpa] *neut* Europe. **Europäer** *m* European. **europäisch** *adj* European. **Europäische Gemeinschaften** (**EG**) European Community. **Europäische Wirtschaftsgemeinschaft** (**EWG**) European Economic Community (EEC).
evakuieren [evaku'iːrən] *v* evacuate.
evangelisch [evan'ɡeɪliʃ] *adj* Protestant. **Evangelium** *neut* gospel.
eventuell [evɛntu'ɛl] *adj* possible. *adv* possibly, if necessary.
ewig ['eɪviç] *adj* eternal, everlasting. **auf ewig** for ever. **Ewigkeit** *f* eternity.
exakt [ɛ'ksakt] *adj* exact, accurate.
Examen [ɛ'ksaɪmən] *neut* (*pl* -, *or* **Examina**) exam(ination).
Exempel [ɛ'ksɛmpəl] *neut* (*pl* -) example.
Exemplar [ɛksɛm'plaɪr] *neut* (*pl* -e) specimen; (*Buch*) copy.
Exil [e'ksiɪl] *neut* (*pl* -e) exile.
Existenz [ɛksis'tɛnts] *f* (*pl* -en) existence; (*Unterhalt*) livelihood. **existieren** *v* exist.
exklusiv [ɛksklu'ziɪf] *adj* exclusive.
exkommunizieren [ɛkskɔmuni'tsiɪrən] *v* excommunicate.
exotisch [ɛ'ksoɪtiʃ] *adj* exotic.
Expedition [ɛkspeditsi'oɪn] *f* (*pl* -en) expedition; (*Versendung*) dispatching.
Experiment [ɛksperi'mɛnt] *neut* (*pl* -e) experiment. **experimentell** *adj* experimental. **experimentieren** *v* experiment.
explodieren [ɛksplo'diɪrən] *v* explode. **Explosion** *f* explosion. **explosiv** *adj* explosive.
Export [ɛks'pɔrt] *m* (*pl* -e) export. **–eur** *m* exporter. **–handel** *m* export trade. **exportieren** *v* export.

extrem [ɛks'treɪm] *adj* extreme. **Extrem∥ismus** *m* extremism. **–ist(in)** extremist.

Exzentriker [ɛk'tsɛntrikər] *m* (*pl* -) eccentric. **exzentrisch** *adj* eccentric.

F

Fabel ['faɪbəl] *f* (*pl* -n) fable; (*Handlungsablauf*) plot. **fabelhaft** *adj* fabulous, marvellous.

Fabrik [fa'briːk] *f* (*pl* -en) factory. **–ant** *m* (*pl* -en) manufacturer. **–arbeiter(in)** factory worker. **–at** *neut* (*pl* -e) manufacture. **fabrizieren** *v* manufacture.

Fach [fax] *neut* (*pl* Fächer) (*Abteil*) compartment, pigeonhole; (*Wissensgebiet*) subject; speciality. **–arbeiter** *m* skilled worker. **–arzt** *m* medical specialist.

fächeln ['fɛçəln] *v* fan. **Fächer** *m* (*pl* -) fan.

Fach∥mann *m* specialist. **–schule** *f* technical college *or* school. **–sprache** *f* technical language, jargon. **–wort** *neut* technical term. **–zeitschrift** *f* technical journal.

Fackel ['fakəl] *f* (*pl* -n) torch.

fade ['faɪdə] *adj* insipid, boring; (*Essen*) tasteless.

Faden ['faɪdən] *m* (*pl* Fäden) thread.

Fagott [fa'gɔt] *neut* (*pl* -e) bassoon.

fähig ['fɛːiç] *adj* capable, able. **Fähigkeit** *f* (*pl* -en) ability.

fahl [faɪl] *adj* pale, sallow.

Fahne ['faɪnə] *f* (*pl* -n) flag, standard; (*mil*) colours. **Fahnen∥flucht** *f* desertion. **–flüchtige(r)** *m* deserter. **–stock** *m* flagstaff.

Fahrbahn ['faɪrbaɪn] *f* (*Mot*) lane. **fahrbar** *adj* passable; (*Wasser*) navigable; (*beweglich*) mobile.

Fähre ['fɛːrə] *f* (*pl* -n) ferry.

*fahren ['faɪrən] *v* go, travel; (*Mot, Zug*) drive; (*Rad, Motorrad*) ride. **Fahrer** *m* driver.

Fahr∥gast *m* passenger. **–geld** *neut* fare. **–gestell** *neut* (*Mot*) chassis; (*Flugzeug*) undercarriage. **–karte** *f* ticket. **–kartenschalter** *m* ticket office.

fahrlässig ['faɪrlɛsiç] *adj* careless, negligent.

Fahr∥plan *m* timetable. **–preis** *m* fare.

–prüfung *f* driving test. **–rad** *neut* bicycle. **–schein** *m* ticket. **–schule** *f* driving school. **–stuhl** *m* lift, (*US*) elevator.

Fahrt [faɪrt] *f* (*pl* en) drive, journey.

Fährte ['fɛːrtə] *f* (*pl* -n) track, trail.

Fahrzeug ['faɪrtsɔyk] *neut* vehicle.

Faktur [fak'tuːr] *f* (*pl* -en) *also* **Faktura** invoice. **fakturieren** *v* invoice.

Fakultät [fakul'tɛɪt] *f* (*pl* -en) faculty.

Falke ['falkə] *m* (*pl* -n) hawk, falcon.

Fall [fal] *m* (*pl* Fälle) (*Sturz*) fall; (*Angelegenheit*) case. **–beil** *neut* guillotine. **–brücke** *f* drawbridge.

Falle ['falə] *f* (*pl* -n) trap, snare; (*umg.*) bed. **in die Falle gehen** go to bed.

*fallen ['falən] *v* fall. **Fallen** *neut* fall, decline.

fällen ['fɛlən] *v* cut down; (*Urteil*) pass; (*Chem*) precipitate.

fällig ['fɛliç] *adj* due.

falls [fals] *conj* if, in case.

Fall∥schirm *m* (*pl* -e) parachute. **–schirmjäger** *m* paratrooper. **–sucht** *f* epilepsy. **–tür** *f* trapdoor.

falsch [falʃ] *adj* false.

fälschen ['fɛlʃən] *v* falsify, fake; (*Geld*) counterfeit. **Fälscher** *m* (*pl* -) counterfeiter, forger.

Falschheit ['falʃhait] *f* (*pl* -en) falsehood.

Fälschung ['fɛʃuŋ] *f* (*pl* -en) falsification; (*Geld*) forgery, counterfeiting.

Falte ['faltə] *f* (*pl* -n) crease, fold. **falten** *v* crease; (*zusammenlegen*) fold.

familiär [famil'jɛːr] *adj* familiar.

Familie [fa'miːliə] *f* (*pl* -n) family. **–stand** *m* personal *or* marital status. **–zulage** *f* family allowance. **Familien∥name** *m* surname.

famos [fa'moːs] *adj* splendid, excellent.

Fanatiker [fa'naːtikər] *m* (*pl* -) fanatic. **fanatisch** *adj* fanatical

Fanfare [fan'faːrə] *f* (*pl* -n) fanfare.

Fang [faŋ] *m* (*pl* Fänge) catch. **fangen** *v* catch.

Farbe ['farbə] *f* (*pl* -n) colour. **Farbe bekennen** show one's colours; (*Karten*) follow suit.

färben ['fɛrbən] *v* colour, tint; (*Stoff*) dye. **farbenblind** ['farbanblint] *adj* colour blind. **Farb∥fernsehen** *neut* colour television. **–film** *m* colour film. **-stoff** *m* dye. **farbig** *adj* coloured. **Farbiger(r)** *m* coloured (man). **farblos** *adj* colourless.

Fasan [fa'zaɪn] *m* (*pl* -e) pheasant.

Fasching ['faʃɪŋ] *m* (*pl* -e) carnival.
Faschismus [fa'ʃɪsmus] *m* (*unz.*) fascism.
Faschist *m* (*pl* -en) fascist. **faschistisch** *adj* fascist.
Faser ['fatzər] *f* (*pl* -n) fibre; (*fein*) filament. **–stoff** *m* synthetic fibre, man-made material.
Faß [fas] *neut* (*pl* **Fässer**) barrel, cask, vat. **–bier** *neut* draught beer.
Fassade [fa'saɪdə] *f* (*pl* -n) façade.
fassen ['fasən] *v* grasp, seize; (*begreifen*) understand. **sich fassen** pull oneself together; (*ausdrücken*) express oneself.
Fassung *f* (*Kleinod*) mounting; (*Gemütsruhe*) composure; (*Wortlaut*) wording; (*Verständnis*) comprehension. **–skraft** *f* (power of) comprehension.
fast [fast] *adv* almost, nearly.
fasten ['fastən] *v* fast. **Fasten** *neut* fasting. **–zeit** *f* Lent. **Fastnacht** *f* Shrove Tuesday.
fatal [fa'taɪl] *adj* disastrous; (*peinlich*) awkward.
faul [faul] *adj* rotten; (*person*) lazy. **–en** *v* rot. **–enzen** *v* idle, be lazy. **Faul||enzer** *m* loafer. **–heit** *f* laziness, sloth.
Fäulnis ['fɔylnɪs] *f* rottenness, putrefaction.
Faust [faust] *f* (*pl* **Fäuste**) fist. **–handschuh** *m* mitten.
Februar ['feːbruaːr] *m* (*pl* -e) February.
***fechten** ['fɛçtən] *v* fence, fight (with swords).
Feder ['feːdər] *f* (*pl* -n) feather; (*tech*) spring; (*schreiben*) pen. **–bett** *neut* featherbed. **–gewicht** *neut* featherweight.
federleicht *adj* light as a feather.
Federung *f* suspension, springs *pl*.
Fee [feː] *f* (*pl* -n) fairy.
fegen ['feːgən] *v* sweep.
Fehde ['feːdə] *f* (*pl* -n) feud.
fehlbar ['feːlbaːr] *adj* fallible. **Fehl||betrag** *m* deficit. **–druck** *m* misprint; (*Briefmarken*) error. **fehlen** *v* (*mangeln*) be missing *or* lacking; (*abwesend*) be absent; (*irren*) make a mistake. **–d** *adj* missing, absent.
Fehler ['feːlər] *m* (*pl* -) mistake; (*Schwäche*) weakness; (*Mangel*) defect. **fehler||frei** *adj* flawless. **–haft** *adj* faulty, defective.
Fehlgeburt ['feːlgəburt] *f* miscarriage. **fehlschlagen** *v* fail, not succeed. **Fehl||tritt** *m* false move *or* step, slip. **–zündung** *f* (*Mot*) misfire.

Feier ['faiər] *f* (*pl* -n) festival. **Feierabend** *m* evening leisure time, free time. **Feierabend machen** finish work (for the day). **feierlich** *adj* solemn, ceremonial. **feiern** *v* celebrate. **Feiertag** *m* holiday; (*Festtag*) festival.
feige ['faigə] *adj* cowardly.
Feige ['faigə] *f* (*pl* -n) fig.
Feig||heit *f* (*unz.*) cowardice. **–ling** *m* coward.
feil [fail] *adj* for sale; (*bestechlich*) venal, corrupt.
Feile ['failə] *f* (*pl* -n) file. **feilen** *v* file.
feilschen ['failʃən] *v* haggle.
fein [fain] *adj* fine.
Feind [faint] *m* (*pl* -e) enemy. **feindlich** *adj* hostile. **Feindschaft** *f* enmity, hostility. **feind/schaftlich** *adj* inimical. **–selig** *adj* hostile.
Fein||gehaltsstempel *m* hallmark (stamp). **–heit** *f* fineness. **–schmecker** *m* gourmet.
Feld [fɛlt] *neut* (*pl* -er) field; (*Schach*) square. **–bau** *m* agriculture. **–blume** *f* wild flower. **–früchte** *f pl* crops. **–herr** *m* commander(-in-chief). **–messer** *m* surveyor. **–zug** *m* campaign.
Fell [fɛl] *neut* (*pl* -e) skin, hide.
Fels [fɛls] *m* (*pl* -en) rock, boulder. **–enklippe** *f* cliff. **–sturz** *m* rockfall.
Femininum [fɛmi'niːnum] *neut* (*pl* **Feminina**) (*Gramm*) feminine (gender).
Fenster ['fɛnstər] *neut* (*pl* -) window.
Ferien ['feːrjən] *neut pl* holiday. **in die Ferien gehen** go on holiday. **–kolonie** *f* holiday-camp. **–ort** *m* holiday resort.
Ferkel ['fɛrkəl] *neut* (*pl* -) piglet.
Ferment [fɛr'mɛnt] *neut* (*pl* -e) enzyme, ferment.
fern [fɛrn] *adj* far(away), distant. **–bleiben** *v* stay away. **Ferne** *f* distance. **ferner** *adj* farther; *adv* further; *conj* in addition. **–hin** *adv* in future.
Fern||gespräch *neut* (*phone*) long-distance call. **–glas** *neut* telescope. **–laster** *m* long-distance lorry. **–lenkung** *f* remote control. **–meldedienst** *m* telecommunications. **–rohr** *neut* telescope. **–schreiber** *m* teletype machine; Telex. **–sehapparat** *m* television (set). **–sehen** *neut* television. *v* watch television. **–sprecher** *m* telephone. **–straße** *f* trunkroad. **–zug** *m* long-distance train.
Ferse ['fɛrzə] *f* (*pl* -n) heel.

fertig ['fɛrtiç] *adj* (*bereit*) ready; (*beendet*) finished. **–en** *v* produce. **Fertigkeit** *f* (*pl* **-en**) skill, proficiency. **fertigmachen** *v* finish; (*umg.*) beat (into submission).
Fessel ['fɛsəl] *f* (*pl* **-n**) fetter, chain. **fesseln** *v* fetter, chain. **–d** *adj* fascinating; (*bezaubernd*) enchanting.
fest [fɛst] *adj* firm, secure; (*dicht*) solid.
Fest [fɛst] *neut* (*pl* **–e**) festival. **–essen** *neut* banquet.
***festhalten** ['fɛsthaltən] *v* hold (tight); (*Bild, Buch*) portray; (*anpacken*) seize.
festigen *v* make firm *or* secure. **Festland** *neut* continent. **festlegen** *v* lay down, fix. **sich festlegen** commit oneself.
festlich ['fɛstliç] *adj* festive. **Festlichkeit** *f* festivity.
fest‖machen *v* fasten; (*vereinbaren*) agree, arrange. **–nehmen** *v* arrest, capture. **–setzen** *v* settle, fix. **Festsetzung** *f* settling, establishment. **fest‖stehen** *v* stand fast. **–stellen** *v* settle; (*herausfinden*) establish, ascertain. **Feststellung** *f* establishment, ascertaining.
Festtag ['fɛsttaːk] *m* holiday.
Festung ['fɛstuŋ] *f* (*pl* **-en**) fortress.
Festzug ['fɛsttsuːk] *m* procession.
fett [fɛt] *adj* fat; (*schmierig*) greasy. **Fett** *neut* (*pl* **-e**) fat; grease. **fettig** *adj* fatty; greasy.
Fetzen ['fɛtsən] *m* (*pl* **-**) rag, shred.
feucht [fɔyçt] *adj* damp, moist. **–en** *v* dampen, moisten. **Feuchtigkeit** *f* dampness, moisture.
Feuer ['fɔyər] *neut* (*pl* **-**) fire. **–alarm** *m* fire alarm. **feuer‖beständig** *or* **–fest** *adj* fireproof. **–gefährlich** *adj* inflammable. **Feuerlöscher** *m* fire extinguisher. **feuern** *v* fire. **Feuer‖schaden** *m* fire damage. **–spritze** *f* fire engine. **–stein** *m* flint. **–waffe** *f* gun. **–wehr** *f* fire brigade, (*US*) fire department. **–wehrmann** *m* fireman. **–zeug** *neut* (cigarette) lighter.
Feuilleton ['fœjətɔ̃] *neut* (*pl* **-s**) newspaper supplement, review section.
feurig ['fɔyriç] *adj* fiery.
Fiber ['fiːbər] *f* (*pl* **-n**) fibre.
Fichte ['fiçtə] *f* (*pl* **-n**) fir, spruce (tree).
Fieber ['fiːbər] *neut* (*pl* **-**) fever. **fieberartig** *adj* feverish. **fieberhaft** *adj* feverish.
Fiedel ['fiːdəl] *f* (*pl* **-n**) fiddle, violin. **fiedeln** *v* (play the) fiddle.
Figur [fi'guːr] *f* (*pl* **-en**) figure; (*Schach*) piece, chessman.

fiktiv [fik'tiːf] *adj* fictitious.
Filiale [fili'aːlə] *f* (*pl* **-n**) (*Komm*) branch.
Film [film] *m* (*pl* **-e**) film.
Filter ['filtər] *m* (*pl* **-**) filter. **filtrieren** *v* filter.
Filz [filts] *m* (*pl* **-e**) felt; (*Geizhals*) miser.
Finanz [fi'nants] *f* (*pl* **-en**) finance. **–amt** *neut* tax office, Inland Revenue. **finanziell** *adj* financial. **Finanzier** *m* (*pl* **-s**) financier. **finanzieren** *v* finance. **Finanz‖jahr** *m* financial year. **–minister** *m* finance minister.
***finden** ['findən] *v* find; (*glauben*) think, believe. **Finder** *m* (*pl* **-**) finder. **findig** *adj* clever, resourceful.
Finger ['fiŋər] *m* (*pl* **-**) finger. **–abdruck** *m* fingerprint. **–hut** *m* thimble; (*Bot*) foxglove. **–nagel** *m* fingernail. **–spitze** *f* fingertip.
Fink [fiŋk] *m* (*pl* **-en**) finch.
Finne ['finə] *m* (*pl* **-**), **Finnin** *f* (*pl* **-nen**) Finn. **finnisch** *adj* Finnish. **Finnland** *neut* Finland. **Finnländer(in)** *f* Finn.
finster ['finstər] *adj* dark; (*düster*) gloomy; (*drohend*) foreboding. **Finsternis** *f* darkness; gloom.
Firma ['firmə] *f* (*pl* **Firmen**) firm, business.
Firnis ['firnis] *m* (*pl* **-se**) varnish.
Fisch [fiʃ] *m* (*pl* **-e**) fish. **Fische** *pl* (*Astrol*) Pisces. **fischen** *v* fish. **Fischer** *m* (*pl* **-**) fisherman. **–boot** *neut* fishing boat. **–ei** *f* fishing. **–korb** *m* creel. **–otter** *m or f* otter. **–reiher** *m* heron. **–zeug** *neut* (*fishing*) tackle.
fix [fiks] *adj* firm; (*fig*) quick.
flach [flax] *adj* flat, even; (*nicht tief*) shallow; (*uninteressant*) dull.
Fläche ['flɛçə] *f* (*pl* **-n**) flatness; (*Gebiet*) area; (*Oberfläche*) surface. **–ninhalt** *m* surface area.
Flachs [flaks] *m* (*unz.*) flax.
flackerig ['flakəriç] *adj* flickering. **flackern** *v* flicker, flare.
Flagge ['flagə] *f* (*pl* **-n**) flag.
Flamme ['flamə] *f* (*pl* **-n**) flame. **flammen** *v* flame, blaze.
Flanell [fla'nɛl] *m* (*pl* **-e**) flannel.
Flanke ['flaŋkə] *f* (*pl* **-n**) flank. **flankieren** *v* (out)flank.
Flasche ['flaʃə] *f* (*pl* **-n**) bottle. **Flaschen–** *adj* cylindrical. **Flaschenöffner** *m* bottle-opener.
flattern ['flatərn] *v* flutter.

flau [flau] *adj* weak; (*Getränke*) flat; (*Komm*) slack, dull.

Flaum [flaum] *m* (*unz.*) down. **flaumig** *adj* downy.

Flaute ['flautə] *f* (*pl* -n) lull, calm; (*Wirtschaft*) recession.

Flechte ['flɛçtə] *f* (*pl* -n) braid; (*Bot*) lichen; (*Med*) ringworm, herpes. **flechten** *v* braid, interweave; (*Korb*) weave.

Flechtkorb *m* wicker basket.

Fleck [flɛk] *m* (*pl* -e) stain, spot; (*Makel*) blemish, flaw. **flecken** *v* stain.

Fledermaus ['fle:dərmaus] *f* bat.

flehen ['fle:ən] *v* implore, entreat (for). **-tlich** *adj* imploring.

Fleisch [flaiʃ] *neut* (*unz.*) meat. **-brühe** *f* (meat) stock. **Fleischer** *m* (*pl* -) butcher. **-ei** *f* (*pl* -en) butcher's (shop). **fleisch‖farbig** *adj* flesh-coloured. **-fressend** *adj* carnivorous. **-ig** *adj* fleshy. **-lich** *adj* carnal. **Fleisch‖topf** *m* meat saucepan; (*fig*) fleshpot. **-werdung** *f* (*Rel*) Incarnation. **-wolf** *m* mincer.

Fleiß [flais] *m* (*unz.*) diligence, industry. **fleißig** *adj* industrious, hard-working.

Flick [flik] *m* (*pl* -en) patch. **-arbeit** *f* patching; (*Pfuscherei*) botch. **flicken** *v* mend, patch.

Fliege ['fli:gə] *f* (*pl* -n) fly. **fliegen** *v* fly. **Flieger** *m* (*pl* -) aviator, flier. **-abwehr** *f* anti-aircraft defence.

*****fliehen** ['fli:ən] *v* flee.

Fließband ['fli:sbant] *neut* conveyor belt, assembly line. **fließen** *v* flow. **fließend** *adj* flowing, running.

flimmern ['flimərn] *v* glimmer, twinkle.

flink [fliŋk] *adj* nimble, agile.

Flinte ['flintə] *f* (*pl* -n) musket; (*Schrot*) shotgun.

flirten ['flirtən] *v* flirt.

Flitterwochen ['flitərvɔxən] *f pl* honeymoon *sing.*

Flocke ['flɔkə] *f* (*pl* -n) flake; (*Wolle, Haar*) flock, tuft. **flocken** *v* fall in flakes. **flockig** *adj* flaky; (*Haar, usw.*) fluffy.

Floh [flo:] *m* (*pl* Flöhe) flea. **-stich** *m* fleabite.

Floskel ['flɔskəl] *f* (*pl* -n) flowery *or* fine phrase.

Floß [flo:s] *neut* (*pl* Flöße) raft.

Flosse ['flɔsə] *f* (*pl* -n) fin.

Flöte ['flø:tə] *f* (*pl* -n) flute. **flöten** *v* play the flute. **Flötist(in)** flautist.

flott [flɔt] *adj* brisk; (*Schnell*) fast;

(*schick*) smart; (*schwimmend*) afloat. **Flotte** *f* fleet, navy.

Flöz [flø:ts] *neut* (*pl* -e) (*Mineralien*) seam.

Fluch [flu:x] *m* (*pl* Flüche) curse; (*Fluchwort*) swear-word. **fluchen** *v* swear, curse.

Flucht [fluxt] *f* (*pl* -en) flight, escape; (*Reihe*) row.

flüchtig ['flyçtiç] *adj* fleeting, cursory. **Flüchtling** *m* (*pl* -e) refugee.

Flug [flu:k] *m* (*pl* Flüge) flight, flying; (*Vögel*) flock. **-bahn** *f* trajectory. **-blatt** *neut* handbill, pamphlet.

Flügel ['fly:gəl] *m* (*pl* -) wing; (*Klavier*) grand piano. **-fenster** *neut* French window.

Flug‖gast *m* air passenger. **-hafen** *m* airport. **-post** *f* air-mail. **-schiff** *m* flyingboat. **-schrift** *f* pamphlet. **-wesen** *neut* aviation, flying. **-zeug** *neut* aeroplane. **-zeug-halle** *f* hangar. **-zeug-träger** *m* aircraft-carrier.

flunkern ['fluŋkərn] *v* fib, lie; (*übertreiben*) exaggerate, brag.

Flur [flu:r] *m* (*pl* -e) floor; (entrance) hall.

Fluß [flus] *m* (*pl* Flüsse) river. **fluß‖abwärts** *adv* downstream. **-aufwärts** *adv* upstream. **Flussfisch** *m* fresh-water fish.

flüssig ['flysiç] *adj* liquid. **Flüssigkeit** *f* liquid.

flüstern ['flystərn] *v* whisper.

Flut [flu:t] *f* (*pl* -en) flood; (*Hochwasser*) (high) tide. **Ebbe und Flut** ebb and flow. **fluten** *v* flood.

Fohlen ['fo:lən] *neut* (*pl* -) foal.

Föhn [fø:n] *m* (*pl* -e) (warm) south wind.

Folge ['fɔlgə] *f* (*pl* -n) succession; (*Wirkung*) consequence. **folgen** *v* follow; (*gehorchen*) obey. **folgend** *adj* (the) following. **-ermaßen** *adv* as follows. **folgerichtig** *adj* consistent, logical. **folgern** *v* conclude, infer. **Folgerung** *f* (*pl* -en) conclusion, inference. **folgewidrig** *adj* inconsistent, illogical. **folglich** *adv* consequently.

Folter ['fɔltər] *f* (*pl* -n) torture; (*Gerät*) rack. **foltern** *v* torture. **Folterung** *f* torture, torturing.

Fön [fø:n] *m* (*pl* -e) hairdrier.

Fonds [fɔ̃:] *m* (*pl* -) fund.

Förderer ['fœrdərər] *m* (*pl* -) promoter, sponsor. **förderlich** *adj* useful, beneficial.

fordern ['fɔrdərn] *v* demand; (*beanspruchen*) claim.
fördern ['fœːrdərn] *v* further, promote.
Forderung ['fɔrdəruŋ] *f* (*pl* -en) demand.
Förderung ['fœːrdəruŋ] *f* (*pl* -en) furtherance, advancement; (*Komm*) promotion; (*Kohle*) mining.
Forelle [foˈrɛlə] *f* (*pl* -n) trout.
Form [fɔrm] *f* (*pl* -en) form; (*tech*, *Kuchen*) mould. **in Form** (*sport*) fit, on form. **Formel** *f* (*pl* -n) formula. **form∥ell** *adj* formal. **-en** *v* form, shape. **-los** *adj* shapeless, formless. **Formular** *neut* (*pl* -e) (*question*) form, (*US*) blank. **formulieren** *v* formulate.
forschen ['fɔrʃən] *v* investigate; (*fragen*) inquire; (*Wissenschaft*) do research. **forschend** *adj* searching. **Forscher** *m* (*pl* -) investigator, enquirer; researcher. **Forschung** *f* (*pl* -en) investigation; research.
Forst [fɔrst] *m* (*pl* -e) forest.
Förster ['fœːrstər] *m* (*pl* -) forester.
Forstwirtschaft ['fɔrstvirtʃaft] *f* forestry.
fort [fɔrt] *adv* away; (*vorwärts*) forward(s); (*weiter*) on.
fortan [fɔrtˈan] *adv* from now on.
*fortbestehen ['fɔrtbəʃteːən] *v* continue (to exist), live on, survive.
Fortbildung ['fɔrtbilduŋ] *f* further education.
*fortbleiben ['fɔrtblaibən] *v* remain away.
fortdauern ['fɔrtdauərn] *v* last, continue. **-d** *adj* continual, incessant.
*fortfahren ['fɔrtfaːrən] *v* drive away, depart; (*weitermachen*) proceed, continue.
*fortgehen ['fɔrtgeːən] *v* go away.
fortgeschritten ['fɔrtgəʃritən] *adj* advanced.
*fortkommen ['fɔrtkɔmən] *v* escape; (*fig*) prosper, make progress.
*fortlaufen ['fɔrtlaufən] *v* run away; (*fortkommen*) escape; (*weiterlaufen*) continue. **-d** *adj* continuous.
fortleben ['fɔrtleːbən] *v* survive. **Fortleben** *neut* survival; (*nach dem Tode*) afterlife.
fortpflanzen ['fɔrtpflantsən] *v* sich **fortpflanzen** reproduce, multiply; (*Krankheit*) spread.
*fortschreiten ['fɔrtʃraitən] *v* go forward, proceed.
Fortschritt ['fɔrtʃrit] *m* (*pl* -e) progress. **fortschrittlich** *adj* progressive.
fortsetzen ['fɔrtzɛtsən] *v* continue. **Fortsetzung** *f* continuation.

fortwährend ['fɔrtvɛɪrənt] *adj* continuous, incessant.
Fossil [fɔˈsiːl] *neut* (*pl* -ien) fossil.
Foto ['foːto] *neut* (*pl* -s) (*umg.*) photo.
Fötus ['fœːtus] *m* (*pl* -se) foetus.
Fracht [fraxt] *f* (*pl* -en) freight. **-brief** *m* consignment *or* dispatch note. **-gut** *neut* cargo, goods. **-schiff** *neut* merchantman.
Frack [frak] *m* (*pl* **Fräcke**) dresscoat, tails. **-hemd** *neut* dress shirt. **-zwang** *m* obligatory evening dress, formal dress.
Frage ['fraːgə] *f* (*pl* -n) question. **-bogen** *m* questionnaire. **fragen** *v* ask. **Fragezeichen** *neut* question mark. **frag∥lich** *adj* in question, doubtful. **-los** *adj* unquestionable.
Fragment [fragˈmɛnt] *neut* (*pl* -e) fragment.
fragwürdig ['fraikvurdiç] *adj* questionable.
Fraktion [fraktsiˈoːn] *f* (*pl* -en) (*Pol*) parliamentary party, faction.
Fraktur [frakˈtuːr] *f* (*pl* -en) fracture; (*Druck*) Gothic type *or* script.
frankieren [fraŋˈkiːrən] *v* (*Brief*) stamp; (*Päckchen*) pre-pay. **franko** *adv* post paid.
Frankreich ['fraŋkraiç] *neut* France.
Franse ['franzə] *f* (*pl* -n) fringe. **fransig** *adj* fringed; (*ausgefasert*) frayed.
Franzose [franˈtsoːzə] *m* (*pl* -n) Frenchman. **Französin** *f* (*pl* -nen) Frenchwoman. **französich** *adj* French.
Fratze ['fratsə] *f* (*pl* -n) grimace. **Fratzen schneiden** make *or* pull faces.
Frau [frau] *f* (*pl* -en) woman; (*Ehefrau*) wife; (*Titel*) Mrs. **Frauen∥arzt** *m* gynaecologist. **-befreiung** *f* women's liberation. **frauenhaft** *adj* womanly. **Frauen∥rechtlerin** *f* (*pl* -nen) feminist. **-welt** *f* womankind, women *pl*.
Fräulein ['frɔylain] *neut* (*pl* -) young lady; (*Titel*) Miss.
frech [frɛç] *adj* cheeky, insolent. **Frechheit** *f* cheek, insolence.
frei [frai] *adj* free; (*nicht besetzt*) vacant, unoccupied; (*offen*) candid.
Freibad ['fraibat] *neut* outdoor swimming pool.
freiberuflich ['fraibərufliç] *adj* freelance, self-employed, professional.
Freibrief ['fraibriːf] *m* charter.
Freie ['fraiə] *neut* (*unz.*) outdoors, open air. **im Freien** in the open air.

Freigabe ['fraigaɪbə] *f* release.
*freigeben ['fraigeɪbən] *v* set free; (Straße, usw.) open; (*Waren, Arznei*) pass, approve, decontrol. **freigebig** *adj* generous.
Freihandel ['fraihandəl] *m* free-trade.
Freiheit ['fraihait] *f* (*pl* -en) freedom, liberty. **freiheitlich** *adj* liberal.
Freiherr ['fraiher] *m* (*pl* -) baron. **–in** *f* (*pl* -nen) baroness.
Freikarte ['fraikaɪrtə] *f* complimentary ticket.
*freilassen ['frailasən] *v* set free.
freilich ['frailiç] *adv* certainly, indeed, of course.
freimachen ['fraimaxən] *v* deliver (from captivity), release.
Freimaurer ['fraimaurər] *m* (*pl* -) freemason.
Freimut ['fraimuːt] *m* (*unz.*) candour, frankness. **freimütig** *adj* candid, frank.
*freisprechen ['fraiʃpreçən] *v* acquit, discharge.
Freitag ['fraitaːk] *m* Friday.
freiwillig ['fraiviliç] *adj* voluntary.
Freizeit ['fraitsait] *f* leisure time, spare time.
fremd [fremt] *adj* strange; (*ausländisch*) foreign. **Fremde(r)** stranger; foreigner. **Fremd‖enzimmer** *neut* guest room. **–heit** *f* strangeness. **–körper** *m* foreign body. **–sprache** *f* foreign language. **–wort** *neut* foreign word, loan word.
Frequenz [freˈkvɛnts] *f* (*pl* -en) frequency.
*fressen ['fresən] *v* eat, devour.
Freude ['frɔydə] *f* (*pl* -n) joy; (*Vergnügen*) delight. **–ntag** *m* red-letter day. **freudig** *adj* joyful, joyous.
freuen ['frɔən] *v* give pleasure to. **es freut mich** I am glad *or* pleased. **sich freuen** be glad, rejoice. **sich freuen auf** look forward to.
Freund [frɔynt] *m* (*pl* -e) friend; (*Liebhaber*) boyfriend. **–in** *f* (*pl* -nen) (girl) friend. **freundlich** *adj* friendly; (*liebenswürdig*) kind. **Freund‖lichkeit** *f* friendliness. **–schaft** *f* friendship. **freundschaftlich** *adj* friendly.
Frevel ['freːfəl] *m* (*pl* -) sacrilege. **frevelhaft** *adj* sacrilegious.
Friede(n) ['friːdə(n)] *m* (*pl* -) peace. **Friedens‖bruch** *m* breach of the peace. **–stifter** *m* peacemaker. **–vertrag** *m* peace (treaty). **Friedhof** *m* cemetary. **friedlich** *adj* peaceful.

*frieren ['friːrən] *v* freeze.
Frikadelle [frikaˈdɛlə] *f* (*pl* -n) rissole.
frisch [friʃ] *adj* fresh; (*lebhaft*) lively. **Frische** *f* freshness; liveliness.
Friseur [friˈzœɪr] *m*, (*pl* -e) **Friseuse** *f* (*pl* -n) hairdresser; (*nur für Herren*) barber. **frisieren** *v* cut *or* style hair; (*Bücher*) cook, falsify; (*Mot*) soup up. **Frisiersalon** *m* hairdressing salon.
Frist [frist] *f* (*pl* -en) period, time; (*Termin*) time limit, deadline.
Frisur [friˈzuːr] *f* (*pl* en) hairstyle; (*umg.*) hairdo.
froh [froː] *adj* glad, cheerful, happy.
fröhlich ['frœːliç] *adj* cheerful, joyous. **Fröhlichkeit** *f* cheerfulness.
frohlocken ['froːlɔkən] *v* rejoice. **Frohsinn** *m* gaiety.
fromm [frɔm] *adj* pious, religious.
frömmelnd ['frœməlnd] *adj* religiose, hypocritical. **Frömmler** *m* hypocritic.
Fronleichnam [froːnˈlaiçnaɪm] *m* Corpus Christi Day.
Front [frɔnt] *f* (*pl* -en) front, face; (*Pol*) front. **–antrieb** *m* front-wheel drive.
Frosch [frɔʃ] *m* (*pl* Frösche) frog; (*Feuerwerk*) squib, banger.
Frost [frɔst] *m* (*pl* Fröste) frost; (*Kälte*) coldness, chill. **–beule** *f* chilblain. **frostig** *adj* chilly, frosty. **Frostschutzmittel** *neut* antifreeze.
Frucht [fruxt] *f* (*pl* Früchte) fruit. **fruchtbar** *adj* fertile. **Fruchtbarkeit** *f* fertility. **fruchtlos** *adj* fruitless. **Fruchtsaft** *m* fruit juice.
früh [fryː] *adj* early. **Frühe** *f* early hour, early morning. **früher** *adj* earlier; (*ehemalig*) former. **frühestens** *adv* earliest.
Früh‖geburt *f* premature birth. **–jahr** *neut* spring. **–ling** *m* spring. **–reife** *f* precocity. **–stück** *neut* breakfast. **früh‖stücken** *v* breakfast. **–zeitig** *adj* premature, untimely; (*rechtzeitig*) early, in good time.
Fuchs [fuks] *m* (*pl* Füchse) fox.
Füchsin ['fyçsin] *f* (*pl* -nen) vixen.
Fuge ['fuːgə] *f* (*pl* -n) joint; (*Musik*) fugue.
fügen ['fyːgən] *v* join together; (*ordnen*) dispose. **sich fügen** submit. **fügsam** *adj* submissive, obedient.
fühlen ['fyːlən] *v* touch, feel. **sich fühlen** feel. **sich glücklich fühlen** feel *or* be hap-

py. **Fühlen** *neut* feeling. **Fühler** *m* feeler. **Fühlung** *f* touch.

führen ['fyːrən] *v* lead, direct; (*Waren*) stock, carry; (*Bücher*) keep. **–d** *adj* prominent, leading. **Führer** *m* leader, guide. **–haus** *neut* (*Zug*) driver's cab. **–schaft** *f* leadership. **–schein** *m* driving licence, (*US*) driver's license. **–sitz** *m* driver's *or* pilot's seat. **Führung** *f* command, management.

Fülle ['fylə] *f* (*pl* -n) abundance, plenty. **Hülle und Fülle** plentiful, in plenty. **füllen** *v* fill (up). **Füll‖feder** *f* fountain-pen. **–ung** *f* (*pl* –en) filling.

Fundament [funda'mɛnt] *neut* (*pl* -e) foundation, base.

fünf [fynf] *adj* five. **fünft** *adj* fifth. **Fünftel** *neut* fifth. **fünf‖zehn** *pron*, *adj* fifteen.

fungieren [fuŋ'giːrən] *v* function (as), act (as).

Funk [fuŋk] *m* (*unz.*) radio, wireless. **–e** *m* (*pl* -n) spark. **funkeln** *v* sparkle. **Funksendung** *f* (*Radio*) programme transmission.

Funktion [fuŋktsi'oːn] *f* (*pl* -en) function. **–är** *m* (*pl* -e) functionary. **funktionieren** *v* function.

für [fyːr] *prep* for.

Furche ['furçə] *f* (*pl* -n) furrow; (*Runzel*) wrinkle. **furchen** *v* furrow.

Furcht [furçt] *f* (*unz.*) fear. **furchtbar** *adj* frightful.

fürchten ['fyrçtən] *v* fear. **sich fürchten vor** be afraid of. **fürchterlich** *adj* terrible, dreadful.

Furnier [fur'niːr] *neut* (*pl* -e) veneer.

Fürsorge ['fyːrzɔrgə] *f* care; (*Hilfstätigkeit*) welfare work; (*Geld*) social security. **–arbeit** *f* social work.

Fürsprecher ['fyːrʃprɛçər] *m* advocate. **fürsprechen** *v* intercede.

Fürst [fyrst] *m* (*pl* -en) prince. **–in** *f* (*pl* -nen) princess. **fürstlich** *adj* princely.

Furz [furts] *m* (*pl* Fürze) (*vulgär*) fart. **furzen** *v* fart.

Fuß [fuːs] *m* (*pl* Füße) foot. **–ball** *m* football. **–boden** *m* floor. **–bremse** *f* footbrake. **–gänger** *m* pedestrian. **–pflege** *f* chiropody. **–steig** *m* pavement, (*US*) sidewalk. **–tritt** *m* kick; (*Gang*) step. **–volk** *neut* infantry. **–weg** *m* footpath.

Futter ['futər] *neut* (*pl* -) feed, fodder; (*Kleider*) lining.

füttern ['fytərn] *v* feed; line. **Fütterung** *f* feeding, fodder; lining.

G

Gabe ['gaːbə] *f* (*pl* -n) gift.

Gabel ['gaːbəl] *f* (*pl* -n) fork. **gabeln** *v* fork. **Gabelung** *f* fork, branching.

gackern ['gakərn] *v* cackle.

gähnen ['gɛːnən] *v* yawn.

galant [ga'lant] *adj* polite, gallant.

Galeere [ga'leːrə] *f* (*pl* -n) galley.

Galerie [galə'riː] *f* (*pl* -n) gallery.

Galgen ['galgən] *m* (*pl* -) gallows *pl*.

Galle ['galə] *f* (*pl* -n) gall, bile; (*fig*) rancour.

Gallen‖blase ['galən‚blaɪzə] *f* gallbladder. **–stein** *m* gallstone.

Galopp [ga'lɔp] *m* (*pl* -e) gallop. **galoppieren** *v* gallop.

galvanisieren [galvani'ziːrən] *v* galvanize.

Gang [gaŋ] *m* (*pl* Gänge) walk; (*Gangart*) gait; (*Flur*) corridor; (*Essen*) course; (*Mot*) gear. **im Gang** in motion. **Gang‖art** *f* gait. **–schalter** *m* gear lever.

Gans [gans] *f* (*pl* Gänse) goose.

Gänse‖blume ['gɛnzəbluːmə] *f* daisy. **–braten** *m* roast goose. **–füßchen** *pl* quotation marks. **–rich** *m* gander.

ganz [gants] *adj* whole, all; (*vollständig*) complete. *adv* quite; (*vollends*) fully. **Ganze** *neut* whole.

gar [gaːr] *adj* (*Kochen*) done, cooked. *adv* very. **gar nicht** not at all. **gar keiner** none whatever.

Garantie [garan'tiː] *f* (*pl* -n) guarantee.

Garde ['gardə] *f* (*pl* -n) guard.

Garderobe [gardə'roːbə] *f* (*pl* -n) cloakroom; (*Kleider*) wardrobe.

Gardine [gar'diːnə] *f* (*pl* -n) curtain.

***gären** ['gɛːrən] *v* ferment.

garnieren [gar'niːrən] *v* garnish; (*Kleidung*) trim.

Garnison [garni'zoːn] *f* (*pl* -en) garrison.

Garnitur [garni'tuːr] *f* (*pl* -en) (*Verzierung*) trimming; (*Satz*) set; (*Ausrüstung*) equipment.

Garten ['gartən] *m* (*pl* Gärten) garden. **–bau** *m* horticulture. **–haus** *neut* summer house. **–laube** *f* arbour.

Gärtner ['gɛrtnər] *m* (*pl* -) gardener. **–ei** *f* (*pl* -en). nursery.

Gärung ['gɛɪruŋ] *f* (*pl* -en) fermentation.
Gas [gaɪs] *neut* (*pl* -e) gas. **-flasche** *f* gas cylinder *or* bottle. **-hebel** *m* accelerator. **-hahn** *m* gas cock. **-herd** *m* gas cooker.
Gasse ['gasa] *f* (*pl* -n) alley, lane.
Gast [gast] *m* (*pl* Gäste) guest. **gastfreundlich** *adj* hospitable. **Gast‖freundschaft** *f* hospitality. **-geber** *m* (*pl* -) host. **-geberin** *f* (*pl* -nen) hostess. **-hof** *m* hotel, inn. **-mahl** *neut* banquet. **-stätte** *f* restaurant, café. **-wirt** *m* landlord, innkeeper.
Gatte ['gata] *m* (*pl* -n) spouse, husband. **gatten** *v* match. **Gattin** *f* (*pl* -nen) spouse, wife.
Gattung ['gatuŋ] *f* (*pl* -en) sort, kind; (*Biol*) species.
gaukeln ['gaukəln] *v* perform tricks, juggle.
Gaul [gaul] *m* (*pl* Gäule) nag.
Gaumen ['gaumən] *m* (*pl* -) palate.
Gauner ['gaunər] *m* (*pl* -) swindler, trickster.
Gaze ['gaɪzə] *f* (*pl* -n) gauze.
Gazelle [ga'tsɛlə] *f* (*pl* -n) gazelle.
geartet [gə'aɪrtət] *adj* constituted, composed.
Gebäck [gə'bɛk] *neut* (*pl* -e) pastry, cakes; (*Keks*) biscuit.
Gebärde [gə'bɛɪrdə] *f* (*pl* -n) gesture.
***gebären** [gə'bɛɪrən] *v* give birth to, bear. **Gebärmutter** *f* womb.
Gebäude [gə'bɔydə] *neut* (*pl* -) building.
***geben** ['geɪbən] *v* give. **sich geben** relent, abate. **es gibt** there is/are. **was gibt es?** what is the matter? **sich zufrieden geben** be content. **das gibt's nicht!** that's impossible! **Geben** *neut* giving. **Geber** *m* (*pl* -), **Geberin** *f* (*pl* -nen) giver, donor.
Gebet [gə'beɪt] *neut* (*pl* -e) prayer. **-buch** *neut* prayerbook.
Gebiet [gə'biɪt] *neut* (*pl* -e) (*Staats-*) territory; (*Gegend*) area, district; (*fig*) field, sphere.
Gebilde [gə'bildə] *neut* (*pl* -) (*Erzeugnis*) product; (*Form*) structure, shape.
gebildet [gə'bildət] *adj* educated, cultured.
Gebirge [gə'birgə] *neut* (*pl* -) mountain range, mountains *pl.*
Gebiß [gə'bis] *neut* (*pl* Gebisse) (set of) teeth; (*Zaum*) bit; (*künstlich*) denture.
Gebläse [gə'blɛɪzə] *neut* (*pl* -) blower, bellows *pl*; (*Mot*) supercharger.
geboren [gə'bɔɪrən] *adj* born. *geborener*

Hamburger native of Hamburg. *Frau Maria Müller, geborene (geb.) Schmidt* Mrs. Maria Müller, *nee* Schmidt.
Gebot [gə'boɪt] *neut* (*pl* -e) order. **die zehn Gebote** the Ten Commandments.
Gebrauch [gə'braux] *neut* (*pl* Gebräuche) custom; (*Benutzen*) use. **gebrauchen** *v* use. **gebräuchlich** *adj* customary. **Gebrauchs‖anweisung** *f or* **-anleitung** *f* instructions (for use). **Gebrauchtwagen** *m* second-hand car.
gebrechlich [gə'brɛçliç] *adj* (*Gegenstand*) fragile; (*Person*) frail.
Gebrüder [gə'bryydər] *m pl* brothers. **Gebrüder Schmidt** Schmidt Bros.
Gebrüll [gə'bryl] *neut* (*unz.*) roar, roaring.
Gebühr [gə'byɪr] **1** *f* (*pl* -en) fee, charge. **2** *f* (*unz.*) decency, propriety. **nach Gebühr** duly. **gebühren** *v* be due. **sich gebühren** be fitting *or* decent. **gebührend** *adj* seemly, proper.
gebunden [gə'bundən] *adj* bound.
Geburt [gə'burt] *f* (*pl* -en) birth. **Geburten‖beschränkung** *f or* **-regelung** *f* birth control. **gebürtig** *adj* born (in). **Geburts‖fehler** *m* congenital defect. **-helfer** *m* obstetrician. **-helferin** *f* midwife; (*Ärztin*) obstetrician. **-hilfe** *f* obstetrics. **-mal** *neut* mole. **-ort** *m* birthplace. **-schein** *m* birth certificate. **-tag** *m* birthday.
Gebüsch [gə'byʃ] *neut* (*pl* -e) (clump of) bushes.
Gedächtnis [gə'dɛçtnis] *neut* (*pl* -se) memory. **-feier** *f* commemoration. **-schwund** *m* loss of memory, amnesia.
Gedanke [gə'daŋkə] *m* (*pl* -n) thought. **sich Gedanken machen über** worry about. **gedankenlos** *adj* thoughtless. **gedanklich** *adj* mental.
Gedeck [gə'dɛk] *neut* (*pl* -e) cover, place-setting; menu.
***gedeihen** [gə'daiən] *v* flourish, thrive.
***gedenken** [gə'dɛŋkən] *v* think (of); (*vorhaben*) intend. **Gendenkfeier** *f* commemoration.
Gedicht [gə'diçt] *neut* (*pl* -e) poem. **-sammlung** *f* anthology (of verse).
gediegen [gə'diɪgən] *adj* (*echt*) genuine; (*rein*) pure; (*solide*) solid; (*sorgfältig*) thorough.
Gedränge [gə'drɛŋə] *neut* (*unz.*) crowd, press; (*Notlage*) difficulty. **gedrängt** *adj* narrow, close; (*Stil*) terse, concise.

gedruckt [gə'drukt] *adj* printed.
gedrückt [gə'drykt] *adj* depressed.
Geduld [gə'dult] *f* patience. **geduldig** *adj* patient. **Geduldspiel** *neut* puzzle.
geehrt [gə'ɛɪrt] *adj* honoured. **sehr geehrter Herr (Smith)** Dear Sir (Dear Mr Smith).
geeignet [gə'aıgnət] *adj* suitable, adapted (to).
Gefahr [gə'faɪr] *f* (*pl* -en) danger. **gefährden** *v* endanger, jeopardize. **gefährlich** *adj* dangerous. **gefahr||los** *adj* safe, without risk. **-voll** *adj* dangerous.
Gefährte [gə'fɛɪrtə] *m* (*pl* -n), **Gefährtin** *f* (*pl* -nen) companion.
*gefallen [gə'falən] *v* please. **es gefällt mir** I like it. **sich nicht gefallen lassen** not put up with it.
Gefallen¹ [gə'falən] *neut* (*unz.*) pleasure.
Gefallen² *m* (*pl* -) favour. **tun Sie mir den Gefallen und . . .** Do me the favour of . . . .
gefällig [gə'fɛlıç] *adj* pleasing; obliging.
gefangen [gə'faŋən] *adj* captive. **Gefangene(r)** *m* prisoner, captive. **Gefangenschaft** *f* captivity.
Gefängnis [gə'fɛŋnıs] *neut* (*pl* -se) prison. **-wärter** *m* warder, prison officer.
Gefäß [gə'fɛıs] *neut* (*pl* -e) container, vessel.
gefaßt [gə'fast] *adj* collected, calm, (*bereit*) ready.
Gefecht [gə'fɛçt] *neut* (*pl* -e) fight, combat.
Gefieder [gə'fiɪdər] *neut* (*unz.*) feathers *pl*, plumage.
Geflügel [gə'flyɪgəl] *neut* (*unz.*) poultry.
Gefolge [gə'fɔlgə] *neut* (*pl* -) followers *pl*, entourage.
gefräßig [gə'frɛısıç] *adj* voracious, gluttonous.
Gefrier||punkt [gə'friɪrpuŋkt] *m* freezing point. **-schutzmittel** *neut* antifreeze.
gefügig [gə'fyɪgıç] *adj* pliant, submissive.
Gefühl [gə'fyɪl] *neut* (*pl* -e) feeling. **gefühllos** *adj* unfeeling. **Gefühlssinn** *m* sense of touch. **gefühlvoll** *adj* full of feeling, emotional.
gegebenenfalls [gə'geɪbənənfals] *adv* if need be, should the need arise. **Gegebenheit** *f* (*pl* -en) reality.
gegen ['geɪgən] *prep* against; (*in Richtung*) towards; (*ungefähr*) about; compared with; (*Tausch*) in exchange for.

Gegen||angriff *m* counterattack. **-besuch** *m* return visit. **-bild** *neut* counterpart.
Gegend ['geɪgənt] *f* (*pl* -en) district, area.
gegeneinander ['geɪgənainandər] *adv* against one another. **-stoßen** *v* collide.
Gegen||gift *neut* antidote. **-leistung** *f* return (service). **-mittel** *neut* remedy. **-satz** *m* opposite, contrary. **gegen||sätzlich** *adj* opposite, contrary. **-seitig** *adj* reciprocal, mutual. **Gegen||stand** *m* object; (*Thema*) subject. **-stück** *neut* counterpart. **-teil** *neut* opposite, contrary. **im Gegenteil zu** contrary to, in contrast to.
gegenüber ['geɪgənybər] *adv*, *prep* opposite. **-liegend** *adj* opposite. **-stehen** *v* stand opposite. **Gegenüberstellung** *f* confrontation; antithesis.
Gegenwart ['geɪgənvaɪrt] *f* (*unz.*) present; (*Anwesenheit*) presence. **gegenwärtig** *adj* present, current.
Gegner ['geɪgnər] *m* (*pl* -) opponent, enemy. **gegnerisch** *adj* antagonistic, hostile.
Gehalt¹ [gə'halt] *m* (*unz.*) contents *pl*; (*Wert*) worth, value.
Gehalt² *neut* (*pl* **Gehälter**) salary, pay. **Gehalts||empfänger** *m* salaried employee. **-erhöhung** *f* rise (in salary).
gehässig [gə'hɛsıç] *adj* spiteful, malicious.
Gehäuse [gə'hɔyzə] *neut* (*pl* -) case, box; (*Tech*) casing.
geheim [gə'haim] *adj* secret. **Geheim||agent** *m* secret agent. **-dienst** *m* secret *or* intelligence service. **geheimhalten** *v* keep secret. **Geheimnis** *neut* (*pl* -se) secret; (*unerklärbar*) mystery. **geheimnisvoll** *adj* mysterious. **Geheim||polizei** *f* secret police. **-schrift** *f* code, cipher. **geheimtuerisch** *adj* secretive.
*gehen ['geɪən] *v* walk, go (on foot); (*Maschine*) go, work. **wie geht es Ihnen?** how are you? **es geht** it's all right. **es geht nicht** it can't be done, that's no good. **sie geht mit ihm** she is going out with him. **an die Arbeit gehen** set to work.
Gehilfe [gə'hilfə] *m* (*pl* -n) assistant, help.
Gehirn [gə'hirn] *neut* (*pl* -e) brain. **-erschütterung** *f* concussion. **-schlag** *m* cerebral apoplexy. **-wäsche** *f* brainwashing.
gehoben [gə'hoɪbən] *adj* high, elevated.
Gehör [gə'hœɪr] *neut* (*unz.*) hearing; (*Musik*) ear.

gehorchen [gə'hɔrçən] *v* obey.

gehören [gə'høːrən] *v* belong (to). **es gehört sich** it is proper *or* fitting. **gehörig** *adj* fit, proper.

gehorsam [gə'hoːrzaɪm] *adj* obedient. **Gehorsam** *m* obedience. **–sverweigerung** *f* insubordination.

Geh‖steig ['geɪʃtaik] *m* (*pl* -e) pavement. **–werk** *neut* movement, works.

Geier ['gaiər] *m* (*pl* -) vulture.

Geifer ['gaifər] *m* (*unz.*) spittle, slaver; (*fig*) venom. **geifern** *v* slaver; (*fig*) rave, foam with rage.

Geige [gaigə] *f* (*pl* -n) violin, fiddle. **–r** *m* violinist.

Geisel ['gaizəl] *m* (*pl* -) hostage.

Geist [gaist] **1** *m* (*unz.*) mind; (*Witzigkeit*) wit; (*nichtmaterielle Eigenschaften*) spirit. **2** *m* (*pl* -er) (Genius) genius; (*Gespenst*) ghost, spirit. **geistesabwesend** *adj* absent-minded. **Geistes‖blitz** *m* brainwave. **–freiheit** *f* freedom of thought. **geisteskrank** *adj* mentally ill, insane. **Geisteskranke(r)** *m* mental patient. **geist‖ig** *adj* intellectual; (*nicht körperlich*) spiritual; (*Getränke*) alcoholic. **–lich** *adj* spiritual, religious; (*kirchlich*) clerical. **Geistliche(r)** *m* cleric, clergyman. **geistreich** *adj* clever, ingenious.

Geiz [gaits] *m* (*unz.*) avarice, miserliness. **geizig** *adj* miserly, avaricious.

Gekicher [gə'kiçər] *neut* (*unz.*) giggling.

Geklapper [ge'klapər] *neut* (*unz.*) clatter(ing).

Geklimper [gə'klimpər] *neut* (*unz.*) jingling, chinking; (*Instrument*) strumming.

Geklingel [gə'kliŋəl] *neut* (*unz.*) tinkling, ringing.

gekünstelt [gə'kynstəlt] *adj* artificial, affected.

Gelächter [gə'lɛçtər] *neut* (*pl* -) laughter.

geladen [gə'laɪdən] *adj* loaded; (*Batterie*) charged.

Gelände [gə'lɛndə] *neut* (*pl* -) tract of land, area; (*Bau-*) site; (*Sport-*) grounds *pl*. **–lauf** *m* cross-country (running).

Geländer [gə'lɛndər] *neut* (*pl* -) railing, banister.

gelangen [gə'laŋən] *v* reach, arrive at; (*Ziel*) attain.

gelassen [gə'lasən] *adj* calm, composed.

geläufig [gə'ɔyfiç] *adj* familiar; (*Sprache*) fluent.

gelaunt [gə'launt] *adj* disposed. **gut**

gelaunt sweet-tempered. **schlecht** *or* **übel gelaunt** bad-tempered.

gelb [gɛlp] *adj* yellow. **Gelb** *neut* yellow. **–sucht** *f* jaundice. **gelbsüchtig** *adj* (*Med*) jaundiced.

Geld [gɛlt] *neut* (*pl* -er) money. **–ausgabe** *f* expenditure. **–beutel** *m* purse. **–geber** *m* financial backer. **geldlich** *adj* pecuniary. **Geld‖nehmer** *m* borrower. **–strafe** *f* fine. **–stück** *neut* coin. **–sucht** *f* avarice.

Gelee [ʒe'leɪ] *neut* (*pl* -s) jelly.

gelegen [gə'leɪgən] *adj* situated; (*günstig*) convenient, opportune. **Gelegenheit** *f* (*pl* -en) opportunity, occasion. **Gelegenheits‖arbeit** *f* casual work. **–kauf** *m* bargain. **gelegentlich** *adj* occasional.

gelehrig [gə'leɪriç] *adj* eager to learn; (*klug*) intelligent. **gelehrt** *adj* learned. **Gelehrte(r)** *m* scholar.

Geleit [gə'lait] *neut* (*pl* -) escort, entourage. **–brief** *m* (letter of) safe conduct. **geleiten** *v* escort, accompany.

Gelenk [gə'lɛŋk] *neut* (*pl* -e) joint. **–entzündung** *f* arthritis.

gelernt [gə'lɛrnt] *adj* skilled, trained.

Geliebte(r) [gə'liːptə] *m* beloved, sweetheart.

gelinde [gə'lində] *adj* gentle, mild.

gelingen [gə'liŋən] *v* succeed, be successful. **es gelingt mir, zu ...** I am able to . . . .

geloben [gə'loːbən] *v* vow, promise solemnly.

*gelten [gɛltən] *v* be worth, cost; (*gültig sein*) be valid; (*betreffen*) concern. **–d** *adj* valid. **geltend machen** urge, insist (on).

Gelübde [gə'lypdə] *neut* (*pl* -) vow.

Gemach [gə'max] *neut* (*pl* Gemächer) room, chamber.

Gemahl [gə'maɪl] *m* (*pl* -e) husband. **–in** *f* (*pl* -nen) wife.

Gemälde [gə'mɛːldə] *neut* (*pl* -) painting, picture. **–galerie** *f* picture gallery.

gemäß [gə'mɛːs] *prep* in accordance with. *adj* suitable.

gemein [gə'main] *adj* common; (*öffentlich*) public; vulgar, low; (*böse*) nasty, mean.

Gemeinde [gə'maində] *f* (*pl* -n) community; (*Kommune*) municipality, town; (*Kirche*) congregation. **–rat** *m* local council; (*Person*) councillor. **–schule** *f* village school. **–steuer** *f* rates *pl*.

Gemeine(r) [gə'mainə(r)] *m (Mil)* private.
Gemeinheit *f* meanness, nastiness; *(Tat)* mean trick, piece of spite. **gemein‖nützig** *adj* charitable. **–sam** *adj* joint, common.
Gemeinschaft *f* community; *(Komm)* partnership. **–serziehung** *f* coeducation. **–sschule** *f* coeducational school.
Gemenge [gə'mɛŋə] *neut (pl -n)* mixture; *(Gewühl)* scuffle.
gemessen [gə'mɛsən] *adj* measured, sedate.
Gemisch [gə'miʃ] *neut (pl -e)* mixture. **gemischt** *adj* mixed.
Gemurmel [gə'murməl] *neut (unz.)* murmuring.
Gemüse [gə'myːzə] *neut (pl -)* vegetable(s). **–gärtner** *m* market gardener. **–händler** *m* greengrocer.
Gemüt [gə'myːt] *neut (pl -er)* disposition, temperament, heart. **gemütlich** *adj* comfortable, cosy; *(leutselig)* good-natured. **Gemütlichkeit** *f* cosiness, comfortableness; good-nature.
Gen [gɛn] *neut (pl -e)* gene.
genannt [gə'nant] *adj* named, called.
genau [gə'nau] *adj* precise, exact. **Genauigkeit** *f* precision, exactness.
genehmigen [gə'neːmiɡən] *v* authorize, permit. **Genehmigung** *f (pl -en)* authorization, permission.
geneigt [gə'naikt] *adj* disposed, inclined.
General [gene'raːl] *m (pl -e)* general. **–police** *f* comprehensive insurance policy. **–probe** *f* dress rehearsal. **–sekretär** *m* secretary-general. **–versammlung** *f* general meeting.
Generation [generatsi'oːn] *f (pl -en)* generation.
*genesen [gə'neːzən] *v* recover, convalesce, get better. **Genesung** *f* recovery. **–sheim** *neut* convalescent home.
Genetik [ge'neːtik] *f* genetics. **genetisch** *adj* genetic.
Genf [gɛnf] *neut* Geneva.
genial [geni'aːl] *adj (Person)* brilliant, gifted; *(Sache)* ingenious, inspired.
Genick [gə'nik] *neut (pl -e)* (nape of the) neck.
Genie [ʒe'niː] *neut (pl -s)* genius.
genieren [ʒe'niːrən] *v* bother, trouble. **sich genieren** be embarrassed.
genießbar [gə'niːsbaːr] *adj* enjoyable; *(Essen, Trinken)* palatable. **genießen** *v* enjoy; eat; drink. **Genießer** *m (pl -)* epicure, gourmet.

Genitalien [geni'taːliən] *pl* genitals.
Genosse [gə'nɔsə] *m (pl -n)*, **Genossin** *f (pl -nen)* comrade; *(Kollege)* colleague. **Genossenschaft** *f* cooperative (society). **genossenschaftlich** *adj* cooperative.
genug [gə'nuːk] *adv, adj* enough, sufficient(ly). **genügen** *v* be enough, suffice. **–d** *adj* sufficient, enough. **genügsam** *adj* easily satisfied. **Genugtuung** *f* satisfaction.
Genuß [gə'nus] *m (pl Genüsse)* pleasure, enjoyment.
Geograph [geo'graːf] *m (pl -en)* geographer. **–ie** *f* geography. **geographisch** *adj* geographical.
Geologe [geo'loːɡə] *m (pl -n)* geologist. **Geologie** *f* geology. **geologisch** *adj* geological.
Geometrie [geome'triː] *f (pl -n)* geometry. **geometrish** *adj* geometrical.
Gepäck [gə'pɛk] *neut (unz.)* baggage, luggage. **–aufbewahrung** *f* left-luggage office. **–netz** *neut* luggage rack. **–träger** *m* porter.
gepflegt [gə'pfleːkt] *adj* well-tended; *(Person)* well-groomed, well-dressed.
gepanzert [gə'pantsərt] *adj* armoured.
Gepflogenheit [gə'pfloːɡənhait] *f (pl -en)* habit, custom.
Geplapper [gə'plapər] *neut (unz.)* chatter.
Geplauder [gə'plaudər] *neut (unz.)* chat, small talk.
Gepräge [gə'prɛːɡə] *neut (pl -)* stamp; *(Münze)* coinage; *(Eigenart)* character.
Geprassel [gə'prasəl] *neut (unz.)* clatter.
gerade [gə'raːdə] *adj* straight; *(direkt)* direct; *(Haltung)* erect; *(Zahl)* even. *adv* just; *(genau)* exactly, precisely; *(direkt)* straight, directly. **–aus** *adv* straight on or ahead. **–so** *adv* just so, just the same. **–stehen** *v* stand erect, stand up straight. **–swegs** *adv* immediately; *(ohne Umwege)* directly. **–zu** *adv* directly; *(freimütig)* plainly, flatly; *(durchaus)* sheer, downright. **Geradheit** *f* straightness; *(Ehrlichkeit)* honesty. **gerad‖läufig** *adj* straight. **–zahlig** *adj* even(-numbered).
Geranie [ge'raːniə] *f (pl -n)* geranium.
Gerassel [gə'rasəl] *neut (unz.)* clatter, rattle.
Gerät [gə'rɛːt] *neut (pl -e)* tool, implement; *(kompliziert)* instrument; *(Maschine)* device, appliance; *(Radio, TV)* set; *(Ausrüstung)* equipment.

geraten [gə'raitən] *v* come upon; (*gel-ingen*) turn out well; (*gedeihen*) thrive. **in Schwierigkeiten geraten** get into difficul-ties. **in Zorn geraten** fly into a rage. **über etwas geraten** come across, stumble upon something.

Geratewohl [gə'raitəvoil] *neut* **aufs Ger-atewohl** at random.

geräumig [gə'rɔymiç] *adj* roomy, spa-cious.

Geräusch [gə'rɔyʃ] *neut* (*pl* -e) noise.

gerben ['gɛrbən] *v* tan. **Gerber** *m* (*pl* -) tanner. **Gerberei** *f* (*pl* -en) tannery.

gerecht [gə'rɛçt] *adj* just, fair; (*geeignet*) suitable. **-fertigt** *adj* justified; (*legitim*) legitimate. **Gerechtigkeit** *f* justice; (*Rechtschaffenheit*) righteousness.

Gerede [gə'reidə] *neut* (*unz.*) gossip.

Gericht¹ [gə'riçt] *neut* (*pl* -e) (*Essen*) dish; (*Gang*) course.

Gericht² *neut* (*pl* -e) law-court; (*fig*) jus-tice, judgment. **gerichtlich** *adj* judicial, legal. **Gerichts‖hof** *m* (law) court. **-kos-ten** *pl* (legal) costs. **-medizin** *f* forensic medicine. **-saal** *m* courtroom. **-schrei-ber** *m* clerk (of the court). **-verfahren** *neut* legal proceedings *pl*. **-vollzieher** *m* bailiff.

gerieben [gə'riibən] *adj* grated.

gering [gə'riŋ] *adj* small; (*Vorrat*) short; (*Preis*) low; (*unbedeutend*) unimportant, insignificant. **-fügig** *adj* trivial, insignifi-cant. **-schätzen** *v* think little of, despise. **-schätzig** *adj* disdainful.

gerinnen [gə'rinən] *v* congeal; (*Blut*) clot. **Gerinnsel** *neut* clot.

Gerippe [gə'ripə] *neut* (*pl* -) skeleton.

Germane [gɛr'mainə] *m* (*pl* -n), **Germanin** *f* (*pl* -nen) German; (*pl*) Germanic (tribes or peoples). **germanisch** *adj* Germanic.

gern(e) ['gɛrn(ə)] *adv* willingly, gladly, readily. **gern haben** *or* **mögen** be fond of, like. **gern tun** like to do. **ich möchte gern ...** I should like .... **gut und gern** easily.

Gerste ['gɛrstə] *f* barley.

Geruch [gə'ruix] *m* (*pl* Gerüche) smell, odour. **-ssinn** *m* (sense of) smell.

Gerücht [gə'ryçt] *neut* (*pl* -e) rumour.

Gerümpel [gə'rympəl] *neut* junk, trash.

Gerüst [gə'ryst] *neut* (*pl* -e) scaffolding.

gesamt [gə'zamt] *adj* whole, entire. **Gesamt‖betrag** *m* total (amount). **-heit** *f* whole, totality. **-schule** comprehensive

school. **-übersicht** *f* overall view. **-ver-sicherung** *f* comprehsive insurance. **-zahl** *f* total (number).

Gesandte(r) [gə'zantə] *m* (*pl* -n) ambassa-dor. **Gesandtschaft** *f* embassy.

Gesang [gə'zaŋ] *m* (*pl* Gesänge) song; (*Singen*) singing. **-buch** *neut* songbook; (*Kirche*) hymnbook.

Gesäß [gə'zeis] *neut* (*pl* -e) seat, bottom.

Geschäft [gə'ʃɛft] *neut* (*pl* -e) business; (*Laden*) shop; (*Handel*) deal. **das Ge-schäft blüht** business is booming. **ein ansauberes Geschäft** a dirty business. **ein gutes Geschäft machen** get a bargain. **geschäftlich** *adj* commercial, business. **Geschäfts‖freund** *m* business associate, customer. **-führer** *m* manager; (*Verein*) secretary. **-haus** *neut* firm. **-jahr** *neut* business year. **-mann** *m* businessman. **-raum** *m* *or* **-räume** *pl* office(s). **ge-schäftsmäßig** *adj* businesslike. **Ge-schäfts‖reisende(r)** *m* commercial travel-ler, representative. **-schluß** *m* closing time. **-stunden** *pl* office hours.

geschehen [gə'ʃeiən] *v* happen.

gescheit [gə'ʃait] *adj* clever, smart.

Geschenk [gə'ʃɛŋk] *neut* (*pl* -e) present, gift.

Geschichte [gə'ʃiçtə] *f* (*pl* -n) (*Erzählung*) story; (*Vergangenheit*) history; (*Angelegenheit*) affair. **Geschichtenbuch** *neut* story book. **geschichtlich** *adj* histori-cal. **Geschichts‖buch** *neut* history book. **-forscher** *m* (research) historian. **-schreiber** *m* historian.

Geschick [gə'ʃik] *neut* (*pl* -e) aptitude; (*Schicksal*) fate. **-lichkeit** *f* skill. **ge-schickt** *adj* able, skilful.

geschieden [gə'ʃiidən] *adj* divorced.

Geschirr [gə'ʃir] *neut* (*pl* -e) crockery, dishes; (*Pferde*) harness. **-tuch** *neut* dishcloth. **-spülmaschine** *f* dishwasher.

Geschlecht [gə'ʃlɛçt] *neut* (*pl* -er) sex; (*Art*) kind, sort; (*Familie*) family, house; (*Gramm*) gender. **geschlechtlich** *adj* sexu-al. **Geschlechts‖krankheit** *f* venereal dis-ease. **-reife** *f* puberty. **-teile** *pl* genitals. **-verkehr** *m* sexual intercourse.

geschlossen [gə'ʃlɔsən] *adj* closed.

Geschmack [gə'ʃmak] *m* (*pl* Geschmäcke) taste. **geschmacklos** *adj* tasteless. **Geschmacks‖sache** *f* matter of taste. **-sinn** *m* sense of taste. **geschmackvoll** *adj* tasteful.

Geschnatter [gə'ʃnatər] *neut* (*unz.*) cackling.

Geschöpf [gə'ʃœpf] *neut* (*pl* **-e**) creature.

Geschoß [gə'ʃɔs] *neut* (*pl* **Geschosse**) projectile, missile; (*Kanone*) shell; (*Stockwerk*) floor, storey.

Geschrei [gə'ʃrai] *neut* (*pl* **-e**) cry, shouting, crying; (*fig*) fuss, noise.

Geschütz [gə'ʃyts] *neut* (*pl* **-e**) gun, cannon.

Geschwätz [gə'ʃvɛts] *neut* idle talk, prattle. **geschwätzig** *adj* talkative.

geschweige [gə'ʃvaigə] *conj* **geschweige denn** let alone, to say nothing of.

geschwind [gə'ʃvint] *adj* quick, fast. **Geschwindigkeit** *f* speed, velocity. **Geschwindigkeits‖grenze** *f* speed limit. **–messer** *m* speedometer.

Geschwister [gə'ʃvistər] *pl* brother(s) and sister(s); siblings. **haben Sie Geschwister?** have you any brothers and sisters?

Geschworene(r) [gə'ʃvoːrənə] *m* (*pl* **-n**) juror. **Geschworenengericht** *neut* (trial by) jury.

Geschwür [gə'ʃvyːr] *neut* (*pl* **-e**) ulcer, sore.

Geselle [gə'zɛlə] *m* (*pl* **-n**) comrade, companion; (*Bursche*) lad, fellow; (*gelehrter Handwerker*) journeyman. **gesellig** *adj* sociable. **Gesellschaft** *f* society; (*Firma*) company; (*Verein*) society, association; (*Abend-, usw.*) party, social gathering; (*Begleitung*) company. **gesellschaftlich** *adj* social. **Gesellschaftsanzug** *m* evening dress. **gesellschaftsfeindlich** *adj* antisocial. **Gesellschafts‖kleid** *neut* party dress. **–steuer** *f* corporation tax. **–tanz** *m* society dance, ball.

Gesetz [gə'zɛts] *neut* (*pl* **-e**) law. **–buch** *neut* statute book, law code. **–entwurf** *m* bill. **gesetzgebend** *adj* legislative. **Gesetzgebung** *f* legislation. **gesetz‖lich** *adj* legal, lawful. **–los** *adj* lawless. **–mäßig** *adj* legal, lawful.

gesetzt [gə'zɛtst] *adj* sedate, quiet.

gesetzwidrig [gə'zɛtsviːdriç] *adj* illegal, unlawful.

Gesicht [gə'ziçt] *neut* (*pl* **-er**) face; (*Miene*) expression. **Gesichts‖ausdruck** *m* (facial) expression. **–farbe** *f* complexion. **–feld** *neut* field of vision. **–punkt** *m* viewpoint.

gesinnt [gə'zint] *adj* disposed, minded. **Gesinnung** *f* opinion, mind, conviction. **gesinnungslos** *adj* unprincipled.

Gespann [gə'ʃpan] *neut* (*pl* **-e**) (*Pferden*) (team of) horses.

gespannt [gə'ʃpant] *adj* tense; (*Verhältnis*) strained. **gespannt sein** be eager or anxious.

Gespenst [gə'ʃpɛnst] *neut* (*pl* **-er**) ghost. **gespenstig** *adj* ghostly.

Gespräch [gə'ʃprɛːç] *neut* (*pl* **-e**) conversation, talk. **Gespräche** *pl* talks, discussion *sing*. **gesprächig** *adj* talkative.

Gestalt [gə'ʃtalt] *f* (*pl* **-en**) form, shape; (*Körper-*) figure, build; (*Literatur*) character. **gestalt‖en** *v* form, shape. **–et** *adj* formed, shaped. **–los** *adj* shapeless. **Gestaltung** *f* (*unz.*) shaping, formation.

Geständnis [gə'ʃtɛntnis] *neut* (*pl* **-se**) confession.

Gestank [gə'ʃtaŋk] *m* stink, stench.

gestatten [gə'ʃtatən] *v* permit, allow.

Geste ['gɛstə] *f* (*pl* **-n**) gesture.

***gestehen** [gə'ʃteːən] *v* confess.

Gestell [gə'ʃtɛl] *neut* (*pl* **-e**) (*Rahmen*) frame, stand; (*Bock*) trestle; (*Regal*) shelf; (*Bett-*) bedstead.

gestern ['gɛstərn] *adv* yesterday.

Gesträuch [gə'ʃtrɔyç] *neut* (*unz.*) shrubbery, bushes *pl*.

gestrichen [gə'ʃtriçən] *adj* painted. **frisch gestrichen** newly painted; wet paint.

gestrig ['gɛstriç] *adj* yesterday's.

Gestrüpp [gə'ʃtryp] *neut* undergrowth, scrub.

Gesuch [gə'zuːx] *neut* (*pl* **-e**) petition. **gesucht** *adj* in demand; (*Person*) wanted.

gesund [gə'zunt] *adj* healthy, well. **Gesundheit** *f* health. *interj* bless you! **gesundheitlich** *adj* sanitary. **gesundheitsförderlich** *adj* wholesome, healthy. **Gesundheitslehre** *f* hygiene. **gesundheitsschädlich** *adj* insanitary, unhealthy.

Getränk [gə'trɛŋk] *neut* (*pl* **-e**) drink.

Getreide [gə'traidə] *neut* (*pl* **-**) grain, cereals *pl*

getreu [gə'trɔy] *adj* loyal, faithful.

Getriebe [gə'triːbə] *neut* (*pl* **-**) commotion, bustle; (*Tech*) transmission, gears *pl*. **–gehäuse** *neut* gearbox.

getrost [gə'trɔist] *adj* confident. *adv* without hesitation.

Getto ['gɛtoi] *neut* (*pl* **-s**) ghetto.

geübt [gə'yːpt] *adj* practised, skilful.

Gewächs [gə'vɛks] *neut* (*pl* **-e**) plant; (*Med*) growth.

gewachsen [gə'vaksən] *adj* grown.
gewachsen sein be equal (to), be up (to).
gewagt [gə'vaːkt] *adj* bold, daring.
gewählt [gə'vɛːlt] *adj* select(ed), choice.
Gewähr [gə'vɛːr] *f* (*unz.*) guarantee, surety. **gewähren** *v* allow, grant. **gewährleisten** *v* guarantee, vouch for.
Gewalt [gə'valt] *f* (*pl* **-en**) force; (*Macht*) power; (*Obrigkeit*) authority; (*Gewalttätigkeit*) violence. **-herrscher** *m* tyrant. **gewalt‖ig** *adj* forceful, powerful; enormous; (*gewalttätig*) violent. **-los** *adj* powerless. **-sam** *adj* violent; *adv* by force. **-tätig** *adj* violent.
Gewand [gə'vant] *neut* (*pl* **Gewänder**) garment, robe.
gewandt [gə'vant] *adj* skilled, skilful. **Gewandtheit** *f* dexterity, skill.
Gewässer [gə'vɛsər] *neut* (*pl* **-**) water(s).
Gewebe [gə'veːbə] *neut* (*pl* **-**) material, textile; (*Biol*) tissue; (*Lügen, usw.*) web, network.
geweckt [gə'vɛkt] *adj* bright, lively.
Gewehr [gə'veːr] *neut* (*pl* **-e**) rifle, gun. **-kugel** *f* (rifle) bullet.
Geweih [gə'vai] *neut* (*pl* **-e**) antlers *pl*.
Gewerbe [gə'vɛrbə] *neut* (*pl* **-**) trade. **-schule** *f* technical school. **gewerb‖lich** *adj* industrial. **-smäßig** *adj* professional. **Gewerkschaft** [gə'vɛrkʃaft] *f* (*pl* **-en**) (trade) union. **-ler** *m* (trade) unionist. **gewerkschaftlich** *adj* trade-union.
Gewicht [gə'viçt] *neut* (*pl* **-e**) weight; (*fig*) importance. **-heben** *neut* weight-lifting. **gewichtig** *adj* heavy; (*fig*) important.
Gewimmel [gə'viməl] *neut* (*pl* **-**) crowd, swarm.
Gewinde [gə'vində] *neut* (*pl* **-**) (*Schraube*) thread.
Gewinn [gə'vin] *m* (*pl* **-e**) profit; (*Ertrag*) yield, returns; (*Preis*) prize; (*Erwerben*) gaining. **-beteiligung** *f* profit-sharing. **gewinn‖bringend** *adj* profitable. **-en** *v* (*Preis*) win; (*erwerben*) gain, acquire; (*siegen*) win. **-süchtig** *adj* acquisitive.
Gewirr [gə'vir] *neut* (*pl* **-e**) confusion, tangle.
gewiß [gə'vis] *adj* certain, sure. *adv* certainly. *ein gewisser Herr Schmidt* a certain Mr Schmidt. *ein gewisses Etwas* a certain something.
Gewissen [gə'visən] *neut* (*unz.*) conscience. **gewissen‖haft** *adj* conscientious. **-los** *adj* unscrupulous. **Gewissens‖bisse**

pl pangs of conscience. **-konflikt** *m* conflict of conscience.
gewissermaßen [gə'visərmaɪsən] *adv* to some extent.
Gewißheit [gə'vishait] *f* (*unz.*) certainty.
Gewitter [gə'vitər] *neut* (*pl* **-**) thunderstorm. **gewitterhaft** *adj* stormy.
gewogen [gə'voɪgən] *adj* well disposed, favourably inclined.
gewöhnen [gə'vœɪnən] *v* accustom. **sich gewöhnen an** become accustomed to, get used to. **Gewohnheit** *f* (*pl* **-en**) habit; (*Brauch*) custom. **gewohnheitsmäßig** *adj* customary. **gewöhnlich** *adj* usual, ordinary; (*unfein*) vulgar. *adv* usually. **gewohnt** *adj* used (to).
Gewölbe [gə'vœlbə] *neut* (*pl* **-**) vault. **gewölbt** *adj* arched, vaulted.
Gewühl [gə'vyːl] *neut* (*unz.*) crowd, tumult.
Gewürz [gə'vyrts] *neut* (*pl* **-e**) spice, seasoning. **gewürzig** *adj* spicy. **gewürzt** *adj* spiced, seasoned.
gezackt [gə'tsakt] *adj* serrated; (*Fels*) jagged.
geziemend [gə'tsiːmənt] *or* **geziemlich** *adj* seemly.
geziert [gə'tsiːrt] *adj* affected.
gezwungen [gə'tsvuŋən] *adj* forced; (*steif*) formal, stiff.
Gicht [giçt] *f* (*unz.*) gout.
Giebel ['giːbəl] *m* (*pl* **-**) gable. **-dach** *neut* gabled roof.
Gier [giːr] *f* greed; (*nach etwas*) craving, burning desire (for). **gierig** *adj* greedy.
*gießen ['giːsən] *v* pour; (*Pflanzen*) water; (*schmelzen*) cast. **Gieß‖erei** *f* (*pl* **-en**) foundry. **-kanne** *f* watering can.
Gift [gift] *neut* (*pl* **-e**) poison. **-gas** *neut* poison gas. **giftig** *adj* poisonous. **Giftschlange** *f* poisonous snake.
Ginster ['ginstər] *m* (*pl* **-**) (*Bot*) broom.
Gipfel ['gipfəl] *m* (*pl* **-**) peak, summit. **-gespräche** *pl* summit talks. **-leistung** *f* record.
Gips [gips] *m* (*pl* **-e**) gypsum; (*erhitzt*) plaster (of Paris). **-verband** *m* plaster cast.
Giraffe [gi'rafə] *f* (*pl* **-n**) giraffe.
Giro ['dʒiːroɪ] *neut* (*pl* **-s**) giro. **-konto** *neut* current account.
Gitarre [gi'tarə] *f* (*pl* **-n**) guitar.
Gitter ['gitər] *neut* (*pl* **-**) grille, grating; (*Fenster*) bars; (*Spalier*) trellis.

Glanz [glants] *m* (*unz.*) shine, brilliance, brightness; (*fig*) splendour.

glänzen ['glɛntsən] *v* gleam, shine; (*fig*) excel, shine. **-d** *adj* brilliant.

Glas [glaːs] *neut* (*pl* Gläser) glass. **-haus** *neut* greenhouse, hothouse. **-perle** *f* bead. **-scheibe** *f* (window) pane. **glasieren** *v* glaze; (*Kuchen*) ice. **Glasur** *f* glaze; (*Kuchen*) icing.

glatt [glat] *adj* smooth; (*glitschig*) slippery. **Glatteis** *neut* (*Mot*) black ice. **glattrasiert** *adj* clean-shaven.

Glaube ['glaubə] *m* (*unz.*) belief; (*Rel*) faith. **glauben** *v* believe; (*vermuten*) think, suppose; (*vertrauen*) trust. **glaubhaft** *adj* credible.

gläubig ['glɔybiç] *adj* believing; (*fromm*) pious. **Gläubige(r)** *m* believer; (*Komm*) creditor.

glaublich ['glaupliç] *adj* credible. **glaubwürdig** *adj* (*Person*) trustworthy; (*Sache*) credible.

gleich [glaiç] *adj* (the) same, equal; (*eben*) level. *adv* equally; (*sofort*) at once; (*schon*) just. **von gleichem Alter** of the same age. **das ist mir gleich** it makes no difference to me. **das gleiche gilt für Dich** the same goes for you. **Ich komme gleich** I'm just coming. **gleich viel** just as much. **gleich‖artig** *adj* similar. **-bedeutend** *adj* synonymous. **-berechtigt** *adj* having equal rights.

***gleichen** ['glaiçən] *v* equal; (*ähnlich sein*) resemble.

gleichermaßen ['glaiçərmasən] *or* **gleicherweise** *adv* likewise.

gleich‖falls *adv* also, likewise. **-gesinnt** *adj* like-minded.

Gleichgewicht ['glaiçgəviçt] *neut* equilibrium, balance.

gleichgültig ['glaiçgyltiç] *adj* unconcerned, indifferent. **Gleichgültigkeit** *f* indifference.

Gleich‖heit *f* equality. **-maß** *neut* proportion, symmetry. **-mut** *m* equanimity. **-nis** *neut* (*pl* -se) simile; (*Erzählung*) parable.

gleichschalten ['glaiçʃaltən] *v* coordinate; (*Tech*) synchronize.

Gleichschritt ['glaiçʃrit] *m* **Gleichschritt halten** keep step.

Gleich‖strom *m* direct current. **-ung** *f* (*pl* -en) equation.

gleich‖viel *adv* no matter. **-wertig** *adj*

equivalent, of the same value. **-wohl** *adv* nonetheless. **-zeitig** *adj* simultaneous.

Gleis [glais] *neut* (*pl* -e) track, platform.

***gleiten** ['glaitən] *v* slide, slip. **Gleitflugzeug** *neut* glider, sailplane.

Gletscher ['glɛtʃər] *m* (*pl* -) glacier. **Gletscherspalte** *f* crevasse.

Glied [gliːt] *neut* (*pl* -er) limb; (*Kette*) link. **gliedern** *v* organize, arrange; divide into. **Gliederung** *f* (*pl* -en) organization, arrangement.

Glocke ['glɔkə] *f* (*pl* -n) bell. **Glocken‖blume** *f* bluebell. **-turm** *m* belltower.

glorreich ['glɔrraiç] *adj* glorious.

Glossar [glɔ'saːr] *neut* (*pl* -e, -ien) glossary. **Glosse** *f* (*pl* -n) comment.

glotzen ['glɔtsən] *v* stare.

Glück [glyk] *neut* luck; (*Geschick*) fortune; (*Freude*) happiness. **glück‖lich** *adj* happy, fortunate. **-licherweise** *adv* fortunately, luckily. **-selig** *adj* blissful. **Glücks‖fall** *m* lucky chance. **-spiel** *neut* game of chance.

glühen ['glyːən] *v* glow. **Glüh‖hitze** *f* white heat. **-wein** *m* mulled wine.

Glut [gluːt] *f* (*pl* -en) glow. **-asche** *f* embers *pl*.

Gnade ['gnaːdə] *f* (*pl* -n) grace, mercy. **Gnaden‖frist** *f* reprieve, period of grace. **-stoß** *m* coup de grâce.

gnädig ['gnɛːdiç] *adj* gracious; kind. **gnädige Frau** Madam.

Gold [gɔlt] *neut* (*unz.*) gold. **-barren** *m* gold bar *or* ingot. **gold‖en** *adj* golden. **-ig** *adj* sweet, lovely.

Golf [gɔlf] *m* (*pl* -e) gulf.

Golf² *neut* (*unz.*) (*Sport*) golf.

gönnen ['gœnən] *v* not begrudge; grant, allow.

Gönner *m* (*pl* -) patron, sponsor. **gönnerhaft** *adj* patronizing; condescending.

Gosse ['gɔsə] *f* (*pl* -n) gutter.

Gott [gɔt] *m* God; (*pl* Götter) god. **grüß Gott!** greetings! God be with you! **Gott sei dank!** thank God! **um Gottes willen!** for God's sake! **Gottes‖dienst** *m* (church) service. **-lästerung** *f* blasphemy. **Gottheit** *f* godhead, divinity.

Göttin ['gœtin] *f* (*pl* -nen) goddess. **göttlich** *adj* divine.

Götze ['gœtsə] *m* (*pl* -n) idol, false god.

Grab [graːp] *neut* (*pl* Gräber) grave. **graben** *v* dig. **Graben** *m* ditch, trench. **Grab‖schrift** *f* epitaph. **-stätte** *f* grave. **-stein** *m* tombstone.

Grad [graːt] *m* (*pl* -e) degree; (*Rang*) rank, grade. **−messer** *m* (*fig*) indication, sign.

graduieren [gradu'iːrən] *v* graduate. **Graduierte(r)** *m* graduate.

Graf [graːf] *m* (*pl* -en) count.

Gräfin ['grɛːfin] *f* (*pl* -en) countess.

Grafschaft ['graːfʃaft] *f* (*pl* -en) county.

Gram [graːm] *m* (*unz.*) grief.

Gramm [gram] *neut* (*pl* -e) gram(me).

Grammatik [gra'matik] *f* (*pl* -en) grammar.

Granatapfel [gra'naːtapfəl] *m* (*pl* Granatäpfel) pomegranate.

Granate [gra'naːtə] *f* (*pl* -n) shell, grenade.

Granit [gra'niːt] *m* (*pl* -e) granite.

Graphik ['graːfik] *f* (*unz.*) graphics. **-er** *m* (*pl* -) designer, commercial artist. **graphisch** *adj* graphic. **graphische Darstellung** *f* graph.

Gras [graːs] *neut* (*pl* Gräser) grass. **grasen** *v* graze.

gräßlich ['grɛsliç] *adj* horrible, ghastly.

Grat [graːt] *m* (*pl* -e) ridge, edge.

Gräte ['grɛːtə] *f* (*pl* -n) fishbone. **−nmuster** *neut* herringbone pattern.

gratulieren [gratu'liːrən] *v* congratulate.

grau [grau] *adj* grey. **Graubrot** *neut* ryebread.

grauen ['grauən] *v* be horrible. *es graut mir vor* I have a horror of. **-haft** *adj* dreadful, horrible.

Graupe ['graupə] *f* (*pl* -n) groats *pl*, pearl barley.

graupeln ['graupəln] *pl* sleet *sing.*

grausam ['grauzaːm] *adj* cruel. **Grausamkeit** *f* cruelty. **grausig** *adj* fearful, dreadful.

gravieren [gra'viːrən] *v* engrave.

greif∥en ['graifən] *v* seize, grasp. **-bar** *adj* (*Waren*) available, at hand; (*fig*) tangible. **greifen an** touch. **greifen in** dip into.

Greis [grais] *m* (*pl* -e) old man.

grell [grɛl] *adj* (*Ton*) shrill, harsh; (*Farbe*) glaring.

Grenze ['grɛntsə] *f* (*pl* -n) (*eines Staates*) border, frontier; (*einer Stadt, Zone*) boundary; (*fig*) limit. **grenzen** border (on). **Grenz∥fall** *m* borderline case. **-übergang** *m* crossing (of a frontier).

Greuel ['grɔyəl] *m* (*pl* -) (*Abscheu*) horror; (*Scheußlichkeit*) atrocity, abomination.

Grieche ['griːçə] *m* (*pl* -n) Greek (man). **Griechenland** *neut* Greece. **Griechin** *f* (*pl* -nen) Greek (woman). **griechisch** *adj* Greek.

Grieß [griːs] *m* (*unz.*) (*Essen*) semolina; (*Kies*) gravel. **-pudding** *m* semolina pudding.

Griff [grif] *m* (*pl* -e) (*Henkel, Knopf, usw.*) handle; (*Greifen*) hold, grip.

Grille ['grilə] *f* (*pl* -n) (*Insekt*) cricket; (*Laune*) whim.

Grimasse [gri'masə] *f* (*pl* -n) grimace.

grimmig ['grimiç] *adj* furious.

grinsen ['grinzən] *v* grin.

Grippe ['gripə] *f* (*pl* -n) influenza.

grob [groːp] *adj* coarse; (*Benehmen*) coarse, rude; (*Scherz*) crude, coarse; (*Fehler*) gross, serious. **Grobheit** *f* coarseness, rudeness.

Groll [grɔl] *m* animosity, rancour. **grollen** *v* be resentful, be angry.

gros [groː] *en gros* wholesale.

Gros[1] [groː] *neut* (*pl* -) (*Armee*) main body.

Gros[2] [grɔs] *neut* (*pl* -e) gross, twelve dozen.

Groschen ['grɔʃən] *m* (*pl* -) (*Österreich*) Groschen; (*BRD*) ten-pfennig piece; (*fig*) penny.

groß [groːs] *adj* big, large; (*wichtig*) great, grand; (*hoch*) tall. **im großen und ganzen** on the whole. **-artig** *adj* splendid, grand.

Großbritannien [groːsbri'taniən] *neut* Great Britain.

Großbuchstabe ['groːsbuːxʃtaːbə] *m* capital (letter).

Großeltern ['groːseltern] *pl* grandparents.

großenteils ['groːsentails] *adv* mostly, for the most part.

Groß∥handel *m* wholesale trade. **-händler** *m* wholesaler.

großherzig ['groːshertsiç] *adj* magnanimous.

Groß∥industrie *f* large-scale industry. **-macht** *f* great power. **-maul** *neut* braggart, big-mouth. **-mutter** *f* grandmother. **-stadt** *f* large town, city.

größtenteils ['grøːstəntails] *adv* mostly, largely.

Groß∥teil *m* bulk. **-tuer** *m* show-off, big-head. **-vater** *m* grandfather.

großzügig ['groːstsyːgiç] *adj* generous; (*weittragend*) large-scale. **Großzügigkeit** *f* generosity; largeness.

grotesk [gro'tɛsk] *adj* grotesque.
Grübchen ['gryːpçən] *neut (pl -)* dimple.
Grube ['gruːbə] *f (pl -n)* pit, hole; (*Bergbau*) mine, pit; (*Höhle, Bau*) hole, burrow; (*Falle*) snare.
grübeln ['gryːbəln] *v* brood, ponder.
grün [gryːn] *adj* green. **Grün** *neut* green.
–anlage *f* public park, open space.
Grund [grunt] *m (pl Gründe)* (*Erdboden*) ground, soil; (*Veranlassung*) reason, grounds *pl*; (*Grundlage*) basis, base; (*Grundbesitz*) land; (*eines Meeres*) bottom. **–bau** *m* foundation. **–besitz** *m* landed property, real estate. **im Grunde (genommen)** basically.
gründen ['gryndən] *v* found, establish. **sich gründen auf** be based on. **Gründer** *m (pl -)* founder.
Grund‖gesetz *neut* basic law; (*Verfassung*) constitution. **–lage** *f* basis, foundation.
gründlich ['gryntliç] *adj* thorough.
grundlos ['gruntloːs] *adj* unfounded, baseless.
Grund‖maß *neut* standard of measurement. **–riß** *m* outline, design. **–satz** *m* principle, axiom. **grundsätzlich** *adj* fundamental.
Grund‖schule *f* primary school. **–stoff** *m* raw material; (*Chem*) element. **–stück** *neut* lot of land.
Gründung ['grynduŋ] *f (pl -en)* establishment, foundation.
Grund‖unterschied *m* basic difference. **–zahl** *f* cardinal number. **–zug** *m* characteristic, feature.
Grünkohl ['gryːnkoːl] *m* kale.
grunzen ['gruntsən] *v* grunt.
Grünzeug ['gryːntsɔyk] *neut* greens *pl*, green vegetables *pl*.
Gruppe ['grupə] *f (pl -n)* group. **–nführer** *m* section leader. **gruppieren** *v* group.
gruselig ['gruːzəliç] *adj* gruesome; (*umg.*) creepy.
Gruß [gruːs] *m (pl Grüße)* greeting; (*Mil*) salute. **herzliche Grüße** kind regards, best wishes.
grüßen ['gryːsən] *v* greet; (*Mil*) salute.
gucken ['gukən] *v* (take a) look, peep.
Gulasch ['guːlaʃ] *neut, m (pl -e)* goulash.
gültig ['gyltiç] *adj* valid; (*Gesetz*) in force. **Gültigkeit** *f* validity, currency. **–sdauer** *f* (period of) validity.
Gummi ['gumi] *neut (pl -s)* rubber; (*Kleb-*

stoff) gum; (*Kau-*) (chewing) gum. **–band** *neut* rubber band. **gummiert** *adj* (*Briefmarke, usw.*) gummed.
Gunst [gunst] *f (unz.)* favour.
günstig ['gynstiç] *adj* favourable, advantageous.
gurgeln ['gurgəln] *v* gargle. **Gurgelwasser** *neut* gargle.
Gurke ['gurkə] *f (pl -n)* cucumber; (*saure*) gherkin.
Gurt [gurt] *m (pl -e)* belt; (*Pferd*) girth.
Gürtel ['gyrtəl] *m (pl -)* belt; (*Geog*) zone. **–reifen** *m* radial-ply tyre, (*umg.*) radial.
Guß [gus] *m (pl Güsse)* (*Regen*) downpour, gush; (*Metall*) casting, founding.
gut [guːt] *adj* good. *adv* well. **gut sein mit** be on good terms with. *es wird schon alles gut werden* everything will be all right. *das tut mir gut* that does me good. *schon gut!* that's all right. **gut aussehen** look good; (*gesund*) look well. **Gut** *neut (pl Güter)* possession; (*Land*) landed estate; (*Ware*) commodity. **gutartig** *adj* good-natured. **Gutdünken** *neut* discretion. **nach (Ihrem) Gutdünken** at your discretion.
Güte ['gyːtə] *f (unz.)* kindness, goodness; (*Qualität*) quality.
Güter‖flugzeug *neut* cargo plane. **–zug** *m* freight train.
gut‖gelaun *adj* good-humoured. **–gesinnt** *adj* friendly, well-disposed. **–gläubig** *adj* acting in good faith, bona-fide; *adv* in good faith.
Guthaben ['guːthaːbən] *neut* credit (balance).
*gut‖heißen *v* approve. **–herzig** *adj* kind-hearted.
gütig ['gyːtiç] *adj* kind.
gutmachen ['guːtmaxən] *v* **wieder gutmachen** make amends for, make good.
gutmütig ['guːtmyːtiç] *adj* good-natured.
Gutschein ['guːtʃain] *m (pl -e)* voucher, credit-note.
Gymnasium [gym'naːzium] *neut (pl Gymnasien)* grammar school.
Gymnastik [gym'nastik] *f* gymnastics. **gymnastisch** *adj* gymnastic.

H

Haag, Den [dein'haik] *m* The Hague.
Haar [hair] *neut* (*pl* -e) hair. **sich die Haare schneiden lassen** have a haircut. **haarig** *adj* hairy. **Haar∥nadelkurve** *f* hairpin bend. **-schnitt** *m* haircut. **haarsträubend** *adj* hair-raising.
Habe ['haibə] *f* (*unz.*) property, possessions *pl*. **haben** *v* have. **habsüchtig** *adj* greedy, (*umg.*) grasping.
Hackbrett ['hakbrɛt] *neut* chopping board. **hacken** *v* chop, hack; (*Fleisch*) mince. **Hackfleisch** *neut* mince, minced meat.
Hafen ['haifən] *m* (*pl* Häfen) port, harbour. **-arbeiter** *m* docker. **-damm** *m* pier, mole. **-sperre** *f* embargo. **-stadt** *f* port.
Hafer ['haifər] *m* (*pl* -) oats *pl*. **-flocken** *f pl* rolled oats, oat-flakes.
Haft [haft] *f* arrest, detention, custody. **haften** *v* adhere, cling. **haften für** be liable for, answer for. **Haftpflichtversicherung** *f* (compulsory) third-party insurance.
Hagel ['haigəl] *m* (*pl* -) hail. **-korn** *neut* hailstone. **hageln** *v* **es hagelt** it is hailing.
hager ['haigər] *adj* lean, haggard.
Hahn [hain] *m* (*pl* Hähne) cock; (*Wasser-, usw.*) tap. **Hahnenkamm** *m* cockscomb.
Hähnchen [hɛinçən] *neut* (*pl* -) cock; (*Wasser-, usw.*) tap.
Hai [hai] *m* (*pl* -e) *or* **Haifisch** *m* shark.
Hain [hain] *m* (*pl* -e) grove.
Häkelarbeit ['heikəlairbait] *f* crochet work. **häkeln** *v* crochet.
haken ['haikən] *v* hook. **sich haken an** catch on, get caught on. **Haken** *m* (*pl* -) hook; (*fig*) snag. **-kreuz** *neut* swastika.
halb [halp] *adj* half. **um halb drei** at half past two. **eine halbe Stunde** half an hour. **-jährlich** *adj* half-yearly. **Halb∥kreis** *m* semicircle. **-kugel** *f* hemisphere. **-messer** *m* radius. **-starke(r)** *m* hooligan. **halbwegs** *adv* halfway. **Halbzeit** *f* halftime.
Hälfte ['hɛlftə] *f* (*pl* -n) half.
Halfter ['halftər] *f or neut* (*pl* -n) halter.
Hall [hal] *m* (*pl* -e) sound, peal.
Halle ['halə] *f* (*pl* -n) hall; (*Hotel*) lobby; (*Flugzeug-*) hangar.
hallen ['halən] *v* sound, resound.
Hallenbad ['halənbait] *neut* indoor swimming-pool *or* baths.
Halm [halm] *m* (*pl* -e) stalk; (*Gras*) blade.

Hals [hals] *m* (*pl* Hälse) neck; (*innerer Hals, Kehle*) throat. **-band** *neut* (*Hund*) collar; (*Frauen*) necklace, choker. **-binde** *f* tie. **-kette** *f* necklace. **-weh** *neut* sore throat.
Halt [halt] *m* (*pl* -e) (*Anhalten*) stop, halt; (*Stütze*) hold, support; (*Standhaftigkeit*) steadiness, firmness. **haltbar** *adj* durable, lasting. **haltbar bis ...** (*Speisen*) use by .... **halten** *v* hold; (*bewahren*) keep; (*dauern*) last, keep; (*Gebot, usw.*) observe; (*anhalten*) stop. **viel halten von** think highly of. **halten für** consider (to be), think of as. **Halte∥stelle** *f* (*Bus*) busstop. **-tau** *neut* guy-rope. **haltmachen** *v* stop. **Haltung** *f* (*pl* -en) attitude; (*Körper-*) bearing, posture.
hämisch ['hɛimiʃ] *adj* spiteful, sardonic.
Hammelfleisch ['haməlflaiʃ] *neut* mutton.
Hammer ['hamər] *m* (*pl* Hämmer) hammer.
hämmern ['hɛmərn] *v* hammer.
Hämorrhoiden [hɛmoro'iidən] *pl* piles, haemorrhoids *pl*.
Hamster ['hamstər] *m* (*pl* -) hamster. **hamstern** *v* hoard.
Hand [hant] *f* (*pl* Hände) hand. **an Hand von** with the aid of. **bei der Hand** ready, at hand. **mit der Hand** by hand. **von Hand gemacht** hand-made. **zur linken/rechten Hand** on the left/right hand side. **Hand∥arbeit** *f* handiwork; (*Nadelarbeit*) needlework. **-becken** *neut* hand basin. **-bremse** *f* handbrake. **-buch** *neut* manual, handbook.
Händedruck ['hɛndədruk] *m* handshake.
Handel ['handəl] *m* trade, commerce; (*Geschäft*) transaction, deal. **handeln** *v* act. **handeln mit** (*Person*) trade *or* deal with; (*Waren*) trade *or* deal in. **handeln von** treat, deal with. **Handels∥beziehungen** *pl* trade relations. **-bilanz** *f* balance of trade. **-schule** *f* business *or* commercial school. **-sperre** *f* (trade) embargo.
handfest ['hantfest] *adj* sturdy, strong.
Hand∥fläche *f* palm. **-gebrauch** *m* everyday use. **-gelenk** *neut* wrist. **-gepäck** *neut* hand luggage.
handhaben ['hanthaibən] *v* (*gebrauchen*) use, employ; (*fig*) handle.
Händler ['hɛntlər] *m* (*pl* -) trader, dealer.
handlich [hantliç] *adj* handy.

Handlung ['hantluŋ] f (pl -en) deed, act; (*Roman, usw.*) plot; (*Geschäft*) business, firm; (*Laden*) shop.

Hand‖schellen pl handcuffs pl. **–schuh** m glove. **–tasche** f handbag. **–tuch** neut towel. **–werk** neut craft, trade. **–werker** m craftsman, workman.

Hang [haŋ] m (pl **Hänge**) slope; (*Neigung*) tendency.

Hängematte ['hɛŋəmatə] f hammock.

***hängen[1]** [hɛŋən] v be suspended, hang; (*sich neigen*) slope; (*unentschieden*) be pending, remain undecided; (*abhängen*) depend.

hängen[2] v hang, suspend; (*hinrichten*) hang.

Hannover [ha'nɔɪfər] neut Hanover.

hantieren [han'tiːrən] v busy oneself, potter around.

Happen ['hapən] m (pl -) mouthful, bite.

Harfe ['harfə] f (pl -n) harp.

harmlos ['harmlɔɪs] adj harmless.

Harmonie [harmɔ'niː] f (pl -n) harmony. **harmonisch** adj harmonic. **harmonisieren** v harmonize.

Harn [harn] m urine. **–blase** f (*Anat*) bladder.

Harnisch ['harniʃ] m (pl -e) armour; harness.

Harpune [har'puːnə] f (pl -n) harpoon.

harren ['harən] v wait for, await.

hart [hart] adj hard; (*fig*) harsh, rough. **Härte** ['hɛrtə] f (pl -n) hardness; (*Strenge*) severity; (*Grausamkeit*) cruelty. **härten** v harden; (*Metall*) temper.

hart‖gekocht adj hard-boiled. **–näckig** adj stubborn.

Harz [harts] neut (pl -e) resin.

Haschisch ['haʃiʃ] neut hashish.

Hase ['haɪzə] m (pl -n) hare.

Haselnuß ['haɪzəlnus] f hazelnut.

Haspe ['haspə] f (pl -n) hinge.

Haß [has] m hate.

hassen ['hasən] v hate. **–swert** adj hateful, odious.

häßlich ['hɛsliç] adj ugly; (*fig*) wicked, nasty. **Häßlichkeit** f ugliness; (*fig*) wickedness.

Hast [hast] f haste. **hasten** v hasten. **hastig** adj hasty.

hätscheln ['hɛtʃəln] v (*liebkosen*) caress, fondle; (*verwöhnen*) pamper.

Haube ['haubə] f (pl -n) bonnet, cap; (*Mot*) bonnet, (*US*) hood.

Hauch [haux] m (pl -e) breath; (*fig*) touch, trace.

Haue ['hauə] f (pl -n) pick; (*umg.*) beating, spanking. **hauen** v hew; (*zerhacken*) chop up; (*umg.*) beat, belt.

Haufen ['haufən] m (pl -) heap, pile; (*umg.*) heaps of, lots of. **häufen** ['hɔyfən] v heap (up), accumulate. **häufig** ['hɔyfiç] adj frequent, numerous. adv frequently.

Haupt [haupt] neut (pl **Häupter**) head; (*Führer*) leader, chief. **–bahnhof** m main railway station, central station. **–buch** neut ledger. **–film** m feature film, main film. **–leitung** f (*Gas, Strom*) mains pl. **–mann** m (*Mil*) captain. **–rolle** f (*Theater*) leading part or role.

Hauptsache ['hauptzaxə] f main thing or point. **hauptsächlich** adj essential. adv principally, mainly.

Haupt‖sitz m head office. **–stadt** f capital (city). **–straße** f main street. **–wort** neut noun.

Haus [haus] neut (pl **Häuser**) house; (*Heim*) home. **zu Hause** at home. **–arbeit** f housework; (*Schule*) homework. **–aufgaben** pl (*Schule*) homework sing.

Häuschen ['hɔsçən] neut (pl -) cottage, small house.

Haus‖frau f housewife. **–halt** m household; (*Budget*) budget. **–hälterin** f housekeeper. **–haltsplan** m budget.

hausieren [hau'ziːrən] v peddle, hawk.

häuslich ['hɔysliç] adj domestic.

Haus‖mädchen neut housemaid. **–meister** m caretaker. **–tür** f front door. **–wart** m caretaker. **–wirt** m landlord. **–wirtin** f landlady. **–wirtschaft** f housekeeping.

Haut [haut] f (pl **Häute**) skin; (*Tier*) hide, pelt. **–auschlag** m rash. **–krem** m skin cream.

Hebamme ['heɪpamə] f (pl -n) midwife.

Hebel ['heɪbəl] m (pl -) lever.

***heben** ['heɪbən] v lift, raise; (*Steuer*) raise, levy. `sich heben rise. **Hebung** f raising; (*Beseitigung*) removal.

Hecht [hɛçt] m (pl -e) pike.

Heck [hɛk] neut (pl -e) stern; (*eines Autos*) rear. **–klappe** f (*Mot*) hatchback, tailgate.

Hecke ['hɛkə] f (pl -n) hedge; (*Brut*) brood, hatch. **–nschütze** m sniper.

Heer [heɪr] *neut* (*pl* -e) army.

Hefe ['heɪfə] *f* yeast.

Heft [heft] *neut* (*pl* -e) notebook, exercise book; (*Zeitschrift*) issue; (*Griff*) handle, haft.

heftig ['heftiç] *adj* violent; (*leidenschaftlich*) passionate, vehement.

hegen ['heɪgən] *v* (*hätscheln*) cherish; (*schützen*) protect; (*Gedanken*) nurture.

Heide¹ ['haidə] *m* (*pl* -n) heathen, pagan.

Heide² *f* (*pl* -n) heath, moor. −**kraut** *neut* heather.

Heidelbeere ['haidəlbeɪrə] *f* bilberry.

heidnisch ['haitniʃ] *adj* heathen, pagan.

heikel ['haikəl] *adj* delicate, awkward.

heil [hail] *adj* safe, uninjured; (*geheilt*) healed; (*ganz*) whole. **Heil** *neut* welfare; (*Kirche*) salvation. −**and** *m* saviour. **heil‖bringend** *adj* salutary. −**en** *v* heal, cure.

heilig ['hailiç] *adj* holy, sacred. **Heiliger Abend** Christmas Eve. **Heilige(r)** *m* saint. **Heiligenschein** *m* halo.

Heil‖kunde *f* medicine, medical science. −**mittel** *neut* remedy, cure.

heim [haim] *adv* home(ward). **Heim** *neut* (*pl* -e) home.

Heimat ['haimaɪt] *f* (*unz.*) home(land), native place. −**land** *neut* homeland. **heimatlos** *adj* homeless. **Heimatstadt** *f* home town.

Heimfahrt ['haimfaɪrt] *f* return journey. **heimisch** *adj* domestic; (*heimatlich*) native. **Heimkehr** *f* return (home).

heim‖lich *adj* secret. −**suchen** *v* plague, afflict. −**tückisch** *adj* malicious, insidious.

Heimweh ['haimveɪ] *neut* homesickness. **Heimweh haben** be homesick.

Heirat ['hairaɪt] *f* (*pl* -en) marriage. **heiraten** *v* marry.

heiser ['haizər] *adj* hoarse.

heiß [hais] *adj* hot.

*****heißen** ['haisən] *v* be called *or* named; (*bedeuten*) mean. **wie heißt Du?** what's your name? **das heißt (d.h.)** that is (i.e.).

heiter ['haitər] *adj* (*Person*) serene; (*Erählung*) happy; (*Wetter*) bright, clear. **Heiterkeit** *f* serenity.

Heiz‖apparat ['haitsaparaɪt] *m* (*pl* -e) heater. −**decke** *f* electric blanket. **heizen** *v* heat. **Heiz‖ung** *f* heating. −**material** *neut* fuel.

Hektar [hɛk'taɪr] *neut* (*pl* -e) hectare.

Held [hɛlt] *m* (*pl* -en) hero. **Helden‖mut** *m* heroism. −**tat** *f* heroic deed, exploit. **Heldin** *f* (*pl* -nen) heroine.

helfen ['hɛlfən] *v* help, assist; (*nützen*) help, do good. **Helfer** *m* (*pl* -), **Helferin** *f* (*pl* -nen) helper, assistant.

hell [hɛl] *adj* (*Licht*) bright; (*Farbe*) light; (*Klang*) clear. **hellblau** *adj* light blue. **Hellseher** *m* (*pl* -), **Hellseherin** *f* (*pl* -nen) clairvoyant.

Helm [hɛlm] *m* (*pl* -e) helmet; (*Naut*) rudder; (*Kuppel*) dome.

Hemd [hɛmt] *neut* (*pl* -en) shirt. −**särmel** *m* shirtsleeve.

hemmen ['hɛmən] *v* restrain, hinder, inhibit; (*Psychol*) inhibit. **Hemmung** *f* (*pl* -en) hindrance, stoppage; (*Psychol*) inhibition. **hemmungslos** *adj* unrestrained.

Hengst [hɛŋst] *m* (*pl* -e) stallion.

Henkel ['hɛŋkəl] *m* (*pl* -) handle.

Henker ['hɛŋkər] *m* (*pl*-) hangman.

her [heɪr] *adv* (to) here; (*zeitlich*) ago, since; (*von*) from. **hin und her** to and fro, back and forth. **komm her!** come here! **wo kommen Sie her?** where do you come from? **schon lange her** a long time ago. **von weit her** from afar.

herab [hɛ'rap] *adv* down(wards). −**hängen** *v* hang down. −**lassen** *v* lower. **sich herablassen** condescend. **herab‖lassend** *adj* patronizing. −**setzen** *v* reduce; (*Person*) degrade. −**setzend** *adj* contemptuous. −**würdigen** *v* debase, degrade.

heran [hɛ'ran] *adv* near, up to; (*hierher*) (to) here. −**gehen** *v* go up to, approach. −**kommen** *v* approach, draw near.

herauf [hɛ'rauf] *adv* (up) here; (*hinauf*) upwards. −**beschwören** *v* conjure up. −**ziehen** *v* pull up.

heraus [hɛ'raus] *adv* out; (*draußen, aus dem Hause*) outside. −**fordern** *v* challenge. **Herausforderung** *f* challenge. **herausgeben** *v* give out; (*Buch, usw.*) publish. **Herausgeber** *m* publisher. **herauswachsen aus** *v* grow out of.

herb [hɛrp] *adj* sharp, tart; (*Wein*) dry; (*fig*) harsh.

herbei [hɛr'bai] *adv* (to) here, this way. −**führen** *v* cause.

Herberge ['hɛrbɛrgə] *f* (*pl* -n) hostel.

Herbst [hɛrpst] *m* (*pl* -e) autumn, (*US*) fall. **herbstlich** *adj* autumnal.

Herd [heɪrt] *m* (*pl* -e) cooker, stove.

Herde ['heɪrdə] *f* (*pl* -n) herd.

herein [hɛˈrain] *adv* in, inside, in here. **–führen** *v* usher in. **–treten** *v* enter.
*hergeben [ˈheːrgeɪbən] *v* hand over.
hergebracht [ˈheɪrgəbraxt] *adj* traditional, customary.
Hering [ˈheːrin] *m* (*pl* -e) herring.
*herkommen [ˈheɪrkɔmən] *v* come here; (*abstammen*) come from. **herkommen von** be caused by, be due to. **herkömmlich** *adj* customary, traditional.
Herkunft [ˈheːrkunft] *f* (*unz*) origin; (*Person*) birth, descent.
herleiten [ˈheːrlaitən] *v* lead here; (*fig*) derive, deduce. **Herleitung** *f* derivation.
Hermelin [hɛrməˈliːn] *neut* (*pl* -e) ermine.
hernach [hɛrˈnaix] *adv* afterwards, after this.
Heroin [heroˈiːn] *neut* heroin.
Herr [hɛr] *m* (*pl* -en) (*Anrede*) Mr; (*Herrscher*) master, lord. **der Herr Gott** Lord God. **dieser Herr** this gentleman. **Herren‖artikel** *pl* men's clothing. **–haus** *neut* manor house. **–toilette** *f* men's lavatory.
herrichten [ˈheːrɪçtən] *v* prepare, arrange.
Herrin [ˈheːrin] *f* (*pl* -nen) lady, mistress.
herr‖isch *adj* overbearing, domineering. **–lich** *adj* splendid, magnificent.
Herr‖lichkeit *f* splendour, magnificence. **–schaft** *f* power, rule; (*fig*) mastery.
herrschen *v* rule, govern; (*vorhanden sein*) prevail. **Herrscher** *m* (*pl* -) ruler.
her‖rühren *v* originate (from). **–stammen** *v* descend (from). **–stellen** *v* manufacture, make; (*reparieren*) repair. **Hersteller** *m* manufacturer, maker. **Herstellung** *f* manufacture.
herüber [hɛˈryːbər] *adv* across, over here.
herum [hɛˈrum] *adv* (a)round, about. **–fahren** *v* drive around. **–pfuschen** *v* tinker, mess around (with). **–streichen** *v* roam about, wander around.
herunter [hɛˈruntər] *adv* downwards, down (here). **–kommen** *v* come down; (*sinken*) decline.
hervor [hɛrˈfoːr] *adv* forth, out. **–bringen** *v* produce; (*Worte*) utter. **–heben** *v* make prominent, bring out. **–ragen** *v* stand out, jut out. **–ragend** *adj* outstanding. **–rufen** *v* arouse; (*verursachen*) cause. **–treten** *v* come forward.
Herz [hɛrts] *neut* (*pl* -en) heart. **–anfall** *m* heart attack. **herz‖erfreuend** *adj* heartening, cheering. **–erschütternd** *adj* appalling. **–haft** *adj* stout-hearted. **–ig** *adj*

lovely. **–lich** *adj* hearty. **–los** *adj* heartless.
Herzog [ˈhɛrtsoɪk] *m* (*pl* Herzöge) duke. **–in** *f* (*pl* -nen) duchess. **Herzogtum** *neut* duchy, dukedom.
herzu [hɛrˈtsuː] *adv* (to) here, towards.
Hessen [ˈhɛsən] *neut* Hesse.
Hetze [ˈhɛtsə] *f* (*pl* -n) hounding, baiting; (*Eile*) mad rush, dash; (*Jagd*) hunt. **hetzen** *v* hound; rush, dash; hunt.
Heu [hɔy] *neut* hay. **Heu‖fieber** *neut* hay fever. **–gabel** *f* pitchfork. **–schober** *m* haystack. **–schrecke** *f* grasshopper, locust.
Heuchelei [hɔyçəˈlai] *f* (*pl* -en) hypocrisy.
heucheln *v* be hypocritical. **Heuchler** *m* (*pl* -), **Heuchlerin** *f* (*pl* -nen) hypocrite.
heuchlerisch *adj* hypocritical.
heulen [ˈhɔylən] *v* cry, howl.
heute [ˈhɔytə] *adv* today. **heutig** *adj* today's; (*gegenwärtig*) present, current. **heutzutage** *adv* nowadays, these days.
Hexe [ˈhɛksə] *f* (*pl* -n) witch.
Hieb [hiːp] *m* (*pl* -e) blow, stroke; (*Schnitt*) cut, slash.
hier [hiːr] *adv* here. **hier und da** now and then. **hier und dort** here and there. **hier‖auf** *adv* then, upon this. **–aus** *adv* from this. **–bei** *adv* hereby, herewith; (*Brief*) enclosed. **–für** *adv* for this.
hi-fi [ˈhaifai] *adj* hi-fi.
Hilfe [ˈhilfə] *f* (*pl* -n) help, assistance. **–ruf** *m* cry for help. **hilf‖los** *adj* helpless. **–reich** *adj* helpful. **–sbereit** *adj* eager to help. **Hilfs‖lehrer** *m* assistant teacher. **–mittel** *neut* remedy, aid.
Himbeere [ˈhimbeːrə] *f* raspberry.
Himmel [ˈhiməl] *m* (*pl* -) sky; (*Paradies*) heaven. **–fahrt** *f* Ascension. **–reich** *neut* heaven. **–skörper** *m* celestial body.
himmlisch [ˈhimliʃ] *adj* celestial, heavenly.
hin [hin] *adv* (to) there, from here, towards. **hin und her** to and fro, back and forth. **hin und wieder** now and again. **hin und zurück** there and back. **vor sich hin** to oneself. **es ist noch lange hin** there's a long time to go.
hinab [hiˈnap] *adv* down(wards). **–lassen** *v* lower, let down. **–steigen** *v* descend.
hinan [hiˈnan] *adv* up (to), upwards.
hinauf [hiˈnauf] *adv* up (there), upwards. **die Treppe hinauf** up the stairs. **–setzen** *v* put up. **–ziehen** *v* pull up, (*umziehen*) move up.

hinaus [hi'naus] *adv* out, forth. **–gehen** *v* go out. **hinausgehen über** surpass, exceed. **hinaus‖kommen** *v* come out. **–werfen** *v* throw out.

Hinblick ['hinblik] *m* **im Hinblick auf** with regard to.

hinderlich ['hindərliç] *adj* restrictive, hindering. **hindern** *v* hinder; (*verhindern*) prevent. **Hindernis** *neut* (*pl* **-se**) obstacle, hindrance.

hindeuten ['hindɔytən] *v* point (at); (*fig*) hint (at).

hindurch [hin'durç] *adv* through, across; (*zeitlich*) throughout.

hinein [hi'nain] *adv* in(to). **sich hineindrängen** *v* force one's way in. **hineinziehen** *v* draw in; (*fig: verwickeln*) involve; (*umziehen*) move to.

hinfahren ['hinfaːrən] *v* drive there; (*hinbringen*) take there. **Hinfahrt** *f* outward journey, way there.

*****hinfallen** ['hinfalən] *v* fall down. **hinfällig** *adj* feeble, frail; (*Meinung*) untenable, invalid.

Hingabe ['hingaːbə] *f* devotion.

*****hingeben** ['hingeːbən] *v* give up. **sich hingeben** devote oneself (to).

hingegen ['hingeːgən] *conj* on the other hand, whereas.

*****hingehen** ['hingeːən] *v* go there; (*Zeit*) pass, elapse. **etwas hingehen lassen** let something pass.

hinken ['hiŋkən] *v* limp.

hin‖kommen *v* arrive, get there; (*umg.*) manage. **–langen** *v* reach. **–länglich** *adj* sufficient. **–legen** *v* put down. **sich hinlegen** lie down. **hin‖nehmen** *v* put up with, bear. **–reichend** *adj* sufficient.

Hinreise ['hinraizə] *f* outward journey, way there.

hinreißen ['hinraisən] *v* carry along; (*entzücken*) charm, transport. **–d** *adj* charming, enchanting.

hinrichten ['hinriçtən] *v* (*Person*) execute. **Hinrichtung** *f* execution.

*****hinschreiben** ['hinʃraibən] *v* write down.

Hinsicht ['hinziçt] *f* **in Hinsicht auf** with regard to. **in dieser Hinsicht** in this regard. **hinsichtlich** *adv* with regard to.

hinten ['hintən] *adv* behind, at the back. **nach hinten** to the back, backwards. **von hinten** from behind.

hinter ['hintər] *prep* behind, after. *adj* rear, back. **Hinter‖achse** *f* rear axle. **–bein** *neut* hind leg. **Hintere(r)** *m* back

part; (*Körper*) bottom, backside. **hintergehen** *v* deceive, fool.

Hinter‖grund *m* background. **–halt** *m* ambush. **aus dem Hinterhalt überfallen** ambush. **Hinterhof** *m* rear court, back yard.

hinter‖lassen *v* leave (behind). **–legen** *v* deposit.

Hintern ['hintərn] *m* (*pl* **-**) bottom, backside.

Hinter‖schiff *neut* stern. **–teil** *m* back part. **–tür** *f* back door.

hinterziehen [hintər'tsiːən] *v* (*Steuern*) evade. **Hinterziehung** *f* (tax) evasion.

hinüber [hi'nyːbər] *adv* over, across, to the other side. **–gehen** *v* cross (over).

hinunter [hi'nuntər] *adv* downwards, down (there). **die Treppe hinunter** downstairs.

hinweg [hin'vɛk] *adv* away (from here), off. **Hinweg** *m* outward journey. **hinwegkommen über** get over.

Hinweis ['hinvais] *m* (*pl* **-e**) indication, hint. **hinweisen** *v* point out, show; (*Person*) direct; (*anspielen*) refer, allude.

*****hinziehen** ['hintsiːən] *v* draw, attract; (*verzögern*) drag out.

hinzu [hin'tsuː] *adv* in addition, as well. **–fügen** *v* add. **–kommen** *v* be added. **–kommend** *adj* additional. **–ziehen** *v* draw *or* bring in; (*Fachmann*) consult.

Hirn [hirn] *neut* (*pl* **-e**) brain.

Hirsch [hirʃ] *m* (*pl* **-e**) stag. **–fleisch** *neut* venison. **–kalb** *neut* fawn. **–kuh** *f* doe, hind.

Hirt [hirt] *m* (*pl* **-en**) shepherd, herdsman. **–in** *f* (*pl* **-nen**) shepherdess.

hissen ['hisən] *v* hoist.

Historiker [hi'stoːrikər] *m* (*pl* **-**) historian. **historisch** *adj* historical; (*bedeutend*) historic.

Hitze ['hitsə] *f* (*unz.*) heat; (*Leidenschaft*) passion. **hitzebeständig** *adj* heat-resistant. **hitzig** *adj* hot; (*fig*) fiery, passionate. **Hitz‖kopf** *m* hothead. **–schlag** *m* heat-stroke.

hoch [hoːx] (**hoher, hohe, hohes, höher, höchst**) *adj* high; (*Baum*) tall; (*Alter*) old, advanced. *adv* highly, greatly. **hohe Blüte** full bloom. **hohe See** high *or* open sea. **10 hoch 4** 10 to the power of 4. **Hoch** *neut* (*pl* **-s**) cheer; (*Hochdruckgebiet*) high-pressure area. **Dreimal hoch** three cheers.

Hochachtung ['hoːxaxtuŋ] *f* respect, esteem. **hochachtungsvoll** respectfully, yours faithfully.

hochdeutsch ['hoxdɔytʃ] *adj* high German, standard German.

Hoch‖druck *m* high pressure. —**ebene** *f* plateau. —**flut** *f* high tide. —**frequenz** *f* high frequency.

*hochhalten ['hoːxhaltən] *v* think highly of, esteem.

Hoch‖haus *neut* tall building, high-rise block. —**konjunktur** *f* boom. —**land** *neut* highland(s). —**leistung**- *adj* heavy-duty. —**mut** *m* pride, arrogance. **hochmütig** *adj* proud, arrogant.

Hoch‖ruf *m* cheer. —**schätzung** *f* (high) esteem. —**schule** *f* college, university; (*technische*) polytechnic. —**spannung** *f* high tension, high voltage. —**sprung** *m* high jump. —**verrat** *m* high treason. —**wasser** *neut* high tide, high water; (*Überschwemmung*) flooding. **Hochzeit** *f* wedding. **hochzeitlich** *adj* nuptial, bridal. **Hochzeitskleid** *neut* wedding dress.

höchst [hœːxst] *adj* highest, greatest. *adv* very (much), greatly, highly.

hochstehend ['hoxʃtɛɪənt] *adj* high-ranking, eminent.

höchstens [hœːxstəns] *adv* at most, at best.

Höchst‖geschwindigkeit *f* maximum speed. —**preis** *m* maximum price.

hocken ['hɔkən] *v* squat, crouch. **Hocker** *m* (*pl* -) stool.

Hode ['hoːdə] *f* (*pl* -n) *or* **Hoden** *m* (*pl* -) testicle.

Hof [hoːf] *m* (*pl* Höfe) (court)yard; (*Landwirtschaft*) farm; (*fürstlich*) court.

hoffen ['hɔfən] *v* hope. **hoffentlich** *adv* I hope (so); let us hope (that). **Hoffnung** *f* (*pl* -en) hope. **hoffnungs‖los** *adj* hopeless. —**voll** *adj* hopeful.

höflich ['hœfliç] *adj* polite, courteous. **Höflichkeit** *f* courtesy, politeness.

hohe(r) ['hoːə(r)] *V* **hoch**.

Höhe ['hœːə] *f* (*pl* -n) height; (*Gipfel*) top; (*Geog*) latitude; (*Hügel*) hill.

Hoheit ['hoːhaɪt] *f* (*unz.*) grandeur, greatness; (*Titel*) Highness. —**sgewässer** *pl* territorial waters.

Höhepunkt ['hœːəpuŋkt] *m* climax.

höher ['hœːər] *V* **hoch**.

hohl [hoːl] *adj* hollow, (*Linse*) concave.

Höhle ['hœːlə] *f* (*pl* -n) cave; (*Loch*) hole;

(*eines Tiers*) burrow, hole. **höhlen** *v* hollow (out).

höhnen ['hœːnən] *v* mock, taunt. **höhnisch** *adj* mocking, scornful.

hold [hɔlt] *adj* charming, gracious. —**selig** *adj* most charming, most gracious.

holen ['hoːlən] *v* fetch. **Atem holen** draw breath. **sich Rat holen bei** ask for advice.

Holländer ['hɔlɛndər] *m* (*pl* -) Dutchman. —**in** *f* (*pl* -nen) Dutchwoman. **holländisch** *adj* Dutch.

Hölle ['hœlə] *f* (*pl* -n) hell.

Holunder [ho'lundər] *m* (*pl* -) elder (tree). —**beere** *f* elderberry.

Holz [hɔlts] *neut* (*pl* Hölzer) wood. —**blasinstrument** *neut* woodwind instrument.

hölzern ['hœltsərn] *adj* wooden; (*fig*) stiff, awkward, clumsy.

holzig ['hɔltsiç] *adj* woody.

Holz‖klotz *m* wooden block. —**kohle** *f* charcoal. —**schnitt** *m* woodcut. —**weg** *m* **auf dem Holzwege sein** be on the wrong track. **Holzwurm** *m* woodworm.

Homosexualität [homozɛksuali'tɛɪt] *f* homosexuality. **homosexuell** *adj* homosexual. **Homosexuelle(r)** *m* homosexual.

Honig ['hoːniç] *m* honey. —**biene** *f* honeybee.

Honorar [hono'raɪr] *neut* (*pl* -e) fee, honorarium; (*eines Autors*) royalties *pl*.

Hopfen ['hɔpfən] *m* (*pl* -) hops *pl*.

hörbar ['hœːrbaɪr] *adj* audible.

horchen ['hɔrçən] *v* listen (to); (*heimlich*) eavesdrop.

Horde ['hɔrdə] *f* (*pl* -n) horde.

hören ['hœːrən] *v* hear; (*Radio*) listen to. **Hören** *neut* (sense of) hearing. —**sagen** *neut* hearsay. **Hörer** *m* hearer; (*Radio*) listener; (*Telef*) receiver; (*pl*) audience. —**schaft** *f* audience. **Hörgerät** *neut* hearing aid.

Horizont [hɔri'tsɔnt] *m* (*pl* -e) horizon. **horizontal** *adj* horizontal.

Hormon [hɔr'moɪn] *neut* (*pl* -e) hormone.

Horn [hɔrn] *neut* (*pl* Hörner) horn. —**brille** *f* horn-rimmed spectacles. —**haut** *f* (*Anat*) cornea.

Horoskop [horo'skoɪp] *neut* (*pl* -e) horoscope.

Hör‖probe *f* audition. —**saal** *m* lecture hall. —**spiel** *neut* radio play.

Hose ['hoːzə] *f* (*pl* -n) trousers. **Hosen‖schlitz** *m* flies, (*US*) fly. —**träger** *pl* braces, (*US*) suspenders.

Höschen ['hœɪsçən] *neut* (*pl* -) knickers
pl; panties *pl*.
Hotel [ho'tɛl] *neut* (*pl* -s) hotel.
Hub [huɪp] *m* (*pl* Hübe) lift; (*Mot*)
stroke. –**raum** *m* cylinder capacity.
hübsch [hypʃ] *adj* pretty, nice; (*Mann*)
good-looking.
Hubschrauber ['hupʃraubər] *m* (*pl* -) helicopter.
Huf [huːf] *m* (*pl* -e) hoof. –**eisen** *neut*
horseshoe.
Hüftbein ['hyftbain] *neut* hipbone. **Hüfte**
f hip.
Hügel ['hyːgəl] *m* (*pl* -) hill. **hügelig** *adj*
hilly.
Huhn [huɪn] *neut* (*pl* Hühner) hen;
(*Küche*) chicken.
Hühner||**auge** *neut* (*Med*) corn. –**braten**
m roast chicken. –**brühe** *f* chicken broth.
–**ei** *neut* hen's egg. –**stall** *m* henhouse.
huldigen ['huldigən] *v* pay homage to;
(*Ansicht*) hold, subscribe to. **Huldigung** *f*
homage.
Hülle ['hylə] *f* covering, wrapping;
(*Umschlag*) envelope; (*Buch*) jacket, cover. **in Hülle und Fülle** in abundance. **hül-
len** *v* wrap, cover.
Hülse ['hylzə] *f* (*pl* -n) husk, shell; (*Erbse*)
pod; (*aus Papier, usw.*) case, casing.
human [hu'maɪn] *adj* humane. **Humanist**
m (*pl* -en) humanist. **humanitär** *adj*
humanitarian.
Hummel ['huməl] *f* (*pl* -n) bumblebee.
Hummer ['humər] *m* (*pl* -) lobster.
Humor [hu'moɪr] *m* (sense of) humour.
humorvoll *adj* humorous.
humpeln ['humpəln] *v* hobble, limp.
Hund [hunt] *m* (*pl* -e) dog. **Hunde**||**hütte** *f*
kennel. –**leine** *f* leash.
hundert ['hundərt] *adj, pron* hundred.
Hundert||**füßler** *m* centipede. –**jahrfeier** *f*
centenary. **hundert**||**mal** *adv* a hundred
times. –**prozentig** *adj* one-hundred-per-
cent, complete.
Hündin ['hyndin] *f* (*pl* -nen) bitch.
Hunger ['huŋər] *m* hunger. **Hunger haben**
be hungry. –**lohn** *m* starvation wages *pl*;
pittance. **hungern** *v* starve; be hungry.
Hungersnot *f* famine. **Hungerstreik** *m*
hungerstrike. **hungrig** *adj* hungry.
Hupe ['huɪpə] *f* (*pl* -n) (*Mot*) horn. **hupen**
v sound the horn, beep.
hüpfen ['hypfən] *v* hop, skip.
Hürde ['hyrdə] *f* (*pl* -n) hurdle; (*Schafe*)
fold, pen.

Hure ['huːrə] *f* (*pl* -n) whore.
hurra [hu'raɪ] *interj* hurrah!
husten ['huːstən] *v* cough. **Husten** *m* (*pl* -)
cough.
Hut[1] [huːt] *m* (*pl* Hüte) hat.
Hut[2] *f* (*unz.*) (*Schutz*) protection; (*Vorsicht*) care; (*Aufsicht*) guard. **auf der Hut
sein** (**vor**) be on one's guard (against).
hüten ['hyɪtən] *v* guard. **sich hüten** (**vor**)
be careful *or* wary (of).
Hütte ['hytə] *f* (*pl* -n) hut, cabin; (*Metall*)
foundry, ironworks. –**nkäse** *m* cottage
cheese.
Hyäne [hy'ɛɪnə] *f* (*pl* -n) hyena.
Hydraulik [hy'draulik] *f* hydraulics.
hydraulisch *adj* hydraulic.
Hygiene [hygi'eɪnə] *f* hygiene. **hygienisch**
adj hygienic.
Hymne ['hymnə] *f* (*pl* -n) hymn.
Hypnose [hyp'noɪzə] *f* (*pl* -n) hypnosis.
hypno||**tisch** *adj* hypnotic. –**tisieren** *v*
hypnotize.
Hypothek [hypo'teɪk] *f* (*pl* -en) mortgage.
Hypothese [hypo'teɪzə] *f* (*pl* -n) hypothesis. **hypothetisch** *adj* hypothetical.
Hysterie [hyste'riɪ] *f* hysteria. **hysterisch**
adj hysterical. **hysterische Anfälle** *pl* hys-
terics.

I

ich [iç] *pron* I. **Ich** *neut* self, ego.
ichbezogen *adj* egocentric.
ideal [ide'aɪl] *adj* ideal. **Ideal** *neut* (*pl* -e)
ideal. **Idealismus** *m* idealism.
Idee [i'deɪ] *f* (*pl* -n) idea.
identifizieren [iˌdɛntifiˈtsiɪrən] *v* identify.
identisch *adj* identical. **Identität** *f* identity.
Idiot [idi'oɪt] *m* (*pl* -en) idiot. **idiotisch** *adj*
idiotic.
Igel ['iɪgəl] *m* (*pl* -) hedgehog.
ignorieren [igno'riɪrən] *v* ignore.
ihm [iɪm] *pron* (*Person*) (to) him; (*Sache*)
(to) it.
ihn [iɪn] *pron* (*Person*) him; (*Sache*) it.
ihnen ['iɪnən] *pron* (to) them. **Ihnen** *pron*
(to) you.
ihr [iɪr] *pron* you; (*Dat*) (to) her. *pron, adj*
(*Person*) her; its; their. **Ihr** *pron, adj*
your. **ihrer, ihre, ihres** *pron* hers; its;
theirs. **Ihrer, Ihre, Ihres** yours. **ihrerseits**
adv for your part. **ihr**||**esgleichen** *adv* like

her (it, them). **–etwegen** *or* **–etwillen** on her (its, their) account. **der, die, das ihrige** *pron* hers; its; theirs.

Illusion [iluzi'oɪn] *f* (*pl* **-en**) illusion. **illusorisch** *adj* illusory.

illustrieren [ilu'striːrən] *v* illustrate. **Illustrierte** *f* (illustrated) magazine.

im [im] *prep + art* in dem.

Imbiß ['imbis] *m* (*pl* **Imbisse**) snack. **–stube** *f* snack bar.

Immatrikulation [imatrikulatsi'oɪn] *f* (*pl* **-en**) matriculation, registration.

immer ['imər] *adv* always. **immer mehr** more and more. **immer noch** still. **immer wieder** again and again. **wenn auch immer** although. **auf immer** forever. **–fort** *adv* constantly. **–grün** *adj* evergreen. **–hin** *adv* nevertheless. **–zu** *adv* all the time.

Immigrant [imi'grant] *m* (*pl* **-en**) immigrant.

Immobilien [imo'biːliən] *pl* real estate *sing*.

Imperialismus [imperia'lismus] *m* imperialism. **Imperialist** *m* (*pl* **-en**) imperialist.

impfen ['impfən] *v* inoculate, vaccinate. **Impfung** *f* (*pl* **-en**) inoculation, vaccination.

imponieren [impo'niːrən] *v* impress. **–d** *adj* impressive.

Import [im'pɔrt] *m* (*pl* **-e**) import(ation); (*Ware*) import. **–eur** *m* (*pl* **-e**) importer. **–handel** *m* import trade. **importieren** *v* import.

impotent ['impɔtɛnt] *adj* impotent.

imprägnieren [imprɛg'niːrən] *v* impregnate, saturate.

improvisieren [improvi'ziːrən] *v* improvise. **improvisiert** *adj* improvized, ad-lib.

imstande [im'ʃtandə] *adv* imstande sein be able *or* capable.

in [in] *prep* (+ *Dat*) in; (+ *Acc*) into, in; (*Zeit*) (with)in.

Inanspruchnahme [in'anʃpruxnaɪmə] *f* demands *pl*.

Inbegriff ['inbəgrif] *m* essence, epitome. **mit Inbegriff von** inclusive of. **inbegriffen** *adj, adv* (*Steuer*) included, inclusive(ly).

Inbrunst ['inbrunst] *f* ardour, fervour.

indem [in'deɪm] *conj* (*dadurch daß*) in that, by; (*während*) while.

Inder ['indər] *m* (*pl* **-**) (Asian) Indian.

indessen [in'dɛsən] *conj* (*inzwischen*) meanwhile, in the meantime; (*immerhin*) however, nevertheless.

Indianer [indi'aɪnər] *m* (*pl* **-**) (American) Indian. **indianisch** *adj* (American) Indian.

Indien ['indiən] *neut* India.

indirekt ['indirɛkt] *adj* indirect.

indisch ['indiʃ] *adj* (Asian) Indian.

indiskret ['indiskrɛt] *adj* indiscreet, tactless.

Individualist [individua'list] *m* (*pl* **-en**) individualist. **individualistisch** *adj* individualist(ic). **individuell** *adj* individual. **Individuum** *neut* (*pl* **-duen**) individual.

industrialisieren [industriali'ziːrən] *v* industrialize. **Industrie** *f* (*pl* **-n**) industry. **–gebiet** *neut* industrial region. **industriell** *adj* industrial. **Industrielle(r)** *m* industrialist.

ineinander [inain'andər] *adv* in(to) each other. **–greifen** *v* (*Tech*) engage; (*fig*) overlap.

Infanterie [infantə'riː] *f* infantry. **Infanterist** *m* (*pl* **-en**) infantryman.

infiltrieren [infil'triːrən] *v* infiltrate.

infizieren [infi'tsiːrən] *v* infect. **sich infizieren** become infected, catch a disease.

Inflation [inflatsi'oɪn] *f* (*Komm*) inflation. **inflationär, inflationistisch** *adj* inflationary.

infolge [in'fɔlgə] *prep* on account of, owing to. **–dessen** *adv* consequently.

Information [infɔrmatsi'oɪn] *f* (*pl* **-en**) information. **eine Information** a piece of information.

informell ['infɔrmɛl] *adj* informal.

informieren [infɔr'miːrən] *v* inform, instruct. **sich informieren über** find out about, gather information about.

Ingenieur [inʒe'njœːr] *m* (*pl* **-e**) engineer. **–schule** *f* engineering college. **–wesen** *neut* engineering.

Ingwer ['iŋvɛr] *m* ginger.

Inhaber ['inhaɪbər] *m* (*pl* **-**) owner; (*Titel, Paß, Patent*) holder.

inhalieren [inha'liːrən] *v* inhale.

Inhalt ['inhalt] *m* (*pl* **-e**) contents *pl*; (*Bedeutung*) meaning, content. **–sverzeichnis** *neut* table of contents.

Initiative [initsia'tiːvə] *f* (*unz.*) initiative. **die Initiative ergreifen** take the initiative.

inklusive [inklu'ziːvə] *prep* including, inclusive of.

inkonsequent ['inkɔnzekvɛnt] *adj* inconsistent.

Inkontinenz ['inkɔntinɛnts] *f* incontinence.

inkorporieren [inkɔrpɔ'riːrən] *v* incorporate.

Inkrafttreten [in'kraftreːtən] *neut* coming into effect.

Inland ['inlant] *neut* inland, interior.

inmitten [in'mitən] *prep* in the midst of, among.

inne ['inə] *adv* within.

innen ['inən] *adv* within, inside. **nach innen** inwards. **Innen‖ausstattung** *f* interior decoration, decor. **–minister** *m* Home Secretary, Minister of the Interior. **–politik** *f* domestic policy. **innenpolitisch** *adj* (relating to) internal affairs. **Innenraum** *m* interior.

inner ['inər] *adj* internal, inner. **Innereien** *pl* offal. **Innere(s)** *neut* (*pl* -(e)n) interior. **inner‖halb** *prep* within. **–lich** *adj* inward, internal. **innerst** *adj* innermost.

innewohnen ['inəvoːnən] *v* be inherent (in).

innig ['iniç] *adj* (*Gefühle*) sincere; (*Freunde*) intimate.

ins [ins] *prep* + *art* in das.

Insasse ['inzasə] *m* (*pl* -n) inmate.

insbesondere [insbə'zɔndərə] *adv* particularly.

Inschrift ['inʃrift] *f* inscription.

Insekt [in'zɛkt] *neut* (*pl* -en) insect. **–enpulver** *neut* insect powder. **–izid** *neut* insecticide.

Insel ['inzəl] *f* (*pl* -n) island.

Inserat [inze'raːt] *neut* (*pl* -e) (newspaper) advertisement.

insgesamt [insgə'zamt] *adv* altogether.

insofern [inzo'fɛrn] *conj* so far as; [in'zofɛrn] (*bis zu diesem Punkt*) to that extent. **insofern als** inasmuch as.

insoweit [inzo'vait] *adv* to that extent.

Inspektor [inspɛk'tɔr] *m* (*pl* -en) inspector.

instand halten [in'ʃtant haltən] *v* maintain (in good order). **instand setzen** *v* repair, overhaul; (*Person*) enable. **Instandhaltung** *f* unkeep, maintenance.

Instanz [in'stants] *f* (*pl* -en) authority. **durch die Instanzen** through official channels.

instinktiv [instiŋk'tiːf] *adj* instinctive.

Institut [insti'tuːt] *neut* (*pl* -e) institute.

Instrument [instru'mɛnt] *neut* (*pl* -e) instrument.

inszenieren [instse'niːrən] *v* (*Film*, *Schauspiel*) produce; (*fig*) create, engineer.

integrieren [inte'griːrən] *v* integrate. **Integration** *f* integration.

intellektuell [intɛlɛktu'ɛl] *adj* intellectual.

intelligent [intɛli'gɛnt] *adj* intelligent, clever.

interessant [intərɛ'sant] *adj* interesting. **Interesse** *neut* interest. **interessieren** *v* interest. **sich interessieren für** take an interest in, be interested in.

intern [in'tɛrn] *adj* internal.

Internat [intər'naɪt] *neut* (*pl* -e) boarding school.

international [intɛrnatsio'naɪl] *adj* international.

Interview [intər'vjuː] *neut* (*pl* -s) interview. **interviewen** *v* interview. **Interviewer** *m* interviewer. **Interviewte(r)** interviewee.

intim [in'tiːm] *adj* intimate.

Intrige [in'triːgə] *f* (*pl* -n) intrigue. **intrigieren** *v* plot, scheme.

Invalide(r) [inva'liːdə(r)] *m* invalid. **Invaliden‖heim** *neut* home for the disabled. **–rente** *f* disability pension. **invalid** *adj* invalid.

Inventar [invɛn'taːr] *neut* (*pl* -e) inventory.

Inventur [invɛn'tuːr] *f* (*pl* -en) stock-taking.

inwendig ['invɛndiç] *adj* inner.

inwiefern [invi'fɛrn] *conj* to what extent, how far.

inzwischen [in'tsviʃən] *adv* meanwhile.

irdisch ['irdiʃ] *adj* earthly, worldly.

Ire ['iːrə] *m* (*pl* -n) Irishman. **Irin** *f* (*pl* -nen) Irishwoman.

irgend ['irgənt] *adv* perhaps, ever. *pron* some, any. **irgend etwas** something, anything. **irgend jemand** someone, anyone. **irgend‖ein** *adj* some, any. **–wann** *adv* (at) sometime (or other). **–was** *pron* something, anything. **–wie** *adv* somehow, anyhow. **–wo** *adv* somewhere, anywhere.

Iris ['iːris] *f* (*pl* -) (*Anat*) iris.

irisch ['iːriʃ] *adj* Irish.

Irland ['irlant] *neut* Ireland. **Irländer** *m* (*pl* -) Irishman. **Irländerin** *f* (*pl* -nen) Irishwoman. **irländisch** *adj* Irish.

Ironie [iro'niː] *f* (*pl* -n) irony. **ironisch** *adj* ironic; (*spöttisch*) ironical.

irre ['irə] *adj* (*geistesgestört*) insane, mad; (*verwirrt*) confused. *adv* (*von Ziel weg*) astray. **irr werden** go insane. **irren** *v* err.

Irre(r) madman/woman). **irreführen** v
lead astray; (täuschen) mislead. **Irrenanstalt** f mental home. **Irrglaube** m heresy.
irrig adj erroneous. **Irrsinn** m insanity,
madness. **irrsinnig** adj insane. **Irrtum** m
(pl **Irrtümer**) error. **irrtümlich** adj erroneous, wrong.
Isolierband [izo'liːrbant] neut insulating
tape; **isolieren** v isolate; (Elek) insulate.
Isolierung f isolation; insulation.
Italien [i'taːliən] neut Italy. **Italiener** m
(pl -). **Italienerin** f (pl -nen) Italian.
italienisch adj Italian.

J

ja [jaː] adv yes. **ja doch** to be sure, but yes.
ja freilich yes indeed. **wenn ja** if so.
Jacht [jaxt] f (pl -en) yacht.
Jacke ['jakə] f (pl -n) jacket.
Jagd [jaːkt] f (pl -en) hunt; (Jagen) hunting. **–flugzeug** neut fighter plane. **–hund**
m hound. **–schloß** neut hunting lodge.
jagen ['jaːgən] v hunt; (treiben) drive
(away); (verfolgen) pursue; (eilen) rush,
race.
Jäger ['jɛːgər] m (pl -) hunter; (Flugzeug)
fighter.
jäh [jɛː] adj steep; (plötzlich) sudden.
Jahr [jaːr] neut (pl -e) year. **–buch** neut
yearbook. **jahrelang** adv for years.
Jahres‖einkommen neut annual income.
–ende neut end of the year. **–tag** m
anniversary. **–viertel** neut quarter.
–wende f New Year, turn of the year.
–zeit f season. **jahreszeitlich** adj seasonal. **Jahrhundert** neut century.
jährig ['jɛːriç] adj lasting a year. **dreijährig**
adj three-year-old.
jährlich ['jɛːrliç] adj yearly, annual.
Jahr‖markt m fair. **–zehnt** neut decade.
Jalousie [ʒalu'ziː] f (pl -n) venetian blind.
Jammer ['jamər] m (unz.) wailing;
(Elend) misery; (Verzweiflung) despair.
jämmerlich ['jɛmərliç] adj pitiable.
jammern ['jamərn] v wail; (klagen) complain.
Januar ['januaːr] m (pl -e) January.
Japan ['jaːpan] neut Japan. **–er** m (pl -),
Japanerin f (pl -nen) Japanese. **japanisch**
adj Japanese.
jauchzen ['jauxtsən] v shout joyfully,
rejoice.

jawohl [ja'voːl] adv, interj yes indeed, certainly.
Jazz [dʒɛs] m jazz.
je [jeː] adv ever. **je und je** always. **je zwei**
two each. conj **je mehr, desto besser** the
more, the better. **je nachdem** that
depends.
jedenfalls ['jeːdənfals] adv in any case.
jeder ['jeːdər], **jede, jedes** pron, adj each,
every. **jedermann** pron everybody.
jederzeit adv always, (at) any time.
jedesmal ['jeːdəsmaːl] adv each time.
jedoch [je'dɔx] adv however, yet.
jemals ['jeːmaːls] adv ever, at any time.
jemand ['jeːmant] pron someone; (Fragen)
anyone.
jener ['jeːnər], **jene, jenes** pron, adj that,
pl those; (zuerst erwähnt) the former.
jenseits adv on the other side. prep on
the other side of, across.
jetzig ['jɛtsiç] adj current, present. **jetzt**
adv now, at present.
jeweilig ['jeːvailiç] adj at the time; (Vergangenheit) at that time, then. **jeweils**
adv at a(ny) given time.
Jiddisch ['jidiʃ] neut Yiddish (language).
Joch [jɔx] neut (pl -e) yoke.
Jockei ['dʒɔki] m (pl -s) jockey.
Jod [jɔt] neut iodine.
jodeln ['jɔːdəln] v yodel.
Joghurt ['jɔgurt] neut (pl -s) yoghurt.
Johannisbeere [jo'hanisbeːrə] f redcurrant. **schwarze Johannisbeere** blackcurrant.
Journalismus [ʒurna'lismus] m journalism. **Journalist** m (pl -en) journalist.
journalistisch adj journalistic.
Jubel ['juːbəl] m rejoicing, jubilation.
jubeln v rejoice. **Jubiläum** neut (pl -äen)
anniversary, jubilee.
jucken ['jukən] v itch. **Jucken** neut itch.
Jude ['juːdə] m (pl -n), **Jüdin** f (pl -nen)
Jew. **jüdisch** adj Jewish.
Judo ['juːdo] neut judo.
Jugend ['juːgənt] f (unz.) youth. **–gericht**
neut juvenile court. **–herberge** f youth
hostel. **–kriminalität** f juvenile delinquency. **jugendlich** adj youthful, young,
juvenile. **jugendlicher Verbrecher** m juvenile delinquent. **Jugendliche(r)** m youth,
juvenile.
Jugoslawe [jugo'slaːvə] m, **Jugoslawin** f
Yugoslav. **Jugoslawien** neut Yugoslavia.
jugoslawisch adj Yugoslav.

Juli ['juːli] *m* (*pl* -s) July.
jung [juŋ] *adj* young. **Junge** *m* (*pl* -n)
boy; (*Lehrling*) apprentice; (*Karten*)
jack. **jungenhaft** *adj* boyish.
jünger ['jyŋər] *adj* younger, junior. **Jünger** *m* (*pl* -) disciple.
Junges ['juŋəs] *neut* (*pl* Jungen) young
(animal), offspring.
Jung‖fer *f* (*pl* -n) virgin; (*Mädchen*) girl.
alte Jungfer old maid, spinster. **–frau** *f*
virgin. **jungfräulich** *adj* maidenly, chaste.
Junggeselle *m* bachelor.
Jüngling ['jyŋliŋ] *m* (*pl* -e) youth, young
man. **–salter** *neut* youth, adolescence.
jüngst [jyŋst] *adj* youngest; (*letzt*) latest.
das jüngste Gericht the Last Judgment.
Juni ['juːni] *m* (*pl* -s) June.
Junker ['juŋkər] *m* (*pl* -) squire; (*jung*)
young aristocrat.
Jura¹ ['juːra] *f* law *sing*. **Jura studieren**
study law.
Jura² *m* (*pl* -s) the Jura, Jura Mountains.
Jurist [ju'rist] *m* (*pl* -en) lawyer.
just [just] *adv* just, exactly.
Justiz [jus'tiːts] *f* (*unz.*) justice, administration of the law. **–irrtum** *m* miscarriage of justice. **–wesen** *neut* legal
affairs, the law.
Juwel [ju'veːl] *neut* (*pl* -en) jewel. **–ier** *m*
(*pl* -e) jeweller.
Jux [juks] *m* (*pl* -e) joke, prank. **aus Jux**
as a joke, for fun.

K

Kabarett [kaba'rɛt] *neut* (*pl* -e) cabaret.
Kabel ['kaːbəl] *neut* (*pl* -) cable.
Kabeljau ['kaːbəljau] *m* (*pl* -e) cod.
kabeln ['kaːbəln] *v* cable, wire.
Kabine [ka'biːnə] *f* (*pl* -n) (*Schiff*) cabin;
(*Umkleide-*) cubicle; (*Seilbahn*) cable-
car.
Kabinett [kabi'nɛt] *neut* (*pl* -e) (*Pol*) cabi-
net; (*Zimmer*) closet.
Kadaver [ka'daːvər] *m* (*pl* -) carcass.
Kadett [ka'dɛt] *m* (*pl* -en) cadet.
Käfer ['kɛːfər] *m* (*pl* -) beetle.
Kaffee [ka'feː] *m* (*pl* -s) coffee. **–bohne** *f*
coffee bean. **–kanne** *f* coffee-pot.
–mühle *f* coffee-grinder. **–satz** *m* coffee
grounds *pl*.
Käfig ['kɛːfiç] *m* (*pl* -e) cage.
kahl [kaːl] *adj* bald; (*Landschaft*) bare,

barren. **Kahlheit** *f* baldness. **kahlköpfig**
adj bald-headed.
Kahn [kaːn] *m* (*pl* Kähne) small boat,
punt; (*Last-*) barge.
Kai [kai] *m* (*pl* -e) quay, wharf.
Kaiser ['kaizər] *m* (*pl* -) emperor. **–in** *f*
empress. **kaiserlich** *adj* imperial. **Kaiser-
reich** *neut* empire.
Kakao [ka'kao] *m* cocoa.
Kaktee [kak'teː] *f*, **Kaktus** *m* (*pl* Kakteen)
cactus.
Kalb [kalp] *neut* (*pl* Kälber) calf. **–fleisch**
neut veal. **–sbraten** *m* roast veal.
Kalender [ka'lɛndər] *m* (*pl* -) calendar.
Kaliber [ka'liːbər] *neut* (*pl* -) calibre.
Kalk [kalk] *m* (*pl* -e) lime. **–stein** *m*
limestone.
Kalorie [kalo'riː] *f* (*pl* -n) calorie.
kalt [kalt] *adj* cold. **–blütig** *adj* cold-
blooded.
Kälte ['kɛltə] *f* (*unz.*) cold(ness).
Kamel [ka'meːl] *neut* (*pl* -e) camel.
Kamera ['kamera] *f* (*pl* -s) camera.
–mann *m* cameraman.
Kamerad [kame'raːt] *m* (*pl* -en) companion, comrade. **–schaft** *f* companionship,
comradeship.
Kamin [ka'miːn] *m* (*pl* -e) (*Feuerstelle*)
hearth, fireplace; (*Schornstein*) chimney.
–feger *m* chimneysweep. **–gesims** *neut*
mantelpiece. **–vorsatz** *m* fireguard, fender.
Kamm [kam] *m* (*pl* Kämme) comb.
(*Vogel*) crest; (*Berg*) ridge, crest.
kämmen ['kɛmən] *v* comb. **sich kämmen**
comb one's hair.
Kammer ['kamər] *f* (*pl* -n) small room,
chamber; (*Mil, Pol*) chamber. **–frau** *f*
chambermaid. **–herr** *m* chamberlain.
–musik *f* chamber music.
Kampf [kampf] *m* (*pl* Kämpfe) fight,
struggle; (*Schlacht*) battle.
kämpfen ['kɛmpfən] *v* fight, struggle.
Kämpfer *m* (*pl* -) fighter.
Kampf‖handlung *f* (*Mil*) engagement;
action. **–platz** *m* battlefield. **–wagen** *m*
(*Mil*) tank.
Kanada ['kanada] *neut* Canada. **Kanadier**
m (*pl* -), **Kanadierin** *f* (*pl* -nen) Canadian.
kanadisch *adj* Canadian.
Kanal [ka'naːl] *m* (*pl* Kanäle) canal;
(*natürlicher, auch Radio, fig*) channel;
(*Abwasser*) drain, sewer. **–inseln** *pl*
Channel Islands.

Kanarienvogel [ka'naːriənfoːgəl] *m* canary.

Kandidat [kandi'daːt] *m* (*pl* -en) candidate. **kandidieren** *v* (*Wahl*) stand (for election); (*Posten*) apply (for).

Känguruh [kɛŋgu'ruː] *neut* (*pl* -s) kangaroo.

Kaninchen [ka'niːnçən] *neut* (*pl* -) rabbit. **–stall** *m* rabbit hutch.

Kanne ['kanə] *n* (*pl* -n) can; (*Kaffee, Tee*) pot; (*Krug*) jug, pitcher.

Kannibale [kani'baːlə] *m* (*pl* -n) cannibal. **kannibalisch** *adj* cannibal.

Kanon ['kanɔn] *m* (*pl* -s) canon.

Kanone [ka'noːnə] *f* (*pl* -n) cannon, gun. **Kanonen‖feuer** *neut* bombardment. **–kugel** *f* cannonball.

Kante ['kantə] *f* (*pl* -n) edge.

Kantine [kan'tiːnə] *f* (*pl* -n) canteen.

Kanton [kan'tom] *m* (*pl* -e) canton.

Kanzel ['kantsəl] *f* (*pl* -n) pulpit. **–rede** *f* sermon.

Kanzlei [kants'lai] *f* (*pl* -en) (*Büro*) office; (*Behörde*) chancellery. **–papier** *neut* foolscap.

Kanzler ['kantslər] *m* (*pl* -s) chancellor.

Kap [kap] *neut* (*pl* -s) cape, headland.

Kapazität [kapatsi'tɛːt] **1** *f* (*unz.*) capacity. **2** *f* (*pl* -en) (*Könner*) authority, expert.

Kapelle [ka'pɛlə] *f* (*pl* -n) chapel; (*Musik*) band.

Kaper ['kaipər] *f* (*pl* -n) (*Gewürz*) caper.

kapieren [ka'piːrən] *v* (*umg.*) understand, catch on, (*umg.*) get.

Kapital [kapi'taːl] *neut* (*Komm*) capital. **–ismus** *m* capitalism. **–ist** *m* capitalist. **kapitalistisch** *adj* capitalist.

Kapitän [kapi'tɛːn] *m* (*pl* -e) (ship's) captain.

Kapitel [ka'pitəl] *neut* (*pl* -) chapter.

kapitulieren [kapitu'liːrən] *v* capitulate, surrender. **Kapitulation** *f* (*pl* -en) capitulation, surrender.

Kaplan [ka'plan] *m* (*pl* Kapläne) chaplain.

Kappe ['kapə] *f* (*pl* -n) cap; (*Deckel*) top; (*Arch*) dome; (*Schuh*) toecap.

Kapriole [kapri'oːlə] *f* (*pl* -n) caper, cartwheel.

kaputt [ka'put] *adj* broken, (*umg.*) bust; (*erschöpft*) exhausted, (*umg.*) shattered. **–machen** *v* break, ruin.

Kapuze [ka'puːtsə] *f* (*pl* -n) hood.

Karaffe [ka'rafə] *f* (*pl* -n) carafe.

Karamelle [kara'mɛlə] *f* (*pl* -n) toffee.

Karat [ka'raːt] *neut* (*pl* -e) carat.

Karate [ka'raːtə] *neut* karate.

Karawane [kara'vaːnə] *f* (*pl* -n) caravan.

Kardinal [kardi'naːl] *m* (*pl* Kardinäle) cardinal.

Karfreitag [kaːr'fraitak] *m* Good Friday.

karg [kark] *adj* meagre, poor; (*geizig*) miserly.

kärglich ['kɛrkliç] *adj* scanty, poor.

kariert [ka'riərt] *adj* chequered, checked.

Karies ['kaːriɛs] *f* (*Med*) caries.

Karikatur [karika'tuːr] *f* (*pl* -en) caricature.

karmesin [karmɛ'ziːn] *adj* crimson.

Karneval ['karnɛval] *m* (*pl* -s) (Shrovetide) carnival.

Karo ['kaːro] *neut* (*pl* -s) square; (*Karten*) diamonds.

Karosserie [karɔsə'riː] *f* (*pl* -n) body, coachwork.

Karotte [ka'rɔtə] *f* (*pl* -n) carrot.

Karpfen ['karpfən] *m* (*pl* -) carp.

Karre ['karə] *f* (*pl* -n), **Karren** *m* (*pl* -) cart.

Karriere [kari'ɛːrə] *f* (*pl* -n) rise, (successful) career; (*Pferd*) full gallop.

Karte ['kartə] *f* (*pl* -n) (*Blatt*) card; (*Land-*) map; (*Eintritt, Reise*) ticket.

Kartei [kar'tai] *f* (*pl* -en) card file, card index.

Kartell [kar'tɛl] *neut* (*pl* -e) cartel, combine.

Karten‖ausgabe *f* ticket office. **–spiel** *neut* card game.

Kartoffel [kar'tɔfəl] *f* (*pl* -n) potato. **–chips** *pl* potato crisps (*US* chips). **–püree** *neut* mashed potatoes *pl*. **–puffer** *m* potato pancake. **–salat** *m* potato salad.

Karton [kar'tõ] *m* (*pl* -s) cardboard; (*Schachtel*) cardboard box, carton; (*Skizze*) cartoon.

Kartusche [kar'tuʃə] *f* (*pl* -n) cartridge.

Karussell [karu'sɛl] *neut* (*pl* -s) roundabout, merry-go-round.

Kaschmir [kaʃ'miːr] *neut* cashmere.

Käse ['kɛːzə] *m* (*pl* -) cheese.

Kaserne [ka'zɛrnə] *f* (*pl* -n) barracks *pl*.

Kasino [ka'ziːno] *neut* (*pl* -s) casino; (*Mil*) (officers') mess; (*Gesellschaftshaus*) club.

Kasse ['kasə] *f* (*pl* -n) cash box, till; (*Laden, Supermarkt*) cash-desk; (*Kino, Theater*) box office; (*Bank*) cashier's window, counter. **gut/schlecht bei Kasse sein** be flush/hard up. **Kassen‖buch** *neut* cash book. **–wart** *m* treasurer.

Kassette [ka'sɛtə] *f (pl* -n) small box, casket; (*Geld*) strong-box; (*Tonband*) cassette. –**nrecorder** *m* cassette recorder.
kassieren [ka'siːrən] *v* (*Geld*) receive; (*Scheck*) cash; (*Urteil*) annul, reverse; (*Mil*) cashier, dismiss. **Kassierer** *m* cashier.
Kastanie [ka'staːniə] *f (pl* -n) chestnut. **kastanienbraun** *adj* chestnut, auburn.
Kasten ['kastən] *m (pl* **Kästen**) box, chest; (*Schrank*) cupboard.
kastrieren [ka'striːrən] castrate.
Kasus ['kaːzus] *m (pl* -n) (*Gramm*) case.
Katalog [kata'loːg] *m (pl* -e) catalogue.
Katarakt¹ [kata'rakt] *m (pl* -e) rapids, waterfall.
Katarakt² *f (pl* -e) (*Med*) cataract.
Katarrh [ka'tar] *m (pl* -e) catarrh.
katastrophal [katastro'faːl] *adj* catastrophic. **Katastrophe** *f (pl* -n) catastrophe.
Kategorie [katego'riː] *f (pl* -n) category. **kategorisch** *adj* categorical.
Kater ['kaːtər] *m (pl* -) tom cat; (*Katzenjammer*) hangover.
Kathedrale [kate'draːlə] *f (pl* -n) cathedral.
Katholik(in) [kato'liːk(in)] Catholic. **katholisch** *adj* Catholic. **Katholizismus** *m* Catholicism.
Kätzchen ['kɛtsçən] *neut* kitten.
Katze ['katsə] *f (pl* -n) cat. **katzenartig** *adj* feline, cat-like. **Katzen‖auge** *neut* (*Rückstrahler*) rear reflector. –**jammer** *m* hangover.
Kauderwelsch ['kaudərvɛlʃ] *neut* gibberish.
kauen ['kauən] *v* chew.
kauern ['kauərn] *v* cower.
Kauf [kauf] *m (pl* **Käufe**) purchase. **einen guten Kauf machen** make a good buy, get a bargain. **kaufen** *v* buy, purchase.
Käufer ['kɔyfər] *m (pl* -) buyer.
Kauf‖haus *neut* department store. –**kraft** *f* purchasing power.
käuflich ['kɔyfliç] *adj* saleable, purchasable; (*bestechlich*) corrupt, venal.
Kaufmann *m* businessman; (*Kleinhandel*) shopkeeper; (*Großhandel*) merchant. **kaufmännisch** *adj* commercial, mercantile. **Kaufpreis** *m* purchase price.
kaum [kaum] *adv* hardly, scarcely.
Kaution [kau'tsioːn] *f (pl* -en) security, deposit. **gegen Kaution freilassen** release on bail.

Kauz [kauts] *m (pl* **Käuze**) screech owl; (*fig*) odd fellow.
Kavaller‖ie [kavalə'riː] *f (pl* -n) cavalry. –**ist** *m* cavalryman.
Kaviar ['kaviar] *m (pl* -e) caviar.
keck [kɛk] *adj* pert, cheeky.
Kegel ['keːgəl] *m (pl* -) cone; (*Spiel*) skittle. –**bahn** *f* bowling alley. **kegel‖förmig** *adj* conical. –**n** *v* play skittles, go bowling. **Kegelspiel** *neut* skittles, bowling.
Kehle ['keːlə] *f (pl* -n) throat. **Kehlkopf** *m* larynx. –**entzündung** *f* laryngitis.
kehren¹ [keːrən] *v* sweep, brush.
kehren² *v* turn. **sich kehren** turn (round). **sich kehren an** pay attention to.
Kehricht ['keːriçt] *m (unz.)* sweepings *pl*.
Kehr‖reim *m* refrain. –**seite** *f* reverse, other side.
Keil [kail] *m (pl* -e) wedge; (*Arch*) keystone. **keilen** *v* wedge; (*werben*) win over. **sich keilen** scuffle.
Keiler ['kailər] *m (pl* -) (wild) boar.
Keilriemen ['kailriːmən] *m* (*Mot*) fanbelt.
Keim [kaim] *m (pl* -e) germ; (*Bot*) bud; embryo; (*Anfang*) origin. **keimen** *v* germinate; bud. **Keim‖träger** *m* carrier. –**ung** *f* germination.
kein [kain] **keine, kein** *pron*, *m, f* no one, nobody; *neut* nothing, none. *adj* no, not any. **kein anderer als** none other than. **keine Ahnung!** (I've) no idea! **keiner von beiden** neither (of the two). **keinerlei** *adj* of no sort. **keines‖falls** *adv* on no account. –**wegs** *adv* not at all.
Keks [keiks] *m (pl* -e) biscuit.
Keller ['kɛlər] *m (pl* -) cellar. –**ei** *f* wine cellar. –**geschoß** *neut* basement.
Kellner ['kɛlnər] *m (pl* -) waiter. –**in** *f* waitress.
****kennen** ['kɛnən] *v* know. –**lernen** *v* get to know, become acquainted with. **Kenner** *m* (*Wein, Kunst*) connoisseur; (*Fachmann*) expert. **kenntlich** *adj* distinguishable, distinct. **Kenntnis** *f* knowledge. **kenntnisreich** *adj* experienced. **Kennwort** *neut* password. **kennzeichnen** *v* (*fig*) characterize, distinguish. –**d** *adj* characteristic. **Kennziffer** *f* reference *or* code number; (*Math*) index.
kentern ['kɛntərn] *v* capsize.
Kerbe ['kɛrbə] *f (pl* -n) notch.
Kerker ['kɛrkər] *m (pl* -) dungeon.

Kerl [kɛrl] *m* (*pl* -e) fellow.
Kern [kɛrn] *m* (*pl* -e) kernel; (*Obst*) stone, pit; (*Atom*) nucleus; (*fig*) core, essence. **kerngesund** *adj* thoroughly healthy. **Kern‖haus** *neut* core. **–reaktion** *f* nuclear reaction. **–waffe** *f* nuclear weapon. **–kraftwerk** *neut* nuclear power station.
Kerze ['kɛrtsə] *f* (*pl* -n) candle. **Kerzen‖leuchter** *neut* candlestick. **–licht** *neut* candlelight.
Kessel ['kɛsəl] *m* (*pl* -) kettle; (*Tech*) boiler; (*Geog*) depression, hollow.
Kette ['kɛtə] *f* (*pl* -n) chain. **ketten** *v* chain, link. **Ketten‖gebirge** *neut* mountain range. **–geschäft** *neut* chain store. **–raucher** *m* chain smoker. **–reaktion** *f* chain reaction.
Ketzer ['kɛtsər] *m* (*pl* -) heretic. **–ei** *f* (*pl* -en) heresy. **ketzerisch** *adj* heretical.
keuchen ['kɔyçən] *v* gasp, pant. **Keuchhusten** *m* whooping cough.
Keule ['kɔylə] *f* (*pl* -n) club, bludgeon; (*Fleisch*) leg.
keusch [kɔyʃ] *adj* chaste, modest. **Keuschheit** *f* chastity.
kichern ['kiçərn] *v* giggle.
Kiefer¹ ['kiːfər] *m* (*pl* -) (*Anat*) jaw.
Kiefer² *f* (*pl* -n) (*Bot*) pine.
Kieferknochen ['kiːfərknɔxən] *m* jawbone.
Kiefern‖holz *neut* pinewood. **–wald** *m* pine forest.
Kiel [kiːl] *m* (*pl* -e) keel.
Kieme [kiːmə] *f* (*pl* -n) gill.
Kies [kiːs] *m* (*pl* -e) gravel. **Kiesel** *m* (*pl* -) pebble, flint. **–stein** *m* pebble. **Kiesgrube** *f* gravelpit.
Kilo ['kiːlo] *neut* (*pl* -) kilo, kilogram(me). **–gramm** *neut* (*pl* -) kilogram(me). **Kilometer** *neut* kilometre. **–zähler** *m* milometer, odometer.
Kind [kint] *neut* (*pl* -er) child. **ein Kind bekommen/erwarten** have/expect a baby.
Kinder‖arzt *m* paediatrician. **–bett** *neut* cot, crib. **–buch** *neut* children's book. **–heilkunde** *f* paediatrics. **–jahre** *pl* childhood *sing*. **–lähmung** *f* polio. **–spiel** *neut* children's game; (*fig*) child's play. **–wagen** *m* pram, (*US*) baby carriage.
Kindheit *f* childhood. **kindisch** *adj* childish. **kindlich** *adj* childlike.
Kinn [kin] *neut* (*pl* -e) chin.
Kino ['kiːno] *neut* (*pl* -s) cinema.

Kiosk ['kiːɔsk] *m* (*pl* -e) kiosk.
kippen ['kipən] *v* tip, tilt. **Kippwagen** *m* tipper, tip cart.
Kirche ['kirçə] *f* (*pl* -n) church. **Kirchen‖gemeinde** *f* parish. **–lied** *neut* hymn. **–schändung** *f* desecration, profanation. **Kirch‖gänger** *m* church-goer. **–hof** *m* churchyard. **kirchlich** *adj* ecclesiastical, church.
Kirsch [kirʃ] *m* kirsch, cherry brandy. **–e** *f* (*pl* -n) cherry.
Kissen ['kisən] *neut* (*pl* -) cushion; (*Kopf-*) pillow; (*pl*) bedding.
Kiste ['kistə] *f* (*pl* -n) chest, case, box.
Kitsch [kitʃ] *m* (tasteless) trash, kitsch. **kitschig** *adj* trashy.
Kittel ['kitəl] *m* (*pl* -) smock.
Kitzel ['kitsəl] *m* (*pl* -) tickle. **kitzeln** *v* tickle. **kitzlig** *adj* ticklish.
klaffen ['klafən] *v* gape, yawn. **–d** *adj* gaping.
Klage ['klaːgə] *f* (*pl* -n) complaint, grievance; (*Jur*) action, lawsuit. **klagen** *v* complain, (*Jur*) bring an action. **Klagende(r)** plaintiff.
kläglich ['klɛːkliç] *adj* miserable, pitiful.
Klammer ['klamər] *f* (*pl* -n) clamp; (*kleine*) clip; (*Wäsche*) peg. **klammern** *v* clamp; (*befestigen*) fasten. **sich klammern an** cling to.
Klamotten [kla'mɔtən] *pl* (*umg.*) gear *sing*, clothes *pl*.
Klang [klaŋ] *m* (*pl* Klänge) sound.
klapp‖en ['klapən] flap, clap; (*umg.*) work out, be all right. **–bar** *adj* collapsible, folding. **Klappe** *f* flap; (*umg.*) mouth, trap. **halt die Klappe!** (*vulgär*) shut up!
Klapper ['klapər] *f* (*pl* -n) rattle. **klapperig** *adj* clattering, rattling. **klappern** *v* rattle, clatter.
Klapp‖messer *neut* jack-knife. **–stuhl** *m* folding chair. **–tür** *f* trapdoor.
klar [klaːr] *adj* clear.
klären ['klɛːrən] *v* clarify.
Klarheit ['klaːrhait] *f* clarity, clearness.
Klarinette [klari'nɛtə] *f* (*pl* -n) clarinet. **Klarinettist** *m* clarinettist.
klarlegen ['klaːrleːgən] *v* clear up.
Klärung ['klɛːruŋ] *f* clarification.
klarwerden ['klaːrveːrdən] *v* become clear.
klasse ['klasə] *adj* (*umg.*) marvellous, splendid. **Klasse** *f* class. **ein Musiker von Klasse** an excellent musician. **ein Restaurant erster Klasse** a first-class restaurant.

klassenbewußt *adj* class-conscious. **Klassenzimmer** *neut* classroom.
Klassik ['klasik] *f* classical era; (*Literatur, Musik*) classicism. **–er** *m* classicist. **klassisch** *adj* classical.
Klatsch [klatʃ] *m* (*pl* **-e**) slap, smack; (*Gerede*) gossip, chatter. **–base** *f* gossip, chatterbox. **klatschen** *v* clap; (*reden*) gossip, chatter.
Klaue ['klauə] *f* (*pl* **-n**) claw; (*Raubvogel*) talon. **klauen** *v* (*umg.*) steal, pinch.
Klausel ['klauzəl] *f* (*pl* **-n**) clause.
Klavier [klaviːr] *neut* (*pl* **-e**) piano. **–spieler(in)** pianist.
Klebeband ['kleɪbəbant] *neut* (adhesive) tape. **kleben** *v* glue, paste; (*anhaften*) stick. **klebrig** *adj* sticky. **Klebstoff** *m* glue.
Klecks [klɛks] *m* (*pl* **-e**) blot, spot.
Klee [kleɪ] *m* clover. **–blatt** *neut* cloverleaf.
Kleid [klait] *neut* (*pl* **-er**) garment; (*Frau*) dress; (*pl*) clothes. **kleiden** *v* clothe. **Kleider‖bügel** *m* coat-hanger. **–bürste** *f* clothes brush. **–schrank** *m* wardrobe. **Kleidung** *f* clothing, clothes. **–sstück** *neut* article of clothing, garment.
klein [klain] *adj* small, little. **der kleine Mann** the ordinary man. **klein stellen** turn down, put on low. **im kleinen** in miniature; (*Komm*) retail.
Klein‖anzeige *f* classified advertisement. **–asien** *neut* Asia Minor. **–bürger** *m* petty bourgeois. **–geld** *neut* (small) change. **–handel** *m* retail trade. **Kleinigkeit** *f* (*pl* **-en**) trifle, trivial matter. **Klein‖kind** *neut* infant. **–lebewesen** *neut* microorganism. **klein‖lich** *adj* petty. **–mütig** *adj* fainthearted, cowardly.
Kleinod ['klainoːt] *neut* (*pl* **-ien**) jewel, gem.
Kleister ['klaistər] *m* (*pl* **-**) paste, gum.
Klemme ['klɛmə] *f* (*pl* **-n**) clamp; (*Haar*) grip; (*Klammer*) clip. **in der Klemme sitzen** be in a dilemma *or* tight corner. **klemmen** *v* squeeze, pinch.
Klempner ['klɛmpnər] *m* (*pl* **-**) plumber; (*Metall*) metalworker. **–ei** *f* plumbing. **klempnern** *v* do plumbing.
Kleriker ['kleːrikər] *m* (*pl* **-**) cleric, clergyman. **Klerus** *m* (*unz.*) clergy.
Kletterer ['klɛtərər] *m* (*pl* **-**) climber. **klettern** *v* climb. **Kletterpflanze** *f* climbing plant, creeper.
Klima ['kliːma] *f* (*pl* **-te**) climate. **–anlage**

f air-conditioning (equipment). **klimatisch** *adj* climatic.
Klinge ['kliŋə] *f* (*pl* **-n**) blade.
Klingel ['kliŋəl] *f* (*pl* **-n**) (door)bell. **klingeln** *v* ring the bell, ring.
klingen ['kliŋən] *v* sound; ring.
Klinik ['kliːnik] *f* (*pl* **-en**) clinic, hospital. **klinisch** *adj* clinical.
Klinke ['kliŋkə] *f* (*pl* **-n**) doorhandle, latch.
Klippe ['klipə] *f* (*pl* **-n**) cliff; (*im Meer*) rocks *pl*, reef.
klirren ['kliːrən] *v* tinkle, jangle.
Klischee [kli'ʃeɪ] *neut* (*pl* **-s**) (*fig*) cliché.
Klo [kloː] *neut* (*pl* **-s**) (*umg.*) toilet, loo.
Kloake [klo'aːkə] *f* (*pl* **-n**) sewer.
klopfen ['klɔpfən] *v* (*Tür*) knock; (*Herz*) beat; (*Schulter*) tap, pat. **Klopfen** *neut* knocking; beating.
Klosett [klo'zɛt] *neut* (*pl* **-s**) toilet. **–papier** *neut* toilet paper.
Kloß [kloːs] *m* (*pl* **Klöße**) dumpling; (*Fleisch*) meatball.
Kloster ['kloːstər] *neut* (*pl* **Klöster**) monastery, abbey, convent. **–gang** *m* cloister.
Klotz [klɔts] *m* (*pl* **Klötze**) block, log.
Klub [klup] *m* (*pl* **-s**) club, association.
Kluft [kluft] *m* (*pl* **Klüfte**) cleft; (*Abgrund*) chasm, abyss; (*fig*) rift.
klug [kluːk] *adj* clever; (*Ansicht, Rat*) sensible, prudent. **Klugheit** *f* cleverness, intelligence.
Klumpen ['klumpən] *m* (*pl* **-**) lump; (*Gold*) nugget.
knabbern ['knabərn] *v* nibble.
Knabe ['knaːbə] *m* (*pl* **-n**) boy. **–nalter** *neut* boyhood, youth. **knabenhaft** *adj* boyish.
Knäckebrot ['knɛkəbroːt] *neut* crispbread.
knacken ['knakən] *v* crack.
Knall [knal] *m* (*pl* **-e**) bang; explosion. **–bonbon** *m* cracker. **knallen** *v* crack, bang; explode. **Knallfrosch** *m* banger, jumping jack.
knapp [knap] *adj* scant, insufficient; (*Kleidung*) tight. **knapp sein** be in short supply. **knapp werden** be running short *or* out. **knapp bei Kasse sein** be hard up. *knapp drei Meter* just under (*or* barely) three metres.
knarren ['knarən] *v* creak.
knattern ['knatərn] *v* crackle, rattle.
Knebel ['kneɪbəl] *m* (*pl* **-**) gag. **knebeln** *v* gag.

Knecht [knɛçt] *m* (*pl* -e) (farm) worker; (*Diener*) servant.
***kneifen** ['knaifən] *v* pinch, nip.
Kneifzange *f* pincers.
Kneipe ['knaipə] *f* (*pl* -n) pub, bar.
kneipen *v* go boozing.
kneten ['kneɪtən] *v* knead; (*Körper*) massage.
Knick ['knik] *m* (*pl* -e) crack; (*Kniff*) crease; (*Kurve*) sharp bend. **knicken** *v* break, crack; fold, crease.
Knicks [kniks] *m* (*pl* -e) curtsey.
Knie [kniɪ] *neut* (*pl* -) knee. **knien** *v* kneel. **-d** *adj* kneeling, on one's knees. **Kniescheibe** *f* kneecap.
Kniff [knif] *m* (*pl* -e) pinch; (*Falte*) crease; trick. **den Kniff heraushaben** get the hang of it.
knipsen ['knipsən] *v* punch, clip; (*Foto*) snap.
knirschen ['knirʃən] *v* gnash.
Knitter ['knitər] *m* (*pl* -) crease. **knitter||frei** *adj* crease-resistant. **-n** *v* crease.
Knoblauch ['knoɪplaux] *m* garlic.
Knöchel ['knœçəl] *m* (*pl* -) (*Finger*) knuckle; (*Bein*) ankle.
Knochen ['knɔxən] *m* (*pl* -) bone. **-bruch** *m* fracture. **-gerüst** *neut* skeleton. **-mark** *neut* (bone) marrow. **knochig** *adj* bony.
Knödel ['knœɪdəl] *m* (*pl* -) dumpling.
Knolle ['knɔlə] *f* (*pl* -n) tuber; (*Zwiebel, Tulpe*) bulb.
Knopf [knɔpf] *m* (*pl* Knöpfe) button.
knöpfen ['knœpfən] *v* button.
Knorpel ['knɔrpəl] *m* (*pl* -) cartilage; (*bei gekochtem Fleisch*) gristle.
Knospe ['knɔspə] *f* (*pl* -n) bud. **knospen** *v* bud.
Knoten ['knoɪtən] *m* (*pl* -) knot; (*Tech*) node. **knoten** *v* knot. **Knotenpunkt** *m* junction.
knüpfen ['knypfən] *v* join, tie.
knusprig ['knuspriç] *adj* crisp.
Koalition [koali'tsioɪn] *f* (*pl* -en) coalition.
Kobold ['koɪbɔlt] *m* (*pl* -e) goblin.
Koch [kɔx] *m* (*pl* Köche) cook. **-buch** *neut* cookery book. **kochen** *v* cook; (*sieden*) boil. **-d** boiling. **Kocher** *m* cooker. **Kochherd** *m* kitchen range.
Köchin ['kœçin] *f* (*pl* -nen) (female) cook.
Koch||platte *f* hotplate, ring. **-topf** *m* saucepan, pot.
Köder ['kœɪdər] *m* (*pl* -) bait. **ködern** *v* lure, entice.

Koexistenz [koɛksi'stɛnts] *f* coexistence. **koexistieren** *v* coexist.
Koffer ['kɔfər] *m* (*pl* -) suitcase; (*Schrankkoffer*) trunk. **-kuli** *m* (luggage) trolley. **-raum** *m* (*Mot*) trunk.
Kohl [koɪl] *m* (*pl* -e) cabbage.
Kohle ['koɪlə] *f* (*pl* -n) coal; (*Holzkohle*) charcoal. **Kohlen||bergwerk** *neut* coal mine, pit. **-säure** *f* carbonic acid; (*in Getränken*) carbon dioxide. **-hydrat** *neut* carbohydrate. **-stoff** *m* carbon. **Kohle||papier** *neut* carbon paper. **-stift** *m* charcoal crayon.
Kohl||rabi [koɪl'rabi] *m* (*pl* -s) kohlrabi. **-rübe** *f* swede.
Koje ['koɪjə] *f* (*pl* -n) bunk, berth; (*Zimmer*) cabin.
kokett [ko'kɛt] *adj* coquettish. **-ieren** *v* flirt.
Kokosnuß ['koɪkɔsnus] *f* coconut.
Koks ['koɪks] *m* (*pl* -e) coke.
Kolben ['kɔlbən] *m* (*pl* -) club; (*Gewehr*) butt; (*Zylinder*) piston.
Kollege [kɔ'leɪgə] *m* (*pl* -n) **Kollegin** *f* (*pl* -nen) colleague.
kollektiv [kɔlɛk'tiɪf] *adj* collective.
Köln [kœln] *neut* Cologne. **-ischwasser** *neut* eau de Cologne.
Kolon ['koɪlɔn] *neut* (*pl* -s) colon.
kolonial [kɔloˈniaɪl] *adj* colonial. **Kolonialwaren** *pl* groceries. **-händler** *m* grocer.
Kolonne [kɔ'lɔnə] *f* (*pl* -n) column.
Kombi ['kɔmbi] *m* (*pl* -s) estate car.
Kombination [kɔmbina'tsioɪn] *f* (*pl* -en) combination; (*Sport*) teamwork; (*Unterkleidung*) combinations *pl*; (*Schützkleidung*) one-piece suit; (*Ideen*) conjecture. **kombinieren** *v* combine.
Komet [ko'meɪt] *m* (*pl* -en) comet.
Komfort [kɔm'foɪr] *m* (*unz.*) comfort. **komfortabel** *adj* comfortable.
Komiker ['koɪmikər] *m* (*pl* -) comedian, comic. **komisch** *adj* funny; (*seltsam*) strange.
Komitee [kɔmi'teɪ] *neut* (*pl* -s) committee.
Komma ['kɔma] *neut* (*pl* -s) comma.
Kommandant [kɔman'dant] *m* (*pl* -en) commander. **kommandieren** *v* command.
Kommanditgesellschaft (**KG**) [kɔman'diɪtgəzɛlʃaft (ka'geɪt)] *f* limited-liability company.
Kommando [kɔ'mandɔt] *neut* (*pl* -s) order, command; (*Abteilung*) squad, detachment, detail. **-truppe** *f* commando (unit).

*kommen ['kɔmən] *v* come. **kommen lassen** send for. **um etwas kommen** lose something. **hinter etwas kommen** get to the bottom of something. **Kommen** *neut* arrival, coming. **kommend** *adj* coming.
Kommentar [kɔmɛn'taɪr] *m* (*pl* -e) commentary. **kommentieren** *v* comment on.
Kommerz [kɔ'mɛrts] *m* commerce. **komerziell** *adj* commercial.
Kommisar [kɔmi'saɪr] *m* (*pl* -e) commissioner; (*Polizei*) inspector. **Kommission** *f* commission.
kommun [kɔ'muɪn] *adj* common. **-al** *adj* municipal. **Kommune** *f* (*pl* -n) commune; (*Gemeinde*) municipality.
Kommunikation [komunika'tsioɪn] *f* (*pl* -en) communication.
Kommuniqué [kɔmyni'keɪ] *neut* (*pl* -s) communiqué.
Kommunismus [kɔmu'nizmus] *m* communism. **Kommunist(in)** (*i*) communist. **kommunistisch** *adj* communist.
Komödie [kɔ'mœɪdiə] *f* (*pl* -n) comedy; (*Ereignis*) farce.
Kompaß ['kɔmpas] *m* (*pl* **Kompasse**) compass. **-strich** *m*: point of the compass.
kompetent [kɔmpe'tɛnt] *adj* competent.
Komplex [kɔm'plɛks] *m* (*pl* -e) complex.
Kompliment [kɔmpli'mɛnt] *neut* (*pl* -e) compliment.
komplizieren [kɔmpli'tsiɪrən] *v* complicate. **kompliziert** *adj* complicated, complex.
Komplott [kɔm'plɔt] *neut* (*pl* --e) plot, conspiracy.
komponieren [kɔmpo'niɪrən] *v* compose. **Komponist** *m* (*pl* -en) composer.
Kompott [kɔm'pɔt] *neut* (*pl* -e) stewed fruit, compote.
Kompresse [kɔm'prɛsə] *f* (*pl* -n) compress.
Kompromiß [kɔmpro'mis] *m* (*pl* **Kompromisse**) compromise. **kompromittieren** *v* compromise.
kondensieren [kɔndɛn'siɪrən] *v* condense. **Kondensmilch** *f* condensed milk.
Konditorei [kɔndito'raɪ] (*pl* -en) patisserie, cake shop. **-waren** *pl* pastries, cakes.
Kondom [kɔn'doɪm] *m* (*pl* -e) condom.
Konferenz [kɔnfe'rɛnts] *f* (*pl* -en) conference.
Konfession [kɔnfe'sioɪn] *f* (*pl* -en) confession, creed, faith.
Konflikt [kɔn'flikt] *m* (*pl* -e) conflict.

konform [kɔn'fɔrm] *adj* in agreement, in accordance.
Konfrontation [kɔnfrɔnta'tsioɪn] *f* (*pl* -en) confrontation. **konfrontieren** *v* confront.
konfus [kɔn'fuɪs] *adj* confused, muddled. **Konfusion** *f* confusion.
Kongreß [kɔŋ'grɛs] *m* (*pl* **Kongresse**) congress.
König ['kœɪniç] *m* (*pl* -e) king. **-in** *f* (*pl* -nen) queen. **-inmutter** *m* queen mother. **königlich** *adj* royal, regal. **Königreich** *neut* kingdom, realm.
Konjunktur [kɔnjuŋk'tuɪr] *f* (*pl* -en) (state of the) economy, economic trends *pl*; (*Aufschwung*) boom.
Konkurrent [kɔnku'rɛnt] *m* (*pl* -en) competitor. **Konkurrenz** *f* (*unz*.) competition. **konkurrenzfähig** *adj* competitive. **konkurrieren** *v* compete.
Konkurs [kɔn'kurs] *m* (*pl* -e) bankruptcy, insolvency. **in Konkurs gehen** become bankrupt.
*können ['kœnən] *v* can, be able (to); (*dürfen*) may, be allowed (to); (*gelernt haben*) know. **tun können** know how to do. **eine Sprache können** speak a language. *Ich kann nicht mehr!* I can't go on. **das kann sein** it may be so. *er kann nichts dafür* it's not his fault, he can't help it. **Können** *neut* ability.
konsequent [kɔnze'kvɛnt] *adj* consistent. **Konsequenz** *f* consistency; (*Folge*) consequence. **die Konsequenzen tragen** bear the consequences. **Konsequenzen ziehen** draw conclusions.
konservativ [kɔnzɛrva'tiːf] *adj* conservative. **Konservative(r)** conservative.
Konserve [kɔn'zɛrvə] *f* (*pl* -n) preserve, tinned *or* bottled food. **Konservenbüchse** *f* tin (of preserves). **konservieren** *v* preserve.
konsolidieren [kɔnzɔli'diɪrən] *v* consolidate.
Konsonant [kɔnzo'nant] *m* (*pl* -en) consonant.
konstant [kɔn'stant] *adj* constant.
konstruieren [kɔnstru'iɪrən] *v* construct. **Konstruktion** *f* (*pl* -en) construction; (*Entwurf*) design.
Konsul [kɔn'zuːl] *m* (*pl* -n) consul. **-at** *neut* (*pl* -e) consulate.
Konsum [kɔn'zuɪm] *m* consumption. **-gesellschaft** *f* consumer society. **konsumieren** *v* consume. **Konsumverein** *m* co-operative society.

Kontakt [kɔn'takt] *m* (*pl* -e) contact.
Kontinent [kɔnti'nɛnt] *m* (*pl* -e) continent.
Konto ['kɔnto] *neut* (*pl* **Konten**) account. **–auszug** *m* (bank) statement. **–buch** *neut* passbook. **–inhaber** *m* accountholder.
Kontrabaß ['kɔntrabas] *m* double bass.
konträr [kɔn'trɛː] *adj* adverse.
Kontrast [kɔn'trast] *m* (*pl* -e) contrast. **kontrastieren** *v* contrast.
Kontrolle [kɔn'trɔlə] *f* (*pl* -n) control, supervision. **–abschnitt** *m* counterfoil. **–eur** *m* controller. **kontrollieren** *v* control, supervise. **Kontrollpunkt** *m* checkpoint. **unter Kontrolle** under control.
konventionell [kɔnvɛntsio'nɛl] *adj* conventional.
Konversation [kɔnvɛrza'tsioːn] *f* (*pl* -en) conversation. **–slexikon** *neut* encyclopedia.
konvertieren [kɔnvɛr'tiːrən] *v* convert.
konvex [kɔn'vɛks] *adj* convex.
Konzentrat [kɔntsən'traːt] *neut* (*pl* -e) concentrate. **–ion** *f* (*pl* -en) concentration. **–ionslager** *neut* concentration camp. **konzentrieren** *v* concentrate.
Konzept [kɔn'tsɛpt] *neut* (*pl* -e) rough draft.
Konzert [kɔn'tsɛrt] *neut* (*pl* -e) concert; (*Stück*) concerto.
Kopf [kɔpf] *m* (*pl* **Köpfe**) head. **auf den Kopf stellen** turn upside down. **pro Kopf** per capita, each. **im Kopf haben** be preoccupied with. **–ball** *m* (*Sport*) header.
köpfen ['kœpfən] *v* behead, decapitate.
Kopf‖haut *f* scalp. **–hörer** *m* headphone. **–kissen** *neut* pillow. **–putz** *m* headdress. **–salat** *m* lettuce. **–schmerzen** *pl* headache *sing*. **–sprung** *m* header. **–stand** *m* headstand. **kopfüber** *adv* headlong, head first.
Kopie [ko'piː] *f* (*pl* -n) copy. **kopieren** *v* copy.
Kopulation [kɔpula'tsioːn] *f* (*pl* -en) copulation. **kopulieren** *v* copulate; (*Bäume*) graft.
Koralle [ko'ralə] *f* (*pl* -n) coral. **–nriff** *neut* coral reef.
Korb [kɔrp] *m* (*pl* **Körbe**) basket. **–ball** *m* basketball. **–geflecht** *neut* basketwork.
Kord [kɔrt] *or* **Kordsamt** *m* cord(uroy). **Kordhose** *f* corduroy trousers; (*umg.*) cords.

Korinthe [ko'rintə] *f* (*pl* -n) currant.
Kork [kɔrk] *m* (*pl* -e) cork. **–enzieher** *m* corkscrew.
Korn [kɔrn] *neut* (*pl* **Körner**) grain, corn.
Körnchen ['kœrnçən] *neut* (*pl* -) granule.
Koronarthrombose [kɔro'naɪrtrɔmbɔɪzə] *f* (*pl* -n) coronary thrombosis.
Körper [kœrpər] *m* (*pl* -) body. **–bau** *m* physique, build. **körperbehindert** *adj* physically handicapped. **Körper‖bildung** *f* body-building. **–geruch** *m* body odour. **–gewicht** *neut* weight. **–haltung** *f* posture.
körperlich ['kœrpərliç] *adj* bodily, physical; (*Strafe*) corporal.
Körper‖maß *neut* cubic measure. **–pflege** *f* hygiene. **–schaft** *f* (*pl* -en) corporation.
Korporal [kɔrpo'raːl] *m* (*pl* -e) corporal.
korrekt [ko'rɛkt] *adj* correct. **Korrektur** *f* (*pl* -en) correction; (*Druck*) proof.
Korrespondent [kɔrɛspɔn'dɛnt] *m* (*pl* -en) correspondent. **Korrespondenz** *f* correspondence.
korrigieren [kɔri'giːrən] *v* correct; (*gedrucktes*) proofread.
Kosename ['koɪzənaːmə] *m* pet name.
Kosmetik [kɔz'mɛɪtik] *f* (*unz.*) cosmetics *pl*. **kosmetisch** *adj* cosmetic.
Kosmos ['kɔsmɔs] *m* (*pl* **Kosmen**) cosmos, universe. **kosmisch** *adj* cosmic.
Kost [kɔst] *f* (*unz.*) food, fare. **Kost und Wohnung** board and lodging. **kräftige Kost** rich diet.
kostbar ['kɔstbaɪr] *adj* expensive; (*sehr wertvoll*) precious.
kosten[1] ['kɔstən] *v* (*probieren*) taste, try, sample.
kosten[2] *v* cost. **Kosten** *pl* costs. **auf meine Kosten** at my expense. **kostenlos** *adj* free (of charge).
köstlich ['kœstliç] *adj* delicious; (*reizend*) charming; (*wertvoll*) precious.
kostspielig ['kɔstʃpiːliç] *adj* expensive.
Kostüm [kɔs'tyɪm] *neut* (*pl* -e) costume; (*Damen-*) suit. **–ball** *m* fancy-dress ball. **–probe** *f* dress rehearsal.
Kot [koɪt] *m* dung, droppings *pl*; (*Schmutz*) dirt, mud.
Kotelett [kɔtə'lɛt] *neut* (*pl* -e) chop, cutlet. **–en** *pl* sideburns, mutton-chop whiskers.
Kotflügel ['koɪtflyːgəl] *m* mudguard, fender.

kotzen ['kɔtsən] v (*vulgär*) puke, be sick. **zum Kotzen** enough to make you sick.
Krabbe ['krabə] f (*pl* -n) shrimp.
krabbeln ['krabəln] v scuttle, scurry.
Krach [krax] m (*pl* -e) noise; (*Streit*) quarrel, row; (*Knall*) crash.
krächzen ['krɛçtsən] v croak.
kraft [kraft] *prep* on the strength of, by virtue of. **Kraft** f (*pl* **Kräfte**) strength; (*Macht*) power. –**fahrer** m driver. –**fahrzeug** *neut* motor vehicle.
kräftig ['krɛftiç] *adj* strong; (*mächtig*) powerful; (*Essen*) substantial. –**en** v strengthen. –**end** *adj* invigorating.
kraftlos *adj* powerless. **Kraft||probe** f trial of strength. –**rad** *neut* motorcycle. –**stoff** m fuel. –**wagen** m motor vehicle. –**werk** *neut* power station.
Kragen ['kraɪgən] m (*pl* -) collar.
Krähe ['krɛɪə] f (*pl* -n) crow. **krähen** v crow.
Kralle ['kralə] f (*pl* -n) claw. **krallen** v claw. **sich krallen an** clutch.
Kram [kraɪm] m stuff, trash; (*umg.*) things, stuff.
Krampf [krampf] m (*pl* **Krämpfe**) cramp, spasm. **krampfhaft** *adj* convulsive; (*heftig*) frenzied, frantic.
Kran [kraɪn] m (*pl* **Kräne**) (*Mech*) crane.
Kranich ['kraɪniç] m (*pl* -e) (*Zool*) crane.
krank [kraŋk] *adj* sick, ill, unwell. **Kranke(r)** patient.
kränken ['krɛŋkən] v vex, annoy.
Kranken||haus *neut* hospital. –**kasse** f health insurance (company). –**schein** m medical certificate. –**schwester** f nurse. –**versicherung** f health insurance. –**wagen** m ambulance. **krankhaft** *adj* diseased, unhealthy. **Krankheit** f (*pl* -en) disease, illness.
Kranz [krants] m (*pl* **Kränze**) wreath, garland.
Krapfen ['krapfən] m (*pl* -) fritter; doughnut.
kraß [kras] *adj* crass, gross.
kratzen ['kratsən] v scratch. **Kratzwunde** f scratch.
kraulen ['kraulən] *or* **kraulschwimmen** v swim the crawl. **Kraulstil** m crawl.
kraus [kraus] *adj* curly, crinkled.
Kraut [kraut] *neut* (*pl* **Kräuter**) herb; (*Kohl*) cabbage; (*grüne Pflanzen*) vegetation.
Kräuter||buch ['krɔytərbuːx] *neut* herbal. –**tee** m herb tea.

Krawall [kra'val] m (*pl* -e) brawl.
Krawatte [kra'vatə] f (*pl* -n) (neck)tie.
Krebs [kreːps] m (*pl* -e) crab; (*Med*) cancer; (*Astrol*) Cancer.
Kredit [kre'diːt] m (*pl* -e) (*Komm*) credit. –**brief** m letter of credit. **kreditieren** v credit.
Kreide ['kraɪdə] f (*pl* -n) chalk. –**fels** m chalk cliff.
Kreis ['krais] m (*pl* -e) circle; (*Gebiet*) district, area. –**bahn** f orbit. –**bewegung** f rotation, revolution. –**bogen** m arc (of a circle).
kreischen ['kraiʃən] v screech, shriek.
Kreisel ['kraizəl] m (*pl* -) (spinning) top. **kreiseln** v spin (like a top).
kreis||en v revolve, rotate. –**förmig** *adj* circular. **Kreis||lauf** m circulation. –**säge** f circular saw. –**umfang** m circumference.
Krem [kreɪm] f (*pl* -s) cream.
Krematorium [krema'toɪrium] *neut* (*pl* **Krematorien**) crematorium.
Kreml ['krɛməl] m Kremlin.
Krempel ['krɛmpəl] m junk, rubbish.
krepieren [kre'piːrən] v burst; (*umg.*) die.
Kresse ['krɛsə] f (*pl* -n) cress.
Kreuz [krɔyts] *neut* (*pl* -e) cross; (*Karten*) club(s); (*Anat*) small of the back. **kreuz und quer** in all directions. **kreuzen** v cross; (*Schiff*) cruise. **sich kreuzen** intersect. **Kreuzer** m (*pl* -) cruiser. **Kreuz||fahrer** m crusader. –**fahrt** f (*Schiff*) cruise; (*Kreuzzug*) crusade.
kreuzigen ['krɔytsigən] v crucify. **Kreuzigung** f (*pl* -en) crucifixion.
Kreuzung ['krɔytsun] f (*pl* -en) crossing.
Kreuz||verhör *neut* cross-examination. –**verweis** m cross-reference. –**weg** m crossroads. –**worträtsel** *neut* crossword puzzle. –**zug** m crusade.
*****kriechen** ['kriːçən] v creep, crawl; (*fig*) cringe, grovel. **kriecherisch** *adj* cringing, servile.
Krieg [kriːk] m (*pl* -e) war. **den Krieg erklären/führen** declare/wage war. **Krieger** m (*pl* -) warrior. **kriegführend** *adj* belligerent. **Kriegs||dienstverweigerer** m conscientious objector. –**gefangene(r)** prisoner of war. –**gericht** *neut* courtmartial. –**hetzer** m warmonger. –**verbrecher** m war criminal. –**zeit** f wartime.
Krimi ['krimi] *neut* (*pl* -s) detective novel, thriller.

kriminal [krimi'naːl] *adj* criminal.
Kriminal‖polizei *f* detective force, CID.
–roman *m* detective novel, thriller.
Krippe ['krɪpə] *f* (*pl* -n) crib; (*Kinder*-) crèche.
Krise ['kriːzə] *f* (*pl* -n) crisis.
Kristall [kri'stal] *m* (*pl* -e) crystal. **kristallisieren** *v* crystallize.
Kritik [kri'tiːk] *f* (*pl* -en) criticism. **–er** *m* critic. **kritisch** *adj* critical. **kritisieren** *v* criticize; (*Buch*, *Film*) review.
Krokodil [kroko'diːl] *neut* (*pl* -e) crocodile.
Krone ['kroːnə] *f* (*pl* -n) crown.
krönen ['krœːnən] *v* crown. **Krönung** *f* coronation.
Kröte ['krœːtə] *f* (*pl* -n) toad.
Krücke ['krykə] *f* (*pl* -n) crutch.
Krug [kruːk] *m* (*pl* Krüge) jug; (*Becher*) mug.
Krume ['kruːmə] *f* (*pl* -n) crumb.
Krümel [kryməl] *m* (*pl* -) crumb.
krümelig ['kryməliç] *adj* crumbly.
krumm [krum] *adj* crooked. **–beinig** *adj* bow-legged.
Krumme ['krumə] *f* (*pl* -n) sickle.
Krümmung ['krymuŋ] *f* (*pl* -en) curve, bend.
Krüppel ['krypəl] *m* (*pl* -) cripple.
Kruste ['krustə] *f* (*pl* -n) crust. **–ntier** *neut* crustacean.
Kruzifix [kruːtsi'fiks] *neut* (*pl* -e) crucifix.
Kubikinhalt [ku'biːkinhalt] *m* volume.
Küche ['kyçə] *f* (*pl* -n) kitchen; cookery, cuisine.
Kuchen ['kuːxən] *m* (*pl* -) cake.
Küchen‖schabe *f* cockroach. **–schrank** *m* kitchen cupboard.
Kuckuck ['kukuk] *m* (*pl* -e) cuckoo.
Kugel ['kuːgəl] *f* (*pl* -n) ball; (*Gewehr*) bullet; (*Math*) sphere. **kugel‖fest** *adj* bullet-proof. **–förmig** *adj* spherical. **Kugel‖lager** *neut* ball-bearing. **–schreiber** *m* ball(point) pen.
Kuh [kuː] *f* (*pl* Kühe) cow.
kühl [kyːl] *adj* cool. **Kühle** *f* coolness. **kühlen** *v* cool. **Kühl‖schrank** *m* refrigerator. **–ung** *f* cooling.
kühn [kyːn] *adj* daring, bold, audacious. **Kühnheit** *f* daring, boldness, audacity.
Kuhstall ['kuːʃtal] *m* cowshed.
Kulissen [ku'lisən] *pl* (*Theater*) scenery *sing.* **hinter den Kulissen** (*fig*) behind the scenes.
Kult [kult] *m* (*pl* -e) cult; (*Verehrung*) worship.

kultivieren [kulti'viːrən] *v* cultivate.
Kultur [kul'tuːr] *f* (*pl* -en) culture; (*Boden*) cultivation; (*Bakterien*) culture. **kulturell** *adj* cultural.
Kümmel ['kyməl] *m* caraway (seed).
Kummer ['kumər] *m* (*unz.*) sorrow, distress.
kümmerlich ['kymərliç] *adj* miserable, poor. **kümmern** *v* grieve; (*angehen*) concern. **sich kümmern um** take care of, look after.
Kumpel ['kumpəl] *m* (*pl* -s) (*umg.*) mate, buddy; (*Bergmann*) miner.
kund [kunt] *adj* (generally) known.
Kunde[1] ['kundə] *f* information, (*Nachrichten*) news.
Kunde[2] *m*, **Kundin** *f* customer, client.
Kundendienst ['kundəndiːnst] *m* after-sales service.
*kundgeben ['kuntgeːbən] *v* make known, declare. **Kundgebung** *f* demonstration; (*Kundgeben*) declaration.
kündigen ['kyndigən] *v* give notice. **Kündigung** *f* notice.
Kundschaft ['kuntʃaft] *f* (*unz.*) customers *pl,* clientele.
künftig ['kynftiç] *adj* future.
Kunst [kunst] *f* (*pl* Künste) art; (*Fertigkeit*) skill. **–akademie** *f* art college. **kunstfertig** *adj* skilled. **Kunst‖gegenstand** *m* objet d'art. **–griff** *m* trick, dodge. **–handwerker** *m* craftsman.
Künstler ['kynstlər] *m* **Künstlerin** *f* artist. **künstlerisch** *adj* artistic.
künstlich ['kynstliç] *adj* artificial. **künstliche Atmung** *f* artificial respiration. **Kunst‖stück** [*neut* stunt, trick. **–werk** *neut* work of art.
Kupfer ['kupfər] *neut* (*pl* -) copper. **kupfer‖farben** *adj* copper(-coloured). **–n** *adj* copper.
Kuppel ['kupəl] *f* (*pl* -n) dome, cupola.
Kuppelei [kupə'lai] *f* (*unz.*) procuring, pimping. **kuppeln** *v* unite, couple; (*Mot*) declutch. **Kuppler** *m* procurer. **Kupplerin** *f* procuress. **Kupplung** *f* coupling; (*Mot*) clutch.
Kur [kuːr] *f* (*pl* -en) (course of) treatment. **–anstalt** *f* sanatorium.
Kurbel ['kurbəl] *f* (*pl* -n) crank, handle. **–welle** *f* crankshaft.
Kürbis ['kyrbis] *m* (*pl* -se) pumpkin.
Kurfürst ['kuːrfyrst] *m* elector, electoral prince.

Kurort *m* spa.

Kurs [kurs] *m* (*pl* -e) course; (*Komm*) rate. −**buch** *neut* railway timetable.

kursiv [kur'ziːf] *adv* in italics.

Kurve ['kurvə] *f* (*pl* -n) curve; (*Straße*) bend.

kurz [kurts] *adj* short. **kurze Hose** shorts *pl*. **kurz und gut** in a word, in short. **sich kurz fassen** be brief, make it short. **Kurz‖arbeit** *f* short time (work). −**ausgabe** *f* abridged edition.

Kürze ['kyrtsə] *f* shortness; (*Zeit*) brevity.

kürzen *v* shorten. **kürzlich** *adv* recently, lately.

Kurz‖meldung *f* news flash. −**schluß** *m* short circuit. −**schrift** *f* shorthand. **kurzsichtig** *adj* nearsighted, shortsighted.

Kürzung ['kyrtsuŋ] *f* (*pl* -en) shortening, reduction.

Kurz‖waren *f pl* haberdashery. −**welle** *f* shortwave.

Kusine [ku'ziːnə] *f* (*pl* -n) (female) cousin.

Kuß [kus] *m* (*pl* **Küsse**) kiss.

küssen ['kysən] *v* kiss.

Küste ['kystə] *f* (*pl* -n) coast, shore. −**nwache** *f* coastguard.

Kutsche ['kutʃə] *f* (*pl* -n) carriage, coach. −**r** *m* (*pl* -) coachman.

L

labil [la'biːl] *adj* unstable; (*oft krank*) delicate, sickly.

Labor [la'bɔːr] *neut* (*pl* -s) (*umg.*) lab.

Laboratorium [labora'toːrium] *neut* (*pl* **Laboratorien**) laboratory, (*umg.*) lab.

lächeln ['lɛçəln] *v* smile. **Lächeln** *neut* smile.

lachen ['laxən] *v* laugh. **Lachen** *neut* laughter, laugh. **zum Lachen bringen** make laugh. **das ist zum Lachen** that's ridiculous.

lächerlich ['lɛçərliç] *adj* ridiculous.

Lachs [laks] *m* (*pl* -e) salmon.

Lack [lak] *m* (*pl* -e) lacquer; (*mit Farbstoff*) (enamel) paint. −**farbe** *f* (enamel) paint. −**leder** *neut* patent leather.

*laden[1] ['laɪdən] *v* load.

*laden[2] *v* invite; (*Jur*) summon.

Laden ['laɪdən] *m* (*pl* **Läden**) shop; (*Fenster*) shutter. −**diebstahl** *m* shoplifting. −**schluß** *m* closing time. −**tisch** *m* counter.

Lade‖platz *m* loading place; (*Schiff*) wharf. −**raum** *m* hold. **Ladung** (*pl* -en) *f* load; (*Schiffe*) cargo.

Lage ['laɪgə] *f* (*pl* -n) situation, position. **in der Lage sein zu** be in a position to.

Lager ['laɪgər] *neut* (*pl* -) camp; (*Speicher*) store(s); (*Tier*) lair; (*Geol*) stratum, layer; (*Tech*) bearing. −**feuer** *neut* campfire. −**haus** *neut* warehouse. **lagern** *v* (*im Freien rasten*) camp; (*aufbewahren*) store; (*einlegen*) lay down, place; (*aufbewahrt werden*) be stored.

Lagune [la'guːnə] *f* (*pl* -n) lagoon.

lahm [laːm] *adj* crippled; (*müde*) exhausted; (*schwach*) lame, feeble.

lähmen ['lɛːmən] *v* cripple, paralyze; (*fig*) obstruct. **Lähmung** *f* (*pl* -en) paralysis.

Laib [laip] *m* (*pl* -e) loaf.

Laie ['laɪə] *m* (*pl* -n) layman. **Laien‖priester** *m* lay preacher. −**stand** *m* laity.

Lakritze [la'kritsə] *f* (*pl* -n) liquorice.

Lamm [lam] *neut* (*pl* **Lämmer**) lamb. −**fleisch** *neut* lamb. −**wolle** *f* lambswool.

Lampe ['lampə] *f* (*pl* -n) lamp.

Land [lant] 1 *neut* (*unz.*) (*Erdboden, Grundstück, Festland*) land; (*Landschaft*) country(side). 2 *neut* (*pl* **Länder**) land, country; (*Provinz*) state, province. **an Land gehen** go ashore, disembark. **Hügeliges Land** hilly country *or* terrain. **auf dem Lande** in the country. **Land‖arbeiter** *m* farmworker. −**besitz** *m* land, property. **landen** *v* land; (*umg.*) land up, end up. **Landenge** *f* isthmus. **Landes‖bank** *f* national bank; regional bank. −**flagge** *f* national flag. −**verrat** *m* high treason. **Land‖gut** *neut* (landed) estate. −**haus** *neut* country house. −**karte** *f* map. −**leute** *pl* country folk.

ländlich ['lɛntliç] *adj* rural.

Land‖mann *m* countryman; (*Bauer*) farmer. −**messer** *m* surveyor. −**mine** *f* landmine. −**schaft** *f* countryside; (*Malerei*) landscape; (*Gebiet*) area, region. −**schule** *f* village school. −**smann** *m* fellow countryman. −**spitze** *f* cape, headland. −**straße** *f* highway, main road. −**streicher** *m* tramp, vagrant.

Landung ['landuŋ] *f* (*pl* -en) landing. −**ssteg** *m* gangway, landing ramp.

Landweg ['lantvɛːk] *m* land route. **auf dem Landwege** by land.

Landwirt ['lantviɪrt] *m* farmer. **landwirt-schaftlich** *adj* agricultural.

lang [laŋ] *adj* long; (*Mensch*) tall. **viele Jahre lang** for many years. **lange** *adv* (for) a long time.

Länge ['lɛŋə] *f* (*pl* -n) length; (*Mensch*) height; (*Größe*) size; (*Geog*) longitude.

langen ['laŋən] *v* suffice. **langen nach** reach for.

länger ['lɛŋər] *adj* longer; taller. **länger machen** lengthen, extend. **auf längere Zeit** for a considerable period.

Langeweile ['laŋəvailə] *f* boredom.

lang‖jährig *adj* of long standing. **–lebig** *adj* long-lived.

länglich ['lɛŋliç] *adj* oblong, longish. **–rund** *adj* oval, elliptical.

längs [lɛŋs] *prep* along.

langsam ['laŋzaɪm] *adj* slow. **Langsamkeit** *f* slowness.

Langspielplatte ['laŋʃpiɪlplatə] *f* long-playing record, LP.

längst [lɛŋst] *adj* longest. *adv* long ago. **–ens** *adv* (*höchstens*) at the most; (*spätestens*) at the latest.

langweilen ['laŋvailən] *v* bore. **sich langweilen** be bored. **langweilig** *adj* boring, tedious.

Lanze ['lantsə] *f* (*pl* -n) lance.

Lappen ['lapən] *m* (*pl* -) rag, (cleaning) cloth; (*Anat, Bot*) lobe. **lappig** *adj* (*umg.*) flabby; (*Anat, Bot*) lobed.

Lärche ['lɛrçə] *f* (*pl* -n) larch.

Lärm [lɛrm] *m* (*unz.*) noise, din. **lärmen** *v* make a noise. **–d** *adj* noisy.

Laser ['leɪzər] *m* (*pl* -) laser.

*lassen ['lasən] *v* (*erlauben*) let, allow; (*unterlassen*) leave, stop; (*überlassen*) leave. **außer Acht lassen** disregard. **bleiben lassen** leave alone. **fallen lassen** (let) drop. **kommen lassen** send for. **sich machen lassen** have done *or* made. **lassen von** renounce. **sich nicht beschreiben lassen** be indescribable *or* beyond words. **laß mich gehen!** let me go! **laß mich in Ruhe!** leave me alone. **es läßt sich nicht machen** it can't be done.

lässig ['lɛsiç] *adj* careless, negligent.

Last [last] *f* (*pl* -en) load; (*Bürde*) burden; (*Gewicht*) weight; (*Fracht*) cargo.

Laster¹ ['lastər] *m* (*pl* -) (*umg.*) lorry, truck.

Laster² *neut* (*pl* -) vice. **lasterhaft** *adj* immoral.

lästern ['lɛstərn] slander. **Lästerung** *f* slander.

lästig ['lɛstiç] *adj* irksome, bothersome.

Last‖kahn *m* barge, lighter. **–kraftwagen (Lkw)** *m* lorry, truck. **–pferd** *neut* packhorse.

Latein [la'tain] *neut* Latin (language). **–amerika** *neut* Latin America. **lateinisch** *adj* Latin.

Laterne [la'tɛrnə] *f* (*pl* -n) lantern. **–npfahl** *m* lamppost.

Latte ['latə] *f* (*pl* -n) lath.

lau [lau] *adj* lukewarm, tepid; (*Wetter*) mild.

Laub [laup] *neut* (*pl* -e) foliage. **–baum** *m* deciduous tree. **–säge** *f* fretsaw. **–wald** *m* deciduous forest. **–werk** *neut* foliage.

Lauch [laux] *m* (*pl* -e) leek.

lauern ['lauərn] *v* lurk, lie in ambush; (*umg.*) hang around, wait impatiently.

Lauf [lauf] *m* (*pl* Läufe) run; (*Sport*) race; (*Fluß*) course; (*Gewehr*) barrel; (*Maschine*) running, operation. **–bahn** *f* career. **laufen** *v* (*Maschine, Wasser, Weg, usw.*) run; (*zu Fuß gehen*) walk. **laufend** *adj* current, running; (*Zahl*) consecutive. **auf dem laufenden** up to date.

Läufer ['lɔyfər] *m* (*pl* -) (*Sport*) runner; (*Schach*) bishop.

läufig ['lɔyfiç] *adj* (*Hündin*) in heat.

Lauf‖planke *f* gangway. **–werk** *neut* mechanism, drive.

Lauge ['laugə] *f* (*pl* -n) lye; (*Seifen-*) suds. **laugenartig** *adj* alkaline, (*Chem*) basic.

Laune ['launə] *f* (*pl* -n) mood, temper; (*Grille*) whim. **launenhaft** *adj* capricious, whimsical. **launig** *adj* humorous, funny. **launisch** *adj* moody, capricious.

Laus [laus] *f* (*pl* Läuse) louse.

lauschen ['lauʃən] *v* listen (to); (*heimlich*) listen in, eavesdrop.

lausig ['lauziç] *adj* lousy.

laut¹ [laut] *adj* loud. *adv* aloud.

laut² *prep* according to.

Laut [laut] *m* (*pl* -e) sound.

Laute ['lautə] *f* (*pl* -n) lute.

lauten ['lautən] *v* read, say; (*klingen*) sound.

läuten ['lɔytən] *v* ring, sound.

lauter ['lautər] *adj* pure; (*echt*) genuine; (*nichts als*) nothing but, sheer.

Laut‖sprecher *m* loudspeaker. **–stärke** *f* volume, loudness.

lauwarm ['lauvarm] *adj* lukewarm.

Lawine [la'viːnə] *f* (*pl* -n) avalanche.
lax [laks] *adj* lax.
leben ['leɪbən] *v* live. **von ... leben** live on
.... **Es lebe die Königin!** Long live the
Queen! **Leben** *neut* (*pl* -) life; (*Geschäftigkeit*) activity, bustle. **am Leben** alive.
ums Leben kommen lose one's life, die.
lebend *adj* living, alive. **-ig** *adj* alive, living; (*munter*) lively.
Lebens∥art *f* lifestyle. **-freude** *f* joy of
life. **-funktion** *f* vital function. **-gefahr** *f*
danger to life. **-haltungskosten** *pl* cost of
living *sing*. **-jahr** *neut* year of one's life.
im 16. Lebensjahr during the sixteenth
year of his/her life.
lebenslänglich ['leɪbənsleŋliç] *adj* lifelong; (*Jur*) for life.
Lebens∥lauf *m* curriculum vitae, c.v.
-mittel *pl* food *sing*. **-standard** *m* standard of living. **-stil** *m* lifestyle.
-unterhalt *m* livelihood. **-versicherung** *f*
life insurance. **-weise** *f* way of life.
Leber ['leɪbər] *f* (*pl* -n) liver. **-fleck** *m*
birthmark. **-wurst** *f* liver sausage.
Lebe∥wesen *neut* living creature, organism. **-wohl** *neut* farewell.
lebhaft ['leɪphaft] *adj* lively. **Lebhaftigkeit**
f liveliness.
leblos ['leɪploːs] *adj* lifeless.
leck [lɛk] *adj* leaky. **Leck** *neut* (*pl* -e)
leak.
lecken ['lɛkən] *v* lick.
lecker ['lɛkər] *adj* delicious. **-bissen** *m*
delicacy, titbit.
Leder ['leɪdər] *neut* (*pl* -) leather. **-hose** *f*
leather shorts *pl*. **ledern** *adj* leather; (*fig*)
dry, boring. **Leder∥riemen** *m* leather
strap. **-waren** *pl* leather goods.
ledig ['leɪdiç] *adj* single, unmarried; (*frei*)
free (of). **lediger Stand** *m* celibacy. **lediglich** *adv* solely.
Lee [leɪ] *f* lee.
leer [leɪr] *adj* empty; (*unbesetzt*) unoccupied; (*Stellung*) open; (*Seite*) blank.
Leere *f* emptiness; (*Physik*) vacuum.
leeren *v* empty. **Leer∥lauf** *m* (*Mot*)
idling, tick-over. **-ung** *f* (*pl* -en) emptying; (*Post*) collection.
legal [le'gaːl] *adj* legal.
legen ['leɪgən] *v* lay, place, put (down);
(*Eier*) lay; (*installieren*) install, fit. **sich
legen** lie down; (*wind*) abate.
Legende [le'gɛndə] *f* (*pl* -n) legend.
legieren [le'giːrən] *v* (*Metalle*) alloy;
(*Suppe*) thicken.

legitim [legi'tiːm] *adj* legitimate.
Lehm [leɪm] *m* (*pl* -e) loam.
Lehne ['leɪnə] *f* (*pl* -n) support, prop;
(*Stuhl*) back. **lehnen** *v* lean, rest. **sich
lehnen** lean, rest. **Lehn∥sessel** *or* **-stuhl**
m armchair, easy chair.
Lehrbuch ['leɪrbux] *neut* textbook. **Lehre**
f (*pl* -n) teaching; (*Lehrzeit*) training.
lehren *v* teach. **Lehrer** *m* (*pl* -) teacher,
schoolmaster. **-in** *f* (*pl* -nen) teacher,
schoolmistress. **Lehr∥film** *m* educational
film. **-gang** *m* curriculum, course of
instruction. **-ling** *m* (*pl* -e) apprentice.
lehrreich *adj* instructive. **Lehr∥satz** *m*
rule, proposition. **-zeit** *f* training,
apprenticeship.
Leib [laip] *m* (*pl* -er) body. **Leibes∥frucht**
f foetus. **-übung** *f* physical exercise.
Leiche ['laiçə] *f* (*pl* -n) corpse.
Leichen∥halle *neut* mortuary. **-schau** *f*
postmortem, autopsy. **Leichnam** *m* (*pl*
-e) corpse.
leicht [laiçt] *adj* light; (*einfach*) easy.
leicht zugänglich easily accessible. **es sich
leicht machen** take it easy. **Leichtathletik**
f athletics. **leichtfertig** *adj* superficial;
(*Antwort*) glib. **Leichtgewichtler** *m* lightweight. **leichtgläubig** *adj* credulous.
Leichtigkeit *f* lightness; (*Mühelosigkeit*)
ease. **leichtlebig** *adj* easy-going. **-sinnig**
adj thoughtless.
leid [lait] *adj* disagreeable, painful. **es ist**
(*or* **es tut**) **mir leid** I am sorry. **Leid** *neut*
(*unz.*) sorrow, grief; (*Schaden*) harm. **leiden** *v* suffer; (*erlauben*) tolerate, allow.
leiden an suffer from. **ich kann ihn nicht
leiden** I can't stand him. **leidend** *adj* suffering; (*kränklich*) sickly.
Leidenschaft ['laidənʃaft] *f* (*pl* -en) passion. **leidenschaft∥lich** *adj* passionate.
-slos *adj* dispassionate.
leider ['laidər] *adv* unfortunately. **leider
muß ich ...** I am afraid I have to ....
leidig [laidiç] *adj* tiresome, disagreeable.
leidlich ['laitliç] *adj* tolerable.
Leier ['laiər] *f* (*pl* -n) lyre. **die alte Leier**
the same old story. **leiern** *v* (*sprechen*)
drawl.
leihen ['laiən] *v* lend; (*borgen*) borrow.
Leihbibliothek *f* lending library.
Leim [laim] *m* (*pl* -e) glue.
Lein [lain] *m* (*pl* -e) flax.
Leine ['lainə] *f* (*pl* -n) line, cord; (*Hund*)
leash.

leinen ['lainən] *adj* linen. **Leinen** *neut* linen.

leise ['laizə] *adj* quiet; *(sanft)* gentle, soft.

Leiste ['laistə] *f (pl -n) (Anat)* groin.

leisten ['laistən] *v* do; *(schaffen)* accomplish, achieve; *(ausführen)* carry out. **Hilfe leisten** help, assist. **sich leisten** allow oneself. *ich kann mir einen neuen Wagen nicht leisten* I cannot afford a new car. **Leistung** *f (pl -en)* achievement, accomplishment; *(Tat)* deed; *(Arbeit)* output. **leistungsfähig** *adj* capable; productive. **Leistungsfähigkeit** *f* ability (to work); productivity.

leiten ['laitən] *v (führen) (Elek, Musik)* conduct. **-d** *adj* guiding, leading; *(Person)* prominent, senior.

Leiter[1] ['laitər] *m (pl -)* leader; manager. **Leiter**[2] *f (pl -n)* ladder.

Leit‖faden *m* clue; *(Lehrbuch)* guide, textbook. **-satz** *m* guiding principle. **-ung** *f (pl -en) (Führung)* leadership; *(Verwaltung)* management; *(Elek)* circuit; *(Draht)* wire; *(Wasser)* pipes *pl*, mains *pl*.

Lektüre lɛk'tyːrə] *f (pl -n)* reading; *(Lesestoff)* reading material, literature.

Lende ['lɛndə] *f (pl -n) (Anat)* lumbar region; *(Fleisch)* loin.

lenken ['lɛŋkən] *v* steer; *(führen)* direct. **Lenk‖er** *m* guide; *(Flugzeug)* pilot; *(Leiter)* manager. **-rad** *m* steering wheel. **-ung** *f (pl -en) (Mot)* steering; *(Leitung)* direction.

Leopard [leo'part] *m (pl -en)* leopard.

lepra ['leɪpra] *f* leprosy. **-kranke(r)** leper.

Lerche ['lɛrçə] *f (pl -n)* lark.

lernen ['lɛrnən] *v* learn. **Lernen** *neut (unz.)* learning.

lesbar ['lɛsbaɪr] *adj* readable. **Lese** *f (pl -n)* vintage. **Lesebuch** *neut* reading book. **lesen** *v* read; lecture; *(sammeln, ernten)* gather, harvest. **Leser** *m (pl -)*, **Leserin** *f (pl -en)* reader. **leserlich** *adj* legible. **Leserschaft** *f* readership, readers. **Lesesaal** *m* reading room.

letzt [lɛtst] *adj* last; *(spätest)* latest, final. **letzte Nummer** current issue. **letztens** *adv* lately; *(zum Schluß)* lastly.

Leuchte ['lɔyçtə] *f (pl -n)* light, lamp. **leuchten** *v* emit light, shine. **-d** *adj* shining, luminous. **Leuchter** *m (pl -)* candlestick. **Leuchtturm** *m* lighthouse.

leugnen ['lɔygnən] *v* deny.

Leukämie [lɔykɛ'miɪ] *f* leukaemia.

Leute ['lɔytə] *pl* people.

Leutnant ['lɔytnant] *m (pl -e)* lieutenant.

leutselig ['lɔytzeɪliç] *adj* affable, sociable.

Lexikon ['lɛksikɔn] *neut (pl Lexika)* dictionary.

Libelle [li'bɛlə] *f (pl -n) (Insekt)* dragonfly; *(Tech)* (spirit) level.

liberal [libe'raɪl] *adj* liberal.

licht [liçt] *adj* bright; *(Farbe)* light; *(Wald)* sparse, thin. **Licht** *neut (pl -er)* light; *(Kerze)* candle. **-bild** *neut* photograph. **lichtdurchlässig** *adj* translucent.

lichten ['liçtən] *v (Wald)* clear; *(Anker)* weigh.

Licht‖jahr *neut* lightyear. **-pause** *f* blueprint. **-signal** *neut* light signal. **lichtundurchlässig** *adj* opaque.

Lichtung ['liçtuŋ] *f (pl -en)* glade, clearing.

Lid [liɪt] *neut (pl -er)* eyelid.

lieb [liɪb] *adj* dear; *(nett)* nice; *(angenehm)* agreeable. *ein liebes Kind* a good child. *es wäre ihm lieb* he would appreciate it. *das ist lieb von Ihnen* that is most kind of you.

Liebchen ['liɪpçən] *neut (pl -)* darling.

Liebe ['liɪbə] *f (pl -n)* love. **Liebelei** *f (pl -en)* flirtation. **lieben** *v* love. **liebens‖wert** *adj* lovable. **-würdig** *adj* amiable, helpful, kind.

lieber ['liɪbər] *adj* dearer. *adv* rather; *(besser)* better. **lieber haben** prefer. **lieber als** rather than. **Ich gehe lieber zu Fuß** I prefer to walk. *das hättest Du lieber nicht sagen sollen* you had better not say that.

Liebes‖affäre *f* (love) affair. **-brief** *m* love letter. **-paar** *neut* lovers *pl*, couple.

liebevoll ['liɪbəfɔl] *adj* affectionate, loving.

*liebhaben ['liɪphaɪbən] *v* love, like. **Liebhaber** *m (pl -)*, **Liebhaberin** *f (pl -nen)* lover.

lieb‖kosen *v* caress, fondle. **-lich** *adj* lovely. **Lieb‖ling** *m* darling; *(Günstling)* favourite. **-reiz** *m* charm, attraction.

liebst [liːpst] *adj* favourite, best-loved. *adv* **am liebsten haben** like best of all. **am liebsten machen** like doing best.

Lied [liɪt] *neut (pl -er)* song. **-erbuch** *neut* songbook; *(Rel)* hymnbook.

liederlich *adj* slovenly; *(sittenlos)* debauched, dissipated.

Lieferant [liɪfə'rant] *m (pl -en)* supplier. **liefern** *v* deliver, supply; *(Ertrag)* yield. **Lieferung** *f (pl -en)* delivery, supply.

Liege ['liːgə] *f* (*pl* -n) couch. **liegen** *v* lie. **-bleiben** *v* remain; (*Waren*) be unsold; (*Arbeit*) remain unfinished; (*Panne haben*) break down. **-lassen** *v* leave (behind). **Liege‖platz** *m* berth. **-stuhl** *m* deckchair.

Liga ['liːga] *f* (*pl* **Ligen**) league.

Likör *m* (*pl* -e) liqueur.

lila ['liːla] *adj* lilac, purple. **Lila** *neut* lilac, purple.

Lilie ['liːliə] *f* (*pl* -n) lily.

Limonade [limo'naːdə] *f* (*pl* -n) lemonade, soda-pop.

Linde ['lində] *f* (*pl* -n) lime tree.

lindern ['lindərn] *v* alleviate, mitigate.

Lineal [line'aːl] *neut* (*pl* -e) ruler, rule.

Linie ['liːniə] *f* (*pl* -n) line.

Linke ['liŋkə] *f* (*pl* -n) left, left(-hand) side; (*Pol*) the Left. **linkisch** *adj* clumsy. **links** *adv* (on *or* to the) left. **Linkshänder** *m* left-hander. **linkshändig** *adj* left-handed. **Links‖radikale(r)** *m* (radical) left-winger. **-steuerung** *f* left-hand drive.

Linse ['linzə] *f* (*pl* -n) (*Foto, Anat*) lens; (Küche) lentil.

Lippe ['lipə] *f* (*pl* -n) lip. **-nstift** *m* lipstick.

lispeln ['lispəln] *v* lisp.

Lissabon ['lissabon] *neut* Lisbon.

List [list] *f* (*pl* -en) (*Schlauheit*) cunning; trick, ruse.

Liste ['listə] *f* (*pl* -n) list.

listig ['listiç] *adj* cunning.

Litanei [lita'nai] *f* (*pl* -en) litany.

Liter ['liːtər] *neut or m* (*pl* -) litre.

literarisch [lite'raːriʃ] *adj* literary. **Literatur** *f* literature.

Live-Sendung ['laifzɛnduŋ] *f* live *or* direct broadcast.

Lizenz [li'tsɛnts] *f* (*pl* -en) licence. **-inhaber** *m* licensee.

Lob [loːp] *neut* (*pl* -e) praise. **loben** *v* praise. **Lob‖gesang** *m* song of praise. **-hudelei** *f* adulation.

Loch [lɔx] *neut* (*pl* **Löcher**) hole; (*Reifen*) puncture. **lochen** *v* pierce, punch; (*perforieren*) perforate.

löcherig ['lœçəriç] *adj* full of holes.

Lochung ['lɔxuŋ] *f* (*pl* -en) perforation.

Locke ['lɔkə] *f* (*pl* -n) curl, lock.

locken ['lɔkən] *v* lure, entice.

locker ['lɔkər] *adj* loose; (*Lebensart*) lax, slack. **lockern** *v* loosen (up). **sich lockern** *v* become loose; (*entspannen*) relax.

lockig ['lɔkiç] *adj* curly.

Lock‖speise *f* bait. **-vogel** *m* decoy.

lodern ['loːdərn] *v* blaze (up); (*fig*) glow, smoulder.

Löffel ['lœfəl] *m* (*pl* -) spoon.

Loge ['loːʒə] *f* (*pl* -n) (*Theater*) box; (*Freimaurer*) lodge.

logieren [lo'ʒiːrən] *v* lodge.

Logik ['loːgik] *f* logic. **logisch** *adj* logical.

Lohn [loːn] *m* (*pl* **Löhne**) (*Gehalt, Bezahlung*) wages *pl*, pay; (*Belohnung*) reward; (*verdiente Strafe*) deserts *pl*. **-arbeiter** *m* wage-earner, (weekly-paid) worker. **lohnen** *v* reward. **es lohnt sich (nicht)** it's (not) worth it. **Lohn‖forderung** *f* wage claim. **-schreiber** *m* hack (writer). **-stopp** *m* wage freeze. **-tag** *m* payday.

lokal [lo'kaːl] *adj* local. **Lokal** *neut* (*pl* -e) pub, tavern.

Lokomotive [lokomo'tiːvə] *f* (*pl* -n) locomotive.

Lorbeer ['lɔrbeːr] *m* (*pl* -en) laurel. **-blatt** *neut* bay leaf. **-kranz** *m* laurel wreath.

los [loːs] *adj* free; (*nicht fest*) loose. *adv* away, off. **los!** go on! off you go! **was ist los?** what's going on? **was ist mit dir los?** what's the matter (with you)? **etwas/jemanden los sein/werden** be/get rid of something/someone.

Los *neut* (*pl* -e) (*Schicksal*) fate, lot; (*Lotterie*) lottery ticket. **das Los ziehen** draw lots.

lösbar ['lœːsbaːr] *adj* soluble.

*los‖binden *v* untie. **-brechen** *v* break loose.

löschen ['lœʃən] *v* (*Feuer*) put out, extinguish; (*Licht*) turn off, switch off; (*Schuld*) cancel, write off; (*Tinte*) blot; (*Firma*) liquidate; (*Durst*) quench. **Löscher** *m* (*Feuer*) extinguisher; (*Tinte*) blotter.

lose ['loːzə] *adj* loose.

Lösegeld ['lœːzəgɛlt] *neut* ransom.

lösen ['lœːzən] *v* loosen; (*Knoten*) unravel (a plot); (*Verschluß*) unfasten; (*Rätsel, Problem*) solve; (*abtrennen*) detach; (*Chem*) dissolve.

*los‖fahren *v* drive off. **-gehen** *v* set out, get going. **-knüpfen** *v* untie. **-kommen** *v* get away *or* free. **-lassen** *v* let go.

löslich ['lœːsliç] *adj* soluble.

los‖lösen *v* free, detach. **-machen** *v* unfasten, release. **-reißen** *v* tear away. **-sagen** *v* **sich lossagen von** renounce.

los‖schießen *v* fire away/off. –schrauben *v* unscrew. –sprechen *v* acquit, release.

Losung ['loːzuŋ] *f* (*pl* -en) password.

Lösung ['løːzuŋ] *f* (*pl* -en) solution; (*Lösen*) loosening. –smittel *neut* solvent.

los‖werden *v* get rid of. –ziehen *v* set out.

Lot [loːt] *neut* (*pl* -e) plumbline; (*zum Löten*) solder. **loten** *v* take soundings.

löten *v* solder.

lotrecht ['loːtrɛçt] *adj* perpendicular, vertical.

Lotse ['loːtsə] *f* (*pl* -n) (*Schiff*) pilot.

Lotterie [lɔtəˈriː] *f* (*pl* -n) lottery.

Löwe ['løːvə] *m* (*pl* -n) lion. –nzahn *m* dandelion. **Löwin** *f* lioness.

Luchs [luks] *m* (*pl* -e) lynx.

Lücke ['lykə] *f* (*pl* -n) gap; (*Auslassung*) omission; (*eines Gesetzes*) loophole. –nbüßer *m* stopgap. **luckenhaft** *adj* defective; (*fig*) patchy, full of gaps.

Luft [luft] *f* (*pl* Lüfte) air. –ansicht *f* aerial view. –bild *neut* aerial photograph. –bremse *f* air brake. –brücke *f* airlift. **luftdicht** *adj* airtight.

lüften ['lyftən] *v* ventilate, air.

Luftfahrt ['luftfaːrt] *f* aviation. **luftgekühlt** *adj* air-cooled. **Lufthafen** *m* airport. **luftig** *adj* airy, breezy. **Luft‖krankheit** *f* airsickness. –krieg *m* aerial warfare. –post *f* airmail. –reifen *m* pneumatic tyre, (*US* tire). –röhre *f* windpipe. –schiff *neut* airship.

Lüftung ['lyftuŋ] *f* (*pl* -en) ventilation.

Luftverkehr ['luftvɛrkɛːr] *m* air traffic. –sgesellschaft *f* airline.

Lüge ['lyːgə] *f* (*pl* -n) lie. **lügen** *v* (tell a) lie. –haft *adj* lying. **Lügner** *m* liar.

Lump [lump] *m* (*pl* -) rag. –händler *m* rag-and-bone man.

Lunge ['luŋə] *f* (*pl* -n) lung. **Lungen‖entzündung** *f* pneumonia. –krebs *m* lung cancer.

Lupe ['luːpə] *f* (*pl* -n) magnifying glass. **unter die Lupe nehmen** scrutinize, examine closely.

Lust [lust] *f* (*pl* Lüste) delight, pleasure; (*Verlangen*) desire; (*Wollust*) lust. **Lust haben an** take pleasure in. **Lust haben (zu tun)** feel like (doing). **keine Lust haben (zu tun)** not be in the mood (to do), not feel like (doing).

lüstern ['lystərn] *adj* (*geil*) lascivious, lecherous.

Lustfahrt ['lustfaːrt] *f* pleasure trip. **lustig** *adj* merry, joyful; (*unterhaltend*) amusing, funny. **sich lustig machen über** make fun of. **Lustigkeit** *f* gaiety, merriment.

lustlos *adj* dull, inactive. **Lust‖mord** *m* sex murder. –spiel *neut* comedy.

lutschen ['lutʃən] *v* suck. **Lutscher** *m* (baby's) dummy, (*US*) pacifier.

Luxus ['luksus] *m* luxury. –artikel *m* luxury item; *pl* luxuries.

Luzern ['luːtsɛrn] *neut* Lucerne.

lyrisch ['lyːriʃ] *adj* lyrical.

M

Maat [maːt] *m* (*pl* -e) mate; (*Kriegsmarine*) petty officer.

machen ['maxən] *v* make; do; (*Rechnung*) come to. **eine Prüfung machen** sit an exam. **fertig machen** get ready. **Licht machen** switch on a light. **(das) macht nichts,** it doesn't matter, never mind. **mach's gut!** good luck! all the best!

Macht [maxt] *f* (*pl* Mächte) power.

mächtig ['mɛçtiç] *adj* powerful; mighty; (*riesig*) immense.

Machtkampf *m* power struggle. **machtlos** *adj* powerless. **Machtprobe** *f* trial of strength.

Mädchen ['mɛːtçən] *neut* (*pl* -) girl. **mädchenhaft** *adj* girlish. **Mädchenname** *m* maiden name.

Made ['maːdə] *f* (*pl* -n) maggot.

Mädel ['mɛːdəl] *neut* (*pl* -) girl.

Magazin [magaˈtsiːn] *neut* (*pl* -e) store(house); (*Zeitschrift, auch Gewehr-*) magazine.

Magd [maːkt] *f* (*pl* Mägde) maid(servant).

Magen ['maːgən] *m* (*pl* -Mägen) stomach. –brennen *neut* heartburn. –schmerzen *pl* stomach-ache *sing*.

mager ['maːgər] *adj* thin, lean.

Magie [maˈgiː] *f* magic. **magisch** *adj* magic(al).

Magnet [magˈneːt] *m* (*pl* -en) magnet. **magnetisch** *adj* magnetic.

Mahagoni [mahaˈgoːni] *neut* (*pl* -s) mahogany.

Mähdrescher ['mɛːdrɛʃər] *m* combine harvester. **mähen** *v* mow.

Mahl [maːl] *neut* (*pl* -e) meal.

***mahlen** ['maːlən] *v* mill, grind.

Mahl‖zahn *m* molar. **–zeit** *f* meal; *interj* good appetite!

Mähne ['mɛːnə] *f* (*pl* -n) mane.

mahnen ['maːnən] *v* remind, admonish; warn. **Mahnung** *f* reminder, warning.

Mai [mai] *m* (*pl* -e) May. **–blume** *f* lily of the valley.

Mais [mais] *m* maize, (*US*) corn. **–kolben** *m* cob of corn. **–mehl** *neut* cornflour.

Majestät [majɛsˈtɛːt] *f* (*pl* -en) majesty. **majestätisch** *adj* majestic.

Majoran [majoˈraːn] *m* marjoram.

Makel ['maːkəl] *m* (*pl* -) stain, spot; (*Fehler*) defect, fault. **makellos** *adj* spotless; faultless.

Makler ['maːklər] *m* (*pl* -) broker.

Makrele [maˈkreːlə] *f* (*pl* -n) mackerel.

mal [maːl] *adv* (*Math*) times; (*einmal*) once, just. **drei mal fünf** three times five. **hör' mal!** just listen!

Mal[1] [maːl] *neut* (*pl* -e) time. **zum ersten Mal** for the first time.

Mal[2] *neut* (*pl* -e *or* **Mäler**) mark, sign; (*Denkmal*) monument; (*Grenzstein*) boundary stone.

Malaria [maˈlaːria] *f* malaria.

malen ['maːlən] *v* paint; (*zeichnen*) draw. **Maler** *m* (*pl* -) painter. **Malerei** *f* (*pl* -en) painting. **malerisch** *adj* picturesque.

Malz [malts] *neut* (*pl* -e) malt. **–bier** *neut* malt beer, stout.

Mama [maˈmaː] *f* (*pl* -s) mamma.

man [man] *pron* one, you; (*die Leute*) people. **man sagt** people say, it is said. *man tut das nicht* that is not done, you shouldn't do that.

Manager ['mɛnidʒər] *m* (*pl* -) manager.

manch [manç] *pron, adj* many a, some. **manche** *pl* several, many. **–mal** *adv* sometimes.

Mandat [manˈdaːt] *neut* (*pl* -e) mandate.

Mandel ['mandəl] *f* (*pl* -n) almond; (*Anat*) tonsil. **–entfernung** *f* tonsillectomy. **–entzündung** *f* tonsillitis.

Mangel[1] ['maŋəl] *f* (*pl* -n) mangle.

Mangel[2] [*m* (*pl* **Mängel**) lack, want; (*Knappheit*) shortage; (*Fehler*) fault. **mangeln** ['maŋəln] *v* lack, want. *es mangelt mir an* I lack.

Manie [maˈniː] *f* (*pl* -n) mania.

Manier [maˈniːr] *f* (*pl* -en) manner, way; (*Stil*) style. **Manieren** *pl* manners. **maniert** *adj* affected, mannered. **manierlich** *adj* well-mannered, civil.

Manifest [maniˈfɛst] *neut* (*pl* -e) manifesto.

manisch ['maːniʃ] *adj* manic.

Mann [man] *m* (*pl* **Männer**) man; (*Ehemann*) husband.

Männchen ['mɛnçən] *neut* (*pl* -) little man; (*Tier*) male.

Mannesalter ['manəsaltər] *neut* (age of) manhood. **mannhaft** *adj* manly.

Mannequin [manəˈkɛ̃] *neut* (*pl* -s) mannequin, fashion model.

mannigfaltig ['maniçfaltiç] *adj* varied, manifold.

männlich ['mɛnliç] *adj* male; (*fig, Gramm*) masculine. **Männlichkeit** *f* manhood; masculinity.

Mannschaft ['manʃaft] *f* (*pl* -en) crew; (*Sport*) team; (*Belegschaft*) personnel. **–führer** *m* (*Sport*) captain.

Manöver [maˈnœrvər] *neut* (*pl* -) manoeuvre. **manövrieren** *v* manoeuvre.

Manschette [manˈʃɛtə] *f* (*pl* -n) cuff.

Mantel ['mantəl] *m* (*pl* **-Mäntel**) coat; (*Umhang*) cloak.

Manuskript [manuˈskript] *neut* (*pl* -e) manuscript.

Mappe ['mapə] *f* (*pl* -n) briefcase; (*Aktenmappe*) folder, portfolio.

Märchen ['mɛːrçən] *neut* (*pl* -) fairytale. **märchenhaft** *adj* fairytale, magical.

Margarine [margaˈriːnə] *f* (*pl* -n) margarine.

Marien‖bild *neut* (picture of the) Madonna. **–käfer** *m* ladybird.

Marine [maˈriːnə] *f* (*pl* -n) (*Kriegsmarine*) navy; (*Handelsmarine*) merchant navy. **–soldat** *m* marine.

marinieren [mariˈniːrən] *v* marinate.

Marionette [marioˈnɛtə] *f* (*pl* -n) marionette.

Mark[1] [mark] *neut* (*unz.*) (bone) marrow. **bis ins Mark** (*fig*) to the core.

Mark[2] *f* (*pl* -) (*Geld*) mark.

Mark[3] *f* (*pl* -en) boundary; (*Grenzgebiet*) marches *pl*, border-country.

Marke ['markə] *f* (*pl* -n) (*Zeichen*) mark, stamp; (*Fabrikat, Sorte*) brand; (*Handelszeichen*) trademark; (*Briefmarke*) (postage) stamp; (*Wertschein*) token. **–nname** *m* tradename, brand-name.

Markt [markt] *m* (*pl* **Märkte**) market. **–halle** *f* covered market, market hall. **–platz** *m* marketplace. **–tag** *m* market day. **–wirtschaft** *f* (free) market economy.

Marmelade [marmə'laɪdə] *f* (*pl* -n) jam.
Marmor ['marmɔr] *m* (*pl* -e) marble.
Mars [maːrs] *m* Mars. –**bewohner** *m* Martian.
Marsch¹ [marʃ] *m* (*pl* **Märsche**) march.
Marsch² [marʃ] *f* (*pl* -en) marsh.
Marschall ['marʃal] *m* (*pl* **Marschälle**) marshal.
marschieren [marˈʃiːrən] *v* march.
Märtyrer ['mɛrtyrər] *m* (*pl* -) martyr. –**tum** *neut* martyrdom.
Märtyrin [mɔɪr'tyrin] *f* (*pl* -nen) martyr.
Marxismus [marˈksismus] *m* (*unz.*) Marxism.
März [mɛrts] *m* (*pl* -e) March.
Masche ['maʃə] *f* (*pl* -n) mesh; (*Stricken*) stitch; (*Trick*) trick.
Maschine [maˈʃiːnə] *f* (*pl* -en) machine; (*Mot*) engine. **Maschinen‖bau** *m* mechanical engineering. –**fabrik** *f* engineering works. –**gewehr** *neut* machine-gun. –**schreiben** *neut* typewriting, typing. –**schreiber(in)** *m* typist.
Maske ['maskə] *f* (*pl* -n) mask. **Masken‖ball** *m* fancy-dress ball. –**kostüm** *neut* fancy dress (costume).
Maß [maːs] *neut* (*pl* -e) measure; (*Mäßigung*) moderation; (*Grenze*) limit; (*Umfang*) extent. **in hohem Maße** to a great extent. **Maß halten** be moderate.
Masse ['masə] *f* (*pl* -n) mass; (*Jur*) estate, assets. **die Massen** the masses. **Massen‖erzeugung** *f* mass production. –**karambolage** *f* multiple collision, (*umg.*) pile-up. –**versammlung** *f* mass meeting. **massenweise** *adv* wholesale, in large numbers.
Maßgabe ['maːsgaɪbə] *f* standard. **maßgeblich** *adj* authoritative.
mäßig ['mɛːsiç] *adj* moderate. **mäßigen** *v* moderate. **Mäßigung** *f* modulation.
massiv [maˈsiːf] *adj* massive.
maßlos ['maːslos] *adj* immoderate. **Maßnahme** *f* (*pl* -n) measure, step. **Maßnahmen treffen** take steps. **Maßstab** *m* measure; (*Tech*) scale; (*fig*) yardstick.
Mast [mast] *m* (*pl* -e *or* -en) mast.
mästen ['mɛstən] *v* fatten.
Material [materi'aːl] *neut* (*pl* -ien) material. –**ismus** *m* materialism. **materialistisch** *adj* materialist(ic).
Materie [maˈteɪriə] *f* (*pl* -n) matter, stuff, substance.
Mathematik [matemaˈtiːk] *f* (*unz.*) mathe-

matics. -**er** *m* (*pl* -) mathematician. **mathematisch** *adj* mathematical.
Matratze [maˈtratsə] *f* (*pl* -n) mattress.
Mätresse [mɛˈtrɛsə] *f* (*pl* -n) mistress.
Matrize [maˈtriːtsə] *f* (*pl* -n) (*Druck*) stencil; (*Math*) matrix.
Matrose [maˈtroːzə] *m* (*pl* -n) sailor.
Matsch [matʃ] *m* mud; (*Schnee-*) slush. **matschig** *adj* muddy; (*breiig*) squashy.
matt [mat] *adj* faint, weary; (*glanzlos*) dull, matt; (*Licht*) dim; (*Schach*) mate.
Matte ['matə] *f* (*pl* -n) mat.
Mattheit ['mathait] *f* weariness; dullness. **mattherzig** *adj* fainthearted.
Mauer ['mauər] *f* (*pl* -n) wall. **mauern** *v* build (a wall). **Mauerwerk** *neut* masonry.
Maul [maul] *neut* (*pl* **Mäuler**) (animals) mouth, snout, muzzle; (*vulgär*) (person's) mouth.
Maurer ['maurər] *m* (*pl* -) bricklayer, building worker.
Maus [maus] *f* (*pl* **Mäuse**) mouse. **Mause‖falle** *f* mousetrap. –**loch** *neut* mousehole.
maximal [maksi'maːl] *adj* maximum. **Maximum** *neut* maximum.
Mechanik [meˈçaːnik] **1** *f* (*unz.*) mechanics. **2** (*pl* -en) (*Mechanismus*) mechanism. –**er** *m* mechanic. **mechanisch** *adj* mechanical.
meckern ['mɛkərn] *v* bleat; (*nörgeln*) grumble, moan.
Medaille [meˈdaijə] *f* (*pl* -n) medal.
Medikament [medika'mɛnt] *neut* (*pl* -e) medicine.
Medizin [medi'tsiːn] *f* (*pl* -en) medicine. –**er** *m* doctor, physician; (*student*) medical student. **medizinisch** *adj* medical.
Meer [meːr] *neut* (*pl* -e) sea. –**enge** *f* straits *pl*. **Meeres‖boden** *m* sea bed. –**spiegel** *m* sea level.
Mehl [meːl] *neut* (*pl* -e) flour. **mehlig** *adj* floury, mealy.
mehr [meːr] *adv, adj* more. **mehr als** more than. **nicht mehr** no longer. **immer mehr** more and more. **noch mehr** still more. **Mehrbetrag** *m* surplus. **mehrdeutig** *adj* ambiguous.
mehrere ['meːrərə] *pl pron, adj* several. **mehrfach** *adj* multiple.
Mehr‖gepäck *neut* excess baggage. –**gewicht** *neut* excess weight. –**heit** *f* majority.
mehr‖mals *adv* repeatedly, several times. –**seitig** *adj* many-sided; (*Math*) polygo-

nal. **–sprachig** adj multilingual. **–stöckig** adj multistoreyed.

Mehr‖wertsteuer (MwSt) f value added tax (VAT). **–zahl** f majority; (Gramm) plural.

*meiden ['maidən] v avoid.

Meierei ['maiərai] f (pl **-en**) farm; (Milchwirtschaft) dairy farm.

Meile ['mailə] f (pl **-n**) mile.

mein [main] adj, pron my; mine. **meinerseits** adv for my part. **meinesgleichen** pron people like me, the likes of me. **meinethalben, meinetwegen, meinetwillen** adv for my sake. **meinige** pron (**der, die, das meinige**) mine.

Meineid ['mainait] m (pl **-e**) perjury.

meinen ['mainən] v mean; (denken) think; (äußern) say; (beabsichtigen) intend. **Meinung** f opinion. **Ich bin der Meinung, daß** I am of the opinion that. **meiner Meinung nach** in my opinion. **Meinungs‖forschung** f opinion research. **–umfrage,** f opinion poll. **–verschiedenheit** f difference of opinion.

Meißel ['maisəl] m (pl **-**) chisel. **meißeln** v chisel.

meist [maist] adj most. **die meisten(Leute)** most people. **am meisten** for the most part. **Meistbietende(r)** m highest bidder. **meistens** adv mostly.

Meister ['maistər] m (pl **-**) master; (Sport) champion. **meisterhaft** adj masterly. **Meisterin** f (Sport) champion. **meistern** v master. **Meister‖schaft** f mastery; (Sport) championship. **–schaftsspiel** neut championship match. **–stück** or **–werk** neut masterpiece.

meistgekauft ['maistgəkauft] adj best-selling.

Meldeamt ['mɛldəamt] neut registration office. **melden** v inform; (ankündigen) announce. **sich melden** report, present oneself; (Stelle) apply. **Meldung** f report; (ankündigung) announcement; (bei der Polizei, usw.) registration.

*melken ['mɛlkən] v milk. **Melkmaschine** f milking machine.

Melodie [melo'diː] f (pl **-n**) melody. **melodisch** adj melodious.

Melone [me'loːnə] f (pl **-n**) melon.

Membran(e) [mem'braːn] f (pl **Membranen**) membrane.

Menge ['mɛŋə] f (pl **-n**) quantity; (Menschen) crowd. **eine (ganze) Menge** a lot (of), lots (of). **mengen** v mix. **sich mengen in** meddle.

Mensa ['mɛnsa] f (pl **Mensen**) student refectory.

Mensch [mɛnʃ] m (pl **-en**) human (being), man, person. **Menschenfeind** m misanthrope. **menschenfeindlich** adj misanthropic. **Menschenfreund** m philanthropist. **menschenfreundlich** adj philanthropic; (gütig) affable. **Menschen‖kunde** f anthropology. **–leben** neut human life; (Lebenszeit) lifetime. **–liebe** f human kindness. **–rechte** pl human rights. **–würde** f human dignity.

Menschheit ['mɛnʃhait] f mankind, human race. **menschlich** adj human; (human) humane. **Menschlichkeit** f humanity.

menstrual [mɛnstru'aːl] adj menstrual. **Menstruation** f (pl **-nen**) menstruation. **menstruieren** v menstruate.

Mentalität [mɛntali'tɛːt] f (pl **-en**) mentality.

merkbar ['mɛrkbaːr] adj noticeable. **merken** v notice, note. **sich etwas merken** make a mental note of something. **merklich** adj evident. **Merkmal** (pl **-e**) neut characteristic, attribute. **merkwürdig** adj remarkable, peculiar.

Meßband ['mɛsbant] neut tape measure. **meßbar** adj measurable.

Messe ['mɛsə] f (pl **-n**) (Rel) mass; (Ausstellung) (trade) fair.

*messen ['mɛsən] v measure. **sich messen mit** compete with.

Messer¹ ['mɛsər] m (pl **-**) (Gerät) gauge, meter.

Messer² neut (pl **-**) knife.

Messing ['mɛsiŋ] neut (pl **-**) brass.

Messung ['mɛsuŋ] f (pl **-en**) measurement; (Messen) measuring.

Metall [me'tal] neut (pl **-e**) metal. **metallisch** adj metallic.

Meteor [mete'oːr] neut (pl **-e**) meteor. **–ologe** m meteorologist. **–ologie** f meteorology. **meteorologisch** adj meteorologist.

Meter ['meːtər] neut (pl **-**) metre.

Methode [me'toːdə] f (pl **-n**) method. **methodisch** adj methodical.

metrisch ['meːtriʃ] adj metric.

Mettwurst ['mɛtvurst] f a type of German sausage.

metzen ['mɛtsəln] v massacre, slaughter.

Metzger *m* (*pl* -) butcher. **–ei** *f* (*pl* -en) butcher's shop.

Meuchelmord ['mɔyçəlmɔrt] *m* assassination.

Meuterei [mɔytə'rai] *f* (*pl* -en) mutiny. **meutern** *v* mutiny.

mich [miç] *pron* me.

Mieder ['miːdər] *neut* (*pl* -) bodice.

Miene ['miːnə] *f* (*pl* -n) expression, look.

mies [miːs] *adj* (*umg.*) nasty, wretched.

Miete ['miːtə] *f* (*pl* -n) hire; (*für Wohnung*) rent. **mieten** *v* (*Haus, Wohnung*) rent; (*Wagen, usw.*) hire. **Mieter** *m* (*pl* -), **Mieterin** *f* (*pl* -nen) tenant, lessee. **Miet‖shaus** *neut* block of flats, tenement. **–wagen** *m* hired car. **–wohnung** *f* rented apartment.

Mikrophon [mikro'foːn] *neut* (*pl* -e) microphone.

Mikroskop [mikro'skoːp] *neut* microscope. **mikroskopisch** *adj* microscopic.

Milbe ['milbə] *f* (*pl* -n) mite.

Milch [milç] *f* milk. **milchig** *adj* milky. **Milchstraße** *f* Milky Way.

mild [milt] *adj* mild; (*sanft*) soft, gentle. **Milde** *f* mildness; gentleness. **mildern** *v* alleviate, moderate. **Milderung** *f* (*pl* -en) alleviation. **mildtätig** *adj* charitable.

Militär [mili'tɛːr] **1** *neut* (*unz.*) army, military. **2** *m* (*pl* -s) military man, soldier.

Milliarde [mil'jardə] *f* (*pl* -n) thousand million, (*US*) billion.

Million [mil'joːn] *f* (*pl* -en) million. **–är** *m* (*pl* -e) millionaire.

Mimik ['miːmik] *f* (*pl* -en) mimicry, miming. **–er** *m* (*pl* -) mimic.

minder ['mindər] *adj* lesser, smaller. *adv* less. **Minderheit** *f* minority. **Minderjährige(r)** minor. **minderjährig** *adj* under age. **minderwertig** *adj* inferior. **Minderwertigkeit** *f* inferiority.

mindest ['mindəst] *adj* least; (*kleinst*) smallest. **–ens** *adv* at least. **Mindestzahl** *f* minimum number; (*Pol*) quorum.

Mine ['miːnə] *f* (*pl* -n) mine.

Mineral [mine'raːl] *neut* (*pl* -ien) mineral. **–wasser** *neut* mineral water.

Miniatur [minia'tuːr] *f* (*pl* -en) miniature.

minimal [mini'maːl] *adj* minimum. **Minimum** *neut* minimum.

Minister [mi'nistər] *m* (*pl* -) minister. **–ium** *neut* ministry. **–präsident** *m* prime minister.

minus ['miːnus] *adv* minus, less.

Minute [mi'nuːtə] *f* (*pl* -n) minute.

mir [miːr] *pron* (to) me.

mischen ['miʃən] *v* mix, blend. **sich mischen in** meddle *or* interfere in. **Misch‖ling** *m* (*Pflanze*) hybrid; (*Tier*) mongrel; (*Mensch*) half-breed. **–sprache** *f* pidgin. **–ung** *f* (*pl* -en) mixture.

mißach‖ten [mis'axtən] *v* disregard. **Mißachtung** *f* disregard.

Mißbildung ['misbilduŋ] *f* deformity.

mißbilligen ['misbiligən] *v* disapprove (of), object (to). **Mißbilligung** *f* disapproval.

Mißbrauch ['misbraux] *m* misuse, abuse. **mißbrauchen** *v* misuse, abuse.

mißdeuten [mis'dɔytən] *v* misinterpret, misunderstand. **Mißdeutung** *f* misinterpretation.

Mißerfolg ['misɛrfɔlk] *m* failure.

Missetat ['misətaːt] *f* misdeed. **Missetäter** *m* wrong-doer; (*Verbrecher*) criminal.

***mißfallen** [mis'falən] *v* displease. **Mißfallen** *neut* displeasure.

Mißgeschick ['misgəʃik] *neut* misfortune.

mißgestaltet ['misgəʃtaltət] *adj* misshapen.

mißhandeln [mis'handəln] *v* maltreat. **Mißhandlung** *f* maltreatment.

Mission [misi'oːn] *f* (*pl* -en) mission. **–ar** *m* (*pl* -e) missionary.

Mißklang ['misklaŋ] *m* discord.

mißlich ['mislıç] *adj* awkward, embarrassing.

***mißlingen** *v* fail. **mißlungen** *adj* failed, unsuccessful.

mißtrauen [mis'trauən] *v* distrust. **Mißtrauen** *neut* distrust. **–svotum** *neut* vote of no confidence.

Mißverständnis ['misferʃtɛntnis] *neut* misunderstanding. **mißverstehen** *v* misunderstand.

Mist [mist] *m* (*pl* -e) dung, manure.

Mistel ['mistəl] *f* (*pl* -n) mistletoe.

mit [mit] *prep* with; (*mittels*) by; (*Zeit*) at. *adv* along with; (*außerdem*) also, as well. *kommst du mit?* are you coming (with us)? *mit 10 Jahren* at the age of ten. **mit einemmal** suddenly. **mit dabei sein** be concerned *or* involved.

Mitarbeiter ['mitarbaitər] *m* colleague, fellow worker; (*Zeitschrift*) contributor.

Mitbestimmung ['mitbəʃtimuŋ] *f* worker participation, co-determination.

mitbeteiligt ['mitbətailiçt] *adj* participating, taking part.

*mitbringen ['mitbriŋən] *v* bring along.

miteinander [mitain'andər] *adv* together, with each other.

miteinbegriffen [mit'ainbəgrifən] *adj* included.

Mitgefühl ['mitgəfyːl] *neut* sympathy.

Mitglied ['mitgliːt] *neut* member. **–schaft** *f* membership.

mithin [mit'hin] *adv* consequently, therefore.

*mitkommen ['mitkɔmən] *v* come along (with); keep up.

Mitlaut ['mitlaut] *m* consonant.

Mitleid ['mitlait] *neut* pity, sympathy. **mitleid haben mit** have pity on, be sorry for.

mitmachen ['mitmaxən] *v* take part in, join in; *(erleben)* go *or* live through.

Mitmensch ['mitmɛnʃ] *m* fellow man.

*mitnehmen ['mitneːmən] *v* take (along); *(im Auto)* give a lift to; *(erschöpfen)* exhaust. **Essen zum Mitnehmen** food to take away.

mitnichten [mit'niçtən] *adv* by no means.

*mitreißen ['mitraisən] *v* drag along; *(fig)* sweep along, transport.

Mittag ['mitaːk] *m* noon, midday. **–essen** *neut* lunch, midday meal. **mittags** *adv* at noon. **Mittagspause** *f* lunch hour.

Mitte ['mitə] *f* (*pl* **-n**) middle, centre; *(Math)* mean.

mitteilen ['mittailən] *v* communicate, inform of, tell. **jemandem etwas mitteilen** inform *or* notify someone of something. **Mitteilung** *f* communication, report.

Mittel ['mitəl] *neut* (*pl* **-**) means, way; *(Ausweg)* remedy; *(Durchschnitt)* average, mean. **–alter** *neut* Middle Ages. **mittelalterlich** *adj* medieval.

Mittel‖amerika *f* Central America. **–gewichtler** *m* middleweight.

mittelgroß ['mitəlgroːs] *adj* of medium size.

Mittelläufer ['mitəllɔyfər] *m* (*Fußball*) centre-half.

mittel‖los *adj* destitute. **–mäßig** *adj* mediocre.

Mittel‖meer *neut* Mediterranean (Sea). **–punkt** *m* centre.

mittels ['mitəls] *prep* by (means of).

Mittel‖stand *m* middle classes *pl*. **–stürmer** *m* (*Fußball*) centre-forward.

mitten ['mitən] *adv* in the middle, midway. **mitten in/auf/unter** in the middle of. **mitten drin** in the middle.

Mitternacht ['mitərnaxt] *f* midnight.

mittler ['mitlər] *adj* **in mittlerem Alter** middle-aged. **mittlerweile** *adv* in the meantime.

Mittwoch ['mitvɔx] *m* (*pl* **-e**) Wednesday.

mitwirken ['mitvirkən] *v* cooperate, take part, participate. **–d** *adj* participating, contributing.

Möbel ['møːbəl] *neut* (*pl* **-**) piece of furniture; *(pl)* furniture *sing*.

mobil [mo'biːl] *adj* movable, mobile; *(flink)* active, lively.

möblieren [mø'bliːrən] *v* furnish. **möbliert** *adj* furnished.

Mode ['moːdə] *f* (*pl* **-n**) fashion, vogue. **in Mode sein** be in fashion. **aus der Mode kommen** become unfashionable. **Modeartikel** *pl* fancy goods, fashions.

Modell [mo'dɛl] *neut* (*pl* **-e**) model; *(Muster)* pattern. **Modellierbogen** *m* cutting-out pattern. **modellieren** *v* model.

Modenschau ['moːdənʃau] *f* fashion show. **Modezeichner** *m* dress *or* fashion designer.

Moder ['moːdər] *m* decay, mould. **moderig** *adj* mouldy, putrid. **modern** *v* rot, decay.

modern [mo'dɛrn] *adj* modern. **modernisieren** *v* modernize.

modifizieren [modifi'tsiːrən] *v* modify.

modisch ['moːdiʃ] *adj* fashionable.

mogeln ['moːgəln] *v* cheat.

*mögen ['møːgən] *v* like; *(wünschen)* wish; *(können)* may, might. **nicht mögen** dislike. **Ich mag ihn** I like him. **das mag sein** that may be so. **Wer mag das sein?** who might that be? **Ich möchte** I would like. **Ich möchte lieber** I would prefer. **Er mag ruhig warten!** let him wait!

möglich ['møːgliç] *adj* possible. **–erweise** *adv* possibly. **Möglichkeit** *f* possibility. **möglichst** *adv* as . . . as possible.

Mohammedaner [mohame'daːnər] *m* (*pl* **-**) Muslim, Mohammedan. **mohammedanisch** *adj* Muslim, Mohammedan.

Mohn [moːn] *m* (*pl* **-e**) poppy; *(Samen)* poppyseed.

Mohr [moːr] *m* (*pl* **-en**) moor, black(man).

Möhre ['møːrə] *f* (*pl* **-n**) carrot.

Mohrrübe ['moːrryːbə] *f* (*pl* **-n**) carrot.

Molekül [moleˈkyːl] *neut* (*pl* -e) molecule.
molekular *adj* molecular.
Molkerei [mɔlkəˈrai] *f* (*pl* -en) dairy.
Moll [mɔl] *neut* (*unz.*) (*Musik*) minor.
Moment[1] [moˈmɛnt] *m* (*pl* -e) moment, instant. **Moment mal!** Just a moment!
Moment[2] *neut* (*unz.*) (*Physik*) moment; (*Anlaß*) motive; (*Umstand*) factor.
Monarch [moˈnarç] *m* (*pl* -en) monarch. **-ie** *f* (*pl* -n) monarchy. **-ist** *m* (*pl* -en) monarchist.
Monat [ˈmoːnat] *m* (*pl* -e) month. **monatelang** *adv* for months. **monatlich** *adj* monthly. **Monats‖blutung** *f* menstruation. **-karte** *f* (monthly) season ticket.
Mönch [mœnç] *m* (*pl* -e) monk.
Mond [moːnt] *m* (*pl* -e) moon. **-finsternis** *f* lunar eclipse. **-schein** *m* moonlight. **-strahl** *m* moonbeam.
Monogramm [monoˈɡram] *neut* (*pl* -e) monogram, initials.
Monopol [monoˈpoːl] *neut* (*pl* -e) monopoly. **monopolisieren** *v* monopolize.
Montag [ˈmoːntaːk] *m* Monday. **montags** *adv* (on) Mondays.
Montage [mɔnˈtaːʒə] *f* (*pl* -n) assembly; installation. **-band** *neut* assembly line.
Monteur [mɔnˈtøːr] *m* (*pl* -e) mechanic, fitter. **montieren** *v* install, assemble.
Moor [moːr] *neut* (*pl* -e) marsh, moor.
Moos [moːs] *neut* (*pl* -e) moss.
Moped [ˈmoːpɛt] *neut* (*pl* -s) moped.
Moral [moˈraːl] *f* (*pl*-en) moral; (*Sittlichkeit*) morality; (*Zuversicht*) morale. **moralisieren** *v* moralize.
Mord [mɔrt] *m* (*pl* -e) murder.
Mörder [ˈmœrdər] *m* (*pl* -) murderer. **mörderisch** *adj* murderous.
morgen [ˈmɔrɡən] *adv* tomorrow. **morgen früh** tomorrow morning. **Morgen** *m* (*pl* -) morning. **-dämmerung** *f* dawn. **-land** *neut* Orient. **-stern** *m* morning star, Venus.
Morphium [ˈmɔrfium] *neut* morphine.
morsch [mɔrʃ] *adj* rotten.
Morseschrift [ˈmɔrzəʃrift] *f* Morse code.
Mörtel [ˈmœrtəl] *m* (*pl* -) mortar, cement.
Mosaik [mozaˈiːk] *neut* (*pl* -e) mosaic.
Moschee [mɔˈʃeː] *f* (*pl* -n) mosque.
Mosel [ˈmoːzəl] *f* Moselle.
Moskau [ˈmɔskau] *neut* Moscow.
Most [mɔst] *m* (*pl* -e) new wine, must.
Motiv [moˈtiːf] *neut* (*pl* -e) (*Antrieb*) motive; (*Kunst, Dichtung*) theme, motif. **motivieren** *v* motivate.
Motor [ˈmoːtɔr] *m* (*pl* -en) motor, engine. **-ausfall** *m* engine failure. **-boot** *neut* motorboat. **-haube** *f* bonnet, (*US*) hood. **-rad** *neut* motorcycle. **-roller** *m* (motor) scooter.
Motte [ˈmɔtə] *f* (*pl* -n) moth.
Möwe [ˈmœːvə] *f* (*pl* -n) seagull.
Mücke [ˈmykə] *f* (*pl* -n) midge, gnat. **Mücken‖netz** *neut* mosquito net. **-stich** *m* midge *or* gnat bite.
müde [ˈmyːdə] *adj* tired. **Müdigkeit** *f* tiredness, fatigue.
Muff[1] [muf] *m* (*unz.*) musty smell.
Muff[2] *m* (*pl* -e) (*Pelz*) muff.
Muffel [ˈmufəl] *m* (*pl* -) grumpy person. **muffelig** *adj* grumpy, sullen.
muffig [ˈmufiç] *adj* (*moderig*) musty.
Mühe [ˈmyːə] *f* (*pl* -n) trouble, pains *pl.* **sich Mühe geben** take pains. **nicht der Mühe wert** not worth the trouble. **mühelos** *adj* effortless. **sich mühen** trouble oneself, take pains. **mühevoll** *adj* laborious, troublesome.
Mühle [ˈmyːlə] *m* (*pl* -n) mill.
mühsam [ˈmyːzaːm] *adj also* **mühselig** troublesome; (*schwierig*) difficult.
Mulde [ˈmuldə] *f* (*pl* -n) trough; (*Landschaft*) depression, hollow.
Mull [mul] *m* (*pl* -e) muslin.
Müll [myl] *m* refuse, rubbish, (*US*) garbage. **-abfuhr** *f* refuse disposal. **-eimer** *m* dustbin.
Müller [ˈmylər] *m* (*pl* -) miller.
Multiplikation [multiplikatsiˈoːn] *f* (*pl* -en) multiplication. **multiplizieren** *v* multiply.
Mumie [ˈmumiə] *f* (*pl* -n) mummy.
Mummenschanz [ˈmumənʃants] *m* (*pl* -e) masquerade.
München [ˈmynçən] *neut* Munich. **Münchner** *adj* (of) Munich.
Mund [munt] *m* (*pl* **Münder**) mouth. **-art** *f* dialect.
münden [ˈmyndən] *v* **münden in** (*Fluß*) flow into; (*Straße*) run into, join.
mund‖faul *adj* taciturn. **-fertig** *adj* glib. **-gerecht** *adj* appetizing. **Mund‖geruch** *m* bad breath, halitosis. **-harmonika** *f* mouth organ, harmonica.
mündig [ˈmyndiç] *adj* of age. **mündig werden** come of age. **Mündigkeit** *f* majority, full legal age.

mündlich ['myntliç] *adj* oral.
Mundstück ['muntstyk] *neut* mouthpiece.
Mündung ['myndoŋ] *f (pl -en) (Fluß)* estuary.
Munition [munitsi'oɪn] *f (pl -en)* ammunition.
munter ['muntər] *adj* lively, cheerful, merry. **Munterkeit** *f* liveliness, cheer.
Münze ['myntsə] *f (pl -n)* coin; *(Anstalt)* mint. **für bare Münze nehmen** take at face value. **Münz||einwurf** *m* coin-slot. **–fernsprecher** *m* pay phone, call box.
mürbe ['myrbə] *adj (Fleisch)* tender; *(morsch)* rotten, soft; *(brüchig)* brittle; *(Gebäck)* crumbly. **Mürbeteig** *m* short pastry.
murmeln ['murməln] *v* murmur.
murren ['murən] *v* grumble.
mürrisch ['myriʃ] *adj* morose, grumpy.
Mus [muɪs] *neut* purée.
Muschel ['muʃəl] *f (pl -n)* mussel; *(Telef)* (telephone) receiver. **–tier** *neut* mollusc.
Museum [mu'zeɪum] *neut (pl Museen)* museum.
Musical ['mjuɪzikəl] *neut (pl -s)* musical.
Musik [mu'ziɪk] *f* music; *(Kapelle)* band. **musikalisch** *adj* musical. **Musik||antenknochen** *m (umg.)* funnybone. **–er** *m (pl -)* musician. **–freund** *m* music-lover. **–instrument** *m* musical instrument.
Muskat [mus'kaɪt] *m (pl -e)* nutmeg. **–blüte** *f* mace. **–nuß** *f* nutmeg.
Muskel ['muskəl] *m (pl -n)* muscle. **–kraft** *f* muscular strength. **–krampf** *m* muscle spasm. **–zerrung** *f* pulled muscle.
Muße ['muɪsə] *f* leisure. **müßig** *adj* idle.
***müssen** ['mysən] *v* must, have to. *ich mußgehen* I must go. *ich muß nicht gehen* I don't have to go. *ich muß fort* I must leave. *ich müßte* I ought to.
Muster ['mustər] *net (pl -)* model, pattern; *(Stoffverzierung)* pattern, design; *(warenprobe)* sample. **–stück** *neut* sample, specimen. **–zeichnung** *f* design.
Mut [muɪt] *m* courage. **mutig** *adj* brave, courageous. **mutlos** *adj* discouraged, despondent.
mutmaßen ['mutmaɪsən] *v* suppose, surmise. **Mutmaßung** *f (pl -en)* conjecture.
Mutter¹ ['mutər] *f (pl Mütter)* mother.
Mutter² *f (pl -n) (Tech)* nut.
mütterlich ['mytərliç] *adj* motherly.

–erseits *adv* on one's mother's side, maternal.
Mutter||liebe *f* mother-love. **–mal** *neut* birthmark. **–schaft** *f* motherhood. **–sprache** *f* mother tongue, native language.
Mütze ['mytsə] *f (pl -n)* cap.
mysteriös [mysteri'œɪs] *adj* mysterious.
Mystik ['mystik] *f (unz.)* mysticism. **–er** *m* mystic. **mystisch** *adj* mystical.
Mythe ['mytə] *f (pl -n)* myth. **mythisch** *adj* mythical.

N

na [na] *interj* well! (come) now!
Nabe ['naɪbə] *f (pl -n)* hub.
Nabel ['naɪbəl] *m (pl -)* navel. **–schnur** *f* umbilical cord.
nach [naɪx] *prep* after; *(örtlich)* to, towards; *(gemäß)* according to, by. *adv* after. **nach und nach** gradually. **der Größe nach** by size. **nach außen** externally.
nachahmen ['naɪxaɪmən] *v* imitate. **Nachahmung** *f* imitation.
Nachbar ['naɪxbaɪr] *m (pl -n)* neighbour. **–land** *neut* neighbouring country. **–schaft** *f* neighbourhood.
Nachbildung ['naɪxbilduŋ] *f* copy, replica.
nachdem [naɪx'deɪm] *adv* afterwards. *conj* after. **je nachdem** according as.
***nachdenken** ['naɪxdɛŋkən] *v* think (over), reflect. **Nachdenken** *neut* reflection, thinking over. **nachdenklich** *adj* reflective, thoughtful.
Nachdruck ['naɪxdruk] *m (Betonung)* emphasis, stress; *(Festigkeit)* vigour. **nachdrücklich** *adj* emphatic; forceful.
nacheifern ['naɪxaifərn] *v* emulate.
nacheinander ['naɪxainandər] *adv* one after another.
Nachfolge ['naɪxfɔlgə] *f* succession. **nachfolgen** *v* succeed, follow. **Nachfolger** *m* successor.
Nachfrage ['naɪxfraɪgə] *f (Erkundigung)* inquiry; *(Komm)* demand.
***nachgeben** ['naɪxgeɪbən] *v* give way or in.
Nachgeburt ['naɪxgəburt] *f* afterbirth.
***nachgehen** ['naɪxgeɪən] *v* follow; *(untersuchen)* investigate; *(Uhr)* be slow.

nachgemacht ['naːxgəmaxt] *adj* imitated, false.

Nachgeschmack ['naːxgəʃmak] *m* aftertaste.

nachgiebig ['naːxgiːbiç] *adj* pliable, flexible; (*Person*) compliant, yielding.

nachher [naːx'heːr] *adv* afterwards.

Nachhilfe ['naːxhilfə] *f* help, assistance. **–stunden** *pl* coaching *sing*, private tuition *sing*.

nachholen ['naːxhoːlən] *v* fetch later; (*fig*) make up for, catch up on.

Nach‖hut ['naːxhuːt] *f* rearguard. **–klang** *m* echo, resonance.

Nachkomme ['naːxkɔmə] *m* (*pl* **-n**) descendant. **nachkommen** *v* follow, come after; (*Verpflichtung*) fulfil. **Nachkommenschaft** *f* posterity, descendants *pl*.

Nachkriegszeit ['naːxkriːkstsait] *f* postwar era.

Nachlaß ['naːxlas] *m* (*pl* **Nachlässe**) (*Preis*) reduction, discount; (*Erbschaft*) inheritance, estate. **nachlassen** *v* slacken, abate; (*aufhören*) cease; (*Strafe*) remit; (*Preis*) reduce. **nachlässig** *adj* careless, negligent.

nachmachen ['naːxmaxən] *v* copy, imitate.

Nachmittag ['naːxmitaːk] *m* afternoon. **nachmittags** *adv* in the afternoon(s).

Nachnahme ['naːxnaːmə] *f* gegen *or* per Nachnahme cash on delivery (COD).

Nachname ['naːxnaːmə] *m* (*pl* **-n**) surname.

nachprüfen ['naːxpryːfən] *v* verify, check again.

Nachricht ['naːxriçt] *f* (*pl* **-en**) report, (item of) news. **Nachrichten** *pl* news *sing*. **Nachrichten‖büro** *neut* news agency. **–dienst** *m* (*Radio*) news service; (*Mil*) intelligence service.

Nachruf ['naːxruːf] *m* (*Zeitung*) obituary; (*Rede*) memorial address.

*nachschlagen ['naːxʃlaːgən] *v* (*Buch*) look up, consult. **Nachschlagebuch** *neut* reference book.

Nach‖schrift ['naːxʃrift] *f* (*Brief*) postscript; (*eines Vortrages*) transcript. **–schub** *m* (*Mil*) reinforcement(s); (*Material*) supplies *pl*.

*nach‖sehen ['naːxzeːən] *v* (*nachblicken*) watch, follow with one's eyes; (*prüfen*) examine, check; (*nachschlagen*) consult; (*verzeihen*) overlook. **–senden** *v* send on; (*Post*) forward.

Nach‖sicht ['naːxziçt] *f* leniency. **–sorge** *f* (medical) aftercare. **–spiel** *neut* epilogue, sequel. **–speise** *f* dessert.

nächst [nɛçst] *adj* next; (*Entfernung*) nearest; (*Verwandte*) close, closest; (*umg: kürzest*) shortest. *adv* next. *prep* next to. **am nächsten** next. **nächste Woche** next week. *das nächste Dorf liegt 10 km von hier entfernt* the nearest village is 10 km away. **Nächste(r)** fellowman, neighbour.

*nach‖stehen ['naːxʃteːən] *v* be inferior to. **–stellen** re-adjust; (*Uhr*) put back; (*Frau*) molest, bother.

Nächstenliebe ['nɛçstənliːbə] *f* charity, love of one's fellow men. **nächstens** *adv* shortly.

Nacht [naxt] *f* (*pl* **Nächte**) night. **heute Nacht** tonight. **über Nacht** overnight.

Nachteil ['naːxtail] *m* disadvantage; (*Schaden*) damage, detriment. **nachteilig** *adj* disadvantageous, unfavourable.

Nachthemd ['naxthɛmt] *neut* nightshirt, nightgown.

Nachtigall ['naxtigal] *f* (*pl* **-en**) nightingale.

Nach‖tisch ['naːxtiʃ] *m* dessert. **–trag** *m* supplement. **nachträglich** *adj* subsequent, later.

nachts [naxts] *adv* at *or* by night. **Nachtwächter** *m* nightwatchman. **nachtwandeln** *v* sleepwalk.

Nach‖untersuchung ['naːxʊntərzuːxʊŋ] *f* check-up. **–wahl** *f* by-election. **–weis** *m* proof, evidence. **nachweisen** *v* prove, demonstrate.

Nach‖wirkung ['naːxvirkʊŋ] *f* after-effect. **–wort** *neut* epilogue. **–wuchs** *m* new *or* young generation.

*nachziehen ['naːxtsiːən] *v* drag, draw along; (*nachzeichnen*) trace; (*folgen*) follow.

Nachzügler ['naːxtsyːklər] *m* (*pl* **-**) straggler, late-comer.

Nacken ['nakən] *m* (*pl* **-**) (nape of the) neck.

nackt [nakt] *adj* naked, bare. **Nacktheit** *f* nakedness.

Nadel ['naːdəl] *f* (*pl* **-n**) needle; (*Stecknadel*) pin. **–baum** *m* conifer. **–öhr** *neut* eye (of a needle). **–wald** *m* coniferous forest.

Nagel ['naːgəl] *m* (*pl* **Nägel**) nail. **–feile** *f* nail-file. **–haut** *f* cuticle. **–lack** *m* nail varnish. **nageln** *v* nail. **nagelneu** *adj* brand-new. **Nagelschere** f nail scissors pl.

nagen ['naɪgən] v gnaw.

Nagetier ['naɪgətiːr] neut rodent.

nah(e) ['naː(ə)] adj, adv near, close. prep near to. **einer Person zu nahe treten** offend a person. **nahe dabei** or **gelegen** nearby. **nahe Freundschaft** close friendship.

Nahaufnahme ['naːaufnaɪmə] f (Foto) close-up.

Nähe ['nɛːə] f nearness; (Sicht-, Hörweite) vicinity. **in der Nähe** close by, in the vicinity.

***nahe‖kommen** v approach. **–liegend** adj obvious; (örtlich) close, nearby.

nähen ['nɛːən] v sew, stitch.

näher ['nɛːər] adj nearer, closer; (ausführlicher) more detailed. **nähere Angaben** further details. **nähere Umstände** exact circumstances. **Nähere(s)** neut particulars pl, details pl. **nähern** v bring near. **sich nähern** approach, draw near.

nahe‖stehend adj close, friendly. **–zu** adv nearly, almost.

Näh‖kasten m sewing box. **–machine** f sewing machine. **–nadel** f sewing needle.

nähren ['nɛːrən] v nourish; (unterhalten) support. **sich nähren von** live on.

nahrhaft ['naːrhaft] adj nutritious.

Nährmittel ['nɛːrmɪtəl] pl foodstuffs, food sing.

Nahrung ['naːruŋ] f (unz.) food; (Unterhalt) support. **–smittel** pl foodstuffs.

Naht ['naːt] f (pl Nähte) seam; (Med) suture.

naiv [na'iːf] adj naive.

Name ['naːmə] or **Namen** m (pl Namen) name. **namens** adv named, by the name of.

nämlich ['nɛːmlɪç] adv that is (to say), namely.

Napf [napf] m (pl Näpfe) basin, bowl.

Narbe ['narbə] f (pl -n) scar.

Narkose [nar'koːzə] f (pl -n) (Betäubung) anaesthesia. **Narkotikum** neut (pl Narkotika) narcotic. **narkotisch** adj narcotic.

Narr [nar] m (pl -en) fool. **zum Narren haben** make a fool of. **Narrheit** f folly, foolishness.

närrisch ['nɛːrɪʃ] adj foolish, crazy, silly.

Nase ['naːzə] f (pl -n) nose. **die Nase voll haben von** be fed up with. **Nasen‖loch** neut nostril. **–höhle** f (anat) sinus. **–spitze** f tip of the nose. **naseweis** adj cheeky.

naß [nas] adj wet; (feucht) moist, damp. **Nässe** ['nɛsə] f wet, wetness.

Nation [natsi'oːn] f (pl -en) nation. **national** adj national. **National‖flagge** f national flag. **–hymne** f national anthem.

nationalisieren [natsionaːli'ziːrən] v nationalize. **Nationalisierung** f nationalization. **Nationalismus** m nationalism. **nationalistisch** adj nationalist(ic).

National‖mannschaft f national team. **–sozialismus** m national socialism, Nazism. **–tracht** f national costume.

Natter ['natər] f (pl -n) adder.

Natur [na'tuːr] f (pl -en) nature. **–anlage** f temperament, disposition. **–forscher** m scientist, naturalist. **–kunde** f natural history. **natürlich** adj natural. **Natur‖schutz** m preservation (of nature). **–trieb** m instinct. **–wissenschaft** f natural science.

Nazi ['naɪtsi] m (pl -s) Nazi.

Nebel ['neːbəl] m (pl -) fog; (dünner) mist. **–horn** neut foghorn. **nebelig** adj foggy; misty.

neben ['neːbən] prep near (to), beside; (im Vergleich zu) compared with, next to. **–an** adv next door. **–bei** adv by the way; (außerdem) besides. **Neben‖beschäftigung** f second job, sideline. **–buhler** m rival.

nebeneinander ['neːbənainandər] adv side by side. **–stellen** v juxtapose.

Neben‖fach neut subsidiary subject. **–fluß** m tributary. **–gebäude** neut annexe. **–kosten** pl extras, additional expenses.

nebensächlich ['neːbənsɛçlɪç] adj incidental.

necken ['nɛkən] v tease.

Neffe ['nɛfə] m (pl -n) nephew.

negativ ['neːgatiːf] adj negative.

Neger ['neːgər] m (pl -) Negro, Black. **–in** f (pl -nen) Black (woman).

***nehmen** ['neːmən] v take.

Neid [naɪt] m envy, jealousy. **neid‖en** v envy. **–isch** adj envious, jealous.

Neige ['naɪgə] f (pl -n) slope, incline. **neigen** v incline. **neigen zu** tend (to), be inclined (to). **sich neigen** incline, slope. **Neigung** f slope; (fig) inclination.

nein [nain] *adv* no.
Nelke ['nɛlkə] *f* (*pl* -n) carnation; (*Gewürz*) clove.
*****nennen** ['nɛnən] *v* call, name. **Nenn‖er** *m* denominator. **–ung** *f* naming; (*Sport*) entry. **–wert** *m* nominal value.
Nerv [nɛrf] *m* (*pl* -en) nerve. **Nerven‖kitzel** *m* thrill. **–krankheit** *f* nervous disease. **nervös** *adj* nervous.
Nessel ['nɛsəl] *f* (*pl* -n) nettle.
Nest [nɛst] *neut* (*pl* -er) nest.
nett [nɛt] *adj* nice; (*gepflegt*) neat.
netto ['nɛtto] *adj* net. **Netto‖gewinn** *m* net profit. **–preis** *m* net price.
Netz [nɛts] *neut* (*pl* -e) net; (*System*) grid, network. **–haut** *f* retina. **–werk** *neut* network.
neu [nɔy] *adj* new; (*modern*) modern. **–artig** *adj* novel.
Neu‖ausgabe *f* new edition. **–bau** *n* new building.
neuerdings ['nɔyərdɪŋs] *adv* recently, lately.
Neuerer ['nɔyərər] *m* (*pl* -) innovator.
Neuerscheinung ['nɔyɛrʃainuŋ] *f* (*pl* -en) new book.
Neu‖erung ['nɔyəruŋ] *f* (*pl* -en) innovation.
neuestens ['nɔyəstəns] *adv* of late.
neu‖geboren *adj* new-born. **–gestalten** *v* reorganize.
Neugier(de) ['nɔygiːr(də)] *f* (*unz.*) curiosity. **neugierig** *adj* curious.
Neu‖heit *f* (*pl* -en) novelty. **–igkeit** *f* (*pl* -en) (item of) news. **–jahr** *neut* New Year. **–jahrstag** *m* New Year's Day.
neulich ['nɔylɪç] *adv* recently, lately.
neun [nɔyn] *pron*, *adj* nine. **neunte** *adj* ninth. **neunzehn** *pron*, *adj* nineteen. **neunzig** *pron*, *adj* ninety.
Neu‖ordnung *f* reorganization. **–reiche(r)** nouveau riche, wealthy parvenu.
Neurologe [nɔyroˈloːgə] *m* (*pl* -n) neurologist. **Neurologie** *f* neurology. **neurologisch** *adj* neurological.
Neurose [nɔyˈroːzə] *f* (*pl* -n) neurosis. **neurotisch** *adj* neurotic.
Neuseeland [nɔyˈzeːlant] *neut* New Zealand.
neutral [nɔyˈtraːl] *adj* neutral. **neutralisieren** *v* neutralize. **Neutralität** *f* neutrality.
neuzeitlich ['nɔytsaitlɪç] *adj* modern.
nicht [nɪçt] *adv* not. **durchaus nicht** not at all. **nicht einmal** not even. **bitte nicht** please don't. **nicht mehr** no longer. **nicht wahr?** isn't it? don't you agree?
Nicht‖achtung *f* disregard. **–annahme** *f* nonacceptance. **–beachtung** *f* nonobservance.
Nichte ['nɪçtə] *f* (*pl* -n) niece.
Nicht‖einmischung *f* nonintervention. **–erscheinen** *neut* nonappearance.
nichtig ['nɪçtɪç] *adj* futile, empty; (*ungültig*) null, void. **Nichtigkeit** *f* futility; invalidity.
Nicht‖mitglied *neut* non-member. **–raucher** *m* non-smoker. **–raucherabteil** *neut* no-smoking compartment.
nichts [nɪçts] *pron* nothing. **nichts daraus machen** not take seriously. **(es) macht nichts** it doesn't matter. **nichts dergleichen** nothing of the kind. **Nichts** *neut* nothing(ness).
nichts‖sagend *adj* meaningless. **–würdig** *adj* worthless, base.
Nicht‖vorhandensein *neut* lack, absence. **–zutreffende(s)** *neut* (that which is) nonapplicable.
Nickel ['nɪkəl] *neut* nickel.
nicken ['nɪkən] *v* nod, bow; doze, nod off. **Nickerchen** *neut* nap.
nie [niː] *adv* never.
nieder ['niːdər] *adj* low; (*fig*) inferior. *adv* down.
*****nieder‖brennen** *v* burn down. **–drücken** *v* depress. **–fallen** *v* fall down.
Nieder‖frequenz *f* low frequency. **–gang** *m* decline, downfall; (*Sonne*) setting.
*****nieder‖gehen** *v* go down; (*Aero*) land. **–geschlagen** *adj* depressed.
Niederlage ['niːdərlaːgə] *f* defeat.
Niederlande ['niːdərlandə] *pl* Netherlands. **Niederländer** *m* Dutchman. **–in** *f* Dutchwoman. **niederländisch** *adj* Dutch.
*****niederlassen** ['niːdərlasən] *v* lower. **sich niederlassen** settle down; (*Vogel*) land, settle. **Niederlassung** *f* (*pl* -en) settlement; (*Komm*) branch.
niederlegen ['niːdərleːgən] *v* lay down.
Niedersachsen ['niːdəzaksən] *neut* Lower Saxony.
Niederschlag ['niːdərʃlaːk] *m* (*Regen, usw.*) precipitation; (*auf Fensterscheiben*) condensation; (*Chem*) sediment, precipitation; (*Boxen*) knock-down.
*****niederschlagen** *v* knock down; (*Augen*) lower; (*Aufstand*) suppress.

nieder‖schmettern v strike down. **–schreiben** v write down. **–setzen** v put down. **–werfen** v throw down. **sich niederwerfen** prostrate oneself.

niedlich ['niːdliç] adj nice, (umg.) cute, dainty.

niedrig ['niːdriç] adj low. **Niedrigkeit** f lowness. **Niedrigwasser** neut low water, low tide.

niemals ['niːmaːls] adv never.

niemand ['niːmant] pron no one, nobody. **Niemandsland** neut no-man's-land.

Niere ['niːrə] f (pl -n) kidney.

nieseln ['niːzəln] v drizzle.

niesen ['niːzən] v sneeze. **Niesen** neut sneeze.

Niet [niːt] neut (pl -e) rivet.

Niete ['niːtə] f (pl -n) (Lotterie) blank (ticket); (Person) nonentity, failure; (Theater) flop.

Nikotin [niko'tiːn] neut nicotine.

Nilpferd ['niːlpfɛrt] neut hippopotamus.

nimmer ['nimər] adv never. **–mehr** adv never again.

nippen ['nipən] v sip.

nirgends ['nirgənts] or **nirgendwo** adv nowhere.

Nische ['niːʃə] f (pl -n) niche, alcove.

nisten ['nistən] v (build a) nest.

Niveau [ni'voː] neut (pl -s) level; (fig) standard; (geistig) culture, good education. **Niveau haben** be cultured or sophisticated.

noch [nox] adv (außerdem) in addition. conj nor. **noch nicht** not yet. **noch einmal** once again. **noch etwas?** anything else? **noch dazu** in addition. **weder ... noch ... neither ... nor .... nochmals** adv once again.

Nockenwelle ['nɔkənvɛlə] f camshaft.

Nomade [no'maːdə] m (pl -n) nomad.

Nominativ ['noːminatiːf] m (pl -e) nominative.

nominell [nomi'nɛl] adj nominal.

Nonne ['nɔnə] f (pl -n) nun. **–nkloster** neut convent, nunnery.

Nord [nɔrt] m north. **–amerika** f North America. **–en** m north. **nordisch** adj northern; (Skandinavisch) nordic. **Nordländer 1** m (pl -) Northerner. **2** pl northern countries.

nördlich ['nœrtliç] adj northern. adv northwards. prep to the north of.

Nordost(en) ['nɔrtɔst(ən)] m northeast. **nordöstlich** adj northeast(ern).

Nord‖pol m North Pole. **–rhein-Westfalen** neut North Rhine-Westphalia. **–see** f North Sea. **nordwärts** adv northwards.

Nordwest(en) ['nɔrtvɛst(ən)] m northwest. **nordwestlich** adj northwest(ern).

nörgeln ['nœrgəln] v grumble, grouse.

Norm [nɔrm] f (pl -en) standard, norm. **normal** adj normal. **–erweise** adv normally. **normalisieren** v normalize. **–maß** neut standard measure. **normgerecht** adj conforming to a standard.

Norwegen ['nɔrveɡən] neut Norway. **Norweger** m (pl -), **Norwegerin** f (pl -nen) Norwegian. **norwegisch** adj Norwegian.

Not [noːt] f (pl Nöte) (Armut) need, want; (Gefahr) danger; (Bedrängnis) distress; (Knappheit) lack, shortage.

Notar [no'taːr] m (pl -e) notary.

Not‖ausgang m emergency exit. **–bremse** f emergency brake. **–durft** f call of nature. **–dürftig** adj scanty; hard up.

Note ['noːtə] f (pl -n) note; (Schul-) mark, grade; banknote, (US) bill; (Musik) note. **–nständer** m music stand.

Not‖fall m emergency. **–hilfe** f emergency service.

notieren [no'tiːrən] v note.

nötig ['nœːtiç] adj necessary. **–en** v compel, force.

Notiz [no'tiːts] f (pl -en) notice; (Vermerk) note. **–buch** neut notebook.

Not‖lage f distress, predicament. **–landung** f emergency landing. **–lüge** f white lie. **notleidend** adj distressed; (arm) needy, destitute.

notorisch [no'toːriʃ] adj notorious.

Not‖ruf m distress call; (Telef) emergency call. **–stand** m emergency.

notwendig ['nɔːtvɛndiç] adj necessary. **Notwendigkeit** f necessity.

Notzucht ['nɔːttsuxt] f rape.

Novelle [no'vɛlə] f (pl -n) short story, short novel.

November [no'vɛmbər] m (pl -) November.

Novize [no'viːtsə] m (pl -n) novice.

Nuance [ny'ãsə] f (pl -n) nuance.

Nüchternheit ['nyçtərnhaɪt] f sobriety; (fig) realism, clear-headedness.

Nudeln ['nuːdəln] pl noodles.

null [nul] adj nil, zero; (ungültig) null. **null und nichtig** null and void. **Null** f (pl -en) nought, zero.

numerieren [numeˈriːrən] v number.
numerisch adj numerical.
Nummer [ˈnumər] f (pl -n) number. **Nummern‖scheibe** f (telephone) dial. – **schild** neut number plate.
nun [nuːn] adv now. interj well! **was nun?** what now? **nun also** why then. – **mehr** adv (by) now.
nur [nuːr] adv only, merely; (eben) just. conj nevertheless, but. **nur noch** only, still. **nicht nur ... sondern auch ...** not only ... but also ... .
Nürnberg [ˈnyrnbɛrk] neut Nuremberg.
Nuß [nus] f (pl Nüsse) nut. – **baum** m walnut tree. **Nuß‖knacker** m nutcracker. – **schale** f nutshell.
nutz [nuts] adj useful. – **bar** adj useful. – **bringend** adj profitable.
nutzen [ˈnutsən] or **nützen** v be of use, be useful; (gebrauchen) make use of, use. **Nutzen** m (pl -) use; (Vorteil) profit, advantage. **Nutzen ziehen aus** derive advantage from, benefit from. **zum Nutzen von** for the benefit of. **Nutzfahrzeug** neut commercial vehicle.
nützlich [ˈnytsliç] adj useful. **Nützlichkeit** f usefulness.
nutzlos [ˈnutsloːs] adj useless. **Nutz‖losigkeit** f uselessness. – **nießer** m beneficiary. – **ung** f use, utilization.
Nylon [ˈnailɔːn] neut (pl -s) nylon.

O

Oase [oˈaːzə] f (pl -n) oasis.
ob [ɔp] conj whether. **als ob** as if, as though.
Obdach [ˈɔpdax] neut (unz.) shelter. **obdachlos** adj homeless.
oben [ˈoːbən] adv above, at the top; (Haus) upstairs. **oben auf** on top of. **von oben** from above.
ober [ˈoːbər] adj upper, higher; (fig) superior; (Dienstgrad) senior, principal. **Ober** m (pl -) (head) waiter. **die Oberen** those in authority.
Ober‖arm m upper arm. – **befehlshaber** m commander-in-chief. – **bürgermeister** m (lord) mayor. – **fläche** f surface (area). **oberflächlich** adj superficial.
oberhalb [ˈoːbərhalp] adv, prep above.
Ober‖hand f upper hand, ascendancy. – **haupt** m chief, head. – **hemd** neut shirt.

– **in** f (pl -nen) (Rel) mother superior; (Krankenschwester) matron.
oberirdisch [ˈoːbərˈirdiʃ] adj above ground; (Leitung) overhead.
Ober‖kellner m head waiter. – **klasse** f upper class. – **schicht** f ruling class, upper classes pl. – **schule** f secondary school. – **schwester** f (Med) sister. – **seite** f upper side.
oberst [ˈoːbərst] adj highest, uppermost; (fig) supreme. **Oberst** m (pl -en) colonel.
obgleich [ɔpˈglaiç] conj although.
Obhut [ˈɔphuːt] f (unz.) care, protection. **in seine Objut nehmen** take care of, take under one's wing.
obig [ˈoːbiç] adj above-mentioned, foregoing.
Objekt [ɔpˈjɛkt] neut (pl -e) object. **objektiv** adj objective.
***obliegen** [ˈɔpliːgən] v (einer Aufgabe) perform, carry out. **es liegt ihm ob, zu** it is his job or duty to. **Obliegenheit** f duty.
obligatorisch [ɔbligaˈtoːriʃ] adj obligatory, compulsory.
Obmann [ˈɔpman] m foreman; (Vorsitzender) chairman; (Sprecher) spokesman.
Oboe [oˈboːə] f (pl -n) oboe. **Oboist** m oboist.
Obrigkeit [ˈoːbriçkait] f (pl -en) authorities pl, government.
obschon [ɔpˈʃoːn] conj although.
Observatorium [ɔpzɛrvaˈtoːrium] neut (pl Observatorien) observatory.
obskur [ɔpsˈkuːr] adj obscure.
Obst [oːpst] neut (unz.) fruit. – **baum** m fruit tree. – **garten** m orchard. – **händler** m fruiterer.
obszön [ɔpsˈtsœːn] adj obscene.
obwohl [ɔpˈvoːl] conj although.
Ochse [ˈɔksə] m (pl -n) ox. **Ochsen‖fleisch** neut beef. – **schwanz** m oxtail.
Ode [ˈoːdə] f (pl -n) ode.
öde [ˈœːdə] adj desolate, bleak; (fig) dull, bleak. **Öde** f (unz.) desert, wasteland; (fig) dullness, tedium.
oder [ˈoːdər] conj or.
Ofen [ˈoːfən] m (pl Öfen) stove; (Back-, Tech) oven.
offen [ˈɔfən] adj open; (freimütig) open, frank; (Stellung) vacant. – **bar** adj obvious. – **baren** v reveal, disclose. **Offenheit** f openness, frankness. **offen‖herzig** adj open-hearted. – **kundig** adj evident. – **sichtlich** adj obvious, evident.

offensiv [ɔfɛn'ziːf] *adj* offensive. **Offensive** *f* (*pl* -n) offensive.
offenstehend ['ɔfənʃteːənt] *adj* open; (*Schuld*) outstanding.
öffentlich ['œfəntliç] *adj* public. **Öffentlichkeit** *f* publicity; (*das Volk*) public.
offiziell [ɔfi'tsjɛl] *adj* official.
Offizier [ɔfi'tsiːr] *m* (*pl* -e) officer. **Offiziers∥messe** *f* officers' mess. **-patent** *neut* (officer's) commission.
offiziös [ɔfitsi'øːs] *adj* semi-official.
öffnen ['œfnən] *v* open. **Öffnung** *f* opening. **-szeiten** *pl* opening hours.
oft [ɔft] *adv* often; frequently. **wie oft?** how many times?
öfter ['œftər] *adj* frequent. *adv* more often *or* frequently. **öfters** *adv* often.
Oheim ['oːhaim] *m* (*pl* -e) uncle.
ohne ['oːnə] *prep*, *conj* without. **ohne daß ich es wußte** without my knowledge. **ohne∥dies** *or* **-hin** *adv* all the same, besides.
Ohnmacht ['oːnmaxt] *f* unconsciousness, faint. **ohnmächtig** *adj* unconscious. **ohnmächtig werden** *v* faint.
Ohr [oːr] *neut* (*pl* -en) ear. **die Ohren spitzen** prick up one's ears. **ganz Ohr sein** be all ears.
Öhr [œːr] *neut* (*pl* -e) eye (of a needle).
Ohren∥schmalz *neut* ear wax. **-schmerz** *m* earache. **Ohrfeige** *f* slap across the face. **ohrfeigen** *v* slap (across the face). **Ohr∥läppchen** *neut* ear lobe. **-muschel** *f* (external) ear. **-ring** *m* earring.
Ökonom [øko'noːm] *m* (*pl* -en) (*Hausverwalter*) caretaker, steward; (*Wirtschaftswissenschaftler*) economist. **-ie** *f* housekeeping; economics. **ökonomisch** *adj* economic; (*sparsam*) economical.
Oktave [ɔk'taːvə] *f* (*pl* -n) octave.
Oktober [ɔk'toːbər] *m* (*pl* -) October.
Okzident ['ɔktsidɛnt] *m* occident.
Öl [œːl] *neut* (*pl* -e) oil. **-baum** *m* olive tree. **ölen** *v* oil, lubricate. **Ölfarbe** *f* oil paint.
Olive [o'liːvə] *f* (*pl* -n) olive. **olivengrün** *adj* olive-green. **olivenöl** *neut* olive oil.
Öl∥leitung *f* (oil) pipeline. **-meßstab** *m* dipstick.
Olympiade [olympi'aːdə] *f* (*pl* -n) Olympiad, Olympic games. **olympisch** *adj* Olympic.
Ölzweig ['œːltsvaik] *m* olive branch.

Oma ['oːma] *f* (*pl* -s) granny, grandma.
Omelett [ɔmə'lɛt] *neut* (*pl* -e) *or* **Omelette** *f* (*pl* -n) omelette.
Ondulieren [ɔndu'liːrən] *v* wave.
Onkel ['ɔŋkəl] *m* (*pl* -) uncle.
Opa ['oːpa] *m* (*pl* -s) grandad, grandpa.
Opal [o'paːl] *m* (*pl* -e) opal.
Oper ['oːpər] *f* (*pl* -n) opera; (*Opernhaus*) opera house.
Operation [operatsi'oːn] *f* (*pl* -en) operation. **-ssaal** *m* operating theatre. **operieren** *v* operate.
Opfer ['ɔpfər] *neut* (*pl* -) (*Verzicht, Gabe*) sacrifice; (*Geopfertes*) victim. **opfern** *v* sacrifice, offer. **Opferung** *f* sacrifice.
Opium ['oːpium] *neut* opium.
opportun [ɔpɔr'tuːn] *adj* opportune.
Opposition [ɔpozitsi'oːn] *f* (*pl* -n) opposition. **-sführer** *m* leader of the opposition.
Optik ['ɔptik] *f* optics. **-er** *m* optician.
optimal [ɔpti'maːl] *adj* optimum. **Optimismus** *m* optimism. **Optimist** *m* optimist. **optimistisch** *adj* optimistic.
optisch ['ɔptiʃ] *adj* optic(al).
Orange [o'rãːʒə] *f* (*pl* -n) orange. **orange** *adj* orange. **Orangensaft** *m* orange juice.
Orchester [ɔr'kɛstər] *neut* (*pl* -) orchestra.
Orchidee [ɔrçi'deːə] *f* (*pl* -n) orchid.
Orden ['ɔrdən] *m* (*pl* -) (*Gesellschaft*) order; (*Ehrenzeichen*) decoration, order. **Ordens∥bruder** *m* member of an order; (*Rel*) monk, friar. **-schwester** *f* nun.
ordentlich ['ɔrdəntliç] *adj* (*ordnungsgemäß*) orderly; (*ordnungsliebend, geordnet*) tidy; (*anständig, auch umg.*) proper, decent. **Ordentlichkeit** *f* orderliness; decency, respectability.
ordinär [ɔrdi'nɛːr] *adj* common, vulgar.
Ordinarius [ɔrdi'naːrius] *m* (*pl* Ordinarien*) professor.
Ordination [ɔrdina'tsioːn] *f* (*pl* -en) ordination. **ordinieren** *v* ordain.
ordnen ['ɔrdnən] *v* put in order, arrange, classify. **Ordner** *m* (*pl* -) organizer; (*Versammlungen*) steward; (*Mappe*) file. **Ordnung** *f* (*pl* -en) order; (*Regel*) regulation. **ordnungs∥gemäß** *or* **-mäßig** *adj* orderly, lawful. *adv* properly, duly. **-widrig** *adj* irregular, illegal.
Organ [ɔr'gaːn] *neut* (*pl* -e) organ. **-isation** *f* organization. **organ∥isch** *adj* organic. **-isieren** *v* organize. **Organismus** *m* (*pl* Organismen) organism.

Orgasmus [ɔr'gazmus] *m* (*pl* **Orgasmen**) orgasm.

Orgel ['ɔrgəl] *f* (*pl* -n) organ. **–spieler** *m* (*pl* -), **–spielerin** *f* (*pl* -nen) organist.

Orgie ['ɔrgiə] *f* (*pl* -n) orgy.

Orient ['ɔriɛnt] *m* Orient. **Orientale** *m* (*pl* -n), **Orientalin** (*pl* -nen) Oriental. **orientalisch** *adj* oriental.

orientieren [ɔriɛn'tiːrən] *v* locate. **sich orientieren** orientate oneself. **Orientierung** *f* orientation. **Orientierungs‖punkt** *m* reference point. **–vermögen** *neut* sense of direction.

original [ɔrigi'naːl] *adj* original. **Original** *neut* (*pl* -e) original.

originell [ɔrigi'nɛl] *adj* original, novel; (*eigenartig*) peculiar.

Orkan [ɔr'kaɪn] *m* (*pl* -e) hurricane.

Ornat [ɔr'naːt] *m* (*pl* -e) (official) robes.

Ort [ɔrt] *m* (*pl* -e) place; (*Ortschaft*) town; (*Dorf*) village; (*Punkt*) point.

orthodox [ɔrto'dɔks] *adj* orthodox.

Orthopädie [ɔrtope'diː] *f* orthopaedics.

örtlich ['œrtliç] *adj* local.

Orts‖gespräch *neut* local call. **–verkehr** *m* local traffic. **–zeit** *f* local time.

Öse ['œːzə] *f* (*pl* -n) eye(let). **Haken und Ösen** hooks and eyes.

Ost(en) ['ɔst(ən)] *m* east. **der Nahe/Ferne Osten** the Middle/Far East. **Ostblock** *m* Eastern bloc, Eastern Europe.

Oster‖ei *neut* Easter egg. **–hase** *m* Easter bunny.

Ostern ['ɔɪstərn] *neut pl* Easter.

Österreich ['œːstərraiç] *neut* Austria. **Österreicher** *m* (*pl* -), *f* **Österreicherin** (*pl* -nen) Austrian. **österreichisch** *adj* Austrian.

Osteuropa ['ɔstɔyropa] *f* Eastern Europe.

östlich ['œstliç] *adj* east(ern).

Ost‖politik *f* East policy, policy towards the Eastern bloc. **–see** *f* Baltic Sea.

Otter ['ɔtər] *m* (*pl* -) or *f* (*pl* -n) otter.

Ouvertüre [uver'tyːrə] *f* (*pl* -n) overture.

Ovarium [o'vaːrium] *neut* (*pl* **Ovarien**) ovary.

oval [o'vaːl] *adj* oval.

Oxyd [ɔ'ksyːt] *neut* (*pl* -e) oxide. **oxydieren** *v* oxidize.

Ozean ['ɔtseaɪn] *m* (*pl* -e) ocean. **ozeanisch** *adj* oceanic.

P

paar [paɪr] *adj* **ein paar** a few. **Paar** *neut* (*pl* -e) pair, couple. **paaren** *v* (*Tiere*) pair, couple; (*vereinigen*) join. **sich paaren** couple, mate. **Paarung** *f* (*pl* -en) mating. **paarweise** *adv* in couples.

Pacht [paxt] *f* (*pl* -en) lease; (*Entgelt*) rent. **–brief** *m* lease. **pachten** *v* lease.

Pächter ['pɛçtər] *m* (*pl* -) leaseholder; (*Bauer*) tenant farmer.

Pack [pak] *m* (*pl* **Päcke**) pack; packet; bundle.

Päckchen ['pɛkçən] *neut* (*pl* -) packet, small parcel.

packen ['pakən] *v* grasp, seize; (*einpacken*) pack. **–d** *adj* thrilling, fascinating. **Pack‖kasten** *m* packing case. **–pferd** *neut* pack-horse. **–esel** *m* (*fig*) drudge. **–stoff** *m* packing (material). **Packung** *f* (*pl* -en) package.

Pädagogik [peda'goːgik] *f* pedagogy, education. **pädagogisch** *adj* pedagogic. **pädagogische Hochschule** teacher-training college.

Paddel ['padəl] *neut* (*pl* -) paddle. **paddeln** *v* paddle.

Page ['paːʒə] *m* (*pl* -n) page(boy).

Paket [pa'keːt] *neut* (*pl* -e) packet, parcel.

Pakt [pakt] *m* (*pl* -e) pact, agreement.

Palast [pa'last] *m* (*pl* **Paläste**) palace.

Palästina [palɛ'stiːna] *neut* Palestine.

Palette [pa'lɛtə] *f* (*pl* -n) palette.

Palme ['palmə] *f* (*pl* -n) palm. **Palmsonntag** *m* Palm Sunday.

Pampelmuse ['pampəlmuːzə] *f* (*pl* -n) grapefruit.

Panda ['panda] *m* (*pl* -) panda.

Paneel [pa'neːl] *neut* (*pl* -e) panel, panelling.

paniert [pa'niːrt] *adj* coated with breadcrumbs.

Panik ['paːnik] *f* (*pl* -en) panic. **panisch** *adj* panic-stricken, panicky.

Panne ['panə] *f* (*pl* -n) breakdown.

Pantoffel [pan'tɔfəl] *m* (*pl* -n) slipper.

Pantomime [panto'miːmə] *f* (*pl* -n) pantomime.

Panzer ['pantsər] *m* (*pl* -) armour; (*Panzerwagen*) tank; (*Tiere*) shell. **–hemd** *neut* coat of mail. **panzern** *v* armour. **Panzer‖ung** *f* (*pl* -en) armour-plating. **–wagen** *m* tank, armoured car. **–weste** *f* bullet-proof vest.

Papa [pa'paɪ, 'papa] *m* (*pl* -s) daddy, papa.

Papagei [papa'gaɪ] *m* (*pl* -en) parrot.

Papier [pa'piːr] *neut* (*pl* -e) paper. **–bogen** *m* sheet of paper. **–korb** *m* wastepaper basket. **–tüte** *f* paper bag. **–waren** *pl* stationery *sing*.

Pappe ['papə] *f* (*pl* -n) cardboard.

Pappel ['papəl] *f* (*pl* -n) poplar.

pappen ['papən] *v* paste (together).

Pappschachtel ['papʃaxtəl] *f* cardboard box.

Paprika ['paprika] *m* (*pl* -s) paprika. **–schote** *f* green *or* red pepper, capsicum.

Papst [paːpst] *m* (*pl* Päpste) pope.

päpstlich ['pɛɪpstliç] *adj* papal.

Parabel [pa'raɪbəl] *f* (*pl* -n) parable; (*Math*) parabola.

Parade [pa'raɪdə] *f* (*pl* -n) parade. **paradieren** *v* parade; (*fig*) make a show, show off.

Paradies [para'diːs] *neut* (*pl* -e) paradise.

paradox [para'dɔks] *adj* paradoxical. **Paradoxie** *f* paradox.

Paragraph [para'graɪf] *m* (*pl* -en) paragraph, section.

parallel [para'leɪl] *adj* parallel. **Parallele** *f* parallel.

Paralyse [para'lyːzə] *f* (*pl* -n) paralysis. **paralysieren** *v* paralyse. **Paralytiker** *m* paralytic. **paralytisch** *adj* paralytic. **Paranuß** ['paranus] *f* Brazil nut.

Parasit [para'ziːt] *m* (*pl* -en) parasite.

Pärchen ['pɛɪrçən] *neut* (*pl* -) couple, lovers.

Parenthese [parɛn'teɪzə] *f* (*pl* -n) parenthesis.

Parfüm [par'fyɪm] *neut* (*pl* -e) perfume. **parfümieren** *v* perfume, scent.

parieren [pa'riːrən] *v* (*Angriff*) parry; (*Pferd*) rein (in); (*gehorchen*) obey, toe the line.

Parität [pari'tɛɪt] *f* (*pl* -en) parity.

Park [park] *m* (*pl* -s) park. **–anlagen** *f pl* park, public gardens. **parken** *v* park.

Parkett [par'kɛt] *neut* (*pl* -e) (*Fußboden*) parquet; (*Theater*) stalls.

Park‖platz *m* car park, (*US*) parking lot. **–uhr** *f* parking meter.

Parlament [parla'mɛnt] *neut* (*pl* -e) parliament. **–arier** *m* (*pl* -) parliamentarian. **parlamentarisch** *adj* parliamentary.

Parodie [paro'diː] *f* (*pl* -n) parody. **parodieren** *v* parody.

Partei [par'tai] *f* (*pl* -en) (*Pol*, *Jur*) party. **–führer** *m* party leader. **partei‖isch** *or* **–lich** *adj* biased, partial. **–los** *adj* impartial. **Partei‖politik** *f* party politics. **–tag** *m* party conference.

Parterre [par'tɛr] *neut* (*pl* -s) ground floor; (*Theater*) pit. **–wohnung** *f* ground-floor flat.

Partie [par'tiː] *f* (*pl* -n) (*Teil*, *Musik*) part; (*Spiel*, *Heirat*) match; (*Jagd*-) party.

Partikel [par'tiːkəl] *f* (*pl* -n) particle.

Partisan [parti'zaɪn] *m* (*pl* -en) partisan.

Partitur [parti'tuːr] *f* (*pl* -en) (*Musik*) score.

Partizip [parti'tsiːp] *neut* (*pl* -ien) participle.

Partizipation [parrtisipa'tsioɪn] *f* participation. **partizipieren** *v* participate.

Partner ['parrtnər] *m* (*pl* -) partner. **Partnerschaft** *f* partnership.

Party ['parrti] *f* (*pl* -s) party.

Parzelle [par'tsɛlə] *f* (*pl* -n) plot (of land).

Paß [pas] *m* (*pl* Pässe) (*Reisepaß*) passport; (*Durchgang*) pass.

passabel [pa'saɪbəl] *adj* tolerable, passable.

Passage [pa'saɪʒə] *f* (*pl* -n) passage. **Passagier** *m* (*pl* -e) passenger.

Passant [pa'sant] *m* (*pl* -en) passer-by.

Paßbild ['pasbilt] *neut* passport photograph.

passen ['pasən] *v* fit, suit; (*Kartenspiel*) pass. **gut zueinander passen** go well together. **das paßt mir nicht** that doesn't suit me. **passend** *adj* fitting, suitable.

passieren [pa'siːrən] *v* (*geschehen*) happen; (*vorübergehen*) pass; (*überqueren*) cross. **Passierschein** *m* permit, pass.

Passion [pasi'oɪn] *f* (*pl* -en) passion. **sich passionieren für** be enthusiastic about. **passioniert** enthusiastic, dedicated. **Passions‖spiel** *neut* Passion Play. **–woche** *f* Holy Week.

passiv ['pasiːf] *adj* passive. **Passiv** *neut* passive.

Paßkontrolle ['paskɔntrolə] *f* passport inspection.

Pastellfarbe [pa'stɛlfaɪrbə] *f* pastel colour.

Pastete [pa'steɪtə] *f* (*pl* -n) (*savoury*) pie, pasty.

pasteurisieren [pastœri'ziɪrən] *v* pasteurize.

Pastille [pa'stilə] *f* (*pl* -n) lozenge.

Pastor ['pastɔr] *m* (*pl* -en) pastor, priest.
Pate ['paːtə] *m* (*pl* -n) godfather. –**nkind**
neut godchild.
Patent [pa'tɛnt] *neut* (*pl* -e) patent;
(*Erlaubnis*) licence; (*Mil*) commission.
patentieren *v* patent. **Patentinhaber** *m*
patentee.
pathetisch [pa'teːtiʃ] *adj* (*feierlich*) solemn, lofty; (*übertrieben*) rhetorical,
flowery.
Pathologe [pato'loːgə] *m* (*pl* -n) pathologist. **Pathologie** *f* pathology. **pathologisch**
adj pathological.
Patient [patsi'ɛnt] *m* (*pl* -en) patient.
Patin ['paːtin] *f* (*pl* -nen) godmother.
Patriot [patri'oːt] *m* (*pl* -en) patriot. **patriotisch** *adj* patriotic. **Patriotismus** *m* patriotism.
Patron [pa'troːn] *m* (*pl* -e) patron; (*umg.*)
fellow, customer.
Patrone [pa'troːnə] *f* (*pl* -n) cartridge.
Patrouille [pa'truljə] *f* (*pl* -n) patrol.
Patt [pat] *neut* (*pl* -s) stalemate.
Pauke ['paukə] *f* (*pl* -n) kettledrum.
pauken *v* (*umg.*) cram, swot. **Pauker** *m*
drummer; (*umg.*) crammer.
pausbackig ['pausbakiç] *adj* chubby(-
faced).
pauschal [pau'ʃaːl] *adj* all-inclusive. **Pauschalsumme** *f* lump sum.
Pause ['pauzə] *f* (*pl* -n) pause, break;
(*Theater*) interval. **Pause machen** take a
break. **pausenlos** *adj* uninterrupted, continuous.
Pavian ['parviaːn] *m* (*pl* -e) baboon.
Pazifik [pa'tsiːfik] *m* Pacific Ocean.
pazifisch *adj* Pacific.
Pazifismus [patsi'fismus] *m* pacifism.
Pazifist *m* (*pl* -en) pacifist.
Pech [pɛç] *neut* (*pl* -e) pitch; (*fig*) bad
luck. **Pech haben** be unlucky. **pechdunkel**
adj pitch dark.
Pedal [pe'daːl] *neut* (*pl* -e) pedal.
Pedant [pe'dant] *m* (*pl* -en) pedant.
pedantisch *adj* pedantic.
peilen ['pailən] *v* take (one's) bearings;
(*loten*) sound; (*umg.*) sound out.
Pein [pain] *f* (*unz.*) pain, torment, agony.
pein‖igen *v* torment; –**lich** *adj* awkward,
embarrassing; (*genau*) (over-)careful,
fussy.
Peitsche ['paitʃə] *f* (*pl* -n) whip, lash.
Pelikan ['peːlikaːn] *m* (*pl* -e) pelican.
Pelle ['pɛlə] *f* (*pl* -n) peel, skin.

Pellkartoffel *pl* potatoes (boiled) in their
jackets.
Pelz [pɛlts] *m* (*pl* -e) fur, pelt. **pelzig** *adj*
furry. **Pelzmantel** *m* fur coat.
Pendel ['pɛndəl] *neut* (*pl* -) pendulum.
pendeln *v* swing, oscillate; (*fig*) commute.
Pendler *m* commuter.
penibel [pe'niːbəl] *adj* meticulous.
pennen ['pɛnən] *v* (*umg.*) doss, kip down.
Penne *f* (*umg.*) school. **Penner** *m* dosser.
Pension [pã'sjoːn] *f* (*pl* -en) guest house,
boarding house; (*Ruhegehalt*) pension.
pensionieren *v* pension off. **Pension-
ierte(r)** pensioner.
per [pɛr] *prep* by, per. **per Adresse** care
of, c/o.
perfekt [pɛr'fɛkt] *adj* perfect. **einen Vertrag perfekt machen** clinch a deal.
perforieren [pɛrfo'riːrən] *v* perforate. **Perforation** *f* perforation.
Pergament [pɛrga'mɛnt] *neut* (*pl* -e)
parchment. –**papier** *neut* greaseproof
paper.
Periode [peri'oːdə] *f* (*pl* -n) period. **periodisch** *adj* periodic.
Perle ['pɛrlə] *f* (*pl* -n) pearl; (*Glas-*) bead.
perlen *v* sparkle. **Perl‖enkette** *f* string of
pearls. –**mutter** *f* mother-of-pearl.
permanent [pɛrma'nɛnt] *adj* permanent.
perplex [pɛr'plɛks] *adj* perplexed, confused.
Person [pɛr'zoːn] *f* (*pl* -en) person.
Personal [pɛrzo'naːl] *neut* staff, personnel. –**abteilung** *f* personnel department.
–**ausweis** *m* pass, ID card. –**chef** *m* personnel manager.
Personen‖kraftwagen (Pkw) *m* (passenger) car. –**verzeichnis** *neut* (*Theater*) dra-
matis personae. –**zug** *m* (local) passenger train.
persönlich [pɛr'zøːnliç] *adj* personal. **Persönlichkeit** *f* personality.
Perspektive [pɛrspɛk'tiːvə] *f* (*pl* -n) perspective.
Perücke [pe'rykə] *f* (*pl* -n) wig.
pervers [pɛr'vɛrs] *adj* perverse. **Perversion**
f perversion.
Pessimismus [pɛsi'mismus] *m* pessimism.
Pessimist *m* (*pl* -en) pessimist. **pessimis-
tisch** *adj* pessimistic.
Pest [pɛst] *f* (*pl* -en) plague.
Petersilie [petər'ziːliə] *f* (*pl* -n) parsley.
Petroleum [pe'troːleum] *neut* petroleum;
(*Kerosin*) paraffin, (*US*) kerosene.

petzen ['pɛtsən] v (*umg.*) tell tales, sneak.
Pfad [pfaɪt] m (*pl* -e) path. **-finder** m
Boy Scout.
Pfahl [pfaɪl] m (*pl* Pfähle), post, stake;
(*Stange*) pole. **-werk** *neut* paling, pali-
sade.
Pfalz [pfalts] f Palatinate.
Pfand [pfant] *neut* (Pfänder) pledge,
security; (*Flaschen, usw.*) deposit. **-brief**
m mortgage (deed). **-leiher** m pawn-
broker.
Pfanne ['pfanə] f (*pl* -n) pan.
Pfannkuchen m pancake.
Pfarrbezirk ['pfaɪrbətsɪrk] m parish. **Pfar-
rer** m parson. **Pfarrhaus** *neut* parsonage.
Pfau [pfau] m (*pl* -en) peacock.
Pfeffer ['pfɛfər] m (*pl* -) pepper. **-kuchen**
m gingerbread. **-minz** *neut* (*pl* -e) peppermint (sweet). **-minze** f (*Bot*) peppermint.
Pfeife ['pfaifə] f (*pl* -n) pipe. **pfeifen** v
whistle. **Pfeifer** m whistler; (*Pfeife*) pip-
er.
Pfeil [pfail] m (*pl* -e) arrow.
Pfeiler ['pfailər] m (*pl* -e) pillar.
pfeilschnell ['pfailʃnɛl] *adj* swift as an
arrow. **Pfeilschütze** m archer.
Pfennig ['pfɛniç] m (*pl* -e) pfennig; (*fig*)
penny.
Pferch [pfɛrç] m (*pl* -e) fold, pen.
pferchen v pen.
Pferd [pfeɪrt] *neut* (*pl* -e) horse.
Pferde||**bremse** f horsefly. **-knecht** m
groom. **-rennbahn** f race course. **-ren-
nen** *neut* horseracing. **-stall** m stable.
-stärke (Ps) f horsepower (hp).
Pfiff [pfif] m (*pl* -e) (*Ton*) whistle; (*Kniff*)
trick.
Pfifferling ['pfɪfərlɪŋ] m (*pl* -e) (*Bot*)
chanterelle (edible mushroom). **das ist
keinen Pfifferling wert** that's (worth)
nothing.
Pfingsten ['pfɪŋstən] *neut* (*pl* -) Whit-
sun(tide).
Pfirsich ['pfirzɪç] m (*pl* -e) peach.
Pflanze ['pflantsə] f (*pl* -n) plant. **pflanzen**
v plant. **-fressend** *adj* herbivorous.
Pflanzen||**fresser** m herbivore. **-öl** *neut*
vegetable oil. **-reich** *neut* vegetable
kingdom.
Pflaster ['pflastər] *neut* (*pl* -) (*Straße*)
pavement; (*Wunden*) plaster. **-stein** m
paving stone.
Pflaume ['pflaumə] f (*pl* -n) plum.

Pflege ['pfleɪgə] f (*pl* -n) care. **-dienst** m
service. **-eltern** *pl* foster parents. **-kind**
neut foster child. **-mutter** f foster mother. **pflegeleicht** *adj* easy-care.
pflegen ['pfleɪgən] v care for; (*Kranken*)
nurse; (*Pflanzen*) cultivate; (*gewohnt
sein*) be accustomed to. **er pflegte zu
sagen** he used to say. **Pfleger** m male
nurse; (*vormund*) guardian. **Pflegerin** f
nurse, sister.
Pflege||**sohn** m foster son. **-mutter** f fos-
ter mother. **-tochter** f foster daughter.
-vater m foster father.
pfleglich ['pfleɪklɪç] *adj* careful. **pfleglich
behandeln** handle with care.
Pflicht [pflɪçt] f (*pl* -en) duty.
pflicht||**bewußt** *adj* conscientious.
-gemäß *adj* dutiful, in accordance with
duty. **-getreu** *adj* dutiful, conscientious.
Pflock [pflɔk] m (*pl* Pflöcke) peg, pin.
pflücken ['pflʏkən] v pluck; gather.
Pflug [pfluɪk] m (*pl* Pflüge) plough.
pflügen ['pflyɪgən] v plough.
Pflüger ['pfleɪrtər] m ploughman.
Pforte ['pfɔrtə] f (*pl* -n) door, gate.
Pförtner ['pfœɪrtnər] m (*pl* -) doorkeeper,
porter.
Pfosten ['pfɔstən] m (*pl* -) post, stake.
Pfote ['pfoɪtə] f (*pl* -n) paw.
Pfropf [pfrɔpf] m (*pl* -e *oder* Pfröpfe)
(*Blutgerinsel*) blood clot; (*Watte*) wad
(of cotton wool). **pfropfen** v (*Flasche*)
cork, stopper; (*Bäume*) graft; (*stopfen*)
pack, stuff. **Pfropf**||**en** m (*pl* -) cork, stop-
per. **-reis** *neut* graft.
pfui [pfui] *interj* pooh, ugh.
Pfund [pfunt] *neut* (*pl* -e) pound.
pfuschen ['pfuʃən] v botch, bungle, make
a mess. **Pfuscher** m botcher, bungler. **-ei**
f bungling; (*Arbeit*) botch-job, botch-up.
Pfütze ['pfʏtsə] f (*pl* -n) puddle.
Phänomen [fɛnoˈmeɪn] *neut* (*pl* -e) phenomenon.
Phantasie [fantaˈziː] f (*pl* -n) (*Einbildung-
skraft*) imagination; (*Trugbild*) fantasy.
phantasie||**los** *adj* unimaginative. **-reich**
'*adj* imaginative. **-ren** v fantasize, daydream; (*Med*) be delirious. **phantastisch**
adj fantastic.
Phantom [fanˈtoɪm] *neut* (*pl* -e) phantom.
Phase ['faɪzə] f (*pl* -n) phase.
Philister [fiˈlistər] m (*pl* -) philistine.
philisterhaft *adj* philistine, narrow-minded.

Philosoph [filo'zo:f] *m* (*pl* -en) philosopher. **-ie** *f* philosophy. **philosophisch** *adj* philosophical.

Phonetik [fo'ne:tik] *f* (*unz.*) phonetics. **phonetisch** *adj* phonetic.

Phosphor ['fɔsfɔr] *m* (*unz.*) phosphorus.

Photo ['fo:to] *neut* (*pl* -s) photo, photograph. **-album** *neut* photograph album. **-apparat** *m* camera. **photogen** *adj* photogenic. **Photograph** *m* (*pl* -en) photographer. **-ie** *f* photography. **photograph‖ieren** *v* photograph. **-isch** *adj* photographic.

Phrase ['fra:zə] *f* (*pl* -n) phrase; (*fig*) empty talk, fine phrases.

Physik [fy'zi:k] *f* physics. **-er** *m* physicist.

Physiologie [fyzio'lo:gi:] *f* physiology. **physiologisch** *adj* physiological.

physisch ['fy:ziʃ] *adj* physical.

Pianist [pia'nist] *m* (*pl* -en), **Pianistin** *f* (*pl* -nen) pianist.

Pickel¹ ['pikəl] *m* (*pl* -), **Picke** *f* (*pl* -n) pickaxe.

Pickel² ['pikəl] *m* (*pl* -) (*Med*) pimple, spot.

piep [pi:p] *interj* cheep. **nicht piep sagen** not say a word. **Piep** *m* (*pl* -se) peep, chirp. **piep‖en** *v* chirp. **-sen** *v* (*Maus*) squeak.

Pietät [pie'tɛ:t] *f* piety; (*Ehrfurcht*) reverence.

Pik [pi:k] *neut* (*pl* -s) spades *pl*.

pikant [pi'kant] *adj* spicy; (*fig*) suggestive, racy.

Pikkoloflöte ['pikoloflœ:tə] *f* piccolo.

Pilger ['pilgər] *m* (*pl* -), **Pilgerin** *f* (*pl* -nen) pilgrim. **Pilgerfahrt** *f* pilgrimage.

Pille ['pilə] *f* (*pl* -n) pill. **die Pille** (*umg.*) the (contraceptive) pill.

Pilot [pi'lo:t] *m* (*pl* -en) pilot.

Pilz [pilts] *m* (*pl* -e) mushroom.

Pinguin [pingu'i:n] *m* (*pl* -e) penguin.

Pinie ['pi:niə] *f* (*pl* -n) stone pine. **-nnuß** *f* pine kernel.

Pinne ['pinə] *f* (*pl* -n) pin, peg; (*Ruder-*) tiller.

Pinsel ['pinzəl] *m* (*pl* -) brush; (*Farbe*) paintbrush. **pinseln** *v* paint, daub.

Pionier [pio'ni:r] *m* (*pl* -e) pioneer.

Pirat [pi'ra:t] *m* (*pl* -en) pirate.

Piste ['pistə] *f* (*pl* -n) track; (*Ski*) ski-run; (*Flugzeug*) runway.

Pistole [pi'sto:lə] *f* (*pl* -n) pistol.

pissen ['pisən] *v* (*vulgär*) piss.

Plackerei [plakə'rai] *f* (*pl* -en) drudgery, toil.

plädieren [plɛ'di:rən] *v* plead. **Plädoyer** *neut* (*pl* -s) (*Jur*) plea.

Plage ['pla:gə] *f* (*pl* -n) nuisance, bother, vexation. **plagen** *v* torment, annoy.

Plagiat [plagi'a:t] *neut* (*pl* -e) plagiarism. **plagiieren** *v* plagiarize.

Plakat [pla'ka:t] *neut* (*pl* -e) poster, placard.

Plan [pla:n] *m* (*pl* **Pläne**) (*Absicht*) plan, intention; (*Zeichnung*) plan, diagram; (*Stadt*) map; (*Skizze*) design, scheme.

Plane ['pla:nə] *f* (*pl* -n) awning.

planen ['pla:nən] *v* plan.

Planet [pla'ne:t] *m* (*pl* -en) planet. **-arium** *neut* (*pl* -arien) planetarium.

planieren [pla'ni:rən] *v* plane, level, smooth. **Planierraupe** *f* grader, bulldozer.

Planke ['plaŋkə] *f* (*pl* -n) plank.

Plänkelei [plɛŋkə'lai] *f* (*pl* -en) (*Gefecht*) skirmish; (*Wortstreit*) bantering.

planmäßig ['pla:nmɛ:siç] *adj* systematic; (*nach einem Plan*) according to plan. **der Zug fährt planmäßig um drei Uhr ab** the train is scheduled to leave at 3 o'clock.

Plantage [plan'ta:ʒə] *f* (*pl* -n) plantation.

Planung ['pla:nuŋ] *f* planning. **Planwirtschaft** *f* planned economy.

plappern ['plapərn] *v* chatter.

plärren ['plɛrən] *v* blubber, cry, sob.

Plastik ['plastik] *f* (*pl* -en) (*Kunst*) sculpture; (*Med*) plastic surgery; (*Kunststoff*) plastic. **plastisch** *adj* plastic.

Platin [pla'ti:n] *neut* platinum.

plätschern ['plɛtʃərn] *v* (*Bach*) babble; (*Regen*) splash, patter; (*planschen*) paddle.

platt [plat] *adj* flat, level; (*Redensart*) silly, trite; (*erstaunt*) tongue-tied, flabbergasted. **Plattdeutsch** *neut* Low German.

Platte ['platə] *f* (*pl* -n) plate, dish; (*Stein*) flag; (*Metall, Holz*) sheet, slab; (*Tisch*) leaf; (*Schallplatte*) record, disc. **-nspieler** *m* record-player.

Platz [plats] *m* (*pl* **Plätze**) place; (*Sitz*) seat; (*Raum*) space, room; (*Stadt*) square. **-anweiser** *m* usher. **-anweiserin** *f* usherette.

platzen ['platsən] *v* burst, split; (*explodieren*) explode; (*Scheck*) bounce.

Platz‖karte *f* seat-reservation ticket. **-patrone** *f* blank cartridge. **-regen** *m* downpour, heavy shower.

plaudern ['plaudərn] v chat.
plausibel [plau'ziːbəl] adj plausible.
Plazenta [pla'sɛnta] f (pl **-s** or **Plazenten**) placenta.
pleite ['plaitə] adj bankrupt; (umg.) broke. **Pleite** f bankruptcy; (fig) flop, wash-out.
plombieren [plɔm'biːrən] v seal; (Zahn) fill.
plötzlich ['plœtsliç] adj sudden.
plump [plump] adj (grob) coarse; (ungeschickt) clumsy. **plumps** Interj bump, thud. **plumpsen** v fall down (with a thud), plump down.
plündern ['plyndərn] v plunder.
Plural ['pluːraːl] m (pl **-e**) plural.
pneumatisch [pnɔy'maːtiʃ] adj pneumatic.
Pöbel ['pœːbəl] m mob, rabble.
pochen ['pɔxən] v knock, tap; (Herz) beat.
Pocken ['pɔkən] pl smallpox sing.
Pokal [po'kaːl] m (pl **-e**) (Sport) cup. **-endspiel** neut (Sport) cup final. **-spiel** neut cup tie.
Pökel ['pœːkəl] m (pl **-**) brine (for pickling). **pökeln** v pickle, salt.
Pol [poːl] m (pl **-e**) pole. **polar** adj polar. **Polarmeer** neut Arctic Ocean. **südliches Polarmeer** Antarctic Ocean.
Polemik [po'leːmik] f (pl **-en**) polemic, controversy. **polemisch** adj polemic(al).
Polen ['poːlən] neut Poland. **Pole** m (pl **-n**), **Polin** f (pl **-nen**) Pole. **polnisch** adj Polish.
Police [po'liːs, po'liːsə] f (pl **-n**) (insurance) policy.
polieren [po'liːrən] v polish. **Poliermittel** neut polish.
Politik [poli'tiːk] f (unz.) (Staatskunst) politics; (Verfahren, Programm) policy. **-er** m (pl **-**) politician. **politisch** adj political.
Politur [poli'tuːr] f (pl **-en**) polish.
Polizei [poli'tsai] f (pl **-en**) police. **-hund** m police dog. **-kommissar** or **-kommissär** m police inspector. **polizeilich** adj police. **Polizei‖präsident** m chief constable, commissioner. **-stunde** f closing time. **-wache** f police station. **Polizist** m (pl **-en**) policeman. **-in** f (pl **-nen**) policewoman.
Polster ['pɔlstər] neut (pl **-**) cushion; (Polsterung) upholstery. **polstern** v upholster. **Polsterung** f upholstery.

Poltergeist ['pɔltərgaist] m poltergeist, hobgoblin.
Polyp [po'lyːp] m (pl **-en**) (umg.) copper.
Polytechnikum [poly'tɛçnikum] neut (pl **Polytechniken**) technical college.
Pommern ['pɔmərn] neut (unz.) Pomerania.
Pommes frites [pɔm'friːt] pl (potato) chips, (US) French fries.
Pomp [pɔmp] m pomp. **pomphaft** adj stately, with pomp.
Pony ['pɔni] neut (pl **-s**) pony; (Frisur) fringe.
Pop-Musik ['pɔp mu'ziːk] f pop (music).
populär [popu'lɛːr] adj popular. **popularisieren** v popularize.
Pore ['poːrə] f (pl **-n**) pore.
Pornographie [pɔrnogra'fiː] f pornography. **pornographisch** adj pornographic.
porös [pɔ'rœːs] adj porous.
Porree ['pɔrə] m (pl **-s**) leek.
Portion [pɔrtsi'oːn] f (pl **-en**) portion, helping.
Porto ['pɔrto] neut (pl **-s**) postage. **portofrei** adv post-free.
Porträt [pɔr'trɛt, pɔr'trɛːt] neut (pl **-s**) portrait.
Portugal ['pɔrtugal] neut Portugal. **Portugiese** m (pl **-n**), **Portugiesin** f (pl **-nen**) Portuguese. **portugiesisch** adj Portuguese.
Porzellan [pɔrtsɛ'laːn] neut (pl **-e**) porcelain, china.
Posaune [po'zaunə] f (pl **-n**) trombone.
Pose ['poːzə] f (pl **-n**) pose, attitude. **Poseur** m poseur. **posieren** v (strike a) pose.
Position [pozitsi'oːn] f (pl **-en**) position.
positiv ['poːzitiːf] adj positive.
Posse ['pɔsə] f (pl **-n**) (Theater) farce. **Possen** m (pl **-**) prank, practical joke, trick. **possenhaft** adj farcical.
possessiv ['pɔsɛsiːf] adj possessive.
Post [pɔst] f (pl **-en**) post (office), postal service; (Briefe) post, mail. **-amt** neut post office. **-anweisung** f postal order. **-beamte(r)** m post office official. **-bote** m postman.
Posten ['pɔstən] m (pl **-**) place, post; (Stellung) position, post; (Mil) sentry; (Ware) item; (Streik-) picket.
Post‖fach ['pɔstfax] neut post-office box, PO box. **-gebühr** f postage. **-karte** f postcard.
postlagernd ['pɔstlaːgərnt] adj poste restante, (US) general delivery.

post‖leitzahl f postal code. **–sparkasse** f post-office savings bank. **–stempel** m postmark.

Postulat [pɔstuˈlaɪt] neut (pl -e) postulate. **postulieren** v postulate.

postwendend [ˈpɔstvɛndənt] adj by return (of) post. **Postwertzeichen** neut postage stamp.

potent [poˈtɛnt] adj capable; (Med) potent.

potential [potɛntsiˈaɪl] adj potential. **Potential** neut potential. **potentiell** adj potential, possible.

Potenz [poˈtɛnts] f (pl -en) power.

Pottasche [ˈpɔtaʃə] f potash.

Pracht [praxt] f splendour, magnificence. **prächtig** [ˈprɛçtiç] adj splendid, magnificent.

Prag [praɪk] neut Prague.

Präge [ˈprɛɪgə] f (pl -n) mint. **prägen** v stamp; (Münze) mint, coin.

pragmatisch [pragˈmatiʃ] adj pragmatic. **Pragmatiker** m (pl -) pragmatist.

prägnant [prɛgˈnant] adj precise, terse.

prahlen [ˈpraɪlən] v brag, boast. **Prahler** m (pl -)braggart. **prahlerisch** adj boastful.

Praktikant [praktiˈkant] m (pl -en), **Praktikantin** f (pl -nen) trainee, probationer. **Praktik‖er** m experienced person, expert. **–um** neut (pl -a) training course, field course. **praktisch** adj practical; (zweckmäßig) useful; (Person) handy.

prall [pral] adj (rund) plump, chubby; (straff) tight; (sonne) blazing. **Prall** m (pl -e) collision, impact. **prallen** v (Ball) bounce, rebound. **prallen gegen** collide with, bump into.

Prämie [ˈprɛmiə] f (pl -n) bonus; (Versicherungs-) premium.

Prämisse [prɛˈmisə] f (pl -n) premise.

Präparat [prɛpaˈraɪt] neut (pl -e) preparation; (Med) medicament.

präsentieren [prɛɪzenˈtiɪrən] v present. **Präsenz** f (pl -en) presence.

Präsident [prɛziˈdɛnt] m (pl -en) president. **–enwahl** f presidential election. **–schaft** f presidency. **präsidieren** v preside, act as chairman.

prasseln [ˈprasəln] v clatter; (Regen) patter, drum; (Feuer) crackle.

präventiv [prɛvenˈtiɪf] adj preventive. **Präventiv‖maßnahme** f preventive measure. **–mittel** neut contraceptive.

Praxis [ˈpraksis] f (pl Praxen) practice.

Präzedenzfall [prɛtseˈdɛntsfal] m precedent.

präzis [prɛˈtsiɪs] adj precise.

predigen [ˈpreɪdigən] v preach. **Prediger** m (pl -) preacher. **Predigt** f (pl -en) sermon.

Preis [prais] m (pl -e) price; (Belohnung) prize; (Lob) praise.

Preißelbeere [ˈpraisəlbeɪrə] f cranberry.

preisgeben [ˈpraisgeɪbən] v give up, abandon; (opfern) sacrifice. **Preisgebung** f surrender; sacrifice.

Preis‖liste f price list. **–senkung** f price reduction. **–steigerung** f price rise. **–stopp** m price freeze. **–sturz** m slump or fall in prices. **preiswert** adj cheap. **Preiszettel** m price tag.

prellen [ˈprɛlən] v (betrügen) swindle, cheat; (Ball) bounce.

Premiere [premˈjeɪrə] f (pl -n) première, first night.

Premierminister [premˈjeɪrministər] prime minister, premier.

Presse [ˈprɛsə] f (pl -n) (Zeitungen) the press; (Druckmaschine) press; (Saft) squeezer. **–agentur** f press agency. **–freiheit** f freedom of the press. **pressen** v press.

Preß‖holz neut chipboard. **–kohle** f briquette. **–luftbohrer** m pneumatic drill.

Preuße [ˈprɔysə] m (pl -n), **Preußin** f (pl -nen) Prussian. **Preußen** neut Prussia. **preußisch** adj Prussian.

prickeln [ˈprikəln] v prickle, tingle. **–d** adj tingling.

Priester [ˈpriɪstər] m (pl -) priest. **–in** f priestess. **priesterlich** adj priestly.

prima [ˈpriɪma] adj (umg.) first-rate, excellent. **Prima** f sixth form.

primär [priˈmɛɪr] adj primary.

Primarschule [priˈmaɪrʃuɪlə] f primary school (in Switzerland).

Primel [ˈpriɪməl] f (pl -n) primrose.

primitiv [primiˈtiɪf] adj primitive.

Prinz [prints] m (pl -en) prince. **-essin** f (pl -nen) princess.

Prinzip [prinˈtsiɪp] f (pl -ien) principle. **aus Prinzip** on principle. **im Prinzip** in principle, theoretically. **Prinzipal** m principal.

Priorität [prioriˈtɛɪt] f (pl -en) priority.

Prise [ˈpriɪzə] f (pl -n) pinch.

Prisma [ˈprisma] neut (pl Prismen) prism.

privat [priˈvaɪt] adj private. **Privat‖adresse**

f home address. **–angelegenheit** *f* personal matter.

Privileg [privi'leɪk] *neut (pl -ien)* privilege. **privilegiert** *adj* privileged.

Probe ['proːbə] *f (pl -n) (Versuch)* test, trial; *(Theater)* rehearsal; *(Muster)* sample, specimen. **auf Probe** on approval. **auf die Probe stellen** put to the test. **Probe‖abzug** *m (Druck)* proof. **–zeit** *f* probationary period. **probieren** *v (versuchen)* try, attempt; *(Speise)* taste, sample.

Problem [pro'bleɪm] *neut (pl -e)* problem. **problematisch** *adj* problematic.

Produkt [pro'dukt] *neut (pl -e)* product; *(Landwirtschaft)* produce. **–ion** *f* production. **produktiv** *adj* productive. **Produzent** *m* producer; *(Landwirtschaft)* grower. **produzieren** *v* produce.

Professor [pro'fɛsɔr] *m (pl -en)* professor. **professorisch** *adj* professorial. **Professur** *f (pl -en)* professorship.

Profil [pro'fiːl] *f (pl -e)* profile; *(Reifen)* tread. **profilieren** *v* outline, sketch.

Profit [pro'fiːt] *m (pl -e)* profit. **profit‖abel** *adj* profitable. **–ieren** *v* profit, gain. **Profitmacher** *m* profiteer.

Prognose [pro'gnoːzə] *f (pl -n) (Med)* prognosis; *(Wetter)* outlook, forecast.

Programm [pro'gram] *neut (pl -e)* programme. **programmgemäß** *adj* according to plan. **programmieren** *v (Computer)* program. **Programm‖ierer** *m (pl -)*, **–ierin** *f (pl -nen)* programmer. **–ierung** *f* programming.

Projekt [pro'jɛkt] *neut (pl -e) (Plan)* plan; *(Entwurf)* scheme. **projektieren** *v* plan; scheme. **Projektionsapparat** *m* projector. **projizieren** [proji'tsiːrən] *v* project.

proklamieren [prokla'miːrən] *v* proclaim.

Proletariat [proletaːri'aɪt] *neut (pl -e)* proletariat. **Proletarier** *m* proletarian. **proletarisch** *adj* proletarian.

Prolog [pro'loɪk] *m (pl -e)* prologue.

Promenade [promə'naːdə] *f (pl -n)* promenade.

Promotion [promotsi'oɪn] *f (pl -en)* (awarding of a) doctorate; *(Komm)* (sales) promotion. **promovieren** *v* be awarded a doctorate.

prompt [prɔmpt] *adj* prompt.

Propaganda [propa'ganda] *f* propaganda. **Propagandist** *m (pl -en)* propagandist.

Propeller [pro'pɛlər] *m (pl -)* propeller.

Prophet [pro'feɪt] *m (pl -en)* prophet. **–ie** *f* prophecy. **prophe‖tisch** *adj* prophetic. **–zeien** *v* prophesy. **Prophezeiung** *f (pl -en)* prophecy.

Proportion [propɔrtsi'oɪn] *f (pl -en)* proportion. **proportional** *adj* proportional.

Prosa ['proɪza] *f* prose.

prosit [ˌ'proːzit] *interj* cheers! your health! **prosit Neujahr!** a Happy New Year!

Prospekt [pro'spɛkt] *m (pl -e)* prospectus, leaflet; *(Ansicht)* prospect.

prostituieren [prostitu'iːrən] *v* prostitute. **Prostituierte** *f (pl -n)* prostitute. **Prostitution** *f* prostitution.

Protest [pro'tɛst] *m (pl -e)* protest. **Protestant** [prote'stant] *m (pl -en)* Protestant. **protest‖antisch** *adj* protestant. **–ieren** *v* protest.

Prothese [pro'teːzə] *f (pl -n)* prosthesis; *(Arm-, Bein-)* artificial limb; *(Zahn-)* denture.

Protokoll [proto'kɔl] *neut (pl -e) (Jur)* record; *(einer Versammlung)* minutes *pl*; *(Diplomatie)* protocol.

Protz [prɔts] *m (pl -en)* snob. **protzen** *v* put on airs, swagger. **–haft** *adj* snobbish.

Proviant [provi'ant] *m* provisions *pl*, victuals *pl*.

Provinz [pro'vints] *f (pl -en)* province. **provinzial** *adj* provincial, regional. **provinziell** *adj* provincial, narrow-minded.

Provision [provizi'oɪn] *f (pl -en) (Komm)* commission.

provisorisch [provi'zoɪriʃ] *adj* provisional.

provozieren [provo'tsiːrən] *v* provoke.

Prozedur [protse'duɪr] *f (pl -e)* procedure.

Prozent [pro'tsɛnt] *neut (pl -e)* percent. **–satz** *m* percentage.

Prozeß [pro'tsɛs] *m (pl Prozesse) (Jur)* lawsuit, trial; *(Vorgang)* process.

Prozession [protsɛsi'oɪn] *f (pl -en)* procession.

prüde ['pryːdə] *adj* prudish.

prüfen ['pryːfən] *v (Kenntnisse)* examine, test; *(erproben)* try, test; *(untersuchen)* inspect, check. **Prüf‖ling** *m (pl -e)* (examination) candidate. **–stein** *m* touchstone. **–ung** *f (pl -en)* examination, test.

Prügel ['pryːgəl] *m (pl -)* cudgel, club; *pl* beating. **prügeln** *v* beat, thrash. **Prügelstrafe** *f* corporal punishment.

Prunk [pruŋk] *m* pomp, show, splendour. **prunken** *v* show off. **Prunkstück** *neut*

showpiece. **prunk‖süchtig** *adj* ostentatious. **–voll** *adj* magnificent, gorgeous.
Psalm [psalm] *m* (*pl* -en) psalm.
Pseudonym [psɔydo'nyːm] *neut* (*pl* -e) pseudonym.
Psychiater [psyki'aːtər] *m* (*pl* -) psychiatrist. **Psychiatrie** *f* psychiatry. **psychiatrisch** *adj* psychiatric. **psychisch** *adj* psychic.
Psycho‖analyse [psyçoana'lyːzə] *f* psychoanalysis. **–loge** *m* (*pl* -n) psychologist. **psychologisch** *adj* psychological.
Psycho‖path *m* (*pl* -en) psychopath. **–therapeut** *m* (*pl* -en) psychotherapist. **–therapie** *f* psychotherapy.
Pubertät [puber'tɛɪt] *f* puberty.
Publikum ['puːblikum] *neut* public; (*Zuhörer*) audience.
publizieren [publi'tsiːrən] *v* publish. **Publizist** *m* journalist.
Pudding ['pudiŋ] *m* (*pl* -s) pudding.
Pudel ['puːdəl] *m* (*pl* -) poodle.
Puder ['puːdər] *m* (*pl* -) powder.
Puff¹ [puf] 1. *m* (*pl* Püffe) push, thump. 2. *m* (*pl* -e) pouffe.
Puff² *neut* (*Spiel*) backgammon.
puffen ['pufən] *v* shove, thump; (*knallen*) pop. **Puffer** *m* buffer; (*Kartoffel-*) pancake, fritter. **Puff‖mais** *m* popcorn. **–spiel** *neut* backgammon.
Pulli ['puli] *m* (*pl* -s) pullover. **Pullover** *m* (*pl* -) pullover.
Puls [puls] *m* (*pl* -e) pulse. **pulsieren** *v* pulsate, throb. **Puls‖schlag** *m* pulse. **–zahl** *f* pulse rate.
Pult [pult] *neut* (*pl* -e) desk. **-dach** *neut* lean-to roof.
Pulver ['pulvər] *neut* (*pl* -) powder. **pulver‖artig** *adj* powdery. **–isieren** *v* pulverize.
Pumpe ['pumpə] *f* (*pl* -n) pump. **pumpen** *v* pump.
Pumpernickel ['pumpərnikəl] *m* black (rye) bread.
Punkt [puŋkt] *m* (*pl* -e) point; (*Ort*) place, spot; (*Gramm*) full stop. **punktieren** *v* punctuate; (*Med*) puncture; (*tüpfeln*) dot. **punktiert** *adj* dotted.
pünktlich ['pyŋktliç] *adj* punctual, on time. **Pünktlichkeit** *f* punctuality.
Pupille [pu'pilə] *f* (*pl* -n) (*Anat*) pupil.
Puppe ['pupə] *f* (*pl* -n) doll; (*Theater*) puppet; (*Insekten*) pupa, chrysalis. **Puppen‖haus** *neut* doll's house. **–theater** *neut* puppet show.

pur [puːr] *adj* pure, unadulterated; (*Getränk*) neat.
Puritaner [puri'taːnər] *m* (*pl* -) Puritan. **puritanisch** *adj* puritan.
Purpur ['purpur] *m* purple. **purpurn** *adj* purple.
Purzelbaum *m* somersault. **purzeln** *v* somersault.
Pustel ['pustəl] *f* (*pl* -n) pustule.
Pute ['puːtə] *f* (*pl* -n) turkey (hen). **Puter** *m* (*pl* -) turkey (cock).
Putsch [putʃ] *m* (*pl* -e) putsch, uprising. **putschen** *v* revolt, rise.
Putz ['puts] *m* (*pl* -e) (*Kleidung*) finery, fine dress; (*Zierat*) ornaments *pl*, trimmings *pl*; (*Bewurf*) plaster. **putzen** *v* clean; (*Schuhe*) polish. **sich putzen** dress up. **sich die Nase putzen** wipe one's nose. **Putzer** *m* (*pl* -), **Putzerin** *f* (*pl* -nen) cleaner. **Putz‖frau** *f* charwoman, cleaner. **–tuch** *f* polishing cloth.
Pyjama [pi'dʒaːma] *m* (*pl* -s) pyjamas *pl*.
Pyramide [pyra'miːdə] *f* (*pl* -n) pyramid.

Q

quabbelig ['kvabəliç] *adj* flabby, wobbly. **quabbeln** *v* wobble, quiver.
Quacksalber ['kvakzalbər] *m* (*pl* -) quack, charlatan.
Quadrat [kva'draːt] *neut* (*pl* -e) square. **–meter** *neut* square metre. **–wurzel** *f* square root. **–zahl** *f* (*Math*) square. **quadrieren** *v* (*Math*) square.
quäken ['kvɛɪkən] *v* squeak.
Qual [kvaːl] *f* (*pl* -en) torment, pain.
quälen ['kvɛɪlən] *v* torment; (*foltern*) torture. **sich quälen** toil. **quälerisch** *adj* tormenting.
Qualifikation [kvalifikatsi'oːn] *f* (*pl* -en) qualification; (*Fähigkeit*) ability, fitness. **qualifizieren** *v* qualify. **sich qualifizieren** be fit (for).
Qualität [kvali'tɛɪt] *f* (*pl* -en) quality.
Qualle ['kvalə] *f* (*pl* -n) jellyfish.
Qualm [kvalm] *m* dense smoke; (*Wasser*) vapour, steam. **qualmen** *v* smoke; (*Wasser*) steam.
qualvoll ['kvaːlfɔl] *adj* painful; agonizing.
Quantität [kvanti'tɛɪt] *f* (*pl* -en) quantity.
Quarantäne [kvaran'tɛɪnə] *f* (*pl* -n) quarantine.

Quark [kvark] *m* curds *pl*, curd cheese; (*fig*) tripe, rubbish. **–käse** *m* curd cheese.

Quartal [kvar'taıl] *neut* (*pl* **-e**) quarter (of a year).

Quartett [kvar'tɛt] *neut* (*pl* **-e**) quartet.

Quartier [kvar'tiːr] *neut* (*pl* **-e**) accommodation; (*Mil*) quarters *pl*; (*Stadt*) quarter, district.

Quarz [kvarts] *m* (*pl* **-e**) quartz.

quasi ['kvaızi] *adv* as it were, in a way.

Quatsch [kvatʃ] *m* (*umg.*) rubbish, nonsense. **quatschen** *v* babble, talk nonsense.

Quecksilber ['kvɛkzilbər] *neut* quicksilver, mercury.

Quelle ['kvɛlə] *f* (*pl* **-n**) (*Wasser*) spring; (*Herkunft*) source, origin; (*Öl*) well. **aus guter Quelle** on good authority. **quellen** *v* spring, gush; arise.

quer [kveːr] *adj* cross, transverse; (*seitlich*) lateral. *adv* across, crosswise. **kreuz und quer** hither and thither. **Quer‖balken** *m* crossbeam. **–baum** *m* crossbar. **querdurch** *adv* (right) across.

quetschen ['kvɛtʃən] *v* squeeze, squash. **Quetschung** *f* (*pl* **-en**) bruise.

quietschen ['kviːtʃən] *v* (*Person, Bremsen*) squeal; (*Tür*) squeak.

Quintett [kvin'tɛt] *neut* (*pl* **-e**) quintet.

Quirl [kvirl] *m* (*pl* **-e**) whisk, beater. **quirlen** *v* whisk, beat.

quitt [kvit] *adj* quits, even.

Quitte [kvitə] *f* (*pl* **-n**) quince.

quittieren [kvi'tiːrən] *v* (*aufgeben*) abandon; (*Rechnung*) give a receipt for. **Quittung** *f* (*pl* **-en**) receipt.

R

Rabatt [ra'bat] *m* (*pl* **-e**) discount, rebate.

Rabbiner [ra'biːnər] *m* (*pl* **-**) rabbi.

Rabe ['raːbə] *m* (*pl* **-n**) raven. **rabenschwarz** *adj* jet-black.

rabiat [rabi'aıt] *adj* furious, raging.

Rache ['raxə] *f* revenge, vengeance. **Rache nehmen an** revenge oneself on.

Rachen ['raxən] *m* (*pl* **-**) throat; (*Maul*) jaws *pl*, mouth.

rächen ['rɛçən] *v* avenge. **sich rächen an** take revenge on.

Rad [raıt] *neut* (*pl* **Räder**) wheel.

Radar ['raıdaır] *neut or m* radar.

Rädchen ['rɛıtçən] *neut* (*pl* **-**) caster.

Rädelsführer ['rɛıdəlzfyırər] *m* ringleader.

*radfahren ['raıtfaırən] *v* cycle. **Radfahrer** *m* (*pl* **-**), **Radfahrerin** *f* (*pl* **-nen**) cyclist.

radieren [ra'diːrən] *v* erase, rub out; (*Kupfer*) etch. **Radiergummi** *m* rubber, eraser.

Radieschen [ra'diːsçən] *neut* (*pl* **-**) radish.

radikal [radi'kaıl] *adj* radical. **Radikal‖e(r)** radical. **–ismus** *m* radicalism.

Radio ['raıdio] *neut* (*pl* **-s**) radio. **radioaktiv** *adj* radioactive. **Radioaktivität** *f* radioactivity.

Radium ['raıdium] *neut* radium. **–therapie** *f* radiotherapy.

raffen ['rafən] *v* snatch (up); (*Stoff*) gather; (*langes Kleid*) take up.

raffinier‖en [rafi'niːrən] *v* refine. **–t** *adj* refined; (*fig*) clever, crafty.

ragen ['raıgən] *v* project, tower up.

Rahm [raım] *m* cream.

rahmen ['raımən] *v* frame. **Rahmen** *m* (*pl* **-**) frame; (*fig*) framework, limit; (*Umgebung*) surroundings *pl*, setting. **im Rahmen von** in the context of.

Rakete [ra'keıtə] *f* (*pl* **-n**) rocket.

Rakett [ra'kɛt] *neut* (*pl* **-s**) (*Sport*) racket.

Ramme ['ramə] *f* (*pl* **-n**) pile-driver.

Rampe ['rampə] *f* (*pl* **-n**) ramp; (*Bühne*) apron. **–nlicht** *neut* footlight.

'ran [ran] *V* **heran**.

Rand [rant] *m* (*pl* **Ränder**) edge; (*Seite*) margin; (*Gefäß, Hut*) brim; (*Grenze*) border, boundary. **–bemerkung** *f* marginal note.

Rang [raŋ] *m* (*pl* **Ränge**) rank, class; (*Theater*) circle.

rangieren [rã'ʒiːrən] *v* rank; (*Eisenbahnwagen*) shunt.

Ranke ['raŋkə] *f* (*pl* **-n**) tendril, shoot.

Ränke ['rɛŋkə] *pl* intrigues *pl*, machinations *pl*.

Ranzen ['rantsən] *m* (*pl* **-**) knapsack; (*Schule*) satchel.

ranzig ['rantsiç] *adj* rancid.

rar [raır] *adj* rare, scarce. **Rarität** *f* (*pl* **-en**) rarity.

rasch [raʃ] *adj* rapid, swift.

rascheln ['raʃəln] *v* rustle.

Raschheit ['raʃhait] *f* swiftness.

rasen ['raızən] *v* rage, storm; (*eilen*) race.

Rasen ['raızən] *m* (*pl* **-**) lawn, grass.

rasend ['raızənt] *adj* furious, raving. **rasend werden** go mad, (*umg.*) blow one's top.

rasieren [ra'ziːrən] v shave. **Rasierapparat** f safety razor. **elektrischer Rasierapparat** electric razor. **sich rasieren** shave (oneself). **Rasier‖klinge** f razor blade. **–krem** f shaving cream. **–messer** neut razor. **–pinsel** m shaving brush.
Raspel ['raspəl] f (pl -n) rasp; (Küche) grater.
Rasse ['rasə] f (pl -n) race; (Tiere) breed. **Rassehund** m pedigree dog.
Rassel ['rasəl] f (pl -n) rattle. **rasseln** v rattle, clatter.
Rassen‖diskriminierung f racial discrimination. **–haß** m racial hatred. **–integration** f racial integration. **–kreuzung** f cross-breeding. **–trennung** f racial segregation.
rassig ['rasiç] adj purebred; (schwungvoll) racy.
rassisch ['rasiʃ] adj racial. **Rassismus** m racialism, (US) racism. **rassistisch** adj racialist, (US) racist.
Rast [rast] f (pl -en) rest; (Pause) halt, break. **rasten** v rest. **rastlos** adj restless; (unermüdlich) unwearying. **Raststätte** f (motorway) service area.
Rasur [razuːr] f (pl -en) (Radieren) erasure; (Rasieren) shave.
Rat [raːt] 1 m (unz.) advice. 2 (pl Räte) (Versammlung) council; (Beamter) councillor. **um Rat fragen** ask for advice. **sich Rat holen bei** consult. **Rat wissen** know what has to be done.
Rate [raːtə] f (pl -n) instalment, payment.
*****raten** ['raːtən] v advise; (mutmaßen) guess.
Ratenkauf ['raːtənkauf] m hire purchase. **ratenweise** adv by instalments.
Rat‖geber(in) adviser, counsellor. **–haus** neut town hall.
ratifizieren [ratifi'tsiːrən] v ratify. **Ratifizierung** f ratification.
Ration [ra'tsioːn] f (pl -en) ration.
rationalisieren [ratsionali'ziːrən] v rationalize. **Rationalisierung** f rationalization. **rationell** adj rational.
rationieren [ratsio'niːrən] v ration.
rat‖los ['raːtloːs] adj helpless, perplexed. **–sam** adj advisable; (nützlich) useful; (förderlich) expedient. **Ratschlag** m (piece of) advice. **ratschlagen** v deliberate, consult together.
Rätsel ['rɛːtsəl] neut (pl -) puzzle, riddle; (Geheimnis) mystery. **rätselhaft** adj puzzling; mysterious.

Rats‖herr ['raːtshɛːr] m (town) councillor. **–keller** m town-hall restaurant. **–versammlung** f council meeting.
Ratte ['ratə] f (pl -n) rat.
Raub [raup] m robbery; (Beute) loot. **–anfall** m (armed) raid. **rauben** v rob; (Person) abduct; (plündern) plunder.
Räuber ['rɔybər] m (pl -) robber.
raubgierig ['raupgiːriç] adj rapacious. **Raub‖tier** m beast of prey. **–vogel** m bird of prey.
Rauch [raux] m smoke. **–rauchen** v smoke. **Rauchen** neut smoking. **Raucher** m (pl -) smoker.
räuchern ['rɔyçərn] v cure, smoke.
Rauch‖fang m chimney. **–fleisch** neut smoked meat. **rauch‖frei** adj smokeless. **–ig** adj smokey.
'rauf [rauf] V herauf.
Raufbold ['raufbɔlt] f (pl -e) ruffian, rowdy. **raufen** v (Haare) tear out. **sich raufen mit** brawl with. **Rauferei** f (pl -en) fight, brawl. **rauflustig** adj quarrelsome.
rauh [rau] adj rough; (grob) coarse; (Klima) inclement. **Rauheit** f roughness; coarseness; harshness.
Raum [raum] 1 m (unz.) room, space. 2 m (pl Räume) room; (Gebiet) area.
räumen ['rɔymən] v evacuate, remove; (Zimmer) vacate.
Raum‖fahrt f space travel. **–inhalt** m volume, capacity.
räumlich ['rɔymliç] adj spatial, of space.
Raumschiff ['raumʃif] neut space ship.
Räumung ['rɔymuŋ] f (pl -en) evacuation, removal; (Gebiet) cleaning.
Raupe [raupə] f (pl -n) caterpillar. **–nkette** f caterpillar track.
'raus [raus] V heraus.
Rausch [rauʃ] m (pl Räusche) intoxication.
rauschen ['rauʃən] v (Blätter) rustle; (Bach) babble, murmur.
Rauschgift ['rauʃgift] neut drug, narcotic. **–sucht** f drug addiction. **–süchtige(r)** (drug) addict.
Reagenzglas [rea'gɛntsglaːs] neut test tube.
reagieren [rea'giːrən] v react.
Reaktion [reaktsi'oːn] f (pl -en) reaction. **reaktionär** adj reactionary.
real [re'aːl] adj real. **–isieren** v realize. **Real‖ismus** m realism. **–ist** m (pl -en) realist. **realistisch** adj realistic.

Rebe ['reɪbə] f (pl -n) vine.
Rebell [re'bɛl] m (pl -en) rebel. **rebellieren** v rebel. **Rebellion** f (pl -en) rebellion. **rebellisch** adj rebellious.
Rebhuhn ['rɛphuːn] neut partridge.
Rebstock ['reɪpʃtɔk] m vine.
rechen ['rɛçən] v rake. **Rechen** m (pl -) rake.
Rechen‖fehler m miscalculation. **–kunst** f arithmetic. **–maschine** f calculating machine. **–schaft** f (unz.) account.
rechnen ['rɛçnən] v calculate. **rechnen auf** count on. **rechnen mit** reckon with. **Rechnen** neut arithmetic. **Rechner** m calculator. **Rechnung** f calculation; (Waren) invoice; (Gaststätte) bill. **Rechnungs‖abschluß** m balancing of accounts. **–führer** m accountant, bookkeeper. **–prüfer** m auditor. **–wesen** neut accountancy, accounting.
recht [rɛçt] adj right. adv (sehr) quite, very. mir ist das recht that suits me. **recht haben** be (in the) right. **ganz recht!** just so! **Recht** neut (pl -e) right; (Gesetze) law. **–e** f right (side), right-hand side; (Pol) the Right. **–eck** neut rectangle. **Rechtfertigung** f justification. **recht‖fertigen** v justify. **–gläubig** adj orthodox. **Rechthaber** m (pl -) dogmatic person, (umg.) know-all. **recht‖haberisch** adj dogmatic, obstinate. **–lich** adj legal, of law; (ehrlich) honest, just. **–mäßig** adj legal, lawful.
rechts [rɛçts] adv on or to(wards) the right.
Rechtsanwalt m lawyer.
Rechtschreibung f spelling.
Rechts‖fall m law suit, case. **–gleichheit** f equality before the law. **–händer** m right-handed person, right-hander. **rechts‖händig** adj right-handed. **–kräftig** adj legally binding, legal. **Rechtsprechung** f (pl -en) judicial decision, verdict; (Gerichtsbarkeit) jurisdiction.
rechtsradikal adj extreme right-wing. **Rechts‖radikale(r)** m right-wing radical. **–spruch** m (Urteil) verdict, judgment; (Strafe) sentence. **–steuerung** f right-hand drive. **–streit** m law suit. **rechtswidrig** adj illegal.
recht‖winklig adj right-angled. **–zeitig** adj timely, opportune; adv in (good) time.

recken ['rɛkən] v stretch.
Redakt‖eur [redak'tøːr] m (pl -) editor. **–ion** f editing; (Arbeitskräfte) editorial staff.
Rede ['reɪdə] f (pl -n) speech, talk. **redefertig** adj fluent, eloquent. **Rede‖freiheit** f freedom of speech. **–kunst** f rhetoric.
reden ['reɪdən] v speak, talk. **offen reden** speak out. **mit sich reden lassen** be open to persuasion, listen to reason. **Reden** neut speech, talking. **–sart** f expression, idiom. **Redewendung** f turn of speech, idiom.
redigieren [redi'giːrən] v edit.
redlich ['reɪtlɪç] adj honest, upright, just. **Redlichkeit** f honesty.
Redner ['reɪdnər] m (pl -) speaker, orator.
reduzieren [redu'tsiːrən] v reduce, decrease. **sich reduzieren** diminish, be reduced.
Reeder ['reɪdər] m (pl -) shipowner.
reell [re'ɛl] adj respectable, honest, reliable.
Referat [refe'raɪt] neut (pl -e) lecture, talk; (Gutachten) report, review. **Referent** m lecturer, speaker; (Fachmann) expert adviser, reviewer.
reflektieren [reflɛk'tiːrən] v reflect.
Reflex [re'flɛks] m (pl -e) reflex. **–bewegung** f reflex action.
Reform [re'fɔrm] f (pl -en) reform. **–ation** f reformation. **–er** m (pl -) reformer. **–haus** neut health-food shop. **reformieren** v reform.
Regal [re'gaɪl] neut (pl -e) (book)shelf.
rege ['reɪgə] adj active, lively.
Regel ['reɪgəl] f (pl -n) rule. **regel‖los** adj irregular (unordentlich) chaotic. **–mäßig** adj regular. **regelmäßigkeit** f regularity. **regeln** v regulate, arrange. **Regelung** f regulation, arrangement. **regelwidrig** adj against the rule(s). **Regelwidrigkeit** f irregularity; (Sport) foul.
Regen ['reɪgən] m rain. **–bogen** m rainbow. **–fall** m rainfall. **–mantel** m raincoat. **–tropfen** m raindrop. **–wetter** neut rainy weather. **–wurm** m earthworm. **–zeit** f rainy season, rains pl.
Regie [re'ʒiː] f (pl -n) (Theater, Film) direction; (Verwaltung) administration, management.
regieren [re'giːrən] v rule, govern. **Regierung** f government.

Regiment [regi'mɛnt] *neut* (*pl* -er) regiment.

Regisseur [reʒi'sœɪr] *m* (*pl* -e) (theatre *or* film) director.

Register [re'gistər] *neut* (*pl* -) register; (*Buch*) index. **registrieren** *v* register. **Registrierkasse** *f* cash register.

Regler ['reiglər] *m* (*pl* -) regulator.

regnen ['reignən] *v* rain. **regnerisch** *adj* rainy.

regulieren [regu'liɪrən] *v* regulate.

Regung ['reiguŋ] *f* (*pl* -en) motion; (*Gefühle*) stirring, emotion; (*Antrieb*) impulse.

Reh [rei] *neut* (*pl* -e) roe deer. **–bock** *m* roebuck. **rehfarben** *adj* fawn. **Reh‖fleisch** *neut* venison. **–kalb** *neut* fawn. **–ziege** *f* doe.

***reiben** ['raibən] *v* rub; (*Käse, usw.*) grate. **Reibung** *f* rubbing; (*fig, Tech*) friction; (*Käse*) grating.

reich [raiç] *adj* rich.

Reich [raiç] *neut* (*pl* -e) empire; (*fig*) realm; (*Tier-, Pflanzen*) kingdom.

reichen ['raiçən] *v* reach; (*überreichen*) pass, hand; (*anbieten*) offer; (*genügen*) be enough.

reich‖haltig *adj* copious; (*Programm*) full. **–lich** *adj* plentiful, ample.

Reichs‖adler *m* (German) imperial eagle. **–tag** *m* (German) Imperial Parliament (1871–1934).

Reichtum ['raiçtuɪm] *m* (*pl* **Reichtümer**) wealth, riches *pl*; (*Fülle*) abundance.

Reichweite ['raiçvaitə] *f* range.

reif [raif] *adj* (*Frucht*) ripe; (*Person*) mature.

Reif [raif] *m* hoarfrost.

Reife ['raifə] *f* (*Frucht*) ripeness; (*Person*) maturity. **reifen** *v* mature.

Reifen ['raifən] *m* (*pl* -) ring, hoop; (*Mot*) tyre. **–druck** *m* tyre pressure.

Reihe ['raiə] *f* (*pl* -n) row; (*Satz*) series, set. *ich bin an der Reihe* it is my turn. *eine ganze Reihe (von)* a lot (of), a whole series (of). **reihen** *v* line up, put in a row; (*Perlen*) string; (*Stoff*) gather; (*heften*) tack. **Reihenfolge** *f* order, sequence.

Reiher ['raiər] *m* (*pl* -) heron.

Reim [raim] *m* (*pl* -e) rhyme. **reimen** *v* rhyme. *sich reimen* make sense.

rein [rain] *adj* pure; (*sauber*) clean; (*vollkommen*) perfect; (*Komm*) net. *ins Reine bringen* clear up, settle. *adv* completely. *die reine Wahrheit* the plain truth.

***rein** [rain] *V* **herein**.

Reinemachen ['rainəmaxən] *neut* cleaning. **Reinheit** *f* purity; cleanness, cleanliness. **reinigen** *v* clean; (*fig*) purify, cleanse. **Reinigung** *f* cleaning; purification. **chemische Reinigung** *f* dry cleaning. **rein‖lich** *adj* clean, neat, tidy. **–rassig** *adj* purebred; (*Pferd*) thoroughbred.

Reis [rais] *m* rice.

Reise ['raizə] *f* (*pl* -n) trip, journey; (*See*) voyage. **–büro** *neut* travel agency. **–leiter(in)** *m* courier. **reisen** *v* travel. **–d** *adj* itinerant, travelling. **Reisende(r)** traveller. **Reise‖paß** *m* passport. **–tasche** *f* travelling bag. **–scheck** *m* traveller's cheque.

Reißbrett ['raisbrɛt] *neut* drawing board. **reißen** *v* tear, rip; (*zerren*) pull. *sich reißen um* fight for. **reißend** *adj* rapid; (*Schmerz*) sharp, shooting. **Reiß‖kohle** *f* charcoal. **–verschluß** *m* zip, zipper.

***reiten** ['raitən] *v* ride. **Reit‖en** *neut* riding. **–er** *m* rider, horseman. **–erin** *f* rider, horsewoman. **–kunst** *f* horsemanship, equitation.

Reiz [raits] *m* (*pl* -e) charm, attractiveness; (*Erregung*) stimulation. **reiz‖bar** *adj* irritable. **–en** *v* excite, stimulate; (*anziehen*) attract, charm; (*zornig machen*) irritate. **–end** *adj* charming, enchanting.

Reklame [re'klaɪmə] *f* (*pl* -n) advertising, publicity; (*einzelne*) advertisement. **Reklame machen für** promote, advertise.

Rekord [re'kɔrt] *m* (*pl* -e) record.

Rekrut [re'kruɪt] *m* (*pl* -en) recruit. **rekrutieren** *v* recruit.

Rektor ['rɛktor] *m* (*pl* -en) (*Universität*) vice-chancellor; (*andere Schulen*) principal, head.

relativ [rela'tiɪf] *adj* relative. **Relativität** *f* relativity.

Relief [rə'ljɛf] *neut* (*pl* -s) (*Kunst*) relief.

Religion [religi'oɪn] *f* (*pl* -en) religion. **–sbekenntnis** *neut* confession of faith. **religiös** *adj* religious.

Ren [rɛn] *neut* (*pl* -e) reindeer.

Rennbahn ['rɛnbaɪn] *f* racecourse. **rennen** *v* run; (*Sport*) race. **Renn‖en** *neut* running; race. **–pferd** *neut* racehorse. **–wagen** *m* racing car.

renovieren [reno'viɪrən] *v* renovate.

rentabel [rɛn'taɪbəl] *adj* profitable.
Rentabilität *f* profitability. **Rente** *f*
(*Alters-*) pension; (*Versicherung*) annuity. **rentieren** *v* **sich rentieren** be profitable. **Rentner** *m* (*pl* -) **Rentnerin** *f* (*pl* -nen) pensioner.
Reparatur [repara'tuːr] *f* (*pl* -en) repair. **–werkstatt** *f* repair shop. **reparieren** *v* repair.
Report [re'pɔrt] *m* (*pl* -e) report. **–age** *f* (*pl* -n) (eye-witness) report. **–er** *m* (*pl* -) reporter.
Repressalien [repre'saɪliən] *pl* reprisals.
Reproduktion [reproduk'tsioːn] *f* (*pl* -en) reproduction. **reproduzieren** *v* reproduce.
Reptil [rep'tiːl] *neut* (*pl* -ien) reptile.
Republik [re'publik] *f* (*pl* -en) republic. **–aner** *m* (*pl* -) republican. **republikanisch** *adj* republican.
Reserve [re'zɛrvə] *f* (*pl* -n) reserve. **–rad** *neut* spare wheel. **reservier‖en** *v* reserve, book. **–t** *adj* reserved.
Residenz [rezi'dɛnts] *f* (*pl* -en) residence.
Resonanz [rezo'nants] *f* (*pl* -en) resonance.
Respekt [re'spɛkt] *m* respect. **respekt‖abel** *adj* respectable. **–ieren** *v* respect. **–los** *adj* disrespectful. **–voll** *adj* respectful.
Rest [rɛst] *m* (*pl* -e) remainder, rest.
Restaurant [resto'rãː] *neut* (*pl* -s) restaurant.
Restbetrag *m* balance, remainder. **restlich** *adj* remaining.
Resultat [rezul'taɪt] *neut* (*pl* -e) result.
retablieren [reta'bliːrən] *v* re-establish.
Retorte [re'tɔrtə] *f* (*pl* -n) retort.
retten ['rɛtən] *v* save. **Retter** *m* (*pl* -) rescuer; (*Rel*) Saviour. **Rettung** *f* (*pl* -en) rescue, deliverance. **Rettungs‖boot** *neut* lifeboat. **–gürtel** *m* lifebelt.
Reue ['rɔyə] *f* remorse, regret. **reuen** *v* regret. *es reut mich, daß ich es getan habe* I regret doing that, I am sorry I did that.
Revanche [re'vãːʃə] *f* (*pl* -n) revenge, vengeance. **sich revanchieren** *v* take one's revenge.
Revers¹ [re'vɛrs] *m* (*pl* -e) (*Rückseite*) reverse, back.
Revers² [re'vɛɪr] *m or neut* (*pl* -) (*Jacke*) lapel.
Revers³ [re'vɛrs] *m* (*pl* -e) written undertaking, bond.
reversibel [revɛr'siːbəl] *adj* (*Med, Chem*) reversible.

revidieren [revi'diːrən] *v* revise.
Revier [re'viːər] *neut* (*pl* -e) district; (*Polizei*) beat; (*Wache*) station.
Revis‖ion [revizi'oɪn] *f* (*pl* -en) revision, (*Jur*) appeal; (*Komm*) auditing. **–or** *m* auditor.
Revolte [re'vɔltə] *f* (*pl* -n) revolt, insurrection.
Revolution [revolutsi'oɪn] *f* (*pl* -en) revolution. **revolutionär** *adj* revolutionary. **Revolutionär** *m* (*pl* -e) revolutionary. **revolutionieren** *v* revolutionize.
Revolver [re'vɔlvər] *m* (*pl* -) revolver.
rezensieren [retsɛn'ziːrən] *v* review.
Rezept [re'tsɛpt] *neut* (*pl* -e) recipe; (*Med*) prescription.
Rhabarber [ra'barbər] *m* rhubarb.
Rhapsodie [rapso'diː] *f* (*pl* -n) rhapsody.
Rhein [rain] *m* Rhine. **–hessen** *neut* Rhenish Hesse. **rheinisch** *adj* Rhine, Rhenish. **Rheinland** *neut* Rhineland. **–-Pfalz** *f* Rhineland-Palatinate. **Rheinwein** *m* hock, Rhine wine.
rhetorisch [re'toːriʃ] *adj* rhetorical.
Rheumatismus [rɔyma'tizmus] *m* (*pl* **Rheumatismen**) rheumatism.
Rhinozeros [ri'noɪtsɛrɔs] *neut* (*pl* -se) rhinoceros.
rhythmisch ['rytmiʃ] *adj* rhythmic(al).
Rhythmus *m* (*pl* **Rhythmen**) rhythm.
richten ['riçtən] *v* (*zurechtmachen*) arrange, prepare; (*einstellen*) adjust, set; (*reparieren*) repair; (*Frage, Brief*) address; (*Gewehr*) aim; (*Jur*) judge. **sich richten an** address oneself to. **sich richten nach** follow. **Richter** *m* (*pl* -) judge.
richtig ['riçtiç] *adj* correct, right. *ein richtiger Berliner* a real Berliner. **Richtigkeit** *f* correctness, rightness. **richtigstellen** *v* correct, set right.
Richt‖linie *f* guideline. **–preis** *m* recommended price.
Richtung [riçtuŋ] *f* (*pl* -en) direction; (*Neigung*) trend, tendency.
Richtweg ['riçtvɛk] *m* short cut.
***riechen** ['riːçən] *v* smell. **riechen nach** smell of. **gut/übel riechen** smell good/bad.
Riegel ['riːgəl] *m* (*pl* -) bolt, bar; (*Seife, Schokolade*) bar. **riegeln** *v* bolt, bar.
Riemen ['riːmən] *m* (*pl* -) strap, belt; (*Gürtel*) belt.
Riese ['riːzə] *m* (*pl* -n) giant. **Riesen-** *adj* colossal, huge. **Riesenerfolg haben** be a great success, (*umg.*) be a smash hit.

Riff   324

riesengroß or **riesig** adj gigantic. huge.
Riesin f (pl **-nen**) giantess.
Riff [rɪf] neut (pl **-e**) reef.
Rille ['rɪlə] f (pl **-n**) groove; (Furche) furrow.
Rind [rɪnt] neut (pl **-er**) (Ochse) ox; (Kuh) cow.
Rinde ['rɪndə] f (pl **-n**) (Baum) bark; (Käse) rind; (Brot) crust.
Rind∥erbraten m roast beef. **–fleisch** neut beef. **–vieh** neut cattle.
Ring [rɪŋ] m (pl **-e**) ring; (Straße) ring road; (Komm) combine, cartel; (Kettenglied) link. **–elchen** neut (pl **-**) ringlet.
***ringen** ['rɪŋən] v wrestle; (Hände) wring. **ringen um** struggle for. **Ringen** neut struggle, battle.
Ringfinger m ring finger. **ringförmig** adj ring-shaped.
Ringkampf m wrestling (match).
rings [rɪŋs] adv around. **–herum** adv all around.
Ringstraße f ring road.
Rinne ['rɪnə] f (pl **-n**) channel, groove; (Dach-) gutter.
Rippchen ['rɪpçən] neut (pl **-**) cutlet, chop. **Rippe** f (pl **-n**) rib.
Risiko ['rɪːziko] neut (pl **-s** or **Risiken**) risk. **risk∥ant** adj risky. **–ieren** v risk.
Riß [rɪs] m (pl **Risse**) (Stoff, Haut) tear; (Mauer) crack; (fig) breach, rift; (Zeichnung) technical drawing, plan.
rissig ['rɪsɪç] adj cracked; (Haut) chapped.
Ritt [rɪt] m (pl **-e**) ride.
Ritter ['rɪtər] m (pl **-**) knight. **ritterlich** adj chivalrous. **Ritterlichkeit** f chivalry.
rittlings ['rɪtlɪŋs] adv astride.
rituell [rɪtu'ɛl] adj ritual. **Ritus** m (pl **Riten**) rite.
Ritz [rɪts] m (pl **-e**) or **Ritze** f (pl **-n**) crack; (Schramme) scratch.
Robbe ['rɔbə] f (pl **-n**) seal.
Roboter ['rɔbɔtər] m (pl **-**) robot.
Rock [rɔk] m (pl **Röcke**) (Frauen) skirt; (Obergewand) cloak; (Jacke) jacket, coat.
Rodel ['rɔɪdəl] m (pl **-**) toboggan. **rodeln** v toboggan.
roden ['rɔɪdən] v clear (land). **Rodung** f (pl **-en**) cleared land.
Rogen ['rɔɪgən] m (pl **-**) (fish) roe.
Roggen ['rɔgən] m rye. **–brot** neut ryebread.
roh [rɔː] adj raw; (grausam) cruel, brutal; (Stein, Person) rough. **rohe Gewalt** brute force. **Roheit** f rawness; brutality; rough-

ness. **Roh∥gewicht** neut gross weight. **–öl** neut crude oil.
Rohr [rɔːr] neut (pl **-e**) tube, pipe; (Gewehr) barrel; (Bot) seed.
Röhre ['rœːrə] f (pl **-n**) tube, pipe; (Radio) valve; (Leitung) conduit, duct.
Rohr∥leitung f pipeline. **–leitungen** pl pipes, plumbing sing. **–stock** m cane, bamboo. **–stuhl** m cane chair. **–zucker** m cane sugar.
Rohstoff m raw material.
Rolladen ['rɔlˌaːdən] m (pl **-** or **Rolläden**) rolling shutter.
Rollbahn f runway.
Rolle ['rɔlə] f (pl **-n**) roll; (Theater, Film) role; (Tech) pulley. **eine Rolle spielen** play a part. **keine Rolle spielen** make no difference, not matter.
rollen ['rɔlən] v roll; (Flugzeug) taxi.
Roll∥mops m pickled herring. **–schuh** m roller skate. **–schuhlaufen** neut rollerskating. **–stuhl** m wheelchair. **–treppe** f escalator. **–tür** f sliding door.
Rom [rɔːm] neut Rome.
Roman [ro'maːn] m (pl **-e**) novel.
Romantik [ro'mantik] f Romanticism. **–er** m (pl **-**) romantic. **romantisch** adj romantic.
Römer ['rœːmər] m (pl **-**) Roman. **römisch** adj Roman. **römisch-katholisch** adj Roman Catholic.
röntgen ['rœntgən] v x-ray. **Röntgen∥behandlung** f radiation therapy. **–bild** neut x-ray (photograph) **–strahlen** pl x-rays.
rosa ['rɔːza] adj pink, rose.
Rose ['rɔːzə] f (pl **-n**) rose. **Rosen∥busch** m rose bush. **–kohl** m Brussels sprouts pl. **–kranz** m rose garland; (Rel) rosary.
Rosine [ro'ziːnə] f (pl **-n**) raisin.
Rosmarin [rozma'riːn] m rosemary.
Roß [rɔs] neut (pl **Rosse**) steed, horse. **–kastanie** f horse chestnut.
Rost¹ [rɔst] m (pl **-e**) grate; (Kochen) grill.
Rost² m rust.
Röstbrot ['rœstbrot] neut toast.
rosten ['rɔstən] v rust.
rost∥beständig adj rustproof. **–braun** adj rust(-brown).
rösten ['rœstən] v roast; (Brot) toast.
rot [rɔt] adj red. **Rot** neut red.
Röte ['rœːtə] f red(ness).
Röteln ['rœːtəln] pl German measles, rubella.

rot‖glühend adj red-hot. **–haarig** adj red-haired. **Rot‖käppchen** neut Little Red Riding Hood. **–kehlchen** neut robin.

rötlich ['rœːtliç] adj reddish.

Rotte ['rɔtə] f (pl -n) gang, band; (Tiere) pack. **sich rotten** v band together, gang up.

Roulade [ruˈlaɪdə] f (pl -n) rolled meat; (Musik) trill.

Rübe ['ryːbə] f (pl -n) (Bot) rape. **weiße/gelbe/rote Rübe** turnip/carrot/beetroot.

Rubin [ruˈbiːn] m (pl -e) ʹruby.

Rubrik ['ruːbrik] f (pl -en) (Titel) title, heading; (Spalte) column; (fig) category.

ruchbar ['ruːxbaɪr] adj notorious.

Ruck [ruk] m (pl -e) jolt, jerk, start.

Rück‖ansicht f rear view. **–blende** f flashback. **–blick** m glance back; (fig) retrospect.

rücken ['rykən] v move, shift; (Platz machen) move up, shift up.

Rücken ['rykən] m (pl -) back. **–lehne** f back (of a chair). **–mark** neut spinal cord. **–schmerzen** pl backache sing. **–schwimmen** neut backstroke.

Rück‖erstattung f return; (Geld) repayment. **–fahrkarte** f return ticket. **–fahrt** f return journey. **–gabe** f return, restoration. **–gang** m decline, retrogression. **rückgängig** adj retrograde. **rückgängig machen** cancel, annul. **Rück‖grat** neut backbone. **–griff** m recourse. **–halt** m support. **–handschlag** m (Tennis) backhand (stroke). **–kehr** f return. **–licht** neut rear light.

Rucksack ['rukzak] m rucksack, pack.

Rück‖schlag m set-back, reverse. **–schritt** m retrogression, relapse. **–seite** f reverse (side), back.

Rücksicht f consideration, regard. **Rücksicht nehmen auf** take into consideration; (Person) show consideration to. **mit Rücksicht auf** with respect to. **Rücksichtnahme** f consideration, regard. **rücksichtslos** adj inconsiderate (hart) ruthless. **Rücksichtslosigkeit** f lack of consideration; ruthlessness.

Rück‖sitz m back seat. **–spiegel** m rearview mirror. **–spiel** neut return match.

Rückstand m rest, remainder. **im Rückstand** in arrears. **rückständig** adj in arrears; (altmodisch) old-fashioned, backward.

Rücktritt m resignation; (in den Ruhestand) retirement.

rückwärts adv back(wards). **–gehen** v decline, retrogress.

Rück‖wirkung f reaction, repercussion. **–zug** m retreat. **–zahlung** f repayment, reimbursement.

Rudel ['ruːdəl] neut (pl -) (Schar) troop; (Hunde) pack; (Rehe, Schafe) herd.

Ruder ['ruːdər] neut (pl -) oar; (Steuer) rudder. **–boot** neut rowing boat. **rudern** v row. **Rudersport** m rowing.

Ruf [ruːf] m (pl -e) call, shout; (Tier) cry; (Vogel) call; (Ruhm) reputation, good name; (Aufforderung) summons. **rufen** v call, shout, cry. **Rufnummer** f telephone number.

Rüge ['ryːgə] f (pl -n) rebuke, reprimand. **rügen** v rebuke, reprimand.

Ruhe ['ruːə] f quiet, stillness; (Erholung) rest; (Gefaßtsein) composure, calm. **in Ruhe lassen** leave alone. **zur Ruhe gehen** go to bed. **ruhelos** adj restless. **Ruhelosigkeit** f restlessness. **ruhen** v rest; (schlafen) sleep; (begründet sein) be based. **–d** adj resting; (Tech) latent. **Ruhe‖pause** f break, rest period. **–platz** m resting place. **–stand** m retirement. **–stätte** f resting place. **–störung** f breach of the peace. **–tag** m day of rest. **ruhig** ['ruːiç] adj still, quiet; (gefaßt) calm, composed.

Ruhm [ruːm] m fame, glory.

rühmen ['ryːmən] v praise. **sich rühmen** boast. **rühmlich** adj glorious.

Ruhr [ruːr] f dysentery.

Rührei ['ryːrai] neut scrambled egg(s). **rühren** v (bewegen) move; (vermischen) stir; (innerlich) move, affect. **sich rühren** stir, move. **rühr‖end** adj (fig) touching, moving. **–selig** adj sentimental. **Rührung** f (unz.) feeling, emotion.

Ruine [ruˈiːnə] f (pl -n) ruin. **ruinieren** v ruin.

Rülps [rylps] m (pl -e) belch. **rülpsen** v belch.

Rum [rum] m (pl -s) rum.

Rumäne [ruˈmɛːnə] m (pl -n) Rumanian. **Rumänien** n Rumania. **Rumänin** f (pl -nen) Rumanian (woman). **rumänisch** adj Rumanian.

Rummel ['ruməl] m (unz.) (umg.) bustle, activity; (Lärm) hubbub, racket. **–platz** m fairground.

Rumpf [rumpf] m (pl Rümpfe) trunk, torso; (Tier) carcass; (Schiff) hull; (Flugzeug) fuselage.

rümpfen [rympfən] v turn up (one's nose).

rund [runt] adj round. adv about. **Rundblick** m panorama. **Runde** f (pl -n) circle; (Boxen) round; (Rennen) lap; (Sport) heat; (Polizist) beat. **runden** v round (off).

Rund‖fahrt f (circular) tour. **–frage** f questionnaire. **–funk** m radio; (Übertragung) broadcasting. **–funksendung** f radio programme. **–gang** m tour (of inspection); (Spaziergang) stroll. **–heit** f roundness.

rund‖heraus adv frankly, flatly. **–lich** adj rotund, plump.

Rund‖schau f panorama; (Zeitschrift) review. **–schreiben** neut circular. **–ung** f curve.

'runter ['runtər] V herunter.

Runzel ['runtsəl] f (pl -n) wrinkle. **runzelig** adj wrinkled. **runzeln** v wrinkle. **die Stirn runzeln** frown.

rupfen ['rupfən] v pluck.

Ruß [rus] m soot.

Russe ['rusə] m (pl -n) Russian.

rußig ['ruːsiç] adj sooty.

Russin ['rusin] f (pl -nen) Russian (woman). **russisch** adj Russian.

Rußland ['ruslant] neut Russia.

rüsten ['rystən] v prepare; (Mil) arm, prepare for war. **sich rüsten (auf)** get ready (for). **Rüstung** f armament; (Kriegsvorbereitung) arming; **Rüstungs‖fabrik** f armaments factory. **–wettbewerb** m arms race.

Rute ['ruːtə] f (pl -n) rod; (Gerte) switch; (Anat) penis.

Rutsch [rutʃ] m (pl -e) slide; (Erde) landslip. **rutsch‖en** v slip; (gleiten) slide. **–ig** adj slippery.

rütteln ['rytəln] v shake (up); (beim Fahren) jolt.

S

Saal [zaːl] m (pl Säle) hall, large room.
Saat [zaːt] f (pl -en) (Samen) seed; (Säen) sowing; (grün) green corn. **–korn** neut seed corn.

Sabbat ['zabat] m (pl -e) Sabbath.
Säbel ['zɛːbəl] m (pl -) sabre.
Sabotage [zabo'taːʒə] f sabotage. **sabotieren** v sabotage.
Saccharin [zaxa'riːn] neut saccharine.
Sachbearbeiter ['zaxbəarbaitər] m executive, official in charge. **Sache** f thing; (Angelegenheit) affair, matter; (Tat) fact. **Sachen** pl things, belongings; (Kleider) things, clothes. **Sach‖kundige(r)** expert. **–lage** f situation, state of affairs. **sachlich** adj businesslike, matter-of-fact; (objektiv) objective.
Sachse ['zaksə] m (pl -n) Saxon. **Sachsen** neut Saxony.
Sächsin ['zɛksin] f (pl -nen) Saxon (woman). **sächsisch** adj Saxon.
sacht(e) [zaxt(ə)] adv softly, gently.
Sack [zak] m (pl Säcke) sack, bag. **–gasse** f cul-de-sac, (US) dead end.
Sadismus [za'dizmus] m sadism. **Sadist** m (pl -en) sadist. **sadistisch** adj sadistic.
säen ['zɛːən] v sow.
Safari [za'faːri] f (pl -s) safari.
Safe [seːf] m (pl -s) safe.
Saft [zaft] m (pl Säfte) juice; (Baum) sap; (umg.: Strom, Benzin) juice. **saftig** adj juicy; (Witz) spicy.
Sage ['zaːgə] f (pl -n) legend, fable.
Säge ['zɛːgə] f (pl -n) saw. **–maschine** f mechanical saw. **–mehl** neut sawdust.
*sagen ['zaːgən] v say; (mitteilen) tell. **was Sie nicht sagen!** you don't say! **sagen wir** let's say, suppose. **wie gesagt** as I said. **das sagt mir etwas** that means something to me.
sägen ['zɛːgən] v saw.
sagenhaft ['zaːgənhaft] adj legendary; (umg.) splendid, great.
Sahne ['zaːnə] f cream. **–kuchen** m cream cake. **sahnig** adj creamy.
Saison [zɛ'zõ] f (pl -s) season. **stille Saison** off-season.
Saite ['zaitə] f (pl -n) string. **–ninstrument** neut stringed instrument.
Sakrament [zakra'mɛnt] neut (pl -e) sacrament.
Salat [za'laːt] m (pl -e) salad; (Kopfsalat) lettuce. **–kopf** m head of lettuce.
Salbe ['zalbə] f (pl -n) ointment, salve.
Salbei [zal'bai] f or m (Bot) sage.
salben ['zalbən] v anoint.
Saldo ['zaldo] m (pl Salden) (Komm) balance.

Salon [za'lɔ̃] *m* (*pl* -e) drawing room. **salonfähig** *adj* presentable (in society).
Salut [za'luːt] *m* (*pl* -e) salute. **salutieren** *v* salute.
Salve ['zalvə] *f* (*pl* -n) volley.
Salz [zalts] *neut* (*pl* -e) salt. **salzen** *v* salt. **Salzfaß** *neut* salt cellar. **salzig** *adj* salty. **Salz‖kartoffeln** *pl* boiled potatoes. **–wasser** *neut* salt water.
Samen ['zaːmən] *m* (*pl* -) seed; (*Tiere*) sperm. **–erguß** *m* ejaculation. **–händler** *m* seed merchant. **–pflanze** *f* seedling. **–staub** *m* pollen.
Sämischleder ['zɛːmiʃleːdər] *neut* chamois (leather).
sammeln ['zaməln] *v* gather; (*Hobby*) collect. **Samm‖elplatz** *m* assembly point. **–ler** *m* collector. **–lung** *f* collection.
Samstag ['zamstaːk] *m* Saturday. **samstags** *adv* on Saturdays.
samt [zamt] *prep* (together) with, including.
Samt [zamt] *m* (*pl* -e) velvet.
sämtlich ['zɛmtliç] *adj* complete, entire; (*alle*) all; (*Werke*) complete.
Sand [zant] *m* (*pl* -e) sand.
Sandale [zan'daːlə] *f* (*pl* -n) sandal.
Sandbank *f* sandbank. **sandfarben** *adj* sandy(-coloured). **Sand‖papier** *neut* sandpaper. **–stein** *m* sandstone.
sanft [zanft] *adj* gentle, soft. **Sanftheit** *f* gentleness, softness. **sanftmütig** *adj* gentle, mild.
Sänger ['zɛŋər] *m* (*pl* -), **Sängerin** *f* (*pl* -nen) singer.
sanieren [za'niːrən] *v* heal; (*Betrieb*) rationalize, make viable; (*Stadt, Viertel*) redevelop. **Sanierung** *f* (*Komm*) reorganization; (*Gebäude*) renovation.
sanitär [zani'tɛːr] *adj* sanitary, hygienic. **sanitäre Anlagen** *pl* sanitation *sing*.
Sankt [zaŋkt] *adj* Saint.
Sanktion [zaŋk'tsioːn] *f* (*pl* -en) sanction. **sanktionieren** *v* sanction.
Saphir [zafiːr] *m* (*pl* -e) sapphire.
Sardelle [zar'dɛlə] *f* (*pl* -n) anchovy.
Sardine [zar'diːnə] *f* (*pl* -n) sardine.
Sarg [zark] *m* (*pl* **Särge**) coffin.
sarkastisch [zar'kastiʃ] *adj* sarcastic.
Satan ['zaːtan] *m* (*pl* -) Satan; (*böser Mensch*) devil, demon. **satanisch** *adj* satanic.
Satellit [zate'liːt] *m* (*pl* -en) satellite.
Satin [za'tɛ̃] *m* (*pl* -s) satin.

Satire [za'tiːrə] *f* (*pl* -n) satire. **Satiriker** *m* (*pl* -) satirist. **satirisch** *adj* satirical.
satt [zat] *adj* satisfied, satiated; (*Farbe*) deep, rich. **satt sein** have had enough; (*nach dem Essen*) be full. **satt haben** have had enough of, be tired of.
Sattel ['zatəl] *m* (*pl* **Sättel**) saddle. **satteln** *v* saddle. **Sattel‖schlepper** *m* (tractor for an) articulated truck. **–tasche** *f* saddlebag.
Satz [zats] *m* (*pl* **Sätze**) (*Sprung*) leap, jump; (*Gramm*) sentence; (*Sammlung, Math*) set; (*Musik*) movement; (*Bodensatz*) sediment; (*Wein*) dregs *pl*; (*Grundsatz*) principle; (*Geld*) price, rate; (*Druck*) composition, setting. **–lehre** *f* syntax.
Satzung ['zatsuŋ] *f* (*pl* -en) statute; (*Vorschrift*) rule. **satzungs‖gemäß** *or* **–mäßig** *adj* statutory.
Sau [zau] *f* (*pl* **Säue**) sow.
sauber ['zaubər] *adj* clean; (*hübsch*) pretty, nice; (*ordentlich*) tidy. **Sauberkeit** *f* cleanliness; niceness; tidiness.
säuberlich ['zɔybərliç] *adj* clean; (*ordentlich*) tidy; (*anständig*) proper.
saubermachen *v* clean (up).
sauer ['zauər] *adj* (*Geschmack*) sour; (*säurehältig*) acid. **Sauerbraten** *m* roast marinated beef.
Sauerei *f* (*pl* -en) (*Unanständigkeit*) smuttiness; (*Pfuscherei*) mess.
Sauerkraut ['zauərkraut] *neut* pickled cabbage, sauerkraut.
Sauerstoff *m* oxygen. **sauersüß** *adj* bittersweet; (*Speise*) sweet-and-sour.
***saufen** ['zaufən] *v* drink; (*umg.*) drink, booze.
Säufer ['zɔyfər] *m* (*pl* -) heavy drinker, boozer.
***saugen** ['zaugən] *v* suck; (*einziehen*) absorb. **Saugen** *neut* suction, sucking.
säugen ['zɔygən] *v* suckle, nurse. **Säug‖en** *neut* suckling, nursing. **–etier** *neut* mammal. **–ling** *m* baby.
Säule ['zɔylə] *f* (*pl* -n) column, pillar.
Saum [zaum] *m* (*pl* **Säume**) seam, hem; (*Rand*) border, margin.
säumen[1] ['zɔymən] *v* (*Kleid*) hem; (*allgemein*) edge; (*fig*) skirt, fringe.
säumen[2] *v* (*zögern*) delay, hesitate.
Säumnis ['zɔymnis] *f* (*pl* -se) *or* *neut* (*pl* -e) delay.
Saumpferd ['zaumpfɛrt] *neut* packhorse.

Sauna ['zauna] *f* (*pl* **-s**) sauna.
Säure ['zɔyrə] *f* (*pl* **-n**) acid; sourness.
Sauregurkenzeit [zaurə'gurkəntsait] *f* silly season.
sausen ['zauzən] *v* (*eilen*) rush, dash, zoom; (*Wind*) howl, whistle.
Saxophon [zakso'foɪn] *neut* (*pl* **-e**) saxophone.
schaben ['ʃaɪbən] *v* scrape; (*Fleisch*) cut into strips.
schäbig ['ʃɛːbiç] *adj* shabby.
Schablone [ʃa'bloɪnə] *f* (*pl* **-n**) stencil, pattern, model.
Schach [ʃax] *neut* (*Spiel*) chess; (*Warnruf*) check. **in Schach halten** keep in check. **Schachbrett** *neut* chessboard.
Schacherei [ʃaxə'rai] *f* haggling, bargaining.
Schachfigur *f* chessman.
Schacht [ʃaxt] *m* (*pl* **-e**) shaft.
Schachtel ['ʃaxtəl] *f* (*pl* **-n**) box.
schade ['ʃaɪdə] *adv* a pity. **es ist schade** it's a pity, it's a shame. **schade, daß Sie ...** what a pity that you ... . **wie schade!** what a pity!
Schädel ['ʃɛːdəl] *m* (*pl* **-**) skull.
schaden ['ʃaɪdən] *v* harm, injure, hurt. **Schaden** *m* damage; (*Verlust*) loss; (*körperlich*) injury, harm. **–ersatz** *m* compensation. **–freude** *f* malicious joy, gloating. **schadenfroh** *adj* malicious, gloating. **schadhaft** *adj* damaged.
schädigen ['ʃɛːdɪgən] *v* harm, damage; (*körperlich*) injure. **Schädigung** *f* damage; injury. **schädlich** *adj* dangerous, injurious.
Schaf [ʃaːf] *neut* (*pl* **-e**) sheep.
Schäfer ['ʃɛːfər] *m* (*pl* **-**) shepherd. **–hund** *m* sheepdog; (*deutscher*) Alsatian (dog). **–in** *f* (*pl* **-nen**) shepherdess.
Schaffell *neut* sheepskin, fleece.
schaffen[1] ['ʃafən] *v* (*hervorbringen, gestalten*) create.
schaffen[2] *v* (*bringen*) bring, convey; (*fertigbringen*) manage, accomplish; (*arbeiten*) work.
Schaffner ['ʃafnər] *m* (*pl* **-**) (*Zug*) guard; (*Bus*) conductor. **–in** *f* (*pl* **-nen**) guard; conductress.
Schaf‖**pelz** *m* sheepskin. **–stall** *m* sheepfold.
Schaft [ʃaft] *m* (*pl* **Schäfte**) shaft; (*Griff*) handle; (*Gewehr*) stock; (*Baum*) trunk.
Schale ['ʃaɪlə] *f* (*pl* **-n**) (*Schüssel*) bowl,

basin; (*Ei, Nuß*) shell; (*Frucht, Gemüse*) peel, skin; (*fig*) cover(ing).
schälen ['ʃɛːlən] *v* shell; peel.
Schalk [ʃalk] *m* (*pl* **-e**) rogue, knave.
schalkhaft *adj* roguish.
Schall [ʃal] *m* (*pl* **-e**) sound. **–dämpfer** *m* silencer. **schallen** *v* sound, resound; (*Glocke*) ring, peal. **Schall**‖**platte** *f* (gramophone) record. **–welle** *f* soundwave.
schalten ['ʃaltən] *v* switch; (*Mot*) change (gear). **Schalt**‖**er** *m* (*Bank, usw.*) counter, window; (*Elek*) switch. **–hebel** *m* control lever, switch; (*Mot*) gear lever. **–jahr** *neut* leap year. **–plan** *m* circuit diagram. **–ung** *f* wiring; (*Mot*) gear-change.
Scham [ʃaːm] *f* shame; (*Scheu*) modesty.
schämen ['ʃɛːmən] *v* **sich schämen** *v* be ashamed.
scham‖**haft** *adj* bashful, modest. **–los** *adj* shameless, immodest.
Schampoo [ʃam'puɪ] *neut* shampoo.
schampoonieren *v* shampoo.
Schande ['ʃandə] *f* (*pl* **-n**) disgrace, shame.
schänden ['ʃɛndən] *v* disgrace; (*verderben*) spoil; (*entheiligen*) desecrate; (*Frau*) rape, violate.
Schandfleck ['ʃantflɛk] *m* blemish, stain.
schändlich ['ʃɛntliç] *adj* shameful, disgraceful.
Schandtat ['ʃanttart] *f* misdeed, crime.
Schank ['ʃaŋk] *m* (*pl* **Schänke**) bar.
Schanze ['ʃantsə] *f* (*pl* **-n**) fortification; (*Erdwall*) earthworks *pl*; (*Skilauf*) skijump.
Schar [ʃaːr] *f* (*pl* **-en**) troop, band; (*Gänse*) flock; (*Hunde*) pack. **sich scharen** *v* gather, congregate.
scharf [ʃarf] *adj* sharp; (*Gewürze*) spicy, hot.
Schärfe ['ʃɛrfə] *f* (*pl* **-n**) sharpness, edge; (*Ätzkraft*) acidity; (*Klarheit*) clarity. **schärfen** *v* sharpen.
Scharfschütze *m* marksman, sharpshooter. **scharfsichtig** *adj* sharpsighted. **Scharfsinn** *m* shrewdness. **scharfsinnig** *adj* shrewd.
Scharlachfieber ['ʃarlaxfiːbər] *neut* scarlet fever. **scharlachrot** *adj* scarlet.
Scharm [ʃarm] *m* charm. **scharmant** *adj* charming, delightful.
Scharnier [ʃar'niːr] *neut* (*pl* **-e**) hinge.
scharren ['ʃarən] *v* scrape, scratch.

Schatten ['ʃatən] m (pl -) shadow;
(*Dunkel*) shade. **in den Schatten stellen**
overshadow. **Schattenbild** neut silhouette. **schatten‖haft** adj shadowy. **-ig** adj
shaded.

Schatz [ʃats] m (pl **Schätze**) treasure;
(*fig*) darling. **-amt** neut treasury.

schätzen ['ʃɛtsən] v value; (*ungefähr*) estimate. **-swert** adj valuable, estimable.

Schatz‖kammer f treasury. **-meister** m
treasurer.

Schätzung ['ʃɛtsuŋ] f (pl -en) estimate;
(*Hochschätzung*) esteem. **schätzungsweise**
adv approximately; at a guess.

Schau [ʃau] f (pl -en) show; (*Ausstellung*)
exhibition; (*Überblick*) survey, review.
zur Schau stellen exhibit.

schaudern ['ʃaudərn] v shudder, shiver.
-haft adj horrible.

schauen ['ʃauən] v look (at), observe.

Schauer ['ʃauər] m (pl -) (*Regen*) shower;
(*Schrecken*) horror; (*Zittern*) thrill.

Schaufel ['ʃaufəl] f (pl -n) shovel; (*Tech*)
blade.

Schaufenster neut shop window.

Schaukel ['ʃaukəl] f (pl -n) (child's)
swing. **-pferd** neut rocking horse. **-stuhl**
m rocking-chair.

Schaum [ʃaum] m (pl **Schäume**) foam;
(*Seife*) lather.

schäumen ['ʃɔymən] v foam; (*Wein*) sparkle.

schaumig ['ʃaumiç] adj foamy.

Schauspiel neut play; drama; (*fig*) spectacle. **-er** m (pl -) actor. **-erin** f (pl
-nen) actress. **-haus** neut theatre.

Scheck [ʃɛk] m (pl -s) check.
-buch neut check book.

Scheibe ['ʃaibə] f (pl -n) disc; (*Brot*,
Wurst) slice; (*Glas*) pane.
Scheiben‖bremse f disc brake. **-wischer**
m windshield wiper.

Scheide ['ʃaidə] f (pl -n) sheath; (*Anat*)
vagina; (*Grenze*) limit. **scheiden** v separate; (*Ehepartner*) divorce. **sich scheiden**
part, separate. **sich scheiden lassen get** a
divorce. **Scheideweg** m crossroads.
Scheidung f separation; (*Ehe*) divorce.

Schein [ʃain] m (pl -e) (*Aussehen*) appearance; (*Licht*) light; (*Glanz*) shine; (*Geld*)
bill (*US*); banknote; (*Bescheinigung*) certificate. **schein‖bar** adj apparent, ostensible. **-en** v (*aussehen*) appear, seem;
(*leuchten*) shine. **-heilig** adj sanctimoni-

ous. **Schein‖heilige(r)** hypocrite.
-krankheit f feigned sickness. **-werfer**
m (pl -) searchlight; (*Reflektor*) reflector;
(*Theater*) spotlight; (*Mot*) headlight.

Scheiße ['ʃaisə] f (*vulgär*) shit. **scheißen** v
shit.

Scheitel ['ʃaitəl] m (pl -) top; (*Kopf*)
crown, top of the head; (*Haar*) parting.

scheitern ['ʃaitərn] v fail, come to
nought; (*Schiff*) be wrecked.

Schelle ['ʃɛlə] f (pl -n) small bell; (*Hand-*)
handcuff.

Schellfisch ['ʃɛlfiʃ] m haddock.

Schelm [ʃɛlm] m (pl -e) rogue.

Schema ['ʃema] neut (pl -ta or **Schemen**)
scheme; (*Muster*) pattern; (*Darstellung*)
diagram.

Schenkel ['ʃɛŋkəl] m (pl -) thigh.
-knochen m thigh-bone, femur.

schenken ['ʃɛŋkən] v give, present;
(*Getränk*) pour (out). **Schenk‖er** m (pl -)
donor, giver. **-ung** f donation.

Scherbe ['ʃɛrbə] f (pl -n) fragment.

Schere ['ʃeirə] f (pl -n) scissors pl; (*große*)
shears pl; (*Krebs*) claw. **scheren** v (*Wolle*)
shear; (*Haare*) cut; (*Hecke*) cut, trim;
(*Rasen*) mow.

Scherz [ʃɛrts] m (pl -e) joke; (*Unterhaltung*) fun. **scherz‖en** v joke, have fun.
-haft adj joking.

scheu [ʃɔy] adj shy.

Scheuche ['ʃɔyçə] f (pl -n) scarecrow.

scheuen ['ʃɔyən] v shy away from, avoid;
(*Pferd*) shy; (*Mühe, usw.*) spare. **sich**
scheuen vor be afraid of.

Scheuerbürste ['ʃɔyərbyrstə] f scrubbing
brush. **scheuern** v scrub, scour.

Scheune ['ʃɔynə] f (pl -n) barn.

Scheusal ['ʃɔyzal] neut (pl -e) monster.

scheußlich ['ʃɔysliç] adj horrible, hideous.
Scheußlichkeit f hideousness.

Schicht [ʃiçt] f (pl -en) layer; (*Arbeit*)
shift; (*Gesellschaft*) class. **-arbeit** f shift
work. **-holz** neut plywood. **-ung** f strat-
ification; (*fig*) classification.

schick [ʃik] adj elegant, chic, smart.

schicken ['ʃikən] v send. **sich schicken**
(*sich gehören*) suit, be becoming; (*sich*
entwickeln) happen.

schicklich ['ʃikliç] adj becoming, fit,
proper. **Schicklichkeit** f fitness, propriety.

Schicksal ['ʃikzal] neut (pl -e) fate,
destiny. **-sschlag** m stroke of fate, blow.

Schiebedach ['ʃiːbədax] *neut* sliding roof; (*Mot*) sun-roof. **schieben** *v* push; (*Schuld*) pass on; (*Arbeit*) put off. **Schiebetür** *f* sliding door.
Schieds‖gericht ['ʃiːtsgəriçt] *neut* arbitration court, tribunal. **–richter** *m* arbitrator; (*Sport*) referee, umpire. **–spruch** *m* arbitration, award.
schief [ʃiːf] *adj* slanting, sloping; (*fig*) wrong, amiss.
Schiefer ['ʃiːfər] *m* (*pl* -) slate.
*schiefgehen *v* go wrong *or* amiss.
schielen ['ʃiːlən] *v* squint. **Schielen** *neut* (*Med*) strabismus, squint.
Schienbein ['ʃiːnbain] *neut* shin(bone).
Schiene ['ʃiːnə] *f* (*pl* -n) rail; (*Med*) splint.
*schießen ['ʃiːsən] *v* shoot. **Schieß‖en** *neut* shooting. **–erei** *f* gunfight.
Schiff [ʃif] *neut* (*pl* -e) ship; (*Kirche*) nave. **–ahrt** *f* navigation; (*Verkehr*) shipping. **–bau** *m* shipbuilding. **–bruch** *m* shipwreck. **–brüchig** *adj* shipwrecked. **Schiffs‖küche** *f* galley. **–raum** *m* hold; (*Inhalt*) tonnage. **–verkehr** *m* shipping. **–werft** *f* shipyard.
Schikane [ʃi'kaːnə] *f* (*pl* -n) chicanery. **schikanieren** *v* make trouble for.
Schild[1] [ʃilt] *m* (*pl* -e) shield.
Schild[2] *neut* (*pl* -er) sign; (*Namen-*) name-plate; (*Flasche*) label; (*Mütze*) peak.
schildern ['ʃildərn] *v* depict, describe. **Schilderung** *f* depiction, description.
Schildkröte *f* turtle; (*Land*) tortoise.
Schilf [ʃilf] *neut* (*pl* -e) reed.
Schilling ['ʃiliŋ] *m* (*pl* -e) (Austrian) Schilling.
Schimmel ['ʃiməl] *m* (*pl* -) mildew, mould. **schimmel‖ig** *adj* mouldy. **–n** *v* become mouldy.
Schimmer ['ʃimər] *m* (*pl* -) glimmer, gleam. **schimmern** *v* gleam, shine.
Schimpanse [ʃim'panzə] *m* (*pl* -n) chimpanzee.
Schimpf [ʃimpf] *m* (*pl* -e) abuse, insult. **schimpfen** *v* swear, curse; (*umg.: tadeln*) curse, scold. **Schimpfwort** *neut* swearword.
*schinden ['ʃindən] *v* (*ausnützen*) exploit. **sich schinden** work hard, slave.
Schinken ['ʃiŋkən] *m* (*pl* -) ham.
Schippe ['ʃipə] *f* (*pl* -n) shovel; (*Karten*) spade(s).
Schirm [ʃirm] *m* (*pl* -e) (*Regen-*) umbrel-

la; (*Lampen-*) shade; (*Bild-*) screen; (*Mütze*) peak; (*fig: Schutz*) protection. **schirmen** *v* protect, screen.
schizophren [ʃitso'freːn] *adj* schizophrenic. **Schizophrenie** *f* schizophrenia.
Schlacht [ʃlaxt] *f* (*pl* -en) battle. **schlachten** *v* slaughter.
Schlächter ['ʃlɛçtər] *m* (*pl* -) butcher.
Schlacht‖feld *neut* battlefield. **–hof** *m* slaughterhouse. **–schiff** *neut* battleship.
Schlaf [ʃlaːf] *m* sleep. **–anzug** *m* pyjamas *pl.* **schlafen** *v* sleep. **–d** *adj* sleeping; (*fig*) dormant. **Schlafenszeit** *f* bedtime.
Schläfer ['ʃlɛːfər] *m* (*pl* -) sleeper.
schlaff [ʃlaf] *adj* slack; (*fig*) lax; (*welk*) limp.
Schlaf‖losigkeit *f* sleeplessness, insomnia. **–mittel** *neut* sleeping pill.
schläfrig ['ʃlɛːfriç] *adj* sleepy.
Schlaf‖wagen *m* sleeping car. **–zimmer** *neut* bedroom.
Schlag [ʃlaːk] *m* (*pl* Schläge) blow, stroke; (*Elek*) shock; (*Med*) stroke; (*Art*) sort, kind. **schlagen** *v* hit, strike; (*besiegen*) beat, defeat; (*mit der Faust*) punch; (*Vögel*) warble, sing; (*Wurzel*) take root. **kurz und klein schlagen** smash to pieces. **Alarm schlagen** sound the alarm. **nach jemandem schlagen** take after someone. **Schlagen** *neut* striking, hitting. **schlagend** *adj* striking; (*fig*) impressive; (*entscheidend*) decisive.
Schlager *m* (*pl* -) (great) success, hit; (*Musik*) hit (song).
Schläger ['ʃlɛːɡər] *m* (*pl* -) (*Tennis*) racket; (*Golf*) club; (*Kochen*) beater; (*Raufbold*) rowdy.
schlagfertig ['ʃlaːkfɛrtiç] *adj* quick-witted. **Schlag‖instrument** *neut* percussion instrument. **–sahne** *f* whipped cream. **–wort** *neut* slogan. **–zeile** *f* headline. **–zeug** *neut* percussion (instruments) *pl.*
Schlamm [ʃlam] *m* (*pl* -e) mud. **schlammig** *adj* muddy.
Schlampe ['ʃlampə] *f* (*pl* -n) slut. **schlampig** *adj* slovenly.
Schlange ['ʃlaŋə] *f* (*pl* -n) snake; (*Reihe Menschen*) queue, (*US*) line. **Schlange stehen** *v* queue, (*US*) line up. **Schlangen‖gift** *neut* snake venom. **–leder** *neut* snakeskin.
schlank [ʃlaŋk] *adj* slender, slim. **Schlank‖heit** *f* slenderness, slimness. **–skur** *f* (reducing) diet.

schlapp [ʃlap] *adj* slack, limp.

schlau [ʃlau] *adj* cunning, sly, clever. **Schlauheit** *f* cunning, slyness.

Schlauch [ʃlaux] *m* (*pl* **Schläuche**) hose; (*Reifen*) inner tube.

schlecht [ʃlɛçt] *adj* bad; (*unwohl*) ill; (*Qualität*) poor, inferior; (*Luft*) stale, foul. **mir ist schlecht** I feel ill. −**gelannt** *adj* bad-tempered. **Schlechtigkeit** *f* wickedness. **Schlechtheit** *f* badness. **schlechthin** *adv* simply, plainly.

Schlegel [ʃleːɡəl] *m* (*pl* -) (wooden) mallet; (*Trommel*) drumstick.

*****schleichen** [ʃlaiçən] *v* creep; (*heimlich*) slink, sneak.

Schleier [ʃlaiər] *m* (*pl* -) veil.

Schleife [ʃlaifə] *f* (*pl* -n) loop, slip-knot; (*Band*) bow.

*****schleifen**[1] [ʃlaifən] *v* slide, glide, slip.

schleifen[2] *v* (*schleppen*) drag; (*Messer*) sharpen, grind; (*Edelstein*) cut.

Schleim [ʃlaim] *m* (*pl* -e) slime; (*Med*) mucus. **schleimig** *adj* slimy; mucous.

*****schleißen** [ʃlaisən] *v* slit; (*spalten*) split; (*reißen*) rip, tear.

schlendern [ʃlɛndərn] *v* saunter. **Schlendrian** *m* (*pl* -) (*umg.*) old routine.

Schleppboot [ʃlɛpboːt] *neut* tug(boat). **schleppen** *v* drag, pull; (*tragen*) carry, lug. **sich schleppen** *v* drag oneself along.

Schlesien [ʃleːziən] *neut* Silesia.

Schleuder [ʃlɔydər] *f* (*pl* -n) sling, catapult; (*Wäsche*) spin-drier, spinner; (*Zentrifuge*) centrifuge. −**preis** *m* cut-price, give-away price. **schleudern** *v* sling, hurl; (*Mot*) skid; (*Wäsche*) spin-dry; (*Komm*) dump, sell off cheap.

schleunig [ʃlɔyniç] *adj* prompt, speedy.

Schleuse [ʃlɔyzə] *f* (*pl* -n) sluice; (*Kanal*) lock.

schlicht [ʃliçt] *adj* simple, plain; (*bescheiden*) modest. −**en** *v* (*glätten*) smooth; (*ebnen*) level; (*Streit*) settle. **Schlichtung** *f* (*pl* -en) settlement.

*****schließen** [ʃliːsən] *v* close, shut; (*mit dem Schlüssel*) close, end, conclude; (*folgern*) conclude, infer. **Schließfach** *neut* (*Bank*) safe-deposit box. **schließlich** *adv* finally, (at) last.

schlimm [ʃlim] *adj* bad. **schlimmstenfalls** *adv* at worst.

Schlinge [ʃliŋə] *f* (*pl* -n) noose, loop; (*Jagd, fig*) snare, trap.

*****schlingen**[1] [ʃliŋən] *v* wind; (*flechten*) twist; (*verknüpfen*) tie, knot.

*****schlingen**[2] *v* (*schlucken*) swallow; (*gierig essen*) devour, wolf.

Schlitten [ʃlitən] *m* (*pl* -) sledge. **Schlittschuh** *m* skate. **Schlittschuh laufen** skate.

Schlitz [ʃlits] *m* (*pl* -e) slit; (*Münzeinwurf*) slot; (*Hosen-*) fly.

Schloß [ʃlɔs] *neut* (*pl* **Schlösser**) lock; (*Burg*) castle.

Schlosser [ʃlɔsər] *m* (*pl* -) fitter, mechanic, locksmith.

Schlot [ʃloːt] *m* (*pl* -e) chimney.

schlott(e)rig [ʃlɔt(ə)riç] *adj* (*wackelig*) wobbly, shaky; (*schlaff*) loose; (*kleider*) baggy.

Schluck [ʃluk] *m* (*pl* -e) sip, gulp, mouthful. −**auf** *m* hiccup. **schlucken** *v* swallow.

Schlund [ʃlunt] *m* (*pl* **Schlünde**) throat; (*geog*) abyss, gorge; (*fig*) gulf.

schlüpfen [ʃlypfən] *v* slip, slide. **Schlüpfer** *m* knickers *pl*. **schlüpfrig** *adj* slippery; (*fig*) lewd.

Schlupfwinkel [ʃlupfviŋkəl] *m* hiding place.

Schluß [ʃlus] *m* (*pl* **Schlüsse**) end, close; (*Folgerung*) inference, conclusion. **zum Schluß** finally. **Schluß machen** stop, finish.

Schlüssel [ʃlysəl] *m* (*pl* -) key; (*Musik*) clef; (*Tech*) spanner, (*US*) wrench. −**bein** *neut* collarbone. −**bund** *m* bunch of keys. −**loch** *neut* keyhole. −**ring** *m* keyring.

Schluß‖prüfung *f* final examination, finals *pl*. −**runde** *f* (*Sport*) final. −**verkauf** *m* end-of-season sale.

Schmach [ʃmax] *f* disgrace, dishonour.

schmächtig [ʃmɛçtiç] *adj* slim, slender.

schmackhaft [ʃmakhaft] *adj* appetizing, delicious.

schmal [ʃmaːl] *adj* narrow, thin, slender; (*fig*) scanty, poor.

Schmalz [ʃmalts] *neut* (*pl* -e) fat, grease, dripping; (*fig*) sentimentality.

schmarotzen [ʃmaˈrɔtsən] *v* (*umg.*) sponge, scrounge. **Schmarotzer** *m* (*Tier, Pflanze*) parasite; (*Person*) scrounger, parasite.

schmatzen [ʃmatsən] *v* smack one's lips, eat noisily; (*küssen*) give a smacking kiss.

schmecken [ʃmɛkən] *v* taste; (*gut*) taste good. **schmecken nach** taste of. (*wie*)

schmeckt es? do you like it? **es schmeckt (mir)** I like it, it's good.
Schmeichelei [ʃmaɪçəˈlaɪ] f (pl **-en**) flattery. **schmeicheln** v flatter. **Schmeichler** m (pl **-**) flatterer. **schmeichlerisch** adj flattering.
***schmeißen** [ˈʃmaɪsən] v throw, cast; (umg.) chuck; (Schlagen) strike, smash.
Schmelz [ʃmɛlts] m (pl **-e**) (Email) enamel; (Glasur) glaze; (Stimme, Töne) mellowness, sweetness. **schmelzen** v melt; (Erz) smelt.
Schmerz [ʃmɛrts] m (pl **-en**) pain; (seelisch) grief, pain. **Schmerzen haben** be in pain. **schmerzen** v hurt; (seelisch) grieve, pain. **schmerz‖haft** adj painful. **-lich** adj painful, hurtful. **-los** adj painless.
Schmetterling [ˈʃmɛtərlɪŋ] m (pl **-e**) butterfly. **-sschwimmen** neut butterfly (stroke).
Schmied [ʃmiːt] m (pl **-e**) (black)smith. **Schmiede** f (pl **-n**) forge, smithy. **-eisen** neut wrought iron. **schmieden** v forge; (Pläne) devise.
Schmiere [ˈʃmiːrə] f (pl **-n**) grease; (Theater, umg.) small (touring) company. **schmieren** v (fetten) grease; (ölen) oil, lubricate; (streichen) spread. **Schmierung** f (pl **-en**) lubrication.
Schminke [ˈʃmɪŋkə] f (pl **-n**) make-up. **schminken** v make up. **sich schminken** put on make-up; make oneself up.
Schmorbraten [ˈʃmoːrbraːtən] m stewed steak, pot roast. **schmoren** v stew, braise.
Schmuck [ʃmʊk] m (pl **-e**) ornament, decoration; (Juwelen) jewellery. **schmücken** [ˈʃmykən] v adorn, decorate; (Kleider) trim.
schmuggeln [ˈʃmʊɡəln] v smuggle. **Schmuggelware** f contraband. **Schmuggler** m (pl **-**) smuggler.
Schmus [ʃmuːs] m (umg.) (empty) chatter, soft-soap; **schmusen** v chatter, soft-soap.
Schmutz [ʃmʊts] m dirt, filth. **schmutzig** adj dirty, filthy. **Schmutzpresse** f gutter press.
Schnabel [ˈʃnaːbəl] m (pl **Schnäbel**) bill, beak.
Schnalle [ˈʃnalə] f (pl **-n**) clasp; (Schuh, Gürtel) buckle; (Tür) latch. **schnallen** v buckle.
schnappen [ˈʃnapən] v snap; (erwischen) grab, catch. **nach Luft schnappen** gasp for air.

Schnaps [ʃnaps] m (pl **Schnäpse**) liqueur, schnaps, brandy.
schnarchen [ˈʃnarçən] v snore.
schnattern [ˈʃnatərn] v (Geflügel) cackle; (Menschen) prattle.
schnaufen [ˈʃnaufən] v pant, puff.
Schnauze [ˈʃnautsə] f (pl **-n**) snout, muzzle; (Kanne) spout. **halt die Schnauze!** (vulgär) shut up! belt up!
Schnecke [ˈʃnɛkə] f (pl **-n**) snail; (nackte) slug.
Schnee [ʃneː] m snow. **-glöckchen** neut snowdrop. **-lawine** f avalanche. **-mann** m snowman. **-schläger** m egg whisk. **-schuh** m ski. **-sturm** m blizzard. **-wehe** f snowdrift.
Schneide [ˈʃnaɪdə] f (pl **-n**) (cutting) edge. **schneiden** v cut; (Braten) carve. **Schneider** m (pl **-**) tailor. **-ei** f (pl **-en**) tailor's shop. **-in** f (pl **-nen**) dressmaker, seamstress.
schneien [ˈʃnaɪən] v snow.
schnell [ʃnɛl] adj fast, quick. **mach schnell!** hurry up! get a move on! **Schnellboot** neut speedboat. **schnellen** v jerk, spring. **Schnell‖gaststätte** f fastfood restaurant, cafeteria. **-igkeit** f speed. **-imbiß** m snack. **-zug** m express train.
schnippisch [ˈʃnɪpɪʃ] adj pert, saucy.
Schnitt [ʃnɪt] m (pl **-e**) cut; (Scheibe) slice; (Art) style; (Math) intersection; (Zeichnung) (cross-)section. **-lauch** m chive(s). **-ling** m (Bot) cutting.
Schnitzel [ˈʃnɪtsəl] neut (pl **-**) chip, shaving; (Fleisch) cutlet, escalope.
schnitzen [ˈʃnɪtsən] v carve (wood). **Schnitzer** m carver; (Fehler) blunder, bloomer.
Schnörkel [ˈʃnœrkəl] m (pl **-**) flourish; (Kunst, Architektur) scroll.
schnüffeln [ˈʃnyfəln] v snuffle, sniff; (fig) snoop, nose around.
Schnuller [ˈʃnʊlər] m (pl **-**) (baby's) dummy, (US) pacifier.
schnupfen [ˈʃnʊpfən] v take snuff. **Schnupfen** m (pl **-**) catarrh, (head) cold. **einen Schnupfen bekommen/haben** catch/have a cold. **Schnupftabak** m snuff.
Schnur [ʃnuːr] f (pl **Schnüre**) string, cord; (Elek) flex, wire.
schnüren [ˈʃnyːrən] v tie (up), fasten.

schnurgerade [ˈʃnuːrɡəraɪdə] *adj, adv* (as) straight (as a die).

Schnurrbart [ˈʃnurbaːrt] *m* moustache.

schnurren [ˈʃnurən] *v* hum, buzz; (*Katze*) purr.

Schock [ʃɔk] *m* (*pl* -s *or* -e) shock.

schokieren *v* shock, scandalize.

Schokolade [ʃokoˈlaɪdə] *f* (*pl* -n) chocolate.

Scholle [ˈʃɔlə] *f* (*pl* -n) (*Erde*) clod, clump; (*Eis*) floe; (*Fisch*) plaice; (*fig*) native soil, home.

schon [ʃoːn] *adv* already; (*bestimmt*) certainly; (*zwar*) indeed. **schon lange** for a long time. **schon lange her** a long time ago. **ich komme schon!** I'm coming! **schon wieder** yet again. **schon der Name** the mere name, the name alone.

schön [ʃœːn] *adj* beautiful, pretty; (*Wetter*) fine, fair. **danke schön** thank you. **bitte schön** (if you) please. **schön machen** beautify.

schonen [ˈʃoːnən] *v* spare; treat carefully, go carefully with. **-d** *adj* considerate, careful.

Schönheit [ˈʃœːnhaɪt] *f* (*pl* -en) beauty. **Schönheits‖fehler** *m* blemish, flaw. **-königin** *f* beauty queen. **-pflege** *f* beauty treatment.

Schonkost [ˈʃoːnkɔst] *f* (bland) diet.

Schopf [ʃɔpf] *m* (*pl* **Schöpfe**) shock, tuft.

schöpfen [ˈʃœpfən] *v* scoop, ladle; (*Atem*) take, draw; (*Mut*) take.

Schöpfer[1] [ˈʃœpfər] *m* (*pl* -) creator.

Schöpfer[2] *m* (*pl* -) (*zum Schöpfen*) scoop.

schöpferisch [ˈʃœpfərɪʃ] *adj* creative.

Schöpflöffel [ˈʃœpflœfəl] *m* ladle.

Schöpfung [ˈʃœpfuŋ] *f* creation.

Schornstein [ˈʃɔrnstaɪn] *m* chimney. **-feger** *m* chimney-sweep. **-kappe** *f* chimney-pot.

Schoß[1] [ʃoːs] *m* (*pl* **Schöße**) lap; (*fig*) bosom. **-hund** *m* lap-dog.

Schoß[2] [ʃɔs] *m* (*pl* **Schosse**) (*Bot*) shoot, sprout.

Schote [ˈʃoːtə] *f* (*pl* -n) pod. **Schoten** *pl* (green) peas.

Schotte [ˈʃɔtə] *m* (*pl* -n) Scot, Scotsman. **Schottin** *f* (*pl* -nen) Scot, Scotswoman. **schottisch** *adj* Scottish, Scots. **Schottland** *neut* Scotland.

schräg [ʃrɛːk] *adj* sloping, slanting, oblique.

Schrank [ʃraŋk] *m* (*pl* **Schränke**) cupboard; (*Kleider*) wardrobe.

Schranke [ˈʃraŋkə] *f* (*pl* -n) barrier, bar. **schrankenlos** *adj* limitless, boundless.

Schraube [ˈʃraubə] *f* (*pl* -n) screw. **Schraubdeckel** *m* screw-cap. **Schrauben‖schlüssel** *m* spanner, (*US*) wrench. **-zieher** *m* screwdriver.

Schrebergarten [ˈʃreːbərɡartən] *m* allotment (garden).

Schreck [ʃrɛk] *m* (*pl* -e) *or* **Schrecken** *m* (*pl* -) fright, terror. **einen Schreck bekommen/kriegen** receive/get a fright. **schrecken** *v* terrify, frighten. **schrecklich** *adj* terrible, frightful.

Schrei [ʃraɪ] *m* (*pl* -e) cry, shout, scream. **schreien** *v* cry, shout; (*kreischen*) shriek, screech; (*weinen*) cry, weep.

*schreiben [ˈʃraɪbən] *v* write; (*buchstabieren*) spell. **schreibfaul** *adj* lazy about writing (letters). **Schreib‖fehler** *m* spelling error. **-krampf** *m* writer's cramp. **-maschine** *f* typewriter. **-tisch** *m* desk. **-ung** *f* (*pl* -en) spelling. **-waren** *pl* stationery *sing*.

Schrein [ʃraɪn] *m* (*pl* -e) (*Kasten*) chest, box; (*Reliquien*) shrine. **-er** *m* (*pl* -) joiner, carpenter.

*schreiten [ˈʃraɪtən] *v* stride, step.

Schrift [ʃrɪft] *f* (*pl* -en) writing; (*Handschrift*) handwriting; (*Geschriebenes*) pamphlet, paper; (*Art*) script, type. **schriftlich** *adj* in writing, written. **Schrift‖steller** *m* (*pl* -), **Schriftstellerin** *f* (*pl* -nen) writer, author. **-stück** *neut* document, paper.

Schritt [ʃrɪt] *m* (*pl* -e) step, stride; (*Gangart*) gait; (*Tempo*) pace. **Schritt halten mit** keep pace with. **Schrittmacher** *m* (*fig*, *Med*) pacemaker. **schrittweise** *adv* step-by-step.

schroff [ʃrɔf] *adj* steep, precipitous; (*fig*) gruff, surly.

Schrot [ʃroːt] *m or neut* (*pl* -e) (*Getreide*) groats *pl*; (*Bleikügelchen*) (buck)shot. **-brot** *neut* wholemeal bread.

Schrott [ʃrɔt] *m* (*pl* -e) scrap (metal).

schrubben [ˈʃrubən] *v* scrub.

schrumpfen [ˈʃrumpfən] *v* shrink. **Schrumpfung** *f* shrinking, contraction.

Schub [ʃuːp] *m* (*pl* **Schübe**) shove, push; (*Tech*) thrust. **-fach** *neut* drawer. **-karren** *m* wheelbarrow. **-lade** *f* drawer.

schüchtern [ˈʃʏçtərn] *adj* shy. **Schüchternheit** *f* shyness.

Schuft [ʃuft] *m* (*pl* -e) rascal, rogue.
schuften *v* (*umg.*) toil, sweat, graft.
Schuh [ʃuː] *m* (*pl* -e) shoe. **–krem** *f* shoe polish. **–macher** *m* shoemaker. **–werk** *neut* footwear.
Schul‖arbeit *f* homework, task. **–buch** *neut* school book.
schuld [ʃult] *adj* guilty. **schuld haben** be guilty. **Schuld** *f* (*pl* -en) (*Geld, fig*) debt; (*Rel, Jur*) guilt. **schuld sein an** be to blame for. **Schulden haben** be in debt. **die Schuld schieben auf** push the blame onto. **schulden** *v* owe. **Schuldgefühl** *neut* sense of guilt. **schuldig** *adj* guilty; (*Geld*) indebted. **Schuldig‖e(r)** guilty person, culprit. **–keit** *f* (*unz.*) obligation; (*Pflicht*) duty. **–sprechung** *f* conviction, verdict of guilty.
Schuldirektor *m* headmaster. **–in** *f* headmistress.
schuldlos ['ʃultloːs] *adj* innocent. **Schuld‖ner** *m* (*pl* -), **–nerin** *f* (*pl* -nen) debtor. **–schein** *m* promissory note, IOU.
Schule ['ʃuːlə] *f* (*pl* -n) school. **schulen** *v* school, train.
Schüler ['ʃyːlə] *m* (*pl* -) schoolboy; (*bei einem Meister*) pupil; (*Rel*) disciple. **–in** *f* (*pl* -nen) schoolgirl; pupil; disciple.
Schul‖fach *neut* (school) subject. **–ferien** *pl* school holidays. **schulfrei haben** have a holiday. **Schul‖freund** *m* school friend. **–geld** *neut* school fees. **–hof** *m* (school) playground. **–junge** *m* schoolboy. **–lehrer** *m* (*pl* -), **–lehrerin** *f* (*pl* -nen) schoolteacher. **–mädchen** *neut* schoolgirl. **–schluß** *m* end of term, breaking-up.
Schulter ['ʃultər] *f* (*pl* -en) shoulder. **–blatt** *neut* shoulder blade.
Schulung ['ʃuːluŋ] *f* (*pl* -en) schooling, training. **Schul‖wesen** *neut* educational system. **–zimmer** *neut* classroom, schoolroom.
Schund [ʃunt] *m* trash, rubbish.
Schuppe ['ʃupə] *f* (*pl* -n) scale. **Schuppen** *pl* dandruff. **schuppig** *adj* scaly.
schüren ['ʃyːrən] *v* stir up, incite; (*Feuer*) poke, stoke.
schürfen ['ʃyrfən] *v* (*Haut*) scratch, graze; (*Metall*) prospect. **Schürfung** *f* (*pl* -en) graze, abrasion; prospecting.
Schurke ['ʃurkə] *m* (*pl* -n) villain, scoundrel.
Schürze ['ʃyrtsə] *f* (*pl* -n) apron.

Schuß [ʃus] *m* (*pl* Schüsse) shot. **–loch** *neut* bullet-hole. **–waffe** *f* firearm. **–weite** *f* range. **–wunde** *f* gunshot wound.
Schüssel ['ʃysəl] *f* (*pl* -n) bowl, dish.
Schuster ['ʃuːstər] *m* (*pl* -) cobbler, shoemaker.
Schutt [ʃut] *m* (*Trümmer*) debris; (*Abfall*) refuse.
schütteln ['ʃytəln] *v* shake.
schütten ['ʃytən] *v* pour (out). **es schüttet** it's pouring (with rain).
schüttern ['ʃytərn] *v* tremble, shake.
Schutz [ʃuts] *m* (*pl* -e) protection; (*Obdach*) shelter; (*Schirm*) screen. **–anzug** *m* protective clothing. **–brille** *f* goggles *pl*.
Schütze ['ʃytsə] *m* (*pl* -n) marksman, sharpshooter; (*Bogen*) archer. **schützen** *v* protect, defend; (*behüten*) guard.
Schutz‖farbe *f* camouflage. **–heilige(r)** *m* patron saint.
Schützling ['ʃytsliŋ] *m* (*pl* -e) protégé(e), charge.
schutzlos ['ʃutslos] *adj* defenceless. **Schutz‖mann** *m* policeman. **–maßnahme** *f* precaution, preventive measure. **–mittel** *neut* preservative. **–umschlag** *m* (Book) jacket, dust cover.
Schwabe ['ʃvaːbə] *m* (*pl* -n) Swabian (man). **–n** *neut* Swabia.
Schwäbin ['ʃvɛːbin] *f* (*pl* -nen) Swabian woman. **schwäbisch** *adj* Swabian.
schwach [ʃvax] *adj* weak; (*kränklich*) delicate, sickly; (*klein*) small; (*gering*) scanty, poor.
Schwäche ['ʃvɛçə] *f* (*pl* -n) weakness. **schwächen** *v* weaken.
Schwachheit ['ʃvaxhait] *f* (*pl* -en) weakness.
schwächlich ['ʃvɛçliç] *adj* feeble, sickly, delicate.
Schwachsinn ['ʃvaxzin] *m* feeblemindedness. **schwachsinnig** *adj* feebleminded.
Schwager ['ʃvaːgər] *m* (*pl* Schwäger) brother-in-law.
Schwägerin ['ʃvɛːgərin] *f* (*pl* -nen) sister-in-law.
Schwalbe ['ʃvalbə] *f* (*pl* -n) (*Vogel*) swallow.
Schwall [ʃval] *m* (*pl* -e) flood, torrent.
Schwamm [ʃvam] *m* (*pl* Schwämme) sponge.
Schwan [ʃvaːn] *m* (*pl* Schwäne) swan.

schwanger [ˈʃvaŋər] *adj* pregnant. **Schwangere** *f* (*pl* **-n**) pregnant woman. **Schwangerschaft** *f* pregnancy. **–vorsorge** *f* ante-natal care.

schwanken [ˈʃvaŋkən] *v* sway, swing; (*taumeln*) stagger, reel; (*zögern*) waver; (*Preise*) fluctuate. **–d** *adj* (*Person*) wavering. **Schwankung** *f* (*pl* **en**) swaying, wavering, fluctuation.

Schwanz [ʃvants] *m* (*pl* **Schwänze**) tail.

Schwarm [ʃvarm] *m* (*pl* **Schwärme**) swarm; (*Vogel*) flock; (*Fische*) shoal; (*Rind, Schaf*) herd; (*Menschen*) crowd; (*fig*) craze.

schwärmen [ˈʃvɛrmən] *v* swarm; (*Mil*) deploy. **schwärmen für** rave about, gush over. **schwärmerisch** *adj* wildly enthusiastic.

schwarz [ʃvarts] *adj* black. **Schwarz** *neut* black (colour). **–brot** *neut* black bread. **–e(r)** Black, Negro.

Schwärze [ˈʃvɛrtsə] *f* (*pl* **-n**) blackness; (*Druck*) printer's ink. **schwärz‖en** *v* blacken. **–lich** *adj* blackish, darkish.

Schwarz‖markt *m* black market. **–wald** *m* Black Forest. **schwarzweiß** *adj* black-and-white.

schwatzen [ˈʃvatsən] *v* *also* **schwätzen** chatter, prattle; (*Geheimnisse*) gossip.

Schwebe [ˈʃveːbə] *f* suspense. **in der Schwebe** *adj* undecided, pending. **schweben** *v* float, hover; (*hängen*) hang, be suspended; (*fig*) remain undecided.

Schwede [ˈʃveːdə] *m* (*pl* **-n**), **Schwedin** *f* (*pl* **-nen**) Swede. **Schweden** *neut* Sweden. **schwedisch** *adj* Swedish.

Schwefel [ˈʃveːfəl] *m* sulphur.

schweifen [ˈʃvaifən] *v* roam, wander.

*schweigen [ˈʃvaigən] *v* be silent. **ganz zu schweigen von** to say nothing of. **Schweigen** *neut* silence. **schweigsam** *adj* silent; (*fig*) secretive.

Schwein [ʃvain] *neut* (*pl* **-e**) pig; (*fig*) (good) luck. **Schweine‖braten** *m* roast pork. **–fett** *neut* lard. **–fleisch** *neut* pork. **–hund** *m* (*vulgär*) bastard, swine. **–rei** *f* filthy mess; (*fig*) dirty trick. **–stall** *m* pigsty. **Schweinsrippchen** *neut* pork chop.

Schweiß [ʃvais] *m* (*pl* **-e**) sweat, perspiration. **schweißen** *v* weld; (*Wild*) bleed.

Schweiz [ʃvaits] *f* **die Schweiz** Switzerland. **Schweizer** *m* (*pl* **-**), **Schweizerin** *f* (*pl* **-nen**) Swiss. **schweizerisch** *adj* Swiss.

Schwelle [ˈʃvɛlə] *f* (*pl* **-n**) threshold; (*Eisenbahn*) sleeper.

*schwellen [ˈʃvɛlən] *v* swell.

schwemmen [ˈʃvɛmən] *v* wash down; (*Vieh*) water.

Schwengel [ˈʃvɛŋəl] *m* (*pl* **-**) (*Glocke*) clapper; (*Pumpe*) pump handle.

schwenken [ˈʃvɛŋkən] *v* turn; (*Fahne, Hut*) wave, flourish.

schwer [ʃveːr] *adj* heavy; (*schwierig*) difficult; (*ernst*) serious. **es ist 2 Kilo schwer** it weighs two kilos. **schwere Arbeit** hard work. **–beschädigt** *adj* seriously disabled. **Schwere** *f* weight. **schwerfällig** *adj* clumsy, awkward. **Schwergewichtler** *m* heavyweight. **schwerhörig** *adj* hard of hearing. **Schwer‖industrie** *f* heavy industry. **–kraft** *f* gravity. **schwer‖lich** *adj* with difficulty, hardly. **–mütig** *adj* melancholy, sad.

Schwert [ʃveːrt] *neut* (*pl* **-er**) sword.

Schwester [ˈʃvɛstər] *f* (*pl* **-n**) sister. **schwesterlich** *adj* sisterly. **Schwesternschaft** *f* sisterhood.

Schwieger‖eltern *pl* parents-in-law; (*umg.*) in-laws. **–mutter** *m* mother-in-law. **–sohn** *m* son-in-law. **–tochter** *f* daughter-in-law. **–vater** *m* father-in-law.

schwierig [ˈʃviːriç] *adj* difficult, hard. **Schwierigkeit** *f* (*pl* **-en**) difficulty.

Schwimmbad [ˈʃvimbat] *neut* swimming pool. **Schwimmbecken** *neut* swimming pool. **schwimmen** *v* swim; (*Gegenstand*) float. **Schwimmen** *neut* swimming. **schwimmend** *adj* swimming; floating. **Schwimmer** *m* (*pl* **-**) swimmer; float.

Schwindel [ˈʃvindəl] *m* (*pl* **-**) giddiness; (*Täuschung*) swindle, fraud. **schwindel‖haft** *adj* giddy; fraudulent. **–ig** *adj* giddy, dizzy. **schwindeln** *v* cheat, swindle. **mir schwindelt** I feel giddy. **Schwindler** *m* (*pl* **-**) swindler, cheat.

*schwingen [ˈʃviŋən] *v* swing; (*Fahne, Waffe*) wave, flourish. **Schwingung** *f* (*pl* **-en**) oscillation, vibration.

schwitzen [ˈʃvitsən] *v* sweat.

*schwören [ˈʃvøːrən] *v* swear.

schwul [ʃvuːl] *adj* (*vulgär*) queer, homosexual.

schwül [ʃvyːl] *adj* sultry, hot and humid.

Schwulst [ʃvulst] *m* (*pl* **Schwülste**) bombast, pomposity. **schwülstig** *adj* bombastic, pompous.

Schwund [ʃvunt] *m* contraction, shrinkage; (*Med*) atrophy.

Schwung [ʃvʊŋ] *m* (*pl* **Schwünge**) impetus, momentum; (*fig*) drive, vitality, verve. **–kraft** *f* centrifugal force; (*fig*) verve. **–rad** *neut* flywheel.

Schwur [ʃvuːr] *m* (*pl* **Schwüre**) oath. **–gericht** *neut* court with jury.

sechs [zɛks] *pron, adj* six. **sechst** *adj* sixth. **Sechstel** *neut* sixth (part).

sechzehn [ˈzɛçtseɪn] *pron, adj* sixteen. **sechzehnte** *adj sixteenth.*

sechzig [ˈzɛçtsiç] *pron, adj* sixty. **die sechziger Jahre** the '60s. **sechzigst** *adj* sixtieth.

See [seɪ] **1** *m* (*pl* **-n**) lake. **2** *f* (*pl* **-n**) sea. **–fahrt** *f* voyage. **–jungfer** *f* mermaid. **seekrank** *adj* seasick.

Seele [ˈzeɪlə] *f* (*pl* **-n**) soul, spirit. **seelisch** *adj* spiritual.

See‖löwe *m* sealion. **–räuber** *m* pirate. **–wasser** *neut* sea water.

Segel [ˈzeɪgəl] *neut* (*pl* **-**) sail. **–boot** *neut* sailing boat. **–flugzeug** *neut* glider, sailplane. **segeln** *v* sail. **Segeltuch** *neut* canvas.

Segen [ˈzeɪgən] *m* (*pl* **-**) blessing; (*Tischgebet*) grace. **segnen** *v* bless. **Segnung** *f* (*pl* **-en**) blessing.

*****sehen** [ˈzeɪən] *v* see; (*anblicken*) look; (*beobachten*) watch, observe. **sehen lassen** display, show. **Sehen** *neut* (eye)sight, vision. **–swürdigkeit** *f* (tourist) sight. **Seh‖feld** *neut* field of vision. **–kraft** *f* eyesight, vision.

Sehne [ˈzeɪnə] *f* (*pl* **-n**) sinew, tendon; (*Bogen*) string.

sehnen [ˈzeɪnən] *v* **sich sehnen nach** long for.

sehr [zeɪr] *adv* very.

Sehweite [ˈzeɪvaɪtə] *f* range of vision.

seicht [zaɪçt] *adj* shallow.

Seide [ˈzaɪdə] *f* (*pl* **-n**) silk.

Seife [ˈzaɪfə] *f* (*pl* **-n**) soap. **Seifen‖schaum** *m* lather. **–wasser** *neut* suds *pl*, soapy water.

Seil [zaɪl] *neut* (*pl* **-e**) rope; (*Kabel*) cable. **–bahn** *f* funicular.

sein¹ [zaɪn] *adj, pron* his, its. **seinerseits** *adv* on *or* for his part. **seinesgleichen** *pron* the likes of him *pl*, people like him *pl*. **seinethalben, seinetwegen,** *or* **seinetwillen** *adv* for his sake. **seinige** *pron* **der, die, das seinige** his.

*****sein²** *v* be. **es sei denn, daß** unless. **kann sein** perhaps. **sein lassen** leave alone. **mir ist kalt/warm** I feel cold/warm.

seit [zaɪt] *prep* since. **–dem** *conj* since; *adv* since then. **seit damals** since then. **seit wann?** since when? **seit zwei Jahren** for two years.

Seite [ˈzaɪtə] *f* (*pl* **-n**) side; (*Buch*) page. **auf die Seite bringen** put aside. **von seiten** on the part (of). **Seiten‖lampe** *f* side lamp. **–schiff** *neut* aisle. **–straße** *f* side street. **–wagen** *m* sidecar.

seither [zaɪtˈheɪr] *adv* since then.

seitlich [ˈzaɪtliç] *adj* lateral, side. **seitwärts** *adv* sideways.

Sekretär [zekreˈteɪr] *m* (*pl* **-e**) secretary; (*Schreibschrank*) bureau, locking desk. **–in** *f* (*pl* **-nen**) secretary.

Sekt [zɛkt] *m* (*pl* **-e**) sparkling wine.

Sekte [ˈzɛktə] *f* (*pl* **-n**) sect. **sektiererisch** *adj* sectarian.

sekundär [zekunˈdeɪr] *adj* secondary.

Sekunde [zeˈkundə] *f* (*pl* **-n**) second.

selber [ˈzɛlbər] *V* **selbst.**

selbst [zɛlpst] *pron* self. *adv* even. **ich selbst** I myself. **von selbst** on one's own accord; (*Sache*) by itself. **sie kann es selbst machen** she can do it by herself. **selbst wenn** even though. **Selbst** *neut* self. **–achtung** *f* self-respect.

selbständig [ˈzɛlpstendiç] *adj* independent. **Selbständigkeit** *f* independence.

Selbst‖bedienung *f* self-service. **–beherrschung** *f* self-control. **–mitleid** *f* self-pity. **–bestimmung** *f* self-determination.

selbstbewußt *adj* self-confident; (*eingebildet*) conceited. **Selbstbewußtsein** *neut* self-confidence; conceit.

Selbsterkenntnis *f* self-knowledge.

selbst‖gebacken *adj* home-made. **–gefällig** *adj* self-satisfied. **–gerecht** *adj* self-righteous.

Selbsthilfe *f* self-help; (*Jur*) self-defence.

selbst‖klebend *adj* adhesive, gummed. **–los** *adj* selfless.

Selbst‖mord *m* suicide. **–mörder** *m* suicide. **–schutz** *m* self-defence.

selbstsicher *adj* self-confident. **Selbstsicherheit** *f* self-confidence.

Selbstsucht *f* selfishness. **selbstsüchtig** *adj* selfish.

Selbst‖täuschung *f* self-deception. **–versorgung** *f* self-sufficiency.

selbstverständlich *adj* self-evident. *adv* obviously, naturally.

Selbstvertrauen *neut* self-confidence.

selig ['zeːlɪç] *adj* blessed; (*verstorben*) late, deceased; (*überglücklich*) blissful, delighted.

Sellerie ['zɛləriː] *f* (*pl* -n) *or m* (*pl* -s) celeriac. **–stangen** *pl* celery *sing*.

selten ['zɛltən] *adj* rare. *adv* rarely, seldom.

seltsam ['zɛltzaɪm] *adj* strange, odd, curious.

Semester [ze'mɛstər] *neut* (*pl* -) semester, (half-yearly) session.

Seminar [zemiˈnaːr] *neut* (*pl* -e) training college; tutorial group.

Semit [ze'miːt] *m* (*pl* -en) Semite. **semitisch** *adj* Semitic.

Semmel ['zɛməl] *f* (*pl* -n) bread roll.

Senat [ze'naːt] *m* (*pl* -e) senate. **–or** *m* (*pl* -en) senator.

***senden** ['zɛndən] *v* send; (*Funk*) transmit, broadcast. **Sender** *m* (*pl* -) (*Gerät*) transmitter; (*Anstalt*) station. **Sendung** *f* (*pl* -en) package; (*Waren*) consignment; (*Funk*) broadcast.

Senf [zɛnf] *m* (*pl* -e) mustard.

sengen ['zɛŋən] *V* singe.

Senkblei ['zɛŋkblai] *neut* plumb-line.

Senkel ['zɛŋkəl] *m* (*pl* -) (shoe)lace.

senken ['zɛŋkən] *v* lower; (*Kopf*) bow; (*Preise*) reduce. **sich senken** sink. **senkrecht** *adj* vertical, perpendicular. **Senkung** *f* (*pl* -en) sinking; (*Preise*) reduction; (*Vertiefung*) depression.

Sensation [zɛnzatsi'oːn] *f* (*pl* -en) sensation. **sensationell** *adj* sensational.

Sense ['zɛnzə] *f* (*pl* -n) scythe.

sensibel [zɛn'ziːbəl] *adj* sensitive.

sentimental [zɛntimɛn'taːl] *adj* sentimental.

separieren [zɛpa'riːrən] *v* separate.

September [zɛp'tɛmbər] *m* (*pl* -) September.

septisch ['zɛptiʃ] *adj* septic.

Serie ['zeːriə] *f* (*pl* -n) series. **–nherstellung** *f* mass production.

seriös [zeri'œːs] *adj* serious, earnest; (*Firma*) reliable, honourable.

Service[1] [zɛr'viːs] *neut* (*pl* -) (dinner) service.

Service[2] *neut or m* (*pl* -s) (customer) service.

servieren [zɛr'viːrən] *v* serve. **Servierwagen** *m* trolley. **Serviette** *f* (*pl* -n) (table) napkin.

Sesam ['zɛzaːm] *m* sesame.

Sessel ['zɛsəl] *m* (*pl* -) armchair. **–lift** *m* chairlift.

seßhaft ['zɛshaft] *adj* settled, established; (*ansässig*) resident.

setzen ['zɛtsən] *v* set, put, place; (*einpflanzen*) plant; (*Druck*) compose, set; (*Spiel*) wager, bet. **in Bewegung setzen** set in motion. **außer Kraft setzen** invalidate. **in die Welt setzen** give birth to. **sich setzen** sit down. **sich in Verbindung setzen mit** get in contact with.

Seuche ['zɔyçə] *f* (*pl* -n) epidemic.

seufzen ['zɔyftsən] *v* sigh. **Seufzer** *m* (*pl* -) sigh.

Sex [zɛks] *m* (*pl* -) sex. **Sexual‖ität** *f* sexuality. **–aufklärung** *f* sex education. **sexuell** *adj* sexual. **sexy** *adj* sexy.

sezieren [ze'tsiːrən] *v* dissect.

sich [zɪç] *pron* himself, herself, itself, yourself, oneself, yourselves; themselves; (*miteinander*) (with) one another, each other. **an (und für) sich** in itself. **bei sich haben** have with one. **sich die Hände waschen** wash one's hands. **sie lieben sich** they love each other.

Sichel ['zɪçəl] *f* (*pl* -n) sickle; (*Mond-*) crescent.

sicher ['zɪçər] *adj* safe, secure; (*gewiß*) sure, certain. *adv* surely, certainly. **Sicherheit** *f* safety; certainty; trustworthiness; (*Pol, Psychol*) security. **Sicherheits‖bestimmungen** *pl* safety regulations. **–gurt** *m* safety belt. **–nadel** *f* safety pin. **sicher‖lich** *adv* surely, certainly. **–n** *v* secure; (*schützen*) protect. **–stellen** *v* secure, guarantee. **Sicherung** *f* (*pl* -en) protection; (*Elek*) fuse; (*Tech*) safety device.

Sicht [zɪçt] *f* (*unz.*) sight; (*Aussicht*) view; (*Sichtbarkeit*) visibility. **sichtbar** *adj* visible. **Sichtbarkeit** *f* visibility.

sickern ['zɪkərn] *v* trickle, seep.

sie [ziː] *pron* she, it; her; they; them. **Sie** *pron* you.

Sieb [ziːp] *neut* (*pl* -e) sieve; (*Tee*) strainer.

sieben[1] ['ziːbən] *v* sift, sieve.

sieben[2] *pron, adj* seven. **siebent** *or* **siebt** *adj* seventh.

siebzehn ['ziːptseːn] *pron, adj* seventeen. **siebzehnt** *adj* seventeenth.

siebzig ['ziːptsɪç] *pron, adj* seventy. **siebzigt** *adj* seventieth.

siedeln ['ziːdəln] *v* settle, colonize.

*sieden ['ziːdən] v boil. **Siedepunkt** m boiling point.

Siedler ['ziːdlər] m (pl -) settler. **Siedlung** f (pl -en) settlement (place); (am Stadtrand) housing estate.

Sieg [ziːk] m (pl -e) victory.

Siegel ['ziːgəl] neut (pl -) seal, signet.

siegen ['ziːgən] v win, triumph, be victorious. **Sieger** m (Mil) conqueror, victor; (Sport) winner. **siegreich** adj victorious.

Signal [zig'naɪl] neut (pl -e) signal. **–feuer** neut beacon. **–rakete** f rocket-flare.

Signatur [zigna'tuːr] f (pl -en) mark, symbol; (Unterschrift) signature.

Silbe ['zilbə] f (pl -n) syllable.

Silber ['zilbər] neut silver. **silbern** adj silver.

Silvesterabend [zil'vɛstəraɪbənt] m New Year's Eve.

simpel ['zimpəl] adj simple.

Sims [zims] neut (pl -e) (Fenster) window-sill.

simulieren [zimu'liːrən] v pretend; (Krankheit) malinger; (Tech) simulate.

Sinfonie [zinfo'niː] f (pl -n) symphony.

*singen ['ziŋən] v sing. **Singvogel** m songbird.

*sinken ['ziŋkən] v sink; (fig) diminish; (Preise) fall. **Sinken** neut fall, drop; (Werte) depreciation; (fig) decline.

Sinn [zin] m (pl -e) sense; (Gedanken) mind, thoughts pl. **es hat keinen Sinn** it makes no sense. **es kam mir in den Sinn, daß** ... it crossed my mind that .... **Sinn für Humor** sense of humour. **Sinn für Literatur** interest in literature. **Sinnbild** neut symbol. **sinn‖bildlich** adj symbolic. **–en** v reflect, think (over). **–lich** adj sensual. **–los** adj senseless. **Sinnspruch** m epigram, maxim.

Sippe ['zipə] f (pl -n) tribe; (Verwandte) kin.

Sirup ['ziːrup] m (pl -e) syrup.

Sitte ['zitə] f (pl -n) custom; (Gewohnheit) habit. **Sitten** pl morals. **Sittenlehre** f ethics. **sittenlos** adj immoral. **sittlich** adj moral. **Sittlichkeit** f morality. **–sverbrechen** neut indecent assault.

Situation [zituatsi'oːn] f (pl -en) situation.

Sitz [zits] m (pl -e) seat; (Kleidung) fit. **–bank** f bench. **sitzen** v sit; (Kleidung) fit. **–bleiben** v remain seated. **Sitzung** f (pl -en) sitting; (Versammlung) session.

Skala ['skaːla] f (pl Skalen) scale. **Skalenscheibe** f dial.

Skandal [skan'daːl] m (pl -e) scandal. **skandalös** adj scandalous.

Skandinavien [skandi'naːvjən] neut Scandinavia. **Skandinavier** m (pl -), **Skandinavierin** f (pl -nen) Scandinavian. **skandinavisch** adj Scandinavian.

Skelett [ske'lɛt] neut (pl -e) skeleton.

Skeptiker ['skɛptikər] m (pl -) sceptic. **skeptisch** adj sceptical.

Ski [ʃiː] m (pl -er) ski. **–fahrer(in)** skier.

Skizze ['skitsə] f (pl -n) sketch. **skizzieren** v sketch.

Sklave ['sklaːvə] m (pl -n) slave. **Sklaverei** f slavery. **Sklavin** f (pl -nen) (female) slave, slave girl.

Skorpion ['skɔrpiɔn] m (pl -e) (Tier) scorpion; (Astrol) Scorpio.

Skrupel ['skruːpəl] m (pl -) scruple. **skrupellos** adj unscrupulous. **skrupulös** adj scrupulous.

Skulptur [skulp'tuːr] f (pl -en) sculpture.

Smaragd [sma'rakt] m (pl -e) emerald. **smaragdgrün** adj emerald(-green).

Smoking ['smɔːkiŋ] m (pl -s) dinner jacket, (US) tuxedo.

so [zoː] adv thus, so, in this way. conj consequently, therefore. **so daß** so that. **so ein** such a. **so sehr** so much. **so ... wie** ... as ... as ... . **um so besser** all the better. **–bald** conj as soon as.

Socke ['zɔkə] f (pl -n) sock.

Sockel ['zɔkəl] m (pl -) pedestal, base.

sodann [zo'dan] adv, conj then, in that case.

Sodawasser ['zoːdavasər] neut soda water.

Sodbrennen ['zoːtbrɛnən] neut heartburn.

soeben [zo'eːbən] adv just (now).

Sofa ['zoːfa] neut (pl -s) sofa.

sofern [zo'fɛrn] conj as or so far as.

sofort [zo'fɔrt] adv at once, immediately. **–ig** adj immediate.

Sog [zoːk] m (pl -e) suction; (Boot) wake.

sogar [zo'gaːr] adv even.

sogenannt ['zoːgənant] adj so-called.

Sohle ['zoːlə] f (pl -n) (Fuß, usw.) sole. **sohlen** v sole.

Sohn [zoːn] m (pl Söhne) son.

solang(e) [zo'laŋ(ə)] conj as long as; (während) while.

solch [zɔlç] pron, adj such. **solcher‖art** adv of this sort, along these lines. **–lei** adj of such a kind. **–weise** adv in such a way.

Soldat [zɔl'daɪt] m (pl **-en**) soldier. **Soldat werden** enlist, join up.

Söldner ['zœldnər] m (pl **-**) mercenary.

solid [zo'liːt] adj also **solide** (Person) reliable, decent; (Leben) decent, respectable; (Gegenstand) solid, robust. **–arisch** adj united, unanimous. **Solidarität** f solidarity.

Solist [zo'list] m (pl **-en**), **Solistin** f (pl **-nen**) soloist.

Soll [zɔl] neut (pl **-s**) (Komm) debit; (Produktion) target. **sollen** v ought to, have to, should; (angeblich) be supposed to be. ich sollte I should. was soll das? what is this supposed to be or mean? sie soll reich sein she is said to be rich. Kinder sollen gehorchen children should be obedient. du sollst nicht töten thou shalt not kill.

Solo ['zoːlo] neut (pl **-s** or **Soli**) solo. **–sänger** m soloist, solo singer.

Sommer ['zɔmər] m (pl **-**) summer. **–ferien** pl summer holidays. **–sprosse** f freckle.

Sonate [zo'naːtə] f (pl **-n**) sonata.

Sonde ['zɔndə] f (pl **-n**) (Tech) probe.

Sonder‖angebot neut special offer. **–ausgabe** f special edition. **sonder‖bar** adj strange, peculiar. **–lich** adj remarkable, special.

sondern¹ ['zɔndərn] v separate.

sondern² conj but. nicht nur ... sondern auch ... not only ... but also ... .

Sonder‖preis m special price. **–ung** f (pl **-en**) separation.

Sonnabend ['zɔnaːbənt] m Saturday. **sonnabends** adv on Saturdays.

Sonne ['zɔnə] f (pl **-n**) sun. **sonnen** v air, put out in the sun. **sich sonnen** sun oneself, lie in the sun.

Sonnen‖aufgang m sunrise. **–blume** f sunflower. **–brand** m sunburn. **–bräune** f suntan. **–finsternis** f solar eclipse. **–schein** m sunshine. **–stich** m sunstroke. **–system** neut solar system. **–untergang** m sunset.

sonnig ['zɔniç] adj sunny.

Sonntag ['zɔntaːk] m Sunday. **sonntags** adv on Sundays.

sonst [zɔnst] adv otherwise, else. **sonst etwas?** anything else? **sonst nichts** nothing else. **wer sonst?** who else? **wie sonst** as usual. **–ig** adj other, miscellaneous. **–wie** adv some other way. **–wo** adv elsewhere.

Sopran [zo'praɪn] m (pl **-e**) soprano. **–istin** f (pl **-nen**) soprano (singer).

Sorge ['zɔrgə] f (pl **-n**) (Kummer) care, worry; (Pflege) care. **sich Sorgen machen (um)** worry (about). **sorgen für** take care of. **dafür sorgen, daß** make sure that, see to it that. **sich sorgen** be anxious, worry. **sorgen‖frei** or **–los** adj carefree. **–voll** adj careworn. **sorg‖lich** adj careful, caring. **–los** adj careless. **–sam** adj careful, cautious.

Sorte ['zɔrtə] f (pl **-n**) sort, kind; (Ware) brand. **sortieren** v sort (out). **Sortiment** neut (pl **-e**) assortment.

Soße ['zoɪsə] f (pl **-n**) sauce; (für Fleisch) gravy.

Souveränität [suvərɛmi'tɛɪt] f sovereignty.

soviel ['zofiːl] conj as far as. adv as or so much. **soviel wie** as much as. **soweit** conj as or so far as; adv so far. **sowenig(wie)** conj as little (as). **sowie** conj as soon as; (außerdem) as well as, and also. **sowieso** adv in any case.

Sowjet [zɔ'vjɛt] m (pl **-e**) Soviet. **sowjetisch** adj Soviet. **Sowjetunion** f Soviet Union.

sowohl [zɔ'voːl] conj as well as. **sowohl ... als auch ...** both ... and ... .

sozial [zotsi'aɪl] adj social. **Sozial‖abgaben** pl national insurance contributions. **–demokrat** m social democrat. **–einrichtungen** pl social services. **–fürsorge** f (social) welfare.

Sozialismus [zotsia'lizmus] m socialism. **Sozialist** m socialist. **sozialistisch** adj socialist.

Sozial‖politik f social policies pl. **–produkt** neut (gross) national product. **–unterstützung** f social security.

Soziologe [zotsio'loːgə] m (pl **-n**) sociologist. **Soziologie** f sociology. **soziologisch** adj sociological.

sozusagen [zotsu'zaːgən] adv so to speak.

spähen ['ʃpɛːən] v look out, watch; (Mil) scout.

Spalt [ʃpalt] m (pl **-e**) crack, slit. **–e** f (Druck) column; crack, crevice. **spalten** v split.

Span [ʃpaːn] m (pl **Späne**) chip, shaving; (Splitter) splinter.

Spange ['ʃpaŋə] f (pl **-n**) clasp; (Schnalle) buckle.

Spanien ['ʃpaːniən] neut Spain. **Spanier** m (pl **-**), **Spanierin** f (pl **-nen**) Spaniard. **spanisch** adj Spanish.

Spann [ʃpan] *m* (*pl* -e) instep.
Spanne [ʃpanə] *f* (*pl* -n) span.
spannen [ʃpanən] *v* stretch; (*straff ziehen*) tighten. **–d** *adj* thrilling, exciting.
Spann‖seil *neut* guy(-rope). **–ung** *f* (*pl* -en) tension.
sparen [ʃpaːrən] *v* save; (*sparsam sein*) economize. **Sparer** *m* (*pl* -) saver.
Spargel [ʃpargəl] *m* (*pl* -) asparagus. **–kohl** *m* broccoli.
Sparkasse [ʃparkasə] *f* savings bank. **–nbuch** *neut* deposit book.
spärlich [ʃpeːrliç] *adj* scanty, meagre. **Spärlichkeit** *f* scarcity.
Sparmaßnahme [ʃparmaːsnaːmə] *f* economy measure.
Spaß [ʃpaːs] *m* (*pl* Späße) fun; (*Scherz*) joke. **Spaß haben an** enjoy. *es macht uns Spaß* it amuses us, it is fun. **spaß‖en** *v* make fun, joke. **–haft** *or* **–ig** *adj* comical. **Spaßvogel** *m* joker, clown.
spät [ʃpeːt] *adj* late. *wie spät ist es?* what is the time?
Spaten [ʃpaːtən] *m* (*pl* -) spade.
später [ʃpeːtər] *adj* later. **spätestens** *adv* at the latest.
Spatz [ʃpats] *m* (*pl* -en) sparrow.
spazieren [ʃpaˈtsiːrən] *v* go for a walk, stroll. **–fahren** *v* go for a drive. **–gehen** *v* go for a walk, walk. **Spazier‖fahrt** *f* drive. **–gang** *m* walk, stroll.
Specht [ʃpeçt] *m* (*pl* -e) woodpecker.
Speck [ʃpɛk] *m* (*pl* -e) bacon; (*Schmalz*) lard, fat. **speckig** *adj* greasy.
spedieren [ʃpeˈdiːrən] *v* forward, transport, ship. **Spediteur** *m* (*pl* -e) shipping agent, haulier, carrier. **Spedition** *f* (*pl* -en) shipping (agency).
Speer [ʃpeːr] *m* (*pl* -e) spear.
Speichel [ʃpaiçəl] *m* spittle, saliva.
Speicher [ʃpaiçər] *m* (*pl* -) warehouse, storehouse; (*Getreide*) granary; (*Computer*) memory. **speichern** *v* store.
Speise [ʃpaizə] *f* (*pl* -n) food; (*Gericht*) dish. **–eis** *neut* ice cream. **–karte** *f* menu. **speisen** *v* dine, eat. **Speise‖röhre** *f* gullet. **–saal** *m* dining room. **–wagen** *m* dining car.
Spektakel [ʃpɛkˈtaːkəl] *m* (*pl* -) spectacle; (*Aufregung*) uproar.
Spekulation [ʃpekulatsiˈoːn] *f* (*pl* -en) speculation. **spekulieren** *v* speculate.
Spende [ʃpɛndə] *f* (*pl* -n) donation. **spenden** *v* contribute, donate. **Spender** *m* (*pl* -), **Spenderin** *f* (*pl* -nen) donor.

Sperre [ʃpɛrə] *f* (*pl* -n) barrier; (*Verbot*) ban. **sperren** *v* close, bar; (*untersagen*) ban; (*Strom*) cut off. **Sperr‖riegel** *m* (door) bolt. **–kette** *f* door chain. **–klinke** *f* safety catch. **–ung** *f* blocking, barring. **–zeit** *f* closing time.
Spesen [ʃpeːzən] *pl* expenses.
Spezialfach [ʃpertsiˈaːlfax] *neut* speciality. **spezialisieren** *v* specialize. **Spezialist** *m* specialist. **speziell** *adj* special.
spezifisch [ʃpeˈtsiːfiʃ] *adj* specific.
Sphäre [ˈsfɛːrə] *f* (*pl* -n) sphere.
Spiegel [ʃpiːgəl] *m* (*pl* -) mirror; (*Schiff*) stern. **–ei** *neut* fried egg. **–glas** *neut* plate glass. **spiegeln** *v* reflect; (*glänzen*) shine. **Spiegelung** *f* (*pl* -en) reflection.
Spiel [ʃpiːl] *neut* (*pl* -e) game; (*Theater*) play; (*Glücksspiel*) gambling. **aufs Spiel setzen** put at stake. **auf dem Spiel stehen** be at stake. **–automat** *m* slot machine. **–bank** *f* casino. **–brett** *neut* board.
spielen [ʃpiːlən] *v* play; (*Geld*) gamble.
Spieler [ʃpiːlər] *m* (*pl* -), **Spielerin** *f* (*pl* -nen) player; (*Schauspiel*) actor *m*, actress *f*; (*Geld*) gambler. **Spielergebnis** *neut* result, (final) score. **spielerisch** *adj* playful. **Spiel‖feld** *neut* playing field. **–karte** *f* playing card. **–platz** *m* playground. **–zeug** *neut* toy.
Spieß [ʃpiːs] *m* (*pl* -e) spear; (*Bratspieß*) spit. **–bürger** *m* philistine.
Spinat [ʃpiˈnaːt] *m* (*pl* -e) spinach.
Spindel [ʃpindəl] *f* (*pl* -n) spindle, axle.
Spinne [ʃpinə] *f* (*pl* -n) spider. **spinnen** *v* spin; (*umg.*) talk nonsense. *du spinnst ja!* you're crazy!
Spion [ʃpiˈoːn] *m* (*pl* -e) spy. **–age** *f* espionage. **spionieren** *v* spy.
Spirale [ʃpiˈraːlə] *f* (*pl* -n) spiral.
Spirituosen [ʃpirituˈoːzən] *pl* spirits, liquor *sing*.
spitz [ʃpits] *adj* sharp, pointed. **Spitze** *f* (*pl* -n) point, tip. **Spitzen** *pl* (*Gewebe*) lace *sing*. **spitzen** *v* sharpen. **Spitzen‖geschwindigkeit** *f* top speed. **–leistung** *f* maximum performance, record. **Spitzer** *m* (*pl* -) pencil-sharpener. **spitzfindig** *adj* shrewd, ingenious; (*haarspalterisch*) over-critical, hair-splitting. **Spitzname** *m* nickname.
Splitter [ʃplitər] *m* (*pl* -) splinter. **–gruppe** *f* splinter group.
spontan [ʃpɔnˈtaːn] *adj* spontaneous.

Spore ['ʃpɔːrə] *f* (*pl* -**n**) spore.

Sporn [ʃpɔrn] *m* (*pl* **Sporen**) spur. **spornen** *v* spur.

Sport [ʃpɔrt] *m* (*pl* -**e**) sport. **Sport treiben** go in for sport(s). **Sport∥feld** *neut* sports ground. –**ler** *m* (*pl* -) sportsman. –**lerin** *f* (*pl* -**nen**) sportswoman. **sportlich** *adj* sporting.

Spott [ʃpɔt] *m* ridicule. **spottbillig** *adj* dirt cheap. **spotten über** ridicule, deride.

spöttisch ['ʃpœtiʃ] *adj* mocking, scornful.

Sprache ['ʃpraːxə] *f* (*pl* -**n**) language, speech. **Sprachfehler** *m* speech defect; (*Gramm*) grammatical error. **sprach∥lich** *adj* linguistic. –**los** *adj* speechless.

***sprechen** ['ʃprɛçən] *v* speak. **sprechen mit** talk to, speak with. **Sprecher** *m* (*pl* -). **Sprecherin** *f* (*pl* -**nen**) speaker; (*offiziell*) spokesman.

sprengen ['ʃprɛŋən] *v* explode, blow up; (*aufbrechen*) burst open; (*bespritzen*) sprinkle. **Spreng∥kopf** *m* warhead. –**stoff** *m* explosive.

Sprichwort ['ʃpriçvɔrt] *neut* (*pl* **Sprichwörter**) proverb.

***sprießen** ['ʃpriːsən] *v* sprout.

Spring [ʃpriŋ] *m* (*pl* -**e**) spring. –**brunnen** *m* fountain. **springen** *v* jump, spring; (*Ball*) bounce; (*platzen*) burst, break; (*Schwimmen*) dive. **Springen** *neut* jumping; (*Schwimmen*) diving. **Springer** *m* (*pl* -) jumper; (*Schach*) knight. **Spring∥feder** *f* spring. –**seil** *neut* skipping rope.

Sprit [ʃprit] *m* (*pl* -**e**) (*umg.*) gas, juice.

Spritze ['ʃpritsə] *f* (*pl* -**n**) syringe; (*Einspritzung*) injection; (*Tech*) spray. **spritzen** *v* squirt; (*besprengen*) sprinkle; (*Med*) inject.

spröde ['ʃprøːdə] *adj* brittle; (*Person*) reserved, cool.

Sproß [ʃprɔs] *m* (*pl* **Sprosse**) shoot, sprout.

Spruch [ʃprux] *m* (*pl* **Sprüche**) saying, aphorism; (*Jur*) sentence.

Sprudel ['ʃpruːdəl] *m* (*pl* -) spring, source (of water); mineral water. **sprudeln** *v* bubble up; (*Mineralwasser, usw.*) sparkle. –**d** *adj* bubbling; sparkling. **Sprudelwasser** *neut* mineral water.

Sprühdose ['ʃpryːdoːzə] *f* spray can, aerosol pack. **sprühen** *v* spray; (*Regen*) drizzle. **Sprühregen** *m* drizzle.

Sprung [ʃpruŋ] *m* (*pl* **Sprünge**) leap, jump; (*Schwimmen*) dive; (*Riß*) crack, split. –**brett** *neut* diving board.

spucken ['ʃpukən] *v* spit.

Spuk [ʃpuːk] *m* (*pl* -**e**) ghost.

Spülbecken ['ʃpyːlbɛkən] *neut* sink.

Spule ['ʃpuːlə] *f* (*pl* -**n**) spool; (*Elek*) coil. **spulen** *v* wind.

spülen ['ʃpyːlən] *v* rinse, wash; (*Geschirr*) wash up; (*WC*) flush. **Spül∥ung** *f* rinsing, washing; flushing. –**wasser** *neut* dishwater.

Spur [ʃpuːr] *f* (*pl* -**en**) track, trail; (*fig*) trace.

spürbar ['ʃpyːrbaɪr] *adj* perceptible, noticeable. **spüren** *v* trace; (*folgen*) track; (*fühlen*) feel. **Spürsinn** *m* shrewdness.

Staat [ʃtaːt] *m* (*pl* -**e**) state. **staatlich** *adj* state. **Staats∥angehörige(r)** *m* citizen, national. –**angehörigkeit** *f* nationality. –**anwalt** *m* public prosecutor. –**bürger** *m* citizen. –**mann** *m* statesman. –**streich** *m* coup d'état.

Stab [ʃtaːp] *m* (*pl* **Stäbe**) staff; (*Metall*) bar; (*Holz*) stick, pole.

stabil [ʃtaˈbiːl] *adj* stable. –**isieren** *v* stabilize. **Stabilität** *f* stability.

Stachel ['ʃtaxəl] *m* (*pl* -**n**) spike, prickle; (*Biene*) sting. –**beere** *f* gooseberry. –**draht** *m* barbed wire. **stachel∥ig** *adj* prickly; stinging. –**n** *v* prick; sting. **Stachelschwein** *neut* porcupine.

Stadion ['ʃtaːdiɔn] *neut* (*pl* **Stadien**) stadium.

Stadt [ʃtat] *f* (*pl* **Städte**) town, city.

städtisch ['ʃtɛtiʃ] *adj* urban; (*Verwaltung*) municipal.

Stadt∥mitte *f* town centre. –**plan** *m* town map. –**rat** *m* town council; (*Person*) councillor.

Staffel ['ʃtafəl] *f* (*pl* -**n**) rung, step; (*Mil*) detachment; (*Lauf*) relay. –**ei** *f* (*pl* -**en**) easel.

Stahl [ʃtaːl] *m* (*pl* -**e**) steel.

Stall [ʃtal] *m* (*pl* **Ställe**) (*Pferde*) stable; (*Hunde*) kennel; (*Schweine*) sty; (*Kuhe*) cowshed.

Stamm [ʃtam] *m* (*pl* **Stämme**) (*Volk*) tribe; (*Baum*) trunk; (*Stengel*) stalk, stem. –**baum** *m* family tree, genealogy; (*Hund*) pedigree. **stammen (von)** *v* (*Ort*) come (from); (*Familie*) be descended (from); (*fig, Gramm*) be derived (from).

stampfen ['ʃtampfən] *v* stamp; (*zerstampfen*) mash, crush.

Stand [ʃtant] *m* (*pl* **Stände**) stand; (*Markt*) stall; (*Höhe*) level, height; (*Stellung*) position, situation.

Standard ['ʃtandart] m (pl -s) standard.
Standbild ['ʃtantbilt] neut statue.
Ständer ['ʃtɛndər] m (pl -) stand.
Standesamt ['ʃtandəzamt] neut registry office.
standhaft ['ʃtandhaft] adj steadfast. **Standhaftigkeit** f steadfastness.
standhalten v stand firm.
ständig ['ʃtɛndiç] adj permanent; (laufend) constant.
Stand‖ort m position, station. **–punkt** m standpoint.
Stange ['ʃtaŋə] f (pl -n) pole, bar.
Stanniol [ʃtani'oːl] neut (pl -e) tinfoil.
Stapel ['ʃtaɪpəl] m (pl -) pile, heap, stack. **stapeln** v pile up.
Star[1] [ʃtaɪr] m (pl -e) (Vogel) starling.
Star[2] m (pl -s) (Film) star.
Star[3] m (pl -e) (Med) cataract.
stark [ʃtark] adj strong; (Zahl) numerous; (dick) thick(set). **starke Erkältung** severe cold. **stark gesucht** in great demand.
Stärke ['ʃtɛrkə] f (pl -n) strength; (Dicke) stoutness; (Gewalt) violence; (Wäsche-, Chem) starch. **stärken** v strengthen.
starr [ʃtar] adj rigid; (Blick) fixed, staring. **starren** v stare. **Starrheit** f rigidity; (Charakter) obstinacy.
Start [ʃtart] m (pl -e) start; (Flugzeug) take-off. **starten** v start; take off. **Starter** m (pl -) (Mot, Sport) starter. **–klappe** f (Mot) choke.
Station [ʃtatsi'oɪn] f (pl -en) station; (Krankenhaus) ward.
Statistik [ʃta'tistik] f (pl -en) statistics. **statistisch** adj statistical.
statt [ʃtat] prep instead of. **Statt** f place, stead.
Stätte ['ʃtɛtə] f (pl -n) place, spot.
statt‖finden v take place. **–haft** adj allowed, permissible. **–lich** adj stately; (Summe) considerable.
Statut [ʃta'tuɪt] neut (pl -en) statute.
Staub [ʃtaup] m dust. **staubig** adj dusty. **Staubtuch** neut duster.
stauen ['ʃtauən] v dam (up); (Ladung) stow (away). **sich stauen** accumulate, pile up.
staunen ['ʃtaunən] v be astonished. **Staunen** neut (pl -) astonishment.
Steak [stɛk] neut (pl -s) steak.
stechen ['ʃtɛçən] v (Insekt) sting; (Dorn) prick; (mit einer Waffe) stab, jab. **–d** adj stinging; (fig) piercing. **Stechpalme** f holly.

Steck‖brief m warrant (for arrest). **–dose** f (Elek) socket.
stecken ['ʃtɛkən] v put, place, insert; (sich befinden) be, lie. **etwas in die Tasche stecken** put something in one's pocket. **in Brand stecken** set fire to. **da steckt er!** there he is! that's where he's hiding! **es steckt etwas dahinter** there's more to it than meets the eye. **steckenbleiben** v be or get stuck. **Steck‖enpferd** neut hobbyhorse; (fig) hobby. **–er** m (pl -) (Elek) plug. **–nadel** f pin.
Steg [ʃtɛk] m (pl -e) (foot)path; (Brücke) (foot)bridge; (Geige) bridge.
stehen ['ʃteɪən] v stand; (sein) be (situated). **in Verdacht stehen** be suspected. **offen stehen** be open. **das Kleid steht dir** (gut) the dress suits you. **stehen‖bleiben** v (nicht weitergehen) come to a standstill, stop; (nicht umfallen) remain standing. **–d** adj standing; (ständig) permanent.
stehlen ['ʃteɪlən] v steal. **Stehlen** neut (unz.) stealing, theft.
steif [ʃtaif] adj stiff. **Steifheit** f stiffness.
Steig [ʃtaik] m (pl -e) path. **–bügel** m stirrup. **steigen** v rise; (klettern) climb. **–d** adj rising; (wachsend) growing.
steigern ['ʃtaigərn] v raise, increase. **Steigerung** f (pl -en) rise, increase.
Steigung ['ʃtaiguŋ] f (pl -en) rise, incline.
steil [ʃtail] adj steep.
Stein [ʃtain] m (pl -e) stone. **–bock** m (Tier) ibex; (Astrol) Capricorn. **–bruch** m quarry. **steinern** adj stone. **Steingut** neut stoneware, pottery. **steinigen** v stone (to death). **Steinzeit** f Stone Age.
Stelle ['ʃtɛlə] f (pl -n) place; (Arbeit) job, position; (in einem Buch) passage. **an Ort und Stelle** on the spot. **an Stelle von** in place of. **eine Stelle bekleiden** hold a position.
stellen ['ʃtɛlən] v put, place; (Frage) ask; (Forderung) make. **zufriedenstellen** satisfy. **eine Falle stellen** set a trap. **sich stellen** present oneself; (vortäuschen) pretend, feign.
Stellen‖angebot neut vacancy, vacant position. **–nachweis** m employment agency.
Stellung ['ʃtɛluŋ] f (pl -en) position; (Arbeit) post, position; (Ansicht) attitude, opinion; (Körperhaltung) posture. **–nahme** f comment, opinion.

stellvertretend *adj* deputy, delegated. **Stellvertret‖er** *m* deputy, representative. **–ung** *f* representation.
Stelze ['ʃtɛltsə] *f* (*pl* -n) stilt.
Stempel ['ʃtɛmpəl] *m* (*pl* -) stamp. **–geld** *neut* (*umg.*) dole money. **stempeln** *v* stamp. **stempeln gehen** (*umg.*) go on the dole.
Stengel ['ʃtɛŋəl] *m* (*pl* -) stalk.
Stenograph [ʃteno'graːf] *m* (*pl* -en) stenographer. **–ie** *f* shorthand. **Stenotypist(in)** shorthand typist.
Steppe ['ʃtɛpə] *f* (*pl* -n) steppe, prairie.
Sterbe‖bett *neut* deathbed. **–fall** *m* a death.
*sterben ['ʃtɛrbən] *v* die. **Sterben** *neut* death. **sterblich** *adj* mortal. **Sterblichkeit** *f* mortality.
Stereoanlage ['ʃtereoanlaːgə] *f* stereo (system).
steril [ʃte'riːl] *adj* sterile. **–isieren** *v* sterilize.
Stern [ʃtɛrn] *m* (*pl* -e) star. **–bild** *neut* constellation. **–chen** *neut* asterisk. **–kunde** *f* astronomy.
stet [ʃtett] *or* **stetig** *adj* constant, continual. **stets** *adv* always, constantly.
Steuer ['ʃtɔyər] *f* (*pl* -n) tax.
Steuer‖behörde *f* inland revenue, (*US*) internal revenue. **–berater** *m* tax consultant. **–erklärung** *f* tax return. **–hinterziehung** *f* tax evasion.
steuern ['ʃtɔyərn] *v* steer.
steuerpflichtig ['ʃtɔyərpfliçtiç] *adj* taxable, subject to taxation.
Steuer‖rad *neut* steering wheel. **–säule** *f* steering column.
Steuerung ['ʃtɔyəruŋ] *f* (*pl* -en) steering.
Steuerzahler ['ʃtɔyərtsaːlər] *m* tax-payer.
Stich [ʃtiç] *m* (*pl* -e) prick; (*Insekt*) sting; (*Messer*) stab; (*Nähen*) stitch; (*Kartenspiel*) trick. **im Stich lassen** abandon, leave in the lurch.
sticken ['ʃtikən] *v* embroider. **Stickerei** *f* embroidery.
Stickstoff ['ʃtikʃtɔf] *m* nitrogen.
Stiefbruder ['ʃtiːfbruːdər] *m* stepbrother.
Stiefel ['ʃtiːfəl] *m* (*pl* -) boot.
Stief‖eltern *pl* step-parents. **–kind** *neut* stepchild. **–mutter** *f* stepmother. **–mütterchen** *neut* pansy. **–schwester** *f* stepsister. **–sohn** *m* stepson.. **–tochter** *f* stepdaughter. **–vater** *m* stepfather.
Stiel [ʃtiːl] *m* (*pl* -e) handle; (*Bot*) stalk.

Stier [ʃtiːr] *m* (*pl* -e) bull. **–kampf** *m* bullfight.
Stift[1] [ʃtift] *m* (*pl* -e) peg; (*Bleistift*) pencil; (*Pflocke*) pin.
Stift[2] *neut* (*pl* -e *or* -er) (charitable) foundation; (*Kloster*) monastery.
stiften ['ʃtiftən] *v* donate; (*gründen*) found, establish; (*Frieden*) make. **Stifter** *m* founder. **Stiftung** *f* (*pl* -en) (charitable) foundation, institution; (*geschenktes Vermögen*) endowment, bequest.
Stil [ʃtiːl] *m* (*pl* -e) style.
still [ʃtil] *adj* quiet, still; (*schweigend*) silent. **Stille** *f* quiet, stillness, silence. **stillen** *v* allay, stop; (*Schmerz*) soothe; (*Durst*) quench; (*Säugling*) nurse. **stillschweigen** *v* be silent. **–d** *adj* silent; (*fig*) implicit, tacit. **Stillstand** *m* standstill. **stillstehen** *v* stand still; (*aufhören*) stop.
Stimme ['ʃtimə] *f* (*pl* -n) voice; (*Wahl*) vote; (*Musik*) part. **seine Stimme abgeben** cast one's vote. **sich der Stimme enthalten** abstain (from voting). **stimmen** *v* (*richtig sein*) be right *or* true, tally; (*Wahl*) vote; (*Instrument*) tune. **hier stimmt etwas nicht!** something's wrong here! **stimmt schon!** that's all right. **Stimm‖enthaltung** *f* abstention. **–recht** *neut* franchise. **–ung** *f* (*pl* -en) mood, atmosphere; (*Musik*) tuning.
*stinken ['ʃtiŋkən] *v* stink.
Stipendium [ʃti'pɛndium] *neut* (*pl* Stipendien) scholarship, (student) grant.
Stirn [ʃtirn] *f* (*pl* -en) forehead. **die Stirn runzeln** frown.
stöbern ['ʃtœːbərn] *v* rummage (about).
Stock [ʃtɔk] *m* (*pl* Stöcke) stick, rod; (*Musik*) baton; (*Etage*) storey. **stockdunkel** *adj* pitch dark.
stocken ['ʃtɔkən] *v* stoop, come to a standstill; (*Milch*) curdle. **Stockung** *f* (*pl* -en) standstill, stop; (*Verkehr*) congestion, jam.
Stockwerk ['ʃtɔkvɛrk] *neut* floor, storey.
Stoff [ʃtɔf] *m* (*pl* -e) matter; (*Gewebe, fig*) material.
stöhnen ['ʃtœːnən] *v* groan.
Stolle ['ʃtɔlə] *f* (*pl* -n) *or* **Stollen** *m* (*pl* -) (German) Christmas cake.
stolpern ['ʃtɔlpərn] *v* stumble.
stolz [ʃtɔlts] *adj* proud. **Stolz** *m* pride.
stopfen ['ʃtɔpfən] *v* stuff, fill; (*Strümpfe*) darn; (*sättigen*) fill up; (*Med*) constipate.

Stopp [ʃtɔp] *m* (*unz.*) hitchhiking.
Stoppel ['ʃtɔpəl] *f* (*pl* -n) stubble.
stoppen ['ʃtɔpən] *v* stop. **Stopplicht** *neut* brake light.
Stöpsel ['ʃtœpsəl] *m* (*pl* -) stopper; (*Elek*) plug.
Storch [ʃtɔrç] *m* (*pl* Störche) stork.
stören ['ʃtœːrən] *v* disturb; (*belästigen*) bother, trouble; (*Radio*) interfere. **-d** *adj* disturbing, troublesome. **Störenfried** *m* troublemaker. **Störung** *f* (*pl* -en) disturbance; trouble; (*Radio*) interference.
Stoß [ʃtoːs] *m* (*pl* Stöße) push, shove; (*Schlag*) blow; (*Tritt*) kick; (*Haufen*) heap. **-dämpfer** *m* shock-absorber. **stoßen** *v* push, shove; knock; (*fig*) take offence. **stoßen an** run across. **sich stoßen an** bump into *or* against; (*fig*) take offence at. **Stoß‖stange** *f* bumper. **-zahn** *m* tusk.
stottern ['ʃtɔtərn] *v* stutter, stammer.
Straf‖anstalt *f* prison, penal institution. **-arbeit** *f* (*Schule*) punishment, lines *pl*. **strafbar** *adj* punishable.
Strafe ['ʃtraːfə] *f* (*pl* -n) punishment; (*fig*) penalty; (*Jur*) sentence. **strafen** *v* punish.
Straferlaß *m* pardon; (*allgemeiner*) amnesty.
straff [ʃtraf] *adj* tight, taught; (*fig*) strict, stern.
Straf‖geld *neut* fine. **-gericht** *neut* criminal court.
sträflich ['ʃtrɛːfliç] *adj* punishable. **Sträfling** *m* prisoner.
Straf‖recht *neut* criminal law. **-tat** *f* offence.
Strahl [ʃtraːl] *m* (*pl* -en) ray, beam; (*Blitz*) flash; (*Wasser*) jet. **strahlen** *v* radiate; (*fig*) beam. **-d** *adj* beaming. **Strahlmotor** *m* jet engine. **Strahlung** *f* radiation.
Strand [ʃtrant] *m* (*pl* -e) beach, shore. **stranden** *v* run aground; (*fig*) founder.
strapazieren [ʃtrapa'tsiːrən] *v* fatigue, tire; (*abnutzen*) wear out.
Straße ['ʃtraːsə] *f* (*pl* -n) street. **Straßen‖bahn** *f* tram, (*US*) street car. **-kreuzung** *f* crossing. **-laterne** *f* street lamp. **-sperre** *f* roadblock. **-überführung** *f* overpass. **-unterführung** *f* underpass.
sträuben ['ʃtrɔybən] *v* ruffle (up). **sich sträuben** (*Haare*) stand up on end; (*fig*) struggle (against), resist.
Strauch [ʃtraux] *m* (*pl* Sträucher) bush.

Strauß[1] [ʃtraus] *m* (*pl* -e) (*Vogel*) ostrich.
Strauß[2] *m* (*pl* Sträuße) bouquet, bunch (of flowers).
streben ['ʃtreːbən] *v* strive.
Strecke ['ʃtrɛkə] *f* (*pl* -n) stretch, distance; (*Math*, *Sport*) distance; (*Teilschnitt*) section. **strecken** *v* stretch (out), extend.
Streich [ʃtraiç] *m* (*pl* -e) stroke, blow; (*Peitsche*) lash; (*Possen*) trick, prank.
streicheln ['ʃtraiçəln] *v* stroke, pet.
*streichen ['ʃtraiçən] *v* stroke, rub; (*Farbe*) paint; (*gehen*) wander, ramble. **Streich‖instrument** *neut* string instrument. **-musik** *f* string music. **-quartett** *neut* string quartet.
Streife ['ʃtraifə] *f* (*pl* -n) patrol; (*Streifzug*) stroll, look around.
Streifen ['ʃtraifən] *m* (*pl* -) stripe; (*Land*) strip.
streifen ['ʃtraifən] *v* streak, stripe; (*berühren*) brush (against), touch; (*wandern*) wander, roam.
Streik [ʃtraik] *m* (*pl* -s) strike. **-brecher** *m* strike-breaker; (*umg.*) scab. **streiken** *v* (go on) strike.
Streit [ʃtrait] *m* (*pl* -e) dispute, quarrel; (*Kampf*) conflict; (*Schlägerei*) fight, brawl. **streiten** *v* dispute, quarrel. **sich streiten um** quarrel about, fight over. **Streitfrage** *f* matter in dispute. **streit‖ig** *adj* contested; (*fraglich*) controversial. **-lustig** *adj* quarrelsome, aggressive.
streng [ʃtrɛŋ] *adj* stern, severe, strict. **Strenge** *f* severity, strictness.
streuen ['ʃtrɔyən] *v* scatter, spread.
Strich [ʃtriç] *m* (*pl* -e) stroke, line; (*Vogel*) flight; (*Gebiet*) district; (*Kompaß*) compass point. **-punkt** *m* semicolon.
Strick [ʃtrik] *m* (*pl* -e) cord, string, (thin) rope; (*Kind*) rascal. **-arbeit** *f* knitting; (*Artikel*) knitwear. **stricken** *v* knit. **Strick‖maschine** *f* knitting machine. **-nadel** *f* knitting needle. **-zeug** *neut* knitting.
strittig ['ʃtritiç] *adj* questionable, debatable; (*Angelegenheit*) disputed.
Stroh [ʃtroː] *neut* straw. **-dach** *neut* thatched roof.
Strolch [ʃtrɔlç] *m* (*pl* -e) tramp, vagabond. **strolchen** *v* roam, stroll about.
Strom [ʃtroːm] *m* (*pl* Ströme) (*Fluß*) (large) river; (*Strömung*, *Elek*) current;

(*fig*) stream. **strom‖abwärts** *adv* downstream. **–aufwärts** *adv* upstream.
strömen [ˈʃtrœːmən] *v* stream, flow; (*Regen*) pour.
Strom‖erzeuger *m* generator. **–sperre** *f* power cut.
Strömung [ˈʃtrœːmuŋ] *f* (*pl* -en) current.
Struktur [ʃtrukˈtuːr] *f* (*pl* -en) structure.
Strumpf [ʃtrumpf] *m* (*pl* **Strümpfe**) stocking; (*Socke*) sock.
Stube [ˈʃtuːbə] *f* (*pl* -n) room, chamber. **stubenrein** *adj* house-trained.
Stück [ʃtyk] *neut* (*pl* -e) piece; (*Theater*) play; (*Vieh*) head. **in Stücke gehen** fall to pieces. **Stückchen** *neut* bit, little piece; (*Papier*) scrap. **stückeln** *v* cut *or* chop into pieces.
Student [ʃtuˈdent] *m* (*pl* -en) student. **–enheim** *neut* hall of residence, (*US*) dorm(itory). **Studentin** *f* (*pl* -nen) (woman) student.
Studien‖direktor *m* headmaster, (*US*) principal. **–plan** *m* syllabus.
studieren [ʃtuˈdiːrən] *v* study. **Studio** *neut* studio. **Studium** *neut* studies *pl*; (*Untersuchung*) study.
Stufe [ˈʃtuːfə] *f* (*pl* -n) step; (*Leiter*) rung; (*fig*) stage. **stufen‖los** *adj* infinitely variable. **–weise** *adv* gradually.
Stuhl [ʃtuːl] *m* (*pl* **Stühle**) chair; (*ohne Lehne*) stool. **–gang** *m* bowel movement.
stumm [ʃtum] *adj* mute, dumb; (*schweigend*) silent. **Stumme(r)** *m* mute, dumb person.
Stummel [ˈʃtuməl] *m* (*pl* -) stump. **Stumm‖film** *m* silent film. **–heit** *f* dumbness.
stumpf [ʃtumpf] *adj* blunt; (*Mensch*) dull. **Stumpf‖heit** *f* bluntness; dullness. **–sinn** *m* stupidity. **stumpfsinnig** *adj* stupid, dull-witted.
Stunde [ˈʃtundə] *f* (*pl* -n) hour; (*Unterricht*) lesson. **Stunden‖plan** *m* timetable. **–satz** *m* hourly rate.
stupid [ʃtuˈpiːt] *adj* half-witted, idiotic.
stur [ʃtuːr] *adj* stubborn.
Sturm [ʃturm] *m* (*pl* **Stürme**) storm; (*Angriff*) attack.
stürmen [ˈʃtyrmən] *v* storm; (*Wind*) blow. **Stürmer** *m* (*pl* -) assailant; (*Fußball*) forward. **stürmisch** *adj* stormy.
Sturz [ʃturts] *m* (*pl* **Stürze**) fall; (*Zusammenbruch*) collapse.
stürzen [ˈʃtyrtsən] *v* (*fallen*) fall (down); (*umkippen*) overturn; (*Regierung*) over-

throw; (*eilen*) dash, rush. **sich stürzen auf** rush at.
Sturzhelm [ˈʃturtshelm] *m* crash-helmet.
Stute [ˈʃtuːtə] *f* (*pl* -n) mare. **–nfüllen** *neut* foal, filly.
Stütze [ˈʃtytsə] *f* (*pl* -n) prop, support.
stutzen[1] [ˈʃtutsən] *v* stop short, be startled.
stutzen[2] *v* (*schneiden*) clip, trim; (*Schwanz*) dock.
stützen [ˈʃtytsən] *v* prop, support. **Stützpunkt** *m* fulcrum; (*Mil*) stronghold.
subjektiv [subjɛkˈtiːf] *adj* subjective.
subtil [zupˈtiːl] *adj* subtle.
Subvention [zupvɛntsiˈoːn] *f* (*pl* -en) subsidy.
Suche [ˈzuːxə] *f* (*pl* -n) search. **suchen** *v* look for, search for. **Sucher** *m* (*pl* -) searcher. **Sucht** *f* (*pl* **Süchte**) addiction; (*fig*) craving, passion.
süchtig [ˈzyçtiç] *adj* addicted. **Süchtige(r)** *m* addict.
Süd(en) [zyt (ˈzyːdən)] *m* south. **Süd‖afrika** *neut* South Africa. **–amerika** *neut* South America. **–länder(in)** southerner.
südlich [ˈzyːtliç] *adj* southern.
Südost(en) [zyːtˈɔst(ən)] *m* southeast. **südöstlich** *adj* southeast(ern); (*Wind, Richtung*) southeasterly.
Südpol [ˈzyːtpoːl] *m* South Pole.
südwärts [ˈzyːtvɛrts] *adv* southwards.
Südwest(en) [zyːtˈvɛst(ən)] *m* southwest. **südwestlich** *adj* southwest(ern); (*Wind, Richtung*) southwesterly.
Sühne [ˈzyːnə] *f* (*pl* -n) atonement. **sühnen** *v* atone for.
Sultanine [zultaˈniːnə] *f* (*pl* -n) sultana.
Sülze [ˈzyltsə] *f* (*pl* -n) brawn.
Summe [ˈzumə] *f* (*pl* -n) sum total; (*Geld*) sum, amount.
summen [ˈzumən] *v* buzz, hum.
summieren [zuˈmiːrən] *v* add up. **Summierung** *f* summation.
Sumpf [zumpf] *m* (*pl* **Sümpfe**) swamp, marsh.
Sund [zunt] *m* (*pl* -e) sound, channel.
Sünde [ˈzyndə] *f* (*pl* -n) sin. **–nbock** *m* scapegoat. **Sünder(in)** sinner. **sündhaft** *adj* sinful.
Suppe [ˈzupə] *f* (*pl* -n) soup.
süß [zyːs] *adj* sweet. **Süße** *f* sweetness. **süßen** *v* sweeten. **Süßigkeit** *f* sweetness. **Süßigkeiten** *pl* sweets, (*US*) candy *sing*. **süßlich** *adj* sweetish; (*fig*) slushy, senti-

mental. **Süß||waren** *pl* sweets, (*US*) candy *sing*. **–wasser** *neut* fresh water.
Symbol [zym'boɪl] *neut* (*pl* -e) symbol.
symbol||isch *adj* symbolic. **–isieren** *v* symbolize.
sympathisch [zym'paɪtiʃ] *adj* likeable, congenial.
Symptom [zymp'toɪm] *neut* (*pl* -e) symptom.
Synagoge [zyna'goɪgə] *f* (*pl* -n) synagogue.
synchron [*'*zynkron] *adj* synchronous. **–isieren** *v* synchronize.
Synthese [zyn'teɪzə] *f* (*pl* -n) synthesis.
Syphilis ['zyɪfilis] *f* syphilis.
System [zys'teɪm] *neut* (*pl* -e) system. **systematisch** *adj* systematic.
Szene ['stseɪnə] *f* (*pl* -n) scene.

T

Tabak ['taɪbak] *m* (*pl* -e) tobacco.
Tabelle [ta'bɛlə] *f* (*pl* -n) table, list. **tabellenförmig** *adj* tabular.
Tablette [ta'blɛtə] *f* (*pl* -n) pill, tablet.
Tadel ['taɪdəl] *m* blame; reproach, reprimand; (*Schule*) bad mark. **tadellos** *adj* faultless. **tadeln** *v* reproach, scold, criticize.
Tafel ['taɪfəl] *f* (*pl* -n) board; (*Schule*) blackboard; (*Schokolade*) bar; (*Tabelle*) table, chart. **die Tafel decken** lay the table.
Tag [taɪk] *m* (*pl* -e) day. **am Tag** by day. **Tages||anbruch** *m* dawn, daybreak. **–licht** *neut* daylight. **–zeitung** *f* daily (newspaper). **täglich** *adj* daily.
Taille ['taljə] *f* waist.
Takelwerk ['taɪkəlverk] *neut* rigging.
Takt [takt] *m* (*Musik*) time, beat; (*Tech*) stroke; (*Höflichkeit*) tact. **Zweitaktmotor** *m* two-stroke engine.
Taktik ['taktik] *f* (*pl* -en) tactics *pl*. **taktisch** *adj* tactical.
taktlos ['taktloɪs] *adj* tactless.
Tal [taɪl] *neut* (*pl* Täler) valley, vale.
Talent [ta'lɛnt] *neut* (*pl* -e) talent, gift. **talentiert** *adj* talented, gifted.
Talk [talk] *m* talcum.
Tampon [tã'pɔ̃] *m* (*pl* -s) (*Med*) swab; (*für Frauen*) tampon.
tändeln ['tɛndəln] *v* flirt; (*langsam gehen*,

usw.) dawdle, dally. **Tändelei** *f* (*pl* -en) flirtation.
Tang [taŋ] *m* (*pl* -e) seaweed.
Tank [taŋk] *m* (*pl* -e) tank. **tanken** *v* (*Mot*) refuel, fill up. **Tank||schiff** *neut* tanker. **–stelle** *f* petrol station.
Tanne ['tanə] *f* fir. **Tannen||baum** *m* fir-tree. **–zapfen** *m* fir-cone.
Tante ['tantə] *f* (*pl* -n) aunt.
Tanz [tants] *m* (*pl* Tänze) dance; (*Tanzen*) dancing. **tanzen** *v* dance. **Tänzer** *m* (*pl* -), **Tänzerin** *f* (*pl* -nen) dancer. **Tanz||lokal** *neut* dancehall. **–platz** *m* dance-floor.
Tapete [ta'petə] *f* (*pl* -n) wallpaper. **tapezieren** *v* paper, decorate.
tapfer ['tapfər] *adj* brave, courageous. **Tapferkeit** *f* bravery, courage.
tappen ['tapən] *v* grope, fumble about.
Tarif [ta'riɪf] *m* (*pl* -e) price list. **–verhandlungen** *pl* collective bargaining *sing*.
tarnen ['tarnən] *v* camouflage. **Tarnung** *f* camouflage.
Tasche ['taʃə] *f* (*pl* -n) pocket; suitcase; handbag; (*Schule*) satchel; (*Aktentasche*) briefcase. **Taschen||dieb** *m* pickpocket. **–geld** *neut* pocket money. **–lampe** *f* torch. **–messer** *neut* penknife.
Tasse ['tasə] *f* (*pl* -n) cup. **eine Tasse Kaffee** a cup of coffee.
Taste ['tastə] *f* (*pl* -n) (*Klavier, Schreibmaschine*) key; (push)button. **tasten** *v* feel, touch. **Tastenbrett** (*Musik*) *neut also* **Tastatur** keyboard.
Tat [taɪt] *f* (*pl* -en) deed, act. **in der Tat** in reality, really.
tätig ['tɛɪtiç] *adj* active, busy, employed. **tätig sein als** be employed as, practise. **tätig sein bei** work for. **Tätigkeit** *f* (*pl* -en) activity; (*Beruf*) work, occupation.
tätowieren [teto'viɪrən] *v* tattoo. **Tätowierung** *f* (*pl* -en) tattoo.
Tatsache ['taɪtzaxə] *f* (*pl* -n) fact. **tatsächlich** *adj* real, actual. *adv* really, actually. *interj* really? is that so?
Tatze ['tatsə] *f* (*pl* -n) paw.
Tau[1] [tau] *neut* (*pl* -e) (*Seil*) rope, cable.
Tau[2] *m* (*unz.*) dew. **Tauwetter** *neut* thaw.
taub [taup] *adj* deaf.
Taube ['taubə] *f* (*pl* -n) pigeon, dove.
taubstumm ['taupʃtum] *adj* deaf and dumb. **Taubstumme(r)** deaf mute.
tauchen ['tauxən] *v* dive, plunge; immerse, dip. **Tauchen** *neut* diving. **Taucher** *m* (*pl* -) diver.

tauen ['tauən] v thaw, melt.
Taufe ['taufə] f (pl -n) baptism, christening. **taufen** v baptize, christen. **Taufname** m Christian name.
taugen ['taugən] v **taugen zu** be good or fit for. **zu nichts taugen** be useless or worthless. **Taugenichts** m (pl -e) good-for-nothing.
taumeln ['tauməln] v stagger, reel.
Tausch [tauʃ] m (pl -e) exchange. **tausch‖bar** adj exchangeable. **–en** v exchange, swap.
täuschen ['tɔyʃən] v deceive, delude. **–d** adj deceptive.
Tauschhandel ['tauʃhandəl] m barter.
Täuschung ['tɔyʃuŋ] f (pl -en) delusion, illusion; (Schwindel) deception, fraud.
tausend ['tauzənt] adj thousand.
Taxe ['taksə] f (pl -n) charge, fee; (Schätzung) valuation. **taxieren** v value, assess.
Taxi ['taksi] neut or m (pl -s) taxi. **–fahrer** m taxi-driver.
Technik ['teçnik] f (pl -n) technique; engineering, technology. **–er** m (pl -) technician. **Technologie** f technology. **technologisch** technological.
Tee [teː] m tea. **–kanne** f teapot. **–löffel** m teaspoon. **–service** neut tea-set.
Teer [teːr] m (pl -e) tar, pitch.
Teich [taiç] m (pl -e) pond.
Teig [taik] m (pl -e) dough; (flüssig) batter. **–waren** f noodles pl.
Teil [tail] m or neut (pl -e) part; share, portion. **teilbar** adj divisible. **Teil‖beschäftigung** f part-time work. **–chen** neut particle. **teil‖en** v divide; share out. **–haben** take part (in). **Teilnahme** f participation; interest; (Mitleid) sympathy. **teil‖nehmen** v take part in. **–s** adv partly. **Teilung** f (pl -en) division, partition; sharing out, distribution. **teilweise** adj partial. adv partly.
Telegramm [tele'gram] neut (pl -e) telegram.
Telephon [tele'foːn] neut (pl -e) telephone. **–buch** neut telephone directory. **telephonieren** v telephone, ring up. **Telephon‖zelle** f call box. **–zentrale** f telephone exchange.
Teleskop [tele'skoːp] neut (pl -e) telescope.
Teller ['tɛlər] m (pl -) plate; (Tech) disc.
Tempel ['tɛmpəl] m (pl -) temple.

Temperament [tɛmpera'mɛnt] neut (pl -e) temperament, disposition. **temperamentvoll** adj high-spirited, lively.
Temperatur [tɛmpera'tuːr] f temperature.
Tempo ['tɛmpo] neut (pl -s or -pi) pace, tempo.
temporär [tɛmpo'rɛːr] adj temporary.
Tendenz [tɛn'dɛnts] f (pl -en) tendency, propensity.
Tennis ['tɛnis] neut tennis. **–platz** m tennis court. **–schläger** m tennis racket.
Tenor [te'noːr] m (pl -e) tenor.
Teppich ['tɛpiç] m (pl -e) carpet, rug; (Wand) tapestry.
Termin [tɛr'miːn] m (pl -e) fixed date; closing date, deadline. **–geschäft** neut (Komm) futures pl.
Terpentinöl [tɛrpɛn'tiːnœːl] neut turpentine.
Terrasse [tɛ'rasə] f (pl -n) terrace.
Terror ['tɛrɔr] m terror. **–ismus** m terrorism. **–ist(in)** terrorist. **terroristisch** adj terrorist.
Testament [tɛsta'mɛnt] neut (pl -e) will; (Bibel) testament. **Testaments‖bestätigung** f probate. **–vollstrecker** m executor.
testieren [tɛs'tiːrən] v make one's will; bequeath.
teuer ['tɔyər] adj expensive, dear; (lieb) dear, cherished. adv dearly. **Teuerung** f (pl -en) rising prices pl, increase in the cost of living. **Teuerungszulage** f cost-of-living bonus.
Teufel ['tɔyfəl] m devil, Satan. **Teufels‖beschwörung** f exorcism. **–skreis** m vicious circle. **teuflisch** adj devilish, diabolical.
Text [tɛkst] m (pl -e) text; (Lied) lyrics pl; (Oper) libretto. **–buch** neut libretto.
Textilien [tɛks'tiːliən] or **Textilwaren** pl textiles.
Theater [te'aːtər] neut (pl -) theatre; (umg.) fuss, to-do. **theatralisch** adj theatrical.
Thema ['teːma] neut (pl Themen) theme, subject.
Theologe [teo'loːgə] m (pl -n) theologian. **Theologie** f theology. **theologisch** adj theological.
Theoretiker [teo'reːtikər] m (pl -) theorist. **theoretisch** adj theoretical. **Theorie** f (pl -n) theory.
Therapie [tera'piː] f (pl -n) therapy.

thermisch ['tɛrmiʃ] *adj* thermal.
Thermometer [tɛrmo'mɛɪtər] *neut* (*pl* -) thermometer.
Thermosflasche ['tɛrmɔsflaʃə] *f* vacuum flask, thermos .
Thermostat [tɛrmo'ʃtaɪt] *m* (*pl* -en) thermostat.
These [teɪzə] *f* (*pl* -n) thesis.
Thrombose [trɔm'boɪzə] *f* (*pl* -n) thrombosis.
Thron [troɪn] *m* (*pl* -e) throne. **–erbe** *m* heir to the throne.
Thunfisch ['tuːnfiʃ] *m* tuna.
Thüringen ['tyːrɪŋən] *neut* Thuringia.
Thymian ['tyːmian] *m* thyme.
ticken ['tikən] *v* tick.
tief [tiːf] *adj* deep; (*Musik*) low(-pitched), bass; (*Stimme*) deep; (*Sinn*) profound; extreme. *adv* deep; (*Atmen*) deeply. **aus tiefstem Herzen** from the bottom of one's heart. **tief in der Nacht** at dead of night. **tiefbewegt** *adj* deeply moved. **Tief‖druckgebeit** *neut* low-pressure area. **–e** *f* depth. **–ebene** *f* lowlands *pl*. **tief‖gekühlt** *adj* deep-frozen. **–greifend** *adj* far-reaching. **Tief‖kühltruhe** *f* freezer, deep freeze. **–punkt** *m* low(est) point.
Tiegel ['tiːgəl] *m* (*pl* -) saucepan.
Tier [tiːr] *neut* (*pl* -e) animal, beast. **hohes Tier** (*umg.*) big shot. **Tier‖arzt** *m* veterinary surgeon, (*umg.*) vet. **–garten** *m* zoological gardens *pl*. **tierisch** *adj* animal; (*brutal*) bestial, brutal. **Tier‖kreis** *m* zodiac. **–welt** *f* animal kingdom, fauna. **–zucht** *f* livestock breeding.
Tiger ['tiːgər] *m* (*pl* -) tiger.
tilgen ['tilgən] *v* (*streichen*) delete, erase; (*ausrotten*) exterminate; (*Schuld*) pay off. **Tilgung** *f* (*pl* -en) deletion; extermination; discharge, repayment.
Tinte ['tintə] *f* ink. **–nklecks** *m* ink-stain.
Tip [tip] *m* (*pl* -s) hint; (*Sport*) tip.
tippen ['tipən] *v* tap; (*mit der Schreibmaschine*) type. **Tippfehler** *m* typing error.
Tisch [tiʃ] *m* (*pl* -e) table. **den Tisch decken/abdecken** lay/clear the table. **Tich‖gast** *m* diner, guest (at table). **–gesellschaft** *f* dinner party.
Tischler ['tiʃlər] *m* carpenter, cabinet-maker. **–arbeit** *f* carpentry.
Titel ['tiɪtəl] *m* (*pl* -) title. **–bild** *neut* frontispiece. **–kopf** *m* heading.
Toast [toɪst] *m* (*pl* -e) toast. **toasten** *v* toast. **Toaster** *m* (*pl* -) toaster.

toben ['toɪbən] *v* rage, rave. **tobsüchtig** *adj* raving, frantic.
Tochter ['tɔxtər] *f* (*pl* **Töchter**) daughter.
Tod [toɪt] *m* (*pl* -e) death. **Todes‖anzeige** *f* obituary. **–fall** *m* (a case of) death. **–kampf** *m* death throes *pl*. **–strafe** *f* death penalty. **–wunde** *f* mortal wound. **Todfeind** *m* deadly enemy. **tödlich** *adj* deadly, fatal, lethal. **todmüde** *adj* dead tired.
Toilette [toa'lɛtə] *f* (*pl* -n) toilet, lavatory; toilette; dressing-table. **–papier** *neut* toilet paper.
tolerant [tole'rant] *adj* tolerant. **Toleranz** *f* toleration. **tolerieren** *v* tolerate.
toll [tɔl] *adj* raving mad, crazy, wild; (*umg.*) fantastic. **Toll‖heit** *f* (*pl* -en) madness; fury. **–wut** *f* rabies.
Tölpel ['tœlpəl] *m* (*pl* -e) awkward person; oaf, boor.
Tomate [to'maɪtə] *f* (*pl* -n) tomato.
Ton[1] [toɪn] *m* (*pl* -e) clay.
Ton[2] *m* (*pl* **Töne**) sound; (*Musik*) tone, note; accent, stress; tone, fashion. **–art** *f* (*Musik*) key, pitch. **–band** *neut* magnetic tape. **–bandgerät** *neut* tape-recorder. **–blende** *f* tone control.
tönen ['tœɪnən] *v* ring, resound; (*Foto*) shade, tint.
Ton‖fall *m* intonation; (*Musik*) cadence. **–fülle** *f* volume (of sound). **–leiter** *f* (musical) scale. **–spur** *f* soundtrack.
Tonne ['tɔnə] *f* (*pl* -n) ton; cask, barrel.
Topf [tɔpf] *m* (*pl* **Töpfe**) pot.
Töpfchen ['tœpfçən] *neut* (*pl* -) (child's) potty. **Töpfer** *m* (*pl* -) potter. **–waren** *pl* pottery *sing*.
Tor[1] [toɪr] *m* (*pl* -en) fool.
Tor[2] *neut* (*pl* -e) gate; (*Sport*) goal. **–schütze** *m* (football) scorer.
Torf [tɔrf] *m* peat.
Torheit ['tɔrhait] *f* (*pl* -en) folly.
töricht ['tœɪriçt] *adj* foolish. **Törin** *f* (*pl* -nen) fool, foolish woman.
torkeln ['tɔrkəln] *v* stagger, reel.
Torpedo [tɔr'peɪdo] *m* (*pl* -s) torpedo. **–boot** *neut* torpedo boat.
Torte ['tɔrtə] *f* (*pl* -n) (fruit) flan, tart, gâteau.
Tor‖waächter *m* (*pl* -) gatekeeper. **–wart** *m* goalkeeper.
tot [toɪt] *adj* dead.
total [to'taɪl] *adj* total, complete.
Tote(r) ['toɪtə(r)] *m* dead person.

töten ['tœɪtən] v kill.
Toten‖bett neut deathbed. **–gräber** m gravedigger. **–hemd** neut shroud. **–wagen** m hearse.
totgeboren ['toɪtgəbɔɪrən] adj stillborn. **sich totlachen** v split one's sides laughing. **totschießen** v shoot dead.
Totschlag ['toɪtʃlak] m manslaughter. **tot‖schlagen** v slay, kill; (Zeit) waste (time). **–schweigen** v hush up. **–sicher** adj absolutely or dead certain.
Tötung ['tœɪtuŋ] f (pl -en) killing.
Tour [tuɪr] f (pl -en) tour, trip. **–ismus** m tourism. **–ist** m (pl -en) tourist.
Trab [traɪp] m trot. **traben** v trot.
Tracht [traxt] f (pl -en) costume, dress.
Tradition [traditsiˈoɪn] f (pl -en) tradition. **traditionell** adj traditional.
träge ['trɛɪgə] adj (faul) lazy; (langsam) ponderous, slow; (schläfrig) sleepy.
*tragen ['traɪgən] v carry; (Kleider) wear; (stützen) support; (ertragen) endure, bear.
Träger ['trɛɪgər] m (pl -) carrier; (Mensch) porter; (Balken) girder.
Trägheit ['trɛɪkhait] f laziness; (Langsamkeit) slowness.
tragisch ['traɪgiʃ] adj tragic. **Tragödie** f (pl -n) tragedy.
Trainer ['trɛɪnər] m (pl -) (Sport) coach, trainer. **trainieren** v train. **Training** neut training. **–sanzug** m track suit.
Traktor ['traktɔr] m (pl -en) tractor.
trampeln ['trampəln] v trample, stamp.
trampen ['trɛmpən] v hitchhike.
Tran [traɪn] m (pl -e) whale oil.
tranchieren [trãˈʃiɪrən] v carve. **Tranchiermesser** neut carving knife.
Träne ['trɛɪnə] f (pl -n) tear.
Trank [traŋk] m (pl Tränke) drink.
tränken ['trɛŋkən] v water; (durchtränken) soak.
transatlantisch [transatˈlantiʃ] adj transatlantic.
Transmission [transmisiˈoɪn] f (pl -en) transmission.
Transport [transˈpɔrt] m (pl -e) transportation. **transportieren** v transport. **Transportunternehmen** neut haulage or shipping company.
Tratte ['tratə] f (pl -n) bill of exchange, draft.
Traube ['traubə] f (pl -n) grape; bunch of grapes. **Trauben‖lese** f vintage. **–saft** m grape juice. **–zucker** m glucose.

trauen ['trauən] v trust; (Ehepaar) marry, join in wedlock. **sich trauen** dare.
Trauer ['trauər] f sorrow, grief; (für Tote) mourning. **–anzeige** f death notice. **–gottesdienst** m funeral service. **trauern** v grieve, mourn. **Trauer‖spiel** neut tragedy. **–weide** f weeping willow. **traurig** adj sad.
Traufe ['traufə] f (pl -n) eaves pl. **aus dem Regen in die Traufe** out of the frying pan into the fire. **Traufrinne** f gutter.
traulich ['trauliç] adj snug, cosy, comfortable.
Traum [traum] m (pl Träume) dream. **–bild** neut vision.
träumen ['trɔymən] v dream. **Träumer** m (pl -) dreamer. **–ei** f (pl -en) daydream, reverie. **träumerisch** adj dreamy.
Trau‖ring m wedding ring.
*treffen ['trɛfən] v (begegnen) meet; (erreichen) hit; (betreffen) concern; (Vorkehrungen) make; (Maßnahmen) take. **sich treffen** meet; (zufällig geschehen) happen. **Treffen** neut meeting. **treffend** adj striking; (Antwort) pertinent. **Treffpunkt** m meeting place.
*treiben ['traibən] v drive, move; (drängen) urge, impel; (Metall) work; (Pflanzen) force; (tun) do, occupy oneself with; (Blüte) blossom; (im Wasser) float. **treibend** adj driving; (im Wasser) floating. **Treib‖er** m driver; (Vieh) drover. **–haus** neut hothouse. **–kraft** f moving force. **–stoff** m fuel.
trennbar ['trɛnbaɪr] adj separable. **trennen** v separate; (abtrennen) sever, cut; (Telef) cut off. **sich trennen** part, separate. **Trennung** f (pl -en) separation.
Treppe ['trɛpə] f (pl -n) staircase, stairs pl. **–ngeländer** neut handrail, banister.
*treten ['treɪtən] v tread, step; (betreten) step on; (stoßen) kick. **Trethebel** m treadle.
treu [trɔy] adj loyal, faithful, true; (redlich) honest, sincere. **Treubruch** m disloyalty, breach of faith. **Treue** f loyalty, faithfulness. **treu‖lich** adj loyal, faithful. **–los** adj disloyal, faithless.
Tribüne [triˈbyɪnə] f (pl -n) platform; (für Zuschauer) gallery.
Trichter ['triçtər] m (pl -) funnel; (Bombe) crater.
Trick [trik] m (pl -s) trick. **–film** m animated cartoon.

Trieb [triːp] *m* (*pl* -e) force, drive; (*Antrieb*) impulse; (*Bot*) shoot; (*Instinkt*) instinct.

***triefen** ['triːfən] *v* trickle, drip. **triefnaß** *adj* dripping wet.

triftig ['triftiç] *adj* convincing, plausible.

Triller ['trilər] *m* (*pl* -) trill. **trillern** *v* trill.

trinkbar ['triŋkbaːr] *adj* drinkable, potable. **trinken** *v* drink. **Trink‖er** *m* (*pl* -) drinker. **–geld** *neut* tip. **–halm** *m* (drinking) straw. **–spruch** *m* toast.

Tripper ['tripər] *m* (*pl* -) gonorrhoea.

Tritt [trit] *m* (*pl* -e) step, tread; (*Stoß*) kick; (*Fußspur*) footprint. **–leiter** *f* step-ladder.

Triumph [tri'umf] *m* (*pl* -e) triumph.

trocken ['trɔkən] *adj* dry. **Trockenheit** *f* dryness. **trocknen** *v* dry. **Trockner** *m* (*pl* -) drier.

Trödel ['trœdəl] *m* junk, rubbish. **trödeln** *v* dawdle; (*handeln*) trade in old junk.

Trommel ['trɔməl] *f* (*pl* -n) drum. **–fell** *neut* drumskin; (*Anat*) eardrum. **trommeln** *v* drum. **Trommler** *m* (*pl* -) drummer.

Trompete [trɔm'peːtə] *f* (*pl* -n) trumpet.

Tropen ['troːpən] *pl* tropics.

tröpfeln ['trœpfəln] *v* trickle, drip.

Tropfen ['trɔpfən] *m* (*pl* -) drop.

tropisch ['troːpiʃ] *adj* tropical.

Trost [troːst] *m* consolation, solace, comfort.

trösten ['trœstən] *v* console, solace, comfort. **sich trösten mit** take comfort in.

trostlos ['troːstloːs] *adj* disconsolate.

Tröstung ['trœstuŋ] *f* (*pl* -en) consolation, comfort.

Trott [trɔt] *m* (*pl* -e) trot.

Trottel ['trɔtəl] *m* (*pl* -) idiot, fool.

trotz [trɔts] *prep* despite, in spite of. **Trotz** *m* defiance; (*Eigensinn*) obstinacy. **trotzdem** *conj, adv* nevertheless. **trotzen** *v* defy; (*widersetzlich sein*) be obstinate. **trotzig** *adj* defiant, obstinate.

trüb(e) ['tryːb(ə)] *adj* cloudy, opaque; (*glanzlos*) dull; (*fig*) gloomy. **trüben** *v* cloud, dim, darken. **Trübsinn** *m* gloom, depression. **trübsinnig** *adj* gloomy, miserable.

Trug [truːk] *m* (*Täuschung*) fraud, deceit; (*Sinnes*) delusion.

***trügen** ['tryːgən] *v* be deceptive; (*betrügen*) deceive. **trügerisch** *adj* treacherous, deceitful.

Truhe ['truːə] *f* (*pl* -n) chest, trunk.

Trümmer *pl* ruins, debris *sing*.

Trumpf [trumpf] *m* (*pl* **Trümpfe**) trump. **–karte** *f* trump (card).

Trunk [truŋk] *m* (*pl* **Trünke**) drink. **–enheit** *f* drunkenness, intoxication. **–sucht** *f* alcoholism.

Trupp [trup] *m* (*pl* -s) troop, gang, band. **Truppe** *f* (*pl* -n) (*Theater*) company; (*Mil*) (combat) troops *pl*. **Truppen** *pl* troops.

Truthahn ['truːthaːn] *m* turkey-cock.

Tscheche ['tʃɛçə] *m* (*pl* -n), **Tschechin** *f* (*pl* -nen) Czech. **tschechisch** *adj* Czech. **Tschechoslowakei** *f* Czechoslovakia.

Tuberkulose [tubɛrku'loːzə] *f* tuberculosis, TB.

Tuch [tuːx] **1** *neut* (*pl* -e) cloth, fabric. **2** *neut* (*pl* **Tücher**) (piece of) cloth; (*zum Trocknen*) towel. **–händler** *m* draper.

tüchtig ['tyçtiç] *adj* capable, able; (*leistungsfähig*) efficient; (*fleißig*) hard-working; (*klug*) clever. **Tüchtigkeit** *f* ability; efficiency; cleverness.

Tücke ['tykə] *f* (*pl* -n) spite, malice. **tückisch** *adj* spiteful.

Tugend ['tuːgənt] *f* (*pl* -en) virtue. **tugendhaft** *adj* virtuous.

Tulpe ['tulpə] *f* (*pl* -n) tulip.

***tun** [tuːn] *v* do; (*machen*) make. **tun als ob** pretend to. **nur so tun** pretend. **zu tun haben** be busy, have things to do. **groß tun** boast. **etwas in etwas tun** put something into something.

Tünche ['tynçə] *f* (*pl* -n) whitewash, distemper.

Tunke ['tuŋkə] *f* (*pl* -n) sauce. **tunken** *v* dip, dunk.

Tunnel ['tunəl] *m* (*pl* -) tunnel.

Tupfen ['tupfən] *m* (*pl* -) dot, spot. **tupfen** *v* dot.

Tür [tyːr] *f* (*pl* -en) door.

Türkis [tyr'kiːs] *m* (*pl* -e) turquoise.

Türklinke ['tyrkliŋkə] *f* doorhandle.

Turm [turm] *m* (*pl* **Türme**) tower; (*Schach*) rook, castle; (*Elek*) pylon. **–spitze** *f* spire, steeple.

turnen ['turnən] *v* do gymnastics. **Turnen** *neut* gymnastics. **Turnhalle** *f* gymnasium.

Turnier [tur'niːr] *neut* (*pl* -e) tournament.

Türschwelle ['tyrʃvelə] *f* threshold.

Tusche ['tuʃə] *f* (*pl* -n) Indian ink, drawing ink.

tuscheln ['tuʃəln] *v* whisper.

Tüte ['tʏtə] *f* (*pl* **-n**) paperbag.
tuten ['tuːtən] *v* hoot, honk.
Typ [tʏp] *m* (*pl* **-en**) type. **-e** *f* (*Druck*) type.
Typhus ['tyːfus] *m* typhoid (fever).
typisch ['tyːpiʃ] *adj* typical.
Tyrann [ty'ran] *m* (*pl* **-en**) tyrant. **-ei** *f* tyranny. **tyrann‖isch** *adj* tyrannical. **-isieren** *v* tyrannize.

U

U-Bahn ['uːbaɪn] *f* underground (railway), (*US*) subway.
übel ['yːbəl] *adj* evil, wicked; (*schlecht*) bad; (*unwohl*) sick, ill. *mir wird übel* I feel sick. *übel daran sein* be in a bad way. **Übel** *neut* (*pl* **-**) evil; (*Mißgeschick*) misfortune; (*Krankheit*) sickness. **übel‖gelaunt** *adj* bad-tempered. **-gesinnt** *adj* evil-minded. **-nehmen** *v* be offended by, take amiss. **-riechen** *v* smell bad.
üben ['yːbən] *v* practise.
über ['yːbər] *prep* over, above; (*quer über*) across; (*während*) during. (*betreffend*) about; (*mehrals*) over; (*weg*) via.
überall [yːbər'al] *adv* everywhere.
überanstrengen [yːbər'anʃtrɛŋən] *v* overwork. *sich überanstrengen* overexert oneself. **Überanstrengung** *f* overexertion.
überarbeiten [yːbər'aɪrbaitən] *v* revise. *sich überarbeiten* overwork, work too hard.
überbelichten ['yːbərbəliçtən] *v* (*Foto*) overexpose.
***überbieten** [yːbər'biːtən] *v* outbid; (*fig*) surpass, beat.
Überbleibsel ['yːbərblaipsəl] *neut* (*pl* **-**) remainder.
Überblick ['yːbərblik] *m* survey, overall view.
***überbringen** [yːbər'briŋən] *v* deliver.
überbrücken [yːbər'brykən] *v* bridge.
überdies [yːbər'diːs] *adv* besides.
überdrüssig ['yːbərdrusiç] *adj* sick (of), disgusted (with).
übereifrig ['yːbəraifriç] *adj* too eager, over-zealous.
übereilen [yːbər'ailən] *v* rush, hurry too much. **übereilt** *adj* hasty; (*Benehmen*) inconsiderate.
übereinander [yːbəraɪn'andər] *adv* one

upon another. **-greifen** *v* overlap. **-legen** *v* lay one upon another.
***übereinkommen** [yːbər'ainkɔmən] *v* agree. **Überein‖kommen** *neut* (*pl* **-**) *or* **kunft** *f* agreement.
übereinstimmen [yːbər'ainʃtimən] *v* concur, agree; (*zueinander passen*) correspond, tally. **Übereinstimmung** *f* agreement, concord.
überempfindlich ['yːbərɛmpfintliç] *adj* hypersensitive.
***überfahren** ['yːbərfaɪrən] take *or* drive across. (*Mot*) run over. **Überfahrt** *f* crossing.
Überfall ['yːbərfal] *m* (sudden) attack, assault. **überfallen** *v* attack (suddenly). **Überfallkommando** *neut* flying squad.
Überfluß ['yːbərflus] *m* excess, overabundance. **überflüssig** *adj* superfluous.
überführen ['yːbərfyɪrən] *v* transport, convey. [-'ryɪrən] (*Jur*) convict. **Überführung** *f* transport; (*Brücke*) viaduct, overpass.
Übergabe ['yːbərgaɪbə] *f* surrender, handing-over.
Übergang ['yːbərgaŋ] *m* crossing, passage; (*fig*) transition.
***übergeben** ['yːbərgeɪbən] *v* deliver, hand over; (*Mil*) surrender. *sich übergeben* vomit.
übergehen ['yːbərgeɪən] *v* cross (over); (*werden*) pass into, become. [-'geɪən] omit, overlook.
Übergewicht ['yːbərgeviçt] *neut* overweight.
***übergreifen** ['yːbərgraifən] *v* overlap. *übergreifen auf* encroach on.
***überhandnehmen** [yːbər'hantneɪmən] *v* increase (rapidly).
überhaupt [yːbər'haupt] *adv* in general. *wenn überhaupt* if at all. *überhaupt nicht* not at all. *überhaupt kein ...* no ... whatever.
***überheben** [yːbər'heɪbən] *v* exempt, spare. *einer Mühe überheben* spare the trouble. **überheblich** *adj* presumptuous, arrogant.
überholen [yːbər'hoɪlən] *v* overtake; (*Tech*) overhaul. **überholt** *adj* outmoded.
überhören [yːbər'hœɪrən] *v* not hear; (*ignorieren*) ignore, let pass.
überirdisch ['yːbərirdiʃ] *adj* celestial; (*übernatürlich*) supernatural.
überkochen ['yːbərkɔxən] *v* boil over.

*überlassen [yːbərˈlasən] v leave.
überlaufen [ˈyːbərlaufən] v overflow; (Mil) defect.
überleben [yːbərˈleːbən] v survive.
überlegen [yːbərˈleɪgən] v consider, reflect. adj superior. Überlegenheit f superiority. überlegt adj considered, deliberate. Überlegung f consideration, reflection.
überleiten [ˈyːbərlaitən] v lead on to; (fig) convert.
überliefern [yːbərˈliːfərn] v deliver; (der Nachwelt) pass on, hand down.
Übermacht [ˈyːbərmaxt] f superiority. übermächtig adj overwhelming, too powerful.
Übermaß [ˈyːbərmaɪs] neut excess. übermäßig adj excessive.
Übermensch [ˈyːbərmɛnʃ] m superman. übermenschlich adj superhuman.
übermitteln [yːbərˈmitəln] v convey.
übermorgen [ˈyːbərmɔrgən] adv the day after tomorrow.
übermüdet [yːbərˈmyːdət] adj overtired.
Übermut [ˈyːbərmuːt] m arrogance; (Ausgelassenheit) high spirits pl. übermütig adj arrogant; high-spirited.
übernächst [yːbərˈnɛːçst] adj the next but one, the one after.
übernachten [yːbərˈnaxtən] v spend the night, stay overnight.
übernatürlich [ˈyːbərnatuːrliç] adj supernatural.
*übernehmen [yːbərˈneːmən] v take over; (Pflicht) undertake.
überprüfen [yːbərˈpryːfən] v verify, check, examine. Überprüfung f verification, check.
überqueren [yːbərˈkveːrən] v cross.
überragen [yːbərˈraːgən] v rise above, tower above; (fig) surpass, outdo. −d adj excellent.
übersinnlich [ˈyːbərzinliç] adj spiritual, transcendental.
überspannen [yːbərˈʃpanən] v overstretch, overtighten; (fig) go too far, exaggerate; (bedecken) stretch over. überspannt adj eccentric.
*überspringen [yːbərˈʃpriŋən] v jump over; (auslassen) omit, skip.
*überstehen [yːbərˈʃteːən] v survive.
*übersteigen [yːbərˈʃtaigən] v climb over, surmount; (fig) exceed.
Überstunden [ˈyːbərʃtundən] pl overtime

sing. Überstunden machen v work overtime. überstürzen [yːbərˈʃtyrtsən] v rush, hurry. sich überstürzen rush, act too hastily. überstürzt adj hasty.
Übertrag [ˈyːbərtraɪk] m (pl Überträge) balance brought forward. übertragen v carry over; (Komm) bring forward; (befördern) transport; (übersetzen) translate; (Radio, Med) transmit. Übertragung f transfer; (Radio, Med) transmission; (Übersetzung) translation.
*übertreffen [yːbərˈtrɛfən] v excel, surpass.
*übertreiben [yːbərˈtraibən] v exaggerate. Übertreibung f exaggeration.
*übertreten [yːbərˈtreːtən] v overstep. [ˈyːbər-] (Fluß) overflow; (Sport) step over.
übertrieben [yːbərˈtriːbən] adj exaggerated.
Übervölkerung [yːbərˈfœlkəruŋ] f overpopulation.
überwachen [yːbərˈvaxən] v supervise. Überwachung f supervision.
überwältigen [yːbərˈvɛltigən] v overpower, overwhelm. −d adj overwhelming. Überwältigung f overpowering, conquest.
*überweisen [yːbərˈvaizən] v transfer. Überweisung f transfer; (Post-) money order.
überwiegend [yːbərˈviːgənt] adj preponderant. adv primarily, mainly.
*überwinden [yːbərˈvindən] v overcome. sich überwinden (zu) bring oneself (to). Überwindung f overcoming, conquest.
überwuchern [yːbərˈvuxərn] v overrun, overgrow.
überzeugen [yːbərˈtsɔygən] v convince. −d adj convincing. überzeugt adj convinced, sure. Überzeugung f conviction.
*überziehen [ˈyːbərtsiːən] v pull over, put on. [-ˈtsiːən] cover; (Konto) overdraw; (Bett) change the sheets of). Überziehung f overdraft.
Überzug [ˈyːbərtsuːk] m cover(ing).
üblich [ˈyːpliç] adj usual.
U-Boot [ˈuːboɪt] neut submarine.
übrig [ˈyːbriç] adj remaining, left(-over). die Übrigen the rest, the others. übrig haben have left (over). −bleiben v remain, be left (over). −ens adv by the way, incidentally.
Übung [ˈyːbuŋ] f (pl -en) exercise; (Üben) practice.

Ufer ['uɪfər] *neut* (*pl* -) bank, shore.
-damm *m* embankment.

Uhr [uɪr] *f* (*pl* -en) clock; (*Armbanduhr*) watch; (*Gas, usw.*) meter; (*Kraftstoff*) gauge. **-armband** *neut* watch strap. **-werk** *neut* clockwork. **-zeiger** *m* (clock) hand. **-zeigersinn** *m* clockwise direction. **im Uhrzeigersinn** *adv* clockwise. **entgegen dem Uhrzeigersinn** *adv* anticlockwise (*US*) counterclockwise.

Ulk [ulk] *m* (*pl* -e) fun, lark. **ulkig** *adj* funny.

Ulme ['ulmə] *f* (*pl* -n) elm.

um [um] *prep* (*zeitlich, örtlich*) around, about; (*wegen*) for; (*Maßangaben*) by; (*ungefähr*) about. *adv* about. *conj* in order to. **um zu** (in order) to. **um diese Zeit** around this time. **um so besser** so much the better. **bitten um** ask for. **um 2 cm länger** longer by 2 cm.

umändern ['umɛndərn] *v* change, alter. **Umänderung** *f* change, alteration.

umarmen [um'armən] *v* embrace. **Umarmung** *f* embrace.

Umbau ['umbau] *m* alteration, rebuilding, conversion. **umbauen** *v* rebuild, alter, convert.

umbilden ['umbildən] *v* transform, remodel. **Umbildung** *f* transformation.

*umbinden** ['umbindən] *v* tie (up), tie around (oneself), put on.

Umblick ['umblik] *m* panorama, survey. **umblicken** *v* (*sich umblicken*) look around.

*umbringen** ['umbriŋən] *v* kill. (*sich umbringen*) commit suicide.

umdrehen ['umdreiən] *v* turn over *or* around. **sich umdrehen** rotate, spin; (*Person*) turn around. **Umdrehung** *f* turn, rotation.

*umfahren** ['umfaɪrən] *v* run over, knock down; [-'faɪrən] drive around.

*umfallen** ['umfalən] *v* fall over.

Umfang ['umfaŋ] *m* (*pl* **Umfänge**) (*Kreis*) circumference; (*Ausdehnung*) extent; (*Größe*) size. **umfangreich** *adj* extensive.

umfassen [um'fasən] *v* put one's arm around, hold, clasp; (*fig*) embrace, cover; (*Mil*) encircle. **-d** *adj* comprehensive.

Umfrage ['umfraɪgə] *f* poll, inquiry.

Umgang ['umgaŋ] *m* circuit, turn; (*Verkehr*) intercourse, (social) contact. **umgänglich** *adj* sociable.

*umgeben** [um'geɪbən] *v* surround.

Umgebung *f* surroundings *pl*, environment.

*umgehen** *v* ['umgeɪən] go around; (*behandeln*) handle, deal with; (*mit Menschen*) associate (with). [-'geɪən] go around; (*vermeiden*) avoid.

umgekehrt ['umgəkeɪrt] *adv* the other way round. *adj* inverted, reverse(d).

umgestalten ['umgəʃtaltən] *v* alter, transform; (*umorganisieren*) reorganize. **Umgestaltung** *f* alteration, transformation; reorganization.

Umhang ['umhaŋ] *m* wrap, cape.

umher [um'heɪr] *adv* about, (a)round. **-blicken** *v* look around. **-laufen** run around.

umhüllen [um'hylən] *v* wrap up.

Umkehr ['umkeɪr] *f* turning back, return; (*fig*) change, conversion. **umkehren** *v* turn back, return; (*umdrehen*) turn over; (*fig*) reform.

umkippen ['umkipən] *v* tip over.

umklammern [um'klamərn] *v* clasp.

umkleiden ['umklaidən] *v* **sich umkleiden** change (one's clothes). **Umkleideraum** *m* changing room.

*umkommen** ['umkɔmən] *v* die, perish, be killed; (*verderben*) go bad.

Umkreis ['umkrais] *m* neighbourhood, vicinity. **umkreisen** *v* (en)circle.

Umlauf ['umlauf] *m* circulation. **im Umlauf** in circulation.

Umlaut ['umlaut] *m* vowel modification.

umleiten ['umlaitən] *v* divert. **Umleitung** *f* diversion.

umlernen ['umlɛrnən] *v* learn anew, relearn.

umliegend ['umliːgənt] *adj* surrounding.

umordnen ['umɔrdnən] *v* rearrange.

umpflanzen ['umpflantsən] *v* transplant.

umrahmen [um'raɪmən] *v* frame.

umrechnen ['umrɛçnən] *v* convert, (ex)change. **Umrechnung** *f* conversion. **-skurs** *m* rate of exchange.

*umreißen** ['umraisən] *v* pull down, demolish. [-'raisən] sketch, outline.

umringen [um'riŋən] *v* surround.

Umriß ['umris] *m* sketch, outline. **umrissen** *adj* defined.

umrühren ['umryɪrən] *v* stir.

ums [ums] *prep* + *art* **um das**.

Umsatz ['umzats] *m* turnover, sales.

umsäumen ['umzɔymən] *v* hem. [-'zɔymən] enclose, surround.

umschalten ['umʃaltən] v (fig) switch or change over. **Umschaltung** f (fig) change-over, switch.

umschauen ['umʃauən] v **sich umschauen** look around.

umschiffen [um'ʃifən] v circumnavigate; trans-ship. **Umschiffung** f circumnavigation.

Umschlag ['umʃlaɪk] m cover; (Brief) envelope; (Buch) wrapper, jacket; (Hose) turn-up; (Kleid) hem; (Veränderung) change; (Komm) turnover. **umschlagen** v change (Boot) capsize; (Wind) veer; (umwenden) turn over; (umwerfen) knock down.

*****umschließen** [um'ʃliːsən] v surround, enclose.

*****umschreiben** ['umʃraibən] v rewrite; transcribe. [-'ʃraibən] paraphrase.

umschulen ['umʃuːlən] v retrain; (neue Schule) send to a new school. **Umschulung** f retraining.

Umschwung ['umʃvuŋ] m turn; (fig) sudden change, reversal.

*****umsehen** ['umzeːən] v **sich umsehen** look around; (rückwärts) look round.

umsetzen ['umzɛtsən] v transpose; (Pflanze) transplant; (verkaufen) sell.

Umsicht ['umzɪçt] f prudence, circumspection. **umsichtig** adj prudent, circumspect.

umsiedeln ['umziːdəln] v resettle. **Umsiedlung** f resettlement.

umsonst [um'zɔnst] adv free (of charge); (vergebens) in vain.

Umstand ['umʃtant] m circumstance. **in anderen Umständen** (umg.) expecting, in the family way. **ohne Umstände** without fuss. **nähere Umstände** further particulars. **unter diesen Umständen** in these circumstances.

*****umsteigen** ['umʃtaigən] v change (trains, buses, etc.). **Umsteiger** m through-ticket.

*****umstoßen** ['umʃtoːsən] v overturn, knock over; (ungültig machen) revoke; (Pläne) upset.

Umsturz ['umʃturts] m overthrow; (Pol) revolution. **umstürzen** v overturn; (Regierung) overthrow; (umfallen) fall over.

Umtausch ['umtauʃ] m exchange. **umtauschen** v exchange, (umg.) swap.

umwälzen ['umvɛltsən] v roll over; (gründlich ändern) revolutionize.

umwandeln ['umwandəln] v change, transform; (Elek) transform, (Komm) convert.

Umweg ['umveːk] m detour, long way round.

Umwelt ['umvɛlt] f environment. **umweltfreundlich** adj non-polluting, conservationist. **Umweltverschmutzung** f (environmental) pollution.

*****umwenden** ['umvɛndən] v turn over; (Wagen) turn round.

*****umwerben** [um'vɛrbən] v court.

*****umwerfen** ['umvɛrfən] v upset, overturn; (Kleider) wrap round oneself.

umwickeln [um'vikəln] v wrap round.

umzäunen [um'tsɔynən] v fence in.

*****umziehen** ['umtsiːən] v move (house); (Kind) change (clothes). **sich umziehen** change (clothes).

Umzug ['umtsuːk] m move, removal; procession.

unabänderlich [unap'ɛndərliç] adj unalterable.

unabhängig ['unaphɛŋiç] adj independent. **Unabhängig‖e(r)** (Pol) independent. **–keit** f independence.

unabkömmlich ['unapkœmliç] adj indispensable.

unablässig ['unaplɛsiç] adj incessant.

unabsichtlich ['unapziçtliç] adj unintentional.

unachtsam ['unaxtsaɪm] adj careless.

unähnlich ['unɛːnliç] adj unlike, dissimilar (to).

unangemessen ['unaŋgəmɛsən] adj unsuitable; (Forderung) unreasonable.

unangenehm ['unaŋgəneɪm] adj unpleasant; (peinlich) awkward.

Unannehmlichkeit ['unannɛɪmliçkait] f unpleasantness; (lästige Mühe) inconvenience.

unansehnlich ['unanzeːnliç] adj unsightly.

unanständig ['unanʃtɛndiç] adj indecent, improper. **Unanständigkeit** f indecency.

unartig ['unaɪrtiç] adj badly-behaved, rude.

unauffällig ['unauffɛliç] adj inconspicuous.

unaufgefordert ['unaufgəfɔrdət] adj unbidden, unasked.

unaufhörlich ['unaufhœɪrliç] adj incessant.

unaufmerksam ['unaufmɛrkzaɪm] adj inattentive.

unaufrichtig ['unaufriçtiç] *adj* insincere.

unausgeglichen ['unausgəgliçən] *adj* uneven, unbalanced.

unbändig ['unbɛndiç] *adj* tremendous.

unbeabsichtigt ['unbəapziçtiçt] *adj* unintentional.

unbeachtet ['unbəaxtət] *adj* unnoticed, unheeded.

unbedacht ['unbədaxt] *adj* inconsiderate, thoughtless, rash.

unbedeutend ['unbədɔytənt] *adj* unimportant, insignificant.

unbedingt ['unbədiŋt] *adj* absolute, unconditional. *adv* by all means.

unbefahrbar ['unbəfaɪrbaɪr] *adj* impassable.

unbefriedigend ['unbəfriːdigənt] *adj* unsatisfactory.

unbefugt ['unbəfukt] *adj* unauthorized.

unbegreiflich ['unbəgraifliç] *adj* incomprehensible, inconceivable.

Unbehagen ['unbəhaɪgən] *neut* uneasiness, discomfort. **unbehaglich** *adj* uneasy, uncomfortable.

unbeholfen ['unbəhɔlfən] *adj* clumsy, awkward.

unbekannt ['unbəkant] *adj* unknown.

unbekümmert [unbə'kymərt] *adj* unconcerned.

unbemerkt ['unbəmɛrkt] *adj* unnoticed, unobserved.

unbemittelt ['unbəmitəlt] *adj* poor, without means.

unbequem ['unbəkveɪm] *adj* uncomfortable.

umberechenbar ['unbəreçənbaɪr] *adj* incalculable.

unberechtigt ['unbəreçtiçt] *adj* (*ungerechtfertigt*) unjustified; (*unbefugt*) unauthorized. *adv* without authority.

unberührt ['unbəryɪrt] *adj* untouched, intact.

unbeschränkt ['unbəʃrɛnkt] *adj* unlimited, unrestricted.

unbeschreiblich ['unbəʃraipliç] *adj* indescribable.

unbesonnen ['unbəzɔnən] *adj* imprudent; (*unüberlegt*) rash, hasty.

unbeständig ['unbəʃtɛndiç] *adj* unsettled, unstable; (*nicht dauernd*) inconstant.

unbestimmt ['unbəʃtimt] *adj* indefinite.

unbestreitbar [unbə'ʃtraitbaɪr] *adj* indisputable.

unbestritten ['unbəʃtritən] *adj* undisputed, uncontested.

unbeteiligt ['unbətailiçt] *adj* unconcerned; (*nicht beteiligt*) uninvolved.

unbeweglich ['unbəveɪkliç] *adj* immovable; (*bewegungslos*) motionless.

unbewußt ['unbəvust] *adj* unconscious.

unbiegsam ['unbiːkzaɪm] *adj* unbending.

unbrauchbar ['unbrauxbaɪr] *adj* useless.

und [unt] *conj* and.

undankbar ['undaŋkbaɪr] *adj* ungrateful; (*Arbeit*) thankless. **Undankbarkeit** *f* ingratitude.

undenkbar [un'dɛŋkbaɪr] *adj* unthinkable.

undeutlich ['undɔytliç] *adj* unclear, indistinct.

undurchdringlich ['undurçdriŋliç] *adj* impenetrable.

undurchlässig ['undurçlɛsiç] *adj* impermeable; (*Wasser-*) water-proof.

undurchsichtig ['undurçziçtiç] *adj* opaque; (*Person*) inscrutable.

uneben ['uneɪbən] *adj* uneven, rough.

unecht ['uneçt] *adj* not genuine, false; (*künstlich*) artificial.

unehelich ['uneːliç] *adj* illegitimate.

unehrlich ['uneɪrliç] *adj* dishonest. **Unehrlichkeit** *f* dishonesty.

unendlich [un'entliç] *adj* endless, infinite.

unentbehrlich [unent'beɪrliç] *adj* indispensable.

unentschieden ['unentʃiːdən] *adj* undecided; (*Fussball*) drawn. **Unentschiedenheit** *f* indecision.

unentschlossen ['unentʃlɔsən] *adj* undecided, irresolute. **Unentschlossenheit** *f* indecision, irresolution.

unentwickelt ['unentvikəlt] *adj* undeveloped.

unentzündbar ['unentzyntbaɪr] *adj* non-flammable.

unerbittlich [unɛr'bitliç] *adj* relentless.

unerfahren ['unɛrfaiərən] *adj* inexperienced.

unerhört [unɛr'hœɪrt] *adj* unheard-of, outrageous.

unerklärbar ['unɛrkleɪrbaɪr] *adj* inexplicable.

unerläßlich [unɛr'lɛsliç] *adj* indispensable.

unerlaubt ['unɛrlaupt] *adj* not permitted; (*ungesetzlich*) forbidden, illegal.

unermeßlich [unɛr'mɛsliç] *adj* immense, immeasurable.

unermüdlich [unɛr'myɪtliç] *adj* indefatigable, untiring.

unerreichbar ['unɛraiçbaːr] *adj* unattainable. **unerreicht** *adj* unequalled, unrivalled.

unersättlich ['unɛrzɛtliç] *adj* insatiable.

unerschrocken ['unɛrʃrɔkən] *adj* fearless, undaunted.

unerschütterlich ['unɛrʃytərliç] *adj* imperturbable, unshakeable.

unersetzlich ['unɛrzɛtsliç] *adj* irreplaceable.

unerträglich ['unɛrtrɛːkliç] *adj* unbearable, intolerable.

unerwartet ['unɛrvaːrtət] *adj* unexpected.

unfähig ['unfɛːiç] *adj* incapable; *(nicht instande)* unable. **Unfähigkeit** *f* incapacity; inability.

unfair ['unfɛːr] *adj* unfair.

Unfall ['unfal] *m* accident. **–station** *f* first-aid post. **–verhütung** *f* accident prevention.

unfaßbar ['unfasbaːr] *adj* inconceivable.

unfehlbar [un'feːlbaːr] *adj* infallible.

unflätig ['unflɛːtiç] *adj* filthy, coarse.

unfreundlich ['unfrɔyntliç] *adj* unfriendly; *(barsch)* rude; *(Wetter)* disagreeable, inclement. **Unfreundlichkeit** *f* unfriendliness, unkindness.

Unfug ['unfuːk] *m* misconduct; *(Dummheiten)* mischief.

unfühlbar ['unfyːlbaːr] *adj* intangible, impalpable.

Ungar ['uŋgar] *m (pl -n)*, **Ungarin** *f (pl -nen)* Hungarian. **ungarisch** *adj* Hungarian. **Ungarn** *neut* Hungary.

ungastlich ['ungastliç] *adj* inhospitable.

ungeachtet ['ungəaxtət] *adj* overlooked, disregarded. *prep* notwithstanding.

ungebeten ['ungəbeːtən] *adj* uninvited.

ungebildet ['ungəbildət] *adj* uneducated; *(Benehmen)* ill-mannered.

ungebührend ['ungəbyːrənt] *or* **ungebührlich** *adj* improper, unbecoming.

ungebunden ['ungəbundən] *adj* unbound; *(fig)* unrestrained, free.

Ungeduld ['ungədult] *f* impatience. **ungeduldig** *adj* impatient.

ungeeignet ['ungəaiknət] *adj* unsuitable.

ungefähr ['ungəfɛːr] *adv* approximately, about, roughly. *adj* approximate.

ungefährlich ['ungəfɛːrliç] *adj* not dangerous.

ungeheuer ['ungəhɔyər] *adj* enormous. **Ungeheuer** *neut (pl -)* monster.

ungehorsam ['ungəhoːrzaːm] *adj* disobedient. **Ungehorsam** *m* disobedience.

ungekünstelt ['ungəkyːnstəlt] *adj* unaffected, natural.

ungelegen ['ungəleːgən] *adj* inconvenient.

ungelernt ['ungəlɛrnt] *adj* unskilled.

ungemächlich ['ingəmɛçliç] *adj* uncomfortable, unpleasant.

ungemein ['ungəmain] *adj* uncommon, extraordinary.

ungemütlich ['ungəmyːtliç] *adj* uncomfortable; *(grob)* unpleasant, nasty.

ungenannt ['ungənant] *adj* unnamed.

ungeniert ['unʒəniːrt] *adj* free and easy, relaxed and informal.

ungenießbar ['ungəniːsbaːr] *adj* inedible, unenjoyable.

ungenügend ['ungənyːgənt] *adj* insufficient; *(Qualität)* inadequate.

ungeraten ['ungəraːtən] *adj (Kind)* spoiled.

ungerecht ['ungəreçt] *adj* unjust.

ungereimt ['ungəraimt] *adj (fig)* nonsensical, absurd.

ungern ['ungɛrn] *adv* unwillingly, reluctantly.

Ungeschick ['ungəʃik] *neut* ineptitude, clumsiness. **ungeschickt** *adj* clumsy, awkward.

ungesellig ['ungəzɛliç] *adj* unsociable.

ungesetzlich ['ungəzɛtsliç] *adj* illegal, unlawful.

ungestüm ['ungəʃtyːm] *adj* impetuous.

ungesund ['ungəzunt] *adj* unhealthy, unwell.

ungewiß ['ungəvis] *adj* uncertain. **Ungewißheit** *f* uncertainty.

ungewöhnlich ['ungəvœːnliç] *adj* unusual, uncommon. **ungewohnt** *adj* unaccustomed.

Ungeziefer ['ungətsiːfər] *neut* vermin.

ungezogen ['ungətsoːgən] *adj* rude; *(Kind)* naughty.

ungezwungen ['ungətsvuŋən] *adj* free, natural, uninhibited.

ungläubig ['unglɔybiç] *adj* incredulous, disbelieving; *(Rel)* unbelieving. **Ungläubige(r)** *m* sceptic; *(Rel)* unbeliever.

unglaublich ['unglaupliç] *adj* incredible, unbelievable. **unglaubwürdig** *adj (Person)* untrustworthy, unreliable; *(Sache)* incredible.

ungleich ['unglaiç] *adj* unequal, uneven; *(verschieden)* different; *(unähnlich)* unlike; *(Zahl)* odd. **Ungleichheit** *f* inequality; difference.

Unglück ['unglyk] *neut* misfortune; (*Katastrophe*) disaster, catastrophe; (*Pech*) bad luck. **unglücklich** *adj* unlucky; (*traurig*) unhappy. **-erweise** *adv* unfortunately. **Unglücksfall** *m* accident.

Ungnade ['ungnaɪdə] *f* disgrace, displeasure. **ungnädig** *adj* ungracious, churlish.

ungünstig ['ungynstiç] *adj* unfavourable.

unhaltbar ['unhaltbaɪr] *adj* untenable.

Unheil ['unhaɪl] *neut* mischief, harm. **unheil∥bar** *adj* incurable. **-bringend** *adj* unlucky, fateful.

unheimlich ['unhaɪmlɪç] *adj* weird, sinister, uncanny. *adv* (*umg.*) tremendously.

unhöflich ['unhœɪflɪç] *adj* impolite, rude. **Unhöflichkeit** *f* rudeness, incivility.

unhörbar ['unhœɪrbaɪr] *adj* inaudible.

uniform [uni'fɔrm] *adj* uniform. **Uniform** *f* (*pl* -en) uniform.

uninteressant ['unintərɛsant] *adj* uninteresting. **uninteressiert** *adj* disinterested.

universal [univɛr'saɪl] *or* **universell** *adj* universal.

Universität [univɛrzi'tɛit] *f* (*pl* -en) university.

Universum [uni'vɛrzum] *neut* universe.

unkenntlich ['unkɛntlɪç] *adj* unrecognizable. **Unkenntnis** *f* ignorance.

unklar ['unklaɪr] *adj* unclear, obscure; (*trübe*) muddy, cloudy.

unklug ['unkluɪk] *adj* unwise, unintelligent.

Unkosten ['unkɔstən] *pl* expenses, costs; (*Komm*) overheads.

Unkraut ['unkraut] *neut* weed.

unlängst ['unlɛŋst] *adv* recently, lately.

unlauter ['unlautər] *adj* impure; (*nicht ehrlich*) unfair, dishonest. **unlauterer Wettbewerb** unfair competition.

unlesbar ['unleɪzbaɪr] *adj* illegible, unreadable.

unlogisch ['unlɔɪgɪʃ] *adj* illogical.

unlösbar ['unlœɪsbaɪr] *adj* insoluble.

unmäßig ['unmɛɪsɪç] *adj* immoderate.

Unmenge ['unmɛŋə] *f* huge quantity.

Unmensch ['unmɛnʃ] *m* brute, monster, barbarian. **unmenschlich** *adj* inhuman, brutal. **Unmenschlichkeit** *f* inhumanity.

unmittelbar ['unmɪtəlbaɪr] *adj* immediate, direct.

unmodisch ['unmɔɪdɪʃ] *adj* unfashionable.

unmöglich ['unmœɪklɪç] *adj* impossible. **Unmöglichkeit** *f* impossibility.

unmoralisch ['unmɔraɪlɪʃ] *adj* immoral.

unmündig ['unmyndɪç] *adj* under age.

unnachgiebig ['innaxgiɪbɪç] *adj* unyielding, uncompromising.

unnatürlich ['unnatyrlɪç] *adj* unnatural.

unnötig ['unnœɪtɪç] *adj* unnecessary.

unnütz ['unnyts] *adj* useless, unprofitable.

unordentlich ['unɔrdəntlɪç] *adj* disorderly, untidy. **Unord∥entlichkeit** *f* untidiness, disorderliness. **-nung** *f* disorder.

unorganisch ['unɔrgaɪnɪʃ] *adj* inorganic.

unpaar ['unpaɪr] *adj* odd.

unparteiisch ['unpartaiɪʃ] *or* **unparteilich** *adj* impartial, unbiased. **Unparteilichkeit** *f* impartiality.

unpassend ['unpasənt] *adj* unsuitable, inappropriate; (*unschicklich*) improper.

unpersönlich ['unpɛrzœɪnlɪç] *adj* impersonal.

unpolitisch ['unpoliɪtɪʃ] *adj* nonpolitical.

Unrat ['unraɪt] *m* refuse, dirt.

unratsam ['unraɪtzaɪm] *adj* inadvisable.

unrecht ['unrɛçt] *adj* wrong; (*ungerecht*) unjust. **Unrecht** *neut* wrong; (*Ungerechtigkeit*) injustice. **unrechtmäßig** *adj* illegal, unlawful, illegitimate.

unregelmäßig ['unreɪgəlmɛɪsɪç] *adj* irregular. **Unregelmäßigkeit** *f* irregularity.

unreif ['unraif] *adj* unripe; (*Mensch*) immature.

unrein ['unrain] *adj* dirty, unclean; (*fig*) impure.

unrentabel ['unrentaɪbəl] *adj* unprofitable.

unrichtig ['unrɪçtɪç] *adj* incorrect.

Unruhe ['unruɪə] *f* restlessness; (*Aufruhr*) unrest. (*Uhr*) balance(-wheel). **unruhig** *adj* restless.

uns [uns] *pron* (to) us; (*Reflexiv*) (to) ourselves.

unsauber ['unzaubər] *adj* unclean, dirty; (*unfair*) unfair.

unschätzbar ['unʃɛtsbaɪr] *adj* inestimable.

unscheinbar ['unʃainbaɪr] *adj* inconspicuous.

unschicklich ['unʃiklɪç] *adj* improper, unseemly.

unschlüssig ['unʃlysɪç] *adj* irresolute.

unschön ['unʃœɪn] *adj* unlovely, unpleasant.

Unschuld ['unʃult] *f* innocence. **unschuldig** *adj* innocent.

unselbständig ['unzɛlpʃtɛndɪç] *adj* dependent.

unselig ['unzeːliç] adj unfortunate, fatal.

unser ['unzər] adj our. pron ours. **unser(er) seits** adv for our part, as for us.

unser(es)gleichen pron people like us.

pron der, die, das uns(e)rige ours.

unserthalben, unsertwegen, unsertwillen for our sakes.

unsicher ['unziçər] adj unsafe, insecure; (zweifelhaft) uncertain. **Unsicherheit** f insecurity, uncertainty.

unsichtbar ['unziçtbaːr] adj invisible.

Unsinn ['unzin] adj nonsense. **unsinnig** adj nonsensical.

unsittlich ['unzitliç] adj indecent, immoral. **Unsittlichkeit** f immorality.

unsre ['unzrə] V unser.

unsrige ['unzrigə] V unser.

unsterblich ['unʃtɛrpliç] adj immortal. **Unsterblichkeit** f immortality.

unstet ['unʃtɛt] adj unsteady, inconstant.

Unstimmigkeit ['unʃtimiçkait] f (pl -en) inconsistency; (Meinungsverschiedenheit) disagreement.

unsympathisch ['unzympaːtiʃ] adj disagreeable, unpleasant.

Untat ['untaːt] f outrage, crime.

untätig ['untɛːtiç] adj inactive, idle. **Untätigkeit** f inactivity, idleness.

untauglich ['untaukliç] adj unfit; (Sache) unusable.

unten ['untən] adv below, at the bottom; (im Hause) downstairs. **nach unten** downwards. **von oben bis unten** from top to bottom. **von unten an** from the bottom (up).

unter ['untər] prep below, under; (zwischen) between, among. adj lower. **unter allen Umständen** under any circumstances. **unter uns** between you and me. **unter vier Augen** in private. **unter der Hand** secretly.

Unterarm ['untərarm] m forearm.

Unterbau ['untərbau] m foundations pl.

unterbelichten ['untərbəliçtən] v (Foto) underexpose.

unterbevölkert ['untərbəfœlkərt] adj underpopulated.

unterbewußt ['untərbəvust] adj subconscious. **Unterbewusstsein** neut subconsciousness.

unterbleiben [untər'blaibən] v not occur.

unterbrechen [untər'brɛçən] v interrupt; (Telef) cut off, disconnect. **Unterbrechung** f interruption.

unterbringen ['untərbriŋən] v accommodate, lodge, shelter; (lagern) store.

unterdrücken [untər'drykən] v suppress. **Unterdrückung** f suppression.

untereinander [untərain'andər] adv with each other, with one another.

unterentwickelt ['untərɛntvikəlt] adj underdeveloped.

Unterführung [untər'fyːruŋ] f underpass.

Untergang ['untərgaŋ] m (Sonne) setting; (Schiff) sinking, wreck; (fig) decline, fall.

Untergebene(r) [untər'geːbənə(r)] m subordinate.

untergehen ['untərgeːən] v sink; (Sonne) set; (fig) perish, be lost.

untergeordnet ['untərgəɔrdnət] adj subordinate.

Untergestell ['untərgəʃtɛl] neut undercarriage.

Untergewicht ['untərgəviçt] neut short weight. **Untergewicht haben** be underweight.

untergraben [untər'graːbən] v undermine.

Untergrund ['untərgrunt] m subsoil. **–bahn** f underground (railway), (US) subway.

unterhalb ['untərhalp] prep below, under(neath).

Unterhalt ['untərhalt] m support, keep; (Instandhaltung) maintenance.

unterhalten v (Person) keep, support; (Instand halten) maintain; (zerstreuen) entertain. **sich unterhalten** enjoy oneself; (reden (mit)) converse (with), talk (to). **unterhaltsam** adj entertaining, amusing. **Unterhaltung** f entertainment, amusement; (Instandhaltung) maintenance. **–skosten** pl maintenance costs.

unterhandeln [untər'handəln] v negotiate.

Unterhaus ['untərhaus] neut lower chamber (of parliament).

Unterhemd ['untərhɛmt] neut vest, (US) undershirt.

Unterholz ['untərholts] neut undergrowth.

Unterhose ['untərhoːzən] f underpants pl.

unterirdisch ['untəːrirdiʃ] adj underground.

unterkommen ['untərkɔmən] v find accommodation or shelter; (Arbeit) find work.

Unterkunft ['untərkunft] f accommodation, lodgings pl.

Unterlage ['untərlaɪgə] *f* base, basis, foundation; (*Beweisstück*) (documentary) evidence.

Unterlaß ['untərlas] *m* **ohne Unterlaß** incessantly, unceasingly.

***unterlassen** [untər'lasən] *v* neglect, fail (to do), omit. **Unterlassung** *f* omission.

unterlegen [untər'leɪgən] *adj* inferior.

Unterleib ['untərlaip] *m* abdomen.

***unterliegen** [untər'liːgən] *v* be defeated. **es unterliegt keinem Zweifel** it is not open to doubt.

Untermieter ['untərmiːtər] *m* lodger.

***unternehmen** [untər'neːmən] *v* undertake, attempt. **Unternehmen** *neut* undertaking, enterprise; (*Firma*) firm. **Unternehmer** *m* entrepreneur, contractor. **unternehmungslustig** *adj* enterprising.

Unteroffizier ['untərɔfitsiːr] *m* noncommissioned officer, NCO.

Unterredung [untər'reːduŋ] *f* (*pl* -en) conversation, discussion.

Unterricht ['untəriçt] *m* (*pl* -e) instruction, lessons *pl*, teaching. **Unterricht geben** teach, give lessons. **unterrichten** *v* teach, give lessons. **unterrichten** *v* instruct, teach; (*benachrichtigen*) inform.

Unterrock ['untərɔk] *m* slip, petticoat.

unters ['untərs] *prep + art* **unter das.**

untersagen [untər'zaːgən] *v* forbid, prohibit.

***unterscheiden** [untər'ʃaidən] *v* distinguish. **sich unterscheiden** differ.

***unterschieben** [untər'ʃiːbən] *v* attribute (to); substitute.

Unterschied ['untərʃiːt] *m* (*pl* -e) difference. **unterschiedlich** *adj* different.

***unterschlagen** [untər'ʃlaːgən] *v* (*Geld*) embezzle; (*Nachricht*) suppress. **Unterschlagung** *f* embezzlement; suppression.

Unterschlupf ['untərʃlupf] *m* (*pl* **Unterschlüpfe**) refuge, hiding place.

***unterschreiben** [untər'ʃraibən] *v* sign. **Unterschrift** ['untərʃrift] *f* signature.

Unterseeboot ['untərzeːboːt] *neut* submarine. **unterseeisch** *adj* submarine.

unterst ['untərst] *adj* lowest, bottom, undermost.

***unterstehen** [untər'ʃteːən] *v* be subordinate (to). **sich unterstehen** dare.

***unterstreichen** [untər'ʃtraiçən] *v* underline.

unterstützen [untər'ʃtytsən] *v* support,

assist. **Unterstützung** *f* (*pl* -en) support, assistance.

untersuchen [untər'zuːxən] *v* examine. **Untersuchung** *f* examination. **–shaft** *f* imprisonment on remand.

Untertan ['untərtaɪn] *m* (*pl* -en) subject.

Untertasse ['untərtasə] *f* saucer.

untertauchen ['untərtauxən] *v* dive; (*verschwinden*) disappear.

Unterteil ['untərtail] *m* bottom (part).

Untertitel ['untərtiːtəl] *m* (*Film*) subtitle.

unterwärts ['untərvɛrts] *adv* downwards.

Unterwäsche ['untərvɛʃə] *f* underwear.

unterwegs [untər'veːks] *adv* on the way, en route.

***unterweisen** [untər'vaizən] *v* instruct, teach. **Unterweisung** *f* instructions *pl*.

Unterwelt ['untərvelt] *f* underworld.

***unterwerfen** [untər'vɛrfən] *v* subject (to); (*besiegen*) subjugate. **sich unterwerfen** submit, surrender. **unterworfen** *adj* subject (to).

unterwürfig [untər'vyrfiç] *adj* obsequious.

unterzeichnen [untər'tsaiçnən] *v* sign. **Unterzeichnung** *f* signature.

***unterziehen** [untər'tsiːən] *v* subject. **sich unterziehen** undergo, submit (to).

untief ['untiːf] *adj* shallow.

untreu ['untrɔy] *adj* unfaithful.

untrüglich [un'tryːkliç] *adj* infallible, certain.

untüchtig ['untyçtiç] *adj* incompetent, incapable.

Untugend ['untuːgənt] *f* vice.

unüberlegt ['unyːbərleɪkt] *adj* ill-considered, hasty.

unüberwindlich ['unyːbərvintliç] *adj* impregnable; insurmountable, insuperable.

ununterbrochen ['ununtərbrɔxən] *adj* uninterrupted.

unveränderlich ['unfɛrɛndərliç] *adj* unchangeable.

unverantwortlich [unfɛr'antvɔrtliç] *adj* irresponsible. **Unverantwortlichkeit** *f* irresponsibility.

unverbesserlich [unfɛr'besərliç] *adj* incorrigible.

unverbindlich ['unfɛrbintliç] *adj* not binding; (*Komm*) without obligation.

unverdaulich ['unfɛrdauliç] *adj* indigestible.

unverderblich ['unfɛrderpliç] *adj* incorruptible.

unverdient ['unfɛrdiːnt] *adj* unearned, undeserved.

unvereinbar [unfɛr'ainbaːr] *adj* incompatible.

unverfroren ['unfɛrfroːrən] *adj* impudent, brazen. **Unverfrorenheit** *f* impudence.

unvergänglich ['unfɛrgɛsliç] *adj* imperishable; immortal.

unvergeßlich [unfɛr'gɛsliç] *adj* unforgettable.

unverhältnismäßig ['unfɛrhɛltnismɛːsiç] *adj* disproportionate.

unverheiratet ['unfɛrhairaːtət] *adj* unmarried.

unvermeidlich [unfɛr'maitliç] *adj* unavoidable.

unvermittelt ['unfɛrmitəlt] *adj* sudden, unexpected.

Unvermögen ['unfɛrmœːgən] *neut* inability, powerlessness.

unvermutet ['unfɛrmuːtət] *adj* unexpected.

unvernünftig ['unfɛrnynftiç] *adj* unreasonable.

unverschämt ['unfɛrʃɛːmt] *adj* impudent, impertinent. **Unverschämtheit** *f* impudence, impertinence.

unversehens ['unfɛrzeːəns] *adv* suddenly, unexpectedly.

unversöhnlich ['unfɛrsœːnliç] *adj* irreconcilable.

unverständlich ['unfɛrʃtɛntliç] *adj* unintelligible.

unverträglich ['unfɛrtrɛːkliç] *adj* incompatible; unsociable.

unverzagt ['unfɛrtsakt] *adj* undaunted, fearless.

unverzüglich ['unfɛrtsyːkliç] *adj* immediate, instant.

unvollkommen ['unfɔlkɔmən] *adj* imperfect.

unvoreingenommen ['unfɔraingənɔmən] *adj* unprejudiced.

unvorsichtig ['unfɔrziçtiç] *adj* careless, incautious; (*unklug*) imprudent.

unvorstellbar ['unfɔrʃtɛlbaːr] *adj* unimaginable.

unvorteilhaft ['unfɔrtailhaft] *adj* unfavourable.

unwahr ['unvaːr] *adj* untrue. **–haftig** *adj* untruthful. **Unwahrheit** *f* untruth, falsehood. **unwahrscheinlich** *adj* unlikely, improbably; (*umg.*) fantastic, incredible. *adv* (*umg.*) incredibly.

unweit ['unvait] *prep, adv* near, not far (from).

Unwetter ['unvɛtər] *neut* storm.

unwichtig ['unviçtiç] *adj* unimportant. **Unwichtigkeit** *f* unimportance; (*Sache*) trifle.

unwiderruflich [unviːdər'ruːfliç] *adj* irrevocable.

unwiderstehlich [unviːdər'ʃteːliç] *adj* irresistible.

unwillig ['unviliç] *adj* indignant; (*widerwillig*) unwilling, reluctant.

unwillkürlich ['unvilkyːrliç] *adj* involuntary; instinctive.

unwirksam ['unviːrkzaːm] *adj* ineffective.

unwissend ['unvisənt] *adj* ignorant. **Unwissenheit** *f* ignorance. **unwissentlich** *adv* unconsciously, unwittingly.

unwürdig ['unvyrdiç] *adj* unworthy.

Unzahl ['untsaːl] *f* endless number.

unzählbar ['untsɛːlbaːr] *or* **unzählig** *adj* innumerable.

unzeitgemäß ['untsaitgəmɛːs] *adj* inopportune; (*unmodisch*) outdated. **unzeitig** *adj* premature; (*Obst*) unripe.

unzerbrechlich [untsɛr'brɛçliç] *adj* unbreakable.

unzertrennlich [untsɛr'trɛnliç] *adj* inseparable.

unziemlich ['untsiːmliç] *adj* unseemly.

Unzucht ['untsuxt] *f* lechery, fornication; (*Jur*) sexual offence. **unzüchtig** *adj* lewd, lecherous.

unzufrieden ['untsufriːdən] *adj* dissatisfied.

unzugänglich ['untsuːgɛnliç] *adj* inaccessible.

unzulänglich ['untsuːlɛnliç] *adj* inadequate, insufficient.

unzulässig ['untsuːlɛsiç] *adj* inadmissible.

unzureichend ['untsuraiçənt] *adj* insufficient, inadequate.

unzuverlässig ['untsufɛrlɛsiç] *adj* unreliable.

unzweifelhaft ['untsfaifəlhaft] *adj* undoubted.

üppig ['ypiç] *adj* abundant, luxuriant; (*blühend*) exuberant; (*wollüstig*) voluptuous.

uralt ['uːralt] *adj* very old, ancient.

Uran [u'raːn] *neut* uranium.

uranfänglich ['uranfɛnliç] *adj* original, premordial.

Uraufführung ['uːrauffyːruŋ] *f* first performance, première.

urban [urˈbaɪn] *adj* urbane.
urbar [ˈurbaɪr] *adj* arable.
Ureinwohner [ˈuɪrainvoɪnər] *m* aboriginal.
Ureltern [ˈuɪrɛltərn] *pl* ancestors.
Urenkel [ˈuɪreŋkəl] *m* (*Kind*) great-grandchild, (*Junge*) great-grandson. **–in** *f* great-granddaughter.
Urgeschichte [ˈurɡəʃɪçtə] *f* prehistory.
Urgroß‖eltern [ˈuɪrɡroɪsɛltərn] *pl* great-grandparents. **–mutter** *f* great-grand-mother. **–vater** *m* great-grandfather.
Urheber [ˈuɪrheɪbər] *m* (*pl* -) author, creator. **–recht** *neut* copyright.
Urin [uˈriɪn] *m* urine. **urinieren** *v* urinate.
Urkunde [ˈurkundə] *f* document, deed; (*Zeugnis*) certificate. **urkundlich** *adj* documentary.
Urlaub [ˈurlaup] *m* (*pl* -e) leave (of absence); (*Ferien*) holiday, vacation. **im** *or* **auf Urlaub** on holiday, on vacation.
Urmensch [ˈurmɛnʃ] *m* primitive man.
Urne [ˈurnə] *f* (*pl* -n) urn.
Ursache [ˈuɪrzaxə] *f* cause. **keine Ursache!** don't mention it!
Ursprung [ˈurʃpruŋ] *m* source, origin. **ursprünglich** *adj* original. **Ursprungsland** *neut* country of origin.
Urteil [ˈurtaɪl] *neut* judgment, verdict; (*Strafmaß*) sentence; (*Urteilskraft*) judgment. **urteilen** *v* judge. **Urteils‖kraft** *f* (power of) judgment, discernment. **–spruch** *m* verdict, sentence.
Urvater [ˈuɪrfaɪtər] *m* forefather.
Urwelt [ˈuɪrvɛlt] *f* primeval world.
Urzeit [ˈuɪrtsaɪt] *f* prehistory, earliest times *pl.* **urzeitlich** *adj* primordial, primeval.
Utopie [utoˈpiɪ] *f* (*pl* -n) Utopia. **utopisch** *adj* utopian.

V

vag [vaɪk] *adj* vague.
Vagabund [vaɡaˈbunt] *m* (*pl* -en) vagabond, tramp.
vakant [vaˈkant] *adj* vacant.
Vakuum [ˈvaɪkuum] *neut* (*pl* Vakua) vacuum.
validieren [valiˈdiɪrən] *v* make valid, validate.
Valuta [vaˈluɪta] *f* (*pl* Valuten) (*Wert*) value; (*Währung*) currency.

Vampir [ˈvampiɪr] *m* (*pl* -e) vampire.
Vandale [vanˈdaɪlə] *m* (*pl* -n) vandal. **Vandalismus** *m* vandalism.
Vanille [vaˈniljə] *f* vanilla.
Varietät [varieˈtɛtt] *f* (*pl* -en) variety.
Variation [variatsiˈoɪn] *f* (*pl* -en) variation.
Vase [ˈvaɪzə] *f* (*pl* -en) vase.
Vater [ˈfaɪtər] *m* (*pl* Väter) father. **–land** *neut* native land, fatherland. **vaterländisch** *adj* national; patriotic. **väterlich** [ˈfɛttərliç] *adj* paternal, fatherly. **väterlicherseits** *adv* on the father's side. **Vaterschaft** [ˈfaɪtərʃaft] *f* (*pl* -en) paternity.
Vegetarier [veɡeˈtaɪriər] *m* (*pl* -) vegetarian. **vegetarisch** *adj* vegetarian.
Veilchen [ˈfailçən] *neut* (*pl* -) violet. **veilchenblau** *adj* violet.
Vene [ˈveɪnə] *f* (*pl* -n) vein. **Venenentzündung** *f* (*Med*) phlebitis.
Venedig [veˈneɪdiç] *neut* Venice. **venezianer** *m* (*pl* -), **Venezianerin** *f* (*pl* -nen) Venetian. **venezianisch** *adj* Venetian.
Ventil [vɛnˈtiɪl] *neut* (*pl* -e) valve. **–ator** *m* (*pl* -en) ventilator; (*Mot*) fan; (*Elek*) electric fan.
verabreden [fɛrˈapreɪdən] *v* agree (upon); (*Ort, Zeitpunkt*) fix, appoint. **Verabredung** *f* agreement; appointment.
verabscheuen [fɛrˈapʃɔyən] *v* abhor, detest.
verabschieden [fɛrˈapʃiɪdən] *v* dismiss; (*Gesetze*) pass. **sich verabschieden von** take one's leave of, say goodbye to.
verachten [fɛrˈaxtən] *v* despise. **verächtlich** *adj* contemptible. **Verachtung** *f* contempt.
verallgemeinern [fɛralɡəˈmainərn] *v* generalize. **Verallgemeinerung** *f* generalization.
veralten [fɛrˈaltən] *v* become outmoded, go out of use. **veraltet** *adj* out-of-date.
veränderlich [fɛrˈɛndərliç] *adj* changeable. **verändern** *v* change, alter. **sich verändern** change, alter. **Veränderung** *f* change, alteration.
verankern [fɛrˈaŋkərn] *v* moor, anchor.
veranlagt [fɛrˈanlaɪkt] *adj* talented, gifted.
veranlassen [fɛrˈanlasən] *v* cause, bring about. **Veranlassung** *f* cause; (*Beweggrund*) motive.
veranschaulichen [fɛrˈanʃauliçən] *v* make clear.

veranstalten [fɛr'anʃtaltən] v organize, arrange. **Veranstalt‖er** m (pl -) organizer. **–ung** f (pl -en) event, function; (Veranstalten) organization.

verantworten [fɛr'antvɔrtən] v take responsibility for, answer for. **verantwortlich** adj responsible. **Verantwort‖lichkeit** f responsibility. **–ung** f (pl -en) responsibility; (Rechtfertigung) justification.

verarbeiten [fɛr'aɪbaitən] v manufacture, make; (bearbeiten) work, process; (durchdenken) assimilate. **Verarbeitung** f manufacture; working; assimilation.

verargen [fɛr'argən] v blame.

verärgern [fɛr'ɛrgərn] v annoy, vex.

verarmen [fɛr'aɪmən] v become poor. **verarmt** adj impoverished.

Verb [vɛrp] neut (pl -en) verb.

Verband [fɛr'bant] m (pl Verbände) (Med) bandage, dressing; (Verein) association, society.

verbannen [fɛr'banən] v banish. **Verbann‖te(r)** exile. **–ung** f banishment, exile.

*verbergen [fɛr'bɛrgən] v hide.

verbessern [fɛr'bɛsərn] v improve; (berichtigen) correct. **Verbesserung** f (pl -en) improvement; correction.

verbeugen [fɛr'bɔygən] v sich verbeugen bow.

*verbieten [fɛr'biːtən] v forbid, prohibit.

*verbinden [fɛr'bindən] v connect, join; (Med) bandage, dress; (Telef) connect, put through. **sich verbinden mit** join up with, combine with. **verbindlich** adj binding, obligatory; (zuvorkommend) obliging. **Verbindung** f connection; (Med) bandage, dressing; (Telef) connection. **in Verbindung mit** in association with. **im Verbindung treten mit** get in touch with. **im Verbindung stehen mit** be in contact with. **in Verbindung setzen mit** put in contact with.

verbissen [fɛr'bisən] adj grim, dogged.

verbittern [fɛr'bitərn] v embitter. **Verbitterung** f bitterness.

verblassen [fɛr'blasən] v turn or grow pale; (Farbe, Erinnerung) fade.

Verbleib [fɛr'blaip] m whereabouts. **verbleiben** v remain.

verblenden [fɛr'blɛndən] v blind, dazzle, delude; (Mauerwerk) face. **Verblendung** f blindness, delusion.

verblüffen [fɛr'blyfən] v dumbfound, nonplus. **verblüfft** adj dumbfounded, nonplussed. **Verblüffung** f amazement, stupefaction.

verbluten [fɛr'bluːtən] v bleed to death.

verbohrt [fɛr'boːrt] adj stubborn.

verborgen [fɛr'bɔrgən] adj hidden. **Verborgenheit** f concealment, secrecy.

Verbot [fɛr'boːt] neut (pl -e) prohibition, ban. **verboten** adj prohibited, forbidden.

Verbrauch [fɛr'braux] m consumption, use. **verbrauchen** v consume, use up. **Verbraucher** m (pl -) consumer. **Verbrauchsgüter** pl consumer goods pl.

Verbrechen [fɛr'brɛçən] neut crime. **–er** m criminal. **verbrechen** v commit a crime. **verbrecherisch** adj criminal.

verbreiten [fɛr'braitən] v spread. **weit verbreitet** adj widespread.

*verbrennen [fɛr'brɛnən] v burn; (Leichen) cremate. **Verbrennung** f burning; cremation. **–smotor** m internal combustion engine.

*verbringen [fɛr'briŋən] v spend (time).

verbrühen [fɛr'bryːən] v scald.

Verbum ['vɛrbum] neut (pl Verben) verb.

verbünden [fɛr'byndən] v sich verbünden mit ally oneself with. **Verbündete(r)** m ally.

verchromt [fɛr'kroːmt] adj chromiumplated. **Verchromung** f chromium plating.

Verdacht [fɛr'daxt] m (pl -e) suspicion. **in Verdacht kommen** arouse suspicion, be suspected. **verdächtig** adj suspicious. **–en** v suspect.

verdammen [fɛr'damən] v condemn, damn. **verdammt** adj damned. interj damn! **Verdammung** f damnation.

verdampfen [fɛr'dampfən] v evaporate, vaporize. **Verdampfung** f evaporation, vaporization.

verdanken [fɛr'daŋkən] v owe.

verdauen [fɛr'dauən] v digest. **verdaulich** adj digestible. **Verdauung** f digestion.

Verdeck [fɛr'dɛk] neut (pl -e) canopy, covering; (Mot) roof; (Schiff) deck. **verdecken** v cover, conceal. **verdeckt** adj masked, concealed.

Verderb [fɛr'dɛrp] m ruin, destruction. **verderben** v spoil, ruin; (verführen) corrupt; (Speisen) spoil, go bad; (Menschen) come to grief, perish. **Verderben** neut ruin, destruction. **verderblich** adj destructive, pernicious; (Waren) perishable. **verderbt** adj corrupt(ed).

verdeutlichen [fɛr'dɔytliçən] v make clear,
elucidate.
verdichten [fɛr'diçtən] v compress.
Verdichtung f compression.
verdicken [fɛr'dikən] v thicken.
verdienen [fɛr'diːnən] v (Geld) earn;
(Beachtung, Lob) deserve. er hat es
verdient he deserves it; (negativ) it serves
him right. **Verdienst 1** m (pl -e) earnings
pl, gains pl. **2** neut (pl -e) deserts pl.
–spanne f margin (of profit).
verdingen [fɛr'diŋən] v hire out.
verdoppeln [fɛr'dɔpəln] v double. Verdoppelung f doubling.
verdorben [fɛr'dɔrbən] adj spoilt; (fig)
corrupted.
verdrängen [fɛr'drɛŋən] v displace, push
out; (vertreiben) drive away; (Psychol)
repress.
verdrehen [fɛr'dreːən] v distort, twist.
*verdrießen [fɛr'driːsən] v vex, annoy.
verdrießlich adj sullen, disgruntled; tiresome irksome.
verdrossen [fɛr'drɔsən] adj sullen.
Verdruß [fɛr'drus] m annoyance.
verdummen [fɛr'dumən] v stupefy;
(dumm werden) grow stupid.
verdunkeln [fɛr'duŋkəln] v darken.
verdünnen [fɛr'dynən] v dilute, thin.
veredeln [fɛr'eːdəln] v ennoble; (fig)
improve, refine.
verehren [fɛr'eːrən] v (Rel) worship;
(lieben) adore; (hochschätzen) venerate,
respect. Verehr∥er m worshipper; adorer; admirer. –ung f worship; adoration;
veneration.
Verein [fɛr'ain] m (pl -e) society, association; (Klub) club. **vereinbar** adj reconcilable, compatible. **vereinbar∥en** v agree
upon. –t adj agreed (upon). Vereinbarung f (pl -en) agreement.
vereinfachen [fɛr'ainfaxən] v simplify.
vereinheitlichen [fɛr'ainhaitliçən] v unify,
standardize.
vereinigen [fɛr'ainigən] v unite, join. sich
vereinigen unite. vereinigt adj united. die
Vereinigten Staaten pl the United States.
Vereinigung f (pl -en) union; association,
society; (Zusammenschluß) combination.
–spunkt m meeting point.
vereint [fɛr'aint] adj united.
vereiteln [fɛr'aitəln] v frustrate. Vereitelung f frustration.
vererben [fɛr'ɛrbən] v leave, bequeath;

(Krankheit, Eigenschaft) transmit. vererblich adj hereditary. Vererbung f heredity.
verewigen [fɛr'eːvigən] v immortalize.
verfahren [fɛr'faːrən] v act, proceed. sich
verfahren lose one's way. Verfahren neut
procedure; (Methode) method; (Tech)
process.
Verfall [fɛr'fal] m ruin; (allmählich)
decline, decay. verfallen v decline, decay.
verfälschen [fɛr'fɛlʃən] v falsify. Verfälschung f falsification.
verfassen [fɛr'fasən] v compose, write;
(Urkunde) draw up. Verfasser m (pl -),
Verfasserin f (pl -nen) author, writer.
*verfechten [fɛr'feʧən] v fight for, defend.
verfehlen [fɛr'feːlən] v miss, not reach;
(versäumen) fail. Verfehlung f mistake,
lapse.
verfeinern [fɛr'fainərn] v refine.
verflechten [fɛr'fleçtən] v interweave; (fig)
involve.
verfluchen [fɛr'fluːxən] v curse. verflucht
adj cursed, damned. interj damn (it)!
verfolgen [fɛr'fɔlgən] v pursue;
(beobachten) follow; (gerichtlich) prosecute; (plagen) persecute. Verfolger m
pursuer; persecutor. Verfolgung f pursuit; prosecution; persecution.
Verformung [fɛr'fɔrmuŋ] f distortion,
warping.
verfügbar [fɛr'fyːkbaɪr] adj available.
verfügen v order, decree. **verfügen über**
have at one's disposal, dispose of.
Verfügung f disposal; (Anordnung) order.
zur Verfügung stehen/stellen be/put at
the disposal (of).
verführen [fɛr'fyːrən] v seduce; (verleiten)
lead astray. Verführ∥er m seducer;
tempter. –ung f seduction; temptation.
vergangen [fɛr'gaŋən] adj past. Vergangenheit f past. vergänglich adj transitory, impermanent.
Vergaser [fɛr'gaːzər] m (pl -) carburettor.
*vergeben [fɛr'geːbən] v (verzeihen) forgive; (verschenken) give away; (verteilen)
distribute. vergeb∥ens adv in vain. –lich
adj vain. adv in vain. Vergebung f forgiveness. interj pardon me!
vergegenwärtigen [fɛrgeːgən'vɛrtigən] v
represent.
*vergehen [fɛr'geːən] v pass. vergehen vor
die of. sich vergehen v commit an
offence, err. Vergehen neut misdeed.

*vergelten [fɛr'gɛltən] v pay back. **Vergeltung** f reward; retaliation.
*vergessen [fɛr'gɛsən] v forget. **Vergessenheit** f oblivion. **vergeßlich** adj forgetful.
vergeuden [fɛr'gɔydən] v waste, squander. **Vergeudung** f waste, dissipation.
vergewaltigen [fɛrgə'valtigən] v rape. **Vergewaltiger** m rapist. **Vergewaltigung** f rape.
*vergießen [fɛr'giːsən] v shed, spill.
vergiften [fɛr'giftən] v poison. **Vergiftung** f poisoning.
Vergißmeinnicht [fɛr'gismainniçt] neut (pl -e) forget-me-not.
verglasen [fɛr'glɑːzən] v glaze.
Vergleich [fɛr'glaiç] m (pl -e) comparison; (Redewendung) simile; (Abkommen) agreement, settlement. **einen Vergleich schließen** come to an agreement. **im Vergleich mit/zu** in comparison with/to. **vergleichbar** adj comparable. **vergleichen** v compare; settle, agree.
Vergnügen [fɛr'gnyːgən] neut enjoyment. **vergnügen** v amuse. **sich vergnügen** amuse oneself. **vergnügt** adj merry, happy. **Vergnügung** f pleasure, enjoyment. **–spark** m amusement park.
vergoldet [fɛr'gɔldət] adj (Metall) gold-plated; (Holz) gilt.
vergöttern [fɛr'gœtərn] v deify; (fig) idolize.
vergraben [fɛr'grɑːbən] v bury.
vergriffen [fɛr'grifən] adj sold out; (Buch) out of print.
vergrößern [fɛr'grœːsərn] v enlarge, magnify. **Vergrößerung** f (pl -en) enlargement.
Vergünstigung [fɛr'gynstiguŋ] f (pl -en) privilege; (Rabatt) discount.
vergüten [fɛr'gyːtən] v compensate (for); (Unkosten) reimburse. **Vergütung** f (pl -en) compensation; reimbursement.
verhaften [fɛr'haftən] v arrest. **verhaftet** adj arrested; (fig) bound, connected. **Verhaftung** f (pl -en) arrest.
*verhalten [fɛr'haltən] v hold back. **sich verhalten** behave, act; (Sache) be. **Verhalten** neut behaviour.
Verhältnis [fɛr'hɛltnis] neut (pl -se) relation, proportion; (Beziehungen) relation; (Liebesaffäre) relationship; liaison. **im Verhältnis zu** in comparison with. **Verhältnisse** pl circumstances. **Verhältn-**

ismäßig adj proportional. adv relatively, comparatively.
verhandeln [fɛr'handəln] v negotiate. **Verhandlung** f negotiation.
Verhängnis [fɛr'hɛŋnis] neut (pl -se) fate, destiny. **verhängnisvoll** adj fateful.
verhaßt [fɛr'hast] adj odious, hated.
verheeren [fɛr'heːrən] v devastate, lay waste.
verheimlichen [fɛr'haimliçən] v conceal, keep secret.
verheiraten [fɛr'hairaːtən] v marry. **sich verheiraten** get married, marry.
*verheißen [fɛr'haisən] v promise.
*verhelfen [fɛr'hɛlfən] v assist, help.
verherrlichen [fɛr'hɛrliçən] v glorify. **Verherrlichung** f glorification.
verhindern [fɛr'hindərn] v prevent. **Verhinderung** f prevention.
verhöhnen [gɛr'hœːnən] v ridicule, mock.
Verhör [fɛr'hœːr] neut (pl -e) interrogation, examination. **verhören** v interrogate, examine. **sich verhören** hear wrongly, misunderstand.
verhungern [fɛr'huŋərn] v starve (to death).
verhüten [fɛr'hyːtən] v prevent, ward off. **–d** adj preventive. **Verhütung** f prevention. **–smittel** neut contraceptive.
verirren [fɛr'irən] v **sich verirren** go astray, get lost.
verjüngen [fɛr'jyŋən] v rejuvenate; (erneuern) renew. **Verjüngung** f rejuvenation; renewal.
Verkauf [fɛr'kauf] m sale. **verkaufen** v sell. **Verkäufer** m seller; (Angestellter) salesman; (im Laden) sales assistant. **–in** f saleswoman, sales assistant. **verkäuflich** adj for sale. **Verkaufs‖abteilung** f sales department. **–automat** m vending machine. **–bedingungen** (pl) terms of sale. **–förderung** f sales promotion. **–preis** m selling price.
Verkehr [fɛr'keːr] m traffic; (Umgang) intercourse; (Handel) trade. **verkehren** v (Bus) run; (verdrehen) distort; (besuchen) frequent; (Menschen) associate (with). **Verkehrs‖ampeln** f pl traffic lights. **–ordnung** f traffic regulation. **–spitze** f rush hour. **–stockung** f traffic jam. **–unfall** m road accident. **verkehrt** adj inverted, wrong way round; (falsch) wrong.
*verkennen [fɛr'kɛnən] v mistake, misjudge; (Person) not recognize.

verklagen [fɛr'klaɪgən] v (Jur) sue (for); (umg.) inform against.

verklären [fɛr'klɛɪrən] v transfigure; (fig) illumine. **Verklärung** f transfiguration; illumination.

verkleiden [fɛr'klaɪdən] v cover, mask; (Wand) face. **sich verkleiden** disguise oneself. **Verkleidung** f (pl -en) disguise; facing, lining.

verkleinern [fɛr'klaɪnərn] v reduce, diminish. **Verkleinerung** f (pl -en) reduction, diminution.

verknüpfen [fɛr'knypfən] v knot (together), join; (fig) connect. **verknüpft** adj connected.

*verkommen [fɛr'kɔmən] v (Person) degenerate, (umg.) go to the dogs; (speisen) go bad; (Gebäude) decay, be neglected.

verkörpern [fɛr'kœrpərn] v embody. **Verkörperung** f embodiment, incarnation.

verkrümmen [fɛr'krymən] v bend, make crooked. **Verkrümmung** f (pl -en) crookedness, distortion; (Rückgrat) curvature.

verkrüppeln [fɛr'krypəln] v cripple.

verkünden [fɛr'kyndən] v announce, proclaim; (Urteil) pronounce. **verkündigen** v proclaim. **Mariä Verkündigung** Annunciation, Lady Day.

verkürzen [fɛr'kyrtsən] v shorten, abbreviate; (Buch) abridge. **sich verkürzen** shrink, diminish. **Verkürzung** f shortening; (Buch) abridgment.

*verladen [fɛr'laɪdən] v load; (verschicken) dispatch. **Verladung** f loading.

Verlag [fɛr'laɪk] m (pl -e) publishing house, publisher.

verlangen [fɛr'laŋən] v demand; (benötigen) require. **verlangen nach** long for. **Verlangen** neut demand; (Wunsch) desire. **auf Verlangen** on demand.

verlängern [fɛr'lɛŋərn] v extend, lengthen; (Gültigkeit, usw.) extend. **Verlängerung** f (pl -en) extension.

verlangsamen [fɛr'laŋzaɪmən] v · slow down.

Verlaß [fɛr'las] m trustworthiness, reliability. **verlassen** v leave; (im Stich lassen) desert, abandon, forsaken. **sich verlassen auf** rely on. **verläßlich** adj reliable.

Verlauf [fɛr'lauf] m course. **verlaufen** v (Zeit) pass; (Angelegenheit) go, turn out; (Weg) run, to. es ist alles gut verlaufen

everything went very well. **sich verlaufen** lose one's way.

verlautbaren [fɛr'lautbaɪrən] v notify.

verlegen [fɛr'leɪgən] v misplace; (Platz ändern) transfer, remove; (Buch) publish; (Termin) postpone. adj embarrassed. **Verleg‖enheit** f embarrassment; (Schwierigkeit) difficulty. **–er** m (pl -) publisher.

*verleihen [fɛr'laɪən] v lend; (Preise) confer, bestow.

verleiten [fɛr'laɪtən] v lead astray, mislead.

verlernen [fɛr'lɛrnən] v forget.

*verlesen [fɛr'leɪzən] v read out; (auslesen) pick. **sich verlesen** misread.

verletzen [fɛr'lɛtsən] v injure, wound; (kränken) hurt, offend; (Gesetze) infringe. **verletzlich** adj vulnerable; (fig) sensitive, touchy. **Verletzung** f (pl -en) injury; (Vergehen) offence.

verleugnen [fɛr'lɔygnən] v deny; (Kind, Freunde) disown.

verleumden [fɛr'lɔymdən] v slander. **Verleumder** m (pl -) slanderer. **verleumderisch** adj slanderous. **Verleumdung** f (pl -en) slander.

verlieben [fɛr'liːbən] v **sich verlieben in** fall in love with.

*verlieren [fɛr'liːrən] v lose. **sich verlieren** get lost.

verloben [fɛr'loɪbən] v **sich verloben mit** get engaged to. **Verlobte** f (pl -n) fiancée. **Verlobter** m (pl -en) fiancé. **Verlobung** f (pl -en) engagement.

verlocken [fɛr'lɔkən] v tempt, entice. **–d** adj tempting. **Verlockung** f (pl -en) enticement, temptation.

verlogen [fɛr'loɪgən] adj untruthful, lying.

verloren [fɛr'loɪrən] adj lost. **–gehen** v be lost.

Verlust [fɛr'lust] m (pl -e) loss. **verlustbringend** adj detrimental.

vermachen [fɛr'maxən] v bequeath, leave. **Vermächtnis** neut (pl -se) (Testament) will; (Vermachtes) legacy, bequest.

vermehren [fɛr'meɪrən] v also **sich vermehren** increase. **Vermehrung** f (pl -en) increase.

*vermeiden [fɛr'maɪdən] v avoid. **vermeidlich** adj avoidable. **Vermeidung** f avoidance.

vermeintlich [fɛr'maɪntlɪç] adj supposed, presumed.

Vermerk [fɛr'mɛrk] *m* (*pl* **-e**) note, remark. **vermerken** *v* note, remark.

*****vermessen** [fɛr'mɛsən] *v* measure; (*Land*) survey. *adj* presumptuous. **Vermess∥er** *m* surveyor. **–ung** *f* measurement; (*Land*) survey.

vermieten [fɛr'miːtən] *v* let, rent (out). **Vermiet∥er** *m* landlord. **–ung** *f* letting.

vermindern [fɛr'mindərn] *v* reduce, decrease. **Verminderung** *f* reduction, decrease.

vermischen [fɛr'miʃən] *v* mix, blend.

vermissen [fɛr'misən] *v* miss. **vermißt** *adj* missing.

vermitteln [fɛr'mitəln] *v* mediate, negotiate; (*verschaffen*) procure, obtain. **Vermittl∥er** *m* mediator, go-between; (*Komm*) agent. **–ung** *f* (*pl* **-en**) mediation, negotiation; (*Telef*) exchange.

*****vermögen** [fɛr'møːɡən] *v* be able (to). **–d** *adj* well-to-do. **Vermögen** *neut* fortune, wealth, property; (*Fähigkeit*) ability. **–sverwalter** *m* trustee (of an estate).

vermuten [fɛr'muːtən] *v* suppose, suspect. **vermutlich** *adj* supposed. *adv* probably, presumably. **Vermutung** *f* (*pl* **-en**) supposition, suspicion.

vernachlässigen [fɛr'naɪxlɛsiɡən] *v* neglect.

vernarren [fɛr'narən] *v* **sich vernarren in** become infatuated with; (*Kind*) dote on.

*****vernehmen** [fɛr'neːmən] *v* perceive; (*Gefangene*) interrogate. **vernehmlich** *adj* perceptible.

verneinen [fɛr'naɪnən] *v* deny; (*Frage*) say no, answer in the negative. **Verneinung** *f* denial; negation.

vernichten [fɛr'niçtən] *v* destroy, annihilate. **–d** *adj* annihilating, crushing. **Vernichtung** *f* destruction, annihilation.

vernieten [fɛr'niːtən] *v* rivet.

Vernunft [fɛr'nunft] *f* reason; (*Besonnenheit*) sense, commonsense. **zur Vernunft kommen** come to one's senses. **vernünftig** *adj* sensible, reasonable.

veröden [fɛr'øːdən] *v* become desolate.

veröffentlichen [fɛr'œfəntliçən] *v* publish. **Veröffentlichung** *f* publication.

verordnen [fɛr'ɔdnən] *v* order; (*Med*) prescribe. **Verordnung** *f* order; prescription.

verpachten [fɛr'paxtən] *v* lease, let.

verpacken [fɛr'pakən] *v* pack.

verpassen [fɛr'pasən] *v* miss.

verpfänden [fɛr'pfɛndən] *v* pawn, pledge.

verpflegen [fɛr'pfleːɡən] *v* feed, cater for. **Verpflegung** *f* food, board.

verpflichten [fɛr'pliçtən] *v* oblige, commit. **sich verpflichten** bind *or* commit oneself. **Verpflichtung** *f* obligation, commitment, duty.

verpfuschen [fɛr'pfuʃən] *v* bungle, botch, make a mess of.

verprügeln [fɛr'pryːɡəln] *v* thrash, beat.

verputzen [fɛr'putsən] *v* plaster; (*umg.*) scoff, put away.

Verrat [fɛr'raɪt] *m* (*unz.*) treachery; (*Pol*) treason; (*eines Gehimnisses*) betrayal. **verraten** *v* betray. **Verräter** *m* (*pl* **-**) traitor. **verräterisch** *adj* treacherous.

verrechnen [fɛr'rɛçnən] *v* reckon up. **sich verrechnen** miscalculate. **Verrechnung** *f* miscalculation.

verreisen [fɛr'raizən] *v* go away (on a journey).

verrenken [fɛr'rɛnkən] *v* dislocate, sprain. **Verrenkung** *f* (*pl* **-en**) dislocation, sprain.

verrichten [fɛr'riçtən] *v* perform, do, execute.

verriegeln [fɛr'riːɡəln] *v* bolt, bar.

verringern [fɛr'riŋərn] *v* reduce, lessen.

verrotten [fɛr'rɔtən] *v* rot. **verrottet** *adj* rotten.

verrücken [fɛr'rykən] *v* shift, displace. **verrückt** *adj* crazy.

Verruf [fɛr'ruːf] *m* ill repute, disrepute. **in Verruf bringen/kommen** bring/fall into disrepute.

Vers [fɛrs] *m* (*pl* **-e**) line; (*Strophe*) verse.

versagen [fɛr'zaːɡən] *v* fail; (*verweigern*) refuse. **Versager** *m* (*pl* **-**) failure.

versammeln [fɛr'zaməln] *v* assemble, gather. **sich versammeln** meet. **Versammlung** *f* (*pl* **-en**) meeting, assembly, convention.

Versand [fɛr'zant] *m* dispatch, shipment, forwarding. **–handel** *m* mail-order (trading).

versäumen [fɛr'zɔymən] *v* neglect, fail; (*verpassen*) miss. **Versäumnis** *f* neglect, omission.

verschaffen [fɛr'ʃafən] *v* obtain, procure.

verschämt [fɛr'ʃɛimt] *adj* bashful, ashamed.

Verschanzung [fɛr'ʃantsuŋ] *f* (*pl* **-en**) fortification, entrenchment.

verschärfen [fɛr'ʃɛrfən] *v* sharpen, intensify.

*****verscheiden** *v* die. **verschieden** *adj* dead.

verschicken [fɛrˈʃikən] v send off, dispatch.

***verschieben** [fɛrˈʃiːbən] v move, shift; (*Termin*) postpone. **Verschiebung** f displacement; postponement.

verschieden [fɛrˈʃiːdən] adj different. **–artig** adj various. **Verschiedenheit** f difference.

verschiffen [fɛrˈʃifən] v ship.

verschimmeln [fɛrˈʃiməln] v moulder, grow mouldy.

***verschlafen** [fɛrˈʃlaːfən] v oversleep; (*Sorgen*) sleep off. adj sleepy.

Verschlag [fɛrˈʃlaːk] m shed.

verschlechtern [fɛrˈʃlɛçtərn] v make worse, aggravate. **sich verschlechtern** deteriorate, get worse. **Verschlechterung** f deterioration.

verschleiern [fɛrˈʃlaiərn] v veil; (*fig*) camouflage, conceal.

Verschleiß [fɛrˈʃlais] m (*pl* -e) wear and tear. **verschließen** v wear out.

verschleudern [fɛrˈʃlɔydərn] v waste, squander.

verschließbar [fɛrˈʃliːsbair] adj lockable. **verschließen** v lock; (*Sachen*) lock up *or* away.

verschlimmern [fɛrˈʃlimərn] v make worse, aggravate. **sich verschlimmern** become worse, deteriorate. **Verschlimmerung** f deterioration.

***verschlingen** [fɛrˈʃliŋən] v devour, gorge; (*verflechten*) twist, intertwine.

verschlossen [fɛrˈʃlɔsən] adj locked; (*Person*) reserved, withdrawn.

verschlucken [fɛrˈʃlukən] v swallow.

Verschluß [fɛrˈʃlus] m fastening; (*Propfen*) stopper, plug; (*Phot*) shutter.

verschmähen [fɛrˈʃmɛiən] v disdain, scorn.

***verschmelzen** [fɛrˈʃmɛltsən] v melt, fuse; (*ineinander*) merge.

***verschneiden** [fɛrˈʃnaidən] v trim, prune; (*Wein*) mix, adulterate; (*kastrieren*) castrate.

verschollen [fɛrˈʃɔlən] adj missing.

verschonen [fɛrˈʃoːnən] v spare.

verschönern [fɛrˈʃœinərn] v beautify.

verschränken [fɛrˈʃrɛŋkən] v fold, cross.

verschulden [fɛrˈʃuldən] v fall into *or* be in debt; (*Übel*) be to blame for. **Verschulden** neut guilt, fault. **verschuldet** adj in debt.

***verschweigen** [fɛrˈʃvaigən] v keep secret, hide. **Verschweigung** f concealment.

verschwenden [fɛrˈʃvɛndən] v waste, squander. **verschwenderisch** adj wasteful. **Verschwendung** f waste.

verschwiegen [fɛrˈʃviːgən] adj discreet; (*Platz*) secluded, quiet. **Verschwiegenheit** f discretion.

***verschwinden** [fɛrˈʃvindən] v disappear.

verschwommen [fɛrˈʃvɔmən] adj blurred, hazy.

verschwören [fɛrˈʃvœirən] v renounce, abjure. **sich verschwören** conspire, plot. **Verschwör‖er** m conspirator, plotter. **–ung** f conspiracy.

***versehen** [fɛrˈzeiən] v (*versorgan*) provide, supply; (*Dienst*) discharge; (*Haus, usw.*) look after. **sich versehen** make a mistake. **Versehen** neut mistake; (*Übersehen*) oversight. **versehentlich** adv by mistake.

***versenden** [fɛrˈzɛndən] v send, dispatch.

versengen [fɛrˈzɛŋən] v singe, scorch.

versenken [fɛrˈzɛŋkən] v lower; (*unter Wasser*) submerge; (*Schiff*) sink. **sich versenken in** become absorbed in.

versessen [fɛrˈzɛsən] adj **versessen auf** mad about *or* on.

versetzen [fɛrˈzɛtsən] v move, transfer; (*verpfänden*) pawn; (*umg.*) leave in the lurch, jilt. **Versetzung** f removal, transfer.

verseuchen [fɛrˈzɔyçən] v contaminate.

versichern [fɛrˈziçərn] v insure; (*überzeugen*) assure. **sich versichern** make certain. **Seien Sie versichert, daß** you may rest assured that. **Versicherung** f insurance. **–spolice** f insurance policy.

versiegeln [fɛrˈziːgəln] v seal.

versöhnen [fɛrˈzœinən] v reconcile. **sich versöhnen mit** become reconciled with. **versöhnlich** adj conciliatory. **Versöhnung** f reconciliation.

versorgen [fɛrˈzɔrgən] v (*Kind, usw.*) provide for. **versorgen mit** provide *or* supply with. **Versorgung** f care, provision; (*staatlich*) maintenance, (public) assistance.

verspäten [fɛrˈʃpɛitən] v delay. **verspätet** adj late, delayed. **Verspätung** f (*pl* -en) delay. **10 Minuten Verspätung haben** be running 10 minutes late.

versperren [fɛrˈʃpɛrən] v bar; obstruct.

verspielen [fɛrˈʃpiːlən] v gamble away, lose.

verspotten [fɛrˈʃpɔtən] v scoff at, ridicule. **Verspottung** f ridicule.

*versprechen [fɛrˈʃprɛçən] v promise. **sich versprechen** make a (verbal) mistake. **Versprechen** neut (pl -) promise.

versprengen [fɛrˈʃprɛŋən] v (Mil) scatter, disperse.

versprochen [fɛrˈʃprɔxən] adj promised.

verstaatlichen [fɛrˈʃtaːtliçən] v nationalize. **Verstaatlichung** f nationalization.

Verstand [fɛrˈʃtant] m understanding; (Geist) mind, intelligence. **den Verstand verlieren** lose one's reason, go out of one's mind. **verständig** adj intelligent; sensible. **verständigen** v inform. **sich verständigen mit (über)** come to an understanding with (about). **Verständigung** f understanding, arrangement. **verständlich** adj intelligible. **Verständnis** neut understanding, comprehension. **verständnis∥los** adj uncomprehending, unappreciative. **-voll** adj understanding, sympathetic.

verstärken [fɛrˈʃtɛrkən] v strengthen; (Ton) amplify; (Farbe, Spannung) intensify. **Verstärk∥er** m amplifier. **-ung** f strengthening; (Ton) amplification; (Mil) reinforcements pl.

Versteck [fɛrˈʃtɛk] neut (pl -e) hiding place. **verstecken** v hide. **sich verstecken** hide. **versteckt** adj hidden; (Anspielung) veiled, implied.

*verstehen [fɛrˈʃteːən] v understand. **zu verstehen geben** give to understand. **sich verstehen mit** come to an understanding with.

Versteigerer [fɛrˈʃtaigərər] m (pl -) auctioneer. **versteigern** v (sell by) auction. **Versteigerung** f (pl -en) auction.

versteinern [fɛrˈʃtainərn] v petrify. **versteinert** adj petrified.

verstellbar [fɛrˈʃtɛlbaːr] adj adjustable, movable. **verstellen** v adjust; (versperren) block, bar; (unkenntlich machen) disguise. **sich verstellen** feign, dissemble. **Verstellung** f (pl -en) adjustment; (fig) pretence.

verstimmt [fɛrˈʃtimt] adj (Musik) out of tune; (Person) bad-tempered; (Magen) upset.

verstockt [fɛrˈʃtɔkt] adj stubborn.

verstohlen [fɛrˈʃtoːlən] adj furtive, stealthy.

verstopfen [fɛrˈʃtɔpfən] v plug, stop up;

(Med) constipate. **Verstopfung** f obstruction; (Med) constipation.

verstorben [fɛrˈʃtɔrbən] adj deceased, late. **Verstorbene(r)** the deceased.

Verstoß [fɛrˈʃtoːs] m offence. **verstoßen** v offend; (von sich stoßen) reject.

verstricken [fɛrˈʃtrikən] v entangle, ensnare.

verstümmeln [fɛrˈʃtyməln] v mutilate, maim.

Versuch [fɛrˈzuːx] m (pl -e) attempt; (Probe) test, trial; (Experiment) experiment. **versuchen** v attempt, try; (kosten) taste, try. **Versuchs∥fahrt** f trial run. **-kaninchen** neut (fig) guinea pig.

vertagen [fɛrˈtaːgən] v adjourn.

vertauschen [fɛrˈtauʃən] v exchange.

verteidigen [fɛrˈtaidigən] v defend. **Verteidig∥er** m (pl -) defender; (Jur) defence counsel. **-ung** f (pl -en) defence.

verteilen [fɛrˈtailən] v distribute; (zerteilen) divide. **Verteil∥er** m (pl -) distributor. **-ung** f (pl -en) distribution.

vertiefen [fɛrˈtiːfən] v deepen. **sich vertiefen in** be absorbed in. **vertieft** adj sunk; (fig) absorbed. **Vertiefung** f depression, hollow; (fig) absorption.

vertikal [vɛrtiˈkaːl] adj vertical.

vertilgen [fɛrˈtilgən] v exterminate; (vernichten) destroy. **Vertilgung** f extermination; destruction.

Vertrag [fɛrˈtraːk] m (pl Verträge) contract; (Pol) treaty. **vertragen** v bear, endure. **sich vertragen mit** get on well with. **vertraglich** adj stipulated, agreed.

verträglich [fɛrˈtrɛːkliç] adj (Person) good-natured, obliging; (Speise) light, digestible.

Vertrags∥bruch m breach of contract. **-nehmer** m contractor.

vertrauen [fɛrˈtrauən] v trust. **vertrauen auf** trust in, have confidence in. **Vertrauen** neut trust, confidence. **Vertrauens∥sache** f confidential affair. **-votum** neut vote ̇ of confidence. **vertrauens∥voll** adj trustful, trusting. **-würdig** adj trustworthy. **vertraulich** adj confidential. **vertraut** adj familiar.

*vertreiben [fɛrˈtraibən] v expel, drive away; (verkaufen) sell. **Vertreibung** f (pl -en) expulsion.

*vertreten [fɛrˈtreːtən] v represent; (vorübergehend) replace, stand in for; (eintreten für) advocate. **Vertret∥er** m (pl

-) representative; (*Komm*) sales representative; **–ung** *f* (*pl* -**en**) representation.
Vertrieb [fɛrˈtriːp] *m* (retail) sale.
***vertun** [fɛrˈtuːn] *v* squander, spend.
vertuschen [fɛrˈtuʃən] *v* hush up.
verunglimpfen [fɛrˈʊnglɪmpfən] *v* defame,
revile.
verunglücken [fɛrˈʊnglykən] *v* be
involved in an accident; (*Angelegenheit*)
fail.
verunreinigen [fɛrˈʊntainigən] *v* pollute,
soil.
verunstalten [fɛrˈʊnʃtaltən] *v* disfigure.
veruntreuen [fɛrˈʊntrɔyən] *v* embezzle.
verursachen [fɛrˈuːrzaxən] *v* cause, bring
about.
verurteilen [fɛrˈuːrtailən] *v* condemn;
(*Jur*) sentence. **Verurteilung** *f* condemnation; conviction.
vervielfältigen [fɛrˈfiːlfɛltigən] *v* duplicate,
copy. **Vervielfältigung** *f* reproduction,
duplication.
vervollkommnen [fɛrˈfɔlkɔmnən] *v* perfect.
vervollständigen [fɛrˈfɔlʃtɛndigən] *v* complete.
***verwachsen** [fɛrˈvaksən] *v* grow togeth-
er; (*Wunde*) heal up; (*bucklig werden*)
become deformed; (*sich verbinden*) be
tied to. *adj* deformed.
verwahren [fɛrˈvaːrən] *v* keep; (*schützen*)
protect, preserve.
verwahrlosen [fɛrˈvaːrloːzən] *v* neglect.
verwahrlost *adj* neglected; (*Kind*) scruffy,
unkempt.
verwalten [fɛrˈvaltən] *v* administer, manage. **Verwalter** *m* administrator; (*Fabrik,
Büro*) manager; (*Gut, Haus*) steward.
Verwaltung *f* administration; management.
verwandeln [fɛrˈvandəln] *v* transform;
(*ändern*) change. **Verwandlung** *f* transformation; change.
verwandt [fɛrˈvant] *adj* related. **Ver-
wandt‖e(r)** relative, relation. **–schaft** *f*
relationship; (*Verwandte*) relatives *pl*.
verwechseln [fɛrˈvɛksəln] *v* confuse.
verwechseln mit mistake for, confuse
with. **Verwechslung** *f* confusion.
verwegen [fɛrˈveːgən] *adj* bold, audacious.
verweichlicht [fɛrˈvaiçlɪçt] *adj* effeminate.
verweigern [fɛrˈvaigərn] *v* refuse.
Verweigerung *f* refusal.
verweilen [fɛrˈvailən] *v* linger, stay.
Verweis [fɛrˈvais] *m* (*pl* -**e**) reprimand,

rebuke; (*Hinweis*) reference. **verweisen** *v*
reprimand, rebuke; (*verbannen*) exile,
banish. **verweisen auf** refer to.
***verwenden** [fɛrˈvɛndən] *v* use, employ;
apply; (*Zeit*) spend. **Verwendung** *f* use;
application.
***verwerfen** [fɛrˈvɛrfən] *v* throw away;
(*zurückweisen*) reject.
verwesen¹ [fɛrˈveːzən] *v* (*verwalten*)
administer.
verwesen² *v* (*verfaulen*) decay.
verwickeln [fɛrˈvikəln] *n* entangle. **sich
verwickeln in** become involved in.
verwickelt *adj* complicated. **Verwicklung**
f (*pl* -**en**) entanglement, complication.
verwirken [fɛrˈvirkən] *v* forfeit.
verwirklichen [fɛrˈvirkliçən] *v* realize. **sich
verwirklichen** come true, materialize.
Verwirklichung *f* realization.
***verwirren** [fɛrˈvirən] *v* confuse, bewilder.
verwirrt *adj* confused. **Verwirrung** *f* confusion.
verwischen [fɛrˈviʃən] *v* blur, smear; (*fig*)
cover up, wipe out.
verwitwet [fɛrˈvitvət] *adj* widowed.
verwöhnen [fɛrˈvøːnən] *v* spoil. **verwöhnt**
adj pampered, spoiled.
verworfen [fɛrˈvɔrfən] *adj* depraved.
verworren [fɛrˈvɔrən] *adj* confused.
verwundbar [fɛrˈvuntbaːr] *adj* vulnerable.
verwunden *v* wound, hurt. **verwundet** *adj*
wounded. **Verwundete(r)** injured person;
(*Mil*) casualty. **Verwundung** *f* wound,
injury.
verwunderlich [fɛrˈvundərliç] *adj* surprising. **verwundern** *v* surprise, astonish.
sich verwundern über be astonished by,
wonder about. **Verwunderung** *f* astonishment.
verwünschen [fɛrˈvynʃən] *v* curse.
verwünscht *adj* cursed, bewitched.
verwüsten [fɛrˈvyːstən] *v* devastate.
Verwüstung *f* devastation.
verzagt [fɛrˈtsaikt] *adj* downcast, despondent.
verzaubern [fɛrˈtsaubərn] *v* enchant,
charm. **verzaubert** *adj* enchanted, magic.
Verzehr [fɛrˈtseːr] *m* consumption (of
food and drink). **verzehren** *v* consume,
take, eat.
verzeichnen [fɛrˈtsaiçnən] *v* note, enter,
write down. **Verzeichnis** *neut* (*pl* -**se**) list,
catalogue; (*Buch*) index; (*Register*) register.

*verzeihen [fɛrˈtsaiən] v pardon, forgive. **verzeihen Sie!** pardon (me)! I'm sorry! **Verzeihung** f pardon, forgiveness. *interj* I beg your pardon! excuse me!

verzerren [fɛrˈtsɛrən] v distort.

Verzicht [fɛrˈtsiçt] m (pl -e) renunciation. **verzichten auf** renounce, do without.

verziehen [fɛrˈtsiːən] v distort; (*Kinder*) spoil.

verzieren [fɛrˈtsiːrən] v decorate, adorn.

verzögern [fɛrˈtsœɪgərn] v delay. **Verzögerung** f (pl -en) delay.

verzollen [fɛrˈtsɔlən] v pay duty on.

verzücken [fɛrˈtsukən] v enrapture. **verzückt** adj enraptured, ecstatic. **Verzückung** f (pl -en) rapture, ecstasy.

verzuckern [fɛrˈtsukərn] v sugar.

Verzug [fɛrˈtsuk] m (unz.) delay.

verzweifeln [fɛrˈtsvaifəln] v despair. **verzweifelt** adj desperate. **Verzweiflung** f despair.

verzwickt [fɛrˈtsvikt] adj complicated, difficult.

veterinär [veteriˈnɛːr] adj veterinary. **Veterinär** m (pl -e) veterinary surgeon.

Vibration [vibratsiˈoːn] f (pl -en) vibration. **vibrieren** v vibrate.

Vieh [fiː] 1 neut (unz.) cattle pl. 2 neut (pl **Viecher**) beast. **viehisch** adj bestial, brutal. **Vieh‖stall** m cowshed. **–treiber** m drover. **–zucht** f cattle-breeding.

viel [fiːl] adj much. **viele** pl adj many. **so viel** so much. **viel besser** much better. **viel mehr als** far more than. **recht viel** a great deal. **viel halten von** think much or highly of. **viel‖fach** adj multiple. adv frequently, many times. **–fältig** adj various, manifold.

vielleicht [fiˈlaiçt] adv perhaps.

viel‖mal(s) adv often, many times. **–mehr** adv, conj rather. **–seitig** adj many-sided. **–versprechend** adj (very) promising.

vier [fiːr] pron, adj four. **Viereck** neut square, rectangle. **viereckig** adj square, rectangular. **viermal(s)** adv four times. **viert** adj fourth. **Viertaktmotor** m four-stroke engine. **Viertel** neut quarter. **–stunde** f quarter (of an) hour. **viertens** adv fourthly.

vierzehn [ˈfiːrtsein] pron, adj fourteen. **vierzehn Tage** fortnight. **vierzehnt** adj fourteenth.

vierzig [ˈfiːrtsiç] pron, adj forty. **vierzigst** adj fortieth.

Villa [ˈvila] f (pl **Villen**) villa.

Viola [viˈoːla] f (pl **Violen**) viola. **Viol‖ine** f violin. **–inist** m (pl -), **–inistin** f (pl -nen) violinist. **–oncello** neut violoncello, cello.

Virtuose [virtuˈoːzə] m (pl -n) virtuoso.

Visite [viˈziːtə] f (pl -n) visit. **–nkarte** f visiting card.

Visum [ˈviːzum] neut (pl **Visa**) visa.

Vitamin [vitaˈmiːn] neut (pl -e) vitamin.

Vlies [fliːs] neut (pl -e) fleece.

Vogel [ˈfoːgəl] m (pl **Vögel**) bird. **–gesang** m bird-song. **–haus** neut aviary. **–kunde** f ornithology. **–perpektive** f or **–schau** f bird's-eye view.

vokal [voˈkaːl] adj vocal. **Vokal** m vowel.

Volk [fɔlk] neut (pl **Völker**) people, folk; nation.

Völker‖kunde f ethnology. **–schaft** people, tribe. **völkisch** adj national.

Volks‖eigentum neut public property. **–entscheid** m plebiscite, referendum. **–gruppe** f ethnic group. **–lied** neut (traditional) folksong. **–menge** f crowd. **–schule** f primary school. **–staat** m republic. **–tanz** m folk dance. **–tracht** f national costume.

volkstümlich [ˈfɔlkstyɪmliç] adj popular.

Volkswirt [ˈfɔlksvirt] m economist. **–schaft** f (political) economy. **volkswirtschaftlich** adj economic.

voll [fɔl] adj full. adv fully. der Topf ist voll Wasser the pot is full of water. ein Glas voll Milch a glassful of milk. in voller Blüte in full bloom. volles Gesicht round face. **voll‖auf** adv in abundance. **–automatisch** adj fully automatic. **–berechtigt** adj fully authorized. **–beschäftigt** adj fully employed. **–blütig** adj full-blooded.

*vollbringen [fɔˈbriŋən] v accomplish. **Vollbringung** f accomplishment.

vollenden [fɔlˈɛndən] v finish, end, complete. **vollendet** adj completed; (*vervollkomnet*) perfect. **Vollendung** f completion; perfection.

voller [ˈfɔlər] adj or **voll von** full (of).

völlig [ˈfœliç] adj complete, entire, whole.

vollkommen [ˈfɔlkɔmən] adj perfect, finished. **Vollkommenheit** f perfection.

Voll‖kornbrot neut wholemeal bread. **–macht** f power of attorney, authority. **–milch** f whole milk.

voll‖ständig *adj* complete. **–stopfen** *v* stuff.

vollstrecken [fɔl'ʃtrɛkən] *v* execute, carry out. **Vollstreck‖er** *m* (*pl* -), **–erin** *f* (*pl* **-nen**) executor. **–ung** *f* (*pl* **-en**) execution.

*vollziehen [fɔl'tsiːən] *v* carry out, execute.

Volontär [vɔlɔn'tɛːr] *m* (*pl* **-e**) volunteer (worker), unpaid helper.

vom [fɔm] *prep* + *art* von dem.

von [fɔn] *prep* from; (*einer Person gehörig*) of; (*einer Person stammend*) by. *das Buch von Peter* Peter's book. *ein Buch von Greene* a book by Greene. *ein Freund von ihm* a friend of his. **von . . . an** starting, from. **von nun an** from now on. *von mir aus* as far as I am concerned. **von selbst** by itself, automatically.

vor [foːr] *prep* in front of; (*zeitlich*) before. *vor acht Tagen* a week ago. *vor allem* above all. *nach wie vor* as ever. *nicht vor* not until. *Viertel vor 12* (a) quarter to twelve. **vor Zeiten** formerly.

Vorabend ['foːraːbənt] *m* eve.

Vorahnung ['foːraːnuŋ] *f* presentiment.

voran [fo'ran] *adv* at the head, in front, first. **–gehen** *v* go ahead, precede. **–kommen** *v* make progress.

Voranschlag ['foːrʔanʃlaːk] *m* rough estimate.

Vorarbeiter ['foːrarbaitər] *m* foreman, supervisor.

voraus [fo'raus] *adv* ahead, in front. **im voraus** in advance. **vorausbestimmen** *v* predetermine. **vorausgesetzt daß** provided that. **Voraussage** *f* prediction. **voraus‖sagen** *v* predict, forecast. **–sehen** *v* foresee. **Voraus‖setzung** *f* assumption; (*Vorbedingung*) prerequisite. **–sicht** *f* foresight. **voraussichtlich** *adv* probably. **Vorauszahlung** *f* advance payment.

vorbedacht ['foːrbədaxt] *adj* premeditated. **Vorbedacht** *m* forethought. **mit Vorbedacht** on purpose, advisedly.

Vorbedingung ['foːrbədiŋuŋ] *f* precondition, prerequisite.

Vorbehalt ['foːrbəhalt] *m* (*pl* **-e**) reservation, proviso. **vorbehalten** *v* hold in reserve, withhold.

vorbei [fɔr'bai] *adv* (*örtlich*) past, by; (*zeitlich*) past, over. **vorbei sein** be all over. **vorbei‖gehen** *v* go past, pass. **–kommen** *v* pass by. **–marschieren** *v* march past.

vorbereiten ['foːrbəraitən] *v* prepare. **Vorbereitungen** *pl* preparations.

vorbestellen ['foːrbəʃtɛlən] *v* book in advance.

Vorbestrafte(r) ['foːrbəʃtraːftə(r)] *m* person with previous conviction.

vorbeugen ['foːrbɔygən] *v* prevent. **Vorbeugung** *f* prevention.

Vorbild ['foːrbilt] *neut* model, example. **vorbildlich** *adj* model, exemplary.

*vorbringen ['foːrbriŋən] *v* bring up, put forward.

vorder ['fɔrdər] *adj* fore(most) front. **Vorder‖bein** *neut* foreleg. **–grund** *m* foreground. **–radantrieb** *m* front-wheel drive. **–seite** *f* façade; obverse; face (of coin). **–teil** *m* front (part). **–tür** *f* front door.

*vordringen ['foːrdriŋən] *v* advance, press forward. **vordringlich** *adj* urgent, pressing.

voreilig ['foːrailiç] *adj* premature, hasty, precipitate.

voreingenommen ['foːraingənɔmən] *adj* prejudiced. **voreingenommen gegen** prejudiced against. **voreingenommen für** biased in favour of. **Voreingenommenheit** *f* prejudice.

*vorenthalten ['foːrʔɛnthaltən] *v* hold back, withhold.

vorerst ['foːreːrst] *adv* for the time being.

vorerwähnt ['foːrʔɛrvɛːnt] *adj* above-mentioned, already mentioned, aforesaid.

Vorfahr ['foːrfaːr] *m* (*pl* **-en**) ancestor.

Vorfahrt ['foːrfaːrt] *f* right-of-way.

Vorfall ['foːrfal] *m* incident.

vorführen ['foːrfyːrən] *v* bring forward, present; (*zeigen*) show; (*Film*) project. **Vorführung** *f* presentation, demonstration; (*Film*) showing.

Vorgang ['foːrgaŋ] *m* event, incident; (*Tech*) process; (*Komm*) file, record. **Vorgänger** *m* predecessor.

*vorgeben ['foːrgeːbən] *v* pretend.

Vorgebirge ['foːrgəbirgə] *neut* foothills *pl*; (*Kap*) promontory.

vorgeblich ['foːrgeːpliç] *adj* alleged, ostensible.

vorgefaßt ['foːrgəfast] *adj* preconceived.

Vorgefühl ['foːrgəfyːl] *neut* presentiment.

*vorgehen ['foːrgeːən] *v* go forward; (*handeln*) act, proceed; (*geschehen*) occur; (*Uhr*) be fast; (*wichtiger sein*) take precedence; (*führen*) lead (on). **Vorgehen** *neut* advance; proceedings *pl*.

vorgenannt ['foːrgənant] *adj* above-mentioned.

Vorgeschichte ['foːrgəʃiçtə] *f* previous history; (*Urgeschichte*) prehistory.

Vorgeschmack ['foːrgəʃmak] *m* foretaste.

Vorgesetzte(r) ['foːrgəzɛtstə] *m* superior.

vorgestern ['foːrgɛstərn] *adv* the day before yesterday.

*****vorhaben** ['foːrhaɪbən] *v* intend, plan. *haben Sie heute etwas vor?* have you anything arranged for today?

Vorhalle ['foːrhalə] *f* vestibule, entrance (hall).

vorhanden ['foːrhandən] *adj* existing, available. **Vorhandensein** *neut* existence, availability.

Vorhang ['foːrhaŋ] *m* (*pl* **Vorhänge**) curtain.

vorher [foːr'heːr] *adv* before(hand), previously. **Vorhersage** *f* prediction. **vorher‖sagen** *v* predict. **–sehen** *v* foresee.

vorherrschend ['foːrhɛrʃənt] *adj* predominant.

vorhin ['foːrhin] *adv* a short while ago, just now.

Vorhut ['foːrhuːt] *f* (*pl* **-en**) vanguard.

vorig ['foːriç] *adj* previous.

Vorjahr ['foːrjaːr] *neut* last year. **vorjährig** *adj* last year's.

vorjammern ['foːrjamərn] *v* lament, complain.

Vorkämpfer ['foːrkɛmpfər] *m* (*pl* **-**) advocate, champion.

Vorkehrung ['foːrkeːruŋ] *f* (*pl* **-en**) precaution.

Vorkenntnis ['foːrkɛntnis] *f* previous knowledge. **Vorkenntnisse** *pl* rudiments, basic knowledge *sing*.

*****vorkommen** ['foːrkɔmən] *v* (*geschehen*) happen, take place; (*sich finden*) occur, be found; (*nach vorn kommen*) come forward; (*scheinen*) seem, appear.

*****vorladen** ['foːrlaːdən] *v* summon. **Vorladung** *f* summons.

Vorlage ['foːrlaːgə] *f* submission, presentation; (*Muster*) model; (*Gesetz*) bill.

Vorläufer ['foːrlɔyfər] *m* forerunner. **vorläufig** *adv* provisional, temporary.

vorlaut ['foːrlaut] *adj* forward, nosy.

vorlegen ['foːrleːgən] *v* present; (*Essen*) serve.

*****vorlesen** ['foːrleːzən] *v* read out, read aloud. **Vorlesung** *f* (*pl* **-en**) lecture.

vorletzt ['foːrlɛtst] *adj* last but one, penultimate.

Vorliebe ['foːrliːbə] *f* preference, liking.

*****vorliegen** ['foːrliːgən] *v* be, exist; (*Arbeit*) be in hand. **der vorliegende Fall** the case in point, the case in question.

Vormachtstellung ['foːrmaxtʃtɛluŋ] *f* hegemony.

vormals ['foːrmaɪls] *adv* formerly.

Vormittag ['foːrmitaɪk] *m* morning. **vormittags** *adv* in the morning.

Vormund ['foːrmunt] *m* guardian.

vorn [fɔrn] *adv* in front, ahead. **nach vorn** forward. **von vorn** from the start.

Vorname ['foːrnaɪmə] *m* first name, Christian name.

vornehm ['foːrneɪm] *adj* (*von höherem Stand*) distinguished; (*edel*) noble; elegant, (*umg.*) posh.

vornherein ['foːrnherain] *adv* **von vornherein** from the start.

Vorort ['foːrɔrt] *m* outpost.

Vorrang ['foːrraŋ] *m* precedence, priority.

Vorrat ['foːrraɪt] *m* supply, stock. **vorrätig** *adj* in stock.

Vorrecht ['foːrrɛçt] *neut* privilege.

Vorrede ['foːrreɪdə] *f* introduction; (*Buch*) preface.

Vorrichtung ['fɔːrriçtuŋ] *f* (*pl* **-en**) device.

vorrücken ['foːrrykən] *v* move forward, advance.

Vorsatz ['foːrzats] *m* intention, purpose. **vorsätzlich** *adj* intentional.

Vorschau ['foːrʃau] *f* preview; (*Film*) trailer.

*****vorschieben** ['foːrʃiːbən] *v* push forward; (*Entschuldigung*) plead (as an excuse).

vorschiessen ['foːrʃiːsən] *v* advance (money).

Vorschlag ['foːrʃlaːk] *m* suggestion, proposal. **vorschlagen** *v* suggest, propose.

Vorschlußrunde ['foːrʃlusrundə] *f* semifinal.

vorschneiden ['fɔːrʃnaidən] *v* carve.

vorschreiben ['foːrʃraibən] *v* prescribe, order.

Vorschrift ['foːrʃrift] *f* rule, regulation; (*Befehl*) order; (*Med*) prescription. **vorschrifts‖gemäß** *adj, adv* in accordance with regulations. **–widrig** *adj, adv* contrary to regulations.

Vorschub ['foːrʃuːp] *m* assistance, support. **Vorschub leisten** assist, support.

Vorschule ['foːrʃuːlə] *f* prep school.

Vorschuß ['foːrʃus] *m* (cash) advance.

vorschützen ['foːrʃytsən] v pretend. **Unwissenheit vorschützen** plead ignorance.

vorsehen ['foːrzeːən] v assign, earmark. **sich vorsehen** take care, mind. **Vorsehung** f providence.

vorsetzen ['foːrzɛtsən] v put (forward); (anbieten) offer, put before.

Vorsicht ['foːrzɪçt] f caution, care. interj be careful! take care! **vorsichtig** adj careful, cautious. **Vorsichtsmaßnahme** f precaution.

Vorsitz ['foːrzits] m chair(manship). **den Vorsitz führen** be in the chair, preside. **Vorsitzende(r)** chairman.

Vorsorge ['foːrzɔrgə] f (unz.) provision, precaution, advance measure. **versorglich** adj provident. adv as a precaution.

Vorspeise ['foːrʃpaizə] f hors d'oeuvre, starter.

vorspiegeln ['foːrʃpiːgəln] v **jemandem etwas vorspiegeln** delude someone with something. **Vorspiegelung** f misrepresentation.

Vorspiel ['foːrʃpiːl] neut prelude.

*vorspringen ['foːrʃpriŋən] v leap forward; (hervorragen) project.

Vorsprung ['foːrʃpruŋ] m (Vorteil) lead, advantage; (Arch) projection.

Vorstadt ['foːrʃtat] f suburb.

Vorstand ['foːrʃtant] m board of directors, management.

*vorstehen ['foːrʃteːən] v protrude; (leiten) manage, be head of. **-d** adj protruding; (vorangehend) preceding. **Vorsteher** m chief, superintendant, manager. **-in** f manageress.

vorstellbar ['foːrʃtɛlbaːr] adj imaginable. **vorstellen** v put forward; (Person) introduce; (bedeuten) mean. **sich vorstellen** introduce oneself. **sich etwas vorstellen** imagine something. **Vorstellung** f introduction; (Begriff) idea; (Theater) performance. **-skraft** f (power of) imagination.

vorstrecken ['foːrʃtrɛkən] v stretch out.

Vorstufe ['foːrʃtuːfə] f first stage.

Vorteil ['foːrtail] m advantage. **vorteilhaft** adj advantageous, favourable.

Vortrag ['foːrtraːk] m (pl Vorträge) (Vorlesung) talk, lecture; (Komm) balance carried forward. **vortragen** v lecture; (Gedicht) recite; (Meinung) express;

(Rede) deliver. **Vortragssaal** m lecture hall.

vortrefflich [foːr'trɛfliç] adj excellent.

*vortreten ['foːrtreːtən] v step forward; (hervorragen) protrude.

Vortritt ['foːrtrit] m precedence.

vorüber [fo'ryːbər] adv past; (Zeit) over, past. **-gehen** v pass. **-gehend** adj passing, temporary.

Vorurteil ['foːrurtail] neut prejudice. **vorurteilsfrei** adj unprejudiced.

Vorverkauf ['foːrfɛrkauf] m advance sale; (Theater) advance booking.

Vorwahl ['foːrvaːl] f preliminary election, (US) primary. **Vorwahlnummer** f (Telef) area code.

Vorwand ['foːrvant] f pretence, pretext, excuse.

vorwärts ['foːrvɛrts] adv forward(s), onward(s). **-bringen** v promote, further. **-gehen** v go ahead. **-kommen** v make progress.

vorweg [for'vɛk] adv in advance. **-nehmen** v anticipate, forestall.

*vorwerfen ['foːrvɛrfən] v reproach with.

vorwiegend ['foːrviːsən] adj preponderant. adv chiefly, mostly.

Vorwissen ['foːrvisən] neut foreknowledge, prescience.

Vorwort ['foːrvɔrt] neut (pl -e) preface, foreword.

Vorwurf ['foːrvurf] m reproach.

Vorzeichen ['foːrtsaiçən] neut omen; (Math) sign.

*vorzeigen ['foːrtsaigən] v produce, display.

Vorzeit ['foːrtsait] f antiquity. **vorzeitig** adj premature, too early.

*vorziehen ['foːrtsiːən] v (bevorzugen) prefer; (hervorziehen) pull forward.

Vorzug ['foːrtsuːk] m preference; (Vorteil) advantage; (Eigenschaft) merit, good quality. **vorzüglich** adj excellent, superb. **Vorzugsrecht** neut priority.

vulgär [vul'gɛːr] adj vulgar.

Vulkan [vul'kaːn] m (pl -e) volcano. **vulkanisch** adj volcanic.

W

Waage ['vaɪgə] f (pl -n) scales pl. **waagerecht** adj horizontal.
wabbelig ['vabəliç] adj wobbly, flabby.
Wabe ['vaɪbə] f (pl -n) honeycomb.
wach [vax] adj awake. **Wache** f (pl -n) watch, guard; (Polizei) station. **wachen** v be awake; (Wache halten) keep watch. **wachen über** watch over.
Wachs [vaks] neut (pl -e) wax.
wachsam ['vaxzaɪm] adj watchful, alert. **Wachsamkeit** f watchfulness, vigilance.
***wachsen** ['vaksən] v grow. **-d** adj increasing, growing. **Wachstum** neut growth.
Wacht [vaxt] f (pl -en) watch, guard.
Wachtel ['vaxtəl] f (pl -n) quail.
Wächter ['vɛçtər] m (pl -) watchman, guard. **Wacht∥hund** neut watchdog. **-meister** m sergeant-major; (Polizist) constable. **-turm** m watchtower.
wackelig ['vakəliç] adj wobbly, shaky. **wackeln** v wobble, shake.
wacker ['vakər] adj brave, stout; (anständig) worthy.
Wade ['vaɪdə] f (pl -n) (Anat) calf.
Waffe ['vafə] f (pl -n) weapon.
Waffel ['vafəl] f (pl -n) waffle; (Eis) wafer.
waffenlos ['vafənloɪs] adj unarmed. **waffnen** v arm. **Waffenstillstand** m armistice.
wagehalsig ['vaɪgəhalsiç] adj reckless, daring. **Wagemut** m daring. **wagen** v dare, risk, venture. **sich wagen** venture.
Wagen ['vaɪgən] m (pl -) (Mot) car; (Kutsche) coach; (Karren) wagon, cart; (Eisenbahn) carriage.
***wägen** ['vɛɪgən] v weigh.
Wagen∥führer m driver. **-heber** m (Mot) jack.
Waggon [va'gɔ̃] m (pl -s) (railway) wagon.
Wagnis ['vaɪknis] neut (pl -se) (Mut) daring; (Unternehmen) venture; (Risiko) risk.
wahl [vaɪl] f (pl -en) choice; (Pol) election. **wahlberechtigt** adj enfranchised, entitled to vote. **Wahl∥bezirk** m constituency, electoral district. **-bude** f polling booth.
wählen ['vɛɪlən] v choose; (Pol) elect; (Telef) dial.
wählerisch ['vɛɪləriʃ] adj particular, fussy, choosy. **Wählerschaft** f electorate, voters pl.
Wahl∥feldzug m (election) campaign.

-gang m ballot. **wahllos** adj indiscriminate. **Wahlrecht** neut franchise, suffrage.
Wählscheibe ['vɛɪlʃaibə] f (telephone) dial.
Wahl∥tag m election day. **-zettel** m ballot (paper).
Wahn [vaɪn] m (unz.) delusion; madness. **-sinn** m insanity, madness. **wahnsinnig** adj insane, mad. **Wahnsinnige(r)** madman, madwoman.
wahr [vaɪr] adj true; (wirklich) real; (echt) genuine.
wahren ['vaɪrən] v take care of; (schützen) protect; (erhalten) maintain.
während ['vɛɪrən] v last.
während ['vɛɪrənt] prep during. conj while.
wahrhaft ['vaɪrhaft] adj true, genuine. adv really, truly. **-ig** adj sincere, truthful. adv really, indeed. **Wahr∥haftigkeit** f truthfulness. **-heit** f (pl -en) truth. **wahr∥nehmen** v perceive; (Interessen) protect; (Gelegenheit) seize, take. **-sagen** v foretell (the future). **-scheinlich** adj likely, probable. **Wahrscheinlichkeit** f probability.
Wahrung ['vaɪruŋ] f preservation, maintenance.
Währung ['vɛɪruŋ] f (pl -en) currency.
Waise ['vaɪzə] (pl -n) orphan. **-nknabe** m orphan boy.
Wal [vaɪl] m (pl -e) whale.
Wald [valt] m (pl Wälder) wood, forest. **-beere** f cranberry. **-brand** m forest fire. **waldig** adj wooded. **Wald∥ung** f (pl -en) woodland. **-wirtschaft** f forestry.
Walfang ['vaɪlfaŋ] m whaling.
Wall [val] m (pl Wälle) earthworks pl, embankment.
wallen ['valən] v boil.
***wallfahren** ['valfaɪrən] v go on a pilgrimage. **Wall∥fahrer** m pilgrim. **-fahrt** f pilgrimage.
Walnuß ['valnus] f walnut.
Wal∥öl neut whale-oil. **-roß** neut walrus.
Walze ['valtsə] f (pl -n) roller. **walzen** v roll; (tanzen) waltz.
wälzen ['vɛltsən] v roll.
Walzer ['valtsər] m (pl -) waltz.
Wand [vant] f (pl Wände) wall.
Wandel ['vandəl] m change. **wandelbar** adj variable; (Person) changeable, fickle. **wandeln** v change. **sich wandeln in** change or turn into.

Wanderer ['vandərər] m (pl -) wanderer; (auf dem Lande) hiker, rambler. **Wanderlust** f wanderlust. **wandern** v wander; ramble, hike. **-d** adj wandering; (Volk, Tiere) migratory. **Wanderung** f (pl -en) (zu Fuß) walking-tour, hike; (Volk, Tiere) migration.

Wandgemälde ['vantgəmɛldə] neut mural.

Wandlung ['vandluŋ] f (pl -en) change; (total) transformation; (Rel) transubstantiation.

Wange ['vaŋə] f (pl -n) cheek.

Wankelmut ['vaŋkəlmuːt] m fickleness, inconstancy. **wankelmütig** adj fickle, inconstant.

wanken ['vaŋkən] v rock, sway; (Person) totter, reel; (fig) waver, vacillate. **-d** adj wavering.

wann [van] adv when.

Wanne ['vanə] f (pl -n) tub; (Badewanne) bath(tub). **-nbad** neut bath.

Wanze ['vantsə] f (pl -n) bug.

Wappen ['vapən] neut (pl -) (coat of) arms. **-kunde** f heraldry.

Ware ['vaːrə] f (pl -n) article, commodity. **Waren** pl goods, wares, merchandise sing. **Waren‖haus** neut department store. **-markt** m commodity market.

warm [varm] adj warm; (Getränk, Essen) hot. **warmer Bruder** (umg.) homosexual. **Wärme** ['vɛrmə] f warmth; temperature; (Physik) heat. **wärmen** v warm (up), heat. **Wärmflasche** f hot-water bottle.

warnen ['varnən] v warn. **Warnung** f (pl -en) warning.

Warschau ['varʃau] neut Warsaw.

warten ['vartən] v wait; (pflegen) care for; (Maschine) service, maintain. **warten auf** wait for.

Wärter ['vɛrtər] m (pl -), **Wärterin** f (pl -nen) attendant; (Kranken) nurse; (Gefängnis) warder.

Warte‖saal m waiting room. **-zimmer** neut waiting room. **Wartung** f maintenance, upkeep.

warum [va'rum] adv why.

Warze ['vartsə] f (pl -n) wart; (Brust) nipple.

was [vas] pron what; (umg.) something. **ach was!** nonsense! **was ist mit ...** how about .... **was für ...** what sort of .... **alles was ich sehe** everything that I see.

Waschbecken ['vaʃbekən] neut wash basin.

Wäsche ['vɛʃə] f (pl -n) washing, laundry.

waschecht [vaʃeçt] adj (Farbe) (colour-) fast; (fig) thorough, dyed-in-the-wool.

Wäsche‖klammer f clothes-peg, (US) clothes-pin. **-korb** m laundry basket. **-leine** f clothes-line.

***waschen** [vaʃən] v wash.

Wäscherei ['vɛʃa'rai] f (pl -en) laundry.

Wasch‖lappen m facecloth. **-maschine** f washing machine. **-mittel** neut detergent, washing powder. **-tag** m wash(ing) day.

Wasser ['vasər] neut (pl -) water. **-abfluß** m drain. **-abfuhr** f drainage. **-behälter** m tank, reservoir. **-dampf** m steam, water vapour.

wasser‖dicht adj waterproof; (Gefäß) watertight. **-fest** adj waterproof.

wässerig ['vɛsəriç] adj watery.

Wasser‖kraftwerk neut hydroelectric plant. **-leitung** f water mains pl. **-mann** m (Astrol) Aquarius.

wässern ['vɛsərn] v water; (bewassern) irrigate; (Erbsen, usw.) soak.

Wasser‖pflanze f aquatic plant. **-rad** neut water wheel. **-stoff** m hydrogen. **-tier** neut aquatic animal.

Wässerung ['vɛsəruŋ] f watering; (Bewässern) irrigation.

Wasser‖versorgung f water supply. **-weg** m waterway. **-werk** neut waterworks pl.

Watte ['vatə] f (pl -n) wadding, cotton wool. **-bausch** m swab.

weben ['veːbən] v weave. **Web‖er** m (pl -), **Weberin** f (pl -nen) weaver. **-stoff** m textile. **-stuhl** m loom.

Wechsel ['vɛksəl] m (pl -) change; (Austausch) exchange; (Komm) bill (of exchange). **-folge** f alternation. **-geld** neut change. **-jahre** pl menopause sing, change of life sing. **wechseln** v (ex)change; (variieren) vary. **wechselseitig** adj alternating; (gegenseitig) mutual, reciprocal. **Wechsel‖strom** m alternating current. **-zahn** f milk tooth.

wecken ['vɛkən] v awaken, wake up. **Wecker** m (pl -) alarm clock.

wedeln ['veːdəln] v (Schwanz) wag.

weder ['veːdər] conj neither. **weder ... noch ...** neither ... nor ....

weg [vɛk] adv away, off, gone. Hände weg! hands off! er ist schon weg he has already left. meine Uhr ist weg my watch has gone. weit weg far off. **Weg** m (pl -e) way; (Straße) road; (Pfad) path.

weg‖bleiben v stay away. —blicken v look away. —bringen v take away, remove.

wegen ['veɪɡən] prep because of, on account of.

weg‖fahren v drive away; (abfahren) leave. —fallen v fall away; (aufhören) stop; (ausgelassen werden) be omitted. —führen v lead away. —gehen v go away. —kommen v get away. —lassen v omit. —müssen v must go, have to leave.

Wegnahme [vɛknaːmə] f (pl -n) confiscation, seizure. wegnehmen v take away; (beschlagnahmen) confiscate, seize; (Zeit, Raum) occupy.

weg‖räumen v clear away. —schaffen v get rid of. —schikken v send away. —schließen v lock away. —treiben v drive off.

Wegweiser [veɪkvaizər] m (pl -) signpost; (Buch, Mensch) guide.

weg‖wenden v turn aside. —werfen v throw away, discard. —werfend adj disdainful. —ziehen v pull aside; (Wohnsitz wechseln) move away.

weh [veɪ] adj sore, painful; (seelisch) sad. interj alas. mein Hals tut mir weh my throat hurts. sich weh tun hurt oneself. jemandem weh tun hurt someone, cause someone pain. Weh neut (pl -e) pain; sorrow.

Wehe ['veːə] f (pl -n) drift (of snow or sand). wehen v blow; (Fahne) flutter.

Wehr[1] [veɪr] f (pl -en) (Waffe) weapon; (Schutz) defence; (Rüstung) armament; (Widerstand) resistance.

Wehr[2] neut (pl -e) weir, dam.

Wehrdienst ['veɪrdiːnst] m military service. —verweigerer m conscientious objector. wehren v restrain. sich wehren gegen defend oneself against. wehrlos adj (waffenlos) unarmed; (schutzlos) defenceless. Wehr‖macht f armed forces pl. —pflicht f compulsory military service. —pflichtige(r) person liable for military service.

Weib [vaip] neut (pl -er) woman; (Gattin) wife. —chen neut (Tier) female. weiblich adj female; (Gramm) feminine.

weich [vaiç] adj soft; (sanft) gentle.

Weiche ['vaiçə] f (pl -n) (Anat) side, flank.

weichen[1] ['vaiçən] v soften; (einweichen) soak.

weichen[2] v give way; (nachgeben) yield; (Preise) fall.

Weichheit ['vaiçhait] f softness. weichherzig adj tender-hearted, gentle. Weichkäse m soft cheese. weichlich adj soft, weak, effeminate.

Weide[1] ['vaidə] f (pl -n) (Baum) willow.

Weide[2] f (pl -n) (Wiese) pasture.

*weiden ['vaidən] v graze. sich weiden an feast one's eyes on.

weigern ['vaigərn] v sich weigern refuse. Weigerung f (pl -en) refusal.

Weihe ['vaiə] f (pl -n) consecration; (Einweihung) initiation. weihen v consecrate.

Weihnachten ['vainaxtən] neut (pl -) Christmas. Weihnachts‖abend m Christmas Eve. —baum m Christmas tree. —geschenk neut Christmas present. —lied neut Christmas carol. —mann m Father Christmas, (US) Santa Claus.

weil [vail] conj because, since.

Weile ['vailə] f while, short time.

Wein [vain] m (pl -e) wine; (Pflanze) vine. —berg m vineyard. —brand m brandy.

weinen ['vainən] v cry, weep. Weinen neut crying, weeping, tears pl. —Wein‖lese f (pl -n) vintage. —stock m vine. —stube f wine bar. —traube f bunch of grapes.

weise ['vaizə] adj wise.

Weise ['vaizə] f (pl -n) manner, way; (Melodie) melody. Art und Weise manner, way. auf diese/jede/kleine Weise in this way/in any case/by no means.

weisen ['vaizən] v show; (Finger, Zeiger) point. weisen auf point to. weisen nach direct to.

Weisheit ['vaishait] f (pl -en) wisdom. —szahn m wisdom tooth.

weiß [vais] adj white. Weißbrot neut white bread. Weiße f whiteness. Weiße(r) White (man/woman). weiß‖en v whitewash. —glühend adj white-hot. Weiß‖kohl m (white) cabbage. —waren pl linens. —wein m white wine.

weit [vait] adj wide; (breit) broad; (geräumig) vast, spacious; (lang) long; (entfernt) far (off). bei weitem by far. von weitem from a distance. weit entfernt (von) far away (from). weit‖ab adv far away. —aus adv by far. Weite f (pl -n) width; (Ausdehnung) extent; (Größe) size. weiten v widen; (vergrößern) enlarge.

weiter ['vaitər] *adj* wider; (*Entfernung*) farther; (*zusätlich*) further. *adv* (*Entfernung*) farther; (*fig*) further; (*sonst*) else; (*weiterhin*) furthermore. **ohne weiteres** directly, immediately. **bis auf weiteres** for the present. **weiter nichts?** nothing else? **und so weiter** and so forth. **es geht weiter** it goes on. **weiter‖bringen** *v* harp on. **–geben** *v* pass (to). **–gehen** *v* move on. **–hin** *adv* moreover, furthermore. **–kommen** *v* make progress, get on. **–machen** *v* carry on.

weit‖gehend *adj* far-reaching. **–her** *adv* from afar. **–hergeholt** *adj* far-fetched. **–herzig** *adj* broad-minded. **–reichend** *adj* far-reaching. **–sichtig** *adj* far-sighted. **–verbreitet** *adj* widespread.

Weizen ['vaitsən] *m* wheat. **–brot** *neut* white bread. **–kleie** *f* bran.

welch [vɛlç] *adj, pron* which, what, who. **welche** *pl* some, any. **welch ein Glück!** what luck! **welches Kind?** which child? **welche schöne Blumen** what beautiful flowers. **möchtest du welche?** would you like some?

welk [vɛlk] *adj* withered. **welken** *v* wither.

Welle ['vɛlə] *f* (*pl* **-n**) wave; (*Tech*) shaft, axle. **wellen** *v* wave; (*rollen*) roll. **Wellen‖länge** *f* wavelength. **–sittich** *m* budgerigar.

Welt [vɛlt] *f* (*pl* **-en**) world. **–all** *neut* universe. **–anschauung** *f* (*pl* **-en**) philosophical outlook. **welt‖berühmt** *adj* world-famous. **–bürgerlich** *adj* cosmopolitan. **–erschütternd** *adj* world-shaking. **–lich** *adj* worldly, mundane. **Welt‖macht** *f* world power. **–raum** *m* (outer) space. **–rekord** *m* world record.

wem [veim] *pron* to whom.

wen [vein] *pron* whom.

Wende ['vɛndə] *f* (*pl* **-n**) turn; (*Änderung*) change. **–l** *f* (*pl* **-n**) coil, spiral. **wenden** *v* turn. **Wendepunkt** *m* turning point. **wendig** *adj* manoeuvrable; (*Person*) agile. **Wendung** *f* (*pl* **-en**) turn; (*Änderung*) change.

wenig ['veiniç] *adj* little. *adv* not much, slightly. **ein wenig** a little. **wenige** *pl* a few. **–er** *adj* less, fewer. **wenigst** *adj* least. **am wenigsten** *adv* least (of all). **wenigstens** *adv* at least.

wenn [vɛn] *conj* (*falls*) if; (*sobald*) when. **auch wenn** even if. **wenn nicht** unless. **wenn nur** if only.

wer [veir] *pron* who; (*derjenige, der*) whoever.

Werbe‖büro *neut* advertising agency. **–feldzug** *m* advertising campaign.

werben ['vɛrbən] *v* advertise, publicize; (*Rekruten*) enlist. **Werb‖esendung** *f* commercial. **–ung** *f* advertising.

***werden** ['vɛrdən] *v* become; (*allmählich*) grow; (*Futurum*) will, shall; (*Passiv*) be. **es wird dunkel** it is growing *or* getting dark. **er wird kommen** he will come. **er will Arzt werden** he wants to be a doctor. **der Baum wurde gefällt** the tree was felled. **würden Sie so freundlich sein?** would you be so kind? **Werden** *neut* development, growth. **werdend** *adj* developing, growing; (*Mutter*) expectant.

***werfen** ['vɛrfən] *v* throw.

Werft [vɛrft] *f* (*pl* **-en**) shipyard, dockyard.

Werk [vɛrk] *neut* (*pl* **-e**) work; (*Fabrik*) factory, works *pl*; (*Getriebe*) mechanism. **–statt** *or* **statte** *f* workshop. **–tag** *m* working day. **–zeug** *neut* tool.

Wermut ['vɛrmuːt] *m* wormwood; (*Wein*) vermouth.

wert [vɛrt] *adj* worth; (*würdig*) worthy; (*lieb*) dear. **für wert halten** consider worthwhile. **nicht der Mühe wert** not worth the bother. **fünf Mark wert** worth five Marks. **Wert** *m* value, worth. **wert‖en** *v* value. **–los** *adj* worthless. **Wert‖sachen** *pl* valuables. **–ung** *f* (*pl* **-en**) (e)valuation.

Wesen ['veizən] *neut* (*pl* **-**) being; (*Kern*) essence; (*Natur*) nature; (*Benehmen*) conduct. **–sart** *f* nature, character. **wesentlich** *adj* essential.

weshalb [vɛs'halp] *adv, conj* why.

Wespe ['vɛspə] *f* (*pl* **-n**) wasp.

wessen ['vɛsən] *pron* (*Person*) whose; (*Sache*) of which.

West [vɛst] *m* west.

Weste ['vɛstə] *f* (*pl* **-n**) waistcoat.

Westen ['vɛstən] *m* west. **West‖europa** *f* western Europe. **–falen** *neut* Westphalia. **–indien** *neut* West Indies *pl*. **westlich** *adj* western; (*Wind, Richtung*) westerly. **Westmark** *f* West German mark.

wett [vɛt] *adj* equal, even.

Wettbewerb ['vɛtbəvɛrp] *m* competition. **–er** *m* competitor. **wettbewerbsfähig** *adj* competitive.

Wette ['vɛtə] *f* (*pl* **-n**) bet. **Wetteifer** *m*

rivalry. **wetteifern mit** vie with, compete with. **wetten** v bet.

Wetter ['vɛtər] neut (pl -) weather. **–bericht** m weather report. **–kunde** f meteorology. **–vorhersage** f weather forecast.

Wett‖kampf m contest, match. **–kämpfer** m contestant. **–lauf** m race. **–streit** m contest.

wichtig ['viçtiç] adj important. **Wichtig‖keit** f importance. **–tuer** m busybody; pompous person.

Widder ['vidər] m (pl -) ram; (Astrol) Aries.

wider ['viːdər] prep against, contrary to. **–fahren** v happen to, befall.

Wider‖haken m barbed hook. **–hall** m response; (Echo) echo. **widerhallen** v echo.

wider‖legen v refute. **–lich** adj repulsive; (ekelhaft) disgusting. **–natürlich** adj unnatural. **–rechtlich** adj unlawful, illegal.

Widerruf ['viːdərruːf] m (Befehl) revocation, countermand; (Nachricht) denial. **widerrufen** v revoke, countermand; deny.

widersetzen [viːdər'zɛtsən] v **sich widersetzen** oppose. **widersetzlich** adj obstructive.

wider‖spenstig adj contrary, difficult, stubborn. **–spiegeln** v reflect. **–sprechen** v contradict. **Widerspruch** m contradiction.

Widerstand ['viːdərʃtant] m resistance, opposition.

*widerstehen [viːdər'ʃteːən] v resist.

Widerstreit ['viːdərʃtrait] m (Kampf) conflict; (Widersprüche) opposition.

widerwärtig ['viːdərvɛrtiç] adj disgusting, repulsive.

Widerwille ['viːdərvilə] m aversion, intense dislike. **widerwillig** adj reluctant, unwilling.

widmen ['vitmən] v devote, dedicate; (Buch) dedicate. **Widmung** f (pl -en) dedication.

widrig ['viːdriç] adj adverse, unfavourable.

wie [viː] adv how. conj as.

wieder ['viːdər] adv again; (zurück) back. **immer wieder** again and again.

Wiederaufbau ['viːdəraufbau] m reconstruction, rebuilding. **wiederaufbauen** v reconstruct, rebuild. **Wiederauf‖erstehung** f resurrection. **–nahme** f resumption. **wiederauf‖nehmen** v resume.

–tauchen v come to light again, resurface.

*wieder‖bringen v bring back, return. **–erkennen** v recognize.

Wiedergabe ['viːdərgaːbə] f reproduction. **wiedergeben** v give back, return; (darbieten) render.

wiedergeboren ['viːdərgəboːrən] adj reborn, regenerated. **Wiedergeburt** f rebirth, regeneration.

*wieder‖gewinnen v recover, retrieve. **–gutmachen** v make up for, compensate for.

wiederholen [viːdər'hoːlən] v repeat. **wiederholt** adj repeated. **Wiederholung** f (pl -en) repetition.

Wiederhören ['viːdərhœːrən] n **auf Wiederhören!** (Telef) goodbye!

wieder‖kehren v return. **–kommen** v come back, return.

*wiedersehen ['viːdərzeːən] v see or meet again. **Wiedersehen** neut reunion. **auf Wiedersehen!** goodbye!

wiederum ['viːdərum] adv (nochmals) again, afresh; (andererseits) on the other hand.

wieder‖vereinigen v reunite; (versöhnen) reconcile. **–verheiraten** v remarry.

Wiege ['viːgə] f (pl -n) cradle.

wiegen¹ ['viːgən] v (Gewicht) weigh.

wiegen² v (sanft schaukeln) rock.

Wiegenlied ['viːgənliːt] neut lullaby.

wiehern ['viːərn] v neigh; (Mensch) guffaw.

Wien [viːn] neut Vienna.

Wiese ['viːzə] f (pl -n) meadow.

Wiesel ['viːzəl] neut (pl -) weasel.

wieso [viː'zoː] adv why.

wieviel [viː'fiːl] adj, adv how much. **wieviele** adj how many.

wild [vilt] adj wild; (unzivilisiert, ungestüm) savage. **Wild** neut game. **–dieb** m poacher. **–heit** f wildness; savageness. **–leder** neut deerskin. **–nis** f wilderness.

Wille ['vilə] m (pl -n) or **Willen** m (pl -) will. **um ... willen** for the sake of. **willens‖schwach** adj weak-willed. **–stark** adj strong-willed. **willig** adj willing.

willkommen ['vilkɔmən] adj welcome. **willkommen heißen** v welcome, greet. **Willkommen** neut welcome.

Willkür ['vilkyːr] f arbitrariness, whim. **willkürlich** adj arbitrary.

wimmeln ['viməln] v **wimmeln von** swarm or teem with.

Wimper ['vimpər] *f* (*pl* -n) eyelash. **ohne mit der Wimper zu zucken** without batting an eyelid.

Wind [vint] *m* (*pl* -e) wind.

Winde ['vində] *f* (*pl* -n) windlass; (*Bot*) bindweed.

Windel ['vindəl] *f* (*pl* -n) nappy, (*US*) diaper.

*winden ['vindən] *v* wind, twist. **sich winden** writhe.

Wind‖hund *m* greyhound. **–mühle** *f* windmill. **–pokken** *pl* chickenpox *sing*. **–schutzscheibe** *f* windscreen, (*US*) windshield. **–stoß** *m* gust, blast of wind.

Windung ['vinduŋ] *f* (*pl* -en) winding, turn.

Wink [viŋk] *m* (*pl* -e) sign; (*Hand*) wave; (*Kopf*) nod; (*Augen*) wink; (*fig*) hint.

Winkel ['viŋkəl] *m* (*pl* -) (*Ecke*) corner; (*Math*) angle. **winkelig** *adj* angular. **winkelrecht** *adj* rectangular.

Winter ['vintər] *m* (*pl* -) winter. **winterlich** *adj* wintry. **Winter‖schlaf** *m* hibernation. **–sport** *m* winter sports *pl*.

winzig ['vintsiç] *adj* tiny.

Wipfel ['vipfəl] *m* (*pl* -) treetop.

Wippe ['vipə] *f* (*pl* -n) seesaw, balance.

wir [viːr] *pron* we.

Wirbel ['virbəl] *m* (*pl* -) whirl; (*Wasser*) whirlpool; (*Luft*) whirlwind; (*Trommeln*) roll; (*Rücken*) vertebra; (*Scheitel*) crown (of head). **wirbel‖los** *adj* spineless; (*Tiere*) invertebrate. **–n** *v* whirl, swirl; (*Trommeln*) roll. **Wirbel‖säule** *f* spine. **–tier** *neut* vertebrate. **–wind** *m* whirlwind.

wirken ['virkən] *v* work (on), act (on). **–d** *adj* active; (*erfolgreich*) effective. **wirklich** *adj* real, actual; (*echt*) genuine. **Wirklichkeit** *f* reality. **wirksam** *adj* effective. **Wirkung** *f* (*pl* -en) effect.

wirr [vir] *adj* tangled, disorderly; (*Haare*) dishevelled. **Wirrwarr** *m* chaos, jumble, disorder.

Wirt [virt] *m* (*pl* -e) innkeeper, landlord; (*Gastgeber*) host; (*Zimmervermieter*) landlord. **–in** *f* (*pl* -nen) innkeeper, landlady; hostess; landlady. **wirtlich** *adj* hospitable.

Wirtschaft ['virtʃaft] *f* (*pl* -en) economy; (*Haushaltung*) housekeeping; (*Gaststätte*) inn, public house. **wirtschaft‖en** *v* manage; (*Haushalt*) keep house. **–lich** *adj* economic; (*sparsam*) economical. **Wirtschafts‖krise** *f* economic crisis. **–politik** *f*

economic policy. **–wunder** *neut* economic miracle.

Wirtshaus ['virtshaus] *neut* inn, public house.

wischen ['viʃən] *v* wipe. **Wischlappen** *m* cloth, duster.

wispeln ['vispəln] *or* **wispern** *v* whisper.

Wißbegier(de) ['visbəgiːr(də)] *f* intellectual curiosity, thirst for learning. **wißbegierig** *adj* inquisitive, eager to learn.

*wissen ['visən] *v* know. **etwas tun wissen** know how to do something. **Wissen** *neut* knowledge.

Wissenschaft ['visənʃaft] *f* (*pl* -en) science, knowledge. **–ler** *m* (*pl* -), **–lerin** *f* (*pl* -nen) scientist. **wissenschaftlich** *adj* scientific.

wissentlich ['visəntliç] *adj* conscious, deliberate. *adv* knowingly, wittingly.

Witterung ['vitəruŋ] *f* (*pl* -en) weather (conditions).

Witwe ['vitvə] *f* (*pl* -n) widow. **Witwer** *m* (*pl* -) widower.

Witz [vits] *m* (*pl* -e) (*Gabe*) wit; (*Spaß*) joke. **–bold** *m* witty fellow, clown. **–blatt** *neut* comic (paper). **witzig** *adj* witty; (*spaßhaft*) humorous, funny. **witzeln** *über* joke about.

wo [voː] *adv* where. *conj* when. **ach wo!** what nonsense! **wo‖anders** *adv* elsewhere. **–bei** *adv* whereby, by which.

Woche ['voxə] *f* (*pl* -n) week. **Wochen‖blatt** *neut* weekly (paper). **–ende** *neut* weekend.

wöchentlich ['vœçtliç] *adj* weekly.

Wodka ['vodkə] *m* (*pl* -s) vodka.

wo‖durch *adv* whereby, by which; (*Frage*) how? by what means? **–für** *adv* for which; (*Frage*) for what? what ... for? **–gegen** *adv* against which. *conj* whereas. **–her** *adv* from where, whence. **–hin** *adv* (to) where, whither.

wohl [voːl] *adv* well; (*vermutend*) probably, I suppose. **Wohl** *neut* well-being, welfare.

wohlauf [voːl'auf] *adv* well. *interj* come on! cheer up!

Wohl‖befinden *neut* well-being, (good) health. **–behagen** *neut* comfort.

wohl‖bekannt *adj* well-known. **–erzogen** *adj* well brought up.

Wohlfahrt ['voːlfaːrt] *f* welfare. **–sstaat** *m* welfare state.

wohl‖gemeint adj well-intentioned. **–geraten** adj well done; (Kind) well-behaved.

Wohl‖geruch m perfume, fragrance. **–geschmack** m pleasant or agreeable taste.

wohlhabend ['voːlhaːbənt] adj well-to-do, well-off.

Wohlklang ['voːlklaŋ] m harmony.

Wohlstand ['voːlʃtant] m prosperity, affluence. **–sgesellschaft** f affluent society.

Wohl‖tat f kindness, kind deed; (Annehmlichkeit) boon, benefit. **–täter** m benefactor. **–täterin** f benefactress. **wohltätig** adj charitable. **Wohltätigkeit** f charity. **–sverein** m charitable association.

*wohltun ['voːltuːn] v do good.

Wohlwollen ['voːlvɔlən] neut good will, benevolence. **wohlwollend** adj benevolent.

wohnen ['voːnən] v live, dwell, reside. **wohnhaft** adj resident. **Wohn‖ort** m place of residence. **–Schlafzimmer** neut bedsitting room, (umg.) bedsit. **–ung** f (pl -en) flat, (US) apartment. **–wagen** m caravan, (US) trailer. **–zimmer** neut living-room, sitting-room.

Wölbung ['vœlbuŋ] f (pl -en) vault, arch, dome.

Wolf [vɔlf] m (pl **Wölfe**) wolf.

Wölfin ['vœlfin] f (pl **-nen**) she-wolf.

Wolke ['vɔlkə] f (pl -n) cloud. **–nkratzer** m skyscraper.

Wolle ['vɔlə] f (pl -n) wool.

*wollen[1] ['vɔlən] v want, wish. ich will gehen I want to go, I intend to go. ich will nicht gehen I don't want to go, I will not go. wollen Sie bitte ... would you please .... tun Sie, was Sie wollen do as you please.

wollen[2] adj woollen, (US) woolen.

wollig ['vɔliç] adj woolly.

Wollust ['vɔlust] f lust, voluptuousness. **wollüstig** adj lustful, voluptuous, sensual.

wo‖mit adv with which; (Frage) with what? **–nach** adv after which, whereupon.

Wonne ['vɔnə] f (pl -n) bliss; (Freude) joy; (Entzücken) rapture.

woran [voˈran] adv on which. **woran denkst du?** what are you thinking about? **woran liegt es, daß ... ?** how is it that ... ? **wo‖rauf** adv upon which, whereup-

on. **–raus** adv from which, whence. **–rin** adv in(to) which.

Wort [vɔrt] **1** neut (pl **Wörter**) word. **2** neut (pl **Worte**) (spoken) word.

Wörterbuch ['vœrtərbux] neut dictionary. **wörtlich** adj literal.

Wort‖schatz m vocabulary. **–spiel** neut pun.

wovon [voˈfɔn] of or from which; (Frage) from what? **wovon lebt er?** what does he live on? **wovon spricht er?** what is he talking about? **wozu** adv to which; (warum) what ... for, why.

Wrack [vrak] neut (pl **-s**) wreck.

*wringen ['vriŋən] v wring.

Wucher ['vuːxər] m profiteering. **wuchern** v profiteer; (Pflanze) proliferate, be rampant. **Wucherpreis** m exorbitant price.

Wuchs [m (pl **Wüchse**) growth; (Körperbau) physique, build.

Wucht [vuxt] f (pl **-en**) weight, impetus, force. **wuchtig** adj heavy, weighty.

wülen ['vyːlən] v root, dig; (durchstöbern) rummage; (Gefühle) well up. **sich wühlen in** burrow into. **wühlerisch** adj subversive.

Wulst [vulst] m (pl **Wülste**) swelling, bulge. **wulstig** adj swollen.

wund [vunt] adj sore. **Wunde** f (pl -n) wound.

Wunder ['vundər] neut (pl -) miracle, wonder. **wunderbar** adj wonderful, marvellous. **Wunder‖kind** neut child prodigy. **–land** neut fairy-land. **wunder‖lich** adj odd, strange, peculiar. **–n** v surprise, astonish. **sich wundern über** be astonished by, wonder at. **wunderschön** adj (very) beautiful. **Wundertat** f miracle, miraculous feat.

Wunsch [vunʃ] m (pl **Wünsche**) wish, desire.

wünschen ['vynʃən] v wish, desire. **–swert** adj desirable.

Würde ['vyrdə] f (pl -n) dignity; (Ehre) honour. **würde‖los** adj undignified. **–voll** adj dignified. **würdig** adj worthy. **–en** v appreciate. **Würdigung** f (pl **-en**) appreciation.

Wurf [vurf] m (pl **Würfe**) throw, cast; (Tiere) litter, brood.

Würfel ['vyrfəl] m (pl -) cube; (Spielstein) die.

würgen ['vyrgən] v choke; (erwürgen) strangle, throttle.

Wurm [vurm] *m* (*pl* **Würmer**) worm.
wurmig *adj* worm-eaten.
Wurst [vurst] *f* (*pl* **Würste**) sausage.
Würstchen ['vyrstçən] *neut* (*pl* -) (small)
sausage; (*Mensch*) little man, insignificant person.
Würze ['vyrtsə] *f* (*pl* -n) seasoning, spice.
Wurzel ['vyrtsəl] *f* (*pl* -n) root. **wurzeln** *v*
take root; (*fig*) be rooted in.
würzen ['vyrtsən] *v* season, spice. **würzig**
adj seasoned, spiced.
wüst [vyːst] *adj* desert, desolate; (*wirr*)
disorderly; (*Person*) coarse, vile. **Wüste**
f (*pl* -n) desert, waste.
wut [vuːt] *f* rage, fury.
wüten ['vyːtən] *v* rage, be furious. **-d** *adj*
furious.

X

X-Beine ['iksbainə] *pl* knock-knees. **X-
beinig** *adj* knock-kneed.
x-mal ['iksmaːl] *adj* (*umg.*) many times, *n*
times.
X-Strahlen ['iksʃtraːlən] *pl* x-rays.

Z

Zacke ['tsakə] *f* (*pl* -n) or **Zacken** *m* (*pl* -)
point, jag; (*Gabel*) prong; (*Kamm*) tooth.
zackig *adj* pointed, jagged; pronged;
toothed.
zaghaft ['tsaːkhaft] *adj* timid.
zäh [tsɛː] *adj* tough; (*Flüssigkeit*) thick;
(*Person*) stubborn.
Zahl [tsaːl] *f* (*pl* -en) number; (*Ziffer*)
figure, numeral. **zahlbar** *adj* payable.
zahlen *v* pay.
zählbar ['tsɛːlbaːr] *adj* countable. **zählen** *v*
count; (*Sport*) keep the score. **zählen auf**
count *or* rely on.
Zahler ['tsaːlər] *m* (*pl* -) payer.
Zähler ['tsɛːlər] *m* (*pl* -) counter; (*Bank*)
teller; (*Gerät*) meter, recorder.
zahl‖los *adj* countless. **-reich** *adj* numerous. **Zahl‖tag** *m* payday. **-ung** *f* (*pl* -en)
payment.
Zählung ['tsɛːluŋ] *f* (*pl* -en) counting;
(*Volkszählung*) census.
zahlungs‖fähig [*adj* (*Komm*) solvent.
-unfähig *adj* insolvent.

zahm [tsaːm] *adj* tame.
zähmen ['tsɛːmən] *v* tame.
Zahn [tsaːn] *m* (*pl* **Zähne**) tooth. **-arzt** *m*
dentist. **-bürste** *f* toothbrush. **-fleisch**
neut gum, gums *pl*. **-paste** *f* toothpaste.
-rad *neut* cogwheel, gearwheel.
-schmerz *m* toothache.
Zange ['tsaŋə] *f* (*pl* -n) pliers *pl*, tongs *pl*;
(*Pinzette*) tweezers *pl*.
Zank [tsaŋk] *m* (*pl* **Zänke**) quarrel.
zanken *v* scold. **sich zanken** quarrel.
Zapfen ['tsapfən] *m* (*pl* -) plug, bung;
(*Bot*) cone.
zappelig ['tsapəliç] *adj* fidgety. **zappeln** *v*
fidget.
Zar [tsaːr] *m* (*pl* -en) tsar, czar. **-in** *f* (*pl*
-nen) tsarina.
zart [tsaːrt] *adj* (*Fleisch, Gemüt*) tender;
(*sanft*) gentle, soft; (*zerbrechlich*) delicate. **-heit** *f* tenderness; gentleness.
zärtlich ['tsɛːrtliç] *adj* tender, loving,
affectionate. **Zärtlichkeit** *f* tenderness,
affection.
Zauber ['tsaubər] *m* (*pl* -) magic. **-bann**
m spell, charm. **-ei** *f* magic, sorcery.
-er *m* (*pl* -) magician, sorcerer. **-erin** *f*
(*pl* -nen) magician, sorcerer. **zauberhaft**
adj magical. **Zauber‖kunst** *f* sorcery;
(*Sinnestäuschung*) conjuring. **-künstler**
m conjurer. **-kunststück** *neut* conjuring
tricks *pl*. **zaubern** *v* practise magic;
(*Zauberkunst*) conjure. **Zauberspruch** *m*
magic spell.
zaudern ['tsaudərn] *v* hesitate, waver.
Zaum [tsaum] *m* (*pl* **Zäume**) rein, bridle.
zäumen ['tsɔymən] *v* (*Pferd*) bridle; (*fig*)
curb, restrain.
Zaun [tsaun] *m* (*pl* **Zäune**) fence; (*Hecke*)
hedge.
Zebra ['tseːbra] *neut* (*pl* -s) zebra.
Zeche ['tsɛçə] *f* (*pl* -n) (*Gasthaus*) bill;
(*Bergwerk*) mine, pit.
Zehe ['tseːə] *f* (*pl* -n) toe. **-nspitze** *f* tip
of the toe.
zehn [tseːn] *pron, adj* ten. **zehnte** *adj*
tenth. **Zehntel** *neut* tenth (part).
zehren ['tseːrən] *v* **zehren an** (*fig*) gnaw
at. **zehren von** live *or* feed on.
Zeichen ['tsaiçən] *neut* (*pl* -) sign;
(*Merkmal*) mark; (*Signal*) signal;
(*Hinweis*) indication. **-brett** *neut* drawing board. **-(trick)film** *m* animated cartoon. **zeichnen** *v* draw; (*kennzeichnen*)
mark; (*unterschreiben*) sign; (*Muster*)

design. **Zeichnung** *f* drawing; marking; (*Muster*) design.

Zeigefinger ['tsaigəfiŋər] *m* forefinger, index finger. **zeigen** *v* point out, show; (*zur Schau stellen*) show, display; (*beweisen*) demonstrate, show. **Zeiger** *m* pointer, indicator; (*Uhr*) hand.

Zeile ['tsailə] *f* (*pl* -n) line.

Zeit [tsait] *f* (*pl* -en) time. **auf Zeit** on credit. **freie Zeit** spare *or* free time. **für alle Zeiten** for all time. **in kurzer Zeit** shortly, soon. **Zeit‖alter** *neut* age, era. **–folge** *f* chronological order. **–geist** *m* spirit of the age.

Zeitgenosse ['tsaitgənosə] *m* (*pl* -n), **Zeitgenossin** *f* (*pl* -nen) contemporary. **zeitgenössisch** *adj* contemporary.

zeitig ['tsaitiç] *adj* early.

Zeit‖karte *f* season ticket. **–lang** *f* while. **ein Zeitlang** for some time, for a while. **Zeitlauf** *m* course of time.

zeitlich ['tsaitliç] *adj* temporal.

Zeit‖punkt *m* (point in) time, moment. **–raum** *m* period. **–schrift** *f* magazine, periodical.

Zeitung ['tsaituŋ] *f* (*pl* -en) newspaper. **Zeitungs‖anzeigt** *f* newspaper advertisement. **–ausschnitt** *m* press cutting. **–händler** *m* newsagent. **–stand** *m* newsstand, kiosk. **–wesen** *neut* the press, journalism.

Zeit‖verschwendung *f* waste of time. **–vertrieb** *m* pastime, diversion. **zeitweilig** *adj* temporary.

Zeitwort ['tsaitvort] *neut* verb.

Zelle ['tsɛlə] *f* (*pl* -n) cell.

Zelt [tsɛlt] *neut* (*pl* -e) tent. **–decke** *f* awning, canopy. **zelten** *v* camp. **Zeltplatz** *m* camp.

Zement [tse'mɛnt] *m* (*pl* -e) cement.

Zensur [tsɛn'zuːr] *f* (*pl* -en) censorship; (*Schule*) mark.

Zentimeter [tsɛnti'meɪtər] *m or neut* centimetre.

Zentner ['tsɛntnər] *m* (*pl* -) hundredweight, 50 kilos.

zentral [tsɛn'traːl] *adj* central. **Zentrale** *f* (*pl* -n) central office; (*Telef*) telephone exchange. **Zentral‖heizung** *f* central heating. **–isierung** *f* centralization. **Zentrum** *neut* (*pl* Zentren) centre.

zerbrechen [tsɛr'brɛçən] *v* break (in pieces), shatter. **zerbrechlich** *adj* fragile, breakable.

zerdrücken [tsɛr'drykən] *v* crush; (*Kleider*) crumple, crease.

Zeremonie [tseremo'niː] *f* (*pl* -n) ceremony. **zeremoniell** *adj* ceremonial.

Zerfall [tsɛr'fal] *m* decay, disintegration; (*Chem*) decomposition. **zerfallen** *v* disintegrate, fall to pieces; (*auflösen*) dissolve. **zer fallen mit** fall out with.

zerfetzen [tsɛr'fɛtsən] *v* shred, tear up.

*****zerfressen** [tsɛr'frɛsən] *v* gnaw; (*Chem*) corrode.

*****zergehen** [tsɛr'geːən] *v* melt.

zergliedern [tsɛr'gliːdərn] *v* dismember; (*fig*) analyse.

zerhacken [tsɛr'hakən] *v* chop up, chop into pieces.

zerkleinern [tsɛr'klainərn] *v* cut up, chop up.

zerlegen [tsɛr'leːgən] *v* take apart, separate; (*Fleisch*) carve; (*fig*) analyse. **Zerlegung** *f* (*pl* -en) taking apart; carving; analysis.

zerlumpt [tsɛr'lumpt] *adj* ragged.

zermahlen [tsɛr'maːlən] *v* grind.

zermürben [tsɛr'myrbən] *v* wear down. **Zermürbung** *f* attrition. **–skrieg** *m* war of attrition.

zerplatzen {tsɛr'platsən] *v* explode, burst.

zerquetschen [tsɛr'kvɛtʃən] *v* squash, crush.

Zerrbild ['tsɛrbilt] *neut* distortion, caricature.

*****zerreißen** [tsɛr'raisən] *v* tear up/to pieces; (*entzweigehen*) rip, tear, break.

zerren ['tsɛrən] *v* tug, pull; (*Med*) strain, pull. **Zerrung** *f* (*pl* -en) (*Med*) strain.

zerschellen [tsɛr'ʃɛlən] *v* be dashed to pieces.

*****zerschlagen** [tsɛr'ʃlaːgən] *v* knock *or* smash to pieces.

zerschlissen [tsɛr'ʃlisən] *adj* tattered, shredded.

*****zerschneiden** [tsɛr'ʃnaidən] *v* cut up.

zersetzen [tsɛr'zɛtsən] *v* disintegrate; (*untergraben*) undermine, demoralize. **sich zersetzen** disintegrate; (*Chem*) decompose. **Zersetzung** *f* disintegration.

zersplittern [tsɛr'ʃplitərn] *v* splinter, shatter; (*fig*) split up. **Zersplitterung** *f* splintering; splitting-up.

zersprengen [tsɛr'ʃprɛŋən] *v* blow up, burst (open).

zerstäuben *v* pulverize; (*Flüssigkeit*) spray, atomize. **Zerstäuber** *m* spray atomizer.

zerstören [tsɛrˈʃtœːrən] v destroy. **–d** adj destructive. **Zerstör‖er** m destroyer. **–ung** f destruction.

zerstreuen [tsɛrˈʃtrɔyən] v disperse, scatter; (unterhalten) amuse, entertain. **zerstreut** adj scattered; (geistig) distracted, absent-minded. **Zerstreuung** f dispersion; distraction; (Unterhaltung) amusement.

zerteilen [tsɛrˈtailən] v divide, separate; (zerstückeln) cut up.

*zertreten [tsɛrˈtreːtən] v tread on, trample on.

zertrümmern [tsɛrˈtrymərn] v smash, wreck; (vernichten) destroy.

zerzausen [tsɛrˈtsauzən] v rumple, tousle. **zerzaust** adj tousled, dishevelled.

zetern [ˈtseːtərn] v cry out, shout (for help).

Zettel [ˈtsɛtəl] m (pl -) slip (of paper); (Merkzettel) note; (Preis) ticket.

Zeug [tsɔyk] neut (pl -e) material, stuff; (Arbeitsgeräte) tools pl; (allerlei Dinge) stuff, things pl.

Zeuge [ˈtsɔygə] m (pl -n) witness.

zeugen[1] [ˈtsɔygən] v testify, give evidence. **von etwas zeugen** be evidence of something.

zeugen[2] v (Kind) procreate, beget; (fig) generate, produce.

Zeugen‖bank f witness box. **–beweis** m evidence. **Zeugin** (pl -nen) f (female) witness. **Zeugnis** neut evidence, testimony; (Bescheinigung) certificate; (Schule) report.

Zeugung [ˈtsɔyguŋ] f (pl -en) generation, procreation.

Zickzack [ˈtsiktsak] m (pl -e) zigzag.

Ziege [ˈtsiːgə] f (pl -n) goat.

Ziegel [ˈtsiːgəl] m (pl -) (Backstein) brick; (Dachziegel) (roof-)tile. **–stein** m brick.

Ziegen‖bock m billy goat. **–leder** neut kid (leather), goatskin. **–milch** f goat's milk.

*ziehen [ˈtsiːən] v pull, draw; (Zeichnen) draw; (strecken) stretch; (wandern) wander; (marschieren) march; (Tee) infuse; (Zigarre) draw or pull (on); (umziehen) move. **es zieht** (Luft) there is a draught. **sich in die Länge ziehen** drag on.

Ziel [tsiːl] neut (pl -e) aim, goal; (Geschoß) target; (Wettlauf) finish. **ziel‖en** v aim (at). **–los** adj aimless. **Zielscheibe** f target.

ziemlich [ˈtsiːmliç] adj considerable. adv rather, moderately.

Zier [tsiːr] f (pl -en) decoration. **zier‖en** v decorate. **sich zieren** be affected, behave with affectation. **–lich** adj dainty; (elegant) elegant.

Ziffer [ˈtsifər] f (pl -n) cipher, numeral. **–blatt** neut clock-face.

Zigarette [tsigaˈrɛtə] f (pl -n) cigarette. **Zigaretten‖etui** neut cigarette case. **–stümmel** m cigarette end. **Zigarre** f (pl -n) cigar.

Zigeuner [tsiˈgɔynər] m (pl -), **Zigeunerin** f (pl -nen) Gipsy.

Zimmer [ˈtsimər] neut (pl -) room. **–arbeit** f carpentry. **–mann** m carpenter. **–spiel** neut (parlour) game.

zimperlich [ˈtsimpərliç] adj prim.

Zimt [tsimt] m (pl -e) cinnamon.

Zink [tsiŋk] neut zinc.

Zinke [ˈtsiŋkə] f (pl -n) prong; (Kamm) tooth.

Zinn [tsin] neut tin. **zinnern** adj tin. **Zinnfolie** f tinfoil.

Zins [tsins] m (pl -en) (Miete) rent; (Abgabe) tax, duty. **Zinsen** pl interest. **Zinsfuß** m rate of interest.

Zipfel [ˈtsipfəl] m (pl -) tip; (Ecke) corner.

Zirkel [ˈtsiːrkəl] m (pl -) (Kreis) circle; (Gerät) (pair of) compasses pl.

Zirkus [ˈtsirkus] m (pl -se) circus.

zirpen [ˈtsirpən] v chirp.

zischen [ˈtsiʃən] v kiss.

Zitat [tsiˈtaːt] neut (pl -e) quotation, quote. **zitieren** v quote, cite; (vorladen) summon.

Zitrone [tsiˈtroːnə] f (pl -n) lemon.

zittern [ˈtsitərn] v tremble, shake.

Zitze [ˈtsitsə] f (pl -n) nipple, teat.

zivil [tsiˈviːl] adj civil. **Zivilisation** f (unz.) civilization. **zivil‖isieren** v civilize. **–isiert** adj civilized, cultured. **Zivil‖ist** m (pl -en) civilian. **–kleidung** f civilian clothes pl.

zögern [ˈtsœːgərn] v hesitate.

Zoll[1] [tsɔl] m (pl -e) (Längenmaß) inch. **Zoll**[2] m (pl Zölle) (customs) duty; (umg.: Zollabfertigungsstelle) customs pl. **Zoll‖abfertigung** f customs clearance. **–beamte(r)** m customs official.

Zone [ˈtsoːnə] f (pl -n) zone.

Zoo [tsoː] m (pl -s) zoo. **–loge** m (pl -n) zoologist. **–logie** f zoology. **zoologisch** adj zoological.

Zopf [tsɔpf] *m* (*pl* **Zöpfe**) plait, pigtail.

Zorn [tsɔrn] *m* anger. **zornig** *adj* angry.

zu [tsuː] *prep* (*Richtung*) to, toward(s); (*Ziel, Ort*) at, in; (*neben*) beside. *adv* too; (*geschlossen*) closed, shut. **zu Hause** at home. **zu verkaufen** for sale. **zu Mittag** at noon. **zu Fuß** on foot. **ab und zu** now and then. **um zu** in order to.

Zubehör ['tsuːbəhœːr] *neut* (*pl* -e) fittings *pl*; (*Tech*) accessories *pl*. **-teil** *neut* attachment, accessory.

zubereiten ['tsuːbəraitən] *v* prepare.

*****zubringen** ['tsuːbriŋən] *v* bring *or* take (to); (*Zeit*) spend.

Zucht [tsuxt] **1** *f* (*unz.*) discipline. (*Pflanzen*) cultivation, breeding; (*Vieh*) rearing, breeding. **2** *f* (*pl* -en) breed.

züchten ['tsʏçtən] *v* breed. **Züchter** *m* breeder; (*Bienen*) beekeeper; (*Pflanzen*) grower.

züchtigen ['tsʏçtigen] *v* punish, discipline. **Züchtigung** *f* (*pl* -en) punishment.

zuchtlos ['tsuxtloːs] *adj* undisciplined.

Zuck [tsuk] *m* (*pl* -e) jerk. **zucken** *v* start, jerk.

Zucker ['tsukər] *m* sugar. **zuckerkrank** *adj* diabetic. **Zucker‖kranke(r)** *m* diabetic. **-krankheit** *f* diabetes. **-rohr** *m* sugarcane.

zudecken ['tsuːdekən] *v* cover (up).

zudem [tsuˈdeːm] *adv* moreover, besides.

zudrehen ['tsuːdreːən] *v* turn off.

zudringlich ['tsuːdriŋliç] *adj* importunate, pushing.

zueinander [tsuainˈandər] *adv* to each other.

zuerst [tsuˈeːrst] *adv* (at) first.

Zufahrt ['tsuːfaːrt] *f* approach, driving in. **-straße** *f* access road; (*Haus*) driveway.

Zufall ['tsuːfal] *m* chance, accident. **glücklicher Zufall** happy coincidence. **zufällig** *adj* accidental, chance; *adv* by chance, accidentally.

Zuflucht ['tsuːfluxt] *f* refuge, shelter.

Zufluß ['tsuːfluːs] *m* influx; (*Fluß*) tributary; (*Waren*) supply.

zufolge [tsuˈfɔlgə] *prep* owing to, in consequence of.

zufrieden [tsuˈfriːdən] *adj* contented. **Zufriedenheit** *f* content(ment). **zufriedenstellen** *v* satisfy.

zufügen ['tsuːfyːgən] *v* add (to); (*Böses*) inflict (on).

Zufuhr ['tsuːfuːr] *f* (*pl* -en) supply.

zuführen *v* supply; (*zuleiten*) lead to.

Zug [tsuːk] *m* (*pl* **Züge**) pull; (*Eisenbahn*) train; (*Charakter*) trait; (*Gesicht*) feature; (*Luft*) draught; (*Schub*) thrust; (*Brettspiel*) move; (*Einatmen*) inhalation; (*Rauchen*) puff, pull; (*Festzug*) procession; (*Zeichnen*) stroke, dash; (*Umriß*) outline; (*Vögel*) migration.

Zugabe ['tsuːgaibə] *f* addition; (*Zuschlag*) extra.

Zugang ['tsuːgaŋ] *m* entry, access; (*Eingang*) entrance; accession. **zugänglich** *adj* accessible; (*Mensch*) approachable.

Zugbrücke ['tsuːgbrykə] *f* drawbridge.

*****zugeben** ['tsuːgeːbən] *v* add; (*einräumen*) admit; (*gestatten*) permit.

zugegen [tsuˈgeːgən] *adj* present.

*****zugehen** ['tsuːgeːən] *v* close, be closed; (*weitergehen*) go on; (*geschehen*) happen.

zugehören ['tsuːgəhœːrən] *v* belong (to).

Zügel ['tsyːgəl] *m* (*pl* -) rein(s); (*fig*) curb. **zügel‖los** *adj* unrestrained, unbridled. **-n** *v* rein; (*beherrschen*) control, curb.

Zugeständnis ['tsuːgəʃtɛntnis] *neut* concession.

*****zugestehen** ['tsuːgəʃteːən] *v* admit, concede.

Zugführer ['tsuːkfyːrər] *m* (*Eisenbahn*) guard, (*US*) conductor.

*****zugießen** ['tsuːgiːsən] *v* pour (in).

zugig ['tsuːgiç] *adj* draughty.

Zugluft ['tsuːkluft] *f* draught.

*****zugreifen** ['tsuːgraifən] *v* grasp, grab; (*helfen*) lend a hand; (*bei Tisch*) help oneself.

zugrunde [tsuˈgrundə] *adv* **zugrunde gehen** *v* perish, be ruined.

zugunsten [tsuˈgunstən] *prep* in favour of.

zugute [tsuˈguːtə] *adv* to one's advantage. **zugute halten** *v* take into consideration, allow for.

*****zuhalten** ['tsuːhaltən] *v* keep shut. **zuhalten auf** head for. **Zuhälter** *m* pimp.

zuhanden [tsuˈhandən] *adj* (ready) at hand, ready.

Zuhause [tsuˈhauzə] *f* (*unz.*) home.

zuhören ['tsuːhœːrən] *v* listen. **Zuhörer** *m* (*pl* -), **Zuhörerin** *f* (*pl* -nen) listener. **Zuhörer** *pl* audience *sing*; (*Radio*) listeners.

zuklappen ['tsuːklapən] *v* slam, clap shut.

zuknöpfen ['tsuːknœpfən] *v* button up.

*****zukommen** ['tsuːkɔmən] *v* (*gebühren*) befit. **zukommen lassen** send, supply. **zukommen auf** come up to.

Zukunft ['tsuːkunft] *f* future. **zukünftig** *adj* future; *adv* in (the) future.

Zulage ['tsuːlaːgə] *f* extra pay, bonus.

zulänglich ['tsuːlɛnliç] *adj* sufficient.

***zulassen** ['tsuːlasən] *v* permit, admit; (*hereinlassen*) let in, admit. **zulässig** *adj* permissible. **Zulassung** *f* permission; admission; (*Mot*) registration. **–sschein** *m* permit, licence.

zuleiten ['tsuːlaitən] *v* lead to.

zuletzt [tsuˈlɛtst] *adv* finally, last.

zuliebe [tsuˈliːbə] *adv* **jemandem zuliebe** to please someone.

Zulieferer ['tsuːliːfərər] *m* (*pl* -) subcontractor.

zum [tsum] *prep + art* **zu dem**.

zumachen ['tsuːmaxən] *v* shut, close.

zumeist [tsuˈmaist] *adv* mostly.

zumindest [tsuˈmindəst] *adv* at least.

zumute [tsuˈmuːtə] *adv* **gut/schlecht zumute sein** be in high/low spirits.

zumuten ['tsuːmuːtən] *v* expect, demand. **Zumutung** *f* presumption, unreasonable expectation.

zunächst [tsuˈnɛːçst] *adv* first (of all). *prep* near, close to.

Zunahme ['tsuːnaːmə] *f* (*pl* -n) increase.

Zuname ['tsuːnaːmə] *m* surname.

zünden ['tsyndən] *v* catch fire, light; (*Mot, Tech*) ignite.

Zunder ['tsundər] *m* (*pl* -) tinder.

Zünder ['tsyndər] *m* (*pl* -) fuse, detonator. **Zünd‖kerze** *f* sparking plug. **–schlüssel** *m* ignition key. **–ung** *f* ignition; (*Sprengladung*) detonation.

***zunehmen** ['tsuːneːmən] *v* increase; (*wachsen*) grow; (*dicker werden*) put on weight. **–d** *adj* increasing, accelerating.

zuneigen ['tsuːnaigən] *v* incline, lean; (*fig*) incline, tend. **Zuneigung** *f* inclination; (*Sympathie*) affection.

Zunft [tsunft] *f* (*pl* **Zünfte**) guild.

Zunge ['tsuŋə] *f* (*pl* -n) tongue. **zungenfertig** *adj* glib, fluent.

zunichte [tsuˈniçtə] *adv* **zunichte machen** (*Hoffnungen*) destroy, shatter; (*Pläne*) frustrate.

zunicken ['tsuːnikən] *v* nod to.

zunutze [tsuˈnutsə] *adv* **sich etwas zunutze machen** utilize something, put something to use.

zuoberst [tsuˈoːbərst] *adv* at the top.

zupfen ['tsupfən] *v* pluck; (*Fasern*) pick.

zur [tsuːr] *prep + art* **zu der**.

zurechnen ['tsuːrɛçnən] *v* (*zuschreiben*) ascribe, attribute. **Zurechnung** *f* attribution.

zurecht [tsuˈrɛçt] *adv* right, correctly, in order. **sich zurechtfinden** *v* find one's way. **zurechtkommen** *v* arrive in time. **zurechtkommen mit** get along with. **zurecht‖machen** *v* prepare. **–weisen** *v* reprimand.

zureden ['tsuːreːdən] *v* urge, coax.

zureichen ['tsuːraiçən] *v* (*ausreichen*) do, be enough; (*hinreichen*) hand, pass. **–d** *adj* sufficient.

zurichten ['tsuːriçtən] *v* prepare, get ready; (*umg.*) mess up, make a mess of.

zürnen ['tsyrnən] *v* be angry.

zurück [tsuˈryk] *adv* back(wards); (*hinten*) behind. **–behalten** *v* keep back, detain. **–bekommen** *v* get back, recover. **–bezahlen** *v* refund, pay back. **–bleiben** *v* remain behind. **–blicken** *v* look back. **–bringen** *v* bring back. **–datieren** *v* backdate; (*stammen aus*) date back. **–erstatten** *v* return, restore; (*ausgelegtes Geld*) reimburse. **–fahren** *v* drive back; (*vor Schreck*) recoil, start.

Zurückgabe [tsuˈrykgaːbə] *f* restitution, restoration. **zurückgeben** *v* give back, restore.

zurück‖gehen *v* go back, return; (*nachlassen*) decrease, fall off. **zurückgehen auf** originate in, go back to. **–gezogen** *adj* retiring, withdrawn.

zurückhalten [tsuˈrykhaltən] *v* (*Person*) keep, detain; (*Sache*) retain, withhold. **–d** *adj* reserved; (*vorsichtig*) cautious. **Zurückhaltung** *f* reserve.

zurück‖kehren *v* return. **–kommen** *v* come back; (*wieder aufgreifen*) revert (to). **–legen** *v* put aside; (*Geld*) put by. **–melden** *v* report back.

Zurücknahme [tsuˈryknaːmə] *f* (*pl* -n) withdrawal, taking back. **zurücknehmen** *v* take back; (*Worte*) withdraw; (*Anordnung, Auftrag*) cancel.

zurück‖scheuen *v* shrink back (from), shy (at). **–schicken** *v* send back. **–setzen** *v* put *or* place back; (*herabsetzen*) reduce; (*Person*) neglect, slight. **–strahlen** *v* reflect. **–reten** *v* step back; (*vom Posten*) resign, retire. **–weisen** *v* refuse, reject. **–zahlen** *v* pay back, repay. **–ziehen** *v* draw back, withdraw. **sich zurückziehen** withdraw, retire.

Zuruf ['tsuːruːf] *m* shout. **zurufen** *v* shout, call.

Zusage ['tsuːzaːgə] *f* promise; (*Bejahung*) assent, consent. **zusagen** *v* (*versprechen*) promise; (*Einladung*) accept, agree to come; (*gefallen*) suit, please.

zusammen [tsu'zamən] *adv* together; (*insgesamt*) all told, all together.

Zusammenarbeit *f* cooperation. **zusammenarbeiten** *v* cooperate.

zusammenballen *v* roll up; (*Faust*) clench. **sich zusammenballen** gather.

*zusammenbrechen *v* collapse, break down. **Zusammenbruch** *m* collapse.

zusammendrängen *v* **sich zusammendrängen** crowd together.

*zusammen‖fahren *v* travel together; (*aufeinanderstoßen*) collide; (*zusammenschrecken*) wince, start. **–fallen** *v* fall down, collapse; coincide.

zusammenfassen *v* summarize. **–d** *adj* comprehensive. **Zusammenfassung** *f* summary.

zusammengesetzt *adj* composed, compounded.

Zusammenhang *m* (*verbindung*) connection; (*Text*) context. **zusammenhängen** *v* (*verbunden sein*) be connected. **–d** *adj* coherent.

zusammenklappen *v* fold up.

Zusammenkunft *f* (*pl* **Zusammenkünfte**) meeting.

zusammen‖legen *v* put together; (*falten*) fold (up); (*vereinigen*) combine; (*Geld*) pool. **–passen** *v* go (well) together; match; (*Menschen*) get on well.

Zusammenprall *m* collision. **zusammenprallen** *v* collide.

*zusammenschließen *v* join together. **sich zusammenschließen** unite. **Zusammenschluß** *m* union, merger.

zusammensetzen *v* put together, construct. **sich zusammensetzen** sit down with one another; (*bestehen*) consist (of). **Zusammensetz‖spiel** *neut* jigsaw puzzle. **–ung** *f* composition.

zusammenstellen *v* (*vereinigen*) join; (*vergleichen*) compare.

Zusammenstoß *m* collision; (*Streit*) clash, conflict. **zusammenstoßen** *v* collide; clash, conflict.

Zusammentreffen *neut* coincidence; (*Begegnung*) encounter, meeting.

*zusammenziehen *v* close, draw together; (*verkürzen*) shorten, contract;

(*verbinden*) join together; (*sammeln*) gather. **sich zusammenziehen** (*Stoff*) shrink. **Zusammenziehung** *f* shrinking; contraction.

Zusatz ['tsuːzats] *m* addition; (*Ergänzung*) supplement; (*Anhang*) appendix. **zusätzlich** *adj* additional, extra.

zuschauen ['tsuːʃauən] *v* watch, look on, observe. **Zuschauer** *m* (*pl* -), **Zuschauerin** *f* (*pl* -nen) spectator, onlooker.

Zuschlag ['tsuːʃlaːk] *m* surcharge, extra charge. **zuschlagen** *v* hit (out); (*Tür*) slam (shut).

*zuschließen ['tsuːʃliːsən] *v* lock (up).

*zuschneiden ['tsuːʃnaidən] *v* cut out. **Zuschnitt** *m* cut, style.

*zuschreiben ['tsuːʃraibən] *v* attribute, ascribe; (*übertragen*) transfer to. *das hast du dir selbst zuzuschreiben* you have yourself to blame for that.

Zuschuß ['tsuːʃus] *m* subsidy, allowance.

*zusehen ['tsuːzeːən] *v* look on, watch. **zusehen, daß** see to it that.

*zusenden ['tsuːzɛndən] *v* send on, forward.

zusetzen ['tsuːzɛtsən] *v* (*hinzufügen*) add; (*verlieren*) lose; (*bedrängen*) press, importune.

Zuspruch ['tsuːʃprux] *m* encouragement, approval.

Zustand ['tsuːʃtant] *m* condition, state.

zustande [tsu'ʃtandə] *adv* **zustande bringen** achieve, bring about. **zustande kommen** come about, materialize.

zuständig ['tsuːʃtɛndiç] *adj* appropriate; competent; responsible.

zustellen ['tsuːʃtɛlən] *v* deliver; (*Klage*) serve on. **Zustellung** *f* (*pl* -en) delivery.

zustimmen ['tsuːʃtimən] *v* consent, agree. **Zustimmung** *f* consent, agreement.

zustopfen ['tsuːʃtɔpfən] *v* plug (up), stop (up); (*flicken*) darn.

*zustoßen ['tsuːʃtoːsən] *v* (*Tür*) push to; (*geschehen*) happen (to), befall.

zutage [tsu'taːgə] *adv* **zutage bringen** bring to light.

Zutaten ['tsuːtaːtən] *f pl* ingredients; (*Beiwerk*) trimmings.

zuteilen ['tsuːtailən] *v* assign, allocate, issue. **Zuteilung** *f* allocation.

zutiefst [tsu'tiːfst] *adv* deeply.

*zutragen ['tsuːtraːgən] *v* carry to. **sich zutragen** happen, take place. **zuträglich** *adj* beneficial.

zutrauen ['tsuɪtrauən] v credit (with), believe (of). **Zutrauen** neut confidence, trust, faith.
***zutreffen** ['tsuɪtrɛfən] v be right, be or hold true. **–d** adj right, accurate.
Zutritt ['tsuɪtrɪt] m access. **Zutritt verboten!** keep out! no admission!
***zutun** ['tsuɪtuɪn] v (hinzutun) add; (schließen) shut.
zuverlässig ['tsuɪfɛrlɛsiç] adj reliable. **Zuverlässigkeit** f reliability.
Zuversicht ['tsuɪferziçt] f confidence, trust. **zuversichtlich** adj confident.
zuviel [tsu'fiɪl] adv too much.
zuvor [tsu'foɪr] adv before, previously. **–kommen** v anticipate.
Zuwachs ['tsuɪvaks] m growth; (Vermehrung) increase.
zuwege [tsu'veɪgə] adv **zuwege bringen** bring about, cause.
zuweilen [tsu'vailən] adv sometimes, at times.
***zuweisen** ['tsuɪvaizən] v assign, allot.
***zuwenden** ['tsuɪvɛndən] v turn (towards); (geben) present, let have. **sich zuwenden** apply oneself (to).
zuwider [tsu'viɪdər] prep (entgegen) contrary to. adj (widerwärtig) repugnant.
zuwinken ['tsuɪvɪŋkən] v wave (to).
***zuziehen** ['tsuɪtsiɪən] v draw together; (Vorhänge) draw; (Wohnung) move in. **sich zuziehen** incur; (Med) contract, catch.
Zwang [tsvaŋ] m (pl Zwänge) compulsion; (Gewalt) force; (Hemmung) restraint.
zwängen ['tsvɛŋən] v force, press.
zwanglos ['tsvaŋloɪs] adj unconstrained; (ohne Förmlichkeit) informal. **Zwangs‖arbeit** f hard labour. **–kauf** m compulsory purchase. **zwangsläufig** adj inevitable.
zwanzig ['tsvantsiç] pron, adj twenty. **zwanzigst** adj twentieth.
zwar [tsvaɪr] adv indeed, certainly. **und zwar** namely, in fact.
Zweck [tsvɛk] m (pl -e) purpose, object; (Ziel) goal. **es hat keinen Zweck** it's pointless, it is of no use.
Zwecke ['tsvɛkə] m (pl -n) tack; (Reißnagel) drawing pin, (US) thumbtack.
zweck‖los adj pointless. **–mäßig** adj expedient, appropriate. **–s** prep for the purpose of.

zwei [tsvai] pron, adj two. **zwei‖deutig** adj ambiguous. **–erlei** adj of two kinds or sorts.
Zweifel ['tsvaifəl] m (pl -) doubt. **zweifel‖haft** adj doubtful. **–los** adj doubtless. **–n** v doubt.
Zweig [tsvaik] m (pl -e) branch, twig; (fig) branch. **–stelle** f branch (office).
zwei‖jährig adj two-year-old; (Bot) biennial. **–jährlich** adj biennial. **–mal** adv twice. **–seitig** adj two-sided; (fig) bilateral. **–sprachig** adj bilingual.
zweit [tsvait] adj second. **–ens** adv secondly. **–klassig** adj second-rate.
zweiwöchentlich ['tsvaivœçəntliç] adj fortnightly.
Zwerchfell ['tsvɛrçfɛl] neut diaphragm.
Zwerg [tsvɛrk] m (pl -e) dwarf. **zwergenhaft** adj dwarf.
Zwetsche ['tsvɛtʃə] or **Zwetschge** f (pl -n) plum.
Zwick [tsvik] m (pl -e) pinch. **zwicken** v pinch; (Fahrschein) punch, clip.
Zwieback ['tsviɪbak] m (pl -e) rusk, biscuit.
Zwiebel ['tsviɪbəl] f (pl -n) onion; (Blumen) bulb.
Zwiegespräch ['tsviɪgərʃprɛç] neut dialogue.
Zwielicht ['tsviɪliçt] neut twilight.
Zwiespalt ['tsviɪʃpalt] m (inner) conflict; (Uneinigkeit) dissension, discord.
Zwietracht ['tsviɪtraxt] f conflict, dissension.
Zwilling ['tsviliŋ] m (pl -e) twin. **Zwillinge** pl (Astrol) Gemini. **Zwillings‖bruder** m twin brother. **–schwester** f twin sister.
Zwinge ['tsviŋə] f (pl -n) vice.
***zwingen** ['tsviŋən] force, compel; (leisten können) manage, cope with.
zwischen ['tsviʃən] prep between; (mitten unter) among. **Zwischen‖bemerkung** f remark, aside. **–händler** m middleman. **–raum** m (intervening) space, interval. **–satz** m insertion. **–stunde** f free period, break, interval. **–zeit** f interim, interval. **in der Zwischenzeit** (in the) meantime.
zwitschern ['tsvitʃərn] v chirp, twitter.
zwo [tsvoɪ] V **zwei**.
zwölf [tsvœlf] pron, adj twelve. **zwölft** adj twelfth.
zyklisch ['tsyɪkliʃ] adj cyclic.
Zyklone [tsy'kloɪnə] f (pl -n) low-pressure area, depression.

Zyklus ['tsyːklus] *m* (*pl* **Zyklen**) cycle.
Zylinder [tsi'lindər] *m* (*pl* -) cylinder;
(*Hut*) top hat. **−kopf** *m* cylinder head.
Zyniker ['tsyːnikər] *m* (*pl* -) cynic. **zynisch**

adj cynical.
Zypern ['tsyːpərn] *neut* Cyprus. **Zyprer** *m*
(*pl* -). **Zyprerin** *f* (*pl* -**nen**) Cypriot.
zyprisch *adj* Cypriot.